HARUKI MURAKAMI

In 1978, Haruki Murakami was 29 and running a jazz bar in downtown Tokyo. One April day, the impulse to write a novel came to him suddenly while watching a baseball game. That first novel, *Hear the Wind Sing*, won a new writers' award and was published the following year. More followed, including *A Wild Sheep Chase* and *Hard-Boiled Wonderland and the End of the World*, but it was *Norwegian Wood*, published in 1987, which turned Murakami from a writer into a phenomenon. His books became bestsellers, have been translated into more than 50 languages, and he has received many honours, including the Franz Kafka Prize.

His works include non-fiction, such as *What I Talk About When I Talk About Running* and *Absolutely On Music*, short story collections, like *Men Without Women*, and the masterful novels *The Wind-Up Bird Chronicle*, *1Q84* and *Colorless Tsukuru Tazaki and his Years of Pilgrimage*. He is one of the world's most acclaimed and well-loved writers.

ALSO BY HARUKI MURAKAMI

Fiction

1Q84
After Dark
After the Quake
Blind Willow, Sleeping Woman
Colorless Tsukuru Tazaki and His Years of Pilgrimage
Dance Dance Dance
The Elephant Vanishes
Hard-Boiled Wonderland and the End of the World
Kafka on the Shore
Men Without Women
Norwegian Wood
South of the Border, West of the Sun
Sputnik Sweetheart
The Strange Library
A Wild Sheep Chase
The Wind-Up Bird Chronicle
Wind/Pinball

Non-Fiction

Absolutely On Music: Conversations with Seiji Ozawa
Underground: The Tokyo Gas Attack and the Japanese Psyche
What I Talk About When I Talk About Running

HARUKI MURAKAMI

Killing Commendatore

TRANSLATED FROM THE JAPANESE BY

Philip Gabriel and Ted Goossen

VINTAGE

2 4 6 8 10 9 7 5 3

Vintage
20 Vauxhall Bridge Road,
London SW1V 2SA

Vintage is part of the Penguin Random House group of companies
whose addresses can be found at global.penguinrandomhouse.com.

First published by Vintage in 2019
First published by Harvill Secker in 2018
First published in Japan in two volumes titled
Kishidancho goroshi: Dai ichi-bu, Arawareru idea hen and
Kishidancho goroshi: Dai ni-bu, Utsurou metafa hen in 2017
by Shinchosha Publishing Co. Ltd., Tokyo

penguin.co.uk/vintage

A CIP catalogue record for this book is available from the British Library

ISBN 9781784707330

Printed and bound in Great Britain by Clays Ltd, Elcograf S.p.A.

Penguin Random House is committed to a sustainable future
for our business, our readers and our planet. This book is made
from Forest Stewardship Council® certified paper.

KILLING COMMENDATORE

PART 1

THE IDEA MADE VISIBLE

Prologue

Today when I awoke from a nap the faceless man was there before me. He was seated on the chair across from the sofa I'd been sleeping on, staring straight at me with a pair of imaginary eyes in a face that wasn't.

The man was tall, and he was dressed the same as when I had seen him last. His face-that-wasn't-a-face was half hidden by a wide-brimmed black hat, and he had on a long, equally dark coat.

"I came here so you could draw my portrait," the faceless man said, after he'd made sure I was fully awake. His voice was low, toneless, flat. "You promised you would. You remember?"

"Yes, I remember. But I couldn't draw it then because I didn't have any paper," I said. My voice, too, was toneless and flat. "So to make up for it I gave you a little penguin charm."

"Yes, I brought it with me," he said, and held out his right hand. In his hand—which was extremely long—he held a small plastic penguin, the kind you often see attached to a cell phone strap as a good-luck charm. He dropped it on top of the glass coffee table, where it landed with a small *clunk*.

"I'm returning this. You probably need it. This little penguin will be the charm that should protect those you love. In exchange, I want you to draw my portrait."

I was perplexed. "I get it, but I've never drawn a portrait of a person without a face."

My throat was parched.

"From what I hear, you're an outstanding portrait artist. And there's a first time for everything," the faceless man said. And then he laughed. At least, I think he did. That laugh-like voice was like the empty sound of wind blowing up from deep inside a cavern.

He took off the hat that hid half of his face. Where the face should have been, there was nothing, just the slow whirl of a fog.

I stood up and retrieved a sketchbook and a soft pencil from my studio. I sat back down on the sofa, ready to draw a portrait of the man with no face. But I had no idea where to begin, or how to get started. There was only a void, and how are you supposed to give form to something that does not exist? And the milky fog that surrounded the void was continually changing shape.

"You'd better hurry," the faceless man said. "I can't stay here for long."

My heart was beating dully inside my chest. I didn't have much time. I had to hurry. But my fingers holding the pencil just hung there in midair, immobilized. It was as though everything from my wrist down into my hand were numb. There were several people I had to protect, and all I was able to do was draw pictures. Even so, there was no way I could draw him. I stared at the whirling fog. "I'm sorry, but your time's up," the man without a face said a little while later. From his faceless mouth, he let out a deep breath, like pale fog hovering over a river.

"Please wait. If you give me just a little more time—"

The man put his black hat back on, once again hiding half of his face. "One day I'll visit you again. Maybe by then you'll be able to draw me. Until then, I'll keep this penguin charm."

Then he vanished. Like a mist suddenly blown away by a freshening breeze, he vanished into thin air. All that remained was the unoccupied chair and the glass table. The penguin charm was gone from the tabletop.

It all seemed like a short dream. But I knew very well that it wasn't.

If this was a dream, then the world I'm living in itself must all be a dream.

Maybe someday I'll be able to draw a portrait of nothingness. Just like another artist was able to complete a painting titled *Killing Commendatore*. But to do so I would need time to get to that point. I would have to have time on my side.

1

IF THE SURFACE IS FOGGED UP

From May until early the following year, I lived on top of a mountain near the entrance to a narrow valley. Deep in the valley it rained constantly in the summer, but outside the valley it was usually sunny. This was due to the southwest wind that blew off the ocean. Moist clouds carried by the wind entered the valley, bringing rain as they made their way up the slopes. The house was built right on the boundary line, so often it would be sunny out in front while heavy rain fell in back. At first I found this disconcerting, but as I got used to it, it came to seem natural.

Low patches of clouds hung over the surrounding mountains. When the wind blew, these cloud fragments, like some wandering spirits from the past, drifted uncertainly along the surface of the mountains, as if in search of lost memories. The pure white rain, like fine snow, silently swirled around on the wind. Since the wind rarely let up, I could even get by in the summer without air conditioning.

The house itself was old and small, but the garden in back was spacious. Left to its own devices it was a riot of tall green weeds, and a family of cats made its home there. When a gardener came over to trim the grass, the cat family moved elsewhere. I imagine they felt too exposed. The family consisted of a striped mother cat and her three kittens. The mother was thin, with a stern look about her, as if life had dealt her a bad hand.

The house was on top of the mountain, and when I went out on the terrace and faced southwest, I could catch a glimpse of the ocean through the woods. From there the ocean was the size of water in a washbowl, a minuscule sliver of the huge Pacific. A real estate agent I know told me that even if you can see a tiny portion of the ocean like I could here, it made all the difference in the price of the land. Not that I cared about an ocean view. From far off, that slice of ocean was nothing more than a dull lump of lead. Why people insisted on having an ocean view was beyond me. I much preferred gazing at the surrounding mountains. The mountains on the opposite side of the valley were in constant flux, transforming with the seasons and the weather, and I never grew tired of these changes.

Back then my wife and I had dissolved our marriage, the divorce papers all signed and sealed, but afterward things happened and we ended up making a go of marriage one more time.

I can't explain it. The cause and effect of how this all came about eluded even those of us directly involved, but if I were to sum it up in a word, it would come down to some overly trite phrase like "we reconciled." Though the nine-month gap before the second time we married (between the dissolution of our first marriage and the beginning of our second marriage, in other words) stood there, a mouth agape like some deep canal carved out of an isthmus.

Nine months—I had no idea if this was a long period or a short period for a separation. Looking back on it later, it sometimes seemed as though it lasted forever, but then again it passed by in an instant. My impression changed depending on the day. When people photograph an object, they often put a pack of cigarettes next to it to give the viewer a sense of the object's actual size, but the pack of cigarettes next to the images in my memory expanded and contracted, depending on my mood at the time. Like the objects and events in constant flux, or perhaps in opposition to them, what should have been a fixed yardstick inside the framework of my memory seemed instead to be in perpetual motion.

Not to imply that all my memories were haphazard, expanding and contracting at will. My life was basically placid, well adjusted, and, for the most part, rational. But those nine months were different, a period of inexplicable chaos and confusion. In all senses of the word that period was the exception, a time unlike any other in my life, as though I were a swimmer in the middle of a calm sea caught up in a mysterious whirlpool that came out of nowhere.

That may be the reason why, when I think back on that time (as you guessed, these events took place some years ago), the importance, perspective, and connections between events sometimes fluctuate, and if I take my eyes off them even for a second, the sequence I apply to them is quickly supplanted by something different. Still, here I want to do my utmost, as far as I can, to set down a systematic, logical account. Maybe it will be a wasted effort, but even so I want to cling tightly to the hypothetical yardstick I've managed to fashion. Like a helpless swimmer who snatches at a scrap of wood that floats his way.

When I moved into that house, the first thing I did was buy a cheap used car. I'd basically driven my previous car into the ground and had to scrap it, so I needed to get a new one. In a suburban town, especially living alone on top of a mountain, a car was a must in order to go shopping. I went to a used Toyota dealership outside Odawara and found a great deal on a Corolla station wagon. The salesman called it powder blue, though it reminded me more of a sick person's pale complexion. It had only twenty-two thousand miles on it, but the car had been in an accident at one point so they'd drastically reduced the sticker price. I took it for a test drive, and the brakes and tires seemed good. Since I didn't plan to drive it on the highway much, I figured it would do fine.

Masahiko Amada was the one who rented the house to me. We'd been in the same class back in art school. He was two years older, and was one of the few people I got along well with, so even after we finished college we'd occasionally get together. After we graduated he gave up on being an artist and worked for an ad agency as a graphic designer. When he heard that my wife and I had split up, and that I'd left home and had nowhere to stay, he told me the house his father owned was vacant and asked if I'd like to stay there as a kind of caretaker. His father was Tomohiko Amada, a famous painter of Japanese-style paintings. His father's house (which had a painting studio) was in the mountains outside Odawara, and after the death of his wife he'd lived there comfortably by himself for about ten years. Recently, though, he'd been diagnosed with dementia, and had been put in a high-end nursing home in Izu Kogen. As a result, the house had been empty for several months.

"It's up all by itself on top of a mountain, definitely not the most convenient location, but it's a quiet place. That I guarantee for sure," Masahiko said. "The perfect environment for painting. No distractions whatsoever."

The rent was nominal.

"If the house is vacant, it'll fall apart, and I'm worried about break-ins and fires. Just having someone there all the time will be a load off my mind. I know you wouldn't feel comfortable not paying any rent, so I'll make it cheap, on one condition: that I might have to ask you to leave on short notice."

Fine by me. Everything I owned would fit in the trunk of a small car, and if he ever asked me to clear out, I could be gone the following day.

I moved into the house in early May, right after the Golden Week holidays. The house was a one-story, Western-style home, more like a cozy cottage, but certainly big enough for one person living alone. It was on top of a midsized mountain, surrounded by woods, and even Masahiko wasn't sure how far the lot extended. There were large pine trees in the back garden, with thick branches that spread out in all directions. Here and there you'd find stepping stones, and there was a splendid banana plant next to a Japanese stone lantern.

Masahiko was right about it being a quiet place. But looking back on it now, I can't say that there were "no distractions whatsoever."

During the eight months after I broke up with my wife and lived in this valley, I slept with two other women, both of whom were married. One was younger than me, the other older. Both were students in the art class I taught.

When I sensed that the timing was right, I invited them to sleep with me (something I would normally never do, since I'm fairly timid and not at all used to that sort of thing). And they didn't turn me down. I'm not sure why, but I had few qualms about asking them to sleep with me, and it seemed to make perfect sense at the time. I felt hardly a twinge of guilt at inviting my students to have sex with me. It seemed as ordinary as asking somebody you passed on the street for the time.

The first woman I slept with was in her late twenties. She was tall with large, dark eyes, a trim waist, and small breasts. A wide forehead, beautiful straight hair, her ears on the large side for her build. Maybe not exactly a beauty, but with such distinctive features that if you were an artist you'd want to draw her. (Actually I am an artist, so I did sketch her a number of times.) She had no children. Her husband taught history at a private high school, and he beat her. Unable to lash out at school, he took his frustrations out at home. He was careful to avoid her face, but when she was naked I saw all the bruises and scars. She hated me to see them and when she took off her clothes, she insisted on turning off the lights.

She had almost no interest in sex. Her vagina was never wet and penetration was painful for her. I made sure there was plenty of foreplay, and we used lubricant gel, but nothing made it better. The pain was terrible, and it wouldn't stop. Sometimes she even screamed in agony.

Even so, she wanted to have sex with me. Or at least she wasn't averse to it. Why, I wonder? Maybe she wanted to feel pain. Or was seeking the *absence* of pleasure. Or perhaps she was after some sort of self-punishment. People seek all kinds of things in their lives. There was one thing, though, that she wasn't looking for. And that was *intimacy*.

She didn't want to come to my house, or have me come to hers, so to have sex we always drove in my car to a love hotel near the shore. We'd meet up in the large parking lot of a chain restaurant, get to the hotel a little after one p.m., and leave before three. She always wore a large pair of sunglasses, even when it was cloudy or raining. One time, though, she didn't show up, and she missed art class too. That was the end of our short, uneventful affair. We slept together four, maybe five times.

The other married woman I had an affair with had a happy home life. At least it didn't seem like her family life was lacking anything. She was forty-one then (as I recall), five years older than me. She was petite, with an attractive face, and she was always well dressed. She practiced yoga every other day at a gym and had a flat, toned stomach. She drove a red Mini Cooper, a new car she'd just purchased, and on sunny days I could spot it from a distance, glinting in the sun. She had two daughters, both of whom attended a pricey private school in upscale Shonan, which the woman was a graduate of too. Her husband ran some sort of company, but I never asked her what kind of firm it was. (Naturally I didn't want to know.)

I have no idea why she didn't flatly turn down my brazen sexual overtures. Maybe at the time I had some special magnetism about me that pulled in her spirit as if (so to speak) it were a scrap of iron. Or maybe it had nothing to do with spirit or magnetism, and she'd simply been needing physical satisfaction outside marriage and I just happened to be the closest man around.

Whatever it was, I seemed able to provide it, openly, naturally, and she commenced sleeping with me without hesitation. The physical aspect of our relationship (not that there was any other aspect) went smoothly. We performed the act in an honest, pure way, the purity almost reaching the level of the abstract. It took me by surprise when I suddenly realized this, in the midst of our affair.

But at some point she must have come to her senses, since one gloomy early-winter morning, she called me and said, "I think we shouldn't meet anymore. There's no future in it." Or something to that effect. She sounded like she was reading from a script.

And she was absolutely right. Not only was there no future in our relationship, there was no real basis for it, no *there* there.

Back when I was in art school I mainly painted abstracts. Abstract art is a hard thing to define, since it covers such a wide range of works. I'm not sure how to explain the form and subject matter, but I guess my definition would be "paintings that are nonfigurative images, done in an unrestrained, free manner." I won a few awards at small exhibitions, and was even featured in some art magazines. Some of my instructors and friends praised my work and encouraged me. Not that anyone pinned his hopes on my future, but I do think I had a fair amount of talent as an artist. Most of my oil paintings were done on very large canvases and required a lot of paint, so they were expensive to create. Needless to say, the possibility of laudable people appearing, ready to purchase an unknown artist's massive painting to hang on the wall at their home, was pretty close to zero.

Since it was impossible to make a living painting what I wanted, once I graduated, I started taking commissions for portraits to make ends meet. Paintings of so-called pillars of society—presidents of companies, influential members of various institutes, Diet members, prominent figures in various locales (there were some differences in the width of these "pillars"), all painted in a figurative way. They were looking for a realistic, dignified, staid style, totally utilitarian types of paintings to be hung on the wall in a reception area or a company president's office. In other words, my job compelled me to paint paintings that ran totally counter to my artistic aims. I could add that I did it *reluctantly,* and that still wouldn't amount to any artistic arrogance on my part.

There was a small company in Yotsuya that specialized in portrait commissions, and through an introduction by one of my art school teachers, I signed an exclusive contract with them. I wasn't paid a fixed salary, but if I turned out enough portraits, I made plenty for a young, single man to live on. It was a modest lifestyle—I was able to rent a small apartment alongside the Seibu Kokubunji railway line, usually managed to afford three meals a day, would buy a bottle of inexpensive wine from time to time, and went out on the occasional date to see a movie. Several years went by, and I decided that I'd focus on portrait painting for a fixed period, and then, once I'd made enough to live on for a while, I'd return to the kind of paintings I really wanted to do. Portraits were just meant to pay the rent. I never planned to paint them forever.

But once I got into it, I discovered that painting *typical* portraits was a pretty easy job. When I was in college I'd worked part-time for a moving company, and at a convenience store, and compared to those jobs, painting portraits was, physically and emotionally, much less of a strain. Once I got the hang of it, it was just a matter of repeating the same process again and again. Before long, I was able to finish a portrait quickly. Like flying a plane on autopilot.

After I'd been rather indifferently doing this work for about a year, I learned that my portraits were gaining some acclaim. My clients were really satisfied with my work. Obviously, if customers complain about the finished portraits, then not much work will come your way, and your contract with the agency might even get terminated. Conversely, if you have a good reputation, you get more work and your fees go up with each painting. The world of portrait painting is a fairly serious profession. I was still a beginner, but I was getting more and more commissions, and could charge higher fees with each work. The agent in charge of my portfolio was impressed, and some of my clients even glowingly commented that I had a "special touch."

I couldn't figure out why the portraits were being received so well. I was less than enthusiastic, just trudging through one assignment after another. Truthfully, I can't recall the face of a single person whose portrait I painted. Still, as my ultimate goal was to become a serious artist, once I took up my brush and faced a canvas I couldn't bring myself to paint something completely worthless, no matter what type of painting it was. To do so would tarnish my sense of artistry, and show contempt for the kind of professional I was hoping to be. Even if I painted a portrait that I didn't love, at least I never felt embarrassed about the work I'd completed. You could call it professional ethics, I suppose. For me, it was just something I felt compelled to do.

One other aspect of my portrait painting was that I insisted on following my own approach. I never used the actual person as a model. When I got a commission I would meet with the client, just the two us, to talk for an hour or so. I wouldn't do any rough sketches at all. I would ask a lot of questions, and the client would respond. When and where were you born? What kind of family did you grow up in? I asked what kind of childhood they had, what school they attended, what sort of work they did, what kind of family they had now, how they had achieved their present position. Typical questions. I'd ask about their daily life and interests, too. Most people were happy, even enthusiastic, to talk about themselves. (Most likely no one else wanted to hear those things.) Sometimes the hour interview would stretch to two, even three hours.

After this I would ask to borrow five or six casual snapshots of the person, just unposed, ordinary snapshots. And occasionally I would use my own small camera and take a few close-ups from different angles. That's it.

Most clients seemed concerned. "Aren't I supposed to sit still and pose for the portrait?" they'd ask. From the outset, they were resigned to enduring a long painting process. Artists—even if no one wore those silly berets anymore—were supposed to stand, brush in hand before the canvas, brow furrowed, as the model sat there, trying to sit up straight. Perfectly still. Clients were imagining the kind of scene they'd seen a million times in movies.

Instead of answering, I would ask them, "Do you want to do it that way? Being a painter's model is hard work if you're not used to it. You have to hold the same pose for a long time, and it's boring and your shoulders will really ache. Of course, if that's how you'd like to do it, I'd be happy to oblige."

Predictably, ninety-nine percent of my clients declined. Most all of them were busy people with busy lives, or else elderly people who had retired. They all preferred, if possible, to avoid such pointless asceticism.

"Meeting you and talking together is all I need," I would say, putting them at ease. "Whether I have a live model or not won't affect the result at all. If you find you're dissatisfied with the painting, I'll be happy to do it over again."

After this I'd spend about two weeks on the portrait (though it would take several months for the paint to fully dry). What I needed was less the actual person in front of me than my vivid memories of that person. (Having the subject present, truth be told, actually interfered with my ability to complete the portrait.) These memories were three-dimensional, and all I had to do was transfer them to canvas. I seem to have been born with that sort of powerful visual memory—a special skill, you might label it—and it was a very effective tool for me as a professional portrait artist.

It was critical to feel a sense of closeness, even just a little, toward the client. That's why during our initial one-hour meeting I tried so hard to discover, as much as I could, some aspects of the client that I could respond to. Naturally, this was easier with some people than with others. There were some I'd never want to have a personal relationship with. But as a *visitor* who was with them for only a short time, in a set place, it wasn't that hard to find one or two appealing qualities. Look deep enough into any person and you will find something shining within. My job was to uncover this and, if the surface is fogged up (which was more often the case), polish it with a cloth to make it shine again. Otherwise the darker side would naturally reveal itself in the portrait.

So, before I knew it, I had become an artist who specialized in portraits. And I became fairly known within this particular, rather narrow field. When I got married, I ended my exclusive contract with the company in Yotsuya, became independent, and—through an agency specializing in the art business—received individual commissions to do portraits for even higher fees. The agent in charge, a capable, ambitious person, was ten years older than me. He encouraged me to be independent and take my work even more seriously. After that point, I painted portraits of numerous people (mostly in the financial and political worlds, celebrities in some cases, though I'd never heard of most of them) and made a decent income. Not that I became a great authority in the field or anything. The world of portraiture is totally different from that of the *artistic* art world. And different from photography too. There are a lot of photographers specializing in portraits who are held in high esteem and whose names are well known, but you don't find that with portrait artists. Very seldom is one of our works seen in the world at large. They aren't featured in art magazines or hung in galleries. Instead they're hung in reception areas somewhere, forgotten, gathering dust. If anyone happens to look at those paintings carefully (someone with time on his hands), they still aren't about to ask about the artist's name.

Occasionally I've thought of myself as a high-priced artistic prostitute. I use all the techniques at my disposal, as conscientiously as I can, in order to satisfy my client. I possess that sort of talent. I'm a professional, but that said, it doesn't mean I mechanically follow a set procedure. I do put a certain amount of feeling into my work. My fees aren't cheap, but my clients all pay without any complaints. The sort of people I take on as clients aren't the kind to worry about price. People learned of my skill through word of mouth, and I had an unending line of clients, my appointment book always jam-packed. But inside me I felt no desire whatsoever. Not a shred.

I hadn't become that sort of artist, or that type of person, because I'd wanted to. Carried along by circumstances, I'd given up doing paintings for myself. I'd married and needed to make a stable income, but that wasn't the only reason. Honestly, I'd already lost the desire to paint for myself. I might have been using marriage as an excuse. I wasn't young anymore, and something—like a flame burning inside me—was steadily fading away. The feeling of that flame warming me from within was receding ever further.

I should have washed my hands of that person I'd become. I should have stood up and done something about it. But I kept putting it off. And before I got around to it, the one who gave up on it all was my wife. I was thirty-six at the time.

2

THEY MIGHT ALL GO TO THE MOON

I am very sorry, but I don't think I can live with you anymore," my wife said in a quiet voice. Then she was silent for a long while.

This announcement took me by complete surprise. It was so unexpected I didn't know how to respond, and I waited for her to go on. What she'd say next wasn't going to be very upbeat—I was certain about that—but waiting for her to continue was the most I could manage.

We were seated across from each other at the kitchen table. A Sunday afternoon in the middle of March. Our sixth wedding anniversary was the middle of the following month. A cold rain had been falling since morning. The first thing I did when I heard her news was turn toward the window and check out the rain. It was a quiet, gentle rain, with hardly any wind. Still, it was the kind of rain that carried with it a chill that slowly but surely seeped into the skin. Cold like this meant that spring was still a long ways off. The orangish Tokyo Tower was visible through the misty rain. The sky was bereft of birds. All of them must have quietly sought shelter.

"I don't want you to ask me why. Can you do that?" my wife asked.

I shook my head slightly. Neither yes nor no. I had no idea what to say, and just reflexively shook my head.

She had on a thin, light purple sweater with a wide neckline. The soft strap of her white camisole was visible beside her collarbone. It looked like some special kind of pasta used in some specific recipe.

Finally, I was able to speak. "I do have one question, though," I said, gazing blankly at that strap. My voice was stiff, dry, and flat.

"I'll answer, if I can."

"Is this my fault?"

She thought this over. Then, like someone who has been underwater for a long time, she finally broke through to the surface and took a deep, slow breath.

"Not directly, no."

"Not *directly*?"

"I don't think so."

I considered the subtle tone of her voice. Like checking the weight of an egg in my palm. "Meaning that I am, *in*directly?"

She didn't answer.

"A few days ago, just before dawn, I had a dream," she said instead. "A very realistic dream, the kind where you can't distinguish between what is real and what's in your mind. And when I woke up that's what I thought. I was certain of it, I mean. That I can't live with you anymore."

"What kind of dream was it?"

She shook her head. "I'm sorry, but I can't tell you that here."

"Because dreams are personal?"

"I suppose."

"Was I in the dream?" I asked.

"No, you weren't. So in that sense, too, it's not your fault."

Just to make sure I got it all, I summarized what she'd just said. When I don't know what to say I have a habit of summarizing. (A habit that, obviously, can be really irritating.)

"So, a few days ago you had a very realistic dream. And when you woke up you were certain you can't live with me anymore. But you can't tell me what the dream was about, since dreams are personal. Did I get that right?"

She nodded. "Yes. That's about the size of it."

"But that doesn't explain a thing."

She rested her hands on the tabletop, staring down at the inside of her coffee cup, as if an oracle was floating there and she was deciphering the message. From the look in her eyes the words must have been very symbolic and ambiguous.

My wife puts great stock in dreams. She often makes decisions based on dreams she had, or changes her decisions accordingly. But no matter how crucial you think dreams can be, you can't just reduce six years of marriage to nothing because of one vivid dream, no matter how memorable.

"The dream was just a trigger, that's all," she said, as if reading my mind. "Having that dream made lots of things clear for me."

"If you pull a trigger, a bullet will come out."

"Excuse me?"

"A trigger is a critical part of a gun. 'Just a trigger' isn't the right expression."

She stared at me silently, as if she couldn't understand what I was getting at. I don't blame her. I couldn't understand it myself.

"Are you seeing someone else?" I asked.

She nodded.

"And you're sleeping with him?"

"Yes, and I feel bad about it."

Maybe I should have asked her who it was, and when it had started. But I didn't want to know. I didn't want to think about those things. So I gazed again outside the window at the falling rain. Why hadn't I noticed all this before?

"This was just one element among many," my wife said.

I looked around the room. I'd lived there a long time, and it should have been familiar, but it had now transformed into a scene from a remote, strange land.

Just one element?

What does that mean, just one? I gave it some thought. She was having sex with some man other than me. But that was "just one element." Then what were all the others?

"I'll move out in a few days," my wife said. "So you don't need to do anything. I'm responsible, so I should be the one who leaves."

"You already decided where you're going to go?"

She didn't answer, but seemed to have already decided on a place. She must have made all kinds of preparations before bringing this up with me. When I realized this, I felt helpless, as if I'd lost my footing in the darkness. Things had been steadily moving forward, and I'd been totally oblivious.

"I'll get the divorce procedures going as quickly as I can," my wife said, "and I'd like you to be responsive. I'm being selfish, I know."

I turned from the rain and gazed at her. And once again it struck me. We'd lived under the same roof for six years, yet I knew next to nothing about this woman. In the same way that people stare up at the sky to see the moon every night, yet understand next to nothing about it.

"I have one request," I ventured. "If you'll grant me this, I'll do whatever you say. And I'll sign the divorce papers."

"What is it?"

"That *I'm* the one who leaves here. And I do it today. I'd like you to stay behind."

"Today?" she asked, surprised.

"The sooner the better, right?"

She thought it over. "If that's what you want," she said.

"It is, and that's *all* I want."

Those were my honest feelings. As long as I wasn't left behind alone in this wretched, cruel place, in the cold March rain, I didn't care what happened.

"And I'll take the car with me. Are you okay with that?"

I really didn't need to ask. The car was an old, stick-shift model a friend of mine had let me have for next to nothing back before I got married. It had well over sixty thousand miles on it. And besides, my wife didn't even have a driver's license.

"I'll come back later to get my painting materials and clothes and things. Does that work for you?"

"Sure, that's fine. By 'later,' how much later do you mean?"

"I have no idea," I said. I couldn't wrap my mind around the future. There was barely any ground left under my feet. Just remaining upright was all I could manage.

"I might not stay here all that long," my wife said, sounding reluctant.

"Everyone might go to the moon," I said.

She seemed not to have caught it. "Sorry?"

"Nothing. It's not important."

• • •

By seven that evening I'd stuffed my belongings into an oversized gym bag and thrown that into the trunk of my red Peugeot 205. Some changes of clothes, toiletries, a few books and diaries. A simple camping set I had always had for hiking. Sketchbooks and a set of drawing pencils. Other than these few items, I had no idea what else to take. It's okay, I told myself, if I need anything I can buy it somewhere. While I packed the gym bag and went in and out of the apartment, she was still seated at the kitchen table. The coffee cup was still on top of the table, and she continued to stare inside it . . .

"I have a request, too," she said. "Even if we break up like this, can we still be friends?"

I couldn't grasp what she was trying to say. I'd finished tugging on my shoes, had shouldered the bag, and stood, one hand on the doorknob, to stare at her.

"Be friends?"

"I'd like to meet and talk sometimes. If possible, I mean."

I still couldn't understand what she meant. Be friends? Meet and talk sometimes? What would we talk about? It's like she'd posed a riddle. What could she be trying to convey to me? That she didn't have any bad feelings toward me? Was that it?

"I'm not sure about that," I said. I couldn't think of anything more to say. If I'd stood there a whole week, running this through my head, I doubt I'd have found anything more to add. So I opened the door and stepped outside.

When I left the apartment I hadn't given any thought to what I was wearing. If I'd had on a bathrobe over pajamas, I probably wouldn't have noticed. Later on, when I looked at myself in a full-length mirror in a restroom at a drive-in, I saw I had on a sweater that I favored while working, a gaudy orange down jacket, jeans, and work boots. And an old knit cap. There were white paint stains here and there on the frayed, green, round-neck sweater. The only new item I had on were the jeans, their bright blue too conspicuous. A random collection of clothes, but not too peculiar. My one regret was not having brought a scarf.

When I pulled the car out from the parking lot underneath the apartment building, the cold March rain was still falling. The Peugeot's wipers sounded like an old man's raspy, hoarse cough.

I had no clue where to go, so for a while I drove aimlessly around Tokyo. At the intersection at Nishi Azabu, I drove down Gaien Boulevard toward Aoyama, turned right at Aoyama Sanchome toward Akasaka, and after a few more turns found myself in Yotsuya. I stopped at a gas station and filled up the tank. I had them check the oil and tire pressure for me, and top off the windshield washer fluid. I might be in for a very long trip. For all I knew I might even go all the way to the moon.

I paid with my credit card, and headed down the road again. A rainy Sunday night, not much traffic. I switched on an FM station, but it was all pointless chatter, a cacophony of shrill voices. Sheryl Crow's first CD was in the CD player, and I listened to the first three songs and then turned it off.

I suddenly realized I was driving down Mejiro Boulevard. It took a while before I could figure out which direction I was going—from Waseda toward Nerima. The silence got to me and I turned on the CD again and listened to Sheryl Crow for a few more songs. And then switched it off again. The silence was too quiet, the music too noisy. Though silence was preferable, a little. The only thing that reached me was the scrape of the worn-out wipers, the endless hiss of the tires on the wet pavement.

In the midst of that silence I imagined my wife in the arms of another man.

I should have picked up on that, at least, a long time ago. *So how come I didn't think of it?* We hadn't had sex for months. Even when I tried to get her to, she'd come up with all kinds of reasons to turn me down. Actually, I think she'd lost interest in having sex for some time before that. But I'd figured it was just a stage. She must be tired from working every day, and wasn't feeling up to it. But now I knew she was sleeping with another man. When had that started? I searched my memory. Probably four or five months ago, would be my guess. Four or five months ago would make it October or November.

But for the life of me I couldn't recall what had happened back in

October or November. I mean, I could barely recall what had happened yesterday.

I paid attention to the road—so as not to run any red lights, or get too close to the car in front of me—and mentally reviewed what had happened last fall. I thought so hard about it that it felt like the core of my brain was going to overheat. My right hand unconsciously changed gears to adjust to the flow of traffic. My left foot stepped on the clutch in time with this. I'd never been so happy that my car was a stick shift. Besides mulling over my wife's affair, it gave me something to do to keep my hands and feet busy.

So what had happened back in October or November?

An autumn evening. I'm picturing my wife on a large bed, and some man undressing her. I thought of the straps on her white camisole. And the pink nipples that lay underneath. I didn't want to visualize all this, but once one image came to me, I couldn't stop. I sighed, and pulled into the parking lot of a drive-in restaurant. I rolled down the driver's-side window, took a deep breath of the damp air outside, and slowly got my heart rate back to normal. I stepped out of the car. With my knit cap on but no umbrella I made my way through the fine drizzle and went inside the restaurant. I sat down in a booth in the back.

The restaurant was nearly empty. A waitress came over and I ordered coffee and a ham-and-cheese sandwich. As I drank the coffee I closed my eyes and calmed down. I tried my best to erase the image of my wife and another man in bed. But the vision wouldn't leave me.

I went to the restroom, gave my hands a good scrub, and checked myself in the mirror over the sink. My eyes looked smaller than usual, and bloodshot, like a woodland animal slowly fading away from famine, gaunt and afraid. I wiped my hands and face with a thick handkerchief, then studied myself in the full-length mirror on the wall. What I saw there was an exhausted thirty-six-year-old man in a shabby, paint-spattered sweater.

As I gazed at my reflection I wondered, *Where am I headed?* Before that, though, the question was *Where have I come to?* Where *is* this place? No, before that even I needed to ask, *Who the hell* am *I?*

As I stared at myself in the mirror, I thought about what it would be like to paint my own portrait. Say I were to try, what sort of self would

I end up painting? Would I be able to find even a shred of affection for myself? Would I be able to discover even one thing shining within me?

These questions unanswered, I returned to my seat. When I finished my coffee the waitress came over and refilled my cup. I asked her for a paper bag and put the untouched sandwich in it. I should be hungry later on. But right now I didn't want to eat anything.

I left the drive-in, and drove down the road until I saw the sign for the entrance to the Kan-Etsu Expressway. I decided to get on the highway and head north. I had no idea what lay north, but somehow I got the sense that heading north was better than going south. I wanted to go somewhere cold and clean. More important than north or south, however, was getting away from this city.

I opened the glove compartment and found five or six CDs inside. One of them was a performance of Mendelssohn's Octet by I Musici. My wife liked to listen to it when we went on drives. An unusual setup with a double string quartet, but a beautiful melody. Mendelssohn was only sixteen when he composed the piece. My wife told me this. A child prodigy.

What were you doing when you were sixteen?

I called up the past. When I was sixteen I was crazy over a girl in my class.

Did you go out with her?

No, I barely said a word to her. I just looked at her from a distance. I wasn't brave enough to speak up. When I went home I used to sketch her. I did quite a few drawings.

So you've done the same thing from way back when, my wife said, laughing.

True, I've done the same thing from way back when.

True, I've done the same thing from way back when, I said, mentally repeating the words I'd spoken to her.

I took the Sheryl Crow CD out of the player and slipped in an MJQ album. *Pyramid.* I listened to Milt Jackson's pleasant, bluesy solo as I headed down the highway toward the north. I'd make the occasional stop at a service area, take a long piss, and drink a couple of cups of hot black coffee, but other than that I drove all night. I drove in the slow lane, only speeding up to pass trucks. I didn't feel sleepy, strangely enough. It felt like I'd never be sleepy again in my whole life. And just before dawn I reached the Japan Sea coast.

In Niigata I turned right and drove north along the coast, from Yamagata to Akita Prefecture, then through Aomori into Hokkaido. I didn't take any highways, and drove leisurely down back roads. In all senses of the word I was in no hurry. When night came I'd check in to a cheap business hotel or run-down Japanese inn, flop down on the narrow bed, and sleep. Thankfully I can fall asleep right away just about anywhere, in any type of bed.

On the morning of the second day, near Murakami City, I phoned my agent and told him I wouldn't be able to do any portrait painting for a while. I had a few commissions I was in the middle of, but wasn't in a place where I could do any work.

"That's a problem, since you've already accepted the commissions," the agent said, his tone harsh.

I apologized. "There's nothing I can do about it. Could you tell the clients I got in a car accident or something? There are other artists who could take over, I'm sure."

My agent was silent for a time. Up till now I'd never missed a deadline. He knew how seriously I took my work.

"Something came up, and I'll be away from Tokyo for a while. I'm sorry, but in the meantime I can't do any painting."

"How long is 'for a while'?"

I couldn't answer. I switched off the cell phone, found a nearby river, parked my car on the bridge over it, and tossed that small communication device into the water. I felt sorry toward him, but I had to get him to give up on me. Have him think I'd gone to the moon or something.

In Akita I stopped at a bank, withdrew some cash, and checked my balance. There was still a decent amount in my personal account. Credit card payments were automatically deducted . . . For the time being I had enough to continue my trip. I wasn't using that much each day. Gas money, nights in business hotels, that's about the size of it.

At an outlet store outside Hakodate I purchased a simple tent and a sleeping bag. Hokkaido in early spring was still cold, so I also bought some thermal underwear. Whenever I arrived in a place, I looked for an open campground, set up my tent, and slept there, in order to save money. Hard snow still covered the ground and the nights were cold, but because I'd been spending nights in cramped, stuffy business hotel rooms I felt relieved and free inside the tent. Hard ground below, the endless sky above. Countless stars sparkling in the sky. That and nothing else.

For the next three weeks I wandered all over Hokkaido in my Peugeot. April came, but it looked like the snow wasn't going to melt anytime soon. Still, the color of the sky visibly changed, and plants began to bud. Whenever I ran across a small town with a hot springs I'd stay in an inn there, enjoy the bath, wash my hair and shave, and have a decent meal. Even so, when I weighed myself I found I'd lost eleven pounds.

I didn't read any newspapers or watch TV. My car radio had started acting up from the time I arrived in Hokkaido, and soon I couldn't hear anything on it at all. I had no clue what was happening in the world at large, and didn't care to know. I stopped once in Tomakomai and did laundry at a laundromat. While I waited for the clothes to finish I went to a nearby barbershop and got a haircut and shave. At the shop I saw the NHK news on TV for the first time in a long while. I say "saw," but even with my eyes closed I could hear the announcer's voice, whether I wanted to or not. From start to finish, though, the news had nothing to do with me, like events happening on some other planet. Or else some fake stories somebody had cooked up for the fun of it.

The only news story that hit home was a report on a seventy-three-year-old man in Hokkaido who'd gone mushroom gathering in the mountains and been attacked and killed by a bear. When bears wake from hibernation, the announcer said, they're hungry and irritable and very dangerous. I slept in my tent sometimes, and when the mood struck me I took walks in the woods, so it wouldn't have been strange if I were the one who'd been attacked. It *just happened* to be that old man who got attacked, and not me. But even hearing that news I felt no sympathy for the old man who'd been so cruelly butchered by a bear. No empathy came to me for the pain and fear and shock he must have experienced. I felt more sympathy for the bear. No, "sympathy" isn't the right word, I thought. It's more like a feeling of complicity.

Something's wrong with me, I thought as I stared at myself in the mirror. I said this aloud, in a small voice. It's like something's messed up with my brain. *Better not get near anyone.* For the time being, at least.

Toward the latter half of April I was sick and tired of the cold, so I bid Hokkaido farewell and crossed back over to the mainland. I drove from Aomori to Iwate, from Iwate to Miyagi, along the Pacific coast. The weather got more springlike the farther south I drove. And all the while I thought about my wife. About her, and the anonymous hands caressing her this very moment in bed somewhere. I didn't want to think about it, but I couldn't think of anything else.

The first time I met my wife was just before I turned thirty. She was three years younger than me. She worked in a small architecture firm in Yotsuya, held a second-level architect certificate, and was a former high school classmate of the girl I was dating at the time. She had straight hair, wore little makeup, and had rather calm-looking features (her personality was not all that calm, but I only understood that later on). My girlfriend and I were on a date and happened to run into her at a restaurant. We were introduced, and I basically fell for her right then and there.

She wasn't exactly a standout in terms of looks. There wasn't anything at all wrong with her appearance, but neither was there anything about her that would turn any heads. She had long eyelashes, a thin nose, was on the small side, and her hair, which fell to her shoulder blades, was beautifully styled. (She was very particular about her hair.) On the right side of her full lips was a small mole, which moved in marvelous ways whenever her expression changed. It lent her a slightly sensual air, but again this was only if you paid close attention. Most people would see the girl I was going out with at the time as far more beautiful. But even so, one look was all it took for me to fall for her, like I'd been struck by lightning. Why? I wondered. It took a few weeks for me to figure out the reason. But then it suddenly hit me. She reminded me of my younger sister, who had died. Reminded me very clearly of her.

Not that they looked alike on the outside. If you were to compare photos of the two of them, most people would be hard-pressed to find any resemblance. Which is why at first I didn't see the connection either. It wasn't anything specific about her looks that made me remember my younger sister, but the way her expression changed, especially the way her eyes moved and sparkled, was amazingly like my sister's. It was like magic or something had brought back the past, right before my very eyes.

My sister had also been three years younger than me, and had a congenital heart valve problem. She'd had numerous operations when she was little, and though they were successful, there were lingering aftereffects. Her doctors had no idea if those aftereffects would get better on their own, or cause some life-threatening issues. In the end, she died when I was fifteen. She'd just entered junior high. All her short life she'd battled those genetic defects, but never failed to be anything other than positive and upbeat. Until the very end she never grumbled or complained, and always made detailed plans for the future. That she would die so young was not something she factored into her plans. She was naturally bright, always with outstanding grades (a lot better a child than I was). She had a strong will, and always stuck to whatever she decided to do, no matter what. If she and I ever quarreled—a pretty rare occurrence—I always gave in. At the end she was terribly thin and drawn, yet her eyes remained animated, and she was still full of life.

It was my wife's eyes, too, that drew me to her. *Something* I could see deep in them. When I first saw those eyes, they jolted me. Not that I was thinking that by making her mine I could restore my dead sister or anything. Even if I'd wanted to, I could imagine the only thing that would lead to was despair. What I wanted, or needed, was the spark of that positive will. That definite source of warmth needed to live. It was something I knew very well, but that was, most likely, missing in me.

I managed to get her contact info, and asked her on a date. She was surprised, of course, and hesitated. I was, after all, her friend's boyfriend. But I kept at it. I just want to see you, and talk, I told her. Just meet and talk, that's all. I'm not looking for anything else. We had dinner in a quiet restaurant, and talked about all kinds of things. Our conversation was a little nervous and awkward at first, but then became more animated. There was so much I wanted to know about her, and I had plenty to talk about. I found out that her birthday and my sister's were only three days apart.

"Do you mind if I sketch you?" I asked.

"Right here?" she asked, glancing around. We were seated at the restaurant, and had just ordered dessert.

"I'll finish before they're back with dessert," I said.

"Then I guess I don't mind," she replied doubtfully.

I took out the small sketchbook I always carried with me, and quickly sketched her face with a 2B pencil. As promised, I finished before our desserts arrived. The important part was, of course, her eyes. That's what I wanted to draw most. Back within those eyes there was a deep world, a world beyond time.

I showed her the sketch, and she seemed to like it.

"It's very full of life."

"That's because *you* are," I said.

She gazed for a long time at the sketch, apparently taken with it. As if she were seeing a self she hadn't known before.

"If you like it, I'll give it to you."

"I can have it?" she said.

"Of course. It's just a quick sketch."

"Thank you."

After this we went on more dates, and eventually became lovers. It all happened so naturally. My girlfriend, though, was shocked that her friend stole me away. She was probably thinking that we might get married. So of course she was upset (though I doubt I ever would have married her). My wife, too, was going out with someone else at the time, and their breakup wasn't easy either. There were other obstacles to overcome, but the upshot was that half a year later we were married. We had a small party with a handful of close friends to celebrate, and settled into a condo in Hiroo. Her uncle owned the condo and gave us a good deal on rent. I used one small room as my studio and focused on my portrait work. This was no longer just a temporary job. Now that I was married I needed a steady income, and other than portrait painting I had no means of earning a decent living. My wife commuted from our place by subway to the architecture firm in Yotsuya. And it sort of naturally came about that I was the one who took care of everyday housework, which I didn't mind at all. I never minded doing housework, and found it a nice break from painting. At any rate it was far more pleasant to do housework than commute every day to a job and be forced to do work behind a desk.

I think for both of us our first few years of marriage were calm and fulfilling. Before long we settled into a pleasant daily rhythm. On weekends and holidays I'd take a break from painting and we'd go out. Sometimes to an art exhibition, sometimes hiking outside the city. At other times we'd just wander around town. We had intimate talks, and for both of us it was important to regularly update each other. We spoke honestly, and openly, about what was going on in our lives, exchanging opinions, sharing feelings.

For me, though, there was one thing I never opened up about to her: the fact that her eyes reminded me so much of my sister who'd died at twelve, and that that was the main reason I'd been attracted to her. Without those eyes I probably never would have tried to win her over as eagerly as I did. But I felt it was better not to tell her that, and until the very end I didn't. That was the sole secret I kept from her. What secrets she may have kept from me—and I imagine there were some—I have no idea.

My wife's name was Yuzu, the name of the citrus fruit used in cooking. Sometimes when we were in bed I'd call her Sudachi, a similar type of fruit, as a joke. I'd whisper this in her ear. She'd always laugh, but it upset her all the same.

"I'm not Sudachi, but Yuzu. They're similar but not the same," she'd insist.

When did things start to go south for us? As I drove on, from one roadside restaurant to another, one business hotel to another, randomly moving from point A to point B, I thought about this. But I couldn't pinpoint where things had begun to go wrong. For a long time I was sure we were doing fine. Of course, like many couples, we had some issues and disagreements. Our main issue was whether or not to have children. But we still had time before we had to make a final decision. Other than that one problem (one we could postpone for the time being), we had a basically healthy marriage, on both an emotional and physical level. I was sure of that.

Why had I been so optimistic? Or so stupid? It's like I'd been born with a blind spot, and was always missing something. And what I missed was always the most important thing of all.

In the mornings, after I saw my wife off to work, I'd focus on my painting, then after lunch would take a walk around the neighborhood, do some shopping while I was at it, and then get things ready for dinner. Two or three times a week I'd go swimming in a nearby sports club. When my wife got back we'd have a beer or some wine together. If she called me saying she had to work overtime and would grab something near the office, I'd sit by myself and have a simple dinner alone. Our six years together were mostly a repeat of those kinds of days. And I was basically okay with that.

Things were busy at the architecture firm, and she often had to work overtime. I gradually had to eat dinner alone more often. Sometimes she wouldn't get back until nearly midnight. "Things have gotten so hectic at work," she'd explain. One of her colleagues suddenly changed jobs, she said, and she had to pick up the slack. The firm was reluctant to hire new staff. Whenever she came home late, she was exhausted and would just take a shower and go to sleep. So the number of times we had sex went way down. Sometimes she even had to go in on days off, too, to finish her work. Of course I believed her. There wasn't any reason not to.

But maybe she wasn't working overtime at all. While I was eating dinner alone at home, she may have been enjoying some intimate time in a hotel bed with a new lover.

My wife was outgoing. She seemed quiet and gentle but was sharp and quick-witted, and needed situations where she could be more social and gregarious. And I wasn't able to provide those. So Yuzu went out to eat a lot with women friends (she had lots of friends) and would go out drinking with work colleagues (she could hold her liquor better than me). And I never complained about her going out on her own and enjoying herself. In fact I might have encouraged it.

When I think about it, my younger sister and I had the same kind of relationship. I've always been more of a stay-at-home type, and when I got back from school I'd hole up in my room to read or draw. My sister was much more sociable and outgoing. So our everyday interests and activities didn't overlap much. But we understood each other well, and valued each other's special qualities. It might have been pretty unusual for an older brother and younger sister the ages we were, but we talked over lots of things together. Summer or winter, we'd climb up to the balcony upstairs where we hung our laundry, and talk forever. We loved to share funny stories, and often had each other in stitches.

I'm not saying that's the reason why, but I felt secure about the relationship my wife and I had. I accepted my role in our marriage—as the silent, auxiliary partner—as natural, self-evident even. But maybe Yuzu didn't. There must have been aspects of our marriage that dissatisfied her. She and my sister were, after all, different people with different personalities. And of course, I wasn't a teenage boy anymore.

By May I was getting tired of driving day after day. And sick of the same thoughts looping endlessly around in my head. The same questions spun around in my brain, with no answers in sight. Sitting all day in the driver's seat had given me a backache, as well. A Peugeot 205 is an economy car, and the seats weren't exactly high quality, the suspension noticeably worn out. All the road glare I'd stared at for hours was giving me chronic eyestrain. I realized I'd been driving pretty much nonstop for over a month and half, restlessly moving from one spot to another as if something were chasing me.

I ran across a small, rustic therapeutic hot springs in the mountains near the border between Miyagi and Iwate, and decided to take a break. An obscure hot springs tucked away deep in a valley, with a small inn that locals would stay in for days to rest and recuperate. The room rate was cheap, and there was a communal kitchen where you could cook simple meals. I enjoyed soaking in the baths and sleeping as much as I wanted. I sprawled on the tatami, read, and recovered from the exhaustion of all that driving. When I got tired of reading I'd take out my sketchbook and draw. It had been a long time since I'd felt like drawing. I started off sketching flowers and trees in the garden, then drew the rabbits they kept there. Just rough pencil sketches, but people were impressed. Some asked me to draw their portraits. Fellow lodgers, and people who worked at the inn. People just passing through my life, people I'd never see again. And if they asked, I'd give them the sketches.

Time to get back to Tokyo, I told myself. Going on like this would get me nowhere. And I wanted to paint again. Not commissioned portraits, or rough sketches, but paintings I could really concentrate on, and undertake for myself. Whether this would work out or not I had no clue, but it was time to take the first step.

I'd planned to drive my Peugeot across the Tohoku region and return to Tokyo, but just before Iwaki, along Highway 6, my car breathed its last. There was a crack in the fuel line and the car wouldn't start. I'd done hardly any maintenance on the car up till then, so I couldn't complain when it gave out. The one lucky thing was that the car gave up the ghost right near a garage where a friendly mechanic worked. It was hard to get parts for an old Peugeot in a place like that, and would take time. Even if we repair it, the mechanic told me, it's likely something else will soon go wrong. The fan belts looked sketchy, the brake pads were ready to go, and the suspension was nearly shot. "My advice? Put it out of its misery," he said. The car had been with me for a month and a half on the road, and now had nearly seventy-five thousand miles on the odometer. It was sad to say goodbye to the Peugeot, but I had to leave it behind. It felt like the car had died in my stead.

To thank him for disposing of the car for me, I gave the mechanic my tent, sleeping bag, and camping equipment. I made one last sketch of the Peugeot, and then, shouldering my gym bag, boarded the Joban Line and went back to Tokyo. From the station I called Masahiko Amada and explained my situation. My marriage fell apart and I went on a trip for a while, I told him, but now I'm back in Tokyo. Do you know of any place I could stay? I asked.

I do know of a good place, he said. It's the house my father lived in for a long time by himself. He's in a nursing home in Izu Kogen, and the house has been unoccupied for a time. It's furnished and has everything you'd need, so you don't have to get anything. It's not exactly a convenient location, but the phone works. If that sounds good, you should try it out.

That's perfect, I told him. I couldn't have asked for more.

And so my new life, in a new place, began.

3

JUST A PHYSICAL REFLECTION

A few days after I'd settled into my new mountaintop house outside Odawara, I got in touch with my wife. I had to call five times before I finally got through. Her job always kept her busy, and apparently she was still getting home late. Or maybe she was with someone. Not that that was my business anymore.

"Where are you now?" Yuzu asked me.

"I've moved into the Amadas' house in Odawara," I said. Briefly I explained how I came to live there.

"I called your cell phone many times," Yuzu said.

"I don't have the cell phone anymore," I said. That phone might have washed into the Japan Sea by then. "I'm calling because I'd like to go pick up the rest of my things. Does that work for you?"

"You still have the key?"

"I do," I said. I'd considered tossing the key into the river, too, but thought better of it since she might want it back. "But you don't mind if I go into the apartment when you're not there?"

"It's your house too. So of course it's okay," she said. "But where have you been all this time?"

Traveling, I told her. I told her how I'd been driving alone, going from one cold place to the next. How the car had finally given out.

"But you're okay, right?"

"I'm alive," I said. "The car was the one that died."

Yuzu was silent for a while. And then she spoke. "I had a dream the other day with you in it."

I didn't ask what kind of dream. I didn't really care to know about me appearing in her dream. She didn't say any more about it.

"I'll leave the key when I go," I said.

"Either way's fine with me. Just do what you like."

"I'll put it in your mailbox when I leave," I said.

There was a short pause before she spoke.

"Do you remember how you sketched my face on our first date?"

"I do."

"I take it out sometimes and look at it. It's really well done. I feel like I'm looking at my real self."

"Your real self?"

"Right."

"But don't you see your face every morning in the mirror?"

"That's different," Yuzu said. "My self in the mirror is just a physical reflection."

After I hung up I went to the bathroom and looked at my face in the mirror. I hadn't looked at myself straight on like that for ages. My self in the mirror is just a physical reflection, she'd said. But to me my face in the mirror looked like a virtual fragment of my self that had been split in two. The self there was the one I *hadn't chosen*. It wasn't even a physical reflection.

In the afternoon two days later I drove my Corolla station wagon to the apartment in Hiroo, and gathered my possessions. It had been raining since morning that day, too. The underground parking lot beneath the building had its usual rainy-day odor.

I took the elevator upstairs and unlocked the door, and when I went inside for the first time in nearly two months I felt like an intruder. I'd lived there almost six years and knew every inch of the place. But I no longer was part of this scene. Dishes were stacked up in the kitchen, all dishes she had used. Laundry was drying in the bathroom, all her clothes. Inside the fridge it was all food I'd never seen before. Most were ready-made food. The milk and orange juice were different brands from what I bought. The freezer was packed with frozen food. I never bought frozen food. A lot of changes in the two months I'd been away.

I was struck by a strong urge to wash the dishes stacked up in the sink, bring in the laundry drying and fold it (and iron it if I could), and neatly rearrange the food in the fridge. But I did none of this. This was someone else's house now. I shouldn't poke my nose in where I didn't belong.

My painting materials were the bulkiest possessions I had. I tossed my easel, canvas, brushes, and paints into a large cardboard box. Then turned to my clothes. I've never been one to need a lot of clothes. I don't mind wearing the same clothes all the time. I don't own a suit or necktie. Other than a thick winter coat, it all fit into one suitcase.

A few books I hadn't read yet, and about a dozen CDs. My favorite coffee cup. Swimsuit, and goggles, and swim cap. That was about all I felt I needed. Even those I could get along without if need be.

In the bathroom my toothbrush and shaving kit were still there, as well as my lotion, sunscreen, and hair tonic. An unopened box of condoms, too. But I didn't feel like taking all that miscellaneous stuff to my new place. She could just get rid of it.

I packed my belongings in the trunk of the car, went back to the kitchen, and boiled water in the kettle. I made tea with a tea bag, and sat at the table and drank it. I figured she wouldn't mind. The room was perfectly still. The silence lent a faint weight to the air. As though I were sitting alone, at the bottom of the sea.

All told, I was there by myself in the apartment for about a half hour. No one came to visit, and the phone didn't ring. The thermostat on the fridge turned off once, then turned back on once. In the midst of the silence I perked up my ears, probing what I sensed in the apartment, as if measuring the depths of the ocean with a sinker. No matter how you looked at it, it was an apartment occupied by a woman living alone. Someone busy at work who had next to no time to do any housework. Someone who took care of any errands on the weekends when she had free time. A quick visual sweep of the place showed that everything there was hers. No evidence of anyone else (hardly any evidence of me anymore, either). No man was stopping by here. That's the impression I got. They must have seen each other elsewhere.

I can't explain it well, but while I was in the apartment I felt like I was being watched. Like someone was observing me through a hidden camera. But that couldn't be. My wife is a major klutz when it comes to equipment. She can't even change the batteries in a remote control. No way could she do something as clever as setting up and operating a surveillance camera. It was just me, on edge.

Even so, while I was in the apartment I acted as if every single action of mine was being recorded. I did nothing extra, nothing untoward. I didn't open Yuzu's desk drawer to see what was inside. I knew that in the back of one of the drawers of her wardrobe, where she had her stockings, she kept a small diary and some important letters, but I didn't touch them. I knew the password for her laptop (assuming she hadn't changed it), but didn't even open it. None of this had anything to do with me anymore. I washed the cup I'd drunk tea in, dried it with a cloth, put it back on the shelf, and turned off the lights. I went over to the window and gazed at the falling rain for a while. The orangish Tokyo Tower loomed up faintly in the distance. Then I dropped the key in the mailbox and drove back to Odawara. The trip was only an hour and a half, but it felt like I'd taken a day trip to a far-off foreign land.

The next day I called my agent. I'm back in Tokyo, I told him, and I'm really sorry, but I don't plan to do any more portrait painting.

"You're never going to do any more portraits? Is that what you're telling me?"

"Most likely," I said.

He didn't say much. No complaints, nothing in the way of advice. He knew that once I said something, I didn't back down.

"If you ever find yourself wanting to do this work again, call me anytime," he said at the end. "I'd welcome it."

"Thank you," I said.

"Maybe it isn't my place to say this, but how are you planning to make a living?"

"I haven't decided," I admitted. "I'm by myself, so I don't need much to live on, and I've got a bit of savings."

"Will you still paint?"

"Probably. There isn't much else I know how to do."

"I hope it works out."

"Thanks," I said once more. And tagged on a question that had just occurred to me. "Is there anything I should make sure to keep in mind?"

"Something you should make sure to keep in mind?"

"In other words—how should I put it—any advice from a pro?"

He thought it over. "You're the type of guy who takes longer than other people to be convinced of anything. But long term, I think time is on your side."

Like the title of an old Rolling Stones song.

"One other thing: I think you really have a special talent for portraiture. An intuitive ability to get straight to the heart of the subject. Other people can't do that. Not using that talent would be a real shame."

"But right now painting portraits isn't what I want to do."

"I get that. But someday that ability will help you again. I hope it works out."

Hope it works out, I thought. Good if time is on your side.

On the first day I visited the house in Odawara, Masahiko Amada—the son of the owner—drove me there in his Volvo. "If you like it, you can move in today," he said.

We took the Odawara-Atsugi Road almost to the end and, when we exited, headed toward the mountains along a narrow, paved farm road. On either side, there were fields, rows of hothouses for growing vegetables, and the occasional grove of plum trees. We saw hardly any houses, and not a single traffic signal. Finally we drove up a steep, winding slope in low gear for a long time, until we came to the end and arrived at the entrance to the house. There were two stately pillars at the entrance, but no gate. And no wall, either. It seemed the owner had planned to add a gate and wall but thought better of it. Maybe halfway through he'd realized there was no need. On one of the pillars was a magnificent nameplate with AMADA on it, almost like some business sign. The house beyond was a small Western-style cottage with a faded brick chimney sticking out of the flat roof. It was a one-story house, but the roof was unexpectedly high. In my imagination I'd been taking it for granted that a famous painter of Japanese-style paintings would live in an old Japanese-style dwelling.

We parked in a spacious covered driveway by the front door, and when we opened the car doors some screeching black birds—jays, I imagine—flew off from a nearby tree branch into the sky. They seemed none too happy about us intruding on their space. The house was pretty, surrounded by woods with a variety of trees, with only the west side of the house open to a broad view of the valley.

"What do you think? Not much here, is there?"

I stood there, gazing around me. He was right, there wasn't much there. I was impressed that his father had built a house in such isolated surroundings. He really must have wanted nothing to do with other people.

"Did you grow up here?" I asked.

"No, I've never lived here very long. Just came to stay over occasionally. Or visited on summer holidays when we were escaping the heat. I had school, and grew up in our house in Mejiro with my mother. When my father wasn't working he'd come to Tokyo and live with us. Then come back here and work by himself. I went out on my own, then ten years ago my mother died, and ever since he's been living here by himself. Like someone who's forsaken the world."

A middle-aged woman who lived nearby had been watching the house, and she came over to explain some things I needed to know. How the kitchen operated, how to order more propane and kerosene, where various items were kept, which days the trash was picked up and where to put it. The artist seemed to have led a very simple solitary existence, with very little equipment or appliances, so there wasn't much for a lecture. If there's anything else you need to know, just give me a call, the woman said (though I actually never called her, not even once).

"I'm very happy someone will be living here now," she said. "Empty houses get dilapidated, and they're unsafe. And when they know no one's at home, the wild boar and monkeys get into the yard."

"You do get the occasional wild boar or monkey around here," Masahiko said.

"Be very careful about the wild boars," the woman explained. "You see a lot of them in the spring around here when they root for bamboo shoots. Female boars with young are always jumpy, and dangerous. And you need to watch out for hornets, too. There've been people who've been stung and died. The hornets build nests in the plum groves."

The central feature of the house was a fairly large living room with an open-hearth fireplace. On the southwest side of the living room was a spacious roofed-in terrace, and on the north side was a square studio. The studio was where the master had done his painting. On the east side of the living room was a compact kitchen with dining area, and a bathroom. Then a comfortable master bedroom and a slightly smaller guest bedroom. There was a writing desk in the guest bedroom. Amada seemed to enjoy reading, as the bookshelves were stuffed with old books. He seemed to have used this room as his study. For an older house, it was fairly neat and clean, and comfortable looking, though strangely enough (or perhaps not so strangely) there was not a single painting hanging on the walls. Every wall was completely bare.

As Masahiko had said, the place had most everything I'd need—furniture, electric appliances, plates and dishes, and bedding. "You don't need to bring anything," he'd told me, and he was right. There was plenty of firewood for the fireplace stacked up under the eaves of the shed. There was no TV in the house (Masahiko's father, I was told, hated TV), though there was a wonderful stereo set in the living room. The speakers were huge Tannoy Autographs, the separate amplifier an original vacuum tube Marantz. And he had an extensive collection of vinyl records. At first glance there seemed to be a lot of boxed sets of opera.

"There's no CD player here," Masahiko told me. "He's the sort of person who hates new devices. He only trusts things from the past. And naturally there's not a trace of anything to do with the Internet. If you need to use it, the only choice is to use the Internet café in town."

"I don't have any real need for the Internet," I told him.

"If you want to know what's going on in the world, then the only choice is to listen to the news on the transistor radio on the shelf in the kitchen. Since we're in the mountains the signal isn't great, but you can at least pick up the NHK station in Shizuoka. Better than nothing, I suppose."

"I'm not that interested in what's going on in the world."

"That's fine. Sounds like you and my father would get along fine."

"Is your father a fan of opera?" I asked.

"Yes, he paints Japanese paintings, but always liked to listen to opera while he painted. He went to the opera house a lot when he was a student in Vienna. Do you listen to opera?"

"A little."

"I'm not into it at all. Way too long and boring for me. There are a lot of records, so feel free to listen to them as much as you'd like. My father has no need of them anymore and I know he'd be happy if you listened to them."

"No need of them?"

"His dementia's getting bad. Right now he doesn't know the difference between an opera and a frying pan."

"Vienna, you said? Did he study Japanese painting in Vienna?"

"Nobody's that eccentric—to go all the way to Vienna to study Japanese painting. My father originally worked on Western painting. That's why he went to study in Vienna. At the time he did very cutting-edge modern oil paintings. But after he came back to Japan he suddenly switched styles, and began painting Japanese-style. Not totally unheard of, I suppose. Going abroad awakens your own ethnic identity or something."

"And he was very successful at it."

Amada made a small shrug. "According to the public he was. But from a child's perspective, he was just a grouchy old man. All he thought about was painting, and did exactly as he pleased. No trace of that now, though."

"How old is he?"

"Ninety-two. When he was young he was apparently pretty wild. I never heard the details."

I thanked him. "Thank you for everything. I'm really grateful. This really helps me out."

"You like it here?"

"Yes, I'm really happy you're letting me stay."

"I'm glad. Though I'm hoping you and Yuzu can get back together again."

I didn't respond. Masahiko himself wasn't married. I'd heard a rumor he was bisexual, though I didn't know if it was true or not. We'd known each other for a long time, but had never spoken about it.

"Are you going to keep doing portraits?" Amada asked as we were leaving.

I explained how I'd made a clean break with portrait painting.

"Then how are you going to make a living?" Amada asked, the same thing my agent had wanted to know.

I'll cut back on expenses and get by on my savings for a while, I replied, echoing my first answer. I also wanted to try painting whatever I wanted, something I hadn't been able to do for ages.

"Sounds good," Amada said. "Do what you like for a while. But would you consider teaching art part time too? There's this arts-and-culture center near Odawara Station and they have painting classes. Most of them are for children, but they have some community art classes for adults set up as well. They teach sketching and watercolor, but not oil painting. The man who runs the school knows my father, he's not really in it for the money. And he needs a teacher. I'm sure he'd be overjoyed if you'd help out. It doesn't pay much, but you could make a little extra to live on. You'd only need to teach twice a week, and it shouldn't be too much trouble."

"But I've never taught painting, and don't know much about watercolors."

"It's simple," he said. "You're not training professionals. You just teach the basics. You'll pick it up in a day. Teaching children should be good for you, too. And if you're going to live up here all by yourself, you have to get down off the mountain a couple of times a week and be with other people, even if you don't want to, or else you'll go a little stir-crazy. Don't want you ending up like *The Shining*."

Masahiko screwed up his face like Jack Nicholson. He's always been good at impressions.

I laughed. "I'll give it a try. Whether I'll do a good job or not, I don't know."

"I'll get in touch with him and let him know," he said.

Then Masahiko drove me to the used Toyota dealership next to the highway, where I paid cash for the Corolla station wagon. My life alone on a mountaintop in Odawara began that day. I'd been on the move for nearly two months, but now I'd take up a sedentary life. It was quite a switch.

Starting the following week, I began teaching art classes on Wednesdays and Fridays at the arts-and-culture center near Odawara Station. There was a perfunctory interview beforehand, but Masahiko's introduction meant that I was as good as hired already. I was to teach two classes for adults, plus one for children on Fridays. I quickly got used to teaching the kids. I enjoyed seeing the paintings they did, and, as Masahiko said, it was a good stimulus for me as well. I quickly got to be friends with the children. All I did was go around the room, check on the paintings they did, give them a few words of technical advice, find good points about their paintings, and praise and encourage them. My approach was to have them paint the same subject matter several times, to instill in them the idea that the same object could appear quite different if viewed from a different angle. Just as people had many facets, so too did objects. The kids immediately picked up on how fascinating this could be.

Teaching adults was a bit more of a challenge. The students were either elderly retirees, or housewives whose children were grown and in school, and had time on their hands. As you might imagine, they weren't as adaptable as the kids, and when I pointed out something, they didn't easily accept my suggestions. A few of them, though, were willing to learn, and there were a couple who did some pretty appealing paintings. Whenever they asked, I gave them helpful pointers, but for the most part I let them paint however they liked. I confined myself to praising them whenever I found something nice about what they'd done. That seemed to please them. I figured it was enough for them to simply enjoy painting.

And I started sleeping with two housewives, both of whom attended the art classes and received my so-called instruction. Both my students, in other words, and incidentally both fairly decent painters. It's hard for me to tell whether that was something permissible for a teacher—even a casual teacher like me with no proper license. I basically think mutually consenting adults having sex isn't a problem, though certainly society might frown at this kind of relationship.

I'm not trying to excuse my actions, but at the time I really didn't have the mental wherewithal to decide whether I was right or wrong. I was desperately clinging to a scrap of wood that had been swept away. In pitch-black darkness, not a single star, or the moon, visible in the sky. As long as I clung to that piece of wood I wouldn't drown, but I had no clue where I was, where I was heading.

It was a couple of months after I'd moved there that I discovered Tomohiko Amada's painting *Killing Commendatore*. I couldn't know it at the time, but that one painting changed my world forever.

4

FROM A DISTANCE, MOST THINGS LOOK BEAUTIFUL

One sunny morning near the end of May I carried all my painting materials into the studio Mr. Amada had been using, and for the first time in what seemed like forever stood before a brand-new canvas. (Nothing of the master's painting materials was left in the studio. I assume that Masahiko had packed them all away somewhere.) The studio was a large, square room sixteen feet on a side, with a wood floor and white walls. The floor was bare wood, with not a single rug. There was a large open window on the north side, with simple white curtains. The window on the east side was smaller, with no curtains. As elsewhere in the house, there was nothing hanging on the walls. In one corner of the room was a large porcelain sink for washing away paint. The sink must have been in long use, for its surface was dyed with a mix of different colors. Next to the sink was an old-fashioned kerosene stove, and there was a large ceiling fan. A worktable and a round wooden stool. A compact stereo set was on a built-in shelf so he could listen to opera while painting. The wind blowing in the open window carried with it the fresh fragrance of trees. This was, without doubt, a space for an artist to focus on his work. Everything you might need was here, and not one thing extra.

Now that I had this environment to work in, the feeling of *wanting to paint something* grew stronger, like a quiet ache. And there were no limits on the amount of time I could spend for myself. No need any longer to paint things I didn't want to in order to earn a living, no more obligation to prepare dinner for my wife when she came home. (Not that I minded making dinner, though that didn't change the fact that it was an obligation.) And it wasn't just preparing meals—I had the right to stop eating altogether and starve if I felt like it. I was utterly free to do exactly what I wanted, without worrying about anybody else.

In the end, though, I couldn't paint a thing. No matter how long I stood in front of the canvas and stared at that white, blank space, not a single idea of what to paint came to me. I had no clue where to begin, how to start. Like a novelist who has lost words, or a musician who has lost his instrument, I stood there in that bare, square studio, at a complete loss.

I'd never felt that way before, not ever. Once I faced a canvas, my mind would immediately leave the horizon of the everyday, and *something* would well up in my imagination. Sometimes it would be a productive image, at other times a useless illusion. But still, something would always come to me. From there, I'd latch onto it, transfer it to the canvas, and continue to develop it, letting my intuition lead the way. If I did it that way, the work completed itself. But now I couldn't see *anything* that would provide the initial spark. You can have all the desire and ache inside you want, but what you really need is a concrete starting point.

I would get up early in the morning (I generally always wake before six), brew coffee in the kitchen, and then, mug in hand, pad off to the studio and sit on the stool in front of the canvas. And focus my feelings. Listen closely to the echoes in my heart, trying to grasp the image of something that had to be there. But this always ended in a fruitless retreat. I'd try concentrating for a while, then plunk down on the studio floor, lean back against the wall, and listen to a Puccini opera. (I'm not sure why, but all I seemed to listen to then was Puccini.) *Turandot*, *La Bohème*. I'd sit there, staring at the languidly rotating ceiling fan, waiting for an idea or motif to come to me. But nothing ever came. Just the early-summer sun that rose sluggishly in the sky.

What was the problem? Maybe it's because I'd spent so many years doing portraits for a living. Maybe that diminished any natural intuition I had. Like sand slowly washed away by the tide. Somehow the flow of my life had gone off in the wrong direction. I needed time, I thought. I had to be patient. *Make time be on my side.* Do that, and I was sure to seize the right flow. That channel would surely come back to me. Truthfully, though, I wasn't sure it ever would.

It was during this period, too, that I slept with the two married women. I think I was looking for some kind of inner breakthrough. Come what may, I wanted to break out of the rut I was in, and the only way for me to do so was to jolt my psyche, give it a prod (it didn't matter what kind). Plus I'd started to tire of being alone. And it had been a long time since I'd slept with a woman.

It occurs to me now that my days back then were pretty strange. I'd wake up early, go into that small square, white-walled studio, have no ideas for what to paint as I stared at the blank canvas, then flop down on the floor and listen to Puccini. When it came to the realm of creativity, I was basically facing a pure nothingness. When Claude Debussy had writer's block while composing an opera, he wrote, "Day after day I produce *rien*—nothingness." That summer was the same for me—day after day I took part in *producing nothingness*. Perhaps I was quite used to facing nothingness day after day—though I wouldn't go so far as to say we were intimate.

About twice a week in the afternoon, the second of the married women would drive to my place in her red Mini. We'd go straight to bed and make love. In the early afternoon we'd devour each other's flesh. What this produced was, of course, not nothingness. No doubt about it, actual flesh-and-blood bodies were involved. Bodies you could actually touch with your hands, every inch, even run your lips over them. In this way, as if I'd flipped a switch on my consciousness, I began moving between an ambiguous, vague *rien* and a vivid, living reality. The woman said her husband hadn't made love to her in nearly two years. He was ten years older than she was, and busy with work, never returning home until late at night. She tried many ways of enticing him, but nothing seemed to rouse his interest.

"I wonder why. I mean, you have such a lovely body," I said.

She gave a small shrug. "We've been married over fifteen years and have two kids. I guess I'm no longer as fresh as I used to be."

"You seem plenty fresh to me."

"Thanks. Though that makes it sound like I'm being recycled or something."

"Like recycling resources?"

"Exactly."

"It's a very precious resource, though," I said. "Contributes to society, too."

She giggled. "As long as you sort everything correctly."

A little while later, we eagerly set out to sort out resources once more.

Truthfully I wasn't all that drawn to her as a person at first. In that sense there was a different tone about our relationship than with the women I'd dated. She and I had almost nothing in common to talk about. There was hardly anything about our present lives, or our personal histories until then, that overlapped. I'm not generally a talkative person, so when we were together, she did most of the talking. She'd tell me personal things and I'd make the appropriate responses, giving my feedback, I guess you'd call it, though it was hardly a real conversation.

This was a first for me. With other women, I'd always been attracted to their personalities. Physical relationships came later, something that accompanied the initial appeal . . . That was the usual pattern. But not with her. With her the physical came first. Not that I'm complaining. When I was with her I could enjoy the act in a pure, unfettered way. And I think she could, too. She came many times as we made love, and I came many times too.

She told me this was the first time since she got married that she'd slept with another man. I had no reason to doubt her. And for me, too, this was the first time I'd slept with another woman since I got married. (No, actually there was one exception, when I shared a bed with another woman. Not that it was something I was looking for. I'll get into that later on.)

"But my friends the same age, all of them are married but most of them are having affairs," she said. "They talk about it a lot."

"Recycling," I said.

"I never imagined I'd join them."

I gazed up at the ceiling and thought about Yuzu. Was she off somewhere, in bed with somebody?

After the woman left, I felt at loose ends. The bed still showed the hollows where she had lain. I didn't feel like doing anything, so I lay out on a lounge chair on the terrace and killed time reading a book. All the books on Mr. Amada's bookshelf were old, among them a few unusual novels that would be hard to get hold of these days. Works that in the past had been pretty popular but had been forgotten, read by no one. I enjoyed reading this kind of out-of-date novel. Doing so let me share—with this old man I'd never met—the feeling of being left behind by time.

As the sun set, I opened a bottle of wine (drinking wine was my one and only luxury at the time, though of course this was inexpensive wine) and listened to some old LPs. The record collection was comprised entirely of classical music, the majority of which was opera and chamber music. All of them looked like they'd been lovingly cared for, without a single scratch. During the day I listened to opera, while at night I favored Beethoven and Schubert string quartets.

Having a relationship with that older married woman, being able to hold a real live woman in my arms regularly, brought me a certain level of calm. The soft touch of a mature woman's skin eased the pent-up emotions I'd had. At the very least, while I made love to her I was able to shelve the doubts and problems I'd been carrying around. Yet I still wasn't able to come up with an idea of what to paint. Occasionally in bed I'd do a pencil sketch of her in the nude. Most of these were pornographic. Pictures of my cock inside her, or her sucking me off. The sketches made her blush, but she enjoyed looking at them. I imagine that if these had been photos most women wouldn't have liked them, and would even have been disgusted with the man who made them, and on their guard. But I found that with rough sketches, if they were done well, women were actually happy to see them. Because they had the warmth of life in them—or, at least, they didn't have a mechanical coldness. But still, no matter how well I managed these sketches, not even a fragment of an image of what I really wanted to paint came to me.

The kind of paintings I did as a student, so-called abstracts, no longer appealed to me. My heart wasn't drawn to them anymore. Looking back on it now, I see that what I'd been wrapped up in back then was nothing more than the pursuit of form. Back when I was young, I was completely drawn to the beauty of form, and to balance. Nothing wrong with that. But in my case I didn't reach the soulful depth that should lie beyond. Now I see it very clearly, but at the time, all I could grasp was the *appeal* of shape at a superficial level. Nothing really moved me. My paintings were *smart* but nothing more.

And now I was thirty-six. Forty was just around the corner. I felt that by the time I turned forty, I'd have to secure my own unique artistic world. Forty was a sort of watershed for people. Once you get past that age, you can't keep going on as you were before. I still had four years to go, but I knew that those four years might flash by in an instant. Painting portraits for a living had taken me on a wide detour. Somehow I had to get time on my side once again.

While I lived in that house in the mountains I found myself wanting to know more about Tomohiko Amada. I'd never been interested in Japanese-style painting, and though I'd heard the name Tomohiko Amada, and he happened to be my friend's father, I had no idea what kind of person he was, or what kind of paintings he did. He might be a heavyweight in the world of Japanese painting, but he had totally stayed out of the limelight, turning his back on his worldly renown, and alone, quietly—or one might say stubbornly—focused on creating his art. This was about the extent of what I knew about him.

But as I listened to his record collection on the stereo he'd left behind, borrowed his books, slept in his bed, made meals every day in his kitchen, and used his studio, I gradually became more interested in Tomohiko Amada as a person. Something close to curiosity, you could say. The path he'd taken aroused my interest—the way he'd been focused on modernist painting, traveled all the way to Vienna to study, then after returning to Japan made a sudden return to Japanese-style painting. I didn't know the details, but in general you would think that it couldn't have been very easy for someone who'd done Western painting for so long to shift over to Japanese-style painting. You'd need to decide to abandon all the techniques you'd spent so much time and effort mastering, and begin again from zero. Despite this, Tomohiko Amada had chosen that arduous path. There must have been a compelling reason.

One day, before my art class, I went to the Odawara city library to search out collections of Tomohiko Amada's artwork. Probably because he was an artist living in the area, the library had three beautiful volumes of his work. One of them included some of the Western paintings he'd done in his twenties as reference material. What surprised me was that the series of Western-style paintings he'd done as a young man reminded me somewhat of the abstract paintings I'd done myself in the past. The style wasn't specifically the same (in the prewar period he'd been heavily influenced by Cubism), yet his stance of "greedily pursuing form" in no small way had something in common with my own approach. As you might expect from someone who went on to become a first-class artist, his paintings also had much more depth and persuasive power than mine. Technically, too, there were things about them that were, simply, astounding. I imagine they must have been highly acclaimed at the time. Still, there was *something missing*.

I sat there in the reading room at the library and carefully examined his works for a long time. So what was it that was lacking from his work? I couldn't pinpoint it. But if I had to give an opinion, I'd say they were paintings that *weren't really necessary*. The kind of paintings that, if they disappeared somewhere forever, wouldn't put anybody out. A cruel way of putting it, perhaps, but it's the truth. From the present perspective, some seventy years on, I could see that quite well.

I turned the pages and followed along, in chronological order, to see how he shifted gears to become a painter of Japanese-style art. In his early period these works were still a bit awkward, imitating the methods of previous artists, but then gradually, and undeniably, he discovered his own unique style. I could see how it progressed. A bit of trial and error at times, but no hesitation. After he took up painting Japanese-style art, his works all had something unique that only he could paint, and he himself was well aware of this. He always strode confidently toward the core of that special *something*. No more did you get the impression, as with his Western paintings, of something missing. It was less a shift and more akin to a conversion.

Like most artists of Japanese-style paintings, at first Tomohiko Amada painted realistic scenery and flowers, but eventually (and there must have been some motive for this) he began painting scenes from ancient Japan. Some were themes from the Heian and Kamakura periods, but what he was most fond of was the Asuka period at the beginning of the seventh century, specifically the period when Prince Shotoku Taishi, the legendary regent, was alive . . . On his canvases he boldly, minutely, reproduced the scenery, historical events, and lives of the people of that period. Naturally he had never witnessed those scenes in reality with his own eyes. But with his inner eye he *saw* them, clearly and vividly. Why he chose the Asuka period, I have no idea. But that became his own special period, done in an inimitable style. And with the passage of time his technique in painting Japanese-style paintings became even more refined.

If you pay close attention you can see that from a certain point on he painted exactly what he wanted to paint. From then on his brush seemed to freely leap across the canvas. The wonderful part about his paintings was the use of blank space. Paradoxically, the best part was what was *not* depicted. By not painting certain things he clearly accentuated what he *did* want to paint. This is undoubtedly one of the areas that Japanese painting excels at. At least I'd never seen such bold use of blank space in any Western paintings. Seeing this, I could somehow understand why Tomohiko Amada converted to painting Japanese art. But what I didn't understand was exactly when and how he made that daring conversion and put it into practice.

According to his brief biography at the end of the book, he was born in the mountainous Aso district in Kumamoto. His father was a great landowner, an influential local figure, and his family was quite affluent. He was always artistically talented and distinguished himself while still quite young. He graduated from the Tokyo Fine Arts School (later Tokyo University of the Arts), and with great expectations for his career studied abroad in Vienna from the end of 1936 to 1939. At the beginning of 1939, before World War Two began, he boarded a passenger ship from Bremen and returned to Japan. Hitler was in power during this time. Austria was annexed by Germany, the so-called *Anschluss* taking place in March 1938. And the young Tomohiko Amada was right there in Vienna in the midst of this turbulent period. He must have witnessed a number of historical events at that time.

So what happened to him then?

I read through a long essay in one of the collections titled "Theory of Tomohiko Amada," only to find that almost nothing was known about his time in Vienna. The essay went into great detail about his career as a painter of Japanese-style paintings after he returned to Japan, yet there was only vague, baseless speculation about the motives and details of the conversion he must have experienced during his time in Vienna. What he had done in Vienna, and what had led him to his dramatic conversion, remained a mystery.

Tomohiko Amada returned to Japan in February 1939, and settled into a rented house in Sendagi in Tokyo. By this point he had completely abandoned Western painting. But he still received an allowance every month from his family, so he wanted for nothing. His mother, in particular, doted on her son. During this period he was, apparently, studying Japanese-style painting on his own. A number of times he tried to have established painters take him under their wing, but it never worked out. Tomohiko was, from the first, not exactly the humblest of people. Maintaining calm, friendly ties with others was not his forte. Isolation from others was a leitmotif that ran through his entire life.

With the attack on Pearl Harbor in 1941, Japan entered an all-out war, and Amada left turbulent Tokyo and moved back to his parents' home in Aso. As the second son, he avoided all the problems involved in succeeding to his father's estate, and was given a small house with a maid, and lived a quiet life there pretty much isolated from the war. For better or worse, he had a congenital lung defect and thus there was no worry he would be drafted. (Though this could have been the excuse they used for the public, and his family may have worked behind the scenes to make sure he didn't have to be a soldier.) He also avoided the severe food shortages and near starvation that plagued most Japanese citizens at the time. Living deep in the mountains of rural Japan, unless some major mistake was made he could also be pretty certain that no U.S. planes would be dropping any bombs on them. So until the surrender in 1945 he lived, holed up alone, deep in the mountains of Aso. His ties with society were severed, and he devoted himself entirely to mastering the techniques of Japanese-style painting. He didn't display a single work during this time.

For Tomohiko Amada, after being in the spotlight as a promising painter of Western art, and then going to study in Vienna, it must have been a trying experience to maintain total silence for over six years, forgotten by the art world. But he was not the type to easily lose heart. When the long war was finally over, and as people struggled to recover from the chaos, a reborn Tomohiko Amada debuted again, this time as an up-and-coming painter in the Japanese style. One by one he displayed the works he'd completed during the war. This was the period when most artists, having painted stirring propaganda pieces, were forced to take responsibility for their actions and, under the watchful eye of the Occupation, were fairly compelled into retirement. Which is precisely why Tomohiko's works, revealing the possibility of a revolution in Japanese painting, garnered so much attention. The times, one could say, were his ally.

There was little to say of his career after this time. Once an artist is successful, his life is often quite boring. Of course there are some artists who, once they are successful, head straight toward a colorful downfall, but Tomohiko Amada wasn't one of them. He won countless awards over the years (though he turned down the Order of Cultural Merit award from the government, claiming it would be "distracting") and became very famous. Over the years the price for his works rose, and most were displayed in public exhibitions. There was no end to the number of commissions, and he gained a high reputation abroad, too. Smooth sailing all around. The artist himself, though, avoided center stage, and turned down any official positions. He also refused any invitations, domestic or international. Instead he stayed holed up alone in the mountaintop house in Odawara (the house I was now living in) painting whatever he liked.

Now he was ninety-two and in a nursing home in Izu Kogen, and no longer knew the difference between an opera and a frying pan.

I shut the book of paintings and returned it to the library counter.

When the weather was good I liked to lie on a lounge chair out on the terrace after dinner and enjoy a glass of white wine. And as I gazed at the twinkling stars to the south, I would consider what lessons I might draw from Tomohiko Amada's life. Naturally there should be a few lessons I should learn. The courage not to fear a change in one's lifestyle, the importance of having time on your side. And above all, discovering your own uniquely creative style and themes. Not an easy thing, of course. Though if you make a living creating things, it's something you have to accomplish no matter what. If possible, before you turn forty . . .

But what kind of experiences did Tomohiko Amada have in Vienna? What scenes did he witness? And most of all, what exactly made him decide to lay down his oil paintbrush forever? I pictured red-and-black Nazi swastika flags fluttering over a street in Vienna, a young Tomohiko Amada walking down that street. For some reason the season is winter. He has on a thick coat, a scarf, and a cloth cap pulled down low. His face isn't visible. A streetcar rounds the corner and approaches in the newly falling sleet. As he walks, he exhales white breath into the air like the very embodiment of silence. The Viennese are in warm cafés, sipping coffee with a spot of rum.

I tried visualizing his later paintings of Japanese scenes in the Asuka period overlapping with this old Viennese street scene. But my imagination was unequal to the task, and I couldn't discover any similarities between the two.

My terrace faced the narrow valley to the west, and across the way was a range of mountains about the same height as mine. And on the slopes of those mountains were a number of houses with generous space separating them, surrounded by lush greenery. To the right, diagonally across from the house I was living in, was a particularly striking modern-style house. The mountaintop house, built of white concrete and plenty of bluish tinted glass, was so elegant and luxurious the word "mansion" seemed a better term. It was built in three levels that ran along the slope. Most likely some first-rate architect had designed it. There are lots of summer homes in this area, but someone seemed to live in this house all year long, with lights on behind the windows every night. Of course it could be that the lights were on timers as a safety precaution. But I gathered otherwise, since the lights came on and turned off at different times, depending on the day. Sometimes all the lights were on at once and the windows were lit like brilliant window displays on a main street, while at other times the whole house sank back into darkness, the only light a faint glow from lanterns in the yard.

Sometimes a person would appear on the deck that faced my direction (the one that resembled the top deck of an ocean liner). At twilight I would often see the figure of whoever lived there. I couldn't tell if it was a man or a woman. The silhouette was small and usually backlit and in shadow. But from the outline of the silhouette, and the movements, my guess was that it was a man. And this person was always alone. Perhaps he didn't have any family.

What kind of person lived in a place like that? In spare moments I tried to imagine. Did this person really live all by himself on this out-of-the-way mountaintop? What sort of work did he do? No doubt his life in that chic, glass-enclosed mansion was one of luxury and ease. He couldn't be commuting every day to Tokyo from such an inconvenient spot. He must be living a life free of worries. But viewed from his perspective, looking at me from his side of the valley, I might appear to also be living a life of ease and leisure. From a distance, most things look beautiful.

That evening the figure appeared again. Like me, he sat, barely moving, in a chair out on the deck. As if he too was gazing at the twinkling stars, mulling over something. Thinking, no doubt, about things for which there was no answer, no matter how hard you thought about them. At least that's how he looked to me. Everybody has something they speculate and wonder about, no matter how blessed their circumstances. I raised my wineglass a couple of inches, a secret gesture of solidarity to this person across the valley.

Naturally at the time I never imagined that this person would soon enter my life and change its direction entirely. Without him, none of the events that happened to me would have ever taken place. At the same time, if he hadn't been there I might very well have lost my life in the darkness, with no one ever the wiser.

Our lives really *do* seem strange and mysterious when you look back on them. Filled with unbelievably bizarre coincidences and unpredictable, zigzagging developments. While they are unfolding, it's hard to see anything weird about them, no matter how closely you pay attention to your surroundings. In the midst of the everyday, these things may strike you as simply ordinary things, a matter of course. They might not be logical, but time has to pass before you can see if something is logical.

Generally speaking, whether something is logical or isn't, what's meaningful about it are the effects. Effects are there for anyone to see, and can have a real influence. But pinpointing the cause that produced the effect isn't easy. It's even harder to show people something concrete that caused it, in a "Look, see?" kind of way. Of course there is a cause somewhere. Can't be an effect without a cause. You can't make an omelet without breaking some eggs. Like falling dominoes, one domino (cause) knocks over the adjacent domino (cause), which then knocks over the domino (cause) next to it. As this sequence continues on and on, you no longer know what was the original cause. Maybe it doesn't matter. Or people don't care to know. And the story comes down to "What happened was, a lot of dominoes fell over." The story I'll be telling here may very well follow a similar route.

In any case, the first things I want to describe—the first two dominoes I have to bring up, in other words—are the mysterious neighbor who lived on the mountaintop across the valley, and the painting titled *Killing Commendatore*. I'll start with the painting.

5

HE HAS STOPPED BREATHING . . . HIS LIMBS ARE COLD

The first thing I found odd after I moved into the house was the utter lack of any paintings. Not only were none hanging on the walls, but there wasn't a single painting of any kind even stuffed away in a shed or closet. No paintings by Tomohiko Amada, but none by any other artists either. Every wall was bare, with no traces even of nails that might have once been used to hang paintings. Artists almost always had at least some paintings around them—their own paintings, or those by other artists. Before they knew what had hit them, they'd be surrounded by all kinds of paintings, like when you endlessly shovel the snow but it keeps on piling up.

Once when I called Masahiko about something else, I happened to raise the topic. How come there's not a painting of any kind in this house? Did somebody take them away, or there weren't any to begin with?

"My father didn't like keeping his own paintings around," Masahiko said. "He'd call up his art dealers when he finished a work and leave it with them. If he wasn't happy with a painting, he burned it in the incinerator in the yard. So it's not so strange that there's not a single one of his paintings there."

"He didn't own any paintings by other artists either?"

"He owned a handful. An old Matisse or Braque and the like. All of them small paintings he bought in Europe before the war. He got them from acquaintances, and they weren't so expensive at the time. Now, of course, they would bring a hefty price. When he went into the nursing home I took all those paintings to an art dealer I know and let him handle them. Can't leave them sitting there in an empty house now, can I? I imagine they're in a special air-conditioned art storage warehouse. Apart from those, I've never seen any other artists' works in the house. To tell the truth, my father didn't much like other artists. And they didn't like him either. A lone wolf, you might call him, or if we're not being nice about it, a misfit."

"Your father was in Vienna from 1936 to 1939, wasn't he?"

"Right, he was there for about two years. I don't know why he chose Vienna, since the artists he liked were mainly French."

"And then he returned to Japan and suddenly switched to Japanese-style paintings," I said. "Why do you think he made such a monumental decision? Did something unusual happen while he was abroad?"

"Hmm. It's a mystery. My father never spoke much about his time in Vienna. Occasionally he'd talk about things nobody cared about—the Vienna zoo, or food, or the opera house. But when it came to talking about himself, he was a man of few words. And I never dared to ask him. We mostly lived apart, and rarely saw each other. He was less like a father to me than an uncle who came to visit every once in a while. When I got to junior high he seemed even more annoying, and I avoided contact with him. When I went into the art institute, too, I never consulted him about it. It's not like our family was complicated, though it wasn't exactly a normal family either. You get the general idea?"

"I do."

"Anyway, my father's memories of the past are all gone now. Or have sunk away into deep mud. He won't answer you, no matter what you ask. He doesn't even know who I am. Probably doesn't even know who *he* is. Sometimes I think I should have asked all kinds of things before he got this way. Well, it's too late now."

Masahiko was silent for a time, lost in thought. "Why do you want to know that?" he finally asked. "Did something spark an interest in him?"

"Not particularly," I said. "It's just that, living in this house, I sense something like your father's shadow lurking about. I also did a little research into his life at the library."

"My father's shadow?"

"Like a reminder of his existence, maybe."

"Don't you find that a little creepy?"

Over the phone I shook my head. "No. Not at all. It's just like the presence of Tomohiko Amada is still hovering over things. Like it's in the air."

Masahiko was lost in thought again. "My father lived in that house for a long time, and did a lot of work there," he said, "so maybe his presence remains. Who knows? To tell the truth, that's why I don't want to go near the place."

I listened without comment.

"Like I said before," he went on, "to me, Tomohiko Amada was basically just a grouchy old man I knew. Always holed up in his studio, painting, with a sour look on his face. He didn't talk much, so I had no idea what was on his mind. When we were under the same roof my mom always told me, 'Don't bother your father when he's working.' I couldn't run around or yell or anything. The world saw him as a famous artist, but to a little kid, he was simply a pain. Plus when I decided to go into art myself, having him as a father was a burden. Every time I introduced myself people would ask if I was related to Tomohiko Amada. I even thought about changing my name. I realize now he wasn't such a bad person, really. I suppose he showed me affection in his own way. Though he wasn't the type to show unconditional love toward a child. But that can't be helped. Painting was always his top priority. That's what artists are like."

"I suppose so," I said.

"I could never be an artist," Masahiko said with a sigh. "That might be the only thing I learned from my father."

"Didn't you tell me before that when he was young he was pretty wild and did whatever he liked?"

"By the time I was big, he wasn't like that anymore, but when he was young he played around a lot apparently. He was tall, good-looking, a young guy from a wealthy family, and a talented painter. How could women not be drawn to him? And he was certainly fond of the ladies. Rumor is that he had some affairs that his family had to pay to clear up. But my relatives said that after he returned from his time abroad, he was a different person."

"A different person?"

"After he returned to Japan, he didn't play around anymore, and just stayed at home focusing on his painting. And he didn't socialize anymore. After he got back to Tokyo he was a bachelor for a long time, but once he could earn a good living painting, like the idea had just occurred to him, he suddenly and unexpectedly married a distant relative back home. For all the world like he was balancing the account book of his life or something. It was a late marriage for him. And then I was born. I have no clue if he ever played around with other women after he got married. Though I can say that he no longer made a show of having a good time."

"Quite a change."

"His parents were really happy, though, at how he'd changed. No more messy affairs for them to clean up. But none of our relatives could tell me what had happened to him in Vienna, or why he rejected Western painting in favor of Japanese-style art. When it came to those things my father's mouth was clamped shut, like an oyster at the bottom of the sea."

And even if you pried open that shell now, there would be nothing inside. I thanked Masahiko and hung up.

It was by total coincidence that I discovered the painting by Tomohiko Amada, the one with the unusual title, *Killing Commendatore*.

Sometimes in the middle of the night I'd hear a faint rustling sound from the attic above the bedroom. At first I thought it must be mice, or a squirrel that had found its way into the attic. But the sound was clearly not that of a rodent's feet scurrying around. Nor that of a slithering snake. It sounded more like oil paper being crumpled up. Not loud enough to keep me from sleeping, but it did concern me that there was some unknown creature in the house. I figured it might be an animal that could cause some damage.

After searching around, I located the opening to the attic in the ceiling in the back of the guest bedroom closet. I lugged over the aluminum ladder from the storage shed and, flashlight in one hand, pushed open the cover. I timidly stuck my head through and looked around. The attic was bigger than I'd thought, and dark. A small amount of sunlight filtered in through the small vent holes on either side. I shone the flashlight around but didn't see anything. At least nothing was moving. I took the plunge and hauled myself up into the attic.

The place smelled dusty, but not enough to bother me. The attic was apparently well ventilated and there wasn't much dust on the floor. Several thick beams hung low on the ceiling, but as long as I avoided them I could walk around okay. I edged forward and checked both vents. Both were covered with screens so no animals could get in, but the screen on the north vent had a gap in it. Something might have knocked against it and ripped it. Or else an animal had intentionally ripped the wire to get inside. Either way, the opening was large enough for a smallish animal to easily scramble in.

I spotted the culprit I'd been hearing at night, silently settled on top of a beam in the dark. It was a small, gray horned owl. The owl's eyes were closed and it seemed to be sleeping. I switched off my flashlight and stood away to silently observe without frightening it. I'd never seen a horned owl up close before. It looked less like an owl than like a cat with wings. It was a beautiful creature.

The owl most likely rested here during the day and then at night went out the vent hole to hunt for prey in the mountains. The sound of it going in and out must have been what woke me. No harm done. Having an owl in the attic also meant I needn't worry about mice and snakes settling in. I figured I should just leave it be. I felt close to the little owl. Both of us just happened to be borrowing this house and sharing it. It could have the run of the attic as far as I was concerned. I enjoyed observing it for a time, then tiptoed back where I'd come from. That's when I discovered the large wrapped package near the entrance.

One look told me it was a wrapped-up painting. About three feet in height and five feet in length, it was wrapped tightly in brown Japanese wrapping paper, with string tied several times around it. Nothing else was in the attic. The faint sunlight filtering in from the vent holes, the gray horned owl on top of a beam, the wrapped painting propped up against a wall. The combination felt magical, somehow, and captivated me.

I gingerly lifted the package. It wasn't heavy—the weight of a painting set in a simple frame. The wrapping paper was slightly dusty. It must have been placed here, out of anyone's sight, quite some time ago. A name tag was attached tightly with wire to the string. In blue ballpoint ink was written *Killing Commendatore*. The writing was done in a very careful hand. Most likely this was the title of the painting.

Naturally, I had no clue why that one painting would be hidden away in the attic. I considered what I should do. Obviously the correct thing to do would be to leave it where it was. This was Tomohiko Amada's house, not mine, the painting clearly his possession (presumably it was one that he himself had painted), one that, for whatever reason, he had hidden away so no one would see it. That being the case, I thought I shouldn't do anything uncalled for, and should let it continue to silently share the attic with the owl. I should just leave it be.

That made the most sense, but still I couldn't suppress the curiosity surging up inside. The words in (what appeared to be) the title—*Killing Commendatore*—grabbed me. What kind of painting could it be? And why did Tomohiko Amada have to hide away *this* painting alone in the attic?

I picked up the painting and tested to see if it could squeeze through the opening to the attic. Logic dictated that a painting that had been brought up here shouldn't have any problem being carried down. And there was no other entrance to the attic. But still I checked to see if it would squeeze through. As expected, it was a tight fit, but when I held it diagonally, it squeezed through the square opening. I imagined Tomohiko Amada carrying the painting up to the attic. He must have been by himself then, carrying around some secret inside him. I could vividly imagine the scene, as if I were actually witnessing it.

I don't think Amada would be angry if he found out I'd brought the painting down from the attic. His mind was buried now in a deep maelstrom, according to his son, "unable to distinguish an opera from a frying pan." He would never be coming back to this home. And if I left this painting in an attic with the screen over the vent hole ripped, mice and squirrels might gnaw away at it someday. Or else bugs might get to it. And if this painting really was by Tomohiko Amada, this would be a substantial loss to the art world.

I lowered the package on top of the shelf in the closet, gave a little wave to the horned owl huddled on the beam, then clambered down and quietly shut the lid to the entrance.

I didn't unwrap the painting right away. I left that brown package propped up against the wall in the studio for several days. And I sat on the floor, gazing vaguely at it. It was hard for me to decide whether I should unwrap it or not. I mean, it belonged to somebody else, and whatever positive spin you might try to put on it, I didn't have the right to unwrap it. If I wanted to, at least I should get permission from his son, Masahiko. I'm not sure why, but I didn't feel like letting Masahiko know the painting existed. I felt like it was something personal, just between me and Tomohiko Amada. I can't explain why. But that's how I felt.

I stared at the painting (my assumption, of course, that it was actually a painting)—wrapped in Japanese paper and tied tightly with string—so hard I almost burned a hole in it, and after running the next step through my mind, over and over, I finally decided to unwrap it. It was no contest: my curiosity won out over any sense of etiquette or common sense. Whether this was the professional curiosity of an artist, or simple personal curiosity, I couldn't say. Whatever, I just had to see what was inside. I don't care what anyone says, I told myself. I brought over scissors, cut the tightly bound string, and peeled away the brown wrapping paper. I took my time, and did it carefully, in case I needed to rewrap it again later on.

Underneath the layers of wrapping paper was a painting in a simple frame, wrapped in a soft white cloth like bleached cotton. I gently lifted off that cloth, as carefully as if I were removing the bandages from a burn victim.

What was revealed under the white cloth was, as expected, a Japanese-style painting. A long, rectangular painting. I stood it up on a shelf, stood back a bit, and studied it.

It was Tomohiko Amada's work, no doubt about it. Clearly done in his style and inimitable technique, with his signature bold use of space and dynamic composition. The painting depicted men and women dressed in the fashions of the Asuka period, the clothes and hairstyles of that age. But the painting startled me nonetheless. What it depicted was so violent it took my breath away.

As far as I knew, Tomohiko Amada hardly ever painted pictures that were harsh and violent. Maybe never. His paintings mostly summoned up feelings of nostalgia, gentleness, and peace. Occasionally they would take up historical events as his theme, but the people depicted in them generally faded away into the overall composition. They were shown as part of a close community in the midst of the abundant natural scenery of ancient times, esteeming harmony above all. Ego was submerged in the collective will, or absorbed into a calm fate. And the circle of life was quietly drawn closed. For Tomohiko Amada that very well may have been utopia. Over the years he continued to depict that world from all sorts of angles, all sorts of perspectives. Many called his style a "rejection of modernity" or a "return to antiquity." Of course there were some who criticized it as escapist. In any case, after he returned to Japan from studying in Vienna he abandoned modernist oil painting, and shut himself away inside that kind of serene world, without a single word of explanation or justification.

But this painting titled *Killing Commendatore* was full of blood. Realistic blood flowing all over. Two men were fighting with heavy, ancient swords, in what seemed to be a duel. One of the men fighting was young, the other old. The young man had plunged his sword deep into the old man's chest. The young man had a thin black mustache and wore tight-fitting light-greenish clothes. The old man was dressed in white and had a lush white beard. Around his neck was a necklace of beads. He had dropped his sword, which had not yet struck the ground. Blood was spewing from his chest. The tip of the sword must have pierced his aorta. The blood had soaked his white clothes, and his mouth was twisted in agony. His eyes were wide open, staring in disbelief into space. He realized he was defeated. But the real pain had yet to hit him.

For his part, the young man's eyes were cold, fixed on his opponent. Not a sign of regret in those eyes, not a hint of confusion or fear, or a trace of agitation. Totally composed, those eyes were simply watching the impending death of another, and his own unmistakable victory.

The gushing blood was nothing more than proof of that, and elicited no emotional reaction whatsoever.

Honestly, until then I had thought of Japanese-style paintings as static and formulaic, their techniques and subject matter ill-suited to the expression of strong emotion. A world that had nothing to do with me. But looking now at Tomohiko Amada's *Killing Commendatore* I realized that had been nothing but prejudice on my part. In Amada's depiction of the two men's violent duel to the death was something that shook the viewer to the core. The man who won, the man who lost. The man who stabbed and the man who was stabbed. My heart was captured by the discrepancy. There is something very special about this painting, I thought.

There were a few other figures nearby watching the duel. One was a young woman. She had on refined, pure white clothes. Her hair was done up, with a large hair ornament. She held one hand in front of her mouth, which was slightly parted. She looked like she was about to take a deep breath and let out a scream. Her lovely eyes were wide open.

And there was another young man there. His clothes were not as splendid. Dark clothes, bereft of any ornaments, the kind of outfit designed to be easy to move around in. On his feet were plain-looking zori sandals. He looked like a servant. He had no long sword, just a short sword hanging from his waist. He was short and thickset, with a scraggly beard. In his left hand he held a kind of account book, like a clipboard that a company employee nowadays might have. His right hand was reaching out in the air as if to grab something. But it couldn't grab anything. You couldn't tell from the painting if he was the servant of the old man, or of the young man, or of the woman. One thing that was clear, though, was that this duel had taken place quickly, and neither the woman nor the servant had expected it to happen. Both of their faces revealed an unmistakable shock at the sudden turn of events.

The only one of the four who wasn't surprised was the young man doing the killing. Probably nothing ever took him by surprise. He was not a born killer, and he didn't enjoy killing. But if it served his purpose he wouldn't hesitate to kill. He was young, burning with idealism (though of what kind I have no idea), a man overflowing with strength.

And he was skilled in the art of wielding a sword. Seeing an old man past his prime dying by his hand didn't surprise him. It was, in fact, a natural, rational act.

There was one other person there, an odd observer. The man was at the bottom left of the painting, much like a footnote in a text. His head was peeking out from a lid in the ground that he had partially pushed open. The lid was square, and made of boards. It reminded me of the attic cover in this house. The shape and size were identical. From there the man was watching the people on the surface.

A hole opening up to the surface? A square manhole? No way. They didn't have sewers back in the Asuka period. And the duel was taking place outdoors, in an empty vacant lot. The only thing visible in the background was a pine tree, with low-hanging branches. Why would there be a hole with a cover there, in the middle of a vacant lot? It didn't make any sense.

The man who was sticking his head out of the hole was weird looking. He had an unusually long face, like a twisted eggplant. His face was overgrown with a black beard, his hair long and tangled. He looked like some sort of vagabond or hermit who'd abandoned the world. In a way he also looked like someone who'd lost his mind. But the glint in his eyes was surprisingly sharp, insightful, even. That said, the insight there wasn't the product of reason, but rather something induced by a sort of deviance—perhaps something akin to madness. I couldn't tell the details of what he was wearing, since all that I could see was from the neck up. He, too, was watching the duel. But unlike the others, he showed no surprise at the turn of events. He was a mere observer of something that was supposed to take place, as if checking all the details of the incident, just to be sure. The young woman and the servant weren't aware of the man with the long face behind them. Their eyes were riveted on the bloody duel. No one was about to turn around.

But who *was* this person? And why was he hiding beneath the ground back in ancient times? What was Tomohiko Amada's purpose in deliberately including this uncanny, mysterious figure in one corner of the painting, and thus forcibly destroying the balance of the overall composition?

And why in the world was this painting given the title *Killing Commendatore*? True, an apparently high-ranking person was being killed in the picture. But that old man in his ancient garb certainly didn't deserve to be called a commendatore—a knight commander. That was a title clearly from the European Middle Ages or the early modern period. There was no position like that in Japanese history. But still Tomohiko Amada gave it this strange-sounding title—*Killing Commendatore*. There had to be a *reason*.

The term "commendatore" sparked a faint memory. I'd heard the word before. I followed that trace of memory, as if tugging a thin thread toward me. I'd run across the word in a novel or drama. And it was a famous work. I knew I'd seen it somewhere . . .

And then it hit me. Mozart's opera *Don Giovanni*. In the beginning of that opera was a scene, I was sure, of *Killing Commendatore*. I went over to the shelf of records in the living room, took out the boxed set of *Don Giovanni*, and read through the accompanying commentary. And sure enough, the person killed in the opening scene was the Commendatore. He didn't have a name. He was simply listed as "Commendatore."

The libretto was in Italian, and the old man killed in the beginning was called *Il Commendatore*. Whoever translated the libretto into Japanese had rendered it as *kishidancho*—literally, "the knight commander"—and that had become the standard term in Japanese. I had no clue what sort of rank or position the term "commendatore" referred to in reality. The commentary in a few other boxed sets didn't elaborate. He was merely a nameless commendatore appearing in the opera with the sole function of being stabbed to death by Don Giovanni in the opening of the opera. And in the end he transformed into an ominous statue that appeared to Don Giovanni and took him down to hell.

Pretty obvious, if you think about it, I thought. The handsome young man in this painting is the rake Don Giovanni (Don Juan in Spanish) and the older man being killed is the honored knight commander. The young woman is the Commendatore's beautiful daughter Donna Anna, the servant is Don Giovanni's man, Leporello. What he had in his hands was the detailed list of all the women Don Giovanni had seduced up until then, a lengthy catalog of names. Don Giovanni had forced himself on Donna Anna, and when her father confronted him with this violation, they had a duel, and Don Giovanni stabbed the older man to death. It's a famous scene. Why hadn't I picked up on that?

Probably because Mozart's opera and a Japanese-style painting depicting the Asuka period were so remote from each other. So of course I hadn't been able to make the connection. But once I did, everything fell into place. Tomohiko Amada had "adapted" the world of Mozart's opera into the Asuka period. A fascinating experiment, for sure. That, I recognized. But why was that adaptation *necessary*? It was so very different from his usual style of painting. And why did he tightly wrap the painting and hide it away in the attic?

And what was the significance of that figure in the bottom left, the man with the long face sticking his head out from underground? In Mozart's *Don Giovanni* no one like that appeared. There must have been a reason Tomohiko Amada had added him. Also in the opera Donna Anna didn't actually witness her father being stabbed to death. She was off asking her lover, the knight Don Ottavio, for help. By the time they got back to the scene, her father had already breathed his last. Amada had—no doubt for dramatic purposes—subtly changed the way the scene played out. But there was no way the man sticking his head out of the ground was Don Ottavio. That man's features weren't anything found in this world. It was impossible that this was the upright, righteous knight who could help Donna Anna.

Was he a demon from hell? Scouting out the situation in anticipation of dragging Don Giovanni down to hell? But he didn't look like a demon or devil. A demon wouldn't have such strangely sparkling eyes. A devil wouldn't push a square wooden lid up and peek out. The figure more resembled a trickster who had come to intervene. "Long Face" is what I called him, for lack of a better term.

For a few weeks I just silently stared at that painting. With it in front of me, I couldn't bring myself to do any painting of my own. I barely even felt like eating. I'd grab whatever vegetables were in the fridge, dip them in mayo, and chew on that, or else heat up a can of whatever I had on hand. That's about the size of it. All day long I'd sit on the floor of the studio, endlessly listening to the record of *Don Giovanni*, staring enthralled at *Killing Commendatore*. When the sun set, I'd have a glass of wine.

The painting was amazing. As far as I knew, though, it wasn't reprinted in any collection of Amada's work, which meant no one else knew it existed. If it were made public it would no doubt become one of his best-known paintings. If they held a retrospective of his art, it wouldn't be surprising if this was the painting used on the promotional poster. This wasn't simply a painting that was wonderfully done, though. The painting was brimming with an extraordinary sort of energy. Anyone with even a little knowledge of art couldn't miss that fact. There was something in this painting that appealed to the deepest part of the viewer's heart, something suggestive that enticed the imagination to another realm.

I couldn't take my eyes off the bearded Long Face on the left side of the painting. It felt like he'd opened the lid to invite me, personally, to the world underground. No one else, just *me*. I couldn't stop thinking about what sort of realm lay beneath. Where in the world had he come from? And what did he do there? Would that lid be closed up again, or would it be left open?

As I stared at the painting I listened to that scene from *Don Giovanni* over and over. Act 1, scene 3, soon after the overture. And I nearly memorized the lyrics and the lines.

DONNA ANNA: *Ah, the assassin*
has struck him down! This blood . . .
this wound . . . his face
discolored with the pallor of death . . .
He has stopped breathing . . . his limbs
are cold.
Oh father, dear father, dearest father!
I'm fainting . . . I'm dying!

6

AT THIS POINT HE'S A FACELESS CLIENT

Summer was winding down when the call came in from my agent. It had been a while since anyone had called me. The summer heat still lingered during the day, though when the sun set the air in the mountains was chilly. The noisy clamor of the summer cicadas was slowly fading away, but now a chorus of other insects had taken their place. Unlike when I lived in the city, I was surrounded by nature now and one season freely chipped away at portions of the preceding one.

We brought each other up to date, though there wasn't much to tell on my end.

"How's your painting coming along?" he asked.

"Slowly but surely," I said. This was a lie, of course. It was more than four months since I'd moved here, yet the canvas I'd prepared was still blank.

"Glad to hear it," he said. "I'd like to see how you're doing sometime. Maybe there's something I can do to help out."

"Thanks. We'll do that sometime."

Then he told me why he'd called. "I have a request. Are you sure you're not willing to do one more portrait? What do you think?"

"I told you I've given up doing portraits."

"I know. But the fee this time is unbelievable."

"Unbelievable?"

"It's amazing."

"How amazing?"

He told me the figure. I nearly let out a whistle of surprise. "There have got to be a lot of other people besides me who specialize in portraits," I replied calmly.

"There aren't all that many, really, though there are a few besides you who are fairly decent."

"Then you should ask them. With a fee like that anybody would jump at the chance."

"The thing is, the other party specifically asked for *you*. That's their condition. No one else will do."

I shifted the phone to my left hand and scratched behind my right ear.

The agent went on. "The person saw several portraits you've done and was very impressed. He felt that the vitality in your paintings can't easily be found elsewhere."

"I don't get it. How could an ordinary person have seen *several* of my portraits? It's not like I have a one-man show at a gallery every year."

"I really don't know the details," he said, sounding perplexed. "I'm just passing along what the other party told me. I told him up front that you were no longer doing portraits. I said you seemed pretty firm about it, and even if I asked you you'd most likely turn him down. But he wouldn't give up. That's when this figure came up."

I mulled over the offer. Honestly, it was a tempting amount. And I felt a bit of pride that someone saw that much value in my paintings—even if it was work I'd done half mechanically for money. But the thing was, I'd sworn I'd never paint commissioned portraits again. When my wife left me it spurred me to start over again, and I couldn't reverse my decision just because somebody was willing to shell out a pile of money.

"Why is he being so generous?" I asked.

"Even though we're in a recession, there are still people who have so much money they don't know what to do with it. There are a lot of people like that—ones who made a killing in online stock trading, or tech entrepreneurs. And getting a portrait done is something they can write off as a business expense."

"Write off?"

"In their accounts a portrait isn't included as a work of art but as office equipment."

"Talk about heartwarming," I said.

But even if they have tons of excess cash, and even if they can write it off as a business expense, I can't see entrepreneurs or people who've made a fortune trading stocks online wanting to have their portraits painted and hung on their company walls as *office equipment*. Most of these are young people decked out at work in faded jeans, sneakers, worn T-shirts, and Banana Republic jackets, proud to be drinking Starbucks from a paper cup. An imposing oil portrait didn't fit their lifestyle. But there are all kinds in the world. You can't generalize. It's not necessarily true that no one wants to be painted sipping Starbucks (or whatever) coffee (Fair Trade beans only, of course) from a paper cup.

"But there's one condition," the agent said. "The other party wants you to use the client as a live model, and paint when you're actually together. They'll make the time to do that."

"But I don't work that way."

"I know. You meet the client but don't have them model for you. That's your way of working. I told them that. They said they understood but they'd like you to make an exception and paint the client live and in person. That's the other party's condition."

"What's the purpose?"

"I don't know."

"That's a pretty odd request. Why would they insist on that? You'd think they'd be happy not to actually have to sit for the portrait."

"I agree it's unconventional. But it's hard to complain about the fee."

"I'm with you there—hard to complain about the fee," I agreed.

"It's all up to you. It's not like you're being asked to sell your soul or anything. You're a very skilled portrait painter, and they're counting on that skill."

"I feel like a retired hit man in the mob," I said. "Like I'm being asked to whack one more target."

"Though no blood's going to be shed. What do you say—will you do it?"

No blood's going to be shed, I silently repeated. The painting *Killing Commendatore* came to mind.

"What sort of person is the one I'd paint?" I asked.

"Actually, I don't know."

"You don't even know if it's a man or a woman?"

"I don't. I haven't heard a thing about the sex or age or name. At this point he's a totally faceless client. A lawyer saying he was representing the client called me. That's the 'other party' I spoke with about it."

"Do you think it's legit?"

"I don't see anything suspect about it. The lawyer works at a reputable firm and said they'll transfer an advance as soon as you accept."

Phone in hand, I sighed. "This is kind of sudden, and I don't think I can give you an answer right away. I need time to think."

"Understood. Think about it as long as you need. It's not an urgent job, the other party said."

I thanked him and hung up. I couldn't think of anything else to do so I went to the studio, turned on the light, plunked myself down on the floor, and stared vaguely at *Killing Commendatore*. After a while I started to get hungry and went to the kitchen, piled a plate with Ritz Crackers and ketchup, and went back to the studio. I dipped the crackers in the ketchup and munched them as I went back to staring at the painting. Nothing about that food tasted good. It was, if anything, pretty awful. But taste wasn't the issue. Keeping hunger at bay for a while was the priority.

That's how much the painting drew me in, from the overall composition to the small details. It truly held me captive. After a few weeks of exhaustive gazing at the painting, I ventured closer to it to inspect each detail. What most caught my attention were the expressions on each of the five people's faces. I did minute pencil sketches of each of them. From the Commendatore, to Don Giovanni, Donna Anna, Leporello, and Long Face. Just like a reader might carefully copy down in a notebook each word and phrase he liked in a book.

This was the first time I'd ever sketched figures from a Japanese-style painting, and it was far more difficult than I'd expected. Japanese painting emphasized lines, and tended to be more flat than three-dimensional. Symbolism was emphasized over reality. It's inherently impossible to transfer a painting done from that perspective into the grammar of Western painting, though after much trial and error I was able to do a fairly decent job of it. Calling it "recasting" might be a bit much, but it was necessary to interpret and translate the painting in my own way. Which necessitated grasping the intent that went into the original painting. I had to come to an understanding of Tomohiko Amada, his viewpoint as an artist, and the kind of person he was. Figuratively speaking, I had to put myself in his shoes.

After I'd done this for a while, the thought struck me: maybe doing a portrait again wasn't such a bad idea. I mean, my painting wasn't going anywhere. I couldn't even get a hint of what I should paint, or what I wanted to paint. Even if I wasn't too keen on the job, getting my hands moving again wouldn't be a bad thing. If I kept on like this, unable to draw a thing, I might find myself unable to paint ever again. *Maybe I wouldn't even be able to paint a portrait.* The fee, of course, was also pretty tempting. My living expenses at this point were minimal, but my pay from the art classes wasn't enough to cover them. I'd gone on that long trip, bought a used Corolla station wagon, and my savings were diminishing. So a sizable fee like the one I'd get from doing the portrait was, admittedly, very appealing.

I called my agent and told him that just this one time, I would take on the job. Naturally, he was happy to hear this.

"But if I have to paint the client in person, that means I need to travel to wherever he is," I said.

"No need to worry about that. The other party will come to your place in Odawara."

"To Odawara?"

"That's right."

"He knows where I'm living?"

"He apparently lives nearby. He even knows that you're living in Tomohiko Amada's place."

This left me speechless. "That's strange. Hardly anybody knows I'm living here. Especially that I'm in Amada's house."

"I didn't know that either," the agent said.

"Then how does that person know?"

"I have no idea. But you can find out just about anything from the Internet these days. For people who know their way around it, privacy is a thing of the past."

"Is it just a coincidence that that person lives near me? Or was the fact that I live nearby one of the reasons he chose me?"

"That, I couldn't say. When you meet the client, if there's something you want to know, you can ask."

"I'll do that," I said.

"So when can you start?" he asked.

"Anytime," I said.

"All right, I'll let them know, and get back to you," the agent said.

After I hung up I went out to the terrace, settled into the lounge chair, and thought about how things had turned out. The more I mulled it over, the more questions I had. First off, it bothered me that the client knew I was living here, in this house. It was like I was under surveillance, with somebody watching my every move. But why would anyone have that much interest in a person like me? Plus the whole thing sounded too good to be true. The portraits I'd done were certainly well received. And I had a certain amount of confidence in them. But these were, ultimately, the kind of portraits you could find anywhere. No way could you ever call them "works of art." And as far as the world was concerned I was a completely unknown artist. No matter how many of my paintings someone had seen and liked (not that I accepted that story at face value), would that person really shell out such an enormous fee?

A thought suddenly struck me, out of nowhere: Could the client be the husband of the woman I was having an affair with? I had no proof to go on, yet the more I thought about it the more it seemed like a real possibility. When it came to an anonymous neighbor who was interested in me, that's all I could come up with. But why would her husband go to the trouble and expense of paying a huge fee to have his wife's lover paint his own portrait? It didn't add up. Unless he was some weird pervert or something.

Fine. If that's how things are working out, then just go with the flow. If the client has some hidden agenda, just let it play out. That was a much more sensible thing to do than remaining as I was, stuck, deadlocked in the mountains. Curiosity was also a factor. What kind of person *was* this client? What did he want from me in exchange for the huge fee? I had to discover what motivated him.

Once I'd made up my mind I felt relieved. That night, for the first time in a while, I fell into a deep sleep right away, with no thoughts buzzing around in my head. At one point I felt like I heard the rustling of the horned owl in the middle of the night. But that might have just been a piece of a fragmentary dream.

7

FOR BETTER OR FOR WORSE, IT'S AN EASY NAME TO REMEMBER

My agent in Tokyo called a few more times, and we decided that I would meet our mystery client on Tuesday afternoon of the following week. (At that point the client's name was still not revealed.) I had them agree to my usual procedure, wherein, on the first day, we simply met and talked together for an hour or so, before we embarked upon a drawing.

As you might imagine, painting a portrait requires the ability to accurately grasp the special features of a person's face. But that's not all. If it were, you'd end up with a caricature. To paint a vibrant portrait you need the skill to discover what lies at the core of the person's face. A face is like reading a palm. More than the features you're born with, a face is gradually formed over the passage of time, through all the experiences a person goes through, and no two faces are alike.

On Tuesday morning I straightened up the house, picked some flowers from the garden and put them in vases, moved the *Killing Commendatore* painting out of the studio into the guest bedroom, and wrapped it up again in brown paper. I didn't want anyone else seeing it.

At five past one p.m. a car drove up the steep slope and parked in the covered driveway at the entrance. A heavy, brazen-sounding engine echoed, like some giant animal giving a satisfied purr from deep inside a cave. A high-powered engine. The engine shut off, and quiet again settled over the valley. The car was a silver Jaguar sports coupe. Sunlight from between the clouds reflected brightly off the long, brightly polished fenders. I'm not that into cars, so I don't know which model this was, but my guess was that it was the latest model, the mileage in the four digits, the price twenty times what I paid for my used Corolla station wagon. Not that this surprised me. The client was, after all, willing to pay such a huge fee to have a portrait done. If he'd appeared at my door in a massive yacht, it wouldn't have been surprising.

The person who got out of the car was a well-dressed middle-aged man. He had on dark-green sunglasses, a long-sleeved white cotton shirt (not simply white, but a pure white), and khaki chinos. His shoes were cream-colored deck shoes. He was probably a shade over five feet seven inches tall. His face had a nice, even tan. He gave off an overall fresh, clean feel. But what struck me most on this first encounter was his hair. Slightly curly and thick, it was white down to the last hair. Not gray or salt-and-pepper, but a pure white, like freshly fallen, virgin snow.

He got out of the car, closed the door (which made that special pleasant *thunk* expensive car doors make when you casually shut them), didn't lock it but put the key in his trouser pocket, and strode toward my front door—all of which I watched from a gap in the curtains. The way he walked was quite lovely. Back straight, the necessary muscles all equally in play. I figured he must work out regularly, and pretty hard training at that. I stepped away from the window, sat in a chair in the living room, and waited for the front doorbell to ring. Once it did, I slowly walked to the door and opened it.

When I opened the door the man took off his sunglasses, slipped them into the breast pocket of his shirt, and without a word held out his hand. Half reflexively I held out my hand, too. He shook it. It was a firm handshake, the way Americans do it. A little too firm for me, not that it hurt or anything.

"My name is Menshiki. It's very nice to meet you," the man said in a clear voice. The sort of tone a lecturer would make at the beginning of his talk to test the microphone and introduce himself at the same time.

"The pleasure's mine," I said. "Mr. Menshiki?"

"The *men* is written with the character in *menzeiten*—the one that means 'avoidance'—and the *shiki* is the character *iro*, for 'color.' "

"Mr. Menshiki," I repeated, lining the two characters up in my mind. A strange combination.

" 'Avoiding colors,' is what it means," the man said. "An unusual name. Other than my relatives I rarely run across anyone who shares it."

"But it's easy to remember."

"Exactly. It's an easy name to remember. For better or for worse." The man smiled. He had faint stubble from his cheeks to his chin, but I don't think he'd simply left off shaving. When he'd shaved he'd left an exact, calculated amount of stubble. Different from his hair, his beard was half black. I found it odd that only his hair was pure white.

"Please come in," I said.

Menshiki gave a small nod, removed his shoes, and stepped inside. The way he carried himself was charming, though I could sense a bit of tension. Like some large cat taken to a new place, each movement was careful and light, his eyes darting quickly around to take in his surroundings.

"A comfortable-looking place," he said after sitting down on the sofa. "Very relaxed and quiet."

"Quiet it certainly is. But kind of inconvenient when you have to go shopping."

"I would imagine for someone in your field it's an ideal environment."

I sat down in the chair across from him.

"I heard that you live nearby, Mr. Menshiki?"

"Yes, that's right. It would take a while to walk here, though as the crow flies it's actually pretty near."

"As the crow flies," I said, repeating his words. There was a somehow strange ring to the expression. "But how near is it, actually?"

"Close enough that if you wave your hand here you could see it."

"You can see your house from here?"

"Exactly."

I wasn't sure how to respond, and Menshiki asked, "Would you like to see my house?"

"If I could, yes," I said.

"Do you mind if we go out on the terrace?"

"Please, go right ahead."

Menshiki got up from the sofa and went straight from the living room to the terrace. He leaned out over the railing and pointed across the valley.

"You see that white concrete house over there? The one on top of the mountain, with the shiny windows?"

I was speechless. That was the house, that smart, elegant house I often looked at when I went out at sunset onto the terrace to enjoy a glass of wine. The large house that stood out from all the rest, diagonally to the right from mine.

"It's a little far, but if you made a big wave with your hand you could say hello," Menshiki said.

"But how did you know I was living here?" I asked, resting my hands on the railing.

He looked puzzled. He wasn't really fazed, just displaying a puzzled look. Not that his expression seemed contrived. He'd simply wanted to throw in a pause before responding.

"One aspect of my job is gathering all kinds of information," he said. "That's the sort of business I'm in."

"Is it tech related?"

"That's right. Or more precisely, that's also one aspect of my work."

"But hardly anyone knows yet that I'm living here."

Menshiki smiled. "Saying hardly anyone knows means, paradoxically, that there are some who *do*."

I looked over again at that exquisite white concrete building across the valley, and once more studied the man beside me. He was, most likely, the one who appeared almost every evening on the deck of that house. When I thought of it, his shape and movements all fit that silhouette perfectly . . . It was hard to figure out his age. That snow-white hair made me think he must be in his late fifties or early sixties, though his skin was lustrous and tight, and wrinkle free. His deep-looking eyes had the youthful twinkle of a man in his late thirties. All of which made guessing his age a tough call. I would have accepted anything between forty-five and sixty.

Menshiki went back to the sofa in the living room, and I sat down again across from him.

"Do you mind if I ask a question?" I finally ventured.

"Ask away," he said, beaming.

"Is there some connection between the fact that I live near your house and your decision to ask me to paint your portrait?"

A slight look of confusion came over him. And when he looked confused, several tiny wrinkles appeared at the corners of his eyes. Charming wrinkles. His features, viewed individually, were all quite attractive—the eyes almond shaped and slightly deep set, the forehead noble and broad, the eyebrows thick and nicely defined, the nose thin and a nice size. Eyes, eyebrows, and nose that perfectly fit his smallish face. His face was a bit small, yet too broad in a way, and from a purely aesthetic viewpoint was a little imbalanced. The vertical and horizontal were out of sync, though this disparity wasn't necessarily a defect. It's what gave his face its distinctiveness, since it was this imbalance that conversely gave the viewer a sense of calm. If his features had been too perfectly symmetrical people might have felt a bit of antipathy, or wariness, toward him. But as it was, his ever-so-slightly unbalanced features had a calming effect on anyone meeting him for the first time. They broadcast, in a friendly way, "It's all good, not to worry. I'm not a bad person. I don't plan to do anything bad to you."

The pointed, largish tips of his ears were slightly visible through his neatly trimmed hair. They conveyed a sense of freshness, of vigor, reminding me of spry little mushrooms in a forest, peeking out from among the fallen leaves on an autumn morning, just after it had rained. His mouth was broad, the thin lips neatly closed in a line, diligently prepared to, at any moment, break into a smile.

One could call him handsome. And he actually was. Yet his features rejected that sort of casual description, neatly circumventing it. His face was too lively, its movements too subtle to simply abide by that label. The expressions that rose on his features weren't calculated, but looked more like they'd arisen naturally, spontaneously. If they weren't, then he was quite the actor. But I got the impression that wasn't the case.

When I observe the face of a person I've met for the first time, from habit I sense all sorts of things. In most cases there's no tangible basis for how I feel. It's nothing more than intuition. But that's what helps me as a portrait artist—that *simple intuition*.

"The answer is yes, and no," Menshiki said. His hands on his knees were wide open, palms up. He turned them over.

I said nothing, waiting for his next words.

"I do worry about who lives in the neighborhood," Menshiki went on. "No, not worry, exactly. It's more like I'm *interested*. Especially when it's someone I see now and then across the valley."

It's a little too great a distance to say we actually *see* each other, I thought, but didn't say anything. Maybe he had high-powered binoculars and had been secretly observing me? I kept that thought to myself. I mean, what possible reason could he have to observe a person like *me*?

"And I learned that you had moved in here," Menshiki continued. "I found out you're a professional portrait artist, and that aroused my interest enough to seek out a few of your paintings. At first I saw them on the Internet. But I wasn't satisfied, so I went to see three actual paintings."

That had me puzzled. "You saw the actual paintings?"

"I went to see the people who had modeled for you and asked them to let me see the portraits. They were happy to show me them. It seems like people who sit for portraits are really pleased to show them off. I got a strange sensation when I saw the actual paintings up close and compared them to the faces of the people. It's like I couldn't tell which one was real anymore. How should I put it? There's something about your paintings that strikes the viewer's heart from an unexpected angle. At first they seem like ordinary, typical portraits, but if you look carefully you see something hidden inside them."

"Something hidden?" I asked.

"I'm not sure how to put it. Maybe the real personality?"

"Personality," I mused. "*My* personality? Or the *subject's*?"

"Both, probably. They're mixed together, so elaborately intertwined they can't be separated. It's not something you can overlook. Even if you just glance at the paintings as you pass by, you feel like you've missed something, and you can't help but come back and study them carefully. It's that indefinable *something* that drew me to them."

I was silent.

"And I had this thought: This is the person I want to paint my portrait. No matter what. I got in touch with your agent right away."

"Through an intermediary."

"Correct. I normally use an intermediary, a law office. It's not that I have a guilty conscience or anything. I just like to protect my anonymity."

"And it's an easy name to remember."

"Exactly," he said, and smiled. His mouth spread wide, the tips of his ears quivered ever so slightly. "There are times when I don't want my name to be known."

"Still, the fee is a little too much," I said.

"Price is always relative, determined by supply and demand. Those are basic market principles. If I want to buy something and you don't want to sell it, the price goes up. And in the opposite case, the price goes down."

"I understand market principles. But is it really necessary for you to go to all that length to have me paint your portrait? Maybe I shouldn't say this, but a portrait isn't something a person really *needs*."

"True enough. It's not something you need. But I'm also curious about what sort of portrait you'd do if you painted me. I want to find that out. You could think of it another way, namely that I'm putting a price on my own curiosity."

"And your curiosity doesn't come cheap."

He smiled happily. "The purer the curiosity is, the stronger it is. And the more money it takes to satisfy it."

"Would you care for some coffee?" I asked.

"That would be nice."

"I made it a little while ago in the coffee maker. Is that okay?"

"That's fine. I'll take it black, if you don't mind."

I went into the kitchen, poured coffee into two cups, and carried them back out.

"I notice you have a lot of opera recordings," Menshiki said as he drank the coffee. "You're a big opera fan?"

"Those aren't mine. The owner of this place left them. Thanks to them, though, I've listened to a lot of opera since I came here."

"By owner you mean Tomohiko Amada?"

"That's right."

"Do you have a favorite?"

I gave it some thought. "These days I've been listening to *Don Giovanni* a lot. There's a bit of a reason for that."

"What kind of reason? I'd like to hear, if you don't mind?"

"Well, it's personal. Nothing important."

"I like *Don Giovanni* too, and listen to it a lot," Menshiki said. "I heard it once in a small opera house in Prague. This was back just after the fall of the communist regime.

"I'm sure you know this," he continued, "but *Don Giovanni* was first performed in Prague. The theater was small, and so was the orchestra, and none of the singers were famous, yet it was a wonderful performance. They didn't have to sing really loud like in a big opera house, and could express their feelings in a very intimate way. Impossible at the Met or La Scala. There you need a well-known singer with a booming voice. Sometimes the arias in those big opera houses remind me of acrobatics. But what operas like Mozart's need is intimacy, like music. Don't you think so? In that sense the performance I heard in Prague was the ideal *Don Giovanni*."

He took another sip of coffee. I said nothing, observing his actions.

"I've had the opportunity to hear performances of *Don Giovanni* all over the world," he went on. "In Vienna, Rome, Milan, London, Paris, at the Met, and even in Tokyo. With Abbado, Levine, Ozawa, Maazel, and who else? . . . Georges Prêtre, I believe. But the *Don Giovanni* I heard in Prague is the one that, strangely enough, has stayed with me. The singers and conductor weren't people I'd ever heard of, but outside, after the performance, Prague was covered in a thick fog. There weren't many lights back then and the streets were pitch black at night. As I wandered down the deserted cobblestone streets I suddenly ran across a bronze statue. Whose statue, I have no idea. But he was dressed as a medieval knight. The thought struck me that I should ask him out to dinner. I didn't, of course."

He smiled again.

"Do you often go abroad?" I asked.

"Sometimes for work I do," he said. As if a thought occurred to him, he remained silent. I surmised that he didn't want to talk specifics about his job.

"So, what do you think?" Menshiki asked, looking me right in the eye. "Did I pass the test? Will you paint my portrait?"

"I'm not testing you. We're just getting together for a talk."

"But before you begin a painting you always meet and talk with the client. I heard that if you don't like the person, you won't paint his portrait."

I glanced over toward the terrace. A large crow had settled on the railing, but as if sensing my gaze, he spread his glossy wings and took off.

"I guess that's possible, but fortunately I haven't met anyone I don't like yet."

"I hope I'm not the first," Menshiki said with a smile. His eyes, though, weren't smiling. He was serious.

"Don't worry. I would be more than pleased to paint your portrait."

"That's wonderful," he said. He paused. "This is kind of selfish of me, but I have a little request myself."

I looked straight at him again. "What kind of request?"

"If possible I'd like you to paint me freely, and not worry about the usual conventions involved in doing a portrait. I mean, if you want to paint a standard portrait, that's fine. If you paint it using your usual techniques, the way you've painted till now, I'm all right with that. But if you do decide to try out a different approach, I'd welcome that."

"A different approach?"

"Whatever style you like is entirely up to you. Paint it any way you like."

"So you're saying that, like Picasso's painting during one period, I could put both eyes on one side of the face and you'd be okay with that?"

"If that's how you want to paint me, I have no objections. I leave it all up to you."

"And you'll hang that on the wall of your office."

"Right now I don't have an office per se. So I'll probably hang it in my study at home. As long as you have no objection."

Of course I had none. All walls were the same as far I was concerned. I mulled all this over before replying.

"Mr. Menshiki, I'm grateful to you for saying that, for telling me to paint in whatever style I want. But honestly nothing specific pops into my head at the moment. You have to understand, I'm merely a portrait painter. For a long time I've followed a set pattern and style. Even if

I'm told to remove any restrictions, to paint as freely as I want, the restrictions themselves are part of the technique. So I think it's likely I'll paint a *standard* portrait, the way I have up till now. I hope that's all right with you?"

Menshiki held both hands wide. "Of course. Do what you think is best. The only thing I want is for you to have a totally free hand."

"One other thing: if you're going to pose for the portrait, I'll need you to come to my studio a number of times and sit in a chair for quite a while. I'm sure your work keeps you quite busy, so do you think that'll be possible?"

"I can clear my schedule anytime. I was the one, after all, who asked that you paint me from real life. I'll come here and sit quietly in the chair as long as I can. We can have a good long talk then. You don't mind talking?"

"No, of course not. Actually, I welcome it. To me, you're a complete mystery. In order to paint you, I might need a little more information about you."

Menshiki laughed and quietly shook his head. When he did so, his pure white hair softly shook, like a winter prairie blowing in the wind.

"I think you overestimate me. There's nothing particularly mysterious about me. I don't talk much about myself because telling all the details would bore people, that's all."

He smiled, the lines at his eyes deepening. A very clean, open smile. But that can't be all, I thought. There was something hidden inside him. A secret locked away in a small box and buried deep down in the ground. Buried a long time ago, with soft green grass now growing above it. And the only person in the world who knew the location of the box was Menshiki. I couldn't help but sense, deep within his smile, a solitude that comes from a certain sort of secret.

We talked for another twenty minutes or so, deciding when he would come here to model, and how much time he could spare. On his way out, at the front door, he once more held out his hand, quite naturally, and I took it without thinking. A firm handshake at the beginning and end of an encounter seemed to be Menshiki's way of doing things. He slipped on his sunglasses, took the car keys from his pocket, boarded the silver Jaguar (which looked like some well-trained, slick, oversized animal), and gracefully eased down the slope, as I watched from the window. I went out on the terrace and gazed at the white house on the mountain he was heading back to.

What an unusual character, I thought. Friendly enough, not overly quiet. But it was as if he hadn't said a single thing about himself. The most I'd learned was that he lived in that elegant house across the valley, did work that partly involved the Internet, and frequently traveled abroad. And that he was a big fan of opera. Beyond that, though, I knew very little. Whether or not he had a family, how old he was, where he was from originally, how long he'd lived on that mountain. He hadn't even told me his first name.

And why be so insistent on me being the one to paint his portrait? I'd like to think it was because I had talent, something obvious to anyone who saw my work. Yet it was clear that this was not his sole motivation for commissioning me to do the painting. It seemed true that portraits I'd done had drawn his attention. That couldn't be a complete lie. But I wasn't naive enough to accept everything he told me at face value.

So—what did this man, Menshiki, want from me? What was his endgame? What sort of scenario had he prepared for me?

Even after we had talked, I still had no idea how to answer these questions. The mystery, in fact, had deepened. Why, for one thing, did he have such amazingly white hair? That kind of white wasn't exactly normal. I recalled an Edgar Allan Poe short story in which a fisherman gets caught up in a massive whirlpool and his hair turns white overnight. Had Menshiki experienced something just as terrifying?

After the sun set, lights came on in the white concrete mansion across the valley. Bright lights, and plenty of them. It looked like the kind of house designed by a self-assured architect unconcerned about things like the electric bill. Or perhaps the client was overly afraid of the dark and requested the architect to build a house where lights could blaze from one end to the other. Either way, viewed from afar, the house looked like a luxury liner silently crossing the ocean at night.

I sprawled out on the chair on the terrace and, sipping white wine, gazed at those lights. I was half expecting Menshiki to come out on his terrace, but that evening he didn't appear. But if he had, how should I have acted? Wave my hand in a big gesture of greeting?

I figured that, in time, my questions would be answered. That's about all I could expect.

8

A BLESSING IN DISGUISE

After my Wednesday-evening art class, when I taught an adult class for about an hour, I stopped by an Internet café near Odawara Station and did a Google search for the name Menshiki. I came up empty-handed. There were lots of online articles with the character *men* in them, as in *unten* men*kyo*—driver's license—and the *shiki* appeared in ones about partial color-blindness—shiki*jaku*. But there didn't seem to be any information out there in the world about a Mr. Menshiki. His statement that he took anonymity seriously seemed, indeed, to be the case. I was assuming, of course, that Menshiki was his real name, but my gut told me he wouldn't lie about something like that. It didn't make sense for him to tell me where he lived but not tell me his real name. And unless he had some compelling reason, it seemed to me that if he were to make up a phony name, he would choose one that was more common and didn't stand out so much.

When I got back home I called Masahiko Amada. After chatting a bit I asked if he knew anything about the man named Menshiki who lived across the valley. I described the white concrete house on the mountain. He had a vague memory of it.

"Menshiki?" Masahiko asked. "What kind of name is that?"

"It's written with the characters that mean 'avoiding colors.' "

"Sounds like a Chinese ink painting."

"But white and black are counted as colors," I pointed out.

"In theory, I suppose. . . . Menshiki? I don't think I've heard the name. I wouldn't know anything about anyone living on a mountain across the valley. I mean, I don't even know the people living on *your* side of the valley. Is there something going on between the two of you?"

"We sort of connected," I said. "And I was wondering if you knew anything about him."

"Did you check online?"

"I did a Google search but struck out."

"How about Facebook or other social media?"

"I don't know much about those."

"While you were asleep with the fish in the Dragon King's palace, like in the fairy tale, culture has forged on ahead. Not to worry—I'll check them for you. If I find anything, I'll give you a call."

"Thanks."

Masahiko was suddenly silent. On the other end of the phone it felt like he was contemplating something.

"Hold on a sec. Did you say Menshiki?" Masahiko asked.

"That's right. Menshiki. The *men* in *menzeiten*—'avoidance'—and the *shiki* in 'color'—*shikisai*."

"*Menshiki . . .* ," he said. "You know, I do remember now hearing that name before. Maybe I'm just imagining it."

"It's such an unusual name I'd think if you heard it once you wouldn't forget it."

"Agreed. Which is why maybe it's stuck in a corner of my mind. But I can't remember when I heard it, or in what context. It feels like when you have a small fishbone stuck in your throat."

If you remember, let me know, I said. Will do, Masahiko promised.

I hung up and then had a light meal. While I was eating, a call came in from the married woman I was having an affair with. Do you mind if I come to your place tomorrow afternoon? she asked. No problem, I replied.

"By the way, do you know anything about a person named Menshiki?" I asked. "He lives in the neighborhood."

"Menshiki?" she repeated. "Is that the last name?"

I explained how it was written.

"I've never heard of him," she said.

"You know that white concrete house across the valley from me? He lives there."

"I remember that house. The one you see from the terrace that really stands out."

"That's his house."

"Mr. Menshiki lives there?"

"That's right."

"So what about him?"

"Nothing, really. I just wanted to know if you knew him or not."

Her voice grew one tone darker. "Does that have something to do with me?"

"No, nothing to do with you."

She sighed, as if in relief. "Well, I'll see you tomorrow afternoon. Probably about one thirty."

"I'm looking forward to it," I said. I hung up and finished eating.

The call from Masahiko came a little while after that.

"It seems like there are a few people with the name Menshiki in Kagawa Prefecture down in Shikoku," Masahiko said. "Perhaps this Mr. Menshiki has roots in Kagawa. But I couldn't find any information anywhere on a Menshiki living now around Odawara. What's his first name?"

"He didn't tell me. I don't know what kind of work he does, either. Something tech related. If his lifestyle is any indication, he must be doing pretty well. That's all I know. I don't even know how old he is."

"I see," Masahiko said. "In that case, that might be the best you can do. Information is, after all, a product, and if you pay enough you can neatly cover your tracks. Even truer if the person knows a lot about technology."

"You mean Mr. Menshiki erased his footprints?"

"Could be. I spent a lot of time online, searching through sites, and didn't get a single hit. It's such an eye-catching name, yet there's not a thing online. Which is all pretty strange. I know you're a little naive when it comes to things like this, but for someone who is fairly active in society to completely block any information about themselves and have nothing at all get out on the web—that's no mean feat. Even information on you, and on me, is out there and available. There's information on me I didn't even know. If that's true for nobodies like us, you can imagine how much harder it is for some big shot to erase their digital presence. Like it or not, that's the world we live in. What about you? Have you checked out the information that's out there on you?"

"No, never."

"You should keep it that way."

"That's the plan," I told him.

One aspect of my job is gathering all kinds of information. That's the sort of business I'm in. Those were Menshiki's own words. If he could get hold of information that easily he could probably erase it as well.

"By the way, Mr. Menshiki said he looked me up on the Internet and saw a few of my portraits there," I said.

"And?"

"And he asked me to paint his portrait. He said he liked the portraits I've done."

"But you turned him down because you're no longer in the portrait business. Correct?"

I was silent.

"Are you telling me you didn't?" he asked.

"Actually, I didn't turn him down."

"How come? Weren't you set on not doing any more?"

"The fee is pretty hefty, that's why. I thought it might be okay to do one more portrait."

"For the money?"

"That's a big reason. I'm making hardly any money anymore, and I have to think about how I'm going to make a living. My expenses right now are minimal, but still, with one thing and another the money keeps flowing out."

"Huh. So, how much is the fee?"

I named the amount. Masahiko let out a whistle.

"Wow," he said. "That certainly makes it worth taking on. I bet you were surprised when you heard how much he'd pay?"

"Yeah, of course I was."

"Maybe I shouldn't say this, but there can't be any other odd people out there willing to pay that much for one of your paintings."

"I know."

"Don't get me wrong, I'm not saying you're not a talented artist. You do solid work, and people recognize that. I think you're about the only one of our classmates from our art school class who's managed to make a living doing oil paintings. What level of living we're talking about, I have no idea, but anyway it's admirable what you've accomplished. But honestly? You're no Rembrandt, or Delacroix. Or even Andy Warhol."

"I'm well aware of that."

"If you are, then you understand how exorbitant that fee is he's offering, right?"

"Of course I do."

"And just *by chance* he lives near you."

"Exactly."

"'By chance' is putting it mildly."

I didn't say anything.

"There might be something else to it. Didn't that cross your mind?" he asked.

"Sure, I thought about it. But what else there could be, I have no clue."

"So you accepted the job?"

"I did. I start the day after tomorrow."

"Because the fee's so good?"

"The fee's a big part of it. But that's not all. There are other reasons," I said. "Honestly, I want to see how things are going to play out. See with my own eyes why he's willing to pay so much. And if there're really other motives at work, I want to find out what they are."

"I see," Masahiko said, and paused. "Well, if there are any new developments, let me know. I'm intrigued."

Just then I recalled the horned owl.

"I forgot to mention it, but there's a horned owl living in the attic," I said. "A little gray horned owl that sleeps on a beam during the day. At night it goes out the vent hole and hunts. I don't know how long it's been here, but it seems to have roosted."

"In the attic?"

"I heard a sound from the ceiling, so I climbed up during the day to check on it."

"Really. I didn't know you could access the attic."

"There's an opening in the closet in the guest bedroom. It's a tight space, though. Smaller than what you might think of as an attic. But just the right size for an owl to roost in."

"That's a good thing, though," Masahiko said. "With an owl there, no mice or snakes will get in. I've heard it's a lucky omen to have an owl roosting in a house."

"Maybe that lucky omen brought me that high portrait fee."

"That would be nice if it did," he laughed. "You know the English expression 'a blessing in disguise'?"

"Languages aren't my strong suit."

"A camouflaged blessing. A blessing that's changed appearance. At first glance it seems unfortunate, but it turns out to bring you happiness. There are things that should be the opposite, too, of course. In theory."

In theory, I repeated to myself.

"Better keep your eyes open," he said.

"Will do," I said.

At one thirty the next day she came to see me, and as always we headed straight for bed. While we had sex we hardly said a word. It was raining that afternoon, an unusually heavy shower for autumn, more like a midsummer downpour. Heavy raindrops, carried on the wind, rapped against the window, and I think there were a few flashes of lightning, too. A thick bank of dark clouds passed over the valley, and when the rain let up, the mountains had taken on a darker hue. Flocks of birds that had taken shelter from the rain somewhere now twittered back and were busily hunting down insects. Right after rain was the perfect lunchtime for them. The sun shone from breaks in the clouds, making the raindrops on all the tree branches sparkle. While it had been raining we were deep into making love, and I had barely given the falling rain a second thought. And just as we were finishing, the rain abruptly stopped. Almost as if it were waiting for us.

We lay naked in bed, wrapped in a thin bedcover, talking. Mostly we talked about the grades her two daughters were getting in school. The older girl was good at school and had very good grades. She was a placid child who never caused any trouble. The younger daughter, in contrast, hated to study and would never settle down at her desk to do homework. But she was cheerful and upbeat, and quite good-looking as well. Self-assured, popular, good at sports. Maybe we should give up on having her do well at school, her mother said, and let her go into the entertainment field? I'm thinking of eventually putting her into one of those schools that train child entertainers, she said.

If you think about it, it was kind of strange. I was lying there next to a woman I'd known for only about three months, listening to her talk about her daughters, whom I'd never laid eyes on. She was even asking me my opinion on what sort of path they should take in life. And the two of us there, without a stitch on. Admittedly, though, not a bad feeling, to take a random peek into the lives of people I hardly knew. Brushing past the lives of people I would never have anything to do with. Their lives felt right before me, yet also far away. As she talked, the woman toyed with my now flaccid penis, which was slowly coming back to life.

"Have you been painting anything these days?" she asked.

"Not really," I answered honestly.

"No creative urge welling up?"

I hesitated. ". . . Well, tomorrow I have to start on a commission I got."

"You're going to paint on commission?"

"That's right. Have to earn some money sometimes."

"What sort of commission?"

"A portrait."

"Is it, by any chance, a portrait of that person you mentioned on the phone yesterday, Mr. Menshiki?"

"It is," I said. She was so sharp at times it took me by surprise.

"And you want to know something about this Mr. Menshiki, right?"

"At this point he's a mystery. I met him once and we talked, but I still have no idea what sort of person he is. I like to know what kind of person I'm going to paint."

"You should just ask him directly."

"He might not give me a straight answer," I said. "He might only tell me what he wants me to know."

"I could look into it for you," she said.

"You can do that?"

"I might have an idea."

"There were zero hits on him on the Internet."

"The Internet doesn't work well in the jungle," she said. "The jungle has its own communications network. Signaling with drums, tying a message around a monkey's neck."

"I don't know much about the jungle, I'm afraid."

"When civilization's devices don't operate, it's worth trying drums or a monkey."

My penis had now grown fully erect under her soft, busy fingers. She skillfully and greedily began to use her lips and tongue, and a meaningful silence descended upon us for a while. As the birds outside chirped and went about the work of making a living, the two of us began a second round of sex.

After our long second bout of lovemaking, punctuated by an intermission, we climbed out of bed, lazily gathered our clothes from the floor, and dressed. We went out to the terrace and, sipping hot herb tea, gazed across the valley at the large white concrete house there. We sat side by side on the weathered wooden deck chairs and breathed in deeply the fresh dampness of the mountain air. Through the woods to the southwest was a small patch of sparkling ocean, a mere fragment of the enormous Pacific. The mountain slopes around were already dyed with autumn colors, minute gradations of yellow and red, with an intrusion of green from the clumps of evergreens. The mix of these vivid colors made the white concrete of Menshiki's house stand out all the more. It was an almost obsessive white that looked like it would never be dirtied or treated with contempt by such things as wind, rain, dust, or even time itself. *White is a color, too*, I thought distractedly. Definitely not the lack of color. We sat there on the lounge chairs for a long time without saying a word, silence an entirely natural companion.

"Mr. Menshiki in his white mansion," she said after a while. "Sounds like the beginning of an amusing fairy tale."

But what awaited me was, of course, not some "amusing fairy tale." Or a blessing in disguise, either. But by the time that became clear to me, there was no turning back.

9

EXCHANGING FRAGMENTS WITH EACH OTHER

On Friday at one thirty Menshiki appeared in the same Jaguar. The deep roar of the engine as it climbed the steep slope grew louder as it approached, and finally came to a stop in front of the house. As before, he shut the door of the car with the same solid sound, and removed his sunglasses and slipped them into the breast pocket of his jacket. An exact repeat of the previous visit. This time, though, he wore a white polo shirt with a blue-gray cotton jacket, cream-colored chinos, and brown leather shoes. He was so impeccably dressed that he could have been a model in a magazine, though he didn't give the impression that it was all *too perfect*. It looked casual, and naturally neat. And that abundant white hair of his was, like the walls of his mansion, a pure, unadulterated white. Just as I had the first time, I watched him approach through a gap in the curtains.

The front doorbell rang and I opened it and let him in. This time he didn't hold his hand out to shake mine. He just looked me in the eye, and gave a small smile and a brief nod of greeting. I breathed a sigh of relief. I'd been a bit anxious that every time we met I'd have to go through one of his firm handshakes. Once again, I showed him into the living room and had him sit on the sofa. And brought out two cups of freshly brewed coffee from the kitchen.

"I didn't know what I should wear," he said, sounding apologetic. "Is this outfit all right?"

"It doesn't matter at this point. We can decide at the end how you should be dressed. A suit, or shorts and sandals, we can adjust the clothes later on however we want."

Or show you holding a Starbucks cup, I added to myself.

"Knowing you're going to be modeling makes you anxious. I know I won't have to take off all my clothes, but it still makes me feel like I'm being stripped down."

"You could be right. Models for paintings sometimes pose nude—in most cases actually nude, in some cases more metaphorically. The artist wants to view the model's essence, meaning he has to strip away the clothed, outer appearance. To do that, of course, takes great powers of observation and a sharp intuition."

Menshiki spread his hands on his lap and seemed to be inspecting them. He then looked up. "I heard that you don't use a live model when you paint a portrait."

"That's right. I meet the subject once and have a long talk with him, but don't have him model live for me."

"Is there a reason for that?"

"No real reason. I've just found, through experience, that things go more smoothly that way. When we first meet I concentrate as much as I can, trying to get a take on the subject's looks, expressions, quirks, and tendencies, and brand those into my memory. Once I've done that, it's just a question of reproducing them from memory."

"That's very intriguing," Menshiki said. "So, days later you take the memory you've burned into your brain, rearrange all that as an image, and reproduce it as a work of art. You must have a gift to do that—to have such extraordinary visual recall."

"I wouldn't call it a gift, exactly. More of a skill set, I'd say."

"Maybe that's why, when I saw some of the portraits you've done, I sensed something unique in them. Compared with other standard portraits—portraits done purely as commodities. The way everything's reproduced so vividly, you might say . . ."

He took a sip of coffee, took a light-cream linen handkerchief from his jacket pocket, and wiped his mouth. "But this time, unusually, you'll be using a model—with me in front of you, in other words—as you do the portrait."

"Exactly. At your request."

He nodded. "Truthfully, I was curious. About how it feels to become part of a painting, right in front of your eyes. I wanted to actually experience it. Not simply have my painting done, but to experience it as a kind of exchange."

"An exchange?"

"Between the two of us, you and me."

I was silent. The meaning of the expression "an exchange" eluded me for a moment.

"We exchange parts of us with each other," Menshiki explained. "I offer something of myself, and you offer something of yourself. It doesn't have to be something valuable. It can be simple, like a kind of sign."

"Like children exchange pretty seashells?"

"Exactly."

I thought about this. "Sounds interesting, but the problem is I don't have any nice seashells to offer you."

"You're not so comfortable doing it this way? Are you intentionally avoiding that kind of exchange? Is that why you don't use live models? If that's true, then I can—"

"No—that's not it. I don't use models because I don't need them. That's all. I'm not trying to avoid an interchange between people. I've studied painting for a long time, and have used live models more times than I can remember. If you don't mind the drudgery of sitting still in a hard chair for hours at a time, I'm totally fine with you posing for me."

"I don't mind," Menshiki said, spreading his palms up, lightly lifting them upward. "Then why don't we commence the drudgery?"

We went into the studio. I brought over a dining room chair and had Menshiki sit in that. I let him assume whatever posture he wanted. I sat on an old wooden stool facing him (no doubt the stool Tomohiko Amada used when he painted), and started sketching with a soft pencil. I needed to decide on a basic approach of how I was going to reproduce his face on canvas.

"Is it boring to sit there? If you'd like, we could listen to some music," I said.

"If it doesn't bother you, I'd love to hear some music," Menshiki said.

"Why don't you choose something from the shelf in the living room."

He spent about five minutes perusing the selection of records and returned with a four-disc boxed set of LPs of Georg Solti conducting a performance of Richard Strauss's *Der Rosenkavalier*. The orchestra was the Vienna Philharmonic, the singers Régine Crespin and Yvonne Minton.

"Do you like *Der Rosenkavalier*?" he asked me.

"I've never heard it."

"It's an unusual opera. The plot's critical, of course, like with all operas, but with this one even if you don't know the plot it's easy to give yourself over to the music and be completely enveloped by that world. The world of supreme bliss Strauss achieved at the peak of his powers. When it was first performed, people criticized it as nostalgic, unadventurous even, where in reality the music is quite progressive and uninhibited. He was influenced by Wagner, but Strauss creates his own strange, unique musical realm. Once you get into this music you can't get enough of it. I usually prefer Karajan's or Erich Kleiber's version, and have never heard Solti's. If it's all right with you, I'd like to take this opportunity to hear it."

"Of course. Let's listen to it."

He placed the record on the turntable, lowered the needle, and carefully adjusted the volume on the amp. He went back to his chair, settled into a proper pose, and concentrated on the music flowing from the speakers. I did some quick sketches in my sketchbook of his face from several angles. His face was overall nicely put together, the features distinctive enough that I didn't find it hard to capture the unique details of each. In the space of thirty minutes I completed five sketches from different angles. But when I examined them again, I was struck by an odd, helpless feeling. My sketches had accurately captured what was distinctive about his face, yet there was nothing about them beyond the sense that they were *well-done drawings*. They were all oddly shallow and superficial, devoid of depth. They were no different from caricatures drawn by some street artist. I tried doing a few more sketches, with basically the same result.

For me, this was pretty unusual. I had years of experience reconstructing people's faces in a drawing, and flattered myself that I was good at it. Whether with a pencil or a paintbrush I could almost always come up with several mental images of what I was after with no trouble. I rarely struggled to decide on the composition of a painting. But now, with Menshiki as my model, not a single image came to me.

Perhaps I was overlooking something important. I couldn't help but think that. Maybe Menshiki was adeptly hiding it from me. Or maybe it didn't exist in him to begin with.

When the B side of the first of the four records in *Der Rosenkavalier* set finished I gave up, shut my sketchbook, and laid down my pencil. I lifted the needle, took the record off the turntable, and returned it to the boxed set. I glanced at my watch and sighed.

"I'm finding it very hard to draw you," I admitted.

He looked at me in surprise. "In what way?" he asked. "Are you saying there's some pictorial issue with the way I look?"

I shook my head slightly. "No, it's not that. Of course there's nothing wrong with your face."

"Then what's making it hard?"

"I wish I could tell you. It just feels that way. Maybe we still haven't *exchanged* enough yet, as you put it. Haven't traded enough seashells."

Menshiki smiled, looking a bit perplexed. "Is there anything I can do to help?"

I stood up from the stool, went over to the window, and watched the birds flying over the woods.

"Mr. Menshiki, if it's all right with you, could you give me a little more information about yourself? I know next to nothing about you."

"Of course. I'm not trying to hide anything. No outrageous secrets or anything I'm trying to keep from you. I can tell you just about everything. What sort of information were you thinking of?"

"Well—for starters, I don't even know your full name."

"That's right!" he said, looking a bit surprised. "Now that you mention it, you're absolutely right. I was so caught up in talking I forgot to give this to you."

He took a black leather holder from a pocket of his chinos and removed a business card. He handed me the card, and I read it. The thick white card simply read:

On the back was an address in Kanagawa Prefecture, a phone number, and an email address. That was all. No company name or title.

"The *wataru* in my name is the character that means 'to cross a river,'" Menshiki said. "I don't know why I was given that name. I've never had much to do with water."

"The name Menshiki isn't one you see very often."

"I heard our family's roots are in Shikoku, but I have no connection to Shikoku at all. I was born and raised in Tokyo, all my schooling was in Tokyo. And I prefer soba noodles to udon, which Shikoku is famous for." Menshiki laughed.

"May I ask how old you are?"

"Of course. I turned fifty-four last month. How old do I look to you?"

I shook my head. "Honestly, I had no idea. That's why I asked."

"It must be this white hair," he said with a smile. "People often tell me they can't tell my age because of the white hair. You often hear about people whose hair turned white overnight because they were terrified. People often ask if that's what happened with me, but I never had such a traumatic experience. I just tended to have a lot of white hair, ever since I was young. By the time I was in my mid-forties it was completely white. It's weird, though, since my grandfather, father, and two older brothers are all bald. In the whole family I'm the only one who has completely white hair."

"If you don't mind me asking, what sort of work are you involved in?"

"I don't mind at all. It's just—hard to talk about."

"If you'd rather not . . ."

"It's a little embarrassing, actually," he said. "Right now I'm not working at all. Not that I'm getting unemployment insurance or anything, but officially I'm unemployed. I spend a few hours each day online in my office in stock trading and currency exchange, though we're not talking large amounts. More a hobby or to kill time. Training to keep my mind active. Like a pianist practices scales every day."

Menshiki took a quiet, deep breath and recrossed his legs. "In the past I started and ran a tech-related company, but not long ago I decided to sell all my stock and step down. The buyer was a major telecommunications company. That sale meant I have enough savings to live on for a while. I used that opportunity to sell my house in Tokyo and move here. Basically, I'm retired. My savings are divided among several overseas banks, and I move those around depending on variable exchange rates, so I make a bit of a profit that way."

"I see," I said. "Do you have a family?"

"No family. I've never been married."

"So you live in that huge house all by yourself?"

He nodded. "I do. At this point I have no household staff. I've lived by myself for a long time and am used to doing housework. But since it's such a big place, I can't clean it all myself, so I hire a cleaning service to come in once a week. Other than that, I pretty much take care of everything. What about you?"

I shook my head. "I've been on my own less than a year. Still an amateur."

Menshiki gave a slight nod, but didn't ask any questions or offer any comments. "Are you close to Tomohiko Amada?" he asked.

"No, I've never even met him. I was with his son in art school, and through that connection he asked me if I wanted to take care of the vacant house. Some things came up in my life and I didn't have any place to live then, so I decided to accept the offer. For the time being."

Menshiki gave a few more small nods. "It's not very convenient for anyone working at a regular job, but for folks like you two, I imagine it's a wonderful environment."

I gave a forced smile. "We might both be painters, but Tomohiko Amada and I are on totally different levels. It's embarrassing to even be mentioned in the same breath as him."

Menshiki raised his head and looked at me, his eyes serious. "It's too soon to say that. You might become a well-known artist someday."

There was nothing I could say to that, so I was silent.

"Sometimes people go through huge transformations," Menshiki said. "They obliterate the style they've worked in, and out of the ruins they rise up again. Tomohiko Amada was that way. When he was young he painted Western-style work. You've heard about this, I'm sure?"

"I have. Before the war he was a promising young painter of Western-style art. But after he came back from studying in Vienna he changed to being a Japanese-style artist, and after the war was amazingly successful."

"The way I see it," Menshiki said, "there's a point in everybody's life where they need a major transformation. And when that time comes you have to grab it by the tail. Grab it hard, and never let go. There are some people who are able to, and others who can't. Tomohiko Amada was one who could."

A major transformation. The words suddenly made me think of *Killing Commendatore*. And the young man stabbing the Commendatore to death.

"Do you know much about Japanese-style painting?" Menshiki asked.

I shook my head. "I'm basically a layman. I attended lectures on it when I was in art school, but that's the extent of my knowledge."

"This is a very basic question, but how is Japanese art defined, professionally?"

"It's not so easy to define. It's usually taken to mean paintings done using glue and pigment and foil leaf. And done not with a paintbrush, but with a writing brush. In other words Japanese paintings are defined mainly by the materials used to paint them. The transmission of ancient, traditional techniques is one feature, though there are lots of Japanese paintings done using avant-garde techniques, and with colors, too, there is a lot of use of new materials. So the definition has steadily become increasingly vague. But as far as Tomohiko Amada's paintings go, they're classic Japanese art. Archetypal, you might call them. They're done in a style that's recognizably his own, of course. I just mean as far as techniques are concerned."

"So you're saying that if the definition based on materials and techniques gets vague, all you're left with is the mental aspect, right?"

"Maybe so. But the mental aspect of Japanese paintings isn't easily defined. They are, from the beginning, rather eclectic."

"By eclectic you mean . . . ?"

I searched the depths of memory and recalled what I'd learned in art history class. "The Meiji Restoration took place in the latter half of the nineteenth century, and along with other aspects of Western culture Western art also was introduced into Japan, but until then the genre of 'Japanese painting' didn't actually exist. The term didn't even exist. Just like up till then the name of the country, Japan, was hardly ever used. With the appearance of Western art from abroad, the concept of Japanese art was born as a way of asserting something that could be distinguished as standing in opposition to Western art. What had existed up until then in various forms and styles was, for the sake of simplicity, lumped together under the new name of 'Japanese painting.' Of course, there were some types of painting that were excluded from that and fell into decline. Chinese ink paintings, for instance. The Meiji government established and cultivated so-called Japanese painting as a kind of national art, as part of Japanese cultural identity that could stand shoulder to shoulder with Western culture—the 'Japanese spirit' part of the popular slogan at the time—'Japanese Spirit with Western Learning.' What had been everyday designs, arts and crafts designs such as paintings on folding screens and *fusuma* sliding doors and bowls and plates, were now set in frames and featured in art exhibitions. To put it another way, items done in a natural style as part of everyday life were now accommodated to the Western system and elevated to the status of 'works of art.' "

I paused for a moment and studied Menshiki's face. He seemed to be listening closely to what I said. I went on.

"Tenshin Okakura and Ernest Fenollosa were at the forefront of this movement. What happened with art could be counted as one of the amazing success stories during this period when aspects of Japanese culture were rapidly being reconfigured. A similar process was taking place in the worlds of music, literature, and thought. It must have been a pretty hectic time for Japanese back then, since they had tons of important work they had to accomplish in a very short period of time. Looking back on it now, I'd say we did a pretty clever and skillful job of it. The merging and compartmentalizing of Western aspects and non-Western aspects took place very smoothly. Maybe Japanese are intrinsically suited to that kind of process.

"So Japanese painting wasn't clearly defined originally. You might say it was a concept based on a vague consensus. There wasn't initially a clear division, and it only came about tangentially, when external and internal pressure created one."

Menshiki seemed to be considering all this. "It might have been vague," he finally said, "but this was a consensus born of necessity, right?"

"Exactly. A consensus arising out of necessity."

"Not having a set framework was both a strength and a weakness of Japanese painting. Could we interpret it this way?"

"I think so."

"But when we look at a painting, in most cases we have the sense whether it's a Japanese painting or not. Right?"

"That's right. There's an intrinsic method used. A kind of trend, or tone. And a tacit, shared understanding. It's hard sometimes to define it, though."

Menshiki was silent for a while. "If a painting is non-Western, then does it have the form of a Japanese painting?"

"Not necessarily," I replied. "In principle there are Western paintings that have a non-Western form."

"I see," he said. He tilted his head ever so slightly. "But if it's a Japanese painting, then to some extent it will have a non-Western form about it. Would that be accurate?"

I gave it some thought. "Put that way, yes, you could say so. I hadn't thought about it that way, to tell you the truth."

"It's self-evident, but still difficult to put into words."

I nodded in agreement.

He paused for a moment, and then went on. "If you think about it, it's akin to defining yourself as compared with another person. The difference is self-evident, but still difficult to verbalize. As you said, you can perhaps only understand it as a kind of tangent produced when external and internal pressure combine to create it."

Menshiki gave a slight smile. "Fascinating," he added in a small voice, as if to himself.

What are we talking about? I suddenly thought. An intriguing topic in its own right, but what significance did this conversation hold for him? Was it mere intellectual curiosity? Or was he testing my intellect? What was the point?

"By the way, I'm left-handed," Menshiki said at one point, as if he'd just recalled this fact. "I don't know if that will be helpful, but it's another piece of information about me. If I'm told to go left or right, I always choose left. It's become a habit."

It was finally near three o'clock, and we set the date and time of our next session. He would come to my house in three days, on Monday at one p.m. As he did this day, we would spend two hours together in my studio, and I would attempt to sketch him again.

"I'm in no rush," Menshiki said. "As I said in the beginning, take as much time as you need. I have all the time in the world."

And then he left. Through the window I watched him get into his Jaguar and drive away. I picked up all the sketches I'd done of him, studied them for a time, then tossed them aside.

A terrible silence descended over the house. Now alone, it was as if the silence had become all the more weighty. I went out on the terrace and there was no wind, the air jelly-thick and chilly. It felt like it was going to rain.

I sat down on the living room sofa, reviewing the conversation Menshiki and I had had, in order. How we'd talked about posing for a portrait. About Strauss's opera *Der Rosenkavalier*. About how Menshiki had started a tech company, sold off his stock, and with the sizable profit retired young. How he lived all alone in that huge house. His first name was Wataru. Written with the character that means "to cross a river." He'd always been a bachelor, and his hair had turned white early on. He was left-handed and was now fifty-four. How Tomohiko Amada had made a bold pivot, how one should grab opportunity by the tail and never let go. The definition of Japanese painting. And finally, about the relationship between Self and Other.

What in the world did he want from me?

And why wasn't I able to do any decent sketches of him?

The answer was simple, really. *Because I had not yet grasped what lay at the core of his being.*

After talking with him I felt uneasy. Yet at the same time, my curiosity about him had grown all the stronger.

Thirty minutes later heavy drops of rain began to fall. The little birds had by then already vanished.

10

AS WE PUSH OUR WAY THROUGH THE LUSH GREEN GRASS

When I was fifteen my younger sister died. It happened very suddenly. She was twelve then, in her first year of junior high. She had been born with a congenital heart problem, but since the time she was in the upper grades of elementary school she hadn't shown any more symptoms, and our family had felt reassured, holding out the faint hope that her life would go on, without incident. But in May of that year her heartbeat became more irregular. It was especially bad when she lay down, and she suffered many sleepless nights. She underwent tests at the university hospital, but no matter how detailed the tests the doctors couldn't pinpoint any changes in her physical condition. The basic issue was supposed to have been resolved back when she'd had her operations, and the doctors were baffled.

"Avoid strenuous exercise, and follow a regular routine, and things should settle down soon," the doctor said. That was probably all he could say. And he wrote out a few prescriptions for her.

But her arrhythmia didn't settle down. As I sat across from her at the dining table I often looked at her chest and imagined the defective heart inside it. Her breasts were beginning to noticeably develop. Her heart might have problems, but her flesh continued growing nonetheless. It felt strange to see my little sister's breasts grow by the day. Up till then she'd just been a little child, but now she'd suddenly had her first period, and her breasts were slowly starting to take shape. Yet within that tiny chest, my sister's heart was defective. And even a specialist couldn't pinpoint the defect. That fact alone had my brain in constant turmoil. I spent my adolescence in a state of anxiety, fearful that, at any moment, I might lose my little sister.

My parents told me to watch over her, since her body was so delicate. While we attended the same elementary school I always kept my eye on her. If need be, I was willing to risk my life to protect her and her tiny heart. Though the opportunity never presented itself.

She was on her way home from junior high one day when she collapsed and lost consciousness while climbing the stairs at Seibu Shinjuku Station. She was rushed by ambulance to the nearest emergency room. By the time I got home and then raced to the hospital, her heart had already stopped. It all happened in the blink of an eye. That morning we'd eaten breakfast together, said goodbye to each other at the front door, me going off to high school, she to junior high. And the next time I saw her she'd stopped breathing. Her large eyes were closed forever, her mouth slightly open as if she were about to say something. Her developing breasts would never grow.

The next time I saw her she was in a coffin. She was dressed in her favorite black velvet dress, with a touch of makeup, her hair neatly combed. She had on black patent-leather shoes and lay faceup in the modestly sized coffin. The dress had a white lace collar, so white it looked unnatural.

Lying there, she appeared to be peacefully sleeping. Shake her lightly and she'd wake up, it seemed. But that was an illusion. Shake her all you want, but she would never awaken again.

I didn't want my sister's delicate little body to be stuffed into that cramped, confining box. Her body should be laid to rest on a much more spacious place. In the middle of a meadow, for instance. We would wordlessly go to visit her, pushing aside the lush green grass as we went. The wind would slowly rustle the grass, and birds and insects would call out from all around her. The raw smell of wildflowers would fill the air, pollen swirling. When night fell, the sky above her would be dotted with countless silvery stars. In the morning a new sun would make the dew on the blades of grass sparkle like jewels. But in reality she was packed away in some ridiculous coffin. The only decorations were ominous white flowers that had been snipped by scissors and stuck in vases. The narrow room had fluorescent lighting that was drained of color. From a small speaker set into the ceiling came the artificial strains of organ music.

I couldn't stand to see her be cremated. When the coffin lid was shut and locked, I couldn't take it anymore and left the cremation room. I didn't help when the family ritually placed her bones inside a vase. I went out into the crematorium courtyard and cried soundlessly by myself. During her all-too-short life, I'd never once helped my little sister, a thought that hurt me deeply.

After my sister's death, our family changed. My father became even more taciturn, my mother even more nervous and jumpy. Basically I kept on with the same life as always. I joined the mountaineering club at school, which kept me busy, and when I wasn't doing that I started oil painting. My art teacher recommended that I find a good instructor and really study painting. And when I finally did start attending art classes, my interest became serious. I think I was trying to keep myself busy so I wouldn't think about my dead sister.

For a long time, I'm not sure how many years, my parents kept her room exactly as it was. Textbooks and study guides, pens, erasers, and paper clips piled on her desk, the sheets, blankets, and pillows on her bed, her laundered and folded pajamas, her junior high school uniform hanging in the closet—all untouched. The calendar on the wall still had her schedule written in her tiny writing. It was left at the month she died, as if time had frozen solid at that point. It felt as if the door would open at any moment and she'd come inside. When no one else was at home I'd sometimes go into her room, sit down on the neatly made bed, and gaze around me. But I never touched anything. I didn't want to disturb, even a little, any of the silent little objects left behind, signs that my sister had once been among the living.

I often tried to imagine what sort of life my sister would have had if she hadn't died at twelve. Though there was no way I could know. I couldn't even picture how my own life would turn out, so I had no idea what her future would have held. But I knew that if only she hadn't had a problem with one of her heart valves, she would have grown to be a capable, attractive adult. I'm sure many men would have loved her, and held her gently in their arms. But I couldn't picture any of that in detail. For me, she was forever my little sister, three years younger, who needed my protection.

For a time after she died I drew sketches of her, over and over. Reproducing in my sketchbook, from all different angles, my memory of her face, so I wouldn't forget it. Not that I was about to forget her face. It will remain etched in my mind until the day I die. What I sought was not to forget the face I remembered at that point in time. In order to do that, I had to give form to it by drawing. I was only fifteen then, and there was so much I didn't know about memory, drawing, and the flow of time. But one thing I did know was that I needed to do something in order to hold on to an accurate record of my memory. Leave it alone, and it would disappear somewhere. No matter how vivid a memory, the power of time was stronger. I knew this instinctively.

I would sit alone in her room on her bed, drawing her, sketching her face over and over. I tried to reproduce onto the blank paper how she looked in my mind's eye. I lacked experience then, and the requisite technical skill, so it wasn't an easy process. I'd draw, rip up my effort, draw and rip up, endlessly. But now when I look at the drawings I did keep (I still treasure my sketchbook from back then), I can see that they are filled with a genuine sense of grief. They may be technically immature, but it was a sincere effort, my own soul trying to awaken my sister's. When I looked at those sketches, I couldn't help but cry. I've done countless drawings since, but never again has anything I've drawn brought me to tears.

There's one other effect my sister's death had on me—a very severe case of claustrophobia. Ever since I saw her be placed in that cramped little coffin, the lid shut and locked tight, and taken away to the crematorium, I haven't been able to go into tight, enclosed places. For a long time I couldn't take elevators. I'd stand in front of an elevator and all I could think about was it automatically shutting down in an earthquake, with me trapped inside that confined space. Just the thought of it was enough to send me into a choking sense of panic.

These symptoms didn't appear right after my sister's death. It took nearly three years for them to surface. The first time I had a panic attack was soon after I started art school, when I had a part-time job with a moving company. I was the driver's assistant in a covered truck, loading boxes and taking them out, and one time I got mistakenly locked inside the empty cargo compartment. Work was done for the day and the driver was checking to see if anything was left behind in the cargo compartment. He forgot to make sure if anyone was still inside, and locked the door from the outside.

About two and half hours passed until the door was opened and I was able to crawl out. That whole time I was locked inside a sealed, cramped, totally dark place. It wasn't a refrigerated truck or anything, so there were gaps where air could get in. If I'd thought about it calmly, I would have known I wouldn't suffocate.

But still, a terrible panic had me in its grip. There was plenty of oxygen, yet no matter how deeply I breathed in, I wasn't able to absorb it. My breathing got more and more ragged and I started hyperventilating. I felt dizzy, like I was choking, and was overwhelmed by an inexplicable panic. It's okay, calm down, I told myself. You'll be able to get out soon. It's impossible to suffocate here. But logic didn't work. The only thing in my mind was my little sister, crammed into a tiny coffin, and hauled off to the crematorium. Completely terrified, I pounded on the walls of the truck.

The truck was in the company parking lot, and all the employees, their workday done, had gone home. Nobody noticed that I wasn't around. I pounded like crazy, but no one seemed to hear. If I was unlucky I might be shut inside until morning. At the thought of that, it felt like all my muscles were about to disintegrate.

It was the night security guard, making his rounds of the parking lot, who finally heard the noise I was making and unlocked the door. When he saw how agitated and exhausted I was, he had me lie down on the bed in the company break room. And gave me a cup of hot tea. I don't know how long I lay there. But finally my breathing became normal again. Dawn was coming, so I thanked the guard and took the first train of the day back home. I slipped into my own bed and lay there, shaking like crazy for the longest time.

Ever since then, riding elevators has triggered the same panic. The incident must have awoken a fear that had been lurking within me. And I have little doubt this was set off by memories of my dead sister. And it wasn't only elevators, but any enclosed space. I couldn't even watch movies with scenes set in submarines or tanks. Just imagining myself shut inside such confined spaces—*merely* imagining it—made me unable to breathe. Often I had to get up and leave the theater. If a scene came on of someone shut away in a confined space, I couldn't stand to watch. That's why I seldom watched movies with anyone else.

One time on a trip to Hokkaido I had no choice but to stay overnight in one of those capsule hotels. My breathing became labored, and I couldn't sleep, so I went outside and spent the night inside my car. It was early spring in Hokkaido, still quite cold, and the whole night was like a nightmare.

My wife often kidded me about my panic attacks. When we had to go to a floor high up in a building she would precede me in the elevator and would wait there, enjoying me huffing and puffing my way up sixteen or so flights of stairs. But I never explained to her why I had that phobia. I just told her I've always had a fear of elevators.

"Well, it might be healthier for you to walk," she said.

I also had a feeling akin to fear about women with larger than normal breasts. I don't know if that has anything to do with my sister, or the way her breasts were just beginning to develop when she died. Still, I've always been attracted to women with more modest breasts, and every time I see them, every time I touch them, I remember my sister . . . Don't get me wrong, I wasn't sexually interested in my sister. I think I was just looking for a certain type of scene. A finite scene, lost and never to return.

On Saturday afternoon my hand was resting on the chest of my married lover. Her breasts weren't particularly small, or large. Just the right size, they fit neatly into my palm. Her nipples were still hard in my hand.

She'd never come to my house on a Saturday. She always spent the weekends with her family. But that weekend her husband was on a business trip to Mumbai and her two daughters were staying over at their cousin's house in Nasu in Tochigi. So she came to my place. And like we did on weekday afternoons, we leisurely enjoyed sex. Afterward we lay there in a lazy, indolent silence. Like always.

"Would you like to hear what the jungle grapevine turned up?" she asked.

"Jungle grapevine?" I suddenly couldn't think of what she was talking about.

"Don't tell me you forgot? The mystery man in the big white house across the valley. You asked me to look into this Mr. Menshiki the other day."

"Ah, that's right. Of course I remember."

"I found out a little bit about him. One of my housewife friends lives near him, and she could gather some info on him. Would you like to hear it?"

"Of course."

"Mr. Menshiki bought that house with the gorgeous view about three years ago. Another family was living in it before then. They're the ones who built the house, but those original owners only lived there about two years. One sunny morning they suddenly packed up all their belongings and left, and Menshiki took their place. He bought the house, which was practically brand-new. How that all came about, though, nobody knows."

"So he didn't build the house himself," I said.

"That's right. He moved into a container that was already there. Like a quick-witted hermit crab."

That was unexpected. I'd been positive he was the one who built that house. That's how closely I'd linked his image—probably corresponding to his wonderfully white hair—with that white mansion on top of the mountain.

She continued. "Nobody knows what kind of work he does. What they do know is that he never commutes to work. He stays in his house all day, probably on his computer. His study is full of those devices. Nowadays if you know what you're doing, you can find out most everything online. A man I know is a surgeon who works entirely from home. He's crazy about surfing and doesn't want to leave the ocean."

"A surgeon can work entirely from home?"

“They send him all the images and information about the patients, which he analyzes and then creates the protocols for the operations, sends these to the on-site staff, and monitors the operations remotely, sometimes giving them advice. Sometimes he uses a remote magic hand device to actually perform operations. That kind of thing.”

“What an age we live in,” I said. “I wouldn’t like to have anyone operate on me like that.”

“I wonder if Mr. Menshiki is doing something similar,” she said. “No matter what kind of work he’s doing, he’s pulling in enough income. He lives alone most of the time in the huge house, occasionally goes on long trips. Probably trips abroad. In his house he has a home gym with lots of exercise machines, where he works out whenever he has a chance. There’s not an ounce of fat on him. He mostly prefers classical music, and has a substantial listening room. A pretty luxurious life, wouldn’t you say?”

“Where’d you get all these details?”

She laughed. “You seem to underestimate women’s information-gathering skills.”

“You could be right.”

“He has four cars altogether. Two Jaguars and a Range Rover. Plus a Mini Cooper. He seems to like British cars.”

“Mini Coopers are made by BMW these days, and I believe Jaguar was purchased by an Indian corporation. So it’s hard to call either of them British cars.”

“The Mini he drives is an older version. And whatever corporation bought Jaguar, it’s still a British car.”

“Did you find out anything else?”

“Hardly anybody ever comes to the house. Mr. Menshiki prefers solitude. He likes to be alone, likes to listen to classical music and read a lot. He’s single and well off, yet almost never brings women home. For all appearances he lives a very simple, orderly life. Makes you think he might be gay. Though there’s some evidence that points in the other direction.”

“I’m thinking you must have a well-placed source of information.”

“She’s not there now, but until not long ago he had a maid who’d come in a few times a week. She's the one who took out the garbage, went shopping for him at the local supermarket, where there were other housewives from the neighborhood and they'd start chatting."

"I see," I said. "That's how the jungle grapevine gets formed."

"You got it. According to her, there's a kind of *forbidden chamber* in the house. He instructed her never to enter it. He made it quite clear."

"Sounds like Bluebeard's castle."

"Exactly. People often say that, right? That every house has a skeleton in the closet."

That reminded me of the painting *Killing Commendatore* hidden away in the attic. That might be a skeleton hidden in a closet too.

She went on. "The woman never did find out what was in that mystery room. It was always locked. But anyway, that maid doesn't work there anymore. Maybe she got fired for being a bit too talkative. He seems to be doing all the housework himself now."

"He told me the same thing. That aside from a once-a-week cleaning service he takes care of all the household chores himself."

"He seems very touchy about his privacy."

"Be that as it may, but isn't the fact that you and I meet like this spreading through your jungle grapevine?"

"I doubt it," she said in a quiet voice. "First of all, I'm very careful that it doesn't. And second, you're a little different from Mr. Menshiki."

"Meaning . . . ," I said, translating this into words that were easy to understand, ". . . that there are things about him that lend themselves to rumor, but not with me."

"We should be thankful for that," she said cheerily.

After my little sister died all kinds of things started to go wrong. The metalworking company my father operated went downhill, and he was so busy dealing with that he hardly ever came home. The atmosphere at home became strained. Long, heavy silences reigned over the house. It hadn't been that way when my sister was still alive. I wanted to get away from it all, and got even more absorbed in painting as a way to escape. Eventually I decided to attend art school and major in painting. My father was dead set against it. You can't earn a decent living painting, he argued. And I don't have the money to help raise an artist. The two of us argued about it. My mother intervened to smooth things over, and though somehow I was able to attend art school, my father and I never did reconcile.

If only my sister hadn't died, I sometimes thought. If she'd lived, my family would have been so much happier. Her sudden disappearance made our family fall apart. Our home became a site where people lashed out and hurt each other. I felt helpless, knowing I could never fill in the hole my sister had left behind.

I stopped drawing pictures of her. After I entered art school the things I wanted to paint were phenomena and objects that didn't have intrinsic meaning. Abstract paintings, in other words. Things in which all sorts of meanings were encoded, where new semantic meaning arose from the interweaving of one sign and another. I plunged into a world that aimed at that type of completeness, and was able to breathe normally for the first time in forever.

Creating those kinds of paintings, though, didn't lead to any decent jobs. I graduated, but as long as I stuck to abstract painting my father was right—I had no hope of earning any money. So in order to make a living (I'd already left my parents' home and needed to earn money for rent and food) I was compelled to take on portrait work. By doing a conventional job, painting those utilitarian paintings, I was somehow able to survive as an artist.

And now I was about to paint a portrait of Wataru Menshiki. The Wataru Menshiki who lived in the white mansion on top of the mountain across the way. The white-haired man the neighbors had heard all sorts of rumors about, this clearly intriguing person. He had picked me out, hired me for a huge fee to paint his portrait. But what I discovered was that at this point I *wasn't even able to paint a portrait.* Even that kind of conventional, utilitarian art was beyond me. I'd truly become hollow, an empty shell.

We should wordlessly go to visit her, pushing our way through the lush green grass. This random thought struck me. If we could, how truly wonderful that would be.

11

THE MOONLIGHT SHONE BEAUTIFULLY ON EVERYTHING

The silence woke me. That happens sometimes. A sudden sound will cut the silence, waking a person, and sometimes a sudden silence will cut through sounds, waking you.

I shot awake and glanced over at my bedside clock. The digital display read 1:45. After a moment I remembered that it was 1:45 a.m. on Saturday night, or rather early Sunday morning. Earlier that afternoon I had spent time with my married lover in this bed. She went home before evening, I'd had a simple dinner, read for a while, and gone to sleep after ten. I'm generally a sound sleeper, and don't wake up until the morning light wakes me. So having my sleep interrupted like that in the middle of the night was unusual.

I lay there in the darkness wondering why I'd awakened at this hour. It was a typical, quiet night. The nearly full moon was a huge round mirror floating in the sky. The scenery on earth was whitish, as if washed with lime. But nothing else seemed out of the ordinary. I half sat up and listened carefully. And finally realized something *was* different from usual. *It was too quiet.* The silence was too deep. It was a fall night, yet no insects were chirping. Since the house was built in the mountains, after sunset the insects invariably started their ear-splitting chirping, a chorus that went on until late at night. (It really surprised me to learn this, since until I lived here I always thought they only chirped early in the evening.) The sound was so piercing it made me think that insects had conquered the world. But this night, when I woke up, there was not a single screech or chirp. It was disconcerting.

Once awake, I found it hard to get back to sleep. I reluctantly crawled out of bed, and threw a light cardigan over my pajama top. I went to the kitchen, poured myself some Scotch, added a few ice cubes from the ice maker, and drank it. I went onto the terrace and gazed at the lights of the houses through the woods. Everyone seemed to be asleep, no lights on anywhere in any houses. All I saw was a scattering of tiny security lights. The area around Menshiki's house across the valley, too, was surrounded by darkness. And like before, there were no insects chirping. Had something happened to them?

After a while I heard a sound I wasn't used to. Or perhaps *felt* like I heard it. A very faint sound. If the insects had been chirping as loudly as usual I probably never would have caught it. But the profound silence that reigned allowed it to reach me, though barely. I held my breath and strained my ears. It wasn't the chirp of any insects. Not a naturally occurring sound. It was the sound some implement or tool might make, a kind of jingling sound. The sound a bell, or something close to it, might make.

There would be a pause, then the sound. A deep silence, then that sound ringing out a few times, then deep silence once more. As if someone were patiently sending out an encoded message. But it wasn't repeated at regular intervals. Sometimes the silence in between rings was longer, sometimes shorter. And it didn't ring the same number of times. I couldn't tell if their regularity was intentional or capricious. At any rate, it was such a faint sound that if I hadn't focused and listened hard I wouldn't have caught it. But once aware of it, in the deep silence of the middle of the night, with the moonlight so unnaturally bright, that unidentified sound irretrievably ate its way into my awareness.

I was flustered, wondering what it could be, then decided to just go outside and see. I wanted to trace the source of that mysterious sound. Someone, somewhere, was ringing *something or other*. I'm not bold. But going out into the dark night alone then didn't frighten me. Curiosity won out over my fears. And the weirdly bright moonlight might have encouraged me, too.

With an oversized flashlight in my hand, I unlocked the front door and stepped outside. A single light above the entrance threw out a yellowish tint. A swarm of flying insects was drawn to that light. I stood there, ears perked up, trying to see what direction that sound was coming from. It really did sound like a bell, but not an ordinary one. It had a deeper, dull, uneven ring. Maybe it was some special percussion instrument. But what was it, and why would someone be ringing it in the middle of the night? The only residence in the vicinity was the house I was living in. If indeed someone nearby was ringing that bell, it meant they were trespassing.

I looked around to see if anything could serve as a weapon. All I had in my hand was a long cylindrical flashlight. Better than nothing. I grasped the flashlight tightly and headed toward the sound.

I turned left from the front door, which led me to a small set of stone steps. I climbed up the seven steps and entered the woods. I walked up the gentle upward-sloping path that cut through the trees, and before long came to a clearing where there was a small shrine. Masahiko had said that the shrine had been there for a very long time. He didn't know the origins of it, but in the mid-1950s when his father had purchased the house and land from an acquaintance, the shrine already existed . . . On top of a flat stone was a sanctuary with a simple triangular roof—or, more accurately, a small wooden box made to look like a sanctuary. It was about two feet high and a foot and a half wide. It had originally been painted, though by now the color had mostly worn off, leaving one to imagine what it had once been. In the front was a small double door, and I had no idea what sort of offering was set up inside. I didn't check, but probably there wasn't anything enshrined inside. In front of the doors was an empty white ceramic pot. Rainwater had accumulated, then evaporated, over and over, leaving a number of dirty stained lines inside. Tomohiko Amada had left the shrine as it was. Not bringing his hands together in prayer as he passed it, not cleaning it, he simply let it be, swept by rain and wind. For him it must have been not a shrine, but just a plain, spare box.

"He had no interest in faith or worship or the like," his son had explained. "He didn't care a wit about things like divine punishment or retribution or anything. He said those were stupid superstitions, and looked down on them. It wasn't that he was brazen about it, it's just that he's always held to an extremely materialist view of things."

Masahiko had shown me the shrine the first time he took me to see the house. "You don't find many houses these days that come with their own shrine," he laughed, and I agreed.

"When I was a kid, though," Masahiko went on, "it creeped me out to have that kind of weird thing on our property. So when I stayed over I avoided coming near here," he said. "Even now, to tell the truth, I'd rather not go near it."

I wasn't a person who often thought in materialistic terms, but just like his father, Tomohiko Amada, having the shrine nearby didn't bother me. People in the past set up shrines in all kinds of places, much like the little Jizo and Dosojin statues you see next to roads in the countryside. This shrine blended naturally into the scenery in the woods, and when I went on walks I often passed in front of it but never gave it much thought. I never prayed to it, or made any offerings. And I didn't feel anything significant about having that sort of thing on the property where I was living. It was just part of the kind of scenery you'd find anywhere.

The bell-like sound seemed to be coming from near that shrine. Once I set foot in the woods, the tree branches above me blocked the moonlight and everything got suddenly darker. I carefully made my way forward, lighting the path with the flashlight. The wind would occasionally pick up, as if remembering to blow, rustling the thin layer of leaves on the ground. The woods at night felt totally different from walking there in the daytime. The place was operating under the principles at work at night, and those principles didn't include me. That said, I didn't feel particularly afraid. Curiosity spurred me on. I felt compelled to locate where that strange sound was coming from. I tightly gripped the heavy cylindrical flashlight, its weight calming me.

The horned owl might be in these woods somewhere, I thought. Hidden in the darkness on a branch, waiting for its prey. It would be nice if it were nearby. In a way that owl was my friend. But I didn't hear anything that sounded like the hooting of an owl. The night birds, like the insects, were keeping quiet.

As I made my way forward, the bell-like sound became ever clearer. It continued to ring out intermittently, irregularly. The sound seemed to be coming from behind the little shrine. It sounded much closer, but was still muffled, like it was filtering out from deep inside a narrow cave. The silence between each ring had grown longer, and the number of rings was decreasing. As if the person ringing the bell had grown weak, become worn out.

The area around the shrine had been cleared and the moonlight shone beautifully on everything. Stepping silently, I walked over behind the shrine. There was a tall thicket of pampas grass and, led by the sound, I pushed my way into the thicket. There I found a small mound of square stones casually piled up, a kind of ancient burial mound. Though perhaps it was too small to be called that. At any rate, I had never noticed it was there before. I'd never gone behind the shrine, and even if I had, the mound was hidden in the midst of the pampas grass. You weren't going to see it unless you had some reason to wade into the thicket.

I approached the mound and shone my flashlight directly upon it. The stones were old, but weren't in their natural form, and had clearly been chiseled into squares. They had been carried up onto the mountain and piled up behind the shrine. The stones were of different sizes, most of them covered in moss. There wasn't any visible writing or designs on them. There were twelve or thirteen stones altogether, by my count. In the past, the mound might have been taller and more orderly, but maybe an earthquake had made part of it crumble. The bell-like sound somehow seemed to be filtering out from the cracks between those stones.

I lightly rested my foot on top of the stones and searched for the source of that sound. But no matter how bright the moonlight, it was next to impossible to locate it in the dark of night. And what if I did happen to locate it? What then? I couldn't lift these heavy stones myself.

At any rate it seemed like someone below the stone mound was ringing the bell. I was sure of it. But *who*? It was at this point that an enigmatic fear began to well up inside me. Instinct told me not to get any closer to the source of that sound.

I left, and with the bell ringing behind me hurried back along the path through the woods. Moonlight filtering through the branches cast a suggestive mottled pattern on my body. I emerged from the woods, rushed down the seven stone steps, got back to the house, went inside, and locked the door. I walked to the kitchen, poured a glass of whiskey straight, no ice, no water, and gulped it down. I could finally breathe a sigh of relief. I took my glass of whiskey out to the terrace.

From the terrace I could hear the bell only faintly. If I hadn't listened carefully I wouldn't have been able to catch it. But the point was, the sound continued. The interval of silence between each ringing of the bell was definitely lengthening. I listened to that irregular repetition for some time.

What in the world lay beneath the stones of that mound? Was there a space there, and somebody locked inside who was ringing that bell, or whatever it was? Maybe it was a signal for help. But no matter how much I thought it over, I couldn't think of a single plausible explanation.

I might have thought about it for a long time. Or maybe it was but a moment. I had no idea. My sense of time had vanished. Glass of whiskey in hand, I sank back into the lounge chair, shuffling back and forth in the maze of consciousness. And then it hit me. The bell had stopped. Everything was enveloped in a profound silence.

I stood up, went into the bedroom, and looked at the digital clock. It was 2:31 a.m. I didn't know the precise time the bell had started ringing, but since it had been 1:45 when I woke up, I surmised the bell had gone on ringing for at least forty-five minutes. Soon after the mysterious sound ceased, the insects began chirping again, as if probing the new silence that had arisen. As if all the insects in the mountains had been patiently waiting for the sound of that bell to stop. Holding their breath, cautiously assessing the situation.

I went back to the kitchen, rinsed out my glass, then slipped back into bed. By this time the autumn insects were a lusty chirping chorus. I should have been too worked up to sleep, but the straight whiskey did the trick and I fell asleep as soon as my head hit the pillow. A long, deep sleep, bereft of dreams. When I woke again it was already bright outside the bedroom.

That day, before ten a.m., I walked out again to the little shrine in the woods. I couldn't hear that enigmatic sound, but I wanted to study the shrine and stone mound once more in the daylight. I found a stout oak walking stick in Tomohiko Amada's umbrella stand and took that with me. It was a sunny, pleasant morning, the clear autumn sunlight throwing the shadows of leaves across the ground. Birds with sharp bills flitted busily from one branch to another, squawking as they searched for fruit. Up above, a straight line of pitch-black crows was winging its way off somewhere.

The little shrine looked worn and shoddy in the daylight. Bathed in the bright, whitish light of the nearly full moon the shrine had looked deeply meaningful, even a bit ominous, yet now in the light of day it seemed like nothing more than a faded, seedy-looking wooden box.

I went behind the shrine, shouldered my way through the tall thicket of pampas grass, and emerged in front of the stone mound. It seemed completely transformed from the night before. What I saw before me now were merely square moss-covered stones long abandoned in the mountains. In the moonlight it had appeared like part of ancient historical ruins, covered with a mythic slime. I stood on top of the mound and perked up my ears, but couldn't hear a thing. Other than the screech of insects and the occasional bird chirp, it was silent all around.

From far away came the bang of what I took to be a shotgun. Someone might be hunting birds in the mountains. Or else it was one of those automatic devices set up by farmers to shoot blanks to scare away sparrows, monkeys, and wild boar. Either way, the sound echoed with the feeling of autumn. The sky was high, the air slightly humid, and sounds carried well. I sat down on top of the stone mound and thought about the space that might exist beneath. Was someone really under there, ringing a bell, calling out for help? Were they like me, back when I worked for the moving company and got locked inside the truck and pounded on the side panels as hard as I could, hoping someone would rescue me? The image of someone locked up in a cramped dark space put me on edge.

After a light lunch I changed into work clothes (and by that I mean things I didn't mind getting dirty), went into the studio, and once more tried my hand at Wataru Menshiki's portrait. I had to dispel the image of someone shut away in an enclosed space, hoping for help, and the chronic sense of suffocation that induced in me. I had to keep my hands busy, and painting was the only solution. This time I put aside my sketchbook and pencil. They wouldn't help, I figured. I readied my paints and paintbrushes, stood facing the canvas, and, gazing deep into that blank space, I focused on Menshiki. I stood erect, focused my concentration, and pruned away any extraneous thoughts.

A white-haired man with young-looking eyes who lived in a white mansion on a mountain. He spent most of his time at home, had what appeared to be a hidden room, and owned four British cars. How had he moved when he was here? What kind of expressions did he have on his face, what was his tone of voice, what did he look at and with what sort of look in his eyes, how did he move his hands? I recalled each and every detail. It took a while, but all the fragments started to fall into place. In my mind now, a three-dimensional, organically constructed sense of the man began to come together.

With small brushstrokes I transferred the image of Menshiki that arose from this directly onto the canvas, without the usual rough sketch. The Menshiki in my mind was facing forward, face slightly tilted to the left, his eyes looking a bit in my direction. For some reason I couldn't picture any other angle his face should be. To me, *that* was Wataru Menshiki. He had to have his face slightly tilted to the left. And had to have both eyes looking a bit in my direction. I'm in his field of vision. No other composition would accurately capture him.

I stepped away from the canvas and studied the simple composition I'd done, pretty much with a single brushstroke. It was just a temporary line drawing, but I could sense from that outline a budding, living organism. With that as the starting point, it would naturally expand from there. Something was reaching out a hand—but what was it?—and had flipped a switch inside me. A sort of vague sensation, as if an animal hibernating deep within me had finally recognized that the season had arrived, and was slowly brushing aside the cobwebs of sleep.

I washed the paint off the brush in the sink and lathered my hands with oil and soap. I was in no hurry. This was plenty for today. It was best to not rush the work. When Mr. Menshiki next came to see me, as a live model, I could then flesh out this outline. I had a premonition that this painting was going to be very different from any portrait I'd ever done before. And this painting required the flesh-and-blood Menshiki.

Which was very odd, I thought.

How had Menshiki known that?

In the middle of the night I suddenly shot awake again. The clock next to my bed read 1:46, almost exactly the same time as the night before. I sat up in bed, listening carefully in the dark. No insects chirping; it was silent all around. As if I were at the bottom of a deep sea. A repeat of the previous night. But now it was dark outside my window. That was the only difference from the night before. Thick clouds covered the sky, completely hiding the nearly full autumn moon.

Everything was in total silence. No, that wasn't entirely true. Of course it wasn't. That silence wasn't total. When I held my breath and listened carefully I could catch the faint sound of the bell wending its way past the deep silence. In the dark of night someone was ringing that bell-like object. As on the night before, it was a fragmented, intermittent sound. And now I knew exactly where the sound was coming from. From the woods, underneath that stone mound. There was no need to check it. What I didn't know, though, was *who was ringing that bell, and to what end?* I got out of bed and padded out to the terrace.

There was no wind, but a fine rain had started to fall. An invisible silent rain wetting the ground. Lights were on over in Mr. Menshiki's mansion. From over here, across the valley, I couldn't see what was going on inside his house, but he seemed to still be awake. It was unusual to see the lights on this late at night. As the fine drizzle wet me, I gazed at those lights, listening to the faint tinkling of the bell.

The rain started to pick up and I went back inside, but couldn't go back to sleep, so I sat on the sofa in the living room and turned the pages of a book I'd been reading. Not a particularly difficult book, but no matter how I focused nothing registered. I was merely tracing the words from one line to the next. Still, it was better than simply sitting there listening to the bell. I guess I could have put on some music to drown out the sound, but I didn't feel like it. I had to hear it. *Because that was a sound directed at me.* I understood that. And as long as I didn't do something about it, it would no doubt go on ringing forever. Suffocating me every night, robbing me of a good night's sleep.

I have to do something. Take some action to stop that sound. To do that, I first had to understand the meaning and purpose of that sound—of that signal that was being sent out. Why was somebody sending out from this mysterious place a signal to me every single night, and who was it? But I felt too choked, my mind too confused, for logical thought. There was no way I could handle this alone. I had to talk to somebody about it. And at this point I could only think of one person.

I went back out on the terrace and looked over at Mr. Menshiki's mansion. Now the lights were all out, with just a glimmer of outdoor lanterns in the garden.

The bell stopped ringing at 2:29 a.m., almost the same time as the night before. Soon after the bell stopped the insects' chirping returned. And as if nothing had happened, the autumn night was once more filled with the clamor of nature's chorus. Everything was a repeat of the previous night.

I went back to bed and went to sleep listening to the insects. I felt confused and anxious, but like on the night before, I soon fell asleep. Plunged into a deep, dreamless sleep.

12

LIKE THAT NAMELESS MAILMAN

Rain started falling early in the morning, and stopped before ten. Slowly, the sun began to peek out. Moist wind from the sea slowly pushed the clouds off to the north. And at one p.m., on the dot, Menshiki showed up at my place. The time signal on the radio and the front doorbell sounded at almost precisely the same moment. Many people are punctual, but seldom do you find anyone that precise. And it wasn't that he stood in front of the door, patiently waiting for the appointed time, timing his ringing of the front doorbell with the second hand on his watch. He drove up the slope, parked in his usual spot, and headed toward the front door at his usual pace and stride, and at almost the same instant he pushed the button for the front doorbell the time signal on the radio chimed. Pretty impressive.

I showed him into the studio, and had him sit on the same dining room chair as before. I put Richard Strauss's *Der Rosenkavalier* on the turntable and lowered the needle. I started at the point we'd ended up with last time. Everything was a repeat of the previous sitting. The only difference was that this time I didn't offer him a drink, and instead had him pose for me. I had him seated on the chair, facing forward, looking to the left, his eyes slightly facing toward me. That's what I wanted from him this time.

He followed my instructions exactly, but it still took a while until he got the position and pose right. The angle and look in his eyes wasn't exactly the way I wanted them. The way the light struck, too, wasn't like my mental image. I don't usually use a model, but once I do, I tend to have a lot of demands. Menshiki very patiently followed my nagging directions. He never looked put out, never complained. I pegged him as a person experienced in putting up with all sorts of trials and difficulties.

When he finally got the pose right I said, "I'm very sorry, but try to hold that pose without moving."

Menshiki said nothing, only his eyes indicating that he understood.

"I'll try to finish as quickly as I can. It might be hard, but please be patient."

Once again he nodded with his eyes. He kept his gaze still, his body unmoving, literally not moving a muscle. He did have to blink a few times, but I couldn't even tell if he was breathing. He was so still he looked like a lifelike statue. I couldn't help but be impressed. Even professional art models find it hard to get to that point.

As Menshiki endured posing, I worked on the canvas as quickly and efficiently as I could. I concentrated, eyeing his figure, and moved my brush as my intuition dictated. I was using black paint on the white canvas, and with a single fine brushstroke fleshed out the outline of his face I'd already drawn. No time even to re-grip the brush. In a limited amount of time I had to capture the various elements that made up his face and get them down on canvas. At a certain point the process switched over to something close to autopilot. It's important to bypass your conscious mind and get your eye and hand movements in sync. There's no time to consciously process every single thing your gaze takes in.

This demanded a very different type of process from me compared with the numerous portraits I'd done up till then—the countless "business items" I'd leisurely painted based solely on memory and photographs. In about fifteen minutes I'd gotten him from the chest up on canvas. It was just a rough, incomplete outline, but at least I was able to capture an image that seemed to breathe a sense of vitality, one that managed to scoop out and capture the sort of internal movement that gave birth to who this person was. If this were an anatomical drawing, though, it would be just the bones and muscles, the internal part alone boldly laid bare. It needed actual flesh and skin laid on over it.

"Thank you, you've been very patient," I said. "That's enough for today. You can take it easy now."

Menshiki smiled and relaxed his pose. He stretched his hands above him and took a deep breath. He slowly massaged his face with his fingers to loosen up the tense muscles. I stood there taking a few deep breaths. It took a while for my breathing to return to normal. I was exhausted, like a sprinter who'd just finished a race. I'd had to work speedily, with intense concentration, and with no room for compromise, something I hadn't experienced for quite some time. I'd had to flex long-dormant muscles, and though I felt tired, it also felt good.

"Like you said, sitting for a painting is a lot harder work than I'd imagined," Menshiki said. "When I think about you painting me, it feels like my insides are slowly being scraped away."

"The official view in the art world is that it's not being scraped away but rather transplanted to a different place," I said.

"Transplanted to a more permanent, lasting place?"

"Yes, if the painting is a true work of art."

"Like, for instance, the nameless mailman who lives on in Van Gogh's portrait of him?"

"Exactly."

"He probably had no idea that, well over a century later, countless people around the world would visit art museums, or look through art books, and gaze intently at his portrait."

"I'm sure he never had a clue."

"It was some odd painting done in a corner of a shabby country kitchen, painted by a man who, whichever way you look at it, was a little off."

I nodded.

"It's kind of weird," Menshiki said. "Something that, on the face of it, shouldn't be so lasting ends up having permanent value."

"Not something that happens every day."

I suddenly thought of *Killing Commendatore*. Through Tomohiko Amada's hand, was the Commendatore given permanent life, even though he was stabbed to death in the painting? And who was this Commendatore anyway?

. . .

I offered Menshiki some coffee. That would be nice, he replied, and I went to the kitchen and made a fresh pot. Menshiki remained on the chair in the studio, listening to the opera record. The coffee was ready as the B side of the record came to an end, and we went into the living room to drink it.

"So, does it look like you can do a good portrait of me?" Menshiki asked as he delicately sipped his coffee.

"I'm not sure yet," I answered honestly. "I don't know if it will turn out well. The way I've painted portraits up till now has been so different from this."

"Because you're using an actual model this time?" Menshiki asked.

"That's one reason, but only a part of it. I don't know why, but it's like I'm not able anymore to paint the sort of conventional portraits I've done up till now. I need a different method and procedure, but those are still out of reach. I'm still fumbling in the dark."

"Which means you really are changing. And I'm the catalyst for that change—wouldn't you say?"

"You may be right."

Menshiki thought for a while before speaking. "As I told you before, it's entirely up to you what style of painting you do. I'm a person who's always seeking change, always in flux. And it's not like I'm hoping you'll paint some conventional portrait. Any style, any concept is fine. What I want is for you to depict me exactly as you see me. The methods and procedure are up to you. I'm not hoping I live on like that mailman from Arles. I'm not that ambitious. I just have a healthy curiosity to see what sort of painting will emerge from this."

"I appreciate your saying that. I just have one request," I said. "If I can't come up with a satisfactory painting, then I'd like to forget the whole thing."

"You won't give me the painting then?"

I nodded. "I'll return the advance, of course."

"All right," Menshiki said. "I'll let you be the final judge. Though I must say I have a strong hunch it's not going to turn out that way."

"I hope your hunch turns out to be correct."

Menshiki looked me in the eyes. "But even if the painting's never completed, I'd be very happy if, in some way, I'm able to help you change. Truly."

"By the way, Mr. Menshiki," I said, broaching the topic a little while later, "there's something I wanted to get your advice on. Something personal, nothing to do with the painting."

"Of course. I'll be happy to help if I can."

I sighed. "It's kind of a weird story. I might not be able to tell the whole story in the right order, so it makes sense."

"Take your time, tell it in whatever order is easiest for you. And then we'll consider it together. The two of us might come up with a good idea that you couldn't come up with on your own."

So I told him the story, start to finish. How I suddenly woke up just before two a.m. and heard a weird sound in the darkness. A faint, far-off sound that I could only catch because the insects had stopped chirping. A sound like someone ringing a bell. When I tried to trace the source, it seemed to be coming from between the cracks in a stone mound in the woods behind my house. That mysterious sound continued for some forty-five minutes, intermittently, with irregular intervals of silence between. Finally it stopped completely. The same thing happened two nights in a row—two nights ago and last night. Someone might be ringing that bell-like thing from underneath the stones. Maybe sending out a distress call. But could that be possible? I was starting to doubt my own sanity a little. Was I just imagining things?

Menshiki listened to my story without comment, and remained silent even after I finished. He'd listened intently to what I'd said, and I could tell he was thinking deeply about it.

"A fascinating story," he said a little while later. He lightly cleared his throat. "As you said, it's certainly out of the ordinary. I wonder . . . if possible, I'd like to hear the sound of that bell myself, so could I come over tonight? If you don't mind?"

This took me by surprise. "Come all the way over here in the dead of night?"

"Of course. If I hear the bell too, that would prove you're not hallucinating. That's the first step. If it is an actual bell, then let's try to locate the source, the two of us. Then we can think about what to do next."

"True enough—"

"If you don't mind, I'll come over here tonight at twelve thirty. Does that work for you?"

"That's fine, but I don't want to put you out—"

A pleasant smile graced his lips. "Not to worry. If I can help you, nothing would make me happier. Plus, I'm a very curious person. What that bell in the middle of the night might mean, and if someone is ringing it, who that is—I'm dying to know. You feel the same way, don't you?"

"Of course—" I said.

"Then let's go with that. I'll see you tonight. And there's something else I thought of."

"Excuse me?"

"I'll tell you about it later. I have to make sure of something first."

Menshiki got up from the sofa and held out his right hand. I shook it. As always, a firm handshake. He looked happier than usual.

After he left I spent the rest of the afternoon in the kitchen cooking. Once a week I prepare all my meals. I put them in the fridge or freezer, then get by on these for the week. This was my meal-prep day. For dinner that evening I added macaroni to some boiled sausage and cabbage. Plus a tomato, avocado, and onion salad. In the evening I lay on the sofa as always, reading while listening to music. After a while I stopped reading and thought about Menshiki.

Why had he looked so happy when we said goodbye? Was he *really* so pleased to be able to help me out? Why? I didn't get it. I was just a poor, unknown artist. My wife of six years had left me, I didn't get along with my parents, had no set place to live, no assets, and was simply hanging out in a friend's father's house. Menshiki, in contrast (not that there was any need to make a comparison), had been successful at business at a young age, and made enough to live comfortably for the rest of his days. At least that's what he had told me. He was good-looking, owned four British cars, and lived in luxury in a huge mountaintop mansion without, apparently, doing any real work. So why would a person like that be interested in someone like me? And why would he make time in the dead of the night to help me out?

I shook my head and went back to reading. Thinking about it wasn't going to get me anywhere. It was like trying to put together a puzzle that was missing some pieces. I could think all I wanted and never arrive at any conclusion. But I couldn't help but think about it. I sighed, and put the book on the tabletop again, closed my eyes, and listened to the music. Schubert's String Quartet no. 15, played by the Vienna Konzerthaus Quartet.

Since coming here, I'd listened to classical music every day, most of it German (or Austrian), since the majority of Tomohiko Amada's record collection consisted of German classical music. His collection included the obligatory nods to Tchaikovsky, Rachmaninoff, Sibelius, Vivaldi, Debussy, and Ravel, but that's all. Since he was an opera fan there were, as you might expect, some recordings by Verdi and Puccini. But compared to the substantial lineup of German opera he didn't seem as enthusiastic about these.

I imagined Amada had intense memories of his time studying in Vienna, which may have accounted for the deep absorption in German music. Or it could have been the opposite. Maybe his love of German music had come first, and that's why he had chosen to study in Vienna instead of France. I had no way of knowing which had come first.

Either way, I was in no position to complain that German music was the preferred type in this house. I was a mere caretaker, and they were kind enough to let me listen to the records there. And I enjoyed listening to the music of Bach, Schubert, Brahms, Schumann, and Beethoven. Not forgetting Mozart, of course. Their music was deep, amazing, and gorgeous. Up to then in my life I'd never had the opportunity to really settle down and listen to that type of music. I'd always been too busy trying to make a living, and didn't have the wherewithal financially. So I decided that, as long as I'd been provided this wonderful opportunity, I'd listen to as much music here as I could.

After eleven I fell asleep for a while on the sofa listening to music. I might have slept for about twenty minutes. When I woke up the record was over, the arm back in its cradle, the turntable not moving. There were two players in the living room, one an automatic, the other an old-school manual type, but to play it safe—so I could fall asleep listening, in other words—I generally used the automatic. I slipped the Schubert record back in its jacket, and returned it to its designated spot on the record shelf. From the open window I could hear the clamor of insects. Since they were still making a racket, I wouldn't be hearing the sound of the bell quite yet.

I warmed up coffee in the kitchen and munched on a few cookies. And listened intently to the noisy insect ensemble that enveloped the mountains. A little before twelve thirty I heard the Jaguar slowly making its way up the slope. As it changed direction, the pair of yellow headlights lit up the window. The engine finally cut out, and I heard the usual solid *thunk* as the door shut. I sat on the sofa, sipping coffee, getting my breathing under control, waiting for the front doorbell to ring.

13

AT THIS POINT IT'S MERELY A HYPOTHESIS

We sat in chairs in the living room, drank our coffee, and talked, killing time until *that time* rolled around. At first we chatted about inconsequential things, but after a curtain of silence descended on us Menshiki, a bit hesitantly, yet resolutely, asked, "Do you have any children?"

The question took me by surprise. He didn't seem the type to ask that kind of question—especially of someone he didn't know well. He seemed more the I-won't-stick-my-nose-in-your-business-if-you-won't-stick-yours-in-mine type of person. At least that's the way I read him. But when I looked up and saw his serious expression, I knew it wasn't an impulsive question. He'd been thinking of asking me this for a long time.

I responded. "I was married for six years, but we didn't have any children."

"You didn't want any?"

"I was fine either way. But my wife didn't want any," I said. I didn't, though, get into the reason she gave. Even now I'm not sure that it reflected her true feelings.

Menshiki seemed hesitant, but forged ahead. "This might sound rude, but have you ever considered that there might be another woman somewhere, other than your wife, who secretly had a child of yours?"

I looked him full in the face again. What a strange question. I rummaged around, pro forma, through a few drawers of memory, but came up empty-handed. I hadn't had sex with all that many women until then, and even if something like that had taken place, I think I would have heard about it.

"I guess it's possible, in theory. But realistically—commonsensically, you might say—it's not."

"I see," Menshiki said. He quietly sipped his coffee, thinking deeply.

"Why do you ask?" I ventured.

He looked out the window, silent for a time. The moon was visible, not as weirdly bright as two days ago, but still plenty bright. Scattered clouds slowly wended their way from the sea toward the mountains.

Menshiki finally spoke up. "As I mentioned before, I've never been married. I've always been a bachelor. Work kept me busy all the time, that's one reason, but it's also because living with someone else didn't fit my personality and lifestyle. I'm sure this sounds pretty stuck-up, but I'm the type who can only live alone. I have almost no interest in lineage or relatives. I've never thought I'd like to have children. There's a personal reason for that, mostly because of my home environment when I was growing up."

He paused, took a breath, then went on.

"But a few years ago I began to think that I might actually have a child. Or I should say, I was compelled to think that way."

No comment from me.

"I find it strange myself that I'm opening up to you, about this kind of personal matter. I mean, we just met." The faintest of smiles rose to Menshiki's lips.

"I'm okay with it, as long as you are."

Ever since I was little, for some reason people have tended to open up to me about the most unexpected topics. Maybe I have an innate ability to draw out secrets from strangers. Or maybe I just seem like a good listener, I don't know. Either way, I don't remember it ever working to my advantage. After people tell me their secrets, they always regret it.

"This is the first time I've ever told anybody this," Menshiki said.

I nodded and waited for more. Everyone says the same thing.

Menshiki began his story. "This happened fifteen years ago, when I was going out with a woman. I was in my late thirties then, she was in her late twenties. She was a beautiful, attractive woman, extremely bright. I was serious about our relationship, though I'd made it clear to her there was no chance of us getting married. I don't plan to ever marry anyone, I told her. I didn't want her to have any false hopes. If she ever found someone else she wanted to marry, I would step aside without a word. She understood exactly how I felt. While we went out—for about two and half years—we got along really well. We never argued, even once. We traveled together to lots of places, and she'd often stay over at my place. She even kept a set of clothes there."

He seemed to be contemplating something, then continued his story.

"If I were a normal person, or closer to being normal, I wouldn't have hesitated to marry her. But—" He paused here and let out a small breath. "But the upshot was I chose the kind of life I have now, a quiet life all by myself, and she chose a healthier life for herself. In other words, she got married to another man who was closer to being normal than me."

Until the very end, however, she didn't disclose to him the fact that she was getting married. The last time he saw her was a week after her twenty-ninth birthday (the two of them had dined out at a restaurant in Ginza on her birthday, and later on he recalled how unusually quiet she'd been). He was working in an office in Akasaka then and she'd called him saying she wanted to see him and talk, and asked if she could see him right away. Of course, he replied. She'd never visited his workplace even once, but he hadn't thought it odd. His office was a small place, just him and a middle-aged woman secretary. So he didn't need to worry about anyone else if she stopped by. There had been a time when he'd managed a large company with lots of employees, but at this point he was developing a new network by himself. His usual approach was to work quietly by himself to develop a new business strategy; then, when he began implementing the plan, he would aggressively employ a broad range of talent.

It was just before five p.m. when his girlfriend showed up. They sat down together on his office sofa to talk. He'd had the secretary in the next room go home. It was his normal routine to continue working alone in the office after his secretary left for the day. Often he'd be so engrossed in his work that he'd stay all night. His idea was for the two of them to go to a nearby restaurant and have dinner, but she turned that down. I don't have time today, she said, I have to meet somebody in Ginza.

"You said you had something you wanted to talk about," he said.

"No, I don't have anything to really talk about," she said. "I just wanted to see you."

"I'm glad you came," he said, smiling. It had been some time since she'd spoken so openly to him. She generally spoke in a more indirect, roundabout way. He had no idea what this portended.

She moved over on the sofa and sat down in his lap. She put her arms around him and kissed him. A serious, deep kiss, tongues entwined. She reached out and undid Menshiki's belt. She took out his already erect penis, holding it in her grasp for a time. Then she leaned forward and wrapped her mouth around it. She slowly ran the tip of her long tongue around it. Her tongue was smooth and hot.

This all came out of nowhere. She was usually more passive when it came to sex—especially oral sex—and when it came to doing it, or having things done to her, he'd always felt a slight resistance on her part. But now here she was taking the lead. What's come over her? he wondered.

She suddenly stood up, tossed aside her expensive black pumps, briskly lowered her stockings and panties, again sat down on his lap, and now guided his penis inside her. Her vagina was wet, and moved smoothly, naturally, like some living being. The whole sequence had happened so quickly (and was so unlike her, since she was always so calm and deliberate). Before he realized it, he was deep inside her, that smooth wall completely enveloping his penis, squeezing him silently yet insistently.

This was unlike any sex he'd ever had with her. It was at once hot and cold, hard and soft. It was a strange, contradictory sensation, as if he were being simultaneously accepted and rejected. He had no idea what that meant. She straddled him, and like a person on a small boat being tossed around by the waves, moved violently up and down. Her black hair tossed about, supple as a willow branch in a strong wind. She lost control, her gasps growing ever louder. Menshiki wasn't sure if he had locked the office door or not. He felt he had, but also that he'd forgotten to. But this wasn't the time to go check.

"Shouldn't we use a condom or something?" he managed to ask. She was always careful about contraception.

"It's okay—today," she gasped in his ear. "Don't worry about a thing."

Everything about her was different from usual, as if a totally different personality dormant inside her had awoken and hijacked her body and soul. Menshiki imagined that today must be some sort of special day for her. There was so much that men can't fathom about women's bodies.

Her movements became increasingly frenzied. There was nothing he could do but make sure not to interfere with what she desired. They neared climax. He couldn't hold back, and ejaculated, and in time with that she let out a short screech like some foreign bird, and her womb, as if waiting for that instant, greedily absorbed his semen. A muddied image occurred to him of himself, in the darkness, being devoured by a greedy beast.

After a while she stood up, as if pushing his body aside, and silently adjusted the hem of her dress, stuffed the stockings and panties that had fallen to the floor in her handbag, and hurried off to the bathroom, bag in hand. She didn't come out for a long time. He was beginning to get worried that something had happened to her when she finally emerged. Her clothing and hair were neatly arranged now, her makeup redone. Her usual calm smile graced her lips.

She gave Menshiki a light peck on the lips, and told him she had to go, since she was already late. And she hurried out of the office, without looking back. He could still recall the click of her pumps as she left.

That was the last time he ever saw her. All contact ceased. He'd call her, and write, but never got a response. And two months later she got married. He heard about this from a mutual friend, after the fact. The friend found it odd that Menshiki was not invited to the wedding ceremony, and, in particular, that he had no idea she was getting married. He'd always thought that Menshiki and the woman were good friends (they'd always been very discreet about their relationship, and no one else had known they were lovers). Menshiki didn't know the man she married. He had never even heard his name. She hadn't told Menshiki she was planning to marry, nor even hinted at it. She just disappeared from his world without a word.

That violent embrace on the sofa at his office, Menshiki realized, must have been her final, farewell act of love. Afterward he went over those events, over and over in his mind. Even after a long time had passed, those memories remained amazingly distinct and clear. The creak of the sofa, her hair whirling around her, her hot breath in his ear—it all came back to him.

So did Menshiki regret losing her? Of course not. He wasn't the type to have regrets. He knew very well he wasn't suited to family life. No matter how much he loved someone, he still couldn't share his life with them. He needed solitary time every day to concentrate, and he couldn't stand it when someone's presence threw off his concentration. If he lived with someone he knew he would end up detesting them. Whether it was his parents, a wife, or children. He feared that above all. He wasn't afraid of loving someone. What he feared was growing to hate someone.

For all that, he had loved her very deeply. He'd never loved any other woman so deeply, and probably never would again. "Even now there's a special spot inside me just for her," Menshiki said. "A very real spot. You might even call it a shrine."

A shrine? This struck me as an odd choice of words. But for him it was likely the right way of putting it.

Menshiki ended his story there. He'd told this private tale in great detail, yet I got little sense of it being sexual. It was more like he'd read aloud from a medical report. Or maybe it really was that sort of dispassionate experience for him.

"Seven months after the wedding she gave birth to a baby girl in a hospital in Tokyo," Menshiki continued. "Thirteen years ago. I heard about this birth much later from someone."

Menshiki stared down at his now empty coffee cup, as if nostalgic for some past age when it had been full of hot coffee.

"And that child might possibly be my own," he said, seemingly forcing out the words. He looked at me, like he wanted to hear my opinion.

It took me a while to grasp what he was trying to say.

"Does the timeline fit?"

"It does. It coincides perfectly. The child was born nine months after she came to my office. She must have picked the day she was most fertile to come see me and—how should I put it?—deliberately *gathered* my sperm. That's my working hypothesis. From the beginning she wasn't expecting to marry me, but had decided to have my child. I figured that's what happened."

"But you can't confirm that," I said.

"Of course. At this point it's merely a hypothesis. But I do have a sort of basis to say this."

"That was a pretty risky experiment for her, wasn't it?" I pointed out. "If the blood types didn't match it might come out that the father was someone else. Would she risk that?"

"My blood is type A. Most Japanese are A, and I think she is too. As long as they didn't have some reason to run a full-blown DNA test, the chances are slim that the secret would come out. That much she could figure out."

"But on the other hand, unless you ran an official DNA test you wouldn't be able to determine if you're the girl's biological father or not. Right? Or else you ask her mother directly."

Menshiki shook his head. "It's no longer possible to ask the mother. She died seven years ago."

"That's terrible. She was still so young," I said.

"She was walking in the woods and was stung by hornets and died. She was allergic to them. By the time they got her to the hospital she'd stopped breathing. Nobody knew she was so allergic to their stings. Maybe she didn't even know herself. She left behind her husband and daughter. Her daughter is thirteen now."

About the same age my little sister was when she died, I thought.

"And you have some sort of basis for conjecturing that this girl is your daughter. Is that what you're saying?"

"Some time after she died I suddenly received a letter from the deceased," Menshiki said in a quiet voice.

• • •

One day a large envelope, with a return receipt, arrived at his office from a law firm he'd never heard of. Inside was a typed two-page letter (with the letterhead of the law firm) and a light pink envelope. The letter from the law firm was signed by a lawyer. The lawyer's letter read: *Ms. **** entrusted me with this letter while she was still alive. Ms. **** left instructions with me to send this letter to you in case of her death. She added a note to the effect that the letter should be for your eyes only.*

That was the gist of the lawyer's letter. The circumstances leading to her death were described simply, in a businesslike manner. Menshiki was speechless, but finally pulled himself together and snipped open the second envelope. The letter inside was handwritten in blue ink, on four sheets of stationery. The handwriting was exquisite.

Dear Mr. Menshiki,

I don't know what month or year it is now, but if you are reading this it means I am no longer among the living. I'm not sure why, but I've always had the feeling I'd depart this world at a relatively young age. Which is why I made full preparations like this for after my death. If all this ends up being wasted, of course nothing could be better—but when all is said and done since you are reading this letter it means that I've already passed away. The thought leaves me very, very sad.

The first thing I'd like to say in advance (maybe it's something I really don't need to say) is that my life has never been of much consequence. I'm well aware of that. So it seems fitting for someone like me to quietly exit the world without making a big deal of things, without any uncalled-for pronouncements. But there is one thing I need to tell you alone. My conscience is telling me that if I don't, I may forever lose the chance to treat you fairly. So I've left this letter with a lawyer I know and trust with instructions to pass it on to you.

Suddenly leaving you like that, and marrying someone else, and not saying a word to you about it beforehand—I am deeply sorry about all of it. I can imagine how shocked and upset you must have been. But you're always so calm, so maybe it didn't shock you, or bother you. At any rate, that was the only path I could follow. I won't get into details here, but I do want you to understand that. I was left with hardly any other choice.

But one choice was left to me. A choice that was condensed in one event, in one act. Do you remember the last time I saw you? That evening in early fall when I suddenly came to your office, maybe I didn't seem like it, but I was at my wit's end then, completely driven into a corner. I no longer felt like I was myself anymore. But even in that confused state of mind, the act I did was utterly intentional. And I've never, ever regretted it. This was something profoundly important in my life. Something far surpassing my own existence.

I am hoping that you will understand my intentions, and ultimately forgive me. And I pray that none of this will cause you, personally, any harm. Since I know very well how much you dislike those kinds of things.

I wish you a long and happy life. And I hope that what a truly wonderful person you were will be passed along, in all its richness, for a long time to come.

* * * *

Menshiki read the letter over so many times that he memorized it all (and he recited it to me without faltering). All sorts of emotions and suggestions played back and forth through the letter—light and dark, shadow and sunlight—creating a complex, hidden picture. Like a linguistics scholar researching an ancient language no one speaks anymore, he spent years considering the possibilities concealed in the letter's contents. Extracting each word and phrasing, recombining them, intertwining them, shifting their order. And he arrived at one conclusion alone: that the baby girl she gave birth to seven months after she got married was, he was now certain, conceived in that office, on that leather sofa, with him.

"I asked a law office I knew to investigate the daughter she left behind," Menshiki said. "Her husband was fifteen years older than she was, worked in real estate. Or, rather, he was the son of a local landowner and managed the land and properties he'd inherited from his father. He had some other real estate holdings, too, of course, but wasn't that ambitious when it came to expanding the business. He had enough assets to live on comfortably without working. The daughter's name was Mariye. The husband had not remarried after his wife's accidental death seven years ago. The husband has an unmarried younger sister who lives with them and takes care of the household. Mariye is in her first year at a local public junior high."

"And have you met this girl, Mariye?"

Menshiki was silent as he chose his words. "I've seen her from a distance many times. But never spoken with her."

"And what did you think when you saw her?"

"Did she look like me? I couldn't say. If I think there's a resemblance then everything about her resembles me, but if I don't think that way then I don't see a resemblance at all."

"Do you have a photo of her?"

Menshiki silently shook his head. "No, I don't. I could get one easily enough, but that's not what I was after. What good is carrying around a photo of her in my wallet going to do? What I'm after is—"

But nothing came after this. He was silent, the quiet buried in the lively buzz of the hordes of insects outside.

"But you told me earlier, Mr. Menshiki, that you were totally uninterested in blood relations."

"True enough. I've never cared about lineage. In fact, I've lived my life trying to avoid that as much as I could. My feelings haven't changed. But still, I find I can't take my eyes off this girl, Mariye. I simply can't stop thinking about her. There's no reason for it, but still . . ."

I couldn't find the right words to say.

Menshiki continued. "I've never had this experience before. I've always been very self-controlled, even proud of it. But sometimes now I find it painful to be alone."

I went ahead and said what was on my mind. "Mr. Menshiki, this is just a hunch on my part, but it seems like there's something you want me to do in regard to Mariye. Or am I overthinking things?"

After a pause Menshiki nodded. "I'm not sure how I should put this—"

I realized at that instant that the clamor of insects had completely stopped. I looked up at the clock on the wall. It was just past one forty. I held a finger up to my lips, and Menshiki stopped in midsentence. And the two of us listened carefully in the still of the night.

14

BUT SOMETHING THIS STRANGE IS A FIRST

Menshiki and I stopped talking, and sat still, listening carefully. The insects had stopped chirping, just like they had two days ago, and again yesterday. In the midst of that deep silence I could again make out the tinkling of the bell. It rang a few times, with uneven periods of silence in between before ringing once again. I looked over at Menshiki, seated across from me on the sofa. I could tell he was hearing the same sound. He was frowning. He lifted up his hands on his lap, his fingers moving slightly in time to the ringing of the bell. So this wasn't an auditory hallucination.

After listening intently to the bell for two or three minutes, Menshiki slowly rose from the sofa.

"Let's go where that sound's coming from," he said drily.

I picked up my flashlight. He went outside and retrieved a large flashlight from his Jaguar. We climbed the seven steps and walked into the woods. Though not as bright as two days before, the autumn moonlight clearly lit the path for us. We walked in back of the little shrine, pushing aside pampas grass as we went, and emerged in front of the stone mound. And again we perked up our ears. No doubt about it, the sound was coming from the cracks between the stones.

Menshiki slowly circled the mound, cautiously shining his flashlight into the cracks between the stones. But nothing was out of the ordinary, just a jumble of old, moss-covered stones. He looked over at me. In the moonlight his face resembled some mask from ancient times. Perhaps my face looked the same?

"When you heard the sound before, was it coming from here?" he whispered.

"The same place," I said. "The exact same spot."

"It sounds like someone underneath the stones is ringing a bell," Menshiki said.

I nodded. I felt relieved to know I wasn't crazy, but I had to admit that the unreality of the situation had now, through Menshiki, taken on a reality, creating a slight gap in the seam of the world.

"What should we do?" I asked Menshiki.

He shone his flashlight on where the sound was coming from, his lips tight as he considered the situation. In the still of the night I could almost hear the wheels turning in his mind.

"Someone might be seeking help," Menshiki said quietly, as if to himself.

"But who could have possibly gotten under these heavy stones?"

Menshiki shook his head. He had no idea either.

"Anyway, let's go back to the house," he said. He lightly touched my shoulders from behind. "At least we've pinpointed the source of the sound. Let's go home and talk it over."

We cut through the woods and came out onto the empty space in front of the house. Menshiki opened the door of his Jaguar and returned the flashlight. In its place he took out a small paper bag. We went back inside the house.

"If you have any whiskey, could I have a glass?" Menshiki asked.

"Regular Scotch okay?"

"Of course. Straight, please. With a separate glass of water, no ice."

I went into the kitchen and took a bottle of White Label from the shelf, poured some into two glasses, and took them and some mineral water out to the living room. We sat across from each other without speaking, and drank our straight whiskey. I went back to the kitchen to get the bottle of White Label and poured him a refill. He picked up the glass but didn't drink any. In the silence of the middle of the night, the bell continued to ring out intermittently. A small sound, but with a delicate weight one couldn't fail to hear.

"I've seen a lot of strange things in my time, but something this strange is a first," Menshiki said. "Pardon me for saying this, but when you first told me about this I only half believed you. It's hard to believe something like this could actually happen."

Something in that expression caught my attention. "What do you mean, could actually happen?"

Menshiki raised his head and looked me in the eyes.

"I read about this sort of thing in a book once," he said.

"You mean hearing a bell from somewhere in the middle of the night?"

"No, what they heard was a gong, not a bell. The kind of gong they would ring along with a drum when searching for a lost child. In the old days it was a small Buddhist altar fitting that you would hit with a wooden bell hammer. You'd strike it rhythmically as you chanted sutras. In the story someone heard that kind of gong ringing out from underground in the middle of the night."

"Was this a ghost story?"

"Closer to what's called a tale of the mysterious. Have you ever read Ueda Akinari's book *Tales of the Spring Rain*?" Menshiki asked.

I shook my head. "I read his *Tales of Moonlight and Rain* a long time ago. But I haven't read that one."

"*Tales of the Spring Rain* is a collection of stories Akinari wrote in his later years. Some forty years after he finished *Tales of Moonlight and Rain*. Compared with that book, which emphasized narrative, *Tales of the Spring Rain* was more an expression of Akinari's philosophy as a man of letters. One strange story in the collection is titled 'Fate over Two Generations.' The main character experiences something like what you're going through. He's the son of a wealthy farmer. He enjoys studying, and one night he's reading late when he hears a sound like a gong coming from underneath a rock in the corner of the garden. Thinking it odd, the next day he has people dig it up, and they find a large stone underneath. When they move that stone they find a kind of coffin with a stone lid. Inside that they discover a fleshless emaciated person, like a dried fish. With hair down to his knees. Only his hands are still moving, striking a gong with a wooden hammer. It was a Buddhist priest who long ago chose his own death in order to achieve enlightenment, and had himself buried alive in the coffin. This act was called *zenjo*. The mummified dead body was unearthed and enshrined in a temple. Another term for *zenjo* is *nyujo*, meaning a deep meditative practice. The man must have originally been quite a highly revered priest. As he had hoped, his soul reached nirvana, and the soul-less physical body alone continued to live on. The main character's family had lived on this plot of land for ten generations, and this burial must have taken place before that. In other words, several centuries before."

Menshiki ended there.

"So you're saying the same sort of thing took place around this house?" I asked.

Menshiki shook his head. "If you think about it, it's not possible. This was just a take on the supernatural written in the Edo period. Akinari knew that this tale had become part of folk legend and he adapted it and created the story 'Fate over Two Generations.' What I'm saying is, the story does have strange parallels with what we're experiencing now."

He lightly shook his glass of whiskey, the amber liquid quietly oscillating in his hand.

"So after he was unearthed, what happened?" I asked.

"The story took off in strange directions," Menshiki replied, sounding hesitant to go into it. "Ueda Akinari's worldview late in his life is deeply reflected in that story. A quite cynical view of the world, really. Akinari had a complicated background, a man who went through a lot of troubles in his life. But rather than hearing me summarize, I suggest you read the story yourself."

Menshiki took an old book out of the paper bag he'd brought inside from the car, and handed it to me. A volume from a collection of classical Japanese literature. The book contained the entire text of Akinari's two most famous books, *Tales of Moonlight and Rain* and *Tales of the Spring Rain*.

"When you told me what was going on here, right away I recalled this story. Just to be sure, I reread the copy I had on my shelves. I'll give you the book. If you'd like, please take a look. It's a short tale and doesn't take long to read."

I thanked him and accepted the book. "It's all pretty strange," I said. "Kind of unbelievable. Of course I'll read it. But apart from all that, what am I actually supposed to *do*? I don't think I can just leave things the way they are. If somebody really is buried beneath those rocks, ringing a bell or gong or whatever, sending out a call for help every night, we have to help get him out."

Menshiki frowned. "But the two of us would never be able to move that pile of stones."

"Should we report it to the police?"

Menshiki shook his head a few times. "The police won't be any help. Once you report that you're hearing a bell ringing from under stones in a woods in the middle of the night, they're not going to take you seriously. They'll just think you're crazy. It could make things worse. Better not go there."

"But if that bell keeps ringing every night, I don't think my nerves can take it. I can't get much sleep. All I can do is move out of this house. That sound is definitely trying to tell us something."

Menshiki considered this. "We'll need a professional's help to move those rocks," he said. "There's a man I know pretty well who's a local landscape designer. He's used to moving heavy rocks in landscaping. If need be, he could arrange for a small backhoe. Then it'd be easy to move the rocks and dig a hole."

"Okay, but I see two problems with that," I said. "First, I'd have to get permission to do that work from the son of the owner. I can't decide anything on my own. And second, I don't have the funds to hire someone to do that kind of job."

Menshiki smiled. "Don't worry about the money. I'll take care of that. What I mean is, that designer owes me one, and I think he'll do it at cost. Don't worry about that. As for Mr. Amada, why don't you get in touch with him? If you explain the situation, I think he'll give permission. If somebody really is shut away underneath those rocks and we just leave him to his fate, Mr. Amada will be liable for it as the property owner."

"But to ask you, an outsider, to go to all that trouble—"

Menshiki spread his hands wide on his lap, as if catching the rain. His voice was quiet.

"I mentioned this before, but I'm a very curious person. I'd like to find out how this odd story will play out. It's not something you run across every day. So, like I said, don't worry about how much it'll cost. I understand you have your own position to consider, but let me arrange everything."

I looked Menshiki in the eye. There was a keen light there I hadn't seen before. Those eyes told me that no matter what happened he was going to pursue it to the very end. If you don't understand something, then stick with it until you do—that seemed to be Menshiki's basic approach to life.

"Okay," I said. "Tomorrow I'll get in touch with Masahiko."

"And I'll contact the landscape designer," Menshiki said. He paused. "By the way, there's one thing I wanted to ask you."

"Yes?"

"Do you often have these kinds of—what should I say?—paranormal experiences?"

"No," I said. "This is a first. I'm a very ordinary person who's lived a very ordinary life. That's why I find it all so confusing. What about you, Mr. Menshiki?"

A faint smile rose to his lips. "I've had many strange experiences. I've seen things common sense can't explain. But something *this* strange is a first."

After this we sat there in silence, listening to the ringing of the bell.

As always the bell stopped completely a little after 2:30. And the mountains were again blasted with the buzz of insects.

"I'd best be going," Menshiki said. "Thank you for the whiskey. I'll get in touch soon."

Under the moonlight Menshiki got into his glossy silver Jaguar and drove off. He gave a short wave out the open window and I waved back. After the sound of his engine had faded away down the slope, I remembered that he'd had a glass of whiskey (the second glass he hadn't touched), but his face hadn't turned red at all, his speech and attitude no different than if he'd drunk water. He must be able to hold his liquor. And he wasn't driving far. It was a road that only local residents used, and at this hour there wouldn't be any cars coming the other direction, or any pedestrians.

I went back inside, rinsed out our glasses in the kitchen sink, and went to bed. I thought about people coming with heavy equipment to move the stones behind the little shrine, and digging a hole. It was hard to picture it as real. Before that happened, I needed to read the Ueda Akinari story he'd mentioned, "Fate over Two Generations." But I'd leave everything for tomorrow. Things would look different in the light of day. I switched off the bedside light, and to the background noise of buzzing insects, I fell asleep.

At ten a.m. I called Masahiko Amada's office and explained the situation. I didn't bring up Ueda Akinari, but told him how I'd had an acquaintance over to make sure that bell ringing in the middle of the night wasn't just an auditory illusion I was having.

"That is really creepy," Masahiko said. "But do you really believe there's someone underneath those stones ringing a bell?"

"I don't know. But I can't just ignore it. I hear it every single night."

"What will you do if, when you dig it all up, something weird emerges?"

"What do you mean, something weird?"

"I don't know," he said. "Some mysterious thing that's best left alone."

"You should come at night sometime and hear that sound. If you heard it yourself you'd understand why I can't just let it be."

Masahiko sighed deeply on the other end of the line. "No thanks," he said, "I'll pass. I've always been a bit of a coward. I hate scary stories, anything frightening. No thanks. I'll leave it all up to you. It's not going to bother anyone if you move those old stones and dig a hole. Do whatever you like. Just make sure not to unearth anything weird, okay?"

"I don't know how it's going to turn out, but once I know, I'll be in touch."

"If it were me, I'd just wear earplugs," Masahiko said.

After I hung up I sat in a chair in the living room and read the Ueda Akinari story. I read it first in the original classical Japanese, then in the contemporary-language version. A couple of details were different, but as Menshiki had said there was a strong resemblance between the story and what I was experiencing here. In the story the character heard the gong sounding at two o'clock in the morning, about the same time. But what I heard wasn't a gong but a bell. In the story the buzz of insects didn't stop. The protagonist hears the gong mixed in with the sound of the insects. But these small details aside, what I experienced was exactly the same as in the story. It left me dumbfounded, in fact, at how close the two were.

The unearthed mummy was completely dried up, just its hand doggedly moving, striking the gong. A terrifying vitality made the hand move almost mechanically. No doubt this priest gave up the ghost while reciting sutras and beating out a rhythm on the gong. The main character put clothes on the mummy and poured water on his lips. Before long he was able to eat some thin rice gruel and gradually put on flesh. Finally he recovered to the point where he looked like a normal human being. But you got no sense from him at all of a priest who had attained enlightenment. No intelligence or wisdom, and not a hint of dignity. And he had lost all memory of his former life. He couldn't recall, even, why he'd gone underground like that for so very long. He ate meat now, and had a considerable sexual appetite. He got married, and managed to make a living doing menial work. People nicknamed him "Nyujo no Josuke"—Josuke, the meditation guy. His pathetic figure made the villagers lose all respect for Buddhism. Is this the kind of wreck you end up as, they wondered, after all the strict ascetic training he went through, risking his life in pursuit of Buddhism? They started to despise faith, and stopped going to temple. That was Ueda's story. As Menshiki had said, the story reflected the author's cynical worldview. It's not merely some tale of the supernatural.

> *For all that, Buddhist teachings were in vain. That man must have been underground, ringing that gong, for well over a hundred years. Yet nothing miraculous came of it, and people were fed up that all that came from it were bones.*

I reread the short story "Fate over Two Generations" several times and found myself utterly confused. Say we used heavy equipment to move the stones, dug up the soil, and what emerged was a bony, pathetic mummy, then how was I supposed to handle that? Would I be responsible for resuscitating him? Was it wiser, as Masahiko had advised, to not meddle, and simply plug up my ears and leave it all alone?

But even if I wanted to do that, I couldn't simply make it go away. I would never be able to escape that sound, no matter how tightly I plugged up my ears. And say I moved somewhere else; that sound might follow me. Plus, like Menshiki, I was curious. I had to find out what lay hidden beneath those stones.

In the afternoon Menshiki called me. "Did you get Mr. Amada's permission?"

I told him pretty much everything about my conversation with Masahiko. And how he'd told me to handle it any way I wanted.

"I'm glad," Menshiki said. "I've arranged things with the landscape designer. I didn't tell him about the mysterious sound. I just asked him to move some stones out in the woods and then dig a hole there. It was a sudden request, but his schedule happened to be free, so if you don't mind, he'd like to come and look over the site this afternoon and start work tomorrow morning. Is it all right with you that he comes to check out the work site?"

"He can come over whenever he wants," I said.

"After he inspects the site, he'll arrange for the equipment he needs. The work itself should be done in a few hours. I'll be present when they're working," Menshiki said.

"I'll be there, too. When you find out what time they'll start, let me know," I said. "By the way," I added, remembering, "about what we were talking about last night, before we heard that sound . . ."

Menshiki didn't seem to follow. "I'm sorry, you mean—"

"It was about the thirteen-year-old girl, Mariye. You said she might be your real daughter. We were talking about her when we heard the bell, and that's as far as we got."

"Ah yes," said Menshiki. "Now that you mention it, we did talk about that. I'd totally forgotten. Yes, we should talk about that again sometime.

But there's no rush. We can talk about it again once we take care of the matter at hand."

After that I couldn't concentrate. I tried reading, listening to music, cooking, but all I could think of was what lay beneath those ancient stones in the woods. I couldn't shake the thought of a blackened mummy, shriveled up like a dried fish.

15

THIS IS ONLY THE BEGINNING

Menshiki called me that night to let me know that the work would begin the next morning, Wednesday, at ten.

Wednesday morning it was drizzling off and on, but not hard enough to delay the work. It was a fine rain, and a hat or raincoat with a hood was enough. No need for an umbrella. Menshiki had on an olive-green rain hat, the kind the British might use for duck hunting. The leaves of the trees, starting to turn fall colors, took on a dull color from the nearly invisible rain that soaked them.

The workers used a flatbed truck to move in a small backhoe. A very compact piece of equipment, with a tight turning radius, made to work in confined spaces. There were four workers altogether—one backhoe operator, one foreman, and two additional workers. The shovel operator and the foreman drove the truck. They all had on matching blue rainwear, jackets and trousers, and muddy thick-soled work boots, and wore protective helmets made of heavy-duty plastic. Menshiki and the foreman were apparently acquainted, and they talked for a while, the two of them beaming, next to the little shrine. I could tell, though, that the foreman remained on his best behavior toward Menshiki.

Menshiki must have had a lot of clout to arrange for this many people and equipment in such a short time. I watched this whole process half impressed, half bewildered. I had a slight sense of resignation, too, as if everything were already out of my hands. Like when I was a child and the little kids would be playing some game and bigger kids would come around and take over. I remembered that feeling.

They started the operation by using shovels and some material and boards to create a flat foothold for the backhoe to move, and then they began to actually remove the stones. The backhoe soon trampled down the thicket of pampas grass surrounding the mound. Menshiki and I stood to one side watching as they lifted the stones from the mound one by one and moved them to a spot a little ways away. There wasn't anything special about the operation. Probably the same sort of operation that takes place every day, all around the world. The workers looked ordinary too, like they were matter-of-factly following procedures they'd done a thousand times. Occasionally the backhoe operator would stop and call out in a loud voice to the foreman, but it didn't seem like there was any problem. They just exchanged a few words, and he didn't switch off the engine.

But I couldn't calmly watch the operation. Each time one of the square stones was removed, my anxiety only deepened. It was like some dark secret that I'd hidden away for years was being revealed, layer by layer, by the powerful, insistent tip of that machine. The problem lay in the fact that even I didn't know what secret I was hiding. Several times I felt I had to get them to stop the operation. Bringing in some large machinery like this backhoe couldn't be the solution. As Masahiko had told me on the phone, all "mysterious things" should be left buried. I was seized by the urge to grab Menshiki's arm and shout, "Let's stop this! Put the stones back where they were."

But of course I couldn't do that. The decision had been made and the work begun. Several other people were already involved. A not-insubstantial sum of money was changing hands (the amount was unclear, but I assumed Menshiki was footing the bill). We couldn't just stop at this point. The work continued, beyond my will.

As if he knew what I was going through, at a certain point Menshiki came over beside me and lightly patted me on the shoulder.

"There's nothing to worry about," he said in a calm voice. "It's going smoothly. It'll all be finished soon."

I nodded in silence.

Before noon all the stones had been moved. The ancient stones that had been piled in a jumble in a crumbling mound were now piled up in a neat, official-looking pyramid a little ways away. The fine drizzle silently fell on the pile. Even after removing all those stones, though, the ground hadn't appeared. Below the stones lay more stone. These stones were flat and had been methodically laid out there like a square stone flooring. The whole thing was about six feet on each side.

"I wonder why it's like that," the foreman said after coming over to where Menshiki was. "I was sure that the stones were just piled up on top of the ground. But they weren't. There seems to be an open space underneath that stone slab. I inserted a thin metal rod into a gap and it went down pretty far. Not sure yet how deep it goes, though."

Menshiki and I gingerly tried standing on top of the freshly uncovered slab. The stones were darkly wet and slippery in spots. Though they'd been artificially cut and evened up over time, the edges had become more rounded off, with gaps between the stones. The nightly sound of the bell must have filtered out through those gaps. And air could probably get in through those too. I crouched down and stared through a gap inside, but it was pitch black and I couldn't make out a thing.

"Maybe they used flagstones to cover up an ancient well. Though for a well, its diameter is a bit big," the foreman said.

"Can you remove these flagstones?" Menshiki asked.

The foreman shrugged. "I'm not sure. We hadn't planned on this. It'll make things a little complicated, but I think we can manage it. Using a crane would be our best bet, but we'd never get one in here. Each stone doesn't look that heavy. And there's a gap between them, so with a little ingenuity I think we can manage with the backhoe. We're coming up on our lunch break, so I'll work out a good plan then and we'll get to work in the afternoon."

Menshiki and I went back to the house and had a light lunch. In the kitchen I threw together some simple ham, lettuce, and pickle sandwiches and we went out on the terrace to eat as we watched the rain.

"This whole operation is delaying what we should be working on, finishing the portrait," I said.

Menshiki shook his head. "There's no rush with the portrait. Our first priority is solving this weird matter. Then you can get back to work on the painting."

Did this man *seriously* want his portrait painted? I couldn't help but wonder. This doubt had been smoldering in a corner of my mind from the very start. Did he *seriously* want me to paint his portrait? Wasn't he just using the portrait as a mere pretext, and had some other reason for getting to know me?

But what could it be? I couldn't figure it out. Was his goal unearthing what was under those stones? This didn't make sense. He hadn't known about them. That was something unforeseen that only came up after we started on the portrait. Still, he seemed overly enthusiastic about digging them up. And he was shelling out quite a bit of money for the operation, even though it had nothing to do with him.

As I was mulling over all this Menshiki asked, "Did you read the story 'Fate over Two Generations'?"

"I did," I told him.

"What did you think? A very strange tale, isn't it?" he said.

"It certainly is," I said.

Menshiki looked at me for a while, then said, "To tell the truth, that story has tugged at me for a long time. It's one of the reasons this discovery has aroused my interest."

I took a sip of coffee and wiped my mouth with a paper napkin. Two crows, cawing at each other, winged their way across the valley, undeterred by the rain. Wet by the rain, their wings would only grow a deeper black.

"I don't know much about Buddhism," I said to Menshiki, "so I don't understand all the details, but doesn't a priest doing a voluntary burial—this *nyujo*—mean he chooses to go into a coffin and die?"

"Exactly. *Nyujo* originally means 'attaining enlightenment,' so they have the term *ikinyujo*—'living *nyujo*'—to distinguish the two. They make a stone-lined underground chamber and insert a bamboo pipe to allow in air. Before a priest does *nyujo* he maintains a fruitarian diet for a set time so his body won't putrefy but will become nicely mummified."

"Fruitarian?"

"Just eating grasses and nuts and berries. They eat no cooked foods whatsoever, starting with grains. In other words, a radical elimination of all fats and moisture from the body. Changing the makeup of the body so it can easily mummify. And after purifying his body, the priest goes underground. In the darkness there the priest fasts and recites sutras, hitting a gong in time to that. Or ringing a bell. And people can hear the sound of that gong or bell through the vent hole. But at some point the sounds stop. That's the sign that he's breathed his last. And over a period of time the body gradually turns into a mummy. The custom is to unearth the body after three years and three months."

"Why would they do that?"

"So the priests could practice austerity to the point of becoming self-mummified. Doing that allows them to reach enlightenment and to arrive at a realm beyond life and death. This also connects up with mankind's salvation. So-called Nirvana. The unearthed enlightened monk, the mummy, is kept at a temple, and through praying to it people are saved."

"In reality it's a kind of suicide."

Menshiki nodded. "Which is why in the Meiji period the practice of self-burial was outlawed. People who helped in the process could be arrested for aiding and abetting suicide. The truth is, though, priests continued to follow the practice in secret. That's why there may be quite a few cases of priests being buried but never unearthed by anyone."

"Are you thinking that stone mound is the remains of a secret burial of that kind?"

Menshiki shook his head. "We won't know until we actually remove the stones. But it's possible. There's no bamboo tube there, but the way it's constructed, air could get in through the gaps, and you can hear sounds from inside too."

"And you're saying that someone is still alive underneath those stones and is ringing a gong or bell every night?"

Menshiki shook his head again. "That obviously doesn't make any sense."

"Reaching Nirvana—is that different from merely dying?"

"It is. I'm not all that familiar with Buddhist doctrine, but as far as I understand, Nirvana is found beyond life and death. You could see it as the idea that even if the flesh dies and disappears, the soul goes over to a place beyond life and death. Worldly flesh is nothing more than a temporary dwelling."

"Even if a priest were, through burial alive, to reach Nirvana, is it possible for him to rejoin his physical body?"

Menshiki said nothing and looked at me for a while. He took a bite of his ham sandwich, and a sip of coffee.

"What you're saying is—"

"I didn't hear that sound until four or five days ago," I said. "I'm certain of that. If the sound had been there I would have noticed. Even if it was small, it's not the kind of sound I would have missed. I only started hearing it a few days ago. What I mean is, even if there's somebody underneath those stones, that person hasn't been ringing the bell for a long time."

Menshiki returned his coffee cup to the saucer and studied the pattern on the cup. "Have you seen a real mummified priest?" he finally said.

I shook my head.

"I've seen several. When I was young I traveled around Yamagata Prefecture on my own and saw a few that were preserved in temples there. For some reason there are a lot of these mummified priests in the Tohoku region, especially in Yamagata. Honestly, they're not very nice to look at. Maybe it's my lack of faith, but I didn't feel very grateful when I saw them. Small, brown, all shriveled up. I probably shouldn't say this, but the color and texture reminded me of beef jerky. The physical body really is nothing more than a fleeting, empty abode. That, at least, is what these mummies teach us. We may do our utmost, but at best we end up as no more than beef jerky."

He picked up the ham sandwich he'd been eating and gazed at it intently for a moment. As if he were seeing a ham sandwich for the first time in his life.

He went on. "At any rate, let's wait till after lunch for them to move those stones. Then we'll know more, whether we want to or not."

We went back to the site in the woods just after one fifteen. The crew had finished lunch and were hard at work. The two workmen put wedge-like metal implements in the gaps between the stones, and the backhoe used a rope to pull those and raise the stones. The workmen then attached ropes to the dug-up stones, and the shovel hauled these up. It was time consuming, but one by one the stones were steadily unearthed and moved off to the side.

Menshiki and the foreman were deep in conversation about something for a while, but then he came back to join me.

"As they thought, the stones aren't all that thick. Looks like they'll be able to remove them," he explained. "There seems to be a lattice-shaped lid underneath all the stones. They don't know what it's made of, but that lid supported the stones. After they remove all the stones on top they'll need to take off that lid. They don't know yet if they can. It's impossible to guess what lies beneath that. It'll take a while for them to remove all the stones, and once they've made more progress they'll call us, so they said they'd like us to wait in the house. If you don't mind, let's do that. Standing around here isn't going to help."

We walked back home. I should have used the extra time to continue work on the portrait, but I didn't feel I'd be able to concentrate on painting. The operation out in the woods had me on edge. The six-foot-square stone flooring that had emerged from underneath the mound of crumbling old stones. The solid lattice lid. And the space that seemed to lie below it. I couldn't erase these images from my mind. Menshiki was right. Until we settled this matter we wouldn't be able to move forward on anything else.

"Do you mind if I listen to music while we wait?" Menshiki asked.

"Not at all," I said. "Play whatever record you'd like. I'll be in the kitchen preparing some food."

He chose a recording of Mozart. A sonata for piano and violin. The Tannoy Autograph speakers weren't very showy, but gave out a deep, steady sound. The perfect speakers for classical music, especially for listening to vinyl records of chamber music. As you might expect of old speakers, they were well suited to a vacuum-tube amp. The pianist was Georg Szell, the violinist Rafael Druian. Menshiki sat on the sofa, eyes closed, and gave himself over to the music. I listened to it from a little ways off, making tomato sauce. I'd bought a lot of tomatoes and had some left over and wanted to make some sauce before they went bad.

I boiled water in a large pan, parboiled the tomatoes and removed the skins, cut them with a knife, removed the seeds, crushed them, put them in a large skillet, added garlic, and simmered it all with olive oil, let it cook well. I carefully removed any scum on the surface. Back when I was married I often made sauce like this. It takes time and effort, but basically it's an easy process. While my wife was at work I'd stand alone in the kitchen, listening to music on a CD while I made it. I liked to cook while listening to old jazz. Thelonious Monk was a particular favorite. *Monk's Music* was my favorite of his albums. Coleman Hawkins and John Coltrane played on it, with amazing solos. But I have to admit that making sauce while listening to Mozart's chamber music wasn't bad either.

It was only a short while ago that I'd been cooking tomato sauce in the afternoon while enjoying Monk's unique offbeat melodies and chords (it was only half a year ago that my wife and I had dissolved our marriage), but it felt like something that had taken place ages ago. A trivial historical episode a generation ago that only a handful of people still remembered. I suddenly wondered how my wife was. Was she living with another man now? Or was she still living by herself in that apartment in Hiroo? Either way, at this time of day she would be at work at the architectural firm. For her, how much of a difference was there between her life when I was there, and her life now without me? And how much interest did she have in that difference? I was sort of half thinking about all this. Did she have the same feeling, that our days spent together seemed like something from the distant past?

The record was over, the needle making a popping sound as it spun in the final groove, and when I went to the living room I found Menshiki asleep on the sofa, arms folded, leaning over slightly to one side. I lifted the needle up from the spinning disc and switched off the turntable. Even when the steady click of the needle stopped, Menshiki continued to sleep. He must have been very tired. He was faintly snoring. I left him where he was. I returned to the kitchen, shut off the gas under the skillet, and drank a big glass of water. I still had time on my hands, so I began to fry some onions.

• • •

When the phone rang Menshiki was already awake. He was in the bathroom, washing his face with soap and gargling. The call was from the foreman at the work site, so I handed the phone to Menshiki. He said a few words, and then said that we would be right over. He handed the phone back.

"They're almost done," he said.

Outside it had stopped raining. Clouds still covered the sky, but it was lighter out now. The weather seemed to be steadily improving. We hurried up the steps and through the woods. Behind the little shrine the four men were standing around a hole, staring down into it. The backhoe's engine was off, nothing was moving, the woods strangely hushed.

The stones had been neatly removed, exposing the hole below. The square lattice lid had been taken off too, and laid to one side. It was a thick, heavy-looking wooden cover. Old, but not rotted at all. After that the circular stone-lined room below was visible. It was under six feet in diameter, about eight feet deep, and was enclosed by a stone wall. The floor seemed to be dirt. Not a single blade of grass grew there. The stone room was completely empty. No one there calling for help, no beef jerky mummy. Just a bell-like object lying on the ground. Actually less like a bell than some ancient musical instrument with a stack of tiny cymbals. A wooden handle was attached, about six inches long. The foreman shone a floodlight down on it.

"Was this all that was in there?" Menshiki asked him.

"Yes, that's it," the foreman said. "Like you asked, we left it just as we found it, after we took off the stones and lid. We haven't touched a thing."

"That's strange," Menshiki said, as if to himself. "So there really wasn't anything else at all?"

"I called you right after we lifted off the lid. I haven't been down inside. This is exactly the way it was when we uncovered it," the foreman said.

"Of course," Menshiki said, in a dry voice.

"It might have been a well originally," the foreman said. "It looks like it was filled in, leaving the hole. But it's too wide for a well, and the stone wall around it is so elaborately constructed. It couldn't have been easy to build. I suppose they must have had some important purpose in mind to construct something that took this much time and effort."

"Can I go down and check it out?" Menshiki asked the foreman.

The foreman was a little unsure. With a hard face, he said, "I think I should go down first. Just in case. If it's all clear, then you can climb on down. Does that sound good?"

"Of course," Menshiki said. "Let's do that."

One of the workmen brought over a folding metal ladder from the truck, opened it up, and lowered it down. The foreman put on his safety helmet and climbed down the eight feet to the dirt floor. He looked around him for a while. He gazed up, then shone his flashlight on the stone wall and the floor, closely checking everything. He carefully observed the bell-like object that lay on the dirt floor. He didn't touch it, though, just observed it. He rubbed the soles of his work boots a few times against the dirt floor, kicking his heel against it. He took a few deep breaths, smelling the air. He was only in the hole for about five or six minutes, then slowly clambered up the ladder to ground level.

"It doesn't seem dangerous. The air's good, and there aren't any weird bugs or anything. And the footing is solid. You can go down now if you'd like," he said.

Menshiki removed his rainwear to make it easier to move around, and in his flannel shirt and chinos, he hung his flashlight by a strap around his neck and climbed down the metal ladder. We watched in silence as he descended. The foreman shone the floodlight below Menshiki's feet. Menshiki stood still at the bottom of the hole for a while, waiting, then reached out and touched the stone wall, and crouched down to check out what the dirt floor felt like. He picked up the bell-like object on the ground, shone his flashlight on it, and gazed at it. Then he shook it a few times. When he did, it was unmistakably the same bell sound I'd heard. No doubt about it. In the middle of the night someone had been ringing it here. But that *someone* was no longer here. Only the bell was left behind. As he studied the bell Menshiki shook his head a few times, evidently puzzled. Then he carefully studied the surrounding wall again, as if looking for a secret entrance and exit. But he found nothing of the sort. He looked up at us at ground level. He seemed totally confused.

He stepped onto the ladder and held out the bell toward me. I bent over and took it from him. A dampness penetrated deep into the ancient wooden handle. As Menshiki had done, I tried shaking it a few times. It sounded louder and clearer than I'd expected. I didn't know what it was made of, but the metal portion wasn't damaged at all. It was dirty, for sure, but not at all rusted. I couldn't figure out how it had remained rust-free despite being underground in damp soil for years.

"What *is* that?" the foreman asked me. He was in his mid-forties, short but with a sturdy build. Suntanned, with a bit of stubble on his face.

"I'm not sure. Maybe some kind of Buddhist implement or something," I said. "Whatever it is, it's certainly from ancient times."

"Is this what you were looking for?" he asked.

I shook my head. "No, we were expecting something else."

"At any rate, it's a strange place," the foreman said. "I can't explain it, but there's a mysterious feeling about it. Who would make this kind of place, I wonder—and why? This was a long time ago, and it must have been quite a task to haul the stones all the way up the mountain and stack them up."

I didn't say anything.

Menshiki finally climbed up out of the hole. He called the foreman over to his side, and they talked for a long time. I stood there, bell in hand, next to the hole. I pondered climbing down into this stone-lined chamber, but then thought better of it. I wasn't as hesitant as Masahiko, but I did decide it was better not to do anything uncalled for. If things could be left alone, the smart thing might be to do so. I placed the bell, for the time being, in front of the little shrine, and wiped my palm on my pants a couple of times.

Menshiki ambled over. "We'll have them do a more thorough examination of that stone-lined chamber," he said. "At first glance it looks like just a hole, but I'll have them check it all out from one end to the other. They might discover something. Though I sort of doubt it." He looked at the bell I'd placed in front of the shrine. "It's odd that this bell's the only thing left. Since someone had to be inside there in the middle of the night ringing the bell."

"Maybe the bell was ringing by itself," I ventured.

Menshiki smiled. "An interesting theory, but I doubt it. For whatever purpose, someone was sending out a message from down inside that hole. A message to you, or maybe to us. Or to people in general. But whoever it was has vanished like smoke. Or else slipped away from there."

"Slipped away?"

"Slipped right past us."

I couldn't understand what he was getting at.

"Because the soul isn't something you can see," Menshiki said.

"You believe in the existence of the soul?"

"Do you?"

I didn't have a good answer.

"I believe that it's not necessary to believe in the soul's existence. But turn that around and you come to the belief that there's no need to *not* believe in its existence. A kind of roundabout way of putting it, but do you understand what I'm getting at?"

"Sort of," I said.

Menshiki picked up the bell from where I'd placed it in front of the shrine. He held it out and rang it several times. "A priest probably breathed his last there, underground, ringing this bell and chanting sutras. All alone, shut away in the pitch-black darkness, that heavy lid in place, in the bottom of a sealed well. And most likely all in secret. I have no idea what sort of priest he was. A respectable priest, or merely some fanatic. Either way, someone constructed a stone tumulus on top of it. I don't know what happened after that, but people then completely forgot he'd been voluntarily buried under here. Then a big earthquake occurred at some point, and the mound collapsed until it was just a pile of stones. It could have been during the Kanto earthquake of 1923, since certain areas around Odawara suffered real damage back then. And everything was swallowed up into oblivion."

"If that's true, then where did the priest who died there—the mummy, I mean—disappear to?"

Menshiki shook his head. "I don't know. Maybe at some point someone dug up the hole and took him away."

"To do that they'd have to move all these stones and then pile them up again," I said. "And then who was ringing the bell yesterday in the middle of the night?"

Menshiki shook his head again, and smiled faintly. "Good grief. We used all this equipment to move the stones and open up the chamber, and in the end all we found out for sure is that we don't know a single thing. All we managed to get was an old bell."

They examined the stone chamber thoroughly, and merely determined that there were no hidden devices anywhere. This was merely a round hole, lined with a stone wall, 8.2 feet deep with a diameter of 5.9 feet (they made precise measurements). Finally, they loaded the backhoe up onto the truck bed, and the workers collected all their tools and left. All that remained was the open hole and the metal ladder. The foreman was kind enough to leave it behind. They also laid several thick boards on top of the hole so no one would fall into it by mistake. They left some heavy stones on top to weigh the boards down so they wouldn't blow away in a strong wind. The wooden lattice cover was too heavy to lift, so they left it on the ground nearby and covered it with a plastic tarp.

Before they left, Menshiki told the foreman not to mention this operation to anyone. It had archaeological significance, and he wanted, he said, to keep it from the public until the time was right to announce the find.

"Understood," the foreman said with a serious expression. "We'll leave it all here. And I'll warn the others not to say anything about it."

After the workers and heavy machinery had left and the mountains were blanketed in their usual stillness again, the dug-up area looked like skin after a major operation, shabby and pitiful. The formerly vigorous clump of pampas grass had been trampled down beyond recognition, the ruts left by the backhoe like stitches left behind in the dark, damp soil. The rain had cleared up completely, though the sky was still covered by an unbroken layer of monotonously gray clouds.

When I looked at the pile of stones now stacked up on another piece of ground, I couldn't help but think, We should never have done this. We should have left them the way they were. On the other hand, though, the indisputable fact was that it was something we *had* to do. I couldn't go on listening to that strange sound night after night. But if I hadn't met Menshiki, I never would have had the means to dig up that hole. It was only because he had arranged for the workers, and had paid for the whole thing—I had no clue how much it cost—that the operation had been possible.

But meeting Menshiki and, as a result, having this large-scale excavation take place—was it really all just coincidence? Had it all just fallen together by chance? Weren't things just a little *too* convenient? Hadn't the scenario been all planned out in advance? With all these unanswered doubts, I went with Menshiki to the house. He carried the bell we'd unearthed. He never let go of it the whole time we were walking. As if trying to read, from the touch of it, some kind of message.

As soon as we got back inside Menshiki asked, "Where should I put this bell?"

Where indeed? I had no idea. For the time being, I decided to place it in the studio. Having that weird object under the same roof didn't sit well with me, but that said, I couldn't just toss it outside. It was, no doubt, a valuable Buddhist implement, imbued with a certain soulfulness, so I couldn't just neglect it. I decided to put it in the sort of neutral zone of the studio, which felt like a separate annex. I cleared a space on the long, narrow shelf used for painting materials and placed it there. Next to the large mug used to hold brushes, it even looked like some specialized painting tool.

"What a strange day," Menshiki said.

"I'm sorry you had to use up your entire day for this," I said.

"No, don't apologize. It's been very interesting," Menshiki said. "And this isn't the end of it, I would imagine."

Menshiki had an odd look on his face, as if gazing far away.

"Meaning something else is going to happen?" I asked.

Menshiki chose his words carefully. "I can't explain it well, but I get the feeling that this is only the beginning."

"Only the beginning?"

He held his palms upward. "I'm not sure, of course. Maybe that'll be it, and we'll just be left thinking what a strange day that was. That would probably be the best outcome. But nothing's been resolved. The same questions remain. And these are *very important* questions. That's why I have a hunch that something else is going to happen."

"Something connected to that stone-lined chamber?"

Menshiki gazed outside for a moment before he spoke. "I don't know what's going to happen. It's just a hunch."

And of course it turned out as he'd felt—or predicted—it might. Like he said, that day was only the beginning.

16

A RELATIVELY GOOD DAY

That night I had trouble sleeping. I was anxious whether the bell I'd left in the studio would start ringing in the middle of the night. If it did, then what would I do? Pull the covers up over my head and pretend not to hear anything until the next morning? Or take my flashlight and go to the studio to check it out? And what would I find there?

Unable to decide how I should react, I lay in bed reading. But even after two a.m. the bell hadn't rung. All I heard was the usual drone of insects. As I read my book I checked the clock next to my bed every five minutes. When the digital display read 2:30 I finally breathed a sigh of relief. The bell wouldn't be ringing tonight, I figured. I closed the book, turned out the bedside light, and went to sleep.

The next morning when I woke up before seven, the first thing I did was go check on the bell. It was as I'd left it the night before, on the shelf. Brilliant sunlight illuminated the mountains, and the crows were in the midst of their usual noisy morning routine. In the light of day the bell didn't look ominous at all. It was nothing more than a simple, well-used Buddhist implement from the past.

I went back to the kitchen, brewed coffee in the coffee maker, and drank it. Heated up a scone that had gotten hard in the toaster and ate it. Then went out to the terrace, breathed in the morning air, leaned against the railing, and looked over at Menshiki's house across the valley. The large tinted windows glistened in the morning sun. Probably one of the tasks included in the once-per-week cleaning service was to clean all the windows. The glass was always clean and shiny. I looked over there for a while, but Menshiki didn't appear. We still hadn't yet reached the point where we waved at each other across the valley.

At ten thirty I drove my car to the supermarket to buy groceries. I came back, put them away, and made a simple lunch, a tofu and tomato salad with a rice ball. After I ate, I had some strong green tea. Then I lay down on the sofa and listened to a Schubert string quartet. It was a beautiful piece. According to the liner notes on the jacket, when it was first performed there was quite a backlash among listeners, who felt it was "too radical." I don't know what part was radical, but something about it must have offended the old-fashioned people of that time.

As one side of the record ended I suddenly got very sleepy, so I pulled a blanket over me and slept for while on the sofa. A short but deep sleep, probably about twenty minutes. It felt like I had a few dreams, but when I woke up I couldn't remember them. Those kinds of dreams—the kind where all sorts of unrelated fragments are mixed together. Each fragment has a certain gravitas, but by intertwining they canceled each other out.

I went to the fridge and drank some cold mineral water straight from the bottle and managed to chase away the dregs of sleep that remained like scraps of clouds in the corners of my body. I felt a renewed awareness of the reality that I was living, alone, in the mountains. I lived here by myself. Some sort of fate had brought me to this special place. I remembered the bell. In the weird stone chamber deep in the woods, who in the world had been ringing that bell? And where on earth was that person now?

By the time I had changed into my painting outfit, gone into the studio, and stood looking at Menshiki's portrait, it was past two p.m. Normally I worked in the morning. From eight to noon was the time I could focus best on painting. I liked the sort of domestic quiet at those times. After moving to the mountains I'd grown fond of the brilliant and pure air that the teeming nature around me provided. Working at the same time in the same place each day has always held a special meaning for me. Repetition created a certain rhythm. But this day, partly because I hadn't slept well the night before, I spent the morning without accomplishing anything. Which is why I went to the studio in the afternoon.

I sat on my round work stool, arms folded, and from a distance of some six feet gazed at the painting I'd begun. I'd started by using a thin brush to outline Menshiki's face, then with him modeling before me for fifteen minutes also used black paint to flesh this out. This was just a rough framework at this point, though it gave rise to a productive flow. A flow that had its source in Wataru Menshiki. This was what I needed most.

As I stared hard at this black-and-white framework, an image of a color I should add came to me. The idea sprang up suddenly, all on its own. The color was like that of a tree with its green leaves dully dyed by rain. I mixed several colors together and created what I wanted on my palette. After much trial and error, I finally arrived at what I'd pictured and, without really thinking, added the color to the line drawing I'd done. I had no idea myself what sort of painting would emerge from this, though I did know that that color was going to be a vital grounding for the work. Gradually this painting was beginning to stray far afield from the format of a typical portrait. But even if it doesn't turn out as a portrait, I told myself, that was okay. As long as there was a set flow, all I could do was go with it. What I wanted now was to paint what *I* wanted to paint, the way *I* wanted to paint it (something Menshiki wanted as well). I could think about the next step later on.

I was simply following ideas that sprang up naturally inside me, with no plan or goal. Like a child, not watching his step, chasing some unusual butterfly fluttering across a field. After adding this color to the canvas I set my palette and brush down, again sat down on the stool six feet away, and studied the painting straight on. This is indeed the right color, I decided. The kind of green found in a forest wet by the rain. I nodded several times to myself. This was the kind of feeling toward a painting I hadn't experienced for ages. Yes—this was it. This was the color I'd wanted. Or maybe the color the framework itself had been seeking. With this color as the base, I mixed some peripheral, variant colors, adding variation and depth to the painting.

And as I gazed at the image I'd done, the next color leaped up at me. Orange. Not just a simple orange, but a flaming orange, a color that had both a strong vitality and also a premonition of decay. Like a fruit slowly rotting away. Creating this color was much more of a challenge than the green. It wasn't simply a color, but had to be connected with a specific emotion, an emotion entwined with fate, but in its own way firm, unfluctuating. Making a color like that was no easy task, of course, but in the end I managed. I took out a new brush and ran it over the surface of the canvas. In places I used a knife, too. *Not thinking* was the priority. I tried to turn off my mind, decisively adding this color to the composition. As I painted, details of reality almost totally vanished from my mind. The sound of the bell, that gaping stone tomb, my ex-wife sleeping with some other man, my married girlfriend, the art classes I taught, the future—I thought of none of it. I didn't even think of Menshiki. What I was painting had, of course, started out as his portrait, but by this point my mind was even clear of the thought of his face. Menshiki was nothing more than a starting point. What I was doing was painting for me, for my sake alone.

I don't remember how much time passed. By the time I looked around, the room had gotten dim. The autumn sun had disappeared behind the western mountains, yet I was so engrossed in my work I'd forgotten to switch on a light. I looked at the canvas and saw five colors there already. Color on top of color, and more color on top of that. In one section the colors were subtly mixed, in another part one color overwhelmed another and prevailed over it.

I turned on the ceiling light, sat down again on the stool, and looked at the painting. I knew the painting was incomplete. There was a wild outburst to it, a type of violence that had propelled me forward. A wildness I had not seen in some time. But something was still missing, a core element to control and quell that raw throng, an idea to bring emotion under control. But I needed more time to discover that. That torrent of color had to rest. That would be a job for tomorrow and beyond, when I could return to it under a fresh, bright light. The passage of the right amount of time would show me what was needed. I had to wait for it, like waiting patiently for the phone to ring. And in order to wait that patiently, I had to put my faith in time. I had to believe that time was on my side.

Seated on the stool, I shut my eyes and took a deep breath. In the autumn twilight I could clearly sense something within me changing. As if the structure of my body had unraveled, then was being recombined in a different way. But why *here*, and why *now*? Did meeting the enigmatic Menshiki and taking on his portrait commission result in this sort of internal transformation? Or had uncovering the weird underground chamber, and being led there by the sound of the bell, acted as a stimulus to my spirit? Or was it that I'd merely reached an unrelated turning point in my life? No matter which explanation I went with, there didn't seem to be any basis for it.

"It feels like this is just the beginning," Menshiki had said as we parted. Had I stepped into this *beginning* he'd spoken about? At any rate, I'd been so worked up by the act of painting in a way I hadn't in years, so absorbed in creating, that I'd literally forgotten the passage of time. As I stowed away my materials, my skin had a feverish flush that felt good.

As I straightened up, the bell on the shelf caught my eye. I picked it up and tried ringing it a couple of times. The familiar sound rang out clearly in the studio. The middle-of-the-night sound that made me anxious. Somehow, though, it didn't frighten me anymore. I merely wondered why such an ancient bell could still make such a clear sound. I put the bell back where it had been, switched off the light, and shut the door to the studio. Back in the kitchen, I poured myself a glass of white wine and sipped it as I prepared dinner.

Just before nine p.m. a call came in from Menshiki.

"How were things last night?" he asked. "Did you hear the bell?"

I'd stayed up until two thirty but hadn't heard the bell at all, I told him. It was a very quiet night.

"Glad to hear it. Since then has anything unusual happened around you?"

"Nothing particularly unusual, no," I replied.

"That's good. I hope it continues that way," Menshiki said. A moment later he added, "Would it be all right for me to stop by tomorrow morning? I'd really like to take another good look at the stone chamber if I could. It's a fascinating place."

"Fine by me," I said. "I have no plans for tomorrow morning."

"Then I'll see you around eleven."

"Looking forward to it," I said.

"By the way, was today a good day for you?" Menshiki asked.

Was today a good day for me? It sounded like a sentence that had been translated mechanically by computer software.

"A relatively good day," I replied, puzzled for a moment. "At least, nothing bad happened. The weather was good, overall a pleasant day. What about you, Mr. Menshiki? Was today a good day for you?"

"It was a day when one good thing happened, and so did one not-so-good thing," Menshiki replied. "The scale is still swinging, unable to decide which one was heavier—the good or the bad."

I didn't know how to respond to that, so I stayed silent.

Menshiki went on. "Sadly, I'm not an artist like you. I live in the business world. The information business, in particular. In that world the only information that has exchange value is that which can be quantified. So I have the habit of always quantifying the good and the bad. If the good outweighs the bad even by a little, that means it's a good day, even if something bad happened. At least numerically."

I still had no idea what he was getting at. So I kept my mouth closed.

"By unearthing that underground chamber like we did yesterday, we must have lost something, and gained something. What did we lose, and what did we gain? That's what concerns me."

He seemed to be waiting for me to reply.

"I don't think we gained anything you could quantify," I said after giving it some thought. "At least right now. The only thing we got was that old Buddhist bell. But that probably doesn't have any actual value. It doesn't have any provenance, and isn't some unique antique. On the other hand, what was lost can be clearly quantified. Before long, you'll be getting a bill from the landscaper, I imagine."

Menshiki chuckled. "It's not that expensive. Don't worry about it. What concerns me is that we haven't yet taken from there *the thing we need to take*."

"The thing we need to take? What's that?"

Menshiki cleared his throat. "As I said, I'm no artist. I have a certain amount of intuition, but unfortunately I don't have the means to make it concrete. No matter how keen that intuition might be, I still can't turn it into art. I don't have the talent."

I was silent, waiting for what came next.

"Which is why I've always pursued quantification as a substitute for an artistic, universal representation. In order to live properly, people need a central axis. Don't you think so? In my case, by quantifying intuition, or something like intuition, through a unique system, I've been able to enjoy a degree of worldly success. And according to my intuition . . ." he said, and was silent for a time. A very dense silence. "According to my intuition, we should have got hold of something from digging up that underground chamber."

"Like what?"

He shook his head. Or at least it seemed that way to me from the other end of the phone line. "I still don't know. But I think we have to know. We need to combine our intuition, allow it to pass through your ability to express things in concrete form, and my ability to quantify them."

I still couldn't really grasp what he was getting at. What was this man talking about?

"Let's see each other again tomorrow at eleven," Menshiki said. And quietly hung up.

Soon after he'd hung up, I got a call from my married girlfriend. I was a little surprised. It wasn't often that she'd get in touch at this time of night.

"Can I see you tomorrow around noon?" she asked.

"I'm sorry, but I have an appointment tomorrow. I made it just a little while ago."

"Not another woman, I hope?"

"No. It's with Mr. Menshiki. I'm painting his portrait."

"You're painting his portrait," she repeated. "Then the day after tomorrow?"

"The day after tomorrow's totally free."

"Great. Is early afternoon okay?"

"Of course. But it's Saturday."

"I'll manage it."

"Did something happen?" I asked.

"Why do you ask?" she said.

"You don't often call me at this time of day."

She made a small sound at the back of her throat, as if making a minor adjustment in her breathing. "I'm in my car now, by myself. I'm calling from my cell."

"What are you doing in the car all alone?"

"I just wanted to be by myself in the car, so that's where I am. Housewives sometimes do these things. Is that a problem?"

"No problem. No problem at all."

She sighed, the kind of sigh that condensed a variety of sighs into one. And then she said, "I wish you were here with me. And that we could do it from behind. I don't need any foreplay. I'm so wet you could slip right inside. I want you to pound me, hard and fast."

"Sounds good to me. But a Mini is too small inside to pound you hard like that."

"Don't expect too much."

"Let's figure out a way."

"I want you to knead my breast with your left hand and rub my clit with your right."

"What should my right foot be doing? I could manage to use it to adjust the car stereo. You don't mind a little Tony Bennett?"

"I'm not joking here. I'm totally serious."

"I know. My bad. Serious. Got it," I said. "Tell me, what are you wearing right now?"

"You want to know what clothes I'm wearing?" she asked enticingly.

"I do. My procedure might change depending on what you have on."

Over the phone she gave me a detailed rundown on the clothes she had on. It always surprised me, the variety of clothes mature women wore. Orally, she took these off, one by one.

"So, did that get you hard?" she asked.

"Like a hammer," I said.

"You could pound a nail?"

"You bet."

There are hammers in the world that need to pound in nails, and nails that need to be pounded by hammers. Now who said that? Nietzsche? Or was it Schopenhauer? Or maybe nobody said it.

Over the phone line, we entwined bodies in a way that felt so real. Phone sex was definitely a first for me, with her—or with anyone, for that matter. Her descriptions were so detailed, so arousing, that these imaginary sex acts were, in part, more sensual than what we could do with our actual bodies. Words can sometimes be so direct, sometimes so erotically suggestive. At the end of this exchange, I unexpectedly climaxed. And she seemed to have an orgasm as well.

We said nothing, catching our breath.

"I'll see you Saturday, then," she said after she seemed to have pulled herself together. "I have something to tell you about our Mr. Menshiki, too."

"You got some new information?"

"A bit of new information I gathered through the jungle grapevine. But I'll wait to see you to tell you. While we're probably doing something naughty."

"You going home now?"

"Of course," she said. "I'd better be getting back."

"Drive carefully."

"Right. I need to take care. I'm still sort of shuddering down there."

I stepped into the shower and used soap to clean my penis. I changed into pajamas, threw on a cardigan, and with a glass of cheap white wine in hand went out onto the terrace and gazed off in the direction of Menshiki's house. The lights were still on in his massive, pure-white mansion across the valley. The lights seemed to be on all over the house. What he was doing over there (most likely) all by himself, I had no idea. Seated at the computer, perhaps, engaged once more in quantifying intuition.

"A relatively good day," I said to myself.

And an odd day at that. What kind of day tomorrow would bring I had no clue. Suddenly I remembered the horned owl up in the attic. Was today a good day for it, too? Then I recalled that for horned owls, the day was now only beginning. During the day they slept in dark places. And come night, they set out to the woods in search of prey. That was a question a horned owl should be asked early in the morning. The question of "Was today a good day?"

I went to bed, read a book for a while, then turned off the light at ten thirty and went to sleep. Since I slept, without waking even once, until just before six the next morning, I imagine that the bell didn't ring during the middle of the night.

17

HOW COULD I MISS SOMETHING THAT IMPORTANT?

I never could forget the last words my wife said when I left our home: "Even if we break up like this, can we still be friends? If possible, I mean." At the time (and for a long time after), I couldn't understand what she was trying to say, what she was hoping for. I was confused, as if I'd put some totally tasteless food into my mouth. The best I could say was, "Well, who knows." And those were the last words I said to her face-to-face. Pretty pathetic, as final words go.

Even after we broke up, it felt like my wife and I were still connected by a single living tube. An invisible tube, but one that was still beating slightly, sending something like hot blood traveling back and forth between our two souls. I still had that sort of organic sensation. But before long, that tube would be severed. And if it was bound to be cut sometime, I needed to drain the life from that faint line connecting us. If the life was drained from it, and it shriveled up like a mummy, the pain of it being severed by a sharp knife would be that much more bearable. To do so, I needed to forget about Yuzu, as soon as I could, as much as I could. That's why I never tried to contact her. After I came back from my trip and went to pick up some belongings back at the apartment, I did call her once. I needed to get all my painting materials I'd left behind. That was the only conversation I had with Yuzu after we broke up, and it didn't last long.

We officially dissolved our marriage, and I couldn't contemplate the thought of us remaining friends. We'd shared so many things during our six years of marriage. A lot of time, emotions, words and silence, lots of confusion and lots of decisions, lots of promises and lots of resignation, lots of pleasure, lots of boredom. Naturally each of us must have had inner secrets, but we even managed to find a way to share the sense of having something hidden from the other. With us there was a gravitas of place that only the passage of time can nurture. We did a good job of accommodating our bodies to that sort of gravity, maintaining a delicate balance. We had our own special local rules that we lived by. And there was no way we could get rid of all that history, jettison the gravitational balance and local rules, and live simply as *good friends*.

I understood that very well. That's the conclusion I came to after thinking about it during that lengthy trip. I invariably came to the same conclusion: it was best to keep Yuzu at a distance and break off contact. That made the most sense. And that's what I did.

And for her part Yuzu didn't contact me either. Not a single phone call, not one letter. Even though she was the one who said she wanted to *remain friends*. That hurt far more than I'd expected. Or more precisely, what hurt me was actually *me*, myself. In the midst of that continuing, unsettled silence my feelings, like a heavy pendulum, a razor-sharp blade, made wide swings between one extreme to the other. That arc of emotions left fresh wounds in my skin. And I had only one way of forgetting the pain. And that was, of course, by painting.

Sunlight filtered in silently through the studio window. From time to time a gentle breeze rustled the white curtains. The room had an autumn-morning scent. After coming to live on the mountain I'd grown sensitive to the changes in smells from one season to another. Back when I lived in the city I'd hardly ever noticed those.

I sat on the stool, and gazed for a long time at the portrait of Menshiki I'd begun. This was the way I always began work, reevaluating with new eyes the work I'd done the previous day. Only then could I pick up my brush.

Not bad, I thought. Not bad at all. The colors I'd created completely enveloped the original framework of Menshiki I'd done. The outline of him in black paint was hidden now behind those colors. Though concealed, I could still make it out. I would have to once more bring that outline into relief. Transform a hint into a statement.

There was no guarantee, of course, that the painting would ever be complete. It was still inchoate, something missing. Something that should be there was appealing to the nonvalidity of absence. And that missing element was rapping on the glass window separating presence and absence. I could make out its wordless cry.

Focusing so hard on the painting had made me thirsty, so I went into the kitchen and drank a large glass of orange juice. I relaxed my shoulders, stretched both arms high above my head, took a deep breath, and exhaled. I went back to the studio and sat down on the stool and studied the painting. Refreshed, I focused again. But something was different from before. The angle I was looking at the painting from was clearly not the same as it had been a few minutes before.

I got down from the stool and checked its location. It was in a slightly different spot from when I'd left the studio earlier. The stool had clearly been moved. But how? When I'd gotten down from the stool, I hadn't moved it. That I was sure of. I'd gotten down gingerly in order not to move the stool, and when I'd come back I'd also been careful not to move it when I sat down. I remembered these details because I'm very sensitive about the position and angle I view paintings from. I have a set position and angle that I always use, and like batters who are very particular about their stance in the batter's box, it bothers me to no end if things are off, even by a fraction.

But now the stool was eighteen inches away from where it had been, the angle that much changed. All I could think was that while I'd been in the kitchen drinking orange juice and taking deep breaths, someone had moved the stool. Someone had gone into the studio, sat on the stool to look at the painting, then got down from the stool before I came back, and silently slipped out of the room. And that's when—whether intentionally or it just worked out that way—they moved the stool. But I'd been out of the studio at most five or six minutes. Who in the world would go out of their way to do something like that—and why? Or had the stool moved on its own?

My memory must be messed up. I'd moved the stool but forgotten that I had. That's all I could think. Maybe I was spending too much time alone. The order of events in my memory was getting muddled.

I left the stool in the spot where I'd found it—in other words, a spot twenty inches away from where it had been, and at a different angle. I sat down on it and studied Menshiki's portrait from that position. What I saw was a slightly different painting. It was the same painting, of course, but it looked ever so different. The way the light struck it was not the same as before, and the texture of the paint, too, looked changed. There was something decidedly animated and alive in the painting. But also something still lacking. The direction of that lack, though, wasn't the same as before.

So what was different about it? I brought my focus to bear on the painting. The difference must be speaking to me, trying to tell me something. I had to discover what was being hinted at by the difference. I took a piece of white chalk and marked the position of the three legs of the stool on the floor (location A). Then I moved the stool back twenty inches to the side to its original position (location B), and marked that, too, with chalk. I moved back and forth between the two positions, studying the one painting from the different angles.

Menshiki was still in both paintings, but I noticed that his appearance was strangely different depending on the two angles. It was as if two different personalities coexisted within him. Yet both versions of Menshiki were missing something. That shared lack unified both the A and B versions of Menshiki. I had to discover what it was, as if it were triangulated between position A, position B, and myself. What could that shared absence be? Was it something that had form, or something formless? If the latter, then how was I to give it form?

Not an easy thing to do, now is it, someone said.

I clearly heard that voice. Not a loud voice, but one that carried. Nothing vague about it. Not high, not low. And it sounded like it was right next to my ear.

I involuntarily gulped and, still seated on the stool, slowly gazed around me. I couldn't see anyone else there, of course. The clear morning light filled the floor like pools of water. The window was open, and from far off I could faintly hear the melody played by a garbage truck. It was playing "Annie Laurie" (why the garbage trucks in Odawara played a Scottish folk song was a mystery to me). Beyond that, I couldn't hear a thing.

Maybe I was just imagining things. Maybe it was my own voice I was hearing, a voice welling up from my unconscious. But what I'd heard sounded odd. *Not an easy thing to do, now, is it?* Even unconsciously, I wouldn't talk to myself like that.

I took a deep breath and from my perch on the stool again looked at the painting, focusing my attention on the work. It must have just been my imagination.

Is it not obvious? someone now said. The voice was right beside my ear.

Obvious? I asked myself. What's so obvious?

What you must discover, can you not see, is what it is about Mr. Menshiki that is not present here, someone said. As before, a clear voice. A voice with no echo, like it was recorded in an anechoic chamber. Each sound clear as crystal. And like an embodied concept, it had no natural inflection.

I looked around again. This time I got down from the stool and went to check in the living room. I checked every room, but nobody else was in the house. The only other creature there was the horned owl in the attic. The horned owl, of course, couldn't talk. And the front door was locked.

First the stool moving on its own, and now this weird voice. A voice from heaven? Or my own voice? Or the voice of some anonymous third party? Something was clearly wrong with my mind. Ever since I had started hearing that bell, I'd begun having doubts about whether my brain was functioning normally. With the bell, at least, Menshiki had been there and had heard the same sound, which proved that it wasn't an auditory hallucination. My hearing was working fine. Okay, so what could this mysterious voice be?

I sat back down on the stool and looked at the painting.

What you must discover, can you see, is what Mr. Menshiki has that is not here. Sounded like a riddle. Like a wise bird deep in the forest showing lost children the way home. *What Menshiki has that is not here*—what could that be?

It took a long time. The clock silently, regularly, ticked away the minutes, the pool of light from the small east-facing window silently shifted. Colorful, agile little birds flew onto the branches of a willow, gracefully searched for something, then flew away with a twitter. White clouds, like round slates, floated over the sky in a row. A single silver plane flew toward the sparkling sea. A four-engine propeller SDF plane, on antisubmarine patrol. Keeping their ears and eyes sharp and watchful, making the latent manifest, was their daily job. I listened as the engine drew closer and then flew away.

And finally, a single fact struck me. Literally as plain as day. Why had I forgotten this? What Menshiki had that my portrait of him did not—it was all clear to me now. *His white hair.* That beautiful white hair, as pure white as newly fallen snow. Menshiki without that white hair was unimaginable. How could I miss something that important?

I leaped up from the stool, went to my paint box and gathered up the white paint, picked a brush, and, without thinking, thickly, vigorously spread it on the canvas. I used a knife too, even my fingertip at one point. For fifteen minutes I painted, then stood back from the canvas, sat down on the stool, and checked out my work.

And there, before me, was Menshiki the person. Without a doubt, he was in the painting now. His personality—no matter what that was made up of—was integrated, manifested in the painting. I had no handle on the person named Wataru Menshiki, and knew barely a thing about him. But as an artist I had captured him on canvas, as a synthesized image, as a single, indivisible package. Alive and breathing within the painting. Even the riddles about him were present.

Still, no matter how you looked at it, this was no *portrait.* I'd succeeded (at least I felt I had) in artistically bringing the presence of Wataru Menshiki into relief on canvas. But the goal wasn't to depict his outer appearance. That wasn't the goal at all. That was the big difference between this work and a portrait. What I'd created was, at heart, a painting I'd done *for my own sake.*

I couldn't predict if Menshiki would accept this painting as his *portrait.* It might be light-years away from the kind of painting he'd been expecting. He'd told me to paint it any way I liked, and didn't have any special requests about the style it was done in. But just *possibly*, there might be some element in the painting, something negative, that he himself didn't want to recognize. Not that I could do anything about that now. Whether he liked the painting or not, it was already out of my hands, beyond my will.

Seated on the stool, I kept staring at the portrait for nearly another half hour. *I* had painted it, that much I knew, but the end product outstripped the bounds of any logic or understanding I possessed. How had I painted something like that? I couldn't even recall now. I stared dumbfounded at the painting, my feelings swinging from intimacy to total alienation. But one thing was sure—the colors and form were perfect.

Maybe I was on the verge of finding an exit, I thought. Finally able to pass through the thick wall that stood in my way. But still, things had only begun. I had only just managed to grasp a kind of clue as to how to proceed. I would have to be extremely careful. Telling myself this, I went over to the sink and methodically cleaned the paint from the brushes and painting knife. I washed my hands with oil and soap. Then I went to the kitchen and drank several glasses of water. I was parched.

All well and good, but who had moved the stool in the studio? (It had most definitely been moved.) And who had spoken in my ear in that strange voice? (I had clearly heard the voice.) And who had suggested to me what was missing from the painting? (A suggestion that had clearly been effective.)

In all likelihood it was me—I'd done this myself. I'd unconsciously moved the stool, and given myself the suggestion about how to proceed. In a strange, roundabout way I must have freely intertwined my conscious and subconscious . . . I couldn't think of any other explanation. Though of course this couldn't be the case.

At eleven, I was seated on a straight-backed chair, sipping hot tea and randomly mulling over things, when Menshiki's silver Jaguar drove up. I'd been so wrapped up in painting that the appointment we'd made the day before had completely slipped my mind. Not to mention the auditory illusion, or the voice I must have imagined.

Menshiki? Why is *he* here?

"I'd really like to take a good look at the stone chamber again if I could," Menshiki had said over the phone. As I listened to the now familiar growl of the V8 engine come to a halt, it all came back to me.

18

CURIOSITY DIDN'T JUST KILL THE CAT

I went outside to greet Menshiki. It was the first time I'd done so. I didn't have any particular reason, it just turned out that way. I wanted to get outside, stretch my legs, breathe some fresh air.

Those round slate-shaped clouds still floated in the sky. Lots of these clouds formed far off in the sea, then were slowly carried on the south-west wind, one by one, toward the mountains. Did those beautiful, perfect circles form naturally, not from any practical design? It was a mystery. For a meteorologist maybe it was no mystery at all, but it was for me. Living on this mountaintop, I found myself attracted to all sorts of natural wonders.

Menshiki had on a collared dark-red sweater, light and elegant. And well-worn jeans, so light blue they looked ready to fade away. The jeans were straight leg, made of soft material. To me (and I might be over-thinking things) he always seemed to intentionally wear colors that made his white hair stand out. This dark-red sweater went very well with his white hair. His hair always was at just the right length. I had no idea how he kept it that way, but it was never any longer or shorter than it was right now.

"I'd like to go and look into the pit right away, if it's okay with you?" Menshiki asked. "See if anything's changed."

"Okay by me," I said. I hadn't been back, either, in the woods since that day. I wanted to see how things were, too.

"Sorry to bother you, but could you bring me the bell?" Menshiki asked.

I went inside, took down the ancient bell from the studio shelf, and returned.

Menshiki took a large flashlight from the trunk of his Jaguar and hung it from a strap around his neck. He set off for the woods, me tagging along. The woods seemed even a deeper color than before. In this season, every day brought changes to the mountains. Some trees were redder, others dyed a deeper yellow, and some stayed forever green. The combination was truly beautiful. Menshiki, though, didn't seem to care.

"I looked into the background of this land a little," he said while he walked. "Who owned it up till now, what it was used for, that sort of thing."

"Did you find out something?"

Menshiki shook his head. "No, next to nothing. I was expecting that it might have been some religious site, but according to what I found that wasn't the case. I couldn't find out any background as to why there would be a small shrine and stone tumulus here. It was apparently just an ordinary piece of mountainous land. Then it was partly cleared and a house was built. Tomohiko Amada purchased the land along with the house in 1955. Prior to that, a politician had used it as a mountain retreat. You probably haven't heard of him, but he held a Cabinet position back before the war. After the war he essentially lived in retirement. I couldn't trace back who owned the place before that."

"It's a little strange that a politician would go to the trouble of having a vacation home in such a remote place."

"A lot of politicians had retreats here back then. Prince Fumimaro Konoe, prime minister just before World War Two, had a summer retreat just a couple of mountains over from here. It's on the way to Hakone and Atami, and must have been a perfect spot for people to gather for secret talks. It's hard to keep it secret when VIPs get together in Tokyo."

We moved the thick boards that lay covering the hole.

"I'm going to go down inside," Menshiki said. "Would you wait for me?"

"I'll be here," I said.

Menshiki climbed down the mental ladder the contractor had left for us. The ladder creaked a bit with each step. I watched him from above.

When he got to the bottom he took the flashlight from around his neck, switched it on, and carefully checked his surroundings. He rubbed the stone wall, and pounded his fist against it.

"This wall is solidly made, and pretty intricate," Menshiki said, looking up at me. "I don't think it's just some well that's been filled in halfway. If it was a well, it would just be a lot of stones piled up on top of each other. They wouldn't have done such a meticulous job."

"You think it was built for some other purpose?"

Menshiki shook his head, indicating that he had no idea. "Anyway, the wall is made so you can't easily climb out. There aren't any spaces to get a foothold. The hole's less than nine feet deep, but scrambling to the top wouldn't be an easy feat."

"You mean it was built that way, to be hard to climb up?"

Menshiki shook his head again. He didn't know. No clue.

"I'd like you to do something for me," Menshiki said.

"What would that be?"

"Would it be an imposition for you to pull up the ladder, and put the cover on tight so no light gets in?"

That left me speechless.

"It's okay. Don't worry," Menshiki said. "I'd like to experience what it's like to be shut up here, in the bottom of the dark pit, by myself. No plans to turn into a mummy yet, though."

"How long do you plan to be down there?"

"When I want to get out, I'll ring the bell. When you hear the bell, take off the cover and lower down the ladder. If an hour passes without you hearing the bell, come and remove the cover. I don't plan to be down here over an hour. Please don't forget that I'm down here. If you did forget, I really *would* turn into a mummy."

"The mummy hunter becomes a mummy."

Menshiki laughed. "Exactly."

"There's no way I'll forget. But are you sure it's okay, doing that?"

"I'm curious. I'd like to try sitting for a while at the bottom of a dark pit. I'll give you the flashlight. And you can hand me the bell."

He climbed halfway up the ladder and held out the flashlight for me. I took it, and held out the bell. He took the bell and gave it a little shake. It rang out clearly.

"But if—just supposing—I were attacked by vicious hornets on the way and fell unconscious, or even died, then you might never be able to get out of here. You never know what's going to happen in this world."

"Curiosity always involves risk. You can't satisfy your curiosity without accepting some risk. Curiosity didn't just kill the cat."

"I'll be back in an hour," I said.

"Watch out for the hornets," Menshiki said.

"And you take care down there in the dark."

Menshiki didn't reply, and just looked up at me, as if trying to decipher some meaning in my expression as I gazed down at him. There was some kind of vagueness in his eyes, like he was straining to focus on my face, but couldn't. It was an uncertain expression, not at all like him. Then, as if reconsidering things, he sat down on the ground and leaned against the curved stone wall. He looked up and raised his hand a little. *All set*, he was telling me. I yanked up the ladder, pulled the thick boards over so they completely covered up the hole, and set some heavy stones on top of that. A small amount of light might filter in through narrow cracks between the boards, though inside the hole should be dark enough. I thought about calling out to Menshiki from on top of the cover, but thought better of it. What he wanted was solitude and silence.

I went back home, boiled water, and made tea. I sat on the sofa and picked up where I'd left off in a book. I couldn't focus on reading, though, since my ears were alert for the sound of the bell. Every five minutes I checked my watch, and imagined Menshiki, alone in the bottom of that dark hole. What an odd person, I thought. He uses his own money to hire a landscape contractor, who uses heavy equipment to move that pile of stones and open up the entrance to that hole. And now Menshiki was confined there, all by himself. Or rather, deliberately *shut away in there* at his own request.

Whatever, I thought. Whatever necessity or intentions motivated it (assuming there was some kind of necessity or intention), that was Menshiki's problem, and I could leave it all up to him. I was an unthinking actor in someone else's plan. I gave up reading the book, lay down on the sofa, closed my eyes, but of course didn't fall asleep. This was no time to be sleeping.

An hour passed without the bell ringing. Or maybe I'd somehow missed the sound. Either way, it was time to get that cover off. I got up off the sofa, slipped on my shoes, and went outside and into the woods. I was a bit apprehensive that hornets or a wild boar might appear, but neither did. Just some tiny birds, Japanese white-eyes, flitted right past me. I walked through the woods and went around behind the shrine. I removed the heavy stones and took off just one of the boards.

"Mr. Menshiki!" I called out into the gap. But there was no response. What I could see of the hole from the gap was pitch dark, and I couldn't make out his figure there.

"Mr. Menshiki!" I called again. But again no answer. I was getting worried. Maybe he'd vanished, like the mummy that should have been there had vanished. I knew it wasn't logically possible, but still I was seriously concerned.

I quickly removed another board, and then another. Finally the sunlight reached to the bottom of the pit. And I could see Menshiki's outline seated there.

"Mr. Menshiki, are you okay?" I asked, relieved.

He looked up, as if finally coming to, and gave a small nod. He covered his face with his hands, as if the light was too bright.

"I'm fine," he answered quietly. "I'd just like to stay here for a little longer. It'll take time for my eyes to adjust to the light."

"It's been exactly an hour. If you'd like to stay there longer I could put the cover on again."

Menshiki shook his head. "No, this is enough. I'm okay now. I can't stay any longer here. It might be too dangerous."

"Too dangerous?"

"I'll explain later," Menshiki said. He stroked his face hard with both hands, as if rubbing something away from his skin.

Five minutes later he slowly got to his feet and clambered up the metal ladder I'd let down. Once again at ground level he brushed the dirt off his pants and looked up at the sky with narrowed eyes. The blue autumn sky was visible through the tree branches. For a long time he gazed lovingly at the sky. We lined up the boards and covered the hole as before, so no one would accidentally fall into it. Then we put the heavy stones on top. I memorized the position of the stones, so I'd know if anyone moved them. The ladder we left inside the pit.

"I didn't hear the bell," I said as we walked along.

Menshiki shook his head. "I didn't shake it."

That's all he said, so I didn't ask anything more.

We walked out of the woods and headed home. Menshiki took the lead as we walked and I followed behind. Without a word he put the flashlight back in the trunk of the Jaguar. We then sat down in the living room and drank hot coffee. Menshiki still hadn't said a thing. He seemed preoccupied. Not that he wore a serious expression or anything, but his mind was clearly in a place far away. A place, no doubt, where only he was allowed to be. I didn't bother him, and let him be. Just like Doctor Watson used to do with Sherlock Holmes.

During this time I mentally went over my schedule. That evening I had to drive down the mountain to teach my classes at the local arts-and-culture center near Odawara Station. I'd look over paintings students had done and give them advice. This was the day when I had back-to-back children's and adults' classes. This was just about the only opportunity I had to see and speak with living people. Without those classes I'd probably live like a hermit up here in the mountains, and if I went on living all alone, I'd likely start to lose my mind, just as Masahiko said.

Which is why I should have been thankful for the chance to come in contact with the real world. But truth be told, I found it hard to feel that way. The people I met in the classroom were less living beings than mere shadows crossing my path. I smiled at each one of them, called them by name, and critiqued their paintings. No, critique isn't the right term. I just praised them. I'd find some good component to each painting—if there wasn't, I'd make up something—and praise them for a job well done.

So I had a pretty good reputation as a teacher. According to the owner of the school, many of the students liked me. I hadn't expected that. I'd never once thought I was suited to teaching. But I didn't really care. It was all the same to me whether people liked me or didn't. I just wanted things to go smoothly in the classroom, without any hitches, so I could repay Masahiko for his kindness.

I'm not saying every person felt like a shadow to me. I'd started seeing two of my students. And after starting a sexual relationship with me, the two women both dropped out of my art class. They must have found it awkward. And I did feel some responsibility for that.

Tomorrow afternoon, I'd see the second girlfriend, the older married woman. We'd hold each other in bed and make love. So she was not just a passing shadow, but an actual presence with a three-dimensional body. Or perhaps a passing shadow with a three-dimensional body. I couldn't decide which.

Menshiki called my name, and I came back to the present with a start. I'd been completely lost in thought, too.

"About the portrait," Menshiki said.

I looked at him. His usual cool expression was back on his face. A handsome face, always calm and thoughtful, the kind that relaxed others.

"If you need me to pose for you, I wouldn't mind doing it now," he said. "Continue from where we left off, maybe? I'm always ready."

I looked at him for a while. *Pose?* It finally dawned on me—he was talking about the portrait. I looked down, took a sip of the coffee, which had cooled down, and after gathering my thoughts, put the cup back on the saucer. A small, dry clatter reached my ears. I looked up, faced Menshiki, and spoke.

"I'm very sorry, but today I have to go teach at the arts-and-culture center."

"Oh, that's right," Menshiki said. He glanced at his watch. "I'd totally forgotten. You teach art at the school near Odawara Station, don't you. Do you need to leave soon?"

"I'm okay, I still have time," I said. "And there's something I need to talk with you about."

"And what would that be?"

"Truthfully, the painting is already finished. In a sense."

Menshiki frowned ever so slightly. He looked straight at me, as if checking out something deep inside my eyes.

"By painting, you mean my portrait?"

"Yes," I said.

"That's wonderful," Menshiki said. A slight smile came to his face. "Really wonderful. But what did you mean by 'in a sense'?"

"It's hard to explain. I've never been good at explaining things."

"Take your time and tell it to me the way you'd like to," Menshiki said. "I'll sit here and listen."

I brought the fingers of both of my hands together on my lap.

Silence descended as I chose my words, the kind of silence that makes you hear the passing of time. Time passed very slowly on top of the mountain.

"I got the commission from you," I said, "and did the painting with you as model. But to tell the truth, it's not a *portrait*, no matter how you look at it. All I can say is it's a *work done with you as model.* I can't say how much value it has, as an artwork, or as a commodity. All I know for sure is it's *a work I had to paint*. Beyond that I'm clueless. Truthfully, I'm pretty confused. Until things become clearer to me it might be best to keep the painting here and not give it to you. I'd like to return the advance you paid. And I am extremely sorry for having used so much of your valuable time."

"In what way is it—not a portrait?" Menshiki asked, choosing his words deliberately.

"Up till now I've made my living as a professional portrait painter. Essentially in portraits you paint the subject the way he wishes to be portrayed. The subject is the client, and if he doesn't like the finished work it's entirely possible he might tell you, 'I'm not going to pay money for this.' So I try not to depict any negative aspects of the person. I pick only the good aspects, emphasize those, and try to make the subject appear in as good a light as I can. In that sense, in most cases it's hard to call portraits works of art. Someone like Rembrandt being the exception, of course. But in this case, I didn't think about you as I painted, but only about myself. To put it another way, I prioritized the ego of the artist—myself—over you, the subject."

"Not a problem," Menshiki said, smiling. "I'm actually happy to hear it. I told you I didn't have any requests, and wanted you to paint it any way you liked."

"I know. I remember it well. What I'm concerned about is less how the painting turned out and more about *what I painted there*. I put my own desires first, so much that I might have painted something I shouldn't have. That's what I'm worried about."

Menshiki observed my face for a time, and then spoke. "You might have painted something inside me that you shouldn't have. And you're worried about that. Do I have that right?"

"That's it," I said. "Since all I thought of was myself, I loosened the restraints that should have been in place."

And maybe extracted something from inside you that I shouldn't have, I was about to say, but thought better of it. I kept those words inside.

Menshiki mulled over what I'd said.

"Interesting," he finally said, sounding like he meant it. "A very intriguing way of looking at things."

I was silent.

"I think my self-restraint is pretty strong," Menshiki said. "I have a lot of self-control, I mean."

"I know," I said.

Menshiki lightly pressed his temple with his fingers, and smiled. "So that painting is finished, you're saying? That *portrait* of me?"

I nodded. "I feel it's finished."

"That's wonderful," Menshiki said. "Can you show me the painting? After I've actually seen it, the two of us can discuss how to proceed. Does that sound all right?"

"Of course," I said.

I led Menshiki to the studio. He stood about six feet in front of the easel, arms folded, and stared at the painting. There was the portrait that he'd posed for. No, less a portrait than what you might call an *image* that formed when a mass of paint hit the canvas. The white hair was a violent burst of pure white. At first glance it didn't look like a face. What should be found in a face was hidden behind a mass of color. Yet beyond any doubt, the reality of Menshiki the person was present. Or at least I thought so.

He stood there, unmoving, gazing at the painting for the longest time. Literally not moving a muscle. I couldn't even tell if he was breathing or not. I stood a little ways away by the window, observing him. I wondered how much time passed. It seemed almost forever. As he observed the painting, his face was totally devoid of expression. His eyes were glazed, flat, clouded, like a still puddle reflecting a cloudy sky. The eyes of someone who wanted to keep others at a distance. I couldn't guess what he might be thinking, deep in his heart.

Then, like when a magician claps his hands to bring a person out of a hypnotic spell, he stood up straight and trembled slightly. His expression returned, as did the light in his eyes. He slowly walked over to me, held out his right hand, and rested it on my shoulder.

"Amazing," he said. "Truly outstanding. I don't know what to say. This is exactly the painting I was hoping for."

I could tell from his eyes that he was saying how he honestly felt. He was truly impressed, and moved, by my painting.

"The painting expresses me perfectly," Menshiki said. "This is a portrait in the real sense of the word. You didn't make any mistake. You did exactly what you should have."

His hand was still resting on my shoulder. It was just resting there, yet I could feel a special power radiating from it.

"But what did you do to discover this painting?" Menshiki asked me.

"Discover?"

"It was you who did this painting, of course. You created it through your own power. But you also discovered it. You found this image buried within you and drew it out. You *unearthed* it, in a way. Don't you think so?"

I suppose so, I thought. Of course I moved my hands, and followed my will in painting it. *I* was the one who chose the paints, the one who used brushes, knives, and fingers to paint the colors onto the canvas. But looked at from a different angle, maybe all I'd done was use Menshiki as a catalyst to locate something buried inside me and dig it up. Just like the heavy equipment that moved aside the rock mound behind the little shrine, lifted off the heavy lattice cover, and unearthed that odd stone-lined chamber. I couldn't help but see an affinity between these two similar operations that took place in tandem. Everything that had happened had started with Menshiki's appearance, and the ringing of the bell in the middle of the night.

Menshiki said, "It's like an earthquake deep under the sea. In an unseen world, a place where light doesn't reach, in the realm of the unconscious. In other words, a major transformation is taking place. It reaches the surface, where it sets off a series of reactions and eventually takes form where we can see it with our own eyes. I'm no artist, but I can grasp the basic idea behind that process. Outstanding ideas in the business world, too, emerge through a similar series of stages. The best ideas are thoughts that appear, unbidden, from out of the dark."

Menshiki once more stood before the painting and stepped closer to examine the surface. Like someone reading a detailed map, he studiously checked out each and every detail. He stepped back nine feet, and with narrowed eyes gazed at the work as a whole. His face wore an expression close to ecstasy. He reminded me of a carnivorous raptor about to latch onto its prey. But what was the prey? Was it my painting, or me myself? Or something else? I had no idea. But soon, like mist hovering over the surface of a river at dawn, that strange expression like ecstasy faded, then vanished. To be filled in by his usual affable, thoughtful expression.

He said, "Generally I avoid saying anything that smacks of self-praise, but honestly I feel kind of proud to know that I didn't misjudge things. I have no artistic talent myself, and have nothing to do with creating original works, but I do know outstanding art when I see it. At least I flatter myself that I do."

Somehow I couldn't easily accept what Menshiki was telling me, or feel happy to hear it. It may have been those sharp, raptor-like eyes that bothered me.

"So you like the painting?" I asked again to make sure.

"That goes without saying. This is truly a valuable painting. I'm overjoyed that you came up with such a powerful work using me as the model, as the motif. And of course it goes without saying that as the one who commissioned the painting, I'll take it. Assuming that's all right with you?"

"Yes. It's just that I—"

Menshiki held up a hand to cut me off. "So, if you don't mind, I'd like to invite you to my house to celebrate its completion. Would that be all right? It will be, like the old expression, a cozy little get-together. As long as this isn't any trouble for you, that is."

"None at all, but you really don't need to do this. You've done so much already—"

"But I'd really like to. I'd like the two of us to celebrate the completion of the painting. So won't you join me for dinner at my place? Nothing fancy, just a simple little dinner, just the two of us. Apart from the cook and bartender, of course."

"Cook and bartender?"

"There's a French restaurant I like near Hayakawa harbor. I'll have the cook and bartender over on their regular day off. He's a great chef. He uses the freshest fish and comes up with some very original recipes. Actually, for quite some time I've been wanting to invite you over, and have been making preparations. But with the painting done, the timing couldn't be better."

It was hard to keep the surprise from showing on my face. I had no idea how much it would cost to arrange something like that, but for Menshiki, it must be a regular occurrence. Or at least something he was accustomed to arranging . . .

Menshiki said, "How would four days from now be? Tuesday evening. If that's good for you, I'll set it up."

"I don't have any particular plans then," I said.

"Tuesday it is, then," he said. "Also, could I take the painting home with me now? I'd like to have it nicely framed and hanging on the wall by the time you come over, if that's possible."

"Mr. Menshiki, do you really see your face within this painting?" I asked again.

"Of course I do," Menshiki said, giving me a wondering look. "Of course I can see my face in the painting. Very distinctly. What else is depicted here?"

"I see," I said. What else could I say? "You're the one who commissioned the work, so if you like the painting, it's already yours. Please do what you'd like with it. The thing is, the paint isn't dry yet, so be extremely careful when you carry it. And I think it's better to wait a little longer before framing it. Best to let it dry for about two weeks before doing that."

"I understand. I'll handle it carefully. And I'll wait to have it framed."

At the front door he held out his hand and we shook hands for the first time in a while. A satisfied smile rose to his face.

"I'll see you Tuesday, then. I'll send a car over around six."

"By the way, you aren't inviting the mummy?" I asked Menshiki. I don't know why I said that. The mummy just suddenly popped into my head, and I couldn't help myself.

Menshiki looked at me searchingly. "Mummy? What do you mean?"

"The mummy that should have been in that chamber. The one that must have been ringing the bell every night, and disappeared, leaving the bell behind. The monk who practiced austerity to the point of being mummified. I was thinking maybe he wanted to be invited to your place. Like the statue of the Commendatore in *Don Giovanni*."

Menshiki thought about this, and a cheerful smile came over him as if he finally got it. "I see! Just like Don Giovanni invited the statue of the Commendatore, you're wondering how would it be if I invited the mummy to our dinner?"

"Exactly. It might be karma, too."

"Sounds good. Fine with me. It's a celebration, after all. If the mummy would care to join us, I will be happy to issue the invitation. Sounds like we'll have a pleasant evening. But what should we have for dessert?" He smiled happily. "The problem is, we can't see him. Makes it hard to invite him."

"Indeed," I said. "But the visible is not the only reality. Wouldn't you agree?"

Menshiki gingerly carried the painting outside. He took an old blanket from the trunk, laid it on the passenger seat, and placed the painting down on top so as not to smear the paint. Then he used some thin rope and two cardboard boxes to secure the painting so it wouldn't move around. It was all cleverly done. He always seemed to carry around a variety of tools and things in his trunk.

"Yes, what you said may be exactly right," Menshiki suddenly murmured as he was leaving. He rested both hands on the leather-covered steering wheel and looked straight up at me.

"What I said?"

"That sometimes in life we can't grasp the boundary between reality and unreality. That boundary always seems to be shifting. As if the border between countries shifts from one day to the next depending on their mood. We need to pay close attention to that movement, otherwise we won't know which side we're on. That's what I meant when I said it might be dangerous for me to remain inside that pit any longer."

I didn't know how to respond, and Menshiki didn't go any further. He waved to me out the window, revving the V8 engine so it rumbled pleasantly, and he and the still-not-dry portrait vanished from sight.

19

CAN YOU SEE ANYTHING BEHIND ME?

At one p.m. on Saturday afternoon my girlfriend drove over in her red Mini. I went out to greet her when she arrived. She had on green sunglasses and a light-gray jacket over a simple beige dress.

"You want to do it in the car? Or do you prefer the bed?" I asked.

"Don't be silly," she laughed.

"Doing it in the car doesn't sound so bad. Figuring out how to manage it in a cramped space."

"Someday soon."

We sat in the living room and drank tea. I told her about how I'd just managed to finish the portrait (or portrait-like painting) of Menshiki I'd been struggling with. And how it was totally different from any of the portraits I'd done professionally. Her interest seemed piqued.

"Can I see the painting?"

I shook my head. "You're a day late. I wanted to get your opinion on it, but Mr. Menshiki already took it home. The paint wasn't completely dry yet, but it seemed like he wanted to take possession as soon as he could. He seemed worried somebody else might take it away."

"So he liked it."

"He said he did, and I don't have any reason to doubt him."

"The painting's successfully completed, and the person who commissioned it likes it. So all's well that ends well?"

"I guess," I said. "And I'm happy with it. I've never done that type of painting before, and I think it's opened up some new possibilities."

"A new style of portrait?"

"I'm not sure. This time, I arrived at that method by using Mr. Menshiki as my model. But maybe it's just coincidence that it was the framework of a portrait that proved to be the entranceway to that. I don't know if the same method would be valid if I tried it again. This might have been a special case. Having Mr. Menshiki as my model may have exerted a special power. But the important thing is I'm dying to do some serious painting now."

"Well, congratulations on finishing the painting."

"Thanks," I said. "I'll also be receiving a fairly hefty payment."

"The munificent Mr. Menshiki," she said.

"And he invited me over to his place to celebrate the painting. Tuesday evening, we'll have dinner together."

I told her about the dinner that was planned. Nothing about inviting the mummy, though. A dinner for two, with a professional cook and bartender.

"So you'll finally set foot in that chalk-white mansion, won't you," she said, sounding impressed. "The mysterious mansion of the man of mystery. I'm so curious. Make sure to keep your eyes open, and observe what kind of place it is."

"As much as my eyes can take in."

"And remember exactly what sort of food was served."

"Will do," I said. "You know, the other day you mentioned getting new information about Mr. Menshiki."

"That's right. Through the jungle grapevine."

"What kind of information?"

She looked a little confused. She picked up her cup and took a sip of tea. "Let's talk about that later," she said. "There's something I'd like to do before that."

"Something you'd like to do?"

"Something I hesitate to put into words."

We moved from the living room into the bedroom. Like always.

During the six years I lived my first married life with Yuzu (my former marriage, is what it might best be called), I never had a sexual relationship with any other women, not even once. Not that the opportunity didn't present itself, but during that period I was much more interested in living a peaceful life with my wife than seeking greener pastures elsewhere. And as far as sex was concerned, regular lovemaking with Yuzu more than satisfied me.

But then at a certain point, out of the blue (to me at least) she announced that she couldn't live with me any longer. An unshakable conclusion, no room for negotiation or compromise. I was shaken, with no clue how to respond. Left speechless. But I did understand one thing: *I can't stay here anymore.*

So I threw some belongings into my old Peugeot 205 and set off on an aimless journey. For a month and a half at the beginning of spring I wandered through northern Japan—Tohoku and Hokkaido—where it was still cold. Until my car finally broke down for good. Every night on the trip I remembered Yuzu's body. Every single detail. How she'd react when I touched certain spots, what sort of cry she made. I didn't want to remember this, but I couldn't help it. Occasionally, as I traced those memories, I'd ejaculate. Another thing I didn't particularly want to do.

But during that long trip I only slept with one actual woman. A truly weird turn of events ended with me spending the night with a young woman I'd never seen before. Not that it was something I was looking for.

This was in a small town in Miyagi Prefecture along the coast. As I recall, it was near the border with Iwate, but I was on the move then and had passed through a number of towns that all blurred into one. My mind wasn't in a place where I could remember their names. I do recall that it had a big fishing harbor. Though most of the towns in that region had harbors. And I remember how everywhere I went the smell of diesel oil and fish tagged along.

On the outskirts of town, near the highway, was a chain restaurant, and I was eating dinner there by myself. It was about eight p.m. Shrimp curry and house salad. There were only a handful of other customers. I was in a table next to the window, reading a paperback book while I ate, when a young woman abruptly sat down across from me. No hesitation, no asking permission, without a word she sat down onto the vinyl-covered seat like it was the most natural thing in the world.

I looked up, surprised. Of course I didn't recognize her. It was the first time I'd ever laid eyes on her. It was all so sudden I didn't know what to think. There were any number of unoccupied tables, and no reason for her to share mine. Maybe that's how they did things in this town? I put down my fork, wiped my mouth with the paper napkin, and gazed at her, bewildered.

"Pretend like you know me," the girl said. "Like we were meeting up here." Her voice was, if anything, a bit husky. Or maybe tension made a voice temporarily hoarse. I detected a slight Tohoku accent.

I put the bookmark in my book and shut it. The woman seemed to be in her mid-twenties. She had on a white blouse with a round collar and a navy-blue cardigan. Neither one very expensive looking, or very fashionable. Ordinary clothes, like what you'd wear when you went shopping at the local supermarket. Her hair was black, cut short, with bangs falling to her forehead. She had on hardly any makeup. On her lap was a black cloth shoulder bag.

There was nothing special about her face. Pleasant enough features, but they didn't leave a strong impression. The kind of face that, if you saw her on the street, you'd forget as soon as you passed by. Her thin lips were taut, and she was breathing through her nose. Her breathing was a bit ragged, the nostrils expanding a tiny bit, then contracting. A small nose, out of balance with the size of her mouth. As if the person molding her out of clay halfway through and decided to scrape some off the nose.

"You understand? Pretend like you know me," she repeated. "Don't look so surprised."

"Okay," I answered, not knowing what was going on.

"Just keep on eating," she said. "And pretend to be talking to me like we know each other?"

"What about?"

"You're from Tokyo?"

I nodded. I picked up my fork and ate a mini tomato. Then drank some water.

"I could tell by the way you talk," the woman said. "But why are you here?"

"Just passing through," I said.

A waitress in a ginger-colored uniform came over, lugging a thick menu. The waitress had mammoth breasts, the buttons on her uniform ready to burst. The girl across from me didn't take the menu. She didn't even glance at the waitress. Staring straight at me she just said, "Coffee and cheesecake." Like she was giving me the order. The waitress nodded without a word. Still lugging the menu, she left.

"Are you in some kind of trouble?" I asked.

She didn't respond. She just stared at me, like she was evaluating my face.

"Can you see anything behind me? Is anybody there?" the woman asked.

I looked behind her. Just ordinary people eating in an ordinary way. No new customers had come in.

"Nothing. Nobody's there," I said.

"Keep an eye out for a little longer," she said. "Tell me if you see anything. Keep on talking like nothing's happened."

Our table looked out on the parking lot. I could see my decrepit, dusty little old Peugeot parked there. There were two other cars. A small silver compact, and a tall black minivan. The minivan looked new. They'd both been parked there for a while. No new cars had driven in. The woman must have walked. Or else someone gave her a ride here.

"Just passing through?" the woman asked.

"That's right."

"Are you on a trip?"

"You could say that," I said.

"What kind of book are you reading?"

I showed her the book. It was Ogai Mori's *Abe Ichizoku,* a samurai tale written over a hundred years before.

"*Abe Ichizoku,*" she intoned. She handed the book back. "How come you're reading such an old book?"

"It was in the lounge of a youth hostel I stayed at in Aomori not long ago. I leafed through it, thought it was interesting, and took it with me. In exchange, I left a couple of books I'd finished reading."

"I've never read *Abe Ichizoku*. Is it interesting?"

I'd read it once and was rereading it. The story was pretty interesting, but I couldn't figure out why, and from what sort of stance, Ogai had written it, or felt compelled to write that kind of tale. But explaining that would take too long. This wasn't a book club. And this woman was just bringing up random topics so our conversation seemed natural (or at least so that it looked that way to the people around us).

"It's worth reading," I said.

"So what sort of work?" she asked.

"You mean the novel?"

She frowned. "No. I don't care about that. I mean *you*. What kind of work do *you* do for a living?"

"I paint pictures," I said.

"You're an artist," she said.

"You could say that."

"What sort of paintings?"

"Portraits," I said.

"By portraits you mean those paintings you see hanging on the wall in the president's office in companies? The ones where big shots look all full of themselves?"

"That's right."

"That's your specialty?"

I nodded.

She said no more about painting. She might have lost interest. Most people in the world, unless they're the ones being painted, have zero interest in portraits.

Right then the automatic door at the entrance slid open and a tall, middle-aged man came in. He had on a black leather jacket and a black golf cap with a golf company's logo on it. He stood at the entrance, gave the whole diner a once-over, chose a table two over from ours, and sat down, facing us. He took off his cap, finger-combed his hair a couple of times, and carefully studied the menu the busty waitress brought over. His hair was cut short, and had some white mixed in. He was thin, with dark, suntanned skin. His forehead was lined with a series of deep, wavy wrinkles.

"A man just came in," I told her.

"What does he look like?"

I gave her a quick description.

"Can you draw him?" she asked.

"You mean a likeness?"

"Yes. You're an artist, aren't you?"

I took a memo pad from my pocket, and, using a mechanical pencil, quickly sketched the man. Even added some shading. While I drew it I didn't need to glance over at him. I have the ability to grasp the features of a person quickly and etch them into my memory. I passed the drawing across the table to her. She took it, and stared at it, eyes narrowed, for a long time, like a bank teller examining dubious handwriting on a check. Finally she laid the memo page on the table.

"You're really good at drawing," she said, looking at me. She sounded genuinely impressed.

"It's what I do," I said. "So, do you know this man?"

She didn't reply, just shook her head. Her lips tight, her expression unchanged. She folded the drawing up twice, and stuffed it away in her shoulder bag. I couldn't figure out why she would keep something like that. She should have just crumpled it up and thrown it away.

"I don't know him," she said.

"But you're being followed by him. Is that what's going on?"

She didn't reply.

The same waitress brought over her coffee and cheesecake. The woman kept quiet until the waitress had left. She sliced a bite of the cheesecake with her fork, then pushed it from side to side on the plate. Like a hockey player practicing on the ice before a game. She finally put the piece in her mouth and, expressionless, chewed slowly. Once she finished it she poured a hint of cream into her coffee and took a sip. She nudged the plate with the cheesecake to one side, as if it was no longer needed.

A white SUV had joined the cars in the parking lot. A stocky, tall car, with solid-looking tires. Apparently driven by the man who'd just come in. He'd parked the car facing in, not backing into the spot as was more usual. On the cover of the spare tire attached to the luggage compartment were the words SUBARU FORESTER. I finished my shrimp curry. The waitress came over to take away the plate, and I ordered coffee.

"Have you been traveling for a long time?" the woman asked.

"It'll be a long trip," I said.

"Is it fun to travel?"

I'm not traveling for fun, is how I should have answered. But that would have made things long and complicated.

"Sort of," I answered.

She stared at me, like studying some rare animal. "You sure are a man of few words."

It depends on who I'm talking with, is how I should have answered. But going there would have also made things long and complicated.

The coffee came, and I drank some. It tasted like coffee, but it wasn't all that good. But at least it was coffee, and piping hot. After this no other customers came in. The salt-and-pepper-haired man in the leather jacket, in a voice that carried, ordered a Salisbury steak and rice.

A string-section version of "Fool on the Hill" came over the sound system. Did John Lennon write that song, or Paul McCartney? I couldn't remember. Probably Lennon. This kind of random thought rattled around in my head. I had no idea what else I should think about.

"Did you come here by car?"

"Um."

"What kind of car?"

"A red Peugeot."

"What district is the license plate?"

"Shinagawa," I said.

Hearing that, she frowned, as if she had a bad memory associated with a red Peugeot with Shinagawa plates. She tugged down the sleeves of her cardigan and checked that the buttons on her white shirt were done all the way up. She wiped her mouth with a paper napkin. "Let's go," she suddenly said.

She drank a half glass of water and stood up. She left her coffee, only one sip taken, and cheesecake, only one bite taken, on the tabletop. Like the remains after a terrible natural disaster.

Not knowing where we were going, I stood up after her, took the bill from the table, and paid at the register. The woman's order was included, but she didn't say a word of thanks, or make a move to pay her share.

As we left, the man with the salt-and-pepper hair was eating his Salisbury steak, seemingly bored by it all. He looked up and glanced in our direction, but that was all. He looked down at his plate again and went on eating, with knife and fork, his face expressionless. The woman didn't look at him at all.

As we passed by the white Subaru Forester, a bumper sticker on it with a picture of a fish caught my eye. Probably a marlin. Of course, I had no idea why he had to have a sticker with a marlin on it on his car. Maybe he worked in the fishing industry, or was a fisherman.

The woman didn't tell me where we were going. She sat in the passenger seat and gave me clipped directions. She seemed to know the roads. She must have been from that town, or else had lived there a long time. I drove the Peugeot where she told me to go. We drove along the highway for a while out of town and came to a love hotel with a gaudy neon sign. I parked there as directed and cut the engine.

"I'm staying here tonight," she announced. "I can't go home. Come with me."

"But I'm staying in another place tonight," I said. "I've already checked in and put my luggage in the room."

"Where?"

I gave the name of a small business hotel near the railway station.

"This place is a lot better than that cheap place," she said. "Your room there must be shabby and no bigger than a closet."

Right she was. A shabby room the size of a closet was an apt description.

"And they don't like women checking in by themselves here. They're on guard against prostitutes. So come with me."

Well, at least she's not a hooker, I thought.

At the front desk I paid in advance for one night (again, no word of thanks from her) and got the key. Once in the room she filled up the bathtub, switched on the TV, and adjusted the lighting. The bathtub was spacious. It was definitely a lot more comfortable than the business hotel. She seemed to have come here—or someplace like it—many times before. She sat on the bed and took off her cardigan. Then removed her white blouse and her wraparound skirt. And took off her stockings. She had on very simple white panties. They weren't particularly new. The kind your ordinary housewife would wear when she went shopping at the neighborhood supermarket. She neatly reached behind her and unhooked her bra, folded it, and set it next to a pillow. Her breasts weren't particularly big, or particularly small.

"Come over here," she said to me. "Since we're in a place like this, let's have sex."

That was the one and only sexual experience of my whole long trip (or wanderings). Wilder sex than I'd expected. She had four orgasms in total, every single one genuine, if you can believe it. I came twice, but oddly enough didn't feel much pleasure. It was like while I was doing it with her, my mind was elsewhere.

"I'm thinking maybe it's been a long time since you had sex?" she asked me.

"Several months," I answered honestly.

"I can tell," she said. "But how come? You can't be that unpopular with women."

"There's a whole bunch of reasons."

"You poor thing," she said, and gently stroked my neck. "You poor thing."

You poor thing, I thought, repeating the words to myself. Put that way I really did feel like I was a person to be pitied. In an unknown town, in some random place, with no clue what was going on, naked in bed with a woman whose name I didn't even know.

We had a few beers from the fridge, in between rounds. It was about one a.m. when we finally slept. When I woke up the next morning she was nowhere to be seen. She left no note or anything behind. I was alone in the overly huge bed. My watch showed seven thirty, and it was light outside. I opened the curtain and saw the highway running alongside the ocean. Huge refrigerated trucks transporting fresh fish roared up and down the road. The world is full of lonely things, but not many could be lonelier than waking up alone in the morning in a love hotel.

A thought suddenly struck me, and I hurriedly checked my wallet in my pants pocket. Everything was still there. Cash, credit cards, ATM card, license, everything. I breathed a sigh of relief. If my wallet had been gone I would have freaked. These sorts of things *did* happen, and I needed to be careful.

She must have left early in the morning, while I was sound asleep. But how had she gotten back to town (or back to where she lived)? Had she walked, or called a taxi? Not that it made any difference to me. Pointless speculation.

I returned the room key at the front desk, paid for the beers we'd drunk, and drove the Peugeot back to town. I needed to get the luggage I'd left at the business hotel near the station, and pay for the one night. Along the way into town I passed by the chain restaurant I'd gone to the night before. I stopped and ate breakfast there. I was starving, and was dying for some coffee. Just before I pulled into the parking lot I saw the white Subaru Forester. Parked nose in, with that marlin bumper sticker. The same Subaru Forester from the night before. The only difference was where it was parked. Which made sense. No one spent the whole night in a place like that.

I went inside the restaurant. As before, hardly any customers. Like I expected, the same man from last night was at a table, eating breakfast. The same table as the night before, wearing the same black leather jacket. Like last night, the same black golf cap with the Yonex logo resting on the tabletop. The only difference from last night was the folded morning newspaper on top of the table. A plate of toast and scrambled eggs was in front of him. It was probably just served, steam still rising from the coffee. As I passed him, the man glanced up and looked me in the face. His eyes were even sharper and colder than the night before. There was a sense of criticism in them, or at least that's what it felt like.

I know exactly where you've been and what you've been up to, he seemed to be telling me.

That's the whole story of what happened to me in that small town along the seacoast in Miyagi. Even now I have no idea what that woman, with her petite nose and perfect teeth, wanted from me. And it was never clear to me if that middle-aged guy with the white Subaru Forester was really following her, or if she was running from him. Whatever was going on, I happened to be there, and through an odd series of events spent the night in a garish love hotel with a woman I'd just met, and had a one-night stand, the wildest sex I'd ever had. But I still can't recall the name of the town.

"Could I get a glass of water?" my married girlfriend said. She'd just woken up from a short postcoital nap.

It was early afternoon, and we were in bed. While she slept I stared at the ceiling and recalled the events in that small fishing town. It was only a half a year before, but it seemed like events from the distant past.

I went to the kitchen, poured mineral water into a large glass, and returned to bed. She drank down half of it in a single gulp.

"Now, about Mr. Menshiki," she said, placing the glass on the nightstand.

"Mr. Menshiki?"

"The new information I got about Mr. Menshiki," she said. "What I said I'd tell you later?"

"Your jungle grapevine."

"Right," she said, and drank more water. "According to my sources, your friend Mr. Menshiki spent quite a long time in Tokyo Prison."

I sat up and looked at her. "Tokyo Prison?"

"Yeah, the one in Kosuge."

"For what crime?"

"I don't know the details, but I imagine it had something to do with money. Tax evasion, money laundering, insider trading—something of that sort, or perhaps all of them. He was imprisoned six or seven years ago. Did Mr. Menshiki tell you what kind of work he does?"

"He said it was dealing with tech, and information," I said. "He started a company, and some years ago sold the stock for a high price. He's living now on the capital gains."

"'Dealing with information' is a pretty vague way of describing it. Nowadays there're hardly any jobs not connected with information."

"Who told you about him being in prison?"

"A friend of mine whose husband's in finance. But I don't know how much of that information is true. Someone heard it from someone, and passed it along to someone else. You know how it is. But from what I can make of it, it doesn't seem groundless."

"If he was in Tokyo Prison that means that he was put there by the Tokyo district prosecutor."

"In the end they found him not guilty, is what I heard," she said. "Still, he was in detention for a long time, and had to endure a very intense investigation. They extended his incarceration a number of times, and wouldn't grant bail."

"But he won in court."

"That's right. He was prosecuted, but wasn't given a jail sentence. He apparently remained totally silent during the investigation."

"My understanding is that the Tokyo district prosecutors are the cream of the crop," I said. "A proud lot. Once they set their sights on someone, they have solid evidence before they arrest them and charge them. Their win rate in court is really high. So the investigation they did while he was in detention couldn't have been half-baked. Most people break down under that kind of scrutiny, and sign whatever the prosecutors want them to. Ordinary people wouldn't be able to stay silent under that kind of pressure."

"Still, that's what Mr. Menshiki did. He must have a strong will and a sharp mind."

Menshiki wasn't your average person, that was for sure . . . A strong will and a sharp mind were indeed part of his repertoire.

"There's one thing I don't get," I said. "Whether it is for tax evasion or money laundering or whatever, once the Tokyo district prosecutor arrests you, it's reported on in the newspapers. And with an unusual name like Menshiki, I would remember the case. I used to be a pretty avid reader of newspapers."

"I don't know about that. There's one other thing—I mentioned it before—but he bought that mountaintop mansion three years ago. Almost forcing the owners to sell. Other people were living there then, and they had no intention at all of selling the house they'd just built. But Mr. Menshiki offered them money—or maybe pressured them in some other way—and drove them out. And then he moved in, like some mean-spirited hermit crab."

"Hermit crabs don't drive away what's living in a shell. They just quietly take over the leftover shell of a dead shellfish."

"But there must be some hermit crabs that are mean."

"I don't get it," I said, trying to avoid a debate over the ecology of hermit crabs. "If what you're saying is true, why would Mr. Menshiki insist so strongly that it had to be *that house*? So much so that he drove the residents out and took over? That must have taken a lot of money and effort. And that mansion is really too gaudy, too conspicuous, to suit him. It's a wonderful house, for sure, but I just don't think it fits his tastes."

"Plus it's too big. He doesn't have a maid, lives alone, hardly ever has guests over. There's no need to live in such a huge place."

She drank the rest of the water.

"There must be some special reason why it had to be that house," she went on. "I have no idea why, though."

"Anyway, he's invited me over to his place on Tuesday. Once I actually visit I might learn more."

"Make sure you check out the secret locked room, the one like Bluebeard's castle."

"I'll remember to," I said.

"For the time being, things have worked out well."

"Meaning—?"

"You finished the painting, Mr. Menshiki liked it, and you got a hefty payment for it."

"I guess so," I said. "I guess it did work out. I'm relieved."

"Felicitations, maestro," she said.

It was no lie to say that I felt relieved. It was true that I'd finished the painting. And true that Menshiki had liked it. And also true that I was happy with the painting. And equally true that this resulted in a nice, healthy amount of money coming my way. For all that, though, I couldn't feel totally pleased with the way things had worked out. So much around me was still up in the air, left as is, with no clues to follow. The more I wanted to simplify my life, the more disjointed it seemed to become.

As if searching for clues, I almost unconsciously reached out to hold my girlfriend. Her body felt soft, and warm. And damp with sweat.

I know exactly where you've been and what you've been up to, the man with the white Subaru Forester said.

20

THE MOMENT WHEN EXISTENCE AND NONEXISTENCE COALESCE

The next morning I woke up at five thirty. It was Sunday morning. It was still pitch dark outside. After a simple breakfast in the kitchen I changed into work clothes and went into the studio. As the eastern sky grew brighter, I switched off the light, threw open the window, and let chilly, fresh morning air into the room. I took out a fresh canvas and set it on the easel. The chirping of birds filtered in through the open window. The rain during the night had thoroughly soaked the trees. The rain had stopped just a while before, bright gaps in the clouds showing. I sat down on the stool, and, sipping hot black coffee from a mug, stared at the empty canvas before me.

I've always enjoyed this time, early in the morning, gazing intently at a pure white canvas. "Canvas Zen" is my term for it. Nothing is painted there yet, but it's more than a simple blank space. Hidden on that white canvas is what must eventually emerge. As I look more closely, I discover various possibilities, which congeal into a perfect clue as to how to proceed. That's the moment I really enjoy. The moment when existence and nonexistence coalesce.

But on this day I knew from the beginning what I would be painting. Emerging from this canvas would be a portrait of the middle-aged man with the white Subaru Forester. Up to this moment the man had been patiently waiting, inside me, to be painted. And I had to paint his portrait not for anyone else (not by commission, not to earn a living) but for myself. Just as I had painted Menshiki's portrait, in order to make visible his reason for being—or at least the meaning it had for me—I had to paint him in my own way. I'm not sure why. But it had to be done.

I closed my eyes and called to mind the figure of the man with the white Subaru Forester. I could distinctly recall the minutest details of his features. Early that second day he'd looked straight at me from his seat in the restaurant. The morning paper on the tabletop was folded, white steam rising from his cup of coffee. The bright morning light shining in the large window, the restaurant filled with the clatter of cheap tableware. That whole scene came back in every detail. And in the midst of that scene the man's face began to show some expression.

I know exactly where you've been and what you've been up to, his eyes told me.

This time I began with a rough draft. I stood up, grabbed a stick of charcoal, and stood before the canvas. On the blank space I created the spot where the man's face would go. With no plan, without thinking, I drew in a single vertical line. A single line, the focal point from which everything else would emerge. What would emerge was the face of a thin, suntanned man, deep wrinkles on his forehead. Thin, piercing eyes. Eyes used to staring at the far-off horizon. Eyes dyed the color of the sky and sea. Hair cut short, dotted with white. My guess, a taciturn, long-suffering man.

Around that central line I used charcoal to add a few supplementary lines, so the outlines of the man's face would appear. I stepped back to look at the lines I'd done, made a few corrections, and added some new lines. What was important was believing in myself. Believing in the power of the lines, in the power of the space the lines divided. I wasn't speaking, but letting the lines and spaces speak. Once the lines and spaces began conversing, then color would finally start to speak. And the flat would gradually transform into the three-dimensional. What I had to do was encourage them all, lend them a hand. And more than anything, not get in their way.

I kept working until ten thirty. The sun had made a slow crawl to the midpoint in the sky, the gray clouds had broken into thin strands, driven away one after another beyond the mountains. No longer did water drip from the tips of the tree branches. I stepped back and examined the rough sketch I'd done from various angles. What I saw was the face of the man I'd remembered. Or rather the framework that should abide in that face. But there were a few too many lines. I needed to do some trimming. Subtraction was the order of the day. But that was for tomorrow. Best to end this day's work here.

I put down the now shorter stick of charcoal, and washed my smudged hands in the sink. As I dried my hands with a towel, my eyes came to rest on the bell on the shelf in front of me, and I picked it up. I shook it, and the sound was terribly light, dry, and outdated. I couldn't believe it was an enigmatic Buddhist implement that had been underground for ages. It sounded so different from what I'd heard in the middle of the night. No doubt the pitch black and stillness had added to the depth and clarity of the sound, and made it carry farther.

The question of who could possibly have been ringing that bell in the middle of the night remained an unsolved mystery. Though someone must have been down in the hole every night ringing it (sending out what had to be some kind of message), whoever it was had vanished. When we uncovered the hole, all that was there was this bell. The whole thing was baffling. I placed the bell back on the shelf.

After lunch I went outside and into the woods out back. I had on a thick gray hooded windbreaker, and paint-stained sweatpants. I followed the damp path to the small shrine, and walked around behind it. The thick board cover over the hole was piled with fallen leaves of different colors and shapes. Leaves soaked by last night's rain. Since Menshiki and I had visited two days before, no one else seemed to have touched the cover. I wanted to make sure of that. I sat down on the damp stones, and, listening to the calls of birds overhead, I gazed for a while at where the hole was.

In the silence of the woods it felt like I could hear the passage of time, of life passing by. One person leaves, another appears. A thought flits away and another takes its place. One image bids farewell and another one appears on the scene. As the days piled up, I wore out, too, and was remade. Nothing stayed still. And time was lost. Behind me, time became dead grains of sand, which one after another gave way and vanished. I just sat there in front of the hole, listening to the sound of time dying.

What would it feel like to sit at the bottom of that hole, all alone,

I wondered. Being shut away by oneself in a cramped dark space. Menshiki had even given up his flashlight and the ladder. Without the ladder, without someone's help (specifically *mine*) it would be nearly impossible to escape from there. Why did he have to go to the trouble of putting himself into such a predicament? Did being down in that dark hole remind him of his solitary time behind bars in Tokyo Prison? There was no way I could know that, of course. Menshiki lived his own life, in his own way.

I could say only one thing for sure. I *would never be able to do that*. Nothing scared me more than dark, confined spaces. Put me in a place like that, and I wouldn't be able to breathe, I'd be so terrified. Even so, I was drawn to that hole. Drawn *very strongly*. So much so it felt like the hole was beckoning to me.

I sat next to the hole for a good half hour. Then I stood up and walked home through the sunlight that filtered down through the trees.

After two p.m. I had a call from Masahiko Amada. He had an errand to run near Odawara and wondered if he might drop by. Of course, I told him. I hadn't seen him in a while. He drove up just before three. He brought a bottle of single-malt whiskey as a present. I thanked him. Good timing, since I'd almost run out of whiskey. As always he was stylishly dressed, neatly shaved, wearing glasses I'd seen before, with shell-rimmed frames. He looked nearly the same as he had in the past, though admittedly his hairline was beating a slow-motion retreat.

We sat in the living room and caught up. I told him how the landscapers had used heavy equipment to dig up the stone mound. How after that, a hole just under six feet in diameter had emerged. Nine feet deep, surrounded by a stone wall. A heavy lattice cover was over it, and when that was removed, all we found was an old Buddhist implement like a bell. He listened intently as I told him the story. But he didn't say he wanted to see the hole. Or the bell.

"After that I take it you didn't hear the bell at night?"

"I don't hear it anymore," I said.

"That's great," he said, sounding a bit relieved. "I can't handle those kind of spooky things. I try to avoid them at all costs."

"Let sleeping dogs lie?"

"Exactly," Masahiko said. "I leave that hole up to you. Do whatever you like."

I told him how now, for the first time in what seemed like forever, I had the urge to paint. How ever since I finished Menshiki's portrait two days ago, it was like some blockage had been removed. I felt like I was discovering a new, original style, using portraits as a motif. I'd started the painting as a portrait, but what had eventually emerged was far from a conventional likeness. Even so, it was in essence still a portrait.

Masahiko wanted to see Menshiki's portrait, but when I told him I'd already given it to him, he was disappointed.

"But the paint can't be dry yet, can it?"

"He said he'd make sure it dries properly," I said. "He seemed eager to have the painting as quickly as possible. I don't know, maybe he was worried I might change my mind and not give it to him."

"Hmm," Masahiko said, impressed. "Do you have any new work, then?"

"I started on something this morning," I said. "But it's still just a charcoal sketch, so even if you saw it, it wouldn't mean anything."

"That's okay. Would you mind showing it to me?"

I took him into the studio and showed him the sketch for *The Man with the White Subaru Forester*. It was just a rough sketch in charcoal, but Masahiko stood in front of the easel, arms folded, a hard look on his face.

"Interesting," he said a little later, squeezing the words out between his teeth.

I was silent.

"It's hard to tell how it's going to develop, but it certainly does look like someone's portrait. Like the root of a portrait. A root buried deep in the ground." He was silent for a time.

"In a very deep, dark place," he went on. "And this man—it *is* a man, right?—is angry about something? What is he blaming?"

"You got me. I haven't got that far."

"You haven't got that far," Masahiko repeated in a monotone. "But there really is a deep anger and sadness here. And he can't spit it out. The anger is swirling around inside him."

In college Masahiko was in the oil painting department, though to be blunt about it, he wasn't known as a great painter. He was skilled enough, but his work lacked depth, something he himself admitted. He was, however, blessed with the skill of being able to instantly evaluate other people's paintings. So whenever I felt stuck doing one of my own paintings, I'd ask his opinion. His advice was always accurate and impartial, as well as practical. And thankfully he had no sense of jealousy or rivalry. I guess this was part of his personality, something he was born with. I always could believe what he told me. He never minced words, but had no ulterior motives, so oddly enough even when his criticism was pretty scathing, I never felt upset.

"When you finish this painting, before you give it to anyone else, could you let me take a look at it, even just for a minute?" he asked, eyes never leaving the painting.

"Sure," I said. "No one commissioned me to do this. I'm just painting it for myself. I don't plan to turn it over to anyone."

"You want to do your *own* painting now, right?"

"Seems that way."

"It's a portrait of sorts, but not a *formal* portrait."

I nodded. "You could put it that way, I suppose."

"You might be . . . discovering a new destination for yourself."

"I'd like to think so," I said.

"I saw Yuzu the other day," Masahiko said as he was leaving. "Happened to bump into her, and we talked for a half hour or so."

I nodded but said nothing. I had no idea what I should say, or how I should react.

"She seemed fine. We didn't talk about you much. It was like we both wanted to avoid the topic. You get it, that feeling? But at the end she did ask about you. What you're doing, that kind of thing. I told her you were painting. I don't know what kind of paintings, I said, but I said you're holed up on a mountaintop and painting something."

"I'm alive, at least," I said.

Masahiko seemed to want to say something more about Yuzu but thought better of it, and clammed up. Yuzu had always liked him and had apparently gone to him for advice. Probably things that had to do with the two of us. Just like I often went to him for advice about paintings. But Masahiko didn't tell me anything. He was that kind of guy. People often sought his advice, but he kept it all inside. Like rain running down a gutter and into a rainwater tank. It doesn't leave there, doesn't spill over the sides. He probably adjusted the amount of water inside as needed.

Masahiko didn't seem to ask anyone else for advice about his own troubles. He must have had plenty, as the son of a famous artist who went to art school but wasn't blessed with much talent as an artist. There must have been things he wanted to talk over. I've known him for a long time, but I don't recall ever hearing him complain about anything, even once. That's the type of man he was.

"Yuzu had a lover, I think," I went ahead and said. "During the last part of our marriage she stopped having sex with me. I should have known something was going on."

It was the first time I'd confessed this to anyone. I had kept it all inside until this moment.

"I see," was all Masahiko said.

"But you already knew that much, didn't you?"

He didn't respond.

"Am I wrong?" I asked again.

"There are things people are better off not knowing. That's all I can say."

"But whether you know it or not, it ends up the same. Sooner or later, suddenly or not suddenly, with a loud knock or a soft one, that's the only difference."

Masahiko sighed. "Yeah. You might be right. Whether you knew about it or not, the end result is the same. But still, there are things I can't talk about."

I was silent.

"No matter how things end up, everything has both a good and bad side. I'm sure breaking up with Yuzu was hard on you. And I feel for you. I really do. But because of that you've finally begun painting what you want to paint. You've discovered your own style. A kind of silver lining, wouldn't you say?"

Maybe he was right. If I hadn't split up with Yuzu—I mean, if Yuzu hadn't left me—I'd probably still be painting run-of-the-mill portraits to make a living. But that wasn't a choice I made *myself*. That's the important point.

"Try to look on the bright side," Masahiko said as he was leaving. "This might sound like dumb advice, but if you're going to walk down a road, it's better to walk down the sunny side, right?"

"And the cup still has one-sixteenth of the water left."

Masahiko laughed. "I like your sense of humor."

I hadn't said it to be humorous, but didn't comment.

Masahiko was silent for a time, and then spoke up. "Do you still love Yuzu?"

"I know I have to forget her, but my heart's still clinging to her and won't let go. That's just the way it is."

"You don't plan to sleep with other women?"

"Even if I did, Yuzu would always come between me and the other woman."

"That's a problem," he said. He rubbed his forehead with his fingertips. He really did look perplexed.

He got in his car and prepared to drive away.

"Thanks for the whiskey," I said. It was not yet five p.m. but the sky was pretty dark. The season when the night gets longer with each passing day.

"Actually, I wanted to have a drink with you," he said, "but I'm driving. Someday soon let's go out and do some serious drinking together. It's been ages."

"We'll do it soon," I said.

There are things people are better off not knowing, Masahiko had said. Maybe so. There are probably things people are better off not hearing, as well. But they can't go forever without hearing them. When the time comes, even if they stop their ears up tight, the air will vibrate and invade a person's heart. You can't prevent it. If you don't like it, then the only solution is to live in a vacuum.

. . .

It was the middle of the night when I woke up. I fumbled for the light next to my bed and looked at the clock. The digital readout showed 1:35. I could hear the bell ringing. *That bell*, no mistake. I sat up and listened to where the sound was coming from.

The bell started ringing again. Someone was ringing it in the middle of the night—and it was much louder, much clearer than ever.

21

IT'S SMALL, BUT SHOULD YOU CUT WITH IT, BLOOD WILL CERTAINLY COME OUT

I sat upright in bed, and in the dark of night I held my breath and listened to the sound of the bell. Where could the sound be coming from? It was louder than before, and clearer. No doubt about it. And it was coming from an entirely new direction.

The bell was ringing inside this house. I could come to no other conclusion. And from a jumble of memories came the recollection that the bell had been resting on a shelf in my studio for a few days. After we uncovered that hole I'd put the bell there myself.

The sound of the bell was coming from the studio.

Absolutely no doubt.

But what should I do? I was shaken, and scared. Something truly weird was taking place inside this house, under the same roof. It was the middle of the night, in an isolated house in the mountains, and I was all alone. I couldn't help but be afraid. When I thought about it later, I think my confusion surpassed my fear at that point. The human brain is probably constructed that way. All the emotions and feelings you have are mobilized to blunt, or mitigate, fear and distress. Like at a fire, where every single container that can hold water is put to use.

I tried to gather my thoughts and figure out what to do. One choice was to pull the covers over my head and go back to sleep. The method Masahiko advocated, to ignore the inexplicable. Switch your mind off, see nothing, hear nothing. The problem was, there was no way I could go back to sleep. Even if I put my head under the covers, stopped up my ears, and switched off my mind, there was no way I could ignore the bell when it rang out this clearly. Because it was ringing inside this very house.

As always, the bell rang intermittently a few times, then came a short silence, then the bell rang out again. The silence in between was never uniform, each time a little shorter or longer than before. There was a strange human feel to that lack of uniformity. The bell wasn't ringing by itself. No device was being used to ring it. Someone was holding it and ringing it. It was sending out a message.

If I can't escape it, then all I can do is get the facts. If this keeps up, then I'll never get to sleep and my life will be totally upended. I decided to take the initiative and find out what was happening in the studio. A bit of anger was included in this—why did I have to go through this? And of course there was a dash of curiosity thrown in as well. I wanted to be certain, with my own eyes, what was going on here.

I got out of bed and threw on a cardigan over my pajamas. I grabbed a flashlight and went out to the front entrance. I grabbed the oak walking stick that Tomohiko Amada had left behind in an umbrella stand. A sturdy, heavy stick. I didn't think it would be useful, but holding something in my hand bucked up my courage. I had to be ready for anything.

Needless to say, I was scared. I was barefoot, but could barely feel the floor. My body was stiff, as if every bone in my body creaked with each step. Someone must have snuck into the house. And that someone was ringing the bell. And it must be the same person who was ringing the bell at the bottom of the hole. Who—or *what*—that was, I couldn't predict. Was it a mummy? Say I set foot in the studio and really did confront a mummy—a shriveled-up man the color of beef jerky—shaking the bell, how should I react? Smack him with Tomohiko Amada's walking stick?

No way, I thought. *I can't do that.* The mummy would have to be a Buddhist priest who'd mummified himself. We weren't talking about a zombie.

Okay, so what should I do? I was still confused. Or rather, my confusion had grown worse. If I had no good way of dealing with the situation, did that mean I'd have to resign myself to sharing the house with a mummy? Putting up with that bell at the same time every night?

I suddenly thought of Menshiki. This problem had arisen because of him. Because he'd done things he shouldn't have. Because he'd used heavy equipment to move the stone mound and uncover the mysterious hole, some unknown being had entered this house along with the bell. I thought of calling him. Despite the late hour I could picture him rushing over in his Jaguar. But I gave up the idea. I didn't have time to wait for him to get ready and drive over. I had to do something *right here, and right now*. I had to make this *my responsibility*.

I steeled myself and stepped into the living room and turned on the light. Even with the light on, the bell kept on ringing. I could clearly hear it coming from beyond the door leading into the studio. I re-gripped the walking stick in my right hand, tiptoed across the large living room, and put my hand on the doorknob of the studio door. I took a deep breath, made up my mind, and turned the knob. As if waiting for me to do that, the second I pushed open the door, the bell stopped cold. A deep silence descended.

The studio was pitch black, and I couldn't see a thing. I reached out to the left-hand wall, fumbled for the light switch, and snapped it on. The pendant light on the ceiling came on and the room was suddenly bathed in light. I stood, legs shoulder-width apart, walking stick in hand, ready to respond to anything, and quickly scanned the room. The tension made my throat so parched that I could hardly swallow.

No one was in the studio. No shriveled-up mummy ringing the bell. No one was there. There was the easel standing by itself in the middle of the room, with a canvas on it. In front of the easel was the old three-legged wooden stool. That was all. The studio was deserted. I couldn't hear a single insect. There was no wind. The white curtain hung down at the window, the whole scene bathed in an unearthly silence. The walking stick was shaking, I was so tense. As it shook, the tip of the stick made an irregular click against the floor.

The bell was still on the shelf. I went over and studied it carefully. I didn't pick the bell up, but I didn't see anything different about it. It was the same as when I'd picked it up in the afternoon and returned it to the shelf, with no evidence of having been moved.

I sat on the stool in front of the easel and once more scanned the room, examining every inch of it. But I still didn't see anyone. It was the same scene I was used to. The painting on the easel was the rough sketch I'd begun of *The Man with the White Subaru Forester*.

I glanced at the clock on the shelf. It was exactly 2 a.m. It was 1:35, as I recall, when the bell woke me up, so twenty-five minutes had passed. It didn't feel like that much time had passed. It felt more like five or six minutes. My sense of time was messed up. Or else the passage of time itself was messed up. One of the two.

I gave up, got down from the stool, turned off the light in the studio, went out, and shut the door. I stood in front of the closed door for a while, my ears perked up, but couldn't hear the bell anymore. I couldn't hear anything, only the silence. Hearing silence—this was no play on words. On an isolated mountaintop, silence had a sound. I stood there before the door to the studio and listened to that sound.

Just then I noticed something on the sofa in the living room I hadn't seen before. It was as big as a cushion or a doll. But I had no memory of putting it there. I looked closer and saw it was no cushion or doll. It was a small, living person, about two feet tall. That little person was wearing odd-looking white clothes. And he was squirming around, like he was uncomfortable in his outfit. I'd seen that ancient, traditional garb before. The kind a high-ranking person would have worn in ancient times in Japan. And it wasn't just the clothes—I remembered the person's face, too.

The Commendatore.

My body felt frozen. As if a fist-sized lump of ice were slowly crawling up my spine. The Commendatore from the painting *Killing Commendatore* was sitting on the sofa in my house—or, more precisely, Tomohiko Amada's house—and looking straight at me. The little man was dressed exactly like in the painting, with the same face. As if he'd escaped directly from the painting.

I tried to recall where I'd put it. That's right, I remembered, it was in the guest bedroom. Not wanting anyone visiting the house to see it, I'd wrapped it in brown washi paper and had hidden it there. If this man had escaped, then what had happened to the painting? Was it solely the Commendatore who had vanished from the canvas?

But was that possible? That a person in a picture could escape from it? Of course not. That's impossible. Obviously. No matter what anybody might think . . .

I stood there, rooted to the spot, the thread of logic lost, random thoughts racing through my head as I gazed at the Commendatore on the sofa. Time temporarily stopped moving forward, shifting back and forth as if waiting for my confusion to subside. I couldn't take my eyes off that bizarre character—all I could think was that he had somehow come from the spirit world. For his part, the Commendatore stared up at me, from the sofa. I had no words, and was silent. The shock must have done it. I was capable of nothing, other than to keep my eyes on him and breathe, my mouth slightly ajar.

The Commendatore didn't take his eyes off me either, and he didn't say a word. His lips were shut tight. On the sofa he flung his short legs out straight in front of him. He leaned back against the sofa, though his head didn't reach to the top. On his feet were oddly shaped shoes. They seemed made out of black leather, the tips pointed and curled upward. At his waist he wore a long sword with a decorated shaft. A long sword, yet of a size to fit his build, so actually nearer in length to a short sword for a normal person. But a lethal weapon all the same. Assuming it was a real sword.

"A real sword it is," the Commendatore said pleasantly, as if reading my mind. His voice carried, despite his small stature. "Affirmative! It's small, but should you cut with it, blood will certainly come out."

Even with this new information, I remained silent. No words came. My first thought was, Oh, so he can talk? My next thought was that he sure had an odd way of speaking. It was not the way ordinary people would speak. But then again, the little two-foot Commendatore was in no way ordinary. So whatever his manner of speech, it shouldn't be surprising.

"In Tomohiko Amada's *Killing Commendatore*, it is indeed me who is impaled by a sword and dies a pitiful death," the Commendatore said. "As my friends are well aware. But have I any wounds that you can see? Negative! No wounds at all. It would be a bother for me to traipse around bleeding, and it would certainly annoy my friends as well. What with blood messing up the carpet and furniture and whatnot. So I left out the stab wound. The one who took the *killing* out of *Killing Commendatore,* that's me. Affirmative! If you need a name for me, my friends can call me the Commendatore."

The way the Commendatore spoke was odd, but he wasn't a poor speaker. In fact he was actually pretty talkative. But I still couldn't get a single word out. Reality and unreality still hadn't come to a mutual understanding inside me.

"Perhaps you will put that stick down?" the Commendatore said. "It is not as though we are about to embark upon a duel . . ."

I looked at my right hand. It was still clutching Amada's walking stick tightly. I let it go . . . The oak stick made a dull *clunk* as it struck the carpet.

"It is not like I escaped from the painting," the Commendatore said, again reading my mind. "Negative! That painting—a fascinating one, by the way—remains intact. The Commendatore is still in the process of being stabbed to death. A huge amount of blood continues to flow from his heart. All I have done is borrow his shape for a while. I need some sort of shape in order to speak with my friends. So for the sake of convenience, I borrowed his form. Is that acceptable to my friends?"

Still not a peep from me.

"Not that anybody really cares. Mr. Amada has gone on to a hazy, peaceful world, and the Commendatore is not trademarked. If I had appeared as Mickey Mouse or Pocahontas, the Walt Disney Company would be only too happy to slap me with a huge lawsuit, but if I am the Commendatore, I think we are safe, my friends."

The Commendatore's shoulders shook as he laughed merrily.

"I would have been okay as a mummy, but if I'd appeared as a mummy all of a sudden in the middle of the night, I am aware that my friends might have been bothered. To see a man all shriveled up like a hunk of beef jerky, ringing a bell in the middle of the night—that would certainly give most people a heart attack."

I nodded almost automatically. True enough—a commendatore was much preferable to a mummy. If he'd been a mummy I might really *have* had a heart attack. But running across Mickey Mouse or Pocahontas ringing a bell in the dark would have been pretty creepy too. A commendatore dressed in Asuka-period costume probably was a better choice.

"Are you a kind of spirit?" I ventured to ask. My voice was hard and hoarse, like a convalescent's.

"An excellent question," the Commendatore said. He held up a tiny white index finger. "An excellent question indeed, my friends. What am I? I am now, for the time being, the Commendatore. Nothing other than the Commendatore. But this form is but temporary. I do not know what I will be next. What am I to begin with? Or I could say, what are *you*, my friends? My friends have your own appearance, but what are *you* to begin with? If you were asked that same question, my friends might indeed be confused, I imagine. It is the same thing with me."

"Can you assume any form you like?" I asked.

"No, it is not that simple. The forms I can take are quite limited. I can't take any form I want. *There is a limit to the wardrobe.* I cannot take on a form unless there is a necessity for it. And the form I could choose now was this pint-sized commendatore. I had to be this small because of the way he was painted. But this attire is highly unpleasant to wear, I am afraid."

He began squirming around in his white costume.

"To return to the pressing question that my friends have pondered—am I a spirit? No, it is nothing like that. I am no spirit. I am just an Idea. A spirit is basically supernaturally free, which I am not. I live under all sorts of restrictions."

I had plenty of questions. Or rather, I *should have had*. But for some reason I couldn't think of a single one. Why did he address me as "my friends"? But that was trivial, not worth asking about. Maybe in the world of an *Idea* there was no second-person singular.

"I have so many kinds of detailed limitations," the Commendatore said. "For instance, I can only take on form for a limited number of hours each day. I prefer the somewhat dubious middle of the night, so mostly shape-shift between one thirty and two thirty a.m. It's too tiring to do it during the day. When I don't have form I take it easy, as a formless Idea, here and there. Like the horned owl in the attic. Also, I cannot go where I am not invited. Whereas when my friends opened the pit and took out the bell for me, I was able to enter this house."

"So you were stuck at the bottom of the pit all this time?" I asked. My voice had improved, but was still a bit hoarse.

"I could not say. I do not have memory, in the exact sense of the term. Though my being stuck in the pit is a fact. I was in the pit and could not escape. But it did not feel inconvenient to me, being shut up in there. I could be stuck in a cramped dark hole for tens of thousands of years and not feel any distress. I am grateful to my friends for getting me out of there. Being free is much more interesting than not being free, needless to say. I am also grateful to that Mr. Menshiki. Without his efforts, the hole never would have been opened up."

I nodded. "That's exactly right."

"I think I must have sensed it. The possibility that the pit would be exhumed, I mean. And must have thought this: The time has come."

"So it was you who began to ring the bell in the middle of the night?"

"Precisely. And the pit was opened. And Mr. Menshiki very kindly invited me to his dinner party."

I nodded again. It was true that Menshiki had invited the Commendatore—though he'd used the word "mummy"—to dinner on Tuesday. Following the example of Don Giovanni's dinner invitation to the bronze statue of Il Commendatore. To him it was probably a bit of a joke. But this was no longer a joke.

"I never take any food," the Commendatore said. "And I do not drink, either. No digestive organs, you see. 'Tis boring if you think about it, since he has gone to the trouble of preparing such a feast. But still I went ahead and accepted. It is not often that an Idea is invited by someone for dinner."

These were the Commendatore's last words that night. He suddenly grew silent and quietly shut both eyes, as if slipping into a meditative state. With his eyes closed, the Commendatore's features took on a contemplative look. His body, too, was completely still. His whole form began to fade, the outline becoming indistinct. And a few seconds later he totally vanished. Reflexively I glanced at the clock. Two fifteen a.m. Most likely his materialization had reached its time limit.

I went over to the sofa and touched the spot where the Commendatore had sat. My hand felt nothing. No warmth, no depression. No evidence at all that anyone had sat there. Ideas most likely had no body heat or weight. That figure was a mere image and nothing more. I sat down next to where he'd been, took a deep breath, and rubbed my face hard.

It felt like it had taken place in a dream. I must have been having a long, very vivid dream. Or maybe this world now was an extension of the dream, one I was shut up inside. But I knew this was no dream. This might not be real, but it wasn't a dream either. Menshiki and I had released the Commendatore—or an Idea taking the appearance of the Commendatore—from the bottom of that strange pit. And that Commendatore—like the horned owl in the attic—had come to inhabit this house. I had no clue what that meant. Or what it would lead to.

I stood up, retrieved Tomohiko Amada's walking stick I'd dropped on the floor, turned off the light in the living room, and returned to my bedroom. It was quiet all around, not a single sound. I took off my cardigan, slipped back into my bed in my pajamas, and lay there thinking about what I should do now. The Commendatore planned to go to Menshiki's house on Tuesday, since Menshiki had invited him to dinner. And what would happen there? The more I thought about it, the more wobbly my brain became, my mind like a dining table with uneven legs.

But before long I grew overpoweringly sleepy. Like every function of my brain was mobilizing to put me to sleep, to pluck me by force from an incoherent, confused reality. And I couldn't resist. Before long I fell asleep. Just before I fell asleep, I thought of the horned owl. How was he doing?

My friends must go to sleep now. It felt like the Commendatore murmured this into my ear.

But that must have been part of a dream.

22

THE INVITATION IS STILL OPEN

The next day was Monday. When I woke up the digital clock showed 6:35. I sat up in bed, and reviewed the middle-of-the-night happenings in the studio. The bell ringing, the miniature Commendatore, the strange conversation with him. I wanted to believe it was all a dream. I'd had a very long, real dream—that's all it was. In the light of morning, that's the only way I could see it. I clearly remembered everything that had taken place, and the more I reviewed each and every detail, the more it felt like something that had happened light-years away from reality.

But no matter how hard I tried to see it all as a dream, I knew that it wasn't. *This might not have been real, but it wasn't a dream.* I didn't know what it was, but at any rate it wasn't a dream. It was something altogether different.

I got out of bed, removed the washi paper wrapping from Tomohiko Amada's *Killing Commendatore,* and carried the painting into the studio. I hung it on the wall, then sat on the stool and studied the painting. Like the Commendatore had said the previous night, nothing about the painting had changed. The Commendatore hadn't escaped from the painting into this world. Like always, the Commendatore was still there, stabbed in the chest, blood pouring out of his heart as he died. He looked up in the air, his mouth open in a grimace, groaning in agony. His hairstyle, the clothes he wore, the long sword he held, even the strange black shoes, were exactly those of the Commendatore who'd appeared here last night. No, to put it in the correct order—chronologically speaking—naturally last night's Commendatore had minutely copied the appearance of the Commendatore in the painting.

It was astounding that the fictional figure that Tomohiko Amada had painted with a Japanese paintbrush and pigment had taken on real form and appeared in reality (or something like reality), moving around under its own willpower in three-dimensional form. But as I stared at the painting, this phenomenon began to seem less and less impossible. That's how vivid and alive Tomohiko Amada's rendering was. The longer I looked at the painting, the less clear was the threshold between reality and unreality, flat and solid, substance and image. Like Van Gogh's mailman, who, the longer you looked, seemed to take on a life of his own. Same with the crows that he painted—nothing but rough black lines, but they really did seem to be soaring through the sky. As I gazed at *Killing Commendatore* I was struck once again with admiration for Amada's gift and craftsmanship as an artist. No doubt that the Commendatore (or Idea, I should say) was equally struck by how amazing and powerful the painting was, and that was why he had "borrowed" the appearance of the Commendatore. Like a hermit crab chooses the prettiest and most sturdy shell to live in.

I studied *Killing Commendatore* for some ten minutes, then went into the kitchen, brewed coffee, and, while listening to the regular news broadcast on the radio, had a simple breakfast. The news was meaningless. Or what I should say is that almost none of the news those days held any meaning for me. Still, listening to the seven a.m. news each day had become part of my routine. It might be a problem if the world was on the brink of destruction and I was the only person unaware of it.

I finished breakfast, and after confirming that that earth, despite all its various troubles, was still spinning away, I headed back to the studio, mug in hand. I drew back the curtain to let in some fresh air, then stood before the canvas and went back to work on my painting. Whether the Commendatore's appearance was real or not, whether he showed up at Menshiki's dinner or not, all I could do in the meantime was focus on the work at hand.

I called to mind the figure of the middle-aged man with the white Subaru Forester. On his table in the restaurant had been a car key with the Subaru logo, a heap of toast, scrambled eggs, and sausage on a plate.

Ketchup (red) and mustard (yellow) containers sat alongside. Knife and fork were lined up on the table. He'd yet to start eating. Morning light shone on the whole tableau. As I passed him, the man raised his suntanned face and stared at me.

I know exactly where you've been and what you've been up to, he was informing me. I recognized that heavy, dispassionate light abiding in his eyes. A light I may have seen somewhere else, though when or where I couldn't say.

I was completing that figure and that wordless message in the form of a painting. I started out using a crust of bread as an eraser to get rid of any excess lines from the charcoal framework I'd sketched the day before. After removing all that I could, I again added some lines in black to the black lines that remained. This process took an hour and a half. What emerged on the canvas was (so to speak) a mummified image of the man who drove the white Subaru Forester. The flesh pruned away, the skin dried up like beef jerky, a figure shrunken one whole size. This was depicted through the rough black charcoal lines alone. Just a preliminary sketch, but I could imagine how it linked up with the full painting to come.

"Nicely done," the Commendatore said.

I spun around. The Commendatore was seated on the shelf near the window, facing me, his silhouette distinctly backlit in the morning light. He had on the same ancient white clothes and the same long sword downsized to fit his height. *This is no dream. Of course it isn't*, I told myself.

"I am no dream, I can tell you. Negative. Of course," the Commendatore said, once again reading my thoughts. "I am closer to wakefulness than dream."

I said nothing. From my perch on the stool I gazed at his silhouette.

"I think I said this last night, but it is pretty exhausting for me to materialize when it is bright out like this," the Commendatore said. "But I wanted to watch my friends painting just this once. So I took the liberty of observing while you worked. I hope this does not offend you?"

I had no answer to this either. Whether it offended me or not, how was a real person supposed to reason with an Idea?

Not waiting for my response (or maybe taking what was in my mind as my response), the Commendatore continued. "You are quite a talented painter. Stroke by stroke, the essence of that man is coming out on that canvas."

"Do you know something about him?" I asked, surprised.

"Affirmative," the Commendatore said. "Of course I do."

"Then could you tell me something about him? What kind of person he is, what work he does, what he's doing now?"

"I wonder," the Commendatore said, slightly inclining his head, a hard look coming over his face. When he made that sort of expression he looked like a goblin. Or like Edward G. Robinson from an old gangster movie. Who knows, maybe the Commendatore had "borrowed" that expression from Edward G. Robinson. That wouldn't be impossible.

"There are things in the world my friends are better off not knowing," the Commendatore said, the Edward G. Robinson look plastered on his face.

The same thing Masahiko Amada had said the other day, I recalled. *There are things people are better off not knowing.*

"In other words, you won't tell me the things I'm better off not knowing," I said.

"Affirmative. Even if you hear it from me, the truth is that my friends *already know it.*"

I was silent.

"As my friends paint that picture, you will be subjectively giving form to what my friends already comprehend. Think of Thelonious Monk. Thelonious Monk did not get those unusual chords as a result of logic or theory. He opened his eyes wide, and scooped those chords out from the darkness of his consciousness. What is important is not creating something out of nothing. What my friends need to do is discover the right thing from what is already there."

So he knew about Thelonious Monk.

"Affirmative! And of course I know Edward whatchamacallit, too," the Commendatore said, grabbing hold of my thoughts.

"No matter," the Commendatore continued. "Ah, there is one thing I must raise at this point, as a matter of courtesy. It is about your lovely girlfriend . . . Right, the married woman who drives a red car. Apologies, but I have been watching all you have been doing here. What you all enjoy doing in bed after you take off your clothes."

I stared at him without a word. *What we enjoy doing in bed . . .* To borrow her words for it, *what one hesitates to mention.*

"But you really should not mind. My apologies, but an Idea watches everything that happens. I cannot choose what I watch. But there is nothing to worry about, at all. Sex, radio exercise routines, chimney sweeping, it is all the same to me. Nothing that interesting to see. I just watch."

"There's no notion of privacy in the world of an Idea?"

"Affirmative," the Commendatore said, rather proudly. "Not a speck of that. So if my friends do not mind, then that is all we need to say. So, are you okay with it?"

I shook my head slightly again. How about it? Was it possible to focus while having sex if you knew somebody else was watching the whole time? Could you call up a healthy sexual desire if you knew you were being observed?

"I have a question for you," I said.

"I would be happy to answer if I can," the Commendatore said.

"Tomorrow, on Tuesday, I'm invited to dinner at Mr. Menshiki's. And you're invited as well. Mr. Menshiki used the expression "inviting a mummy," which actually means you. Since at that point you hadn't yet appeared as the Commendatore."

"That does not matter. If I decide to be a mummy, I can do that in a flash."

"No, stay as you are," I said hurriedly. "I would appreciate it if you stay the way you are."

"I will accompany you to Menshiki's house. You will be able to see me, but Menshiki will not. So it does not matter if I am a mummy or a commendatore. Though there is one thing I would like my friends to do."

"And what would that be?"

"My friends should call Menshiki now and make sure the invitation for Tuesday night is still open. When you do, make sure to say, 'It will not be a mummy coming with me that day, but the Commendatore.

Would that still be all right?' As I mentioned, I cannot set foot in a place unless I have been invited. The other party needs to invite me, in some form or other say 'Please, come on in.' Once I have been invited, then I can go whenever I feel like it. For this house, that bell over there acted as a substitute invitation."

"I see," I said. The one thing I couldn't have was him turning into a mummy. "I'll call Mr. Menshiki, see if the invitation is still on, and tell him I'd like him to revise the guest list from mummy to Commendatore."

"Affirmative. I would be grateful. Receiving an invitation to a dinner party is quite unexpected."

"I have another question," I said. "Weren't you originally a priest who undertook certain death austerities? A priest who voluntarily was buried underground, stopped eating and drinking, and chanted the sutras until you passed away? Didn't you die in the pit while you continued to ring the bell, and eventually turned into a mummy?"

"Hmm," the Commendatore said, and shook his head a little. "Unclear. I can't say, really. At a certain point I became a pure Idea. But I have no linear memory of what I was before that, where I was or what I did."

The Commendatore was silent, staring fixedly into space.

"Anyway, I have to disappear soon," the Commendatore said in a quiet, slightly hoarse voice. "The time during which I can materialize is nearly over. The morning is not my time. Darkness is my friend. A vacuum is my breath. I must be saying goodbye soon. So, thank you in advance for calling Mr. Menshiki."

As if meditating, the Commendatore closed his eyes. His lips were tightly sealed, his fingers locked together, as he steadily grew fainter and then disappeared. Just like the night before. Like fleeting smoke, he silently vanished in the air. In the bright morning sunshine, all that was left was me and the painting I'd started. The outline of the man with the white Subaru Forester glaring at me.

I know exactly where you've been and what you've been up to.

After noon I called Menshiki. I realized this was the first time I'd ever phoned his home. He was the one who always called me. He picked up after six rings.

"I'm glad you called," he said. "I was just about to call you. But I didn't want to bother you while you're working, so was waiting until the afternoon. I remember you mainly work in the morning."

"I just finished for the day," I said.

"Is it going well?" Menshiki asked.

"Yes, I started a new painting. Though I've barely begun."

"That's wonderful. I'm so glad to hear it. By the way, I hung the portrait you painted on the wall of my study, not yet framed. I'm letting it dry there. Even without a frame it looks wonderful."

"About tomorrow . . . ," I said.

"I'll send a car to pick you up at six," he said. "The same car will take you back. It'll just be the two of us, so you don't need to dress up, or bring a gift or anything. Please just come as you are."

"There's one thing I wanted to check with you."

"Yes?"

"The other day you said you wouldn't mind having a mummy join us for dinner, right?"

"I did say that, yes. I remember."

"Is that invitation still open?"

Menshiki considered this for a moment and then gave a cheery laugh. "Of course it is. I meant what I said. The invitation is still open."

"Something happened and the mummy won't be able to come, but instead the Commendatore says he'd like to. Is it all right to invite the Commendatore?"

"Of course," Menshiki said without hesitation. "Like Don Giovanni invited the statue to dinner, I would be pleased to have the Commendatore come to dinner in my humble abode. But unlike Don Giovanni in the opera, I haven't done anything so bad that I deserve to be thrown into hell. At least I don't think I have. After dinner I'm not going to be pulled into hell or anything, I hope?"

"That won't happen," I replied. Though honestly I wasn't all that confident. I couldn't predict anymore what was going to happen next.

"Good. I'm not ready for hell quite yet," Menshiki said cheerily. As you might expect, he was taking it all as a clever joke. "One question, though. As a dead person, Don Giovanni's Commendatore wasn't able to eat earthly food, but what about *this* Commendatore? Should I prepare food for him? Or does he not take any worldly food?"

"There's no need to prepare food for him. He doesn't eat or drink. But it wouldn't be a problem if you set a place for him."

"Because he's basically a spiritual being?"

"I believe so." An Idea and a spirit were a little different, I thought, but I didn't want to get into it.

"I'm fine with that," Menshiki said. "I'll make sure the Commendatore has his own seat at the table. It's an unexpected pleasure to be able to invite the famous Commendatore to dinner in my humble home. It's too bad, though, that he won't be able to sample the food. We'll have some delicious wine as well."

I thanked Menshiki.

"Until tomorrow, then," Menshiki said, and hung up.

That night, the bell didn't ring. The Commendatore must have been tired out from materializing during the day (and answering my questions). Or maybe he no longer felt the need to summon me to the studio. At any rate, I slept a deep, dreamless sleep until morning.

The next morning as I painted in the studio the Commendatore didn't make an appearance. So for two hours, I was able to forget everything and focus on painting. The first thing I did that day was paint over the outline, like spreading a thick slab of butter on toast.

I started with a deep red, an edgy, offbeat green, and a grayish black. These were the colors the man wanted. It took a while to mix the right colors. As I went through this process I put on the record of Mozart's *Don Giovanni*. With that music playing, it felt like the Commendatore would appear behind me at any minute, though he didn't.

That day, Tuesday, the Commendatore, like the horned owl up in the attic, maintained a deep silence. But that didn't bother me particularly. As a flesh-and-blood person, I couldn't worry about an Idea. Ideas had their own way of doing things. And I had my own life. I focused on completing *The Man with the White Subaru Forester*. Whether I was in the studio or out, standing before the canvas or not, the image of the painting was never far from my mind.

According to the radio weather report, there was supposed to be heavy rain that night in the Kanto-Tokai region. And off to the west the weather was indeed taking a turn for the worse. In southern Kyushu torrential rains had made rivers overflow, and people living in low-lying areas had had to evacuate. People in higher areas were warned to watch out for landslides.

A dinner party on a night when it's going to be pouring, I thought.

I thought of that dark hole in the middle of the woods. That weird stone-lined little chamber that Menshiki and I had exposed to the light of day when we moved the heavy rocks of the mound. I pictured myself sitting alone at the bottom of that pitch-dark hole listening to rain pounding on the wooden cover. I'm shut up inside that hole, unable to escape. The ladder's been taken away, the heavy cover shut tight right above me. And everyone in the world has completely forgotten I've been left behind. Or perhaps they think I'm long dead. But I am still alive. Lonely, but still breathing. All I can hear is the downpour. There's no light. Not a single ray reaches me. The stone wall I'm leaning against is damply cold. It's the middle of the night. All sorts of bugs might ooze their way out.

As this scene took shape in my mind, I gradually found it hard to breathe. I went out to the terrace, leaned against the railing, slowly breathed in the fresh air through my nose, and slowly exhaled through my mouth. As always, I counted the number of breaths and repeated this process at regular intervals. After repeating this for a while, I was able to breathe normally again. The twilight sky was covered in heavy, leaden clouds. The rain was getting closer.

Menshiki's white mansion appeared faintly across the valley. This evening that's where I'll be having dinner, I thought. Menshiki, me, and the famous Commendatore—three of us seated around the dining table.

Affirmative. That is real blood I'm talking about, you know, the Commendatore whispered in my ear.

23

THEY ALL REALLY EXIST

When I was thirteen and my little sister was ten, the two of us traveled by ourselves to Yamanashi Prefecture during summer vacation. Our mother's brother worked in a research lab at a university in Yamanashi and we went to stay with him. This was the first trip we kids had taken by ourselves. My sister was feeling relatively good then, so our parents gave us permission to travel alone.

Our uncle was single (and still is single, even now), and had just turned thirty, I think, at that time. He was doing gene research (and still is), was very quiet and kind of unworldly, though a very open, straightforward person. He loved reading and knew everything about nature. He enjoyed taking walks in the mountains more than anything, which, he said, was why he had taken a university job in rural, mountainous Yamanashi. My sister and I liked our uncle a lot.

Backpacks in tow, we boarded an express train at Shinjuku Station bound for Matsumoto, and got off at Kofu. Our uncle came to pick us up at Kofu Station. He was spectacularly tall, and even in the crowded station, we spotted him right away. He was renting a small house in Kofu along with a friend of his, but his roommate was abroad so we were given our own room to sleep in. We stayed in that house for one week. And almost every day we took walks with our uncle in the nearby mountains. He taught us the names of all kinds of flowers and insects. We cherished our memories of that summer.

One day we hiked a bit farther than usual and visited a wind cave near Mt. Fuji. Among the numerous wind caves around Mt. Fuji there was one in particular that was fairly large. Our uncle told us about how these holes were formed. The caves were made of basalt, so inside you heard hardly any echoes at all, he said. Even in the summer the temperature remained low inside, so in the past people would store ice they'd cut in winter inside the caves. He explained the distinction between the two types of holes: *fuketsu*, the larger ones that were big enough for people to go into, and *kaza-ana*, the smaller ones that people couldn't enter. Both terms were alternate readings of the same Chinese characters meaning "wind" and "hole." Our uncle seemed to know everything.

At the large wind hole, you paid an entrance fee and went inside. Our uncle didn't go with us. He'd been there numerous times, plus he was so tall and the ceiling of the cave so low, he'd end up with a backache. It's not dangerous, he said, so you two go on ahead. I'll stay by the entrance and read a book. At the entrance the person in charge handed us each a flashlight and put yellow plastic helmets on us. There were lights on the ceiling of the cave, but it was still pretty dark inside. The deeper we went inside the cave, the lower the ceiling got. No wonder our lanky uncle had bowed out.

My kid sister and I shone the flashlights at our feet as we went. It was midsummer outside but inside the cave it was chilly. It was ninety degrees Fahrenheit outside, but inside it was under fifty. Following our uncle's advice, we were both wearing thick windbreakers we'd brought along. My sister held my hand tightly, either wanting me to protect her, or else hoping to protect me, one or the other (or maybe she just didn't want to get separated). The whole time we were inside the cave that small, warm hand was in mine. The only other visitors were a middle-aged couple. But they soon left, and it was just the two of us.

My little sister's name was Komichi, but everyone in the family called her Komi. Her friends called her Micchi or Micchan. As far as I know, no one called her by her full name, Komichi. She was a small, slim girl. She had straight black hair, neatly cut just above her shoulders. Her eyes were big for the size of her face (with large pupils), which made her resemble a fairy. That day she wore a white T-shirt, faded jeans, and pink sneakers.

After we'd made our way deeper into the cave my sister discovered a small side cave a little ways off from the prescribed path. Its mouth was hidden in the shadows of the rocks. She was very interested in that little cave. "Don't you think it looks like Alice's rabbit hole?" she asked me.

My sister was a big fan of Lewis Carroll's *Alice in Wonderland*. I don't know how many times she had me read the book to her. Must have been at least a hundred. She had been able to read since she was little, but she liked me to read that book aloud to her. She'd memorized the story, but each time I read it, she still got excited. Her favorite part was the Lobster Quadrille. Even now I remember that part, word for word.

"No rabbit, though," I said.

"I'm going to peek inside," she said.

"Be careful," I said.

It really was a narrow hole (close to a *kaza-ana,* in my uncle's definition), but my little sister was able to slip through it with no trouble. Her upper half was inside, just the bottom half of her legs sticking out. She seemed to be shining her flashlight inside the hole. Then she slowly edged out backward.

"It gets really deep in back," she reported. "The floor drops off sharply. Just like Alice's rabbit hole. I'm going to check out the far end."

"No, don't do it. It's too dangerous," I said.

"It's okay. I'm small and I can get out okay."

She took off her windbreaker, so that she was wearing just her T-shirt, and handed the jacket to me along with her helmet. Before I could get in a word of protest, she'd wriggled into the cave, flashlight in hand. In an instant she'd vanished.

A long time passed, but she still didn't come out. I couldn't hear a sound.

"Komi," I called into the hole. "Komi! Are you okay?"

There was no answer. Without any echo my voice was sucked right up into the darkness. I was starting to get concerned. She might be stuck inside the hole, unable to more forward or back. Or maybe she had had a convulsion inside the hole and lost consciousness. If that had happened I wouldn't be able to help her. All kinds of terrible scenarios ran through my head, and I felt choked by the darkness surrounding me.

If my little sister really did disappear in the hole, never to return to this world again, how would I ever explain that to my parents? Should

I run and tell my uncle, waiting outside the entrance? Or should I sit tight and wait for her to emerge? I crouched down and peered into that hole. But the beam from my flashlight didn't reach far. It was a tiny hole, and the darkness inside was overwhelming.

"Komi," I called out again. No response. *"Komi,"* I called more loudly. Still no answer. A wave of cold chilled me to the core. I might lose my sister forever. She might have been sucked into Alice's hole and vanished. Into the world of the Mock Turtle, the Cheshire Cat, and the Queen of Hearts. A place where worldly logic didn't apply. No matter what, we never should have come here.

But finally my sister did return. She didn't back out like before, but crawled out headfirst. First her black hair appeared from the hole, then her shoulders and arms. She wriggled out her waist, and finally her pink sneakers emerged. She stood in front of me, without a word, stretched, slowly took a deep breath, and brushed the dirt off her jeans.

My heart was still pounding. I reached out and straightened her disheveled hair. I couldn't quite make it out in the weak light inside the cave, but there seemed to be dirt and dust and other debris clinging to her white T-shirt. I put the windbreaker on her. And handed back her yellow helmet.

"I didn't think you were coming back," I said, hugging her to me.

"Were you worried?"

"A lot."

She grabbed my hand tightly again. And in an excited voice she said, "I managed to squeeze through the narrow part, and then deeper in it suddenly got lower, and down from there it was like a small room. A round room, like a ball. The ceiling's round, the walls are round, and the floor too. And it was so, so silent there, like you could search the whole world and never find any place that silent. Like I was at the bottom of an ocean, in a hollow going even deeper. I turned off the flashlight and it was pitch dark, but I didn't feel scared or lonely. That room was a special place that only I'm allowed into. A room *just for me*. No one else can get there. You can't go in either."

"'Cause I'm too big."

My little sister bobbed her head. "Right. You've gotten too big to get in. And what's really amazing about that place is that it's darker than anything could ever be. So dark that when you turn off the flashlight it feels like you can grab the darkness with your hands. And when you're there in the dark by yourself, it's like your body is gradually coming apart and disappearing. But since it's dark you can't see it happen. You don't know if you still have a body or not. But even if, say, my body completely disappeared, I'd still remain there. Like the Cheshire Cat's grin remaining after he vanished. Pretty weird, huh? But when I was there I didn't think it was weird at all. I wanted to stay there forever, but I thought you'd be worried, so I came out."

"Let's get out of here," I said. She was so worked up it seemed as if she was going to go on talking forever, and I had to put a stop to that. "I can't breathe well in here."

"Are you okay?" my sister asked, worried.

"I'm okay. I just want to go outside."

Holding hands, we headed for the exit.

"Do you know?" my sister said in a small voice as we walked so no one else would hear (though there wasn't anyone else around). "Alice really existed. It wasn't made up, it was real. The March Hare, the Walrus, the Cheshire Cat, the Playing Card soldiers—they all really exist."

"Maybe so," I said.

We emerged from the wind hole, back to the bright real world. There was a thin layer of clouds in the sky that afternoon, but I remember how strong the sunlight seemed. The screech of the cicadas was overpowering, like a violent squall drowning everything out. My uncle was seated on a bench near the entrance, absorbed in a book. When he saw us, he grinned and stood up.

Two years later, my sister died. And was put in a tiny coffin and cremated. I was fifteen, and she was twelve. While she was being cremated I went off, apart from the rest of the family, sat on a bench in the courtyard of the crematorium, and remembered what had happened in that wind hole. The weight of time as I waited by that small cave for my little sister to come out, the thickness of the darkness enveloping me, the chill I felt to my core. Her black hair emerging from the hole, then her shoulders. All the random dirt and dust stuck to her white T-shirt.

At that time a thought struck me: that maybe even before the doctor at the hospital officially pronounced her dead two years later, her life had already been snatched from her while she was deep inside that cave. I was actually convinced of it. She'd already been lost within that hole, and left this world, but I, mistakenly thinking she was still alive, had put her on the train with me and taken her back to Tokyo. Holding her hand tightly. And we'd lived as brother and sister for two more years. But that was nothing more than a fleeting grace period. Two years later, death had crawled out of that cave to grab hold of my sister's soul. As if time was up, it was necessary to pay for what had been lent, and the owner had come to take back what was his.

At any rate now, at thirty-six, I realized again that what my little sister had confided to me in a quiet voice in that wind hole was indeed true. Alice really does exist in the world. The March Hare, the Walrus, the Cheshire Cat—they all *really exist.* And the Commendatore too, of course.

The weather report was off the mark and we didn't have a rainstorm. Just after five a very light rain began—so fine that you could hardly tell if it was falling or not—and continued till the next morning. Right at six p.m. a large, shiny black sedan slowly made its way up the slope. It reminded me of a hearse, but of course it wasn't one, but the limousine Menshiki had sent for me. A Nissan Infiniti. The driver, in black uniform and hat, alighted from the car and, umbrella in one hand, came over to the front door and rang the bell. I opened the door and he took off his hat and made sure of my name. I left the house and got into the car. I declined the umbrella. It wasn't raining hard enough for one. The driver opened the rear door for me. Once I was inside, he closed it with a solid *thunk* (a little different from the sound of Menshiki's Jaguar). I wore a black, light, round-necked sweater, gray herringbone jacket, dark-gray wool trousers, and black suede shoes. The most formal outfit I owned. At least it didn't have paint stains.

Even after the limo came, the Commendatore still hadn't appeared. And I hadn't heard his voice. So I had no way of making sure he'd remembered the invitation from Menshiki. But he must have. He'd been looking forward to it so much there was no way he'd forgotten.

But I worried for nothing. Soon after the car had set off, I suddenly found the Commendatore, with a nonchalant look on his face, seated beside me. He was dressed in his usual white outfit (looking like it had just come from the cleaners, without a single stain), with the jewel-encrusted long sword at his waist. He was, as always, about two feet high. The whiteness and purity of his clothes stood out even more against the black leather seats of the Infiniti. He stared straight ahead, his arms folded.

"Do not say anything to me," the Commendatore said, as if reminding me. "My friends can see me, but others cannot. My friends can hear me, but others cannot. If you talk to something that cannot be seen, people will think you are very strange. Affirmative? Nod, please, if you understand."

I nodded slightly one time. The Commendatore bobbed his head in response, and afterward sat there silently, his arms folded.

It was dark out. The crows had already withdrawn to their mountain roosts. The Infiniti slowly descended the slope, drove down the road in the valley, and came to a steep slope. It wasn't that long a distance (we were just going to the other side of a narrow valley, after all), but the road was narrow, with plenty of curves. The type of road a driver of a large sedan would not be happy to navigate. The type of road more suited to a four-wheel-drive military vehicle. But the driver's expression didn't change a bit as he calmly handled the car, and we arrived safely at Menshiki's mansion.

The mansion was surrounded by a high white wall, with a solid gate in front. Large wooden double doors painted a dark brown. Like the castle gate in an Akira Kurosawa film set in the Middle Ages. The kind that would look good with a couple of arrows embedded in it. The inside was completely hidden from view. Next to the gate was a plate with the house number, but no nameplate. Probably no need to have one. If someone was going to go to the trouble of coming all the way up to the top of this mountain, they would automatically know this was Menshiki's mansion. The area around the gate was brightly lit by mercury lamps. The driver got out, rang the bell, and spoke for a moment with someone on the intercom. Then he got back in his seat and waited for the gate to open remotely. There were two movable security cameras, one on each side of the gate.

The double doors slowly opened inward, and the driver entered, proceeding leisurely down the curving road on the grounds. The road was a gentle downward slope. I heard the doors close behind us—a heavy sound, as if informing us that there was no return to the world from which we had come. Pine trees lined both sides of the road, all neatly trimmed. The branches were beautifully arranged, like bonsai, and careful measures were obviously taken to keep them from getting any disease. Along the road was also a trim hedge of azaleas. Beyond this there were Japanese roses, and a clump of camellias. The house might be new, but the trees and plants all seemed to have been there since long ago. All of these were beautifully illuminated by garden lanterns.

The road ended in a circular asphalt-covered driveway. As soon as the driver parked, he leaped out the driver's side and opened the back door for me. I looked beside me but didn't see the Commendatore. But I wasn't particularly surprised, and didn't mind. He had his own patterns of behavior.

The taillights of the Infiniti politely and gracefully disappeared into the twilight darkness, leaving me standing there alone. Seen from the front like this, the house looked much cozier and less imposing than I'd expected. When I'd looked at it from across the valley it seemed like an overbearing, gaudy structure. Perhaps the impression changed depending on the angle. The front gate was at the highest point of the mountain, and then, descending the slope, the house was built as if to deliberately make use of the angle of inclination of the land.

On either side of the front door were two old stone statues, a pair of the *komainu* guardian dog figures found in Shinto shrines. On pedestals as well. They might actually have been real *komainu* brought over from somewhere. There were plantings of azaleas at the entrance, too. In May the place must be pretty colorful.

As I slowly walked toward the front door, it opened from inside and Menshiki appeared. He had on a dark-green cardigan over a white button-down shirt, and cream-colored chinos. His pure white hair was, as always, neatly combed and arranged naturally. It felt strange to see

Menshiki welcoming me to his own house. I'd always seen Menshiki when he roared up to my house in his Jaguar.

He invited me in and closed the front door. The entrance foyer was spacious and nearly square, with a high ceiling. A squash court could fit inside. The indirect lighting on the wall pleasantly lit the room, and on top of a large octagonal parquet table in the middle of the foyer was a large flower vase, Ming dynasty by the look of it, overflowing with a fresh flower arrangement. A mix of three different types of large flowers (I don't know much about plants so don't know the names). Probably he'd had them specially arranged just for this evening. A frugal college student could manage to live for a month on what Menshiki probably paid the florist. At least I could have, back when I was a student. There were no windows in the foyer, just a skylight in the ceiling. The floor was well-polished marble.

The living room was down three wide steps, and though not quite big enough for a soccer field was definitely large enough for a tennis court. The southeast side was all tinted glass, with a large deck outside. It was dark, so I couldn't tell if you could see the ocean from here, but I imagine you could. On the opposite wall was an open fireplace. It wasn't the cold season yet so there was no fire lit, but firewood was neatly stacked up beside it, so a fire could be started at any time. I don't know who had stacked it up, but it was placed so beautifully it looked like a work of art in itself. There was a mantelpiece above the fireplace, with a row of old Meissen figurines.

The living room floor was also marble, but covered with a variety of rugs. Antique Persian rugs, with such exquisite patterns and colors they looked less like practical objects than artistic handicrafts. I hesitated to step on them. There were several low tables and a scattering of flower vases, all full of fresh flowers. Each vase looked like a valuable antique. It was all in nice taste, and expensive. Here's hoping we don't have a big earthquake, was my thought.

The ceiling was high, the lighting subdued. Refined indirect lighting on the walls, a few floor lamps, and reading lamps on the tables. At the back of the room was a black grand piano. I'd never seen a Steinway concert grand piano in a room like this, one that made it seem smaller than it was. On top of the piano was a metronome and sheet music.

Perhaps Menshiki played. Or maybe he invited Maurizio Pollini over for dinner every once in a while.

Overall, though, the room was modestly decorated, and I felt relieved. There was nothing excessive, but it didn't have an *empty* feeling. A comfortable room, despite the size. There was a certain sense of warmth about it, you might say. Half a dozen tasteful paintings graced the walls, all modestly displayed. One of them looked like a real Léger, but I could have been mistaken.

Menshiki motioned me to a large brown leather sofa. He sat on a matching easy chair across from me. The sofa was extremely comfortable, neither too hard nor too soft. The kind of sofa that naturally adjusted to whoever sat on it. Of course if you think about it (not that it was something one had to think about), Menshiki wasn't about to put an uncomfortable sofa in his living room.

As if he'd been waiting for us to get settled, as soon as we did, a man glided in from somewhere. A stunningly handsome young man. He wasn't so tall, but was slim and had a refined bearing about him. His skin was evenly tanned, with lustrous hair done up in a ponytail. He would look good at the beach, in surfing shorts, carrying a shortboard, though today he was dressed in a clean white shirt and black bow tie. A pleasant smile played about his lips.

"Would you care for a cocktail?" he asked me. "Please order whatever you'd like."

"I'll have a Balalaika," I said, after considering it for a few seconds. Not that I really wanted a Balalaika, but I wanted to test the young bartender to see if he really could make any kind of drink.

"I'll have the same," Menshiki said.

The young man smiled pleasantly and soundlessly withdrew.

I glanced at the spot next to me on the sofa but didn't see the Commendatore. But he had to be here somewhere in the house. He'd ridden with me in the car up to the house, and had come along with me.

"Is something the matter?" Menshiki asked me. He'd followed my glance.

"No, just admiring your gorgeous house."

"It's a little too much, don't you think?" Menshiki said, a smile rising to his face.

"No, it's much more serene than I imagined," I answered honestly. "From a distance it does look a bit luxurious. Like a luxury cruise ship on the ocean. But inside it's surprisingly relaxed. My impression's completely changed."

Menshiki listened and nodded. "I'm happy to hear that, but it took quite a lot of work to get it to that point. I bought the house already built, and when I purchased it, it was pretty gaudy. Flashy, you might say. A man who ran a big-box store built it. The extremes of bad taste of the nouveau riche, you could say, and not my style at all. So I did a huge renovation after I bought it. Which took a lot of time, effort, and money."

As if remembering all that work, Menshiki looked down and sighed. It really must not have suited his taste at all.

"Wouldn't it have been a lot cheaper to build your own house?" I asked.

Menshiki smiled, his white teeth peeking from between his lips. "You're absolutely right. That would have been the sensible thing to do. But I had my own reasons. Reasons why it had to be this house and no other."

I waited for the story to go on, but it didn't.

"Wasn't the Commendatore supposed to be with you tonight?" Menshiki asked.

"I think he'll be along later," I said. "We were together on the trip up to your house and then he suddenly vanished. I think he must be taking a tour of your house. You don't mind, do you?"

Menshiki spread his hands wide. "Of course. Of course I don't mind. He's welcome to look around as much as he likes."

The young man from before appeared, carrying two cocktails on a silver tray. The cocktail glasses were exquisitely cut crystal. Baccarat, would be my guess. They glittered in the light from the floor lamp. Next to them was a Koimari ceramic plate with slices of various cheeses and cashews. There were small monogrammed linen napkins and a set of silver knives and forks. Everything well thought out.

Menshiki and I picked up our cocktail glasses and made a toast. He toasted the completion of his portrait, and I thanked him. We lightly put our lips to the rim of the glasses. A Balalaika is made of one part each of vodka, Cointreau, and lemon juice. A simple concoction, but unless it's as bitingly freezing as the North Pole, it doesn't taste good. If somebody who doesn't have the right touch mixes it, it ends up tasting diluted, watery. This Balalaika was amazingly delicious, with an almost perfect bite to it.

"This is delicious," I said, impressed.

"He's quite good," Menshiki said lightly.

Of course he is, I thought. Menshiki wasn't about to hire a bad bartender. And of course he had Cointreau on hand, antique crystal glasses, and a Koimari serving plate.

As we sipped our cocktails and munched on some nuts, we talked about various topics. Mainly about my painting. He asked what I was working on now and I explained. I told him I was working on a portrait of a man whose name and background I knew nothing about, someone I had encountered in a distant town.

"A portrait?" Menshiki asked, sounding surprised.

"A portrait, but not a typical commercial portrait. More of an abstract-style portrait, one in which I let my imagination run free. But the motif is definitely a portrait. You might say it's the foundation of the painting."

"Like when you painted my portrait?"

"Exactly. Though this time I wasn't commissioned. It's something I decided to paint on my own."

Menshiki considered this. "Maybe my portrait inspired you to be more creative?"

"No doubt. Though I'm only at the point where my creativity is finally starting to kick in."

Menshiki took another soundless sip of his cocktail, with what I took to be a satisfied gleam deep in his eyes.

"Nothing could make me happier," he said. "The fact that I may have been of help to you, that is. If you don't mind, could I see that new painting when it's finished?"

"I'd be happy to show it to you, provided I'm happy with the result."

I looked over at the grand piano in a corner of the room. "Do you play piano, Mr. Menshiki? That's a beautiful instrument."

Menshiki nodded slightly. "I'm not good, but I do play a little. I took piano lessons as a child. Five or six years from the time I entered elementary school until I graduated. Then I got busy with schoolwork and quit taking lessons. I wish I hadn't, but the piano lessons had worn me out. So my fingers don't move the way I'd like them to, but I'm good at reading sheet music. I play some simple pieces every once in a while just for my own amusement, for a change of pace. I'm not good enough to play for other people, and I never touch the keys when other people are here."

I went ahead and asked a question I'd been wanting to ask for a long time. "Doesn't it feel a little too spacious for you, living in such a big house all by yourself?"

"No, I don't think so," Menshiki replied immediately. "Not at all. I've always preferred being by myself. Consider the cerebral cortex for a moment. Humans are provided with a wonderfully precise and efficient cerebral cortex. But normally we use, at most, less than ten percent of it. We've been divinely provided with this amazing, highly efficient organ, but sadly we haven't the ability to use it completely. You could compare it to a four-person family living in a magnificent, grand mansion but using only one small room. All the other rooms are unused and neglected. When you think that way, it's not so unnatural that I live in this house by myself."

"When you put it that way, I suppose it makes sense," I said. It was an interesting analogy.

Menshiki rolled a few cashews around in his hand for a moment and then spoke. "That highly efficient cerebral cortex might seem wasted at first, but without it we wouldn't be able to think abstract thoughts, or enter the realm of the metaphysical. Even though we use but a small part of it, the cerebral cortex has that capacity. If we could use all the rest of it, what would we be capable of, I wonder. Isn't it fascinating to consider?"

"But in exchange for that efficient brain—the price we paid for that magnificent mansion, in other words—mankind had to neglect all kinds of basic abilities. Right?"

"Exactly," Menshiki said. "Even without abstract thought or metaphysical theorizing, just standing on two legs and using clubs gave mankind more than enough skill to win the race for survival on earth. These other abilities aren't that necessary. And in exchange for our hyper-capable cerebral cortexes, of necessity we have to give up lots of other physical abilities. For example, dogs have a sense of smell several thousand times better than humans, and a sense of hearing tens of times better. But we're able to amass complex hypotheses. We're able to compare and contrast the cosmos and the microcosmos, and appreciate Van Gogh and Mozart. We can read Proust—if you want to, that is—and collect Koimari porcelain and Persian rugs. Not something a dog can do."

"Marcel Proust used a sense of smell inferior to that of a dog's to write his lengthy novel."

Menshiki laughed. "That he did. I'm just speaking in generalities."

"The question then is whether or not an idea can be treated as an autonomous entity or not, right?"

"Exactly."

Exactly, the Commendatore whispered into my ear. But following his earlier warning, I didn't look around me.

After this, Menshiki led me into his study. There were broad stairs that led out of the living room, and we took them to the floor below. Somehow these stairs seemed more than stairs, and part of the habitable space in the house. We went down the hallway past several bedrooms (I didn't count how many, but maybe one of them was the locked "Bluebeard's secret room" my girlfriend spoke of), and at the end was the study. It wasn't an especially big room, but of course, it wasn't cramped either. Built to be just the right amount of space. There were few windows in the study, just long, narrow windows like skylights near the ceiling on one wall. All that was visible from the windows were pine branches and the sky visible through the branches. (The room didn't seem to particularly require sunlight or a view.) Without many windows, the walls were that much bigger. One wall was floor-to-ceiling built-in bookcases, one section of which was for a shelf for CDs. The bookshelves were packed with books of all sizes. There was a wooden stepladder to reach the books on the upper shelves. All the books seemed to have been used at one time or another. It was clear that this was a practical collection used by a devoted reader, not decorative bookshelves.

A large office desk faced away from one wall, with two computers on top, a desktop model and a laptop. There were a couple of cups holding pens and pencils, and a neat pile of paperwork. On another wall was a beautiful, expensive-looking stereo set, and on the opposite wall, facing directly across from the desk, sat a pair of tall, narrow speakers. They were about my height (five feet eight), the cases made of high-quality mahogany. An Art Deco armchair for reading and listening to music was in the middle of the room, and next to it a stainless-steel standing lamp for reading. I imagined that Menshiki spent a large part of his days alone in this room.

My portrait of Menshiki was hanging on the wall, at about eye level, exactly between the two speakers. Bare, not yet framed. It looked like a natural part of the room, as if it had been hanging there for a long time. A painting I'd basically created in one intense sitting, yet in this study that uninhibited aspect of it felt, strangely enough, neatly contained. The unique feeling of the place comfortably stilled the painting's plunge-ahead vigor. And unmistakably concealed within that painting was Menshiki's face. To me, in fact, it looked like Menshiki himself was contained within.

I had most definitely painted that painting, but once it had left my hands and become Menshiki's possession, hanging on his study wall, it had transformed into something beyond my reach. Now it was *Menshiki's painting*, not mine. Even if I tried to comprehend something within it, like a slippery, nimble fish the painting would slip out of my hands. Like a woman who'd once been mine but was now someone else's.

"What do you think? Doesn't it fit this room perfectly?"

Menshiki was referring to the painting, of course. I nodded without a word.

"I tried putting it in lots of different rooms. But in the end I knew this was the best room and the perfect spot for it. The amount of space, the way the light hits it, the whole atmosphere is perfect. What I enjoy most is gazing at the picture from that reading chair."

"Could I give it a try?" I said, pointing to the reading chair.

"Of course. Go right ahead."

I sat down on that leather chair, leaned back into the gentle curve it inscribed, and rested my legs on the ottoman. I brought my hands together on my chest and once more gazed at the painting. As Menshiki said, this was the ideal spot from which to appreciate it. Seen from that chair (a chair so comfortable it left nothing to be desired), my painting hanging on the wall in front of me had a quiet, calm persuasiveness that took me by surprise. It looked like almost a completely different work from when it was in my studio, as if it had acquired, since coming here, its rightful life force. Or something like that. And at the same time it seemed to have severed any contact with me, its creator.

Menshiki used a remote control to turn on some music at just the right low volume. A Schubert string quartet I was familiar with. Composition D804. The sound coming out of those speakers was clear, fine-grained, refined, and elegant. Compared with the sound from the speakers in Tomohiko Amada's home, which had a simpler, unadorned tone, it seemed like different music altogether.

Suddenly the Commendatore was in the room. He was seated on the stepladder in front of the bookshelves, his arms folded, looking at my painting. When I glanced at him he shook his head slightly, signaling that I shouldn't look at him. I returned my gaze to the painting.

"Thank you very much," I said to Menshiki as I rose from the chair. "That's the perfect place to hang it."

Menshiki beamed and shook his head. "No, I should be the one thanking *you*. Now that it's found a home here, I'm liking it more and more. When I look at it, I feel like I'm standing in front of . . . a special mirror. I'm inside there, but that's not me, entirely. It's a little different me. When I stare at it for a while, a strange feeling comes over me."

As he listened to the Schubert, Menshiki again turned his attention to a silent appraisal of the painting. The Commendatore, still seated on the stepladder, likewise gazed at the painting with narrowed eyes, as if teasingly imitating him (though I doubt that was his intention).

Menshiki glanced over at the clock on the wall. "Let's go to the dining room. Dinner should be just about ready. I do hope the Commendatore shows up."

I looked at the stepladder. The Commendatore was no longer there.

"I think he's already here," I said.

"I'm glad," Menshiki said, sounding relieved. He touched the remote control and stopped the Schubert. "There's a place prepared for him, of course. It's really a shame, though, that he won't be able to enjoy eating the meal."

Menshiki explained that on the floor below where we were currently seated, there was a storehouse, a laundry room, and a gym. The gym was outfitted with all sorts of workout equipment. It had a sound system so he could enjoy music while he exercised. Once a week a trainer came and led him through strength-training exercises. There was also an efficiency-sized residence for a live-in maid. It had a simple kitchen and small bathroom, though nobody was using it at present. There used to be a small indoor pool, but it wasn't very practical and took a lot of upkeep, so he had had it filled in and made into a greenhouse. Someday he might build a two-lane twenty-five-meter lap pool, he said. If I do, he said, I'd love for you to come over and swim. That would be wonderful, I said.

We headed to the dining room.

24

MERELY GATHERING RAW DATA

The dining room was on the same floor as the study. The kitchen was in back of it. The dining room was a long room, with a large, long table in the middle. The oak table was about four inches thick, and big enough for ten people. A solid table that would look good hosting a banquet for Robin Hood and his men. But it was simply the two of us, Menshiki and myself, not a merry band of outlaws. A place was set for the Commendatore, but he wasn't there. A place mat, silverware, and an empty glass were ready for him, but they were just for show. A courtesy to indicate that was his place.

Like in the living room, one long wall was entirely glass. It looked out over the mountain range beyond the valley. Just as I could see Menshiki's house from mine, my house should be visible from his. The house I lived in, though, was nowhere as big as Menshiki's mansion, and it was a wooden building whose subdued color didn't stand out, so in the dark I couldn't make out where it was. There weren't many homes built here, but in each of the houses that dotted the mountains there were clearly lights on inside. It was dinnertime. People were with their families at the dinner table, about to enjoy a hot meal. I could sense that slight warmth in those lights.

In contrast, on the other side of the valley, Menshiki, I, and the Commendatore were seated at that large table, about to begin an eccentric, formal dinner party. Outside a fine rain continued to silently fall. But there was almost no wind, and it was a typically hushed autumn night. I looked out the window and thought again about the hole. About the lonely stone-lined chamber behind the little shrine. Even as we sat here the hole was there, dark and dank. Memories of that scene brought a special chill to me, deep inside.

"I found this table while traveling in Italy," Menshiki said after I'd complimented it. He didn't sound like he was bragging, simply stating facts. "I ran across it in a furniture store in Lucca, purchased it, and had it shipped here. It's so heavy it was quite a task to transport it."

"Do you go abroad very often?"

His lips twisted up a bit, then relaxed. "I used to. Part business, part pleasure. Not so many opportunities to do so these days. I'm doing a different sort of work now. Plus I no longer like to go out much anymore. Most of the time I'm here."

To indicate more clearly what he meant by "here," he motioned toward the house with his hand. I expected him to add more about this change in his work, but that's all he said. As always, he didn't seem eager to say much about his work, and I didn't press him about it.

"I thought we'd start with some well-chilled champagne, if that's all right with you. You don't mind?"

"Of course not," I said. "I'll leave it all up to you."

Menshiki made a faint motion, and the ponytailed young man came over and poured cold champagne into long narrow flutes. Pleasant little bubbles fizzed up in the glasses, so light and thin they seemed made of high-quality paper. We toasted each other across the table. Then Menshiki respectfully lifted his glass to the unoccupied seat for the Commendatore.

"Thank you so much for coming, Commendatore," he said.

There was, naturally, no reply from the Commendatore.

As he enjoyed the champagne, Menshiki talked about opera. About how, on a trip to Sicily, he saw a spectacular performance of Verdi's *Ernani* at the Catania opera house. The person seated next to him sang along with the performers, all the while snacking on mandarin oranges. And how he'd had some amazing champagne there.

The Commendatore finally made an appearance in the dining room, though not at the seat at the table prepared for him. Given his short stature, he would have only come up to nose level, hidden by the table. Instead he plunked himself down on a kind of display shelf diagonally behind Menshiki. He was about five feet off the floor, lightly swinging his feet clad in those oddly shaped black shoes. I raised my glass slightly to him so that Menshiki wouldn't see. As expected, the Commendatore acted as if he didn't notice.

The meal was served at this point. There was an open serving slot between the kitchen and the dining room and the bow-tied, ponytailed young man brought each dish placed there one by one to our table. For a first course, we had a beautiful dish of organic vegetables and fresh isaki fish. Accompanied by white wine. The ponytailed young man uncorked the bottle as carefully as if he were an explosives expert handling a land mine. No explanation of what kind of wine it was or where it was from, though of course it was superb. Menshiki wasn't about to serve a less-than-perfect wine.

After that we were served a salad of lotus root, calamari, and white beans. Then a sea turtle soup. The fish dish was monkfish.

"It's a bit early in the season for it, but I heard that down at the harbor they got hold of some excellent monkfish," Menshiki said. The fish was certainly fresh and amazing. Firm texture, a refined sweetness, but still a clean aftertaste. Lightly steamed, then served with (what I took to be) a tarragon sauce.

Next came thick venison steaks. There was again an explanation of the special sauce, but it was so full of specialized terms I couldn't remember half of it. At any rate, a wonderfully fragrant sauce.

The ponytailed young man poured red wine into our glasses. Menshiki explained that the bottle had been opened an hour before and decanted.

"It's breathed nicely, and it should be just the peak time to drink it."

I knew nothing about aerating wine, but it had a deep flavor. When your tongue first encountered it, then when you held it in your mouth, and finally when you drank it down, the flavor was different each time. It was like a mysterious woman whose beauty changes slightly depending on the angle and light. The wine left a pleasant aftertaste.

"It's Bordeaux," Menshiki said. "I won't sing its praises. Just know it's a Bordeaux."

"It's the kind of wine that once you started listing its good points, you'd have a long list."

Menshiki smiled. Pleasant wrinkles formed at the corners of his eyes.

"You're exactly right. It would be very long if you listed its merits. But I don't particularly like to do that with wines. I'm not good at enumerating the merits of things, no matter what they are. It's just a delicious wine—that's enough, right?"

I had no objections to that.

All this time the Commendatore watched us drinking and eating from his perch on the display shelf. He sat there, unmoving, diligently observing the scene there down to the smallest detail, but didn't seem to have any reaction to what he was seeing. Like he told me once, he merely observes. He doesn't judge, or have any partiality toward it. He's merely gathering raw data.

This might be how he observed me and my girlfriend making love in bed in the afternoons. The thought unsettled me. He'd told me that watching people have sex was for him no different from watching morning radio exercise routines or someone sweeping a chimney. And that might very well be the case. But the fact remained that it was disconcerting to think of being observed.

An hour and a half later, Menshiki and I finally arrived at dessert (a soufflé) and espresso. A long but fulfilling journey. For the first time, the chef came out of the kitchen and over to the dining table. A tall man, in a white chef's outfit. In his mid-thirties would be my guess, with a sparse black beard. He greeted me politely.

"The food was amazing," I told him. "I've hardly ever had anything so delicious."

Those were my honest feelings. I still couldn't believe that a chef who made such exquisite dishes ran a small, unknown French restaurant near the harbor in Odawara.

"Thank you very much," he said, smiling brightly. "Mr. Menshiki's always been very kind to me."

He bowed and returned to the kitchen.

"I wonder if the Commendatore was satisfied, too?" Menshiki said after the chef had left, a concerned look on his face. He didn't appear to be playacting. He seemed genuinely concerned.

"I'm sure he is," I replied with a straight face. "It's a shame, of course, that he couldn't enjoy the fabulous meal, but he must have enjoyed the atmosphere."

"I do hope so."

Of course I enjoyed it, the Commendatore whispered in my ear.

Menshiki suggested an after-dinner drink, but I declined. I was so full I really couldn't manage anything else. He had a brandy.

"There was something that I wanted to ask you," Menshiki said as he slowly swirled the brandy in the oversized glass. "It's an odd question, and I hope you're not offended."

"Feel free to ask me anything."

He took a small sip of brandy, tasting it. Then quietly laid his glass on the table.

"It's about the pit in the woods," Menshiki said. "The other day I spent about an hour in that stone chamber. No flashlight, seated alone at the bottom of the pit. The cover was on top, and rocks on top of that to hold it down. And I told you, 'Please come back in an hour and get me out of here.' Correct?"

"That's right."

"Why do you think I did that?"

"I have no idea," I answered honestly.

"I needed to do that," Menshiki said. "I can't explain it, but sometimes I need to do *that*. Be left all alone in a cramped, dark, completely silent space."

I was silent, waiting for his next words.

Menshiki continued. "Here's my question to you. During that hour did you ever find yourself, even for a moment, wanting to abandon me in that pit? Tempted to just leave me behind at the bottom of that dark hole?"

I couldn't grasp what he was getting at. "*Abandon* you?"

Menshiki touched his right temple and rubbed it, as if checking out a scar. "This is what I mean. I was at the bottom of that pit, a little less than nine feet deep and six feet across. The ladder had been pulled up. The stones in the wall were all densely laid together, and there was no way to climb up. And the cover was on tight. In mountains like these I could yell at the top of my voice or ring the bell, but no one would ever hear me—though of course *you* might. In other words, I couldn't get back to the surface on my own. If you hadn't come back, I'd have had to stay in the pit forever. Isn't that so?"

"That could be."

The fingers of his right hand were still at his temple. He'd stopped rubbing. "What I'd like to know is whether during that hour the thought ever occurred to you, even for a moment, *I'll just leave that man inside the pit. Leave him the way he is*. Tell me the truth, it won't offend me."

He took his fingers from his temple, reached for the glass of brandy, and again slowly held it up and swirled it. This time, though, he didn't take a sip. Eyes narrowed, he inhaled the aroma and put the glass back on the table.

"That thought never occurred to me," I answered honestly. "*Even for a moment.* All I thought about was that after an hour I had to take the cover off and get you out of there."

"Really?"

"One hundred percent."

"Well, if I had been in your position . . ." Menshiki said, sounding confessional. His voice was quite calm. "I'm sure I would have thought of that. I definitely would have been tempted to leave you inside that pit forever. I would have thought, This is the chance of a lifetime."

No words came to me.

Menshiki said, "Down at the bottom of the pit that's what I was thinking about the whole time. That if I was in your position I would definitely consider it. It's a strange thing. You were the one on the surface and I was the one at the bottom of the pit, but all that time I was picturing me on the surface and you at the bottom."

"But if you'd actually abandoned me in the pit I might have starved to death. I might have turned into an actual mummy, ringing a bell. You're saying you'd be okay with that?"

"It's just a fantasy. Or delusion, perhaps. *Of course* I would never actually do that. I was just imagining the scenario. Just mentally playing with the concept of death. So don't worry. What I mean is, I find it hard to fathom that you didn't feel the same temptation."

I said, "Weren't you afraid, Mr. Menshiki, being down at the bottom of that dark pit all alone? Thinking that I might be tempted to abandon you there?"

Menshiki shook his head. "No, I wasn't afraid. Deep inside me I may have actually been hoping you would."

"*Hoping* I would?" I said, surprised. "That I would leave you down in that pit?"

"Exactly."

"In other words, you were okay with being abandoned down there?"

"Don't get me wrong, it wasn't that I was okay with dying. Even I still have some attachment to this life. And starving to death or dying of lack of water aren't the ways I'd like to go. All I wanted was to *try to get closer to death,* even if just a little more. I know that boundary is a very fine line."

I thought about what he said, though I still couldn't grasp what he meant. I casually glanced over at the Commendatore, still seated on the display shelf. His face was bereft of expression.

Menshiki went on. "When you're locked up alone in a cramped, dark place, the most frightening thing isn't death. The most terrifying thought is that *I might have to live here forever.* Once you think that, the terror makes it hard to breathe. The walls close in on you and the delusion grabs you that you're going to be crushed. In order to survive, a person has to overcome that fear. Which means conquering yourself. And in order to do that, you need to get as close to death as you possibly can."

"But there's a danger to that."

"Like when Icarus flew close to the sun. It's not easy to know how close you can go, where that line is. You put your life at risk doing it."

"But if you avoid approaching it, you can't overcome fear and conquer yourself."

"Precisely. If you can't do that, you can't take yourself to the next level," Menshiki said. He seemed to be considering something. And then suddenly—at least it seemed sudden to me—he stood up, went over to the window, and looked out.

"It's still raining a little, but not so hard. Do you mind going out on the deck? There's something I want to show you."

We walked up the steps from the dining room to the living room and then out to the deck. It was a large deck, with a Mediterranean tiled floor. We went over to the wooden railing and gazed out at the valley. It was like a tourist lookout, and we were afforded a view of the entire valley. A fine rain was still falling, more like mist at this point. The lights were still on in people's homes across the valley. It was the same valley, but viewed from the opposite side like this, the scenery looked transformed.

A section of the deck was roofed over, with a chaise longue beneath it, for sunbathing or perhaps reading. Next to it was a low glass-topped table to put drinks or books on. And also a large planter with a decorative green plant, and a tall piece of equipment of some kind, covered in plastic. There was a spotlight on the wall, but it wasn't turned on. The lights in the living room were turned down low.

"I wonder which direction my house is?" I asked Menshiki.

Menshiki pointed to the right. "It's over there."

I stared hard in that direction, but with the lights out and the misty rain I couldn't locate it.

"I can't see it," I told him.

"Just a moment," Menshiki said, and walked over to where the chaise longue was. He removed the plastic cover from the piece of equipment and carried it over. It looked like a pair of binoculars on a tripod. The binoculars weren't big, but looked odd, different from normal ones. They were a drab olive green and the crude shape made it appear like some optical instrument for surveying. He placed this beside the railing, pointed it, and carefully focused.

"Here, take a look. This is where you live," he said.

I squinted through the binoculars. They had a clear field of vision, with high magnification. Not your typical binoculars that you find in a store. Through the faint vale of misty rain the far-off scenery looked close enough to touch. And it definitely was the house I was living in. The terrace was there, the lounge chair I always sat in. Beyond that was the living room, and next to it, my painting studio. With the lights off I couldn't make out the interior, though during the day you probably could. It felt strange to see (or peek into) the place where I lived.

"Don't worry," Menshiki said from behind me, as if reading my mind. "No need to be concerned. I don't encroach on your privacy. I mean, I hardly ever turn these binoculars on your house. Trust me. What I want to see is *something else*."

"What do you want to see?" I said. I took my eye from the binoculars, turned around, and looked at him. His face was cool, inscrutable as always. At night on the deck, though, his hair looked whiter than ever.

"I'll show you," Menshiki said. With a practiced hand he swung the binoculars slightly to the north and swiftly refocused. He took a step back and said, "Please take a look."

I looked through the binoculars. In the circular field of vision I saw an elegant wooden house halfway up the mountain. A two-story building also constructed to take advantage of the slope, with a terrace facing this direction. On a map it would be my nearest neighbor, but because of the topography there was no road linking us, so one would have to go down to the bottom of the mountain and ascend once more on a separate road to access it. Lights were on in the windows, but the curtains were drawn, and I couldn't see inside. If the curtains were open, though, and the lights on, you would be able to see the people inside. Very possible with binoculars this powerful.

"These are NATO-issue military binoculars. They're not sold anywhere, so it wasn't easy to get hold of them. They're bright, so you can make out images well even in the dark."

I took my eyes away from the binoculars and looked at Menshiki. "This house is *what you want to see*?"

"Correct. But don't get the wrong idea. I'm no voyeur."

He glanced through the binoculars one last time, then put them and the tripod back where they were and placed the plastic cover over them.

"Let's go inside. We don't want to catch cold," Menshiki said. We went back into the living room, and sat on the sofa and armchair. The ponytailed young man sidled over and asked if we'd like anything to drink, but both of us declined.

"Thank you very much for tonight," Menshiki said to the young man. "Feel free to go now." The young man bowed and withdrew.

The Commendatore was now seated on top of the piano. The black Steinway full grand. He looked like he preferred this spot to where he had been sitting before. The jewels on the top handle of his long sword caught the light with a proud glint.

"In that house over there," Menshiki began, "lives the girl who *may be my daughter*. I like to see her, even if it's from a distance."

For quite some time I was speechless.

"Do you remember? What I told you about the daughter my former girlfriend had, after she married another man? That she might be mine?"

"Of course. The woman who was stung by hornets and died. Her daughter would be thirteen. Right?"

Menshiki gave a short, concise nod. "She lives in *that house* with her father. In that house across the valley."

It took a while to put the myriad questions that welled up in my mind in some kind of order. Menshiki waited silently all this time, patiently waiting for my reaction.

I said, "In other words, in order to see that young girl who might be your daughter through the binoculars every day, you bought this mansion directly across the valley. You paid a lot of money and a great deal to renovate this house *for that sole purpose*. Is that what you're saying?"

Menshiki said, "Yes, that's it. This is the ideal spot to be able to observe her house. I had to get this mansion no matter what. There was no other lot around here that I could get a building permit for. And ever since, I've been looking for her across the valley through my binoculars, almost every day. Though I should say that the days I can't see her far outnumber the days I can."

"So you live alone, keeping people out as much as you can, so no one interferes with that pursuit."

Menshiki nodded again. "That's right. I don't want anyone to bother me. No one to disturb things. That's what I'm looking for. I need unlimited solitude. You're the only other person in the world who knows this secret. It wouldn't be good to confess this kind of delicate thing to people."

You got that right, I thought. And this thought occurred to me as well: Then why did you just tell *me*?

"Then why did you just tell me?" I asked Menshiki. "Is there some special reason?"

Menshiki recrossed his legs and looked straight at me. His voice was soft. "Yes, of course there's a reason. I have a special favor to ask of you."

25

HOW MUCH LONELINESS THE TRUTH CAN CAUSE

"I have a special favor to ask of you," Menshiki said.

From his tone I guessed he'd been waiting for the right moment to bring this up. And that this was the real reason he had invited me (and the Commendatore) to dinner. In order to reveal his secret and bring up this request.

"If it's something I can help with, of course," I said.

Menshiki gazed into my eyes, and then spoke. "More than something you can help with, it's something only *you* can help with."

I was suddenly dying for a cigarette. When I got married I used that as the incentive to stop smoking, and in the nearly seven years since, I hadn't smoked a single cigarette. It was tough quitting—I'd been a pretty heavy smoker—but nowadays I never had the urge. But at that instant, for the first time in forever, I thought about how great it would be to have a cigarette between my lips and light it. I could hear the scratch of the match.

"What could that possibly be?" I asked. Not that I particularly wanted to know—I'd prefer to get by not knowing—but the way the conversation was going, I had to ask.

"Well, I'd like you to paint her portrait," Menshiki said.

In my head I had to dismantle the context of his words, then reassemble it all. Though it was a very simple context.

"You mean you want me to paint the portrait of this girl who *may be* your daughter."

Menshiki nodded. "Exactly. That's what I want you to do. And not from a photograph, but actually have her pose for you and paint the picture with her as the model. Have her come to your studio, like when you painted me. That's my only condition. How you paint her is up to you—do it any way you want. I promise I won't have any other requests later on."

I was at a loss for words. Several questions immediately occurred to me, and I asked the first one that came to mind. "But how can I convince the girl to do that? I might be her neighbor, but I can't very well just suggest to a young girl I don't know that *I want to paint your portrait, so would you model for me?*"

"No, of course not. That would make her suspicious for sure."

"Then do you have any good ideas?"

Menshiki looked at me for a time, then, like quietly opening a door and tiptoeing into a back room of a house, he slowly opened his mouth. "Actually, you already know her. And she knows you very well."

"I already know her?"

"You do. Her name is Mariye—Mariye Akikawa. *Aki*—the character for 'autumn'—and *kawa*, 'river.' *Mariye* is spelled out in hiragana. You do know her, right?"

Mariye Akikawa. I'd heard the name before, but it felt like some temporary obstruction was keeping me from putting name and face together. Finally the pieces fell into place.

I said, "Mariye Akikawa is in my children's art class in Odawara, isn't she?"

Menshiki nodded. "That's right. Exactly. You're her painting teacher."

Mariye Akikawa was a small, quiet thirteen-year-old girl in the children's art class I taught. The class was for elementary school children, and as a junior high student, she was the eldest, but she was so reserved she didn't stand out at all, even though she was with the younger children. She always sat in a corner, trying to stay under the radar. I remembered her because something about her reminded me of my late sister, and she was about the same age as my sister when she passed away.

Mariye Akikawa hardly ever spoke in class. If I said something to her she just nodded, with barely a word in response. When she absolutely had to say something, she spoke it in such a small voice I often had to ask her to repeat herself. She seemed tense, unable to look me straight in the eye. But she loved painting, and the expression in her eyes radically transformed whenever she held a brush and was working on a canvas. Her gaze became focused, her eyes filled with an intense gleam. And her paintings were quite appealing. Not skilled, exactly, but eye-catching. Her use of colors was especially unique. All in all, a curious sort of girl.

Her glossy black hair fell straight down, her features as lovely as a doll's. So beautiful, in fact, when you looked at her whole face, there was the sense of it being detached from reality. Her features were objectively attractive, but most people would hesitate to label her beautiful. Something—perhaps that special raw, unpolished aspect that certain young girls exude in adolescence—interfered with the flow of beauty that should have been there. But someday that blockage might be removed and she would turn into a truly lovely girl. That was still a ways off, though. Now that I thought of it, my sister's features were similar in that way. I often used to think she didn't appear as beautiful as I knew she could be.

"So Mariye Akikawa *might* be your real daughter. And she lives in the house across the valley," I said. "And I'm to paint a portrait with her as model. That's what you're asking?"

"I'd prefer to see it as a *request,* rather than that I'm *commissioning* the work. And if you're okay with it, once the painting is finished I'd like to buy it and hang it on the wall in this house. That's what I want. Or rather what I'm requesting."

Still, there was something about all this I couldn't quite swallow. I had a faint apprehension that things wouldn't simply end there.

"And that's it? That's all you want?" I asked.

Menshiki slowly inhaled and breathed out. "Honestly, there's one other thing I'd like you to do."

"Which is—?"

"A very small thing." His voice was quiet, but with a certain force behind it. "When she's sitting for the portrait, I'd like to visit you. Make it seem like I just happened to stop by. Once is enough. And it can be for just a short time, I don't mind. Just let me be in the same room as her, and breathe the same air. I won't ask for anything more. And I can assure you I won't do anything to get in your way."

I thought about it. And the more I did, the more uncomfortable I felt.

I've never been cut out to act as an intermediary. I don't enjoy getting caught up in the flow of somebody else's strong emotions—no matter what emotions they might be. The role didn't suit me. But the fact was that I also wanted to do something for Menshiki. I had to think carefully about my reply.

"We can talk about that later on," I said. "The first thing is whether or not Mariye will agree to sit for the painting. That's the first step. She's a very quiet girl, like a bashful cat. She might not want to model. Or else her parents might not give permission. They don't really know my background, so they'll be pretty wary, I would imagine."

"I know Mr. Matsushima very well, the man who runs the arts-and-culture center," Menshiki said coolly. "And I'm also, coincidentally, an investor, a financial supporter of the school. I think if Mr. Matsushima puts in a good word, things will go smoothly. You're an upright person, an artist with a solid career, and if he recommends you, I think it will assuage any concerns that her parents might have."

He's already got it all mapped out, I thought. He's already anticipated what might happen, like the opening moves of a game of go. Nothing *coincidental* about it.

Menshiki went on. "Mariye Akikawa's unmarried aunt takes care of her. Her father's younger sister. I believe I mentioned this before, but after Mariye's mother died, this aunt came to live with them and has been like a mother to Mariye. Her father is too busy with work to be very involved. So as long as the aunt is persuaded, things should work out fine. Once she agrees to have Mariye model, I would expect the aunt to accompany her to your house as her guardian. There's no way she'd allow a young girl to go by herself to the house of a man living alone."

"But will she really give permission for Mariye to model?"

"Let me handle that. As long as you agree to paint her portrait, I'll take care of any other practical issues that come up."

I had little doubt he'd be able to "take care of" any of these other "practical issues." That was his forte. But was it good for me to get so deeply involved in those problems—all these complex interpersonal relations? Didn't Menshiki have his own plans and intentions that went beyond what he was revealing to me?

"Can I be totally honest with you?" I said. "Maybe it isn't my place to say this, but I'd like you to hear me out."

"Of course. Say whatever you want."

"Isn't it better, before you put this plan into action, that you determine whether or not Mariye Akikawa really *is* your child? If you find out she isn't, then there's no need to go to all this trouble. It might not be easy, but there has to be a way. I think if anyone could discover that, you could. Even if I paint her portrait, and it's hanging next to yours, that's not going to solve anything."

Menshiki paused before replying. "If I wanted to scientifically determine if Mariye Akikawa is related by blood to me, I could. It might take some effort, but it's not impossible. The thing is—I don't want to."

"Why not?"

"Because whether she's my child or not isn't a determining factor."

I gazed at him, mouth shut. He shook his head, his abundant white hair waving, like it was fluttering in the breeze. When he spoke, his voice was calm, like he was explaining to some large, intelligent dog how to conjugate simple verbs.

"I'm not saying either way is fine. It's just that I don't feel like determining the facts. Maybe Mariye Akikawa is my biological child. And maybc she isn't. But what if I do determine that she's my real child—then what? I announce to her that I'm her real father? Try to get custody? I can't do that."

Menshiki shook his head again, rubbing his hands together on his lap like it was a cold night and he was warming himself before a fireplace. He continued.

"Mariye Akikawa is living a peaceful life in that house with her father and her aunt. Yes, her mother died, but the family—despite some issues her father has—is relatively healthy and functional. She's close to her aunt. She's made a life for herself. If I suddenly appear on the scene announcing that I'm her real father, even if I could prove it scientifically, will that solve anything? The truth will actually confuse things. And it's not going to make anyone happy. Including me."

"So you'd prefer to keep things the way they are, rather than let the truth come out."

Menshiki spread his hands on his lap. "In a word, yes. It took some time for me to arrive at that conclusion, but my feelings are firm. I plan to live the rest of my life holding on to the possibility that *Mariye Akikawa is my real child*. Watching, from a distance, as she grows up. That's enough. Even if I knew for sure she was my child, that wouldn't make me happy. The sense of loss would be all the more painful. And if I knew she *wasn't* my child, that would, in a different sense, also deepen the sense of loss. Or maybe crush me. Either way there's no happy result. Can you follow what I'm trying to say?"

"I think so. At least in theory. But if I were in your position, I'd want to know the truth. Theory aside, it's natural for people to want to know the truth."

Menshiki smiled. "You're still young, so that's why you say that. When you get to be my age, you'll understand how I feel. How much loneliness the truth can cause sometimes."

"So what you're after is not to know the unmitigated truth, but to hang her portrait on your wall, gaze at it every day, and ponder the possibilities. Are you sure that's enough?"

Menshiki nodded. "It is. Instead of a stable truth, I choose unstable possibilities. I choose to surrender myself to that instability. Do you think that's unnatural?"

I did indeed. Or at least I didn't see it as natural. I wouldn't go so far as to call it unhealthy, though. But that was Menshiki's problem, not mine.

I glanced over at the Commendatore seated on top of the Steinway. Our eyes met. He raised both index fingers upward and spread them apart, as if to say, *Let's put that answer on hold*. Then he pointed with his right index finger to a watch on his left wrist. Of course the Commendatore wasn't wearing a watch. He was just pointing to where one would be. And of course what that meant was, *We should be leaving soon*. The Commendatore's advice to me, as well as a warning. I decided to heed it.

"Could I have a little time to get back to you on this? It's a delicate matter, and I need time to consider it."

Menshiki held up his hands from his lap. "Of course. Consider it as long as you'd like. I'm not trying to rush you. I know I may be asking too much."

I stood up and thanked him for the dinner.

"Ah, there's one thing I forgot to tell you," Menshiki said, as if suddenly remembering. "It's about Tomohiko Amada. We talked earlier, didn't we, about how he'd studied abroad, in Austria? About how, just before World War Two broke out, he rushed back home?"

"Yes, I remember."

"I researched it a bit. I'm interested, too, in what was behind all that. It happened a long time ago, and I don't have all the facts, but there were rumors then of some sort of scandal."

"A scandal?"

"That's right. Amada was apparently caught up in an aborted assassination attempt in Vienna. It turned into a political crisis, and the Japanese embassy in Berlin got involved and secreted him back to Japan. According to certain rumors. This was right after the *Anschluss*. You know about the *Anschluss*, I assume?"

"That was when Germany annexed Austria in 1938."

"Correct. Hitler incorporated Austria into Germany. There was a lot of chaos, and the Nazis finally took over all of Austria pretty much by force, and the nation of Austria vanished. This was in March 1938. The place was in turmoil, and in the confusion of the moment a lot of people were murdered. Assassinated, or murdered and made to look like suicides. Or else sent to concentration camps. It was during this time that Tomohiko Amada studied in Vienna. Rumor had it that he fell in love with an Austrian woman and got mixed up with an underground resistance group comprised largely of college students, who plotted to assassinate a high-ranking Nazi official. Not the sort of thing either the German government or the Japanese government would condone, for they'd signed a mutual defense pact only a year and a half before this, and the relationship between the two countries was growing closer all the time. Both were dead set on avoiding anything that would hinder their pact. Though Tomohiko Amada was still young, he had already made a name for himself as an artist in Japan, and his father was a large landowner, a locally politically influential person. A person like that couldn't just be secretly blotted out."

"So Tomohiko Amada was sent back to Japan?"

"Correct. Rescued is more like it. Thanks to the political considerations of higher-ups, he narrowly escaped getting killed. If the Gestapo had gotten hold of him under suspicion of something that serious—even if they hadn't had any clear-cut evidence—that would have been the end of him."

"But the assassination didn't happen?"

"No, it was abortive. There was an informant in the group, and the plan was leaked to the Gestapo. There was a wholesale arrest of the members."

"There would have been a real uproar if they'd gone through with it."

"The strange thing is, there was no talk of it at the time," Menshiki said. "There were whispers about a scandal, but there doesn't seem to be any public record of it. For various reasons, it was covered up."

So the Commendatore in the painting *Killing Commendatore* might represent that Nazi official. The painting might be a hypothetical depiction of the assassination that never actually happened in Vienna in 1938. Amada and his lover were connected with this plot, and then it was discovered by the authorities. The two of them were torn apart, and the woman most likely killed. And after he returned to Japan Amada transferred that horrific experience in Vienna onto the very symbolic canvas of a Japanese-style painting. *Adapting* it, in other words, into a scene from the Asuka period, set over a thousand years ago. *Killing Commendatore* was a painting Tomohiko Amada painted for himself alone. He felt compelled for his own sake to paint it to preserve that awful, bloody memory from his youth. Which is precisely why he never made the painting public, why he wrapped it up tightly and hid it away in the attic.

Perhaps that incident in Vienna was one reason he made a clean break with his career as an artist of Western paintings and converted to Japanese-style painting. He might have wanted to decisively separate himself from the self he used to be.

"How did you find out about all this?" I asked.

"It didn't take a lot of effort on my part. I asked an organization run by an acquaintance to investigate it for me. But it happened such a long time ago, and they can't be held responsible for how much of it is really true. They did check with multiple sources, though, so I think the information can basically be trusted."

"Tomohiko Amada had an Austrian lover. She was a member of an underground resistance group. And he was involved in that assassination plot."

Menshiki inclined his head a bit and then spoke. "If that's true, then it's a pretty dramatic series of events. But most of the people involved are dead by now, so there's no way for us to really know what happened. Facts have a tendency to get embellished, too. At any rate, though, it's pretty melodramatic."

"No one knows how deeply he was involved in that plot?"

"No. We don't know. I've just given it my own dramatic touch. Amada was deported from Vienna, bid his lover farewell—or maybe wasn't even able to do that—was put on a ship in Bremen, and returned to Japan. During the war he remained silent, holed up in rural Aso, then debuted as a painter of Japanese-style paintings soon after the end of the war. Which took people by complete surprise. Another pretty dramatic development."

Thus ended the story of Tomohiko Amada.

The same black Infiniti I'd arrived in was quietly awaiting me in front of the house. A faint drizzle was still intermittently falling, the air wet and chilly. The season when you needed a coat was just around the corner.

"Thank you so much for coming," Menshiki said. "My thanks, too, to the Commendatore."

It is I *who should be doing the thanking*, the Commendatore murmured in my ear. His voice, of course, was only for me to hear. I thanked Menshiki once more for dinner. It was an amazing meal, I said. I couldn't be more satisfied. The Commendatore seemed grateful as well.

"I hope bringing up all of those boring details after dinner didn't spoil the evening," Menshiki said.

"Not at all. But about your request: I need some time to think about it."

"Of course."

"It takes me time to consider things."

"It's the same for me," Menshiki said. "My motto is: Thinking three times is better than two. And if time allows, thinking four times is better than three."

The driver had the rear door open, waiting. I got inside. The Commendatore should have boarded at the same time, though I didn't see him. The car started up the asphalt slope, drove out the open gate, then proceeded slowly down the mountain. Once the white mansion disappeared from view, everything that happened that night seemed like part of a dream. It was getting harder to distinguish what was normal from what was not, what was real and what was not.

What you can see is real, the Commendatore whispered in my ear. *What you need to do is open your eyes wide and look at it. You can judge it later on.*

Even with my eyes wide open, there could be many things I was overlooking, I thought. I may have actually murmured this aloud, since the chauffeur shot me a glance in the rearview mirror. I closed my eyes and leaned back against the seat. And thought this: How wonderful it would be to put off judging things forever.

I got home a little before ten p.m. I brushed my teeth in the bathroom, changed into pajamas, slid into bed, and fell right asleep. Predictably, I had a million dreams, all of them strange, disconcerting. Swastika flags flying over the streets of Vienna, a huge passenger ship easing out of Bremen harbor, a brass band playing on the pier, Bluebeard's unopened room, Menshiki playing the Steinway.

26

THE COMPOSITION COULDN'T BE IMPROVED

Two days later I got a call from my agent in Tokyo. They'd received the transfer of funds from Mr. Menshiki, the payment for the painting, and after taking the agent's fee out of it the rest had been deposited into my bank account. When I heard the total amount I was astonished. It was much higher than what I'd originally heard.

"The finished painting was better than he'd anticipated, so he added a bonus. There was a message from Mr. Menshiki requesting that you accept this as a token of his gratitude," my agent said.

I groaned faintly, but no words would come.

"I haven't seen the actual painting, though Mr. Menshiki attached a photo. From the photo, at least, it looks like an amazing work. Something that goes beyond the boundaries of portrait painting, yet remains a convincing portrait."

I thanked him and hung up.

A little while later my girlfriend called. Did I mind if she came over tomorrow morning? That would be fine, I told her. Friday was when I taught art class, but I'd have enough time to make it.

"Did you have dinner at Mr. Menshiki's place?" she asked.

"Yes, a really excellent meal."

"Did it taste good?"

"It was amazing. The wine was great, too, and the food was outstanding."

"What was the house like inside?"

"Beautiful," I said. "It'd take me half a day to describe it all."

"Could you tell me all about it when I see you?"

"Before? Or after?"

"After's good," she said simply.

After I hung up the phone, I went into the studio and looked at Tomohiko Amada's *Killing Commendatore*. I'd seen it so many times, but now, after what Menshiki told me, it took on a strangely graphic reality. This was not simply some historical picture of a past event, reproduced in an old-fashioned format. It felt—from the expressions and movements of each of the four characters (excluding Long Face)—like you could read their reactions to the situation. The young man piercing the Commendatore with his long sword was perfectly expressionless. He'd shut away his heart, hiding his emotions. In the Commendatore's face, one could read the agony as his chest was stabbed, but also a sense of pure surprise, the sense of *How could this possibly be happening?* The young woman watching this take place (in the opera, this character is Donna Anna) was torn apart by violently conflicting emotions. Her lovely face was contorted in anguish, her lovely white hand held to her mouth. The stocky man, a servant by the look of him (Leporello), was gasping for breath, gazing up at the sky. His hand was stretched out as if trying to reach something.

The organization was perfect. The composition couldn't be improved. It was a superb, polished arrangement. Each character maintained a vivid dynamism in their actions, instantaneously frozen in time. And now I saw the events of the aborted assassination that *may* have occurred in 1938 Vienna overlaying the painting. The Commendatore was dressed not in Asuka period costume but in a Nazi uniform. Maybe the black uniform of the SS. And in his chest was a saber or perhaps a dagger. *Perhaps* the one stabbing him was Tomohiko Amada himself. And who was the woman gasping nearby? Was this Amada's Austrian lover? And what was it that was rending her heart in two like that?

I sat on the stool, gazing for a long time at *Killing Commendatore*. My imagination could come up with all sorts of allegories and messages contained therein, but these were, in the final analysis, nothing more than unsubstantiated hypotheses. The background—what I took as background, that is—that Menshiki had talked about was not historical fact, but nothing more than rumor. Or else just a melodrama. Everything remained on the level of *perhaps*.

A thought suddenly struck me: I wish my sister were here.

If Komi were with me, I'd tell her everything that had happened, and she'd listen quietly, adding an occasional short question. Even with an incomprehensible, mixed-up story like this, I doubt she'd frown or show any surprise. Her calm, thoughtful expression wouldn't change. And after I finished, she'd pause, then give me some useful advice. Ever since we were little we'd had that kind of interaction. But I realized now she'd never come to *me* for advice. As far as I could recall, that had never happened. Why? Maybe she didn't have any major emotional issues? Or maybe she'd decided asking me for advice wasn't going to help? Maybe both, or half of each.

But even if she had been healthy and hadn't died at twelve, the intimate brother-sister relationship we had shared might not have lasted. Komi might have ended up marrying some boring guy, gone to live in a town far away, been run ragged by everyday life, exhausted by raising children, lost her sparkle, and no longer retained the energy to give me advice. No one could say how our lives would have worked out.

The problems my wife and I had had might have stemmed from me unconsciously wanting Yuzu to stand in for Komi. That was never my intention, of course, but now that I thought of it, ever since I lost my sister I may have been seeking, somewhere inside me, a substitute partner I could lean on whenever I was struggling. Needless to say, though, Yuzu wasn't Komi. Their positions, and roles, were vastly different. And so was the history we'd shared.

As I thought about this, I remembered the visit I'd made to Yuzu's parents' home in Kinuta in Setagaya in Tokyo, before we got married.

Yuzu's father was the branch manager of a large bank. His son—Yuzu's older brother—was also a banker, and worked for the same bank. Both were graduates of the elite economics department of Tokyo University. There seemed to be a lot of bankers in her family. I wanted to marry Yuzu (and of course she wanted to marry me, too), and the visit was for me to convey my intentions to her parents. Any way you looked at it, it was hard to call the half-hour interview I had with her father a friendly visit. I was an unknown artist who worked part-time painting portraits and didn't make what could be called a regular income. A guy with little in the way of future prospects. Not at all the sort of man a top banker like her father would view favorably. I'd anticipated this ahead of time and was dead set on not losing my cool no matter what he said, or how much criticism he heaped upon me. And I was basically the kind of person who could put up with a lot.

Yet as I listened to her father's long-winded sermon, a kind of physical revulsion welled up in me, and I lost it. I felt sick, like I was going to throw up. I stood up before he'd finished and said, I'm sorry, but I need to use the bathroom. I knelt down in front of the toilet bowl, trying to vomit up the contents of my stomach. But I couldn't vomit. Because there was hardly anything in my stomach. Even the gastric juices wouldn't come out. I took some deep breaths and calmed down. I gargled with water to get rid of the bad taste in my mouth, wiped the sweat from my face with a handkerchief, and went back to the living room.

"Are you all right?" Yuzu asked, looking concerned. I must have looked awful.

"A successful marriage is up to the people involved, but I can tell you, this one won't last long. Four, five years at the most." These were her father's parting words to me that day. (I didn't respond.) His spiteful words stayed with me, a kind of curse that remained for a long time to come.

Her parents never did agree to our marriage, but we went ahead and registered it, and officially became a married couple. By this time, I had very little contact with my own parents. Yuzu and I didn't have a wedding ceremony. Our friends rented a small place and held a simple party to celebrate, but that was it. (The person who did the most to make that happen was Masahiko, who was always good at taking care of others.) Despite the inauspicious beginning, we were happy. At least for the first few years, we were definitely happy together. For four or five years, we had no problems between us. But then, like a huge cruising ship in the middle of the ocean turning its rudder, there was a gradual change. I still don't know why. I can't even pinpoint when things began to move in a different direction. What she hoped for in marriage, and what I was looking for, must have been different, and that gap only grew more pronounced over time. And then, before I knew it, she was seeing another man. In the end our marriage only lasted some six years.

I imagine that when her father learned that our marriage had failed, he'd chuckled to himself and thought, I told you so. (Though we had stayed together a year or two beyond what he'd predicted.) It must have pleased him no end that Yuzu had left me. After we'd broken up, had Yuzu reconciled with her family? I had no way of knowing, and didn't really want to know, at that point. This was her business, not mine. But still her father's curse continued to hang over me. Even now, I sensed the vague weight of its presence. I'd been hurt, more than I cared to admit, and had bled. Like the pierced heart of the Commendatore in Tomohiko Amada's painting.

Late afternoon came on, and with it, the early-autumn twilight. The sky turned dark in the twinkling of an eye, the glossy black crows squawking their way across the valley, heading for their roosts. I went out on the terrace, leaned against the railing, and gazed over at Menshiki's house across the way. Several mercury lights were on in his garden, the whiteness of the house rising up in the dusk. I pictured Menshiki out there every night, searching through his high-powered binoculars for Mariye Akikawa. He'd purchased that white house, almost by force, for the sole purpose of doing that. Spent a huge amount of money, made a great deal of effort, all for an overly large house that didn't suit his tastes.

And strangely enough (at least to me it felt strange), I'd begun to feel a closeness to Menshiki, a closeness I'd never felt to anyone before. An affinity—no, a sense of solidarity, really. In a sense, we were very similar—that's what I thought. The two of us were motivated not by what we had got hold of, or were trying to get, but by what we'd lost, what we *did not now have*. I can't say I understood his actions. They were beyond my comprehension. But I could understand what had spurred him on.

I went to the kitchen, took the single malt that Masahiko had given me, and poured a glass on the rocks. I carried the drink out to the living room sofa and selected a record of a Schubert string quartet from

Tomohiko Amada's collection, and put it on the turntable. A piece titled "Rosamunde." The same music that had been playing in Menshiki's study. I listened to the music, occasionally clinking the ice in my glass.

The Commendatore never showed up that day. Maybe, like the horned owl, he was quietly resting up in the attic. Even Ideas needed some time off. I didn't do any painting that day, either. I needed some time off as well.

I raised my glass to the Commendatore.

27

EVEN THOUGH YOU REMEMBER EXACTLY WHAT IT LOOKED LIKE

When my girlfriend came over I told her all about the dinner party at Menshiki's. Leaving out, of course, any mention of Mariye Akikawa, the high-powered binoculars, and the Commendatore having secretly accompanied me. What I described was the dinner menu, the way the rooms were laid out in the house, the kind of furniture—safe subjects. We were in bed, completely naked, after making love for about a half hour. At first it was hard to relax, knowing that the Commendatore must be observing us, but as we got into it, I forgot all about him. If he wanted to watch, let him.

Like a rabid sports fan is dying to know how his favorite team scored in the game the night before, my girlfriend panted over every detail of the dishes we had at dinner. I painstakingly went over the details, as far as I could remember them, from the hors d'oeuvres to dessert, from the wine to the coffee. Even the tableware. I've always been blessed with great visual recall. If I focus on something, even a trivial thing, I can recall the minutest details, even after time has passed. I could reproduce the special features of every dish that was served, as if I were doing a quick sketch. She listened to my descriptions, a spellbound look in her eyes, at times actually gulping back her desire.

"Sounds amazing," she said dreamily. "Someday I'd love to have a wonderful meal like that."

"To tell the truth, though, I don't remember much of what it tasted like," I said.

"You don't remember how the food tasted? But you liked it, right?"

"Yes. It was delicious. That much I remember. But I can't recall the flavors, can't explain it in words."

"Even though you remember exactly what it looked like?"

"I could reproduce exactly what it looked like. I'm a painter—it's what I do. But I can't explain what went into it. Maybe a writer would be able to describe the flavors."

"Weird," she said. "So even when we do *this* together, you could paint a painting of it later on, but you wouldn't be able to reproduce the feeling in words?"

I gathered my thoughts. "You're talking about sexual pleasure?"

"Yes."

"Hmm. You may be right. But I think describing the flavor of a dish is harder than describing sexual pleasure."

"So what you're saying," she said, in a voice as chilly as an early-winter nightfall, "is that the taste of the dishes Mr. Menshiki served you is more exquisite, and deeper, than the sexual pleasure I provide?"

"That's not what I'm saying," I said hurriedly. "It's not a comparison of the quality of the two, but a question of the degree of difficulty of explaining them. In a technical sense."

"All right," she said. "What I give you isn't so bad, is it? In a technical sense?"

"Of course," I said. "It's amazing. In a technical sense, and all other senses, so amazing I couldn't paint it."

Truthfully the physical pleasure she provided me left nothing to be desired. Up till then I'd had sexual relationships with a number of women—not so many I could brag about it—but her vagina was more exquisite, more wondrously varied, than *any other* I'd ever known. And it was a deplorable thing that it had lain there, unused, for so many years. When I told her this, she didn't look as dissatisfied as you might have thought.

"Really?"

"Really."

She looked at me, dubiously, then seemed to take me at my word.

"So, did he show you the garage?" she asked.

"The garage?"

"His legendary garage with its four British cars."

"No, I didn't see it," I said. "It's such a huge place, and I didn't get a chance to see the garage."

"Hm," she said. "You didn't ask him if he really does own a Jaguar XK-E?"

"No. I didn't think of it. I mean, I'm not really into cars."

"You're happy with a used Corolla station wagon?"

"You got it."

"I'd love to be able to touch a Jaguar XK-E sometime. It's such a gorgeous car. I've been in love with that car ever since I saw it in a film with Audrey Hepburn and Peter O'Toole when I was a child. Peter O'Toole was driving a bright, shiny Jaguar E. Now what color was it? Yellow, as I recall."

Her thoughts drifted to that sports car she'd seen as a young girl, while what came to my mind was that Subaru Forester. The white Subaru parked in the parking lot on the edge of that tiny town along the coast in Miyagi. Not a particularly attractive vehicle. A typical small SUV, a squat little utilitarian machine. I doubt there'd be many people who would unconsciously feel like touching it. Unlike with a Jaguar XK-E.

"So you didn't get to see the greenhouse or the gym either?" she asked me. She was talking about Menshiki's house again.

"No such luck. Didn't get to see the greenhouse, the gym, or the laundry room, the maid's quarters, the kitchen, or the spacious walk-in closet, or the game room with the billiard table. He didn't show them to me."

That evening Menshiki had an important matter he had to talk with me about. He was far too preoccupied to give me a leisurely tour of the house.

"Does he really have a huge walk-in closet, and a game room with a billiard table?"

"I don't know. I'm just guessing. It wouldn't be strange if he did, though."

"He didn't show you any of the other rooms besides the study?"

"Yeah. It's not like I'm interested in interior design. What he showed me were the foyer, the living room, the study, and the dining room."

"You didn't try to spot Bluebeard's secret chamber?"

"Didn't have the chance to. And I wasn't about to ask Menshiki, 'By the way, where is the famous Bluebeard's secret chamber?' "

She shook her head a few times, clicking her tongue in frustration. "I tell you, that's what's wrong with men. Don't you have any curiosity? If it were me, I'd want to see every nook and cranny."

"The things men and women are curious about must be different."

"It seems like it," she said, resigned to it. "But that's okay. I should be happy to have gotten a lot of new info about the interior of Mr. Menshiki's house."

I was getting increasingly uneasy. "Getting information is one thing, but it wouldn't be good if this got out to others. Through your jungle grapevine . . ."

"It's all right. No need for you to worry about every little thing," she said cheerily.

She took my hand and guided it to her clitoris. In this way, our two spheres of curiosity once more significantly overlapped. I still had time before I had to go teach. At that point I thought I heard the bell in the studio faintly ringing, but I was probably just hearing things.

After she drove away in the red Mini just before three, I went into the studio, and picked up the bell from the shelf. I couldn't see anything different about it. It had just been quietly lying there. I looked around, but the Commendatore was nowhere to be seen.

I went over to the canvas, sat down on the stool, and gazed at the portrait of the man with the white Subaru Forester that I'd begun. I wanted to consider the direction I should take it in now. But here I made an unexpected discovery.

The painting was *already complete*.

Needless to say, the painting was still unfinished. I had a few ideas I planned to incorporate into it. At this point the painting was nothing more than a rough prototype of the man's face done with the three colors I'd mixed, the colors riotously slapped on over the rough charcoal sketch. In my eyes, of course, I could detect the ideal form of *The Man with the White Subaru Forester*. His face was there in the painting in a latent, trompe l'oeil type of way. But this was only visible to me. It was, at this point, only the foundation for a painting. Merely the hint and suggestion of things to come. But that man—the person I had been trying to paint from memory—was already satisfied with his taciturn form presented there. And maybe dead set against his likeness being made any clearer than it was now.

Don't you touch anything, the man was saying—or maybe commanding—from the canvas. *Don't you add a single thing more.*

The painting was complete as is, incomplete. The man actually existed, completely, in that inchoate form. A contradiction in terms, but there was no other way to describe it. And that man's hidden form looked out to me from the canvas as if signaling some hard-and-fast idea. Trying hard to get me to understand something. But I still had no idea what that was. This man is alive, I felt. Actually alive and moving.

The paint on the picture was still wet, but I took the canvas down from the easel, turned it facing away, and propped it up against the studio wall, careful not to get paint on the wall. It was harder and harder for me to stand seeing the painting. There was something ominous about it—something I shouldn't know about.

Hovering around the painting was the air of a fishing port. In that air was a mix of smells—the smell of the tide, of fish scales, of diesel engines, of fishing boats. Flocks of birds were screeching, slowly circling on the strong wind. The black golf cap of a middle-aged man who'd probably never played a round of golf in his life. The darkly tanned face, the stringy nape of the neck, the short-clipped hair mixed with gray. The well-used leather jacket. The clatter of knives and forks in the restaurant—that impersonal sound found at chain restaurants around the world. And the white Subaru Forester quietly parked in the lot out front. The sticker of a marlin on the rear bumper.

"Hit me," the woman had said in the middle of sex. Her fingernails were digging deep into my back. There was a strong smell of sweat. I did as she asked, smacking her face with an open hand.

"Not like that. Don't hold back, hit me harder," the woman said, shaking her head violently. "Harder, *much* harder. Really hit me. I don't care if there's a bruise. Hard enough so my nose bleeds."

I had no desire to hit her. I never had those kind of violent tendencies. Hardly any at all. But she was *seriously* hoping I would *seriously* hit her. What she needed was real pain. So I reluctantly hit her again, a little harder this time. Hard enough to leave a red mark on her. Every time I struck her, her flesh squeezed my penis like a vise. Like a starving animal pouncing on some food.

"Would you choke me a little?" she whispered a little while later. "Use this."

The sound seemed to be coming from another realm. She pulled out a white bathrobe belt from under her pillow. She'd had it there, ready to use.

I refused. I could never do something like that. It was too dangerous. Mess up, and she could die.

"Just pretend," she pleaded, gasping. "You don't need to really choke me, just pretend like you are. Wrap this around my neck and tighten it a little."

I couldn't refuse.

The impersonal clatter of silverware in a chain restaurant.

I shook my head, trying to drive away those memories. It was an incident I didn't care to recall, a memory I'd like to throw away and never have again. But the feel of that bathrobe belt lingered in my hands. The way her neck felt, too. For whatever reason, these stayed with me.

And this man knew. Where I'd been the night before, what I'd done. What I'd been thinking.

What should I do with this painting? Keep it here in the studio, turned toward the wall? Even turned around like that, it still made me uneasy. The only other place to keep it was the attic. The same place Tomohiko Amada had hidden away *Killing Commendatore*. The place to hide away what was in your heart.

In my mind, the words I'd spoken aloud came back to me.

I could reproduce exactly what it looked like. I'm a painter—it's what I do. But I can't explain what went into it.

All sorts of things I couldn't explain were insidiously grabbing hold of me. Tomohiko Amada's *Killing Commendatore* that I'd discovered in the attic, the strange bell left behind inside the gaping stone chamber in the woods, the Idea that appeared to me in the guise of the Commendatore, and the middle-aged man with the white Subaru Forester. And that odd white-haired person who lived across the valley. Menshiki seemed to be enlisting me into some kind of plan he had in mind.

The whirlpool swirling around me was gradually picking up speed. And there was no way for me to turn back. It was too late. That whirlpool was totally soundless. And that weird silence had me scared.

28

FRANZ KAFKA WAS QUITE FOND OF SLOPES

That evening I taught a children's art class. The assignment that day was to do rough sketches of people. The children worked in pairs, selecting the type of drawing instruments they wanted from the ones the school had prepared ahead of time (charcoal or various types of soft pencils), and took turns sketching each other in their notebooks. They were limited to fifteen minutes per drawing (I used a kitchen timer to accurately time them). They were supposed to use an eraser as little as they could, and limit themselves to one sheet of paper, if possible.

One by one the children then came to the front of the class, showed us their sketches, and got feedback from the other children. It was a small class, and the atmosphere was congenial. Afterward I went forward and taught them some simple techniques for rough sketches. I explained in general the difference between *croquis*—rough sketches—and *dessan*. A dessan is more of a blueprint for a painting, and requires a certain accuracy. Compared with that, a croquis is a free first impression. You get an impression in your mind and trace the rough outline of it before it disappears. More than accuracy, croquis require balance and speed. Many famous painters actually weren't very skilled at doing croquis. I've always prided myself on being good at drawing these kind of quick sketches.

Finally I chose one of the children to model for me and did a rough sketch of her on the blackboard in white chalk, to show them an actual example. *Wow! You're so fast! It looks just like her!* the children called out, impressed. One of a teacher's important duties is to get children to be genuinely impressed.

Next, I had them change partners and do another croquis, and the second time they were much improved. They absorbed knowledge quickly. This time, the instructor was impressed. Of course some of them were better than others, but that didn't matter. What I was teaching them was less how to draw than a way to view the world.

On this day I selected Mariye Akikawa (intentionally, of course) to serve as model when I drew an example. I did a simple sketch of her from the waist up on the blackboard. It wasn't exactly a croquis, though the elements were the same. I finished quickly, in three minutes. I wanted to use the class to test what kind of painting I could do of her. What I discovered in doing this was that, as a model for a painting, she had a lot of unique possibilities hidden away inside.

I'd never really consciously observed her before, but now, looking at her carefully as the subject of a drawing, I found her face far more intriguing than my original vague impression. It wasn't just that she had lovely features. She was, indeed, a beautiful girl, but a closer observation showed a kind of imbalance at work. And behind that unstable expression there was a latent energy, like some agile animal lurking in the tall grass.

I wanted to see if I could capture that impression, but it was next to impossible to do that in three minutes, in chalk on a blackboard. Basically impossible, I should say. I needed more time to observe her face and dissect all the elements. And I had to know more about this young girl.

I left the chalk sketch of her on the blackboard, and after the children had all left, I stayed behind, arms folded, studying the sketch. I tried to determine if there was anything of Menshiki in her features. But I couldn't decide. I could detect a resemblance in certain features, in others not so much—it could go either way. But if I had to give one feature it would be the eyes, a shared look in their eyes. The distinctive way their eyes would flash for an instant.

If you stare long enough deep into the bottom of a clear spring you discover a kind of lump that emits light. You can't see it unless you look very closely. That lump soon wavers and loses shape. The more carefully you look, the more you start to wonder if it might all be an illusion. But something there is unmistakably glowing. Having done countless portraits of people, occasionally I'll sense someone giving off that *glow*. Not many people have it. But this girl and Menshiki were among these rare few.

The middle-aged receptionist at the school came into the classroom to straighten up and stood beside me, admiring the drawing.

"That's Mariye Akikawa, isn't it," she said at first glance. "A very nice likeness. It looks like she's about to start moving. It's a waste to have to erase it."

"Thank you," I said. I got up from my desk, picked an eraser, and completely wiped the sketch away.

The Commendatore finally made an appearance the next day (Saturday). It was the first time since Tuesday night at the dinner at Menshiki's that he—to borrow his phrase—*materialized*. I was back from food shopping, in the living room reading a book, when I heard the sound of the bell tinkling from the studio. I went into the studio and found the Commendatore seated on the shelf, lightly shaking the bell next to his ear. As if making sure of the subtle sound. When he spotted me he stopped ringing the bell.

"It's been a while," I said.

"Negative. It has been nothing of the kind," the Commendatore said curtly. "An Idea travels around the world in units of hundreds, thousands of years. A day or two does not count as time."

"How did you like Mr. Menshiki's dinner party?"

"Ah, yes, an interesting dinner that was. I could not partake of the food, of course, but did feast my eyes on it. And Menshiki is a fascinating fellow. Always thinking several steps ahead. And there is much pent up inside him."

"He asked me to do a favor for him."

"Affirmative." The Commendatore gazed at the ancient bell in his hand. He did not seem interested. "I heard it all quite clearly. But it is not something that has much to do with me. It is a practical matter—a worldly matter, you could say—that is between my friends and Menshiki."

"Is it all right if I ask a question?" I said.

The Commendatore rubbed his goatee with his palm. "Affirmative. But I do not know if I will be able to answer."

"It's about Tomohiko Amada's painting *Killing Commendatore*. I assume you know the painting, since you borrowed one of the figures. The painting seems based on an incident in Vienna in 1938. Something Tomohiko Amada himself was involved in. Do you know anything about that?"

Arms folded, the Commendatore thought this over. Finally he narrowed his eyes and spoke.

"There are *plenty* of things in history that are best left in the shadows. Accurate knowledge does not improve people's lives. The objective does not necessarily surpass the subjective, you know. Reality does not necessarily extinguish fantasy."

"Generally speaking," I said, "that might be so. But that painting is calling out to anyone who sees it. I get the sense that Tomohiko Amada painted it to privately capture an event that was essential to him but that he could not share with others. He changed the characters and setting to another age, and made a metaphorical confession, using his newly acquired skills in Japanese-style painting. I even get the feeling that that was the sole reason he abandoned Western painting and converted to Japanese art."

"Cannot you just let the painting speak for itself?" the Commendatore said softly. "If that painting wants to say something, then best to let it speak. Let metaphors be metaphors, a code a code, a sieve a sieve. Is there something wrong with that?"

A sieve? But I let it go.

"No, nothing's wrong with that," I said. "I'd just like to know what made Tomohiko Amada paint it. It's clear that the painting is expecting something. The picture was, without a doubt, painted for a specific purpose."

The Commendatore continued to rub his beard with his palm as if recalling something. "Franz Kafka was quite fond of slopes," he said. "He was drawn to all sorts of slopes. He loved to gaze at homes built on the middle of a slope. He would sit by the side of the street for hours, staring at houses built like that. He never grew tired of it and would sit there, tilting his head to one side, then straightening it up again. A kind of strange fellow. Did you know this?"

Franz Kafka and slopes?

"No, I didn't," I said. I'd never heard of that.

"But does knowing that make one appreciate his works more?"

I didn't respond to his question.

"So you knew Franz Kafka, too? Personally?"

"He does not know about me personally, of course," the Commendatore said. He chuckled, as if recalling something. This might have been the first time I'd seen him laugh out loud. Was there something about Franz Kafka to make him chuckle?

His expression returned to normal and he went on.

"The truth is a symbol, and symbols are the truth. It is best to grasp symbols the way they are. There's no logic or facts, no pig's belly button or ant's balls. When people try to use a method other than the truth to follow along the path of understanding, it is like trying to use a sieve to hold water. I am telling you this for your own good. Better to give it up. Sadly, what Menshiki is doing is similar to that."

"So no matter what, it's a wasted effort?"

"No one can ever float something full of holes on water."

"So what exactly is Mr. Menshiki trying to do?"

The Commendatore lightly shrugged. Charming lines formed between his eyebrows that reminded me of a young Marlon Brando. I seriously doubted the Commendatore had ever seen Elia Kazan's *On the Waterfront*, but those lines were exactly like Marlon Brando's. Though I had no way of knowing how far he went, when it came to referencing his appearance and features.

He said, "There is very little I can explain to my friends about Tomohiko Amada's *Killing Commendatore*. That is because it is, in essence, allegory and metaphor. Allegories and metaphors are not something you should explain in words. You just grasp them and accept them."

The Commendatore scratched behind his ear with his little finger. Just like a cat will scratch behind its ear before it rains.

"I will, however, tell my friends one thing. Nothing that is enormously significant, but tomorrow night you'll get a phone call. A call from Menshiki. Think things over *very carefully* before you answer. Your answer will be the same no matter how much you think it over, but it is still best to think it over very carefully."

"And it's very important to let the other person know you're thinking things over carefully, isn't it. As a gesture."

"Affirmative. A hard-and-fast rule in business is to never accept the first offer. Remember that, and you will never go wrong." The Commendatore chuckled again. He seemed in an especially good mood today. "Changing topics, but I wondered, is it interesting to touch a clitoris?"

"I don't think you touch it because it's interesting," I said honestly.

"From the sidelines it is hard to understand."

"I don't think I get it, either," I said. So an Idea, too, doesn't necessarily understand everything.

"About time for me to disappear," the Commendatore said. "I have someplace else I need to go. Do not have much time."

And with that the Commendatore vanished. A gradual, phased disappearance, like the Cheshire Cat's. I went to the kitchen, made a simple dinner, and ate. I considered for a moment what "someplace else" an Idea would need to go to. And naturally had no clue.

Like the Commendatore had prophesized, at just past eight the following evening, I got a phone call from Menshiki.

I thanked him again for the dinner party. The food was amazing, I said. It was nothing, he replied. I want to thank *you*, Menshiki said, for letting me have such an enjoyable time. I also thanked him for the payment for the portrait, which was way more than we'd agreed to. Please don't worry about it, Menshiki said modestly. That's only to be expected, for such a wonderful painting. Once we'd finished all these polite exchanges there was a moment of silence.

"By the way, about Mariye Akikawa," Menshiki began, as casually as if discussing the weather. "You remember the other day when I asked if you would have her model for a painting?"

"Of course I remember."

"Yesterday I asked Mariye—actually Mr. Matsushima, the owner of the arts-and-culture center, asked her aunt—if it might be possible—and she agreed to model."

"I see," I said.

"So all the pieces are in place, if you'll agree to paint the portrait."

"But Mr. Menshiki, isn't Mr. Matsushima a bit suspicious that you're involved in this?"

"I've been very careful, so no need to worry. He sees me as acting as your patron of sorts. I hope you're not offended . . ."

"I don't mind," I said. "But I'm surprised Mariye Akikawa agreed. She's so quiet and docile, and strikes me as a timid girl."

"Honestly, her aunt didn't like the idea at first. She felt nothing good could come from modeling for a painting. I'm sorry if this offends you, as an artist."

"No, most people would feel that way."

"But Mariye herself seemed quite interested in modeling for the painting. She said if you'd paint her she'd be happy to pose. She's the one who persuaded her aunt to agree."

Why, I wondered? Was there some connection with the sketch of her I did on the blackboard? I didn't venture to bring this up with Menshiki.

"Things have worked out perfectly, haven't they?" Menshiki said.

I thought it over. Was this really the perfect way for things to go? Menshiki seemed to be waiting for my opinion.

"Could you tell me more about how this would unfold?"

Menshiki said, "It's very simple. You're looking for a model for a painting. And you think that Mariye Akikawa, from your art class, would be perfect. So you had the owner of the arts-and-culture center, Mr. Matsushima, sound out the girl's guardian, her aunt. That's the story. Mr. Matsushima personally recommended you. Said you have a sterling character, are an enthusiastic teacher, that you're a talented artist with a promising future. I don't appear anywhere in this. I made sure my name didn't come up. Naturally she'll be clothed when she models, and her aunt will accompany her. And you'll finish the sessions by noon. Those are the conditions they laid down. What do you think?"

Following the Commendatore's advice ("Always turn down first offers"), I put on the brakes.

"I don't have any problem with the conditions, but can I have a bit more time to think about this?"

"Of course," Menshiki said calmly. "Think about it as much as you'd like. I'm not trying to rush you. Obviously you're the one who would paint the picture, and if you don't feel like doing it, that's the end of it. I just wanted to let you know that everything's all set, as far as I'm concerned. One more thing, perhaps a little off topic, but I'm planning to pay you fully for the painting."

Things are really moving along here, I thought. Everything's evolving amazingly quickly and smoothly, like a ball rolling down a slope . . . I pictured Franz Kafka seated halfway down the slope, watching the ball roll by. I needed to be cautious.

"Can you give me two days?" I asked. "I should be able to give you an answer then."

"That's fine. I'll call you again in two days," Menshiki said.

We ended the call.

Truth be told, I really didn't need two days to give a reply. I'd already made up my mind. I was dying to paint Mariye Akikawa's portrait. Even if someone tried to stop me, I'd take on the task. The only reason for asking for two extra days was that I didn't want anyone else to dictate the pace of events. I needed to stop and take a deep breath, something instinct—and the Commendatore—had taught me.

It is like trying to use a sieve to hold water, the Commendatore said. *No one ever can float something full of holes on water.*

His words hinted at something, something to come.

29

ANY UNNATURAL ELEMENTS

I spent those two days gazing, back and forth, at the two paintings in my studio—Tomohiko Amada's *Killing Commendatore* and my own painting of the man with the white Subaru Forester. *Killing Commendatore* was hanging now on the white wall of the studio. *The Man with the White Subaru Forester* was in a corner of the studio facing the wall (only when I wanted to look at it did I return it to the easel). Other than gaze at those paintings, I killed time reading books, listening to music, cooking, cleaning, weeding the garden, taking walks nearby. I didn't feel like taking up my paintbrush. The Commendatore didn't appear, and maintained his silence.

As I hiked the mountain roads nearby, I tried to find a place from which I could view Mariye Akikawa's house. But I could never find it. When I saw it from Menshiki's house, I gathered it wasn't far from me, but the topography obstructed my view. As I hiked through the woods I unconsciously was on the lookout for hornets.

What I rediscovered, spending two days gazing at the paintings, was that my feelings were spot on. *Killing Commendatore* wanted me to break its "code," and *The Man with the White Subaru Forester* wanted the artist (namely me) to not make any more revisions. And both of these appeals were very strong—at least I felt them strongly—and I had to obey. I left *The Man with the White Subaru Forester* as it was (though I did try to fathom the basis for why it wanted to be left as is), and struggled to decipher *Killing Commendatore*. But both paintings were enveloped in an enigma, as hard as a walnut shell, and I couldn't find the means to crack the shell open.

Without the upcoming portrait of Mariye Akikawa to deal with, I might very well have spent my days, ad infinitum, gazing back and forth between these paintings. But in the evening of the second day Menshiki called, and for the time being, at least, the spell was broken.

"Did you make a decision?" Menshiki said, after we'd greeted each other. He was, of course, asking about painting Mariye Akikawa's portrait.

"I'll accept the offer," I replied. "But I do have one condition."

"Which is?"

"I can't predict what kind of painting it will turn out to be. I can't know what style I'll paint it in until Mariye is actually here and I actually begin. If no good ideas come to me, I might not finish. Or it might be finished, but I might not like it. Or you might not like it. So I'd like to do it spontaneously, not because you commissioned it, or because you suggested I do it."

A momentary pause, then Menshiki said, probingly, "In other words, if you're not satisfied with the finished painting it won't end up mine, under any circumstances. Is that what you're saying?"

"That's a possibility. Anyway, I'd like to be the one who decides what to do with the painting. That's my condition."

Menshiki gave it some thought before he spoke. "The only thing I can do, I think, is agree. If not accepting that condition means you won't paint it."

"I'm sorry about that."

"So you want to be more free artistically, not bound by the painting being on commission by me, or having any suggestions from me, is that it? Or is the financial aspect the issue?"

"A little bit of both. But what's really important is that I want to do it all more naturally."

"Naturally?"

"I want to get rid of any unnatural elements, as much as I can."

"Meaning . . . ," Menshiki said. His voice had grown a little hard. "That there's something unnatural in my asking you to paint Mariye's portrait?"

It is like trying to use a sieve to hold water, the Commendatore said. *No one can ever float something full of holes on water.*

I said, "What I mean is, with this painting I'd like to be on an equal footing with you, not in a relationship that's mixed up with questions of individual interests. I'm sorry if this sounds rude."

"No, it's not rude at all. It's only natural for people to be on an equal footing. Feel free to say anything you'd like to me."

"In other words, I'd like to paint the portrait of Mariye Akikawa as a spontaneous act, not one that you had a hand in. Unless I do that, I might not come up with any good ideas about how to paint her. That sort of thing might be a shackle, visible or otherwise."

Menshiki thought about this. "I understand completely," he finally said. "Let's forget about it being a commission. And please forget that I mentioned payment. That was me being overeager, I'm afraid. We can revisit the question of what to do with the painting once it's finished and you show it to me. Of course I'll honor your desires as the artist above all. But how about the other request I had? Do you remember?"

"About you casually stopping by my studio while Mariye is modeling for me?"

"Correct."

I thought it over. "I have no problem with that. I'm acquainted with you, you live in the neighborhood, and just happened to drop by while out for a Sunday stroll. And we just chat for a while. That strikes me as completely natural."

Menshiki seemed relieved. "I'd be very grateful if you'd arrange it. I'll make sure not to get in the way. So can I plan things so that Mariye comes over to your place this Sunday morning, and you'll paint her portrait? Actually Mr. Matsushima will act as intermediary and arrange things between you and the Akikawas."

"That would be fine. Go ahead and set it up. We'll plan on the two of them coming over on Sunday morning at ten, and Mariye will sit for the portrait. I'll be sure to finish up by twelve. It'll take several weeks to finish. Maybe five or six. That's about the size of it."

"I'll be in touch once everything's set."

We'd finished discussing all we needed to.

"Ah, yes," he said, as if suddenly remembering. "I found out a few more things about Tomohiko Amada's time in Vienna. I told you that the failed assassination attempt he was involved in took place right about the time of the *Anschluss,* but actually it was in the early fall of 1938. About half a year after the *Anschluss,* in other words. You know the facts about the *Anschluss*, right?"

"Not in much detail."

"On March 12, 1938, the Wehrmacht smashed across the border with Austria, invaded the country, and soon gained control of Vienna. They threatened President Miklas and made him designate Seyss-Inquart, head of the Austrian Nazi Party, as prime minister. Hitler came to Vienna two days later. On April tenth there was a national referendum, a vote on whether Austria should be annexed by Germany. On the surface it was a free, secret ballot, but the Nazis rigged things so any voter would have to be pretty courageous to vote *nein*. The vote was 99.75 percent *ja* for the annexation. That's how Austria as a nation vanished, reduced to being a part of Germany. Have you ever been to Vienna?"

I'd never been out of the country, let alone to Vienna. I'd never even had a passport.

"Vienna's like no other city in the world," Menshiki said. "You sense it even after being there for a short time. Vienna's different from Germany. The air's different, the people are different. Same with the food and the music. It's a special place for people to enjoy themselves, to love the arts. But back then Vienna was in total chaos, a brutal storm blowing violently through it. And it was exactly this period of upheaval in Vienna that Tomohiko Amada lived through. The Nazis behaved themselves until the national referendum, but after that they revealed their true, brutal nature. The first thing Hitler did after the *Anschluss* was build the Mauthausen concentration camp in northern Austria. It took only a few weeks to complete it. Building it was the Nazis' top priority. In a short space of time, tens of thousands of political prisoners were arrested and shipped off to the camp. Most of those sent to Mauthausen were so-called incorrigible political prisoners or antisocial elements. So their treatment was especially cruel. Lots of people were executed there, or died doing harsh physical labor in the quarries. The label "incorrigible" meant that once you were thrown into that camp, you'd never come out alive. Many anti-Nazi activists weren't sent to the camp, but were tortured and murdered during interrogation, their fate covered up. The aborted assassination attempt that Tomohiko Amada was involved in took place during this chaotic period following the *Anschluss*."

I listened to Menshiki's story without comment.

"But as I mentioned before, there's no public record at all of any abortive assassination attempt on any Nazi VIP from the summer to fall of 1938. Which is pretty strange, if you think about it. If such a plot had really existed, Hitler and Goebbels would have spread the news far and wide and used it for political purposes. Like they did with *Kristallnacht*. You know about *Kristallnacht,* right?"

"The basic facts, yes," I said. I'd seen a movie once that dealt with it. "A German embassy official in Paris was shot and killed by an anti-Nazi Jew, and the Nazis used that as an excuse for fomenting anti-Jewish riots throughout Germany. Lots of businesses run by Jews were destroyed, and quite a few people were murdered. The name comes from the way that the glass from the shattered shop windows glittered like crystals."

"Exactly. That was in November 1938. The German government announced it as spontaneous rioting, when in reality the Nazi government, with Goebbels leading the way, used the assassination to systematically plan this brutality. The assassin, Herschel Grynszpan, carried out the act to protest the cruel treatment of his family as Jews back in Germany. At first he planned to assassinate the German ambassador, but when he couldn't, he instead shot one of the embassy staff who just happened to be there. Ironically, Vom Rath, the staff member he shot, was under surveillance by authorities for anti-Nazi sympathies. At any rate, if there had been a plot at the time to assassinate a Nazi official in Vienna, a similar campaign would definitely have taken place. They would have used it as an excuse to increase the suppression of anti-Nazi forces. At least, they wouldn't have quietly covered up the incident."

"Was there some reason they didn't want it made public?"

"It seems a fact that the incident did take place. Most of the people involved were Viennese college students, and they were all arrested and either executed or murdered. To seal their lips about the plot. One theory is that one of the resistance members was the daughter of a high-ranking Nazi official, and that's why they kept it under wraps. But the facts aren't clear. After the war there was some testimony given about it, but this was all circumstantial evidence, and it's unsure whether any of it is reliable. By the way, the resistance group's name was Candela. In Latin it means a candle shining in the darkness underground. The Japanese word for lantern—*kantera*—derives from this."

"If all those involved in the plot were killed, that means the only survivor is Tomohiko Amada?"

"It does seem that way. Just before the end of the war, the Reich Main Security Office ordered that all secret documents relating to the incident be burned, and the plot was lost to the darkness of history. It would be nice if we could question Tomohiko Amada about the details of what took place, but that would be pretty difficult now."

It would, I said. Up till now Tomohiko Amada had never spoken of the incident, and his memory had now sunk deep into the thick mud of oblivion.

I thanked Menshiki and hung up.

Even while his memory was still solid, Tomohiko Amada had maintained a firm silence about the incident. He must have had some private reasons for why he couldn't talk about it. Or perhaps when he left the country the authorities had forced him to agree to never speak of it. In place of maintaining a lifelong silence, though, he'd left the painting *Killing Commendatore*. He'd entrusted that painting with the truth he was forbidden to ever speak about, and his feelings about what had occurred.

The next evening Menshiki called again. Mariye Akikawa would be coming to my house the following Sunday at ten a.m., he reported. As he'd mentioned, her aunt would be accompanying her. Menshiki wouldn't be there that first day.

"I'll come by after some time has passed, after she's gotten used to posing for you. I'm sure she'll be nervous at first, and it's better that I don't bother you," he said.

His voice was a little unsteady. That tone put me on edge as well.

"Yes, that sounds like a good idea," I replied.

"Come to think of it, though, I might be the one who's the most nervous," Menshiki said after a little hesitation, sounding as if he were revealing a secret. "I think I said this before, but I've never been near Mariye Akikawa, not even once. I've only seen her from a distance."

"But if you wanted to get close to her, you could have created an opportunity to do so."

"Yes, of course. If I'd wanted to I could have made any number of opportunities."

"But you didn't. Why not?"

Uncharacteristically, Menshiki took time to choose his words. He said, "I couldn't predict how I'd feel, or what I'd say, if I was close to her. That's why I've intentionally stayed away. I've been satisfied with being on the other side of the valley, secretly watching her from a distance with high-powered binoculars. Is that a warped way of thinking?"

"Not particularly," I said. "But I do find it a bit odd. But now you've decided to actually meet her at my house. Why?"

Menshiki was silent for a time, and then spoke. "That's because you're here, and can act as an intermediary."

"Me?" I said in surprise. "Why me? Not to be rude or anything, but you hardly know me. And I don't know you well either. We only met about a month ago. We live across the valley from each other, but our lifestyles couldn't be more different. So why did you trust me that much? And tell me your secrets? You don't seem the type to give away your inner feelings so easily."

"Exactly. Once I have a secret I lock it away in a safe and swallow the key. I don't seek advice from others or reveal things to them."

"Then how come—I'm not sure how to put this—you've confided in me?"

Menshiki was silent for a time. "It's hard to explain, but I got the feeling the first day I met you that it's all right to let my guard down. Call it intuition. And that feeling only grew stronger after I saw my portrait. I decided, *This is a trustworthy person*. Someone who would accept my way of seeing things, my way of thinking. Even if I have a slightly odd and twisted way of seeing and thinking."

A slightly odd and twisted way of seeing and thinking, I thought.

"I'm really happy you'd say that," I said. "But I don't think I understand you as a person. You go way beyond the scope of my comprehension. Frankly, many things about you simply surprise me. Sometimes I'm at a loss for words."

"But you never try to judge me. Am I right?"

That was true, now that he'd said it. I'd never tried to apply some standard to judge Menshiki's words and actions. I didn't praise them, and didn't criticize them. They simply left me, as I'd said, at a loss for words.

"You might be right," I admitted.

"And you remember when I went down to the bottom of that hole? When I was down there by myself for an hour?"

"Of course."

"It never even occurred to you to leave me there forever, in that dark, dank hole. Right?"

"True. But that sort of idea wouldn't occur to a normal person."

"Are you sure about that?"

What could I say? I couldn't imagine what lay deep in other people's minds.

"I have another request," Menshiki said.

"And what is that?"

"It's about next Sunday, when Mariye and her aunt come to your place," Menshiki said. "I'd like to watch your house then with my binoculars, if you don't mind?"

"I don't mind," I said. I mean, the Commendatore had watched my girlfriend and me, right beside us, when we'd had sex. Having someone watch my terrace from afar wasn't about to faze me now.

"I thought it'd be best to tell you in advance," Menshiki said, as if excusing himself.

I was impressed all over again how strangely honest he was. We finished talking and hung up the phone. I'd been holding the phone tightly against me, and the spot above my ear ached.

The next morning I received a certified letter. I signed the receipt the mailman held out for me, and got a large envelope. Getting it didn't exactly make me feel cheerful. My experience is that certified mail is never good news.

And as expected, the mail was from a law office in Tokyo, and inside were two sets of divorce papers. There was also a stamped, self-addressed envelope. The only thing accompanying the forms was a letter with businesslike instructions from the lawyer. It said that all I needed to do was read over the forms, check them, and, if I didn't have any objections, sign and seal one set and send it back. If there are any points that you're uncertain about, the letter said, feel free to contact the attorney in charge. I glanced through the forms, filled in the date, signed them, and affixed my seal. I didn't particularly have any *points that were uncertain*. Neither of us had any financial obligations toward the other, no estate worth dividing up, no children to fight a custody battle over. A very simple, easy-to-understand divorce. Divorce 101, you could say. Two lives had overlapped into one, and six years later had split apart again, that was it. I slipped the documents inside the return envelope and put the envelope on top of the dining room table. Tomorrow when I went to town to teach my art class all I'd need to do was toss it inside the mailbox in front of the station.

That whole afternoon I sort of half-gazed at the envelope on the table, and gradually came to feel like the entire weight of six years of married life was crammed inside that envelope. All that time—time tinged with all kinds of memories and emotions—was stuffed inside an ordinary business envelope, gradually suffocating to death. I felt a weight pressing down on my chest, and my breathing grew ragged. I picked up the envelope, took it to the studio, and placed it on the shelf, next to the dingy ancient bell. I shut the studio door, returned to the kitchen, poured a glass of the whiskey Masahiko had given me, and drank it. My rule was not to drink while it was still light out, but I figured it was okay sometimes. The kitchen was totally still and silent. No wind outside, no sound of cars. Not even any birds chirping.

I had no particular problem about getting divorced. For all intents and purposes we already were divorced. And I had no emotional hang-up about signing and sealing the official documents. If that's what she wanted, fine. It was a legal formality, nothing more.

But when it came to why, and how, things had turned out this way, the sequence of events was beyond me. I understood, of course, that over time, and as circumstances changed, a couple could grow closer, or move apart. Changes in a person's feelings aren't regulated by custom, logic, or the law. They're fluid, unstable, free to spread their wings and fly away. Like migratory birds have no concept of borders between countries.

But these were all just generalizations, and I couldn't easily grasp the individual case here—that *this woman,* Yuzu, refused to love *this man,* me, and chose instead to be loved by someone else. It felt terribly absurd, a horribly ugly way to be treated. There wasn't any anger involved (I think). I mean, what was I supposed to be angry with? What I was feeling was a fundamental numbness. The numbness your heart automatically activates to lessen the awful pain when you want somebody desperately and they reject you. A kind of emotional morphine.

I couldn't easily forget Yuzu. I still wanted her. But say she were living in a place across the valley from my house, and say I owned a pair of high-powered binoculars—would I really try to peer into her daily life through those lenses? I sincerely doubted it. What I mean is, in the first place I wouldn't pick that sort of place to live in. It would be like building a torture rack just for me.

The whiskey did its job and I went to bed before eight and fell asleep. At one thirty a.m. I woke up and couldn't get back to sleep. It was a long, lonely haul until dawn. I didn't read, didn't listen to music, just sat on the sofa in the living room blankly staring out into the empty, dark space. All sorts of thoughts swirled through my head. Most of which I shouldn't have thought about.

I wish the Commendatore were with me, I thought. I wish we could talk about something together. *Anything.* The topic didn't matter. Just hearing his voice would be enough.

But the Commendatore was nowhere to be seen. And I had no way to summon him.

30

IT REALLY DEPENDS ON THE PERSON

The next afternoon I mailed the divorce papers I'd signed and sealed. I didn't include any letter. I simply tossed the stamped return envelope with the documents into the mailbox in front of the station. Just having that envelope out of the house felt like a burden had been lifted. I had no idea what legal route these documents would take next. Not that it mattered. They could follow whatever path they liked.

And Sunday morning, just before ten, Mariye Akikawa came to my house. A bright-blue Toyota Prius climbed the slope with barely a sound and came to a stop near my front door. In the bright Sunday sunlight, the car sparkled, grandly, vibrantly. Like it was brand-new, just unwrapped. A lot of different cars had found their way to my place recently—Menshiki's silver Jaguar, my girlfriend's red Mini, the chauffeur-driven black Infiniti that Menshiki had sent for me, Masahiko's old black Volvo, and now the blue Toyota Prius that belonged to Mariye Akikawa's aunt. And of course my own Toyota Corolla station wagon (covered with dust for so long I couldn't recall what the original color had been). I imagine people have all sorts of reasons for choosing the car they drive, and of course I had no clue why Mariye's aunt had chosen a blue Toyota Prius. It looked less like a car than a giant vacuum cleaner.

The quiet Prius engine shut off, and the surroundings grew *that much* quieter. The doors opened, and Mariye Akikawa and the woman I took to be her aunt got out. The aunt looked young, though early forties would have been my guess. She had on dark sunglasses and a gray cardigan over a simple light-blue dress. She carried a shiny black handbag and had on low, dark-gray shoes. Good shoes for driving. She shut her door, removed the sunglasses, and put them in her handbag. Her hair fell to her shoulders and was neatly curled (though not with the excessive perfection of someone just emerged from a hair salon). No accessories, other than a gold brooch on her collar.

Mariye had on a black cotton sweater and a brown, knee-length wool skirt. I'd only seen her in her school uniform up till then, and she seemed different. Side by side they looked like a mother and child from a refined, elegant household. Though I knew from Menshiki that they weren't actually mother and child.

As always I observed them through a gap in the curtain. And when the bell rang I went to the entrance and opened the front door.

Mariye's aunt had a very tranquil, calm way of speaking. She had lovely features. Not the kind of beautiful woman that would turn heads, but neat, regular features. A natural, subdued smile graced her lips, like the pale moon at dawn. She was carrying a box of cookies as a present. I was the one who had asked to have Mariye model for me, so there was no reason for her to bring me anything, but she was probably the type of person who'd had it drummed into her since she was little that when you visit someone's house you always should bring along a present. So I simply thanked her and accepted it, and showed the two of them into the living room.

"Our house isn't so far from here, a stone's throw, really, but when you drive it's a roundabout road to get here," the aunt said. (Her name was Shoko Akikawa, she told me, the *sho* written with the character that meant a traditional Japanese pan flute.) "I knew of course that this was Tomohiko Amada's house, but this is the first time I've ever been up here even though we live next door."

"I've been living here, taking care of the place, since this spring," I explained.

"Yes, I heard. I'm glad it turned out we're neighbors. I look forward to getting to know you better."

Shoko bowed deeply and thanked me for teaching Mariye. "My niece really enjoys going to the school, thanks to you," she said.

"I wouldn't say I'm exactly teaching her," I said. "Basically I just enjoy drawing together with all the pupils."

"But I understand you're a very skilled instructor. I've heard many people say that."

That I found hard to believe, but I made no comment, letting these words of praise pass unremarked. Shoko was raised well, a woman who put a premium on social niceties.

Seated side by side like this, the first thing anyone would notice about Mariye Akikawa and her aunt is that their features didn't resemble each other in the slightest. From a little ways off they seemed a well-matched mother and child, but up close it was hard to find anything in common in their appearance. Mariye had lovely features, too, and Shoko Akikawa was without doubt quite attractive, but their features were poles apart. If Shoko Akikawa's features were aiming at gaining a wonderful balance, Mariye Akikawa's aimed at destroying equilibrium, demolishing a set framework. If Shoko Akikawa aimed at a gentle, overarching harmony and stability, Mariye Akikawa sought an asymmetrical friction. Still, one could sense from the mood between them that despite all this they had a warm, healthy relationship. In a sense they were more relaxed around each other than a real mother and daughter. They seemed to maintain a comfortable distance. At least that's the impression I got.

Of course I knew nothing about why a woman like Shoko, beautiful and refined, was still single, and put up with living far off in the hills like this in her older brother's home. Perhaps she'd had a lover, a mountain climber who'd perished in an attempt to reach the summit of Mt. Everest by the most arduous route, and had pledged to remain single forever, cherishing beautiful memories of her lover in her heart. Or perhaps she was having a long-term affair with a charming married man. In any event, it wasn't my business.

Shoko walked over to the windows on the west side and gazed with great interest at the view of the valley from there.

"It's the same mountain we see from our place, but this is a slightly different angle and it doesn't look the same at all," she said, sounding impressed.

Menshiki's huge white mansion glittered on top of that mountain (and he was probably over there watching my house now through his binoculars). How did that mansion appear from her house? I wanted to ask, but it seemed risky to broach that topic right off the bat. It was hard to tell what that might lead to.

Wanting to steer clear of that, I quickly led them into the studio.

"This is where I'll have Mariye model for me," I said to them.

"This must be where Tomohiko Amada did his painting," Shoko said, gazing with great interest around the studio.

"I believe so," I said.

"There's a different feeling here, even from the rest of your house. Don't you think?"

"I'm not sure. Living here day to day, I don't really get that sense."

"What do you think, Mari-chan?" Shoko asked Mariye. "Don't you find there's an unusual sort of feeling to the room?"

Mariye was busy looking around the studio and didn't reply. She probably hadn't heard her aunt's question. I wanted to hear her reply as well.

"While the two of you are working here, I'll wait in the living room, if that's all right?" Shoko asked.

"It's all up to Mariye. The most important thing is creating an environment where she can feel relaxed. Whether you stay here or not, either way is fine with me."

"I don't want Auntie to be here," Mariye said, the first time she'd opened her mouth that day. She spoke quietly, but it was a terse announcement with no room for negotiation.

"That's fine. I'll do as you'd prefer. I figured that's how it would be, so I brought a book to read," Shoko replied calmly, not bothered by her niece's stern tone. She was probably used to that sort of exchange.

Mariye completely ignored what her aunt said, and crouched down a bit, gazing steadily at Tomohiko Amada's *Killing Commendatore* hanging on the wall. The look in her eyes as she studied this rectangular Japanese painting was intense. She examined each and every detail of the painting, as if etching every element of it in her memory. Come to think of it (I thought), this might be the first time anyone else had ever laid eyes on this painting. It had totally slipped my mind to move the painting somewhere out of sight. Too late now, I thought.

"Do you like that painting?" I asked the girl.

Mariye didn't reply. She was concentrating so much on the painting that she didn't hear my voice. Or did she hear it but was just ignoring me?

"I'm sorry. She really goes her own way sometimes," Shoko said, interceding. "She focuses so hard sometimes she blocks out everything else. She's always been that way. With books and music, paintings and movies."

I don't know why, but neither Shoko nor Mariye asked whether the painting was by Tomohiko Amada, so I didn't venture to explain. And of course I didn't tell them the title, *Killing Commendatore*, either. I wasn't too worried that they'd both seen the painting. Neither one probably would notice that this was a special work not included in Amada's oeuvre. Things would be different if Menshiki or Masahiko spotted it.

I let Mariye examine *Killing Commendatore* to her heart's content. I went to the kitchen, boiled water, and made tea. I put cups and the teapot on a tray and carried it to the living room. I added the cookies Shoko had brought as a gift. Shoko and I sat on chairs in the living room and sipped tea while chatting about life in the mountains, the weather in the valley, etc. This kind of relaxed conversation was necessary before I began to work in earnest.

Mariye kept studying *Killing Commendatore* by herself for a while, then finally, like a very curious cat, slowly made her way around the studio, picking things up and checking them out along the way. Brushes, tubes of paint, a canvas, and even the old bell that had been exhumed from underground. She held the bell and shook it a few times. It made its usual light jingling sound.

"How come there's an old bell here?" Mariye, facing a blank space, didn't seem to be addressing her question to anyone in particular. She was asking me, of course.

"The bell came nearby, from out of the ground," I said. "I just happened across it. I think it's connected with Buddhism somehow. Like a priest would ring it as he recited sutras."

She rang it again next to her ear. "Kind of a strange sound," she commented.

Once more I was impressed that such a faint sound could have reached out from underground in the woods and found me in the house. Maybe there was some special way of shaking it.

"You shouldn't touch someone else's things without permission," Shoko Akikawa cautioned her niece.

"I don't mind," I said. "It's not valuable."

Mariye seemed to quickly lose interest in the bell. She returned it to the shelf, plunked down on the stool in the middle of the room, and gazed at the scenery out the window.

"If you don't mind, I was thinking of starting," I said.

"All right, then I'll stay here and read," Shoko said, an elegant smile rising to her lips. From her black bag she took out a thick paperback with a bookstore's paper cover. I left her there, went into the studio, and shut the door between it and the living room. Mariye and I were alone in the room.

I had Mariye sit in a dining room chair, one with a backrest. And I sat on my usual stool. We were about six feet apart.

"Could you sit there for a while for me? You can sit however you'd like. As long as you don't change your position too much, it's okay to move around. No need to sit completely still."

"Is it okay for me to talk while you're painting?" Mariye asked probingly.

"No problem at all," I said. "Let's talk."

"That drawing of me you did the other day was great."

"The one in chalk on the blackboard?"

"Too bad it got erased."

I laughed. "Can't keep it on the blackboard forever. But if you like that kind of thing I can do as many as you want. It's simple."

She didn't reply.

I picked up a thick pencil and used it as a kind of ruler to measure the various elements of her facial features. Different from a croquis, when drawing a dessan you need to take time and make sure you have an accurate grasp of the model's features. No matter what kind of painting it ends up being.

"I think you have a real talent for drawing," Mariye said after a period of silence, as if remembering.

"Thank you," I said. "Hearing that gives me courage."

"You need courage?"

"Sure I do. Everybody needs to have courage."

I picked up a large sketchbook and opened it.

"I'm going to sketch dessan of you today. I enjoy painting with oils directly on a blank canvas, but today I'll stick to drawing detailed dessan. That way I can gradually understand the kind of person you are."

"Understand me?"

"Drawing someone means understanding and interpreting another person. Not with words, but with lines, shapes, and colors."

"I wish I could understand myself," Mariye said.

"I feel the same way," I agreed. "I wish I could understand myself, too. But it's not easy. That's why I paint."

Using a pencil, I quickly sketched her face and figure from the waist up. How to transfer her depth to a flat medium was critical. And how to transplant her subtle movements to something static—that too was vital. A dessan sketch determines the outline of those.

"My breasts are really small, don't you think?" Mariye asked, out of nowhere.

"I wonder," I said.

"They're like bread that didn't rise."

I laughed. "You've just started junior high. I'm sure they'll get bigger. It's nothing to worry about."

"I don't even really need a bra. The other girls in my class all wear bras."

Certainly it was hard to see any development through her sweater. "If it really bothers you, you could always pad your bra," I said.

"You want me to?"

"Either way's fine with me. It's not like I'm painting you to capture your breasts. You should do whatever you like."

"But don't men like women with big breasts?"

"Not necessarily," I said. "When my younger sister was about your age, her breasts were small too. But that didn't seem to bother her."

"Maybe it bothered her, but she just didn't mention it."

"Could be," I said. But I don't think that bothered Komi. She had other things to worry about.

"Did your sister's breasts get bigger after that?"

My hand continued to move the pencil swiftly across the page. I didn't respond to her question. Mariye watched my hand glide along the paper.

"Did her breasts get bigger after that?" Mariye asked again.

"No, they didn't," I finally gave up and answered. "My sister died the year she entered junior high. She was only twelve."

Mariye didn't say anything for a while.

"Don't you think my aunt's really beautiful?" Mariye said, abruptly changing subjects.

"Yes, she's a very lovely person."

"Are you single?"

"Ah—*nearly,*" I responded. Once that envelope arrived at the law office it'd be completely.

"Would you like to go on a date with her?"

"That would be nice."

"She has big breasts, too."

"I hadn't noticed."

"And they're really nicely shaped. We bathe together sometimes, so I know."

I looked at Mariye's face again. "Do you get along well with your aunt?"

"We fight sometimes," she said.

"About what?"

"All kinds of things. When we have a difference of opinion, or when she makes me mad."

"You're an unusual girl," I said. "You're quite different from when you're in art class. I got the impression you were very quiet."

"In places where I don't want to talk, I don't," she said simply. "Am I talking too much? Would it be better if I stayed quiet?"

"No, not at all. I like talking. Feel free to talk as much as you like."

Of course I welcomed a lively conversation. I wasn't about to stay totally silent for nearly two hours and just paint.

"I can't help thinking about my breasts," Mariye said after a while. "That's all I think about, pretty much. Is that weird?"

"Not particularly," I said. "You're at that age. When I was your age all I thought about was my penis. Whether it was shaped funny, or was too small, whether it was working wrong."

"What about now?"

"You're asking what I think about my penis now?"

"Yeah."

I thought about it. "I don't give it much thought. It's pretty ordinary, I guess, and hasn't given me any problems."

"Do women admire it?"

"Occasionally there might be one who does. But that might just be flattery. Like when people praise paintings."

Mariye pondered this for a while. Finally she said, "You may be a little strange."

"Really?"

"Normal men don't talk like that. Even my father doesn't say things like that to me."

"I doubt fathers in normal families want to talk about penises with their daughters," I said. All the while my hand continued to move busily over the paper.

"At what age do nipples get bigger?" Mariye asked.

"I'm not really sure. Since I'm a guy. I'd say it really depends on the person."

"Did you have a girlfriend when you were a kid?"

"I had my first girlfriend when I was seventeen. A girl in the same class in high school."

"What high school?"

I told her the name of a public high school in Toshima, in Tokyo. Outside of people who lived in Toshima, probably no one had ever heard of it.

"Did you like school?"

I shook my head. "Not particularly."

"Did you ever see that girlfriend's nipples?"

"Yeah," I said. "She showed them to me."

"How big were they?"

I remembered the girl's nipples. "They weren't especially small, or big. Normal size, I guess."

"Did she pad her bra?"

I tried to recall the bra my girlfriend had worn back then. All I had was a very vague memory of it. What I did recall was how much trouble I had slipping my hand behind her and unhooking it. "No, I don't think she padded it."

"What's she doing now?"

What *was* she doing now? "I don't know. I haven't seen her for a long time. I imagine she's married, maybe with some children."

"How come you don't see her?"

"The last time I saw her, she said she never wanted to see me again."

Mariye frowned. "Was this because there was something wrong with you?"

"I guess," I said. Of course the problem lay with me. No room for doubt there.

Actually, I'd recently had two dreams about this high school girlfriend. In one dream we were strolling along a river on a summer's evening. I tried to kiss her, but her long black hair formed a curtain in front of her face and my lips couldn't touch hers. In the dream she was still seventeen, but I had already turned thirty-six, something I suddenly noticed. And that's when I woke up. It was such a vivid dream. I could still feel her hair on my lips. Before this, I hadn't thought about her for years.

"How much younger than you was your younger sister?" Mariye said, again suddenly changing topics.

"Three years younger."

"You said she died when she was twelve?"

"That's right."

"So that would make you fifteen then."

"Right. I was fifteen. I'd just started high school. And she'd just started junior high. Just like you."

Now that I thought about it, Komi was now twenty-four years younger than me. Since she'd died, every year the age gap only increased between us.

"I was six when my mother died," Mariye said. "She got stung by hornets. When she was walking in the mountains nearby."

"I'm very sorry," I said.

"She had an allergy to hornet stings. They took her by ambulance to the hospital but she was already in shock and went into cardiac arrest."

"Your aunt moved in with you after that?"

"Yeah," Mariye said. "She's my father's younger sister. I wish I'd had an older brother. A brother three years older."

I finished up the first dessan and began a second. I wanted to draw her from several angles. This first day I planned to devote just to sketches.

"Did you ever fight with your sister?" she asked.

"No, I don't recall ever fighting."

"So you got along well?"

"I suppose so. I never considered whether we did or not."

"What does 'nearly single' mean?" Mariye asked, again shifting subjects.

"I'll soon be officially divorced," I said. "We're in the midst of handling all the paperwork, so that's why it's 'nearly.' "

She narrowed her eyes. "I don't get *divorce*. Nobody I know has ever divorced."

"I don't get it either. I mean, it's the first time I ever got divorced."

"What does it feel like?"

"A bit bizarre, I guess. Like you're walking along as always, sure you're on the right path, when the path suddenly vanishes, and you're facing an empty space, no sense of direction, no clue where to go, and you just keep trudging along. That's what it feels like."

"How long were you married?"

"About six years."

"How old is your wife?"

"She's three years younger." Just a coincidence, but the same age difference as with my sister.

"Do you think you wasted those six years?"

I thought about it. "No, I don't think so. I don't want to think it was all for nothing. We had a lot of good times, too."

"Does your wife think so too?"

I shook my head. "I don't know. I'd hope she would, of course."

"You didn't ask her?"

"No. If I have a chance, maybe I will sometime."

Silence reigned between us for a while. I focused on the dessan, and Mariye Akikawa was lost in serious thought—thoughts about the size of nipples, perhaps, or divorce, or hornets, or maybe something else entirely. Eyes narrowed, lips tight, both hands tightly holding her knees. She'd shifted into that mode, apparently, as I was capturing her earnest expression on the white page of my sketchbook.

Every day, exactly at noon, I could hear a chime from down the mountain. Ringing from some government office, or maybe a school, to announce the time. When I heard it now, I glanced at the clock and finished drawing. I'd managed to complete three dessan during this first session. All of them pretty interesting compositions, each one hinting at something to come. Not bad for a day's work.

Mariye Akikawa had sat on the chair in the studio, posing for me, for over an hour and a half. For the first day, that was enough. For someone not used to it—especially an active, growing child—posing for a painting wasn't easy.

Shoko Akikawa had put on black-framed glasses and was seated on the living room sofa absorbed in reading her paperback. When I came in she took off the glasses and stowed the paperback in her bag. The glasses made her look quite intellectual.

"We're all finished for the day," I said. "If it's all right, could you come again the same day next week?"

"Yes, of course," Shoko said. "It feels really nice to read here. Maybe because the sofa's so comfortable?"

"You don't mind?" I asked Mariye.

Mariye nodded silently. *I don't mind*, it meant. In front of her aunt she was totally changed, and had become taciturn again. Maybe she didn't like when the three of us were together.

They got into their blue Toyota Prius and drove away. I saw them off at the front door. Shoko, sunglasses on, reached a hand out the window and gave a few short waves goodbye. A small, pale hand. I raised my hand in reply. Mariye tucked in her chin and stared straight ahead.

Once the car had disappeared from view down the slope, I went back inside. The house seemed suddenly barren. Like something that should be there wasn't anymore.

An odd pair, I thought, as I stared at the teacups still on the table. There was something peculiar about them. But what, exactly?

I remembered Menshiki. Maybe I should have taken Mariye out on the terrace so he could get a good look at her through his binoculars. But then I rethought that. Why did I have to go out of my way to do that, when he hadn't even asked me to?

Other opportunities would present themselves. No need to rush. Probably.

31

MAYBE A LITTLE TOO PERFECT

That night I got a call from Menshiki. The clock showed that it was past nine. He apologized for calling so late. Something silly came up and I couldn't get free until now, he said. I'm not going to bed for a while, I said, so don't worry about the time.

"So how did things go today? Did it work out well?" he asked.

"It did. I completed a few dessan of Mariye. The two of them will be coming over the same time next Sunday."

"I'm glad," Menshiki said. "By the way, was the aunt favorably disposed toward you?"

Favorably disposed? What a strange way of putting it.

I said, "Yes, she seems like a very nice woman. I don't know if 'favorably disposed' is the right term, but she didn't seem particularly wary."

I summed up what had taken place that morning. Menshiki listened with what seemed like bated breath, apparently trying to absorb as much detailed information as he could. Other than a couple of questions, he hardly said a word, and just listened intently. What sort of clothes the two had on, how they had arrived. How they appeared, what they'd said. And how I'd gone about sketching Mariye Akikawa. I told Menshiki all this, piece by piece. I didn't, though, delve into Mariye's obsession with the size of her breasts. That was best kept between us.

"It might be a little early, then, for me to show up next week?" Menshiki asked me.

"It's up to you. I can't say. I don't have a problem if you come over next week."

On the other end of the line Menshiki was silent. "I'll have to think about it. It's kind of delicate."

"Take your time. It's going to take a while to finish the painting, and there should be plenty of opportunities. Next week, or the week after that—either way's fine with me."

I'd never seen Menshiki so hesitant before. Quickly decisive and never wavering—that was the Menshiki I knew.

I was thinking of asking him if he'd been watching my house with his binoculars this morning. Whether he'd been able to observe Mariye and her aunt. But I thought better of it. As long as he didn't bring it up, it seemed smarter not to mention that topic. Even if the place under surveillance was the house I was living in.

Menshiki thanked me again. "I'm really sorry to ask you to go to all this trouble for me."

I said, "I'm not doing anything for your sake. I'm simply doing a painting of Mariye Akikawa. I'm painting it because I want to. I thought that's how we decided things were going to be. Both the private and public reasons for it. So there's no reason for you to thank me."

"Still, I'm very grateful," Menshiki said quietly. "In *a lot of ways*."

I didn't really understand what he meant by "a lot of ways," but didn't ask. It was getting late. We said a quick goodbye and hung up. But after I put the phone down, it suddenly occurred to me that Menshiki might be spending a long, sleepless night tonight. I could sense the tension in his voice. He probably had lots of things on his mind.

Not much happened that week. The Commendatore didn't make an appearance, and my girlfriend didn't get in touch. A very quiet week altogether. Autumn steadily deepened around me. The sky opened up, the air clear and crisp, the clouds like beautiful white brushstrokes.

I often studied the three dessan I'd done of Mariye. The different poses, the different angles. I found them fascinating, and suggestive. Though from the beginning I hadn't planned to choose one of them to use as the preliminary design for the painting. The point of doing those three sketches, as she herself had said, was so I could understand the totality of this girl. To internally assimilate her.

I looked at those three dessan over and over again, intently focusing, trying to construct a concrete picture of the girl in my mind. As I did this, I got the distinct sense of Mariye Akikawa's figure and that of my sister getting mixed into one. Was this appropriate? I couldn't say. But the spirits of these two young girls nearly the same age were already, somewhere—probably in some deep internal recesses I shouldn't access—blended and combined. I could no longer unravel those two intertwined spirits.

That Thursday I received a letter from my wife. This was the first time since I'd left home in March that she'd gotten in touch. My name and address and hers were written on the envelope in her familiar, beautiful, steady handwriting. She was still using my last name, I saw. Maybe it was more convenient, somehow, until the divorce became official, to continue to use her husband's last name.

I used scissors to neatly snip open the envelope. Inside was a postcard with a photo of a polar bear standing on top of an iceberg. On the card she'd written a simple message thanking me for signing the divorce papers and mailing them back so quickly.

How are you? I'm managing to get by, nothing to report. I'm still living in the same place. Thank you for mailing back the papers so quickly. I appreciate it. I'll get in touch when there's been progress in the process.

If there's anything you left at the house you need, please let me know. I'll send it to you. At any rate, I hope both our new lives work out.

Yuzu

I reread the letter many times, straining to decipher the feelings hidden behind those lines. But I couldn't detect any implied emotion or intention. She just seemed to be transmitting the clearly stated message that the words conveyed.

One other thing I didn't understand was why it had taken her so long to prepare the divorce papers. It's not that much trouble to get them ready. And she must have wanted to dissolve our relationship as fast as possible. Even so, half a year had passed since I'd left our house. What had she been doing all that time? What had been going through her mind?

I gazed at the postcard with the polar bear, but couldn't read any intentions in that either. Why a polar bear from the North Pole? She probably just happened to have the polar bear card on hand and used it. Most likely that's the case, I figured. Or was she suggesting that my future was like that of the polar bear, stuck on a tiny iceberg, directionless, carried away by the whims of the current? No—that was reading too much into it.

I tossed the card into the envelope and put it inside the top drawer of my desk. Once I shut the drawer it felt like things had progressed one step forward. Like with a *click* the scale had moved one line up. Not that this was my doing. Someone, something, had prepared this new stage in my stead, and I was simply going along with the program.

I recalled how on Sunday I'd talked to Mariye Akikawa about life after divorce.

Like you're walking along as always, sure you're on the right path, when the path suddenly vanishes, and you're facing an empty space, no sense of direction, no clue where to go, and you just keep trudging along. That's what it feels like.

A directionless ocean current, a road to nowhere, it didn't matter much. They were both the same. Just metaphors. I was experiencing the real thing, and being swallowed up by reality. If I had that, who needs a metaphor?

If I could, I wanted to write a letter to Yuzu to explain the situation I found myself in now. I didn't think I could write something vague like *I'm managing to get by, nothing to report*. Far from it. My honest sense was there was *too much to report*. But if I started writing about every single thing that had happened to me since I started living here, it would spin out of control. The biggest problem was that I couldn't explain well to myself what was happening. At least I knew I couldn't find a consistent, logical context in which to *explain* it all.

So I decided not to write back to Yuzu. If I did start writing there were only two ways to go: either explain everything that had taken place (ignoring logic and consistency), or write nothing. I chose the latter. In a sense I really was the lonely polar bear left behind to drift on an iceberg. Not a single mailbox as far as the eye could see. A polar bear has no way to send a letter, now does he.

I remember very well when Yuzu and I first met, and started dating.

On our first date we had dinner, talked about all kinds of things, and she seemed to like me. She said I could see her again. From the first our minds seemed to inexplicably click. Simply put, we seemed a good match.

But it took some time before I actually became her lover. Yuzu had another man she'd been seeing for two years. Not that she was head over heels in love with him.

"He's really handsome. Though a bit boring sometimes," she said.

Very handsome but boring . . . There was no one I knew like that, so I couldn't picture that type of person. What came to mind was a dish of food that looked delicious but ended up tasting bland. Would anyone be happy with that kind of food?

"I've always had a weakness for good-looking men," she said, as if making a confession. "Whenever I meet a handsome man it's like my brain goes out the window. I know that's a problem, but I can't do anything about it. I can't get over that. That might be my biggest weakness."

"A chronic disease," I said.

She nodded. "That could be. An incurable disorder. A chronic disease."

"Not exactly great news for me," I said. Handsome features weren't my strongest selling point.

She didn't deny that, and just laughed happily. At least she didn't seem bored when we were together. She had a lot to say, and laughed a lot.

So I waited patiently for things to not work out between her and this handsome boyfriend. (He wasn't merely good-looking, but had graduated from a top university and had a high-paying job at a top corporation. I bet he and Yuzu's father got along famously.) All this time she and I talked over all sorts of things, went to all sorts of places. We got to understand each other better. We kissed, held each other, but didn't have sex. Having a physical relationship with several partners at the same time wasn't her style. "I'm a bit old-fashioned that way," she said. So all I could do was bide my time.

This went on for about half a year. For me, it felt like eternity. Sometimes I just wanted to give up. But I managed to hang in there, convinced that someday soon she would be mine.

And finally she and her handsome boyfriend broke up (at least I think they broke up—she never said a word about it, so it was conjecture on my part), and she chose me—not much to look at, not much of a breadwinner—as her lover. Soon after we decided to get married.

I remember very well the first time we made love. We'd gone to stay at a small hot-springs town in the country, and spent our first night together there. Everything went really well. Almost perfect, you could even say. Maybe a little too perfect. Her skin was soft and pale, and silky smooth. The somewhat slick hot mineral water of the hot springs bath, combined with the pale glow of the early-autumn moonlight, may have contributed to the beauty and smoothness of her skin. I held her naked body for the first time, went inside her, she moaned quietly in my ear, and dug her nails hard into my back. The autumn insects were in full chorus then, too. A cool mountain stream burbled in the background. I made a firm pledge to myself then: *Never, ever, let this woman go*. This may have been the most sublime moment of my life up till then. Finally making Yuzu mine.

After I got the short letter from Yuzu I thought about her for a long time. About when we'd first met, that autumn night when we first made love. About how my feelings for her had basically never changed, from the first moment up to the present. Even now I didn't want to lose her. That much was clear to me. I'd signed and sealed the divorce papers, but that didn't change things. No matter how I felt about it, though, the fact was that she'd suddenly left me. Gone far away—probably very far away—where even the most powerful binoculars couldn't afford me a glimpse of her.

Somewhere, while I was oblivious to it, she must have found a new, handsome lover. As always, her *brain went out the window*. I should have picked up on this when she started refusing to sleep with me. *Having a physical relationship with several partners at the same time wasn't her style.* If only I'd thought about it, I soon would have realized that.

A chronic disease, I thought. A serious illness with no prospects for a cure. A physical inclination that doesn't respond to reason.

That night (a rainy Thursday night) I had a long, dark dream.

In that small seaside town in Miyagi I was driving the white Subaru Forester (it was now my car). I had on an old black leather jacket, and a black golf cap with a Yonex logo. I was tall, deeply suntanned, my salt-and-pepper hair short and stiff. In other words, I was the man with the white Subaru Forester. I was stealthily following my wife and the small car (a red Peugeot 205) the man she was having an affair with was driving. We were on the highway that ran along the coast. I saw the two of them go into a tacky love hotel on the outskirts of town. The next day I came up behind my wife and strangled her with a narrow, white belt from a bathrobe. I was used to physical labor and had powerful arms. And as I strangled her with all my might, I screamed something. I couldn't hear what I'd yelled out—a meaningless roar of pure rage. A horrific rage I'd never experienced before had control over my mind and body. White spittle flew as I roared out.

As she desperately gasped for air, I saw my wife's temples convulse a little. I saw her pink tongue ball up and twist inside her mouth. Blue veins rose up on her skin like an invisible-ink map. I smelled my own sweat. An unpleasant smell I'd never smelled before rose up from my body like steam from a hot springs. It reminded me of the stink of some hairy beast.

Don't you dare paint me, I ordered myself. I violently thrust out an index finger at myself in the mirror on the wall. *Don't paint me anymore!*

And there I snapped awake.

I knew now what had frightened me most in bed in that love hotel in the seaside town. Deep in my heart I feared that in the last instant I really would have strangled to death that girl (the young girl whose name I didn't even know). "You can just pretend," she said. But it might not have ended with just that. It might not have ended with *just pretend*. And the reason for that lay inside me.

I wish I could understand myself, too. But it's not easy.

This is what I'd told Mariye Akikawa. I remembered this as I wiped the sweat away with a towel.

The rain let up on Friday morning, the sky turning beautifully sunny. I hadn't slept well, felt worked up, and to calm down went for an hour's walk around the neighborhood later in the morning. I went into the woods, walked behind the little shrine, and checked out the hole for the first time in a long while. It was November now and the wind was much colder than before. The ground was covered with damp, fallen leaves. The hole was, as before, tightly covered over with several boards. Many-colored leaves had piled up on the boards, and there were several heavy stones to hold the boards down. But the way the stones were lined up seemed a little different from when I'd last seen them. Nearly the same, yet ever so slightly positioned differently.

I didn't worry about it. There wouldn't be anyone else other than Menshiki and me who would tramp all the way out here. I pulled away one of the boards and peered down inside, but no one was there. The ladder was leaned up against the wall like before. Like always, that dark, stone-lined chamber lay there, deep and silent, at my feet. I put the board back on top and placed the stone back where it had been.

It didn't bother me, either, that the Commendatore hadn't appeared for a good two weeks. Like he said, an Idea has a lot of business to attend to. Business that transcended time and space.

The following Sunday finally came. A lot of things happened that day. It turned out to be a very hectic day.

32

HIS SKILLS WERE IN GREAT DEMAND

Another prisoner approached us as we talked. He was a professional painter from Warsaw, a man of medium height with a hawk nose and a very black mustache on his fair-skinned face . . . His distinctive figure stood out from afar, and his professional status (his skills were in great demand in the camp) was evident. He was certainly no one's nonentity. He often talked to me at length about his work.

"I do color paintings, portraits, for the Germans. They bring me photos of their relatives, wives, mothers and children. Everyone wants to have pictures of their closest kin. The SS describe their families to me with emotion and love—the color of their eyes, their hair. I produce family portraits from amateurish, blurry black-and-white photos. Believe me, I would rather paint black-and-white pictures of the children in the piles of corpses in the *Lazarett* than the Germans' families. Give 'em pictures of the people they murdered; let 'em take them home and hang them on the wall, the sons of bitches."

The artist was especially distraught on this occasion.

—SAMUEL WILLENBERG, *Revolt in Treblinka*, p. 96.

Lazarett was another name for the execution facility in the Treblinka concentration camp.

PART 2

THE SHIFTING METAPHOR

33

I LIKE THINGS I CAN SEE AS MUCH AS THINGS I CAN'T

Sunday was another fine clear day. No wind to speak of, and the fall colors in the valley sparkling in the sunlight. Small white-breasted birds hopped from one branch to the next, deftly pecking the red berries. I sat on the terrace, soaking it all in. Nature grants its beauty to us all, drawing no line between rich and poor. Like time—no, scratch that, time could be a different story. Money may help us buy a little extra of that.

The bright blue Toyota Prius rolled up the slope to my door at ten on the dot. Shoko Akikawa was decked out in a thin beige turtleneck and snug-fitting slacks of pale green. Around her neck, a modest gold chain gave off a muted glow. As on her past visit, her hair was perfectly done. When it swayed I could catch a glimpse of the lovely line of her neck. Today, though, she had a leather bag, not a purse, slung over her shoulder. She wore brown loafers. It was a casual outfit, yet she had clearly spent time choosing each piece. And the swell of her breasts was very attractive too. I had the inside scoop from her niece that "no padding" was involved. I felt quite drawn to those breasts—in a purely aesthetic way, of course.

Mariye was dressed in straight-cut faded blue jeans and white Converse sneakers, a 180-degree turnaround from the formality of her first visit. Her jeans had holes in them (strategically placed, of course). She had on the sort of plaid shirt a lumberjack might wear in the woods, with a thin gray windbreaker draped over her shoulders. Underneath the shirt, as before, her chest was flat. And, just as before, she had a sour expression on her face. Like a cat whose dish has been whisked away halfway through its meal.

Just as I'd done the previous week, I went into the kitchen, made a pot of tea, and brought it to the living room. Then I showed them the three dessan I had made.

Shoko seemed to like them. "They're all so full of life," she exclaimed. "So much more like Mariye than photographs."

"Can I keep them?" Mariye asked.

"Sure," I answered. "Once your portrait is finished. I may need them until then."

Her aunt looked worried. "Really? Aren't you being too— . . ."

"Not at all," I said. "They're of no use to me once the portrait's done."

"Will you use one of these dessan for your underdrawing?" Mariye asked.

"No." I shook my head. "I did them just to get a three-dimensional feel for who you are. The you who I put on canvas will be altogether different."

"Can you tell what that's going to look like?"

"No, not yet. The two of us still have to figure that one out."

"Figure out how I look three-dimensionally?" Mariye asked.

"That's right. A painting is a flat surface, but it still has to have three dimensions. Do you follow me?"

Mariye frowned. I guessed she might somehow associate the word "three-dimensional" with her flat chest. In fact, she shot a glance at the curves beneath her aunt's thin sweater before looking at me.

"How can somebody learn to draw this well?" Mariye asked.

"You mean like these dessan?"

She nodded. "Yeah, like dessan, croquis, things like that."

"It's all practice. The more you practice the better you get."

"I think there are a lot of people," she said, "who don't improve, no matter how much they practice."

She sure hit that one on the head. I had attended art school, but loads of my classmates couldn't paint their way out of a paper bag. However we thrash about, we are all thrown in one direction or another by our natural talent, or lack of it. That's a basic truth we all have to learn to live with.

"Fair enough, but you still have to practice. If you don't, any gifts or talents you do have won't emerge where people can see them."

Shoko gave an emphatic nod. Mariye looked dubious.

"You want to learn to paint well, correct?" I asked her.

Mariye nodded. "I like things I can see as much as things I can't," she said.

I looked in her eyes. A light was shining there. I wasn't sure I understood exactly what she meant. But that inner light was drawing me in.

"What a strange thing to say," Shoko said. "Like you were speaking in riddles."

Mariye didn't respond, just studied her hands. When she did look up a short while later, the light was gone. It had only been there a moment.

Mariye and I went to the studio. Shoko had already pulled out the same thick paperback—at least, it looked identical to the one she had brought the previous week—and settled down on the sofa to read. She seemed totally engrossed in the book. I was even more curious than before as to what it might be, but I didn't ask.

Mariye and I sat across from each other about six feet apart, just as we had the last time. The only difference was that now I had an easel and canvas in front of me. No paints or brush, though—my hands were empty. My eyes hopped back and forth, from Mariye to the canvas to Mariye again. All the while, the question of how best to portray her "three-dimensionally" was running through my mind. I needed a *story* of some sort to work from. It wasn't enough to just look at the person I happened to be painting. Nothing good could result from that. The portrait might be a passable likeness, but no more. To turn out a true portrait, I had to discover *the story that must be painted*. Only that could get the ball rolling.

We sat there for some time, me on the stool, Mariye on a straight-backed chair, as I studied her face. She stared back at me without blinking, never averting her eyes. She didn't look defiant so much as ready to stand her ground. Her pretty, almost doll-like, appearance sent people the wrong signal—at her core, she had a strong sense of herself, and her own unshakable way of doing things. Once she'd drawn a straight line, good luck getting her to bend it.

There was something in Mariye's eyes that reminded me of Menshiki, though I had to look closely to see it. I had felt the similarity before, but it still surprised me. Their gaze had a strange radiance—"a frozen flame" was the phrase that leapt to mind. That flame had warmth, but at the same time, it was cool and collected. Like a rare jewel whose glow came from deep within. That light expressed naked yearning when projected outside. Focused inward, it strove for completion. These two sides were equally strong, and at perpetual war with each other.

Did Menshiki's revelation that his blood might be running through Mariye's veins influence me? Perhaps that had led me to unconsciously link the two of them together.

Whatever the case, I had to transfer that glow in her eyes to the canvas, to capture how *special* it was. The core element in her expression, the thing that cut through her modulated exterior. Yet I still hadn't located the context that made such a transfer possible. If I failed, that warm light would come across as an icy jewel, nothing more. Where was the heat coming from, and where was it headed? I had to find out.

I sat there for fifteen minutes, gazing at her face, then at the canvas and back again, before finally giving up. I pushed the easel aside and took a few slow, deep breaths.

"Let's talk," I said.

"Um, sure," she answered. "What do you want to talk about?"

"I want to know more about you. If that's okay."

"Like?"

"Well, what sort of person is your father?"

Mariye gave a small smirk. "I don't know him very well."

"You don't talk?"

"We hardly see each other."

"Because he's busy with work?"

"I don't know anything about his work," Mariye said. "I don't think he cares about me that much."

"Doesn't care?"

"That's why he handed me over to my aunt to raise."

I took a pass on that one.

"How about your mother—can you remember her? You were six when she passed away, right?"

"I can only remember her in patches."

"What do you mean, in patches?"

"My mom disappeared all of a sudden. I was too little to understand what dying meant, so I didn't really know what had happened. She was there and then she just *wasn't*. Like smoke."

Mariye was quiet for a moment.

"It happened so quickly, and I couldn't understand the reason," she said at last. "That's why I can't remember much about that part of my life, like right before and after her death."

"You must have been pretty confused."

"It's like there's this high wall that divides when she was with me and when she was gone. I can't connect the two parts together." She chewed her lip for a moment. "Do you get what I mean?"

"I think so," I said. "My sister died when she was twelve. I told you that before, right?"

Mariye nodded.

"She was born with a defective valve in her heart. She had a big operation, and everything was supposed to be okay, but for some reason there was still a problem. So she lived with a time bomb ticking inside her body. As a result, everyone in our family was more or less prepared for the worst. Her death didn't hit us like a bolt from the blue, like when your mother was stung by hornets."

"A bolt . . . ?"

"A bolt from the blue," I said. "A bolt of lightning that strikes from a cloudless sky. Something sudden and unexpected."

"A bolt from the blue," she said. "What characters is it written with?"

"The 'blue' is written with characters for 'blue sky.' 'Bolt' is really complicated—I can't write it myself. In fact, I've never written it. If you're curious, you should look it up in a dictionary when you get back home."

"A bolt from the blue," she repeated. She seemed to be storing the phrase in her mental filing cabinet.

"At any rate," I went on, "we all had an idea what might happen. When it actually did, though—when she had a sudden heart attack and died, all in one day—our preparations didn't make a bit of difference. Her death paralyzed me. And not just me, my whole family."

"Did something change inside you after that?"

"Yes, completely. Both *inside* and *outside*. Time didn't pass as it had before—it flowed differently. And, like you said, I had a problem connecting how things were before her death with the way they were after."

Mariye stared at me without speaking for a full ten seconds. "Your sister meant a lot to you, didn't she?" she said at last.

"Yes," I nodded. "She did."

Mariye studied her lap for a moment. "It's because my memory is blocked," she said, looking up, "that I have trouble recalling my mom. The kind of person she was, her face, the things she said to me. My dad doesn't talk much about her either."

All I knew about Mariye's mother was the blow-by-blow account Menshiki had given me of the last time they had had sex. It had been on his office couch—the moment of Mariye's conception, perhaps—and it was violent. Not a big help at the moment.

"You must remember something, even if it's not much. After all, you lived with her till you were six."

"Just the smell."

"The smell of her body?"

"No, the smell of rain."

"Rain?"

"It was raining then. So hard I could hear the drops hit the ground. But my mother was walking outside without an umbrella. So we walked through the rain together, holding hands. I think it was summer."

"A summer shower, then?"

"I guess so. The pavement was hot from the sun, so it gave off that smell. That's what I remember. We were high in the mountains, on some kind of observation deck. And my mother was singing a song."

"What kind of song?"

"I can't remember the melody. But I do remember some of the words. They were like, 'The sun's shining on a big green field across the river, but it's been raining on this side for so long.' Have you ever heard a song like that?"

It didn't ring a bell. "No," I replied. "I don't think so."

Mariye gave a little shrug. "I've asked different people, but no one knows it. I wonder why. Do you think maybe I made it up in my head?"

"Maybe she invented it there on the spot. For you."

Mariye looked up at me and smiled. "I never thought about it like that before. If that's true—it's pretty cool."

I think it was the first time I'd seen her smile. It was as if a ray of sunlight had shot through a crack in an overcast sky to illuminate one special spot. It was that kind of smile.

"Could you recognize the place if you went there again?" I asked. "Back to that same observation deck in the mountains?"

"Maybe," Mariye said. "I'm not sure, but maybe."

"I think it's pretty cool that you carry that scene inside you."

Mariye just nodded.

After that, we just sat back and listened to the birds chirping. The autumn sky outside the window was perfectly clear. Not a wisp of cloud anywhere. We were each in our own inner world, pursuing our own random thoughts.

It was Mariye who broke the silence. "Why's that painting facing the wrong way?" she asked.

She was pointing at my oil painting (to be more precise, my attempted painting) of the man with the white Subaru Forester. The canvas was sitting on the floor, turned to the wall so that I wouldn't have to look at it.

"I'm trying to paint a certain man. It's a work in progress, but it's not progressing right now."

"Can I see it?"

"Sure. I've just started it, though. I have a long way to go."

I turned the canvas around and placed it on the easel. Mariye got up from her chair, walked over, and stood before it with her arms folded. The sharp gleam in her eyes had returned. Her lips were set in a straight line.

I had used three colors—red, green, and black—but still hadn't given the man a distinct shape. My initial charcoal sketch was now totally obscured. He refused to be fleshed out any further, to have more color added to his form. But I knew he was there. I had grasped the essence of who he was. He was like a fish caught in a net. I had been trying to pull him out of the depths, and he was fighting me at every turn. At that point in our tug of war I had set the painting aside.

"This is where you stopped?" Mariye asked.

"That's right. I couldn't find a way to push it past this stage."

"It looks pretty finished to me," she murmured.

I stood next to her and looked at the painting again from her angle. Could she really see the man lurking there in the darkness?

"You mean I don't need to add anything more?" I asked.

"Yeah, I think you should just leave it like this."

I swallowed. She was echoing what the man with the white Subaru Forester had said almost word for word. *Leave the painting alone. Don't touch it again.*

"Why do you think that?" I pressed.

Mariye didn't answer right away. Instead, she studied the painting some more. She unfolded her arms and pressed her hands to her cheeks. As if they were hot, and she was trying to cool them.

"This painting is more than powerful enough as it is," she said at last.

"More than powerful enough?"

"I think so."

"You mean a *not so good kind* of power?"

Mariye didn't answer. Her hands were still pressed to her cheeks.

"Do you know the man in the painting well?"

I shook my head. "No, to tell the truth he's a complete stranger. I ran across him a while back. In a faraway town when I was on a long trip. We never talked, so I don't know his name."

"I can't tell if the power is good or not. Maybe it could be either good or bad, depending on the situation. You know, like the way we see things changes depending on where we're standing."

"And you don't think I should let that power come to the surface, right?"

She looked me in the eye. "Suppose you did and it turned out to be a *not so good thing*, what would you do? What if it tried to grab you?"

She was right. If it turned out to be a *not so good thing*, or indeed an *evil thing*, and it reached for me, what would I do then?

I took the canvas from the easel and set it back down on the floor, facing the wall. The moment its surface was hidden, the tension in the studio released its grip. It was a tangible sensation.

Perhaps I should pack it up and shut it away in the attic, I thought. Just as Tomohiko Amada had stashed *Killing Commendatore* there, to make sure no one could see it.

"All right, so then what do you think of that painting?" I asked, pointing to *Killing Commendatore* hanging on the wall.

"I like it," Mariye said immediately. "Who did it?"

"It was painted by Tomohiko Amada, the man who owns this house."

"It's calling out to me. Like a caged bird crying to be set free. That's the feeling I get."

I looked at her. "Bird? What kind of bird?"

"I don't know what kind of bird. Or what kind of cage. Or what they look like. It's just my feeling. I think maybe this painting's a little too difficult for me."

"You're not the only one. It's too difficult for me, too. But I'm sure you're right. There is a cry in this painting, a plea that the artist desperately wanted people to hear. I react the same way you do. But for the life of me, I can't figure out what that plea is."

"Someone is murdering someone else. Out of passion."

"Exactly. The young man has plunged a knife into the older man's chest, exactly as he planned. The man being murdered can't believe what's happening. The others are in total shock at what's taking place before their eyes."

"Can there be a proper murder?"

I thought for a moment. "I'm not sure. It depends how you define 'proper' and 'improper.' Many people regard the death penalty as a proper form of murder." Or assassination, I thought.

Mariye took a moment to respond. "It's funny, a man's being killed, and his blood is flying all over the place, but it's not depressing. It's like the painting is trying to take me someplace else. Someplace where things like 'proper' and 'improper' don't matter."

• • •

I didn't pick up a brush that day. Instead, Mariye and I sat there in the bright studio talking about whatever crossed our minds. I kept a close eye on her, though, filing each expression and mannerism away in my mind. That stock of memories would become the flesh and blood of the portrait I wanted to paint.

"You didn't draw anything today," Mariye commented.

"There are days like this," I said. "Time steals some things, but it gives us back others. Making time our ally is an important part of our work."

Mariye said nothing, just studied my eyes. As if she was peering into a house, her face pressed against the window. She was contemplating the meaning of time.

When the chimes rang as always at noon, Mariye and I moved from the studio to the living room. Shoko Akikawa was sitting on the sofa, wearing her black-rimmed glasses, reading her paperback. She was so deep in the book it was hard to tell if she was breathing.

"What are you reading?" I asked, unable to bear the suspense any longer.

"If I told you what it was," she said with a smile, marking her spot and closing the book, "it would jinx it. For some reason, every time I tell someone what I'm reading, I'm unable to finish. Something unexpected happens, and I have to break off partway through. It's strange, but it's true. So I've made it my policy not to reveal the title to anyone. I'd love to tell you about the book once I'm done, though."

"No worries. I'm quite happy to wait until you're finished. I could see how much you're enjoying it, so I got curious."

"It's a fascinating book. Once I get into it I can't stop. That's why I've decided to read it only when I'm here. This way, two hours pass before I know it."

"My aunt reads tons of books," Mariye chimed in.

"I don't have that much to do these days," her aunt said. "So books are how I get by."

"Do you have a job?" I asked.

She removed her glasses and gently massaged the crease between her eyebrows. "I volunteer at our local library once a week. I used to work at a private medical college in Tokyo. I was secretary to the president there. But I gave it up when I moved here."

"That was when Mariye's mother passed away, wasn't it?"

"At the time, I thought it would just be temporary. That I would stay only until things got sorted out. But once I started living with Mariye it became hard to leave. So I've been here ever since. Of course, if my brother remarried, I would move back to the city."

"I'd go with you if that happened," Mariye said.

Shoko smiled politely but didn't say anything.

"Why don't you stay for lunch?" I asked the two of them. "I can whip up a pasta and salad in no time."

Shoko hesitated, as I knew she would, but Mariye seemed excited by the idea.

"Why not?" she told her aunt. "Dad isn't home."

"It's really no problem," I said. "I've got lots of sauce already made, so it's no more trouble to cook for three than for one."

"Are you sure?" Shoko said, looking doubtful.

"Of course. Please do stay. I eat alone all the time. Breakfast, lunch, and dinner, every day. I'd like to share a meal with others for a change."

Mariye looked at her aunt.

"Well, in that case we'll take you up on your kind invitation," Shoko said. "You're quite sure we're not imposing?"

"Not at all," I said. "Please make yourself at home."

The three of us moved to the dining area. They sat at the table, while I prepared the meal. I set the water to boil, warmed the asparagus-and-bacon sauce in a pan, and threw together a quick salad of lettuce, tomato, onion, and green peppers. When the water boiled, I tossed in the pasta and diced some parsley while it cooked. I took the iced tea from the fridge and filled three glasses. Mariye and her aunt watched me bustle about as if witnessing a rare and strange event. Shoko asked if there was something she could do. No, I replied, she should just relax—I had everything under control.

"You seem so at home in the kitchen," she said, impressed.

"That's because I do this every day."

I don't mind cooking at all. In fact, I've always liked working with my hands. Cooking, simple carpentry, bicycle repair, yard work. I'm useless when it comes to abstract, mathematical thought. Mental games like chess and puzzles are just too taxing for my simple brain.

We sat down at the table and began to eat. A carefree lunch on a sunny Sunday afternoon in autumn. And Shoko was a perfect lunch-time companion. She was gracious and witty, full of things to talk about and with a great sense of humor. Her table manners were elegant, yet there was nothing pretentious about her. I could tell she came from a good family and had attended the most expensive schools. Mariye left all the talking to her aunt and concentrated on her meal. Later, Shoko asked for my recipe for the sauce.

We had almost finished our lunch when the front doorbell gave a cheerful ring. It was no surprise to me, for just a moment earlier I thought I had heard the deep purr of a Jaguar engine. That sound—the polar opposite of the whisper of the Toyota Prius—had registered in that narrow layer between my conscious and unconscious minds. So it was hardly a "bolt from the blue" when the bell chimed.

"Excuse me for a second," I said, rising from my chair and putting my napkin down. Leaving the two of them at the table, I went to the front door. What would happen now? I didn't have a clue.

34

I COULDN'T RECALL THE LAST TIME I CHECKED MY TIRES' AIR PRESSURE

I opened the door, and there stood Menshiki.

He was wearing a white button-down shirt, a fancy wool vest with an intricate pattern, and a bluish-gray tweed jacket. His chinos were a light mustard color, his suede shoes brown. A coordinated and comfortable outfit, as always. His white hair glowed in the autumn sun. The silver Jaguar was behind him, parked next to the blue Toyota Prius. Side by side, the two cars resembled someone with crooked teeth laughing with his mouth wide open.

I gestured for him to enter. He was so tense his face looked frozen, like a plastered wall only half dry. Needless to say, I had never seen him like this before. He was always so cool, holding himself in check with his feelings packed out of sight. He had been that way even after an hour entombed in a pitch-black pit. Yet now he was as white as a sheet.

"Do you mind if I come in?" he said.

"Of course not," I answered. "We're almost through with lunch. So do come in."

"I really don't want to interrupt your meal," he said, glancing at his watch in what seemed a reflex motion. He stared at it for a long time, his face blank. As if he had a quarrel with how the second hand was moving.

"We'll be done soon," I said again. "It's a very basic meal. Let's have coffee together afterward. Please wait in the living room. I'll make the introductions there."

Menshiki shook his head. "Introductions might be premature at this stage. I stopped by assuming they'd already left. I wasn't planning to meet them. But I saw an unfamiliar car parked in front and wasn't sure what to do, so I—"

"You came at the perfect time," I said, cutting him off. "Nothing could be more natural. Just leave everything to me."

Menshiki nodded and began to take off his shoes. Yet for some reason he seemed to have forgotten how. I waited until he had struggled through the procedure and showed him into the living room. He'd been there several times before, yet he stared at the room as though it was his first visit.

"Please wait here," I said, patting him on the shoulder. "Just sit down and relax. It shouldn't take more than ten minutes."

I left Menshiki sitting there by himself—though it worried me a bit—and went back to the dining area. Shoko and Mariye had finished their meal in my absence. Their forks rested on empty plates.

"Do you have a visitor?" Shoko asked in a worried voice.

"Yes, but it's all right. Someone from the neighborhood just happened to stop by. I asked him to wait in the living room. We're on friendly terms, so there's no need for formality. I'll just finish my meal first."

I ate what remained of my lunch. Then I brewed a pot of coffee while the two women cleaned up the dishes.

"Shall we have our coffee in the living room?" I asked Shoko.

"But won't we be intruding on you and your guest?"

I shook my head no. "Not in the slightest. It's a stroke of luck—this way, I can introduce you to each other. He lives on top of the slope on the other side of the valley, so I doubt you've ever met."

"What is his name?"

"Menshiki. It's written with the characters for 'avoidance' and 'color.' 'Avoiding colors,' in other words."

"What an unusual name!" Shoko exclaimed. "I've never heard anyone mention a Mr. Menshiki before. The addresses of people across the valley are close to ours, but there's little coming and going between the two sides."

We placed the pot of coffee, four cups, and some milk and sugar on a tray and carried it out to the living room. To my surprise, Menshiki was nowhere to be seen. The room was deserted. He wasn't on the terrace, either. And I doubted he was in the bathroom.

"Where did he disappear to?" I said to no one in particular.

"Was he here earlier?" Shoko asked.

"Until a few minutes ago."

His suede shoes were gone from the entranceway. I slipped on my sandals and opened the front door. The silver Jaguar was parked exactly where he had left it. So he hadn't returned home. The sun reflecting off the Jaguar's windows made it impossible to tell if anyone was inside. I walked over to check. Menshiki was sitting in the driver's seat, rummaging around for something. I tapped on the window, and he rolled it down. He looked lost.

"What happened?" I asked.

"I want to check the air pressure in my tires, but I can't find the gauge. It should be in the glove compartment, but it's gone."

"Is there some kind of rush?"

"No, not really. I was sitting there in your living room when it started to bother me. Couldn't recall the last time I checked."

"So there's no trouble with them?"

"No, nothing in particular. They seem normal."

"Then why don't you forget about the tires for now and come back in? The coffee is made, and two people are waiting."

"Waiting for me?" he said in a hoarse voice. "Are they waiting for me?"

"Yes, I told them I'd introduce you."

"Oh dear," he said.

"Why oh dear?"

"Because I'm not ready for introductions yet. Not emotionally prepared."

He had the baffled, fearful look of someone ordered to jump from the sixteenth floor of a burning building to a net that looked the size of a drink coaster.

"You should come," I said, not mincing words. "It's really not a big deal."

Menshiki nodded and got out, closing the car door behind him. He started to lock it before realizing how unnecessary that was (what thief would stray up here?), so he stuffed the key in the pocket of his chinos.

Shoko and Mariye were waiting in the living room. They rose to greet us as we entered. My introductions were simple and straightforward. A common human courtesy.

"Mr. Menshiki has also modeled for me. I painted his portrait. He happens to live nearby, and we've been friends since we met."

"I understand you live on the other side of the valley. Have you been there long?" Shoko inquired.

Menshiki blanched at the mention of his home. "Yes, I've been living there for a few years. Let's see, how many is it now—three years perhaps? Or is it four?"

He turned to me as if for confirmation, but I didn't respond.

"Can we see your home from here?" Shoko asked.

"Yes," Menshiki said. "But it's really nothing to brag about," he added. "It's awfully out of the way."

"It's the same on this side," Shoko said affably. "Simple shopping is a major expedition. Cell phone service and radios are hit-or-miss. And the road is terribly steep. When the snow is thick, it gets so slippery I'm afraid to take the car out. Luckily, it doesn't happen that often—just once, five years ago."

"You're right," Menshiki said. "It rarely snows here. It has to do with the warmth of the wind coming off the ocean. The ocean exerts a powerful influence on our climate. You see . . ."

"In any case," I broke in, "we should be thankful it snows so rarely here." I feared he was about to launch into a lecture on the structure and effects of the warm sea currents along the coast of Japan—that's how wound up he was.

Mariye was looking back and forth at her aunt and Menshiki throughout this exchange. She seemed to have formed no opinion about Menshiki as of yet. Menshiki, for his part, acted as though Mariye wasn't there, focusing on her aunt as though bewitched.

"Mariye here is letting me paint her portrait," I said to him. "I asked her to model for me."

"I drive her here every Sunday morning," Shoko said. "It's not far as the crow flies—from your eyes to your nose, you might say—but the road twists and turns so much we have to take the car."

Menshiki finally turned to look at Mariye Akikawa. But his eyes didn't focus on any part of her face—they buzzed about nervously like a fly in winter, searching for a place to land. Yet they never seemed to find one.

"These are what I've drawn so far," I said, coming to his aid. I handed him my sketchbook. "I haven't started painting yet—we've just wrapped up the preliminary stage."

Menshiki stared at the three dessan for a long time, devouring them with his eyes. As if the drawings of Mariye somehow meant more to him than Mariye herself. This wasn't true, of course—he simply couldn't bring himself to face her. The dessan were a substitute, nothing more. It was the first time he had been close to her, and he was having a hard time controlling his feelings. Mariye, for her part, regarded the floundering Menshiki as though he were some kind of strange animal.

"They're superb," Menshiki said. He turned to Shoko. "Each is so full of life. He's really captured her!"

"I totally agree," she said, beaming.

"All the same, Mariye is a very difficult subject," I said to Menshiki. "Painting her is a challenge. Her expression is constantly changing, so it takes time to grasp what's at the core. That's why I haven't gotten around to the actual painting stage yet."

"Difficult?" Menshiki said. He looked at Mariye a second time, squinting as though dazzled by her light.

"The three dessan should show very different expressions," I said. "The slightest facial movement radically transforms the whole atmosphere. When I paint her portrait, I have to get past those superficial differences to grasp the essence of her personality. Otherwise, I'd be conveying only part of the whole."

"I see," Menshiki said, dutifully impressed. He looked back and forth between the three sketches and Mariye, comparing them. In the process, his face, which had been so pale, began to regain some of its color. Red dots popped up at first, then the dots grew to blotches the size of ping-pong balls, then baseballs, until in the end his whole face had turned rosy. Mariye watched him, fascinated, but her aunt politely turned away. I grabbed the coffee pot and poured myself another cup.

I felt I had to break the silence. "I'm thinking of starting the actual portrait next week. You know, on canvas with real paint," I said to no one in particular.

"Do you have a clear image what it will look like?" asked Shoko.

"Not yet," I said, shaking my head. "I won't know in any concrete way until I'm sitting in front of the canvas with a brush in my hand. Hopefully, the inspiration will hit me then."

"You painted Mr. Menshiki's picture as well, didn't you?" Shoko asked me.

"Yes, last month."

"It's a beautiful portrait," Menshiki said emphatically. "The paint has to dry a bit more before it can be framed, but it's hanging on the wall of my study. I'm not sure 'portrait' does it justice, though. It's a painting of me, but of something other than me, too. I don't know how to put it—I guess you could say it has *depth*. I never get tired of looking at it."

"You say it's you, yet it's not you at the same time?" Shoko asked.

"I mean it's a step beyond your typical portrait—it's deeper, more profound."

"I want to see it," Mariye said. They were the first words she had spoken since we had moved to the living room.

"But Mariye . . . you shouldn't invite yourself into someone's—"

"That's perfectly all right!" Menshiki said, cutting off her aunt's rebuke as if with a sharp hatchet. His tone was so jarring that we all—including Menshiki himself—were stunned.

"Please do come take a look," he continued after a moment's regrouping. "It's so rare for me to meet someone from the neighborhood. I live alone, so you needn't worry about disturbing anyone. Any time at all would be fine."

Menshiki's face was even redder by the time he finished. It appeared that we hadn't been the only ones shocked by the urgency in his voice.

"Do you like paintings?" Menshiki asked, this time directing his question to Mariye. His voice was back to normal.

Mariye gave a small nod.

"If it's all right with you, why don't I stop by again at this time next

Sunday?" Menshiki said. "I could escort you to my home and we could all look at the painting together."

"But we shouldn't inconvenience you—" Shoko said.

"I want to see the painting!" Mariye was firm.

In the end it was agreed that Menshiki would come to pick up the two of them the following Sunday afternoon. I was invited too, but I declined, citing an important errand. The last thing I wanted was to get sucked in any deeper. From now on, let those who were involved look after things. I would remain the outsider, however the situation turned out. I would be the mediator, nothing more—though even that had not been my intention.

Menshiki and I accompanied the beautiful aunt and her niece outside to give them a proper send-off. Shoko looked for some time at the silver Jaguar parked next to her Prius. Like a dog lover appraising another person's dog.

"This is the latest model, isn't it?" she asked Menshiki.

"Yes, this is their newest coupe on the market," he answered. "Do you like cars?"

"No, it's not that. It's just that my late father drove a Jaguar sedan. I used to sit next to him, and every so often he'd let me hold the wheel. The Jaguar hood ornament takes me back to those times. Was it an XJ6? It had four round headlights, I think. And an inline six-cylinder 4.2-liter engine."

"That is the III series, I believe. A truly beautiful model."

"My father drove that car for ages, so he must have really liked it. Although he complained about the terrible mileage. And it had one minor malfunction after the other."

"That model in particular is a real gas guzzler. And the wiring was probably faulty. The electrical system has always been the Jaguar's Achilles' heel. But if it's running smoothly, and if you don't mind shelling out for gas, you can't beat a Jaguar. For driving comfort and handling, no other car matches it—it's got a charm all its own. Most people, though, are really turned off by things like gas consumption and mechanical glitches, which is why the Toyota Prius is the one flying off the lots."

"I didn't buy this car," Shoko said, as if by way of apology, gesturing toward her Prius. "My brother bought it for me because it's safe and easy to drive, and gentle on the environment."

"The Prius is an excellent car," Menshiki said. "I've thought of buying one myself."

Was he kidding? Menshiki behind the wheel of a Toyota Prius was as hard to picture as a leopard ordering a salade Niçoise.

"This is very rude of me," Shoko said, peering into the Jaguar's interior, "but would it be all right if I sat in it for a minute? I just want to try out the driver's seat."

"Of course," Menshiki answered. He coughed lightly, as if to bring his voice under control. "Sit there as long as you like. Take it for a spin if you wish."

I was flabbergasted by how interested she was in Menshiki's Jaguar. On the surface she was so cool and poised, not my image of a car person at all. Yet her eyes were shining when she climbed into the driver's seat. She snuggled into the cream-colored leather upholstery, studied the dashboard with care, and took the steering wheel in both hands. Then she placed her left hand on the gearshift. Menshiki took the car key from his pocket and passed it to her through the window.

"Turn it on if you like."

Shoko took the key, inserted it into the ignition next to the wheel, and rotated it clockwise. Instantly, the great feline awoke. She sat there entranced for a moment, listening to the deep purr of the engine.

"I remember this sound well," she said.

"It's a 4.2-liter V8 engine. Your father's XJ6 had six cylinders, and the number of valves and the compression ratio were different too, but they may well sound alike. Both are sinful, though—they squander fossil fuel like there's no tomorrow. Jaguars haven't changed a bit on that score."

Shoko flipped on the right-turn signal. I heard a cheerful clicking sound.

"This really brings back memories."

Menshiki smiled. "Only a Jaguar's turn signal sounds like this. It's unlike that of any other automobile."

"When I was young, I secretly practiced on the XJ6 to get my driver's license," she said. "The first time I drove another car I was totally confused—the parking brake wasn't where I expected. I had no idea what to do."

"I know just what you mean," Menshiki grinned. "The Brits are fussy about the funniest things."

"I think the interior smells a bit different than my father's car, though."

"Sadly, you're right. For a variety of reasons, Jaguar can't use the exact same materials on its newer models. The smell changed after 2002, when Connolly Leather stopped supplying their upholstery. In fact, the Connolly company went out of business at that point."

"How too bad. I loved that smell. I connect it to the smell of my father."

"To tell the truth," Menshiki said hesitantly, "I own another Jaguar as well, an older model. It may well have the same odor as your father's car."

"Is it an XJ6?"

"No, it's an E type."

"Does that mean it's a convertible?"

"Correct. It's a Series 1 roadster, made back in the mid-sixties. It still runs well, though. It's also equipped with a six-cylinder 4.2-liter engine. An original two-seater. The top has been replaced, of course, so it's not exactly in mint condition."

Most of this flew over my head—I know nothing about cars—but Menshiki's words seemed to have made a deep impression on Shoko. They clearly shared an interest, and a fairly specialized interest at that, in Jaguars. That made me feel a little calmer. No longer did I have to think up topics to help them through their first meeting. Mariye's boredom was palpable, though—she seemed even less into cars than me.

Shoko got out of the Jaguar, shut the car door, and handed the key to Menshiki, who returned it to the pocket of his chinos. Then she and Mariye got in the blue Prius. Menshiki closed the door after Mariye. I was struck by the different *thunk* it made as it closed, nothing like the Jaguar. In this world, what we think of as a single sound can have so many permutations. Just as we know, from one note struck on the open string of a double bass, whether it's Charlie Mingus or Ray Brown.

"So we'll meet again next Sunday," Menshiki said.

Shoko gave Menshiki a big smile, took the steering wheel, and drove off. Menshiki and I waited until the squat rear of the Toyota Prius was out of sight before returning to the house. We sat in the living room sipping cold coffee. Neither of us spoke for some time. Menshiki looked exhausted. Like a long-distance runner who had just crossed the finish line.

"She's a beautiful girl," I said at last. "Mariye, I mean."

"You're right. She'll be even prettier when she grows up," Menshiki said. His mind seemed elsewhere.

"What did you think, seeing her up close?" I asked.

Menshiki smiled an uncomfortable smile. "I didn't get a very good look, to tell the truth. I was too nervous."

"But you must have seen something."

"Of course," he said, nodding. He paused for a long moment. "What did you think?" he asked at last, his eyes serious.

"What do you mean, what do I think?"

Menshiki's face flushed again. "Do you see any similarity between Mariye's features and mine? As an artist who has painted people's portraits for many years, I'm interested in your professional opinion."

I shook my head no. "You're right, I'm trained to take quick note of people's facial characteristics. But that doesn't mean I can tell whose child is whose. Some parents and children don't look alike at all, while total strangers can appear almost identical."

Menshiki gave a long, deep sigh. It sounded wrenched from his entire body. He rubbed his palms together.

"I'm not asking for a definitive judgment. I'm just asking for your *personal impressions*. Even the most trivial ones. I'd like to know if you noticed something, anything at all."

I thought for a moment. "As far as facial structure goes, I don't see much concrete similarity. But your eyes do have something in common. In fact, it startles me every so often."

He looked at me, his thin lips pressed together. "You're saying there's something similar in our eyes?"

"Maybe it's because they reflect your true feelings. Curiosity, enthusiasm, surprise, suspicion, reluctance—I can see those subtle emotions in both your eyes and hers. Your faces aren't all that expressive, but your eyes really are the windows to your hearts. Most people are the opposite. Their faces are expressive, but their eyes aren't nearly so lively."

Menshiki appeared surprised. "Is that how my eyes look to you?"

I nodded.

"I was never aware of that."

"You couldn't control it if you tried. Maybe it's because your feelings are on such a tight leash that your eyes are so expressive. It's not that obvious, though—you have to pay really, really close attention to read them. Most people wouldn't notice."

"But you can."

"Reading faces is my profession."

Menshiki considered that for a minute. "So she and I have that in common. But you still can't tell if we're father and daughter, right?"

"I do have certain impressions when I look at people, and I value those. But artistic impressions and objective reality are separate things. Impressions don't prove anything. They're like a butterfly in the wind—totally useless. But how about you? Did you feel anything special?"

He shook his head several times. "I couldn't tell anything in one brief meeting. I need to see her more. I have to get used to being around her first."

He shook his head again, this time more slowly. He plunged his hands into his jacket pockets as though searching for something, then pulled them out again. As though he'd forgotten what he was looking for.

"No, maybe it's not the number of times," he went on. "It could be the more we meet the more confused I'll get, the farther from any conclusion. It's *possible* she's my daughter, but then it's possible she isn't. But either way makes no difference to me. Her presence alone allows me to consider that possibility, to physically experience that hypothesis. When that happens, I feel fresh blood coursing through my body. Maybe I've never understood the true meaning of being alive until now."

I held my peace. What could I say about the feelings he was experiencing, or about his definition of being alive? Menshiki glanced at his thin, expensive-looking wristwatch and awkwardly struggled to his feet from the sofa.

"I owe you my thanks. I couldn't have done a thing if you hadn't given me a push."

With these few words he stumbled toward the door, struggled a bit to put on his shoes, and stepped outside. From the door, I watched him climb in his car and drive away. When his Jaguar was out of sight, the peaceful quiet of a Sunday afternoon enfolded me once again.

The clock said a little after two p.m. I was dead tired. I pulled an old blanket from the closet, lay on the sofa, and slept with it tucked over me. It was past three when I awoke. The angle of the sunlight in the room had shifted somewhat. What a strange day! I couldn't be sure if I had moved forward or fallen behind, or if I was just circling over the same spot. My sense of direction had gone haywire. There was Shoko and Mariye, and then there was Menshiki. Each had a special magnetism. And I had landed smack in the middle of it all. Lacking any magnetism of my own to speak of.

However exhausted I might feel, though, Sunday was far from over. The hands of the clock had only just passed three. The sun was still in the sky. Loads of time remained before a new day dawned and Sunday became a thing of the past. Yet I didn't feel like doing anything. I had taken a nap, but my head was muddled. It felt like a ball of yarn had been crammed into the back of a narrow desk drawer, and now the drawer wouldn't close properly. Maybe this was the sort of day I should check the air pressure in my tires. Anyone feeling this blah should be able to rouse himself to do that much.

Come to think of it, though, I had never checked the air pressure myself. Whenever a gas station attendant said that the air in my tires "looked a little low," I always asked him to take care of it. Which means I don't own an air pressure gauge. In fact, I don't even know what one looks like. If it fits in a glove compartment, it can't be all that big. Nor so expensive as to require monthly payments. Maybe I should buy one, just to see.

When it began to get dark, I went to the kitchen, cracked open a can of beer, and began preparing dinner. In the oven, I broiled a piece of yellowtail that I'd marinated in sake lees, then sliced pickles, made a cucumber-and-seaweed salad with vinegar, and fixed some miso soup with radishes and deep-fried tofu. Then I sat down and ate my silent meal. There was no one there to talk to, and nothing in particular I could think of to talk about. Just when I was finishing my simple, solitary dinner, the front doorbell rang. There seemed to be a conspiracy afoot to interrupt me toward the end of every meal.

So this day hasn't ended after all, I thought. I had the premonition it would be a long Sunday. I got up from the table and walked slowly to the door.

35

YOU SHOULD HAVE JUST LEFT THAT PLACE ALONE

I walked slowly to the door. Who could possibly be ringing the bell? Had a car pulled up in front without my knowledge? The dining area was toward the rear of the house, but it was a quiet night, so I should have heard the crunch of gravel and the rumble of an engine. Even the vaunted "silent" hybrid engine of a Prius. Still, my ears had picked up nothing.

No one would climb such a long, steep slope on foot at night on a lark. The road was unlit, and deserted. My house had been plopped down on top of an isolated mountain, with no neighbors close by.

For a moment, I thought it might be the Commendatore. But that didn't make much sense. I mean, he could come and go whenever he wanted, so why ring the bell?

I unlocked and opened the door without bothering to check who it was. Mariye Akikawa was standing there. She was wearing the same clothes she had worn that afternoon, only now a thin navy-blue down jacket covered her windbreaker. Naturally, it got chillier once the sun was down. She had a Cleveland Indians cap on her head (why Cleveland?) and a large flashlight in her right hand.

"Can I come in?" she asked. There was no "Good evening," no "Sorry for the surprise visit."

"Sure," I said. "Come on in." That was it. My mental desk drawer wasn't closing properly yet. That ball of yarn was still jammed in there.

I showed her into the dining room.

"I'm still eating dinner. Mind if I finish?" I said.

She nodded silently. She was free of all the tiresome social graces—they meant nothing to her.

"Want some tea?" I asked.

She nodded again. She took off her down jacket, removed her cap, and straightened her hair. I set the kettle to boil, and put some green tea in a small teapot. I wanted a cup of tea myself.

With her elbows on the table, Mariye watched me polish off the broiled yellowtail, miso soup, and salad as if she had come across something very strange. She could have been sitting on a rock in the jungle, watching a python swallow a baby badger.

"I marinated the yellowtail myself," I explained, breaking the silence. "It keeps a lot longer that way."

She didn't respond. I couldn't tell if my words had reached her or not.

"Immanuel Kant was a man of punctual habits," I said. "So punctual that people set their clocks by when he passed on his strolls."

Absolutely meaningless, of course. I just wanted to see how she'd react to something so totally random. If she was really listening or not. Again, no response. The silence around us only deepened further. Immanuel Kant continued strolling through the streets of Königsberg, leading his regulated and taciturn life. His last words were "This is good" (*Es ist gut*). Some people can live like that.

I finished dinner and carried the dishes to the sink. Then I made tea. I returned with the teapot and two cups. Mariye sat there at the table watching me throughout. She was eyeballing me intently—like a historian meticulously checking the footnotes of a text.

"You didn't come by car, did you?" I asked.

At last she opened her mouth. "I walked," she said.

"All the way from your house, by yourself?"

"Uh-huh."

I waited for her to go on. But she didn't. We sat there across from each other at the table for a while without speaking. I'm pretty good at long silences, though. No accident I'm holed up by myself on top of a mountain.

"There's a secret passageway," Mariye said at last. "It's a long way by car, but not far if you take the passageway."

"I've walked all over this area but I've never seen anything like that."

"You don't know how to look," she shot back. "You really have to pay attention to find it. It's well hidden."

"You hid it, right?"

She nodded. "I've lived here since I was small. The whole mountain is my playground. I know every part of it."

"So the passageway is really well concealed."

She gave another firm nod.

"And you used it to come here."

"Uh-huh."

I sighed. "Have you had dinner?"

"I ate already."

"What did you eat?"

"My aunt isn't a very good cook," the girl said. Not a real answer to my question—it was clear she wanted to let the matter drop. Maybe she didn't want to recall what she'd eaten for dinner.

"Does your aunt know you came here by yourself?"

Mariye didn't reply. Her lips were set in a straight line. I chose to answer my own question.

"Of course she doesn't. What responsible adult would let a thirteen-year-old girl wander the mountains after dark? Right?"

There followed another period of silence.

"She's not aware of the passageway?"

Mariye shook her head several times. So her aunt didn't know.

"And you're the only one who knows about it?"

Mariye nodded several times.

"In any event," I said, "given where you live, once you left the passageway you probably went through the woods and past an old shrine to get here. Right?"

Mariye nodded again. "I know that shrine. And I know that someone used a big machine to dig up the pile of rocks behind it."

"Did you watch?"

Mariye shook her head. "I didn't see them digging. I was at school that day. But I saw the tracks. The ground was covered with them. Why did you do it?"

"I had reasons."

"What kind of reasons?"

"If I tried to explain from the beginning it would take too long," I said. So I didn't try. The last thing I wanted was for her to find out that Menshiki was involved.

"It was wrong to dig it up like that," Mariye said, abruptly.

"Why do you say that?"

She gave what looked like a shrug. "You should have just left that place alone. Everyone else did."

"Everyone else?"

"It's been there like forever, but no one touched it until now."

The girl was right, I thought. Perhaps we shouldn't have touched it. Perhaps we should have behaved like "everyone else" had. It was too late to change that now, though. The stones had been moved, the pit exposed, the Commendatore set free.

"Were you the one who removed the lid?" I asked. "Let me guess: you looked inside, then you replaced the boards and the stones that held them down. Am I right?"

Mariye raised her head and looked me straight in the eye. As if to say: How did you know?

"The rocks on the lid had been rearranged. My visual memory is pretty good, always has been. I could see the difference right away."

"Wow," she murmured, impressed.

"But the hole was empty. Nothing but darkness and damp air, right?"

"A ladder was there too."

"You didn't climb down it, did you?"

Mariye shook her head vigorously. As if to say: No way!

"And now," I said, "you've come here at this time of night for a particular reason, haven't you? I mean, this isn't just a social visit, is it."

"A social visit?"

"You know, an 'I happened to be in the neighborhood so I thought I'd stop by' kind of thing."

She thought for a moment before shaking her head. "No, it's not 'a social visit.' "

"Then what is it?" I asked. "I'm more than happy to have you visit me, but if your aunt or your father found out, it could lead to a bizarre misunderstanding."

"What kind of misunderstanding?"

"There are all sorts of misunderstandings in this world," I said. "Some go far beyond what you and I can imagine. In this case, it could make it impossible for me to paint your portrait. That would bother me a lot. Wouldn't it bother you?"

"My aunt won't find out," she said emphatically. "I go to my room after dinner and she never follows me. It's like an agreement we have. I leave through my window and no one knows. No one's ever caught on."

"So you've been walking the mountain at night for a long time?"

Mariye nodded.

"Isn't it scary all by yourself after dark?"

"Other things are a lot scarier."

"Like what, for example?"

Mariye shrugged her shoulders slightly but said nothing.

"Your aunt may not be a problem, but how about your father?"

"He's not back yet."

"Even though today's Sunday?"

Mariye didn't answer. I guessed she wanted to avoid talking about her father.

"Anyway, you don't have to worry," she said. "No one knows when I leave the house. Even if they found out I'd never give your name."

"All right then, I'll stop worrying," I said. "But why did you come here tonight of all nights?"

"Because I wanted to talk to you about something."

"Like what?"

Mariye picked up her cup and took a sip of hot tea. She looked warily around the room as if to make sure no one would overhear. Of course nobody was there but the two of us. That is, unless the Commendatore had returned and was listening in. I looked around as well. But the Commendatore wasn't there. If he was, he hadn't assumed bodily form.

"Your friend who showed up this afternoon, the guy with the pretty white hair," she said. "What was his name? It was kind of weird."

"Menshiki."

"That's right, Mr. Menshiki."

"He's not really a friend. I met him just a short while ago."

"Whatever."

"So what is it about Mr. Menshiki?"

She narrowed her eyes and looked at me. "I think," she said, lowering her voice, "that man is hiding something. In his heart."

"What sort of thing?"

"I don't know. But I don't believe he showed up this afternoon by accident, like he said. I think he came for a very specific purpose."

"What purpose is that?" I asked, a little shocked by how observant she was.

She fixed me with her gaze. "I'm not sure. Don't you know?"

"I have no idea," I lied, praying that Mariye wouldn't see through my deception. I have never been a good liar. When I lie it's written on my face. But there was no way I could tell her the truth.

"For real?"

"For real," I said. "I had no idea he would show up today."

Mariye seemed to buy my story. Menshiki had not told me he would be coming, and his sudden visit had taken me by surprise. So I wasn't really lying after all.

"His eyes are weird," Mariye said.

"Weird in what way?"

"It's like he's always *scheming* about something. Like the wolf in 'Little Red Riding Hood.' When the wolf dresses up like the grandmother and lies in bed, you can tell it's him by his eyes."

Like the wolf in "Little Red Riding Hood"?

"So you had an adverse reaction to Mr. Menshiki, right?"

"Adverse reaction?"

"A negative impression. A feeling he might harm you."

"Adverse reaction," she said. She seemed to be storing the phrase in her mental filing cabinet. Alongside "a bolt from the blue," no doubt.

"It's not like that," Mariye said. "I don't think he's planning anything bad. I just think Mr. Menshiki with the pretty white hair is hiding something."

"And you sense it, right?"

Mariye nodded. "That's why I came to see you. I thought you might be able to tell me more about him."

"Does your aunt feel the same way?" I asked, trying to deflect her question.

"No," she answered, tilting her head to one side. "That's not what she's like. She seldom has an adverse reaction to people. And I think she's interested in him. He's a bit older, but he's handsome and well dressed and I guess very rich and living all by himself . . ."

"So you think she's taken to him?"

"I guess so. She really lit up when she talked to him. Her face, and her voice—it got higher. She wasn't like usual. I bet he felt the change too."

I said nothing, just poured us both a fresh cup of tea. I took a sip.

Mariye seemed to be turning something over in her mind. "I wonder, how did he know we were going to be here today?" she asked. "Did you tell him?"

"I don't think Mr. Menshiki came planning to meet your aunt." I chose my words with care, hoping to avoid another lie. "In fact, he tried to leave when he realized the two of you were here, but I talked him into staying. He *happened* to stop by when your aunt *happened* to be here, and when he saw her he got interested. Your aunt is a very attractive woman, you know."

Mariye didn't look entirely convinced, but she didn't push the issue any further. She just sat there frowning, elbows on the table.

"In any case, the two of you are going to visit his home next Sunday," I said.

Mariye nodded. "Yes, to see your portrait of him. My aunt seems to be really looking forward to it. To paying Mr. Menshiki a visit, I mean."

"I don't blame her for getting excited," I said. "After all, she's living in the mountains with no other people around. Not like in the city, where she'd have opportunities to meet all sorts of men."

Mariye pressed her lips together for a moment.

"My aunt used to have a boyfriend," she said, as if letting me in on a big secret. "A man she saw for a really long time. When she was a secretary in Tokyo. But a lot of things happened, and in the end they broke up. It hurt her a lot. Then my mother died, and she came to look after me. She didn't tell me any of this, of course."

"I don't think she's seeing anyone now, is she?"

Mariye shook her head. "I don't think so."

"So you're a little concerned that your aunt is interested in Mr. Menshiki, and that she may be experiencing the first stirrings of something. So you came to talk to me about it. Is that right?"

"Tell me, do you think he's trying to seduce her?"

"Seduce her?"

"I mean, that he isn't serious?"

"There's no way for me to tell," I said. "I don't know Mr. Menshiki that well. They just met this afternoon, so nothing has happened between them yet. When two people's feelings are involved like this, things can change in subtle ways. What begins as a small feeling can grow into something really big, or the opposite can happen."

"But I have a kind of hunch this time," she asserted.

I sensed that I should believe her "kind of hunch," baseless though it was. For I had a similar kind of hunch.

"So you're worried something could occur that might harm your aunt psychologically," I said.

Mariye gave a quick nod. "My aunt's not a very cautious person, and she's not used to being hurt."

"It sounds like you're the one looking after her, and not the other way around," I said.

"In a way," Mariye said seriously.

"How about you, then? Are you used to being hurt?"

"I don't know," Mariye said. "At least I'm not about to fall in love."

"You will someday, though."

"But not now. Not until my chest gets a little bigger anyway."

"That may happen sooner than you expect."

Mariye made a wry face. I guessed she didn't believe me.

I felt a seed of doubt sprout in my own chest. Would Menshiki draw close to Shoko Akikawa to establish a firm connection with Mariye?

After all, he had said to me, *I couldn't tell anything in one brief meeting. I need to see her more.*

Shoko would be an important intermediary—through her, Menshiki could see Mariye on a regular basis. After all, she was the one looking after the girl. To a greater or lesser extent, therefore, Menshiki had to place Shoko under his thumb. That shouldn't be too hard for a man of Menshiki's talents. Not child's play, perhaps, but close to it. I didn't like to think that Menshiki was harboring a plan of that sort. Yet perhaps the Commendatore had been right, and he was a man who couldn't help fabricating some scheme or other. From what I had seen, however, he wasn't that cunning.

"Mr. Menshiki's house is really impressive," I said to Mariye. "You may or may not like it, but it wouldn't hurt to take a look."

"Have you been there?"

"Only once. I went there for dinner."

"It's on the other side of the valley?"

"Right across from us."

"Can you see it from here?"

I pretended to think for a moment. "Yes, but it's far away, of course."

"Show me."

I led her to the terrace and pointed out Menshiki's mansion on top of the mountain across the valley. Bathed in the light from the garden lanterns, the building floated white in the distance like an elegant ocean liner sailing the night sea. Several of the windows were also lit up. The lights burning there were small and unobtrusive.

"That enormous white house?" Mariye exclaimed in surprise. She stared at me for a moment. Then, wordlessly, she turned back to the distant mansion.

"I can see it from my house, too," she said eventually. "The angle's a bit different, though. I've always wondered who would live in a place like that."

"It does stand out, that's for sure," I said. "Anyway, that's Mr. Menshiki's home."

Mariye spent a long time leaning over the railing looking at the house. A handful of stars twinkled above its roof. There was no wind, and a small, sharp-edged cloud hung there motionless. Like a paper cutout nailed to a plywood backdrop in a play. Each time the girl moved her head, her straight black hair glittered in the moonlight.

"Does Mr. Menshiki really live there all by himself?" Mariye asked, turning to me.

"Yes, he does. All alone, in that big house."

"And he's not married?"

"He told me he has never married."

"What kind of work does he do?"

"I'm not sure. Something connected to the information business, he said. Maybe having to do with tech. He doesn't have a regular job right now, though. He lives on the money he made from selling his old business, and from stock dividends and so forth. I don't know the details."

"So he doesn't work?" Mariye said, wrinkling her forehead.

"That's what he said. Seldom leaves his home, apparently."

He might well be standing on his terrace, watching the two of us through his high-powered binoculars just as we were watching him. What would run through his mind if he saw us standing side by side like this?

"You'd better head home," I told Mariye. "It's getting late."

"Besides asking about Mr. Menshiki," she said softly, as if confiding something, "I wanted to tell you I'm really happy that you're painting my picture. I can't wait to see it."

"I hope it turns out well," I said. Her words moved me more than a little. It was strange how much this girl opened up when painting was involved.

I walked her to the door. Mariye put on her tight-fitting down jacket and crammed her Indians cap down over her head. Now she looked like a boy.

"Shall I walk with you partway?" I asked.

"I'm fine. I know the path."

"See you next Sunday, then."

But instead of leaving, she paused for a moment with her hand on the doorframe.

"One thing bothers me," she said. "It's that bell."

"The bell?"

"I thought I heard it ringing on my way here. The same kind of jingling sound that the bell in your studio made."

I was at a loss for words. Mariye's eyes were on my face.

"Where was it exactly?" I asked.

"In the woods. It came from behind the shrine."

I listened to the dark. But I heard no bell. I heard no sound at all. Just the quiet of the night.

"Weren't you scared?" I asked.

Mariye shook her head. "If I leave it alone, there's nothing to be scared of."

"Wait here just a second," I told Mariye. I ran back to the studio. The bell was not where I had left it. It had vanished from the shelf.

36

WHAT I WANT IS NOT TO HAVE TO DISCUSS THE RULES OF THE GAME

After seeing Mariye off, I went into the studio, turned on all the lights, and combed every inch of the room. But the old bell was nowhere to be found. It had vanished from sight.

When had I last seen it? The previous Sunday, on her first visit, Mariye had taken the bell down and shaken it. Then she had returned it to the shelf. I remembered that. But had I laid eyes on the bell since? I couldn't recall. I had hardly set foot in the studio all week. Not once had I picked up my brush. *The Man with the White Subaru Forester* had stalled, and I hadn't yet started Mariye's portrait. I was what you might call "between paintings."

Then, without my knowledge, the bell had disappeared.

But Mariye had heard it ringing behind the shrine when she passed through the woods. Could someone have returned it to the pit? Should I rush there now, see if I could hear the bell with my own ears?

Yet the prospect of hurrying off into the dark woods alone didn't appeal to me. Too many surprises in one day had worn me out. Whatever one might say, I had more than filled my quota of "unforeseen events."

I went into the kitchen, pulled out the ice tray, plunked a few cubes in a glass, and doused them with whiskey. It was only eight thirty. Had Mariye safely navigated the woods and returned home through her passageway? I felt sure she had. No need for me to worry. This mountain had been her playground since she was small, she had said. And she was a lot tougher than she looked.

I took my time working my way through two glasses of Scotch, munched a few crackers, brushed my teeth, and went to bed. For all I knew, I might be roused in the middle of the night by a ringing bell. Around two a.m., as before. Nothing much I could do about that. If it happened, I would deal with it then. But nothing happened. As far as I knew, anyway. I slept like a log until half past six the next morning.

When I awoke, it was raining outside. A chilly rain, signaling the approach of winter. Quiet and persistent. It reminded me of the rain that had been falling that day in March when my wife announced that our marriage was over. I hadn't faced her as she spoke. For the most part, I had looked out the window at the rain.

After breakfast, I put on my vinyl poncho and rain hat (both purchased on my trip, at a sporting-goods store in Hakodate) and walked into the woods. I didn't take an umbrella. I circled the shrine and removed half the boards covering the pit. I made a careful search with my flashlight, but it was empty. No bell, and no sign of the Commendatore. Just to make sure, I decided to descend the metal ladder to check. I had never entered the pit before. The rungs sagged and gave an ominous creak with each step down. In the end, however, I found nothing. It was just an uninhabited hole in the ground. Perfectly round, it might have been a well were it not so wide. Had its builders intended to draw water from it, they would have made its circumference much smaller. And the construction of the wall was too intricate. It was just as the landscaper had said.

I stood in the pit for some time, lost in thought. I didn't feel trapped since I could see a cleanly severed half-moon of sky above. I flicked off my flashlight, leaned my back against the damp, dark stone wall, and closed my eyes as the rain pattered overhead. *Something* was running through my mind, but I couldn't grasp what it was. One thought would link to another, which in turn would link to still another thought. That chain was bizarre somehow, though I couldn't say exactly why. It was as if I had been swallowed by the act of thinking, if that makes sense.

The pit was thinking too, I could tell. It was alive—I could feel it breathing. My thoughts and those of the pit were like trees grown together: our roots joined in the dark, our sap intermingled. In this condition, self and other blended like the paints on my palette, their borders ever more indistinct.

At a certain point, it felt as though the walls of the pit were beginning to close in. My heart made a dry sound as it expanded and contracted in my chest. I felt I could hear its valves open and close. The sensation chilled me, as if I were approaching the realm of the dead. That world didn't strike me as altogether unpleasant, but it was not yet my time to enter.

I returned to my senses with a start. I untangled myself from my train of thought, which had run on without me, then flicked on my flashlight and looked around. The ladder was still where it had been. The sky above my head was the same. I breathed a sigh of relief. For all I knew, the sky could have vanished and the ladder disappeared. Anything could happen in this place.

With great care, I climbed from the pit one rung at a time. Only when I had emerged and was standing on the wet ground did my breathing finally return to normal. It took even longer to get my heartbeat under control. I peered down into the pit one last time. With my flashlight, I illuminated every inch of the dirt floor. But it was just a normal, everyday kind of pit. It was not breathing or thinking, nor were its walls closing in. It just sat there in silence, absorbing the chilly mid-November rain.

I moved the boards back into place and set the rocks on top. I arranged them with care, making sure that they were exactly as they had been before. That way I would know if someone moved them. Then I stuck my rain hat back on my head and walked home along the same path I had come on.

As I walked through the woods, I wondered where the Commendatore had gone. I hadn't seen him for at least two weeks. Strangely, I missed having him around. Without realizing it, I had come to feel a certain kinship with the two-foot man with the tiny sword at his side, despite his odd way of speaking, his voyeurism when my girlfriend and I were making love, and the fact that I had no clear idea what he was. I hoped nothing bad had happened to him.

When I got home, I went straight to the studio, sat down on the ancient wooden stool (the stool Tomohiko Amada must have used when he was working), and studied *Killing Commendatore* hanging there on the wall. I often did that when I wasn't sure what to do—in fact, I studied it endlessly. It was a painting I never tired of, no matter how often I looked at it. It should have been displayed in a museum as a prized example of Japanese art, but instead, it graced the wall of this small studio, and I was the only one who could enjoy it. Before me, it had been hidden in the attic, unseen by anyone.

It's calling out to me, Mariye had said. *Like a caged bird crying to be set free.*

The more I studied the painting the more I realized Mariye had hit the nail square on the head—something was desperately struggling to escape that enclosed space. It longed for a place less confined, for freedom. It was the strength of that will that gave the painting its impact. Whether we understood the meaning of the bird and the cage or not.

I felt the urge to paint something that day. Powerfully. I could feel it mounting within me. Like the evening tide coming in. It was still too early, though, to work on Mariye's portrait. That could wait until next Sunday. And I didn't feel like going back to *The Man with the White Subaru Forester* either. As Mariye had pointed out, a dangerous force lurked beneath its surface.

A new canvas sat on the easel, ready for Mariye's portrait. I sat on the stool studying it for a long time. Yet nothing came to me—no image of what to paint. The blank stayed blank. What should be my subject matter? After a while, at last, the answer rose to my mind.

I stepped away from the easel and took out my big sketchbook. Then I sat on the floor, crossed my legs, leaned back against the wall, and began to draw a chamber of stone in pencil. Not my usual soft pencil but a much harder one. It was a sketch of the strange pit we had found under the pile of rocks in the woods. I had just come from there, so it was fresh in my mind, and I rendered it in as much detail as possible. I drew the intricately fitted wall of stones. I drew the ground around the pit, and the beautiful pattern of the wet fallen leaves. The stand of pampas grass that had once hidden the pit lay flattened by the backhoe.

As I sketched, the eerie sensation that I was merging with the pit returned. It wanted me to draw it. Accurately, and in great detail. In response, my hand moved without conscious guidance. It was a pure act of creation, and it brought with it a kind of joy. When I returned to my senses, I realized that a length of time had passed (I had no idea how much), and that the page in my notebook was covered with pencil lines.

I went to the kitchen, gulped down several glasses of cold water, reheated the coffee, and carried a cup back to the studio. I placed the open sketchbook on the easel and sat down to take a second look, this time from farther away. There was the pit in the woods, in realistic detail. It looked somehow alive. Even *more* alive than the real thing. I got off the stool and examined it up close, then studied it again from a different angle. Only then did it hit me how much it looked like a woman's genitals. The clump of pampas grass flattened by the backhoe resembled her pubic hair to a T.

I shook my head and smiled a wry smile. I mean, how Freudian can you get? I imagined some egghead critic fulminating on the drawing's psychological implications: "This black, gaping hole, so reminiscent of a woman's solitary genitalia, must be understood functionally, as a symbolic representation of the artist's memories and unconscious desires." Or something of the sort. Seriously!

Yet try as I might, I couldn't get the connection between the strange circular pit in the woods and a woman's sex out of my head. So when the phone rang a short while later, I had a hunch it would be my married girlfriend.

And it was.

"Hi," she said. "Some free time just opened up, and I was wondering if I might stop by."

I glanced at my watch. "Sounds good. Let's have lunch together."

"I'll pick up something simple on the way," she said.

"Great idea. I've been working since morning, so I haven't prepared anything."

She ended the call. I made the bed, picked my clothes up off the floor, folded them, and returned them to the chest of drawers. I washed the breakfast dishes in the sink and put them away.

Then I went to the living room, placed my usual record—Richard Strauss's *Der Rosenkavalier*, conducted by Georg Solti—on the turntable, and read on the sofa while I waited for her to arrive. What kind of book was Shoko Akikawa reading, I wondered? What could have so captivated her?

My girlfriend showed up at twelve fifteen. Her red Mini pulled up in front of my house and she got out, a paper bag from the grocery store in her arms. Although a quiet rain was still falling, she carried no umbrella. Wearing a yellow vinyl raincoat with a hood, she walked quickly to my door. I met her there, took the bag, and brought it to the kitchen. She removed the raincoat, exposing the brilliant green turtleneck underneath. Beneath the sweater were two very attractive bulges. Her breasts weren't as large as Shoko's, but they suited me just fine.

"Have you been at it all morning?"

"Yeah," I said. "But it's not a commission. I felt like drawing, so I came up with something on my own, just for fun."

"Just passing the time, huh?"

"Yeah, a bit like that."

"Are you hungry?"

"Not all that much."

"That's good," she said. "Why don't we eat afterward, then?"

"Fine by me," I said.

"You were awfully passionate today. Is there a special reason?" she asked. It was afterward, and we were lying in bed.

"I wonder," I said. What I might have said was, maybe it was because I spent the whole morning madly sketching a strange six-foot-wide hole in the ground and, partway through, my mind made a connection between the hole and a woman's vagina, which must have turned me on . . . But I couldn't.

"It was because I haven't seen you for so long," I said instead.

"You're sweet," she said, tracing a line on my chest with her fingertips. "But be honest—sometimes don't you want a younger woman?"

"No, I've never thought about that."

"Really?"

"Not once," I said. I was being truthful. Our sexual relationship was pure pleasure for me, and I had no desire to seek out anyone else. (My desire for Yuzu, of course, was of a wholly different order.)

I decided not to tell her about Mariye Akikawa. If she learned that a beautiful thirteen-year-old girl was modeling for me, it would only spark her jealousy. It seemed a woman at any age—thirteen, forty-one, you name it—felt she was facing a delicate time in her life. This was one thing my modest experience with the opposite sex had taught me.

"Still," she said. "Don't you think it's strange, the way women and men hook up?"

"Strange in what way?"

"I mean, look at us. We haven't known each other that long, yet here we are lying together naked, making love like this. Completely vulnerable, with no sense of shame. Don't you think it's weird?"

"Maybe you're right," I murmured.

"Try to think of it as a game. Maybe not only that, but a kind of game all the same. Otherwise what I'm saying won't make any sense."

"Okay, I'll try," I said.

"A game has to have rules, right?"

"Yeah, you need those."

"Baseball, soccer, all the sports have a thick rule book, right, where the rules are written down to the tiniest detail, and then umpires and players have to memorize them all. Without that, the game can't take place. Isn't that so?"

"You're absolutely right."

She paused, waiting for the image to sink in.

"So what I'm trying to say is, have we ever sat down and discussed the rules of *this game* that we're playing? Have we?"

I thought for a moment. "Possibly not," I said finally.

"Yet despite that, we are playing the game by a set of hypothetical rules. Right?"

"When you put it that way, I guess you have a point."

"So this is what I think," she said. "I'm playing the game according to my set of rules. And you're playing according to yours. The two of us *instinctively* respect each other's rules. As long as the two sets don't conflict and mess things up, we can go on like this without a hitch. Don't you agree?"

I considered what she had said. "Maybe you're right. We basically respect each other's rules."

"But you know, I think there's something even more important than respect and trust. And that's etiquette."

"Etiquette?"

"Etiquette's big."

"You may be right there," I agreed.

"If all those things—trust, respect, etiquette—stop functioning, the rules clash and the game breaks down. Then we either suspend the game and come up with a new set of rules we can both follow, or we end it and leave the playing field. The big question then would be which of those two routes we decide to follow."

That was precisely what had happened to my marriage. I had called a halt to the game and walked off the field. On that cold and rainy Sunday afternoon in March.

"So are you suggesting that we should talk out the rules of our relationship?"

"You don't get what I'm saying at all," she said, shaking her head. "What I want is *not* to have to discuss the rules of the game. That's why I'm able to be naked with you like this. You don't mind, do you?"

"Not a bit," I said.

"So that leaves us with trust and respect. And most of all etiquette."

"And most of all etiquette," I repeated.

She reached down and squeezed a part of my body.

"It's getting hard again," she whispered in my ear.

"Maybe that's because today is Monday," I said.

"What does Monday have to do with it?"

"Or maybe because it's raining. Or winter is coming. Or we're starting to see migrating birds. Or there's a bumper crop of mushrooms this year. Or my cup is a sixteenth full of water. Or the shape of your breasts under your green sweater turns me on."

She giggled. My answer appeared to have done the trick.

. . .

Menshiki called that evening. He thanked me for the day before.

I had done nothing worthy of his gratitude, I replied. All I had done was introduce him to two people. What developed after that, and how, had nothing to do with me—in that sense, I was a mere outsider. And I would like to keep it that way (though I had a premonition things might not work out so conveniently).

"Actually, I'm calling about something else," Menshiki said once the pleasantries were over. "I've received some new information about Tomohiko Amada."

So he was continuing his investigation. He might not be doing it himself, but arranging for such detailed work was certainly costing him a lot. Menshiki was a man who poured money into anything he thought necessary, sparing no expense. But why, and to what degree, was tracking down Tomohiko Amada's experiences in Vienna necessary to him? I didn't have a clue.

"What we've turned up may not have a direct connection with Amada's stay in Vienna," Menshiki went on. "But it overlaps with that time, and it's clear that it had a huge personal impact on him. So I thought you would like to hear about it."

"It overlapped with that time?"

"As I told you before, Tomohiko Amada returned to Japan from Vienna in early 1939. On paper, he was deported, but in fact he was rescued by the Gestapo. Officials from the foreign ministries of Japan and Nazi Germany had met in secret, and agreed that he be extradited but not charged with any crime. The failed assassination attempt had taken place in 1938, but it was linked to two other important events of that year: the *Anschluss*—Hitler's annexation of Austria—and *Kristallnacht*. The *Anschluss* took place in March, and *Kristallnacht* in November. Once they occurred, the brutality of Hitler's plan was obvious to everyone. Austria was firmly installed as a part of the Nazi war effort. An inextricable cog in the machine. Hoping to block this flow of events, students organized an underground resistance movement, and in the same year, Tomohiko Amada was arrested for his role in the assassination plot. Get the picture?"

"In a general sort of way, yes," I said.

"Do you like history?"

"I'm no expert, but I love books that deal with history," I said.

"A number of important events were taking place in Japan that year as well. Fatal, irrevocable events, which led to eventual disaster. Does anything spring to mind?"

I dusted off my store of historical knowledge, so long untouched. What had taken place in 1938? In Europe, the Spanish Civil War had intensified. German Condor bombers had flattened Guernica. But in Japan . . . ?

"Did the Marco Polo Bridge Incident take place that year?" I asked.

"That was the year before," Menshiki said. "On July 7, 1937. With the Marco Polo Bridge Incident, the war between China and Japan went into full swing. Then in December of that year, another serious event took place."

What had happened in December of 1937?

"The fall of Nanjing?" I asked.

"That's right. What's known today as the Nanjing Massacre. After a hard-fought battle, Japanese troops occupied the city, and many people were killed. Some died in the fighting, others after the fighting ended. The Japanese army lacked the means to keep prisoners, so they killed the Chinese soldiers who surrendered as well as thousands of civilians. Historians disagree on exactly how many died, but no one can deny that a massive number of noncombatants were sucked into the conflict and lost their lives. Some say 400,000, others 100,000. But what difference is there really between 400,000 lives and 100,000?"

He had me on that one.

"So Nanjing fell in December, and many were killed. But what does that have to do with what happened to Tomohiko Amada in Vienna?" I asked.

"I'm getting to that," Menshiki said. "The Anti-Comintern Pact was signed by Japan and Germany in November of 1936, cementing their alliance, but Vienna and Nanjing were so far apart it's doubtful much news about Japan's war in China was getting through to Vienna. In fact, however, Tomohiko Amada's younger brother, Tsuguhiko, had been part of the assault on Nanjing as a private in the Japanese army. He had been drafted and assigned to one of the units fighting there. He was twenty, and a full-time student at the Tokyo Music School, now the Faculty of Music at the Tokyo University of the Arts. He studied the piano."

"That's strange," I said. "To my knowledge, full-time university students were exempt from the draft at that time."

"You're absolutely right. Full-time students were given a deferment until graduation. Yet for some reason Tsuguhiko was drafted and sent to China. In any case, he was inducted in June of 1937 and spent the next twelve months as a private second-class in the army. He was living in Tokyo, but his birth was registered in Kumamoto, so he was assigned to the 6th Division based there. That much is documented. After basic training, he was sent to China, and participated in the December assault on Nanjing. He was demobilized in June of the following year, and was expected to return to the conservatory."

I waited for Menshiki to continue.

"Not long after his discharge, however, Tsuguhiko Amada took his own life. He slit his wrists with a razor in the attic of the family home, which was where they found him. Right around the end of summer."

Slit his wrists in the attic?

"If it was toward the end of summer in 1938 . . . then Tomohiko was still an exchange student in Vienna when his brother Tsuguhiko slit his wrists, right?"

"That's correct. He didn't return home for the funeral. Commercial air travel was still in its infancy. You could only travel between Austria and Japan by rail and ship. There was no way he could have made it back in time."

"Are you suggesting that there's a connection between Tomohiko's involvement in the failed assassination and his brother's suicide? They seem to have happened almost simultaneously."

"Maybe yes, maybe no," Menshiki said. "That's in the realm of conjecture. What I'm reporting to you now are the facts our investigation was able to uncover."

"Did Tomohiko Amada have any other siblings?"

"There was an older brother. Tomohiko was the second son. Tsuguhiko was the third and last. The manner of his death was concealed, though, to protect the family's honor. Kumamoto's 6th Division was celebrated as a band of fearless warriors. If word had gotten out that their son had returned from the battlefield bathed in glory only to turn around and kill himself, they could not have faced the world. Still, as you know, rumors have a way of spreading."

I thanked Menshiki for updating me. Though what the new information meant in concrete terms escaped me.

"I'm planning to dig a bit deeper into this," he said. "I'll let you know if we turn up something more."

"Please do."

"So then I'll stop by next Sunday shortly after noon," Menshiki said. "I'll drive the Akikawas over to my place. To show them your painting. That's okay with you, right?"

"Of course. The painting is yours now. You're free to show it or not to whomever you like."

Menshiki paused. As if searching for just the right words. "To tell you the honest truth," he said. "Sometimes I'm very envious of you." There was resignation in his voice.

Envious? Of me?

What could he possibly be talking about? Why would Menshiki envy me? It made no sense. He had everything, while I had nothing to my name.

"What could you possibly be envious about?" I asked.

"I see you as the kind of person who doesn't really envy anyone. Am I right?"

I thought for a moment before replying. "You have a point. I don't think I've ever envied another person."

"That's what I'm trying to say."

All the same, I don't have Yuzu, I thought. She had left me for the arms of another man. There were times I felt abandoned at the edge of the world. Yet even then I felt no envy toward that other man. Did that make me strange?

. . .

After our phone call, I sat on the sofa and thought about Tomohiko Amada's brother slitting his wrists in the attic. It wasn't the attic of this house, that was for sure. Tomohiko had bought this place after the war. No, Tsuguhiko Amada had committed suicide in the attic of their family home. In Aso, no doubt. Nevertheless, the brother's death and the painting *Killing Commendatore* might be connected by that dark, secret room above the ceiling. Sure, it might have been pure coincidence. Or perhaps Tomohiko had his brother in mind when he hid the painting in the attic here. Still, why was Tsuguhiko compelled to take his own life so soon after returning from the front? After all, he had survived the bloody conflict in China and come home with all his limbs intact.

I picked up the phone and dialed Masahiko's number.

"Let's get together in Tokyo," I said. "I have to visit the art supply shop soon to stock up on paints. Maybe we could meet and talk then."

"Sure thing," he said, checking his schedule. Thursday just after noon was best for him, so we arranged to have lunch together.

"The art supply store in Yotsuya, correct?"

"That's the one. I've got to pick up fresh canvases, too, and I'm running out of linseed oil. It'll be quite a load, so I'll take the car."

"There's a quiet restaurant not far from my office. We could have a nice relaxed chat over lunch."

"By the way," I said, "divorce papers from Yuzu came in the mail, so I signed and returned them. It looks like our divorce will become official pretty soon."

"Is that so," Masahiko said in a subdued voice.

"What can you do? It was just a matter of time."

"Still, from where I stand it's a real shame. You guys seemed like such a good match."

"It was great as long as things were going well," I said. Just like an old-model Jaguar. A wonderful ride until the problems start.

"So what will you do now?"

"No big changes. Just keep on as I am for the time being. Can't think of what else to do."

"Are you painting?"

"Yeah, I've got a couple of paintings I'm working on. Not sure what will happen with them, but at least I'm at it."

"That's the way to go." Masahiko hesitated before adding, "I'm glad you called. There's something I want to discuss with you as well."

"Something good?"

"It's just the facts—I can't say if they're good or bad."

"Does it have to do with Yuzu?"

"It's hard to talk about over the phone."

"Okay, on Thursday then."

I ended the call and walked out to the terrace. The rain had stopped, and the cool night air was clear and bracing. I could see stars peeping from the cracks between the clouds. They looked like scattered crystals of ice. Hard crystals, millions of years old, never melting. Hard to their very core. Across the valley, Menshiki's house glimmered in the cool light of its lanterns.

As I looked at his house, I thought of trust, respect, and etiquette. Especially etiquette. As I expected, though, none of those thoughts led me to any definite conclusions.

37

EVERY CLOUD HAS A SILVER LINING

It turned out to be a long haul from my mountaintop perch on the outskirts of Odawara to downtown Tokyo. I took several wrong turns en route, which ate up a lot of time. My old used car had no navigation system or electronic pass for the highway tolls. (I guess I should have been grateful it came with a cup holder!) It took me ages to find the Odawara-Atsugi Road, and when I moved from the Tomei Expressway onto the Metropolitan Expressway it was jammed, so I opted to get off at the Shibuya exit and drive to Yotsuya via Aoyama Avenue. Even the city roads were crowded, though—just choosing the correct lane was a huge pain in the ass. Parking the car wasn't easy, either. It seems as if, year after year, the world becomes a more difficult place to live.

By the time I picked up what I needed at the art supply store, loaded it into the trunk, drove to Masahiko Amada's office in Aoyama, and found a parking spot, I was exhausted. I felt like the country mouse visiting his city cousin. When I reached his office it was past one by my watch, which meant I was more than a half hour late.

I asked the receptionist to call Masahiko. He came right down. I apologized for being so tardy.

"Don't worry about it," he laughed. "My office can adjust, and so can the restaurant."

Masahiko took me to an Italian place in the neighborhood, located in the basement of a small building. Masahiko was obviously well known there, for no sooner had they seen his face than we were guided to a private room in the back. It was very quiet: the sound of voices did not reach us and no music was playing. A quite passable landscape painting hung on the wall. It showed a white lighthouse on a green peninsula under a blue sky. Super-ordinary scene, sure, but done well enough to let the viewer think, "Hey, that place might be nice to check out."

Masahiko ordered a glass of white wine, while I asked for Perrier.

"I've got to drive back after this," I explained. "It's quite a trek."

"No kidding," said Masahiko. "Still, it's a heck of a lot better than Hayama or Zushi. I lived in Hayama once, and driving back and forth to Tokyo in the summer was awful. The whole route was jammed with people heading to the ocean from the city. A round trip was a half day's work. Compared to that, driving in from Odawara is nothing."

The menus arrived and we ordered the prix fixe lunch: prosciutto as appetizer followed by asparagus salad and spaghetti with Japanese lobster.

"So you finally decided to do some serious painting," Masahiko said.

"Well, I'm living alone now, and I don't need commissions to get by. Maybe that's why the urge to paint my own stuff hit me."

Masahiko nodded. "Everything has a bright side," he said. "The top of even the blackest, thickest cloud shines like silver."

"Yeah, but getting up there to see it is no picnic."

"I was speaking more theoretically," Masahiko said.

"I think living on top of a mountain may be affecting me too. It's the perfect spot to focus on my art."

"Yeah, when no one's there to distract you and it's that quiet, you can really concentrate. A more normal person might get a bit lonely, but I figured you're the kind of guy who can handle it."

The door opened and the appetizer was brought in. We fell quiet as the plates were laid out.

"I think the studio has a lot to do with it as well," I said once the waiter had gone. "There's something about being in that room that makes me want to paint. At times it feels like the center of the whole house."

"If the house were human, it'd be the heart, perhaps."

"Yeah, or the consciousness."

"Body and Mind," Masahiko said in English. "To tell the truth, though, it's hard for me to spend time in his studio. *His* smell has sunk in too deep. I can still feel him in the air. When I was a boy, he'd isolate

himself in that room almost all day, painting away without a word to anyone. It was his sanctum, off-limits to a kid like me. I tend to steer clear of the studio when I'm there, even now. You should be careful too."

"Be careful? Why?"

"So you don't become possessed by his spirit. It's a strong one."

"Spirit?"

"Maybe 'psychic energy' is a better term. Or 'flow of being.' His is intense enough to sweep you away. At any rate, when someone like him spends a long time in a particular place, it soaks in his aura. Like particles of smell."

"And that's what could possess me?"

"Maybe 'possessed' isn't the best way to put it. 'Absorb his influence,' perhaps? It's like he invested that room with some special *power*."

"I wonder. I'm only looking after his home, and I never met him. So maybe it won't weigh on me as much."

"You're probably right," Masahiko said. He took a sip of white wine. "Being related to him may make me more sensitive to those things. And if it turns out that his 'aura' inspires you in your work, so much the better."

"So how's he doing these days?"

"Nothing in particular is wrong with him. He's past ninety, so I can't say he's the picture of health, and his mind is confused, but he can still manage to get around with a cane, his appetite's fine, and his eyes and teeth are in good shape. You know, his teeth are better than mine—never had a cavity!"

"How bad is his memory? Can he recall anything?"

"Not a whole lot. He doesn't recognize me. He's lost the concept of family, of father and son. Even the distinction between himself and other people may have blurred. Still, maybe it's easier when those things are swept away, and you don't have to think about them anymore."

I sipped my slender glass of Perrier and nodded. So Tomohiko Amada had forgotten even his son's face. Memories of student days in Vienna must have set sail for the far shore of forgetfulness some time ago.

"All the same, what I called his 'flow of being' is still strong," Masahiko said, as if in wonder. "It's strange: he remembers almost nothing, but his will is the same as always. It's obvious when you look at him. That psychic power is what makes him who he is. I feel a bit guilty sometimes that I didn't inherit that temperament, but there's nothing I can do about it. We're all born with different abilities. Being linked to someone by blood doesn't mean you have similar gifts."

I looked in his face. It was rare to see Masahiko bare his true feelings.

"It must be awfully hard to have such a famous father," I said. "I can't even imagine what it's like. My dad was nothing special, just a small businessman."

"There are some benefits to having a famous father, but there are times that it really sucks. I think the latter are a bit more frequent, actually. You're lucky you don't have to deal with that. You're free to be who you want."

"You look like the one with a free life."

"In a sense," Masahiko said. He turned his wineglass around in his hand. "But in another sense, no."

Masahiko possessed a keen artistic sensibility of his own. He had taken a job with a medium-sized ad agency after finishing school. By now, his salary had increased, and he looked for all the world like a bachelor enjoying everything city life had to offer. I had no way of knowing if that was true, however.

"I was hoping to ask you a few things about your father," I said, broaching the reason for my visit.

"What sort of things? You know, I really don't know that much about him."

"I heard that he had a younger brother named Tsuguhiko."

"Yeah, that's true. That would be my uncle, I guess. But he died a long time ago. Before Pearl Harbor."

"I heard he committed suicide."

A shadow passed across Masahiko's face. "That's supposed to be a family secret, but it happened so long ago, and part of it's public knowledge now anyway. So I guess it's okay to tell you. He cut his wrists with a razor. He was only twenty."

"What made him do it?"

"Why do you want to know something like that?"

"I've been trying to learn more about your father. I stumbled across your uncle's story when I was looking through some documents."

"You want to learn more about my father?"

"I wanted to learn more about his paintings, but as I looked at his career I became more and more interested in his personal life. I'd like to know the kind of man he was."

Masahiko studied my face from across the table. "All right," he said. "You've taken an interest in my father's life. There may be some significance in that. Living in that house has created some sort of bond between the two of you."

He took a swallow of white wine before launching into his story.

"My uncle, Tsuguhiko Amada, was a student at the Tokyo Music School back then. A talented pianist, they say. He loved Chopin and Debussy, and high hopes were held for his future. Forgive me for sounding arrogant, but artistic talent seems to run in our family. To varying degrees, of course. However, in the midst of his studies my uncle was drafted. He should have received a student deferment, but his papers had been mishandled when he enrolled in the conservatory. If those forms had been properly filed, he could have put off military service until graduation, and probably avoided it altogether. My grandfather was a big landowner in the area, and influential in political circles. But there was a slip-up in the paperwork. It came as a great shock to my uncle. But once the system grinds into motion there's not a whole lot anyone can do to stop it. Protest was futile: the army grabbed him, gave him his basic training in Japan, and then loaded him onto a troop transport and shipped him off to Hangzhou. At the time, his elder brother Tomohiko—in other words, my father—was studying painting under a famous artist in Vienna."

I didn't say anything.

"Everyone knew that my uncle wasn't cut out for the rugged life of a soldier or the carnage of the battlefield—he was a high-strung young man, and physically weak. To make matters worse, the young men of southern Kyushu who made up the 6th Division were a rough group, known for their violence. My father agonized over the news that his brother had been drafted and sent off to war. My father was egotistic and highly competitive, a typical second son, but his younger brother was shy and retiring, the somewhat pampered baby of the family. As a pianist, he had to be careful to protect his hands. Even as a child, my father learned to look out for his little brother, who was three years younger, and shield him from the outside world. It became second nature to him—he was his brother's protector. But all he could do in faraway Vienna was sit and fret. The only information he got came in his brother's letters from the front.

"Of course those letters were strictly censored, but the two brothers were so close that the elder could read the younger's feelings between the lines. Moreover, the true meaning of those lines was skillfully camouflaged, so only he could figure it out. My uncle's regiment had fought their way from Shanghai to Nanjing, engaging in fierce battles in the towns and cities en route, and leaving a trail of murder and plunder in their wake. Those bloody events left my high-strung uncle with deep emotional scars.

"One of my uncle's letters described a beautiful pipe organ they had come across in a church in occupied Nanjing. It had survived the fighting in perfect shape. For some unfathomable reason, though, the long description of the organ that followed had been inked out. What military secrets could an organ in a Christian church possibly have compromised? The standards used by the censor attached to their regiment were impossible to fathom. As a matter of fact, it was common for him to black out the most innocuous and unthreatening passages of a letter while overlooking the parts that really might have put troops at risk. As a consequence, my father was left in the dark as to whether his brother had been able to play that organ or not.

"Uncle Tsuguhiko's year in the army ended in June of 1938," Masahiko continued. "Although he had arranged to reenter the conservatory right after his return, he went back to Kyushu instead and committed suicide in the attic of the family home. He sharpened a straight razor to a fine edge and slit his wrists. It must have taken tremendous resolve for a pianist to do that to his hands. I mean, if he had survived, he might never have been able to play again, right? They found him in a pool of blood. The fact that he had killed himself was kept a deep, dark secret.

To the world, the official cause of death was heart failure or something like that.

"In fact, though, it was clear to everyone why Uncle Tsuguhiko had taken his own life—his war experience had ruined his nerves, and wrecked him psychologically. I mean, here was a delicate young man of twenty, whose entire world was playing the piano, thrown into the bloodbath of the Nanjing campaign, surrounded by heaps of corpses. Today we talk about post-traumatic stress disorder, but that phrase—even that concept—was unknown then. In that deeply militaristic society, people like my uncle were dismissed as lacking courage, or patriotism, or strength of character. In wartime Japan, such 'weakness' was neither understood nor accepted. So the family buried what had happened, as evidence of their shame."

"Did he leave a suicide note?" I asked.

"Yes, they found a personal testament in his desk drawer. It was quite long, closer to a memoir, really. In it, Uncle Tsuguhiko recorded his war experiences in excruciating detail. The only people who saw it were his parents—my grandparents, in other words—his eldest brother, and my father. When my father returned from Vienna and read it, he burned it while the other three watched."

I waited for him to go on.

"My father kept his lips sealed about what that testament contained," Masahiko continued. "It was the family's darkest secret: to use a metaphor, it was nailed shut, weighted with heavy stones, and sent to the bottom of the ocean. However, my father did tell me the gist of what was in it once, when he was drunk. I was in grade school, and it was the first time I learned that I had an uncle who committed suicide. To this day, I have no idea whether it was the alcohol that loosened my father's lips, or if he figured that I had to hear the story at some point."

Our salad plates were cleared, replaced by the spaghetti with Japanese lobster.

Masahiko took his fork and stared at it for a moment. As if inspecting an implement used for some special task.

"Hey man," he said. "This isn't really something I want to talk about when I'm eating."

"No problem. Let's talk about something else."

"Like what, for example."

"Something as far removed from your uncle's testament as possible."

So we talked golf as we ate our spaghetti. Of course, I had never played the game. No one around me had either. I didn't even know the rules. Masahiko, however, had taken it up in order to play with the people he did business with. And to get back into some kind of shape after years of inactivity. He had purchased a set of clubs, and spent his weekends on the golf course.

"You may not know this," he told me, "but golf is the oddest game you can imagine. As weird as it gets. You could say it's a sport unto itself. Yet I'm not even sure if it can be called a true sport. The funny thing is, once you get used to its weirdness you can't go back."

Masahiko went on and on about the strangeness of golf, telling me one off-the-wall story after another. A great conversationalist, he made our lunch extremely entertaining. We laughed together as we hadn't in ages.

Our plates were cleared away and coffee was brought in, although Masahiko opted for another glass of white wine.

"Anyway, back to my uncle's suicide letter," he said, his voice abruptly serious. "According to my father, Uncle Tsuguhiko wrote about being forced to behead a Chinese prisoner. He described it in painful detail. Of course, a common soldier like him didn't carry a sword. In fact, he had never touched a sword up to that point. I mean, he was a pianist, right? He could read a complex musical score, but wielding an executioner's sword was beyond him. But his commanding officer handed him one and ordered, 'Chop off his head!' The prisoner wasn't in uniform and had no weapon when he was picked up. Nor was he a young man. He claimed he was a civilian, not a soldier. But the army was grabbing any likely men they could find and dragging them in to be killed. If your palms were callused, you were deemed a peasant and might be released. If they were soft, however, it was assumed that you were a soldier who'd tossed his uniform to pass as a civilian, and you were summarily executed. Arguing the sentence was a waste of breath. The method of execution was either being gutted by a bayonet or decapitated by a sword. If a machine gun unit was in the area, prisoners might be lined up in a row and shot, but there was a general reluctance to 'waste' ammunition that way—bullets were always in short supply—so bayonets and swords were used. The bodies were collected and dumped in the Yangtze River, where they fed the many catfish who lived there. I don't know if it's fact or fiction, but it was said that some grew as big as ponies on that diet.

"My uncle took the sword from the officer, a young second lieutenant who had just completed officer training school, and prepared to cut off the prisoner's head. Of course, he didn't want to do it. But it was unthinkable to refuse an order. Not something corrected by a simple reprimand. An order from an officer in Japan's Imperial Army was an order from the Emperor himself. My uncle's hands were shaking. He wasn't a strong man, and to make matters worse it was a crummy, mass-produced sword. The human neck isn't that easy to sever. His attempt failed. Blood sprayed everywhere, the prisoner thrashed about—it was gruesome."

Masahiko shook his head. I sipped my coffee.

"When it was finally over my uncle started puking. When there was nothing left he puked gastric juice, and when that was gone he puked air. His comrades ridiculed him. The officer called him a 'pitiful excuse for a soldier' and kicked him hard in the side with his army boots. No one sympathized. Instead, he was ordered to decapitate two more prisoners. This was for *practice*, to help him become *accustomed* to cutting off people's heads. A soldier's rite of passage, it was thought. Participating in such carnage made a man a 'true warrior.' But my uncle was never meant to be a warrior in the first place. He wasn't put on this earth for that. He was born to make beautiful music, to perform Chopin and Debussy. Not to chop the heads off other human beings."

"Are some people born to chop off heads?" I asked.

Masahiko shook his head again. "I can't answer that. But I do know there must be quite a few who are able to *get used to it*. People can become accustomed to almost anything, especially when they're pushed to the limit. It may become surprisingly easy then."

"Or when they're given justification for their actions."

"You're right there," Masahiko said. "In most cases, they're provided with some justification for what they do. I'm not confident that I'd be any different, to tell the truth. I might not be strong enough to stand up and say no if I were thrown into a system as violent as the military, even if I knew the order was horribly wrong or inhuman."

I thought of myself. Would I be any different if I were in his uncle's shoes? The image of the strange woman I had spent the night with in the port town in Miyagi popped into my head. The young woman who had handed me the belt of her bathrobe and asked me to strangle her in the middle of sex. I still remembered how the belt felt wrapped tight around my hands. Probably I would never forget.

"Uncle Tsuguhiko couldn't refuse his superior's order," Masahiko said. "He lacked the guts to do that. Yet later he was able to sharpen a razor and use it to kill himself. In that sense, I don't think he was weak at all. Only by taking his own life was my uncle able to recover his humanity."

"The news must have been a terrible shock to your father in Vienna."

"That hardly needs saying," Masahiko replied.

"I've heard that your father got caught up in some political events in Vienna that got him deported back to Japan. Did those have any connection to his brother's suicide?"

Masahiko folded his arms and frowned. "It's hard for me to say. You see, my father never said a word about what happened."

"What I heard was that your father fell in love with a girl who belonged to a resistance organization, and that she was involved in a failed assassination attempt."

"Yes, I know about that. Apparently she was an Austrian student at the university, and they were planning to get married. But when the plot came to light, she was arrested and sent to the concentration camp at Mauthausen. She probably died there. My father was arrested by the Gestapo and forcibly repatriated as an 'undesirable alien' in early 1939. Of course, this didn't come from my father but from someone in the family—a credible source."

"Do you think someone somewhere prevented your father from speaking about what had happened in Vienna?"

"Yeah, I'm sure that's true. I'm sure authorities on both sides—Japan and Germany—laid down the law in no uncertain terms when they arranged his deportation. He knew he had to keep his mouth shut—

that was the price he paid for saving his own neck. But I don't think he wanted to talk about those events, either. Otherwise he wouldn't have remained so close-mouthed when the war ended and the threat was gone."

Masahiko paused for a moment before continuing.

"I think it's entirely possible that Uncle Tsuguhiko's suicide played a role in my father's involvement in the anti-Nazi resistance in Vienna. The Munich Conference removed the threat of war for the time being, but it also strengthened the Berlin-Tokyo axis, and set the world moving in an even more dangerous direction. My guess is that my father was determined to try to put the brakes on that movement. He was a man who prized freedom above all else. Fascism and militarism ran against everything he believed. The death of his younger brother could only have strengthened those convictions."

"Do we know anything more?"

"My father never talked to anyone about his life. He did no interviews with the media, and left nothing written down for posterity. He was like someone who walks backward, erasing his own footsteps with a broom."

"He kept his silence as a painter too, didn't he," I said. "He exhibited none of his work from the time he returned from Vienna to the end of the war."

"Yeah, eight years in total, from 1939 until 1947. All that time, he stayed as far removed as possible from what we might call 'artistic circles.' He couldn't stand that crowd anyway, and their 'nationalist art' glorifying the war effort made him like them even less. Lucky for him, his family was well off, so he didn't have to worry about getting by. And, thankfully, he wasn't drafted to be a soldier during the war. In any case, once the postwar chaos had settled down, Tomohiko Amada reemerged, having metamorphosed into a purely Japanese-style painter. He had jettisoned his old style and adopted a totally new one."

"And thus was born a legend."

"That's right," Masahiko said. "The rest is legend." He waved his hand, as if shooing something away. As if the legend were a mote in the air, interfering with his breathing.

"As I hear you tell the story," I said, "I begin to think your father's student days in Vienna cast a shadow over his whole life. Whatever the exact circumstances may have been."

Masahiko nodded. "Yeah, I think that too. Those events changed the course of his life in a drastic way. The failure of the assassination plot must have led to a number of dreadful things. Things too horrible to speak of."

"Still, we don't know the details."

"No, we don't. I didn't know them growing up, and it's an even bigger riddle now. The man in question can't have a clue either."

Perhaps, I thought. People can forget what they should remember, and remember what by all rights and purposes they should forget. Especially when death approaches.

Masahiko polished off his second glass of white wine and glanced at his watch. He gave a slight frown.

"I've got to head back to the office," he said.

"Wasn't there something you wanted to tell me?" I asked, suddenly remembering.

He rapped his knuckles on the tabletop as if to echo my feeling. "You're right," he said. "There is something. But we spent all our time talking about my father. It'll have to be next time. It's nothing that urgent."

I looked at his face again as we were about to get up. "Why are you being so open with me?" I asked. "Showing me the skeletons in your family's closet."

He spread his hands on the table and thought for a minute. He scratched his ear.

"Let's see. For one thing, I'm getting a little tired carrying these 'family skeletons' around all by myself. Maybe I wanted to share them with someone. Someone who has nothing to gain from them, and who'll keep his mouth shut. In that sense, you're an ideal person to unburden myself to. Also, to tell the truth I'm feeling a little guilty where you're concerned, so this may be my way of trying to pay you back."

"Guilty?" I burst out. "In what way?"

Masahiko half closed his eyes. "I'd intended to tell you about that," he said. "But there's no more time today. My next appointment is one I can't miss. Let's meet again soon. Then we can talk all we want."

Masahiko paid the tab. "Don't worry," he said. "This much I can write off." I accepted with gratitude.

After that, I drove the Corolla station wagon back to Odawara. By the time I parked the dusty old heap in front of the house, the sun had almost reached the ridge of the western mountains. A large flock of cawing crows was winging across the valley, heading to their nests.

38

HE COULD NEVER BE A DOLPHIN

By the time Sunday rolled around, I had a pretty good idea how to attack the canvas I'd set aside for Mariye Akikawa's portrait. I still wasn't sure exactly what form the painting would take. But I did know *how I should begin*. Those first steps—which brush to use, what color, the direction of the first stroke—had come to me out of nowhere: they had gained a foothold in my mind and, bit by bit, taken on a tangible reality of their own. I loved this process.

It was a chilly morning. The kind of morning that heralds the coming of winter. I brewed coffee, ate a simple breakfast, went to the studio, laid out what I needed to paint, and then stood before my easel, which held the empty canvas. In front of the canvas, however, sat my sketchbook, open to the detailed pencil drawing I had done of the pit in the woods. I had tossed it off several mornings earlier without giving it much thought. I had even forgotten I had drawn it.

Nevertheless, the longer I stood there facing the drawing, the more it sucked me in. The mysterious stone chamber in the woods, the secret opening. The sodden earth, the patchwork of fallen leaves. The sunlight filtering through the branches. As my imagination filled in the penciled sketch, I began to see it as a colorful painting. I could breathe in the air of the place, smell the grass, hear the birds singing.

The pit I had drawn with such precision in my big sketchbook was beckoning me, luring me toward something—or was it somewhere? *The pit was demanding that I paint it.* I seldom thought of painting landscapes. I mean, I'd done virtually nothing but portraits for nearly ten years. But maybe a landscape painting wasn't such a bad idea.

The Pit in the Woods. This pencil sketch could be a first step in that direction.

I removed my sketchbook and closed it. The unblemished white canvas remained on the easel. The canvas that would soon be graced by my portrait of Mariye.

At a few minutes before ten, as before, the blue Toyota Prius rolled silently up the slope. The doors opened, and Mariye and her aunt Shoko stepped out. Shoko Akikawa was wearing a long, dark-gray herringbone jacket, a light-gray wool skirt, and patterned black stockings. Wrapped around her neck was a bright Missoni scarf. A chic late-fall outfit. Mariye was dressed much like before: a baggy varsity jacket, a windbreaker, jeans with holes in them, and dark-blue Converse sneakers. Her head was bare. The air was chilly, and a thin blanket of clouds covered the sky.

After a simple exchange of greetings, Shoko curled up on the sofa and, once again, immersed herself in her thick paperback. Mariye and I left her there and went into the studio. I sat on the same wooden stool, Mariye on the same simple straight-backed chair. Six feet or so separated us. Mariye took off her jacket, folded it, and laid it next to her chair. Then she removed her windbreaker. Underneath was a blue short-sleeved T-shirt and, beneath that, a gray long-sleeved T-shirt. Her chest was as flat as ever. She ran her fingers through her straight black hair.

"Aren't you cold?" I asked. There was an old-fashioned kerosene space heater in the studio, but it was unlit.

Mariye gave a slight shake of her head. As if to say *No, not particularly*.

"I'll start painting today," I said. "You don't have to do anything. It's enough if you just sit there. You can leave the rest to me."

"I can't not do anything," she said, looking me straight in the eye.

"What does that mean?" I asked, my hands on my knees.

"Like, I'm living and breathing and thinking all kinds of stuff."

"Of course," I said. "Please, breathe as much as you want and think as many thoughts as you can. All I meant was, there's nothing special you have to do. I just want you to be yourself."

Yet Mariye continued to stare straight at me. As if my explanation was too simple to swallow.

"But I want to do something," she said.

"Like what?"

"I want to help you paint."

"I appreciate that, but what do you mean exactly? Help me in what way?"

"Mentally, of course."

"I see," I said. Yet I couldn't think of anything specific she could do "mentally" to help.

"I'd like to see things as you see them," she said. "Look at myself through your eyes while you're painting me. I think I'd understand myself better if I did that. And you'd probably understand me better, too."

"I'd love that," I said.

"Really?"

"Yes, really."

"It might get pretty scary sometimes."

"Knowing more about yourself, you mean?"

Mariye nodded. "If you want to know yourself better you have to bring in something different from someplace else."

"Are you saying you can't know yourself unless you add a third-person perspective?"

"A third-person perspective?"

"In other words," I explained, "to understand the relationship between A and B you might need C, a third point of view. What we call 'triangulation.'"

Mariye thought for a moment. "Maybe," she said with a shrug.

"Are you saying that what you bring in might be scary, depending on the situation?"

Mariye nodded.

"Have you had that scary feeling before?"

Mariye didn't respond.

"If I can draw you the right way, maybe you'll be able to see yourself through my eyes," I said. "If all goes well, of course."

"That's why we need pictures."

"You're right—that's why we need pictures. Or literature, or music, or anything of that sort."

If all goes well, I said to myself.

"So let's get started," I said to Mariye. Looking at her face, I started mixing the brown for the underdrawing. Then I selected the first brush I would use on the painting.

The work progressed slowly but smoothly. The painting would show her from the waist up. She was a beautiful girl, but beauty wasn't what I was after. Instead, I had to find what was hidden beneath the surface. What underlay her personality—what allowed it to subsist. I had to find that *something* and bring it to the canvas. It didn't have to be pretty. Sometimes it might even be ugly. In either case, though, I had to know her well enough to discover what that something was. Not through words or logic, but as a singular form, a composite of light and shadow.

I concentrated on layering lines and color on the canvas. Rapidly at times, at other times with painstaking care. Mariye sat, unmoving, on the straight-backed chair, her expression never wavering. She had mustered her willpower, I sensed, and was sustaining it for as long as necessary. I could feel her strength. "I can't not do anything," she had said. And indeed, she was *doing something*. To help me, most likely. An unmistakable current of some kind was flowing between this thirteen-year-old girl and myself.

I recalled my sister's hands. She had taken my hand in hers when we entered the chilly darkness of the wind cave on Mt. Fuji. Her hand was small and warm—yet her fingers were surprisingly strong. A definite life force connected us. Each was giving something to the other, and at the same moment receiving something. It was an exchange limited to a particular time and place. It was bound to fade and disappear. But the memory remained. Memory can give warmth to time. And art can—when it goes well—give shape to that memory, even fix it in history. Much as Van Gogh inscribed the figure of a country mailman on our collective memory so well that he lives on, even today.

• • •

For the next two hours, we focused on our respective jobs without exchanging a word.

Thinning the paint with linseed oil, I began by roughing in her form in a single color. That would be the portrait's underdrawing. Mariye sat quietly in the chair, continuing to be herself. At noon, as they did every day, chimes rang in the distance, announcing that our time was up. I put down my palette and paintbrush, straightened my back, and stretched. Only then did I realize how tired I was. I took a deep breath to break my concentration, whereupon Mariye finally let her body relax.

The monochrome outline of Mariye's head and shoulders was there on the canvas before me. This was the structure upon which the portrait would be built. It was skeletal, but at its core was the source of the heat that made her who she was. That was still hidden, but if I could grasp its general location I would be able to make adjustments further down the line. Then all that would be left was fleshing out the skeleton.

Mariye didn't ask anything about what I had painted, nor did she ask to see it. I said little on my part, as well. I was just too worn out. We left the studio together and moved to the living room without a word. Shoko was still absorbed in her paperback. She marked her spot, closed the book, removed her black-rimmed reading glasses, and looked up at us. I could see that she was a bit alarmed. Our fatigue must have been written on our faces.

"Did it go all right?" she asked in a slightly worried tone.

"We're only partway through the process, but we're right on schedule."

"That's so good to hear," she said. "Would you mind if I made some nice hot tea? I've already set the water to boil. And I know where you keep the tea leaves."

Taken somewhat aback, I glanced down at her. Her lips were curved in a refined smile.

"I fear I'm being a poor host, but yes, that would be wonderful," I said. I was dying for some hot tea, but getting up and going to the kitchen to boil water was beyond me. I was exhausted. It had been ages since I'd gotten so tired painting. It felt good, though.

Shoko returned to the living room ten minutes later with three cups and a pot on a tray. We sat there quietly, each drinking our black tea. Mariye hadn't uttered a word since we left the studio. Every so often she'd reach up to push the hair back from her forehead. She had put her heavy jacket on again. As if she needed it to protect her from something.

The three of us sat there politely sipping our tea (not one of us slurped) and enjoying the lazy flow of the Sunday afternoon. No one spoke. The silence was easy and unforced, as if in accordance with the laws of nature. At a certain point, I heard a familiar sound, like waves on a distant shore, a listless and reluctant, yet somehow obligatory, lapping. Soon, however, the sound took on the unmistakable rhythm of a well-tuned engine. An eight-cylinder, 4.2-liter engine with power to spare burning (most elegantly, of course) high-octane fossil fuel. I got up from my chair, went to the window, and watched the approach of the silver car through a crack in the curtain.

Menshiki was wearing a lime-green cardigan over a cream-colored shirt. His pants were gray wool. They were clean and wrinkle-free, as if just back from the cleaners. None of his clothes appeared to be new—they all looked comfortably worn. That made them seem even cleaner. His hair, as always, was a glowing white. It seemed impervious to the seasons and the weather. I guessed that in summer or in winter, on sunny or cloudy days, its radiance would never fade. Only its tone would vary.

Menshiki got out of the car, closed the door, and looked up at the cloudy sky. He thought about the weather for a moment (at least that's how it looked to me), composed himself, and walked slowly to the front door. Then he rang the doorbell. Slowly and deliberately, like a poet selecting the precise word for a crucial passage. However you looked at it, though, it was just a common old doorbell.

I opened the door and showed Menshiki into the living room. Smiling, he greeted the two women. Shoko rose to welcome him. Mariye remained on the sofa, twirling her hair. She barely glanced his way. At my bidding, we all sat down. Would you like some tea, I asked Menshiki. Please don't bother, he replied, shaking his head several times and waving his hand in refusal.

"How is your work going?" he asked me.

Moving along as usual, I replied.

"Modeling is tiring, isn't it?" Menshiki asked Mariye. I couldn't remember him addressing her while looking her in the eye before. His tone was still a bit tense, but today at least he wasn't paling or blushing in her presence. His face looked almost normal. He was doing a good job controlling his emotions. I bet he'd been training hard to pull that off.

Mariye didn't answer. She seemed to mumble something, but it was entirely inaudible. Her hands were clasped tightly on her knees.

"You know she really looks forward to coming here Sunday mornings," Shoko remarked, breaking the silence.

"Modeling is hard work," I said, doing my humble best to back her up. "Mariye is doing a great job."

"I served as a model here for a while," Menshiki said. "I found it odd somehow. There were times it felt like my soul was being stolen from me." He laughed.

"It's not like that at all," Mariye said, in what was little more than a whisper.

The three of us turned in her direction.

Shoko looked as though she had popped something she shouldn't have into her mouth and bitten down on it. Menshiki's face registered unadulterated curiosity. I remained, as ever, the impartial observer.

"What do you mean?" asked Menshiki.

"Nothing's being stolen from me," Mariye said in a monotone. "I'm giving something, and I'm getting something in return."

"You're absolutely right," Menshiki said quietly. He seemed impressed. "I was being too simplistic. There has to be an exchange. Artistic creation can never be a one-way street."

Mariye was silent, her eyes fixed on the teapot on the table. She looked like a lone night heron motionless on the shore, glaring at the water's surface for hours on end. The teapot was simple white ceramic, the kind you can find anywhere. It was old (Tomohiko Amada had used it), and eminently practical, but apart from a small chip on the rim, nothing about it warranted close examination. Mariye just needed something to stare at right then.

The room fell silent. Like a blank, white billboard.

Artistic creation, I thought to myself. Those words had a pull to them that drew all the silence in the vicinity into a single spot. Like air filling a vacuum. No, more like a vacuum sucking up all the air.

"If you're coming to my house," Menshiki said gingerly, facing Shoko, "then perhaps we should go in my car. I'll bring you back here afterward. The backseat is a bit cramped, but the drive is so full of twists and turns—you'll find this much easier."

"Of course," Shoko said at once. "We'll ride in your car."

Mariye's eyes were still on the white teapot. She seemed deep in thought. Of course, I had no idea what was on her mind, or in her heart. I had no idea what the three of them would do for lunch, either. But Menshiki was smart. He had it all planned—there was no need for me to sweat the details.

Shoko sat in the passenger seat, while Mariye settled in the back. Adults in front, kids in back. The natural way of the world—no prior consultation necessary. I watched from my front door as the car slipped down the slope and out of sight. I went back into the house, took the teacups and teapot into the kitchen, and washed them.

When I finished, I placed Richard Strauss's *Rosenkavalier* on the turntable, stretched out on the sofa, and listened. *Der Rosenkavalier* had become my fallback when I had nothing else to do. A habit implanted in me by Menshiki. The music was somehow addictive, as he had warned. An uninterrupted stream of emotion. Musical instruments in colorful profusion. It was Strauss who boasted, "I can describe anything in music, even a common broom." Maybe he didn't say "broom"—it could have been something else. At any rate, there was something painterly about his music. Though what I was aiming for in my painting was very different.

When I opened my eyes a while later, there was the Commendatore. He was sitting in the leather easy chair across from me wearing the same Asuka-period clothing, his sword still on his hip. Perched on the chair, his two-foot frame looked quite demure.

"It's been a while," I said. My voice sounded strained and forced, as if coming from somewhere else. "How have you been?"

"As I have told my friends in the past, time is a concept foreign to

Ideas," he said in a small but clear voice. " 'A while' thus lies outside my understanding."

"It's a customary phrase. Please don't let it bother you."

"I cannot fathom 'customary' either."

Fair enough. Where there is no "time" there can be no "custom." I stood up and walked to the stereo, lifted the needle, and returned the record to its sleeve.

"As you may have surmised," the Commendatore said, reading my mind, "in a realm where time flows freely in both directions such things as customs cannot exist."

"Don't Ideas require an energy source of some kind?" I asked him. The question had been puzzling me for some time.

"It is a thorny question," the Commendatore answered, frowning dramatically. "All beings require energy—to be brought into this world and to survive. It is a principle that holds true throughout the universe."

"So what you're saying is, Ideas have to have a source of energy too. Right? In accordance with the universal principle."

"Affirmative! It is an undisputed fact. Universal law binds us one and all—there can be no exceptions. Ideas are felicitous insofar as we possess no form of our own. We materialize when others become aware of us—only then do we take shape. Though that shape is but a borrowed thing, for the sake of convenience."

"So then Ideas can't exist unless people are cognizant of them."

The Commendatore closed one eye and pointed his right index finger in the air. "And what principle can be deduced from that, my friends?"

It took a long moment to wrap my head around that one. The Commendatore waited patiently.

"This is what I think," I said at last. "Ideas take their energy from the perceptions of others."

"Affirmative!" the Commendatore said cheerfully. He nodded several times. "You have a good head on your shoulders. Ideas cannot exist outside the perceptions of others—those perceptions are our sole source of energy."

"So then if I think, 'The Commendatore doesn't exist,' you cease to exist. Right?"

"Negative! In theory, you have a point," the Commendatore said. "But only in theory. In reality, that is quite unrealistic. One is hard put to will oneself to cease thinking about a given matter. Namely, to determine to 'stop thinking' about something is itself a thought—as long as one follows that path, that something continues to exist. In the end, to stop thinking about something means to stop thinking about stopping thinking."

"In other words," I said, "it's impossible for people to escape Ideas unless they lose either their memory or their interest in Ideas."

"Truly, dolphins have that power," the Commendatore said.

"Dolphins?"

"Dolphins have the power to put the right or left half of their brain to sleep. Did my friends not know that?"

"No, I didn't."

"Affirmative! It is why dolphins have so little time for Ideas. It is why they stopped evolving, too. We Ideas tried our hardest, but I am sad to say that all of our efforts led nowhere. It was such a promising species, too. Proportionate to their size, they had the biggest brains of all the mammals until humankind reached its full development."

"So then you managed to establish a rewarding relationship with humans?"

"It is a known fact that, unlike the dolphin brain, the brain of the human species runs along a single track. Hence, an Idea that enters such a brain cannot be easily brushed aside. That allows us to draw energy therein, and thus sustain ourselves."

"Like parasites," I said.

"Nonsense!" said the Commendatore, wagging his finger like a schoolmaster scolding his wards. "When I say 'drawing energy,' I mean the tiniest amount. A shred so infinitesimal the members of my friends' species are unaware. Too small to affect health, or hinder lives in any way."

"But you told me that Ideas possess nothing like morality. Ideas are an entirely neutral concept, neither good nor bad. It all depends on how humans use them. In which case Ideas can have a beneficial effect in some cases, and a negative effect in others. Isn't that so?"

"$E = mc^2$ is neutral in itself, yet that Idea led to the creation of the atomic bomb. Then the bomb was dropped on Hiroshima and Nagasaki. In reality. Is that what you are trying to say, my friends?"

I nodded.

"My heart bleeds for you—figuratively, of course; we Ideas have no bodies, and hence no hearts. But then again, my friends, all is caveat emptor in this universe."

"What?"

"The Latin for 'buyer beware.' To wit, a vendor is not responsible for how the buyer uses his wares. Can a shopkeeper determine what manner of man will wear the suit hanging in his window?"

"That argument sounds pretty fishy to me."

"$E = mc^2$ gave birth to the atomic bomb, but by the same token it spawned a host of good things as well."

"Like what, for instance?"

The Commendatore thought about this for a moment. He seemed to be having trouble coming up with a good example, however, for he said nothing, just vigorously rubbed his face with the palms of his hands. Then again, perhaps he simply saw no point in pursuing the discussion any further.

"By the way," I asked, suddenly remembering. "Do you have any inkling where the bell in the studio disappeared to?"

"Bell?" the Commendatore asked, looking up. "What bell?"

"The old bell you were ringing at the bottom of the pit. I put it on the shelf in the studio, but when I looked the other day it was gone."

The Commendatore shook his head in an emphatic no. "Oh, that bell. Negative! I have not laid hands on it recently."

"So who do you think might have taken it?"

"How should I know?"

"Whoever it was has started ringing it somewhere."

"Hmm. It is nothing to do with me. I have no use for it anymore. The bell was never mine alone. It belongs to the place, to be shared by everyone. So if it has disappeared, there must be a reason. No need to worry—it will show up sooner or later. Just wait."

"The bell belongs to the place?" I said. "You mean it belongs to the pit?"

"By the way," he said, not answering my question. "If my friends are waiting for Shoko and Mariye's return, it will not happen soon. At least not until nightfall."

"And do you think Menshiki has something up his sleeve?" I asked my final question.

"Affirmative! Menshiki has an ulterior motive for everything. Never wastes a move, that fellow. It is the only way he knows. Using both sides of his brain, all the time. He could never be a dolphin."

The Commendatore's form faded little by little, and then, like mist on a windless midwinter morning, it thinned and spread until it was completely gone. All that sat facing me now was an old empty armchair. His absence was so absolute, so profound, I had trouble believing that, until a moment earlier, he had been there at all. Perhaps I had been sitting across from empty space, nothing more. Perhaps I had only been talking to myself.

As the Commendatore had predicted, Menshiki's silver Jaguar took a long time to show up. The two beautiful ladies seemed in no rush to leave his home. I stepped onto my terrace and looked across the valley at the white house. But I could spot no one. To kill time, I went inside and started preparing dinner. I made soup stock, parboiled the vegetables, and froze what I would not be using. I kept myself busy doing whatever I could think of, but when I finished, I still had time on my hands. I returned to the living room, put Richard Strauss's *Rosenkavalier* back on the turntable, stretched out on the sofa, and read a book.

Shoko was charmed by Menshiki. That much was certain. She looked at him differently than she looked at me. Her eyes shone. He was a most attractive middle-aged man, to say the least. A handsome and wealthy bachelor, well dressed and well mannered, a man who lived in the mountains in a huge mansion with four English automobiles stored in its garage. It was no mystery why so many women in this world might find him charming (to the same degree they might find me less than desirable). Yet it was equally certain that Mariye had a deep distrust of Menshiki. She was a girl of keen instincts. Perhaps she had intuitively divined that he was concealing the reasons for his behavior. Thus she maintained a careful distance. At least that was how it appeared to me.

What was going to happen? I was naturally curious, yet at the same time I had vague misgivings. My curiosity and those misgivings were therefore in direct opposition. Like an incoming tide meeting the outgoing current at the mouth of a river.

It was shortly after five thirty when Menshiki's Jaguar made its way back up the slope. As the Commendatore had predicted, it was already dark outside.

39

A CAMOUFLAGED CONTAINER, DESIGNED FOR A SPECIFIC PURPOSE

The Jaguar eased to a stop in front of my house, and Menshiki emerged. He walked around the car to open the door for Mariye and Shoko Akikawa, lowering the passenger seat so that Mariye could climb out of the back. The girl and the woman got into the blue Prius. Shoko rolled down the window and politely thanked Menshiki (Mariye, of course, turned the other way). Then the two drove home without stopping by to say hello. Menshiki watched them until they were out of sight, took a moment to (I assumed) recalibrate his mind and adjust his expression, and walked to my front door.

"I know it's late, but do you mind if I drop in for a few minutes?" he asked rather shyly.

"Sure, please do. I'm not busy right now," I said, showing him in.

We went to the living room; he sat on the sofa, while I sat in the easy chair that the Commendatore had just vacated. I thought I could feel the Commendatore's shrill voice still reverberating in the air.

"Thank you so much for today," Menshiki said to me. "I owe you a lot."

No thanks were necessary, I said. I really hadn't done anything.

"But if it hadn't been for your portrait—indeed, if it hadn't been for you, period—this chance would have passed me by. I would never have met Mariye face-to-face, never come this close to her. Everything has hinged on you—you're like the base of a folding fan. I'm concerned that you may not be enjoying that role, however."

"Nothing could make me happier than helping you out like this," I said. "But I must confess, it's hard to figure out how much is accidental and how much is planned. That part of it does bother me."

Menshiki thought for a moment. "You may not believe this," he said, nodding, "but I didn't plan any of this. Maybe it's not all pure coincidence, but almost everything has unfolded quite naturally."

"So I'm the catalyst that happened to set those events in motion? Has that been my role?" I inquired.

"Catalyst? Yes, maybe you could say that."

"To tell the truth, though, I feel more like a Trojan horse."

Menshiki looked up at me, as if squinting into a bright light. "What do you mean?"

"You know, the hollow wooden horse the Greeks built. They hid their warriors inside and presented it as a gift to the clueless Trojans, who dragged it inside their fortress. A camouflaged container, designed for a specific purpose."

Menshiki took a moment to respond. "In other words," he said, choosing his words carefully, "you think I may have exploited you, used you as a kind of Trojan horse? To get close to Mariye?"

"At the risk of offending you, I do feel a little that way."

Menshiki narrowed his eyes, and the corners of his mouth curled in the beginnings of a smile.

"I guess that can't be helped. But as I just said, this has been a series of unexpected coincidences. To be honest, I like you. My affection for you is personal, and very natural. I don't find myself liking many people, so when it does happen I try to take it seriously. I would never exploit you for my sole convenience. I know I can be selfish, but I'd like to think that I'm able to draw a line between friendship and self-interest. You're not being used as a Trojan horse—not now, not ever. So please don't worry."

He didn't seem to be making this up—his words had the ring of truth.

"So did you have a chance to show them the painting?" I asked. "My portrait of you in your study?"

"Of course. That's why they came in the first place. They loved it. Though Mariye didn't say anything. She's a girl of few words, as you know. But I could tell how strongly she felt. It showed in her face. She stood in front of the portrait for a very long time. Just stood there, not speaking or moving."

In fact, I couldn't remember the portrait very well, though I had finished it only a few weeks before. That was my pattern—the moment I launched into a new painting, the one I had just finished slipped from my mind. Only a vague and general image remained. I did retain a physical memory, however, of the sense of achievement I got from working on it. That palpable sensation meant more to me than the completed work.

"Their visit sure lasted a long time," I said.

Menshiki gave an embarrassed shrug. "After they'd seen your painting, I gave them a light lunch and showed them around. A tour of my house and the grounds. Shoko seemed interested, you see. The time flew by."

"I bet they were impressed."

"Shoko was, I think," Menshiki said. "Especially by my Jaguar XKE. But Mariye didn't say anything. Maybe she didn't like my house. Or maybe she's not interested in houses in general."

I guessed she probably couldn't care less.

"Did you have a chance to talk to her?" I asked.

Menshiki shook his head no. "She opened her mouth two or three times at most. And what she said was almost meaningless. She generally ignores me."

I kept quiet. I had no special thoughts on the matter, but I could picture the scene. Whenever he tried to start a conversation with Mariye, she would clam up, just mumble a word or two. Once Mariye made up her mind not to speak, trying to reach her was like ladling water onto a parched desert.

Menshiki picked up an ornament from the table, a glossy ceramic snail, and inspected it from a variety of angles. The snail had been one of the very few decorative objects left in the house. Probably a piece of Dresden china. The size of a smallish egg. Purchased long ago, perhaps, by Tomohiko Amada himself. Menshiki gingerly returned the snail to the table. Then he raised his head and looked across at me.

"I guess it will take her a while to get used to me," he said, as if addressing himself. "I mean, we've only just met. She's a quiet child to begin with, and thirteen is said to be a difficult age, the beginning of puberty. All the same, being with her in the same room, breathing the same air—it was a precious experience, priceless really."

"So then your feeling hasn't changed?"

Menshiki's eyes narrowed slightly. "What feeling do you mean?"

"That you don't care to know if Mariye is your child."

"No, that hasn't changed a bit," Menshiki said without hesitation. He chewed his lip for a moment before continuing. "It's hard to explain. But when she's near, and I look at her face and watch her move, this odd feeling comes over me. The sense that somehow my life up to now may have been wasted. That I no longer understand the purpose of my existence, the reason I'm here. As if values I'd thought were certain were turning out to be not so certain after all."

"And for you these sorts of feelings are extremely odd, am I right?" For me, they were par for the course.

"That's right. I've never experienced them before."

"And they started after spending several hours with Mariye?"

"Yes. You must think I'm some kind of idiot."

I shook my head no. "Not at all. I felt the same way when I hit puberty and met a girl I liked."

Menshiki gave a small smile. There was something rueful in it. "That's when the pointlessness of all my accomplishments and successes, and all the money I've accumulated, hit me. That I'm no more than an expedient and transitory vehicle meant to pass a set of genes on to someone else. What other function do I serve? Beyond that, I'm just a clod of earth."

"A clod of earth." I tried saying the words. They had a strange ring.

"To tell the truth, I was down in the pit when that realization hit me. Remember, that pit we uncovered behind the shrine, underneath the pile of rocks?"

"How could I forget?"

"If you'd felt like it, you could have abandoned me there. Without food and water, my body would have shriveled and returned to the soil. I would have been no more than a clod of earth in the end."

I didn't know what to say, so I remained silent.

"It's enough for me," Menshiki said, "that the *possibility* exists that Mariye and I are related by blood. I feel no compulsion to find out if it's true or not. That mere possibility has sent a beam of light into my life—now I can look at myself in a new way."

"I think I understand," I said. "Maybe not every step in your reasoning, but the way you feel. What I don't get is what you're expecting from Mariye. In concrete terms."

"It's not that I haven't given that question any thought," Menshiki said. He looked down at his hands. They were beautiful hands, with long fingers. "People devote a lot of energy to thinking about things. Whether they want to or not. Yet in the end we all just have to wait—only time can tell how events play out. The answers lie ahead."

I remained quiet. I had no clear idea what he had in mind, and no compelling desire to find out. Were I to know, my position might become even more difficult.

"I've heard Mariye is much more forthcoming with you," Menshiki said after a long pause. "That's what Shoko said, at least."

"That's probably true," I said cautiously. "We seem to be able to talk quite naturally when we're in the studio."

Of course, I didn't tell him that Mariye had come to visit me from the adjoining mountain through a hidden passageway. That was our secret.

"Do you think it's because she's gotten comfortable with you? Or because she feels some personal connection?"

"The girl is fascinated by painting, maybe artistic expression in general," I explained. "If a painting is involved, there are occasions—not always, mind you—when she's quite comfortable talking. She's not a typical child, that's for sure. When I taught her at the community center, she didn't speak much to the other kids."

"So she doesn't get along with children her own age?"

"Maybe. Her aunt says she doesn't make many friends at school."

Menshiki pondered that for a moment.

"She opens up with Shoko to some extent, I guess," he said.

"So it seems. From what I've heard, she's much closer to her aunt than she is to her father."

Menshiki merely nodded. His silence seemed charged with implication.

"What sort of man is her father?" I asked him. "Have you checked?"

Menshiki looked to the side and narrowed his eyes. "He was fifteen years older than she was," he finally said. "By 'she' I mean his late wife."

Of course, "late wife" meant Menshiki's former lover.

"I don't know how they got together, or why they married. I have no interest in those things," he said. "Whatever the case, though, it's clear he loved his wife dearly. Her death was a terrible shock. They say he was a changed man after that."

According to Menshiki, the Akikawas were a big landowning family in the area (much as Tomohiko Amada's family was in Kyushu). Although they had lost nearly half of their property in the land reform that followed World War Two, they retained many assets, enough that the family could get along comfortably on the income they produced. Yoshinobu Akikawa, Mariye's father, was the first of two children and the only son, so when his father passed away at an early age he became the head of the family. He built a house for himself at the top of the mountain they owned, and set up an office in one of their buildings in Odawara. From that office, he managed the family properties in the city and its environs: several commercial and apartment buildings, and a number of rental houses and lots. He also dabbled in real estate. In other words, while he kept the business going, he made no attempt to broaden its scale. The core of his enterprise consisted of looking after the family's assets when the need arose.

Yoshinobu married late in life. He was in his mid-forties when he tied the knot, and his daughter (Mariye) was born the following year. Then, six years later, his wife was stung to death. It was early spring, and she had been walking alone through a big plum grove they owned when she was attacked by a swarm of large hornets. Her death hit him hard. To wipe away anything that could remind him of the tragedy, as soon as the funeral was over he hired men to raze the plum trees, and yank their roots from the earth. What was left was a dreary and barren plot of land. It had been a beautiful grove, so its destruction was painful for many. Moreover, for generations those living nearby had been permitted to pick a portion of the abundant fruit to make pickled plums and plum wine. As a result, Yoshinobu Akikawa's barbaric act of retaliation deprived many local residents of one of the small pleasures they could look forward to each year. Still, it was his mountain, the plum grove was *his*, and no one could fail to understand his fury—at the hornets and the trees. As a consequence, those complaints were never voiced in public.

Yoshinobu Akikawa turned into a rather morose man after his wife's death. He hadn't been particularly social or gregarious to begin with, and now his introverted side only grew stronger. His interest in spiritual things deepened, and he became involved with a religious sect whose name was unknown to me. It is said that at one point he spent some time in India. At great personal expense, he built a grand hall for the sect's use on the outskirts of town, where he began spending much of his time. It's not clear exactly what takes place there. But it appears that a daily regimen of stringent religious "austerities" and the study of reincarnation helped him find a new purpose in life after his wife's death.

These activities reduced his involvement in the business, but his duties hadn't been all that demanding in the first place. There were three longtime employees more than capable of managing things when the boss failed to show up. His visits home became more infrequent. When he did return it was usually just to sleep. His relationship with his only daughter had, for some reason, grown more distant after his wife's death. Perhaps she reminded him of his dead wife. Or perhaps he had never really cared for children. In any case, as a result the child never really took to her father. The responsibility for looking after Mariye went to his younger sister, Shoko. She had taken leave from her job as secretary for the president of a medical college in Tokyo and moved to the house atop the mountain near Odawara on what she expected to be a temporary break to look after the child. In the end, though, the arrangement became permanent. Perhaps she came to love the girl. Or perhaps she couldn't stand idly by when her little niece needed her so much.

Having reached that point in his account, Menshiki stopped to touch his fingers to his lips.

"Do you happen to have any whiskey in the house?" he asked.

"There's about a half a bottle of single malt," I said.

"I don't want to impose, but could I have some? On the rocks."

"My pleasure. But aren't you driving?"

"I'll call a cab," he said. "No point in losing my license."

I went to the kitchen and came back with a whiskey bottle, a ceramic bowl of ice, and two glasses. In the meantime, Menshiki put the record of *Der Rosenkavalier* that I had been listening to on the turntable. We sat back and listened to the lush strains of Richard Strauss as we sipped our whiskey.

"Are you a devotee of single malt?" Menshiki asked.

"No, this was a gift. A friend brought it. Sure tastes good, though."

"I have a bottle of rare Scotch at home that a friend in Scotland sent to me. A single malt from the island of Islay. It's from a cask sealed by the Prince of Wales himself on his visit to the distillery there. I'll bring it on my next visit."

"You needn't make such a fuss on my account," I said.

"There's a small island near Islay called Jura," he said. "Have you heard of it?"

"No," I replied.

"It's practically uninhabited. More deer than people. Lots of other wildlife, too—rabbits, pheasants, seals. And one very old distillery. There's a spring of freshwater nearby, just perfect for making whiskey. If you mix the single malt with that water, the flavor is absolutely amazing. You can't find it anywhere else."

"It sounds delicious," I said.

"Jura is also known as the place where George Orwell wrote *1984*. Orwell rented a small house on the northern end of the island, really the middle of nowhere, but the winter took a terrible toll on his body. It was a primitive place, with none of the modern amenities. I guess he needed that kind of Spartan environment to write. I spent a week on that island myself. Huddled next to the fireplace each night, drinking that marvelous whiskey."

"Why did you spend a whole week in such an out-of-the-way place all by yourself?"

"Business," Menshiki said simply. He smiled.

Apparently, he wasn't going to let me in on what sort of business was involved. And I had no particular desire to find out.

"I really needed a drink today," he said. "To settle myself down. That's why I'm imposing on you like this. I'll come and pick up my car tomorrow, if that's all right with you."

"Of course, I don't mind at all."

We sat there awhile without talking.

"Do you mind if I ask something personal?" Menshiki broke the silence. "I hope you won't take offense."

"Don't worry, I'm not a guy who gets offended. I'll answer you if I can."

"You've been married, correct?"

I nodded. "Yes, I was married. As a matter of fact, I just mailed off the divorce papers, signed and sealed. So I'm not sure if I'm officially married now or not. Still, it's safe to say that I *was* married. For six years."

Menshiki was studying the ice cubes in his glass as if deep in thought.

"Sorry to pry," he said. "But do you have any regrets about the way your marriage ended?"

I took another sip of whiskey. "How does one say 'buyer beware' in Latin?" I asked.

" 'Caveat emptor,' " Menshiki said without hesitation.

"I have a hard time remembering how to say it. But I know what it means."

Menshiki laughed.

"Sure, I have regrets," I replied. "But even if I could go back and rectify one of my mistakes, I doubt it would change the outcome."

"Do you think there's something in you that's impervious to change, something that became a stumbling block in your marriage?"

"Perhaps it's my *lack* of something impervious to change that was the stumbling block."

"But you have the desire to paint. That must be closely connected to your appetite for life."

"There may be something I have to get past first before I can really get started with my painting, though. That's my feeling, anyway."

"We all have ordeals we must face," Menshiki said. "It's through them that we find a new direction in our lives. The more grueling the ordeal, the more it can help us down the road."

"As long as it doesn't grind us into the ground."

Menshiki smiled. He had finished his questions about my divorce.

I brought a jar of olives in from the kitchen to accompany our drinks. We nibbled on them while sipping our whiskey. When the record finished, Menshiki flipped it over. Georg Solti continued conducting the Vienna Philharmonic.

Menshiki has an ulterior motive for everything. Never wastes a move, that fellow. It is the only way he knows.

If the Commendatore was correct, what move was Menshiki making—or about to make—now? I hadn't a clue. Perhaps he was holding back for the moment, waiting for his opportunity. He said that he had "no intention" of exploiting me. Probably he was speaking the truth. Yet intentions were, in the end, just intentions. He was a savvy guy who had managed to survive and thrive in the most cutting-edge sector of the business world. If he was harboring an ulterior motive, even if it was dormant now, it would be next to impossible for me to avoid getting sucked in.

"You're thirty-six years old, right?" Menshiki said out of the blue.

"Yes, that's correct."

"That's the best age."

I didn't see it that way at all. But I didn't say so.

"I'm fifty-four. Too old to be fighting on the front lines in the business I was in, but still a little too young to be considered a legend. That's why you see me dawdling around like this."

"Some become legends in their youth, though."

"Sure, there are a few. But there's no great merit in that. In fact, it could be a real nightmare. Once you're considered a legend, you can only trace the pattern of your rise for the rest of your life. I can't think of anything more boring than that."

"Don't you ever get bored?"

Menshiki smiled. "I can't remember ever being bored. I've been too busy."

I could only shake my head in admiration.

"How about you?" he asked. "Have you ever been bored?"

"Of course. It happens a lot. In my case, however, boredom is an indispensable part of life."

"Don't you find it painful?"

"I guess I've gotten used to it. So it doesn't feel like pain."

"I bet that's because painting is so central to your existence. That's your core—your passion to create is born out of what you call boredom. Without that core, I'm sure you'd find boredom unendurable."

"So you're not working these days, are you?"

"That's right, I'm basically retired. I do a little computer trading on the stock markets, as I've told you, but that's not out of necessity. It's more like a game, a form of mental discipline."

"And you live in that big house all by yourself."

"Correct."

"And you still never get bored?"

Menshiki shook his head. "I have so many things to occupy my mind. Books I should read, music I should listen to. Data to gather, sort, and analyze. I'm used to staying active—it's a daily habit. I work out too, and when I need a change of pace, I practice the piano. And there's housework, of course. I haven't time to be bored."

"Don't you ever worry about growing old? About becoming a lonely old man?"

"No question, I will age," Menshiki said. "My body will decline, and I'll probably grow more and more solitary. But I'm not there yet. I have an idea what it will be like. But I'm the kind of guy who doesn't believe something until he's seen it. So I have to wait until it's sitting right in front of me. I'm not especially afraid of aging. I can't say I'm looking forward to it, but I am a little curious."

Menshiki slowly swirled the whiskey in his glass.

"How about you?" he asked, looking me in the eye. "Are you afraid of getting old?"

"I was married for six years, and it didn't turn out so well. I didn't paint a single painting for myself during all that time. I guess people would say I squandered those years. After all, I was turning out one painting after another of a sort I don't especially like. Yet, in a way, maybe I was fortunate to have gone through that. That's how I feel these days."

"I think I understand what you're trying to say. That there's a time in life when you have to discard your ego. Is that it?"

Perhaps, I thought. But maybe in my case it simply took me that long to discover what I'd been lugging around all that time. Had I dragged Yuzu along on that pointless, roundabout journey?

Am I afraid of growing old? I wondered to myself. Did I dread the advent of old age?

"I still have a hard time imagining it," I said. "It may sound foolish for a man in his mid-thirties to say this, but I feel as if my life is just beginning."

"That's not foolish at all," Menshiki said, smiling. "You're probably right—you're just getting started."

"You mentioned genes a few minutes ago," I said. "That you felt you're just a vehicle receiving a set of genes from one generation and transmitting it to the next. And beyond that duty, you're no more than a clod of earth. Right?"

Menshiki nodded. "That's what I said."

"But you don't find being a clod of earth particularly frightening, do you?"

"I may be a clod of earth," Menshiki said, laughing, "but as clods go I'm pretty good. It may sound conceited, but I think I may even be a superior clod. I've been blessed with certain abilities. Those have limits, I know, but they're abilities nonetheless. That's why I go all out in whatever I do. I want to stretch myself as far as I can, to see what I'm capable of. I have no time to be bored. That's the best way I know of keeping fear and emptiness at arm's length."

We drank until almost eight o'clock, at which point the bottle ran out. Menshiki stood up to leave.

"I should be on my way," he said. "I've imposed on you for too long."

I called for a taxi. "Tomohiko Amada's house" was all it took to identify our location. He was a famous man. The dispatcher said it would be fifteen minutes. I thanked him and hung up.

Menshiki used that time to tell me something.

"I told you earlier that Mariye's father had become deeply involved in a religious sect, didn't I?" he began.

I nodded.

"Well, it turns out that it's one of the new religions, and a shady one at that. I checked online and found out they've got a really bad track record. A number of civil suits have been filed against them. Their so-called doctrine is a pile of rubbish unworthy of the name 'religion.' Of course, Mr. Akikawa is free to subscribe to whatever beliefs he likes. That goes without saying. But he has sunk quite a lot of money into this group. His money, company money. He had considerable wealth in the beginning, was able to manage on the monthly rents he collected. But there was a clear limit to how much he could withdraw without selling property and other assets. Now he's way past that limit—he's sold a lot of those. Clearly, an unhealthy situation. Like an octopus trying to survive by devouring its own legs."

"Are you saying he's being preyed on by that cult?"

"Exactly. He's a real pigeon. When a group like that squeezes you, they take everything they can get. Right down to the last drop. Forgive me for saying so, but Mr. Akikawa's privileged upbringing may make him more vulnerable to that kind of thing."

"So you're concerned about this situation."

Menshiki sighed. "It's Mr. Akikawa's responsibility how he ends up. He's a mature adult, aware of his actions. It's not so simple for his family, though—they have no idea what's going on. Not that my worrying about them will make a bit of difference."

"The study of reincarnation," I said.

"It's a fascinating hypothesis," Menshiki said. He quietly shook his head.

The taxi finally arrived. Before getting in, he offered a most courteous thanks. His complexion and his decorum were a constant, no matter how much he drank.

40

I COULD NOT MISTAKE THE FACE

After Menshiki left, I brushed my teeth, climbed into bed, and fell asleep immediately. I drop off in no time at all under normal circumstances, and whiskey only accentuates that tendency.

In the middle of the night, however, a loud sound jolted me awake. I think the sound was real. Possibly, though, it took place in my dream. Its source could have been my own unconscious. Whatever its origins, it was a huge crash, as though an earthquake had struck. The impact lifted me into the air. That part was real, for sure, not a dream or a product of my imagination. I had been fast asleep, and now, an instant later, I was on the verge of tumbling from my bed, my mind on high alert.

According to the clock on the bedside table, it was past two. The time of night when the bell had usually rung. But I could not hear a bell. With winter approaching, there were no insect voices. A deep hush had fallen over the house. Outside, thick, dark clouds covered the sky. If I listened hard enough, I could hear the wind.

I felt for the lamp, switched it on, and slipped a sweater over my pajamas. I would take a quick look around the house. Something very strange had happened, or so it seemed. Had a wild boar crashed through one of the windows? Or had a small meteorite hit the roof? Probably not, but it was still a good idea to make sure. I was, after all, the caretaker of the house. And I would have a hard time falling back to sleep if I didn't find out. The crash had left me wide awake, my heart pounding.

I walked through the house flicking on lights, checking room by room. As far as I could tell, nothing was out of place. All was in order.

It wasn't a big house, so I would have noticed if something was amiss. When I finished my inspection, I headed to the studio. I stepped through the door connecting it to the living room and reached for the wall switch. But some thing stopped me. *Don't turn on the light*, the thing whispered in my ear. In a small but clear voice. *Better to leave it dark.* Following its instructions, I removed my hand from the switch and closed the door behind me without a sound. Quieting my own breathing, I peered into the darkened studio.

As my eyes adjusted to the light, I became aware that someone else was in the room. The signs were unmistakable. And that someone was sitting on the wooden stool that I used when I was painting. At first, I thought it was the Commendatore. That he had materialized and returned. But this person was much bigger. The silhouette looming in the dark was that of a tall, gaunt man. The Commendatore was two feet tall, if that, but this man was close to six feet in height. He was sitting somewhat hunched over, as tall people often do. And not moving at all.

I didn't move either as I stood there looking at his back, with my own back pressed against the doorframe and my left hand near the light switch, just in case. There in the dark, in the middle of the night, we were frozen, like two statues. For some reason, I wasn't scared. My breathing was shallow and the sound of my heartbeat was hard and dry. But I felt no fear. Someone I had never seen before had come barging into my house in the middle of the night. For all I knew, it could have been a burglar. Or perhaps a ghost. Either should have frightened me. Yet for some reason, I felt neither danger nor dread.

Perhaps all the strange happenings I had been experiencing—starting with the appearance of the Commendatore—had made me immune to such weirdness. Yet there was more to it than that. What was the mysterious intruder doing there in the studio so late at night? My curiosity trumped my fear. He seemed to be lost in thought. Or maybe he was staring hard at something. The intensity of his focus was obvious, even to an observer. He had no idea that I had entered the room. Or, perhaps, my presence was beneath his notice.

I tried to quiet my breathing and control the pounding of my heart against my ribs as I waited for my eyes to adjust to the dark. After a while, I began to realize what he was regarding with such ferocity. It was something hanging on the opposite wall. Which meant it had to be Tomohiko Amada's painting *Killing Commendatore*. He was sitting stock-still on the wooden stool, bent slightly forward, staring at that painting. His hands were on his knees.

At last the dark clouds covering the sky began to part, and a shaft of moonlight entered the room. It was as if an ancient tombstone had been bathed in pure, silent water, baring the secrets carved on its surface. Then the darkness returned. But only for a short time. The clouds parted again, and a pale blue light filled the room for a full ten seconds. Now, at last, I could determine the identity of the person on the stool.

His white hair fell to his shoulders. It had been uncombed for some time, for wisps jutted in every direction. Judging from his bearing, he was quite old. And withered, like a dead tree. Once, he must have had a powerful and manly physique. But now he was skeletal, wasted by age and possibly illness. That much I could tell.

His face was so emaciated it took me a while to figure out who he was. But there, in the hushed moonlight, I finally realized. I had seen only a few photographs, yet I could not mistake the face. The profile of his aquiline nose and the powerful physical aura were undeniable proof. Though the night was cold, sweat streamed from my armpits. My heart pounded even faster and harder. It seemed impossible to believe, but there was no room for doubt.

The old man was Tomohiko Amada, the artist who had created the painting. Tomohiko Amada had returned to his studio.

41

ONLY AS LONG AS I DIDN'T TURN AROUND

It couldn't be the flesh-and-blood Tomohiko Amada. That "real" Tomohiko Amada was confined to a nursing home in Izu Kogen. He suffered from advanced dementia and seldom left his bed. There was no way he could have come that far under his own steam. What I was looking at, therefore, could only be his ghost. Yet as far as I knew, Amada was still alive. Which meant I was looking at his "living spirit." Of course, he could have drawn his last breath just moments earlier. In which case, this would indeed be his ghost.

Whichever the case, this was no hallucination. It was far too real, too dense, for that. It projected an unmistakable humanity and the workings of a conscious mind. Tomohiko Amada had, through some special agency, returned to *his* studio, and was sitting on *his* stool regarding *his* painting *Killing Commendatore*. He was staring straight at it—his eyes seemed to cut through the dark. He was indifferent to my presence. I doubt he even realized I was in the room.

As the clouds rolled by, the moonlight through the window came and went, allowing me brief glimpses of his silhouette. He was sitting so I could see his profile, and wearing what could have been an old bathrobe or nightgown. His feet were bare. No stockings, no slippers. Disheveled white hair, jaw covered with a white grizzle. A haggard face, but clear and penetrating eyes.

I wasn't afraid so much as bewildered. The scene before me defied common sense. My hand hovered near the light switch on the wall. I had no intention of turning it on—I was just frozen in that posture. I didn't want to disturb Tomohiko Amada—be he ghost or phantasm—in any way. This studio was his proper place. Where he *truly belonged.* I was the intruder, with no right to interfere in whatever he wanted to do.

I waited until my breath calmed down and my body relaxed, then quietly backed out of the studio. I eased the door shut. Tomohiko Amada remained motionless on his stool throughout. Had I tripped over the table and sent the vase crashing to the floor, though, I doubt he would have noticed. His concentration was that fierce. The moon had broken through the clouds again, illuminating his skeletal frame. That last image engraved itself in my mind—embraced by the delicate shadows of night, that silhouette seemed to distill his entire life. *You must never forget this*, I told myself. I had to preserve in my memory what my eyes had seen, in all its detail.

I sat at the dining room table and drank glass after glass of mineral water. I really wanted a shot of whiskey, but the bottle was empty. Menshiki and I had drained it the previous evening. No other liquor was left in the house. There were a few bottles of beer in the fridge, but they wouldn't do the trick.

It was past four a.m. when sleep finally came calling. Until then, I just sat at the table while one thought after another passed through my head. I was too keyed up to be capable of any kind of action. All I could do was close my eyes and let my mind wander. Nothing cohered. For several hours, I followed those fragmented, meandering thoughts. Like a kitten chasing its tail.

When I grew tired, I mentally called up the image of Tomohiko Amada that I had seen mere hours before. To ensure its accuracy, I sketched it in my mind. I opened my imaginary sketchbook, pulled out my imaginary pencil, and drew the old man's silhouette. This was something I often did when I had time to spare. Actual paper and pencil weren't necessary. In fact, it was easier without them. Mathematicians go through a similar process, I imagine, when they picture a formula on an imaginary blackboard. Someday I might commit what I had seen to canvas.

I didn't really want to check the studio again. Of course, I was curious. Was Tomohiko Amada—or, more likely, his double—still there? Still sitting on his stool with his eyes riveted on *Killing Commendatore*? Sure, the possibility intrigued me. I had encountered a most rare and precious event, had seen it with my own eyes. Might it provide the key—several keys, actually—to help unravel the secrets of Tomohiko Amada's life?

All the same, I didn't want to interfere with what he was doing. He had come so far, transcending space and reason, to reexamine his *Killing Commendatore,* poring over it to find—what? He had to have sacrificed much of his dwindling store of energy just to make it here. Drained his life force. Yet something had compelled him to return to the painting one last time, at whatever cost. To study it to his heart's content.

When I opened my eyes it was already past ten o'clock. Rare for an early bird like me. I washed my face, brewed coffee, and ate breakfast. For some reason, I was famished. I ate nearly double my usual amount. Three slices of toast, two boiled eggs, and a tomato salad. Not to mention two big cups of coffee.

I checked the studio after breakfast just to be sure, but of course Tomohiko Amada was gone. What remained was the empty, silent room in the morning. An easel with a canvas (my painting of Mariye Akikawa), a round stool in front of it, and the straight-backed chair Mariye used when she posed for me. *Killing Commendatore* hanging on the wall. The bell still missing from the shelf. The sky over the valley blue, the air cold and crystal clear. The piercing calls of birds, awaiting winter's arrival.

I picked up the phone and called Masahiko's office. His voice was sleepy, though it was almost noon. A clear case of the Monday-morning blahs. After our hellos, I casually inquired about his father. I wanted to know if he had died, and if the apparition I had seen was his ghost. If Tomohiko Amada had passed away the night before, surely his son would have been notified.

"How's your father?" I asked.

"I went to see him a few days ago. His mind has passed the point of no return, I'm afraid, but he's all right physically, I guess. At least he doesn't look like he's at death's door."

So Tomohiko Amada was still alive. What I had seen wasn't a ghost. It was the fleeting embodiment of a living person's will.

"It's a strange question, I know, but have you noticed anything unusual about your father recently?"

"My father?"

"Yeah."

"Why do you want to know that all of a sudden?"

I followed the script I had prepared. "To tell the truth, I had this weird dream last night where your father visited this place. I bumped into him while he was here. It felt very real. Real enough to make me jump out of bed. That's why I wondered if something had happened to him."

"Wow," he said. "That's wild. What was my father doing while he was there?"

"He just sat on the stool in the studio."

"That's all?"

"That's it. Nothing but that."

"By stool you mean that old three-legged chair, the round one?"

"Yeah, that's the one."

Masahiko thought for a moment.

"Maybe he is reaching the end," he said in a flat voice. "They say that in our last hours, our spirit returns to where we feel we've left something undone. From what I know of my father, that would be the studio."

"But from what you've told me, he has no memory left."

"Yes, memory in the conventional sense, anyway. But his spirit's still there. His brain just can't access it any longer. The circuit's broken—his mind isn't connected. But his spirit remains, behind the scenes. It's probably the same as ever."

"That makes sense," I said.

"Weren't you scared?"

"By the dream?"

"Yeah. I mean it sounds awfully real."

"No, I wasn't afraid. But it did feel very strange. Like the man himself was right there."

"Maybe it really was him," Masahiko said.

I didn't say anything. I couldn't let on that Tomohiko Amada had likely returned specifically to view *Killing Commendatore* (actually, *I* might have invited him—had I not unwrapped the painting, he might not have shown up). If I told his son, I would have had to explain the whole story, from the moment I stumbled across the painting in the attic to when I opened it without permission and, even more blatantly, chose to hang it on the studio wall. I knew I would have to let Masahiko know eventually, but I didn't want to raise the issue at this juncture.

"Anyway," he said, "last time we met I mentioned there was a matter I needed to talk to you about? But we didn't have enough time then. Remember?"

"Yeah."

"So why don't I stop by one of these days and fill you in. Okay?"

"This house is yours, you know. Come whenever you like."

"How about this weekend? I'm thinking of visiting my father in Izu Kogen, so I could stop by on my trip back. It's right on the way."

I told him he was welcome anytime except Wednesday and Friday nights and Sunday morning. My art class was on Wednesday and Friday and Mariye's sitting was on Sunday.

He figured he'd be able to make it Saturday night. "I'll let you know beforehand," he said.

After our phone call, I went into the studio and sat on the stool. The wooden stool that Tomohiko Amada had occupied the night before. As soon as I sat down, it hit me—this stool was no longer *mine*. No, the long years Tomohiko Amada had spent sitting on it painting made it *his*, now and forever. To the uninformed, it looked like no more than an old dinged-up, three-legged chair, but it was infused with his will. I had borrowed it without permission, that was all.

I sat there and studied *Killing Commendatore* on the wall, as I had done countless times before. It rewarded multiple viewings—its depth allowed for so many different ways of looking at it. This time, though, I felt I wanted to inspect it from an entirely new angle. What was there that had made Tomohiko Amada return to it at the end of his life, to see it one last time?

I spent a long time sitting there, just studying the painting. I chose the same position, the same angle, even adopted the same posture that Tomohiko Amada's living spirit or alter ego had taken the night before, and tried to focus on it with the same intense concentration. Yet I couldn't find that *something* I had previously missed.

• • •

When I grew tired of thinking, I went outside. Menshiki's silver Jaguar was still parked in front of my house, at a slight remove from my Toyota Corolla station wagon. It had been sitting there all night, waiting quietly for its master's return, like an intelligent, well-trained pet.

I strolled on past the house, musing about *Killing Commendatore* in a vague sort of way. Walking the little path through the woods, I had the distinct impression that someone was spying on me from behind. As if Long Face had pushed up the square lid of his hole and was secretly observing me from the corner of the painting. I whipped around and looked back. But nothing was to be seen. No hole in the ground, no Long Face. Just a deserted leaf-strewn path wending through the quiet woods. This pattern repeated itself a number of times. But each time I spun around no one was there.

Then again, it might well be that the hole and Long Face were there *only as long as I didn't turn around*. Perhaps they could tell when I was about to look back, and hid themselves at that moment. Like a child playing a game.

I passed through the woods to the very end of the path, the first time I'd gone that far. I figured the entrance to Mariye's secret passageway had to be nearby. Yet I couldn't locate it. "You really have to pay attention to find it," she had said, and it did seem to be well camouflaged. In any case, she had taken the passageway after dark to reach my place from the adjoining mountain, alone and on foot. Past the thickets and through the woods.

The path came to an abrupt end at a small, circular clearing. The overhanging trees thinned out, so I could see pieces of sky. I found a flat stone bathed in a small pool of light, sat down, and looked through the tree trunks at the valley below. I imagined that at any minute Mariye might pop up out of her secret passageway, wherever that was. But of course no one appeared. My only companions were birds, who hopped from limb to limb and then flew off again. They moved about in pairs, each chirping loudly to let the other know where they were. I had once read an article describing how certain birds mate for life, and how when one died, the survivor spent the rest of their days alone. It goes without saying that they never had to sign and seal official divorce papers sent by certified mail from a lawyer's office.

A truck selling fresh produce passed in the distance, its driver listlessly broadcasting his wares over its loudspeaker. No sooner was his voice out of earshot than there was a loud rustle in the bushes nearby. What was it? It didn't sound human. A wild animal was more likely. For a scary second I thought it might be a wild boar (boars and hornets were the most dangerous things in the area), but then the sound abruptly stopped.

I stood up and started walking back to the house. When I passed the small shrine I checked the pit, just to make sure. The planks were in place, the stone weights neatly arranged on top. They hadn't been moved, as far as I could tell. Fallen leaves covered the boards. They had lost their bright colors and turned sodden in the rain. So young and fresh in spring, their quiet death had come now, in late autumn.

As I stared at the planks, I began to feel that Long Face might poke his elongated, eggplant-shaped head out of the pit at any minute. But the planks didn't budge. Obviously. Long Face's hole was square, not round, and was smaller and more personal in scale. Moreover, *this* hole was home to the Commendatore, not Long Face. Or at least home to the Idea that had borrowed the Commendatore's form. It had been the Commendatore that had rung the bell to call me here, and had made me open the pit.

Everything started with this pit. After Menshiki and I had pried open the lid with a backhoe, strange things had started happening one after another. Then again, it might have all begun when I had found *Killing Commendatore* in the attic and removed it from its packaging. That was the correct sequence. Or perhaps the two events acted in tandem. *Killing Commendatore* could have been what called the Idea to the house. The appearance of the Commendatore could have been my reward for liberating the painting. Try as I might, I couldn't tell what was the cause, and what was the result.

Menshiki's Jaguar was gone when I got back to the house. He had probably come by taxi to pick it up. Or else sent one of the people who worked for him to collect it. Whichever the case, my mud-spattered Toyota Corolla was left there, parked forlornly outside my front door.

Menshiki had been right—I should check the tires one of these days, though I hadn't bought an air pressure gauge and probably never would.

I went to the kitchen to start making lunch, but no sooner had I picked up a knife than I realized I was no longer ravenously hungry. Instead, I was very sleepy. I got a blanket, stretched out on the living room sofa, and promptly drifted off. I had a dream, a short one. It was clear and very vivid. But I couldn't remember anything about it. Just that it was clear and vivid. It felt as though a fragment of real life had slipped into my sleeping mind by mistake. Then the moment I awoke, it fled like a quick-footed animal, leaving no trace behind.

42

IF IT BREAKS WHEN YOU DROP IT, IT'S AN EGG

The next week flew by. I spent my mornings focused on my painting, and my afternoons reading, taking walks, and doing whatever housework needed to be done. One day blended into the next. My girlfriend showed up on Wednesday and we spent the afternoon making love. The constant creaking of my old bed really cracked her up.

"It's going to fall to pieces before long," she predicted during a pause in our exertions. "There'll be nothing left but splinters—we won't be able to tell if they're wood or pretzel sticks."

"Maybe we should try to make love more quietly."

"Maybe Captain Ahab should have hunted sardines," she said.

I thought about that for a moment. "Are you saying some things in this world can't be changed?"

"Kind of."

A short time later, we were back on the rolling seas, in pursuit of the great white whale. Some things really can't be changed so easily.

Each day, I worked a little on Mariye Akikawa's portrait. My initial sketch had established the skeleton, and now I was filling it out. I tried combining various colors to come up with the right tone for the background. Her face had to sit naturally over that foundation. These tasks tided me over as I waited for her next visit to the studio on Sunday. Some parts of my job were carried out while the model was present, while other preparatory work had to be done before the model's arrival. I loved both. I could take my time mulling over the various elements, and experiment to find just the right color, just the right style. I enjoyed the hands-on nature of this work, and the challenge of creating an environment from which the subject would spring to life.

While preparing Mariye's portrait, I began working on a different canvas—a painting of the pit behind the shrine. The pit had etched itself in my mind with such force that I didn't need it in front of me. I painted the scene in minute detail. The style was purely realistic, the viewpoint objective. I avoided objective representation in my art (except, of course, the portraits that were my "day job"), but that didn't mean I couldn't do it. When I wanted to, I could paint so precisely that the result could be mistaken for a photograph. I used that hyperrealistic style occasionally to change my mood, or refresh the fundamentals of my craft. I never showed those paintings to anyone, though—they were for my private enjoyment, nothing more.

In this way, the pit in the woods began to appear before me, more vivid and alive with each passing day. A mysterious round aperture half covered by thick planks. This was the pit that had given birth to the Commendatore. There were no human figures in the painting, however, just a black hole. Fallen leaves covered the earth surrounding it. A scene of perfect tranquility. Yet it felt as if someone (or something) might come crawling out of that hole any minute. The longer I pictured the scene, the stronger that premonition grew. Looking at it made my spine tingle, although I was the one who had painted it.

I worked like this every day, spending all morning alone in the studio. Palette and brush in hand, I moved back and forth between *A Portrait of Mariye Akikawa* and *The Pit in the Woods*—two more different paintings would be hard to imagine—as the mood struck me. I applied myself to the canvases while sitting on the same stool Tomohiko Amada had occupied in the dead of night the previous Sunday. Perhaps because my focus was so great, the dense presence I had felt the next morning had at some point disappeared. The old stool was once again a mere piece of furniture, there for my use. It seemed that Tomohiko Amada had gone back to where he belonged.

There were nights that week when I opened the studio door a crack to peek inside. But no one was ever there. Not Tomohiko Amada, not the Commendatore. Just an old stool parked in front of two easels. The moon cast its dim light over the objects in the room. All was quiet. *Killing Commendatore* hung on one wall. My unfinished work, *The Man with the White Subaru Forester*, was turned around so no one could see it. The two paintings I was working on, *A Portrait of Mariye Akikawa* and *The Pit in the Woods*, sat side by side on two easels. The smell of oil paint, turpentine, and poppyseed oil hung in the air. It never left, no matter how long the windows were left open. It was a special aroma, one I breathed every day, and would probably go on breathing for the rest of my life. I inhaled the air of the studio as if to confirm its presence, then quietly closed the door.

Masahiko called Friday night to say he was coming the next afternoon. He'd buy fresh fish from the market nearby, so I needn't worry about dinner. I could look forward to a special treat.

"Anything more I should bring?" he asked. "I can pick up what you want on my way."

"Can't think of anything," I answered. Then I remembered. "Now that you mention it, I'm out of whiskey. A friend and I polished off what you brought last time. Could you pick up another bottle? Any brand is okay."

"I like Chivas myself. Would that do?"

"You bet," I said. Masahiko had always been picky about food and drink. I was a different story. I ate and drank whatever was put in front of me.

When our phone call ended, I went to the studio, took *Killing Commendatore* down from the wall, carried it to my bedroom, and covered it. It wouldn't do to have Tomohiko Amada's son see the painting his father had hidden in the attic. For the time being, at least.

Now a visitor to the studio would see only *A Portrait of Mariye Akikawa* and *The Pit in the Woods*. I stood there looking back and forth at the two works in progress, comparing them. An image rose to my mind: I could see Mariye walking behind the shrine to the pit. I had a distinct sense that *something* might begin then. The lid was half open. The darkness was calling. Was Long Face there waiting for her? Or the Commendatore?

Could these two paintings be connected in some way?

Since moving to this house, I had been painting almost nonstop. I had completed Menshiki's portrait on commission, then started *The Man with the White Subaru Forester* (brought to a halt when I had just begun to add color), and now was working on *A Portrait of Mariye Akikawa* and *The Pit in the Woods* in tandem. It struck me that the four paintings might fit together to form the beginning of a story of some kind.

Then again, perhaps I was documenting the story through my painting. That's what it felt like, anyway. Had someone given me the role or the right to be that chronicler? If so, *who*? Why was I chosen, of all people?

Masahiko's black Volvo station wagon came trundling up the slope shortly before four o'clock on Saturday afternoon. He loved the toughness and reliability of those old boxy cars. He'd driven this one seemingly forever, put a ton of miles on it, yet showed no inclination to trade it in for a new one. On this occasion, he brought along the special carving knife he used for fish. As always, it was razor sharp. In my kitchen, he used it to prepare the large, fresh sea bream he had just bought in Itoh. Masahiko had always been good with his hands, a man of many talents. Without a wasted motion, he filleted the fish, sliced the flesh into sashimi, and boiled the bones for broth. He lightly grilled the skin to nibble on with our drinks. I just stood there, enjoying the show. Who knows, he might have been a famous chef had he taken that route.

"Actually, it's best to let sashimi sit a day until the flesh softens and the flavor comes out, but what the hell," he said, deftly plying the knife. "You can handle it, right?"

"No problem—I'm not picky," I said.

"You can eat any leftovers tomorrow."

"Will do."

"Hey, do you mind if I crash here tonight?" Masahiko asked. "I'd like to stay the evening so we can hang out and drink without feeling rushed. Drinking and driving is no good, right? I can sleep on the sofa in the living room."

"Sure," I said. "It's your house, after all. Stay as long as you like."

"Are you sure some woman won't show up in the middle of the night?"

"No plans as of now," I replied, shaking my head.

"Okay, then I'll stay."

"You don't have to crash on the sofa—there's a bed in the guest room."

"No, I prefer the sofa. It's a lot more comfortable than it looks. Slept like a baby on it back in the old days."

He pulled out a bottle of Chivas Regal, cut the seal, and opened it. I brought ice from the refrigerator and two glasses. The gurgle of whiskey pouring into the glass was music to my ears. Like an old friend opening his heart to me. We sipped the whiskey as we finished preparing dinner.

"It's been a hell of a long time since you and I drank like this," Masahiko said.

"It sure feels that way. I remember us putting back a lot."

"*I* put back a lot, you mean," he said. "You never drank that much."

I laughed. "Maybe not from your point of view, but it was a lot for me."

I never got totally drunk. I always fell asleep first. But he was a different kind of drinker. Once he settled in for the long haul, he went all the way.

We sat across from each other at the table, sipping whiskey and eating the seafood. For starters, we shared the eight raw oysters he had bought with the sea bream. Then we dug into the sashimi. It was a bit too firm, as he had predicted, but it was delicious nonetheless, especially with the whiskey. By the end, we had polished it all off. We were already pretty full. The only other food was the crispy fish skin, small chunks of wasabi mixed with sake lees, and a dish of tofu. We topped off the meal with the soup he had prepared.

"I haven't had a feast like this in ages," I said.

"You can't eat like this in Tokyo," he said. "Living around here wouldn't be half bad. Fresh fish anytime."

"I bet you'd find life here boring eventually, though."

"Are you bored?"

"Am I? I guess I've never found boredom that painful. And besides, there's quite a lot going on here."

That was for sure. I had met Menshiki soon after my arrival in early summer, we had dug up the pit behind the shrine, then the Commendatore had made his appearance, and finally Mariye Akikawa and her aunt Shoko had entered my life. I had a girlfriend, a housewife in her sexual prime, who came to comfort me. Tomohiko Amada's living spirit had paid me a visit. There was hardly time to be bored.

"I might not be bored here either," Masahiko said. "Did you know I used to be into surfing? I rode the waves all up and down this coast."

That was news to me, I told him. He'd never mentioned it before.

"I've been thinking of leaving Tokyo, of going back to that kind of life. I'd check out the ocean when I woke up, then grab my board and head out if the surf was up."

The idea of that kind of life left me cold.

"What about your job?" I asked.

"I only need to go to Tokyo twice a week to take care of business. Most of my work is done on computer anyway, so it wouldn't be that hard to live outside the city. The world's changing, right?"

"I wouldn't know."

He looked at me in amazement. "This is the twenty-first century, man. Haven't you heard?"

"I've heard talk."

After dinner, we moved to the living room to continue drinking. Autumn was almost over, but it wasn't so cold that we needed to light a fire.

"So then, how's your father doing these days?" I asked.

Masahiko let out a small sigh. "Same as always. His mind is shot. Can't tell the difference between his balls and a pair of eggs."

"If it breaks when you drop it, it's an egg," I said.

He laughed. "People are strange creatures, aren't they? I mean, my father was as solid as a rock until just a few years ago. Mind as clear as the night sky in winter. To an almost disgusting degree. And now his memory is like a black hole. This dark, unfathomable hole that popped up out of nowhere in the middle of the cosmos."

Masahiko shook his head.

"Who was it that said, 'The greatest surprise in life is old age'?" he asked.

I couldn't help him with that one. I'd never heard the saying. But it was probably true. Old age must be an even bigger shock than death. Far beyond what we can imagine. The day someone tells you that you're flat-out useless, that your existence is irrelevant—biologically (and socially)—in this world.

"So tell me about this dream you had of my father," Masahiko asked me. "Was it really as lifelike as you said?"

"Yeah, so lifelike it hardly seemed a dream."

"And he was in the studio?"

I took him to the studio.

"Your father was sitting there," I said, pointing to the stool in the middle of the room.

Masahiko walked over to the stool. "Just sitting?" he asked, placing his palm on its seat.

"That's right. He wasn't doing anything."

In fact, his father had been staring at *Killing Commendatore* on the wall, but I didn't tell him that.

"My father loved this stool," he said. "It was just a common old thing, but he never got rid of it. He sat on it to paint, and to think."

"It's relaxing to sit on," I said. "You'd be surprised."

Masahiko stood there with his hand on the stool, lost in thought. But he didn't sit down. After a minute, he turned his attention to the two canvases facing it. *A Portrait of Mariye Akikawa* and *The Pit in the Woods,* my two works in progress. He examined them slowly and carefully, like a doctor looking for a trace of shadow on a patient's X-ray.

"These are great," he said. "Really interesting."

"Both of them?"

"Yes, both. When you place them side by side like this, you feel a strange kind of movement between them. Their styles are totally different, but you get a sense they're somehow linked."

I nodded. I'd been thinking the same thing for a few days, in a vague sort of way.

"It seems to me that, little by little, you're finding a new direction," he went on. "Like you've finally emerged from a deep forest. You should take this really seriously, old friend."

He raised his glass and took a swallow of whiskey. The ice cubes tinkled.

I felt an urge to show Masahiko his father's *Killing Commendatore*. What would he have to say about it? His comments might provide a valuable clue. But I suppressed the impulse. Something was holding me back.

It's still too early, it said. Still too early.

We left the studio and went back to the living room. The wind had picked up—through the window I could see thick clouds edging their way north. The moon was hidden from view.

"So about what brought me here," Masahiko said, not wasting any more time. He seemed to be steeling himself for what he was about to say.

"It sounds like something that's not easy to discuss," I said.

"You're right, it's hard. *Quite* hard, in fact."

"But it's something that I need to know."

Masahiko rubbed his hands together. Like a man preparing to lift a heavy object.

"It's about Yuzu," he said, cutting to the chase. "She and I have met up a number of times. Before you left this spring, and afterward, too. She calls me when she wants to talk, and then we meet somewhere. She asked me not to tell you. I hated hiding it from you, but, well, I promised her."

I nodded. "It's important to keep our promises."

"Yuzu and I were friends too, you know."

"I know," I said. Masahiko put great stock in friendship. It could be a weakness of his.

"She had another man. Apart from you, that is."

"I know that too. *Now,* at least."

He nodded. "It started about six months before you walked out. Their relationship, that is. It hurts me to tell you this, but the guy is someone I know. A colleague of mine at work."

I let out a small sigh. "I imagine he's really handsome, right?"

"Yeah, you got it. Classic features. An agency scouted him in high school, and he modeled part-time for a while. He's that good-looking. And, well, it seems that I was the one who introduced them."

I didn't say anything.

"At least that's how it worked out," Masahiko said.

"Yuzu always had a thing for handsome men. It was almost pathological. She knew it too."

"You're not bad-looking yourself," he said.

"Thanks, man. Now I can sleep better tonight."

We didn't speak for a time. Finally, he broke the silence.

"Anyway, he's a really good-looking guy. A nice guy, too. I know this doesn't help you very much, but he's not violent, or a womanizer, or vain about his looks. He's not that type."

"That's nice to hear," I said. My voice was tinged with sarcasm, though I hadn't meant it to sound that way.

"It all started in September a year ago," Masahiko said. "He and I were out together when we bumped into Yuzu, and since it was about noon, the three of us stopped for lunch nearby. Believe me, I had absolutely no idea things would turn out this way. He's five years younger than she is."

"So the two of them didn't waste much time."

Masahiko gave a small shrug. Things must have progressed very quickly indeed.

"The guy talked to me about what was going on," he said. "Your wife did as well. It put me in a very difficult position."

I kept quiet. Anything I said would just make me look foolish.

Masahiko was silent for a moment. Then he spoke. "The fact is, Yuzu is pregnant."

I was speechless for a moment. "Yuzu? Pregnant?"

"Yeah, seven months gone already."

"She did it on purpose?"

"I don't know," Masahiko said, shaking his head. "But she's planning to have the baby. After seven months there's not much choice, is there."

"She always told me she wasn't ready for kids."

He winced slightly. "There's no chance the child could be yours, is there?" he said, looking into his glass.

I did a quick mental calculation. "No. I don't know the legal side of it, but biologically the chances are zero. I left eight months ago, and we haven't seen each other since."

"That's good," Masahiko said. "At any rate, she asked me to tell you she's going to have a baby. And that it shouldn't cause you any problems."

"But then why tell me at all?"

He shook his head. "I guess she's informing you out of courtesy."

I said nothing. *Out of courtesy?*

"I've been waiting for the chance to apologize for all this. I knew what was going on between Yuzu and my colleague, and I kept it from you. It was inexcusable. Under any circumstances."

"Then was letting me stay in this house your way of making amends?"

"Not at all—there's no connection between that and Yuzu. My father lived and painted in this house for a great many years. I figured you could keep that tradition alive. It's not something I could have asked anybody else, not like that at all."

Again, I said nothing. He sounded sincere.

"In any case," Masahiko continued, "you signed and sealed the divorce papers you received and sent them back to Yuzu, right?"

"More precisely, to her lawyer. So our divorce should be official by now. I guess those two will choose a date for their own wedding now that's taken care of."

And go on to have a happy marriage. A tall, handsome man, a small child, and little Yuzu. The three of them strolling happily through the park on a sunny Sunday morning. Heartwarming.

Masahiko added some ice and poured us more whiskey. He took a swig from his glass.

I went out to the terrace and looked across the valley at Menshiki's white house. Lights were on in some of the windows. What was Menshiki doing at this minute? What was he thinking about?

The night air was chilly. The leafless branches quivered in the wind. I went back to the living room and sat down.

"Can you forgive me?"

"It's not like you meant to hurt me," I said, shaking my head.

"I for one am sorry it turned out this way. You and Yuzu looked so well matched, and you seemed happy together. It's sad that it fell apart."

"You drop them both—the one that breaks is the egg," I said.

Masahiko laughed weakly. "So how are things now? Is there a woman in your life?"

"Yeah, there's someone."

"But not the same as Yuzu?"

"It's different. I've been looking for the same thing in women my whole life. Whatever that is, Yuzu had it."

"And you can't find that in anyone else?"

"Not so far," I said, shaking my head again.

"You have my sympathy," Masahiko said. "So what is it exactly that you've been looking for?"

"It's hard to put into words. I feel as if I lost track of something along the way, and have been searching for it ever since. Don't you think that's how everyone falls in love?"

"I don't think you can say 'everyone,'" he said with a slight frown. "You may actually be in the minority. But if you can't find the right words, why not paint it? You are an artist, after all."

"If you can't say it, paint it. That's easy to say. Not so easy to do, though."

"But it may be important to try, don't you think?"

"And perhaps Captain Ahab should have set out after sardines."

Masahiko laughed. "Sure, from a safety standpoint. But that's not how art is born."

"Hey, give me a break. Mention art, and the conversation comes to a screeching halt."

"Looks like we need some more whiskey," he said, shaking his head. He poured us another drink.

"I can't drink too much. I've got to work tomorrow morning."

"Tomorrow is tomorrow. Today is all we have right now," Masahiko said.

I found this idea strangely compelling.

"Can I ask you a favor?" I said to Masahiko. Our conversation was wrapping up, and we were about to get ready for bed. The hands on the clock pointed to a little before eleven.

"Sure, anything at all."

"I'd like to meet your father. Could you take me with you the next time you go to Izu?"

Masahiko regarded me as he might a strange animal. "You want to meet my father?"

"If it's not too much trouble."

"It's no trouble at all. But my father's in no shape to talk to you. He's quite incoherent. His mind is chaotic—a mud swamp, really. So if you have any expectations—if you're hoping to gain some insight into the person known as Tomohiko Amada—you'll only be disappointed."

"No, I'm not expecting anything like that. I just want to take one good look at him, that's all."

"But why?"

I took a breath and looked around the room. "I've been living in this house for six months now," I said. "Sitting on the stool he sat on, painting in his studio. Eating off his dishes, listening to his records. I feel his presence all over the place. That's why I have to meet the flesh-and-blood Tomohiko Amada. Once is enough. It doesn't matter a bit if we can't talk to each other."

"Then it's all right," Masahiko said, seemingly persuaded. "He won't be thrilled to see you, but he won't be ticked off either. He can't tell one person from another, you see. So there's no problem if you come along. I plan to visit the nursing home again pretty soon. According to the doctor, he doesn't have much longer—the end could come at any time. So join me on my next visit, if you're free."

I brought a spare blanket, pillow, and futon and made up a bed on the sofa in the living room. I looked around the room to make sure the Commendatore wasn't there. If Masahiko woke up in the middle of the night and saw him—two feet tall and dressed in ancient Asuka garb—he'd freak out. He'd figure he had become a real alcoholic.

Besides the Commendatore, there was *The Man with the White Subaru Forester* to worry about. I had turned the painting around so no one could see it. Still, I had no idea what strangeness might happen without my knowledge in the middle of the night.

So I wasn't kidding when I wished Masahiko a sound sleep.

I gave him a spare pair of pajamas to wear. He and I were more or less the same size, so there was no problem with the fit. He took off his clothes, put on the pajamas, and climbed under the bedding I had laid out. The air in the room was a bit chilly, but he looked snug and warm under the covers.

"You're sure you're not angry?" he asked before I left.

"No, I'm not angry," I answered.

"It must hurt a little, though."

"Maybe a little." I had the right to be a little hurt, I thought.

"But the cup is still one-sixteenth full."

"You've got it there," I said.

I turned off the living room light and retired to my bedroom. Before long I had fallen asleep, together with my slightly wounded feelings.

43

IT COULDN'T END LIKE ANY OTHER DREAM

When I woke it was already light outside. Thin gray clouds covered the sky from end to end, but the sun's benevolent rays still quietly filtered through. It was not quite seven.

I washed my face, turned on the coffee maker, and went to check the living room. Wrapped in blankets, Masahiko was fast asleep on the sofa. He appeared unlikely to wake up any time soon. The almost empty bottle of Chivas Regal sat on the table. I managed to tidy up the bottle and glasses without disturbing him.

I must have drunk quite a lot the night before, but I wasn't a bit hungover. My mind was as sharp as it was every morning. No heartburn, either. I've never had a hangover in my life. Why, I don't know. Probably it's just the way I was born. One night's sleep and all traces of alcohol vanish from my system, however much I drink. I eat breakfast and I'm ready to go.

I toasted two slices of bread, fried two eggs, and ate them while listening to the news and weather on the radio. The stock market was fluctuating wildly, a new parliamentary scandal had been uncovered, and a terrorist bombing in the Middle East had killed and wounded many people. Nothing to brighten my day. Yet none of these events was likely to affect my immediate circumstances. For now, at least, they were limited to distant places and people I had never met. I felt bad, but there was nothing I could do. The weather forecast promised nothing new either. Not a particularly gorgeous day, but not particularly awful either. Overcast, but no rain. Maybe not, anyway. But the forecasters and media types were clever—they never used vague words like "maybe." No, they stuck with convenient terms for which no one could be held accountable, like "probability of precipitation."

When the news and weather ended, I turned off the radio and cleaned up the breakfast dishes. Then I sat down again at the table, drank a second cup of coffee, and thought. Most people would have used that time to read the Sunday paper, but I didn't subscribe. So I just sipped my coffee, looked at the magnificent willow tree outside the window, and thought.

First, I thought about my wife, who, I had been told, was about to give birth. Then it hit me—she wasn't my wife any longer. No connection between us remained. Not contractual, not personal. From where she stood, I was now in all likelihood a virtual stranger, a person of no special consequence. It felt weird. Until a few months ago we had eaten breakfast together, shared the same soap and towel, walked around naked in front of each other, slept in the same bed. Now our lives bore no relationship to each other.

As I followed this train of thought, gradually I began to feel a stranger to myself as well. I placed my hands on the table and studied them for a while. These were my hands, no doubt. Right and left a symmetrical pair. I used these hands to paint, to cook, to eat, sometimes to caress a woman's body. But this morning, for some reason, they didn't look like my hands at all. They had become a stranger's hands—the palms, the backs, the fingernails.

I quit studying my hands. And thinking about the woman who had formerly been my wife. I got up from the table and went to the bath, where I removed my pajamas and took a hot shower. I carefully washed my hair and shaved in the bathroom sink. When I finished, I thought about the baby Yuzu was about to have—the baby who was not my child—again. I didn't want to, but there was nothing I could do about it.

She was about seven months pregnant. Seven months ago had been the second half of April. Where was I then, and what was I doing? I had left home and set out on a long, solitary trip in mid-March, driving my antique Peugeot 205 more or less at random all across Hokkaido and northeastern Japan. By the time my trip ended and I returned to Tokyo it was already early May. In late April I had crossed over from Hokkaido to Aomori in northern Honshu on the ferry that ran from Hakodate to Oma on the Shimokita Peninsula.

I pulled the simple diary I had kept out of a desk drawer and checked. At that time I had been traveling in the mountains of Aomori, far from the sea. Although it was well into the second half of April, it was still cold, and snow was everywhere. Why on earth had I chosen such a cold place? I couldn't remember the precise location, but I did recall a small, almost deserted lakefront hotel where I had stayed for a few days. It was an unprepossessing old building made of concrete, where they offered simple (but not bad) meals and amazingly cheap rates. There was even a small outdoor hot springs bath in a corner of the garden that was available twenty-four hours a day. The hotel had just reopened for the spring season, and I was practically the only guest.

For some reason, my recollections of that trip were vague. All I recorded in the notebook I used as a diary were the names of the places I visited, where I stayed, what I ate, the distance I had driven, and how much I spent. It was a brief, very hit-and-miss record. I could find no mention of my thoughts and feelings, or anything else along those lines. I guess there was nothing to write about. One day just flowed into another, with no distinction between them. I had jotted down the names of the places, but couldn't remember much about any of them. Many times, even their names had been left out. Looking back, I could only recall that feeling of repetition: the same scenery day after day, the same food, the same weather ("cold" and "not so cold" were my only categories).

The little sketchbook I had carried did a better job of bringing the trip back to life. (I carried no camera, so I hadn't taken a single photograph. Instead, I had sketched.) Even so, there weren't that many sketches to look at. When I had spare time, I had just whipped off simple drawings of what was before my eyes with an old pencil or ballpoint pen. Flowers and plants on the roadside, dogs and cats, mountain peaks, things like that. Now and then I would sketch someone I met along the way, but I almost always gave those pictures to whomever I had drawn.

Beneath the diary entry for April 19 I had written the words "Dream last night." That was all. I had been staying at the small lakefront hotel on that date. The words were underlined with a thick pencil. It must have been a special kind of dream to warrant such emphasis. It took me a while to remember what the dream had been about. When the memory returned, though, it arrived all at once.

The dream had come to me shortly before dawn that day. It was vivid, and very erotic.

In the dream I was back in the apartment in Hiroo. The one Yuzu and I had shared for six years. There was a bed, and my wife was sleeping in it. I was looking down at her from the ceiling. In other words, I was hovering above her. I didn't find that at all out of the ordinary. In fact, the me in the dream found floating in the air to be perfectly normal. Nothing unnatural about it. Of course, I had no idea I was dreaming. What was happening felt totally real.

Quietly, so as not to wake Yuzu, I descended from the ceiling to stand at the foot of the bed. I was sexually aroused, powerfully so. I hadn't made love to her for ages. Bit by bit, I peeled back the quilt covering her. She was fast asleep (had she taken a sleeping pill before retiring?) and showed no signs of waking up, even when I removed the quilt. She never even twitched. This made me more daring. Taking my time, I slipped off her pajama bottoms, then her panties. Her pajamas were a pale blue, her tiny cotton panties pure white. Still she did not wake. There was no resistance, no sound.

I gently parted her legs and caressed her vagina with my finger. It was warm and wet, and opened to my touch. As if it had been waiting for me. I couldn't stand it any longer—I slipped my erect penis inside. Or, from another angle, that part of her actively swallowed my penis, immersing it in what felt like warm butter. Yuzu did not open her eyes, but she sighed and let out a small moan. As if she had been impatient for this to happen. Her nipples were as hard as cherry pits when I touched them.

She might be deep in a dream, I thought. If she was dreaming of someone, though, it was surely not me. For a long while now she had resisted sex with me. Whatever dream she might be having, though, whoever she was mistaking me for, it was too late to turn back, for I was already inside her. It could be a terrible shock if she woke up in the midst of the act and saw who it was. She might well be furious. If that were to happen, I would deal with it then. Now all I could do was take it to the limit. My desire raged like a river through a broken dam, carrying me along.

At the beginning, I moved my penis slowly, trying not to arouse her so much as to wake her up, but, naturally, the pace quickened as I went on. I could tell from the way her body welcomed me that she wanted me to be more forceful. Soon, though, I reached the moment of climax. I wanted to remain inside her, but I couldn't control myself any longer. It had been ages since we had last had sex, and, though asleep, she was responding to our lovemaking with more passion than ever before.

My ejaculation was violent, and repeated. Again and again, semen poured from me, overflowing her vagina, turning the sheets sticky. There was nothing I could do to make it stop. If it continued, I worried, I would be completely emptied out. Yuzu slept deeply through it all without making a sound, her breathing even. Her sex, though, had contracted around mine, and would not let go. As if it had an unshakable will of its own and was determined to wring every last drop from my body.

I woke up at this point. I had indeed ejaculated. My underwear was drenched in semen. I quickly slipped it off to avoid soiling the bed, carried it to the sink, and washed it. Then I went out through the hotel's back door to bathe in the hot springs. As the bath was entirely exposed to the elements, with no ceiling or walls, I was freezing by the time I reached it. Once I got in, however, the water warmed me to the core.

I soaked there alone in the predawn hush, listening to the water drip as steam melted the ice, replaying the dream over and over in my head. The memory was so vivid and physical it didn't feel like a dream at all. I had *actually* visited the Hiroo apartment and had *actually* made love to Yuzu—that was the only way I could think about it. My hands remembered the touch of her silky skin and my penis could still feel her vagina. It had clung to my penis, had embraced it with a violent passion (true, Yuzu may have mistaken me for someone else, but it was me nonetheless). She had wrung me out, taking every last drop of my semen for her own.

I could not help but feel a kind of shame for having such a dream (if dream indeed it was). After all, I had raped my own wife in my imagination. I had undressed and entered her while she was sleeping, without her consent. In the eyes of the law, a man who does that to a woman—even his wife—is guilty of sexual assault. In that sense, my conduct was far from praiseworthy. Still, objectively speaking, *it was a dream*. Something experienced in sleep. I had not created it on purpose. I had not written the script.

Yet in it I had played out my truest hopes and desires. There was no question on that score. Had I been placed in a similar situation in real life—not in a dream—I might well have acted the same. I might have stripped and forcibly entered her. I wanted Yuzu's body, longed to penetrate it. I was possessed by that desire. I had been able to realize it in exaggerated form in my dream (conversely, only in a dream could it have been realized).

As I continued on my solitary journey, this "real" erotic dream provided me with a provisional kind of happiness. You might say it buoyed me up. By recalling it, I could feel that I was a living creature organically connected to the world. Linked to my surroundings not through logical or conceptual thought, but carnally, through my body.

At the same time, though, the thought that someone else—some other man—was *actually* enjoying Yuzu as I had in my dream was agony. That someone was caressing her stiffened nipples, removing her tiny white panties, and thrusting himself into her until he came, again and again. When I imagined that, it felt as though I were torn and bleeding inside. Nothing (as far as I could remember) had ever made me feel that way before.

That was the strange dream I had experienced shortly before dawn on April 19. Noted in my diary as "Dream last night" and thickly underlined in pencil.

. . .

It was right around that time that Yuzu had conceived. Of course, the precise date could not be known. But it would not be odd if it were that day.

The similarity between my situation and the story Menshiki had told me was striking. The difference was that he had made love to a flesh-and-blood woman on his office sofa *in reality*. That had not taken place in a dream. And it had been right around then that she had conceived. Immediately thereafter she had married a man of substantial means, and had subsequently given birth to Mariye. Menshiki's belief that Mariye might be his child therefore had a basis in fact. It was a long shot, perhaps, but at least it was possible. My lovemaking with Yuzu, on the other hand, had taken place in a dream. I was in the mountains of Aomori, while Yuzu was (probably) in the heart of Tokyo. Thus her child could not possibly be mine. That was the only logical conclusion. The odds were not low, they were zero. *If, that is, one was thinking logically.*

But my dream was too vivid to be so easily dismissed on logical grounds. Moreover, the pleasure I had felt during our lovemaking was greater, and far more memorable, than at any time during our six years of marriage. When I came again and again inside her, the fuses in my brain seemed to have all blown at once, melting what had been distinct layers of reality into a single heavy, turbid mass. As in the primal chaos of the earth.

So graphic an occurrence must have consequences—it couldn't end like any other dream. I felt that strongly. It had to be connected to *something*. To have some sort of impact on the present.

Masahiko woke up shortly before nine. He padded into the dining room in his pajamas and drank a cup of hot black coffee. No breakfast, thanks, he said—just coffee, if you don't mind. There were bags under his eyes.

"Are you okay?" I asked.

"I'm fine," he said, rubbing his eyelids. "I've had much worse hangovers. This is mild."

"Why don't you stick around for a while?" I said.

"Don't you have a guest coming?"

"That's at ten. There's still time. And there's no problem if you're here when they arrive. I'll introduce you. They're both very attractive."

"Both? I thought there was just one model."

"Her aunt is her chaperone."

"Her chaperone? So they still do things the old-fashioned way in this neck of the woods? Like in a Jane Austen novel. They don't wear corsets and ride in a horse-drawn carriage, do they?"

"Not a horse-drawn carriage. A Toyota Prius. And no corsets. When I'm painting the girl, the aunt sits in the living room and reads for the whole two hours. 'Aunt' makes her sound old, though—she's pretty young."

"What sort of books is she into?"

"I don't know. I asked, but she wouldn't tell me."

"No kidding," he said. "Oh yeah, speaking of books, remember the character in Dostoevsky's *The Possessed*, the guy who shoots himself with a pistol just to prove how free he is? What's his name? I figured you might know."

"Kirillov," I said.

"That's right, Kirillov. I've been trying to remember, but it keeps slipping my mind."

"Why do you want to know?"

"No special reason," Masahiko said, shaking his head. "He popped into my head, and when I tried to recall his name, I couldn't. It's been bugging me. Like a fish bone caught in my throat. But man, those Russians. They come up with the weirdest ideas, don't they?"

"There are lots of characters in Dostoevsky who do crazy things just to prove that they are free people, unconstrained by God and society. Though looking at Russia back then, maybe they weren't so crazy after all."

"Then how about you?" Masahiko asked. "You and Yuzu are formally divorced, which means you're now a lawfully unwedded man. So what comes next? Even if it wasn't your choice, freedom is still freedom, right? Why not run out and do something crazy, now that you have the opportunity?"

I laughed. "I'm not planning anything at present. Sure, I may be free for the moment, but that doesn't mean I've got to go out and prove it to the world, does it?"

"So that's how you look at it," Masahiko said in a disappointed tone. "But hey, you're a painter, right? An artist. Artists flaunt the rules left and right—they make a great show of it. But you've always walked the straight and narrow. The path of reason, I guess. So why not let loose now, throw off the restraints and do something wild?"

"Like murdering an old moneylender with an axe?"

"Yeah, that might work."

"Or falling for a prostitute with a heart of gold?"

"Even better."

"I'll think about it," I said. "But you know, it seems to me that reality itself has a screw loose somewhere. That's why I try to keep at least myself in line as much as possible."

"Well, I guess that's one way of looking at it," Masahiko said resignedly.

It's more than just "one way of looking at it," I wanted to tell him. Indeed, it felt like everything around me was becoming unscrewed—that reality was losing its grip. If I lost my grip too, then the craziness would get completely out of hand. But I couldn't tell Masahiko the whole story at this stage of the game.

"At any rate, I've got to be going," he said. "I'd love to meet the two women, but I've got work waiting for me back in Tokyo."

Masahiko finished his coffee, got dressed, and drove off in his boxy jet-black Volvo. Baggy eyes and all. "Glad we finally had a chance to talk," were his parting words.

One thing that morning completely stumped me. Masahiko's knife, the one he'd brought to prepare the fish, had gone missing. It had been carefully washed, and neither of us remembered touching it afterward, but we searched the kitchen high and low and still couldn't find it.

"Forget it," he said. "It's probably out for a walk. Grab it for me when it comes back. I'll pick it up on my next visit—I don't use it all that often."

I'll keep looking, I told him.

. . .

I checked my watch once the Volvo was out of sight. The Akikawas would be showing up before long. I removed the bedding from the living room sofa, and flung the windows wide open to let fresh air in. The sky was still faintly overcast and gray. There was no wind.

I took *Killing Commendatore* from my bedroom and hung it back where it had been on the studio wall. Then I sat down on the stool to examine the painting one more time. Red blood still gushed from the Commendatore's chest, while Long Face's sharp eyes still glittered in the lower left-hand corner of the canvas. Nothing had changed.

Even as I studied *Killing Commendatore,* though, I couldn't erase Yuzu from my mind. It had been no dream, of that much I felt sure. *I had truly visited our apartment that night.* I was as sure of that as I was that Tomohiko Amada had visited the studio several days before. Like him, I had overcome the laws of physics by some means to make my way to our Hiroo apartment, penetrate her, and discharge my semen inside her body. People can accomplish anything, I thought, if they want it badly enough. There are channels through which reality can become unreal. Or unreality can enter the realm of the real. If we desire it that strongly. Deep in our heart. But that didn't mean that we were free. It might demonstrate quite the opposite.

If I had the chance, I wanted to ask Yuzu if *she* had experienced a similar dream in late April of this year. If she had dreamed shortly before dawn that I had come to ravish her while she was fast asleep (or else somehow deprived her of her freedom). In other words, was my dream something I alone experienced, or was it a two-way street? That's what I wanted to confirm. Yet if the dream was one we had shared, wouldn't she view me as sinister, a villain? Could such a presence exist within me? I hated to think of myself in that way.

Was I free? As far as I was concerned, the question was wholly irrelevant. What I needed now more than anything was a firm reality to hold on to. A solid foundation on which to stand. Not the sort of freedom that allowed me to rape my own wife in my dreams.

44

THE TRAITS THAT MAKE A PERSON WHO THEY ARE

Mariye didn't speak that morning. She just sat there, the perfect model, in the simple straight-backed chair, and gazed at me as if at some distant landscape. Since my stool was taller than her chair, she was looking up at a slight angle. I made no special attempt to talk to her. There was nothing I had to say, nor did I feel any particular need. So I plied my brush across the canvas in silence.

I was painting Mariye's portrait, yet I could sense elements of my dead sister Komi and my former wife Yuzu creeping into the work. This wasn't intentional—they worked their way in quite naturally. Perhaps I was searching within Mariye for reminders of those two women, so important to me, whom I had lost. I couldn't say if this was healthy or not. But that was the only way I could paint at the time. No, to say "at the time" is off the mark. When I thought about it, I had operated like this from the very beginning. Giving form to what eluded me in reality. Inscribing secret signals only I could decipher.

Whatever the case, I was able to push Mariye's portrait forward with relative ease. Step by step, it moved steadily toward completion. Like a river, it followed the contours of the land, pooling in the hollows until it overflowed the final barrier to stream unobstructed to the sea. I could feel it circulate through my body, like blood.

"Can I come visit you later," Mariye said in a small voice just before we finished our morning's work. The lack of inflection made it sound like an assertion, but it was a clear question.

"You mean through your secret passageway?"

"Yes."

"I don't mind at all, but around what time?"

"I don't know yet."

"I don't think you should come after dark," I said. "You can never tell what's in these mountains at night."

All sorts of weird things could be lurking out there: the Commendatore, Long Face, the man with the white Subaru Forester, Tomohiko Amada's living spirit. Even the incubus that was my sexual alter ego. Yes, depending on the circumstances, I might turn into one of those sinister creatures that prowled the night. The thought gave me a chill.

"I'll try to come before dark," Mariye said. "I want to talk to you about something. Just the two of us."

"I'll be waiting."

We wrapped up for the day not long after the noon-hour chimes sounded.

Shoko was sitting on the sofa, once again focused on her reading. She appeared to have almost finished the thick paperback. Taking off her glasses, she noted her place with a bookmark and looked up at us.

"We made good progress today," I told her. "One or two more sessions and we should be done. I'm sorry to be taking so much of your time."

Shoko smiled. It was a beautiful smile. "Not at all," she answered. "Mariye seems to enjoy sitting for you, and I so look forward to seeing the finished portrait. And this sofa is the perfect place to read. I'm never bored in the slightest. In fact, it's a welcome change of pace for me to come here—I always feel better afterward."

I wanted to ask her how their visit to Menshiki's house had gone the previous Sunday. Had his fine mansion impressed her? What had she thought of him as a person? But asking questions like that would have been a breach of etiquette—I had to wait for her to raise the subject first.

Once again, Shoko had dressed for the occasion. It was most definitely not what a regular person would put on to visit a neighbor on a Sunday morning. A perfectly pressed camel hair skirt, a fancy white silk blouse with a big ribbon, and a dark blue-gray jacket with a gold pin adorning the collar. The pin had a jewel embedded in it, which I took to be a real diamond. The whole outfit seemed rather too fashionable to wear behind the wheel of a Toyota Prius. But who was I to say? Toyota's director of marketing would likely have a very different opinion.

Mariye was dressed as usual. The same old varsity jacket, her hole-studded jeans, and a pair of white sneakers even dirtier than the ones she usually wore (the backs of these were stomped flat).

When they were heading out the door, Mariye looked back and gave me a wink, a secret sign that said "See you later." I flashed a quick smile in response.

When Shoko and Mariye had gone, I went to the living room, lay down on the sofa, and slept. I had no appetite, so I skipped lunch. It was a brief nap, about thirty minutes, deep and dreamless. I was grateful for that. It was more than a little scary to think what I might do in my dreams, and even scarier to think *what I might become.*

My mood that Sunday afternoon was as unfocused as the weather. It was a quiet, slightly overcast day with no wind to speak of. I read a little, listened to a little music, cooked a little, but nothing helped me work out my feelings. It promised to be one of those afternoons where nothing gets resolved. Giving up, I ran a hot bath, got in, and soaked for a long time. I tried to remember the names of the characters in Dostoevsky's *The Possessed.* I was able to come up with seven, including Kirillov. For some reason, since my high school days I've had a knack for memorizing lengthy Russian names. Maybe now was a good opportunity to go back and reread *The Possessed.* I was free, with time on my hands and nothing that had to be done. The perfect conditions for reading long Russian classics.

I thought about Yuzu some more. Her belly would probably be showing after seven months. I pictured how that would look. What would she be doing now? What would she be thinking? Was she happy? Of course, I had no way to know any of those things.

Perhaps it was as Masahiko had said. Perhaps, like a nineteenth-century Russian intellectual, I should do something out-and-out crazy just to prove I was a free man. But what? Something like . . . spend an hour shut up at the bottom of a pitch-black pit? *That* was what Menshiki had done. True, his actions might not fit the category "out-and-out crazy." But they were definitely beyond the pale, to put it mildly.

It was after four when Mariye showed up. The doorbell rang, I opened the door, and there she was. She slipped through the half-open door like a wisp of cloud and looked around warily.

"No one's here."

"Nobody's here, that's true," I said.

"Someone was here yesterday."

That was a question. "Yes, a friend of mine stayed over," I said.

"A man."

"Yes, a man. A male friend. But how did you know?"

"There was an old car I'd never seen before parked in front of your house. It looked like a black box."

That would be Masahiko's ancient Volvo station wagon, what he called his "Swedish lunch box." Convenient for hauling reindeer carcasses.

"So you came yesterday."

Mariye nodded. It appeared that she was using her passageway to come and check on the house whenever she had time. She'd probably been doing this since long before my arrival. After all, it was her playground. Or "hunting ground" might be more accurate. I was just someone who had chanced to move in. In which case, could she have come face-to-face with Tomohiko Amada at some point? I had to ask her about that sometime.

I led her into the living room. We sat down together, she on the sofa, me in the armchair. I offered her something to drink, but she said no.

"The guy who stayed over is a friend from my college days," I said.

"A good friend?"

"I think so," I said. "In fact, he may be the only person I can call a true friend."

Such a good friend that he could introduce his colleague to my wife and keep me in the dark when they started sleeping together—a situation that had led to my just concluded divorce—without casting a cloud over our relationship. To call us friends would hardly be stretching the truth.

"Do you have any good friends?" I asked her.

Mariye didn't answer. In fact, she didn't bat an eye, just acted as if she hadn't heard what I'd said. I guessed it was something I shouldn't have asked.

"Mr. Menshiki isn't a good friend of yours," she said. I knew it was a question, though her intonation was flat. *Do you mean Mr. Menshiki isn't a good friend of yours?* was what she meant.

"As I've told you," I said, "I haven't known Mr. Menshiki long enough to call him a real friend. I started talking with him after I moved here, and that was only six months ago. It takes longer than that for people to become close. Still, he strikes me as a very interesting person."

"Interesting."

"How can I explain? His disposition strikes me as a little different than the average guy. Maybe more than a little, actually. He's not an easy person to figure out."

"Disposition."

"Personality. The traits that make a person who they are."

Mariye stared at me for a while. As if selecting the exact words she ought to use.

"He can see my home from his deck—it's right across the valley."

It took me a moment to respond to that. "Yes, you're right. That's the lay of the land. But he can see my house just as clearly. Not yours alone."

"Still, I think that man is *spying on* us."

"What do you mean, spying on you?"

"He's got something like a pair of big binoculars on the terrace, though he hides them with a cover. They're on a kind of tripod. He can see us really clearly if he uses those."

So the girl found him out, I thought. Watchful, observant. Eyes that missed nothing of importance.

"So you think that Mr. Menshiki has been observing you through those binoculars?"

Mariye gave a terse nod.

I took a deep breath, then let it out. "Still, that's just a guess on your part, right? They don't necessarily mean he's peeking into your house. He could be observing the moon and stars."

Mariye's gaze didn't waver. "I've had this feeling like I'm *being watched*," she said. "For a while. But I didn't know who was watching me, or from where. But now I know. It's *that person,* for sure."

I took another long, slow breath. Mariye's supposition was on the money. Menshiki was watching her through his high-powered military binoculars on a nightly basis. Yet to my knowledge—and this was not to defend Menshiki—his motives for being a peeping Tom were far from nefarious. He just wanted to see the girl. This beautiful thirteen-year-old girl who might be his biological daughter. For that reason, and that reason alone, he had purchased the mansion on the other side of the valley. Wresting it from the family living there and booting them out. Yet I couldn't reveal that to Mariye.

"Let's say you're right," I said. "But then what's his motive? Why is he so fixated on your home?"

"I don't know. Maybe he has a crush on my aunt."

"Has a crush on your aunt?"

She gave a brief shrug of her shoulders.

Mariye couldn't imagine she was the target. She hadn't yet reached the stage where she could see herself as an object of male desire. I found it strange, yet I didn't dare call her version of events into question. If that was how she read the situation, better perhaps to let it ride.

"I think Mr. Menshiki is hiding something," Mariye said.

"What, for example?"

"My aunt is seeing Mr. Menshiki," she said, not answering my question. "They met twice this week." Her tone suggested that she was passing on highly sensitive state secrets.

"On dates?"

"I think she went to his house."

"Alone?"

"She left a little after noon and didn't return until late."

"But you can't be sure she went to Mr. Menshiki's, can you?"

"I can tell," she said.

"How can you tell?"

"My aunt doesn't leave the house that much," she said. "Sure, she'll volunteer at the library or go shopping, but then she doesn't take a long shower, or paint her nails, or put on perfume and her fanciest underwear."

"You really have sharp eyes, don't you," I said, impressed. "You see everything. But are you sure the man she's meeting is Mr. Menshiki? Couldn't it be someone else?"

Mariye narrowed her eyes at me. She gave a small shake of her head. As in, *Do you think I'm that stupid?* After all, under the circumstances it was unlikely to be anyone but Menshiki. And Mariye was anything but stupid.

"So your aunt spends quite a bit of time at Mr. Menshiki's house, just the two of them together."

Mariye nodded.

"And the two of them—how should I put this?—are engaged in what we might call a very intimate relationship."

She nodded again. "Yes, a very intimate relationship," she said, her cheeks turning a faint pink.

"But you're in school all day. Not at home. So how can you know these things?"

"I can tell. I can tell that much from a woman's face."

But I couldn't tell. Yuzu had carried on an extended affair while we were living together, and I was clueless. Looking back, I should have been able to figure out that much. How could a thirteen-year-old girl pick up on something I couldn't that quickly?

"So things really moved fast between those two, didn't they," I said.

"My aunt's no dummy—there's nothing wrong with her head. But her heart has a weak spot. And Mr. Menshiki is stronger than normal people. A lot stronger—she's no match for him."

She's probably right, I thought. Menshiki did have some special power. Once he made his move, it would be almost impossible for an average person to resist. Myself included. I doubted he would find it difficult to make a woman his, if that was his goal.

"So you're worried about your aunt, right? That Mr. Menshiki is using her for some reason."

Mariye swept her hair back with her hand, exposing her ear. It was small and white, and its shape was lovely. She nodded.

"But it's not that easy to stop a relationship of this sort once it's gotten started," I said.

Not that easy at all, I said to myself. It would move forward, crushing everything in its path, like the Hindus' great wheel of karma. There could be no turning back.

"That's why I had to talk to you," Mariye said. Then she looked me square in the eye.

When it began to get dark, I took my flashlight and walked Mariye almost as far as her passageway. She said she had to be home by dinner. They usually ate around seven.

She had come to ask me for advice. Yet I hadn't been able to offer anything useful. All I could tell her was to wait and see how things developed. I knew Menshiki and Shoko might be having sex, but they were two unmarried and consenting adults. What was I supposed to do? Sure, I had some background information, but I couldn't reveal it, not to Mariye, and not to her aunt. That meant that I couldn't give useful advice to anyone. I was like a boxer trying to fight with his best arm tied behind his back.

Mariye and I walked side by side through the woods, hardly exchanging a word. We had gone partway along the path when she reached down and took my hand. Her hand was small, but its grip was unexpectedly firm. I was surprised at first, but then I had often walked this way with my sister, so it didn't put me off. Instead, it felt normal, a kind of return to my youth.

Mariye's hand was very smooth to the touch. Warm but not at all sweaty. She must have been thinking about something, for her hand squeezed mine and relaxed, squeezed and relaxed, depending, I guess, on what she was thinking. My sister had done the same thing back in the old days.

When we reached the shrine, she let go of my hand and, without a word, circled around to the back. I followed her.

The pampas grass still bore the tread marks of the backhoe. Within lay the silent pit. Its cover was made of sturdy boards, weighted down by a row of stones. I shone my flashlight on them to confirm that they hadn't been moved. They hadn't.

"Is it okay if I look in?" Mariye asked me.

"Just look."

"Just look," Mariye said.

I set some of the stones to the side and removed one of the boards. Mariye knelt and peered through the opening. I trained the flashlight on the floor of the pit. Of course, nobody was there. Only a metal ladder leaning against the wall. If one so chose, one could use it to climb down and then back up again. It would be next to impossible to get out without the ladder, although the pit was less than nine feet deep. The walls were just too smooth and slick to be scaled.

Holding her hair back with one hand, Mariye stared inside the pit for a long time. Intently, as if searching for something in the dark. I had no idea what was down there to capture her attention.

"Who built this?" she asked, looking up at last.

"I don't know. At first I thought it might be a well, but now I'm not so sure. I mean, who would dig a well in such an out-of-the-way place? Anyway, it looks very old. And it's very well put together. It must have taken a long time to build."

Mariye looked at me steadily without saying anything.

"This area has been your playground for quite a while, hasn't it?" I said.

She nodded.

"But you didn't know this pit was behind the shrine until recently."

She shook her head. No, she hadn't known.

"You found it and opened it, didn't you?" she asked.

"That's right, I may have been the one who discovered it. I didn't know it was a pit, but I figured *something* had to be under that pile of rocks. The person who arranged for the rocks to be moved and the pit to be opened, though, was Mr. Menshiki." I wanted to let her in on this much, at least. It was better to be honest.

A bird cried in the trees. It was a sharp, piercing call, as if to warn its fellow creatures. I looked up but couldn't catch sight of it. All I could see were the layered branches of the leafless trees. And beyond those the evening sky of approaching winter, flat, expressionless, and gray.

Mariye winced slightly. But she didn't respond.

"It's hard to explain," I said. "I felt as if the pit was demanding that someone open it. And that I had been bidden to perform that task."

"Bidden?"

"Invited. Called upon to."

She looked up at me. "It wanted you to open it?"

"Yes."

"*This pit* asked you to open it?"

"It could have been anyone, perhaps. Maybe I just happened to be around."

"But it was Mr. Menshiki who actually did it."

"Yes. I brought him here. I couldn't have uncovered it without him. The rocks were too heavy to move by hand, and I didn't have the cash to bring in heavy equipment. It was a fortunate coincidence."

"Maybe you shouldn't have done it," she said after a moment's thought. "I think I told you that before."

"So you think I should have left it as it was?"

Mariye didn't answer immediately. She stood up and brushed the dirt off the knees of her jeans. Not once but several times. She and I replaced the board, and the stones that held it down. Once again, I committed their location to memory.

"Yes, I think so," she said at last, lightly rubbing her palms against each other.

"I think this place may have had some kind of religious background. There might be legends or stories connected to it."

Mariye shook her head. She didn't know of any. "Maybe my father knows something."

The whole area had been owned by her father's family since before the Meiji period. The adjoining mountain was also in their hands. He might have a good idea of what the pit and shrine meant.

"Could you ask him?"

Mariye winced slightly. "I'll try," she said in a small voice. She hesitated. "If I have a chance."

"It would be a big help if we knew who built it when, and for what purpose."

"Maybe they shut up something inside, and put heavy stones on top to make sure it didn't get out," she offered.

"So you think maybe they heaped on the stones to prevent whatever it was from escaping, and then built the little shrine to ward off its curse?"

"Maybe."

"And then we went and pried it open anyway."

Mariye gave a small shrug.

I accompanied her to where the woods ended. She'd go on from there by herself, she said. The darkness was no problem—she knew the way. She wanted no one to see the passage that led to her home. It was a shortcut that she alone should know. So I turned back, leaving her there. Only a glimmer of light remained in the sky. The cold blackness was descending.

The same bird made the same piercing call when I passed before the shrine. This time, though, I didn't look up. I headed straight home, leaving the shrine behind. As I prepared dinner I sipped a glass of Chivas Regal and water. There was only enough left in the bottle for one more drink. The night was deathly silent. As if the clouds were absorbing every living sound.

You shouldn't have opened the pit.

Perhaps Mariye was right. I should have steered clear of the pit. It seemed that everything I did these days was off the mark.

I imagined Menshiki making love to Shoko. The two of them naked, entwined on a big bed in a room somewhere in that sprawling white mansion. That event was taking place in another world, of course, one that bore no connection to me. Yet the thought of the two of them together left me bereft. As if I were standing in a station watching a long, empty train pass by.

Finally, I fell asleep and my Sunday ended. A deep dreamless sleep, undisturbed by anyone.

45

SOMETHING IS ABOUT TO HAPPEN

Of the two paintings I was working on, *The Pit in the Woods* was the one I knocked off first. It was Friday afternoon when I finished it. Paintings are strange things: as they near the end they acquire their own will, their own viewpoint, even their own powers of speech. They tell the artist when they are done (at least that's the way it works for me). A spectator to the process—if one is present—can't tell the difference between a painting in process and a completed painting, for the line is virtually invisible to the naked eye. But the artist knows. He or she can hear the painting say, *Hands off, I'm done*. The artist has only to heed that voice.

So it was with *The Pit in the Woods*. At a certain point, it announced itself finished and refused my brush. Like a sexually satisfied woman. I took the canvas from the easel and leaned it against the wall. Then I sat down on the floor and regarded it at length. My painting of a half-covered hole in the ground.

I couldn't pin down my motive for painting it, or its meaning. It had just grabbed me. I couldn't come up with anything beyond that. These things happen. When something strikes me in that way—a landscape, an object, a person—I pick up my brush and am off to the races. No meaning, no motive. I just go where my gut tells me, pure and simple.

But wait, I thought. This time was different. This wasn't mere impulse. *Something* had demanded that I paint this painting. Urgently. That was why I had finished it so quickly—whatever it was, that demand had fired me up, sent me to my easel, and propelled me forward, like a hand on my back. Or maybe the pit was the agent, pushing me to draw its portrait, leaving me to guess its motive. In the same way that Menshiki, likely in pursuit of some larger plan, had enlisted me to paint his portrait.

Judged in a fair and objective way, the painting wasn't bad. I couldn't tell whether it could be called a work of art or not. (Not to make excuses, but I hadn't begun with that goal in mind.) From the standpoint of pure technique, though, it was a success. The composition was flawless, and I had captured both the light streaming through the trees and the colors of the fallen leaves. It was realistic right down to its tiniest detail, yet, nevertheless, a mysterious, symbolic aura hovered over it.

As I sat there staring at the finished work, a feeling came over me, what might be called a *premonition of impending movement*. On the surface at least, it was just as its title said: a landscape painting of the pit in the woods. It was so accurate, in fact, that "reproduction" might be closer to the truth. As someone who had been developing his craft, however imperfectly, for so long, I had the artistic skill to reproduce an exact likeness of the scene on canvas. I had not painted the scene so much as I had *documented* it.

Nevertheless, that *premonition* was there. Something was about to take place within that landscape. The painting was telling me that. Then I realized. What I had been trying to get across, or what that *something* had been trying to get me to paint, was precisely that premonition, those signs.

Sitting there on the floor, I straightened my back and looked at the painting anew.

What was about to happen? Was someone or something about to come crawling out from the darkness that lay beneath the half-open cover? Or, conversely, was someone about to climb down into the hole? Though I looked long and hard, I couldn't guess what would take place. I only knew some sort of movement was about to occur. The strength of my premonition left no doubt.

Why did the pit so badly want me to paint it? To try to tell me something? To warn me? It was a game of riddles. So many riddles, and not a single answer. I wanted to show the painting to Mariye and hear what she had to say. Maybe she could see what I couldn't.

• • •

Friday was the day I taught drawing near Odawara Station. Mariye was one of the students, so she would be there. Perhaps I could have a word with her afterward. I hopped in my car and headed to town.

There was still plenty of time when I arrived, so I parked and went to get my customary cup of coffee. No gleaming, functional Starbucks for me—my coffee shop was untouched by time, a back-alley spot run by a man on the cusp of old age who served a jet-black, muddy brew in a cup that weighed a ton. Jazz from a former era played on the ancient speakers. Billie Holiday, Clifford Brown, and other classics. As I still had time to spare when I finished my coffee, I wandered down the shopping street. I was low on coffee filters, so I bought a pack. I found a used-record store, and browsed through their old LPs. I realized I hadn't listened to anything other than classical music for a very long time. Tomohiko Amada's shelves contained no other kinds of records. If I listened to the radio, it was only to catch the news and weather on the AM dial (my location meant almost no FM reception).

I had left my records and CDs—not that there were a lot of them—in the Hiroo apartment. It would have been painful to sort out which books and records belonged to Yuzu and which to me. Impossible, really. Who did Bob Dylan's *Nashville Skyline* belong to? How about the Doors album with "Alabama Song" on it? What difference did it make who had shelled out the money? We'd shared the same music for a period of time, lived our life together listening to it. Even if we had been able to divide the records, we could never have separated the memories attached to them. I had to leave them all behind.

I looked for *Nashville Skyline* and the first album by the Doors, but couldn't find either. They may have been available on CD, but I wanted to hear them on an old-style phonograph. There was no CD player in Tomohiko Amada's house anyway. And no cassette deck. Just a couple of record players. Tomohiko Amada likely had no interest in new technology. He'd probably never come within six feet of a microwave oven.

In the end, I bought two records. Bruce Springsteen's *The River* and a collection of duets by Roberta Flack and Donny Hathaway. Both were old favorites of mine. At some point in my life, I had given up on new music. Instead, I listened to the old stuff over and over again. Books were the same. I reread books from my past, often more than once, but ignored books that had just come out. Somewhere along the way, time seemed to have come to a screeching halt.

Perhaps time really had stopped. Then again, maybe it kept nudging forward despite the fact that evolution, or anything resembling it, had ended. Like a restaurant approaching closing time that has stopped taking orders. And I was the only one who hadn't figured it out.

The shop assistant put the two records in a bag, and I paid. Then I went to a nearby liquor store to buy some whiskey. I wasn't sure what to get, but finally settled on Chivas Regal. It was a little more expensive, but would be a big hit with Masahiko the next time he stopped by.

My starting time for class was approaching, so I stashed the records, coffee filters, and whiskey in my car and entered the building where classes were held. The kids were first, starting at five o'clock. Mariye was part of that group. But I couldn't spot her. This was a first. She was passionate about the class, had never skipped it before, as far as I knew. Her absence unsettled me. I found it somehow alarming, even threatening. Was she all right? Was she ill, or had something unexpected happened to her?

Nevertheless, I carried on as though nothing was wrong, assigning simple exercises, offering comments on each child's drawing, giving advice. When class ended, the children went home and the adult class began. It too passed without incident. I exchanged good-natured pleasantries with the people there (hardly my strong point, but I can do it when required). After that, I had a brief meeting with the workshop organizer about future plans. He had no idea why Mariye was absent. There had been no word from her family.

After work, I went to a nearby noodle shop and ate a hot bowl of tempura soba. This too was my weekly habit. Always the same shop, and always tempura soba. One of life's little pleasures. Then I drove back to my house on the mountain. It was almost nine when I arrived.

I couldn't tell if anyone had tried to contact me while I was gone, for there was no answering machine (such a "clever" device probably numbered among Tomohiko Amada's bêtes noires). I gave the simple, old-fashioned telephone a long look, but it didn't speak. It just sat there, in black silence.

I had a long soak in a hot bath. Then I poured what was left of the original bottle of Chivas Regal into a glass, added two ice cubes from the fridge, and took the drink to the living room, where I sipped it while listening to one of the records I had just bought. At first, it seemed somehow *inappropriate* to be playing anything other than classical in my mountaintop domicile. The air in the room had been conditioned to that type of music for a very long time. Still, I was playing my music, so that now, song by song, a familiarity overcame the feeling of inappropriateness. As I listened, I could feel my body start to relax. I must have been tense without being aware of it.

The A side of the Roberta Flack and Donny Hathaway record had ended and the first song on the B side ("For All We Know," a really cool performance) had just begun when the phone rang. The clock said 10:30. Who on earth would be calling me so late? I didn't want to answer. Yet the ring sounded urgent. I put down my glass, rose from the sofa, lifted the needle off the record, and picked up the phone.

"Hello?" It was Shoko Akikawa.

I greeted her.

"I'm so terribly sorry to be phoning this late," she said. I had never heard her sound so anxious. "But I needed to ask you something. Mariye didn't show up at art class today, did she?"

No, I replied, she didn't. The question was a strange one. Normally, Mariye came straight from school (the public junior high in the area) in her uniform. When class ended, her aunt picked her up in the car, and the two went home together. That pattern never varied.

"I haven't seen Mariye anywhere," Shoko said.

"Haven't seen her?"

"She's missing."

"Since what time?" I asked.

"Since this morning, when she left for school. I offered to drive her to the station, but she said she'd walk. She likes walking. Much more than riding in the car. So I give her a lift when she's running late, but otherwise she walks down the hill to the bus stop and takes the bus to the station. This morning she left the house at seven thirty, as usual."

Shoko said all this in a single breath, then stopped. I could hear her trying to control her breathing. I used the pause to put what she had just told me into some kind of order.

"Today is Friday," Shoko continued. "When school lets out on Fridays, she goes directly to art class. And then I pick her up afterward. But today Mariye said she'd take the bus home instead. So I didn't go. When she says something like that, it's pointless to argue. But she still gets back by seven or seven thirty. Then she has dinner. But tonight, it turned to eight and then eight thirty and she still hadn't returned. So I called the center and asked whether she had come to class or not. They checked and said she hadn't shown up. That's when I got really worried. Now it's ten thirty and she's still not back. I've heard nothing. That's why I'm calling you—I thought perhaps you might know something."

"I haven't a clue where she is," I said. "I was rather surprised when I showed up for class and Mariye wasn't there. She's never skipped before."

Shoko gave a deep sigh. "My brother's not back yet. I don't know when to expect him—he hasn't contacted me. I'm not sure if he'll return tonight or not. I'm here all alone, and I don't know what to do."

"She was wearing her school uniform when she left this morning, correct?"

"Yes, she left in her uniform, with a bag over her shoulder. The same as always. A blazer and skirt. I don't know if she ever made it to school, though. It's late, so there's no way to check. But I'm quite sure she got there. The school contacts us if there's an unexplained absence. She was carrying enough money for a single day's expenses, no more. I make her take a cell phone just in case, but it's been shut off all day. She doesn't like cell phones. She'll use hers to call me, but she usually keeps it off the rest of the time. I've warned her about that over and over, begged her not to turn it off, explained that we may need to reach her if something important comes up, but she doesn't—"

"Has this ever happened before? Her coming home late?"

"This is the first time, really. Mariye is very dependable. She has no close friends she hangs out with, and once she's agreed to do something, she follows through, even though she doesn't like school all that much. She won a prize for perfect attendance in elementary school. She always comes straight home after school. She never loiters along the way."

Mariye's aunt was clearly in the dark about her nighttime forays.

"Was there anything she said or did this morning that was out of the ordinary?"

"No, nothing. It was a regular morning. The same as always. She drinks a glass of warm milk, eats a slice of toast, and heads out the door. Every day is identical. I made her breakfast today as I usually do. She didn't say a great deal. But that's normal. She can talk a blue streak once she gets started, but most of the time, you can't get much out of her."

I was beginning to worry. It was almost eleven at night, and it was pitch dark outside. The moon was hiding behind the clouds. What on earth had happened to Mariye Akikawa?

"I'll wait one more hour. If Mariye still hasn't contacted me by then, I'll call the police," Shoko said.

"That's a good idea," I said. "And let me know if there's anything I can do. Any time is all right—please don't hesitate, no matter how late it is."

Shoko thanked me and hung up. I drained what was left of the whiskey and washed the glass in the sink.

After that I went to the studio. I turned on all the lights and stood there in the bright room, taking another lingering look at my unfinished *Portrait of Mariye Akikawa* on the easel. It was close to done—only a little work remained. It showed a version of what a quiet thirteen-year-old girl would ideally look like. Yet there were other elements too, aspects of her that could not be seen, that made her who she was. What I was attempting in all my painting—though not, of course, in the portraits I did on commission—was to try to capture those things which lay outside my field of vision and communicate their message in a different form. Mariye was, in that sense, a most fascinating subject. There was just so much that was hidden, like a trompe l'oeil. And now as of this morning she herself had disappeared. As if swallowed by that very trompe l'oeil.

I turned to look again at *The Pit in the Woods* leaning against the wall. I had just completed it that afternoon. I could feel that painting calling out to me too, though in another way, and from a different direction, than *A Portrait of Mariye Akikawa*.

Something is about to happen. I felt this again as I looked at the landscape. Until that afternoon it had been a premonition of sorts, but now it was encroaching on reality. *The movement was already under way.* Mariye's disappearance and the pit in the woods were linked in some way. I could sense it. By finishing the painting I had set the gears in motion. And Mariye's vanishing act was the likely result.

Yet I could tell Shoko none of this. All that would do was confuse her even more.

I went back to the kitchen and rinsed the whiskey taste from my mouth with several glasses of water. When that was done, I picked up the phone and called Menshiki. I called three times before he picked up. I detected a slight edge to his voice, as if he were waiting for an important call. That it was me on the line seemed to surprise him. It only took a second, though, for the edge to disappear and the voice to turn cool and collected, as always.

"I'm very sorry to call so late," I said.

"Not at all. I stay up late, and I've got plenty of time. I'm always happy to hear your voice."

Skipping the normal pleasantries, I gave him a brief report of Mariye's disappearance. The girl had left home for school in the morning but hadn't returned. Nor had she shown up at my painting class. The news seemed to throw Menshiki for a loop. He took a moment to reply.

"And you have no idea where she might have gone, right?" he asked me.

"None at all," I replied. "It came out of left field. How about you?"

"I have no idea either, of course. She barely says a word to me."

There was no anger or regret in his voice. He was simply relating the way she treated him.

"That's just how she is—she's like that with everybody," I said. "But Shoko is at her wit's end. Mariye's father isn't home either, so she's all alone and unsure what to do."

Menshiki paused again. It was rare to see him at a loss for words—in fact, I had never witnessed it before.

"Is there anything I can do?" he said at last.

"I know it's sudden," I said, "but is there any chance you could drop by now?"

"To your home?"

"Yes. There's something in this connection that I need to talk to you about."

Menshiki took a moment to respond. "All right," he said. "I'll leave right away."

"Are you sure you don't have to take care of a matter there first?"

"It's not big enough to call a 'matter.' It's just a trivial thing," he said. He cleared his throat. He seemed to be checking his watch. "I can be there in about fifteen minutes."

When the phone call ended, I got ready to go out. I laid out a sweater and my leather jacket, and placed the big flashlight within easy reach. Then I sat on the sofa and waited for the purr of Menshiki's Jaguar rolling up the hill.

46

PEOPLE ARE POWERLESS BEFORE A STURDY, TOWERING WALL

Menshiki arrived at eleven twenty. The moment I heard his Jaguar, I slipped on my leather jacket and headed out the door. He stepped from the car wearing a padded, dark-blue windbreaker, narrow-cut black jeans, and leather sneakers. A light scarf was draped around his neck. His mane of white hair glowed in the dark.

"If it's okay, I'd like you to come with me to check out the pit in the woods," I said.

"Of course," Menshiki said. "Do you think it's connected to Mariye's disappearance?"

"I'm not sure. But I've had a premonition for a while that something bad was going to happen. Something connected to that pit."

Menshiki asked no more questions after that. "Fine," he said. "Let's go take a look."

He opened the trunk of his Jaguar and pulled out what looked like a lantern. Then he closed the trunk and set off with me toward the woods. Neither moon nor stars were out, so it was very dark. There was no wind.

"Sorry to ask you to venture out so late," I said. "But it seemed safer to have you come along. If something went wrong, I might not be able to handle it alone."

He patted my arm. As though to encourage me. "It's no trouble at all—I'm happy to do what I can."

We picked our way through the trees, shining the flashlight and lantern on our feet to avoid tripping over the roots. The only sound was the crunch of dry leaves underfoot. Otherwise it was dead silent. I sensed the animals of the woods silently watching us from their hiding places. The dark depths of midnight give rise to illusions like that. Had someone seen us, they might have mistaken us for a pair of grave robbers on their way to ransack a tomb.

"There's just one thing I'd like to ask," Menshiki said.

"What's that?"

"Why do you think Mariye's disappearance and the pit might be connected?"

I explained that she and I had visited the pit together not long before. That she had already known about its existence. That the whole area was her playground. That nothing happened here without her knowledge. Then I told him what she had said: *You should have left the place as it was. You should never have opened it up.*

"When she stood in front of the pit she seemed to have experienced something," I said. "A special feeling . . . I guess you could call it spiritual."

"And she was drawn to it?"

"Yes. She was leery, but at the same time something about the pit was drawing her in. That's why I worry it might have played a role. That she might be down there, unable to get out."

Menshiki thought for a moment. "Did you tell her aunt this?" he asked. "Does Shoko know?"

"No, I haven't said anything yet. If I mentioned the pit to her, I'd have to go back to the beginning. To how we opened it, and why you were involved. It would turn into a very long story, and I doubt I could explain myself very well."

"Yes, it would cause her a lot of needless worry."

"It would be even more awkward if the police got involved. If they grew interested in the pit."

Menshiki looked at me. "Are they investigating already?"

"She hadn't contacted them yet when I talked to her. But she could have put in a search request by now. After all, it's getting pretty late."

Menshiki nodded several times. "Yes, it's only natural. It's almost midnight, and a thirteen-year-old girl hasn't come home. No one knows where she's gone. What can her family do but call the cops?"

I could tell from his tone that Menshiki wasn't too thrilled that the police would be entering the picture.

"Let's keep the pit between ourselves if we can," he said. "The fewer people know, the better. Otherwise we could run into problems." I agreed.

The biggest problem for me was the Commendatore. It was almost impossible to explain the significance of the pit without bringing him—as an Idea, no less—into the mix. Yes, as Menshiki said, mentioning the pit would only make things worse. (And even if I did reveal the existence of the Commendatore, who would believe me? They'd just question my sanity.)

We emerged from the trees in front of the small shrine and circled around to the back. Stepping across the clump of pampas grass, whose plumes still lay cruelly flattened by the backhoe's treads, we arrived at the pit. The first thing we did was shine our lights on the boards covering the hole and the row of stones that held them down. I checked the placement of the stones. The change was subtle, but I could tell they had been moved. Someone had come after Mariye and me, removed the stones and several boards, and then, when they left, tried to return everything to its original position. My eyes could spot that slight difference.

"Someone moved the stones," I said. "There are signs that the pit has been opened."

Menshiki glanced at me. "Do you think it was Mariye?" he asked.

"I wonder. It's not a place anyone would stumble upon, and apart from you and me, she's the only one who knows about it. So the chances are good it was Mariye."

The Commendatore knew about the pit, of course. After all, that was where he had come from. Yet in the end he was an Idea. He had no fixed shape. He wouldn't have had to move those heavy stones if he wanted to go back inside.

We removed the stones and took the boards away. Once again, the hole was exposed. It was perfectly round and not quite six feet across, but it looked bigger now, and blacker, too. I imagined that the darkness was what created the illusion.

Menshiki and I leaned over the hole and directed our lights inside. No one was there. There was nothing at all. Just that empty cylindrical space surrounded by the same stone wall. There was one difference, however. The ladder had vanished. The collapsible metal ladder that the landscaper had considerately left behind after moving the pile of boulders. I had last seen it leaning against the wall of the pit.

"Where did the ladder go?" I wondered out loud.

It didn't take us long to find it lying on its side some distance away in a stand of pampas grass that the backhoe hadn't flattened. Someone had taken it from the hole and chucked it there. It wasn't heavy, so moving it required no great strength. We returned the ladder to the hole and leaned it back against the wall.

"I'm going down to take a look," Menshiki said. "Maybe I'll find something."

"Are you sure you'll be okay?"

"Don't worry, I've been down there before."

Menshiki descended the ladder with ease, lantern in hand.

"By the way, do you know the height of the Berlin Wall?" he asked as he descended.

"No."

"Ten feet," he said looking up at me. "It varied depending on the location, but that was the standard height. A little taller than this hole is deep. It was about a hundred miles long, too. I saw it with my own eyes. When Berlin was still divided into East and West. A pitiful sight."

When Menshiki reached the bottom, he inspected the pit in the light from his lantern. Even then, though, he kept on talking to me.

"Walls were originally erected to protect people. From external enemies, storms, and floods. Sometimes, though, they were used to keep people in. People are powerless before a sturdy, towering wall. Visually and psychologically. Some walls were constructed for that specific purpose."

Menshiki broke off at that point. Holding his lantern aloft, he examined every inch of the wall and the ground. Intently and carefully, like an archaeologist poring over the inner sanctum of an Egyptian pyramid. His lantern was stronger than my flashlight, so it illuminated a much wider area. He seemed to have found something on the floor of the pit, for he knelt down and examined it closely. I couldn't make it out from above, though. Menshiki said nothing. Whatever it was, it must have been very small. He stood up, wrapped it in his handkerchief, and deposited it in the pocket of his windbreaker. He looked up at me.

"I'm coming out," he said, raising his lantern into the air.

"Did you find something?" I asked.

Menshiki didn't answer. Carefully, he ascended the ladder. Each rung gave a dull creak under his weight. I kept close watch, my flashlight trained on him. The vantage point made me realize how well his daily routine had trained his body. Not a motion was wasted. Each muscle played its role perfectly. When he was back on the ground he gave a big stretch and then brushed the dirt from his trousers with care. Not that there was much to brush off.

"You can feel how intimidating the height of those walls is from down there. You really feel powerless. I saw something similar in Palestine a while ago. Israel erected a twenty-five-foot concrete wall there, with high-voltage wires running along the top. That wall is almost three hundred miles long. I guess the Israelis figured ten feet was too low, but that's enough to do the job."

He set the lantern down. Now the ground around our feet was illuminated.

"Come to think of it, the walls of the solitary cells in Tokyo prison measure about ten feet as well," Menshiki said. "I don't know why they made them so high. All you had to look at were those blank walls, day after day. Nothing else to lay your eyes on. No pictures or anything like that, of course. Just those damned walls. You start feeling like you've been thrown into a pit."

I listened in silence.

"I did some time in that place a while back. I haven't told you about that, have I?"

"No, you haven't." My girlfriend had told me he had spent time in prison, but of course I didn't mention that.

"I figure I should be the one to tell you. You know how gossips love to twist facts to spice up their stories. So it's better if I give it to you straight. It's not pretty, but this might be a good time to tell you. In passing, so to speak. Do you mind?"

"Not at all. Tell me."

"I'm not making excuses," he said after a moment's pause, "but I've done nothing to feel guilty about. I've tried my hand at many things in my life. Borne many risks. Still, I'm not stupid, and I am cautious by nature, so I've always been careful to avoid anything illegal. I know where to draw the line. In this case, though, I happened to take on a partner who was careless. Because of him, I suffered a great deal. That experience taught me never to join forces with anyone again. To take responsibility for myself and no one else."

"What were you charged with?"

"Insider trading and tax evasion. What they call 'economic crimes.' I was indicted and tried, but in the end they found me not guilty. All the same, the investigation was grueling, and I spent a pretty long time in prison. They found one reason after another to keep me locked up. I was in there for so long that now being surrounded by walls makes me a little nostalgic. As I said, I had done nothing to warrant punishment. My hands were clean. But the prosecutors had already concocted their scenario, and in it, I was guilty as sin. They had no desire to go back and rewrite it. That's how bureaucracies work. It's practically impossible to change something once it's been decided. Going against the current means that someone, somewhere down the line, has to take responsibility. As a result, I spent a long time in solitary."

"How long?"

"Four hundred and thirty-five days," Menshiki said, as if it were nothing. "A number I'll never forget, no matter how long I live."

It wasn't hard to imagine what spending that much time in solitary meant.

"Have you ever been confined in a small space for a long time?" Menshiki asked me.

"No," I said. My experience being locked in the back of the moving van had given me a bad case of claustrophobia. Now I couldn't even ride in an elevator. I'd fall apart if I were confined as he had been.

"I learned how to endure it," Menshiki said. "I spent the days training myself. In the process, I learned several foreign languages. Spanish, Turkish, and Chinese. They limit how many books you can keep in solitary, but those restrictions don't apply to dictionaries. In that sense, it's the ideal place to study languages. I'm blessed with good powers of concentration, so when I was focused on a language I could forget the walls. There's a bright side to everything."

Even the darkest, thickest cloud shines silver when viewed from above.

Menshiki continued. "What terrified me was the thought of earthquake and fire. Trapped like that, I could never have escaped. Imagining myself crushed or burned to death in that tiny space scared me so much sometimes I couldn't breathe. That was the one fear I couldn't overcome. It woke me up some nights."

"But you got through it."

"Of course. I'd be damned if I'd let those bastards beat me. Or let their system grind me down. If I had signed the papers they laid in front of me, I could have walked out of my cell and returned to the world. But signing them would have meant my utter defeat. I would have admitted to crimes I hadn't committed. So I decided to treat the experience as an ordeal sent from above, an opportunity to test my strength."

"Did you think about your time in prison when you spent that hour alone down in the pit?"

"Yes. I need to return to that experience once in a while—it's my starting point, so to speak. Where the person I am today was formed. It's easy to get soft when life is comfortable."

What a peculiar guy, I thought again. How would another person react to treatment that harsh—wouldn't they try to forget it as soon as possible?

As if remembering, Menshiki reached into the pocket of his windbreaker and pulled out something wrapped in a handkerchief.

"I found this at the bottom of the pit," he said. He unfolded the handkerchief, took out a small plastic object, and handed it to me.

I examined it under my flashlight. It was a black-and-white penguin, barely half an inch long, with a tiny black strap attached to it. The kind of thing that schoolgirls like to attach to their cell phones and schoolbags. It was clean and looked quite new.

"It wasn't there the first time I went into the pit," Menshiki said. "I'm sure of that."

"So it must have been dropped by someone afterward, when they were down there."

"I wonder. It looks like a cell phone ornament. And the strap isn't broken. So someone had to unhook it first. Doesn't that suggest it wasn't dropped—that whoever left it did so intentionally?"

"You mean they entered the pit just to leave it there?"

"Or dropped it down from above."

"Why would anyone do that?" I asked.

Menshiki shook his head. As if he couldn't understand either. "It's possible that whoever it was left it as a charm or talisman. That's just a guess, though."

"You mean Mariye?"

"Probably. After all, it's doubtful anyone else was near the pit."

"So she left it as a kind of charm?"

Menshiki shook his head again. "I don't know," he said. "It's hard to read a thirteen-year-old girl—their minds can come up with all sorts of stuff, can't they?"

I looked again at the tiny penguin in my hand. Now it struck me as a charm or amulet of some kind. An aura of innocence clung to it.

"Then who pulled out the ladder and dragged it over there? What was the reason for that?" I said.

Menshiki shook his head again. He had no idea either.

"Anyway," I said, "let's call Shoko when we get back and find out if Mariye has a penguin charm on her cell phone. She should know one way or the other."

"You hold on to the penguin for now," Menshiki said. I nodded and put it in my trouser pocket.

We replaced the boards, leaving the ladder resting against the wall of the pit. When we put the stones back I registered their exact positions in my mind. Then we headed home through the woods along the same path we had come on. I glanced at my watch—it was already past midnight. We said nothing, just shone our lights on our feet. We were both lost in thought.

As soon as we got back, Menshiki went to his Jaguar, opened the big trunk, and placed the lantern inside. Then he shut the trunk and, as if finally allowing himself to relax, leaned against it and looked up at the sky. The black sky in which nothing was visible.

"Do you mind if I come in for a few minutes?" he said. "It'd be hard for me to relax at home."

"By all means. I don't think I can sleep yet either."

Menshiki's eyes were still fixed on the sky. He seemed lost in thought.

"I can't explain why," I said, "but I can't get rid of this feeling that something bad is happening to Mariye. And that she's nearby."

"But not in the pit, right?"

"I guess not."

"What kind of bad thing?" Menshiki asked.

"That I don't know. But I feel she's in some kind of physical danger."

"And that the danger is lurking *somewhere close to here*, right?"

"Right," I said. "Near here. And it bothers me that the ladder was removed from the pit. Who took it, and why did they hide it in the grass? What does it all mean?"

Menshiki stood up and gave me another pat on the shoulder. "You're right. I don't know either. But worrying about it won't get us anywhere. Let's go inside."

47

"IT IS NOW FRIDAY, IS IT NOT?"

The moment we walked in the house I threw off my leather jacket and called Shoko. She picked up on the third ring.

"Anything new?" I asked.

"Mariye still hasn't called." I could hear her struggling to breathe normally.

"Have you contacted the police?"

"No, not yet. It still feels too early somehow. I keep thinking she'll come wandering in the door . . ."

I described the plastic penguin we had found at the bottom of the pit. Without detailing how we'd found it, I asked if Mariye carried such an object with her.

"Yes, Mariye had a penguin attached to her cell phone. It was a penguin, I'm sure . . . yes. A penguin. Without doubt. A tiny plastic figurine. She got it in a donut shop. It came free with her order, but she treasured it. As if it were a kind of protective charm."

"And she carried her phone wherever she went, correct?"

"Yes. It was turned off most of the time, but she always had it with her, yes. She didn't receive calls, but occasionally she'd call to let me know when something came up." Shoko paused for a moment. "Did you find it somewhere?"

I struggled to come up with an answer. If I told the truth, I'd have to tell her about the pit in the woods. If the police got involved, I would have to explain it to them as well—in a way they could swallow. Since the penguin was something she carried, they would comb the pit, even search the whole woods for further evidence. I would get the third degree, and Menshiki's past would be brought into it. I couldn't see how any of that would help. As Menshiki had said, it would just complicate things.

"I found it in the studio," I said. I hated to lie, but I had to. "When I was sweeping the floor. I thought that it might be Mariye's."

"Yes, it's hers. I'm sure," said the girl's aunt. "But then what should I do? Should I call the police?"

"Have you heard from your brother—I mean, Mariye's father?"

"No, I haven't been able to reach him," she said hesitantly. "I have no idea where he is. He's not someone who follows a regular schedule—I'm never sure if he's coming home or not."

The situation sounded complicated, but now wasn't the time to worry about that. I simply told her to inform the police of Mariye's disappearance. It was after midnight, and the date had changed. It was possible that Mariye had been in some kind of accident. She said she'd call them right away.

"So Mariye still isn't answering her cell phone?"

"No, she isn't answering, though I've called her many times. It seems to be turned off. Or the batteries are dead. One or the other."

"She left this morning for school, and she's been missing ever since. Right?"

"That's right."

"Which means she should be in her school uniform, correct?"

"Yes, she should be. A navy-blue blazer and vest, a white blouse, a knee-length plaid skirt, white socks, and black loafers. Oh, and a plastic shoulder bag with the school's name and emblem on it. She wasn't wearing a coat."

"Didn't she have another bag for her art supplies?"

"She keeps that in her locker at school. She uses it when they have art class, and then takes it to your class on Fridays. She doesn't bring it from home."

That was the outfit she always wore to my class—blue jacket, white blouse, tartan plaid skirt, plastic shoulder bag, and a white canvas bag with her paints and brushes. I could picture her perfectly.

"Was she carrying anything else?"

"No, not today. So I doubt she was going very far."

"Please call me if you hear anything," I said. "Any time of the day or night."

She said she would.

I hung up the phone.

Menshiki was standing beside me throughout this conversation. Only after I put down the phone did he shed his windbreaker. Underneath was a black V-neck sweater.

"So the penguin was Mariye's after all," Menshiki said.

"Seems so."

"In which case, it's likely that she went into the pit at some point—we don't know when—and left her treasured penguin there. That's what we have so far."

"So you think she left it there on purpose, as a protective talisman."

"Probably."

"But if that's so, who or what was it protecting?"

Menshiki shook his head. "I'm not sure. But it was clearly her lucky charm. So she must have left it behind for a reason. People don't part with things they value so easily."

"Unless it's to protect something they value more than themselves."

"For example?" Menshiki said.

Neither of us could answer that one.

We sat there in silence. Slowly but surely, the hands of the clock inched ahead. Each tick pushed the world that much further forward. Outside the window stretched a vast darkness. Nothing moved there. It seemed nothing could.

I suddenly recalled what the Commendatore had said about the missing bell. "The bell was never mine alone. It belonged to the place, to be shared by everyone. So if it disappeared there must have been a reason for it."

Belonged to the place?

"Just maybe Mariye didn't leave this penguin in the pit. Couldn't the pit be connected to some other location? Perhaps it isn't a sealed-off space but a conduit of some kind. If that's the case, it might be able to summon all sorts of things."

That is what I had been thinking, but said aloud it sounded ludicrous. The Commendatore might have understood. But not anyone from *this world*.

A deep silence settled over the room.

"So what could the bottom of the pit be connected to?" Menshiki said at last, as if addressing himself. "Remember, not so long ago I spent an hour alone down there. In the dark, without a light or a ladder. I tried to use the silence to focus my mind. To extinguish my physical existence and become pure consciousness. I figured if I could do that, I could transcend those stone walls and go wherever I liked. I used to try the same sort of thing when I was in solitary. But I couldn't find a way out of the pit. In the end, those walls allowed me no escape."

Perhaps the pit chose whom it wanted, I thought. The Commendatore had come to me when he left the pit. Chosen me as his lodgings, so to speak. Mariye too might have been chosen. But the pit hadn't chosen Menshiki—for whatever reason.

"In any case," I said, "we're agreed—we won't tell the police about the pit. At *this* stage, anyway. Still, we're clearly concealing evidence if we keep our mouths shut about finding the penguin there. If they find that out, we could be in a sticky position."

Menshiki thought for a moment. "So we'll keep our lips sealed—that's all there is to it!" he said at last. "You found it on your studio floor. We'll go with that."

"Maybe one of us should be with Shoko," I said. "She's home by herself with no idea what to do. Lost and confused. She's heard nothing from Mariye's father. Doesn't she need someone there?"

Menshiki furrowed his brow. "I'm in no position to do that," he said at last, shaking his head. "Her brother and I are total strangers, so if he came back . . ."

Menshiki lapsed into silence.

I had nothing to say either.

Menshiki sat there, lightly drumming his fingers on the arm of the sofa. Whatever he was thinking brought a slight flush to his cheeks.

"Would you mind if I stayed a little longer?" he asked a while later. "Shoko may try to get in touch with us."

"By all means, please do," I said. "I don't think I'll be going to bed any time soon. Stay as long as you like. You can sleep here too. I'll lay out some bedding for you."

Menshiki said he might take me up on my offer.

"Shall I make coffee?" I asked.

"Sounds good," Menshiki said.

I went to the kitchen, ground the beans, and started the coffee maker. When the coffee was ready, I took it out to the living room. Then Menshiki and I drank it together.

"I think I'll build a fire," I said. The room had grown markedly colder once midnight passed. It was already December. An appropriate time for the first fire of the season.

I filled the cast-iron grate in the fireplace with the small stack of firewood I had set aside in the corner of the living room. Then I inserted paper under the grate and lit a match. The wood appeared to be dry, for it caught right away. I was worried that the fireplace might back up—Masahiko had said it was set to go, but you never knew until you used it. A bird could have nested in the chimney. Fortunately, however, it worked beautifully. We moved our chairs in front of the fireplace and sat there in the warmth.

"Nothing beats a wood fire," Menshiki said.

I thought of offering him some whiskey but changed my mind. Tonight we should stay sober. Who knows, we might have to drive somewhere. So we listened to records and watched the flames dance. Menshiki selected a Beethoven violin sonata and put it on the turntable. Georg Kulenkampff on violin, with Wilhelm Kempff on piano. Perfect music for an early-winter night before a fire. It was hard to enjoy it, though, with Mariye out there shivering in the cold.

Shoko called half an hour later. Her brother had just come home and had already contacted the police. They would be there any moment to investigate. (The Akikawas were an old and wealthy family in the area, so the possibility that it was a kidnapping was making them move quickly.) There was no word from Mariye, and calling her cell phone still didn't work. They had contacted every likely person they could think of (there weren't that many) with no luck. No one knew where Mariye had gone.

"Let's hope she's all right," I said. I asked her to let me know if there was any progress, and hung up the phone.

We sat before the fire and listened to another record. Richard Strauss's Oboe Concerto. Menshiki plucked that off the shelf as well. It was the first time I had heard it. We sat there side by side as it played, watching the fire and thinking our solitary thoughts.

At one thirty, I suddenly grew terribly sleepy. I could barely keep my eyes open. I've always been an early-to-bed, early-to-rise kind of guy, so late nights are hard on me.

"Go ahead and turn in," Menshiki said, looking directly at me. "Shoko may call again, so I'll stay up a while longer. I don't need much sleep. I can skip a night without any problem. Always been that way. So please don't worry about me. I'll keep the fire burning. I can watch it while I listen to music. Do you mind?"

Of course not, I said. I brought in another load of firewood from the shed outside the kitchen and stacked it next to the fireplace. More than enough, I thought, to last until morning.

"Well then, I'm off to bed," I said to Menshiki.

"Sleep tight," he answered. "Let's rotate. I'll probably sleep for a bit around daybreak. Could you lend me a blanket or something?"

I went and got the blanket Masahiko had used, a down duvet, and a pillow, and arranged them on the sofa. Menshiki thanked me.

"I have whiskey if you'd like some," I added.

Menshiki gave a brusque shake of his head. "No, no alcohol for me tonight. We don't know what could happen."

"If you get hungry, please help yourself to the food in the fridge. There's not much, but there's crackers and cheese at least."

"Thanks," Menshiki said.

Leaving him there, I retired to my room. I slipped under the covers, flicked off the bedside light, and tried to go to sleep. Yet sleep didn't come. I was exhausted, but a tiny bug was whirring in my brain. This happens sometimes. I gave up, switched the light back on, and got out of bed.

"What might be the problem, my friends?" the Commendatore said. "You cannot sleep?"

I looked around the room. There he was, sitting on the windowsill, clad in the same white garment. Strange pointy-toed shoes, a miniature sword by his side. His hair neatly tied back. As always, a perfect replica of the Commendatore who was stabbed to death in Tomohiko Amada's painting.

"You're right, I can't sleep," I said.

"There is indeed a great deal happening these days," said the Commendatore. "No wonder people struggle so to drift off, to no avail."

"It's been a long time, hasn't it," I said.

"I cannot attest to that. I think I told my friends before, but 'long time' is lost on us Ideas. We cannot fathom 'It's been a long time,' or 'Sorry not to have written in so long.' "

"Still, your timing is perfect. There's something I need to ask you."

"And what, then, is the question?"

"Mariye Akikawa went missing this morning, and everyone is out looking for her. Where on earth could she have gone?"

The Commendatore cocked his head to one side and thought for a moment.

"As my friends know," he said, choosing his words carefully, "the human realm is ruled by three elements: time, space, and probability. Ideas, by contrast, must remain independent of all three. I cannot, therefore, concern myself with matters of the sort that my friends have just described."

"I can't entirely follow you—is the problem that you can't foresee the outcome?"

The Commendatore didn't answer.

"Or is it that you know, but can't tell me?"

The Commendatore narrowed his eyes in thought. "I am not evading responsibility—Ideas have our own constraints."

I stiffened my back and looked him square in the face.

"Let's get things straight. I must save Mariye Akikawa. She may be in great danger, and needing my help. She has likely wandered into a place from which she cannot escape. That's the feeling I get, anyway. Still, I'm at a loss how to find her. And I think her disappearance is linked in some way to the pit in the woods. I can't give you a rational explanation, but I'm quite sure there's a connection. Now, you spent a very long time confined in that same hole. I have no idea what led you to be shut up there. Nevertheless, whatever may have been the case, Menshiki and I brought in heavy equipment, moved the pile of boulders, and opened the pit. We *set you free*. That's true, isn't it? Thanks to us, you are now able to move throughout time and space, with no restriction. Appear and disappear as you like. You can even watch me making love to my girlfriend. All this is as I say, isn't it?"

"Affirmative, my friends. Affirmative!"

"I'm not demanding that you tell me precisely how Mariye can be saved. I'm not asking the impossible—I can see that the world of Ideas has its own restrictions. But can't you give me a hint? After all I've done for you, don't you think you owe me at least that much?"

The Commendatore gave a deep sigh.

"An indirect, roundabout hint is enough. I'm not trying to accomplish anything earthshaking here, like putting a stop to ethnic cleansing or global warming, or saving the African elephant. All I'm trying to do is find one thirteen-year-old girl who's likely caught somewhere, in some small, dark place, and return her to this world."

The Commendatore sat there for a long time lost in thought, his arms folded. He seemed to be having second thoughts.

"Affirmative, my friends," he said, with resignation. "When you speak in such a fashion, there is not much I can do. I will give my friends but a single hint. Yet be warned—*several sacrifices* may be required. Are you willing nonetheless?"

"What sort of sacrifices?"

"I cannot speak much of that yet. But they will be inevitable. Metaphorically speaking, *there will be blood*. That is an inevitable fact. What sorts of sacrifices are involved should grow clearer as time passes. Someone may have to risk his life."

"I don't care. Give me the hint."

"Affirmative!" the Commendatore said. "It is now Friday, is it not?"

I checked my bedside clock. "Yes, it's still Friday. No, wait a minute, it's Saturday already."

"On Saturday morning, before noon, my friends will receive a phone call," the Commendatore said. "For an invitation somewhere. No matter the circumstances, my friends must not decline that invitation. Do you understand?"

I mechanically repeated what he had just said. "Someone will call me this morning and invite me somewhere. I must not decline."

"Hold those words close," said the Commendatore. "For it is the only hint I am able to share. It traverses the narrow line that divides 'public' and 'private' parlance."

With those final words, the Commendatore began to fade away. Before I knew it, his form had disappeared from the window ledge.

I turned off the bedside lamp and this time fell asleep with relative ease. The whir of insect wings in my head was gone. A moment before I went under, I imagined Menshiki sitting in front of the fire, absorbed in his thoughts. I guessed he would keep the fire burning all night. I had no idea what those thoughts might be, of course. He was a strange man. But it went without saying that his life was bounded by time, space, and probability. Like everyone else's in this world. None of us could escape those constraints, as long as we lived. Each of us was enclosed by sturdy walls that stretched high in the air, surrounding us on all sides. Probably.

"Someone will call me this morning and invite me somewhere. I must not decline." I parroted the Commendatore's words one more time in my head. Then I slept.

48

THE SPANIARDS SIMPLY COULDN'T NAVIGATE THE ANGRY SEAS OFF THE IRISH COAST

I woke shortly after five. It was still dark outside. I slipped a cardigan over my pajamas and went to check the living room. Menshiki was sleeping on the sofa. He hadn't been asleep for long—the fire was out but the room was still warm. The stack of firewood had shrunk. He was sleeping peacefully on his side, breathing quietly with the duvet draped over his body. Not snoring at all. His manners governed even the way he slept. The room seemed to be holding its breath so as not to disturb him.

Leaving him there, I went into the kitchen and brewed coffee. I made some toast as well. Then I carried the toast and coffee into the dining area and sat there, munching and sipping, as I read my book. It was about the Spanish Armada. About the unfolding of the brutal conflict upon which Queen Elizabeth and Philip II had staked the fortunes of their nations. Why did I feel compelled to read an account of that late-sixteenth-century sea battle off the coast of Great Britain at that particular moment? All I knew was that, once I started reading, I couldn't stop. It was an old book I had found on Tomohiko Amada's shelf.

While standard accounts claim that faulty strategy caused the Armada's decimation by the English fleet, a defeat that changed the course of history, this book argued that most of the damage was caused not by direct fire from English cannon (volleys by both sides, it appeared, missed their targets to fall harmlessly into the ocean), but by shipwreck. Accustomed to the calm waters of the Mediterranean, the Spaniards simply couldn't navigate the angry seas off the Irish coast, and thus ran vessel after vessel against the dark reefs.

As I followed the sad fate of the Spanish navy and sipped my second cup of black coffee, the sky gradually brightened in the east. It was Saturday morning.

Someone will phone you, my friends, this morning, and invite you somewhere. You must not decline.

I mentally repeated what the Commendatore had told me. Then I looked at the phone. It preserved its silence. But it would ring at some point, I was sure of that. The Commendatore was not one to lie. All I could do was be patient and wait.

I thought of Mariye. I wanted to call her aunt to find out if she was safe, but it was still too early. I should wait until seven o'clock at least. Her aunt would contact me if Mariye was found. She knew how worried I was. No word from her meant no progress. So I sat at the dining table reading about the invincible Armada and, when I tired of reading, staring at the phone. But the phone maintained its silence.

I called Shoko shortly after seven. She answered immediately. As if she had been sitting beside the phone, waiting for it to ring.

"We haven't heard from her. She's still missing," she said right away. She sounded as if she'd had little (or maybe no) sleep. Fatigue filled her voice.

"Are the police looking?" I asked.

"Yes, two officers came last night. We gave them photographs of Mariye, described what she was wearing . . . We explained that she isn't the kind of girl who would run away or stay out late partying. They spread the word, and by now I'm sure it's been broadcast to all the precincts. I've asked them not to make the search public yet, of course."

"But nothing so far, correct?"

"That's right, no leads up to this point. I'm sure they're working very hard on it, though."

I did my best to console her and asked her to let me know the moment something did turn up. She promised she would.

When our call ended, Menshiki had already risen and was scrubbing his face in the bathroom sink. After brushing his teeth with the toothbrush I had set aside for him, he sat across from me at the dining room table and drank his black coffee. I offered him toast, but he declined.

Sleeping on the sofa had mussed his luxuriant hair a bit more than usual, but then his "usual" was super neat. The man sitting there was the same coolheaded, well-groomed guy as always.

I related my conversation with Shoko. "This is just my gut feeling," he said when I finished, "but I doubt the police will be very much help."

"Why is that?"

"Mariye is no typical teenager, and her disappearance is no typical disappearance. I don't think she was kidnapped, either. That means the usual police methods are likely to hit a wall."

I didn't offer an opinion. But I figured he was right. We had been given an equation with multiple functions but almost no solid numbers. To make any progress, we had to nail down as many numbers as possible.

"Shall we go take another look at the pit?" I asked. "Who knows—there might be some change."

"Let's go," Menshiki said.

We were operating under the tacit assumption that *nothing else was to be done.* I knew that the phone could ring, and that Shoko Akikawa or the person behind the "invitation" the Commendatore had mentioned might be on the other end. But I was pretty sure neither would call this early. Call it a vague premonition on my part.

We put on our jackets and headed out. It was a sunny day. A southwesterly wind had swept away the cloud cover of the previous night, leaving behind a sky almost unnaturally high and transparent. Indeed, when I raised my eyes to the sky, I had the feeling that up and down had been reversed, and that I was peering down into a spring of clear water. I could hear the faint drone of a long train running along a faraway track. When the air was like this, you could pick up distant sounds on the wind with great clarity. That's the sort of morning it was.

Without exchanging a word, we cut through the woods and around the little shrine. The plank cover of the pit was exactly as we had left it the night before. Nor had the stones holding it down been moved. When we took off the boards, the ladder was still leaning against the wall, its position unchanged. No one was in the pit. This time, Menshiki didn't offer to go down to search the floor. The bright sunlight made that unnecessary—we could see that nothing had changed. The pit looked altogether different in the light of day than it had at night. There was nothing at all unsettling about it.

We replaced the lid and rearranged the stones that held it down. Then we walked back through the woods. In front of my house, Menshiki's spotless silver Jaguar sat reticently beside my dusty, unpretentious Toyota Corolla.

When he reached his car, Menshiki came to a halt. "I think I'll head home," he said. "I'll just be in your way if I presume on your hospitality any longer, and there's nothing I can do now anyway. Do you mind?"

"Of course not. Please go home and rest. I'll let you know right away if there's any change."

"Today is Saturday, isn't it?"

"That's right. It's Saturday."

Menshiki reached into his windbreaker pocket and pulled out his key. He stood there staring at it for a moment, thinking. Trying to make his mind up about something, perhaps. I waited for him to reach a conclusion.

"There's one thing I should probably tell you," he said at last.

I leaned on the door of my Corolla as he figured out what to say.

"It's actually quite personal, so I wasn't sure if it was appropriate, but then I thought perhaps I should, for courtesy's sake. I don't want to cause any needless misunderstandings . . . Anyway, the thing is, Shoko and I have become—what's the correct word?—quite intimately involved."

"You mean you and she are lovers?" I asked, cutting to the chase.

"Exactly," Menshiki replied after a moment's pause. I thought I saw a faint blush rise to his cheeks. "You may think it quite hasty."

"No, the speed isn't the problem."

"That's correct," Menshiki acknowledged. "The speed is not the problem."

"The problem is—" I began.

"My motives, you were going to say. Am I correct?"

I didn't respond. Yet it was clear that my silence meant yes.

"You should know," he said, "that none of this was planned from the beginning. It was an entirely natural development. In fact, it happened without me being conscious of it. You may find that hard to believe, of course."

I sighed. Then I spoke frankly. "All I know is that if you started with that plan in mind, it would have been pretty easy to carry out. I'm not being sarcastic, either."

"You're probably right," Menshiki said. "I recognize that. Easy, or at least not all that difficult. *Perhaps*. But that's not how it was."

"So are you saying that you met Shoko Akikawa for the first time and fell in love right off the bat, or something like that?"

Menshiki pursed his lips as if embarrassed. "Fell in love? No, I can't make that claim. To be honest, the last time I fell in love—I think that's probably what it was—was ages ago. I can't even remember what it was like. But I can say with confidence that I find myself powerfully attracted to Shoko, as a man is attracted to a woman."

"Leaving Mariye out of the picture?"

"That's hard to know. Mariye was the reason for our first meeting, after all. But had Mariye never existed, I think I still would have been attracted to her aunt."

I wondered about that. Would a man whose mind was as complicated as Menshiki's be so "powerfully attracted" to a woman as simple and easygoing as Shoko Akikawa? Still, I was in no position to judge. The workings of the human heart are impossible to predict. Especially when sex is involved.

"I understand," I said. "At any rate, thank you for speaking so honestly. Honesty is always best, I think."

"I hope you're right."

"To tell you the truth, Mariye already knew. That you and Shoko had begun that sort of relationship. In fact, she came to talk to me about it. A few days ago."

The news seemed to catch Menshiki by surprise.

"She's a perceptive child," he said. "We tried our best not to let her find out."

"Yes, a *very* perceptive child. But she didn't find out from you. It was the things her aunt said and did that tipped her off."

Shoko was a well-brought-up, intelligent woman, but while she could conceal her feelings to a degree, her mask was bound to slip sooner or later. Menshiki was aware of that, no question.

"If that's the case . . . do you think Mariye's disappearance is connected to her discovery of our relationship?"

I shook my head. "I can't tell for sure. But I can tell you that you and Shoko ought to talk through everything together. She's beside herself with worry, and she's confused. She must be in need of your encouragement and support. Urgently in need."

"You're right. I'll contact her the minute I get home."

Menshiki wasn't finished. Something else appeared to be on his mind.

He sighed. "To tell the truth, I don't think I've fallen in love. I'm not cut out for that. Haven't been from the beginning. I don't know why I feel as I do. Would I have been so attracted to Shoko if not for Mariye? The connection between the two of them isn't clear to me at all."

I said nothing.

"But I swear I didn't plan any of it in advance. Can you believe me?"

"Mr. Menshiki," I said. "I can't explain why, but I think you're an honest man at heart."

"Thank you," he said. The corners of his mouth edged upward. It was a somewhat uncomfortable smile, but not an altogether unhappy one.

"Can I go on being honest?" he said.

"Of course."

"Sometimes I think I'm empty," he confessed. The smile still lingered on his lips.

"Empty?"

"Hollow inside. I know it sounds arrogant, but I've always operated on the assumption that I was a lot brighter and more capable than other people. More perceptive and discerning, with greater powers of judgment. Physically stronger, too. I figured I could succeed at whatever I turned my mind to. And I did. Put my hands on whatever I wanted to possess. Being locked up in Tokyo prison was a clear setback, of course, but I considered that an exception to the rule. When I was young, I saw no limits to what I could achieve. I thought I could attain a state close to perfection. Climb and climb until I reached a height where I could gaze down on everyone else. But when I passed fifty, I looked at myself in the mirror and discovered nothing but emptiness. A zero. What T. S. Eliot called a 'straw man.' "

I couldn't think of anything to say.

"My whole life may have been a mistake up till now," Menshiki went on. "I feel that way sometimes. That I took a wrong turn somewhere. That nothing I've done has any real meaning. That's why I told you I often find myself envying you."

"Envying what, for example?"

"You have the strength to wish for what you cannot have. While I have only wished for those things I can possess."

I assumed he was talking about Mariye. She was the one thing that had evaded his grasp. Yet there wasn't much I could say about that.

Menshiki slowly got into his car. Then he rolled down the window, said goodbye, and drove off. When his car was out of sight I went back into the house. It was just past eight.

The telephone rang at shortly after ten. The call was from Masahiko.

"I know it's sudden," he said, "but I'm on my way to Izu to see my father. Would you like to come along? You mentioned the other day that you'd like to meet him."

Someone will phone my friends tomorrow morning and invite you somewhere. You must not decline.

"That's great. I'd love to go."

"I just got on the Tokyo-Nagoya Expressway. I'm at the Kohoku parking area now. I think it'll take me about an hour to reach you. I'll pick you up and we can drive to Izu Kogen."

"Did something happen to your father?"

"Yeah, the nursing home called. Seems he's taken a turn for the worse. So I'm going to check on him. I'm more or less free today anyway."

"Are you sure it's all right if I go along? Aren't times like this for family only?"

"Don't worry. It's perfectly okay. No other relatives will be there, so the more the merrier." He hung up.

I put down the phone and scanned the room. Was the Commendatore around? But he was nowhere to be seen. Prophecy dispensed, he had disappeared. Probably to a realm where the dictates of time, space, and probability did not apply. Nevertheless, there had been a morning phone call, and I had been invited somewhere. So far, at least, that prophecy had been accurate. It bothered me to leave with Mariye still unaccounted for, but I couldn't do much about that. The Commendatore had instructed me, "No matter the circumstances, my friends must not decline that invitation." I could leave Shoko in Menshiki's hands. After all, she was his responsibility, to some extent.

I sat back in the easy chair in the living room and resumed the story of the invincible Armada as I waited for Masahiko. Almost all the Spanish soldiers and seamen who had managed to escape their shipwrecked vessels and crawl onto the shores of Ireland more dead than alive were murdered by those who lived along the coast. The poverty-stricken locals had slaughtered them for their possessions. It had been the Spaniards' hope that, as fellow Catholics, the Irish might show them mercy, but they were out of luck. Religious solidarity was no match for the fear of starvation. Sadly, the Spanish ship carrying the war chest holding the gold and silver intended to buy off England's powerful nobility sank as well. No one knew where all that wealth had gone.

It was shortly before eleven in the morning when Masahiko's old black Volvo pulled up in front of my house. I was still thinking about all those gold coins lying at the bottom of the sea as I threw on my leather jacket and headed out the door.

The route Masahiko chose took us from the Hakone Turnpike to the Izu Skyline highway and then down from the Amagi highlands to Izu. He explained that this way would be faster—that the weekend meant the coastal roads would be jammed—but nevertheless our route was crowded with people out on excursions. The leaf-viewing season had not yet ended, and many of those on the road were weekenders unfamiliar with mountain driving, so the trip took a lot longer than expected.

"Is your father really in bad shape?" I asked.

"He's not long for this world, that's for sure," Masahiko said lightly. "A matter of days, to be more precise. Age has whittled him down to almost nothing. He has trouble eating, and pneumonia is a constant threat. But the patient's orders are that under no circumstances are IV lines and feeding tubes to be used. In other words, he demands that he be allowed to go quietly once he can no longer eat. He arranged this with his lawyer when he was still mentally competent, signed the forms and everything. So there will be no interventions. That means he could go at any time."

"So I guess you have to be prepared for the worst."

"That's about right."

"It must be rough."

"Hey, it's a big deal when someone dies. I can hardly complain."

The old Volvo was equipped with a tape deck, and the glove compartment was stuffed with cassettes. Masahiko stuck his hand in, grabbed one, and inserted it without checking to see what it was. It turned out to be a collection of hits from the 1980s. Duran Duran, Huey Lewis, and so on. When ABC's "The Look of Love" came on, I turned to him.

"Sure feels like time has stopped in this car," I said.

"I don't like CDs. They're too shiny—they'd scare crows away if I hung them outside my house, but they're hardly something to listen to music on. The sound is tinny and the mixing is unnatural. Having no A and B sides is a drag too. That's why I still drive this car—so I can listen to my cassettes. Newer models don't have tape decks, right? Everyone thinks I'm nuts. But I'm stuck. I have a huge collection of songs I recorded off the radio and I don't want them to go to waste."

"Man, I never thought I'd hear ABC's 'Look of Love' again in this lifetime."

"Don't you think it's amazing?" Masahiko said, casting me a quizzical glance.

We went on talking about the music of the eighties, songs we'd heard on the radio, as we tooled through the mountains of Hakone. The blue slopes of Mt. Fuji loomed around each curve.

"You and your dad are quite a pair," I said. "The father listens only to records, and the son is stuck on cassettes."

"You should talk. You're just as behind the times. Worse than us, maybe. I mean, you don't even have a cell phone. And you hardly ever go online, right? I've always got my cell phone with me, and anything I need to know, I Google. I design stuff on my Mac at work. Socially, I'm light-years ahead of you."

Bertie Higgins's rendition of "Key Largo" came on. An interesting selection indeed for a guy claiming to be socially evolved.

"Are you seeing anyone these days?" I asked, changing the subject.

"You mean, like a woman?"

"Yeah."

Masahiko gave a small shrug. "I can't say it's going all that well. As usual. And things have gotten even rockier since I made this weird breakthrough."

"What kind of breakthrough?"

"That the right and left sides of a woman's face don't match up. Did you know that?"

"People aren't perfectly symmetrical," I said. "Whether it's breasts or balls, the size and shape of the two sides are always going to be different. Every artist knows that much. That lack of symmetry is one of the things that makes the human form so interesting."

Masahiko shook his head several times without taking his eyes off the road. "Of course I know that. But what I'm saying is a little different. I'm talking about personality, not form."

I waited for him to go on.

"About two months ago, I took a photo of this woman I was seeing with a digital camera. A close-up of her face from the front. I put it on the big office computer. Then I managed to divide the screen down the middle and look at the two halves of her face separately. Removing the right half to look at the left, and vice versa . . . You get the idea, right?"

"Yeah, I get it."

"That's when I realized that her left side and her right side looked like two separate people. Like Two-Face, the bad guy in *Batman*."

"I missed that one."

"You should watch it sometime. It's pretty good. Anyway, it freaked me out a bit. I should have left things alone at that point, but I went ahead and tried reversing each side to make a composite face. That way, I could double the right side to create a complete face, and do the same with the left side. Computers make that sort of stuff easy. What I was left with was images of what could only be seen as two women with two totally distinct personalities. It shocked me. I mean, there were actually two women inside every woman I met. Have you ever looked at women that way?"

"Nope," I said.

"I tested my idea on several other women. Took head shots and created left- and right-side composites on the computer. That made it even clearer. That women literally have two faces. Once I knew that, I found I couldn't figure out women at all. For example, if I was with a woman and we were having sex, I didn't know if it was her right side or her left that I was embracing. If it was the right side, then where had the left side gone—what was it doing, and what was it thinking?—and if it was the left side, then what was the right side thinking? Once I reached that point, things got really messy. Get what I'm saying?"

"Not completely, but I can see that it must be messy."

"You bet. Really messy."

"Did you try it on men's faces?"

"Yeah, I did. But it didn't work the same way. The only drastic changes were with women's faces."

"Maybe you should go see a psychologist or therapist about this," I said.

Masahiko sighed. "You know, I've always believed myself to be a totally normal sort of guy."

"That could be a dangerous belief."

"To believe that I'm normal?"

"I think it was F. Scott Fitzgerald who wrote that one should never trust people who claim they're normal. It's in one of his novels."

Masahiko thought about that for a moment. "So even a commonplace man is irreplaceable?"

"I guess that's another way of putting it."

Masahiko thought for a while, his hands on the steering wheel.

"At any rate," he said, "could you try it just once and see?"

"You know I've been a portrait painter for a long time. So I think I'm more skilled than most when it comes to examining faces. You could even say I'm an expert at it. But I've never thought that the difference between the right and left sides reflected a disparity in personality. Not once."

"But almost all the subjects you painted were men, correct?"

Masahiko had a point. I'd never been commissioned to paint a woman. For whatever reason, my portraits were all of men. The only exception was Mariye Akikawa, and she was more child than woman. And I hadn't finished her portrait, either.

"Men and women are different," Masahiko insisted. "Completely."

"So then let me ask you," I said. "Are you claiming this personality difference on the right and left sides applies to almost all women?"

"Yeah, that's my conclusion."

"So then do you find yourself attracted to one side or the other? Or do you find you like both sides *less*?"

Masahiko pondered this question for a moment. "No," he said at last. "That's not how it works. It's not that I prefer one side to the other. That I find one side cheerful and the other gloomy, or that one side is prettier. The problem is at another level: it's simply that the two sides are *different*. It's that *sheer fact* that shakes me up. Sometimes it scares me."

"It sounds to me like a kind of obsessive-compulsive disorder," I said.

"It sounds like that to me too," Masahiko said. "Just listening to myself. But it's *the truth*. I ask you, just check it out for yourself."

I promised him I would. But I had no intention of following through. That could only add to my troubles. My life was messy enough as it was.

Then we talked about Tomohiko Amada. About Tomohiko Amada in Vienna.

"My father said he heard Richard Strauss conduct one of Beethoven's symphonies," Masahiko said. "With the Vienna Philharmonic, of course. He said it was out of this world. That's one of the few stories he told me about his days in Vienna."

"What else did he say about his time there?"

"Nothing at all remarkable. He mentioned the food, the drink, the music. Stuff like that. He really loved music, you know. That was all he talked about. He never mentioned painting or politics or things of that sort. Or women either."

Masahiko paused before continuing.

"Maybe someone should write my father's biography. It could be a really interesting book. But the reality is, no one will ever take a shot at it. Why? Because there's hardly any personal information out there. My father had no friends, his family members were virtual strangers—he just spent his time shut away by himself on a mountain, painting. His only acquaintances, if you could call them that, were a handful of art dealers. He hardly spoke to anyone. He wrote no letters. So if someone did try to write his biography, they'd have almost nothing to work with. It's not just that there are a few holes in his life story, it's that his life is riddled with them. Think of Swiss cheese with more holes than cheese."

"All he's leaving behind is his work."

"You're right, his paintings and almost nothing else. That's probably the way he wanted it."

"And you. You're a part of his legacy too," I said.

"Me?" Masahiko looked at me in surprise. Then he turned back to the road. "You're right there. If I stop to think of it, I'm part of his legacy too. Not a particularly shining part, though."

"But irreplaceable."

"True enough. Run of the mill, but nonetheless irreplaceable," Masahiko said. "You know what I think sometimes? That you should have been Tomohiko Amada's son. If that were the case, things would have gone so much more smoothly."

"Give me a break!" I said with a laugh. "No one was fit for that role!"

"Maybe not," Masahiko said. "But you might have been his spiritual successor, if you can call it that. You're a lot more qualified in that area than I am—that's my gut feeling anyway."

Killing Commendatore popped into my mind. Was that painting something I had "inherited" from Tomohiko Amada? Had he led me to that attic room to discover it? Was he using it to demand something of me?

Deborah Harry was singing "French Kissin' in the USA" on the car stereo. It was hard to think of less appropriate background music for our conversation.

"I guess it must have been tough having a father like Tomohiko Amada," I said bluntly.

"I reached a point years ago where I had to make a clean break and move on with my life," Masahiko said. "Once I had done that, it wasn't as hard on me as everyone thought. I make a living from art as well, but the scale of my father's talent and the scale of mine are so dramatically different. When the gap is that huge, it stops being a problem. My father's fame as an artist doesn't hurt anymore. What hurts is the kind of human being he was, the fact that until the very end, he never opened up to me, his own son. That he didn't pass a single bit of information about himself on to me."

"So he showed nothing of his inner world, even to you?"

"Not a glimpse. His attitude was: 'I gave you half my DNA, so what more do you want? The rest is up to you.' But a relationship is based on more than DNA. Right? I never asked him to act as my guide through life. I didn't demand that. But it still should have been possible to have something like a father-son conversation once in a while. He could have filled me in just a little on what he had experienced, what he thought. Even bits and pieces would have helped."

I listened quietly to what he had to say.

When we stopped at a long red light, Masahiko took off his dark Ray-Ban sunglasses and wiped them with his handkerchief.

"My guess," he said, turning in my direction, "is that my father is hiding heavy secrets of some kind, personal secrets he has borne entirely alone and intends to take with him when he drifts from this world. It's like there's this metal safe in his heart where he stored them. He locked them all in there, and then he either threw the key away or hid it somewhere. Now he can't remember where he stashed it."

In that case, the unsolved riddle of what had taken place in Vienna in 1938 would be buried in darkness. Then again, perhaps *Killing Commendatore* itself was the hidden key. The idea struck me all of a sudden. Were that true, it would explain why, at the end of his life, Tomohiko's living spirit had returned to his mountaintop to confirm the painting's existence.

I swiveled around to look in the backseat. Just maybe, the Commendatore was sitting there. But the seat was empty.

"Is something wrong?" Masahiko said, glancing behind him.

"No, nothing at all," I said.

When the light turned green, he stepped on the accelerator.

49

FILLED WITH JUST AS MANY DEATHS

On our way to check in on his father, we stopped at a roadside restaurant so that Masahiko could use the toilet. We were shown to a table next to the window, where we ordered coffee. As it was already noon, I ordered a roast beef sandwich, too. Masahiko asked for the same thing. Then he headed for the men's room. While he was gone I stared blankly out the window. The parking lot was packed with cars. Most had come with families. The number of minivans really stood out. All minivans look identical to me. Like cans of tasteless biscuits. There was an observation deck at the end of the lot where people were using small digital cameras and cell phones to snap photos of Mt. Fuji, which towered right in front of them. It's dumb, I know, but I've never really gotten comfortable with phones taking pictures. I'm even less cool with cameras making phone calls.

While I was sitting there looking at nothing in particular, a white Subaru Forester turned off the road and into the lot. I don't know much about cars (and the Subaru Forester is hardly distinctive), but I could tell at a glance that it was the model the man with the white Subaru Forester had been driving. It trolled up and down the rows before finally nosing into an empty space. Sure enough, the logo on the spare-tire cover read SUBARU FORESTER. It appeared to be the same model as the car I had seen in the little seaside town in Miyagi Prefecture. I couldn't make out the license plate, but the more I looked, the more I was sure it was the same car I had seen that spring. Not just the same model. I mean the *exact same car*.

My visual memory is sharper than most—and more durable. As a result, I could tell that the stains and other markings were strikingly similar to those of *that car* as I remembered it. I could hardly breathe. But just when I was straining to identify the driver as he stepped out, a large tour bus pulled into the lot and blocked my view. Unable to move past the jam of cars, it just sat there. I jumped up and hurried out of the restaurant. I rushed around the bus, which had stopped dead in its tracks, and approached the spot where the white Subaru Forester was parked. But the car was empty. Its driver had gone off somewhere. He might be in the restaurant, or perhaps was taking pictures on the observation deck. I scanned the area but couldn't spot the man with the white Subaru Forester anywhere. Of course, the driver could have been someone else.

I checked the license plate. Sure enough, it read "Miyagi Prefecture." On the rear bumper was a sticker with a picture of a marlin on it. It was the same car, no question. *That man had come here.* A chill ran down my spine. I decided to search for him. I wanted to see his face one more time. To figure out why I couldn't finish his portrait. Perhaps I had overlooked something basic about him. First, though, I memorized the license plate number. It might prove useful. Then again, it might be of no use at all.

I walked around the parking lot, keeping an eye out for someone who resembled him. I checked the observation deck. But the man with the white Subaru Forester was nowhere to be seen. A man of middle age, deeply tanned, with a salt-and-pepper crew cut. On the tall side. When last seen, wearing a battered black leather jacket and a Yonex golf cap. I had whipped off a quick sketch on my memo pad and shown it to the young woman sitting across from me. "You're really good at drawing!" she had enthused.

Once I was sure no one matching his description was outside, I looked inside the restaurant. I circled the place, but he was nowhere to be seen. The seats were almost full. Masahiko was back at our table, drinking his coffee. The sandwiches hadn't shown up yet.

"Where'd you disappear to?" he asked me.

"I thought I saw someone I knew. So I went outside to check."

"Did you find them?"

"No. Probably a case of mistaken identity," I said.

After that, I kept a close eye on the white Subaru Forester outside. Yet if the man in question did come back, what should I do? Go out and talk to him? Tell him I was sure I had bumped into him twice this past spring in a small coastal town in Miyagi? *Is that so? Well, I don't remember you*, he'd probably shoot back.

Well then, why are you following me? I would ask. *What are you talking about?* he would reply. *Why the hell would I be tailing someone I don't even know?* End of conversation.

In any event, the driver of the white Subaru Forester never went back to his car. It just sat there in the lot, short and squat, silently awaiting its owner's return. We finished our sandwiches and coffee, but he still hadn't shown.

"We'd better be going," Masahiko said, glancing at his watch. "We don't have a whole lot of time." He picked up his Ray-Bans from the table.

We stood, paid the bill, and walked out. Then we climbed into the Volvo and drove out of the jammed parking lot. I wanted to wait for the man with the white Subaru Forester to return, but meeting Masahiko's father had to be my top priority. The Commendatore had driven home that message with absolute clarity: *My friends will be invited somewhere. You must not decline that invitation.*

I was left with the fact that the man with the white Subaru Forester had shown up once again. He had known where to find me and had made it clear that *he was there*. His intent was obvious. His appearance could be no accident. Nor, of course, was the tour bus that had hidden him from view.

To reach the facility where Tomohiko Amada was being cared for, we had to leave the Izu Skyline and drive down a long, winding road. The area had recently been turned into a summer retreat for city folk: we passed stylish coffee shops, fancy inns built to resemble log cabins, stands selling local produce, and small museums aimed at passing tourists. Each time we went around a curve, I gripped the door handle and thought of the man with the white Subaru Forester. Something was blocking me from finishing his portrait. A key element, something that made him who he was, had escaped me. A missing piece of the puzzle, as it were. This was new for me. I always gathered together everything I knew I would need before I started a portrait. In the case of the man with the white Subaru Forester, though, I had not been able to do that. Probably the man himself was standing in my way. He didn't like having his portrait painted, for whatever reason. In fact, he seemed dead set against it.

At a certain point, the Volvo turned off the road and passed through a big, open steel gate. The gate was marked only by a very small sign. Someone could easily drive right by if they weren't paying attention. It appeared to be an institution that didn't feel compelled to announce its presence to the world. Masahiko stopped at the small guardhouse beside the gate and gave his name and the name of the resident he was visiting to the uniformed security guard on duty. The guard made a phone call to confirm the resident's identity. Once through the gate, we entered a dense grove of trees. Most were tall evergreens, which cast a chilly shadow. We drove up the freshly paved road to the circle set atop the rise, where cars could be parked. A bed of ornamental cabbages surrounding a circle of bright red flowers sat at the center. The flowers were being tended with care.

Masahiko drove to the far end of the circle and parked his car in one of the visitor spots. Two other cars had preceded us. A white Honda minivan and a dark blue Audi sedan. Both were sparkling new—between them his Volvo looked like an aged workhorse. Masahiko, however, didn't seem to mind a bit (his Bananarama cassette tape took clear precedence). Below, the Pacific Ocean gleamed dully in the early-winter sun. A few midsized fishing vessels were plying its waters. A small humped island sat just offshore, and beyond it the Manazuru Peninsula. The hands of my watch pointed to 1:45.

We got out of the car and walked toward the entrance. The building looked quite new. It was a clean and stylish concrete structure, yet nothing was distinctive about it. Perhaps the architect who designed it lacked imaginative oomph. Or else the client, considering its function, had demanded that the building be as simple and conservative as possible. It was three stories high, and quite square—a structure made up entirely of straight lines. The blueprints could have been drawn up with a single ruler. The ground floor was mainly glass, to create as bright an impression as possible. Jutting out from the front of the building was a large wooden balcony with about a dozen deck chairs, but it was winter, so no one would be sunbathing, however bright and pleasant the day. The cafeteria had glass walls that soared from floor to ceiling. I could see five or six people inside, all well along in years, from the look of them. Two were in wheelchairs. I couldn't tell what they were doing. Perhaps watching television on the big screen on the wall. They weren't playing leapfrog, that's for sure.

Masahiko walked through the entranceway and up to a young woman stationed at the front desk. She was round-cheeked and friendly, with beautiful long black hair. A name tag was affixed to her dark blue blazer. She seemed to know Masahiko by sight, for the two of them chatted for a few minutes. I stood a short distance away and waited for them to finish. A large vase sat in the entranceway, overflowing with a lavish assortment of fresh flowers, arranged, I assumed, by an ikebana expert. At a certain point, Masahiko signed the guest register with a pen and, consulting his watch, added the precise time. He left the desk and walked over to me, hands in pockets.

"My father's condition seems to have stabilized," he said. "Apparently, he was coughing all morning and very short of breath, so they worried that he was developing pneumonia. But they got his cough under control a short while ago, and now he's fast asleep."

"Is it really okay for me to go in with you?"

"Of course," Masahiko said. "You came all this way to see him, didn't you?"

He and I took the elevator to the third floor. The corridor there was also simple and conservative. Decoration kept to a bare minimum. The one exception, as if by way of concession, was a row of oil paintings hanging on the long, white wall. All were coastal landscapes. They seemed to be a series by a single artist, who had painted spots along the same stretch of coast from a number of angles. They weren't especially well done, but at least the artist had been generous in his use of paint, and I could applaud the way his paintings disrupted the strict minimalism of the architecture. The rubber soles of my shoes squeaked ostentatiously on the smooth linoleum floor. A little old white-haired lady in a wheelchair pushed by a male attendant passed us in the corridor. She stared straight ahead, her gaze so fixed and rigid it did not even flicker when we went by. As if she was determined not to lose sight of a crucial sign suspended in the air before her.

Tomohiko Amada was in a big room at the very end of the corridor. The name card on the door had been left blank. Most likely to protect his privacy. He was, after all, famous. The room was the size of a small hotel suite, with a basic set of living room furniture in addition to the bed. A folded wheelchair rested against the bed's foot. A large southeast-facing window looked out over the Pacific Ocean. It was a magnificent, unobstructed view. A hotel room with a view like that would cost an arm and a leg. No paintings hung on the walls. Just a mirror and a round clock. A medium-sized vase filled with purple cut flowers sat on the table. There was no odor at all. Not of a sick old person, nor of medicine, nor of flowers, nor of sun-drenched curtains. Nothing. That's what surprised me most—the room's utter lack of smell. It was so striking I thought something had happened to my nose. How could odor be erased so completely?

Tomohiko Amada was fast asleep near the window, oblivious to the view outside. He slept on his back facing the ceiling, his eyes tightly shut. Bushy white eyebrows overhung his aged eyelids like a natural canopy. Deep wrinkles furrowed his forehead. His quilt was pulled up to his neck—I couldn't tell if he was breathing or not. If he was, they were extremely shallow breaths.

I knew right away that this was the mysterious old man who had visited my studio. I had seen him for only a moment or two in the shifting moonlight, but the shape of his head and his wild, white hair left no doubt: it had been Tomohiko Amada. The fact didn't surprise me in the least. It had been clear all along.

"He's dead to the world," Masahiko said to me. "We'll just have to wait for him to wake up. *If* he wakes up, that is."

"All the same, it's a blessing that he's sleeping peacefully," I said. I glanced at the clock on the wall. It said five minutes before two. I suddenly thought of Menshiki. Had he called Shoko Akikawa? Had there been any developments in Mariye's case? Right now, however, I had to focus on Tomohiko Amada.

Masahiko and I sat across from each other on matching chairs, sipping the canned coffee we had bought from the vending machine in the corridor, while we waited for Tomohiko Amada to wake up. In the meantime, Masahiko told me a few things about Yuzu. That her pregnancy was progressing nicely. That her due date was sometime in the first half of January. That her handsome boyfriend was thrilled about becoming a father.

"The only problem—from his perspective, anyway—is that she seems to have no intention of marrying him," Masahiko said.

"Huh?" I couldn't believe what I had just heard. "You mean she plans to be a single mom?"

"Yuzu intends to have the baby. But she doesn't want to marry the father, or live with him, or share custody of the child . . . that seems to be the story. He can't figure out what's going on. He assumed they'd be properly married once the divorce was final, but she completely rejected his proposal."

I thought about that for a moment. The more I thought, though, the more confused I got.

"I can't wrap my head around it," I said. "Yuzu always said she didn't want kids. Whenever I said I thought the time was right, she said it was still too early. So why does she want a child so badly now?"

"Maybe she didn't plan on a baby, but changed her mind once she got pregnant. Women can do that, you know."

"Still, it'll be tough to look after the child all by herself. Hard to hang on to her job, for one thing. So why not marry him? He is the child's father, right?"

"Yeah, he doesn't understand either. He thought they were getting along just great. And he was happy a child was coming. That's why he's so confused. He asked me about it, but I'm stumped too."

"Have you talked to Yuzu directly?" I inquired.

Masahiko frowned. "To tell you the truth, I'm trying hard not to get too sucked in. I like Yuzu, but he's my colleague at work. And of course you and I have been friends for ages. I'm in a tough spot. The more I become involved, the less I know what to do."

I didn't say anything.

"I always enjoyed seeing the two of you together—you seemed like such a happy couple," Masahiko said, looking perplexed.

"You said that before."

"Yeah, maybe I did," Masahiko said. "But it's the truth."

After that, we sat there without speaking, looking at the clock on the wall, or the ocean outside the window. Tomohiko Amada lay on his back in a deep sleep, not moving a muscle. He was so still, in fact, that I worried whether he was alive or not. No one else seemed concerned, though, so I figured his stillness was normal.

Watching him lying there, I tried to imagine how he might have looked as a young exchange student in Vienna. But of course I couldn't. This was an old man with furrowed skin and white hair, experiencing the slow but steady annihilation of his physical existence. All of us are, without exception, born to die, and now he was face-to-face with that final stage.

"Aren't you planning to contact Yuzu?" Masahiko asked me.

"Not at present, no," I said, shaking my head.

"I think it might be a good idea for you two to get together and talk things over. Have a good heart-to-heart, so to speak."

"Our formal divorce proceedings were handled through our lawyers. That's the way Yuzu wanted it. Now she's about to give birth to another man's child. Whether she wants to marry him or not is her problem. I'm in no position to say anything about it. So what exactly are the *things* we should talk over?"

"Don't you want to know what's going on?"

I shook my head no. "I don't want to know any more than I have to. It's not like what took place didn't hurt."

"Of course," Masahiko said.

All the same, to be honest there were times I couldn't tell if I had been hurt or not. Did I really have the right? I wasn't clear enough about things to know. Of course, people can't help feeling hurt in certain situations, whether they have the right to or not.

"The guy is a colleague of mine," Masahiko said after a pause. "He's a serious guy, hard worker, good personality."

"Yeah, and handsome, too."

"True. Women love him. Only natural, I guess. Sure wish they flocked to me like that. But he has this tendency that always left us all shaking our heads."

I waited for him to go on.

"You see, we've never been able to figure out why he's chosen the women he has. I mean, he always has lots of women to pick from, and yet he comes up with these losers. I'm not talking about Yuzu, of course. She's probably the first good choice he's made. But the women before her were real disasters. I still can't figure it out."

He shook his head, remembering those women.

"He almost got married a few years back. They'd printed the invitations, reserved the venue for the ceremony, and were heading off to Fiji or someplace like that for their honeymoon. He'd gotten leave from work, bought the airplane tickets. The bride-to-be wasn't at all attractive. When he introduced us, I remember being shocked by how homely she was. Of course, you can't judge a book by its cover, but from what I could see, her personality was nothing special, either. Yet for some reason he was head over heels in love. Anyway, they seemed poorly matched. Everyone who knew them felt that way, though no one said so. Then, just before the wedding, she skipped out. In other words, it was *the woman* who split. I couldn't tell if that was good or bad for him, but all the same it blew my mind."

"Was there some kind of reason?"

"Not that I know of. I felt sorry for the guy, so I never asked. But I don't think he ever understood why she did what she did. I mean she just *ran*. Couldn't stand the thought of marrying him. Something must have bothered her."

"So what's the point of your story?"

"The point is," Masahiko said, "it still may be possible for you and Yuzu to get back together. Assuming that's what you want, of course."

"But she's about to have another man's child."

"Yeah, I can see that might be a problem."

We fell silent again.

. . .

Tomohiko Amada woke up shortly before three. His body twitched at first. Then he took a deep breath—I could see the quilt over his chest rise and fall. Masahiko stood and went to his father's bedside. He looked down on his face. The old man's eyes slowly opened. His bushy white eyebrows quivered in the air.

Masahiko took a slender glass funnel cup from the bedside table and moistened his father's lips. He mopped the corners of his mouth with a piece of what looked like gauze. His father wanted more, so he repeated the process several times. He seemed comfortable with the job—it appeared that he had done it many times before. The old man's Adam's apple bobbed up and down with each swallow. Only when I saw that movement was I sure he was still alive.

"Father," Masahiko said, pointing at me. "This is the guy who moved into the Odawara house. He's a painter who's working in your studio. He's a friend of mine from college. He's not too bright, and his beautiful wife ran out on him, but he's still a great artist."

It wasn't clear how much Masahiko's father comprehended. But he slowly turned his head in my direction as if following his son's finger. His face was blank. He seemed to be looking at something, but that *something* carried no particular meaning for him. Nevertheless, I thought I could detect a surprisingly clear and lucid light deep within those bleary eyes. That light seemed to be biding its time, waiting for that which might hold real significance. At least that was my impression.

"I doubt he understands a word I say," Masahiko said. "But his doctor instructed us to talk to him in a free and natural way, as if he was able to follow. No one knows how much he's picking up anyway. So I talk to him normally. That's easier for me too. Now you say something. The way you usually talk."

"It's nice to meet you, Mr. Amada," I said. I told him my name. "Your son has been kind enough to let me live in your home in Odawara."

Tomohiko Amada was looking at me, but his expression hadn't changed. Masahiko gestured: *Just keep talking—anything is okay.*

"I'm an oil painter," I went on. "I specialized in portraits for a long time, but I gave that up and now I paint my own stuff. I still accept occasional commissions for portraits, though. The human face fascinates me, I guess. Masahiko and I have been friends since art school."

Tomohiko Amada's eyes were still pointed in my direction. They were coated by a thin membrane, a kind of layered lace curtain hanging between life and death. What sat behind the curtain would fade from view as the layers increased, until finally the last, heavy curtain would fall.

"I love your house," I said. "My work is steadily progressing. I hope you don't mind, but I've been listening to your records. Masahiko told me that was all right. You have a great collection. I enjoy the operas especially. Oh yes, and recently I went up and looked in the attic."

I thought I saw a sparkle in his eyes when I said the word "attic." It was just a quick flash—no one would have noticed it unless they were paying attention. But I was keeping close watch. Thus I didn't miss it. Clearly, "attic" had a charge that caused some part of his memory to kick in.

"A horned owl has moved into the attic," I went on. "I kept hearing these rustling sounds at night. I thought it was a rat, so I went up to check during the day. And there the owl was, sitting under the beams. It's a beautiful bird. The screen on the air vent has a hole, so it can go in and out at will. The attic makes a perfect daytime hideout for a horned owl, don't you think?"

The eyes were still fixed on me. As if waiting to hear more.

"Horned owls don't cause any damage," Masahiko put in. "In fact, they're said to bring good luck."

"I love the bird," I added. "And the attic is a fascinating place too."

Tomohiko Amada stared at me from the bed, not moving a muscle. His breathing had turned shallow again. That thin membrane still coated his eyes, but the secret light within seemed to have brightened.

I wanted to talk more about the attic, but Masahiko was beside me, so there was no way I could bring up what I had found there. It would only prick Masahiko's curiosity. So I let the topic hang in the air while Tomohiko Amada and I stared into each other's eyes.

I chose my words with care. "The attic suits owls, but it might suit paintings too. It could be a perfect place to store them. Japanese-style paintings, especially—they're really tricky to preserve. Attics aren't damp like basements—they're well ventilated, and you don't have to worry about sunlight. Of course, there's always the danger of wind and rain getting in, but if you wrap it up carefully enough a painting should keep for quite a while up there."

"You know, I've never even looked in the attic," Masahiko said. "Dusty places creep me out."

I was watching Tomohiko Amada's face. His gaze was fixed on me as well. I felt him trying to construct a coherent line of thought. Owl, attic, stored paintings . . . these familiar words all needed to be strung together. In his current state, this was no easy thing. No easy thing *at all*. Like trying to pick through a labyrinth blindfolded. But I sensed that making those connections was important to him. *Extremely* important. I stood by quietly watching him concentrate on that urgent yet solitary task.

I considered bringing up the shrine in the woods, and the strange pit behind it. To describe to him the steps that had led to it being opened, and the shape of its interior. But I changed my mind. I shouldn't give him too much to think about at one time. His level of awareness was so diminished that even one topic placed a heavy burden on his shoulders. What little he had left hung by a single, easily severed thread.

"Would you like more water?" Masahiko asked, funnel cup in hand. But his father didn't react. It was as if he hadn't heard his son's question. Masahiko drew nearer and asked again, but when his father still didn't respond, he gave up. The son was invisible in his father's eyes.

"Dad seems to have taken a real shine to you," Masahiko marveled. "He can't stop looking at you. It's been quite a while since anyone or anything held his interest like this."

I continued to look into Tomohiko Amada's eyes.

"It's strange. When I talk to him he won't turn to me, no matter what I say, but in your case he won't turn away. His eyes are riveted on you."

I couldn't help notice a mild envy in Masahiko's voice. He wanted his father to *see* him. That had probably been a common theme in his life, ever since childhood.

"Maybe he smells paint on me," I said. "The smell may be triggering his memories."

"You're right, that could be it. Come to think of it, it's been ages since I touched actual paint."

Regret no longer tinged his words. He was back to being the same old easygoing Masahiko. Just then, his cell phone began buzzing on the table.

Masahiko looked up with a start. "Damn, I forgot to turn the thing off. Cell phones are against the rules in this place. I'll have to go outside. You don't mind, do you?"

"Of course not," I said.

Masahiko picked up the cell phone and walked to the door. "This may take a while," he said, checking the caller's name on his screen. "Please talk to my father while I'm gone."

He was already whispering into the phone as he left, closing the door quietly behind him.

Tomohiko Amada and I were now alone. His eyes remained fixed on my face. No doubt he was struggling to figure out who I was. Feeling a bit suffocated, I circled the foot of his bed and went to the southeast-facing window. Bringing my face close to the glass, I looked out at the wide expanse of ocean. The horizon seemed to be pushing up against the sky. I followed the line where the sky met the water from end to end. No human being could draw a line so beautiful, whatever ruler they might use. Below that long, straight line, countless lives were thriving. The world was filled with so many lives, and just as many deaths.

Something else had entered the room—I felt its presence. I turned around and, sure enough, Tomohiko Amada and I were no longer alone.

"Affirmative, my friends. The two of you are alone no more," said the Commendatore.

50

IT WILL INVOLVE ORDEAL AND SACRIFICE

"Affirmative, my friends. The two of you are alone no more," said the Commendatore.

The Commendatore was sitting on the same upholstered chair that Masahiko had occupied a moment earlier. He hadn't changed a bit: same getup, same hairstyle, same sword, same tiny physique. I stared at him without saying anything.

"The friend of my friends will not return anytime soon," the Commendatore said, raising his right forefinger as though to pierce the sky. "His phone call promises to be a long one. So please do not worry. Instead, converse with Tomohiko Amada for as long as you desire. There are questions that my friends would like to ask him, are there not? How many he can answer, however, is a matter for debate."

"Did you send Masahiko away?"

"Certainly not," the Commendatore said. "I fear my friends have overestimated my powers. They are of a lesser sort. But company men are always at someone's beck and call. Those poor men have no weekends."

"Have you been here the whole time? Did you come with us in the car?"

The Commendatore shook his head. "Negative. It is a dreadfully long way from Odawara, and I am prone to carsickness."

"But still you came. Though you weren't invited, correct?"

"Affirmative! I was not invited. Technically, at least. But I was needed. There is a fine line between being invited and being needed, my friends.

But leaving that aside, this time it was Tomohiko Amada who needed me. And I thought I could be of use to my friends as well."

"Of use to me?"

"Indeed. I am somewhat beholden to you, my friends. You freed me from that place beneath the ground. It was thanks to you that I was able to rejoin the world as an Idea. As my friends asserted. So it is only proper that I repay that debt. Even Ideas can fathom the import of moral obligation."

Moral obligation?

"Oh well, never mind. *Something like that*," the Commendatore said, reading my mind. "In any case, my friends wish with all your heart to track down Mariye Akikawa and bring her back from the other side. Affirmative?"

I nodded. Yes, that was true.

"Do you know where she is?" I asked.

"Indeed, I met her not long ago."

"Met her?"

"We exchanged a few words."

"Then please tell me where she is."

"I know, but cannot speak."

"You cannot say?"

"I do not have the right."

"But you just said that you came here today to help me."

"Affirmative, I said that."

"But still you can't tell me where Mariye is?"

The Commendatore shook his head. "That is not my role. I am most regretful."

"Then whose role is it?"

The Commendatore pointed his right forefinger directly at me. "It is your role, my friends. You, yourself. My friends must tell yourself where Mariye Akikawa is. It is the only path that leads to her."

"I have to tell myself?" I said. "But I haven't the faintest idea where she is."

The Commendatore gave a long sigh. "My friends know. But my friends do not yet know that they know."

"That sounds like a circular argument to me."

"Negative! It is not circular. My friends will know in due course. In a place that is not here."

Now it was my turn to let out a sigh.

"Please tell me one thing. Was Mariye kidnapped? Or did she wander off on her own?"

"That is something my friends can only know after my friends have found her and brought her back to this world."

"Is she in great danger?"

The Commendatore shook his head. "Determining what constitutes great danger is a role that humans, not Ideas, must play. If my friends truly wish to bring her back, however, my friends must find the road and move quickly."

Find the road? What road was he talking about? I looked at the Commendatore for a moment. It was as though he was playing a riddle game. Assuming his riddles had answers, that is.

"So what is it that you are offering me by way of assistance?"

"What I can do for my friends," the Commendatore said, "is to send you to a place wherein my friends encounter yourself. But that is not as easy as it may sound. It will involve considerable sacrifice, and an excruciating ordeal. More specifically, the sacrifice will be made by the Idea, while the ordeal will be endured by my friends. Do I have your approval?"

What could I say? I hadn't a clue what he was talking about.

"So what is it exactly that I have to do?"

"It is simple," the Commendatore said. "My friends must slay me."

51

NOW IS THE TIME

"It is simple," the Commendatore said. "My friends must slay me."

"Slay you?" I said.

"Slay me, as in *Killing Commendatore*—let the painting be your model."

"I should slay you with a sword—is that what you mean?"

"Precisely. As luck would have it, I happen to have a sword with me. It is the real thing—as I told my friends once before, if it cuts you, then you will bleed. It is not full-sized, but I am not full-sized either, so it should suffice."

I stood at the foot of the bed facing the Commendatore. I wanted to say something but had no idea what it should be. So I just stood there, rooted to the spot. Tomohiko Amada was staring in the Commendatore's direction too, from where he lay stretched out on the bed. Whether he could make him out or not was another story. The Commendatore was able to choose who could see him, and who couldn't.

At last I pulled myself together enough to pose a question. "If I kill you with that sword, will I learn where Mariye Akikawa is?"

"Negative. Not exactly. First, my friends must dispose of me. Wipe me off the face of this earth. A chain of events will follow that could well lead my friends to the girl's location."

I struggled to decipher what he meant.

"I'm not sure what sort of chain of events you're talking about, but can I be certain they will lead me in the direction you anticipate? Even if I kill you, there's no guarantee. In which case, yours would be a pointless death."

The Commendatore raised one eyebrow and stared at me. Now he looked like Lee Marvin in *Point Blank*. Super cool. There wasn't the ghost of a chance that the Commendatore had seen *Point Blank*, of course.

"Affirmative! It is as my friends say. Maybe the chain of events will not flow so smoothly in reality. Maybe my hypothesis is based on mere supposition and conjecture. Just maybe, there are too many maybes. But there is no alternative. There is not the luxury of choice."

"So if I kill you, will you be dead to *me*? Will you vanish from my sight forever?"

"Affirmative! As far as my friends are concerned, I shall be dead and gone. One of the countless deaths an Idea must undergo."

"Isn't there a danger that the world itself will be altered when an Idea is killed?"

"How could it be otherwise?" the Commendatore said. Again, he raised one eyebrow, Lee Marvin–style. "What would be the meaning of a world that did *not* change when an Idea was extinguished? Can an Idea be so insignificant?"

"But you think I should still kill you, even though the world would be altered as a result."

"My friends set me free. And now my friends must kill me. Should my friends fail in that task, the circle would remain open. And a circle once opened must then be closed. There are no other options."

I looked at Tomohiko Amada, lying on the bed. His eyes seemed to be trained on the chair where the Commendatore was sitting.

"Can Mr. Amada see you?"

"It is about now that he should be seeing me," the Commendatore said. "And hearing our voices too. A few moments hence, he will begin to grasp the import of our discourse. He is marshaling all his remaining strength to that end."

"What do you think he was trying to convey in *Killing Commendatore*?"

"That is not for me to say. My friends should ask the artist," the Commendatore said. "Since he is right before you."

I sat back down in my chair and drew close to the man stretched out on the bed.

"Mr. Amada, I found the painting you stored in the attic. I am quite sure you meant to hide it. You would not have wrapped it so thoroughly had you planned to show it to anyone. But I unwrapped it. I know that may displease you, but my curiosity got the better of me. And once I discovered how superb *Killing Commendatore* was, I couldn't let it out of my sight. It is a great painting. One of your best, no question. At this moment, almost no one knows of its existence. Even Masahiko hasn't seen it yet. A thirteen-year-old girl named Mariye Akikawa has, though. And she went missing yesterday."

The Commendatore raised his hand. "Please, let him rest. His brain is easily overtaxed—it cannot handle more than this at one time."

I stopped talking and studied Tomohiko Amada's face. I couldn't tell how much had sunk in. His face was still expressionless. But when I looked more closely I could see a glitter in the depths of his eyes. Like the glint of a sharp penknife at the bottom of a deep spring.

I began talking again, this time with frequent pauses. "My question is, what was your purpose in painting that picture? Its subject matter, its structure, and its style are so different from your other works. It makes me think you were using it to communicate a very personal message. What is the painting's underlying meaning? Who is killing whom? Who is the Commendatore? Who is the murderer Don Giovanni? And who is that mysterious bearded fellow with the long face poking his head out of the ground in the lower left-hand corner?"

The Commendatore raised his hand again. I drew up short.

"Enough questions," he said. "It will take a while for those to permeate."

"Will he be able to answer? Does he have enough strength left?"

"No," the Commendatore said, shaking his head. "I doubt my friends will obtain answers. He does not have the energy for that."

"Then why did you have me ask?"

"What my friends imparted were not questions, but information. That my friends had found *Killing Commendatore* in the attic, that its existence was known to my friends. It is the first step. Everything begins from there."

"Then what is the second step?"

"When my friends slay me, of course. It is the second step."

"And is there a third step?"

"There should be, of course."

"Then what is it?"

"Have you still not yet figured this out, my friends?"

"No, I haven't."

"By reenacting the allegory contained within that painting, we shall lure Long Face into the open. Into this room. By dragging him out, my friends shall win back Mariye Akikawa."

I was speechless. What world had I stepped into? There seemed no rhyme or reason to it.

"It is a hard thing, without question," the Commendatore intoned. "Yet there is no alternative. Hence my friends must dispatch me now, without further ado."

We waited for the information I had given Tomohiko Amada to complete its journey to his brain. That took some time. Meanwhile, I tried to put to rest some of my doubts by peppering the Commendatore with questions.

"Why," I asked, "did Tomohiko Amada remain silent about what had happened in Vienna even after the war had ended? I mean, no one was standing in his way at that point."

"The woman he loved was brutally executed by the Nazis," the Commendatore answered. "Slowly tortured to death. Their comrades were slain in a similar fashion. In the end, their plot was a wretched failure. Only through the offices of the Japanese and German governments did he barely escape with his life. The experience savaged him. He had been arrested and detained by the Gestapo for two months. They subjected him to extreme torture. Their violence was unspeakable, but they took care not to kill him, nor to leave any physical scars. Yet their sadism left his nerves in tatters—and as a result, something within him was extinguished. Placed under the strictest orders, he bowed to the inevitable and remained silent. Then he was forcibly repatriated to Japan."

"Not long before," I said, "Tomohiko Amada's younger brother had taken his own life, probably because of the trauma of his own war experience. He had been part of the Nanjing Massacre, and committed suicide right after his discharge from the army. Correct?"

"Affirmative. Tomohiko Amada lost many loved ones in the whirlpool of those years. He himself was sorely damaged. As a result, his anger and grief put down deep roots. The hopeless, impotent realization that, no matter what he did, he could not stand against the torrent of history. As the sole survivor, he must also have felt an immense guilt. Hence he never spoke a word of what happened in Vienna, even after the gag was removed. It is as though he was unable to speak."

I looked at Tomohiko Amada's face. But I could detect no reaction as yet. I couldn't tell if he heard us or not.

I spoke. "Then at some point—we don't know exactly when—he created *Killing Commendatore*. An allegorical painting that expressed all he could not say. He put everything into it. A brilliant tour de force."

"He took that which he had been unable to accomplish in reality," the Commendatore said, "and gave it another form. What we might call 'camouflaged expression.' Not of what had in fact happened, but of *what should have happened*."

"Nevertheless, he bundled the painting up tight and hid it in the attic, out of public view," I said. "Although he had radically transformed the events, they were still too raw to reveal. Is that what you mean?"

"Precisely. It distills the pure essence of his living spirit. Then, one day, my friends happened upon it."

"So are you saying all of this began when I brought the painting out into the light? Is that what you meant by 'opening the circle'?"

The Commendatore said nothing, just extended his hands palms up.

Not long after, we noticed Tomohiko Amada's face turning pink. (The Commendatore and I had been watching him closely for any change.) At the same time, as if in response, the small, mysterious light that had been flickering deep in his eyes began to rise slowly to the surface. Like an ascending deep-sea diver gauging the effects of the water pressure on his body. The veil covering Amada's eyes also lifted, until, finally, both were wide open. The person lying before us was no longer a frail, desiccated old man on the verge of death. Instead, he was someone whose eyes brimmed with a determination to hang on to this world as long as he could.

"He is gathering his remaining strength," the Commendatore said to me. "Recovering as much of his conscious mind as he is able. But the more he regains mentally, the greater the physical torment. His body has been secreting a special substance to blot out that pain. It is thanks to the existence of such a substance that people can die in peace, not in agony. When consciousness returns, so does the pain. Nevertheless, he is trying to recover as much as he can. This is a mission he must fulfill here and now, however great the suffering."

As if to reinforce the Commendatore's words, Tomohiko Amada's face began to contort with agony. Age and infirmity had eaten away at his body until it was ready to shut down—he could feel that now. There was no way to avoid it. The end of his allotted time was fast approaching. It was painful to watch him suffer. Instead of calling him back, I might better have let him die a peaceful, painless death in a semiconscious haze.

"But he chose this way himself," the Commendatore said, again reading my mind. "It is painful to witness, but beyond our control."

"Won't Masahiko be returning soon?" I asked the Commendatore.

"Negative. Not for some time," he said with a small shake of his head. "His call was work related, something important. He will be gone a considerable time."

Tomohiko's eyes were wide open. They had been sunk within their wrinkled sockets, but now his eyeballs protruded like a person leaning out of a window. His breathing was deeper, and more ragged. It rasped as it passed in and out of his throat. And he was staring straight at the Commendatore. There was no doubt. The Commendatore was visible to him. Amazement was written in his face. He couldn't believe what was sitting in front of him. How could a figure produced by his imagination appear before him in reality?

"Negative, that is not the case," the Commendatore said. "What he sees and what my friends see are completely different."

"You mean you don't look the same way to him?"

"My friends, keep in mind that I am an Idea. My form changes depending on the person and the situation."

"Then how do you look to Mr. Amada?"

"That is something even I do not know. I am like a mirror that reflects what is in a person's heart. Nothing more."

"But you assumed this form for me on purpose, didn't you? Choosing to appear as the Commendatore?"

"To be precise, I did not choose this form. Cause and effect are hard to separate here. Because I took the form of the Commendatore, a sequence of events was set in motion. But at the same time, my form is the necessary consequence of that very sequence. It is hard to explain using the concept of time that governs the world you live in, my friends, but it might be summed up as: *All these events have been determined beforehand*."

"If an Idea is a mirror, then is Tomohiko Amada now seeing what he wishes to see?"

"Negative! He is seeing what he *must* see," the Commendatore corrected me. "It may be excruciating. Yet he must look. Now, at the end of his life."

I examined Tomohiko Amada's face again. Mixed with the amazement, I could discern an intense loathing. And almost unendurable torment. The return to consciousness carried with it not only the agony of the flesh. It brought with it the agony of the soul.

"He is squeezing out every last ounce of strength to ascertain who I am. Despite the pain. He is striving to return to his twenties."

Tomohiko Amada's face had turned a fiery red. Hot blood coursed through his veins. His thin, dry lips trembled, he gasped violently. His long, skeletal fingers clutched at the sheets.

"Stop dithering, my friends, and kill me now, while his mind is whole," the Commendatore said. "The quicker, the better. He may not be able to hold himself together much longer."

The Commendatore drew his sword from its scabbard. It was just eight inches long, but it looked very sharp indeed. Despite its dimensions, it was a weapon capable of ending a person's life.

"Stab me with this," the Commendatore said. "We shall re-create the scene from *Killing Commendatore*. But hurry. There is no time to dawdle."

I looked back and forth from the Commendatore to Tomohiko

Amada, struggling to make up my mind. All I could be remotely sure of was that Tomohiko Amada was in desperate need, and the Commendatore's resolve was firm. I alone wallowed in indecision, caught between the two of them.

I felt the rush of owl wings, and heard a bell ring in the dark.

Everything was connected somewhere.

"Affirmative! Everything is connected somewhere," said the Commendatore. "And my friends cannot escape that connection, however my friends may try. So steel yourself, and kill me. There is no room for guilt. Tomohiko Amada needs your help. By slaying me, my friends can save him. Make happen here what should have happened in the past. Now is the time. Only my friends can grant him salvation before he breathes his last."

I rose from my chair and strode to where the Commendatore was seated. I took his unsheathed sword in hand. I was past the point of determining what was just and unjust. In a world outside space and time, all dualities—before and after, up and down—ceased to exist. In such a world, I could no longer perceive myself as myself. I and myself were being torn apart.

The instant I took the sword in hand, however, I realized its handle was too small. It was a miniature sword for a tiny hand. There was simply no way could I kill the Commendatore with it, however keen its blade. The realization brought with it a sense of relief.

"The sword is too small. I can't grip it," I said to the Commendatore.

"That is a shame," he said with a sigh. "Well, there is nothing to be done. We must use something else, although that means diverging further from the painting."

"Something else?"

The Commendatore pointed to a small chest of drawers in the corner of the room. "Look inside the top drawer."

I went to the chest and slid open the uppermost drawer.

"Within is a knife for filleting fish," the Commendatore said.

Sure enough, a knife lay atop a small stack of neatly folded washcloths. The knife that Masahiko had used to prepare the sea bream he had brought to my home. An eight-inch blade honed to a razor's edge.

Masahiko always kept his tools in perfect shape. This knife was no exception.

"Now take that knife and plunge it into my chest," said the Commendatore. "Sword or knife, what is the difference. We can still reenact the scene in *Killing Commendatore*. But we must make haste. There is little time."

I took the knife in hand. It was as heavy as stone. The tip of the blade shone cold and white in the light streaming from the window. The knife had vanished from my kitchen and come to wait for me here, in the chest of drawers. Masahiko had sharpened the blade, as it turned out, for the sake of his own father. There seemed no way to avoid my fate.

I still couldn't come to a decision. Nevertheless, I stepped behind the Commendatore's chair, gripping the knife tightly in my right hand. From his bed, Tomohiko Amada stared at us with eyes as big as saucers. As if watching history unfold before his eyes. His mouth was open, exposing his yellowed teeth and whitish tongue, a tongue that lolled in his mouth as though trying to form words. Words this world would never hear.

"My friends do not have a violent bone in your body," the Commendatore said, as if to admonish me. "It is obvious. My friends are not built to kill. But sometimes people must act against their nature, to rescue something important or for some greater purpose. Now is one of those times. So kill me! I am not big, as my friends can see, and I will not resist. I am merely an Idea. Just insert the tip of the knife into my heart. What could be more straightforward?"

The Commendatore pointed his tiny index finger at the spot where his heart was. But the thought of that heart inevitably recalled my sister's. I could remember her operation as if it were yesterday. How delicate and difficult it had been. Saving a malfunctioning heart was a formidable task. It required a team of specialists and gallons of blood. Yet destroying a heart was *so easy*.

"Such thinking will get us nowhere," the Commendatore said. "If my friends wish to save Mariye Akikawa, then do the deed. Even if my friends do not want to. Trust me. Jettison all feelings, and close your mind. But not your eyes. My friends must keep them open."

I stepped behind the Commendatore and raised the knife. But I couldn't bring it down. Sure, it might be only one of a thousand deaths for an Idea, but it was still extinguishing a life as far as I was concerned. Was this not the same order the young lieutenant had given Tsuguhiko Amada in Nanjing?

"Negative! It is not the same," said the Commendatore. "My friends are doing this at my behest. It is I who am asking my friends to kill me. So that I may be reborn. Be strong. Close the circle at once."

I closed my eyes and thought of the girl I had throttled in the love hotel in Miyagi. Of course, she and I had been pretending. I had squeezed her throat gently, so as not to kill her. I had been unable to do it long enough to satisfy her. Had I continued, I might indeed have strangled her to death. On the bed of that love hotel, I had glimpsed the deep rage within myself for the first time. It had churned in my chest like blood-soaked mud, pushing me closer and closer to real murder.

I know where you were and what you were doing, the man had said.

"All right, now bring it down," the Commendatore said. "I know my friends can do it. Remember, my friends will not be killing me. My friends will be slaying your evil father. The blood of your evil father shall soak into the earth."

My evil father?

Where did that come from?

"Who is the evil father of my friends?" the Commendatore said, reading my mind. "I believe your path crossed with his not long ago. Am I mistaken?"

Do not paint my portrait any further, the man had said. He had pointed his finger at me from within the dark mirror. It had pierced my chest like the tip of a sharp sword.

Spurred by that pain, I reflexively closed my heart and opened my eyes wide. I cleared all thought from my mind (as Don Giovanni had done in *Killing Commendatore*), buried my emotions, made my face a blank mask, and brought the knife down with all my might. The sharp blade entered the Commendatore's tiny chest precisely where he had pointed. I felt the living flesh resist. But the Commendatore himself made no attempt to fend off the blow. His fingers clutched at the air, but apart from that he did not react. Still, the body he inhabited did all that it could to avoid its looming extinction. The Commendatore was an Idea, but his body was not. An Idea may have borrowed it for its own purposes, but that body would not meekly submit to death. It possessed its own rationale. I had to overcome that resistance through brute force, severing its life at the roots. "Kill me," the Commendatore had said. But I was actually dispatching another *someone*'s body.

I wanted to drop the knife, drop everything, and run from the room. But the Commendatore's words echoed in my ears. "If my friends wish to save Mariye Akikawa, then do the deed. Even if my friends do not want to."

So I pushed the blade even farther into the Commendatore's heart. If you're stabbing someone to death, there's no halfway. The tip of the knife emerged from his back—I had run him through. His white garment was dyed crimson. My hands were drenched in blood. But the blood did not spew into the air as it did in *Killing Commendatore*. This is an illusion, I tried to convince myself. I was murdering a mere phantom. My act was purely symbolic.

Yet I knew I was fooling myself. Perhaps the act was symbolic. But it was no phantom that I was killing. Without question, my victim was made of flesh and blood. It may have been barely two feet tall, a fabrication created by Tomohiko Amada's brush, but its life force was unexpectedly strong. The point of my blade had broken the skin and several ribs on its way to the heart, then passed through to the back of the chair. No way that was an illusion.

Tomohiko Amada's eyes were open even wider now, riveted on the scene unfolding before him. My murder of the Commendatore. No, for him it must have been the murder of someone else. Who was he seeing? The Nazi official whose assassination he had helped plot in Vienna? The young lieutenant who had given his brother a Japanese sword and ordered him to behead three Chinese prisoners in Nanjing? Or that evil *something*, something more fundamental, that lay at the root of those events? I could only guess. I could not read the expression on Tomohiko Amada's face. Though his mouth gaped open, his lips were motionless. Only his tongue continued its futile quest to form words of some kind.

At last, the strength left the Commendatore's neck and arms. His whole body went slack, like a marionette whose strings had been cut. I responded by pushing the knife even farther into his heart. All movement in the room came to a standstill; the scene was now a frozen tableau. It stayed that way for a long time.

Tomohiko Amada was the first to move. Once the Commendatore had lost consciousness and collapsed, the strength to focus his mind evaporated. He sighed deeply and closed his eyes. Slowly and solemnly, like lowering the shutters. As if to confirm: *Now I have seen what I needed to see.* His mouth was still open, but his lolling tongue was tucked out of sight. Only his yellow teeth were visible, like a ramshackle fence circling an empty house. His face was free of pain. The torment had passed. He looked peaceful and relaxed. I guessed he was back in the twilight world, where thought and pain did not exist. I was happy for him.

I finally relaxed my arm and drew the blade from the Commendatore's body. Blood spewed from the wound. Exactly as in *Killing Commendatore.* The Commendatore himself spilled lifelessly into the chair. His eyes were open, his mouth contorted in agony. His ten tiny fingers clawed the air. Dark blood pooled around his feet. He was dead. How much blood had come from that tiny body!

Thus did the Commendatore—or the Idea that had taken his form—meet his end. Tomohiko Amada had sunk back into his deep sleep. Standing next to the Commendatore's body, Masahiko's bloody knife in my right hand, I was the only conscious person left in the room. My labored breathing should have been the only sound. Should have been. But something was moving. I sensed it as much as I heard it, to my alarm. *Keep your ears open*, the Commendatore had told me. I did as he had instructed.

Something is in the room. I could hear it moving. Bloody knife in hand, I stood frozen like a statue, scanning the room, searching for the source of the sound. Out of the corner of one eye, I spotted something near the far wall.

Long Face was there.

Killing the Commendatore had lured Long Face into this world.

52

THE MAN IN THE ORANGE CONE HAT

The scene in the room now matched the lower left-hand corner of Tomohiko Amada's *Killing Commendatore.* Long Face had poked his head out of a hole, and was raising its square cover with one hand as he peeked at what was taking place. His hair was long and tangled, and a thick black beard covered much of his face. His elongated head was shaped like a Japanese eggplant, narrow with a jutting chin and bulging eyes. The bridge of his nose was flat. For some reason, his lips glistened like a piece of fruit. His body was small but well proportioned, as if a normal person had been shrunk in size. Just as the Commendatore made you think of a scaled-down copy of a human being.

The big difference between the Long Face in *Killing Commendatore* and here was his expression—now he looked stunned as he stared at the lifeless body of the Commendatore. His mouth gaped in disbelief. How long had he been watching us? I had no idea. I had been so focused on snuffing out the Commendatore's life, and gauging Tomohiko Amada's reaction to his death, that I had been oblivious to the odd-looking man in the corner of the room. Yet I bet he hadn't missed a thing. After all, that was the scene in *Killing Commendatore.*

Long Face remained completely still, there in the corner of our tableau. As if assigned a fixed position. I moved slightly to see how he would respond. But Long Face didn't react. He maintained the same position he had in the painting—one hand holding up the square lid, his eyes round as he gawked at the slain Commendatore. He didn't even blink.

As the tension drained from my body, I moved from my own assigned position. I edged cautiously toward Long Face, deadening my footsteps like a cat, the bloody knife in one hand. I could not let him slip back underground. To save Mariye Akikawa, the Commendatore had given his life to re-create the scene in the painting, and drawn Long Face out into the open. I must not allow that sacrifice to be in vain.

Yet how could I wrest from Long Face what I needed to know about Mariye? I was at a loss. *Who* or *what* was Long Face? How was his presence linked to Mariye's disappearance? What the Commendatore had told me was more riddle than information. One thing was clear, though: I had to get my hands on him. I could figure the rest out later.

The lid that Long Face was holding was about two feet square, made of the same lime-green linoleum as the rest of the floor. When closed, it would blend in perfectly, perhaps even disappear altogether.

Long Face did not move a muscle as I approached. He seemed rooted to the spot. Like a cat in the headlights. Or maybe he was just fulfilling his designated role—to maintain the composition of the painting for as long as possible. Whichever, it was lucky for me. Otherwise, he would have sensed me behind him and slipped back underground for good. Once the lid had been closed, I doubted it would open again.

I crept behind him, softly laid down the knife, and snatched his collar with both hands. He was wearing drab, snug-fitting clothes. Work clothes, from the look of it. Clearly different from the fine cloth of the Commendatore's garments. These looked rough to the touch and were covered in patches.

Jolted from his trance, Long Face thrashed about, desperately attempting to flee down his hole. I held tight to his collar. There was no way I was going to let him escape. I gathered my strength and tried to yank him all the way out. He fought back, grabbing the sides of the hole with both hands. He was much stronger than I'd anticipated. He even tried to bite my arm. What could I do—I slammed his eggplant-shaped head against the corner of the opening. Then I did it again, this time more violently. The second blow knocked him out cold. I could feel his body go limp. At last I could drag him out into the light.

Long Face was a little bigger than the Commendatore. Two and a half feet tall was my guess. He was wearing what a farmer might have worn in the fields, or a manservant sweeping the yard. A stiff, rough jacket over baggy work pants cinched at the ankles. His belt was a thick piece of rope. He wore no shoes, and his soles were thickly callused and stained black with dirt. His long hair showed no sign of having been recently washed or combed. Half his face was covered by a black beard. The other half was a sickly white. Nothing about him looked clean, yet, strangely, his body had no odor.

Based on appearance, I figured the Commendatore belonged to the aristocracy of his time, while Long Face was lower-class. Perhaps he was dressed the way commoners did back then. Or maybe Tomohiko Amada had imagined, *This is how people might have dressed in the Asuka period.* Historical accuracy, however, was beside the point. What I needed to do was squeeze from this man with the strange face any information that would lead me to Mariye.

I rolled Long Face over onto his stomach and tied his hands behind him with the belt of a bathrobe hanging close by. Then I dragged his motionless body to the center of the room. Because of his size, he wasn't very heavy. About the weight of a medium-sized dog. I grabbed a curtain tie and bound one of his legs to the bed. Now he had no way to flee.

Stretched out unconscious in the bright afternoon light, Long Face just looked pitiful. Gone was the weirdness that had alarmed me when he had poked his head up out of his hole, observing events with those glittering eyes. I could find nothing sinister about him. He didn't look bright enough to be evil. Instead, he looked honest in a dull-witted sort of way. And timid, too. Not like someone who concocted plans and made decisions, but, rather, the type who meekly followed his superiors' orders.

Tomohiko Amada was still stretched out on the bed, his eyes closed. He was completely still. I couldn't tell, looking at him, if he was alive or dead. I leaned down and put my ear less than an inch from his mouth. His breathing was faint, like a distant surf. He wasn't dead yet, just sleeping on the floor of his twilight world. I felt relieved. I didn't like the idea of Masahiko returning from his phone call to find that his father had died in his absence. Tomohiko's face, as he lay on his side, looked far more peaceful and satisfied than before. Maybe witnessing the slaying of the Commendatore (or someone else he wished to see killed) had put some of his painful memories to rest.

The Commendatore was slumped in his cloth chair. His eyes were wide open, and I could see his tiny tongue curled behind his parted lips. Blood was still seeping from the wound in his chest, but the flow was weaker than before. His right hand flopped lifelessly when I took it. Although his skin retained some warmth, it felt remote and somehow detached. The kind of detachment life acquires as it moves steadily toward its own end. I felt like straightening his limbs and placing him in a proper-sized coffin, one made for a small child. I would lay the coffin in the pit behind the shrine, where no one could bother him again. But all I could do now was gently close his eyes.

I sat in the chair and watched Long Face on the floor as I waited for him to regain his senses. Outside the window, the broad Pacific sparkled. A few fishing boats were still plying the waters. I could see the sleek fuselage of an airplane shining in the sun as it slowly made its way south. A four-prop plane with an antenna jutting up from its tail—probably an antisubmarine aircraft from the Japanese Maritime Self-Defense Force base in Atsugi. Some of us were quietly going about our business on a Saturday afternoon. I, for one, was in a sunlit room in an upscale nursing home, having just slain the Commendatore and fished out and tied up Long Face in my quest to find a beautiful thirteen-year-old girl. It takes all kinds, I guess.

Long Face didn't regain consciousness for some time. I checked my watch again.

What would Masahiko think if he came back now? The Commendatore in a pool of blood, Long Face bound and unconscious on the floor. Both in the unfamiliar garb of an ancient time, neither standing even three feet tall. Tomohiko Amada comatose on the bed, a faint but satisfied smile (if that's what it was) on his lips. A square, black hole gaping in a corner of the room. How could I explain what had led to this scene?

Of course, Masahiko didn't come back. He was tied up in a work-related phone call of great importance, as the Commendatore had said. He would be dealing with it for some time yet. Everything had been arranged in advance. No one would bother us. I sat on the chair, eyeing the unconscious Long Face. I had whacked his head pretty hard on the edge of the hole, but it shouldn't take him that long to come to. He'd have a fair-sized lump on his head, that's all.

At last, Long Face woke up. He twisted and turned a bit on the floor, and uttered a few incomprehensible words. Then, slowly, he opened his eyes a crack. Like a child looking at something scary—something he didn't want to see, but must.

I went and knelt beside him.

"There's very little time," I said, looking down at him. "I need you to tell me where I can find Mariye Akikawa. If you do, I'll untie you, and you can go back."

I pointed to the square hole in the corner. The lid was still raised. I couldn't tell if he understood what I was saying or not. But I decided to keep talking. All I could do was give it a shot.

Long Face violently shook his head back and forth several times. I couldn't tell if he was saying that he didn't know anything, or that my language was foreign to him.

"If you don't tell me, I'll kill you," I said. "You saw me stab the Commendatore, I bet. Well, there's no big difference between one murder and two."

I pressed the bloody blade of my knife against his dirty throat. I thought of the fishermen and the pilot of the southbound airplane. *We all have jobs we have to do.* And this was mine. I wasn't going to kill him, of course, but the knife was real, and very sharp. Long Face quivered in fear.

"Wait!" he gasped in a husky voice. "Stay your hand."

His way of speaking was strange, but I could understand him. I eased off on the knife.

"Where is Mariye Akikawa?" I pressed him. "Come on, spit it out!"

"No, sir, I do not know. I swear it."

I studied his eyes. They were big and easy to read. He seemed to be telling the truth.

"All right then, tell me, what are you doing here?" I asked.

"I am enjoined to verify and record these events. I do only what I am told to do. You have my word."

"Why must you verify them?"

"Because I was so bidden. I know nothing beyond that."

"So what on earth are you? Another kind of Idea?"

"Goodness no! I am a Metaphor, nothing more."

"A Metaphor?"

"Yes. A mere Metaphor. Used to link two things together. So please, untie my bonds, please, I beseech you."

I was getting confused. "If you are as you say, then give me a metaphor now, off the top of your head."

"I am the most humble and lowly form of Metaphor, sir. I cannot devise anything of quality."

"A metaphor of any kind is all right—it doesn't have to be brilliant."

"He was someone who stood out," he said after a moment's pause, "like a man wearing an orange cone hat in a packed commuter train."

Not an impressive metaphor, to be sure. In fact, not really a metaphor at all.

"That's a simile, not a metaphor," I pointed out.

"A million pardons," he said, sweat pouring from his forehead. "Let me try again. 'He lived as though he were wearing an orange cone hat in a crowded train.' "

"That makes no sense. It's still not a true metaphor. Your story doesn't hold. I'll just have to kill you."

Long Face's lips trembled with fear. His beard may have been manly, but he was short on guts.

"My sincerest apologies, sir. I am yet but an apprentice. I cannot think of a witty example. Forgive me. But I assure you that I am the genuine article, a true Metaphor."

"Then who is your superior—who commands you?"

"I have no superior, per se. Well, perhaps I do, but I have never laid eyes on him. I only follow orders—acting as a link between phenomena and language. Like a helpless jellyfish adrift on the ocean. So please do not kill me. I implore you."

"I can spare your life," I said, my knife still on his throat. "But only if you agree to guide me to where you came from."

"That is something I cannot do," Long Face said in a firm voice. It was the first time he had used that tone. "The road I took to get here is the Path of Metaphor. It is different for each one who traverses it. It is not a single road. Thus I cannot guide you, sir, on your way."

"Let me get this straight. I must follow this path alone, and I must discover it for myself—is that what you're saying?"

Long Face nodded vigorously. "The Path of Metaphor is rife with perils. Should a mortal like you stray from the path even once, you could find yourself in danger. And there are Double Metaphors everywhere."

"Double Metaphors?"

Long Face shuddered with fear. "Yes, Double Metaphors lurking in the darkness. The most *vile* and dangerous of creatures."

"It's all the same to me," I said. "I'm already mixed up in a whole lot of craziness. So it's no skin off my nose if the craziness grows or shrinks. I killed the Commendatore with my own hands. I don't want his death to be in vain."

"I see I have no choice. So let me offer you a word of warning before you set out."

"What kind of warning?"

"Take a light of some kind with you. You will pass through many dark places on your way. You will come across a river. It is a metaphorical river, but the water is very real. It is cold and deep, and the current is strong. You cannot cross without a boat. You will find a boat at the ferrying spot."

"How about after I cross the river—what should I do then?"

Long Face rolled his bulging eyes. "The world that awaits you on the other side, like this one, is subject to the principle of connectivity. You will have to see for yourself."

I checked Tomohiko Amada's bedside table. Sure enough, a flashlight was there. A facility like this one was sure to store one in each room in case of fire or earthquake. I flicked it on. The light was strong. The batteries weren't dead. I slipped on my leather jacket, which I had draped over a chair, and started for the hole in the corner, flashlight in hand.

"Please, sir," Long Face begged. "Will you not loosen my bonds? I fear what may transpire should I be left in this state."

"If you're a true Metaphor, untying yourself should be easy. Aren't Concepts and Ideas and others like you able to move through space and time?"

"No, you overrate me. I am blessed with no such marvelous powers. Concepts and Ideas are Metaphors of a much higher order."

"Like those with orange cone hats?"

Long Face looked stricken. "Please do not mock me, sir. My feelings can be hurt too, you know."

After a moment's hesitation, I decided to untie his hands and feet. I had bound them so tightly they took time to undo. Now that we had talked, he didn't appear to be such a bad fellow. True, he didn't know where Mariye was, but he had volunteered other information. I doubted that he would interfere or cause me any harm if I untied him. And I certainly couldn't leave him bound and trussed where he was. Should anyone find him like that, it would only make things worse. When I finished, he sat there for a moment, rubbing his chafed wrists with his tiny hands. Then he felt his forehead. It appeared a lump had already sprouted.

"Thank you, sir. Now I can return to my world."

"Go ahead," I said, gesturing to the hole in the corner. "I'll follow later."

"I shall now make my departure. Please ensure that the lid is securely closed when you follow. Otherwise, someone might trip and fall in. Or grow curious and climb down. Then I would be held responsible."

"Understood. I will make sure it's closed."

Long Face trotted to the hole and climbed inside. Then his head and shoulders popped up again. His saucer eyes had an eerie glow. As they did in *Killing Commendatore*.

"I wish you a safe journey," Long Face said to me. "I hope you can find *What's-her-name*. Was it Komichi?"

"No, her name isn't Komichi," I said. A chill ran down my spine. My throat turned to sandpaper. I couldn't speak for a moment. "The name was Mariye Akikawa. Do you know something about Komichi?"

"No, I know nothing at all." Long Face seemed to realize that he'd let drop something he shouldn't. "The name just slipped into my clumsy metaphorical brain. A simple mistake. Forgive me, please, sir."

Long Face vanished down the hole. Like smoke in the wind.

I stood there for a moment, plastic flashlight in hand. Komichi? How could my sister's name come up here, of all places? Could she be connected to this strangeness? But I had no time to ponder that question. I switched the flashlight on and entered the hole, feetfirst. It was dark below, and there seemed to be a long path sloping downward. That was odd, too, come to think of it. The room was on the third floor, so the second floor should be directly beneath. I trained the flashlight on the path, but couldn't make out where it led. I lowered the rest of my body inside and closed the lid tight behind me. Now everything was black.

The darkness was so complete that my five senses were useless. As if the links between my body and my mind had been severed, and no information was passing between them. It was the strangest feeling. As if I were no longer myself. Nevertheless, I had to go on.

"If my friends wish to save Mariye Akikawa, then do the deed."

Those had been the Commendatore's words. He had made the sacrifice. Now it was my turn to face the ordeal. I had to push forward. With the flashlight my only ally, I stepped down into the inky blackness of the Path of Metaphor.

MAYBE A FIREPLACE POKER

The blackness enfolding me was so thick, so complete, it seemed to have a will of its own. It felt like walking on the ocean floor, where not even a particle of light could penetrate. Only the yellow beam of my flashlight connected me to the world, and barely, at that. The passageway descended at a steady angle. The surface beneath my feet was hard and smooth—it felt like walking down a tunnel bored into solid rock. The ceiling was so low I had to stoop to keep from hitting my head. The air was chilly and odorless, and the total lack of smell disturbed me. Perhaps even the air was different here than above ground.

How long would my flashlight hold out? Its beam was strong and steady for now, but when the batteries failed (as they would eventually) I would be stranded in the dark. And if I were to believe Long Face, dangerous Double Metaphors were lurking out there, ready to pounce.

The palm of my hand that held the flashlight was sweaty from the tension. My heartbeat was a dull, hard thump. It sounded threatening, like a drumbeat would to someone lost in the jungle. Long Face had warned me: "Take a light of some kind with you. You will pass through many dark places on your way." So not everything in this passageway was pitch black. I wished it would brighten soon. I wished too that the ceiling would rise. I had always felt panicky in dark, constricted spaces. If this continued for much longer, I would soon have trouble breathing.

To calm myself, I tried to focus on other things. I needed to find something, anything, to occupy my mind. What popped into my head was an open-faced grilled cheese sandwich. Why a grilled cheese sandwich? Go figure. That's what came up first, for whatever reason. Perfectly melted cheese on a square of beautifully browned toast. Sitting on a pure white plate. So real I could reach out and touch it. And beside it a cup of piping-hot coffee. Coffee as black as a moonless night. A window opening onto a tall willow, on whose supple branches a small flock of chirping birds perched precariously, like a troupe of tightrope walkers. Everything at an immeasurable distance from where I was now.

Then, for some reason, I thought of the opera *Der Rosenkavalier*. I would listen to it as I sipped my coffee and nibbled my grilled cheese sandwich. That jet-black vinyl disk, released by Decca Records in Great Britain. I placed the heavy record on the turntable and gently lowered the needle. Georg Solti conducting the Vienna Philharmonic. The music elegant, intricate. When Richard Strauss had boasted he could describe even a broom musically, he was in his heyday. But was it a broom? I still couldn't remember. Perhaps it was an umbrella, or then again maybe a fireplace poker. In any case, how could one describe a broom in music? Or a hot grilled cheese sandwich, or someone's callused feet, or the difference between a simile and a metaphor? Could music really depict those things?

Richard Strauss conducted the same orchestra in prewar Vienna. (Was it before the *Anschluss*? After?) The program on this given day was Beethoven's 7th, a resolute yet quiet and well-groomed symphony, squeezed between its bright, uninhibited older sister (the 6th) and its bashful and beautiful younger sister (the 8th). A youthful Tomohiko Amada was in attendance. A pretty young woman sat beside him. Most likely, he was in love with her.

I imagined the city of Vienna on that day. The waltzes, the sweet Sacher tortes, the red-and-black swastikas fluttering from the roofs.

I could feel my thoughts veering off in a pointless direction. Or, more accurately perhaps, in a directionless direction. Yet I was powerless to rein them in. They were no longer under my control. It's no simple matter to hold on to your mind in total blackness. Your thoughts become a tree of riddles whose branches trail off into the dark. (A metaphor.) Nevertheless, I had to focus on *something* to hold myself together. Any old *something* would do. Otherwise, I would start to hyperventilate.

One absurdity after another sauntered through my mind as I pushed down the endless slope. The passageway was as straight as an arrow, with no bends or forks. However far I walked, nothing changed—not the height of the ceiling, or the depth of the darkness, or the quality of the air, or the angle of the slope. My sense of time was foggy, but based on how long I had been walking, I must have been deep underground. Yet in the end, that "depth" had to be a fabrication. After all, I had entered this tunnel from the third floor of a building. The darkness too had to be fabricated. Everything was either concept or metaphor, nothing more. That's what I told myself, anyway. The problem was that the darkness enfolding me was real darkness, the depth pressing down on me real depth.

Just when my neck and back were firing off warning signals about my hunched-over posture, a dim light appeared ahead. Then came a series of twists and turns. With each, my surroundings grew a little brighter, as if the night sky was giving way to day. Now I could make out where I was. I switched off my flashlight to conserve the batteries.

It was growing light, but still I smelled nothing, heard nothing. Then, at last, the cramped passage abruptly ended, and I stepped out into the open. Yet I could see no sky above me, only what looked like a milky-white ceiling, far overheard. A pale glow covered everything, as if the world was lit by a host of luminous insects. It felt odd. Yet it was a relief to say goodbye to the darkness, and to be able to walk upright again. I could relax a bit.

Outside the tunnel, the ground was rough underfoot. There was no path, only a barren, rocky plain that stretched as far as the eye could see. The downward slope had ended, and I was walking up a gentle rise. I picked my way forward, unsure of my direction. I checked my watch, but its hands held no meaning. One glance told me that much. In fact, nothing I carried—key ring, wallet, driver's license, loose change, handkerchief—promised to be of any use at all.

The incline grew steeper and steeper. After a while, I was literally crawling up the slope on my hands and knees. If I could only reach the top, then maybe I could see where I was. I pushed on without pausing to catch my breath. The only sound was the sound I was making, and even that seemed artificial, not like real sound at all. There was nothing alive that I could see. Not a tree, not a clump of grass, not a solitary bird. Not even a puff of wind. Only I moved—all else was still. It was as if time itself had come to a halt.

I finally reached the top of the rise. I could see in all directions from there, as I had anticipated. Yet my view was limited. For there was a whitish mist that hung over everything. All I could make out was what amounted to a lifeless wasteland, a craggy, barren wilderness that stretched in every direction. There was no true sky, just that milky-white ceiling. I felt like an astronaut who had crashed, and landed on an uninhabited planet. Well, at least there was some light, and air that I could breathe. I should be grateful for those.

I could find no sign of life. Finally, though, I was able to make out a faint sound. I thought it might be a hallucination at first, or possibly coming from my own body. Yet it gradually became clear that the noise was continuous, and caused by some kind of natural phenomenon. In fact, it sounded like flowing water. Perhaps it was the river that Long Face had spoken of. Bathed in the pale light, I picked my way down the bumpy slope in the direction of the sound.

The sound of water made me terribly thirsty. Come to think of it, I had been walking a very long time with nothing to drink. Yet I had been so anxious that water had never crossed my mind. Now I craved it desperately. But was the water in that river—if that was where the sound was coming from—drinkable? It might be thick with mud, or filled with dangerous toxins. Or perhaps it was metaphorical water, which my hands could not scoop up. Oh well, I would find out when I got there.

The noise grew louder and clearer as I went along. It sounded like a fast-flowing river, tumbling through rocks. Yet I still could not see it. As I headed toward the sound, the ground on both sides of me rose until I was walking between two rock walls about thirty feet in height. The path cut between those towering cliffs, though its serpentine twists and turns made it impossible to know what lay ahead. It was not a man-made trail. Rather, it appeared to have been fashioned by the forces of nature. From what I could tell, the river lay at its end.

I hurried along the walled path. I passed no tree, no blade of grass. Not a living thing. The silent cliffs were all that I could see. A sterile, monochrome world. It was as if an artist had lost interest in painting a landscape, and had abandoned it before adding the colors. I could barely hear my own footsteps. The rocks seemed to absorb sound.

At a certain point the path, which had been flat for the most part, began to slope upward again. It took some time, but at last I reached the crest, which ran like a spine along the top of the cliffs. When I leaned forward, I could see the river. Now the rush of water was even more audible.

The river was not especially wide. Maybe fifteen or twenty feet across. But its current was swift. I couldn't tell its depth. Judging from the whitecaps it sent up here and there, boulders and other hidden obstacles lay beneath the surface. The river carved a straight line through the rocky terrain. I crossed the ridge and headed down the slope in its direction.

When I reached the river, and saw it rushing past from right to left, I felt much better. At the very least, a large quantity of water was on the move. It had originated somewhere and was flowing somewhere else, following the contours of the land. In a place where nothing stirred, and no wind blew, the sound of rushing water reverberated around me. No, this world was not wholly absent of motion. That fact alone gave me some comfort.

The moment I reached the river, I knelt on the bank and scooped up water in my cupped hands. It was pleasantly cold. The river seemed snow-fed. Its water was crystal clear and appeared pure. Of course, I couldn't tell by looking at it if it was safe to drink. It might contain a deadly poison. Or bacteria that would ravage my body.

I sniffed the water in my hands. It had no odor (that is, if my sense of smell was still functioning). I took a sip. It had no flavor (that is, if I hadn't lost my sense of taste). I braced myself and swallowed deeply. I was too thirsty to resist, whatever the consequences. The water was indeed entirely tasteless and odorless. It might be real or fabricated, but thankfully, it would quench my thirst.

I knelt there, blissfully gulping mouthful after mouthful. I was thirstier than I had realized. Yet it was strange somehow to drink water lacking in taste and odor. Cold water when we are thirsty is *delicious* more than anything else. Our body sucks it in greedily. Our cells rejoice, our muscles regain their strength. Yet drinking the water from this river brought none of those feelings. It did no more than quench my thirst at a simple, physical level.

When I had drunk my fill, I stood up and looked at my surroundings one more time. Long Face had said that there would be a boat landing somewhere along the riverbank. That one of the boats could ferry me to the other side. There I would (probably) find information relating to Mariye Akikawa's whereabouts. But I could see nothing that looked like a landing, either upstream or downstream. I would have to search for it. A boat was crucial. Fording the river unaided was too dangerous. "The water is cold and deep, and the current is strong. You cannot cross without a boat," Long Face had told me. But which way should I turn to find that boat? Upriver or downriver? I had to choose one or the other.

Then I remembered Menshiki's given name, "Wataru," written with the kanji for traversing water. "The *wataru* in my name is the character that means 'to cross a river,'" Menshiki had said, when he introduced himself. "I don't know why I was given that name. I've never had much to do with water." A short while later he had added, "By the way, I'm left-handed. If I'm told to go left or right, I always choose left. It's become a habit."

It was a random comment quite disconnected to what we were talking about—I couldn't figure out why he would blurt out something like that. Which is probably why it stuck in my mind.

Maybe his comment had no special significance. It could have been mere happenstance. Yet (according to Long Face) this was a land built upon the conjunction of phenomena and expression. I ought to be able to handle the *happenstance* of any hints that came in my direction. I stood before the river and made up my mind. I would go left. If I took the unconscious tip that "colorless" Menshiki had provided and followed the tasteless, odorless river downstream, it might provide a further hint of some sort. Then again, it might not.

As I walked along the riverbank, I wondered what, if anything, lived in the water. It didn't seem likely anything did. I couldn't confirm this, of course. Nevertheless, I could see no signs of life. What organism would live in water that had neither taste nor odor? The river appeared wholly concentrated on its own identity. "I am river," it said. "I am that which flows." Certainly it possessed the form of a river, but beyond that *state of being* there was nothing. Not a thing floated on its surface, not a twig, not a blade of grass. It was simply a great quantity of water cutting across the land.

I pushed on through that boundless, cottony mist. It gently resisted me as I moved, like a filmy curtain of white lace. After a while, my gut began to react to the water I had drunk. It didn't feel unpleasant or ominous, but neither was it cause for rejoicing. A neutral feeling, whose true nature eluded my understanding. I felt I was being somehow changed, as if I were no longer the same person. It was a strange sensation. Could the water be turning me into someone physically adapted to this world?

For some reason, though, I was able to stay calm. I thought, optimistically, that there could be no real harm. My optimism had no firm basis. Nevertheless, I had passed without mishap through the narrow pitch-black passageway. With neither map nor compass, I had crossed a rocky wilderness to find this river. I had quenched my thirst with its water. I had avoided a close encounter with a lurking Double Metaphor. Dumb luck? Or perhaps it was predetermined. Whichever the case, I was heading in a good direction. So I thought. Or at least so I tried to convince myself.

Finally, a vague shape appeared through the haze. It was not a natural object—its straight lines meant it had to be human-made. As I drew nearer I saw that it was a boat landing. A small wooden jetty extending from the shore. Turning left had been the correct decision. Then again, it was possible that, in a world governed by connectivity, things would shift to accommodate whatever action I chose. Apparently, Menshiki's unconscious hint had helped steer me through to this point.

I could see the figure of a man, shrouded in the mist. He was tall. In fact, after the tiny Commendatore and Long Face, he looked like a giant. He was standing very still at the end of the jetty, as if lost in thought, leaning against some kind of dark machine. The swift-flowing river bubbled over his feet. He was the first human being I had encountered in this land. Or human-shaped being, perhaps. I approached him with trepidation.

I couldn't see him clearly, so I took a chance and called out, "Hello!"

through that cottony veil. But there was no reply. He just adjusted his posture slightly. I could see his dark silhouette shift in the mist. Perhaps my voice hadn't reached him. The sound of the river might have blotted it out. Or the air in these parts might not carry sound very well.

"Hello!" I said again, moving somewhat closer. In a louder voice this time. Still, he didn't speak. All I could hear was the unbroken rush of water. Perhaps he couldn't understand what I was saying.

"I can hear you. And I do understand," he said, as if reading my mind. His voice was deep and low, befitting his height. But it was also flat, utterly devoid of feeling. Just as the river was devoid of odor and taste.

54

ETERNITY IS A VERY LONG TIME

The tall man standing before me had no face. He did have a head, of course. It sat on his shoulders in a normal way. But the head lacked a face. Where a face should have been was blank. A milky blankness, like pale smoke. His voice emerged from within that emptiness like wind from a deep cavern.

The man was wearing what looked like a dark raincoat. The coat ended just short of the ground, so I could see the tips of his boots peeking out. Its buttons were fastened up to his neck. It was as if there was a storm on the horizon, and he had dressed for it.

I stood there, rooted to the spot, unable to speak. From a distance, he had reminded me of the man with the white Subaru Forester, or Tomohiko Amada the night he had visited my studio. Or again, the young man who slayed the Commendatore with his sword in *Killing Commendatore*. All were similarly tall. A closer look, however, told me he was none of them. He was just the *faceless man*. A broad-brimmed black hat was pulled low over his eyes. The brim half concealed the milky emptiness.

"I can hear you. And I do understand," he repeated. I didn't see his lips move, of course. He had none.

"Is this the boat landing?" I asked.

"Yes," the faceless man replied. "This is the boat landing. Only from here can one cross the river."

"I must travel to the other side."

"As must all."

"Do many come?"

The man did not reply. My question was sucked into the void. There followed an interminable silence.

"What is on the other side?" I asked. The white mist over the river concealed the far shore.

I could feel the faceless man studying my face from within the emptiness. "What is on the other side depends on what you are seeking. It is different for everyone."

"I am trying to locate the whereabouts of a young girl named Mariye Akikawa."

"So that is what you seek on the other side, correct?"

"Yes. That is what I seek. That is why I have come."

"And how was it, then, that you were able to find the entrance?"

"I killed an Idea that had taken the form of the Commendatore. I killed him with a carving knife in a nursing home in Izu Kogen. I did so with his permission. His death summoned Long Face, the Metaphor who opened the hole to the underground passageway. I forced him to let me in."

The man fixed his empty countenance on me for some time. He didn't speak. Had he understood me or not? I couldn't tell.

"Was there blood?"

"A great deal," I answered.

"Actual blood, I take it."

"So it seemed."

"Look at your hands."

I looked. But no trace of blood remained. Perhaps it had been washed away when I drank from the river. There ought to have been a lot, though.

"No matter," the faceless man said. "I have a boat, and I will ferry you across. But there is one condition."

I waited to be told what that might be.

"You must pay me an appropriate fee. That is the rule."

"And if I can't pay, am I unable to cross to the far shore?"

"Yes. You would have to remain here for eternity. The river is cold and deep, and the current is strong. And eternity is a very long time. That is no figure of speech, I assure you."

"But I have nothing to pay you with."

"Show me what is in your pockets," the faceless man said, in a quiet voice.

I emptied my jacket and pants pockets. My wallet containing slightly less than 20,000 yen. My credit card, my bank card, my driver's license, and a gas station discount coupon. My key ring with three keys on it. A cream-colored handkerchief and a disposable ballpoint pen. Five or six coins. And that was it. Minus the flashlight, of course.

The faceless man shook his head. "I'm sorry, but I see nothing that can pay for your passage. Money has no meaning here. Don't you have something else?"

I had nothing more in my possession. A cheap watch was on my left wrist, but time had no value here either.

"If you give me paper, I can portray your likeness. My skill as a painter is the only other thing I carry with me."

The faceless man laughed. At least I think he did. A faint trill echoed in the emptiness.

"In the first place, I have no face. How can you sketch the likeness of a man with no face? Can you draw a void?"

"I am a professional," I said. "I have no need of a face to draw your portrait."

I wasn't at all sure I could pull it off. But I figured it was worth a shot.

"I would be most interested to see what you come up with," the faceless man said. "Unfortunately there is no paper in these parts."

I looked down at the ground. Perhaps I could scratch something on its surface with a stick. But it was solid rock. I shook my head.

"Are you certain that is all you carry with you?"

I carefully searched a second time. The pockets of my leather jacket were empty. Completely. I did find something small tucked in the bottom of one of my jeans pockets, though. A tiny plastic penguin. Menshiki had picked it up from the floor of the pit and given it to me. It had an even tinier strap, which Mariye had used to fasten it to her cell phone. It was her lucky charm. Somehow, it had fallen into the pit.

"Show me what is in your hand," the faceless man said.

I opened my hand, revealing the figurine.

The faceless man stared at it with empty eyes.

"This will do," he said after a moment. "I will accept this as payment."

Should I hand it over or not? It was Mariye's precious lucky charm, after all. It wasn't mine. Could I just give it away? What if something bad happened to her as a result?

But I had no choice. If I failed to turn it over, I would never reach the opposite shore, and if I didn't reach the shore, then I would never find Mariye. The Commendatore's death would have been in vain.

"I will give you the penguin as my fare of passage," I said. "Please take me to the other side of the river."

The faceless man nodded. "The day may come when you can draw my likeness," he said. "If that day arrives, I will return the penguin to you."

The faceless man strode to the end of the wooden jetty and stepped down into the small boat moored there. It was a rectangular vessel, shaped like a pastry box. Barely six feet long and narrow, and made of heavy wooden boards. I doubted it could carry many passengers at a time. There was a thick mast in the middle of the boat, at the top of which stood a metal ring about four inches in diameter. A sturdy rope was threaded through that ring. The rope stretched across the river to the far shore in a straight line—it barely sagged at all. It appeared that the boat ran back and forth along that rope, which kept it from being swept away by the swift current. The boat looked as if it had been in use for ages. It had no visible means of propulsion, or even a proper prow. It was just a shallow wooden box floating on the water.

I followed the faceless man into the boat and seated myself on the horizontal plank that ran from side to side. He leaned against the thick mast with his eyes closed, as if waiting for something. Neither of us spoke. After a few minutes, as if it had made up its own mind, the boat began its slow departure. I had no idea what was propelling us, but we were moving silently toward the far shore. There was no sound of an engine, nor of any other machinery. All I could hear was the steady slapping of water against the hull. We moved at roughly the pace of someone walking. Our boat was dashed from side to side by the current, but the sturdy rope prevented us from being washed downstream. It was just as the faceless man had said—no one could cross the river without a boat. He leaned calmly against the mast, unperturbed even when it felt like our craft might capsize.

"Will I be able to find Mariye Akikawa when we reach the other side?" I asked, when we were about halfway across.

"I am here to ferry you across the river," the faceless man said. "To help you navigate the interstice between presence and absence. After that, it's up to you—my job is done."

Not long after, we hit the jetty on the far shore with a small bump. The faceless man's posture, however, did not change. He leaned against the mast, as if confirming some sort of internal process. When that was done, he expelled a great, empty breath and stepped up onto the jetty. I followed him out of the boat. The jetty and the winch-like mechanism attached to it were the same as those on the opposite bank. So similar, in fact, it felt as if we had made a round-trip, and ended back where we started. That feeling disappeared, however, the moment I stepped onshore. For the ground on this side was normal earth, not solid rock.

"You must proceed alone from here," the faceless man announced.

"But I don't know which path to take. Or which direction to go."

"Such things are inconsequential here," came the rumble from the milky void. "You have drunk from the river, have you not? Now each of your actions will generate an equivalent response, in accordance with the principle of connectivity. Such is the place you have come to."

With these words, the faceless man adjusted his wide-brimmed hat, turned on his heel, and walked back to his boat. Once he was aboard, it returned as it had come, following the rope to the other side. Slow and sure, like a well-trained animal. The faceless man and the boat were one as they vanished into the mist.

I decided to leave the jetty behind and walk downstream along the bank. I could have gone in any direction, but it seemed best to follow the river. That way, there was water to drink when I got thirsty. A short while later, I turned to look back at the jetty, but it was already cloaked in white mist. As though it had never existed.

The farther I walked, the wider the river became, and the gentler the current. There were no more whitecaps, and the sound of rushing water had practically disappeared. Why hadn't they put the pier here, instead of where the flow was so swift? True, the distance would have been greater, but the crossing would have been so much easier where the water was calm. All the same, this world probably operated according to its own principles, its own way of thinking. Even greater danger might lurk beneath the placid surface.

I searched my pockets. Sure enough, the penguin was gone. That the protective charm had been lost (most likely for all eternity) was hardly reassuring. Perhaps I had made the wrong choice. Yet what other option did I have? I could only hope Mariye would be all right without it. At this point, hope was all I had.

I made my way along the riverbank, the flashlight from Tomohiko Amada's bedside in one hand. I kept it turned off. This dusky world was not so dim as to require a light. I could see where I was walking, and for about twelve or fifteen feet ahead. The river flowed to my left, slow and silent. Once in a while, I could glimpse the far shore through the haze.

The farther on I pushed, the more the ground beneath my feet came to resemble a path. Not a well-defined path, yet something that fulfilled the function of a path. There were vague signs that people had passed this way before. Gradually, the path was leading me away from the river. At a certain point, I drew up short. Should I stick to the river? Or allow this *presumed path* to take me in another direction?

After some thought, I elected to follow the path and leave the river behind. I had a feeling it would lead me somewhere. *Now each of your actions will generate an equivalent response, in accordance with the principle of connectivity*, the ferryman had said. This path could well be an example. I decided to follow the plausible suggestion, if that's what it was, that had been presented to me.

The farther I moved from the river, the more the path turned uphill. Eventually, I realized I could no longer hear the rush of water. The slope was easy and the path almost straight, so my steps fell into a steady rhythm. The mist was melting away, but the light remained pale and somewhat opaque. There was no way to tell what lay ahead. I kept my eyes on my feet, and my breathing regular and systematic.

How long had I been walking? I had lost all sense of time. All sense of direction, too. And the thoughts running through my head were distracting me. I had so much to figure out, yet my thoughts had become so terribly fragmented. When I tried to focus on one thought, a new thought would appear to gulp it down, and my mind would careen in the wrong direction. Each time, I lost track of what I had just been thinking about.

I was so distracted, in fact, that I almost bumped right into *that*. I tripped on something, and raised my eyes as I was regaining my balance. In that instant, the air around me was transformed—I could feel it on my skin. I snapped back to reality. An enormous black mass loomed directly ahead. My jaw dropped in surprise. What was it? It took a moment to register that a huge forest stood in my path. It had materialized without warning in a terrain that, until that point, had had no vegetation, not a single leaf or blade of grass. No mystery, then, why I was so shocked.

It was a forest—no question there. A tangle of branches with thick leaves that formed a solid wall. Within the forest was darkness. More accurate than forest, perhaps, might have been "sea of trees." I stood before it and listened, but could hear nothing. No birdsongs, no branches rustling in the wind. A complete absence of sound.

I was afraid to step inside the forest. Instinctively. The trees were too dense, the darkness inside too deep. I had no way to gauge the scale, or how far the path would continue. It might well split into a labyrinth of side trails. If I got lost in that maze, my chances of escaping were practically zero. Still, I had no other real options. The path I had chosen headed straight into the forest (or, more accurately, was sucked into it, like train tracks are sucked into a tunnel). It made no sense, having come this far, to turn around and head back to the river. Who knows, the river might not even be there anymore. No, I had made my choice, and now I had to live with it. I would press on, at whatever cost.

Mustering my courage, I stepped into the trees. It was impossible to tell the time of day—it could have been dawn, or midday, or evening. The half-light never seemed to vary, no matter how much time passed. Then again, time might not exist in this world. In which case, this dusk could persist, day in and day out, forever.

Sure enough, it was dark inside. The layered branches above my head blocked out almost all light. Yet I left my flashlight off. Once my eyes adjusted, I could see enough to walk, and I didn't want to waste the batteries. I plunged through the forest, trying hard to empty my mind. Any thoughts would likely lead me to an even darker place. The path continued its gentle rise. All I could hear were my own footsteps, and those were more and more faint, as if their sound was slowly being sucked away. I hoped my thirst wouldn't return. By this time, the river would be far indeed. No chance of heading back for a drink, however thirsty I got.

How long did I walk? The forest was deep and dark, the view unchanging. The light never changed, either. My footsteps were all I could hear, and barely at that. The air was tasteless and odorless, as always. Thick trees walled both sides of the path. I could see nothing else. Did anything live here? Perhaps not. I had noticed no birds or insects.

Yet I could feel something watching me—the sensation was clear and very unpleasant. Sharp eyes were being trained in my direction from behind the wall of foliage. Every movement I made was under surveillance. My skin burned, as if under a magnifying glass in the sun. *What was I doing there?* they demanded. This was their domain, and I was a lone invader. Yet I never actually saw any of those eyes. I may have imagined them. Fear and suspicion can fashion eyes in the dark.

Then again, Mariye had felt Menshiki's eyes on her from across a valley, and through a telescope, no less. She had guessed that someone was keeping constant watch on her. And she was right. Those eyes were no fantasy.

Nevertheless, I decided to dismiss the eyes I felt scrutinizing me. There was no way that they were real. They had to be hallucinations, created by my fears. I needed to think that way. I had to make it through the great forest (though its actual size was a mystery). While retaining as much of my sanity as possible.

Luckily, there were no side trails. Thus I wasn't forced to make a choice that might take me into a maze that led nowhere. No thorny thickets blocked my way. All I had to do was push forward along a single path.

I couldn't tell how long I had been walking, yet I didn't feel especially tired. Perhaps I was under too much stress to register fatigue.

Just when my legs were getting a little heavy, however, I spied a yellow point of light in the distance. At first, I thought it was a firefly. But I was mistaken. The light didn't move, or flicker on and off. Its fixed position suggested that it was human-made. The farther I went, little by little, the light grew larger and brighter. There could be no doubt. *I was approaching something.*

Was it something good, or something bad? Would it help or harm me? Whichever, I was out of options. For better or for worse, I had to find out what that light was. If I didn't have the guts to do that, I never should have embarked on this journey in the first place. Step by step, I advanced toward the light.

Then, just as suddenly as it had appeared before me, the forest ended. The trees that had lined the path on both sides vanished, and before I knew it, I had stepped out into a broad clearing. The clearing was the shape of a half-moon, and perfectly level. Now I could see the sky once more, and view my surroundings in that dusky light. Directly across from me rose a sheer cliff, and at the base of that cliff was the open mouth of a dark cave. The yellow light I had been following streamed directly from that opening.

The gloomy sea of trees was behind me, the towering cliff (much too steep for me to climb) straight ahead. The mouth of the cave opened directly before me. I looked up at the sky a second time, then around at my surroundings. Nothing looked like a path. My next move had to be to enter the cave—there was no alternative. Before going in, I took several deep breaths, to brace myself. By moving forward, I would generate a new reality in accordance with the principle of connectivity. So the faceless man had said. I would navigate the interstice between presence and absence. I could only entrust myself to his words.

Warily, I stepped into the cave. Then it struck me—*I had been here before*. I knew this cave by sight. The air inside was familiar, too. Memories came flooding back. The wind cave on Mt. Fuji. The cave where our young uncle had taken Komichi and me during our summer break, back when we were kids. She had slipped into a narrow side tunnel and disappeared for a long while. I had been scared to death that she was gone for good. Had she been sucked into an underground maze for all eternity?

Eternity is a very long time, the faceless man had said.

I walked slowly through the cave toward the yellow light, deadening my footsteps and trying to quiet my pounding heart. I rounded a corner, and there it was: the source of the light. An old lantern with a black metal rim, the sort that coal miners once carried, hanging on a thick nail driven into the stone wall. A fat candle burned inside the lantern.

Lantern, I thought. The word had come up not long before. It was part of the name of the anti-Nazi underground student organization that Tomohiko Amada was presumed to have joined. Things seemed to be converging.

A woman was standing beneath the lantern. I didn't see her at first because she was so tiny. Less than two feet tall. Her black hair was coiled atop her head in a neat bun, and she wore a white gown from some ancient time. Its elegance was apparent at a glance. Another character lifted from *Killing Commendatore*. The beautiful maiden who looks on in horror, her hand over her mouth, as the Commendatore is slain. In Mozart's *Don Giovanni,* she is Donna Anna. The daughter of the Commendatore.

Magnified by the light of the lantern, her sharp black shadow trembled on the wall of the cave.

"I have been awaiting you," the miniature Donna Anna said.

55

A CLEAR CONTRAVENTION OF BASIC PRINCIPLES

"I have been awaiting you," said Donna Anna. She was tiny, but her voice was clear and bright.

Nothing could have surprised me by that point. It even seemed natural for her to be there waiting for me. She was a beautiful woman, with an innate elegance, and the way she spoke had a majestic ring. She might be only two feet tall, but she clearly had that special something that could captivate a man.

"I will be your guide," she said to me. "Please be so kind as to take that lantern."

I unhooked the lantern from the wall. I didn't know who had put it there, so far beyond her reach. Its circular metal handle allowed it to be hung on a nail or carried by hand.

"You were waiting for me?" I asked.

"Yes," she said. "For a very long time."

Could she be another form of Metaphor? I hesitated to pose such a bold question.

"Do you live in these parts?"

"Live here?" she said, casting a dubious glance in my direction. "No, I am *here* to meet you. And I'm afraid I don't understand what you mean by 'these parts.'"

I gave up asking questions after that. She was Donna Anna, and she had been waiting for me.

She wore the same sort of ancient garb as the Commendatore. In her case, a white garment, most likely made of fine silk. Draped in layers over the top half of her body, with loose-fitting pantaloons below. Though her shape was therefore hidden, I guessed she was slender but strong. Her small black shoes were fashioned of leather of some kind.

"Then let us commence," Donna Anna said to me. "Not much time remains. The path is narrowing as we speak. Please follow me. And be so good as to hold the lantern."

I followed in her wake, holding the lantern above her head. She walked toward the back of the cave with quick, practiced steps. The candle's flame fluttered as we moved, casting a dancing mosaic of shadows on the pitted walls.

"This looks like a wind cave on Mt. Fuji that I once visited," I said. "Is that possible?"

"All that is here *looks like* something," Donna Anna declaimed without turning around. As though she were addressing the darkness ahead.

"Do you mean to say nothing here is the real thing?"

"No one can tell what is or is not the real thing," she stated flatly. "All that we see is a product of connectivity. Light here is a metaphor for shadow, shadow a metaphor for light. You know this already, I believe."

I didn't think I knew, at least not all that well, but I refrained from inquiring further. That could only lead to more knotty abstractions.

The cave grew narrower the farther back we went. The roof became lower too, so that I had to stoop as I walked. Just as I had done in the Mt. Fuji wind cave. Finally, Donna Anna drew to a halt and turned to face me. Her small, flashing eyes stared up into mine.

"I can guide you this far. Now you must take the lead. I will follow, but only to a certain point. After that, you are on your own."

Take the lead? I shook my head in disbelief—from what I could see, we had reached the very back of the cave. A dark stone wall blocked our way. I passed the lantern across its face. But it appeared that we had hit a dead end.

"It seems we can't go any farther," I said.

"Please look again. There should be an opening in the corner to your left," Donna Anna said.

I shone the lantern on that section of the cave wall once more. When I stuck my head out and looked more closely, I could make out a dark depression on the far side of a large boulder. I squeezed myself between the wall and the boulder to inspect it. It certainly did appear to be an opening. I remembered my sister slipping into an even narrower crack.

I turned back to Donna Anna.

"You must enter there," the two-foot-tall woman said.

I looked at her lovely face, wondering what to say. On the wall, her elongated shadow flickered in the lantern's yellow light.

"I am fully aware," she said, "that you have been terrified of small, dark places all your life. In such places, you can no longer breathe normally. I am correct, am I not? Nevertheless, you must force yourself to enter. Only in such a manner can you grasp that which you seek."

"Where does this opening lead?"

"I do not know. The destination is something you yourself must determine by following your own heart."

"But fear is in my heart as well," I said. "That's what worries me. That my fear will distort what I see and push me in the wrong direction."

"Once again, it is you who determines the path. You are the one who chose the proper route to reach this world. You paid a great price for that, and have crossed the river by boat. You cannot turn back now."

I looked again at the opening. I shuddered to think I would have to crawl into that dark, cramped tunnel. Yet that was what I had to do. She was right—I couldn't turn back now. I placed the lantern on the ground and took the flashlight from my pocket. A lantern would be much too cumbersome in that tiny space.

"Believe in yourself," Donna Anna said, her voice small but penetrating. "You have drunk from the river, have you not?"

"Yes, I was very thirsty."

"It is good that you did so," Donna Anna said. "That river flows along the interstice between presence and absence. It is filled with hidden possibilities that only the finest metaphors can bring to the surface. Just as a great poet can use one scene to bring another new, unknown vista into view. It should be obvious, but the best metaphors make the best poems. Take good care not to avert your eyes from the new, unknown vistas you will encounter."

Tomohiko Amada's *Killing Commendatore* might be seen as one such "unknown vista." Like a great poem, the painting was a perfect metaphor, one that launched a new reality into the world.

I switched on the flashlight and checked its beam. It was bright and unwavering. The batteries should last for some time yet. I removed my leather jacket. It was too bulky to fit into such a tight space. That left me wearing a light sweater and jeans. The cave wasn't especially cold, but neither was it all that warm.

Bracing myself, I crouched until I was almost on all fours and squeezed headfirst into the opening. Inside I found what appeared to be a tunnel sunk into solid rock. It was smooth to the touch, as if worn by water over the course of many years. There were almost no jagged or protruding edges. As a result, despite its narrowness, I was able to progress more easily than I had expected. The rock was cool and slightly damp. I inched forward on my stomach like a worm, the flashlight illuminating my way. I figured that the tunnel must have functioned as a waterway at some point in the past.

The tunnel was about two feet high and three feet across. Crawling was the only option. It looked like it would go on forever, a dark, natural pipe that expanded and contracted by small degrees. Sometimes it curved to the side. At other times it sloped up or down. Thankfully, though, there were no abrupt rises or falls. Then it hit me. If this was an underground conduit, water could flood the tunnel at any moment, and I would surely drown. My legs stopped moving, paralyzed by fear.

I wanted to turn around and go back the way I had come. But it was impossible to reverse course in such a cramped space. The tunnel seemed to have grown even narrower. Crawling backward to where I had begun was out of the question. Terror engulfed me. I was literally nailed to the spot. I couldn't move forward, and I couldn't retreat. Every cell in my body cried out for fresh air. Forsaken by light, I felt powerless and alone.

"Do not stop. You must push on." Donna Anna's command was irrefutable. I couldn't tell if I was hearing things or if she was really behind me, urging me on.

"I can't move," I gasped, squeezing out the words. "And I can't breathe."

"Make fast your heart," said Donna Anna. "Do not let it flounder. Should that happen, you will surely fall prey to a Double Metaphor."

"What are Double Metaphors?" I asked.

"You should know the answer to that already."

"I should know?"

"That is because they are within you," said Donna Anna. "They grab hold of your true thoughts and feelings and devour them one after another, fattening themselves. That is what Double Metaphors are. They have been dwelling in the depths of your psyche since ancient times."

Unbidden, the man with the white Subaru Forester entered my mind. I didn't want him there. But there was no way around it. It was he who had pushed me to throttle that young woman, forcing me to look into the darkness of my own heart. He had reappeared more than once, to make sure I would remember that darkness.

I know where you were and what you were doing, he was announcing to me. Of course he knew everything. Because he lived inside me.

My heart was in chaos. I closed my eyes and tried to anchor it, to hold it in one place. I ground my teeth with the effort. But how should I go about securing my heart? Where was its true location, anyway? I looked within myself, searching one place after another. But it didn't turn up. Where could it be?

"Your true heart lives in your memory. It is nourished by the images it contains—that's how it lives," a woman said. This time, however, it was not Donna Anna speaking. It was Komi. My sister, dead at age twelve.

"Search your memory," said that dear voice. "Find something concrete. Something you can touch."

"Komi?" I said.

There was no answer.

"Komi, where are you?" I said.

Still no reply.

There in the dark, I searched my memory. Like rummaging through an old duffel bag. But it seemed to have been emptied. I couldn't even recall exactly what memory was.

"Turn off your light and listen to the wind," Komi said.

I switched off the flashlight. But I couldn't hear the wind, though

I tried. All I could make out was the restless pounding of my heart, a screen door banging in a gale.

"Listen to the wind," Komi repeated.

Once again, I held my breath and focused. This time, I could hear, lying beyond my heartbeat, a faint humming. A wind seemed to be blowing somewhere far away. A wisp of a breeze brushed my face. Air was entering the tunnel ahead. Air I could smell. The unmistakable odor of damp soil. The first odor I had encountered since setting foot in this Land of Metaphor. The tunnel was leading somewhere. To a place I could smell. In short, to the real world.

"All right then, on you go," said Donna Anna. "There isn't much time left."

With my flashlight turned off, I crawled on into the blackness. As I moved forward, I tried to draw even the slightest whiff of that real air into my lungs.

"Komi?" I asked again.

There was no answer.

I ransacked my store of memories. Komi and I had raised a pet cat. A smart black tomcat. We named it Koyasu, though why we gave it that name escapes me. Komi had picked it up as a kitten on her way home from school. One day, however, it disappeared. We scoured our neighborhood looking for it. We stopped countless people and showed them Koyasu's photograph. But in the end the cat never turned up.

I crawled on, the image of the black cat vivid in my mind. I tried to imagine my sister and me together, searching for it. I strained my eyes to catch a glimpse of the cat at the end of the dark tunnel. I pricked my ears to hear its mewing. The black cat was solid and concrete, something I could touch. I could feel its fur, its warmth, the firmness of its body—even hear it purr—as if it were yesterday.

"That's right," Komi said. "Just keep remembering like that."

I know where you were and what you were doing, the man with the white Subaru Forester called out of nowhere. He wore a black leather jacket and a golf cap with the Yonex logo. His voice was hoarse from the sea wind. Caught by surprise, I recoiled in fear.

I tried to find my memories of the cat. To draw the fragrance of damp earth into my lungs. I seemed to recall that smell from somewhere. From a time not so far away. But I couldn't remember, try as I might. Where had it been? As I struggled to recall, once again, my memories began to fade away.

Strangle me with this, the girl had said. Her pink tongue peeked out at me from between her lips. The belt of her bathrobe lay beside her pillow, ready to be used. Her pubic hair glistened like grass in the rain.

"Come on," Komi urged me. "Call up a favorite memory. Hurry!"

I tried to bring back the black cat. But Koyasu was gone. Why couldn't I remember him? Perhaps the darkness had snatched him away while I was distracted. Its power had devoured him. I had to come up with something else, and fast. I had the horrid sense that the tunnel was tightening around me. It seemed alive. *There is not much time*, Donna Anna had said. Cold sweat trickled from my armpits.

"Come on now, remember something," Komi's voice said behind me. "Something you can physically touch. Something you can draw."

Like a drowning man clutching a buoy, I latched onto my old Peugeot 205. My little French car. I remembered the feeling of the steering wheel as I toured northeastern Japan and Hokkaido. It felt like ages ago, yet I could still hear the rattle of that primitive four-cylinder engine, and the way the clutch growled when I shifted from second into third. For a month and a half, the car had been my constant comrade, my only friend. Now it was probably sitting in a scrap yard somewhere.

The tunnel was definitely narrowing. My head kept banging against the roof. I reached for the flashlight.

"Do not turn on the light," Donna Anna commanded.

"But I can't see where I'm going."

"You must not see," she said. *"Not with your eyes."*

"The hole is closing in. If I go on I won't be able to move."

There was no answer.

"I can't go any farther," I said. "What should I do?"

Again no answer.

I could no longer hear Donna Anna and Komi. I sensed they were gone. All that remained was a deep silence.

The tunnel continued to shrink, making it even harder for me to advance. Panic was setting in. My limbs felt paralyzed—just drawing a breath was growing difficult. A voice whispered in my ear. *You are trapped*, it said. *This is your coffin. You cannot move forward. You cannot move backward. You will lie buried here forever. Forsaken by humanity, in this dark and narrow tomb.*

I sensed something approaching from behind. A flattish thing, crawling toward me through the dark. It wasn't Donna Anna, nor was it Komi. In fact, it wasn't human. I could hear the scraping of its many feet and its ragged breathing. It stopped when it reached me. There followed a few moments of silence. It seemed to be holding its breath, planning its next move. Then something cold and slimy touched my bare ankle. The end of a long tentacle, it seemed. Sheer terror coursed up my back.

Could this be a Double Metaphor? That which stemmed from the darkness within me?

I know where you were and what you were doing.

I couldn't recall a thing. Not the black cat, not the Peugeot 205, not the Commendatore—everything was gone. My memory had been wiped clean a second time.

I squirmed and twisted, frantically trying to escape the tentacle. The tunnel had contracted even farther—I could barely move. I was trying to force myself into a space smaller than my body. That was a clear contravention of basic principles. It didn't take a genius to figure out it was physically impossible.

Nevertheless, I kept on thrusting, pushing myself forward. As Donna Anna had said, this was the path I had chosen, and it was too late to choose another. The Commendatore had died to make my quest possible. I had stabbed him with my own hands. His body had sunk in a pool of blood. I couldn't allow him to die for nothing. And the owner of that clammy tentacle was trying to get me in its grips.

Rallying my spirits, I pressed on. I could feel my sweater unravel as it caught and tore on the rock. I awkwardly squirmed ahead, loosening my joints like an escape artist slipping his bonds. My pace was no faster than that of a caterpillar. The narrow tunnel was squeezing me like a giant vise. My bones and muscles screamed. The slimy tentacle slithered farther up my ankle. Soon it would cover me, as I lay there in the impenetrable dark, unable to move. I would no longer be the person I was.

Jettisoning all reason, I mustered what strength I had left and forced myself into the ever-narrowing space. Every part of my body shrieked in pain. Yet I had to push forward, whatever the consequences. Even if I had to dislocate every joint. However agonizing that would be. For everything around me was the product of connectivity. Nothing was absolute. Pain was a metaphor. The tentacle clutching my leg was a metaphor. All was relative. Light was shadow, shadow was light. I had no choice but to believe. What else could I do?

The tunnel ended without warning, spitting me out like a clump of grass from a clogged drainpipe. I flew through the air, utterly defenseless. There was no time to think. I must have fallen at least six feet before I hit the ground. Luckily, it wasn't solid rock, but relatively soft earth. I curled and rolled as I fell, tucking in my head to protect it from the impact. A judo move, done without thinking. I whacked my shoulder and hip on landing, but I barely felt it.

Darkness surrounded me. And my flashlight was gone. I seemed to have dropped it when I tumbled out. I remained on all fours, not moving. I couldn't see anything. I couldn't think anything. I was only aware, and barely at that, of a growing pain in my joints. Every tendon, every bone wailed in protest at what it had been put through during my escape.

Yes—I had escaped that dreadful tunnel! The realization hit me at last. I could still feel the eerie tentacle sliding over my ankle. I was grateful to have eluded that thing, whatever it was.

But then, where was I now?

There was no breeze. But there was smell. The odor I had caught a whiff of in the tunnel was everywhere. I couldn't recall where I had encountered it before. Nevertheless, this place was dead quiet. Not a sound anywhere.

I needed to find my flashlight. I carefully searched the ground where I had fallen. On all fours, in a widening circle. The earth was moist. I was scared that I might touch something creepy in the dark, but there was nothing, not even a pebble. Just ground so perfectly flat it must have been leveled by human hands.

After a long search, I finally found the flashlight lying about three feet from where I had landed. The moment my hand touched its plastic casing was one of the happiest of my life.

But I didn't switch it on right away. Instead, I closed my eyes and took a number of deep breaths. As if I were patiently unraveling a stubborn knot. My breathing slowed. My heartbeat did, too, and my muscles began to return to normal. I slowly exhaled the last deep breath and switched on the flashlight. Its yellow light raced through the darkness. But I couldn't look yet. My eyes had grown too used to the dark—the tiniest light made my head split with pain.

I shielded my eyes with one hand until I could open my fingers enough to peer through the cracks. From what I could see, I had landed on the floor of a circular-shaped room. A room of modest size, with walls of stone. I shone the flashlight above my head. The room had a ceiling. No, not exactly that. Something more like a lid. No light seeped through.

I realized where I was: in the pit in the woods, behind the little shrine. I had crawled into the tunnel in Donna Anna's cave and tumbled out onto the floor of this stone chamber. I was in a real pit in the real world. I had no idea how that could have happened. But it had. I was back at the beginning, so to speak. But why was there no light? The lid was made of wooden boards. There were cracks between those boards, through which some light should enter. Yet none did.

I was stumped.

At least I knew where I was. The smell was a dead giveaway. Why had it taken me so long to figure out? I carefully examined my surroundings with my flashlight. The metal ladder that should have been standing there was gone. Someone must have pulled it out and carted it off. Which meant there was no means of escape.

What I found strange—it should have been strange, I guess—was that I could find no trace of the opening, no matter how hard I looked. I had exited the narrow tunnel and fallen onto the floor of this pit. Like a newborn baby pushed out in midair. Yet I couldn't find the aperture. It was as if it had closed after it spit me out.

Eventually, the flashlight's beam illuminated an object on the ground. Something I recognized. It was the old bell the Commendatore had rung—hearing it had led me to discover the pit. Everything had begun with this bell. I had left it on the shelf in the studio—then at some point it had vanished. I picked it up and examined it under the flashlight. It had an old wooden handle. There could be no doubt—it was *that bell.*

I stared at it for some time, trying to understand. Had someone brought it back? Had it returned under its own power? The Commendatore had told me the bell belonged to the pit. What did that mean—belonged to the pit? But I was too tired to figure out the principles that might explain what was taking place. And there was no pillar of logic I could lean on.

I sat down, back against the stone wall, and switched off the flashlight. I had to figure out how to escape from this pit. I didn't need light for that. And it was important to conserve the batteries.

So what should I do now?

56

IT APPEARS THAT SEVERAL BLANKS NEED FILLING IN

A number of things made no sense. Most troubling of all was the total absence of light. Someone had sealed the pit's opening. But who would do such a thing, and why?

I prayed that someone (whoever it was) hadn't piled boulders on top of the lid, returning it to how it had been in the beginning. That would mean my chances of getting out were practically zero.

A thought struck me—I clicked on the flashlight and checked my watch. It read 4:32. The second hand was circling the face, doing its job. Time was passing, no doubt about it. At least I was back where time flowed at a set pace, and in a single direction.

Yet what was time, when you got right down to it? We measured its passage with the hands of a clock for convenience's sake. But was that appropriate? Did time really flow in such a steady and linear way? Couldn't this be a mistaken way of thinking, an error of major proportions?

I clicked off the flashlight and, with a long sigh, returned to absolute darkness. Enough pondering time. Enough pondering space. Thinking about stuff like that led nowhere. It only added to my stress. I had to think about things that were concrete, things I could see and touch.

So I thought about Yuzu. She was certainly something I could see with my eyes and touch with my hands (if I was ever given that opportunity again). Now she was pregnant. This coming January, the child—not my child, but that of some other man—would be born. That situation continued without my involvement, in a place far removed from me. A new life with which I had no connection would enter this world. Yuzu had asked nothing of me. So why was she refusing to marry the father? I couldn't figure it out. If she planned to be a single mother, odds were she'd have to quit her job at the architectural firm. I doubted that a small business like that could extend a lengthy maternity leave to a new mother.

I could find no convincing answers to these questions, though I tried. I was stumped. And the darkness made me feel even more powerless.

If I ever got out of this pit, I would put aside my hesitations and go see Yuzu. No question about it, I was hurt when she left me for someone else. It angered me, too (although it took me a very long time to realize that). But why carry around my resentments for the rest of my life? I would go meet her and we could talk things out. I needed to know, from Yuzu herself, what she was thinking, and what she wanted. Before it was too late. Once I made that decision, I felt a little easier. If she wanted to be friends, well, maybe I could give it a shot. It wasn't beyond the realm of possibility, at least. Perhaps we could resolve things that way. If I managed to get out of the pit, that is.

After this I fell asleep. I had shed my leather jacket before entering the tunnel (what fate lay in store for that jacket of mine?), and the cold was starting to get to me. The thin sweater I had on over my T-shirt had been so shredded by the walls of the tunnel that it was a sweater in name only. Moreover, I had returned to the real world from the Land of Metaphor. In other words, I was back where time and temperature played their proper roles. Yet my need for sleep won out. I drifted off, sitting there on the ground, leaning against the hard stone wall. It was a pure sleep, free of dream or deception. A solitary sleep beyond anyone's reach, like the Spanish gold resting on the floor of the Irish Sea.

It was still pitch black when I woke up. I couldn't see my finger when I waved it in front of my face. The darkness blotted out the line between sleep and wakefulness as well. Where did one end and the other begin, and which side was I on? I dragged out my bag of memories and began flipping through them, as if counting a stack of gold coins: the black cat that had been our pet; my old Peugeot 205; Menshiki's white mansion; the record *Der Rosenkavalier;* the plastic penguin. I was able to call up memories of each, in great detail. My mind was working okay—the Double Metaphor hadn't devoured it. It's just that I had been in total darkness for so long that I was having trouble drawing a line between the world of sleep and the waking world.

I switched on the flashlight, covered it with my hand, and read my watch in the light leaking between my fingers: 1:18. Last time I looked, it was 4:32. Could I have been sleeping in such an uncomfortable position for nine hours? That was hard to believe. If that were true, I should be a lot stiffer. It seemed more reasonable to assume that, unbeknownst to me, time had traveled backward three hours. But I couldn't be certain either way. Being immersed in the dark for so long had obliterated my sense of time.

In any case, the cold had grown more penetrating. And I had to pee. Badly. Resigning myself, I shuffled to the other side of the pit and let it all out. It was a long pee that the ground quickly absorbed. A faint smell of ammonia lingered, but only for a moment. Once the need to pee had been taken care of, hunger stepped in to take its place. By slow and steady degrees, it seemed, my body was readapting to the real world. Perhaps the effects of the water I had drunk from the River of Metaphor were wearing off.

I had to get out of the pit as soon as possible. I felt that more urgently now. If I didn't, it wouldn't take long to starve to death. Human beings can only sustain life if provided with food and water—that was a basic rule of the real world. And my present location had neither. All I had was air (though the lid was closed, air seemed to be leaking in from somewhere). Air, love, and ideals were important, no argument there, but you couldn't survive on them alone.

I pulled myself off the ground and attempted to scale the pit's smooth stone wall. I tried from a number of spots, but, as I expected, it was a waste of energy. The wall was less than nine feet high, but it was straight up and down, with nothing at all to grab onto. It would take superhuman ability to climb, and even if I reached the top, there was still that heavy lid to deal with. I would need a solid foothold to push that aside.

I sat back down, resigned. Only one option presented itself. I could ring the bell. As the Commendatore had done. But there was one big difference between the Commendatore and me. He was an Idea, while

I was a flesh-and-blood human being. An Idea never felt hunger, while I did. An Idea wouldn't starve to death, whereas I would, relatively quickly. The Commendatore could ring the bell for a hundred years (though the concept of time was foreign to him) and not get tired, while my limit without food and water was probably three or four days. After that, I wouldn't have the strength, though the bell was light.

So I began ringing the bell there in the dark. There was nothing else to do. Of course I could call out for help. But the pit was in the middle of a deserted woods. Since the woods was the private property of the Amada family, under normal circumstances there would be no one around. To make matters worse, the cover of the pit had been sealed tight. I could shout at the top of my lungs and no one would hear. My voice would just grow hoarse, and I would become even thirstier. At least shaking the bell was better than nothing.

Moreover, there was something out of the ordinary about the bell's ring. It seemed to have some special power. In physical terms, it wasn't very loud. Yet I had heard it from my distant bed in the middle of the night. The autumn insects had fallen silent the moment they heard that ringing. As if commanded to stop their racket.

So I sat there at the bottom of the pit, my back against the stone wall, and rang the bell. I shook my wrist from side to side and emptied my mind as best I could. When I got tired, I took a break and then started again. As the Commendatore had done before me. It wasn't hard to clear my mind. When I listened to the bell I felt, quite naturally, that I didn't have to think about anything else. The ringing sounded different in the dark than in the light. I'm pretty sure that difference was real. I was stuck in a black hole with no way out, but as long as I was shaking the bell, I felt neither fear nor anxiety. I could forget cold and hunger, as well. For the most part, I could even set aside my need to analyze what was taking place. This was a welcome change, as you can imagine.

When I tired of ringing the bell, I dozed off leaning against the stone wall. When I awoke, I switched on the flashlight and checked my watch. Time, I discovered, was behaving in a very haphazard manner. Of course, this may have had more to do with me than the watch. No question there. But that haphazardness was fine with me. I just went on mindlessly ringing the bell, then falling asleep, then waking up to ring the bell again. An endless repetition. With the repetition, my consciousness grew ever more thin and rarified.

Not a single sound made its way into the pit. I couldn't hear the birds, or the wind. What could explain that? This was supposed to be the real world. I was back in a place where people felt hunger, and the need to pee. The real world ought to be filled with all kinds of noises.

I had no idea how much time had passed. I had given up checking my watch. The passing of days made even less sense than the passage of minutes and hours. How could it be otherwise in a place that lacked day and night? Not just time, either—I was losing contact with my own self. My body had become a stranger to me. I was finding it harder and harder to understand what my physical existence meant. Or perhaps I didn't care to understand. All I could do was keep ringing that bell. Until my wrist was almost numb.

After what felt like an eternity (or after time had surged and ebbed like waves pounding the shore), and my hunger became unbearable, finally I heard something above my head. It sounded as if someone had grabbed hold of a corner of the world and was trying to peel back its skin. But the sound didn't strike my ear as real. I mean, how could anyone do that? And if they succeeded, what would follow? A fresh new world, or an endless nothing? In truth, though, I didn't care one way or the other. The final result would probably be more or less the same.

There in the dark, I closed my eyes and waited for the peeling of the world to conclude. But the world wasn't to be peeled so easily, it seemed, and the din only mounted. Maybe it was real, after all. An actual object undergoing a process that produced an actual physical sound. Steeling myself, I opened my eyes and looked up. I trained the beam of my flashlight on the ceiling. Someone was up there making an awful racket. I didn't know why, but it was an ear-splitting grinding noise.

I couldn't tell if the sound threatened me, or was being made *on my behalf*. Whichever the case, I just sat there at the bottom of the pit shaking my bell, waiting to see how things would turn out. At last, a thin sheet of light shot through a crack between the boards and into the pit. Like the broad, sharp blade of a guillotine gliding through a mass of gelatin, it swept down through the darkness to land on my ankle. I dropped the bell and covered my face to protect my eyes.

Next, one of the boards was moved to the side and even more sunlight flooded in. Though my eyes were closed and my palms were pressed against them, I could feel the darkness turn to light. Then new air flowed in from above. It was fresh and cold, and filled with the fragrance of early winter. I loved that smell. I remembered how I had felt as a child wrapping a scarf around my neck on the first cold morning of the year. The softness of the wool against my skin.

Someone was calling my name from the top of the pit. At least, it seemed to be my name. I had forgotten I had one. Names possessed no meaning in the world where I had been for so long.

It took me a while to connect the *someone* calling my name with Wataru Menshiki. I shouted back. But no words emerged. All I could produce was a sort of growl, a signal that I was still alive. I wasn't sure my voice was strong enough to reach him, but at least I could hear it. The strange, harsh call of some imaginary beast.

"Are you all right?" Menshiki called down.

"Menshiki?"

"Yes, it's me," Menshiki said. "Are you hurt?"

"No, I'm all right," I said. My voice had returned. "I think," I added.

"How long have you been down there?"

"I don't know. It just happened."

"Can you climb the ladder if I lower it to you?"

"I think so," I said. Probably.

"Wait just a minute. I'll go get it."

My eyes began to adjust to the sunlight as I waited. I still couldn't open them all the way, but at least I didn't have to cover them with my hands. As luck would have it, it wasn't that bright. I could tell it was daytime, but the sky was probably blanketed with clouds. Or else dusk was approaching. At last, I heard the metal ladder being lowered.

"Please give me a little more time," I said. "My eyes aren't used to the light, so I have to be careful."

"Of course, take all the time you want," said Menshiki.

"Why was the pit so dark? There was no light at all."

"I covered it two days ago. It looked like someone had been monkeying with the lid, so I brought a heavy tarp from my house and tied it down with metal pegs and twine so it wouldn't budge. I didn't want a child to slip and fall in. I checked first to be sure no one was inside. It was empty then, I'm sure of it."

It made perfect sense. Menshiki had covered the lid. That's why it had been so dark.

"There were no signs that anyone had tampered with the tarp. It was just as I left it. So how did you get in? I don't understand," Menshiki said.

"I don't understand either," I said. "It just happened."

There was nothing more I could tell him. And I had no intention of trying to explain, either.

"Shall I come down?" Menshiki asked.

"No, please stay where you are. I'll come up."

I could keep my eyes half open now. Mysterious images were churning behind them, but at least my mind was functioning. I lined up the ladder against the wall, put my foot on the lowest rung, and tried to push myself up. But my legs were weak. They didn't feel like my legs at all. Still, I was able to gingerly climb up the ladder, one rung at a time. The air grew fresher the closer I got to the surface. I could hear birds chirping.

When I reached the top, Menshiki took my wrist in an iron grip and pulled me out. He was much stronger than I expected. Strong enough that I gave myself over to his hands without a second thought. Gratitude was all I felt. Out of the hole, I flopped onto my back and looked up at the dim sky. Sure enough, it was covered by gray clouds. I couldn't tell the time of day. Tiny pellets of rain struck my cheeks and forehead. I found the irregular way they landed on my face exhilarating. I had never realized what a blessing rain could be. It was so full of life. Even the first cold rain of winter.

"I'm starving. And thirsty. And cold. I'm freezing," I said. That's all I could get out. My teeth were chattering.

Menshiki guided me through the woods, his arm wrapped around my shoulder. I was having a hard time putting one foot in front of the other—by the end, he was pulling me along. He was a lot more powerful than he looked. Those daily workouts of his were paying off.

"Do you have the key?" Menshiki asked.

"It's under the potted plant to the right of the front door. Probably." The "probably" was necessary. Nothing in this world could be stated with absolute certainty. I was still shaking with cold. The chattering of my teeth was so loud I could barely hear myself talk.

"You'll be happy to hear Mariye returned home safe and sound early this afternoon," Menshiki said. "What a relief. I got a call from Shoko about an hour ago. I'd been calling you, but no one ever picked up. That worried me, so I came over. I could hear the faint ring of a bell coming from the woods. So on a hunch, I came out and removed the tarp."

The view opened up as we emerged from the trees. I could see Menshiki's silver Jaguar parked demurely in front of my house. It was as spotless as ever.

"Why is your car always so beautiful?" I asked Menshiki. Not a fitting question under the circumstances, perhaps, but something I had long wanted to ask.

"I don't know," he said in a disinterested tone. "Maybe it's because I wash it when I have nothing else to do. From front to back. Then once a month, a pro comes and waxes it. And my garage protects it from the elements. That's all."

That's all? If my poor Toyota Corolla wagon heard that, after six months spent languishing in wind and rain, its shoulders would sag in dismay. It might even pass out.

Menshiki took the key from under the flowerpot and opened the door.

"By the way, what day of the week is it?" I asked him.

"Today? Today is Tuesday."

"Tuesday? Are you sure?"

Menshiki double-checked his memory. "I put out the empty bottles and cans yesterday, so it must have been Monday. Therefore today is Tuesday, without a doubt."

It had been Saturday when I had visited Tomohiko Amada's room. So three days had passed. It wouldn't have surprised me had it been three weeks, or three months, or even three years. I made a mental note. I rubbed my jaw with my palm. But there was no three-day stubble. Instead, my chin was smooth. What explained that?

Menshiki took me to the bath straightaway. He put me in a hot shower and brought me a fresh change of clothes. The clothes I had been wearing were tattered and filthy. I rolled them up in a ball and threw them in the garbage. There were red contusions all over my body but no visible injuries. I wasn't bleeding.

Then he led me to the kitchen, sat me down, and slowly fed me water. By the end I had drained a big bottle of mineral water. While I was drinking he found several apples in the fridge and peeled them. I just sat there, admiring his skill with a knife. The plate of peeled apples looked beautiful, elegant even.

I ate three or four apples in all. It was a moving experience—I had never realized how delicious apples were. I wanted to thank their creator for inventing such a marvelous fruit. When I finished the apples, Menshiki dug up a carton of crackers and gave it to me. I emptied the box. The crackers were a bit soggy, but they still tasted like the best in the world. In the meantime, he boiled water, made tea, and mixed it with honey. I drank a number of cups. The tea and honey warmed me from the inside.

There wasn't much in my fridge. It was, however, well stocked with eggs.

"How about an omelet?" Menshiki asked.

"I'd love one," I said. I needed to fill my stomach—anything would do.

Menshiki took four eggs from the fridge, broke them in a bowl, whipped them with chopsticks, and added milk, salt, and pepper. Then he whipped them again. It was clear he knew what he was doing. Then he turned on the gas, chose a small frying pan, and melted some butter in it. He located a spatula in one of my drawers and deftly cooked the omelet.

His technique was remarkable, as I would have expected. He could have been featured on a TV cooking show. Housewives across the nation would have sighed with envy. When it came to omelets—when it came to *anything*, I should say—Menshiki was precise, efficient, and incredibly stylish. I could only look on in admiration. He slid the finished omelet onto a plate and gave it to me with a dollop of ketchup.

The finished omelet was so beautiful I wanted to sketch it. But instead

I grabbed my knife and started eating. The omelet wasn't just pretty to look at—it was delicious.

"This omelet is perfection," I said.

Menshiki laughed. "Not really. I've made better."

What sort of omelet could that have been? One that sprouted wings and flew from Tokyo to Osaka in under two hours?

When I had polished off the omelet, he took my plate to the sink. At last my stomach felt comfortable. Menshiki sat down across the table from me.

"Can we talk a little?" he asked me.

"Certainly," I said.

"Aren't you tired?"

"Maybe so. But we have lots to talk about."

Menshiki nodded. "It appears that several blanks need filling in."

If they can be filled in, I thought.

"Actually, I stopped by Sunday afternoon," Menshiki said. "I'd called many times but you never picked up, so I was a little worried. I got here around one."

I nodded. I had been *somewhere else* around then.

"I rang the bell and Tomohiko Amada's son came to the door. Masahiko, is that right?"

"Yes, Masahiko Amada. An old friend. He owns this house, and he's got a key so he can get in when I'm not here."

"He was—how should I put this—very worried about you. He said the two of you were visiting his father's room in the nursing home last Saturday when all of a sudden, you disappeared."

I nodded, but didn't say anything.

"He said you vanished into thin air while he was out of the room making a phone call. The nursing home is in Izu Kogen, so the nearest station is too far to reach on foot. But there were no signs that anyone had called a taxi. And the receptionist and the security guard hadn't seen you leave, either. Masahiko called your home later, but no one answered. He was so alarmed that he drove all the way here to check. He was concerned about your safety. Worried something bad had happened to you."

I sighed. "I'll try to explain things to Masahiko. His father's in bad shape, and I only added to his worries. How is his father, by the way? Did he say anything?"

"It seems he's been in a coma. Hasn't regained consciousness at all. His son has taken a room near the home. He was on his way back to Tokyo when he stopped by here."

"I should call him right away," I said, shaking my head.

"That's true," Menshiki said, placing his hands on the table. "But first I think you need to come up with a coherent story about where you've been and what you've been doing the past few days. Including an explanation of how you disappeared from the nursing home. No one's going to buy it if you tell them you just woke up and found yourself back here."

"You're right," I said. "But how about you? Can you buy my story?"

Menshiki thought for a moment. His brow was puckered, as if he was having trouble deciding what to say. "I've always been a man who thought along rational lines," he said at last. "That's how I was trained. To be honest, though, I can't be logical where the pit behind the shrine is concerned. Anything could happen there and it wouldn't feel strange in the least. Spending an hour inside the pit brought that home all the more. That place is more than just a hole in the ground. But I doubt anyone who hasn't experienced it could understand."

I couldn't find the right words to respond, so I stayed silent.

"I think you should take the position 'I don't remember anything' and then stick with it," Menshiki said. "I don't know how many people will believe you, but from what I can see, that's your only option."

I nodded. Yes, that could well be my only option.

"There are some things that can't be explained in this life," Menshiki went on, "and some others that probably *shouldn't* be explained. Especially when putting them into words ignores what is most crucial."

"You've experienced that, correct?"

"Of course," Menshiki said with a small smile. "More than once."

I drained what was left in my teacup.

"So Mariye wasn't hurt at all?" I asked.

"She was muddy and scratched up, but had no serious injuries. Not much more than a skinned knee. Just like you."

Just like me? "Where was she these past few days?"

Menshiki looked perplexed. "I'm pretty much in the dark about that, too. What I do know is that she returned home a short while ago. Dirty and banged up. That's all I was told. Shoko was in such a state she couldn't explain much over the phone. You should probably ask her yourself when things have settled down. Or, if possible, ask Mariye directly."

I nodded. "You're right. I'll do that."

"Don't you think you should get some sleep?" Menshiki asked.

No sooner had these words left his mouth than sleepiness hit me. I had slept deeply while I was in the pit (at least I think I had), but now I could barely keep my eyes open.

"Yes, you're right. I think I'll go lie down," I said, looking at the backs of his clasped hands, perfectly aligned on the table.

"Have a good sleep. That's what you need right now. Is there anything else I can do for you?"

I shook my head. "No, I can't think of anything. But thanks."

"Then I'll take off. Please don't hesitate to call me for whatever reason. I should be at home for the next little while." He slowly rose to his feet. "Thank goodness Mariye got home safely. And that I was able to help you out of a tough spot. To tell the truth, I haven't had much sleep these days either. So I think I'll go home and rest."

With that he left. As always, I heard the solid *thunk* of his car door slamming shut, and the engine starting up. I waited until the car was out of earshot before heading for bed. When my head hit the pillow, I remembered the old bell (I had left it and the flashlight in the pit!) for a split second. Then I descended into a deep sleep.

57

SOMETHING I HAVE TO DO EVENTUALLY

I awoke at two fifteen. Again surrounded by total darkness. For a split second, I was under the illusion that I was still in the pit, but I realized my mistake right away. There was a clear difference between the darkness here and there. Above ground, there was always a vestige of light, even on the blackest night. Not like underground, where no light could enter. It may have been two fifteen, but the sun was still in the sky, albeit on the other side of the planet. That was the size of it.

I turned on the light, went to the bathroom, and drank glass after glass of cold water. The house was hushed. Too hushed, in fact. I listened carefully, but could hear nothing. No breeze. No insect voices, since it was winter. No night birds. No bell. Come to think of it, I had first heard the bell ringing at precisely this time of night. The time when events outside the normal are most likely to occur.

I was no longer sleepy. I was wide awake. Draping a sweater over my pajamas, I headed for the studio. I hadn't set foot in there since returning home. And I was concerned about the paintings I had left. Especially *Killing Commendatore*. Menshiki had said that Masahiko had visited the house in my absence. If he had gone into the studio, he might have stumbled upon it. He would have known right away that it was his father's work. Fortunately, however, I had covered it. I'd worried about leaving it exposed, so I had taken it down from the wall and wrapped a sheet around it to hide it from inquisitive eyes. If the sheet hadn't been removed, Masahiko ought not to have seen it.

I walked in and flipped on the wall switch. The studio was dead quiet as well. Needless to say, no one was there. Not the Commendatore, not Tomohiko Amada. I was all alone.

Killing Commendatore was where I had left it on the floor, the sheet still in place. It didn't seem that anyone had touched it. I couldn't be sure, of course. But nothing suggested otherwise. I unwrapped the painting. It looked the same as always. There was the Commendatore. And Don Giovanni, who had run him through with his sword. And the shocked servant, Leporello. And the beautiful Donna Anna, covering her mouth in astonishment. And in the lower left-hand corner of the painting, poking his head through the square opening, the creepy-looking Long Face.

In truth, I had been harboring some misgivings. Might the painting have been altered by the series of events in which I had played a part? Long Face deleted from the scene, for example, because I had shut the lid? Or the Commendatore killed, not with a sword, but with a carving knife? Yet search as I might, I could find nothing changed. Long Face still poked his grotesque face out of his hole, the raised lid in one hand. His saucer eyes still surveyed the scene. The Commendatore was still impaled on a long sword, blood spewing from his heart. The painting remained a perfectly composed work of art. I admired it for a while, then put the sheet back over it.

I turned to look at the two paintings I was working on. They sat side by side on two easels. One, *The Pit in the Woods*, was wider than it was tall. The other, *A Portrait of Mariye Akikawa*, was taller than it was wide. I looked at them carefully. Both were exactly as I had left them. Nothing had been changed. One was finished, while the other awaited a final go-around.

Then I turned *The Man with the White Subaru Forester*, which had been facing the wall, sat on the floor, and took another good look at it. The man with the white Subaru Forester stared back at me from behind the thick layers of paint, which I had applied with my palette knife in several colors. He had no concrete shape, but I could see him there nonetheless. He was looking straight at me with the piercing eyes of a nocturnal bird of prey, his face empty of expression. He was dead set against the completion of his portrait—the exposure of his true form to the world. Against being hauled from the dark into the light.

But I was determined to reveal who he was. I had to drag him out into full view. However much he might resist. The time might not yet have come. But when it did, I had to be ready to follow through.

I returned to *A Portrait of Mariye Akikawa*. It was far enough along that I didn't need Mariye to model for me anymore. Only a series of final, technical operations remained. Then the portrait would be basically done. I thought it might turn out to be my most accomplished work to date. At the very least, it would capture the freshness of that beautiful thirteen-year-old girl. I was confident of that. But I knew I would never take those last steps. By leaving it unfinished I was shielding something within her, even though I didn't know what that something was. That much was clear.

I needed to look after a few things right away. I had to call Shoko and hear the full story of Mariye's return. I had to call Yuzu and tell her I wanted to see her to talk things out, as I'd resolved at the bottom of the pit. That it was time for us to meet. Then, of course, I had to talk to Masahiko. To explain how it was that I had vanished suddenly from his father's room at the nursing home, and tell him where I had been for the three days I was missing and unaccounted for (though what I would say—what was *possible* to say—escaped me).

Clearly, I couldn't call any of them now. I had to wait for a more appropriate time. That would come in due course—assuming, that is, that time was behaving normally. I drank a glass of warm milk that I heated on the stove and nibbled some biscuits as I sat and looked out the window. It was pitch black outside. No stars were out. Daybreak was still a while off. It was the time of year when nights were the longest.

How should I pass the time? The proper thing would be to climb back into bed. But I wasn't at all sleepy. I didn't feel like reading or working. With nothing better to do, I decided to run a bath. While the bathtub was filling, I lay on my back and stared at the ceiling.

Why had it been necessary to pass through that underground world? To make that trip, I had been forced to kill the Commendatore with my own hands. He had sacrificed his life, and I had been compelled to endure one ordeal after another in a world of darkness. There had to have been a reason. The underground realm was full of unmistakable danger, and real fear. Down there, the most outlandish occurrences weren't strange at all. By successfully navigating that realm, I seemed to have freed Mariye *from somewhere*. At least she had returned home safely. As the Commendatore had foretold. But what connected my experiences underground and her safe return? Were they somehow parallel?

Perhaps the river water I had ingested was an important piece of the puzzle. It could have altered something in me. I felt that at an intuitive and physical level, though it made no rational sense. Thanks to that change, I had passed through a tunnel clearly too small for my body. Cheered on by Donna Anna and Komi, I had managed to overcome my deep-rooted claustrophobia. No, Donna Anna and Komi could have been *a single entity*, Donna Anna at one moment, Komi at the next. Together, perhaps, they had shielded me from the dark powers, and protected Mariye Akikawa at the same time.

But where had Mariye been confined? Had she been confined in the first place? When I had given her penguin charm (though "given" didn't really cover it) to the faceless man, had I harmed her? Or, conversely, had the charm in some shape or form protected her in the end?

The questions only mounted.

Perhaps I would understand the events of the past few days better once I met Mariye in person. I would have to wait. True, things might be no clearer even after we talked. Mariye might recall nothing. Or she might remember, but (like me) be unwilling to share her story.

At any rate, I had to see her once more in this real world, and have a good long talk. We needed to share our stories about what had happened to us. If at all possible.

But was *this the real world?*

I looked around. So much was familiar. The breeze through the window carried a familiar smell, the sounds outside were familiar sounds.

Just because it looked like the real world at first glance, however, didn't mean that was necessarily the case. It might be no more than my assumption. I might well have descended through one hole in Izu and traveled the underworld only to be spit out three days later through the wrong hole in the mountains of Odawara. There was no guarantee that the world I had left and the world I had returned to were one and the same.

I rose from the sofa, stripped off my clothes, and stepped into the bathroom. Once again, I soaped and scrubbed every inch of my body. I thoroughly washed my hair. I brushed my teeth, swabbed my ears with cotton, trimmed my nails. I shaved (though there wasn't much beard to shave). I put on another set of clean underwear. A freshly ironed white cotton shirt and a pair of khaki pants with a sharp crease. I strove to make myself look as acceptable as I could to the real world. But the night still hadn't ended. Outside was pitch black. So black I felt morning might never arrive, not for all eternity.

But morning did come. I brewed some fresh coffee and made some buttered toast. The fridge was almost bare. Two eggs, some sour milk, and a few limp vegetables. I made a mental note to go shopping later.

I was washing the coffee cup when it struck me that I hadn't seen my girlfriend in some time. How long had it been? I couldn't count the exact number of days without checking my calendar. But I knew quite a while had passed. So many things had been going on—a number of them literally not in this world—that I hadn't noticed her failure to contact me.

Why was that? She called me at least twice every week. "How's it going?" she would say. I couldn't call her, though. She couldn't give me her cell phone number, and I didn't use email. When I wanted to see her, I had to wait for her call.

Sure enough, my girlfriend did call around nine that morning, when she was still in the back of my mind.

"I've got to talk to you about something," she said, skipping the pleasantries.

"Fine, let's talk," I said.

I leaned against the kitchen counter, phone to my ear. The clouds outside were starting to break up, and the early-winter sun was peeking through the gaps. The weather at least was improving. From the sound of it, though, what she had to say wasn't going to be all that pleasant.

"I think it's best if we don't see each other again," she said. "It's too bad, but . . ."

Her tone was flat and dispassionate. I couldn't tell if she really felt it was too bad or not.

"There are a number of reasons," she said.

"A number of reasons," I echoed.

"To begin with, I think my husband is catching on. He's noticed some signs."

"Signs," I repeated.

"Women leave certain signs in situations like this. Like they start paying more attention to their makeup and their clothes, or change their perfume, or start a serious diet. I've tried to be careful, but even so."

"I see."

"The main thing is, we can't go on like this."

"Like this," I repeated.

"With no future. No hope of resolution."

She had it there. Our relationship had no "future," no "hope of resolution." The risks were too large if we continued as we were. I didn't have all that much to lose, but she had a family and two teenage daughters attending private school.

"There's more," she went on. "I'm having a serious problem with my daughter. The older one."

Her elder daughter. If I remembered correctly, she was the obedient child who never talked back to her parents and got good grades.

"A serious problem?"

"She can't get out of bed in the morning."

"Can't get out of bed?"

"Hey, will you please stop repeating everything I say?"

"Sorry," I apologized. "But what is her specific problem? She can't get out of bed?"

"That's right. It's been going on for about two weeks. She doesn't try to get up. She doesn't go to school. She just lies in bed in her pajamas all day. Doesn't answer when spoken to. I take food to her, but she barely touches it."

"Has she seen a counselor?"

"Of course," she said. "There's a school counselor. No help at all."

I thought for a minute. But there was nothing I could say. I'd never even met the girl.

"So that's why I can't see you," she said.

"Because you have to stay home and look after her?"

"There's that. But that's not all."

She didn't go on, but I understood how she felt. She was terrified, and blaming herself as a mother for our affair.

"It's really too bad," I said.

"It's fine for you to say that, but it's even worse for me."

She could be right, I thought.

"There's one last thing I wanted to tell you," she said. She took a quick, deep breath.

"What's that?"

"I think you can become a really good artist. Even better than now."

"Thank you," I said. "That gives me some confidence."

"Goodbye."

"Take care," I said.

When our phone call ended, I went to the living room, stretched out on the sofa, and thought about her as I looked at the ceiling. We had been together so many times, yet never had I thought of painting her portrait. Somehow, that feeling had never arisen. Instead I had sketched her over and over again. In a small sketchbook with a thick pencil, so quickly I hardly removed pencil from paper. In most she was naked, and posing lewdly. Spreading her legs to show her vagina, for example. Or I sketched her in the act of making love. Simple drawings but still very real. And very vulgar. She loved looking at them.

"You're really good at drawing naughty pictures, huh? You toss them off, but they're super dirty."

"It's just for fun," I said.

I drew her again and again, then threw the drawings away. Someone might see them, and it didn't make sense to keep them. Still, maybe I should have secretly held on to at least one. To prove to myself she had really existed.

I got up slowly from the sofa. The day was only beginning. There were many conversations ahead.

58

LIKE HEARING ABOUT THE BEAUTIFUL CANALS OF MARS

I called Shoko Akikawa. It was just after nine thirty. A time when most people are already up and about. But no one picked up the phone. It rang on and on until the answering machine kicked in. *We're sorry, but we can't come to the phone right now. Please leave your message after the tone* . . . I left no message. She must be scrambling to deal with her niece's disappearance and sudden return. I kept calling at intervals, but no one answered.

I thought of calling Yuzu after that, but I didn't want to bother her while she was working. I could call during her lunch break. With luck, I would get to have a brief talk with her. It wasn't like our conversation would be a long one. I would simply ask if we could meet sometime soon—that was the gist of it. A yes-or-no question. If the answer was yes, we would set a date and a place to meet. If it was no, that was that.

Then, with a heavy heart, I called Masahiko. He picked up right away. He let out a huge sigh when he heard my voice.

"Are you home now?" he asked.

I told him I was.

"Can I call you back in a couple of minutes?"

Sure, I said. He called fifteen minutes later. He seemed to be using his cell phone on the roof of an office building, or someplace like that.

"Where the hell have you been?" he said, his voice uncharacteristically stern. "You disappeared from my father's room without a word—no one knew where you were. I drove all the way to Odawara looking for you."

"I'm really sorry," I said.

"When did you get home?"

"Last night."

"So you were traipsing around from Saturday afternoon until Tuesday night? Where did you go?"

"To be honest, I have no memory of where I was or what I was doing," I lied.

"So you just woke up and found yourself back home—is that it?"

"Yeah, that's it."

"For real? Are you serious?"

"There's no other way to explain it."

"Sorry, man. I can't buy it. Sounds fake to me."

"Come on, you've seen this sort of thing in movies and novels."

"Give me a break. Whenever they pull that amnesia bit I turn off the TV. It's so contrived."

"Alfred Hitchcock used it."

"You mean *Spellbound*? That's one of his second-rate films," Masahiko said. "So tell me what *really* happened."

"I don't know myself at this point. Like there are these fragments floating around, and I can't figure out how to piece them together. Maybe my memory will return in stages. I'll let you know if that happens. But I can't tell you anything right now. I'm sorry, but you'll have to wait a little longer."

Masahiko paused to digest what I had just said. "All right then, let's call it amnesia for now," he said in a resigned voice. "I gather your story doesn't involve drugs or alcohol or a mental breakdown or a femme fatale or abduction by aliens or anything along those lines."

"No. Nothing illegal or contrary to public morals."

"Public morals be damned," Masahiko said. "But clue me in on one thing, would you?"

"What's that?"

"How did you manage to slip out of the nursing home Saturday afternoon? They keep a really strict eye on who comes and goes. A number of famous people are staying there, so they're paranoid about leaks. They've got a receptionist stationed at the entrance, a guard on-site twenty-four seven, and security cameras. All the same, you managed to vanish in broad daylight without being spotted or caught on film. How?"

"There's a secret passage," I said.

"Secret passage?"

"An exit no one knows about."

"How did you find that? It was your first time there."

"Your father let me know. Or I should say, he gave me a hint. In a very indirect way."

"My father?" Masahiko said. "You must be kidding. His mind's as mushy as boiled cauliflower these days."

"That's one of the things I can't explain."

"What to do," Masahiko said with a sigh. "If it were anyone else I'd say, 'Cut the crap.' But it's you, so I guess I have to put up with it. Put up with this crazy, no-good bum who spends his whole life painting."

"Thanks," I said. "By the way, how's your father doing?"

"When I got back to the room after my phone call, you were nowhere to be seen and Dad was unconscious and barely breathing. I panicked, man. I couldn't figure out what was going on. I knew it wasn't your fault, but I couldn't help blaming you anyway."

"I really am sorry," I said. I wasn't kidding, either. Still, I felt a wave of relief that there was no trace of the Commendatore's body, or of the pool of blood on the floor.

"Yeah, you should be sorry. Anyway, I rented a room nearby to be with him, but his breathing stabilized and his condition improved slightly, so I came back to Tokyo the next afternoon. Work was piling up. I'm heading back this weekend, though."

"It's hard on you."

"There's nothing to be done. Like I told you, dying is a major undertaking. It's the person dying who has it hardest, though, so I really can't complain."

"Is there anything I can do?" I asked.

"No, there's nothing," Masahiko said. "But it would help if you didn't dump any more problems on me . . . Oh yeah, I almost forgot. When I was at your house on my way back to Tokyo your friend Menshiki stopped by. The handsome, white-haired guy in the snazzy silver Jaguar."

"Yes, I met him after that. He said you were there, and that you and he had talked."

"Just a few words at your doorstep. He seemed like an interesting guy."

"A *very* interesting guy," I said, putting it mildly.

"What does he do?"

"Not much of anything. He's so loaded he doesn't have to work. He trades stocks and plays the currency market online, but it's more like a hobby for him, a profitable way to kill time."

"That's really cool," Masahiko said, impressed. "It's like hearing about the beautiful canals of Mars. Where Martians row gondolas with golden oars. While imbibing honeyed tobacco through their ears. Warms my heart just hearing about it . . . Oh yeah, while we're at it, did you ever find the knife I left at your place?"

"Sorry, but no, I haven't come across it," I said. "I don't have a clue where it went. I'll buy you a new one."

"Don't sweat it. It probably had a bout of amnesia, just like you. It'll wander back before too long."

"Probably," I said. So the knife hadn't remained in Tomohiko Amada's room either. It had vanished somewhere, just like the Commendatore's corpse and the pool of blood. It might show up here, though, as Masahiko had said.

Our conversation ended there. We vowed to get together again soon and hung up.

After that, I drove my dusty old Corolla station wagon down the mountain to the shopping plaza. I went to the supermarket, where I toured the aisles with the neighborhood housewives. From the looks on their faces, they weren't thrilled by their morning shopping. Not a whole lot of excitement in their lives. No ferryboat rides in the Land of Metaphor, that's for sure.

I tossed what I needed—meat, fish, vegetables, milk, tofu, the whole lot—into my shopping cart and paid at the register. I saved five yen by bringing my own bag. Then I went to a discount liquor store and bought a twenty-four pack of Sapporo. Back home, I arranged most of what I had purchased in the fridge, including six cans of beer. I wrapped what needed to be frozen in plastic and stuck it in the freezer. I set a big pot of water on the stove and parboiled the asparagus and broccoli for salads. I boiled a few eggs, too. In the process, I managed to kill most of the morning. Nevertheless, there was still time to spare. I considered following Menshiki's example and washing my car, then realized it would get dirty again in no time flat, and tossed the idea. Parboiling vegetables was much more productive.

I called Yuzu's architectural firm shortly after noon. Actually, I wanted to wait until my feelings had settled down before talking to her, but at the same time I didn't want to delay acting on what I had decided in the darkness of the pit, even for a single day. Otherwise, something might cause my feelings to change. Yet the receiver weighed a ton in my hand. A cheerful-sounding young woman answered. I gave her my name, and asked to talk to Yuzu.

"Are you her husband?" she chirped.

Yes, I replied. To be precise I wasn't, of course, but there was no reason to go into details over the phone.

"Please hold on," she said.

I waited for quite a long time. I had nothing in particular to do, so I stood there leaning on the kitchen counter, receiver to my ear, biding my time until Yuzu came to the phone. A big black crow passed right in front of the window. Its glossy feathers gleamed in the sunlight.

"Hello," said Yuzu.

We exchanged a simple greeting. I had no idea how a just-divorced couple was supposed to address each other, how much distance was appropriate. So I kept it as brief and conventional as possible. How have you been? I've been fine. And you? Like a summer shower, our words were sucked up the moment they struck the parched soil of reality.

I mustered my courage. "I thought we should get together and talk about a number of things face-to-face," I said.

"What sorts of things are you talking about?" Yuzu asked. I hadn't expected that response (why hadn't I?), so I was at a loss for words. What did I mean by "things"?

"I . . . I haven't thought it through that far," I stammered.

"But you want to talk about a number of things, correct?"

"That's right. It occurred to me that we ended up like this without ever having talked."

She thought for a moment. "To tell the truth," she said, "I'm pregnant. I'm happy to see you, but don't be shocked to see how big my belly's grown."

"I know. Masahiko told me. He said you asked him to."

"That I did," she said.

"I don't know how big you've gotten, but I'd like to see you in any case. If it's not too much of an imposition."

"Can you wait a moment?" she asked.

I waited. She appeared to be leafing through her appointment book. Meanwhile, I tried hard to remember what kind of songs the Go-Go's sang. I doubted they were as good as Masahiko had claimed, but then maybe he was right, and my view was perverse.

"Next Monday evening is good for me," Yuzu said.

I did the calculation in my head. Today was Wednesday. So Monday was five days away. The day Menshiki took his empty bottles and cans to the pickup spot. A day I didn't have to teach drawing in town. That meant I was free—no need to check my schedule. What did Menshiki wear when he took out his garbage, I wondered.

"It's good for me too," I said. "Just give me a time and place and I'll be there."

She named a coffee shop not far from the Shinjuku Gyoen-mae Station. The name brought back memories. It was not far from her office, and we had met there often when we were still living together as a married couple. After she finished work, usually before we went out someplace for dinner. There was a little oyster bar a short distance away, which offered fresh oysters at a reasonable price. She loved eating their small oysters loaded with horseradish, and washed down with chilled Chablis. Was the restaurant still in the same spot?

"Can we meet there shortly after six?"

I said that'd be fine.

"I'll try not to be late."

"That's all right. I'll wait."

"Okay, see you then," she said, and hung up.

I stared at the receiver in my hand for a moment. So I would see Yuzu again. My estranged wife, soon to bear another man's child. The place and time had been set. Our conversation had gone without a hitch. Yet had I done the right thing? I wasn't at all sure. The receiver still weighed heavy in my hand. Like a phone built back in the Stone Age.

When it came down to it, though, could anything be completely correct, or completely incorrect? We lived in a world where rain might fall thirty percent, or seventy percent, of the time. Truth was probably no different. There could be thirty percent or seventy percent truth. Crows had it a lot easier. For them, it was either raining or not raining, one or the other. Percentages never crossed their minds.

Talking to Yuzu had left me at loose ends. I sat in the dining room for an hour, mostly looking at the clock on the wall. I would see her on Monday and we would talk about "a number of things." We hadn't seen each other since March. It had been a chilly Sunday afternoon then, rain quietly falling. Now she was seven months pregnant. A major change in her life. I, on the other hand, was still just me. True, I had drunk the water of the Land of Metaphor only a few days earlier, and had crossed the river that divided presence and absence, but I wasn't sure if the experience had changed me or not.

Finally, I called Shoko again. But no one came to the phone. Instead it switched to the answering machine. I gave up and sat down on the sofa. I had made all my calls, and nothing more needed to be done. I hadn't set foot in the studio in what felt like ages, and part of me wanted to get back to my easel, but I couldn't think of anything in particular that I wanted to paint.

I put Bruce Springsteen's *The River* on the turntable. Then I lay on the sofa, closed my eyes, and listened. When the A side of the first LP had finished, I turned it over and listened to the B side. Albums like

The River have to be heard in this fashion. After "Independence Day" wraps up the A side, you take the record in both hands, turn it over, and carefully lower the stylus. "Hungry Heart" fills the room. What was the point of listening to *The River* any other way? In my personal opinion, when CDs strung together the sides of records like *The River*, they spoiled the experience. The same was true of *Rubber Soul* and *Pet Sounds*. Great music should be presented in its proper form. And listened to in a proper manner.

Whatever the case, the E Street Band's performance was a knockout. The band revved up the singer, and the singer inspired the band. As I zoned in on the music, I could feel my worries fading.

I was lifting the needle from the first record when I realized that, perhaps, I should give Menshiki a call. We hadn't spoken since the day before, when he had rescued me from the pit. Yet somehow I didn't really feel like it. This happened on occasion. He was a fascinating guy, but there were times I really didn't want to talk to him. The gap between us was vast. Why should that be? At any rate, I didn't feel like hearing his voice at that particular moment.

So I gave up. I'd call him later. After all, the day had just begun. I put the second record of *The River* on the stereo. But just when I was settling back to listen to "Cadillac Ranch" ("All gonna meet down at the Cadillac Ranch"), the telephone rang. I lifted the needle and went into the dining room to answer it. I figured it was Menshiki. As it turned out, it was Shoko.

"Have you been trying to reach me this morning?" she began.

That's right, I replied, I had tried on several occasions. "I heard yesterday from Mr. Menshiki that Mariye had returned home, so I wondered how she was."

"Yes, she came back safe and sound. Yesterday afternoon. I called you a number of times to let you know but there was no answer, so I tried contacting Mr. Menshiki. Did you go somewhere?"

"Yes, I had to look after urgent business some distance from here. I got back last night. I wanted to contact you earlier, but there was no phone where I was, and I don't carry a cell phone," I said. It wasn't a complete lie.

"Mariye returned all by herself yesterday afternoon, covered in mud. But no serious injuries, thank goodness."

"Where was she all that time?"

"We don't know yet," she said in a hushed voice. As if afraid that her phone was tapped. "Mariye won't tell us what happened. We had filed a missing person's report, so the police came and asked her all sorts of questions, but she wouldn't tell them anything. Not a single word. So they gave up and left, saying that they'd come back when she'd had more time to recover. That at least she had made it home, and that she was safe. But she won't tell either her father or me anything. You know how stubborn she can be."

"But she was covered in mud, correct?"

"Yes, her whole body. Her school uniform was torn up too, and her arms and legs were scratched. We didn't have to take her to the hospital, though—none of her injuries was that serious."

Just like me, I thought. Muddy, clothing in tatters. Could we have wormed our way back to this world through the same narrow tunnel?

"And she won't speak?" I asked.

"No, not a single word since she came home. Not just words, either—she hasn't made a sound. As if someone had stolen her tongue."

"Do you think some kind of trauma might have left her in shock? Taken away her voice?"

"No, I don't think so. I think she's made up her mind not to say anything, a vow of silence, if you will. She's done this kind of thing before. When she's furious about something, for example. Once she's made up her mind like this she tends to stick to it—that's the sort of child she is."

"There's no question of criminal acts, right? Like kidnapping, or unlawful confinement?"

"I can't tell. The police say they'll come back to ask more questions once she's had a chance to calm down, so maybe we'll find out then," Shoko said. "But I do have a favor to ask, if it's not too much of an imposition."

"What might that be?"

"Would you try to talk to her? Just the two of you? There may be things she'll only open up to you about. She might reveal more about what happened if you're there."

I stood there with the receiver in my right hand, considering her suggestion. If Mariye and I were alone together, what was there to discuss? I couldn't begin to imagine. I had my own riddles to unravel and she (most likely) had hers. If we laid one set of riddles over the other, what answers could possibly emerge? Still, I had to see her. There were things we had to talk about.

"Of course. I'd be happy to," I said. "Where would you like me to go?"

"Oh no, please let us come to you, as always. I think that's best. If you don't mind, of course."

"No, that's fine with me," I said. "I'm free all day. Please come when it's convenient for you."

"Would it be all right if we came now? She's home from school today. If she's willing, of course."

"Please tell her she doesn't have to talk. That there are things on my end that I'd like to tell her," I said.

"Very well. I'll tell her exactly that. I'm dreadfully sorry to keep imposing on you like this," said the beautiful aunt. Then she quietly hung up the phone.

The phone rang again twenty minutes later. It was Shoko.

"We'll be coming at three o'clock," she said. "Mariye has said she's willing. Well, she gave a small nod, is more accurate."

I said I would expect them at three.

"Thank you so much," she said. "I'm at my wit's end. I don't understand what's going on, or what I should be doing."

I wanted to tell her I felt the same way, but I didn't. That's not the response she was seeking.

"I'll do what I can. I can't be sure if it will work, but I'll try my best," I said. Then I hung up.

I stole a look around the room as I put down the receiver. On the off chance that the Commendatore might be in the vicinity. But he was nowhere to be seen. I missed him. The way he looked, and his odd way of speaking. But I would never lay eyes on him again. With my own hand, I had driven a knife through his tiny heart. The razor-sharp carving knife Masahiko had brought to my house. All for the purpose of rescuing Mariye from someplace. I had to find out where that *someplace* was.

59

UNTIL DEATH SEPARATED US

Before Mariye arrived, I took another look at her portrait, so close to done. I could picture exactly what it would look like if I ever finished it. Sad to say, though, I never would. There was no way around that. I had no good explanation for why I couldn't complete the painting. No logical argument. Just the strong feeling that *it had to be that way*. The reason, I expected, would reveal itself in stages. What was clear now was that I was fighting a very dangerous opponent. I had to be on my toes every second.

I went out to the terrace, sat in a deck chair, and stared across the valley at Menshiki's white mansion. Handsome, colorless Menshiki, he of the white hair. "We only talked for a moment at your door, but he seemed like an interesting guy," Masahiko had said. "*A very* interesting guy," I had corrected him. At this stage of the game, though, I would have to say *a very, very, very* interesting guy.

A few minutes before three, the familiar blue Toyota Prius rolled up the slope and parked in its usual spot in front of my house. The engine stopped, the driver's door opened, and Shoko Akikawa got out. Most elegantly, pivoting in her seat, knees tight together. A moment later, Mariye emerged from the passenger's seat. Most reluctantly, her movements slow and sluggish. The morning clouds had sailed off somewhere, and the sky was the clear blue of early winter. The soft hair of the two women danced in the cold wind coming off the mountain. Mariye brushed the hair from her eyes in an impatient gesture.

Mariye was in a skirt, unusual for her. A wool skirt of navy blue, it reached her knees. Beneath was a pair of dark blue tights. Her white blouse was covered by a cashmere V-neck sweater. The sweater was a deep purple, the color of grapes. Her shoes were dark brown loafers. In that outfit, Mariye looked like a well-brought-up child from a well-off family, a healthy, pretty, utterly conventional girl. You could see nothing eccentric about her. Just that her chest was almost flat.

Shoko was wearing snug light-gray slacks. Gleaming black low-heeled shoes. A long white cardigan, fixed with a belt around her waist. Her breasts stood out proudly beneath the cardigan. She was carrying a black purse made of what looked like enamel. The sort women commonly carry, though their contents have always mystified me. Mariye appeared a bit at a loss with no pockets to plunge her hands into.

They were so different in age and stage of maturity, this young aunt and her niece, yet both were so lovely. I observed their approach through the parted curtains. When they walked side by side, the world brightened a little. As when Christmas and New Year's arrive in tandem each year.

The doorbell chimed, and I went to open the door. Shoko greeted me politely, and I ushered them inside. Mariye said nothing. Her lips were set in a straight line, as if someone had stitched them together. She was a strong-willed girl. Once she made up her mind about something, she never backed down.

As before, I led them to the living room. Shoko launched into a string of apologies, but I cut her off. This was no time for social niceties.

"If you don't mind, could you leave Mariye and me alone for a while?" I said, getting straight to the point. "I think that's best. Please come back in about two hours. Would that be possible?"

"Oh, well, certainly," the young aunt said. She seemed a little flustered. "If it's all right with Mariye, then it's all right with me."

Mariye gave a slight nod. It was all right with her.

Shoko Akikawa consulted her small silver watch.

"Then I'll come back at five o'clock. I'll be waiting at home, so please call if you need anything."

I told her we would.

Looking worried, Shoko paused uncertainly, clutching her black purse. Then she appeared to make up her mind, for she took a deep breath, smiled a bright smile, and left. There was the sound of the Prius's engine starting (I couldn't really hear it, but I assume it did), and the car disappeared down the slope. Mariye and I were left alone in the house.

The girl sat on the sofa and looked down at her lap, her lips still set in a stubborn line and her knees pressed together. Her pleated blouse was neatly ironed.

A deep silence followed. Finally, I spoke up.

"You don't have to say a word," I began. "You can stay quiet as long as you want. So try to relax. I'll do the talking—all you have to do is listen. All right?"

Mariye raised her eyes and looked at me. But she didn't speak. Nor did she nod or shake her head. She merely stared in my direction. Her face showed no emotion. I felt as if I were gazing at the full moon in winter. Perhaps she had made her heart like the moon for the time being. An icy mass of rock floating in the sky.

"First, I need your help with something," I said. "Can you come with me?"

I rose and headed to the studio. A moment later she got up and followed. The room was chilly, so I lit the kerosene stove. When I pulled back the curtains, the mountainside was bright in the sun. Mariye's portrait-in-progress was sitting on an easel, close to finished. She glanced at it but then quickly looked away, as if she had glimpsed something she shouldn't have.

I crouched down, removed the cloth I had draped over *Killing Commendatore*, and hung the painting on the wall. I asked Mariye to sit on the stool to observe it more closely.

"You've seen this painting before, right?"

Mariye gave a small nod.

"It's called *Killing Commendatore*. At least that's what was written on its wrapping. It's one of Tomohiko Amada's most perfect works, though we don't know exactly when he painted it. It's beautifully composed and masterfully drawn. Each character is fully realized and utterly convincing."

I paused for a moment, waiting for my words to sink in.

"Yet this painting was wrapped up and closeted away in the attic of this house," I went on, "where no one would ever see it. When I stumbled upon it and brought it downstairs, it had been gathering dust for a very long time. Apart from the artist, you and I are probably the only people who have ever looked at it. Your aunt could have too on your first visit, but for some reason it didn't catch her eye. I don't know what made Tomohiko Amada hide it in the attic. It's such a brilliant work, one of his true masterpieces, so why would he keep it from the world?"

Mariye didn't respond. She sat on the stool, her eyes fixed on *Killing Commendatore.*

I continued. "As if on cue, weird things have happened one after another since I stumbled on this painting. First, Mr. Menshiki went out of his way to make my acquaintance."

Mariye nodded slightly.

"Then I uncovered that strange hole behind the shrine in the woods. I heard a bell ringing in the middle of the night and traced it to that spot. It was coming from beneath a pile of stones. They couldn't be moved by hand—they were too big and too heavy. So Menshiki arranged for a landscaper to come in with his backhoe. I didn't understand why Menshiki would go to such lengths, and I still don't. At any rate, the stones were moved at great cost of time and money. Underneath them was a hole. A round pit about six feet across, made of smaller stones tightly set together in a perfect circle. Who built it, and for what purpose, is a mystery. Of course you know about the pit."

Mariye nodded.

"The Commendatore came out of that opened pit. This guy."

I went up to the painting and pointed to the figure. Mariye looked at him. But her expression didn't change.

"He looked exactly the same as you see here, same face, same clothes. But he was only two feet tall. Very compact. And with a peculiar way of speaking. For some reason, I seem to be the only person able to see him. He called himself an 'Idea.' And said he had been stuck in that pit. In other words, Mr. Menshiki and I had set him free. Do you get what he meant by 'Idea'?"

Mariye shook her head no.

"It's hard for me, too. The way I understand it, an idea is a type of concept. But not all concepts are ideas. Love, for example, is not an idea. But ideas are what make love possible. Without ideas, love cannot exist. This discussion can go on forever, though. And to tell you the truth, I'm not even sure of the correct definitions. Anyway, an idea is a concept, and concepts have no physical shape. They are pure abstractions. Nevertheless, this Idea temporarily borrowed the form of the Commendatore in the painting to make itself visible to me. Do you follow me so far?"

"Pretty much," Mariye broke her silence for the first time. "I met him too."

"You did?" I exclaimed. I looked at her in stunned silence. Then I recalled what the Commendatore had said to me in the Izu nursing home. *I met her not long ago*, he had told me. *We exchanged a few words*.

"So you met the Commendatore too."

Mariye nodded.

"When? Where?"

"At Mr. Menshiki's," she said.

"What did he say?"

Mariye clamped her lips together again. To signal, it seemed, that she didn't want to talk any more for the moment. I didn't push her further.

"Other characters in this painting have appeared as well," I said. "For example, the man in the lower left-hand corner of the painting, the bearded guy with the strangely shaped face. Right here."

I pointed to Long Face.

"I call him 'Long Face,' and he's a weird one, all right. He's about two and a half feet tall. He slipped out from the painting too—I caught him holding up the cover of his hole just as he is doing here, and he helped me reach the underground world. I had to get a bit rough, though, before he gave me directions."

Mariye looked at Long Face for some time. But she didn't say anything.

I continued. "I walked through that dim world, climbing hills, crossing a rapid river, until I met the pretty young woman you see right here. This person. I call her 'Donna Anna,' after the character in Mozart's opera *Don Giovanni*. She's also very small. She led me to a tunnel in the back of a cave. Then she and my dead sister helped me worm my way through to where it ended. If they hadn't cheered me on I never would have made it—I'd have been trapped in the underworld forever. My hunch—though of course it's pure guesswork—is that Donna Anna in this painting may be the young woman Tomohiko Amada loved when he was a student in Vienna. She was executed as a political prisoner seventy years ago."

Mariye looked at Donna Anna in the painting. Her face still as impassive as the white winter moon.

Then again, Donna Anna could have been Mariye's mother, stung to death by a swarm of hornets. Perhaps she was the one who had protected Mariye. Depending on who was looking at her, Donna Anna might embody many things. Of course, I didn't say this out loud.

"Then we have this man here," I said. I turned the painting leaning against the wall around so we could see its front. It was my portrait in progress, *The Man with the White Subaru Forester*. On the surface, it was just thick layers of paint, three colors in all. Behind those layers, though, was the Subaru Forester guy. I could see him. Though other people couldn't.

"I showed you this before, didn't I?"

Mariye gave a firm nod, but said nothing.

"You told me it was finished as it was."

Mariye nodded again.

"I call the person portrayed here—or the person I must eventually portray—'the man with the white Subaru Forester.' I ran across him in a small coastal village in Miyagi Prefecture. Our paths crossed twice. In a very mysterious and meaningful way. I have no idea what sort of person he is. I don't even know his name. But a moment came when I realized I had to paint him. I was compelled to. I started painting him from memory, but had to stop when I reached a certain point. So I painted over him like this."

Mariye's lips were still set in a straight line.

Then she shook her head from side to side.

"That man is really scary," she said.

"That man?" I said. I followed her eyes. They were fixed on *The Man with the White Subaru Forester*. "Do you mean the painting? Or the man?"

She gave another firm nod. Despite her fear, she seemed unable to look away.

"Can you see him?"

She nodded. "I can see him behind the paint. He's standing there looking at me. Wearing a black cap."

I turned it around and set it back, face against the wall.

"You have the ability to see the man with the Subaru Forester standing there. Most people don't," I said. "But I think it's better if you don't look at him anymore. There's probably no need at this stage."

Mariye nodded as if in agreement.

"I don't know if the man with the white Subaru Forester is of this world or not. It's possible that someone, or something, merely borrowed his form. In the same way an Idea borrowed the form of the Commendatore. Or it could be that I saw part of myself reflected in him. But when I was surrounded by real darkness, it was no mere reflection, believe me. It was a tangible, living, moving *thing*. The people in that land call it a 'Double Metaphor.' I do plan to finish the painting someday. But not yet—it's still too early. And too dangerous. Some things shouldn't be recklessly dragged into the light. But I may not be . . ."

Mariye was looking straight at me without saying a word. I found it difficult to continue.

"Anyway, thanks to the help of many people, I was somehow able to cross the underworld and squeeze through a narrow, black tunnel to make my way back to this world. At virtually the same moment, you were freed *from somewhere*. I can't believe that was a mere stroke of luck. On Friday, you disappeared somewhere for four days. Then on Saturday I disappeared for three days. On Tuesday, we both *returned*. There has to be a connection. My guess is that the Commendatore connected us. And now he's gone from this world. He fulfilled his role and moved on. Only you and I are left. We're the only ones who can close the circle. Do you believe what I'm saying?"

Mariye nodded.

"That's what I wanted to tell you. Why I asked to talk to you alone."

Mariye's eyes were trained on my face.

"No one else would believe me," I went on, "even if I told the truth. They'd think I was nuts. I mean the story just doesn't fly—it's too far removed from reality—though I figured you'd believe me. And then I'd have to show them *Killing Commendatore*. Without that painting, nothing I said would make sense. But I don't want anyone else to see it. Only you."

Mariye kept looking at me. She didn't speak. But I could see the sparkle slowly returning to her eyes.

"Tomohiko Amada invested everything, all of himself, in this painting. It's filled with his emotion. As though he painted it with his own blood and flesh. Truly a once-in-a-lifetime work of art. He did it for himself, but also for those who were no longer of this world, a kind of requiem to their memory. To purify the blood they had shed."

"Requiem?"

"A work to bring peace to the spirits of the dead and heal their wounds. That's why he didn't expose it to public view. The critical reception, the accolades, the financial rewards—they had no meaning. He wanted none of those things for this painting. It was enough for him to know that he had created it, and that it existed somewhere. Even if it was wrapped up in paper and hidden in an attic where no one would ever see it. I want to respect his feelings."

The room was quiet for a while.

"You've played around here since you were small, right? Using that secret passageway of yours. Isn't that so?"

Mariye nodded.

"Did you ever meet Tomohiko Amada?"

"I saw the old guy. But I never talked to him. I just hid and looked at him from far away. When he was painting. I mean, I was trespassing, right?"

I nodded. The image was all too real. Mariye in the shrubbery, peeking into the studio. Tomohiko Amada on his stool, intently wielding his brush. The thought that he was being observed a million miles from his mind.

"You asked me to help you with something," Mariye said.

"So I did. There's one thing," I said. "I'd like you to help me wrap up these two paintings and hide them in the attic where no one can see them. *Killing Commendatore* and *The Man with the White Subaru Forester*. I don't think we need them right now. That's where I could use your help."

Mariye nodded but didn't say anything. Truth be told, this was a task I really didn't want to do alone. More than help, I needed someone to act as observer and witness. Someone tight-lipped, whom I could trust to share the secret.

I went to the kitchen and got some twine and a utility knife. Then Mariye and I packed up *Killing Commendatore*. We wrapped it carefully in the same brown washi, the traditional Japanese paper it had been in before, bound it with twine, draped it in a white cloth, and then tied it again. Firmly, to make it difficult for anyone to unwrap. The thick paint on *The Man with the White Subaru Forester* wasn't quite dry, so we wrapped it more loosely. Then we carried the two paintings to the closet of the guest bedroom. I climbed to the top of the stepladder, raised the trap door to the attic (much like Long Face had pushed up the square lid to his hole, come to think of it), and climbed up. The air was chilly there, but a pleasant kind of chilly. Mariye handed the paintings up to me. *Killing Commendatore* went first, followed by *The Man with the White Subaru Forester*. I leaned them next to each other against the wall.

All of a sudden, I sensed I had company. I gulped. Someone was there—I could feel a presence. Then I saw the horned owl. Probably the same owl I had seen the first time. The night bird was perched on the same beam as before, still as a statue. He didn't seem particularly concerned when I moved in his direction. Also like the first time.

"Hey. Come up and see something," I whispered to Mariye. "Something very cool. Try not to make any noise."

Looking curious, Mariye mounted the ladder and crawled through the opening into the attic. I pulled her up the last step with both hands. The floor of the attic was covered with a fine white dust, but she didn't show any concern that it would get on her wool skirt. I sat down and pointed out the horned owl to her. She knelt beside me and looked at the bird, entranced. It was very beautiful. Like a cat that had sprouted wings. "It's been living here the whole while," I whispered to her. "It goes out to hunt in the forest in the evening, and flies back in the morning to sleep. That's its entrance there."

I pointed at the air vent with the hole in its screen. Mariye nodded. I could hear the faint sound of her breathing.

We sat there side by side without speaking, looking at the owl. Showing little interest in us, the owl sat there quietly, a model of discretion. The owl and I had a tacit understanding that we would share the house. One of us was active during the day, the other at night—in that way, the domain of consciousness was shared equally, half and half.

Mariye reached over and took my hand in hers. Her head came to rest on my shoulder. I gently squeezed her hand back. Komi and I had spent long hours together like this. We were close as brother and sister. Our feelings had flowed back and forth in a very natural way. Until death separated us.

I could feel the tension drain from Mariye's body. Little by little, that part of her that had become so rigid was beginning to unclench. I stroked her head on my shoulder. Her soft, straight hair. When my hand touched her cheek, I realized she was crying. The tears were so warm it felt as if blood was spilling from her heart. I continued to hold her like that. The girl had needed to cry. But she hadn't been able to. Probably for a very long time. The horned owl and I kept watch over her as she wept.

The rays of the afternoon sun angled through the hole in the broken vent. White dust and silence surrounded us, nothing more. Dust and silence that seemed to have been passed down from antiquity. We could hear no wind. On his beam, the horned owl mutely preserved the wisdom of the forest. A wisdom also bequeathed from the distant past.

Mariye wept for a long time. She made no sound, but the trembling of her body told me she was still crying. I kept stroking her hair. As if she and I were heading upstream along the river of time.

60

IF THAT PERSON HAD PRETTY LONG ARMS

I was at Mr. Menshiki's house," Mariye said. "The whole four days." She had stopped crying, and was talking again.

She and I were in the studio. Mariye was perched on the round stool, her knees touching as they peeked out from beneath her skirt. I was leaning on the windowsill. I could see how pretty her legs were. Her bulky tights couldn't hide that. When she matured a bit more, those legs would attract the gaze of many men. By then, her chest would have filled out too. Now, however, she was just a lost and confused girl, wavering on the threshold of adulthood.

"You were at Mr. Menshiki's?" I asked. "I'm not sure I understand. Can you fill me in a little?"

"I needed to know more about him, so I went to his house. I had to find out why he was watching our home through those binoculars every night. I think he bought the big house across the valley just to do that. To spy on us. I couldn't understand why he would do something like that. I mean, it was so not normal. I thought there had to be some kind of reason."

"So you went to pay him a visit?"

Mariye shook her head no. "I didn't pay him a visit. I snuck in. Secretly. And then I couldn't get out."

"You snuck in?"

"Yes, like a burglar. I didn't plan it like that, though."

When her morning classes ended on Friday, Mariye slipped out the back door of the school. If a student was unexpectedly absent in the morning, the school called their family. But no phone call was made when a student missed his or her afternoon classes. There was no clear reason for this policy—that's just the way things were done. Mariye had never skipped out before, so she figured if she got caught she could talk her way out of trouble. She hopped on a bus and got off close to where she lived. But instead of heading home, she turned up the opposite slope, toward Menshiki's house.

At first, Mariye had no intention of sneaking in. The idea never crossed her mind. Yet she wasn't planning to ring Menshiki's doorbell and invite herself in, either. The fact was, she went there with no plan in mind. She was simply drawn to the white mansion like a metal filing to a powerful magnet. She couldn't solve the mystery of Menshiki's behavior merely by standing outside his wall. She knew that much. Yet she couldn't stifle her curiosity. Her legs carried her to his gate under their own volition.

It was a very long climb. When she turned and looked back, she could see the ocean sparkling between the mountains. His house was surrounded by a high wall with a sturdy electrically operated gate positioned at the entrance. Security cameras were set on each side. One of the gate's pillars had a security company's logo stuck to it. She had to approach with care. She hid behind some bushes and took stock of the situation. She could spot no movement, either inside or outside the house. No one entered or left, and no noise of any kind came from within.

After wasting half an hour hanging around with nothing to do, she had given up and was preparing to leave when she saw a van roll up the hill. A minivan, from a parcel delivery service. It stopped in front of the gate, a door opened, and a uniformed young man jumped out, clipboard in hand. He walked to the gate and rang the bell. There was a brief exchange with someone over the intercom. When the big wooden gate started to slowly swing in, the young man hurried back to his van and drove inside.

Mariye had no time to think things through. The moment the van entered, she leapt from the bushes and sprinted as fast as she could through the closing gate. It was pretty close, but she managed to slip through a split second before it shut. The security cameras might have picked her up. But no one came out to challenge her. Dogs, though, were a scarier proposition. A guard dog might be prowling the grounds. She hadn't considered that before racing in. The instant the gate closed behind her, though, the possibility occurred to her. A property this extensive could easily have a Doberman or a German shepherd running loose. A big dog like that would be a problem. Mariye was afraid of dogs. But as luck would have it, none appeared. She heard no barking, either. Now that she thought of it, there had been no talk of a dog when she and her aunt had paid their visit.

Having made her way inside the wall, she hid behind some shrubs and appraised her situation. Her throat was dry. I stole in here like a burglar, she thought. I'm breaking the law—this is trespassing, no doubt about it. The cameras have recorded proof of my guilt.

Had she made the right move? She wasn't sure. When she had seen the delivery van pass through the gate, her response had been automatic. She'd had no time to consider the possible consequences. Now's my one and only chance, she'd thought, and acted on the spur of the moment. Her body had moved before her mind clicked in. Yet for some reason, even now, she had no second thoughts.

From her hiding place she saw the delivery van roll back up the driveway. Once again, the gate slowly swung open and the van passed through. If she was going to leave, now was the time. Just run out before the gate closed. Return to the world of safety. She wouldn't be a criminal. But she didn't move. Instead, she remained there, hidden in the shadows, and watched the gate close again. Intently biting her lower lip.

She waited there for precisely ten minutes, measuring the time on her small Casio G-Shock watch. When the ten minutes were up, she emerged from the shrubbery. Bending low so the cameras would have difficulty spotting her, she hurried down the gentle slope toward the front door of the house. It was two thirty.

What if Menshiki discovered her? She thought about that for a moment. Well, she decided, if that happened she'd wriggle out of it somehow. Menshiki seemed to have a keen interest (or something like that) in her. So if she told him she'd just come to say hi and, seeing the gate open, had walked in, and made it all seem like a kid's game, he would trust her. He wants to believe in something, she thought, so he'll swallow what I say. The problem was, where did his "keen interest" come from, and did he have good intentions, or was he dangerous?

The front door of the mansion was around the bend, at the bottom of the sloping driveway. There was a bell beside the door. Needless to say, she didn't push it. Instead, she moved clockwise around the building, hiding behind trees and shrubs, hugging the concrete wall and giving the roundabout where guests parked a wide berth. A two-car garage sat to the left of the entranceway. Its door was rolled down and locked. A little farther on sat a stylish little building that looked like a cottage. That must be the guesthouse, she thought. Beyond that was a tennis court. She had never seen a home with a tennis court before. Who did Mr. Menshiki play tennis with? The court, however, appeared to have been long ignored. It had no net, its all-weather surface was strewn with leaves, and the white lines were so faded they were almost invisible.

All the windows facing the mountainside were small and tightly shuttered, so nothing inside could be seen. As before, the house was absolutely quiet. No barking dogs. From time to time she could hear birds chirping high in the trees, but that was all. At the back of the house was another garage. Also with space for two cars. It seemed to have been added after the house was built. Menshiki sure could store an awful lot of cars!

The slope behind the house had been turned into a large Japanese-style garden. She could see a descending flight of steps, and below that a path weaving through a number of large rocks. The azalea bushes were pruned to perfection, the pine branches overhead an array of bright greens. What looked like an arbor lay just beyond. A reclining chair where one could stretch out and read sat under the arbor. Beside it was a coffee table. Lanterns and lights were scattered here and there.

Mariye worked her way around the house to the back. The house's broad deck looked from there out over the valley. She had walked out onto that deck on her first visit. It was from there that Menshiki kept watch on her home. The second she set foot on it she knew that was true. She felt it in her bones.

Mariye squinted as she looked over at her home. It was right across from her. So close it seemed a person could reach out and touch it (if that person had pretty long arms, that is). From this vantage point, the house looked utterly defenseless. At the time it was built, there had been no homes on this side of the valley. Only recently (though more than ten years ago) had building restrictions been eased and houses erected on this slope. That was why, when her home was designed, no attempt had been made to shield it from those across the way. That made it a sitting duck for prying eyes. A high-powered telescope or even a pair of good binoculars would give one a clear view of what was going on inside. The window to her bedroom was a perfect example. To be sure, she was a cautious girl. She always closed the curtain before taking off her clothes. But that didn't mean there were no unguarded moments. What had Menshiki seen?

Mariye descended the outside steps to the next floor where the study was, but the windows were shuttered there too. She couldn't peek in at all. So she kept walking down to the lowest level. Most of that floor was occupied by a large utility area. She could see a washing machine, a place for an ironing board, a room that seemed to be set aside for a live-in maid, and, on the far end, a sizable gym containing five or six exercise machines. Unlike the tennis court, these appeared to be well used. They all looked clean and well oiled. A heavy punching bag hung from the ceiling. Compared with the upper floors, this floor was less tightly guarded. Many of the windows lacked curtains, so she could peer inside. Nevertheless, both the windows and the sliding glass doors were securely locked from within. Here too the security company had pasted their stickers to scare off intruders. An alarm would sound in their offices if anyone tried to force their way in.

The mansion was huge. She found it impossible to believe that a single person could inhabit such a big space. It must be a lonely life. The concrete walls were thick, and every precaution had been taken to block anyone from gaining entry. True, there was no guard dog (maybe he didn't like dogs either), but apart from that every antiburglar device under the sun had been employed.

What should be her next step? Nothing came to mind. There was no way to get inside, and no way to breach the wall to get out. Menshiki was home, she knew that. He had pushed the button that opened the gate and taken delivery of the parcel. And he lived there by himself.

Once a week, a cleaning service came, but apart from that the house was off-limits to outsiders. That was his basic principle—he had told them that on their visit.

Since she couldn't gain access to the house, she had to find a place to hide outside. If she kept poking around she might locate a likely spot. After a long search, she finally came across what seemed to be a small storage shed at the far corner of the garden. The door was unlocked. Inside were a bunch of garden tools and stacked bags of fertilizer. She slipped in and sat down on the bags. The shed was far from inviting. But at least the security cameras wouldn't find her here. And it was unlikely anyone would show up. Sooner or later, things would change. All she could do was wait.

Although she was stuck in one place, she felt full of energy. After her shower that morning, she had noticed swellings on her chest in the mirror. It was an exciting development. Of course, she might be deluding herself. It could just be wishful thinking. She had inspected her chest from a number of angles, and touched it with her hands. There did seem to be two soft protuberances that had not been there before. Her nipples were still tiny (a far cry from her aunt's, which resembled olive pits), but there was a hint they might be about to sprout.

Mariye passed her time in the storage shed thinking about her budding breasts. She pictured how they might look when they grew. What would it feel like to live your life with really big ones? She imagined strapping on the kind of underwire bra her aunt used. That day was still miles away, however. After all, her periods had only begun that spring.

She was a little thirsty, but she could bear that. She consulted her chunky G-Shock watch. It was five minutes past three. Her painting class was on Fridays, but she'd been planning to skip that anyway. She hadn't brought her bag of painting supplies with her. Yet her aunt was sure to worry if she didn't get home by dinnertime. She could come up with a good excuse later.

She seemed to have fallen asleep. It was hard to believe that she could have slept in this place, and under these circumstances. Yet she had managed to drop off without realizing it. It hadn't been for very long.

Ten or fifteen minutes. Maybe less. But a deep sleep, nonetheless. She was disoriented when she awoke, her mind at loose ends. For a moment she didn't know where she was or what she was doing. It seemed she had been dreaming. A vague dream, something to do with full breasts and milk chocolate. Her mouth was filled with saliva. Then it hit her. I snuck into Menshiki's, she remembered, and now I'm hiding in his storage shed.

A noise had roused her. A repetitive, mechanical noise. To be more precise, a garage door clattering open. The door of the garage near the entrance. Menshiki was probably in his car and about to head off somewhere. Mariye hurried from the shed and ran around to the front, making as little sound as possible. When the door was fully open the clattering stopped. She heard a car start up, and then the front of Menshiki's silver Jaguar slowly emerged. Menshiki was sitting in the driver's seat. The driver's window was down, and his pure white hair glowed in the afternoon sun. She watched from behind the shrubbery.

Had Menshiki looked to his right, he could have glimpsed her there in the shadows. The shrubs were too small to provide full cover. But his eyes were trained straight ahead. Hands on the wheel, he seemed lost in thought. The Jaguar moved up the driveway, passed around the curve, and disappeared. The remote control–activated metal door began to clatter down again. The second before it closed, Mariye raced from her hiding place and slipped under the door. Like Indiana Jones in *Raiders of the Lost Ark*. Another reflex action. Without really thinking, she had decided to gain access to the house through the garage. The automatic door hesitated when it sensed her slide underneath, then resumed its descent until it was tightly shut.

Another car was in the garage. A stylish blue convertible with a beige hood, the sports car her aunt had admired on their previous visit. Mariye couldn't care less about cars, so she'd barely glanced at it then. It had a very long nose, and, here too, the Jaguar crest. Even someone who knew as little about cars as Mariye could tell it was worth a lot of money. A collector's piece, in all likelihood.

A person could pass into the house through a door in the garage. She tried the knob with some trepidation, but it turned easily. She sighed with relief. Few people would lock a door like that during the day, but Menshiki was such a cautious man she couldn't be sure. Perhaps something had been on his mind to make him forget. She'd been lucky.

She walked through the door and into the house. Should she take her shoes off or keep them on? In the end, she decided to carry them with her. Leaving them on the doorstep didn't seem like a good option. The house was hushed when she entered. As if everything in it was holding its breath. Menshiki was gone, and she was positive no one else was there. I'm alone in this huge house, she thought. For the next little while, I am free to go wherever, and do whatever, I want.

Menshiki had given them a basic guided tour on their first visit. She remembered it well enough. The general layout was fixed in her head. She entered the big living room that took up almost the entire first floor. From there, one could go out to the broad deck through a sliding glass door. She hesitated, though. Menshiki might have activated the security system before leaving. If he had, an alarm would go off when she tried to slide it open. A light would flash in the agency's office. They would phone the house to check. A password would be necessary to end the alert. Mariye stood before the sliding door, black loafers in hand, pondering the situation.

Finally, she reached the conclusion that Menshiki hadn't set the alarm. The fact that he had left the inner door in the garage unlocked suggested that he wasn't heading off on a long trip. Odds were he had gone shopping, or was running some sort of errand. Mariye made up her mind. She unlocked the door, slid it open, and waited to see what would happen. No alarm went off, and the security agency did not phone. She heaved a sigh of relief (had security guards found her there she couldn't have joked her way out of it) and stepped out onto the deck. Putting down her shoes, she went over to the binoculars and removed their plastic cover. They were too heavy to hold, so she tried balancing them on the railing, but that didn't work very well. Looking around, she noticed what looked like a stand leaning against the wall. It resembled a camera tripod and was the same olive color as the binoculars. The binoculars could be screwed onto the stand. She stuck them together, pulled up the low metal stool left nearby, sat down, and looked through them. Now using the binoculars was easy. Moreover, they were positioned so that she couldn't be observed from the other side of the valley. This had to be how Menshiki spent much of his time.

She was shocked at how clearly the inside of her house could be seen. Everything was a notch brighter—one of the binoculars' special features, she assumed. Some of the curtains in the rooms facing the valley hadn't been drawn. The view within was so distinct she felt she could reach out and touch what she was looking at. A vase of flowers, for example, or even a magazine on the table. Her aunt should be home at this hour. But she couldn't locate her anywhere.

It was weird to look inside her own house from such a distance, and in such naked detail. It felt as if she had become one of the dead (how was unclear) and now was viewing her home from their vantage point. She had belonged there for so long, yet it was hers no more. She knew it so intimately but could never go back. It was a strange, dissociated sensation.

She trained the binoculars on her own room. It faced in her direction, but the curtain was drawn. Shut tight, without a crack. Her familiar curtain, with its orange pattern. The orange bleached by the sun. She couldn't see behind it. But her shadow was probably visible at night, when the light was on. How visible, though, could only be known after dark. Mariye panned across the house, looking for her aunt. She ought to be there. But she was nowhere to be seen. Perhaps she was preparing dinner in the kitchen in the back. Or resting in her room. Wherever she was, she wasn't visible from this angle.

Mariye felt a powerful urge to go back to that house. Right away. She longed to sit in her familiar chair at the dining room table and sip hot tea in her very own cup. To watch her aunt preparing dinner in the kitchen. How wonderful that would be, she thought. Until that point, she had never imagined missing her home this way. Not for a second. To her, the house had always been an ugly, barren monstrosity. She had hated living there. In fact, she was impatient for the day when she was old enough to move into her own place, one that suited her. Yet now, looking at its interior from the other side of the valley through the clear lens, she wanted to return at any cost. *It was where she belonged.* Where she would be protected.

Just then she heard a faint droning sound. Prying her eyes from the binoculars, she saw something black circling above her. A large bee with a long body, probably a hornet. The kind of hostile, aggressive hornet with a sharp stinger that had killed her mother. Mariye ran back into the house, forcefully slid the door shut, and locked it. The hornet buzzed around the door for a while, as if to pen her in. It struck the glass several times, then finally gave up and flew away. Mariye gave a great sigh of relief. Her heart was pounding, her breathing ragged. Nothing scared her more than hornets. Her father had lectured her time and again how dangerous they were. Mariye had looked at many photographs so that she knew exactly how they looked. In the process, she had conceived the terrifying idea that she, like her mother, would be stung to death. She might well have the same allergic reaction. One couldn't escape death, but it should come later—she wanted to know what it felt like to have full breasts and a woman's nipples at least once before she died. It would really suck if hornets killed her before she had that chance.

It was better to stay in the house a while, for safety's sake. That savage insect would still be flying about. Moreover, it appeared to be targeting her. She decided to search inside the mansion and forget about going outside for the time being.

Her first step was to tour the sprawling living room. She could see no particular change since her first visit. There was the big Steinway grand piano. A small stack of musical scores was piled on top of it. A Bach invention, a Mozart sonata, one of Chopin's études, that sort of thing. Nothing that required advanced technical skill. Still, being able to play them at all was impressive. Mariye could tell that much. She had taken piano lessons when she was younger. (She hadn't gone very far—art was what had grabbed her.)

A number of books were scattered on the coffee table's marble top. Judging from the bookmarks stuck in them, all were in the process of being read. One was on philosophy, one was historical, and two were novels (one of which was in English). She recognized none of the titles and had heard of none of the authors' names. She flipped through several, but they weren't her thing. The master of the house loved difficult books and classical music. Between those pursuits, he looked into her home across the valley through high-powered binoculars.

Was he just a perv? Or was there a logical reason or purpose for his behavior? Did he have the hots for her aunt? Or for her? Or for both of them? (Was such a thing possible?)

Next she went to take a look at the lower levels. First she made her way to Menshiki's study. His portrait hung on the wall. She stood in the middle of the room and studied it for a moment. Of course, she had seen it before (that had been the purpose of their first visit). This time, though, the longer she looked at it, the more it felt as if Menshiki were there with her. So she turned away from the painting. Trying her best to ignore it, she went over to inspect his desk. There was a state-of-the-art Apple desktop computer, but she didn't switch it on. She knew without trying that it was secured. There would be no way she could gain access. Not much else was on the desk. There was a deskpad calendar with almost nothing written on it. Just a few incomprehensible symbols and numbers here and there. He would have input his daily schedule into the computer, and then shared it with his other devices. All would be locked. Mr. Menshiki was a cautious man. He would leave no traces.

The other things on the desk were the sort of work-related materials you would expect to find in anyone's study. The pencils were all of the same length, and sharpened to a fine point. Paper clips were arranged according to size. The white memo pad waited patiently for someone to write on it. The digital clock faithfully clicked off the time. The desk was in such perfect order it was frightening. Unless he's a well-made android, Mariye thought to herself, something sure is funny about Mr. Menshiki.

As she expected, every desk drawer was locked. That was only natural. No way he would neglect securing them. The study held little else that she wanted to see. She had no special interest in the shelves of books, or the CD collection, or the new, obviously expensive stereo system. Those did no more than reflect his range of tastes. They didn't help her understand who he was as a person. They had no connection to the secret he was (most likely) concealing.

Mariye left the study and walked down the dim hallway, checking the rooms as she went. All were unlocked. None had been included in the house tour. She and her aunt had only been shown the living room, the study, the dining room, and the kitchen (she had also used the guest bathroom on the first floor). Mariye opened the doors to these unknown rooms one by one. The first was Menshiki's bedroom. As the so-called master bedroom (she assumed), it was very big. It had a walk-in closet and a private bathroom. Its large bed was neatly turned out, with a quilted duvet. Since there was no live-in maid, she assumed Menshiki had made the bed. If so, its neatness didn't surprise her. A pair of plain dark brown pajamas lay next to the pillow, also neatly folded. A number of prints hung on the wall. A set by a single artist, from the looks of it. A half-read book rested on the bedside table. He certainly was an avid reader. The window faced the valley, but it wasn't very large and its blinds had been drawn.

She opened the door to the big walk-in closet. Rows of clothes were hanging there. Lots of jackets and blazers, but not many suits. Not many neckties, either. She guessed he seldom needed to dress for formal occasions. All the shirts had plastic covers, and appeared to have just come back from the cleaners. Shoes and sneakers were lined up on shelves in neat rows. Coats of varied thicknesses occupied another part of the closet. Everything in the closet was looked after with care and reflected the good taste of its owner. Indeed, the whole closet could have been featured as it was in a menswear magazine. There were not too many clothes, nor too few. Moderation governed everything.

His drawers contained socks, handkerchiefs, and underwear. All were pressed and folded, and arranged in perfect order. There were more drawers for his jeans, polo shirts, sweatshirts, and so forth. One large drawer had been entirely given over to a colorful array of beautiful sweaters. None had patterns. Yet Mariye could find nothing in any of these drawers to help her unravel Menshiki's secret. Everything was immaculate and divided according to its function. Not a speck of dust was on the floor, and all the picture frames were level on the walls.

Mariye did reach one clear conclusion about Menshiki, however: this man would be impossible to live with. No normal person could meet his standard. Her aunt was something of a neat freak, but even she wasn't this meticulous.

The next door opened onto what appeared to be the guest room. It had a double bed, made up and ready to be used. A writing desk and office chair sat near the window. There was also a small television set. But there was no sign that anyone had ever slept there—the room felt as if it had been forsaken for eternity. Mr. Menshiki was not in the habit of entertaining guests, it seemed. Instead, this room was apparently to be used in emergencies (though she couldn't imagine what those might be).

The room next door was more like a storeroom. It had no furniture, and at least ten cardboard boxes were stacked on the green carpet. Judging by their weight, they contained documents. Each had a label, with markings in ballpoint pen. All were carefully sealed with tape. Mariye imagined they were filled with work-related documents. Those might contain important secrets. But they were business secrets, not the sort of thing that she was after.

None of these rooms was locked. Though their windows faced the valley, their blinds were closed. No one was there to delight in the bright sunlight and the majestic view. They were dimly lit and smelled of abandonment.

The fourth room fascinated her. Not so much the room itself, though. The furnishings were sparse—just a single straight-backed chair and a small, plain wooden table. No pictures graced the bare walls. Without decoration of any kind, it felt barren and empty. A room no one ever used. Yet when she checked the walk-in closet, she found an assortment of women's clothes hanging there. Not a huge number. But everything a woman would need, more or less, for a stay of several days. Mariye guessed the clothes had been set aside for someone who came to visit Menshiki on a regular basis. She scowled. Did her aunt know a woman like that was in the picture?

She quickly realized her mistake, however. The clothes were all out of style, designs from a different era. The dresses and skirts and blouses sported name brands, and were very fashionable and expensive, but not the sort that women wore these days. Mariye wasn't that up-to-date on current trends, but even she could tell that much. They had probably been in style before she was born. And all were permeated with the smell of mothballs. It appeared that the clothes had been hanging there for quite some time. They were being well looked after, though. She saw no moth holes. And the colors hadn't faded, which meant that care had been taken not to expose them to extreme heat or cold. The dresses were size 5. That indicated that the woman was about five feet tall. And very slender, looking at the skirts. She wore a size 5 shoe.

An assortment of women's undergarments, socks, and nightgowns were stored in the closet drawers. All were in plastic bags to ward off dust. She pulled a few out to examine. The bras were a 32C. Mariye pictured the shape of the breasts they had held. Slightly smaller than her aunt's, she estimated (it was impossible to guess the shape of the nipples, of course). The panties were dainty and elegant. Some were on the sexy side. All in all, they spoke of a woman of some means, who shopped in lingerie boutiques while savoring the thought of embracing the man she loved. They were made of silk and lace and had to be washed by hand in lukewarm water. Not the sort of panties one wore to weed the garden. Here too the odor of mothballs was strong. She folded the panties up carefully, returned them to the plastic bag, and put it back in the drawer.

This was the wardrobe of a woman whom Menshiki had been seeing some time before—fifteen or twenty years ago, most likely. That was the conclusion Mariye drew. Then something had happened that caused the woman to leave her stylish clothes—her size 5 dresses, size 5 shoes, and 32C bras—behind. She had never come back. Why would she have left such an expensive collection behind? If they had separated for some reason, wouldn't the normal thing have been to take the clothes with her? Mariye couldn't figure it out. Moreover, Menshiki had preserved that small collection with such care. Like the river sprites of the Rhine, who took pains to preserve their legendary gold for posterity. He probably visited this room on occasion to look at the clothes and take them in his hands. When the seasons changed, he would replace the mothballs (she couldn't imagine him letting anyone else do this).

Where was that woman today? Perhaps she had married another man. Or died of illness, or in some kind of accident. Nevertheless, he held her in his memory, even now.

(Of course, Mariye had no way of knowing that woman was her

mother, and *I* could find no compelling reason to tell her. That right, I thought, belonged to Menshiki alone.)

Mariye pondered this new knowledge. Should she think more generously of a man who had treasured the memory of a woman for so long? Or was the fact that he had preserved her clothing with such care a little creepy?

Mariye was still thinking this through when, all at once, she heard the garage door clattering up. Menshiki had come home. She had been so absorbed in the clothes that she hadn't heard the front gate open, or the car in the driveway. She had to get away as quickly as possible. She needed to find a safe place to hide. Then she realized. Something of *vital importance*. Panic grabbed her.

She had forgotten her shoes on the deck. And the binoculars were out of their case and attached to their stand. The hornet had scared her so much that she had fled into the house without covering her tracks. Everything was out in the open. When Menshiki went out to the deck and saw those things (as he would sooner or later), he would know right away that someone had invaded his home in his absence. The black loafers would tell him that the invader was a girl. Menshiki was no dummy. It wouldn't take long for him to figure out it was Mariye. He would comb the house, searching every nook and cranny, until he found her hiding place. It would be child's play for him.

There wasn't time enough to run outside up to the deck, collect her shoes, and put the binoculars back where they belonged. She was certain to bump into Menshiki somewhere along the way. She couldn't think of a next step. Her heart pounded, her breathing became labored, her limbs froze with fear.

The car engine stopped and the garage door started clattering shut. Any minute now Menshiki would enter the house. What should she do? What should she . . . Her mind was a blank. She sat on the floor, her head in her hands and her eyes squeezed shut.

"It is best to remain where you are," someone said.

Was she hearing things? No, she wasn't. Pulling herself together, she opened her eyes. There was a little old man no more than two feet tall, perched on a low chest of drawers. His salt-and-pepper hair was tied in a bun on top of his head. He wore white garments from a bygone age and carried a tiny sword at his waist. Naturally, she thought she was hallucinating. Her panic was making her imagine things that weren't there.

"No, this is no hallucination," the little old man said in a small but resonant voice. "I am the Commendatore. And I am here to aid my young friends."

61

I HAVE TO BE A BRAVE, SMART GIRL

"This is no hallucination," the Commendatore repeated. "There are sundry opinions as to whether I exist, but a hallucination I am not. I have come to aid my friends. You are in need of aid, are you not?"

"My friends" referred to her, Mariye assumed. She nodded. His manner of speech was strange indeed, but what he said was true. She needed help, no question there.

"My friends cannot retrieve your shoes from the deck," the Commendatore said. "And it is best to forget the binoculars as well. But quell your fears. I will strive my utmost to ensure that Menshiki does not go there. For the time being, at least. Once the sun sets, however, I cannot prevent him. When darkness falls, he will venture out to watch the home of my friends. This is his custom. We must fix the problem before that happens. Can my friends understand the import of my words?"

Mariye could only nod. Somehow, she did understand.

"My friends must hide in this closet awhile," said the Commendatore. "Be as quiet as a mouse. Give no sign that you are here. When the time is propitious I will let you know. Until then, do not move or make a sound. No matter what happens. Do my friends understand?"

Mariye nodded again. Was this a dream? Could he be an elf or sprite of some kind?

"I am neither dream nor sprite," the Commendatore read her thoughts. "I am an Idea, and thus lack shape of my own. It would be very inconvenient if my friends could not see me, so I have taken the form of the Commendatore for the time being."

Idea, the Commendatore . . . Mariye repeated the words in her mind without voicing them. He can tell what I am thinking. Then she remembered. He was a figure in that very wide Japanese-style painting by Tomohiko Amada that she had seen in his studio. Somehow he had slipped out of the painting and come here. That explained his tiny size.

"Affirmative," the Commendatore said. "I am borrowing the form of that character. The Commendatore—I myself do not know his significance. But I am called by that sobriquet now. Wait here in silence. I will come for my friends at the proper time. Do not fear. These raiments will shelter you."

These raiments will shelter me? What did that mean? But he did not respond to her unspoken question. A moment later he was gone. Vanished into thin air, like vapor.

Mariye did as the Commendatore said. She quieted her breathing and didn't move a muscle. Menshiki was home—she had heard him enter the house. He seemed to have been shopping, for she could make out the rustle of paper bags. Her breathing almost stopped when his slippered feet padded slowly past the room where she was hiding.

The closet door was a Venetian blind, so some light seeped upward through the slats. But only a tiny bit. The closet would grow very dark when the daylight faded. She could see only the carpeted floor through the cracks. The closet was cramped, and filled with the sharp odor of mothballs. With walls on all sides, there was nowhere to hide. And no way to escape. The lack of an escape route scared her to death.

The Commendatore had promised to come and get her when the right time came. She had no choice but to believe him. He had said, "These raiments will shelter you," too. He must have meant the clothes there in the closet. Old clothes worn by some unknown woman, likely before Mariye was even born. How could they protect her? She reached out and stroked a dress with a flower pattern. The pink cloth was soft to the touch. She let her fingertips linger for a while. She couldn't explain why, but there was something comforting about it.

I bet this dress would fit, Mariye thought. Its owner wasn't that much bigger than me. I can wear a size 5. Of course my chest hasn't filled out yet, so I'd have to figure a way to conceal that. But I could wear most of these clothes if I wanted to, or if I had to for some reason. The thought made her heart skip a beat.

Time was passing. Slowly but surely, the room was growing darker. Evening was approaching, minute by minute. She looked at her watch. But she couldn't read it in the gloom. She pressed a button and the face lit up. It was almost four thirty. The sun would be going down soon. The days were getting shorter. And when night did come, Menshiki would head out to the deck. It would take him but a second to realize that someone had invaded his home. She had to find some way to deal with the shoes and binoculars before that happened.

Mariye waited impatiently for the Commendatore to arrive, her heart in her mouth. Yet he never did. Perhaps there had been some kind of hitch. Menshiki might have left him no opening. She hadn't a clue how extensive the actual powers of a person—or an Idea—like the Commendatore were, in fact, or how far she could depend on him. Yet he was her only hope. She had nowhere else to turn. Mariye sat holding her knees on the floor of the closet, staring through the slats at the carpet. From time to time she reached up to stroke the flowery dress. As though it were a lifeline of some kind.

When the room had grown quite dark, she heard footsteps in the hall a second time. Once again, they were slow and soft. The footsteps came to an abrupt halt in front of the room where she was hiding. As if whoever it was had sniffed out something. A moment later she heard the door open. There could be no doubt. Her heart froze in her mouth. Then she heard the person (Menshiki, she presumed—no one else was in the house) step inside and gently close the door behind him. It clicked shut. *The man is in the room. For sure.* Like her, he held his breath and listened carefully, trying to pick up the slightest sign. She could tell. But the man did not turn on the light. Instead he carried out his search in the dark. Why? Anyone else would have switched on the light the moment they came in. It baffled her.

Mariye stared at the floor through the slats. If he came close enough, his toes would come into view. She couldn't see them yet. Yet his presence felt very real. It was definitely a man. Moreover, that man (it had to be Menshiki!) was staring at the closet door in the dark. He had picked up signs of something. Something different than usual. Next he would open the door. It couldn't be otherwise. It would be easy, since of course it wasn't locked. All he had to do was reach out, grab the knob, and pull.

The footsteps drew even closer. Fear gripped her. Cold sweat dripped from her armpits. I should never have come, she thought. I should have stayed home like a good girl. In my dear home across the valley. There is something really scary about this place. Something I should never have approached so recklessly. Some kind of consciousness operated here. The hornets were a part of it. Now she was within arm's reach of that *something*. She could see the toe of a slipper through the blinds. She could tell that the slipper was brown and made of leather, but it was too dark to see anything more.

Mariye instinctively reached up and grabbed the dress. The size 5 dress with the flower pattern. *Please help me! Protect me!* she prayed.

The man stood in front of the closet's double doors for some time. He didn't make a sound. She couldn't even hear him breathe. Still as a stone statue, he stood there gauging the situation. The silence grew heavier, the dark more impenetrable. She huddled on the floor, quivering. Her teeth chattered faintly. Mariye longed to shut her eyes and ears. To put her mind in a totally different place. But she didn't. She somehow knew how dangerous that would be. She must never give in to fear, however great. Never abandon her senses. Never stop thinking. With her ears pricked and her eyes fastened on the toes of the leather slippers, she fiercely clutched the hem of the soft pink dress.

The clothes would protect her. The whole wardrobe was her ally. The size 5 dresses, the size 5 shoes, the 32C bras—they would enfold her in a cloak of invisibility. I am not here, she told herself. *I am not here.*

How much time passed? She had no way of knowing. Time was no longer uniform, nor did it flow in sequence. Nevertheless, a fixed period seemed to have elapsed. At one point, the man had been on the verge of opening the door. Mariye felt that strongly. She braced herself. When it opened he would see her. She would see him. Then what? She had no clue. *Perhaps it's not Menshiki at all*—the thought popped into her head. *But then who could it be?*

Yet the man never opened the door. After some hesitation, he pulled back his hand and moved away. Why had he changed his mind at the last minute? *Something* must have held him back. He stepped out into the hallway and closed the door behind him. The room was empty again. For certain. It was no ruse. She was alone. She was certain of that. Mariye closed her eyes and expelled all the air she had been holding in a great sigh.

Her heart was still pounding. Like a tom-tom—that's how a novelist might describe it. What was a tom-tom, anyway? She had no clear picture. She had been in great peril. At the very last moment, however, something had intervened to protect her. Even so, this place was too dangerous—that much was obvious. Whoever it was, that *someone* had sensed her presence. Beyond a doubt. She couldn't hide in this room forever. This time, she had squeaked through. Next time she might not be so lucky.

She kept waiting. The room grew even darker. But she didn't make a sound. She was fearful, she was anxious, but she persevered. The Commendatore would not forget her. She believed what he had told her. She had no other options—she had to rely on the little guy with the funny way of talking.

Then, before she knew it, the Commendatore was there.

"My friends must leave immediately," he whispered. "Now, at this very moment. Wake up, it is now time."

Mariye was at a loss. It was hard to stand up. When she imagined leaving the closet she was assaulted by a new fear. Even greater dangers might await her in the world outside.

"Menshiki is in the shower," the Commendatore said. "You know what a clean person he is. So he should linger there awhile. But he will come out by and by. This is the one and only chance that my friends will have. Make haste!"

Marshaling her strength, Mariye pulled herself to her feet. She pushed the door of the closet open. The room was dark and empty.

Before she stepped out, she turned to take one last look at the clothes hanging there. She inhaled the smell of mothballs. She might never see these clothes again. For some reason, they had become so close to her, so dear.

"My friends must go now," said the Commendatore. "There is not much time. Go into the hallway and turn left."

With her bag over her shoulder, Mariye walked out the door and down the corridor. She ran up the stairs, cut across the big living room, and slid open the glass door to the deck terrace. The hornet might still be around. Or he might have retired for the night. He could be the kind of insect that wasn't fazed by the dark. But she couldn't dwell on that now. She stepped out, unscrewed the binoculars from their stand, and returned them to their plastic cover. She folded the stand and leaned it back against the wall. Her nerves made her hands fumble, so it took longer than she had expected. Then she picked her black loafers up off the deck. All the while, the Commendatore sat on the stool and watched her. The hornet never showed itself. To Mariye's great relief.

"Well done," said the Commendatore, with a nod. "Now go back inside, shut the door, and descend the stairs to the very bottom."

Down two flights of stairs? That would mean plunging into the depths of the house. Wasn't she trying to escape?

"There is no chance of escaping now," the Commendatore said, reading her mind. He shook his head from side to side. "The gate is strictly barred. My friends are constrained to hide a while longer. I beseech you to listen."

Mariye had no choice but to believe the Commendatore. She hurried through the living room and down the two flights of stairs.

The maid's room was at the bottom. Beside it was the laundry room and next to that a storeroom. At the end of the hallway was the gym with its row of exercise machines. The Commendatore pointed to the maid's room.

"This is your hiding place," he said. "Menshiki seldom ventures into that room. He descends once a day to do his laundry and to exercise, but he almost never enters there. It is unlikely he will find my friends, should you remain quiet. The room has a sink and a refrigerator. In case of earthquake, an ample store of food and mineral water has been set aside. So my friends will not starve. There is enough to live in relative safety for a number of days."

A number of days? Mariye asked (albeit without speaking) incredulously, her shoes in hand. I must remain *here* that long?

"Affirmative. It is a shame, but my friends are obliged to stay here for such a time," the Commendatore said, shaking his tiny head. "This house is kept under tight guard. In more than one way. This is a fact I cannot alter. An Idea's powers are limited, I am sad to say."

"How long will I have to stay here?" Mariye asked in a small voice. "I have to go home soon. My aunt will worry about me. If I'm missing too long, she'll have to report it to the police. Then there'll be a real mess."

The Commendatore shook his head. "A million pardons, but this is outside my control. My friends must wait here."

"Is Mr. Menshiki dangerous?"

"A very hard question to answer," the Commendatore said. He made an exaggerated frown. "Menshiki himself is not an evil man. He is a decent sort, one could say, with abilities that exceed those of most people. There is even a hint of nobility in him, if one looks hard enough. Yet there is a gap in his heart, an empty space that attracts the abnormal and the dangerous. It is there that the problem lies."

Mariye wasn't clear what all of this meant, of course. *The abnormal?*

"Who was the person standing outside the closet door?" she asked. "Was that Menshiki?"

"It was Menshiki, but at the same time it was not Menshiki."

"Is he aware of any of this?"

"Most likely," the Commendatore said. "Most likely. But there is nothing he can do about it."

The abnormal and the dangerous? Perhaps the hornet she had seen was one of the forms those things took, Mariye thought.

"Affirmative. Beware of those hornets. They are most virulent creatures," the Commendatore read her mind.

"Virulent?"

"They have the power to kill my friends," the Commendatore explained. "For now, my friends have no choice but to stay here. Do not go outside."

"Virulent," Mariye repeated in her mind. The word sure had a sinister ring.

Mariye opened the door of the maid's room and went in. It was little larger than Menshiki's bedroom closet. There was a kitchenette with a fridge, a hot plate, a small microwave oven, and a sink and faucet. There was also a bed and a tiny bathroom. The bed was bare, but there were blankets, quilts, and a pillow on the shelf, and a simple table and chair for meals. Only a single chair, though. A small window faced the valley. She could look out across it through a crack in the curtain.

"It is best to make as little noise as possible," the Commendatore said. "Do my friends understand?"

Mariye nodded.

"You are a brave girl, my friends," said the Commendatore. "A touch reckless, perhaps, but brave nonetheless. It is an admirable quality. But while you are here, you must be *very* alert. Never be caught off guard. This is no ordinary place. Sinister things are skulking out there that could cause you harm."

"Skulking?"

"Prowling about, in short."

Mariye nodded. In what way was this "no ordinary place," and what sort of sinister things were skulking? She wanted to know, but couldn't think how to ask. Where to begin? There was just so much she couldn't understand.

"I may not be able to come again," the Commendatore said, as if imparting a secret. "There is another place I must go, and another task I must look after. A very important task, if I may say. So I fear I cannot help my friends any further. Hereafter, my friends must manage on your own."

"But how can I escape this place by myself?"

The Commendatore narrowed his eyes and looked squarely at Mariye. "Be sure your ears are open and your eyes are peeled. And keep your wits about you. It is the only way. Then you will know when the right moment comes. As in, 'Aha, now is the time!' You are a brave, smart girl, my friends. Just stay alert."

Mariye nodded. I have to be a brave, smart girl, she thought.

"I wish my friends all the very best," the Commendatore said, encouraging her. Then, as if by afterthought, "And worry not, my friends. Your chest will soon fill out."

"Enough to fill a C-cup bra?"

The Commendatore gave an embarrassed shrug. "I fear I am a mere Idea. I know not how the undergarments of women are measured. But all the same, I can assure you that your breasts will grow. No need to worry. Time is the remedy for your concerns. It is the key for all things that possess form. True, time does not last forever, but as long as you have it, it is remarkably efficacious. So look forward to the future, my friends!"

"Thank you," Mariye said. It was certainly good to hear. She needed every bit of support to be the brave girl she knew she had to be.

Then the Commendatore vanished. Again, like vapor into thin air. The silence around her deepened the moment he was gone. The thought that she might never see him again left her sad and lonely. I have no one to rely on now, she thought. She sprawled out on the bare mattress and stared at the ceiling. It was low, and made of white plasterboard. In its exact center was a fluorescent light. But of course she couldn't turn it on. That was a definite no-brainer.

How long would she be stuck in this room? It was almost dinnertime. If she wasn't home by seven thirty, her aunt would call the arts-and-culture center. They would inform her that she'd been absent that day. The thought hurt. Her aunt would be hysterical, terrified that something bad had happened to her. Somehow, she needed to let her know she was all right. Then she remembered—there was a cell phone in the pocket of her school blazer. She had left it turned off.

She pulled it out and switched it on. The words "Low Battery" flashed on the screen. A split second later the screen went black. Her phone was dead. She could hardly blame the phone: she hadn't used it in ages (she seldom needed it in her daily life, and had little interest in—or affection for—cell phones), so no surprise the battery was drained.

She heaved a sigh. She should have recharged it once in a while at least. Just in case something happened. But there was no use crying over spilt milk. She stuck the cell phone back in her blazer pocket. But something had caught her attention, and she pulled it out again. The plastic penguin attached to it was gone! It had been her lucky charm since she had won it on points at a donut shop. The strap must have broken. But where on earth could she have dropped it? It was hard to imagine. She hardly ever took it out of her pocket.

At first, she felt uneasy without her lucky charm. Then she thought some more. Her own carelessness was probably to blame for losing it. But a new kind of talisman had appeared in its place—that closetful of clothes—and those clothes had protected her. And that little man with the funny way of talking, the Commendatore, had led her to this place. So *something*, she thought, is still looking out for me. No need to mope about the missing penguin.

Mariye wasn't carrying much. Wallet, handkerchief, change purse, house key, and a half a pack of Cool Mint gum—that was about it. Her shoulder bag contained pencils and pens and a few school textbooks. None were likely to be very useful.

She slipped out of the maid's room and went to check the storage room. As the Commendatore had said, it was stocked with provisions in case of earthquake. The ground was comparatively stable in this mountainous part of Odawara, so an earthquake shouldn't be that serious. The great Kanto earthquake of 1923 had devastated the city of Odawara, but here in the hills, the damage had been relatively minor (she'd done a summer project in grade school on the impact of the earthquake on the Odawara region). Nevertheless, it would be very difficult afterward to get food and water way up here. Thus Menshiki had taken pains to stock up on both. His caution knew no bounds.

She selected two bottles of mineral water, a box of crackers, and a bar of chocolate and carried them back to her room. She was pretty sure Menshiki wouldn't miss such a small amount. However meticulous he might be, he wouldn't keep tabs on how many bottles he had stored. The water was necessary because she didn't want to turn on the tap in her room if at all possible. That would make the pipes in the house gurgle. It is best to make as little noise as possible, the Commendatore had said. She had to be careful.

Mariye returned to the maid's room and locked the door from the inside. In a sense, it was a useless gesture, since Menshiki had keys to all the rooms in the house. Yet it might earn her a little time. At the very least, it eased her mind a bit.

She wasn't hungry at all, but she ate a few crackers and drank some of the water just to check. The crackers were mediocre, as was the water. She checked the labels—neither had reached its best-before date. I'm okay, she thought. I won't starve.

Outside was now completely dark. She pulled the curtain back a little farther and looked across the valley. She could see her house. She couldn't see what was going on inside without the binoculars, but she could tell lights were burning in some of the rooms. If she looked hard, she might be able to observe someone moving around. Her aunt was there, freaking out, she was sure, because she hadn't come home. Wasn't there a way to call her? Menshiki must have a phone somewhere. All she had to do was say, "Please don't worry. I'm all right," and hang up. If she kept it short, Menshiki probably wouldn't find out. But her room had no phone, nor had she seen one in that part of the house.

Could she escape under cover of darkness? Find a ladder somewhere and scale the wall to freedom? She recalled seeing a fold-up ladder in the garden shed. Then she recalled the Commendatore's words: *This place is kept under tight guard. In more than one way.* She was pretty sure that "tight guard" didn't refer to the security company's alarm system alone.

I should believe the Commendatore, Mariye thought. This is no normal place. Many things are lurking about. I have to be super cautious. Super patient. This is no time to be rash or willful. I should sit back and wait for the right opportunity, like the Commendatore said.

You will know when the right moment comes. As in, "Aha, now is the time!" You are a brave, smart girl, my friends. Just stay alert.

That's right, I have to be a brave, smart girl. Survive all this in good shape and then watch my breasts get bigger and bigger.

So she thought as she lay there on the bare mattress. All around was growing darker. She could tell that darkness of a different order was about to arrive.

62

ONE CAN STUMBLE INTO A LABYRINTH

Time followed its own principles, paying no heed to her thoughts. She lay there on the bare mattress in her little room, watching it sluggishly shuffle past. She had nothing else to do. It would be nice to have a book to read, she thought. But there were no books at hand, and even if there had been she couldn't switch on the light. All she could do was lie there in the dark. She had found flashlights and spare batteries in the storeroom but had decided to use those as little as possible.

The night deepened, and she fell asleep. She was nervous and apprehensive in such an unfamiliar place, and she wanted to stay awake, but at a certain point fatigue overcame her and she dropped off. She simply couldn't keep her eyes open. The coverless bed was cold, so she took a quilt and blankets from the closet, wrapped herself up in them like a Swiss Roll, and closed her eyes. There was no space heater in the room, and she couldn't use the central system for obvious reasons.

(A note here on the time frame: Menshiki would have left to visit me while Mariye was asleep. He stayed over and went back the following morning. In other words, he wasn't at home that night. The house was empty. But Mariye had no way of knowing that.)

Mariye woke up once that night to use the bathroom, but didn't flush the toilet. During the day was one thing, but in the still, wee hours of the morning the sound of running water could attract attention. Menshiki was without question a cautious and meticulous individual. He would notice even the slightest change. So why risk discovery?

Her watch said two in the morning. Saturday morning, that was. Friday had passed. When she peeped through the curtain she could see her home across the valley. The lights in the living room were blazing. It was after midnight and she still hadn't returned, so the people there—at night that would mean her father and her aunt—were unable to sleep. I've done an awful thing, Mariye thought. She even felt sorry for her father (very rare for her). I shouldn't have been so reckless—it wasn't my intention. This is what I get for acting so impulsively.

Yet whatever her regrets, however much she might blame herself, she couldn't transport herself across the valley. She was not a crow. She couldn't sprout wings and fly through the air. Nor could she disappear and reappear like the Commendatore. She was confined within her still-growing body, and shackled by time and space. Hers was a clumsy, awkward existence. Look at her chest—as flat as a board. Her breasts still pancakes that had failed to rise.

Naturally, Mariye was scared alone there in the dark. Her powerlessness pained her. She wished the Commendatore were there. She had so many things to ask him. Whether he answered them or not, at least she would have someone to talk to. To be sure, his way of speaking was odd, somewhat different from modern Japanese, but she could still understand his general meaning. But he might never come back. "There is another place I must go, and another task I must look after," he had told her. She was desolate to have lost him, perhaps forever.

From outside the window came the resonant cry of a night bird. It sounded like an owl, perhaps a horned owl. They were cloistered in the dark forests, honing their wisdom. I must be as wise as they are, she thought. Be a smart, brave girl. But sleep overtook her a second time. She couldn't keep her eyes open. Pulling the bedding around her once again, she lay down on the mattress and closed her eyes. It was a deep and dreamless sleep. When she woke up it was already growing light outside. Her watch said half past six.

The world was welcoming a new Saturday.

Mariye spent all that day holed up in the maid's room. In place of breakfast, she had more crackers, a few chocolates, and mineral water. She crept into the gym and borrowed several issues from a small mountain of Japanese editions of *National Geographic*. She guessed Menshiki read them when he was working out on his exercise bike, since they were stained here and there with what appeared to be his sweat. She read through them several times. There were articles on the habitat of the Alaskan wolf, the mysteries of the rising and ebbing of the tides, the life of the Inuit, and the gradual shrinking of the Amazon rain forest. Not Mariye's usual reading material by any means, but now, with nothing else to look at, she read them over and over until she had them practically memorized. She bored holes in the illustrations with her eyes.

When she tired of reading, she napped. On occasion, she looked through the curtain at her home across the valley. I wish I had that telescope now, she thought. Then I'd really be able to see inside, even watch people moving around. She wanted to be back inside her room with the orange curtains. Scrub every inch of her body in a nice hot bath, change into fresh pajamas, and curl up in her warm bed with her cat.

Just after nine in the morning, she heard the sound of someone coming down the stairs. The footsteps of a man in slippers. Menshiki, most likely. His way of walking was somehow distinctive. She wanted to peek through the keyhole, but the door didn't have one. She huddled over her knees in a corner of the room, her body rigid. Escape would be impossible if he opened the door and came in. The Commendatore had said that shouldn't happen, and she had taken him at his word. But nothing was a hundred percent sure thing in this world. Making herself as invisible as possible, she thought of the clothes in the closet and prayed, *Don't let anything happen to me.* Her throat was as dry as cotton.

Menshiki seemed to have brought down his dirty laundry. He probably washed a day's worth of clothes at this time each morning. He tossed them in, added detergent, set the timer and mode, and turned the washer on. She could tell by listening that his movements were practiced. She was surprised how well she could hear. The washer began to churn. Menshiki then moved to the gym and began working out on his exercise machines. That seemed to be his ritual—to work out while his clothes were spinning in the washer. While listening to classical music. She could hear strains of Baroque music coming from the speakers attached to the gym's ceiling. It sounded like Bach, or Handel, or Vivaldi. Mariye didn't know much about classical music, though, so it could have been any one of those three.

Mariye spent a full hour with her ears tuned to the churn of the washer, the systematic whirring of the exercise machines, and the music of either Bach, Handel, or Vivaldi. It was a nerve-wracking hour. True, Menshiki probably wouldn't notice that his pile of *National Geographic*s was short a few issues, or that his stash of crackers and chocolate in the storeroom was shrinking bit by bit. She had taken only a tiny fraction of what he had laid away. Nevertheless, there was no telling what might happen. She had to guard against carelessness. To stay on her toes.

Eventually, a buzzer went off and the washer stopped. Menshiki walked slowly back to the laundry room, took the clothes from the washer, put them in the dryer, and turned it on. The dryer began to turn. Satisfied that all was in order, Menshiki ambled up the stairs. It appeared that his workout had ended. Now he would probably take a long shower.

Mariye closed her eyes and sighed with relief. Menshiki would likely come back down in an hour or so. To remove his clothes from the dryer. Yet the most dangerous period had passed. At least it felt that way. He hadn't sensed her hiding there in the room. Hadn't felt her presence at all. She could breathe more freely now.

Then who had it been in front of the closet? The Commendatore had said it was Menshiki, but then again it wasn't him at all. What had that meant? She couldn't understand what he had been trying to say. It was just too difficult for her. Whatever the case, that *someone* had been able to tell that she (or at least a person) was in the closet. They had sensed her there, no doubt. Yet, *for some reason*, that someone was unable to open the closet door. What could that reason have been? Had that assembly of beautiful old clothes really protected her?

She longed to ask the Commendatore. But he had gone off somewhere. There was no one left who could explain things to her.

Menshiki did not set foot outside the house all that Saturday. As far as she knew, the garage door hadn't opened, nor had a car engine started up. He had come down to pick up his laundry, and then walked slowly back up the stairs. That was it. No one had visited the house at the top of the hill where the road came to an end. No parcels or registered documents had been delivered. The doorbell had remained silent. She had heard the telephone ring twice. The ring was faint and distant, but she could still make it out. It was picked up on the second ring the first time, and the third ring the time after that (that was how she knew Menshiki was in the house). The town garbage truck crawled up the slope to the melody of "Annie Laurie" and then crawled back down again (Saturday was garbage pickup day). Otherwise, she heard no sounds. The house was perfectly still.

The morning passed, afternoon rolled on, and soon evening was drawing near.

(A second note on the time frame: While Mariye was hiding in the maid's tiny room, I killed the Commendatore in the Izu nursing home, tied up Long Face, and descended into the underworld.)

But she never found the perfect time to escape. She had to be patient and wait for "the right moment," the Commendatore had told her. *You will know when the right moment comes. As in, "Aha, now is the time!"*

However, the "right moment" never came. Mariye grew more and more tired of waiting. Patience was not her strength. How long, she wondered, must I stay holed up here?

Menshiki began playing the piano not long before nightfall. Apparently, he kept the living room window open when he practiced, so Mariye could hear the music in her hiding place. It sounded like Mozart. One of his sonatas, in a major key. She had noticed the score on the piano. Menshiki ran through the slow-paced movement, then went back to repeat several sections, adjusting his fingering until he was satisfied. It was difficult, though, and he seemed to be having trouble balancing the sound. For the most part, Mozart's sonatas aren't all that hard, but a pianist who tries to master one can stumble into a labyrinth. That labyrinth, however, didn't seem to faze Menshiki in the least. Mariye listened to him patiently walk back and forth over the thorny passages. He practiced that way for about an hour. At the end, he closed the lid with a bang. She sensed he was frustrated. But not all that much. Rather, it was a moderate, elegant frustration. Even when he was alone (or at least, when he thought he was alone) in his sprawling mansion, he kept a tight rein on his feelings.

What followed was a repeat of the previous day. The sun set, the sky darkened, and the crows flew cawing back to their nests in the mountains. One by one, the lights of the houses across the valley went on.

The Akikawas' lights did too, and stayed lit even after midnight. Those lights signaled to Mariye just how worried her family was. At least it felt that way to her. It hurt not to be able to ease their pain.

In stark contrast, not a single light went on at Tomohiko Amada's house (in short, the house *I* inhabited). To all appearances, it looked abandoned. Night came, yet it remained black. It seemed that no one was home. Mariye thought it strange. Where had her teacher gone? Did he know that she was missing?

At a certain hour, sleep again attacked Mariye. The sandman showed no mercy. Shivering in her school blazer, she wrapped herself in blankets and quilts and closed her eyes. I wish my cat were here, she thought as she drifted off. For some reason, her cat—it was a she—seldom mewed or yowled. She only purred. Mariye could have kept her with her without fear of discovery. But of course she wasn't there. Mariye was all alone. In a small pitch-black room with no means of escape.

Sunday morning dawned. When Mariye opened her eyes it was still quite dark. Her watch said before six. The days were getting shorter. Rain was falling outside. A hushed, winter rain. She didn't realize it was raining until she noticed water dripping off the branches. The air in the room was chilly and damp. If only she had a sweater, she thought. All she was wearing under her blazer was a thin knitted vest, a cotton blouse, and beneath that a T-shirt. An outfit for a warm afternoon. A wool sweater would sure come in handy.

Then she remembered—she'd seen a sweater in *that closet*. An off-white cashmere that looked nice and warm. She could trot up the stairs and get it. Put it under her blazer, and she'd be warm as toast. But slipping out the door and climbing the stairs was just too dangerous. *Especially to that room*. She had to make do with what she had on. After all, this cold wasn't unbearable. Nothing like the brutal cold the Inuit had to deal with. This was the outskirts of Odawara, in early December.

Yet the rainy winter morning chilled her to the bone. She could feel the icy damp seep into her body. So Mariye closed her eyes and turned her thoughts to Hawaii instead. When she was small, she and her aunt, and her aunt's old school friend, had visited Hawaii. They rented a small surfboard for her on the beach at Waikiki, and she played in the waves—when she tired of that, she basked in the sun on the white sand. It was so warm, and so harmonious. High above her, the fronds of the palms swayed in the trade winds. White clouds sailed out to sea. She lay there and sipped a glass of lemonade, so cold her temples hurt. Mariye remembered the trip in detail. Would she ever see a place like that again? She'd give anything for that chance.

Once again, a little after nine, Menshiki came padding down the stairs in his slippers. The washer started, the classical music kicked in (this time it sounded like a Brahms symphony), and the rhythm of the exercise machines began. This lasted a full hour. A perfect repeat of the day before. Only the composer was different. The master of the house was certainly a creature of habit. He transferred the laundry from the washer to the dryer, and returned exactly an hour later to pick it up. He didn't come downstairs after that, and showed no interest at all in the maid's room.

(Another note on the time frame: Menshiki went to my home that afternoon, where he bumped into Masahiko and they had a brief conversation. For some reason, though, Mariye was again unaware that he had left the house.)

Menshiki's unwavering routine was useful to Mariye. She could prepare herself emotionally, and plan her movements in advance. Unexpected events would have made it much harder on her nerves. She had grown familiar with Menshiki's pattern, and adapted herself to it. He almost never went out (at least to her knowledge). He worked in his study, washed his own clothes, cooked his own meals, and, in the evening, sat down in front of his Steinway and practiced. Sometimes there was a phone call, but those were infrequent. She could count them on her fingers. For some reason, he didn't seem to like phones all that much. He appeared to take care of his work-related communications—she had no idea how extensive they were—on the computer in his study.

Menshiki took care of the basic cleaning, but once a week he had a cleaning service come to him. Mariye remembered him mentioning that on their previous visit. I don't mind doing it myself, he had said. Cleaning can cheer me up, just like cooking. But it was clearly beyond him to keep such a big house tidy on his own. Thus the need for professional help. He had said he left the house for half a day when they came. What day of the week would it be? Maybe that's when I can make my getaway, Mariye thought. People will be bringing equipment, so the gate should be opening and closing as their vehicles come and go. Menshiki should be absent. So getting out might not be all that hard. That could be my one and only chance.

Yet there was no sign that the cleaners were coming. Monday was much the same as Sunday. Menshiki was making good progress with Mozart: his mistakes were fewer, and the whole piece was coming together musically. He was a careful and patient man. Once he set a goal, he stuck to it. Mariye had to admit she was impressed. Even if he could make it through without a hitch, though, how pleasing would his Mozart be to the ear? Listening to what was coming from upstairs, she had her doubts.

She was surviving on crackers, chocolate, and mineral water. She also polished off an energy bar full of nuts. And a can of tuna fish. Since she had no toothbrush, she brushed her teeth with mineral water, using her finger. She read issue after issue of the Japanese version of *National Geographic*. In the process, she learned about a number of further topics: the man-eating tigers of Bengal; the lemurs of Madagascar; the shifting topography of the Grand Canyon; natural-gas extraction in Siberia; the life expectancy of the penguins of Antarctica; the world of the highland nomads of Afghanistan; the grueling initiation rituals of New Guinean youth. She learned the basics about AIDS, and Ebola. Such miscellaneous information about nature might prove useful one day. Then again, it might be entirely useless. Whatever the case, no other books were on hand. She devoured back issues of *National Geographic* like there was no tomorrow.

Once in a while, she would slip her hand under her T-shirt to check the status of her breasts. But they didn't appear to be growing at all. If anything, they seemed to be getting smaller. She was also concerned about her period. According to her calculations, the next was due in about ten days. She had found nothing related to that condition in the storeroom. (Plenty of toilet paper was stockpiled in case of earthquake, but no sanitary napkins or tampons. It seemed that women and their needs didn't register with the owner of the house.) She'd be in big trouble if it started while she was in hiding. Probably, though, she would have escaped by then. *Probably.* It was hard to imagine putting up with another ten days of this.

The cleaners finally showed up on Tuesday morning. She could hear the lively chatter of women in the upper garden as they unloaded equipment from the back of their van. Menshiki had not done his laundry that morning, nor performed his exercise routine. In fact, he hadn't come downstairs at all. She had wondered if this could be why (Menshiki wouldn't change his daily schedule without a reason), and, sure enough, it was as she had guessed. Menshiki had probably driven his Jaguar out the gate at the same moment the cleaners' big van pulled in.

Mariye rushed to tidy up the maid's room. She gathered the empty water bottles and cracker packets and put them in a garbage bag, which she set out in a visible place. The cleaners would look after it. She neatly folded the blanket and quilt and returned them to the closet. She took care to erase every trace of her presence. Now no one could tell that someone had been living there for days. Then she slung her bag over her shoulder and crept up the stairs. Timing her moves, she darted through the hallway without attracting the cleaners' attention. Her heart pounded at the thought of the dangers of *that room*. At the same time, though, she missed the clothes hanging in its closet. She wanted to go back for one last look. Touch them with her hands. But there was no time for that. She had to hurry.

She slipped through the front door undetected, and ran up the curved driveway. The gate had been left open, as she had anticipated. It made no sense for anyone working there to open and close it each time they passed through. Her face as she stepped out onto the road was a picture of normality.

Should I really be able to leave this easily? she thought outside the gate. Shouldn't I have to pay a higher price? Go through some sort of painful rite of passage, like the teenage tribesmen of New Guinea? Endure a ritual like that as a badge of courage? Those thoughts did not linger, however. They were dwarfed by the liberation she felt at having made her getaway.

The day was overcast, with low-lying clouds that threatened cold rain at any minute. But Mariye's face was raised to the sky. As if she were on the beach at Waikiki, gazing up at the swaying palm trees. She took several deep breaths, giddy with her good fortune. I am free, she thought. My feet will take me anywhere I want to go. My nights spent trembling in the dark are over. That fact alone made her grateful to be alive. It had been only four days, but now the world appeared so fresh, each tree, every blade of grass charged with such wonderful vitality. She found the smell of the wind exhilarating.

Yet this was no time to dawdle. Menshiki could have forgotten something and come driving back at any time. I should get away from here, she thought, and fast. Adopting what she hoped was a nonchalant expression, Mariye tried to smooth her wrinkled school uniform (she had been sleeping in it for days) and straighten her hair to avoid arousing suspicion as she trotted down the mountain.

At the foot of the slope, she turned up the road on the other side. But she did not take her usual route home—rather, she headed for my place. She had something in mind. But the house was empty. She rang the bell repeatedly, but no one came to the door.

Giving up, she went around to the back and took the path through the woods to the pit behind the little shrine. Now, however, a blue plastic sheet covered the pit. The sheet hadn't been there before. It was held firmly in place by cords attached to stakes driven into the ground. Stone weights were lined up on top. It was no longer possible to peek inside. In her absence, someone—who, she didn't know—had sealed it. Probably they considered it a safety hazard. She stood in front of the pit and listened for a while. But she heard nothing.

(My note: The fact she didn't hear the bell could have meant that I hadn't arrived yet. Or possibly that I had fallen asleep.)

Cold drops of rain began to fall. I should go home, she thought. My family is worried about me. But how could she explain the last four days? She had to think of something. She couldn't let on that she had been hiding at Menshiki's all that time—that was out of the question. It would create an even bigger mess. The police had probably been notified of her disappearance. If they knew that she had broken into Menshiki's home, she'd be charged with trespassing. She would be punished.

What if she claimed that she had fallen into the pit by accident, and had been unable to get out for four days? That only when her teacher—*me,* in other words—came by was she able to climb to safety. Mariye had expected me to play along with this scenario. But I hadn't been home, and the pit's opening had been secured with a plastic tarp. Thus her plan fell through. (Had that scenario unfolded, I would have had to explain to the police why Menshiki and I had brought in heavy equipment to uncover the pit, which might have led to even thornier problems.)

Claiming temporary amnesia was the only other story she could think of. Nothing else came to mind. She would say that those four days were a blank. That she couldn't remember a thing. That when she came to, she was lying alone on the mountain. She would stick with that—there was no other way. She had seen a TV show that hinged on that idea. She wasn't sure if people would swallow an excuse like that. The police and her family would grill her. They might send her to a psychiatrist or counselor of some kind. Even so, a claim of amnesia was the only option. She would have to mess up her hair, splatter mud on her legs and arms, and add a few scattered cuts and bruises to make it look as if she had spent all that time in the mountains. It would be an act she would have to carry through to the very end.

And in fact that was what she did. It was hardly a masterful performance, but she could come up with no alternative.

This was what Mariye revealed to me. She had just finished her account when Shoko Akikawa returned. I heard her Toyota Prius pull up in front of my house.

"I think you should keep quiet about what really happened," I said to Mariye. "Don't tell anyone but me. It will be our secret."

"Of course," Mariye said. "Of course I won't tell anyone. Even if I did, they wouldn't believe me."

"I believe you."

"Does this mean the circle is closed?"

"I don't know," I said. "Maybe not all the way. But I think we can rest easy. The dangerous part is over."

"The virulent part."

"That's right," I said. "The virulent part."

Mariye studied my face for a full ten seconds. "The Commendatore," she said in a small voice. "He really exists."

"That's right," I replied. "He really does." And I killed him with these hands. *Really.* But of course I couldn't tell her that.

Mariye gave a single nod. I knew she would keep our secret. It was a secret we would share forever.

I wished I could have told Mariye that the clothes that had protected her from that *something* had been worn by her late mother before she married. But I couldn't. I didn't have the right. Neither did the Commendatore. There was but one person in the world who did, and that was Menshiki. But he would never exercise it.

We all live our lives carrying secrets we cannot disclose.

63

BUT IT'S NOT WHAT YOU'RE THINKING

Mariye and I had a secret. An important secret shared by the two of us alone. I described my time in the underworld, and she told me exactly what had happened to her at Menshiki's mansion. We wrapped up the two paintings, *Killing Commendatore* and *The Man with the White Subaru Forester*, as tightly as we could and stored them in the attic of Tomohiko Amada's house. Nobody else knew about that, either. The owl did, of course, but it wasn't going to talk. It would hold our secret in perfect silence.

Mariye came to visit from time to time (she hid it from her aunt, using her secret passageway). We put our heads together to try to figure out what our experiences had in common, comparing the timelines right down to the smallest detail.

At first, I worried that Shoko would suspect that Mariye's four-day disappearance and my three-day "long-distance trip" were somehow related, but the idea seems never to have entered her head. Nor did the police direct their attention to that coincidence. They were ignorant of the passageway, so they dismissed my home as just another house on the next ridge over. Since I did not number among the Akikawas' "neighbors," they never came to interview me. Nor did it appear that Shoko had told them I was painting Mariye's portrait. She probably didn't see it as relevant. Had the police put Mariye's absence and my trip together, I could have been placed in a delicate situation.

· · ·

I never completed my portrait of Mariye Akikawa. It was almost done, but I feared where finishing it might lead. Menshiki, for one, would move heaven and earth to put his hands on it. That much was clear, no matter what he might say to the contrary. I had no intention, however, of letting him install the painting in his private "sanctuary." That could be dangerous. So in the end I left it unfinished. Mariye, however, loved the painting ("It shows how I think these days," was how she put it), and wanted to keep it near her if possible. So I readily gave it to her in its unfinished state (along with the three sketches I had promised earlier).

"I think it's cool," Mariye said. "It's a work in progress, and I'm a work in progress too, now and forever."

"None of us are ever finished. Everyone is always a work in progress."

"How about Mr. Menshiki?" Mariye asked. "He looks very finished to me."

"I think he's a work in progress too," I said.

Menshiki was far from being a completed human being. From what I could tell, anyway. That is why, night after night, under cloak of darkness, he reached out to Mariye Akikawa across the valley on his high-powered binoculars. He couldn't help himself. That secret allowed him to maintain some sort of personal equilibrium. It was for him the equivalent of the long balancing pole that tightrope walkers carry.

Of course, Mariye was aware that Menshiki was peeking into her house. But she never revealed it to anyone (apart from me). She never told her aunt. What possessed him to do something like that? It mystified her. Yet for some reason she didn't feel like pursuing it any further. All she did was keep her curtain closed. The sun-bleached orange curtain stayed tightly shut at all times. She also made sure that the light in her room was off when she changed for bed at night. Elsewhere in the house, however, his voyeurism didn't bother her. Sometimes she even thought she enjoyed it. Perhaps she found some meaning in the fact that *she alone* knew what was going on.

According to Mariye, Shoko and Menshiki were still seeing each other. Her aunt would jump in the car and drive off to his house once or twice a week. Their relationship appeared to be sexual (Mariye hinted at this in a very roundabout way). Her young aunt never said where she was going, but Mariye knew. When she came back, her complexion was rosier than usual. In any case—whatever the nature of that peculiar void within Menshiki—Mariye was powerless to interfere in their affair. She could only let them continue on as they were. All she wished was not to be drawn into whatever was going on between the two of them. That she be allowed to stand at a safe distance, outside the whirlpool of their relationship.

I doubted that she could pull that off. Without realizing it, she would be sucked in sooner or later, to a greater or lesser degree. From the periphery, unavoidably toward the center. Menshiki was wooing Shoko Akikawa, but always with Mariye in mind. Whether he had planned it all from the start or not, he couldn't help himself—that's the kind of man he was. And, like it or not, I had brought them together. He had met Shoko in this house. That's what he had wanted. And when Menshiki wanted something, the guy knew how to put his hands on it.

Mariye wasn't sure what Menshiki would do with that closetful of shoes and size 5 dresses. She guessed he would keep them—whether they were stored in that closet or in another place. However his relationship with Shoko Akikawa turned out, he wouldn't be able to discard them, or burn them. That was because the wardrobe had become a part of his psyche. The clothes would be forever enshrined within his spiritual sanctuary.

I decided to quit teaching my painting class near Odawara Station. "I'm sorry, but I need to focus on my art," was how I put it to the director. He took it in stride. "It's a shame," he said. "Everyone says you're a wonderful teacher." His words didn't sound altogether false, either. I thanked him, and promised to stick it out till year's end. By then, he had located a good replacement, a retired high school art instructor in her mid-sixties. She struck me as a very nice woman, with eyes that resembled those of an elephant.

Menshiki called from time to time. No practical matter was ever involved—we just chatted. Each time he would ask if there had been any change in the pit behind the shrine, and each time I would tell him no, there hadn't. That was the honest truth. The blue plastic sheet was still stretched across the opening. I went to check sometimes when I was out for a walk, but never saw any sign that it had been tampered with. The stones holding it down hadn't been moved either. There were no more strange or suspicious events connected to the pit. I never heard the bell in the middle of the night, nor did the Commendatore (or anything else) emerge from it. It was just a big hole sitting quietly in the middle of the woods. The clump of tall pampas grass flattened by the backhoe was growing back, concealing the area around the pit once again.

As far as Menshiki knew, I had been in the pit the whole time I was missing. True, he couldn't explain how I had gotten inside. Yet he had found me there—that was an indisputable fact. As a result, he never connected Mariye's disappearance and mine. He could only see the overlap of the two events as some kind of strange coincidence.

Discreetly, I probed to see if he had an inkling that someone had been hiding in his house for four days. But he had seen no telltale signs. He was wholly in the dark. In which case, whoever had been standing outside the closet in the *forbidden chamber* was most likely not him. But then who had it been?

Although Menshiki called, he no longer came by for visits. Perhaps he no longer needed to hang out now that Shoko was in his grasp. Or maybe he had lost interest in me. Or both. It didn't matter to me one way or the other (though there were times I missed the sound of his Jaguar V8 purring up the slope).

Nevertheless, the occasional phone calls (always before eight in the evening) suggested that Menshiki felt we should stay connected in some way. Perhaps the fact that he had revealed to me that he *might* be Mariye's biological father weighed on his mind to some extent. I don't think he worried that I would blurt it out—to either Mariye or Shoko Akikawa—somewhere down the line. He was sure I would guard his secret. He could read me well enough to know that, like he could read all people. Yet it was *so foreign* to Menshiki to have bared his heart to anyone, whoever they might be. He had an iron will, but maybe even he found it exhausting to keep secrets to himself all the time. He must have really needed me on his side when he made his confession. And I had struck him as relatively harmless.

Whether or not he had exploited me from the beginning, however, I still owed him my gratitude. It was he who had rescued me from the pit. Had he not come along, if he hadn't lowered the ladder and then yanked me up to the surface, I would have become a dried-up corpse. In a sense, then, Menshiki and I had each placed our lives in the other's hands. That meant that our accounts were even.

Menshiki just nodded when I told him that I had given *A Portrait of Mariye Akikawa* to Mariye in its unfinished state. I guess he no longer needed the painting that much, though he had commissioned it. Or he saw no meaning in an unfinished work. Or his mind was on other things.

A few days after Menshiki and I had this conversation, I put a simple frame on *The Pit in the Woods*, placed the painting in the trunk of my Corolla, and took it to his house. This was the last time we would meet face-to-face.

"This is for saving my life. Please accept it," I said.

He seemed to like the painting a lot. (I thought it was pretty good myself.) He offered to pay me for it, but I turned him down. I had received too much money from him as it stood. There was no need for further obligations on either side. We had become neighbors who lived across the valley from each other, no more, and I wanted to keep it that way.

Tomohiko Amada passed away the Saturday of the week I was rescued from the pit. He had been in a coma for three days, and in the end his heart simply stopped beating. It shut down quietly and naturally, like a locomotive pulling into the last station. Masahiko was by his side throughout. He called me soon after.

"He went peacefully," he said. "That's the way I would like to go. I thought I could even detect a smile."

"A smile?" I asked.

"Maybe it wasn't a true smile, strictly speaking. But that's the way it looked. To me, anyway."

"I'm very sorry about your father," I said, choosing my words, "but I'm glad he went peacefully."

"He was semiconscious until midweek, but he didn't seem to want to leave any parting words," Masahiko said. "I guess he had no regrets—he lived his ninety years to the fullest, doing what he wanted to do."

You're wrong, I thought. He had regrets. In fact, he bore a very heavy burden. Yet only he knew what that burden was. Now there was no one left who knew, and it would remain like that forever.

"I'm afraid I'll be out of touch for a while," Masahiko said. "Dad was famous in his own way, which means I have to take care of all kinds of things. I'm the son and heir, so I can't say no. Let's get together and talk after things have settled down a little."

I thanked him for taking the trouble to let me know, and we hung up.

Tomohiko Amada's death cast an even deeper hush over my home. But that was only natural. He had lived there for a long time, after all. I shared the house with that silence for several days. It was intense, but not unpleasant. You could call it a pure silence, in that it was not connected to anything else. A chain of events had come to an end. That's how it felt, anyway. It was the kind of hush that comes when matters of major importance are finally resolved.

One night about two weeks after Tomohiko Amada's death, Mariye came to talk to me, stealing to my house in secret like a cautious cat. She didn't stay very long. Her family was keeping close watch on her, so she didn't have the freedom to come and go that she had enjoyed before.

"My breasts seem to be getting bigger," she said. "My aunt and I went shopping for a bra. The stores carry something called a 'beginner's bra.' Did you know that?"

No, I said, I didn't. I glanced at her chest but saw nothing new beneath her green Shetland sweater.

"I don't see much difference," I said.

"That's because the padding is thin. If it were any thicker, people would see the change right away and think you stuffed something inside. So you start thin and then work up from there. It's more complicated than I thought."

Mariye told me that a female police officer had questioned her at length about where she had been those four days. The questioning had been gentle most of the time, yet on occasion the woman had become very firm. But Mariye had stuck with her story: she could remember only that she'd been roaming the mountain and had gotten lost. The rest was a complete blank. She thought she'd survived on the mineral water and chocolate she always carried in her schoolbag. That was all she would say. Otherwise, she kept her mouth clamped shut. She was good at keeping quiet. Once the police were sure that she had not been kidnapped and held for ransom, they took her to a hospital to have her cuts and bruises examined. They wanted to know if she had been sexually abused in any way. When it was clear that no abuse had taken place, the police lost interest. She was just another runaway kid who had gone missing for a couple of days. Hardly a rare occurrence.

Mariye threw away everything she had been wearing during that time: her dark blue blazer, checked skirt, white blouse, knitted vest, loafers—everything. She bought a whole new set of school clothes to replace them. She wanted to start fresh. Then she went back to her life as if nothing had happened. The only difference was that she quit attending the painting class (she was too old for the children's class anyway). She hung my (unfinished) portrait of her on her wall.

It was hard to imagine what kind of woman she would grow up to be. Girls of that age can change in the blink of an eye, physically and emotionally. I might not even be able to recognize her in a few years. I was thus very happy to have painted her picture (unfinished though it was) as she was at thirteen, freezing her image in time. In this real world of ours, after all, nothing remains the same forever.

I called my former agent in Tokyo and told him I wanted to go back to portrait painting. He couldn't have been happier. They were always short of skilled artists.

"But you told me you were through with the business, didn't you?" he said.

"I changed my mind," I answered. Why exactly, I didn't say. He didn't ask, either.

I wanted to live without thinking about anything for a while, to let my hands move on their own, churning out normal, "commercial" portraits one after the other. In the process, I could gain some financial stability. I didn't know how long I could keep that up. I couldn't predict the future. But for the time being, at least, that's what I wanted. To use my hard-won skills without calling up any complicated thoughts. To avoid getting mixed up with Ideas, or Metaphors, or anything along those lines. To keep a safe distance from the messy private affairs of the wealthy, mysterious man who lived across the valley. Not to be dragged into any more dark tunnels for having brought hidden masterpieces into the light. More than anything, that's what I desired.

I met Yuzu. We talked over coffee and Perrier at a café not far from her office. Her belly wasn't as big as I had imagined.

"You're not planning to marry the father?" I asked her right off the bat.

She shook her head. "No, not at the present time."

"Why?"

"I just feel that's for the best."

"But you plan to have the child, right?"

She gave a little nod. "Of course. Can't turn back now."

"Are you living with him?"

"No, I'm not. Since you left I've lived alone."

"How come?"

"For one thing, we're not divorced yet."

"But I sent you the divorce papers a while ago, signed and sealed. So I assumed we were already divorced."

Yuzu was quiet for a moment. "To be honest, I never submitted them," she said at last. "I couldn't somehow, so I let them sit. You and I have been legally married all this time. That means the baby will legally be your child, whether we get divorced or not. You won't bear any responsibility for it, of course."

I couldn't grasp what she meant. "But biologically speaking, the baby is his, correct?"

Yuzu looked me in the eye. "It's not that simple," she said at last.

"What do you mean?"

"How can I put this? I'm not a hundred percent certain the baby is his."

Now it was my turn to look her in the eye. "Are you saying you don't know who got you pregnant?"

She nodded. *I don't know.*

"But it's not what you're thinking," she said. "I wasn't sleeping around. I can only have a sexual relationship with one man at a time. That's why I stopped sleeping with you. Right?"

I nodded.

"I felt sorry for you, though."

I nodded again.

"But I was careful to use protection with him. I didn't want a child. You know how I felt. I was ultra-cautious about those things. And yet I got pregnant, just like that."

"There can always be slipups, no matter how careful we try to be."

"Women know when something like that happens," Yuzu said, shaking her head. "We have a sixth sense that tells us. I don't think men have it."

Of course, I didn't.

"At any rate, you're planning to have the baby," I said.

Yuzu nodded.

"But you never wanted one. At least as long as we were together."

"That's true," she said. "I didn't want one with you. I didn't want one with anybody."

"And yet now you're going to go ahead and bring a child into the world without knowing who the father is. Why didn't you have an abortion? You could have done so earlier."

"I thought about it, of course. And part of me wanted one."

"But you didn't."

"This is how I think these days," Yuzu said. "This is my life, sure, but in the end almost all that happens in it may be decided arbitrarily, quite apart from me. In other words, although I may presume I have free will, in fact I may not be making any of the major decisions that affect me. I've come to think my pregnancy is an example of that."

I listened to her without saying anything.

"I know this sounds fatalistic, but it's what I have *truly* come to feel. Honestly and deeply. So then I thought, if that's how things work, why not have the child and raise it on my own. See it through, and find out what happens. That's come to seem terribly important."

"There's just one thing I need to ask," I said, diving in.

"What is it?"

"It's a simple question, one that requires a mere yes or no. I won't say anything more."

"No problem. Ask away."

"Can I return to you—would you take me back?"

Her brow furrowed slightly. She looked me hard in the face for a moment. "Do you mean you wish to live once more as husband and wife?"

"If that's possible."

"I'd like that," she said quietly. There was no hesitation in her voice. "You are still my husband, and your room is as you left it. You can come back anytime you wish."

"Are you still seeing the other man?" I inquired.

Yuzu quietly shook her head. "No, that's over."

"Why?"

"I didn't want to allow him parental rights—that's the main reason."

I said nothing.

"It seems to have come as a great shock to him. Only natural, I guess," she said. She rubbed her cheeks with her hands.

"But you would allow me?"

She rested her hands on the table and once again looked at me closely.

"You've changed a little, haven't you? Your features, or maybe your expression?"

"I don't know how I look, but I have learned a few things, I think."

"I may have learned a few things myself."

I picked up my cup and drained what was left of my coffee.

"Masahiko's father just passed away," I said, "so he's got a lot to deal with right now. When things have settled down for him, I'll pack my bags and return to our apartment in Hiroo, probably sometime early in the New Year. Assuming that's all right with you, of course."

She studied my face. As if gazing at a landscape she had missed for a very long time. Finally, she reached across the table and gently covered my hand with hers.

"I'd like to give it another try," she said. "In fact, I've been thinking that for a while."

"I've been thinking the same thing," I said.

"I don't know if it will work out or not."

"I don't know either. But it's worth a shot."

"I'm about to have a baby without knowing who the father is. Is that going to be all right with you?"

"I don't have a problem with that," I said. "I know you're going to think I'm crazy, but there's a possibility that I could be the baby's father—potentially. That's my feeling, anyway. I could have somehow gotten you pregnant, mentally, from a distance. As a concept, using a special route."

"As a concept?"

"That's one hypothesis."

Yuzu considered that for a minute. "If that's true," she said, "then that's one heck of a hypothesis."

"Perhaps nothing can be certain in this world," I said. "But at least we can believe in something."

She smiled. That was the end of our conversation that day. She took the subway home, while I climbed into my dusty old Toyota Corolla station wagon and drove back to my home on the mountain.

64

AS A FORM OF GRACE

It was several years after I moved back in with my wife that, on March 11, a huge earthquake devastated northeastern Japan. I sat in front of the television as, one after another, coastal villages and towns from Iwate all the way down to Miyagi were laid to waste before my eyes. That was the very same region I had driven through in my old Peugeot 205. I had encountered the man with the white Subaru Forester in one of those towns. Yet now all I could see were the remains of communities leveled by a tsunami that had fallen on them like some giant beast, leaving nothing in its wake but drowned wreckage. Try as I might, I could find no visible connection to *that town*. Since I couldn't remember the name of the place, I had no way of learning how much damage it had suffered, or how it had been changed.

I couldn't bring myself to do anything—I just sat staring at the TV screen for days on end in stunned silence. I was transfixed. I prayed to find something, anything, connected to my memories. If I failed, I feared, something stored within me, something very important, would be lost for good, carried off to some distant, unknown place. I wanted to hop in my car and drive to the stricken region. See for myself what had survived the disaster. That was out of the question, of course. The main roads had been torn to pieces, which meant that towns and villages were cut off from the world. Electricity, gas, water—all lifelines had been severed. Farther south, on the coast of Fukushima (where I had abandoned my Peugeot when it gave up the ghost), several nuclear reactors were in meltdown. It was impossible to venture into that part of the country.

I had not been a happy man when I had traveled there. It had been a lonely, painful, thoroughly wretched period in my life. I think I was lost in a number of ways. Nevertheless, the trip had allowed me to spend time among unfamiliar people, and witness their lives. I had not imagined then how valuable that would turn out to be. In the process—usually unconsciously—I had discarded some things and picked up others. By the time I passed through all those places I had become a somewhat different person.

I thought of *The Man with the White Subaru Forester* hidden in the attic of the Odawara house. Had that man—whether he belonged to the real world or not—still been living in the same town when disaster struck? What about the skinny young woman with whom I had spent that strange night. Had they and the other inhabitants been able to escape the earthquake and tsunami? Were they still alive? What was the fate of the love hotel and the roadside restaurant?

When five o'clock came around, I would go to pick up our daughter at the nursery school. This was my designated role (my wife having gone back to work at the architectural firm). On an adult's legs, the school was a ten-minute walk away. Then the two of us would slowly stroll home, hand in hand. If the weather was good, we would stop by a park on the way to sit on a bench and watch the neighborhood dogs pass by. Our daughter wanted a little dog of her own, but no pets were permitted in our apartment building, so she had to make do with looking at them in the park. Every so often, someone would let her pet their small, unthreatening dog.

Our daughter's name was Muro. Yuzu had chosen it. She had seen the name in a dream shortly before the baby was born. In the dream, she had been in a large Japanese-style room that looked out over a spacious and beautiful garden. There was a low, old-fashioned writing desk, and on top of that a sheet of white paper. On the paper a single character, 室 (Muro), had been written in bright black ink. The calligraphy was magnificent. That was Yuzu's dream. It stayed stuck in her mind even after she awoke. Thus, she decided, Muro had to be the baby's name. I was fine with that, of course. After all, she was the one having the baby.

The idea that the calligrapher might be Tomohiko Amada popped into my head. But that was just a passing thought. When you came right down to it, it was only a dream, nothing more.

I was happy the child was a girl. I had grown up with my younger sister Komi, so I found it relaxing to have a little girl around. It felt as natural as could be. I was happy, too, that she came into this world with her name already settled. Names are important, whatever one might say.

When we got home, Muro and I watched the news together. I tried to shield her from shots of towns being swallowed by the tsunami. I thought the images were too disturbing for a young child. I was quick to cover her eyes when they came on the screen.

"Why, Daddy?" Muro asked me.

"Because you're still too young."

"But it's real, isn't it?"

"Yes, it is. It's really happening somewhere far from here. But just because it's real doesn't mean you have to see it."

Muro thought about that for a while. But of course she couldn't wrap her head around what I had said. She couldn't understand tsunamis and earthquakes yet, or the meaning of death. All the same, I blocked her vision whenever the tsunami appeared on the screen. Understanding something and seeing it are two different things.

One time, I saw the man with the white Subaru Forester on TV. Or at least I thought I did. They were shooting a large fishing vessel stranded on a bluff some distance from shore, and *he* was standing nearby. Like an elephant keeper beside an elephant that had outlived its usefulness. But that shot was quickly followed by another. I couldn't be sure if it was really the man with the white Subaru Forester or not. But to me the tall fellow in the black windbreaker and black cap with a Yonex logo could be no one else.

His image came and went. There was only a brief second before the camera angle shifted.

Besides watching news about the earthquake, I painted "commercial" portraits on commission to shore up our finances. It was something I could do without thinking—when I sat before the canvas, my hands moved almost automatically. I had been seeking just that sort of life.

And that's what people had been seeking from me. The work provided a steady income. I needed that too. I had a family to take into account.

Two months after the earthquake, my old home in Odawara burned down. The house on the mountain where Tomohiko Amada had spent half his life. Masahiko called with the news. He had been tearing his hair out over how to look after it once I had left, and it turned out his fears were well founded. It had caught fire just before dawn at the end of the May holidays, and although firemen had rushed to the scene, the old wooden structure had almost burned to the ground by the time they arrived (the fire trucks had trouble navigating the steep and twisting road). Luckily, it had rained the night before, so flames hadn't spread to the surrounding trees. The fire department investigated, but to no avail. It might have been an electrical short circuit, but then again it could have been arson.

The first thing that came to mind when I heard the news was *Killing Commendatore*. It must have been incinerated along with the house. Same with *The Man with the White Subaru Forester*. And the record collection. Had the owl in the attic managed to escape?

Killing Commendatore was without a doubt one of Tomohiko Amada's best works, its demise a great loss to Japan's art world. Yet only a few people had laid eyes on it. Just Mariye Akikawa and me. Shoko Akikawa, very briefly. Its creator, Tomohiko Amada, of course. After that, possibly no one. Now it was gone forever, swallowed by the flames. I couldn't shake the feeling that I was somehow to blame. Shouldn't I have made public Tomohiko Amada's hidden masterpiece? Instead, I had bundled it up and stuck it back in the attic. Now it was just a pile of ashes. (I had carefully copied the characters who appeared in it in my sketchbook, all that remained of *Killing Commendatore*.) As a self-respecting artist myself, the idea pained me. The painting was so wonderful, I thought. Perhaps I had committed a crime against art itself.

Yet it also struck me that it might have been a work that *had to be lost*. Tomohiko Amada had poured just too much of his passion, his soul, into it for it to be exposed to public view. It was filled with his spirit. Thus, although it was a superb painting, it possessed some sort of vicious power—it could summon things from *the other side*. By discovering it, I had set a cycle of some kind in motion. Dragging a painting like that out into the light could well have been a big mistake. Wasn't that what the artist himself had thought? Wasn't that why he had hidden it in the attic, away from view? If so, then I had respected his wishes. Whichever the case, it had been lost to the flames, and there was no way anyone could turn back time to recover it.

I didn't regret the loss of *The Man with the White Subaru Forester* for a moment. I knew I would tackle that subject again in the future. By then, though, I would have become a more resolute man, and an artist of greater integrity. When it came time to create my own art again, I should be able to paint *The Man with the White Subaru Forester* from a whole new angle. Perhaps that work would become my own *Killing Commendatore*. If that happened, it would be the greatest legacy I could receive from Tomohiko Amada.

Mariye called me right after the fire, and we talked for half an hour about the little old house it had left in ashes. That house had been important to her. Not so much the building, perhaps, as the world it encompassed, and the time when it was an essential part of her life. That would include Tomohiko Amada, back in the days when he still lived there. Whenever she saw him, the painter was always immersed in his work. From Mariye's experience, an artist was someone who holed up for days painting in his studio. She had watched Amada through the window of that house. Now it was gone, and she had lost that world forever. I shared her sadness. That house held deep meaning for me as well, though I had lived there less than eight months.

At the end of our call, Mariye told me that her breasts were much bigger than before. By now, she was in her second year of high school. I had not seen her once since my departure. Our relationship consisted of an occasional phone call. I didn't particularly want to revisit the house, nor had I any compelling reason to go there. It was always Mariye who called me.

"They haven't filled out yet, but they're definitely growing," she whispered confidentially. It took me a while to register what she was talking about.

"Just as the Commendatore prophesied," she said.

That's wonderful, I said. I considered asking if she had a boyfriend, but decided against it.

Her aunt was still seeing Menshiki. She had revealed that to Mariye at some point. That they were *very close indeed*. And that they might get married before too long.

"Would you live with us if that happened?" her aunt had asked.

Mariye had pretended she hadn't heard. She was good at that.

I found the idea a bit unsettling. "Are you intending to live with Mr. Menshiki?" I asked her.

"I don't think so," she said. "But I'm not so sure."

Not so sure?

"I thought you had some pretty bad memories of his house," I said, my bafflement showing.

"All of that happened when I was a kid. It seems so long ago. And there's no way I'm going to live alone with my father."

So long ago?

It felt like yesterday to me. When I said that to Mariye, though, she didn't respond. Perhaps she wanted to forget those days, and what had taken place then. Or maybe she already had. Now that she was older, she might even have started to develop an interest in Menshiki, however slight. Maybe she had come to see something special in him, a blood tie of some sort.

"I really want to see what happened to that closetful of clothes," Mariye said.

"That room attracts you, doesn't it?"

"That's because those clothes protected me," she said. "But who knows, I may live on my own when I go to college."

Sounds good to me, I said.

"So what's the situation with the pit behind the shrine?" I asked.

"No change," Mariye replied. "The blue plastic sheet's still on it, even after the fire. Leaves will cover it eventually. Then maybe no one will know it's even there."

The little old bell would be lying on the floor of the pit. Together with the flashlight I had taken from Tomohiko Amada's room at the nursing home.

"Have you seen the Commendatore?" I asked.

"No, not once. It's hard to believe he really existed."

"He did, all right," I said. "You'd better believe it."

All the same, I figured that, little by little, that realm would disappear from Mariye's mind. Her life would grow busier and more complicated as she moved into her late teens. She would no longer have time to consider crazy things like Ideas and Metaphors.

Every so often, I found myself wondering about the plastic penguin. I had given it to the faceless man as payment for ferrying me across the river. There had been no alternative, given the swiftness of the current. I could only pray that little penguin was watching over Mariye from somewhere—probably as it shuttled back and forth between presence and absence.

I still can't be sure about the identity of Muro's father. A DNA test would tell me, but I have no desire to know the result. Perhaps we'll find out somewhere along the way. The truth may be revealed. But what meaning would that "truth" carry? Muro is my child in the legal sense, and I love her deeply. I treasure the time we spend together. I couldn't care less who her biological father is or isn't. The question is inconsequential. It can change nothing.

I went to Yuzu in a dream as I wandered from town to town in northeastern Japan. I made love to her while she was asleep, stealing into her dream and impregnating her, so that nine months and a few days later she bore a child. I love this idea (although I hold it in secret). That child's father is me as Idea, or perhaps me as Metaphor. Just as the Commendatore visited me, or as Donna Anna guided me through the dark, so did I, in some alternate world, deposit my seed in Yuzu's womb.

But I will not become like Menshiki. He has built his life by balancing the possibility that Mariye Akikawa is his child with the possibility that she isn't. It is through the subtle and unending oscillation between those two poles that he seeks to find the meaning of his own existence.

I have no need, though, to challenge my life in such a troublesome (or, at the least, unnatural) way. That is because I am endowed with the capacity *to believe*. I believe in all honesty that something will appear to guide me through the darkest and narrowest tunnel, or across the most desolate plain. That's what I learned from the strange events I experienced while living in that mountaintop house on the outskirts of Odawara.

Killing Commendatore may have been lost forever in the flames that hour before dawn, yet its beauty and power live within me even now. I can call up the images of the Commendatore, Donna Anna, the faceless man, and the rest with perfect clarity. They look so tangible, so real, I feel as though I could reach out and touch them. Contemplating them affords me perfect tranquility, as though I were watching raindrops fall on the surface of a broad reservoir. That soundless rain will fall forever in my heart.

I will probably live the rest of my life in their company. My little daughter Muro is their gift to me. A form of grace. I am convinced of this.

"The Commendatore was truly there," I say to Muro as she lies sleeping. "You'd better believe it."

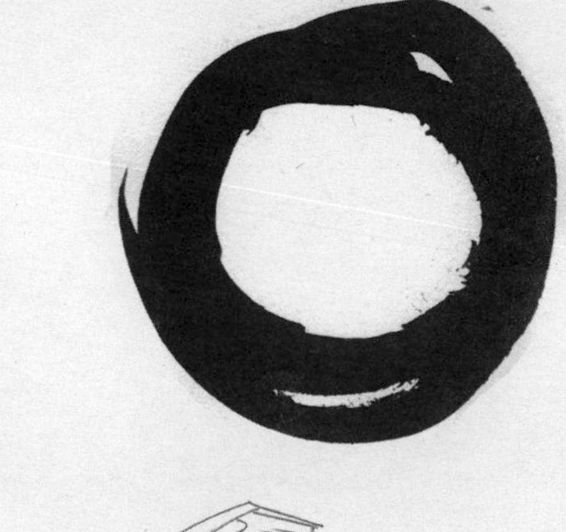

Pauline A. Smith
17, Jordan Lane
Morningside
Edinburgh, 10.

A History of England
in Eight Volumes
Founder Editor: SIR CHARLES OMAN

ENGLAND UNDER THE TUDORS

A History of England

in Eight Volumes

Founder Editor: **SIR CHARLES OMAN**

I England before the Norman Conquest †
(Beginning-1066)
By Sir Charles Oman

II England under the Normans and Angevins
(1066-1272)
By H. W. C. Davis

III England in the Later Middle Ages
(1272-1485)
By Kenneth H. Vickers

IV England under the Tudors*
(1485-1603)
By G. R. Elton

V England under the Stuarts
(1603-1714)
By G. M. Trevelyan

VI England under the Hanoverians
(1714-1815)
By Sir Charles Grant Robertson

VII England since Waterloo
(1815-1900)
By Sir J. A. R. Marriott

VIII Modern England (1885-1945)
By Sir J. A. R. Marriott

* Replacing the original volume of the same title by A. D. Innes.
† Out of print.

England under the Tudors

by

G. R. ELTON

Fellow of Clare College, Cambridge

METHUEN & CO LTD
11 NEW FETTER LANE LONDON E.C.4.

First published September 8th 1955
Reprinted with minor corrections 1956, 1957 and 1958
Reprinted 1959 and 1960
Reprinted with a new bibliography 1962
Reprinted 1963, 1965 and 1967
Printed in Great Britain by
Cox & Wyman Ltd., London, Reading and Fakenham
and bound by James Burn and Co. Ltd., Esher

CATALOGUE NO: 02/5780/33 [METHUEN]

I-II

PREFACE

THE writing of yet another history of the sixteenth century may seem to require justification; I can only say that I should not have written this book if I had thought so. There is much yet to discover about that well-worked period, and —more important—much of what has been discovered in the last thirty years has not yet reached the more general accounts. Only Professor Bindoff's brilliant short study of *Tudor England* provides an introduction to modern views; and he has left room for a book on a somewhat larger scale, with rather more detail in. Inevitably the different aspects of that crowded century could not all be given equal treatment: I can only hope that there is enough of them all to avoid at least the charge of deliberate obtuseness. To me it seems that what matters most in the story is the condition, reconstruction, and gradual moulding of a state—the history of a nation and its leaders in political action and therefore the history of government in the widest sense Other matters—economic, social, literary, military—are dealt with but more succinctly; this could not be helped. The needs of a book of this sort demanded a framework of fairly detailed narrative, and the analysis has had to concentra e on what seemed most important to the author. Tudor history can be written round such topics as religion, the maritime expansion, or Shakespeare,but I have chosen the constitutional problems of politics and government, in part because they attract me most and in part because I think that they involve less omission or falsification by emphasis than any other central theme.

More serious is the fact that in some parts of the story I have gone rather farther in being up-to-date than may be generally liked. I have come to some conclusions, especially about the place of Thomas Cromwell, the importance of the 1530s, and the nature of the Tudor polity, which—though by no means necessarily original—go counter to some accepted notions. I have elaborated some of these points elsewhere and hope to do so for others, but so far this has not been possible. I would therefore ask pardon for this preview, saying only that, confronted with a choice between writing what I think to be true and repeating what I believe to be doubtful, I could not but choose the former. The evidence exists, but much of it is not the kind that can be recited here.

Anyone who writes about the Tudor century puts his head into a number of untamed lions' mouths. Some of the issues—especially in religion—are still alive. Here dissension does not matter because agreement is impossible while people continue to be personally engaged. More troublesome are the difficulties which historians have created for themselves. Conflicts over the use of terms like modern and medieval, Renaissance and new learning, reflect a very real doubt as to the meaning of the century as a whole. I have tried to avoid the pitfalls, very probably without success: one may agree (as I am inclined to do) that modern and medieval are meaningless terms, but one cannot do without them. Where I have used them I have tried to make them say, respectively, 'more like what came after' and 'more like what came before', without prejudice as to what it was that came before and after. I happen to think that in my main theme—the nature of the English polity—changes took place in this period which cannot be described without the use of these terms, but I do not for one moment suppose that the differences between them are those between antitheses. If I speak of a 'Tudor revolution', I also know that the 'after' came out of the 'before'; but there was so much deliberate change crowded into the 1530s that a genuinely new state emerged, however closely it was linked to the old.

The fundamental difficulty arises from the attempt to treat the century as a unit, which it was not. In many ways the date 1485 matters less than almost any of the dates picked by historians as landmarks for guidance through the jungle and desert of events. It had only one real significance and that dynastic: it so happens that the family of Henry Tudor, unlike that of York which he overthrew or that of Lancaster which he claimed to represent, maintained itself on the throne for long enough to set its mark indelibly on the country over which it ruled. 1485 is the beginning of Tudor rule, and 1603 the end of it, and since the dates so conveniently circumscribe the life of one dynasty they have proved long-lived illusions. In the history of England nothing decisive happened in either 1485 or 1603. It may be natural to contrast 'the Tudors' with 'the Yorkists' who came before them and 'the Stuarts' who followed them, but once one can free oneself of these schematic dynastic preoccupations and look at events and people individually, one soon discovers that there are points of more profound significance in the sixteenth century than the accession of Henry VII or the death of Elizabeth. But it is better to accept these old categories and make them do new work than attempt to set up new categories which will only create new confusions and quarrels. In 1485 Henry VII and no one else ascended the throne, and in 1603 a foreign king full of a kind of shrewd stupidity succeeded a wise and native queen: for such not very deep reasons these two dates continue to have some point as the limits of the tale. But let us remember that the potentialities for change contained in so long a period as a hundred and twenty years are not lessened by the simple device of giving those years a family name.

I should like to record my very real gratitude to all those who have helped in the writing of this book. In particular Dr P. J. Jones is responsible for some of the above reflections, though he must not be thought to agree with a word of them; Mr John Saltmarsh gave me most generously of his precious time and great knowledge to save Chapter IX from serious error, though, once again, he is not in any way answerable for what I have there written; and I have profited greatly from Mr J. J. Scarisbrick's unpublished researches concerning the bishops of Henry VIII and from Dr W. Ullmann's conversation on the subject of papal powers. Most of my many debts to others are implicitly acknowledged in the Bibliography.

Cambridge, July 1954 G. R. E.

Though the occasion of an early reprint seemed hardly to call for major alterations or revisions, it has given me the opportunity of correcting some misprints and one or two errors of fact to which reviewers have kindly drawn my attention. I have also added a few items at the end of the Bibliography: in particular, I am glad to be able to supply now two articles in which I have given grounds for my interpretation of the career of Thomas Cromwell, grounds whose absence I had to regret in my original preface.

Cambridge, December 1955

This reprint includes an entirely revised bibliography, a step made necessary by the recent flood of Tudor studies. I hope it will not be regarded as arrogance or delusion if I say that nevertheless I cannot yet see any need to revise the book itself. Though occasionally a minor point has been rendered doubtful by research, and though I have changed my own mind on occasion, a real reconsideration of the account and interpretation here put forward does not, I think, seem so far to be called for.

Cambridge, October 1961

CONTENTS

MAPS AND DIAGRAMS

Chapter I

THE TUDOR PROBLEM

ON 22 August 1485 Henry, earl of Richmond, won one of the successive battles of the wars of the Roses near the Leicestershire township of Market Bosworth. His opponent, who commanded a stronger army halved by treason, was killed, and the throne thus left vacant by Richard III fell to the earl who became Henry VII. With this event, somewhat fortuitous in itself, there began the years of Tudor rule which were in the end to produce an England changed in many essentials—wealthier, more firmly unified, more fully national, more modern in her outlook, and properly equipped to play her part in the wider world which had also emerged in the course of the sixteenth century.

The England which Henry VII came to rule was the product of war and plague. Ever since Edward III set forth, in 1338, to claim the crown of France, Englishmen had been fighting—first the enemy on the continent and then, after a hundred years, each other in the squabbles for the English throne which really began with Richard II's deposition in 1399, burst into open war in 1450, and ended only when another Richard was killed on Bosworth Field. A period of war extending over nearly a century and a half was bound to leave a profound mark, though even by contemporary standards England suffered little in the fighting. The wars were far from continuous; even the thirty years' internecine struggle which we call the wars of the Roses was interrupted by long stretches of official peace. The war with France left that country exhausted and in misery, anxious for 'the naked, poor, and mangled Peace' for which Shakespeare's duke of Burgundy pleads so eloquently; the English, on the other hand, though they knew and disliked the noisy brawling soldier, back from France and eager to spend his loot on drink and women, were unacquainted with the real horrors of war—the ravaged countryside, the burning farm and town, the murder, rape, and brutalisation of the populace. They had, in fact, made considerable profit out of loot and ransoms, though more legitimate trading suffered. One might suppose that the civil wars had taught the country more of the realities, and indeed the wars of the Roses did cause distress here and there where marching columns passed or met for action; on the whole, however, events followed the pattern of English civil disturbances which tend to be transacted in a gentler fashion than those of other countries. The peasant and yeoman tilled the soil, the merchant—recovering from the trading depression of the mid-century—went about his business; life carried on in many parts of the country as though the kings and claimants, the great nobles and their riotous retainers, the politicians and soldiers, had not been busy cutting each other's throats on the public stage on which history must concentrate her attention.

The evil effects of the wars did not lie in material destruction or any stagnation of life. More subtle, less easily seen, and for that reason much more dangerous, they consisted in the growth of an unstable social structure thriving on disorder and lawlessness, and in the rapidly increasing weakness of the crown. The reign of Edward I (1272-1307) marked the transition from a society which was properly feudal to one which is now commonly described as bastard feudalism, a name which signifies not simply a corrupted or decaying form of feudalism but a social structure different and new in essentials. Feudalism embodied the link between lord and vassal in a system of land tenure; services were rendered in return for land held, and the tie was one carefully established in the law. The tenant had rights as well as duties, the lord duties as well as rights. Land is a real thing and does not move; a system taking it for its criterion is bound to have great fixity and stability. The feudal principle, evaded though it was, that land cannot be sold, though it can be granted away in return for services to be performed, added to this permanency. The origins of the system lay in the needs of military defence, but the military basis which had given it reality and strength vanished within a hundred years of the Norman Conquest. Men who owed services for the land they held were bound to be farmers or landlords before they were anything else; however loyal they might be to their lord, they had to see to the management of their estates. They might, reluctant and grumbling, come and do some military service if called upon to do so, but they could never become the nucleus of a private army.

In fact, they could not become the nucleus of any army, and as soon as the kings realised this fact they began to undermine the reality of feudalism by hiring their soldiers. This had happened as early as the middle of the twelfth century. A hundred years later Edward I unwittingly accelerated the break-up when he tried to safeguard the feudal rights of the crown by prohibiting subinfeudation—the creation of new rungs in the feudal ladder—which made it impossible for any man but the king to reward services done, or ensure future services to be done, by the grant of lands. The fourteenth century, from the Scottish wars of Edward I through the civil wars of Edward II to the French wars of Edward III, added the urgent problem of finding a military force which could be relied upon against professional opponents, which could be kept in the field, and which could be paid in some fashion other than in land. Services were paid for as rendered—as a rule in cash—instead of being incumbent upon certain units of land whose tenant had to perform them. There grew up a system by which men took service with someone—the king or a great nobleman or, for that matter, any little knight. The nexus of lord and vassal, whose means of exchange was land and whose essence was direct and individual relationship between two men, was replaced by that of master and man, whose means of exchange was money and whose essence was patronage and affinity, that is membership of a group gathered round one man. Feudalism, stable on its basis of the land and firm in its scheme of known rights and duties, gave way to the patronage system of bastard feudalism where men's ambitions and needs were satisfied by him who could pay for services and at whose order and discretion they were done. It was essentially a less stable system, and at times it grew frighteningly fluid.

Bastard feudalism began in military organisation, with the indentures for service through which fourteenth-century armies were recruited. The captains of the wars gathered round them men eager to fight and make a profit, and they retained them by indentures which specified the services to be done and rewards to be given. In the course of time the system invaded other spheres, and great nobles, from the king downwards, acquired ever growing households of servants and retainers who held either indentures or letters patent of grants outlining their rights and duties. Superficially the relationship continued to be feudal, relying on personal loyalties. In fact it was based on payment, though the unstable tendencies inherent in it were balanced by the persistence of personal and family ties; successive generations of one family, or men of the same locality, would often adhere with remarkable fidelity to the fortunes of one great house such as Lancaster or York or Warwick. It was the military side of it which made the arrangement really dangerous, for there it amounted to the creation of private magnate armies within the kingdom. The companies formed to fight in France were bound together by service to the captain or patron whose retinue they composed; when the wars in France were over, and chances of war offered in England herself, it was fatally easy for these magnate employers of armed bands to engage each other, in despite of the crown. But that this chance offered was less the fault of bastard feudalism than of that other consequence of the wars, the declining power and authority of the crown.

The strength of her kings was once the special glory and distinction of England. No other country in the West achieved so early the unification, the relative national consciousness, the common law and common administration, the efficient and fatherly care, which William I, Henry I, Henry II, and Edward I imposed on their dominions. In the high middle ages England was almost the model of a monarchy, resting indeed on a feudal social order and animated by feudal concepts, but remarkably free from the destructive centrifugal forces which feudalism released in France and Germany. She owed this happy dispensation to the accident of the Norman Conquest which made possible a virtually fresh start; but even more she owed it to the kings who, intent on their own interests, profited the country by the creation of a strong central authority. From the land policy of the Conqueror to the legislation of Edward I, English kings worked hard at preserving the interests of the crown, and with it of the nation at large, against the encroachments of individuals or classes whose potential strength was kept in check only by the exercise of the royal prerogative in the hands of determined rulers. The death of Edward I marked an epoch. His son was the worst king since the Conquest. Richard I had been an absentee, John a man who made enemies with undue ease, Henry III a near-mediocrity who never caught up with the losses incurred in his minority. But Edward II was vicious, unstable, and fatally given to favourites; also, he lacked the warlike prowess which alone could control the incipient phenomenon of bastard feudalism. In his reign, the killing of Gaveston began the long series of political murders, the ambitions of Thomas of Lancaster foreshadowed the future 'overmighty subject', the Ordainers displayed the effective class opposition of the baronage to the crown which was to end in the destruction of Edward I's monarchy, the Dispensers and Mortimer introduced the untamed passions and disorganised liberties of the Welsh Marches into English politics which they were to dominate until the accession of the Tudors, and Edward II's own deposition and shameful death administered a profound shock to the concept of kingship which his ancestors had represented.

In the rest of the fourteenth century things went from bad to worse. Edward III could maintain a pretence of strong kingship only by means of the wars which sidetracked turbulence but themselves gave the danger teeth when armed retainers were formed into small armies; moreover, his policy of lavish grants and generous patronage, while it saved the peace for a time, made sure that when trouble came the strength would not be on the king's side. It was unfortunate that Edward III lived too long and had too many children, that the Black Prince died before his father, that Richard II was a spoiled young man with high notions of his prerogative and little ability to support them. Such accidents shape history as much as the more majestic currents of economic forces or social changes. By endowing his family with the inheritance of the declining Norman nobility, by creating for them dukedoms and powers, Edward III called into being magnates related by blood to the king and ultimately intent on making their claim to the throne effective. The blood of Edward III ramified through too many veins; at the distance of two centuries it was still to prove fatal to the Pole family and the Courtenays in the reign of Henry VIII.

The weakness and arrogance of Richard II precipitated these latent troubles. The revolution of 1399 put on the throne a dynasty with a doubtful title and dependent on a party in the kingdom. In the reign of Henry IV the real power of the nobility came out in the influence of the great council of magnates whose virtual clients and spokesmen sat in the house of commons and gave to opposition that falsely modern air which led nineteenth-century historians to speak of the Lancastrian constitutional experiment. Henry V tried the old expedient of a French war; being himself an able soldier, and a strong man who could command violent men's loyalties, he had a measure of success, but he did nothing to solve the growing problems of the crown. His early death and Henry VI's long minority opened the flood gates. The magnates captured the king's permanent council, the very centre of the royal government; the wars went wrong, the house of Lancaster took the blame, and the house of York came forward to assert a claim which—according to the strict principles of inheritance—was slightly the better. And so the wars of the Roses followed upon the minority of Henry VI, to set the seal on the decay of royal power. The crown was a plaything of forces it did not control; when a great nobleman (of recent vintage) like the earl of Warwick disposed of the throne at his pleasure, English kingship had reached its nadir. For a time the house of York looked capable of restoring the position; that it failed was again due to a variety of largely personal reasons. Edward IV's character was one: his marriage to Elizabeth Woodville created the fatal divisions within his own party which led directly to the usurpation of Richard III and so to Henry Tudor's chance. More important, perhaps, was the accident of Edward's death before his heir was old enough to take over. The minority of Henry VI ruined Lancaster; that of Edward V ruined York. Finally, the Yorkist link with Burgundy and failure in European diplomacy preserved the life of the earl of Richmond, protected as he was by Brittany and France, and made possible the invasion of 1485.

Until then, the accession of Henry VII, the crown continued weak and uncertain, though both Yorkist kings had made quite a creditable start on restoring it to strength. The decline of English kingship in the fourteenth century ended in the wild murders and civil wars of the fifteenth, and no dynasty tied up with these excesses, and dependent for victory on its armed and rebellious followers, could hope to arrest the fatal movement. At the very time when the disruptive and anti-social forces inherent in the master-man relationship of bastard feudalism and nourished by war to extraordinary proportions were at their most dangerous, that part of the body politic which had both the interest and the potential power to control them was in decay. Government at the centre relinquished the reins, and the institutions of law and order fell under the sway of over-powerful individuals with armed men at their backs. The famous evils of the time were all the result of this. Livery (the equipping of armed retainers with their lord's uniform and badge to signify their sole allegiance), maintenance (the lord's support of his followers in courts of law; by force if necessary and irrespective of the merits of the case), embracery (the corruption or intimidation of juries)—these abuses undermined the whole system of law-enforcement and compelled men to resort to violence in order to fight violence. Not all retainers wielded the sword and buckler; others did as acceptable service by sitting on juries, acting as justices of the peace, or even as sheriffs, controlling commissions of enquiry and the like—all in the interest of the magnate to whose 'affinity' or following they belonged. The magnates did not destroy the system of law but perverted it to the service of injustice. Intimidation and chicanery supplanted impartiality and the king's peace.

These were the effects—in the last resort—of 150 years of war, and while they were very serious they were still restricted to those who had law suits to fight or happened to be involved in the faction struggles which spread from the centre outwards and alternatively from the shires inwards to the throne. A man might live a lifetime without coming in touch with these troubles, though he was very lucky if he did; nothing, however, could save him from the mysterious workings of the plague. The Black Death of 1349 was only the first, though also by far the most violent, of a recurring series of outbreaks; from the middle of the fourteenth century to about the middle of the seventeenth, bubonic plague was epidemic in England. As is the manner with the disease, its first onslaught proved the most killing; thereafter it occurred at gradually increasing intervals, withdrew from the countryside into the towns, and declined as a killer. But throughout the fourteenth and fifteenth centuries, men were dying from plague, and the mortality was sufficiently high to cause a permanent decline in population. This naturally had far-reaching economic effects. The increasing population of the thirteenth century had pressed hard on the available land, so that labour was cheap, lords found it easy to enforce the burdens of villeinage, and marginal land and waste were being broken up by the plough. In the fifteenth century the process was reversed. Much of the newly cultivated land was again given back to the wilderness; a land glut succeeded to the land hunger. Farming, with the market for produce declining, lost its attraction; lords preferred to let out their demesne lands rather than work them, but it was increasingly difficult to find tenants ready to enter upon the vacant holdings. Labour grew precious, and serfdom collapsed as lords found it impossible to enforce duties on men who could always escape elsewhere, for workmen were welcome and no one enquired too closely into antecedents. The payment of money wages—practised off and on for a long time—now became the rule, and the whole structure of rural society cracked. Lords who lived on rents from their lands lost contact both with the land and with the people; the old ties disappeared, and with them the basis of true feudalism—service in return for land, land granted in return for services.

Thus among the people who lived on and by the land—nine-tenths of the population—the long-term effects of the plague and the agricultural depression were to assist that change from feudalism to bastard feudalism which other factors in social and political life were producing. On the whole the upper classes suffered most; peasants and yeomen, exploiting their rarity value, could get land on very advantageous terms—easy rents, reduced fines on entry—and were emancipating themselves from legal bondage. During this period the foundations were being laid for many of the new fortunes of the next century; the great house of Russell rose from such humble villein origins. The lords, on the other hand, found their incomes decaying and their assets in land deteriorating, a fact which helps to explain their violent unrest, cut-throat competition, and lawless and ruthless fight for advantages. Long before the wars of the Roses reduced the numbers of the English aristocracy, the agricultural depression was at work sapping their strength and preparing their downfall. A new nobility grew up in the sixteenth century out of the gentry and merchants—or lesser men still—of the fifteenth: they had neither the same commitments nor the same expenses as their betters, and being better able to adjust themselves to the depression they survived more easily.

Trade, too, languished throughout most of the fifteenth century. It was a time when English merchants found their range contracting as the wars destroyed much of the important trade with France, and as the North German Hanse drove them from the Baltic and Iceland. The civil war completed the disaster both because trade always suffers worst from internecine disturbances, and because Edward IV only obtained the throne with the financial assistance of the Hanse who exacted valuable privileges in return. For a time, English merchants were at a disadvantage in their own country compared with the foreigner. The safe old stand-by, the export of wool, was stagnating in the hands of the Staplers of Calais who held a near-monopoly, while the trade in English cloth—mainly in the hands of the rising Merchant Adventurers of London—was still comparatively young and also more open to hazards. Wool was sold at Calais, that is in territory under English control; English cloth, on the other hand, had to fight competition in the markets of Flanders and Central Europe where English merchants were themselves foreigners and therefore at a disadvantage. England was in the awkward position of having relied on one main produce for her export trade; though she also sold tin, leather, hides, and some other goods, and though she imported wine and manufactures, it was on the sheep's backs that her prosperity grew. For that reason it was the more easily upset, and there is no need to look further than the war and the competition of foreign merchants for the cause of the slump which lasted till about 1475. It must be pointed out that the recovery began under Edward IV and was probably due to his restoration of peace; a country which produced the greater part of Europe's wool and exported it either raw or made up could not remain poor for long. But life was difficult at the best of times for the merchant with his overseas enterprises, and war made the risks of commerce impossibly great.

Henry VII thus succeeded to a much depleted inheritance. Just how depleted it was must now be discussed, if his achievement is to be seen in its true light. The country had been suffering from a gradually decreasing population for over a century, with all the depressing effects which such a development has on the spirit of a nation as well as, more obviously, on economic life. The despondent—one is tempted to say decadent—preoccupation with death indulged in by the fifteenth century, with the line 'Timor mortis conturbat me' running through many poems, is very different from the grim and often cynical interest in death displayed by the Elizabethans and Jacobeans. It mirrored a people who had found the medieval commonplace 'In media vita in morte sumus' only too true; they saw in recurrent plague the natural and inescapable punishment for sin, with the result that their spiritual needs found refuge in a rather spineless mysticism and resignation. One must be careful of generalising about the minds and morals of a whole people (even if there were barely three millions of them) and a whole century; there were many vigorous and crude characters about who paid no more regard to morbid fancies than their like in any generation. But it is hard to escape the conclusion that in the fifteenth century England displayed the characteristics of a stagnant and declining civilisation. The fundamental trouble was a spiritual malaise induced by plague and general uncertainty; among the more important symptoms were the disintegration of society, the violence of public life, the decay of law and order, and the weakness of the crown. But no one could cure the malaise—time and changing circumstances were miraculously to do that; it was to the symptoms that a ruler had to turn his attention.

There was, of course, nothing that anyone could then do about the epidemic disease which was undermining mental and physical resistance, but as it happened Henry VII came to the throne after the worst of it was over. Sporadic outbreaks were to recur until 1665: the Great Plague of London is so well remembered because it was the last fling of that particular plague cycle. But nothing like the disaster of the fourteenth-century Black Death, or the heavy mortality of the mid-fifteenth-century outbreak in London and other towns was to happen again. The decline in numbers was arrested and the nation recovering before the first Tudor won the crown. That it not to say that the problem was solved, but that the

Tudors found it at a stage when man-made solutions had a hope of succeeding.

However, it was on the effects of the wars that a strong king would have to start, and once peace was restored natural resilience could be trusted to look to the other matters. A poor and weak crown was confronted by wealthy and arrogant magnates: there lay the crux of the problem, as Edward IV, Richard III, and Henry VII after them, saw clearly enough.[1] The first cause of weakness at the top was the uncertainty of the succession; there was no hope of restoring an effective monarchy until the monarchs could feel reasonably safe on the throne. There had to be an end to dynastic war before any dynasty could set about rebuilding the kingdom. So much is obvious, and we shall see how Henry VII, and Henry VIII as well, were to deal with this question. Once firmly on the throne, what was to be the next step? Was it necessary to create a 'new monarchy', a name once fashionably bestowed on the Tudors, in order to produce an effective sort of kingship? That used to be the common view, and on the whole, with few exceptions, most books seem still to subscribe to it, only differing about the date of its inception and the name of its founder. Henry VII is to be displaced by Edward IV, incidentally a much more romantic figure; that one of them started something fresh—strong, energetic kingship with despotic leanings and practices (often deplorably enough graced with the quite meaningless title of a Renaissance kingship)—that is not doubted. This attitude is a relic of the view which saw in the fourteenth and fifteenth centuries a brave rehearsal of modern constitutionalism; if one believes that Edward III and Henry IV confronted parliaments like those faced by Charles I and James II, one must indeed speak of an incongruous period of despotism and the decline of parliament in the sixteenth century. But no one today seriously holds views on the 'Lancastrian Constitution' which make it necessary to speak of Yorkist or Tudor 'despotism'; those who have abandoned the first term should realise that the second has thereby become meaningless.

It is, thus, futile to argue whether Edward IV or Henry VII founded a monarchy new in that it displayed altogether new

[1] They did not need the teaching of the egregious Sir John Fortescue whose writings (recently at last described as 'overrated and misleading' by Mr K. B. Macfarlane) have for too long been allowed to usurp the credit for an analysis which statesmen could make for themselves. Historians, being literary craftsmen themselves, have a natural disposition to see undue importance in writers and writings. Few men of action ever learned their jobs or ideas from books.

tendencies of centralised control and royal power; there was nothing new in such attributes of kingship. We shall better understand what happened if we remember that the strong English monarchy had suffered first a decline and then a catastrophe in the waning middle ages, and that the task of the new dynasty essentially consisted in getting back to heights already reached 200 years earlier. Of course, the intervening centuries could not be wiped off the slate; in many ways Henry VII's monarchy differed from that of Edward I. But it was not essentially different: it fulfilled much the same ambitions and purpose with much the same instruments. The troubles of the fifteenth century had not destroyed the government of the country; they had merely overlaid it with an alluvial slime of individual lawlessness and general corruption. The weapons of the crown—the institutions through which the kings of England governed—had to be restored to their earlier effectiveness. The key to the problem was the personal action of the king and the ministers and agents who, surrounding him, formed the royal household. But if this is to be clear it will be necessary to give a very brief outline of English medieval government.

English government in the middle ages was truly the king's government. All action centred upon his person, and all action started from his court. The *curia regis* (king's court) of the Anglo-Norman kings contained the ministers, advisers, and servants on whom the king relied for the administration of revenue, the writing of letters and grants, the speaking of justice. But the king and his retinue were always moving about from place to place, while an ever more complicated machinery of government with its growing collections of archives and its need to be readily accessible to the king's subjects had to find some permanent residence. Thus departments began to specialise out of the *curia regis* and to acquire independent status: as the phrase goes, they 'went out of court'. The exchequer or financial department led the way in the middle of the twelfth century, to be followed by the courts of the common law (common pleas and king's bench) and the chancery in the course of the thirteenth. But this raised a new problem. A king who was very much the active ruler and administrator of his dominions now found himself often far from the instruments of his will. No document, for instance, was authentic unless issued under the great seal which was kept by the chancellor, but how was the king, writing perhaps from Chester or Carlisle, to convince a chancellor at Westminster of the genuineness of his instructions, especially since he himself could not write? The obvious answer was to evolve another seal—soon called the privy seal—with which all authorisations (warrants) sent to the chancery had to be sealed.

This process of duplication by which the royal household (as we call the king's retinue after the twelfth century) put out further institutions to supplement those which, having originally grown up in the same way, had already gone out of court and become departments of state, is the characteristic administrative development of the middle ages. The reason already mentioned—convenience and the king's uncertain movements—was reinforced from the thirteenth century onwards by the ambitions of the baronage to control the kingdom through control of the offices of state. When they succeeded in securing the appointment of chancellors, treasurers, and even keepers of the privy seal under their influence, the king could and did counter by developing such parts of his household as the wardrobe and chamber to do the work of departments of state. Henry III, for instance, employed his wardrobe in finance because the exchequer was in baronial hands, while Edward I greatly augmented its use because he found he could govern better through officials directly under his eye and entirely dependent upon him. The king remained the real ruler, in fact if he was capable, and in theory if he was not. Whatever departments might go out of court, there remained full power in the crown to create new instruments of government, and this power was naturally exercised through the king's immediate entourage, his household. Thus, the privy seal and later the signet came to take their place by the side of the great seal; the finances of the kingdom were often administered in wardrobe or chamber even when the official accounts were kept at the exchequer; the courts of common law were supplemented by the more elastic and adaptable jurisdiction of the king in his council, exercised either in ordinary council meetings, or (in the fourteenth century) when parliament met, or (in the fifteenth) by the chancellor who came to take over most of the council's judicial business.

Throughout the later middle ages, then, there were really two systems of administration, or—better—two layers to the royal administration, for both parts were very much the king's. Behind the obvious and manifest set of institutions which had left the retinue and become true departments of state there stood the royal household which not only did much independent work but actively inspired the official part of the administration. It was on these hidden springs that government really depended. The records of the offices of state show no decay or decline in the fifteenth century when the country was notoriously ill-governed or even ungoverned, but because the household did nothing government was in eclipse. As one would expect, the decline of the household went hand in hand with the decline of the crown; the king's increasing dependence on the power of his great nobles was displayed administratively in the gradual disappearance of that second layer of government from the reign of Henry IV onwards. Richard II had tried to set up a despotism through his signet and his chamber; naturally, the reaction against him stressed the need for the crown to work through those public seals and departments over which the magnates could exercise a measure of control. They came near to perfecting that control when during Henry VI's minority they captured the king's perpetual council, ordinarily a body of advisers chosen by the king and entirely his servants. But the household potential in government was not destroyed; it was only left to rust. The official parts of the machinery were in perfect working order even when they either did no effective work, or (like the exchequer) badly needed reconstructing to cope with new conditions, or (like the courts of law) needed supplementing with something less rigid if justice was to be done. Yet the motive power contained in the king's household—dormant not dead—only needed reviving. A new vigour of spirit was urgently necessary, but there was no call for a new kind of king or a new machinery of government.

This outline sketch has omitted two points—parliament, and the so-called franchises. We shall have more to say about parliament in the course of this book; here it will be enough to note that until the Tudor period parliament did not form a regular part of the government of the country. It met at the king's discretion and for his purposes. Its very composition was still in doubt. The clear distinction which the books make between great councils (of nobles, with no representatives from shires and boroughs) and parliaments proper does not appear to have been fully grasped even as late as the reign of Henry VII. The essence of parliament was the king and his council—his professional council, reinforced by such hereditary councillors (barons) as he chose to call, and if he liked by the commons. In practice, the commons were ordinarily necessary to make a parliament, and by the fifteenth century they had acquired sufficient corporateness to form a 'house'; the lords, on the other hand, were still simply a great council and not a 'house' of parliament. Edward III's wars and consequent need for money had promoted parliament to precocious importance; the weakness of the Lancastrian title and the magnates' influence in the great council and, through their clients, in the commons had continued its spuriously 'modern' activity. The need for taxation by parliamentary consent, in any case demanded by the practical problem of collection, was coming to be recognised, and by the late fifteenth century it was generally accepted that statutes enacted in parliament were laws of special authority. But these were vague gropings still. The old view which saw in the Tudor period an interruption to the natural growth of representative institutions in England is simply untenable, and most scholars now agree that parliament entered upon its proper career in the sixteenth century. Building upon medieval foundations but erecting something quite new on them, the Tudors and their ministers produced the composite sovereign body of the king in parliament which has ever since been the supreme authority in England.

Henry VII did not, then, take over a country without administrative institutions or the means of government; nor did he perhaps succeed to a parliamentary state which had broken down and needed rebuilding by despotism. He was faced with a machine which had been allowed to stop, though its components were sound, and these components consisted of departments of state in working order and departments of the royal household (including the council) which it needed only a strong king to revive. Only one problem could not be solved by mere restoration or revival, and that was the problem of franchises and feudal courts. All that has been said so far applies to the king's government only, but it was one of the leading medieval characteristics that the king's government did not cover everything. The state—for the king is only the embodiment of the state—had not yet entered upon its career of exclusive and all-embracing power; there were bodies and areas within the kingdom over which the king's control was limited or even nil. Some of these bodies with special rights were vexatious without being really objectionable, such as the municipal gilds whose regulations represented an obstacle to trade and industry, but an obstacle which the flood was certainly getting over and around. There was, however, nothing but trouble in the noble franchises—the special rights and immunities enjoyed by certain of the crown's subjects. There were palatinates like Durham and Lancaster, liberties like Ripon and Richmond, and plenty of smaller individual privileges and exemptions claimed by noblemen and knights, all of which limited the power of the crown. They involved rights to hold courts and rights to escape from the royal jurisdiction which made it very difficult to discipline the turbulent element. The biggest franchise of all was that of the Church, with its own system of courts, its rights of benefit of clergy which meant in effect that anyone in orders had his first crime free, its powers of granting sanctuary and staying the king's writ. The Church, subject to the international monarchy of the pope at Rome, formed a state within the state; how that problem came to a head in the reign of Henry VIII shall be shown later. In the reign of Henry VII the Church was loyal to the crown, the king a good son of the Church, and no problem arose.

The real trouble, then, were the franchises of the nobility. The early palatinates, Durham and Chester, had not mattered because Durham was episcopal (and bishops were chosen with the king's approval) and Chester soon fell to the crown. The same applied to the large franchise of Lancaster, united with the crown from 1399 when Henry of Lancaster became king. But there were many small franchises, and there were in particular the rights, privileges, and claims of the marcher lords. The powers of frontier nobles are always rather special; in this case, many of them also held lands and rights in Wales which had its own customs and was barely amenable to royal control at any time in the middle ages. The problem was complicated by the typical respect for property, or even mere possession, which the common law of the middle ages imposed upon the English mind until the early twentieth century. It was a principle of the law that no franchise was valid except by grant of the crown, but the reverse of this was that a franchise proven to be by grant of the crown was virtually indefeasible. In practice, it was very difficult to deal with a recalcitrant franchise holder who could prove crown grant. Edward I instituted proceedings known as *quo warranto*—by what warrant do you claim?—to enquire into the origins of rights asserted by his subjects; but the weaker kings who succeeded him could not hope to exercise such a measure of supervision. In the fifteenth century the decay of the crown and the disturbed state of the country produced, in practice, a vast increase in the independence and obstinacy of those claiming to hold franchises. The whole question of the medieval franchise was blown wide open by the abuses of the fifteenth century; ultimately there could be no solution except for the crown to assert the exclusive and general competence of the state. Though something may have been lost in variety and local independence, the gain in law-abiding orderliness and national unity produced by the centralising policy was enormous. It is easy to be romantic at this distance; the men of the sixteenth century who remembered the disturbed time, or remembered their fathers telling them about it, knew well enough why they allowed the Tudor kings to ride fairly roughshod over the petty kingdoms in the marches in the north and west, in Wales and Ireland.

These were the problems; what of the man who in 1485 took over the task of solving them? In many ways, Henry VII was eminently fitted for the job. Born in 1457, he was only twenty-eight when he came to the throne, and only fifty-two when he died in 1509; yet one never thinks of him as a young man. The common picture of him was painted by Francis Bacon in one of the great biographies in the language, and though Bacon wrote the book in a few weeks and without access to any material not now available his book has survived—perhaps too easily. Henry was undoubtedly shrewd, calculating, and long-headed; he seems never to have been overcome by passion. Yet if he had even a touch of the temper so noticeable in his descendants, this exercise of self-restraint must have cost him a great deal. Probably the hard training of a youth spent in wars, danger of execution, and long exile tamed the Tudor propensity to violence and taught the young earl of Richmond to hide his feelings and veil his purposes. That he was eager for money is certain; so, for that matter, were all the Tudors. He was not, however, a miser; where it served his purpose money was spent freely, and he saved and extorted only in the interests of a crown whose solvency was the basis of sound government and peace in the country. Some of the austerity which hangs about him may have been due to the school of exile; more, one suspects, came from the influence of that formidable old lady, his mother Margaret Beaufort, who ruled his court with a rod of iron.

Exile and his own patient nature seem to have taught Henry VII the most important lesson of all. If England was to recover order and the throne stability, the civil wars would have to be ended once and for all. That meant not only the cessation of hostilities, but the healing of wounds left by them, the assuaging of tempers heated by the long controversy. Perhaps the most important quality now required in a king, next to inflexible resolution, was judicious mercy, the mercy of head not heart. Henry VII was to display both resolution and clemency. It was remarked how hard the king was to persuade of conspiracies against him; no doubt the graduate of exile and conspiracies knew just how futile most of such enterprises were. But his reluctance to proceed to extremes and his readiness to accept old enemies into the fold display his determination to show that the wars were over. It is difficult to think that there was anything fundamentally kind-hearted about Henry VII, though he had a sly sardonic humour which both contemporaries and later historians have sometimes mistaken for spite. Perhaps we do him an injustice. If, as his honest partisans grumbled, he refused to listen to information and charged accusers with ill will and malice, it was not that he would not see the obvious but rather that he rated the danger at its true value and preferred to overlook any doings, however hostile, that did not constitute a present danger. Henry VII's famous mercy was the calculated product of statesmanlike common sense, and none the less creditable for that.

But—merciful, slow to wrath, hard-headed, and unemotional though he was—there was nothing at all of the procrastinator about this king. He proved himself a man of action and a soldier before he was twenty-eight, a fact which is commonly forgotten; if he refused to fight thereafter it was because he knew better than most that the need for peace overrode all other considerations. To the establishment of this peace, the preservation of law and order, the security of the realm, the creation of conditions in which men could follow their avocations in safety and with thought for the future, he applied all his high intelligence and tenacity of will, his shrewdness and his steady and daily interest in affairs. Like all his family he had an uncanny gift for picking men to serve him, and not even the great Elizabeth surrounded herself with a brighter galaxy of first-rate ministers than did her grandfather. Cardinal Morton, Bishop Fox, William Warham, Sir Reginald Bray, Sir Thomas Lovell, Sir John Heron, Sir Edward Belknap, Richard Empson, and Edmund Dudley—and others, many of whom are only now being painfully resuscitated by a process of historical exhumation—all these men were loyal and ardent servants of an exacting but worthy master. Much of what we have been accustomed to call the work of Henry VII probably sprang from the brains of these men, but the king himself was the active head of government, and in the last resort the recovery made must stand to his credit. The task was indeed formidable, but the intelligence, stubbornness, and sound sense assembled to deal with it were more formidable still.

Chapter II

HENRY VII: SECURING THE DYNASTY

1. HENRY'S CLAIM TO THE CROWN

WHEN victory was won at Bosworth, Lord Stanley, whose timely desertion of Richard III had made Henry's triumph possible, picked up the crown and put it on the victor's head; according to the chronicler, people rejoiced and clapped their hands and cried, 'King Henry, King Henry'. But while this acclamation must have been pleasant to his ears, it did not make the gold circlet sit any more securely on his head. Henry VII's first task was to convince the country and the world that he really was king. Though he could feel the task somewhat eased as his journey to London assumed the proportions of a triumph, there was probably no need to remind him of men's fickleness. The city of London, in particular, had distinguished itself by the readiness with which it had hailed each successive conqueror of the crown.

Henry's own claim to the crown was far from straightforward. Fifteenth-century England knew no proper law of succession. The judges had repeatedly declared that the common law did not extend to such exalted matters; they had, in fact, been too scared of the consequences to attempt a definition in the middle of the dynastic struggles. Henry IV, in 1399, had put forward a claim compounded of the (false) assertion that he represented the true line of succession, the proof of divine favour contained in his actual victory, and the duty of removing a lawless monarch like Richard II. There were points here which Henry VII might profitably remember. Richard, duke of York, in 1450, and his son Edward IV after him, opposed an out-and-out theory of legitimacy to the claims which the oath of allegiance gave to Henry VI, the king in possession. Legitimacy—the doctrine that the crown can descend only to one man at any given time and that this succession is determined by primogeniture—was the centre of the Yorkist position; being descended from John of Gaunt's elder brother, they found in it a useful weapon against Gaunt's issue. Richard III exploited it further when he took the crown by the simple step of declaring his nephews bastardised; this left him as the only legitimate heir of the only legitimate line. There was then in existence a general idea that the succession should pass to the eldest son, but the strict theory of legitimacy was still the property of a party, and the Lancastrians had never subscribed to it.

The theory was of no use at all to Henry VII. He claimed to represent the line of Lancaster; his mother Margaret was the last of the Beauforts, John of Gaunt's illegitimate descendants who had been legitimised by the pope and by Richard II. However, an insertion, itself of doubtful validity, in Henry IV's confirmation of his predecessor's grant had denied them the right to succeed to the crown. On the male side, Henry had no royal ancestry; if direct descent from Edward III was to be decisive, the young earl of Warwick, son of the late duke of Clarence, had undoubtedly the best claim. Legitimacy was thus valueless to the Tudor king. Nor did he intend to base his right on the much-mooted marriage to Elizabeth, daughter of Edward IV: it might be useful in appeasing the Yorkist faction, but Henry meant to be king in his own right. He therefore deliberately postponed the marriage until he had established himself on the throne. In actual fact, he adopted the simplest solution of all: he said that he was king. In November 1485 he told his first parliament that he had come to the crown by inheritance (leaving the details studiously vague) and by the proof of God's will expressed in his victory: his right was, in his own view, divine to this extent that divine approval had clearly been given on the field of battle. This Tudor kind of divine right is the exact opposite to the Stuart brand. The Tudors appealed to fact—God spoke through the arbitrament of war. The Stuarts believed in an indefeasible right which no amount of adverse circumstances could lessen or destroy.

Thus Henry certainly thought and acted as king of England as soon as Richard III was dead. Indeed, he arbitrarily fixed the beginning of his reign as the day before Bosworth, but this was only a typical piece of sharp practice designed to enable him to deal with Richard's supporters on that day as traitors to himself. There was no question of parliament conferring or even confirming his title. The very fact that the body which met in November 1485 counts as a real parliament is proof enough; only a true king can summon a true parliament, and the writs of summons went out early in September. Henry VII merely followed a precedent set in 1406 by Henry IV who had the succession after him registered in parliament, and he did it for the same reason—to avoid all ambiguity and pave the way for a stable continuance of his dynasty. It was 'ordained, established, and enacted' by the parliament, not that Henry was king, but that the inheritance of the crown of England, with every right and possession belonging to it, should remain and abide with 'our now sovereign lord king Henry' and his heirs. The act thus recognised that Henry was king, and that therefore rightly the succession must pass to his line; its purpose, like that of many Tudor acts, was to put a matter beyond doubt by putting it on record. It served the ends of propaganda the importance of which all the Tudors understood very well.

These were matters of theory, but of legal theory and therefore important. The care with which Henry made sure that his title should not rest on parliament, nor, on the other hand, be too thoroughly investigated, shows that he knew the value of theory. But practical considerations mattered even more. Henry might allege his claim to be beyond cavil, but there were others who would dispute this hotly. It was therefore only sound policy to make sure of all who could possibly raise a rival claim. Richard III had happily died without direct heirs and had—despite doubts, the point remains probable—eased Henry's way further by putting Edward IV's sons out of the way. There remained the daughters of Edward IV and the son of Clarence, the ten-year-old earl of Warwick. Henry dealt with the former by marrying Elizabeth, the eldest of them, in January 1486, and with the latter by securing his body in the Tower. The unfortunate boy was to live out his life there till the conspiracies of others of which he had neither knowledge nor part brought him to the block. There remained the claim of John de la Pole, earl of Lincoln, nephew of Edward IV and nominated as his successor by Richard III, but for the present he submitted to Henry. The marriage with Elizabeth of York also helped to keep quiet that section of Yorkists that had joined Henry against Richard III's usurpation and had made his victory possible; ultimately, in producing heirs to the claims of both Lancaster and York, it brought about that 'Union of the Two Noble and Illustrious Families' which the Tudor historian Edward Hall took for the subject of his discourse. For the moment, however, there remained many dissatisfied with the new king and many more to whom violent ups and downs in public life, with the chances they offered to the enterprising and unscrupulous, had become the normal state of things. Not until 1500 could the Spanish ambassador de Puebla report that no doubtful royal blood remained to unsettle the Tudor claim, and even a year or two later some royal officials at Calais, discussing politics and the king's illness, foresaw further dynastic difficulties. The reign was never quite free from the fact or threat of conspiracy, and for several years Henry VII had to defend his throne against the kind of enterprise which had secured it to him in the first place.

2. CONSPIRACIES

One of the purposes for which the parliament of November 1485 assembled was to dispose of the king's late adversaries. The usual crop of attainders[1] ruined a number of leading Yorkist supporters; so far, Henry VII showed no special mercy or any intention to end the wars by composing the feuds. There was, in any case, another good reason behind these acts which deprived some of the richest men in the kingdom of their property. The great act of resumption of the same year declared void all crown grants made since the death of Henry VI and recovered for Henry VII a vast deal of land; clearly, the king was from the first determined to improve his finances. In the true spirit of the civil wars, each stage of which had been signalled by the attainder of the defeated and the reversal of attainders previously inflicted on the victors, the parliament marked a Tudor, or even a Lancastrian, triumph. For the time being the Yorkists—even those who, hating Richard as a usurper, had supported Henry's bid for the crown—were left rather in the cold; the long overdue marriage to Elizabeth of York, so often promised, came none too soon to prevent the complete alienation of moderate Yorkist sentiment.

Moreover, there were still the extremists. In March 1486, having married his queen and seeing the south at peace, Henry travelled north into the Yorkist stronghold of Yorkshire, to show his face and overcome opposition. At Lincoln he heard that Francis, Lord Lovell, Richard III's friend and chamberlain, had broken sanctuary at Colchester, together with Humphrey and Thomas Stafford, and had fled to unknown parts. As the king continued into Yorkshire, news came in of armed bands raised by the fugitives and of threatened risings in Henry's path. But nothing happened. York, which recently had recorded an official lament at Richard III's overthrow, received his conqueror with pageantry and pomp; a local conspiracy was promptly scotched, and Lovell's forces melted away before the promise of a pardon. Lovell fled abroad; the Staffords, who had failed to raise the west country against the king, were dragged from sanctuary and taken to the Tower. The question arose whether they ought to escape justice because the Church's right of sanctuary had been violated. In his natural desire to prevent an acquittal, Henry tried to get the judges' opinion before the case came to trial, but since they were

[1] Attainders were acts of parliament registering somebody's conviction for treason and declaring all his property forfeit to the king and his blood 'corrupted'; only in 1539 did they come to be used in lieu of trials.

reluctant to commit themselves in advance he had to be content with requesting a rapid decision. In the end the court of king's bench decided that sanctuary was a common-law matter in which the pope could not interfere—certainly a striking instance of the growing spirit of resistance to ecclesiastical pretensions—and that the privilege did not cover treasonable offences. Humphrey Stafford was executed, though Thomas benefited from Henry VII's awakening mercifulness. The rising itself was utterly insignificant, but the case deserves attention because it illustrates the Tudor principle of relying on the decisions of common-law judges, the Tudor readiness to respect the judges' independence, and the Tudor disregard for ancient franchises and immunities.

In September 1486, Henry's heart was gladdened by the birth of a son—Arthur (the revival of the ancient British name was meant to be significant)—who seemed to make the dynasty secure. The king himself was not yet thirty; there seemed no question that he would live long enough to see his heir of age. However, just at this juncture the first of the serious conspiracies of the reign came into the open. The country was much unsettled by rumours: many believed that the princes in the Tower were still alive and had perhaps managed to escape, or that the earl of Warwick, the true Yorkist claimant if Richard III had really disposed of Edward IV's sons, was again at large. There was plenty of credulity, plenty of Yorkist sentiment, and plenty of plain superstition for a skilful man to exploit. An Oxford priest of no birth but some brains, Richard Symonds, was the first to realise this. He planned to pass off a pupil of his, a harmless gentle boy called Lambert Simnel, as Richard of York, the younger of Edward's sons; soon after, when it was rumoured that Warwick had died in the Tower, Simnel's impersonation was changed to Warwick on the grounds that the government would not be able to disprove the fraud by exhibiting the real earl. The very fact that such a wildcat scheme could spring from an obscure priest's brain—and that it came within measurable distance of success—indicates the state of the country and the size of Henry's problem. Symonds found favour with the leaders of the Yorkist party—Margaret, the dowager duchess of Burgundy, sister of Edward IV and the centre of all the plots against the Tudors, and the exiled Lord Lovell who had taken refuge with her. John de la Pole, earl of Lincoln, Richard III's successor-designate whom Henry VII had treated with kindness, repaid the king by fleeing to join the rebels who had raised the White Rose in Ireland. That country had always nursed Yorkist sympathies, and its most powerful noble, the earl of Kildare, welcomed any opportunity to throw off English control.

Thus Henry was suddenly faced with a major threat, all the more dangerous in that it centred upon Ireland where he could not touch it. Subsidiary moves in Lancashire and Cornwall could be disregarded, but the menace from across the Irish channel demanded immediate action. In vain the real Warwick was paraded through London; in May 1487, the false Warwick was proclaimed Edward VI in Dublin, and all Ireland except the city of Waterford went over to him. His power rested on Kildare, the Yorkist leaders Lincoln and Lovell, and 2,000 German mercenaries contributed by Margaret of Burgundy. In June they landed in Lancashire and began their march on London. The familiar story of the Wars of the Roses seemed about to re-open. However, the country showed how tired it was of it all: even Yorkshire gave little support to the White Rose, and the rest of the country remained loyal to Henry. It is probable, also, that the inclusion in Lincoln's army of many wild Irishmen served to lose him much support. The decision came at Stoke, on 16 June 1487, where all the Yorkist leaders were killed, or disappeared never to be heard of again; Symonds and Simnel fell into the king's hands. Henry proved merciful in a politic manner; his treatment of Simnel, taken into the royal household where he made a career from scullion to falconer, bore an air of sardonic but not unkindly humour. Symonds was confined for life; there was no general proscription or holocaust of executions such as was to disgrace later Tudor victories, though a number of Simnel's followers paid for their treason in sizeable fines. One of the victims of the affair, for reasons which have remained obscure, was Henry's mother-in-law, the foolish and meddling Elizabeth Woodville; she ended her days in a convent. Throughout it is clear that Henry tried to play down the whole business, an endeavour in which he succeeded.

Before the next serious threat to Henry's throne arose, England became involved in a war with France. The full story is extremely complicated, and almost equally immaterial. But its main lines are important, for they indicate both Henry's VII's aims in foreign affairs and the European diplomatic situation which was to determine England's attitude to the continent until the fall of Wolsey in 1529. In the last twenty years of the fifteenth century Western Europe assumed a new aspect. France, consolidated by Louis XI (who died in 1483), and Spain, created by the personal union of Ferdinand of Aragon and Isabella of Castile (1469), took over the leadership of affairs, and their quarrels form the story of European diplomacy to which the machinations of Maximilian.

king of the Romans, of Italian princes including the pope, and of the kings of England are quite subsidiary. Henry VII's immediate attitude in 1487 was decided by several factors. The traditional hostility to France was far from dead; indeed, it was kept alive by the king's retention of a claim to the French throne which feeling in the country would not have allowed him to surrender even if he had felt so inclined. More materially, England's continued possession of Calais provided both a gateway into France and a permanent irritant to relations between the two countries. Furthermore, Henry earnestly wished to secure visible recognition for his dynasty from some European power, and common interests, mostly commercial, suggested the rising power of Spain. In 1488-9 he negotiated a treaty of marriage between his son Arthur and Catherine, the younger daughter of Ferdinand and Isabella. In return, Spain—who had ambitions for two French provinces in the Pyrenees—secured a promise of English help against France. The occasion of the quarrel was provided by the affairs of Brittany. That duchy alone had escaped the centralising activities of Louis XI, but his daughter (Anne of Beaujeu) and later his son (Charles VIII) were determined to remedy the omission. Though the French won a great victory in 1488 they lost its gains when the duke of Brittany died soon after, to be succeeded by his daughter Anne, aged twelve. Anne of Brittany was an important heiress whose hand was worth fighting for; Spain saw a chance of embarrassing France, and Anne of Beaujeu a chance of asserting French control of the duchy by claiming the wardship of the young duchess; the war revived.

England's part was decided for her by the danger of letting the Breton ports fall into French hands, by the fact that English volunteers had been killed in hundreds in the previous Breton defeat, and by Spanish pressure. In 1489 Henry prepared for war. With some difficulty he obtained a parliamentary grant of £100,000, only part of which was ever paid; its collection led to a major riot in the north in which the king's lieutenant, the earl of Northumberland, was killed. The garrison at Calais was reinforced. The treaty of Medina del Campo with Spain, in March 1489, bound England to the war. Henry gained big trading concessions, but Spain had much the best of the political bargain: either side could withdraw when it had achieved its ends, but since Spain wanted only the Pyrenean provinces while England spoke of recovering Henry V's conquests, it is plain where the advantage lay. However, Henry got what he wanted—trade on favoured terms and the betrothal of Arthur and Catherine; as events were to show, he had no intention of wasting blood or treasure over the affairs of Brittany or Spain. He fulfilled the terms of the treaty and assisted his other ally, Maximilian, in his struggle with Flemish rebels. Otherwise neither he nor anyone else made any move until in 1490 Maximilian suddenly married Anne of Brittany. Henry occupied 1491 in extracting money from his country by benevolences, that is, by forced gifts described as voluntary, a method declared illegal in 1484; but no one resisted Charles VIII when, stung to action by Anne's marriage, he proceeded gradually to conquer Brittany and in the end himself married Anne after she had secured the necessary dispensation from her non-consummated previous marriage.

The situation was now handsomely confused. Spain showed no intention of supporting her ally; not for the last time did kings of England regret an alliance with Ferdinand of Aragon. Brittany was irrevocably French, and the vast English ambitions for the recovery of Henry V's conquests were merely ridiculous. It need not be thought that the king shared them. But he could not afford to associate the Tudors with the surrender of claims so tenaciously held by Lancaster and York, nor did he wish to write off the considerable loans he had made to Brittany earlier in the war. He therefore spent 1492 in making demonstrations designed to impress France with the gravity of the English threat. He even crossed the channel in person and took an army to besiege Boulogne, an action which came to be considered the *sine qua non* of Tudor generalship in Northern France. Charles VIII had no reason for continuing the war, the more so as his restless ambition was turning to thoughts of Italy. Thus in December 1492 the two powers signed the treaty of Etaples by which Henry agreed to hold his claim to France in abeyance and received in return a sum which he could and did call a tribute, as well as repayment of the Breton debts. At relatively small expense he had obtained an honourable peace and a sizeable pension to compensate him for his outlay. He had thrown over Spain—but Ferdinand and Isabella had themselves been contemplating a separate peace, so that Henry had merely beaten them at their own game. His other ally, Maximilian, also felt himself deserted, but his own conduct had been extremely shifty, and no one ever at any time had any scruples in neglecting Maximilian. The war had demonstrated that England was once again a power to be reckoned with and entitled to play a part in European diplomacy. It had led to the official recognition of the Tudor dynasty by France and Spain, with both of whom Henry had concluded treaties. The king could feel that he had manœuvred well in his first essay in this tricky game.

The treaty of Etaples came not a minute too soon, for Henry had to turn his attention to the most serious threat he was to face in his whole reign. In the year 1491, a young man of seventeen, servant to a Breton merchant, was walking up and down the streets of Cork, displaying on his person the silk clothes in which his master traded. His bearing and splendour made a great impression on the rather backward townsfolk, unsettled as they already were by tales of Plantagenet princes escaping hither and thither. They told the young man that he was the earl of Warwick, and when he denied this they obligingly changed him into a bastard of Richard III. He continued his denials, but they only turned him into Richard, duke of York, the younger son of Edward IV. Worn out by their importunity he agreed. This at least was the tale which the pretender later told in his confession which is now accepted as largely true, though it may still appear doubtful whether a man who for eight years pertinaciously maintained his identity as Richard of York really came by the imposture in so casual a manner. His real name was Perkin Warbeck—his parents were still alive in Tournai in 1497—and he had been travelling in the service of various merchants since he was eleven. The supposed miracle of his knowing the details which convinced others of his Plantagenet descent has been made too much of: it does not appear that he ever convinced anyone except people eager to use him against Henry VII. This also goes for his supposed aunt, Margaret of Burgundy, who was perfectly capable of taking up a pretender and swearing to his identity once she felt sure that no genuine Yorkist claimants survived at liberty. That she later coached him in his part is likely.

Warbeck's career as Richard of York was crowded and various; the story has been told often and at sufficient length, and only its salient points need concern us here. His appearance which had so impressed the Irish at Cork is known from a good drawing: his charm and intelligence cannot disguise a blatant weakness. Everything he undertook by himself ended in dismal failure; anyone less like the brutal and efficient Yorkist strain it is hard to imagine. It seems that of all the men who had to do with him only Henry VII, who treated him with weary contempt and almost offensive leniency, judged him fairly; others were too blinded by his usefulness to take his just measure. In consequence he served as the peg on which hung the events of eight disturbed years.

After the Irish lords had approved of him in their rough Irish fashion which counted not the truth when trouble could be stirred up against England, Warbeck's first protector was Charles

VIII of France, then at war with Henry VII. The treaty of Etaples put a stop to this, and in 1493 Warbeck passed into Burgundy, there to find favour with the dowager duchess Margaret and gather round him the Yorkist exiles and their hopes. The support he received annoyed Henry VII to the point of breaking off all trade with the Low Countries, a boycott which hit the Flemish cloth industry very hard, dependent as it was on English wool and unfinished cloth. However, the embargo was naturally also unpopular with English merchants and could not be prolonged unduly; it was lifted after two years though it had not achieved the end for which it was imposed. Warbeck had sought and found a better protector than Margaret; late in 1493 he was at Vienna, winning over the unstable and foolish Maximilian who saw a chance of paying Henry VII out for his alleged treachery in the treaty of Etaples. Maximilian went so far as to recognise Warbeck as Richard IV, the rightful king of England, and to promise him full support in the recovery of the crown. In return, Warbeck signed a document in January 1495 which made Maximilian his heir, so that—should Warbeck die in the attempt to win the throne of England—the king of the Romans would succeed to the full Yorkist claim. Maximilian was himself good at making worthless promises, but one feels that on this occasion he had met his match. However, the mere fact that the pretender found all this support was significant. Maximilian and his son, the Archduke Philip, ruler of the Netherlands, made the Low Countries the centre of Warbeck's conspiracy to which many flocked even from England in hopes of a Yorkist revival. By this time Warbeck knew his part to perfection, and it is not surprising that he imposed on those eager partisans of the White Rose.

More dangerous still was the fact that the conspiracy had developed a branch in England—indeed, in the very court itself. One of those who had gone to Flanders to join Richard IV was Sir Robert Clifford who, however, had second thoughts on arrival—unless, as is possible, he was secretly in the service of Henry VII. At any rate, in December 1494 he officially made his peace with the king, received a pardon and reward, and returned to lay detailed information against the heads of disaffection in England. Probably Henry had had his eye on the men involved for some time, and Clifford's testimony only served to clinch matters. A number of lesser men, led by Lord Fitzwalter, died on block and gallows, their property being subsequently confiscated and their blood attainted in the parliament of 1495. One man fell with a crash: Clifford accused Sir William Stanley, lord chamberlain of the household and the man who had made the victory at Bosworth possible, of complicity in the plot. Nothing is known about the whole affair, but from the testimony of contemporaries we know that Henry VII was not easily persuaded of anyone's treasonable activity. It therefore seems likely that Stanley had aroused suspicion long before Clifford denounced him. After all, the Stanleys had changed sides in 1485 only after much hesitation; it is possible that Sir William did not think even a chamberlain's staff sufficient reward for his services.

The arrests and executions broke the conspiracy in England and made Warbeck's projected invasion hopeless. Nevertheless, it was attempted. In July 1495 he appeared off Deal and landed gradually the better part of his forces; he himself remained prudently on board ship. The royal officers were ready: the men who had landed were killed or taken, and the affair collapsed in ridicule as Warbeck sailed rapidly off to Ireland. Here he failed to take the loyal town of Waterford in an eleven days' siege and decided to try Scotland. King James IV had come to the throne as the head of the party bitterly hostile to England, after his mildly Anglophil father had been murdered. He was therefore more than ready to receive the pretender and offer him assistance. But this business too came to nothing. In January 1496 a Scottish force crossed the border and burnt and looted savagely—distressing Warbeck not a little, it must be added, much to the amazement of both Scots and English. They then withdrew again. Border raids were one thing; an expedition to put Richard IV on the throne of England was quite another. Henry VII was the less inclined to take serious countermeasures because his natural dislike of war was being encouraged by Spain who wanted his alliance against France (then too successful in Italy) and therefore tried to arrange peace between England and Scotland. Moreover, the heavy war taxation led to a really serious rising in Cornwall. The Cornishmen had no interest in Warbeck; what they wanted was relief from exactions demanded by affairs on the far northern border which they did not consider concerned them. They therefore rose in 1497, under the leadership of the blacksmith Joseph and the lawyer Flamank, to march to London and state their case. They were peaceable enough at first but killed a tax-collector at Taunton, probably thinking little of so obvious a deed. Then, led by Lord Audley, an impoverished peer, they marched right across England, for with the king's forces tied up on the border there was no one to oppose them. In June 1497 they sat down at Blackheath, but instead of being overawed—Henry never parleyed with rebels under arms—

the king proceeded to surround and attack them. Two thousand died on the day; of the survivors only the leaders were hanged. All this, however, did not make the problem of Perkin Warbeck easier for Henry.

In actual fact Perkin left Scotland, where he was kept as a potential but unused asset, in July 1497, hoping to try his luck once more in Ireland. But things had changed there; Kildare was, for the moment, loyal; and Warbeck thought it better to follow an invitation from Cornwall where the king's clemency had by some been misinterpreted as weakness. Opposed by the new lord chamberlain, Giles Lord Daubeney, Perkin once again lost heart; at Taunton he stole away at midnight with some sixty leading followers, leaving his forces unofficered. Though he reached sanctuary at Beaulieu monastery, he was persuaded to throw himself on Henry's mercy, and so in August 1497 the king at last had the troublesome adventurer in his hands. It was now that the famous confession appeared, telling of Warbeck's true identity and early life; but there is sound proof that Henry knew all these details as early as 1493, and corroborative evidence exists to establish the truth of the confession. Warbeck was kept at court in honourable custody; once again Henry VII refused to make martyrs. In 1498, however, he tried to escape and on his recapture suffered a harsher confinement. Finally, he made another attempt in November 1499, as is supposed with the king's connivance, for now the government hoped to get at the real Yorkist, the earl of Warwick, through the pretended one. Warwick seems to have been quite innocent of any attempt against Henry VII, but for some reason of which we are ignorant the government had decided that his very existence constituted a danger. Indeed, the career of Perkin Warbeck, and that of Lambert Simnel before him, gave grounds for such a belief, and it may be that diplomatic difficulties—the insistence of Spain on a safe Tudor title before they would let Catherine of Aragon go to England—forced Henry's hand. At any rate, the government produced some sort of evidence of a conspiracy; Warbeck was hanged and Warwick beheaded; and the Tudor could sleep more easily. There is nothing to be said in extenuation of such judicial murders of which the reign of Henry VIII was to produce many more, except that those who saw a danger in so perfectly innocent a man as Edward of Warwick were far from wrong. It was not what he did or thought but what he stood for in other men's minds that brought him to his death. For Warbeck one may feel sorry, but he had certainly earned his fate several times over.

3. IRELAND AND SCOTLAND

The stories of Lambert Simnel and Perkin Warbeck have served to underline an important truth: there was danger for the English crown within the British isles themselves. Ireland and Scotland were both trouble spots. The Norman conquest of Ireland in the twelfth century had imposed upon the native Celtic population a feudal ruling class, but though the kings of England might claim to be lords of Ireland they never, in fact, effectively ruled much of it. The so-called English Pale—a strip of coast stretching some 50 miles northwards from Dublin—was the real limit of English influence, though the few towns in the south, especially Waterford and Cork, also provided precarious centres of civilisation in a country not far removed from tribal barbarism. The Irish nobility, Anglo-Norman in origin, had long since suffered the common fate of English settlers in Ireland and become as Irish as the Irish, so that there was little to choose, from the king's point of view, between Anglo-Irish families like the Geraldines or Butlers and the purely Irish chieftains. Even within the Pale, Englishry was losing ground to Irish speech, dress, and habits. The wars of the Roses had further weakened the hold of the crown. The local feuds adopted the terminology of the English dynastic struggles: thus the Geraldines, led by the earls of Kildare and Desmond, championed the Yorkist cause, while their enemies, the Butlers under the earl of Ormond, espoused the side of Lancaster. The Geraldines won, with the result that Ireland became something of a Yorkist stronghold. But on the whole these were phrases rather than realities; what mattered to the Irish lords was independence from royal control and the fighting of their own internecine quarrels. The better part of the wild, wooded, boggy, and hilly country of the north and west had never so much as seen an English soldier or administrator.

The recovery and reduction of Ireland proved to be a general Tudor problem; to Henry VII its urgency was brought home by the fact that the country offered a safe and friendly springboard to any claimant, however absurd. In 1485 the power of Fitzgerald was paramount. The elder branch of the Butlers had moved to England, and though Henry VII restored them to their forfeited lands in Ireland, this did not affect the position of the great earl of Kildare whose many links with native families and wide personal possessions made him the virtual ruler of the country. He held the title of lord deputy and his brother was chancellor of Ireland; for the moment, Henry VII could not attempt to attack these strongholds of Geraldine power. Kildare was a curious character: arrogant and restless, he was yet gifted with some political skill, little rancour, and a roughish humour which, as it happened, appealed to the king. The support which the earl gave to Lambert Simnel was blatant and avowed, but Henry deliberately ignored it and permitted the two Fitzgeralds to continue in office when they admitted that they had been mistaken about the pretender. But forbearance was not the right treatment for a man who had earned the title of 'the great earl' by invariably getting his own way. In 1491, when Perkin Warbeck was acclaimed at Cork, Kildare showed himself cautiously ready to side with him, and in June 1492 Henry at last deprived him of the deputyship. Thomas Fitzgerald lost the great seal of Ireland, and the offices went instead to the archbishop of Dublin and Alexander Plunket, ancestor of a noble Irish line.

Kildare was sufficiently taken aback to seek the king's pardon, even asking his old enemy Ormond for help, but it was a full year before Henry would grant it (1493), and then only after the earl had come in person to seek it. The display of energy had at least produced signs of humility. Nothing, however, had been done to settle or even improve the state of Ireland. Government there was at the time managed at two removes: the king, as lord of Ireland, appointed a lord lieutenant (his uncle, the duke of Bedford) whose office was exercised for him by a lord deputy. More was required than the replacement of Kildare by a sequence of mediocrities, and in September 1494 Henry made his most determined attempt to solve the problem. He transferred the title of lord lieutenant to the infant prince Henry, his second son, so as to match in Ireland the nominal headship exercised by his elder son in Wales, and appointed as deputy Sir Edward Poynings, one of his most trusted and able ministers. The offices of chancellor and treasurer, too, were filled by Englishmen; the new policy announced itself from the first as hostile to all things Irish and determined to reduce the country to obedience to England.

Poynings was an experienced soldier and statesman, and the plan he had been sent to execute required the qualities of both. He was to conquer Ulster, the wildest part of the country where rebellion had always found safe refuge, and he was to impose on Ireland a constitution which would secure the full control of the English government. In the first he failed outright; in the second he succeeded after a fashion. His expedition against the tribesmen of the north got literally bogged down, and he had in the end to content himself with buying the clans off. The only positive result was the fall of Kildare, who had accompanied Poynings' forces, on a suspicion of treason to which his family's actions (Desmond assisted Warbeck in the siege of Waterford) and Ormond's whispers gave colour. The parliament of Drogheda, summoned by Poynings in December 1494, attainted him, thus mightily impressing the Irish to whom the earl had seemed an almost more than human figure. The deputy promptly arrested him and shipped him to the Tower. Some other acts of this parliament, commonly known as Poynings' laws, were designed to achieve the second of Henry's aims. Their total effect was to decree that an Irish parliament could only be summoned, and could only legislate, with the king's previous approval; no future laws were to be discussed unless first agreed to by the king in council. Furthermore, all laws made in England were automatically to apply to Ireland. Poynings' laws thus destroyed the legislative independence of the Irish parliament and, in law at least, gave the king vastly greater powers in Ireland than he had in England. It may be noticed that when these and other acts against the lawlessness and wild violence of Irish conditions were passed, they had the approval of the English colonist element which in later years was to be foremost in the attack on Poynings' laws.

However, Henry VII's success proved illusory. The failure to subdue the wild Irish increased the Irish budget enormously by forcing Poynings to pay blackmail for peace, and though he had been so far successful as to deal easily with Warbeck's attack on Waterford, the king was not satisfied. Henry VII now showed one side of the Tudor character not often in evidence in his reign. When new difficulties rendered a pre-arranged policy doubtful or expensive, these inspired opportunists were always ready to give up, even though in consequence the work already done might be put in jeopardy. In effect Henry despaired of the success of the measures initiated in 1494 when in 1496 he recalled Poynings and restored Kildare to favour and the office of deputy. If—as is reported—he answered the bishop of Meath's complaint that all Ireland could not rule Kildare by saying that in that case Kildare had better rule all Ireland, he may have proved his wit but hardly his sagacity. The problem of Ireland had turned out to be too big for solution; the return of Kildare meant the end of effective English control, despite the operation of Poynings' laws; and Henry VIII, Elizabeth, and Oliver Cromwell had to face a problem grown ever bigger in the interval. Henry VII had the best chance of all to win success, before the Reformation came to complicate matters; but parsimony (however necessary) and opportunism triumphed. There were no claimants about to disturb the peace from Ireland; why, then, waste good money on a probably futile policy of direct rule? Henry VII was lucky to die before the Irish problem revived, but revive it did—and largely because he gave up the fight.

Scotland constituted a very different problem—more serious and threatening on the face of it, though ultimately to prove much less insidious. The presence on one small island of two hostile powers had the most disastrous effects on both, but particularly on the politically more advanced kingdom of England. Since Edward I's ill-judged attempts to subdue Scotland, the northern kingdom had been persistently opposed to its larger neighbour, and by dint of its ancient alliance with France had managed to remain a very painful thorn in England's side. The border from Berwick to Carlisle was practically never at peace as raiding parties crossed from either side, to kill, rob, and burn on the other. Far too often these 'rodes' provided the ready pretext for more formal war. Truce followed truce with monotonous and pointless regularity. Compared with Scotland, harassed by perpetual feuds, gang warfare, murders, and dynastic upsets, even the England of the wars of the Roses was almost a law-abiding and peaceful state, and in Scotland such troubles were considered by the nobility as not only pleasurable but a necessity of life. One such conflagration resulted, in 1488, in the overthrow and murder of king James III, elevating to the throne a young king of romantically warlike ambitions, James IV. Little purpose would be served by reciting in detail his various attempts to instigate action on the border and the repeated treaties for a cessation of the trouble, now for three years and now for nine, none of which ever endured their appointed length. The revolution which had put James IV on the throne left, as was usual in Scotland, a powerful and dissatisfied opposition of nobles who intrigued with England and afforded Henry VII an opportunity to keep Scotland from getting dangerous. The French war of 1489-92 passed off without active interference from the north, but when Perkin Warbeck's wanderings took him to Scotland James IV seized upon this providential opportunity of embarrassing the enemy. The story of Scotland's share in Warbeck's Odyssey has already been told. At one time, in 1497, it looked as though Henry VII would accept the challenge and attempt serious war in the north, but the Cornish rebellion came just in time to save James IV from his ill-regulated combativeness. If one may judge from later events in Henry VIII's reign, the

Scottish army would have stood but a poor chance against the forces which the earl of Surrey was marshalling on the border.

As it was, Henry VII preserved his peaceful reputation unsullied, to prove once more how well he could exploit difficult situations without precipitating war. Surrey did cross the border once to teach James a sharp lesson, incidentally refusing a typically chivalrous but unrealistic offer of single combat. The end of Warbeck left James rather at a loss, and his own position in a country some of whose chief lords were ready to throw in their lot with the enemy was none too comfortable. Henry even hinted that two could play at the game of supporting pretenders and showed signs of adopting the cause of a Stuart claimant, the duke of Albany, then living in France. All these things working together, and Henry still continuing to offer real peace, an agreement was finally arrived at in December 1497. It was to endure as long as both sovereigns lived. But this truce suffered the common fate of these border treaties; it was broken in the following year by a Scottish raid and English counter-raid. Something more permanent was required, and Henry VII, seriously intent on settling these tiresome difficulties, therefore proposed to marry his daughter Margaret to the king of Scots. Margaret, born in 1490, was of course too young for a real marriage, and the negotiations were dragged out not only by James's reluctance to make peace but also by a chance he thought he had of marrying a Spanish princess of rather riper years. However, in the end things fell out as Henry had designed. In July 1499, a treaty of peace and alliance was concluded between England and Scotland, and in September serious negotiations began for the marriage. After further delays James IV finally agreed to it in January 1502. The dynastic marriages of the time were commonly concluded when one party or both were yet children; one result of this was the frequent annulment of such unions and remarriage of these diplomatic pawns. However, the union of James of Scotland and Margaret Tudor was destined to be successful. It turned into a proper marriage agreeable to both parties before James crowned a warlike life by getting killed at Flodden, in 1513, fighting his wife's brother as he had once fought his wife's father. The real significance of the marriage lay in the distant future. If Henry VII had hoped to settle Anglo-Scottish difficulties at once he was disappointed; Scotland continued persistently hostile, and Henry VIII was twice at war with her. In the end, however, the marriage provided England with her Stuart kings; though this was to prove anything but a blessing to her constitutional development, it did end the ancient feud on the border and opened the way to a union which was to be fruitful to both countries. Henry VII's Irish policy was right but not pursued long enough; his policy towards Scotland was wise and farseeing, and in the end completely successful.

4. THE DYNASTY SECURED

As has been seen, the first year of the reign showed no indication that Henry VII understood the necessity of ending the wars by overlooking past differences, and of healing the breach by generous and long-suffering mercy. But then the first few months after victory in a ferocious enough struggle were hardly the time for such statesmanlike forbearance; his own followers would not have understood it, and Henry—even if he already desired it—could not have afforded it. After the first proscriptions and attainders his policy changed. For the rest of the reign he did his best to make men forget the past and join as one nation under the Tudor ægis; so far from suspiciously seeking out imaginary conspiracies (as one might have expected), he proved uncommonly hard to convince of real ones, and the statute book began to record the reversal of past attainders rather than the further pursuit of vengeance. It was after the suppression of Simnel's revolt and Warbeck's failure to land in Kent that Henry felt safe enough to put the new policy into practice. The parliament of 1491 reversed the attainder passed on the earl of Surrey, originally a Yorkist supporter but now a loyal follower of Henry's whose best general he proved to be; in 1495, the same was done for a number of Yorkists or their heirs. Those who had shown themselves trustworthy were to be reprieved.

The parliament of 1495 went further: it passed an act designed to draw a line under the past. This was the so-called *de facto* act (11 Henry VII, c.1) which declared that no subject attending upon a king of England 'for the time being' in a war and doing him faithful service should suffer for it in his person or possessions, any future act of parliament to the contrary notwithstanding. This act was exaggerated by Bacon into a far-seeing major piece of statesmanship, outlining a theory of kingship in that it made a king *de facto* equivalent to one *de jure*. But the words *de facto* and *de jure* do not occur in the document, in strong contrast to many acts of the wars which were careful to refer to any defeated predecessor asking in deed though not of right. The distinction was devised as a part of the struggle, and its omission in this act is significant because it marks Henry's intention to let it be forgotten. The act's main purpose was to assure the yet unpunished members of the Yorkist faction that the past was dead; it was, in A. F. Pollard's words, a 'measure of temporary expediency very limited in scope'. It also served to reassure Henry's own followers about a possible reversal of fortune. No one ever invoked it on occasions when, on the common interpretation, it could have been useful. Nor did it make opposition to Henry VII himself venial in any circumstances, for a short but important proviso at the end excepted all men who would 'hereafter decline from his or their said allegiance'. The act was a notable step in closing the chapter of the wars, but no more. The attempt to bind future parliaments serves as a useful reminder that in 1495 the doctrine of parliament's omnicompetence was yet far from fully realised. In the cause of right reason one parliament could commit all its successors.

The policy of pacification continued through the rest of the reign, though interrupted at times by the activities of the irreconcilables. The last parliament of the reign (1504) empowered the king to reverse attainders made in his own reign and that of Richard III, on the grounds that parliamentary action was too dilatory; but this pointer towards Henry's real intentions was accompanied by an act attainting those who had been executed for their part in the Cornish rebellion and the treasons of Warbeck and Suffolk. Edmund de la Pole, earl of Suffolk, was the brother of that earl of Lincoln who had died in the battle of Stoke. A romantic but unimpressive figure, popular but without either sense or purpose, he was allowed to live at Henry's court—in comfort, but under the king's eye. After Warbeck's and Warwick's deaths he seems to have decided that the time had come for him to assert his own claims. In 1499 he fled abroad, without licence and therefore criminally. Though he returned when the king's messengers caught up with him and once more appeared at court, he finally broke with Henry when he absconded a second time, in the autumn of 1501, while assisting in the journey of Catherine of Aragon to England. He took refuge with Maximilian, now Holy Roman Emperor. But Maximilian was busy against the Turks and in Italy, and Henry experienced little difficulty in dealing with this last claimant of the reign. Indeed, one feels that he went through a familiar routine almost with an air of weariness. The normal by-plot in England was easily discovered and suppressed, with only a very few executions; among those to die was Sir James Tyrrell, the murderer of the princes in the Tower, who had since made a career as captain of Guisnes near Calais. Suffolk in exile was soon surrounded by a band of genuine supporters among whom there were also Henry's spies: the king knew all that went on. In June 1502 Maximilian signed a treaty in which he agreed to expel the earl from his dominions in return for £10,000. Suffolk went to Aix-la-Chapelle, technically outside Maximilian's jurisdiction, where he lived miserably on borrowed money. But though all Europe refused him countenance, Prince Arthur's death (1502) and Prince Henry's youth were far from reassuring to the Tudor dynasty, and the king could not feel safe until Suffolk was in his hands. At last, by an agreement of 1506, the Archduke Philip of Burgundy agreed to surrender the earl whose life Henry had promised to spare. Suffolk continued in the Tower until, in 1513, when Henry VIII undertook the first of his several clearances of that depository of awkward personalities, another member of the White Rose paid with his blood for his blood and the mistaken ambitions it encouraged. His brother, Richard de la Pole, left behind in Aix, managed with difficulty to get away from Suffolk's creditors, travelled and fought all over Europe, persuaded France to recognise him as king of England when war broke out again in 1512, and died at the battle of Pavia in 1525, fighting by the side of Francis I of France. A strange and wonderful career ended in an even stranger relief to the Tudor king who had no part in the battle.

The ease with which Henry VII disposed of the earl of Suffolk sufficiently illustrates the fact that the days of an uneasy crown were over. Warbeck had been discredited and removed from the neighbourhood of foreign kings who might use him as a pawn in diplomacy; Warwick's death had ended the chances of further impersonations; and now the last serious rival was lodged in the Tower. The Tudor throne was pretty safe after some seventeen years of Henry's rule. But there was every sign that its safety depended too exclusively on Henry's own life. Prince Arthur died suddenly in 1502, and—as if to underline the persistent and fatal sickliness of the Tudor stock—the king himself fell ill soon after. The continuance of the dynasty was suddenly in doubt; discussions between great men centred on the subject of the succession and the possibility of a dispute; and it is on record that on one occasion, when the problem was argued, people put forward the claims of Buckingham and Suffolk, but ignored those of Prince Henry. This sole male heir to an ailing king was born in 1491; no doubt few wished to see the throne in the hands of a child of twelve or thirteen. For Henry VII himself, assuring the succession after his death had superseded the maintenance of his own rule as the premier problem of his policy, and the diplomacy of his last ten years was dominated by matrimonial projects designed both to perpetuate the dynasty and to make capital out of the bridegrooms he had to offer. After the queen's death in 1503, these included even himself, an extravagance which has produced much moral censure and speculation as to his deteriorating character; yet he was only forty-six, and he may well have thought that with but one male heir he could not afford the luxury of widowerhood.

The triumph of Henry VII's earlier diplomacy was the marriage of Arthur to Catherine of Aragon. The project, first made part of the treaty which involved England in the French war of 1489-92, dragged on interminably. Both Henry and Ferdinand of Aragon were expert bargainers and chafferers; the negotiations over the bride's marriage portion and dower, and the commercial concessions to be made by England, were both lengthy and repellent. Agreement was also prevented by the Spanish ambition to turn Henry into an active ally against France, and by Spanish reluctance to commit the princess to a dynasty as yet threatened by pretenders. However, the two parties finally came to terms in October 1496; it was agreed that Catherine was to come to England in 1500, when Arthur would be fourteen, and that she would not lose her proper (though remote) claim to the throne of Castile if she were the only survivor of her family. The financial side of the transaction was complicated by Ferdinand's promise to pay Catherine's marriage portion in instalments; eighteen years later Henry VIII was still to try to secure payments due to England upon his wife's first marriage. Despite slight delays, the princess arrived in England in October 1501, and the marriage a month later was one of the occasions when Henry VII did not count the cost. For ten days the capital was the scene of festivities for all and sundry, with jousting and dancing, archery and fancy mermaids, singing and play-acting, and many other amusements provided to encourage proper rejoicing at so auspicious an event. Not only was there a prospect of the dynasty being propagated, thus ensuring a continuance of the peace and prosperity which Henry's reign had brought, but the king's son had been married to the daughter of one of the oldest houses in Europe and a princess from what was already obviously one of the great powers. No one could now call the Tudors upstart—or, if upstarts, they had arrived in society.

Five months after the marriage the young bridegroom died, and Catherine was left a widow in a foreign land, nothing now but a diplomatic counter to her unsympathetic father-in-law. Henry, who disliked waste, almost immediately proposed her remarriage to his other son Henry, and though Ferdinand haggled for some time the English king won his way. Since Henry VII would neither repay that part of the marriage portion which he had already received nor permit Catherine to leave the country, and since moreover Spain's affairs were going far from well in 1503, Ferdinand preferred to cut his losses. In June 1503 the younger Henry, now prince of Wales, was betrothed to his brother's widow; in December, the dispensation which their affinity by the bride's previous marriage necessitated was received from Pope Julius II; and though the wedding itself was to be postponed for another six years, with many tribulations to the unfortunate princess in the interval, the fateful union was in the end celebrated. It was delayed by a shift in the European system of alliances which ensued upon the death of Queen Isabella in 1504. The realm of Spain existed so far only through the personal union of the sovereigns of Castile and Aragon, and Isabella's demise threatened to dissolve it. The throne of Castile should have passed to her daughter Joanna, who was insane; Ferdinand, determined to preserve the achievements of a lifetime, made himself master of his late wife's kingdom, but found himself opposed by Joanna's husband, Archduke Philip of Burgundy, son of the Emperor Maximilian. In consequence the natural alliance between the Habsburgs and the house of Aragon, cemented by common hostility to France, collapsed, and in 1505 Ferdinand veered to the side of his old enemy, the king of France. This was to have far-reaching consequences in Italy where the Republic of Venice discovered, in 1508, that she could not withstand the joint forces of France and Spain, assisted by the papacy; in England, it led to some very peculiar twists and turns of matrimonial policy, much at variance with Henry VII's usual prudent treatment of such matters.

Henry intended to re-marry, or at least he said he did in order to attract allies. For it seems clear that after 1506, with Suffolk put away and the dynasty assured, the king desired to discard the self-restraint of earlier years and to play the game of diplomacy for its own sake. Now that he no longer needed to get his throne recognised by the powers, he wished to make the influence of England felt. It seems likely that the ambitious diplomacy later pursued by Wolsey and the young Henry VIII can be traced back to the last years of Henry VII. The habits of a lifetime and a proper regard for the value of money kept the older king from involving himself in wars, but at heart his policy was no less mistaken than Wolsey's because it overrated the weight he could put in the balance. Circumstances assisted him: like Wolsey, he found that the idiotically complicated diplomacy of the powers made possible the spinning of unsubstantial but strong-seeming webs, and like Wolsey he was to discover their real weakness before he died. In the process, however, he almost acquired a reputation either for goatishness or for senility, for his projected marriages included, at one time and another, his own daughter-in-law Catherine, the young queen of Naples whose physical description he told his ambassadors to list in great detail, the Habsburg princess Margaret of Savoy, and her sister-in-law, the mad Joanna of Castile. Whether he was serious in any of these approaches we cannot tell; perhaps he still feared for his house, perhaps he was merely overstressing the common matrimonial aspect of contemporary diplomacy. At any rate, all his foreign policy from 1503 to 1509 was marked by such futility that a very brief summary will be quite sufficient.

The death of Isabella, and the rivalry of Ferdinand and Philip for her inheritance, forced Henry to choose between his two allies. Ordinarily, the king of Aragon—more reliable and powerful as well as the father of Henry's prospective daughter-in-law—would have had the higher claim, but in 1505, as things were going wrong for him, his value as an ally grew doubtful. The marriage of Prince Henry and Catherine was delayed, the prince even making a secret certificate to the effect that he would disavow a contract made during his minority. The presence of Suffolk in Burgundian lands suggested the wisdom of keeping in with Philip, and the Franco-Spanish alliance of October 1505 decided Henry's mind. An accident enabled him to make the most of his new line of action. In January 1506, Philip, on his way to Castile, was driven ashore on the Dorset coast, and Henry at once enveloped his involuntary guest in a mixture of lavish entertainment and diplomatic pressure. In February, the king and archduke signed the treaty of Windsor which renewed their alliance, gave Henry the body of Suffolk, and guaranteed Philip English support against Ferdinand. But when Philip died soon after arriving in Spain, Henry decided to invade the field of Castilian castles himself. He ignored his Habsburg ties and resumed negotiations with Ferdinand, proposing that he himself should marry Joanna; even Catherine was ordered to recommend this fantastic match to her father, and—being little better than a prisoner—she complied. It has been thought that Henry toyed with a plan of ultimately pressing a claim to the kingdom of Castile, a worse madness than any of his predecessors' enterprises in France. To hurry up the hesitating Aragonese, Henry succeeded in 1507 in concluding another alliance with

Maximilian by which the emperor's grandson Charles, heir to all Spanish and Habsburg dominions, was betrothed to Henry VII's daughter Mary. The Tudors were certainly aiming high. It looked as if Ferdinand, confronted by a general European coalition and the threat that Henry might seek another match for his son, would have to give way, agree to everything, pay what he owed of the old marriage portion, and even permit Henry VII's marriage with Joanna. But the whole wonderful structure collapsed at a touch when Pope Julius II, who cared only for Italian affairs, managed to combine France, the Empire, and Spain in the league of Cambrai against Venice (December 1508). So far from isolating Spain, Henry had only succeeded in demonstrating the essential isolation of England at a time when interests centred upon the Mediterranean. For the last half year of his life he played no part in European affairs, though the betrothal of Charles to Mary was celebrated—but only because Maximilian needed the 50,000 crowns which Henry was prepared to lend him in return.

The degree to which Henry's caution, parsimony, and sound sense had been affected by surprising dreams of European influence and ambitions is perhaps best indicated by this loan to a notoriously bad debtor. But Henry VII did not long survive the League of Cambrai and the collapse of his less reasonable hopes. He died on 21 April 1509, only fifty-two years old, and after twenty-four years of ruling as king of England. In those twenty-four years he had fought off all rivals, secured the recognition of his dynasty in Europe, and made its fortunes safe. This was achievement, but he deserves to be judged by his much more important work in restoring the king's government and the country's prosperity which went on behind these details of rebellions, diplomacy, and marriages.

Chapter III

HENRY VII: RESTORATION OF GOVERNMENT

1. HENRY VII'S KINGSHIP

AS has been seen, the decay of good government was not due to any fundamental troubles in the body politic: it sprang from no deep-seated social disruption, but only from the weakness of the crown. A king strong and independent enough to re-assert the inherent powers of the English crown would find the means all ready to hand, only waiting to be used. Henry VII was such a king, but it is not easy to say in what his strength lay. Certainly he did not, like the king of France and the sovereigns of Spain, dispose of an armed force on which to raise his pre-eminence; but then, unlike them, he did not have to create a united state out of militarily powerful particles, so that his need of an army was the less marked. Henry VII possessed the only siege-train of artillery in England, and though these guns were never used at home they had some value as a deterrent. But when rebellion had to be suppressed, Henry VII, with the military conservatism which characterised his house, preferred to rely on the bowmen of the shire levies and the forces raised by his supporters; that he could do so is in itself a sufficient commentary on the kind of opposition he had to overcome. The guard of 200 yeomen which he instituted on his accession (supposedly after the example of France) was never more than a ceremonial body useful in adding dignity to the royal person and in policing the court. Henry promoted the interests of his nascent navy, himself building six king's ships and encouraging the development of the merchant marine on which he depended in time of war, but the fleet was of little importance in the suppression of internal troubles. If Henry VII had depended for his success on physical force he would not have lasted many years.

Fundamental to his dynasty was, as is commonly recognised, the support of his people, a support which the Tudors rarely endangered and never lost. Most Englishmen had little interest in noble faction and were ready to welcome any king as long as he was king; those who suffered from the disturbed times only wanted a king who would restore order, no matter if his rose were white or red. The lesser gentry on their estates, the merchants and craftsmen in the towns, needed peace for their developing activities; what one can only call the middle sort of people—neither great landed magnates with their virtually dynastic politics, nor peasantry who played no part in affairs—were always to be the most reliable of Tudor subjects. To call them a middle class is to define them much more precisely than is proper for the fifteenth and sixteenth centuries; to lay the stress too heavily on the merchants is to forget that at least nine-tenths of England's population lived on and by the land. It was the landed gentry—a vague but unexceptionable term—who formed the bulk of the politically conscious and active population, and whose support had to be kept secure.

It would, however, be quite wrong to suppose, on the one hand, that Henry VII made himself a deliberately 'middle-class' king (though the books too readily suggest this), or—on the other—that he invariably deferred to the interests of gentry and merchants. The most obvious way in which Henry's kingship differed from that of his predecessors was in the greater stress he laid upon it. Even this far from impressive-looking man fostered the visible dignity of the office and took good care that the greatest of his subjects should appear small by his side. The Tudor court, with its red-coated guard and its vast expenditure on silks, satins, and velvets was always a gorgeous affair, and ceremonial was one thing on which Henry invariably spent in a prodigal manner. The feasts and joustings and displays which attended the visits of foreign potentates, the coronations and weddings of the reign, were things to marvel at, impressive even to the cynical eyes of Venetian and Milanese ambassadors. Henry also insisted on that special deference to the royal name which later deteriorated into the king-worship of Henry VIII's court and the Gloriana cult of Elizabeth's. He was still commonly 'his grace' and not yet 'his majesty', but his acts of parliament included references to 'his most gracious disposition', his 'most noble grace', and his 'great wisdom'. These touches were not altogether new—Richard II especially had anticipated the Tudor elevation of the estate of king—but Henry VII built up the formal and ceremonial element in medieval kingship to new heights, even as in other ways he greatly developed its practical attributes. The cheapening of the crown in the wars rendered such insistence on its dignity especially necessary and impressive.

The task was made easier by the relative decline of the nearest rivals, the great men of the kingdom. The nobility suffered a blood-letting in the wars of the Roses, though they were not (as is often assumed) virtually destroyed. Most significant was the disappearance of magnates closely related by blood to the ruling house, a disappearance which automatically increased the distance between the king and the highest rank of his subjects. Edward IV, with his marriage to Elizabeth Woodville, had protracted the entanglement of the royal family with the leading magnates; Henry VII made it quite plain that however magnificent a nobleman might be he could not compare with the blood royal. The Tudors might be upstart and *parvenu*, as indeed many of their deeds and attitudes proclaimed them to be, but by the simple fact of kingship they assumed an eminence which the oldest noble house in England must not rival. The economic decline of the baronage—more marked than the actual failure of lines—assisted further. Tudor society was not egalitarian, though it offered its chance to talent, of however humble an origin. Men who made a career aspired to the dignity and profits of nobility, and the Tudors were soon to surround themselves with many men of title. But the title was recent and conferred by the pre-eminent king, and men promoted at the king's pleasure knew where their loyalties must lie. The elevation of kingship made possible a greater fluidity in the ranks below: he whom the king delighted to honour could hold his own with the descendants of generations of nobility, whether they liked it or not. (They generally disliked it greatly.) What held society together, at the top as well as throughout all the layers of local and family loyalties, was the outstanding position of the king who personified the state. But it was still medieval kingship, no different in essence from that of Edward I and Richard II.

It is also commonly asserted that Henry VII innovated when he surrounded himself with a council of men from the 'middle class'. As a matter of fact, Henry's council included noblemen—Lancastrians like the earls of Oxford and Ormond, and reprieved Yorkists like the earl of Surrey. It included new creations like Giles Lord Daubeney who came from the upper ranks of the gentry. It included ecclesiastics like Cardinal Morton and Bishop Fox. The bulk of it was composed of new men, that is men whose families had not so far made an official career—gentlemen like Bray, Lovell, Poynings, and Belknap, though there were also men of humbler descent. Such a council was typical of nothing new, but of the older, pre-Lancastrian councils. While kings could pick their advisers—before, that is, the magnates conquered the king's council—they naturally picked men loyal to themselves who were useful for their practical qualities, and they had always had councils in which some nobles mixed with the churchmen and knights who supplied the administrative and professional elements of the middle ages. When Henry VII chose advisers from non-magnate ranks, he was following not only Yorkist example but the general practice which was only abandoned when the crown lost control of the government. There was no new kind of advisers—though new men there were inasmuch as they still had to make a name for themselves and their families—to serve a monarchy which it would be utterly misleading to describe as 'new'.

In any case, the prevalent impression that Henry VII, and the other Tudors after him, had only to suppress the nobility and elevate lesser men whose interests they protected, dangerously oversimplifies a pretty complex situation. The Tudors were not against aristocracy as such; they were against obstreperous men, whether noble or gentle or common. Henry VII's military commanders were mostly noblemen of pre-Tudor vintage—men like Oxford and Surrey—a detail which forcibly indicates how little the traditional view will explain. Nor could he rely on his so-called middle-class supporters with the certainty which that view supposes. Even among his immediate servants—that is, among those representatives of the lesser men who had the best reason to remain faithful—loyalty was inevitably tempered by self-interest. As late as 1503, the officers of Calais debated among themselves the best way of re-insuring against the king's death and the collapse of the Tudor dynasty. Sir James Tyrell, a typical 'new man' and as captain of Guisnes clearly a man trusted with a responsible task, deserted to the harebrained Suffolk at the first provocation, when none of the supposedly depressed nobility thought of raising a finger to assist their own return to power. Tudor legislation depended for its effectiveness on unpaid local gentlemen enforcing the law: this fact is taken to support the view that the kings depended on the wishes of that class. But (as we shall see) this dependence was much less than is supposed: in general even unpopular statutes were put into practice, though there were limits to what the crown could do.[1] Henry VII's policy of encouraging trade may have been intended to conciliate special interests, but it was also designed to advance national prosperity. In any case, the king was perfectly capable of using the diplomatic weapon of trade embargos, thus cutting off his merchants' noses to spite a foreign face. All told, the story of Henry VII's reign, like that of his successors', will not support the assumption that the Tudors had to defer to a class of their subjects on which they depended for power. Though they exercised great political skill in knowing the limits of their strength, they exercised as much in

[1] There always are.

going to those limits even against opposition from the very people who ordinarily formed the safest support of the monarchy.

The truth is that Tudor kingship was strong in itself. To listen to some historians, one might think that large-scale rebellion is the kind of thing men devise over breakfast and carry out between lunch and dinner. By being king, and by exploiting the great inherent strength of that office, Henry VII put himself into a position of such power that disagreement had to reach a very considerable pitch before it would translate itself into resistance. The name of king was great, and men obeyed whatever king there was, unless they saw the chance of a better candidate or were driven too far. Henry VII removed all other candidates, walked with some delicacy to avoid driving anyone to extremes, and augmented his strength. He sought national support: he did not wish to be ruler by the grace of any one class or section: and if the policy he pursued suited and benefited especially the middle sort of people, that was because it was a rational and national policy bound to profit those who eschewed factious ambitions. The king expected support from all layers of society, and he got it, though some individuals in all layers he had to overcome. The power of the king rested upon his rights and prerogatives. Not for nothing did Henry VII elevate the word prerogative to the first place in his political vocabulary, a habit which endured until the end of the dynasty. No one could say exactly what the king's prerogative amounted to, but all agreed that it included fixed rights and an indefinite reserve of power vested in the crown. No Tudor wished to define it: its vagueness was its worth. It was the essence of regality, capable of acting in the interests of the state and equipped with rights and privileges which none gainsaid because all understood their necessity and most approved their use. By making himself king Henry VII had taken the longest step towards the restoration of royal power; by putting himself upon his just prerogative he made that power effective. It remains to see how he used his prerogative to create strength out of wealth and to enforce the law upon a violent and turbulent people.

2. REVENUE

The Lancastrians were weak, in great part at least, because they were poor. Edward IV succeeded in returning to solvency, but no more. The crown could not be strong while it had to seek financial support from others, and while the resources of great nobles overshadowed its own. Henry VII realised from the start that in order to be strong he had to be rich. The king came to the throne a poor man and heavily in debt to his French and Breton backers; he found it necessary at first to live on short-term loans contracted as best he might; yet within a few years he could lend sufficient money to Anne of Brittany to make the Breton debts a factor in the French war and the peace of Etaples. Henry understood the value of a good name and sound credit, and he scrupulously repaid the early loans taken up before he could tap the resources of the crown; he was able to do so because these resources were really very large. Once he had ascended the throne, a vast potential treasure-house opened to his touch; it only remained to secure all that was due to him, and to husband his resources in a sensible manner by careful management and controlled spending.

The kings of England disposed of an income derived from two basic sources. There was the ordinary revenue of the crown which came in year by year, and the extraordinary revenue from grants and loans made both in and out of parliament. The latter, however, was meant to assist only in emergencies. The famous theory that the king 'should live of his own'—that is, on his regular revenue and without recourse to special grants—found favour both with a people reluctant to part with its substance and with a king desirous of making himself independent. The politic Tudor reluctance to tax frequently helped to disguise what had already become fact. Most of the expenditure of the crown was no longer in any sense personal to the king; it was for purposes of state, and the nation in whose interests the money was spent ought to have contributed more formally to its supply. But since the Tudors did not wish to follow the Lancastrian precedent of surrendering freedom of action in exchange for votes of money, nor the Yorkist precedent of getting contributions without consent, the English people could continue to indulge their natural dislike of paying taxes and their predilection for starving government of the means to govern. The theory that the king was entitled to ask for money on special occasions was faithfully followed in the reign of Henry VII. Henry received votes after the battle of Stoke (1487) to cover that operation, in 1489 to assist in the French war, and in 1496 when he was preparing for action against Scotland; in 1491 he succeeded in having an illegal benevolence endorsed by parliament. The votes were as a rule for one or more 'tenths and fifteenths'; this, originally an assessment on moveables, had become a fixed sum of about £30,000 unconnected with the true distribution of property. It is difficult to say how much Henry received from parliamentary taxation since the money actually collected often bore little relation to that voted. For the French war, for instance, parliament voted about £100,000, but only something less than £60,000 ever came in, about enough to pay for the cost of the few weeks' invasion of France. This factor has to be taken into account when Henry is accused of cheating his subjects by demanding money for wars which he had no intention of undertaking. War was a terribly expensive business which no responsible king could face without the necessary ready cash in hand—and this he could never have saved from his ordinary revenue. Nevertheless, it is perfectly true that Henry turned the difficulty into an advantage when, for instance, he saved the whole grant for the Scottish war except the not inconsiderable sum spent in suppressing the Cornish rising, or when he allowed himself to be bought off at Etaples for an annual pension of £5,000.

These grants and pensions were only the decorative frills on Henry VII's revenue system: he naturally took what he could get, but as his finances grew sound, and as the danger of war or rebellion receded, he dispensed with parliamentary grants and relied exclusively on his proper revenue. Leaving aside some small and incidental items, the sources of this were four: the crown lands, the customs, profits of justice, and the profits of the feudal prerogative. Between them they yielded a large income capable of remarkable expansion, as Henry VII was to prove. Land he made the basis of his wealth; like any landowner of the age, he found it to be a safe and reliable source of income since it could be let at adequate rents which only needed collecting. Coming after the disturbances of the wars, Henry VII was in the happy position of inheriting from all sides. Repeated attainders and forfeitures had greatly increased even the Yorkist crown lands; these—with the earldoms of March and Warwick—now fell to the king by Richard III's overthrow, to be added to the inheritance of Lancaster (the great duchy) and of Tudor (the earldom of Richmond). As king, Henry VII automatically enjoyed the revenues of the duchy of Cornwall and the earldom of Chester. There were many other parcels of lands acquired through escheats—where men had died without heirs—and through the successive attainders of the reign. The fall of Sir William Stanley alone is supposed to have increased the royal revenues by £1,000 a year. Henry, being solvent, could reverse the earlier policy of alienation: where his predecessors had sold crown lands for ready cash, or granted them away as rewardsfor favours and services either received or solicited, he spent a profitable twenty-three years collecting land. In 1495 an act of parliament confirmed to him all the lands of Richard III, even where no special inquest had found that the lands claimed had ever in fact been Richard's, and various acts of resumption declared void grants of crown lands made as far back as the reign of Edward III. Though Henry's policy of mercy returned to private hands some lands which had been forfeited by attainder, this was a small matter compared with the acquisitions made. Thus the crown lands, once a meagre though sound source of revenue, soon took first place in the list. From a clear annual income[1] of about £10,000 in the early part of the reign, their yield rose to about £35,000. The duchy of Lancaster accounted separately; is, revenues went in the first place to pay for its own administrationt but the surplus available for general purposes grew from £650 to £6,500. This land revenue formed a solid and calculable foundation for the royal finances.

The customs, at first a larger part of the king's income, were in this reign just overtaken by the crown lands. The king enjoyed the export duties (*magna* and *parva custuma*) on wool, woolfells, and leather by virtue of his prerogative, while the import and export duties of tunnage (on wine) and poundage (on certain merchandise) were granted to him for life in the first parliament of the reign. The customs revenue was, however, never as great as it ought to have been. Collection in the various ports was difficult and smuggling flourished; especially in the more distant ports, the underpaid customs-service habitually joined in the illegal traffic. Henry tried several methods of increasing the yield: he vainly attempted by legislation to stop evasions, as by the act prohibiting coastal trading without customers' certificates (1487); he attempted to reduce some of the advantages which foreign merchants enjoyed by earlier treaties (1496); twice he revised the book of rates (1503 and 1507) to bring the assessment more into accord with contemporary conditions; and he encouraged trade for fiscal reasons. Medina del Campo (1491) remained the basis of Anglo-Spanish trade for forty years. The treaty known as the *Magnus Intercursus* of 1496 ended the embargo on trade with the Netherlands and put that vital commerce on a safe and permanent footing which profited both the countries concerned. An attempt of 1506 to take advantage of the Archduke Philip's predicament to extort concessions for the English cloth exporters (the *Malus Intercursus*) failed, but it showed whose interests Henry had at heart. The king assisted the merchants' struggles to break into the territories monopolised by

[1] Clear revenue means the sum left after payments charged on individual groups of lands in fees, wages, annuities, pensions, and expenses had been paid by the individual receivers.

the Hanse (the Baltic and north-eastern Europe) and Venice (Italy and the Mediterranean); commercial treaties concluded in 1490 with Denmark and Florence did something to open up those regions. As Henry's chief activity in foreign trade was to encourage the export of cloth, so he attempted to promote and protect the industry at home. Acts were passed to forbid the export of unfinished cloth by foreigners (1487), to encourage the weaving and finishing of cloth (1489), to prevent bad practices in the manufacture of fustian (1495), and to prohibit the import of silken goods (1504). Together with the navigation act of 1490, which in the interests of English shipping and the navy forbade the import of certain goods in foreign vessels, these statutes certainly amounted to a policy of protection. However, it must remain doubtful whether they were really the expression of a consistent policy of economic nationalism. The king did not interfere with the privileges of the Hanse in England and paid little attention to English interests when he used the cloth trade to put pressure on the Netherlands. His own chief interest lay in increasing the customs revenue: the more English trade flourished, the greater would be the cut enjoyed by the crown. The only thing he did not like about foreign merchants were the exemptions from customs payments they had extorted, and these he revoked; it did not concern him that they might perhaps deprive English merchants of some trade. Yet it is true that the measures of the reign greatly assisted commercial revival while their effect on the customs revenue was small. That revenue expanded immediately after Henry's accession, as one would expect at the conclusion of a civil war, and the average of just over £33,000 a year then attained was increased to no more than about £38,000 twenty years later. Smuggling, the difficulties of administration, and the occasional trade wars prevented the full exploitation of this source of money.

The revenue derived from the profits of justice and the feudal incidents is naturally less easily defined in accurate figures. It varied too much year by year, in accordance with events. However, it was here that an energetic king and council could apply the greatest pressure with the best hope of success, and it was here also that re-assertion of the king's rights was most necessary after the wars had lost the crown so much. The king's courts contributed in two ways to the king's finances. There were the fees paid for the writs without which no action could start or carry on; these, together with the fees payable on letters patent of grants and the like, were accounted for by the hanaper, the financial department of chancery, and formed a safe, continuous, and not inconsiderable income which an official of Henry VIII's time once described as a sheet-anchor. Secondly, there were the fines and amercements levied in the courts by way of punishment. Henry made it a general policy to punish by fine even those whose treasonable activities had earned them the death penalty, and each rising or disturbance in the reign was followed not by a forest of gallows but by an invasion of commissioners assessing and collecting fines. Great men paid heavily for contravening the laws against retainers, even though the story of £10,000 exacted from the earl of Oxford is probably apocryphal; merchants paid for attempts to smuggle goods; landed men were fined for breaches of the forest laws, and crown and borough officials for not doing their duty. New penal legislation punished offences by stated fines. In all this Henry VII did not revive obsolete legislation and rules, as Charles I was to do in a similar attempt to make lawlessness pay; in the later fifteenth century many laws had been disobeyed, but they had not become out of date. It is also certain that the policy of imposing heavy fines was, in part at least, political in intent and designed to weaken potential opponents: it was part of Henry VII's attack on overmighty subjects. Not uncommonly fines were remitted, wholly or in part, which shows that they were often intended to be deterrent rather than punitive. This fact makes it difficult to know what profit the king derived from them. They were not usually collected in cash: the victim gave a bond for his debt which he might take years to pay off. The policy was much resented, but it is by no means clear that it was unjust or even unduly harsh.

With it went the exploitation of the king's feudal rights. In the parliament of 1504 Henry managed to collect a feudal aid for the knighting of Prince Arthur (knighted long before and since dead) and for the marriage of his eldest daughter Margaret (married two years earlier). But this spectacular if belated revival of a legitimate claim was much less important than the searching out and enforcing of the rights which the king enjoyed over his tenants-in-chief. The feudal tenure by knight's service involved a number of financial commitments which lay heavily on the tenant and greatly profited the lord, and since the king was far and away the greatest lord his potential revenue from these rights was large. An heir, on taking over his lands, paid a fine known as relief. If he was under age, he and his lands were subject to wardship (that is, they were in the king's hands until he came of age) and livery (the fine paid to recover the lands out of wardship). An heiress's marriage, a marketable asset, was at the lord's disposal. Wardships could be sold for cash, often to the ward's family who wished to save them from the depredations which a temporary administrator would commonly inflict. Lands in the hands of widows and idiots, incapable of doing military service, also reverted to the lord for administration. No heir at all meant escheat—the complete return of the lands to the lord. Lands could not be alienated (sold) or granted in mortmain (to the Church) without royal licence, which had to be paid for. All these rights had one thing in common: it was in the tenant's interest to conceal their occurrence if he could. The disturbed times had given him his chance, and when Henry VII came to the throne the king's rights were generally speaking in a bad way. His first task was to establish what he could claim, and he therefore set up commissions which in the years 1486-92, and again later after the main attainders of the reign (1497-1500), investigated the king's rights by inquests on lands. Henry's careful attention to inquisitions *post mortem*, which established the possessions of a deceased tenant, was part of the same policy; as has been seen, the feudal incidents fell due when one tenant died and another took over. The work of these commissions was naturally much resented by those who had managed to break the law with impunity and were now forced to pay up. Together with the imposition of fines for breaches of statutes, these exactions created Henry VII's reputation for extortion and rapacity. Solidly entrenched though this reputation is, one may doubt whether it is borne out by the facts. He was getting his due at a time when that was difficult. It is argued that he acquired a liking for money for its own sake, but he never acted like a miser; his bad name grew out of the grouses of discovered offenders whose view prevailed with the chroniclers and was accepted by Bacon.[1] The simple truth is that Henry, faced with the task of replenishing an empty treasury and restoring the strength of royal government, from the beginning to the end of his reign enforced his feudal rights and punished offenders where they felt it most—in their pockets. It was the more necessary that he should do so because another period of evasions and concealments would have resulted in the obsolescence of just claims, the collapse of the royal finances, and consequently anarchy.

Among the lesser sources of revenue a few may be mentioned. The revenues of vacant episcopal sees came to the crown, and Henry only perfected an old policy when he habitually permitted such sees to remain vacant for one year. There are signs that

[1] We read such incredible sentimentalities as the view which ascribes an imaginary deterioration of the king to the death of his queen who played very little part in his life. The idea that Henry's policy turned from just to unjust exactions was based only on insufficient knowledge of the facts.

offices were sometimes sold, and that suitors offered money to buy the king's favour in law-suits; these methods would deserve all the execration heaped upon them if one could be sure of what was involved.[1] Henry sold pardons for offences, especially for murder, which, on the face of it, looks like a very bad practice indeed. But it probably meant only that he collected the fees due upon such pardons (as upon any document under the great seal), a practice common throughout the century and earlier; it need not mean that genuine criminals got off. In those violent times—and life was to remain violent well into the eighteenth century—many affrays ended in killings which resulted in accusations of murder when manslaughter or even self-defence would have been a more appropriate description. A pardon was thus commonly obtained before matters came to trial, not after conviction. One need only recall the affair in which Christopher Marlowe found his death; his killers were accused of murder but pardoned upon investigation by the council. Here, too, Henry's reputation has probably suffered through failure to grasp the meaning behind the phrases in the account books.

All this is not to deny that Henry VII eagerly augmented the royal revenues, as indeed he had to if he was to make his government effective, and that he husbanded his resources with the greatest care. Having started in debt, he balanced his accounts by about 1492 and began to show a sizeable surplus from about 1497 onwards. In the end the erstwhile debtor was making large loans to other European potentates and smaller ones to merchants and entrepreneurs. The total result may be summed up by quoting some more figures. Income rose in the reign from about £52,000 to about £142,000 a year; expenditure, which at first had greatly exceeded the regular revenue, was about £138,000 at the end. Much of this was in the nature of investment: money was freely spent on the jewels and plate in which the age generally laid up its treasure, and on loans and trading enterprises which would show a return in the future. Henry died possessed of a treasure worth between one and two millions; the evidence does not permit a more precise statement. Most of this was not in cash or bullion but in jewelry and plate. Such a reserve was essential in a period when

[1] Offices can only have been sold in the sense that people offered money for the appointment; one wants to know if they got it. And did the king favour those who offered him money? The taking of such sums was certainly undignified; whether it was corrupt is quite another question. One must also remember the circumstances of a time which habitually dealt in favours and rewards.

the government's biggest problem was not how to increase its potential revenue but how to have cash in hand when it was needed. Difficulties arose when payments fell due and the money to pay them was not yet in, as happened constantly. The reserve itself was of course gratifying, but it may be doubted whether it really merits all the admiration which it has excited. After all, it took only two years of by no means extravagant war in the next reign to wipe it out. As always, war was far and away the most expensive of government activities, and Henry's pacifism is easily explained by his financial circumstances. The truth is that no government dependent on 'the king's own' and on ready cash could hope to be solvent for any length of time in the new conditions of European diplomacy and internal centralisation, but that problem—staved off with difficulty by the Tudors—was not solved until modern national methods of finance were developed after the Restoration.

3. FINANCIAL ADMINISTRATION

Henry VII's real difficulty was not to find new sources of revenue but to make sure that he got his due. He had to see that the revenues of his lands did not stick to the fingers of the various receivers, that customs were paid and handed over, that the law with its profitable by-products was enforced, and that the feudal rights of the crown were discovered and exacted. This problem of administration forms one of the most complicated and recondite, but also one of the fundamental, aspects of Tudor government; here it will not be possible to give more than a bare outline.

The financial department of state was the exchequer, developed as a separate institution in the later twelfth century and therefore already 300 years old when Henry VII came to the throne. Its two parts—the exchequer of receipt where the money was received, stored, and disbursed, and the exchequer of audit where accounts were audited and unpaid sums driven in—reflected a thorough desire for safety in bureaucracy. A multiplicity of officials and records, designed to prevent fraud and collusion, dealt with the finances. But while the king could be sure that the work of the exchequer was honest, he often had to wait a long time for the creaking machinery to do its work; accounts were audited years after they were due, and it took even longer to collect outstanding items. The records were so designed as to make knowledge of what was coming in, going out, or still in hand very hard to come by. These shortcomings had caused earlier kings to rival the exchequer machinery by financial departments developed in the royal household where the king could exercise personal and direct supervision, keep clear of baronial interference which at times affected offices of state, and handle the cash needed in daily administration without recourse to the cumbersome machinery of the exchequer. Henry III and Edward I had built up an office of finance out of the wardrobe, the accounting department of the household, while Edward II and Edward III had used the king's chamber, the innermost part of the household out of which the exchequer had originally grown. The decline of royal power in the fifteenth century was reflected in the decline of the dynamic household activity in national government which characterised the middle ages; wardrobe and chamber were reduced to purely household departments. Thus when Henry VII attacked the problem of a shrunken revenue, he was confronted with an administration which could be of little use in the expansion and exploitation of his resources.

Like the 'medieval' king that he was, Henry VII found the answer to his problem in the household. Richard III, building up on the rudimentary practice of his brother, had already outlined a plan by which the king's chamber might become the centre of the royal finances, and Henry VII adopted and developed the idea. The details are unimportant: the result was to make the treasurer of the chamber the chief financial officer of the crown from about 1487 onwards. The office was in the hands of such trained, loyal, and efficient men as Sir Thomas Lovell (1485-92) and Sir John Heron (1492-1524), and they were responsible solely to the king. The basis of this 'chamber-system' was the transferring of the crown-lands revenue from exchequer to chamber, local receivers paying directly to its treasurer. In the course of time other items were added, until the exchequer retained only the 'ancient revenue' (the farms of the counties and towns collected by the sheriffs) and the customs. The latter were left with the inefficient old administration because their collection involved a detailed knowledge and complicated array of officers and records not available to the treasurer of the chamber. But everything else—except the revenues of the self-administered duchy of Lancaster—went to the chamber: land revenue, the profits of wardship and other feudal dues, the profits of the hanaper, the fines and other income from courts of law, the French pension—even parliamentary taxes, though their collection continued to be supervised by the exchequer.

Before the end of the reign the treasurer of the chamber thus handled an annual turnover of well over £100,000. He had taken the place of the exchequer of receipt as the chief treasury of the realm, but since he was not to be responsible to the exchequer of audit some other agency had to be created to supervise his affairs and scrutinise his accounts. In the reign of Henry VII, little progress was made in systematising this side of the new machinery, for the king took the responsibility largely upon himself. He personally checked the treasurer's account books, signing each page with his monogram, while for the periodic audit he appointed some of his councillors who were also to audit the accounts of other receivers of revenue removed from the survey of the exchequer. In course of time, the task came to be a specialised one, but there is no sign that anything like an organisation was set up; everything was still much too fluid and personal, in the true spirit of 'household' administration. The accession of Henry VIII, however, produced some changes which crystallised his father's system and allow one to see it more clearly. Unlike the old king, his successor did not wish to be bothered with the detailed work of government. Moreover, the change of ruler encouraged the exchequer to protest against the use of the chamber; attempts were made to distrain on revenue officials for sums they had long since paid to the chamber, but which in the view of the exchequer had never been officially received. A number of acts of parliament therefore appointed two general surveyors of crown lands to act as a department of audit. Therewith the so-called chamber-system was complete: a household treasurer as chief collector and paymaster of revenue, with a semi-household department of audit to supervise him and help in securing his revenues. The general surveyors were not as yet free of the household or given sufficient organisation to make them independent; the exchequer, a true department of state, kept their records and supplied means for legal process against defaulters.

Especially in the reign of Henry VII it was not enough to have a treasury and an audit office; equally necessary was an agency for the ascertaining of outstanding, and the discovery of concealed, sources of revenue. The commissions, already mentioned, which did this work early in the reign under the general supervision of Sir Reginald Bray were later superseded by more permanent officials. A master of the wards (Sir John Hussey) was appointed in 1503, to secure the revenue from wardships which he paid to the chamber. In 1508, in an attempt to exploit to the full the fiscal rights of the crown, the shortlived office of the surveyor of the king's prerogative was created and given to Sir Edward Belknap; again, the money was to go to the chamber. It is in connection with these agencies that one must explain the work of the notorious Richard Empson and Edmund Dudley. These men, crown officials who were trained lawyers rather than pure administrators like Bray or Lovell, formed the mainstay of the rather obscure 'king's legal counsel', organised under the chairmanship of the chancellor of the duchy of Lancaster, an office Empson held from 1504. Their task was in particular the taking of bonds (recognisances and obligations) in which men promised to pay fines imposed for breaches of the law, or debts contracted, or sums in case of non-performance of certain duties. It was a development of the earlier methods of Bray and Lovell, though the energy with which Empson and Dudley pursued their unpopular tasks gave them a worse reputation. It did not help matters that both men—unlike Bray—rapaciously lined their own pockets. Their activities do not deserve the name of extortion: this has already been explained. However, the fact that they acted as the agents of an energetic and pitiless financial policy left them wide open to attack when their royal protector died. Henry VIII found it an easy way to quick popularity to throw over his father's ministers, and it seems that people, happy to see Empson and Dudley die, overlooked the fact that Empson's and Dudley's policy was soon revived, though on the whole less stringently.

Apart from some small but useful changes in the exchequer of receipt, these were Henry VII's reforms in the financial machinery. He made no innovations in the means and principles employed, for chamber finance and the use of household officers had a long and respectable history. The degree to which he developed the system, however, was something new. No king before him had disposed of so efficient an agency so firmly under his personal control, for the collection of so large a revenue. But the system depended very much on his personal action; Henry VIII's lack of interest doomed it, though Wolsey continued to work a more bureaucratic form of it. In the last analysis, Henry VII, because he used the old household methods, failed to lay the foundations of a really reformed administration.

4. LAW AND ORDER

The financial measures of Henry VII restored strength to the crown, but what would ultimately matter was, of course, the use to which that strength was put. From the first the king took up the tasks of enforcing the law and suppressing those whose improper power had threatened the peace of the country. Some of the financial measures were themselves a means towards that end. The recovery of the king's feudal rights remedied one large-scale breach of the law, while the weapon of heavy fines proved most useful in breaking the power and spirit of 'overmighty subjects'. The turbulent noble and knight who had to redeem evasions of wardships and the like, and to pay for violent dispossessions or excessive retaining, were both taught the strength of the king's arm and rendered too weak to make their resentment felt. On the whole, the existing laws against violence sufficed: the courts needed only to be enabled to apply them sternly and impartially. Though Henry found it desirable to legislate against some symptoms of trouble, remarkably few statutes were passed providing against the kind of offences which had been common, in itself an indication that the disturbances grew out of weakness at the top, and arrogance and corruption lower down, and not out of any fundamental evils in the body politic. In 1485 hunting in disguise was prohibited, since it allegedly offered occasion for riots and murders. In 1487, several acts tightened up the procedure employed in catching and punishing murderers, stopped a gap by forbidding the taking away of women (heiresses) without their consent, and hoped to end the undermining of the king's own tenants' loyalty by forbidding other men to retain them for any service. Four separate acts of 1495 attempted to solve one of the greatest problems of all, the failure of a legal system which depended, both for evidence in property cases and for verdicts on crimes, on juries that had grown intimidated or—more commonly—corrupt. The returning of blatantly false verdicts by local juries, from which there was no appeal, continued to be the principal bane of Tudor law-enforcement, and the acts of 1495—though they spoke bravely against perjury, maintenance, and the empanelling of insufficient and thus easily corrupted jurors—achieved very little. One aspect of the problem lay in the powers of the sheriff whose connections with the local magnates tended to make him useless to the government. Sheriffs empanelled juries and kept prisoners in custody; in both they had often failed, and laws recalling them to their duty had to be passed in 1495 and 1504. In the end, the misdeeds of fifteenth-century sheriffs resulted in the fall from grace and power of their sixteenth-century successors.

In 1504 there was also passed Henry VII's great statute against retaining, not of course the first act against this fundamental evil, but rather a general codified statement on the subject. It ordered the enforcement of existing acts, appointed penalties both for those who retained men except as household servants and for those who allowed themselves to be so retained, placed the burden of searching out offenders on the justices of the peace, clarified the position of the king's council in the enforcement of the law, and provided a procedure which secured convictions even when juries refused to indict patent transgressors.[1] The act remained the decisive pronouncement on the subject; if enforced, it was bound to end the existence of the armed bands on which the great supplanters of royal authority had relied. But laws against retaining had been passed before; what was needed was energetic enforcement. The restoration of order depended not only on the suppression of the overmighty subject; there had never been many of those, the wars had thinned their ranks further, and the task was relatively straightforward. It also required that the lesser men be taught to take their quarrels to the law and not settle them by force. Until the creation of a regular police force in the nineteenth century, England remained a country of ready violence. Every dispute turned too easily to bloodshed; in the Tudor age, men were far too quick to draw daggers, wield clubs, break heads, and raise riots. The sum of hundreds of such small affrays and quarrels year by year was a far more pressing problem to the government than the very occasional major risings or the remoter dangers of private warfare, even though these latter could prove fatal. In the absence of a police force there could be no hope of preventing trouble; one could only make the consequences so unpleasant that people would learn to curb their tempers and to seek satisfaction for their claims and grievances in the long-drawn agony of the law courts instead of the sharp exhilaration of the riot.

Henry VII found in existence a system of local government which needed only fresh vigour and development. The justices of the peace, local and (virtually) unpaid gentlemen appointed and supervised by the crown, were the mainstay of the Tudor system of law-enforcement. With the decline of the sheriff, the decay of the old popular courts of hundred and shire, and the deliberate attack made on the feudal and franchisal courts, they were rapidly promoted to exclusive control of the countryside. Henry VII legislated both to enlarge their duties and to keep them up to the mark. They were empowered to take bail (1487) and to punish on information without indictment (1495); disguised hunters,

[1] Strictly speaking, before the statute no man could be proceeded against for illegal retaining unless he was indicted by a jury of presentment. These juries having failed in their duty, the council were to act on information received (from J.Ps., as a rule), summoning offenders by writs of *subpoena*; the chancellor could also order such *subpoenas* on his own initiative, without formal information being laid. The procedure here outlined was practised by the council before 1504; the act merely legalised it.

vagabonds, thieves of swans' eggs, and many others were put under their jurisdiction; they were given special powers to investigate and punish the transgressions of sheriffs (1495). This was only the beginning of those 'stacks of statutes' whose execution, as the Elizabethan antiquary William Lambarde said, was laid upon their shoulders. Henry VII seems to have begun the practice of invariably including leading councillors in the commissions for the individual shires: this both raised the standing of the office and ensured that some of the justices at least would always be loyal servants of the royal will.

No system of local government is worth having unless it obeys the orders of the central government. The Tudor system suffered in any case from reliance on unpaid and therefore relatively independent agents; there was no choice in the matter. However, the independence of these J.Ps. has been greatly exaggerated. Legislation which went clean contrary to their sectional interests—the interests of the rural gentry—might, indeed, be difficult to enforce: enclosures of common land proceeded in the early Tudor period despite laws forbidding it, and in catholic Lancashire the recusancy laws of Elizabeth were readily flouted. On the other hand, the office of J.P. was not hereditary or held for life; the annual re-issue of the commission gave the government quite sufficient control, for no gentleman could afford being put out of it. With the commission he would lose his standing in his own county society; the consequences would be almost as bad for him as dismissal would be for a salaried official. If proof of their essential dependence and obedience to orders be sought, it will easily be found in the overbearing and peremptory manner in which the council addressed any justice who was thought to have failed in his duty. There was neither thought nor need of tact in these dealings. Henry VII could safely take up the office of justice of the peace, adapt it to his needs, and develop it into the mainstay of local government. But he could do so only because government at the centre fully recovered its vitality.

The centre of Henry VII's government, as of all medieval government, was the king himself, assisted by those with whom he chose to surround himself—that is, his council. The rather fluid permanent council of the fourteenth century consolidated in the reign of Richard II into an organised body. This council, with its small membership, its rules of procedure, and its regular term-time meetings, fell before the magnate onslaught under the Lancastrians; it ceased to be an instrument at the king's disposal. Following Yorkist practice, Henry VII, who chose a number of his own followers to be his councillors, reverted to a more primitive and less organised council. The number of the men described as councillors in his reign is large—over 150—and individual meetings could be attended, on occasion, by forty or more of them. They included great nobles like Oxford and Dorset, and later Surrey; great prelates like Morton and Fox and Warham; great administrators of the stamp of Bray and Lovell; but also the judges and legal advisers, and many lesser men whom one can at best describe as leading civil servants. Generally speaking, Henry's councillors were office-holders, but many of the offices held were minor, and Sir Reginald Bray's importance is not to be measured by the comparatively insignificant post of the chancellor of the duchy of Lancaster which he held.[1] The one qualification which embraces them all was that the king had chosen them; they were his men and did his will.

Naturally, however, there were grades and distinctions among them—even up to a point signs of differentiation in function. The legal council, who in Henry's last years employed themselves in collection of fines and bonds, are a case in point; the court of requests is another. Nevertheless it should be made plain once and for all that never in Tudor times was there more than one council in existence at the centre: there was always only one body to which men called councillors could belong. The separation of star chamber and privy council is hard to trace because in personnel no such separation ever took place. It is wrong to see in the council groupings of Henry VII's reign the origin of any subdivision of the council. In a body as large as this council there were, of course, some men of greater influence; some may be called ministers where others were only leading administrators. Naturally also, since the centre of government was with the king at court, the king tended to take his more important councillors with him on his travels; of all the peripatetic Tudor sovereigns, Henry VII was the most active. Thus there existed an 'inner ring' of more important, more influential, more powerful councillors, commonly in attendance on the king and forming the active ministry (as it were) within the larger body. The king's absence from the seat of the permanent departments of state at Westminister naturally suggested the advisability of leaving some councillors on call in the council room of that palace, the famous star chamber. It was desirable that his subjects or foreign visitors should at all times be able to find part of the government at Westminster. But the 'council attendant'

[1] This office enjoyed a temporary importance between 1485 and 1529 for which neither its earlier nor its later history seem to cast it.

and 'council at Westminster' of the books never existed, though councillors attendant or at Westminster there were. These terms describe the location of individuals, not the differentiation of institutions: a man would change his description as he travelled with the king or stayed behind, and there was no fixity about selection. If the king returned to Westminster all the councillors were there, except those detached on individual business and those away looking after their own affairs. Some men were apparently delegated during term to hear the petitions of poor persons and of the king's servants in the court specially developed for them by the reign of Richard III and known as that of requests; but even this differentiation was far from complete, and men technically allocated to the 'court' of requests are found at work in the 'court' of star chamber. Requests itself underwent frequent re-establishment until it emerged settled late in Henry VIII's reign.[1] Everything was very indeterminate: fluidity and lack of specialisation characterised Henry VII's council.

The council's function was threefold. It existed to advise the king in matters of policy, to administer the realm, and to adjudicate upon cases brought before it by petition. Of the first duty no evidence has survived, for advice was given by word of mouth after debate; the second has left a few traces here and there in writs and orders emanating from king and council; the third, however, is well-documented because it was essentially a task which called for record-keeping. In consequence, the importance of the council's functions has commonly been seen in inverse order to that which really applied, and its most formal business—judicial matters—has been allowed to obscure activities which have to be largely guessed at. In the reign of Henry VII this false stress is less injurious than later. The judicial work of the council was the centre and mainspring of that activity in restoring obedience to the law which gives the reign its chief claim to fame. However, if we are to understand the part the council played it will be necessary to outline briefly the regular courts of the realm—the courts of the common law.

Out of the undifferentiated *curia regis* of the twelfth century there grew, among other institutions, two courts of law which became established in Westminster Hall and separated from the king's entourage: the court of common pleas late in the twelfth century, and the court of king's bench early in the fourteenth. The first dealt with civil cases between party and party; the second with criminal matters and all cases affecting the king's interests.

[1] For the court of requests cf. also below, p. 83.

To them must be added the exchequer sitting as a court and handling revenue cases. These central courts made their influence felt by delegation. Civil cases were heard by justices doing circuits at regular intervals out of the legal terms; criminal jurisdiction was carried out locally by judges or justices of the peace armed with commissions of oyer and terminer and gaol delivery which were made out as need arose.[1] This system administered the common law of England, grown out of custom, judges' decisions (case law), and occasional acts of legislation like Henry II's 'assizes' or, later, parliamentary statutes. They were staffed by men trained at the inns of court who had made a career as counsel at the bar before promotion to the bench.

The common law is certainly one of the glories of England, and it was perhaps the chief legacy of the middle ages. But by the late fifteenth century the courts were in a bad way. The law had grown rigid while circumstances changed, and there were common and necessary practices in affairs of property which the courts did not recognise and therefore failed to protect. Their procedure was slow, highly technical, and very expensive: a trivial mistake in pleading could lose a good case, and a clever lawyer could drive a coach and four through the law by exploiting technicalities. Worst of all, in the wars the system failed because what is commonly regarded as its most praiseworthy component collapsed. The common law relied on the jury. In cases concerning property, for instance, there was no examination of witnesses; instead, a local jury would be empanelled to render a verdict on questions of just possession or rights of property from their own local knowledge. And juries could be intimidated or bribed or packed. In criminal matters, too, a defendant who 'put himself upon the country' (asked to be tried by a jury) could generally be sure of an acquittal if he knew the right people. With the jury proving an obstacle to justice, the whole common-law system, in any case careful rather to save the innocent than convict the guilty, was helpless in the face of the increasing violence.

But the growth of the common-law courts had not exhausted the reservoir of speaking justice which was the king's. The principle had always been that those who failed to get justice at law, or could not afford to seek it there, were entitled to appeal to the

[1] Oyer and terminer (to hear and determine) was originally issued for some specific case reported to the king's bench; gaol delivery was designed to deal with a number of men held in custody in a local gaol till one of the king's judges should arrive to dispose of them. By the sixteenth century the commissions were generally combined and tended to include one central judge together with several local J.Ps.

king for special intervention. In the reign of Edward I the practice grew up of collecting such petitions when the council met local representatives, that is in parliament. Parliaments soon became rather too busy with matters of general interest to attend to individual petitions; the council found their daily work hampered by this flood of requests for redress; and in the fifteenth century one of their number, the chancellor, began to specialise in dealing with petitions. Out of this activity, enormously increased when the chancellor let it be seen that he would enforce the contract known as 'feoffment to uses' or 'the use',[1] there grew the court of chancery, administering a system of law known as equity which was meant to supplement the common law. Thus, by the accession of Henry VII, the sphere of the chancellor in his nascent court of chancery was defined within wide limits: chancery as a court dealt only with civil cases. The judicial powers of the king's council remained untouched by its growth, and it was to them that Henry turned when he wished to enforce the law. People were encouraged to send their bills of complaint to the lords of the council—a technical term meaning councillors and nothing to do with peerage—though not much encouragement was in fact needed. Furthermore, the council began to act on its own initiative, either upon information being laid (usually by the king's attorney-general) or even without this. It enjoyed a number of advantages over the courts of the common law. It did not have to rely on juries but could summon witnesses to establish the truth, or have enquiries made by local magistrates. Plaintiff and defendant were upon oath, and there was no nonsense about allowing them to remain silent rather than incriminate themselves. The council represented the king; it naturally embodied the majesty of the law to a higher degree than the discredited common-law courts. Councillors were king's servants and amenable only to influence from the crown: towards all subjects, regardless of rank, they could be—and generally were—fearlessly impartial. The council could inflict penalties such as imprisonment and confiscation of property which were not open to the common law with its reliance on fines. On the other hand, felony and treason were beyond its competence

[1] Feoffment to uses was a device to transfer the legal property in land to a trustee, so as to avoid the feudal incidents which arose upon inheritance. If A wished his son B to succeed without payment of fines, etc., he would enfeoff C (the trustee) with his lands, to the use of B; the legal seisin (possession) would be in C when A died, though A and B enjoyed the profits from the land. There were more complicated forms of the use. Until the chancellor proved ready to protect such agreements, there was no remedy against defaulting trustees.

because it could not touch life or member—it could not order execution or mutilation.

In this judicial activity of the council lay the origin of the later court of star chamber. It was desirable that men should have some fixed place to resort to if the council was to act as a court, and in turn, once the council began to sit in one place at stated times and deal with judicial business in a regular manner, it developed all the characteristics of a court. It was the councillors at Westminster, meeting in the star chamber which had been the council room since Edward III's time, that dealt with the judicial work. But there was so far no division into court and council; there was only the council which—as it had done for at least a century—would meet in open session to adjudicate upon petitions. Henry VII only added pressure of work; the development into a court came later. The crown recovered strength; therefore the council, the crown's agent, also recovered strength; and thus it was able to deal with the pressing problem of disorder. But let it be noted that the councillors in the star chamber never administered a law of their own, as did chancery. They saw to it that the existing law was observed, a task they could discharge the more easily because their standing and procedure gave them marked advantages both over the ordinary courts and over the criminal. In consequence, the council in the star chamber—strong, impartial, energetic, and incorruptible—soon grew popular with suitors, and business increased steadily. In this reign it was largely concerned with matters of riot—any forcible breach of the peace, for whatever cause—and retained a touch of the tribunal of state, protecting the interests of the king and realm against law-breakers.

The conciliar principle which led to the growth of the court of requests and the development of the council in star chamber produced two more institutions which must be briefly mentioned. The country as a whole was lawless and disturbed enough, but this was as nothing compared with the state of the northern and Welsh borders. Scottish raids in the north, the franchises and violent practices of the marcher lords in the west, kept those parts in a turmoil of primitive lawlessness which the rest of the country had long outgrown. The ordinary institutions of local government exercised little influence in an area where violence was the order of the day and relations between men depended on personal allegiance to some great nobleman. The expansion of these conditions from the marches of Wales across the whole of England had put the country back into an anarchy unknown for centuries; now conditions returned to normal in the settled parts, but the borders remained anarchic. Henry VII produced no far-reaching solution. In the north, Richard III, as duke of Gloucester, had governed during his brother's reign, and like any great nobleman he had been surrounded by a council. After his death, and after the death of the earl of Northumberland (1487) on whom Henry had at first relied to keep the border country quiet, the king made the child Arthur warden of the Scottish marches with the earl of Surrey as his lieutenant. Surrey, too, had a council which, in the Tudor manner, was filled with officials rather than feudal retainers, and out of this the council of the north was ultimately to grow. In Wales and the Welsh marches, the Tudors were well placed by their descent; Henry found it unnecessary to do more than appoint a council technically in attendance on the prince of Wales who himself, of course, was a child and absent. This council administered the principality but played no part in the affairs of the marches where the organisation of the earldom of March (inherited from the Yorkists) was continued. Altogether, these gropings after administrative arrangements on the borders illustrate the conservatism of Henry VII's policy. Every baron had his council, and therefore the barons (or princes) appointed to local control had theirs; one might make sure that these councils were staffed by loyal and skilled administrators—as one made sure of the king's own council—but that was all. So far there was no sign of those later institutions, the council of the north and the council in the marches of Wales; old and tried expedients, personal and temporary in character, were the limits of Henry VII's inventiveness. He restored but did not innovate.

5. PARLIAMENT AND THE CHURCH

We have traced the government of the country from a crown rendered strong by financial independence, through the central council and courts, and through the local institution of justices of the peace; we have shown how Henry VII restored sound government by infusing new life into institutions which he found ready to hand, and in particular by restoring its earlier vigour to the royal household as an agency of national administration. In all this, we have had no occasion to say a word about parliament. The reason is simple: parliament, though by this time recognised as a specific institution, was not part of the ordinary government of the realm. It met when the king called it, and no king called it unless he had a special reason to do so, either to obtain supplies or to pass those formulations of existing or new law that are known as statutes.

Two things were already accepted about parliament: taxes could only be imposed with its consent, and the laws declared there were superior to all other laws. The first point arose originally from the convenience of getting the consent of the realm in one place and at one time; it was the more easily adhered to because a strong king like Henry VII preferred to 'live of his own' and not to trouble his parliaments. The second point arose out of parliament's character as a high court—the highest in the realm—whose decisions were binding on inferior courts; several times in the fifteenth century, the judges declared that certain matters were outside their competence, having been made the subject of parliamentary statute. The roots of parliament's two modern pillars—control of taxation and the supremacy of parliamentary legislation—had taken hold, though the institution was still very 'medieval'. The core of parliament was a meeting of the king with his council in the widest sense, a council consisting both of his barons and of his professional or permanent council. The parliament chamber, with its throne on the cloth of state, its benches for lords spiritual and temporal, and its woolsacks for councillors and judges, signified the true essence of parliament. In addition, there were the representatives of the communities—the knights of the shires and the burgesses of the boroughs. These had no right of access to the parliament chamber; they were outside the high court of parliament and for that very reason had organised themselves into a house of commons under the guidance of the Speaker who alone could address the king in his parliament. In the sixteenth century the meetings of the great council in the parliament were to develop into the house of lords, even as the meetings of the ordinary council in the star chamber developed into the court of star chamber. But this was yet in the future when Henry VII sat on the throne.

Henry VII's parliaments conformed generally to the medieval pattern. The Lancastrians in their weakness had had to rely on parliamentary support and taxes; the frequent meetings then held had certainly established the commons as an essential part of a proper parliament. But even the Lancastrian commons had appeared stronger than they were because the magnate opposition in the great council had employed them as mouthpieces. Henry VII had to fear no opposition from his lords of whom a majority (about forty) were bishops and abbots whose appointments he virtually controlled, while the lay peers were in part at least those he had promoted. Among the commons, too, there were never any signs of opposition. It was not fear, then, which caused Henry

VII to call but six parliaments in twenty-three years,[1] five of them in the first ten years of his reign—a fact for which he claimed credit, since he had thus saved his subjects' pockets. He looked on parliament as a medieval king: it was a weapon he could employ when he felt it to be useful, but with which he could dispense at his pleasure. He would have to call it only if he needed taxes; but he made his ordinary revenue suffice. It was a high court where the grievances of the subject could find redress at the hands of king and council; but the council sessions in the star chamber were doing this more efficiently. It could declare what the law was (as Henry's age still saw it) or, to our way of thinking, make laws by its decisions; but he had little fresh law to make. Thus he called only one parliament between 1497 and his death, and no one thought anything of it. It is not true that this long break, after the frequency of meetings early in the reign, in any way signified a danger to the very existence of parliament: it was not wanted for the present, but it would be called again if and when the king should need it. In the meantime, there was reason to be pleased at a policy which saved many men much bother and expense.

However, while Henry's attitude to parliament was essentially medieval and shared by his subjects, there were signs that the fifteenth-century development had not gone unnoticed and that things might be different in the future. When the king tried to get a money grant out of an irregular assembly called in 1496, he met strenuous opposition on the grounds that only a proper parliament could vote taxes; he called a parliament next year and got his supplies without difficulty. More important still, Henry exploited the dominating position of the high court of parliament to attack the lesser privileges and franchises which were so troublesome to the Tudors. Some parts, such as Tynedale, had their rights taken away by statute. An act of 1504 attacked the immunities of corporations and gilds. Several acts defined the limits of 'benefit of clergy'—the privilege enjoyed by those claiming to be members of the Church to escape the consequences of wrongdoing. Parliament interfered with an ordinance made by the city of London and authorised (in the statute of retainers) the persecution of offenders by methods unknown to the common law. All this legislation purported to state what the true law ought to be and only to clarify a position and elaborate details of procedure. As the phrase goes, it was declaratory rather than legislative. The form was not a disguise for deeper things; this was really the way in which both king and nation looked upon the matter. Nevertheless, when such

[1] 1485, 1487, 1489, 1491, 1495, 1497, 1504.

plain law as accusation by indictment was set aside, when privileges grounded in good prescription were destroyed in a few words without even the pretence that they had never existed, it is clear that the modern doctrine of legislation by parliamentary statute was on the way. These were the foundations, half-realised as yet, on which the full Tudor doctrine of the sovereignty of the king in parliament was to be built. But in the reign of the first Tudor, parliament was still an occasional rather than a permanent part of a government which was in the hands of the king and his courts—institutions of which parliament, though the most solemn, was the least frequent and in practice therefore the least important.

There remains one institution, the church. However, a full discussion of this large subject had best be left till a later chapter. In the reign of Henry VII the church enjoyed a kind of medieval Indian summer. Relations with the lay power—the king—were excellent; Henry was a pious son of the church, and the clergy supplied many of his leading ministers and servants. The troubles of the fourteenth century, to be discussed hereafter, were as if forgotten by common consent. Henry's work in restoring order necessitated a pruning of the privileges of benefit of clergy and sanctuary of which unscrupulous men had taken undue advantage; but the Church did not feel inclined to resent an invasion of its rights which only promoted peace and good order. From these it itself profited greatly. And so, while Henry stopped the violence of greater and lesser troublemakers and asserted the supreme authority of the crown over the laity, the problem of the relations of Church and state never came up and remained unsolved. The king was content to deal with the difficulties that existed, and in this he was of course completely right. It was enough that he should restore good and permanent government, an end he achieved by putting new life into old institutions and, in particular, by himself working night and day at the task of king. His reward came when he could hand to his son a safe throne, a full treasury, a functioning machine of government, and a reasonably ordered and prosperous country.

Chapter IV

THE GREAT CARDINAL

1. THE EARLY YEARS OF HENRY VIII

THE reign of Henry VIII opened in a blaze of glory. Contemporaries were ready to be impressed; Henry VII had never been an inspiring figure, and in his later years—order having been restored—a cold, calculating, and cautious government held little to attract the livelier members of a nation which remembered an heroic past. Legitimate demands were termed exaction, and a foreign policy based on matrimony rather than war roused no enthusiasm. By contrast the new king, not quite eighteen when he ascended the throne on 21 April 1509, promised wonders. In his young days, Henry was a handsome giant with a predilection for athletics; he hunted and shot, played tennis and wrestled, with the best of them. In addition he was intelligent, a capable musician, quite well-seen in theology, a patron of the arts and learning. Foreign ambassadors as well as his own subjects praised him to the skies. Parts of this chorus may be discounted as the sort of exercise in Ciceronian Latin of which the age was fond, and as the kind of adulation which a king-conscious generation offered to a youthful monarch as a matter of course. But scepticism can be taken too far. Undoubtedly Henry was an impressive figure; he remained one throughout a long reign even in later days when muscle had turned to fat. Undoubtedly, too, his mental powers were considerable. At eighteen his character was yet forming, and precisely what his abilities were can only be decided when his life's work has been considered. There is no doubt, however, that many men both high and low, both commonplace and exceptional, expected great things. A month after his father's death, Henry fulfilled his dying wish by marrying Catherine of Aragon, six years older than himself. The scene seemed set for a happy and prosperous reign.

The very fact of Henry's peaceful accession was a triumph for his father's policy; the blood of both the Roses had at last mingled in one unquestioned claimant to the throne. The change of kings made little immediate difference in affairs, for the government continued to be dominated by the previous reign. Henry VII's chief councillors composed Henry VIII's first council: no one else was yet available. To two men the change proved fatal. Both Henry and his council wished to add some concrete foundation to the popularity which so far rested largely on hopes. A gesture proved easy to find. Hatred of Henry VII's policy concentrated on his 'fiscal judges', Empson and Dudley; their sacrifice would cleanse the dead king's name and earn the new king golden opinions. A proclamation asked all who would to come and charge the late king's servants with unjust extortion; many came. Since, however, the intended victims could prove that they had only acted under instructions, it became necessary to arraign them on an entirely fictitious charge of treason. Empson and Dudley went to the scaffold, predecessors of many in this blood-stained reign. The whole story is highly instructive and has been too little regarded. The fact that Empson and Dudley were thrown to the wolves is not significant in itself; it was an obvious way of cementing popularity. But the method employed deserves attention. A fictitious charge of treason brought against two loyal servants marked a notable break with the conciliatory practices of Henry VII who had used that dubious weapon only once—against the earl of Warwick who, however innocent, represented a real threat to the dynasty. Under Henry VIII many were to be caught in that trap. That the reign should have started in this fashion makes it difficult to agree with the view that Henry VIII began as a strong, even wilful, man of sound character who deteriorated through the exercise of power into a suspicious and bloodthirsty autocrat. From the first, he was utterly sure of himself as only a man born to the purple can be, passionately devoted to his own interests and inclinations, unscrupulous but careful of legal form, and clever. Moreover, as this business shows, he was good at picking up the ideas of others. The newcomer to the throne, though he could of himself think of killing two innocent men as a way to quick popularity, cannot possibly have thought of the expedient adopted in face of their inviolability on the real charge. Whoever suggested the treason trial of Empson and Dudley had much to answer for when Henry remembered the lesson on later occasions. The affair also displayed the king's inherent cruelty. This is something so strikingly different from his father's clemency that one is tempted to see here an inheritance from his grandfather, Edward IV, whom Henry VIII resembled physically and in more than one unfortunate aspect of his character.

At any rate, the trick worked. The first parliament of the reign (January 1510) readily endorsed the murders by an act of attainder and voted the supplies which a cessation of the late king's activities made doubly necessary. Therewith the reign was under way; it remained to exploit the momentum gained. Affairs were dominated by the war in Italy where the assault of the League of Cambrai on Venice, begun in 1508, had been rather too successful for its architect, Pope Julius II. French victories threatened to engulf the whole north of the peninsula, with dangerous consequences to the independence of the Holy See. Julius II therefore, reviving the papal policy of holding the balance even between the French in the north and the Spaniards in the south, succeeded in October 1511 in forming the Holy League with Spain and Venice against France. England's adherence was something of a foregone conclusion. There was the memory of Cambrai to wipe out, when England had been left in the cold. France was still the traditional enemy, and many, from the king downwards, were bitterly jealous of her successes. The king, indeed, was the decisive factor. A good papalist, he could not listen unmoved to appeals from Rome; an almost uxorious husband, he was exposed to the influence of Ferdinand of Aragon, since Catherine thought herself in duty bound to manage her husband in her father's interest. Everything was in favour of war, except the tradition of Henry VII, and that was crumbling even in the minds of councillors trained under him. The council was not united: Surrey, an old soldier, resented the priest-ridden peace policy of Warham (archbishop of Canterbury), Fox (bishop of Winchester), and Ruthal (bishop of Durham). The king was bent on war, his wife and father-in-law were egging him on, the treasury was full, the country willing, the pope calling; thus, some sixty years after England had last fought on the continent, Henry VIII went to war against France, in search of glory and for no genuine interests of his own or his nation's. The parliament summoned in February 1512 supplied the necessary grants and listened approvingly to propaganda against the kings of France and Scotland. From the first it was taken into account that the northern border would not remain quiet while the king of England disported himself on the continent.

The war so lightly entered into proved suitably confused, with fortunes as wavering as Henry's allies and results as puny as his reasons for fighting. 1512 produced an expedition to assist Ferdinand in Spain: an English army under the marquess of Dorset landed near Bayonne and occupied the attention of the French while the king of Aragon overran Navarre. The Spaniards made no secret of the fact that the English force was only a pawn in a Spanish game; the reconquest of Guienne, mooted once again, was never a serious possibility. Dorset's men were ill looked after;

dysentery and wine killed numbers, and the rest returned home, refusing to obey their feeble commander's orders. At sea, England at first did well, but attempts to direct action from a distance ended with Henry sending his navy and admiral (Sir Edward Howard) to disaster at Brest (April 1513). Failure and disgrace only spurred Henry to further action. Early in 1513 Ferdinand deserted his allies, but the pope, who unlike Spain had not yet obtained his ends, was eager to carry on. Henry VIII now determined to invade France in person and from the north. Having succeeded in postponing the expected Scottish intervention, for which the king of France was pressing, he crossed with a large army to Calais and from there undertook the siege of the little town of Thérouanne. A French relieving force was beaten off in the 'Battle of the Spurs' (August 1513), so called because of the French speed in reverse, a victory which yielded a fair harvest of important prisoners, including the great but aged Bayard. Thérouanne fell late in August, and Tournai was captured a month later. Leaving garrisons in these towns, Henry returned in triumph, only to find that much more substantial successes had been won during his absence on the Scottish border, by an army under the earl of Surrey. James IV declared war in July and crossed the border in August. After some minor successes he met the main English army, assembled with commendable speed and well led by the old earl, at Flodden Edge on 7 September. The Scottish army was rather the larger and its position exceedingly strong; but Surrey, assisted by James's lack of generalship, forced the Scots from their stronghold and into action on disadvantageous terms. Flodden was a major English triumph: among the 10,000 or more killed that the Scots lost were their king himself and many lords. The accession of a child (James V) whose mother and regent was Henry VIII's own sister Margaret, ended the danger from Scotland for most of Henry's reign.

The war was near its end. Julius II was dead, succeeded by Leo X who wanted peace; Ferdinand continued his game of joining alliances and then repudiating his word; both he and Maximilian were negotiating behind Henry's back. But Henry was not a Tudor for nothing. Early in 1514 he himself opened negotiations with France and, much to their surprise, stole a march on his treacherous allies. The treaty of July 1514 gave England possession of Tournai and a larger pension from France; it was sealed by the marriage of Henry's younger sister Mary to the elderly Louis XII of France. Henry's fury with his father-in-law vented itself in futile dreams of allying with France to drive Ferdinand from

Navarre and assert Catherine of Aragon's claims to Castile. But these were idle thoughts; the facts sufficed to satisfy both king and country. The war had been successful, graced by two major victories and an acquisition of territory, though the victories were petty compared with the battles in Italy, and Tournai proved nothing but a liability. England had asserted her right and power to play a leading part in European affairs; Henry had won some personal renown and learned—very rapidly—how to conduct himself in the treacherous diplomacy of the time which so largely consisted in switching allies at the right moment. But the outstanding result of the war was very different: it provided Henry with the first of the two great ministers who were to give purpose and importance to his reign.

2. WOLSEY'S RULE IN ENGLAND

Thomas Wolsey was born in about 1473, son of a butcher and cattle-dealer of Ipswich.[1] He showed early intellectual promise which he followed up in the traditional way, by going to Oxford and into the Church. Taking his B.A. at fifteen, he became a fellow and then bursar of Magdalen, leaving the college—it is said—when the authorities protested at his high-handed dealings with the college funds. He continued an ordinarily successful career as chaplain to Archbishop Deane of Canterbury and Sir Richard Nanfan, deputy at Calais; in 1507 the latter's death and recommendation transferred him to the service of Henry VII who at once discovered his new chaplain's diplomatic ability. The king's death nearly wrecked a promising start, but late in 1509 Henry VIII made Wolsey almoner and a member of the council. The coming of the war gave him his opportunity. Always careful, at this time, to remain near the king and so augment his influence, he took upon himself the better part of the enormous burden of work involved in raising, equipping, dispatching, and maintaining the 30,000 or so men that Henry took to France. His zeal and ability in administration, his outstanding powers of work, and his assertive self-confidence soon made him indispensable, and from 1512 onwards he rapidly ousted all other men from Henry's confidence. Soon the council of the early years vanished. Surrey—now, as the victor of Flodden, restored to the Howard dukedom of

[1] The snobbery of the sixteenth century insisted on Wolsey's low birth and made his father a common butcher; the snobbery of the nineteenth found this unpalatable and elevated old Wolsey to the status of a 'prosperous grazier'.

Norfolk—was too old to fight the upstart, and his son (who succeeded to the title in 1524) was as yet too young to do so. In 1515 Warham resigned the chancellorship and Wolsey stepped into his shoes; in 1516 Fox retired from the privy seal to devote himself to his episcopal duties at Winchester, and Wolsey obtained the office for Thomas Ruthal, a faithful follower. From 1515 to 1529 Wolsey was not only the king's chief minister but virtually his only one. Though Henry never surrendered ultimate control over affairs, it was Wolsey who ruled. He devised the policy which Henry endorsed, and he saw that it was carried out. Henry was still only twenty-four years old in 1515; his tastes did not alter while vigour remained, and he could never be induced to devote himself consistently to business and affairs. As one of his secretaries put it, he turned the pursuit of hunting into a martyrdom, often spending all day on horseback with the few who could keep up with such prowess; but when it came to the reading of dispatches or signing of instructions, all sorts of excuses were snatched at, and exasperated secretaries often had to pursue him for days before things got attended to. Wolsey owed his advancement to his ability to take these tedious tasks from the royal shoulders; in consequence the reality of power was his—until the king should choose to assert himself.

Wolsey's rapid rise was marked by an equally rapid accumulation of preferments and offices. Dean of Lincoln in 1509, he added several other deaneries by 1513, the bishopric of Tournai in that year, and then—after a brief interlude as bishop of Lincoln—the archbishopric of York in 1514. The next year he obtained a cardinalate from Leo X and the chancellorship from Henry VIII. The only office he thereafter added was that of papal legate *a latere* (1518), which will be discussed hereafter; as far as possessions went, he acquired the abbey of St Albans and exchanged subsidiary bishoprics in succession—Bath and Wells in 1518, Durham in 1524, Winchester in 1529. These appointments were taken for their revenues—St Albans was the richest abbey in England and Winchester the wealthiest see—so as to enable him to support his inordinate love of pomp and display. Wolsey was arrogant by nature and unbelievably fond of showing off his estate, so much so that he far eclipsed even the showiness of the Tudor court and angered nobility and gentry by his intolerable pretensions. He built palaces, dressed and ate and drank lavishly, surrounded himself with a huge household, and developed great skill in adding to his income from extortions and bribes. With all his high intelligence and valour, he was vain, shallow, and greedy.

For many years the king did not mind: Henry's devotion to the favourite or confidant of the moment was invariably complete, a fact in which lies much of the secret of his success. Where he trusted he trusted without reservations; when trust ceased, it ceased at a blow. Wolsey's self-glorification only once took a turn which deserves some respect. In 1525 he began to build two colleges at Ipswich and Oxford: even here he aimed characteristically high, for he was deliberately copying the royal foundations of Eton and King's College, Cambridge. The Ipswich school was abandoned at his fall, but Cardinal College at Oxford was refounded by Henry VIII as Christ Church. It is comforting to think that that college continues to remember Wolsey rather than the king as its true benefactor.

Though he was an able administrator, Wolsey displayed surprisingly little interest in the details of the administrative machine. It was, on the whole, running well under the impetus given by Henry VII's revival of household activity, and the cardinal found it unnecessary to tamper with it. Sir John Heron held the crucial office of treasurer of the chamber until his death in 1524; he was succeeded by two experienced civil servants in Sir Henry Wyatt (1524-8) and Sir Brian Tuke (1528-45). The only change which Wolsey made arose directly out of Henry VIII's refusal to work hard at the business of government. The supervision of the 'chamber system of finance' had been in the hands of the king in person and such individuals as he entrusted with the task; now a more formal arrangement became necessary. Successive acts of parliament therefore appointed two general surveyors of crown lands who were to administer the revenues from these properties and to audit other revenue accounts. The system was still based on 'household' ideas inasmuch as the general surveyors did not preside over a proper department of state; their office existed only from one parliament to another, a new act being required in each case to continue it. Such changes as there were in the rest of the administration only reflected Wolsey's all-powerful position. Thus he controlled the royal seals, either directly or through his nominees; he caused difficulties by taking the great seal abroad with him on his diplomatic missions, and on at least one occasion improperly retained the signet which should have been with the principal secretary. Most important of all, he virtually destroyed the inner ring of the council by concentrating its powers in himself; councillors rarely knew what went on until the cardinal deigned to inform them, and—if Sir Thomas More is to be believed—the king himself was at times in a like state of ignorance.

The history of the council under Wolsey is the history of the star chamber where the cardinal presided, holding his court among the admiring sycophants before whom he displayed his talents. The king meanwhile was accompanied by his boon-companions, his fellow wrestlers and card players and dicers; though at times he complained at being left without a sufficiency of councillors, Wolsey never relaxed his determined hold on his exclusive powers.

Wolsey contemplated administrative reforms: in 1519 he drew up, at Henry's instigation, plans which would have enabled the king to take an active share in government, and in 1526 the great Ordinance of Eltham projected a thorough overhaul of the king's household establishment as well as the consolidation of a small advisory council of leading ministers. But these plans remained plans; to have made them a reality would have destroyed the basis of Wolsey's unrivalled position. Though Henry might stir in an occasional access of zeal he always returned quickly enough to his harts and hounds, to his wife and his occasional mistresses, to his cards and dice, his music and dancing; for many years the cardinal knew how to handle this king who hid behind a bluff façade and frivolous preoccupations an inflexible will and a powerful if intermittent intelligence. During Wolsey's supremacy observers as a rule underestimated his dependence on the king and took him at his own exalted valuation; the insecurity of the cardinal's position was not seen till the test came. Still, it remains true that from 1515 to 1529 Wolsey and not Henry was the effective ruler of the country.

Wolsey's greatest weakness lay in the realm of finance. He knew how to spend money to the best purpose: except in his own affairs he was not extravagant, but he was a bad financier because he could neither make do with the existing revenue nor effectively increase it. He had little understanding of economic facts. His intervention in the anti-foreign riots in London on 'Evil May Day', 1517, when a crowd of apprentices tried to kill and plunder the rich alien merchants, was prompted by his dislike of disorder rather than by any appreciation of the great part played by foreigners in the economy of England. Wolsey never grasped the importance of trade or attempted to manage and exploit it. Worst of all, his autocratic temper would not let him manage parliaments; yet he expected them to supply the means for his dizzy foreign policy. In 1513 he secured a novel tax called a subsidy, a levy of 1*s*. in the £ on income from land and wages; this, because it was based on a realistic assessment, was to remain the chief direct tax under the Tudors, though it soon lost that advantage. The next parliament (1515) had to be dismissed before it made a grant because Wolsey wished to stop its attacks on clerical privilege and administration. When war broke out again in 1522, the coffers were empty and emergency measures had to be taken. In 1522 Wolsey collected a forced loan from (it seems) the wealthy which doubled the yield of the 1514 subsidy to bring in £200,000. In 1523 he at last again confronted a parliament from which he demanded a tax of *4s.* in the £; after a stormy and prolonged session they granted *2s.* and arranged for the levy to be spread over several years. Wolsey got round this by his so-called 'anticipation': holding out promise of certain reliefs, he ordered individuals to pay their share at once. In 1524, when the cardinal tried to supplement the revenue by an arbitrary forced loan from all men owning property in land and goods, a levy which he described as an Amicable Grant, things came to a head. Collectors were still out for the loan of 1522; other commissioners were trying to obtain payment of the 1523 subsidy; and now a third lot of commissioners added their exactions. There was no prospect of the loan-money being repaid, though the subsidy of 1523 had been granted after a promise that it would be used to redeem the previous year's loans. The result might have been foreseen. Both the laity and the clergy began by muttering and ended by violently resisting the demands; in East Anglia and Kent there were signs of armed rebellion—against Wolsey, not against the king—and there was no hope at all of collecting a penny of the Amicable Grant. Only Henry's personal intervention saved the situation: he ordered the collection to cease and granted a general pardon to all who had resisted, thus proving that his common sense and political instinct could overcome even his high pride. For Henry hated giving in under pressure, especially to his own subjects. It availed Wolsey little that he pretended to have secured the remission of the grant by his own intercession; people knew who had been behind the demand, and for the first time Henry's confidence in his minister was seriously shaken.

Wolsey's taxation made enemies of many whose hostility could be dangerous. Another of his attempts to cope with economic difficulties, commendable though it may have been, was equally impolitic. He tried to solve the great problem of depopulation and enclosures, the standard complaint of contemporary moralists and amateur economists. The agrarian difficulties of the sixteenth century were caused directly by the vast inflationary movement known as the price rise which took effect soon after Henry VII's death.[1] The amount of money in circulation increased, with the result that goods became dearer. Men living on fixed incomes were in difficulties, and landlords found it necessary to increase their incomes by various practices of which enclosure for sheep-farming (wool being a profitable crop) and the raising of rents and fines on entry (rack-renting) were the most hated. Contemporaries put it all down to greed and wickedness; the search for scapegoats is ever popular in times of distress. They painted a picture of vast areas stripped of their peasantry, turned into parks for the pleasure of nobility and gentry, and exploited as sheep-runs by lords who found the market for wool more attractive than the maintenance of a stable rural society. This picture continues to be accepted, though most of the bases for it have disappeared. It is quite true that economic pressure forced many gentlemen to obtain better returns from their lands, but it is also true that the inflation profited the primary producer—the small yeoman farmer or even peasant who had a surplus to sell on a rising market, and who could thus afford to pay a higher rent for his land even if he did not much like to do so. A little inexcusable imparking took place, but the whole amount of enclosure was astonishingly small—astonishingly, that is, if one has listened to the false prophets of the day. It has been calculated that some 2 or 3 per cent. of the affected counties (mostly in the Midlands) was enclosed before 1525, and much of this enclosure—often the work of small farmers and yeomen—was designed for better farming and not for pasture at all. The main corn-growing areas remained untouched until the eighteenth century.

That there was a problem cannot and need not be denied. There was an increase in vagrancy, that is in rural unemployment, though here, too, the fact that Tudor governments tried to do something about an evil which earlier governments had ignored has served to distort the picture. There was a certain 'decay of ploughs': here and there the fusing of holdings was replacing several hovels by one homestead. Distinct from this, some towns had decayed—for instance Coventry whose industries had fallen on evil days. There was an increase in sheep-farming, but it really amounted to little more than a return to the great wool-days of the twelfth and thirteenth centuries. Since then the area under sheep had declined; now it increased again; there is every reason to suppose that the increase left the acreage of good arable land virtually undiminished. There was some raising of rents and fines, for the reasons already mentioned, and it naturally caused some

[1] For a full discussion of the price rise see below, Ch. IX.

hardship. How difficult it is to understand the truth is illustrated by the fact that some writers will speak of the decay of the yeoman at this time and others of his golden days. The agrarian revolution laid the foundations of the characteristic structure of the English countryside (landlord, tenant farmer, landless labourer) and destroyed the true land-holding peasant. But the categories developed according to circumstance and individual fate: some yeomen bettered themselves and some fell by the wayside, some gentlemen prospered and some decayed, by no means all peasants were depressed. No class rose or fell as a class; a man's fate depended on whether he succeeded in sharing the advantages which the inflation offered to the enterprising and lucky, or joined those whom rising prices and static or declining incomes were pauperising. Individual greed and stupidity might aggravate the difficulties on occasion; they certainly did not cause them.

The problem was simple at heart. After nearly two centuries of stable or declining prices, and a stable or declining population, both prices and population were now rising. Why the population rose we do not know (population changes are commonly mysterious), nor can we give figures of the increase; but that it rose is plain from many signs and symptoms. Interacting upon each other, these forces, not understood at all at the time and in any case uncontrollable, produced the familiar evils of the sixteenth-century countryside. No industries existed to absorb the surplus of money and men; the result was inflation and unemployment. It struck people with special force because the fifteenth century had been a time of depression and static conditions, thus assisting the notion that economic life in the past had always been stable. They did not know the real reasons for the change, but they saw some of the symptoms (such as enclosing and rack-renting) and argued that these must be the causes of a transformation which—since they believed in the past and held no brief for progress—they thought to be necessarily evil. Thus from the reign of Henry VII onwards, legislation was passed prohibiting enclosure and compelling the upkeep of houses and ploughs in accordance with the conditions of a vanishing age. The laws would have been futile at the best of times because they treated superficial aspects of a profound change; they were rendered merely silly by having to be enforced by the very men—the gentry as justices of the peace—whom inflation was forcing to exploit their assets or go under. Wolsey, eager to champion the poor and humble against the rich who refused to recognise him as one of themselves, determined to make the law effective. In 1517, 1518, and 1526, he appointed commissions to enquire into enclosures made since their prohibition in 1488. The returns showed a good deal of petty and a little major enclosing, but—as we have said—when properly studied they also reveal the essential falseness of the contemporary view. However, Wolsey proceeded to a spasmodic destruction of illegal enclosures; hedges were pulled down here and there, and some open fields restored. It did nothing to relieve the economic problem—naturally not, since it did not tackle that problem. The only result was to enrage the landed gentry still further against the upstart minister, while enclosing went on because, in fact, it did good to more people than it harmed. But Wolsey had succeeded in adding to his enemies.

At home, then, despite his abilities and display, Wolsey proved a singularly ill-advised minister who ruined the finances, exasperated those people whose support was essential to the monarchy, and could not translate his boundless energy into anything profitable to the commonwealth. The one exception to this sad tale lies in his judicial activities. Wolsey gloried in the majesty of a judge, and though he had no legal training that we know of he possessed a remarkable natural ability for the task. His office of lord chancellor gave him a wide sweep of judicial competence, and there are signs, though it is difficult to be sure, that he did much to establish the regular court of chancery. He certainly increased the amount of business transacted there, speeded up decisions, and enforced them by the weight of the authority he derived from his general position: he may be said to have put on a solid basis the system of equity jurisdiction which came first to supplement, then to rival, and finally to accompany the common law. Wolsey did not found the court or its principles of justice: the fifteenth century did that. Nor was he the man who classified these principles and saved them from the accidents of an individual chancellor's whim: that was not to be done until the seventeenth century. But since equity, like the common law, was to grow out of case-law—judges' decisions, that is—the fourteen years of case-law which Wolsey made and on which he impressed the features of a strong and penetrating mind were to have great influence on equity as it ultimately developed. The great chancellors-judges of the sixteenth century—Wolsey, More, Audley, Nicholas Bacon, and Ellesmere—defined and developed the principles on which the seventeenth century erected a coherent system of law.

Chancery was a court of civil jurisdiction: it handled matters of property, contract, trusts, wills, and the like, and since its decisions still depended on the chancellor's private sense of justice the law here made owed a good deal to the Roman law which was then sweeping the board in the other countries of Western Europe.[1] Things were different in the other of Wolsey's courts, the one that may be called the chancellor's court for criminal cases. This was star chamber. Sir Thomas Smith, professor of civil law at Cambridge, diplomatist, and principal secretary to Queen Elizabeth—a man who knew what he was talking about—said in his book on English government, written in 1565, that star chamber, though it began long before, 'took great augmentation and authority' under Wolsey, so much so that some even then thought him to be the inventor of that court. As has already been said, the star chamber originally derived its judicial authority from the fact that it was the king's council meeting to adjudicate upon petitions; to the end of its days, its official title remained 'the lords of the council in the star chamber at Westminster'. Wolsey revived this judicial activity which appears to have been languishing since Henry VII's death, monopolised its authority, and vastly increased its business. He used it, as Henry VII had done, to suppress the riots and disturbances raised by men who thought themselves above the law and whom he taught, as he put it, 'the law of star chamber'. By this he meant not a different kind of law but the powers of enforcement (of statutes, proclamations, and the common law) which the authority of king and council gave to star chamber. To jurisdiction in riots and violent disputes, he added perjury, libel, and forgery. These the medieval common law left to the Church courts which were by now quite incapable of making their decisions effective. It was easy for a prince of the Church to do what no layman could have done and transfer these matters to an efficient secular court. He also punished contempt of court, wherever committed, and continued to deal with false juries; thus he enlarged star chamber's capacity to supervise the whole enforcement of the law. His main achievement was to turn star chamber from a tribunal of state into a court used freely by the king's subjects in the settlement of their affairs; it was under Wolsey that it became (what it remained until its abolition) a part of the regular system of law-administration in

[1] The theory once prevailed, and is still to be found, that in the early sixteenth century the English common law was in danger of being superseded by the Roman or civil law which is more amenable to authoritarian interpretation; this view has, however, been disproved (cf. W. S. Holdsworth, *History of English Law*, iv. 217-83, and below, p. 169). Chancery was saved from Romanisation by the fact that Wolsey's successors, from Sir Thomas More onwards, were as a rule common lawyers.

England. Probably we must not yet speak of a court of star chamber as a separate institution,[1] but Wolsey's work there certainly prepared the ground for just such a development. He left the distinction between the council in star chamber and the court of star chamber in so shadowy a state that modern scholars have been much confused.

Not content with so wide and effective an application of conciliar jurisdiction, Wolsey attempted further to draw all legal business within his orbit; if the common law was ever in danger it was during the cardinal's ascendancy, though the danger was never very serious. That protean institution, the court of requests for poor men's causes, revived together with the council's activity in star chamber; it became subject to Wolsey's machinations when the chancellor tried to extend his powers by commissions. In 1518 he established four conciliar committees to do what was in fact requests' work: they heard poor men's suits concerning civil disputes. Of these four only the committee in the White Hall survived into the 1530s; this became the court of requests proper. Throughout his ascendancy, Wolsey issued commissions to hear individual cases, a common conciliar practice which, however, in Wolsey's generous hands seriously encroached on the business of the common-law courts. In 1524-5 he attempted a general delegation by commission. Cases in the north and in the marches of Wales were committed to the councils there; fresh commissions to individuals issued to relieve pressure at the centre; even the council of the duchy of Lancaster was to be employed more fully in general litigation. The truth was that Wolsey had overreached himself. He had encouraged people to bring their suits to him, and he had found them respond only too readily. There is a familiar story that he announced his willingness to give justice to poor men and then had to change his mind in disgust when he discovered that he was being imposed upon with a flood of unjust claims. True or not, the tale reflects the position: Wolsey had to give up trying to concentrate all justice in his person, as he would have liked to do. He virtually admitted defeat when in 1528 he ordered all minor matters brought before star chamber to be heard on assize; the common law could not be dispensed with.

However, though according to his habit Wolsey cherished plans beyond his or any man's capacity, he did much good and praiseworthy work in his judicial employments, and it was work that endured. He put the court of chancery on a solid foundation and made the fortunes of star chamber; he endeavoured, with

[1] Cf. below, p. 184.

much success, to enforce the law on people who thought themselves free of it; and he gave good justice to all men, many of them weak and poor, who brought their suits before him. The common lawyers, of course, hated him as a rival, and he gained no popularity with the nobles and gentlemen whom he humbled before the law, but it seems that with the poor and the generality this part of his work gained him some credit. It was unfortunate, from his point of view, that the friends thus made were generally weak and without influence, while those he added to his enemies were powerful and dangerous.

3. WOLSEY AND THE CHURCH

As chancellor, Wolsey dominated the state; in the Church he ruled as cardinal and legate. Wolsey's ambitions always reached for the highest goal, and throughout his life he never lost hope of one day being pope. That hope had no reality outside his own mind: the circumstances of European and Italian politics rendered the election of an Englishman quite out of the question. Failure to reach the heights left Wolsey with only the smaller field of England in which to exercise his power and his love of autocracy, but what he lost in scope he made up for in intensity. The first thing to understand about the English Church in the middle ages is that it never existed. There was no one authority in ecclesiastical affairs co-terminous with the king's in secular affairs. Instead, there were only two provinces of the Universal Church—the provinces of Canterbury and York. Each was quite independent of the other; each had its own organisation and its own convocation; the only link between them was their common allegiance and subjection to the papacy at Rome. Naturally, this rigid division could not in practice be maintained in face of a secular organisation which comprehended both provinces. That of Canterbury was much larger and its archbishop the senior of the two; some aspects of their relations with each other were determined by common allegiance and subjection to the crown in temporal matters. The situation was complex and unresolved, giving rise to much bickering and rivalry between the two archbishops. Some ecclesiastical bodies in England—especially many monasteries—were exempt from all episcopal and archiepiscopal authority and came directly under Rome. No priest, of whatever rank, could claim to be in charge of all the clergy in England—except the pope whose authority was distant and foreign. On the other hand, the Church, with its hierarchical organisation, offered a better chance to an autocrat than did the state with its parliaments and franchises; Wolsey, who delighted in personal power, could hardly be expected to forego it in a sphere to which his profession drew him as strongly as his tastes drew him to secular politics.

It would have been something to have obtained the highest ecclesiastical honour in England, but here fate was against him. When Cardinal Bainbridge died at Rome in 1514—of poison, it was said, but then every cardinal's death was at this time followed by that rumour—Wolsey immediately obtained his see of York and a year later the cardinalate. But the road to Canterbury was blocked by Warham who, though born about 1450 and therefore due to die in an age when sixty years were a respectable limit to a man's life, in the end outlived Wolsey. But for this accident it is likely that Wolsey would have added Canterbury to York and thus created an unprecedented unification of the English Church by means of existing offices. Instead he was forced to resort to methods which involved him in objectionable innovation, conflict with the English clergy, uncalled-for dependence on papal authority, and ultimately the king's deadly displeasure. He decided to have himself made a permanent papal legate *a latere*. Papal legates had always been of two kinds. Every archbishop was a *legatus natus*, exercising certain aspects of his authority by grant from Rome. In addition, the pope could send envoys with specific powers on separate occasions; these *legati a latere* might be no more than ambassadors, or they might be sent with a commission superseding for a time all other ecclesiastical authority in the region affected. Wolsey turned the occasional expedient into regular practice and used an office ordinarily confined to genuine envoys from Rome to make himself the permanently resident ruler of the Church in England. His powers were circumscribed by the bulls granting them, and he was always, from the first grant of the legacy in 1518, appealing for renewals and extensions; but the limitations proved theoretical only, for pressure at Rome secured a steady enlargement of scope and, in 1524, a grant for life. His legateship made Wolsey what no one had ever been before: the ecclesiastical ruler of the two provinces of the Church which between them covered the realm of England.

The ostensible purpose behind his demands was his desire to reform the Church. Church reform was very much in the air at this time; many, both churchmen and laymen, admitted that there were things in the conduct of individual priests and the state of the monasteries that needed attention. Wolsey himself was very free with pronouncements and promises on that score. Unfortunately, however, it would have been difficult to find a better example of most of the glaring abuses in the Church than the cardinal himself. He exemplified pluralism at its worst: he always held at least one other bishopric in addition to York, and—most improperly of all—he, a secular priest, was abbot of St Albans. No one could have excelled him in non-residence: he never visited the seats of any of his sees, and until his fall he never attempted to deal with their affairs. As for simony, his income from improper bribes and patronage was large and notorious. No priest was richer or displayed the fact more proudly. Celibacy sat lightly on the man who had probably several daughters and certainly one son whom he promoted rapidly to some valuable benefices in his extreme youth (nepotism and the ordination of minors). This was the would-be reformer of clerical morals and affairs. His plans were considerable. He wished to dissolve decayed monasteries and to found new bishoprics which were badly needed; he wished to throw his whole power and energy into a campaign for the reform of abuses. Out of these dreams came nothing but the dissolution of a few small houses whose property he employed in the founding of his colleges. We need not think that he never meant to do the things he so freely talked about, but apart from his personal unsuitability there was also the fact that Wolsey never knew how to confine himself to the possible. He tried to do the work of ten men and not surprisingly failed. Foreign affairs and star chamber came first; Church reform very definitely last.

In any case, he had in mind a more clearly defined purpose for his legateship. It enabled him to exercise a supreme authority over the Church in England, and this he intended to exploit. With vigour and success he superseded the powers of others—abbots, bishops, archbishops, and convocation. His agents carried out visitations of some small monasteries, reported unfavourably, and dissolved them—altogether an admirable training for the later wholesale destruction which was to be managed by Thomas Cromwell, Wolsey's chief instrument in these matters. His attack on the liberties and independence of the episcopal bench went much further still. He permitted long vacancies on the deaths of bishops, reserving the profits to himself. He encouraged the appointment of foreigners who never visited their titular sees or took care of their charges; Wolsey then paid them a fixed stipend and administered the temporalities to his own advantage. When he fell, five English bishoprics were in foreign hands, and the effective number of bishops was thus seriously reduced. Over those that remained, the cardinal-legate exercised almost despotic powers. He interfered in the administration of sees. He drew cases from episcopal courts to his own legatine court, thus reducing the bishops to cyphers. He compelled some bishops to enter into contracts by which they made over part of their revenues to him. Even Canterbury fell before the onslaught. As early as 1519, Warham had occasion to complain of interference by Wolsey's commissioners, and a long drawn out quarrel over Canterbury's traditional rights in matters of probate ended in the legate's victory. It was proper and usual for a legate *a latere* to supersede a *legatus natus* (which Warham was), but Wolsey's legacy was unprecedented in being permanent, and his claim therefore threatened to extinguish all lawful episcopal jurisdiction except his own. Nor can he be said to have acted in the interests of reform or good practice. His sense of justice and delight in legal matters may have resulted in occasional advantages to litigants, but his greed was more to the fore. Especially obnoxious were the heavy exactions he made on probate of wills, the more so since these affected the laity. But the clergy, too, had no love for the all-powerful cardinal. Though he ought to have been their natural protector and representative, he seemed more like a destroyer; eager as he was to concentrate power over the Church in his own hand, he overrode all other authority and made himself more enemies. Never had the Church been so little able to order its own affairs. The two provincial convocations ceased to meet, except at parliament time when they were treated even more haughtily and mulcted more heavily than their secular counterpart. Wolsey's legatine council, ostensibly designed to represent the English Church, was a fictitious body which never met. He simply took all power to himself and governed as a despot.

The consequences of this energetic but misguided policy were seen at Wolsey's fall. The cardinal, prince of the Church though he was and equipped with the most far-reaching powers for reform, did only two things for the Church. He lessened its allegiance to Rome and weakened it past hope of recovery. Wolsey's legatine powers were papal; the hatred excited by their exercise reflected on the pope. An authority which was tolerable in a pope too weak in his own troubles and at so great a distance to make it felt became quite insupportable when wielded by the restless, interfering, forceful, and tactless cardinal. Wolsey's activities left many clergy, especially in the higher ranks, with the feeling that if subjection to Rome involved such interference with established rights and such heavy and constant demands for money there was little to be said for it. When the attack on the Church came after Wolsey's fall, resistance was in part weakened by the thought that the king's rule could not be worse—must indeed be lighter—than papal rule as exemplified by the pope's legate. By the time the Church realised its mistake the matter was beyond remedy. Furthermore, by accumulating the Church's powers and jurisdiction in himself, Wolsey bound the fate of the Roman Church in England to the fate of Rome's legate; the legate's fall dragged down the legate's superior. Lastly, a bench of bishops weakened in numbers and authority, united only in hatred of Wolsey but kept by him from all corporate action for some twelve years, was in no condition to lead opposition to the king's demands.[1] In one way and another, therefore, Wolsey dug the grave of the institution from which he derived his own greatest glory. Creditably enough, he did not try to build up support among the clergy in face of the hostility which he excited among the nobility and gentry, but it was surely overweening folly that insisted on adding the bishops to his most virulent enemies.

4. WOLSEY'S FOREIGN POLICY

It may be thought that the picture painted here is getting a little too dark. After all, Wolsey was a man of great mental powers, enormous application and assiduity in business, a wide grasp and firm intentions. Yet, with the exception of his judicial activities, nothing has so far been found in his work that can be called successful or deserves praise on other grounds; indeed, all his doings were attended by folly, arrogance, false aims, and final failure. However, it still remains to discuss that part of his work for which he is primarily remembered: his foreign policy. We must therefore go back to the beginning of his career as chief minister and take up the tale where we left it, at the victorious conclusion of the French war in 1514. For fifteen years Wolsey occupied himself with the details and the greater conception of diplomacy, but there has been much doubt about his purpose. At one time it was usual to credit him with the invention of the so-called balance of power. However, as has been pointed out repeatedly, the policy which tries to prevent any one power from becoming too great by forming alliances with its potential enemies is too obvious to be 'invented' by any statesman; moreover, it is

[1] It is a curious and significant fact that among the clergy whose opposition Wolsey had to combat there were some who later offered equally strong resistance to the crown, as for instance Bishop Fisher and Rowland Phillips, vicar of Croydon.

plain that Wolsey did not always pursue it, often allying himself with the stronger power. Bishop Creighton thought he was inspired by the highest patriotism—that he wished to dominate Europe in the interests of England and give England the leadership on the European stage. It is difficult to see why one should praise a goal which was not only not achieved but at the time was manifestly impossible of achievement; but then Creighton, influenced by his (the late Victorian) age, seems to have thought of Wolsey as an earlier and better Bismarck. A. F. Pollard, whose assessment is not only the most recent but also the coolest and best supported, concluded that Wolsey's main principle in foreign policy was to serve the interests of the papacy whose great servant he was and to which he always hoped to succeed. Wolsey was not an anachronistic English patriot, but the true late-medieval Churchman, deriving his glory from Rome and creditably enough convinced that Rome had a claim on his services.

In 1514, the French war ended with a treaty which marked a notable victory for England. But on the last day of that year, Louis XII died, and with him died the marriage alliance which had given reality to the treaty. Henry and Wolsey immediately planned to give the widow to the new French king, Francis I, but the 'French Queen' (as she was known till her death in 1533) put a spoke in that wheel by secretly marrying Charles Brandon, duke of Suffolk, Henry's personal friend and her own previous choice before she had been forced into the French match. For a time the young couple were in danger of death from Henry's fury, but in the end the king was content with exacting money. Wolsey always claimed that his intercession had saved Suffolk, but there is nothing except his unreliable word to support this, and Henry may well have felt merciful towards his favourite sister and his special friend. In any case, no prospect of Mary Tudor's hand could have stopped Francis I from a course of action that was highly displeasing to England. He was young, active, vigorously athletic, and vainglorious—that is, he had all the qualities of the young Henry VIII himself; the king of England soon felt violently jealous of this younger man who supplanted him in the adulation of men. His own temper, if not the interest of his country, drove Francis to renew the Italian wars, and so he set about pacifying his northern border while engaged in the south. A treaty with the young Archduke Charles of Burgundy removed all threat from that quarter; as for England, Francis was not content with renewing his predecessor's treaty of alliance but made sure by sending the Scottish claimant, the duke of Albany, to stir up trouble in

England's northern neighbour. Albany was fully successful: he overthrew the government of the regent, Henry's sister Margaret, who fled to England with her second husband, the earl of Angus, and Henry—breathing fire—thought seriously of restoring her by force of arms. In the meantime, Francis crossed the Alps and won the great victory of Marignano against the Swiss and Milanese (September 1515); at one stroke all the north of Italy was French again and Rome itself under the French shadow.

Marignano annoyed Henry intensely: it wiped out the memories of his own petty triumphs and displayed Francis as Europe's first knight and conqueror. But there was little England could do about it. The country had not yet recovered from the earlier war, and the parliament of 1515 would vote only enough supplies to make up for the fact that the previous grants had never been collected in full. Yet there was an even more compelling reason for intervention than Henry's jealousy of Francis and his resentment at events in Scotland. Marignano and its consequences threatened to turn the papacy into a French chaplaincy, and Wolsey—with his eye ever fixed upon attaining the see of Rome himself—could not permit a situation which destroyed his hopes. Leo X himself, wishing to be free of French predominance, played the papal game of restoring the balance of power in Italy; on this occasion Wolsey's policy of following the papacy and preserving it intact for himself led him to fight for the European balance. The means he adopted were feeble: unable to start a war, the cardinal tried to use the Swiss and the Emperor Maximilian by paying them secret subsidies. This policy, for which Wolsey took all the credit and which, it seems, led to the retirement from the council of Warham and Fox, proved a failure when Maximilian took the money but no action. Wolsey then tried to build up an alliance against France, with Rome, Venice, Spain, and the Empire. Here fate intervened, for in January 1516 Ferdinand died, and the concert of Europe began to look very different. Of the men who had directed affairs in the 1490's only Maximilian remained, and he was old and ever ineffectual.

Ferdinand was succeeded by the Archduke Charles, then in his Flemish dominions but aware that he would have to visit Spain in person to assure his inheritance. Since for the moment neither he nor Francis wanted trouble, they had no difficulty in coming to terms at Noyon (1516). Francis renounced his claim to Naples, while Charles promised to restore Navarre and marry the infant princess of France. Wolsey tried hard to prevent Maximilian from acceding to this treaty, throwing further good money after the bad already wasted on the insatiable emperor, but in 1517 Maximilian joined his grandson in the French alliance, with a comment that remains worth quoting although it is so well known. 'Mon fils,' said the veteran of a dozen betrayals, 'vous allez tromper les Français, et moi je vais tromper les Anglais.' It was an adequate summing-up of the situation. Wolsey's policy had failed all along the line. France was secure in Italy, Noyon seemed to make certain that the balance there between her and Spain would stay stable, the pope himself was tired of wars and negotiations, England had been treated with scarcely concealed contempt.

A dozen years later this sort of failure was to cost Wolsey the king's favour, but in 1517 he had another chance. Charles had no sooner got safely to Spain than he began to feel his way towards breaking the treaty. It became obvious to Francis that the amity with Spain would not endure, and he was only too glad to seek an alliance of which Wolsey, like Leo X, held out hopes. Albany, who had incautiously returned to France, was detained there as a friendly gesture towards England. But Charles, too, had cause to woo England who thus, so recently ignored and isolated, found herself the object of solicitations from both France and Spain. The negotiations were prolonged; but in October 1518 Wolsey celebrated his great triumph in the treaty of London, a compact of universal Christian peace in which the pope, the emperor, Spain, France, and England bound themselves in common action against the Turk. Throughout Wolsey had taken every opportunity to display his master's power and his own glory. The papal envoy, Cardinal Campeggio, was kept waiting for months at Calais, until Wolsey received his own commission as legate *a latere*, and the summer and autumn were full of feasting and display. But there was some cause for congratulation: in the material sphere, the tiresome conquest of Tournai was given up in return for large annual payments to the king and to Wolsey himself;[1] in the matter of prestige, Wolsey made London the centre of Europe, his king its foremost prince, and himself its arbiter.

However, gorgeous though it all appeared, it was but illusion with nothing solid behind it. The conference had hardly broken up before yet another diplomatic edifice crumbled into nothing. In October 1518 something like a concert of Europe was engineered by Wolsey; in January 1519, the death of the emperor Maximilian was enough to shatter these dreams and entirely recast the state-system of Europe. The election, on which Francis I spent vast

[1] By a separate treaty with France, concluded a few days after the treaty of London.

sums in bootless bribes while even Henry VIII toyed for a time with the idea of standing, resulted in the elevation of the obvious candidate, Charles of Spain and Burgundy, grandson of the late emperor, and hereafter the emperor Charles V. The conflict between Habsburg and Valois now stood out stark and unencumbered by other considerations. France, apparently weaker and encircled but—as events were to prove—fully a match for her rival, faced the vast but heterogeneous and troubled empire of Charles. While there had been more counters to move about, Wolsey could play the game of exercising influence from outside; after 1519 England was really out of her class in this contest of heavyweights. Unfortunately for himself, Wolsey failed to realise how circumstances had changed: his own skill and delight in diplomatic manœuvres, his attachment to Rome and persistent hope of becoming pope, and the vanity which prevented him from understanding the true state of affairs kept England in the running. Vital tasks at home were neglected: Irish pacification, administrative reform, financial recovery were all planned in 1519, and all had to be shelved until the cardinal had time to spare from foreign affairs—which in the end proved to be never. Trade was interrupted and the country unsettled by the wars and rumours of wars in which Wolsey's activities resulted. Most telling of all, even in the narrow field of foreign affairs itself there is nothing to record but failure. From the triumph of 1518, Wolsey's influence in Europe declined steadily; bolstered at first by reputation and by the needs of Charles V, it collapsed ruinously after 1525.

From 1519 onwards all diplomacy was governed by the impending struggle between Francis I and Charles V. While the Turks advanced into Europe, conquering Rhodes (1522) and Hungary (1526), and threatening Vienna (1529), eyes in the West remained fixed on the battlefields of Italy and Northern France. This is no place to enter into the reasons for the conflict; suffice it to say that everybody expected it, and that it came in 1520 when French satellites attacked Spanish territory. Both sides had cause to wish England friendly or at least neutral, and as usual it was the imperial interest which stood the better chance. Partly there was the ancient hostility to France and the commercial link with Flanders, partly the policy of a pope (Leo X) who continued to resent the French ascendancy in Northern Italy, partly Wolsey's hopes of being elected pope with imperial support as soon as the declining Leo should die. But before the Anglo-Spanish alliance could be renewed and bear fruit, there were some displays to get through. In 1518 Henry and Francis had arranged to meet, and in the summer of 1520 the arrangement took effect in the joustings and festivities of the famous pageantry of the Field of Cloth of Gold, held near Calais but in French territory. The sovereigns' amity was troubled not only by unexorcisable suspicions, but also by the fact that Charles V had previously paid a visit to England, to make sure that the meeting should not result in hostility to himself; as soon as the Field dispersed, Henry and Charles met once more on Burgundian soil. In July 1521, Wolsey arranged a conference at Calais, to arbitrate between France and Spain, but this sounded better than it was. Though the very appearance of acting as umpire gratified Wolsey deeply, he was in fact already committed to the imperial cause, and late in the year a treaty of alliance and for common war against France was signed with Charles V. Soon after, Leo X died, but neither then nor two years later on the occasion of another vacancy did Wolsey achieve his great ambition. His very energy, his comparative youth, his English birth and allegiance, made him an impossible candidate to the largely Italian cardinals; and whatever Charles V might promise in the worthy cause of tricking Wolsey, he had at his disposal more convenient candidates for the papal throne.

Thus in 1522 England stood committed to a war in which her interests were not involved, while her ally intended to use her for his own concerns only. Trouble immediately appeared on the northern border. Albany, once again unleashed upon Scotland, renewed the attack; prevailed upon to observe a truce when no defence of the marches was possible, he let slip his opportunity through sheer ineptitude. In 1524 he sailed for France, never to trouble Scotland or England more, but the English escape was due entirely to Albany's incompetence and the skill of Lord Dacre, warden of the west march. It owed nothing to Henry or Wolsey who had left the north unprotected in their rash concentration on war in France. As for this war, the activities of the earl of Surrey, who ravaged Normandy and Picardy in a campaign in 1522 without retaining a foot of land on his return to Calais, and a futile expedition by Suffolk in 1523 which was supposed to be part of a general assault from all sides, amounted to the whole English contribution. There was no enthusiasm in the country, as there had been ten years earlier, the more so because this time there was no inherited treasure to spend and the government attempted to extract heavy taxation. Wolsey's expedients in these years have already been discussed. The parliament of 1523 sat for over four months—a very long spell indeed—and spent nearly all that time in refusing Wolsey's demands—despite all that the

Speaker, Sir Thomas More, could do, despite an ill-judged personal intervention on the cardinal's part, and despite the ordinarily attractive prospect of a French war and reconquest. The commons' stubbornness induced Wolsey unfairly to curse the day he had jockeyed More into the speakership, and next year to attempt the expedient of the Amicable Grant with its dire consequences. The war was paying impressive dividends. Apart from the customary protestations of poverty the commons even dared attack the general purpose of Wolsey's policy. A speech reliably ascribed to Thomas Cromwell, which may or may not have been delivered, passed the whole policy of French war and domestic neglect under a reasoned and—with all its courteous language—devastating review. This, together with Cromwell's own report that in this parliament the commons discussed among other things peace and war and the reform of the realm, is good proof that in the reign of Henry VIII the lower house freely debated things which later governments tried to withhold from it.

The war conferred thus neither glory nor material advantage upon England, and it threatened the king with a resistance from his subjects not seen since Henry VII defeated Lambert Simnel. The murmurs of 1523 were a roar in 1524, and Henry's calling off of the Amicable Grant left him without means to play his part in the alliance. It was reserved to the year 1525 to show up Wolsey's false foreign policy in the field of foreign affairs itself. In February that year, imperial arms won the overwhelming victory of Pavia: the French army was destroyed, the French king taken prisoner, and Italy—and, it might seem, all Europe—passed under the ascendancy of Charles V. In the long run Charles's victory destroyed Wolsey's policy and ultimately Wolsey himself. At first, indeed, the cardinal saw no reason why England should not profit greatly from her ally's triumph: he suggested an immediate invasion of France, and Henry VIII seems to have dreamt of reviving his claims to the French crown. However, despite his victory, Charles—short of money with which to pay even the army of Pavia—was in no position for such enterprises; he remembered Wolsey's dubious dealing after the failure of the projected invasions of 1523 and felt no duty to cut his partner in on his gains. Turning away from the northern theatre he concentrated on Italy, while Wolsey for his part began seriously to contemplate the advantages of coming to terms with France. There ensued something like a diplomatic revolution. In August 1525 Wolsey concluded a treaty with France who was forced to buy peace by greatly increasing the pensions she paid to both Henry and the cardinal; further negotiations resulted in the treaty of Cognac (May 1526) in which England, France, and several Italian states agreed to oppose Charles's dominance in the peninsula.

It is on this change of front that Wolsey's reputation as protector of the balance of power chiefly rests; up to then he had commonly supported Spain and the emperor, even when they were manifestly stronger. But in 1526, too, he was not especially concerned with attempting to redress the balance upset by Pavia. In part he followed self-interest: the imperial alliance lost much of its attraction when it failed to give Wolsey the papacy and to yield the pensions which could always be obtained from France. The rebuff which his plans received in 1525 played a powerful part: there was much personal animosity between Wolsey and the emperor. Certainly he had first tried to tilt the balance still further against France; it was Charles's refusal or inability to comply that changed the cardinal's mind. Probably the most powerful inducement, however, was the example of the pope. Clement VII wanted peace on two counts: he, alone of all the rulers, remembered the Turkish menace, and he more than anyone else dreaded the predominance of one power in Italy. Clement's advice and guidance led to the League of Cognac, and Wolsey once again showed himself a consistent follower of the papacy. Though in throwing over the emperor and embracing the cause of defeated France he may in fact have acted in agreement with some principle of preventing the ascendancy of one great power, there is no sign that this consideration weighed with him. Personal grievances, particular causes, and the diplomacy of Rome were instrumental in producing the new alignment. From England's point of view it was disastrous, as might be expected from a policy shaped to the needs and interests of an Italian power. The country's attitude to foreign affairs was dominated by two factors, one emotional—hatred of France—and one realistic—the imperial alliance protecting the vital cloth trade with Spain and the Low Countries. Wolsey was soon to discover how lamentably he had blundered. The League of Cognac achieved nothing; so far from moderating his policy in Italy, Charles V was driven further in 1527 when his mutinous armies, eager for pay, loot, and—some say—Lutheranism, seized and sacked Rome itself. The event burst upon Europe with devastating effect: that Rome should be treated like any conquered city was shattering enough, but the special extent and savagery of the sack made a lasting impression.

The balance of power was now properly upset, and the old fears of the papacy were at last realised. Clement VII, a prisoner in imperial hands, lost control of the destinies of Italy and of the fortunes of the Church everywhere. Wolsey had three good reasons for trying to rescue the pope. The league of 1526 bound him to an anti-imperial policy; he genuinely and passionately resented the fate of the papacy from which he derived his most cherished powers; and—most pressing of all—things had happened at home which made it essential that Clement should be delivered out of Charles V's hands as quickly as possible. In 1527, the king's private and matrimonial life had reached a crisis; the next six years were dominated by his desire to divorce his first wife, Catherine of Aragon. Catherine was the emperor's aunt, and the pope alone was competent to pronounce the marriage void: it was most unfortunate for Henry, tragic for Wolsey, and fatal to the papacy in England that events in Italy had produced conditions which made a straightforward solution of Henry's troubles impossible. Thus Wolsey threw himself into the rescue of the pope. He failed to find support for a desperate plan to establish a deputy-papacy under himself on French soil during Clement's captivity. Only four cardinals obeyed his call, and Charles permitted Clement to escape to Orvieto, a move which continued his virtual subjection to the emperor without justifying action based on the view that he was a prisoner. Nothing but war remained, and this Wolsey declared in January 1528. It was a useless step: the country refused to fight, and threats against the cardinal mingled with complaints of interrupted trade. Nor did it avail Wolsey's personal position that he arranged a local truce which allowed the cloth trade to continue while the sovereigns were at war. For a time, French successes in Italy bolstered up Wolsey's hopes, but Charles's victory at Landriano (in June 1529) settled the question. Clement VII, in whose interest Wolsey had gone to war, resigned himself to the inevitable and came to terms with the emperor, and in August 1529 the final blow fell. Without consulting or informing Wolsey, France and Spain signed the peace of Cambrai which left Charles dominant in Italy and England isolated.

Wolsey took his fate hard. He refused to believe the news of Cambrai, for he knew well enough what it meant for him; he could not think that Europe should have acted without its arbiter. He had spent two desperate years trying to get Henry his divorce; his own fate, as he was fully aware, depended entirely on his being able to do so. Reluctantly and wondering, but still—after so many years and apparent successes—relying on him, the king had followed his minister's manœuvres. Wolsey's promised success depended on the French alliance and the ultimate defeat of the emperor; it depended on the impossibility of agreement between France and Spain. Cambrai shattered the dream, and—since the parties to the peace completely ignored the cardinal and his high opinion of his place in their counsels—it shattered it in a specially brutal manner. Two months after the complete failure of his foreign policy Wolsey had fallen from his high power. It is time to turn to the circumstances which tied his personal fate so closely to the rivalries of France and Spain.

Chapter V

THE KING'S GREAT MATTER

1. THE ORIGINS OF THE DIVORCE

WHEN Henry VIII, a few months after his accession, married Catherine of Aragon, he married his brother's widow: in the momentous story of Henry's first divorce this is almost the only statement one can make without fear of contradiction from some quarter. Catherine's previous marriage had put her into a prohibited degree of relationship with her second husband, and the contracting parties had therefore obtained a dispensation from Pope Julius II. Since this original dispensation was so badly phrased as to leave room for much doubt, Julius allegedly satisfied further questions from Spain with an additional letter or brief in which he resolved the doubtful points. The dispensation was not nearly so matter of course as is sometimes assumed; it was a difficult point of theology and canon law whether the pope could in fact dispense in this particular case. For the authority of Holy Writ was involved: Henry's marriage contravened Leviticus xx. 21, which verse declared that a man who marries his brother's widow shall be childless.[1] It is, however, likely that the papal dispensation would never have been questioned but for the events that followed.

The marriage seems to have been a happy one in the early years, but a sad blight rested upon its children. One after another they were still-born or died within a few days of birth; the queen had several miscarriages; and by 1525, when all hope of further issue had to be given up (Catherine was by then forty and there had been no pregnancy for seven years), Henry's sole heir was a girl, Mary, born in 1516. The Tudor stock was always unhealthy and childbed invariably dangerous in the sixteenth century; but it is not surprising that an amateur theologian and fervent formal Christian like Henry VIII should have remembered the curse in Leviticus. Nor did the doubts arise suddenly. Henry had registered

[1] On an unbiased interpretation the verse appears rather to refer to a man's adultery with his sister-in-law; the verse really applicable to Henry's case is Deuteronomy xxv. 5 which orders a man to marry his brother's widow if she is childless. However, the canonical prohibition against a man so marrying rests on Leviticus (though the Jewish law adheres to Deuteronomy), and Henry therefore had a case in canon law.

a politic protest as early as 1505 when his father wanted to retain a chance of repudiating the marriage; this had never been altogether forgotten. Catherine was the visible sign of the Anglo-Spanish alliance with which her personal fortunes were always bound up. In the later years of Henry VII she had a very miserable time indeed while her father and father-in-law haggled over her second marriage, and in 1514, when Henry VIII fell out with Ferdinand, he vented his anger on his wife, good husband to her though he commonly was. As early as this, rumours began to circulate that the king was thinking of divorcing the queen.[1] These rumours came to nothing, but as the years passed two things combined to revive the king's early doubts about the validity of his marriage. One was the interest of the realm—the danger of a disputed succession; the other Henry's own concupiscence—his falling in love with Anne Boleyn. Which of the two played the greater part in settling his determination is a fascinating problem, often debated, but really insoluble. Nor, in the last resort, does it greatly matter, except that with the divorce, and the Reformation that ensued upon it, we enter a field where 400 years after the event historians' passions are still far from spent.[2]

Fear of succession troubles was ingrained in sixteenth-century England: nation as well as statesmen never forgot the history of the wars of the Roses. How this question affected Henry VII's foreign policy has already been seen. Now it came to plague his

[1] This is the place to dispose of one point. We are often told that no divorce was involved since no such thing exists in canon law, and that one should speak of nullity—for what Henry always claimed was that his marriage had been unlawful and therefore void from the first. That is a perfectly accurate description of the law, but the matter was called a divorce by contemporaries simply because they could declare a marriage fully dissolved only if it had never properly taken place, and—provided the implications are understood—it is quite proper to retain the shorter and traditional term.

[2] It is as well to know where to find the more reputable versions of the different points of view. The Roman Catholic point of view appears moderately in John Lingard's *History of England* (1819-30), with a great deal of partisanship and error in F. A. Gasquet's *Henry VIII and the Monasteries* (1888) and *The Eve of the Reformation* (1900), and judiciously in P. Hughes' *The Reformation in England* (1950). High Anglicanism finds expression in R. W. Dixon's *History of the Church of England* (1878-1902) and briefly in J. Gairdner's *English Church in the Sixteenth Century* (1902). The Protestant interpretation in its extreme form is still best read in J. A. Froude's *History of England* (1862-70); more temperately Protestant is A. F. Pollard's *Henry VIII* (1902). It is fair to say that no full-scale review of the evidence has ever been made by anyone free from evident religious bias, nor has there been a modern appraisal (in the last fifty years) except Dr Hughes'.

son: it looked as though the safety of the Tudor throne, and with it the tranquillity of the country, depended on the life of one girl. These uncertainties accounted, in 1521, for the execution of Edmund Stafford, duke of Buckingham, on a dubious charge of treason; it was probably Buckingham's descent from Edward III's youngest son and his arrogance in displaying the fact, rather than Wolsey's hatred of the disdainful duke, that led to his death. The same fears also promoted to public place Henry's illegitimate son, Henry Fitzroy (born in 1519), who in 1525 was made duke of Richmond and given offices which recalled his father's early distinctions. When the divorce got under way there were even suggestions from Rome that Richmond should marry his half-sister Mary and thus clarify the succession; but Henry—always rather a simple man in matters of morality—drew the line at that.

This policy, which could hope to put a Tudor bastard on the English throne, indicates how desperate the position looked to the king. Even if Mary survived (and who could be sure of that?) it would only mean the accession of a female sovereign, for which undesirable event the sole dubious precedent lay in the unsuccessful attempt to seize the throne by Henry I's daughter Matilda (in the twelfth century). That had meant civil war; there was little hope of better things when men still alive had assisted in wars for the crown, and when a queen regnant was bound to raise a whole crop of questions connected both with her right and power to rule, and with her own subsequent marriage. As we shall see, Mary's reign later bore out all these fears; we find them less comprehensible only because we know in how daring a manner Elizabeth I disproved them. Considering solely the interests of his dynasty and his nation, Henry VIII had reason to wish to end a marriage from which no further issue could be expected. But the problem did not appear in such straightforward terms either to the king himself or to onlookers then or since. Some time between 1525 and 1527 Henry fell violently in love with one of the ladies at court, Anne, daughter of the courtier and minister Sir Thomas Boleyn and sister to one of Henry's earlier mistresses. His infatuation is fully attested by the famous love-letters which he laboriously wrote in his own hand; it is also a little difficult to understand, both from her portraits and from contemporary descriptions. Historians, who like to rationalise, speak learnedly and a little absurdly of Anne's French ways (she was brought up at the dissolute court of France) and her skilful use of the great eyes which seem to have been her chief attraction. But perhaps there is little mystery in the passion for a lively girl of a man of thirty-five whose wife had grown old and ugly with confinements and disappointments and was moreover displaying a growing addiction to Spanish piety.

Be that as it may, Henry determined to win Anne, and the shock which this first appearance of his inflexible will must have occasioned may well be imagined when it is remembered that most people then thought the king a mere cypher behind the overpowering cardinal—a mistake into which Wolsey himself fell at times, to his destruction. It is alleged that Anne played her royal lover skilfully, for she wanted the crown and not the status of a mistress. Perhaps she did: certainly the allegations of enemies that Henry overcame her resistance as early as 1529 deserve no credit. But the decisive point was that nothing short of marriage would do for the king who wanted a legitimate heir to the throne. Thus by the beginning of 1527 the stage was set. Old doubts reinforced by the deaths of his children led Henry to question the validity of his marriage; the problem of the succession intervened to represent the matter as urgent; and Anne Boleyn was there to inflame a naturally imperious temper to volcanic heat. It all fused in the king's conscientious scruples. For Henry did not argue the matter out: he was convinced in his conscience that his marriage to Catherine had been a great sin. Henry's conscience is, indeed, the clue to the whole affair. Extreme and uncompromising egoist that he was, he possessed to perfection that most dangerous weapon—a complete conviction of his own rightness. When Henry told the cardinal, the pope, and the world that his conscience was violently troubled by the illegality of his marriage he was not being hypocritical. He did not, in his heart, admit that he wished to see the succession settled or to get him a new and more attractive wife, but he genuinely knew that his life with Catherine was a sin. Therein lay his strength: it was this unshakable conviction into which all the arguments of policy and passion had been transformed by the forces of his self-centred nature that carried him through the setbacks of six tiresome years, through the break with Rome and the creation of a new polity, through the vast and profound revolution which grew out of Catherine's childlessness and Anne's winning ways.

Of course, the view that these personal and accidental factors were really behind the Reformation has found little favour with the writers of history who rightly argue that things of such magnitude do not happen in so superficial a manner. The part played by Henry's personal ends can only be understood against the state of affairs upon which his fierce determination impinged. Henry's passionate will can explain why the king drove the country along the path of war with Rome; it cannot explain his success or how he came to take the country with him. For it is most certainly true that he could not simply force the nation to his will; for one thing, he lacked all physical means of coercion. He had to have, at best, their enthusiastic support, or at worst their ready acquiescence. In order to understand the singular and rapid success of Henry VIII's political Reformation we must look at the condition and reputation of the Church and papacy in England.

2. STATE AND CHURCH IN ENGLAND

One ought not to generalise about whole nations, but if one thing can be said of the English people early in the sixteenth century it is that they thought little of priests. They were not alone in this: popular opinion all over Western Europe, though it preserved some respect for the Church as an institution, often treated its members with ribaldry. The literature of the later middle ages is full of stories which rely for their point on the peccadilloes of the priesthood; the hero of one discreditable adventure after another turns out to be a monk or a clerk in secular orders. In a way, this does no more than reflect the natural feelings of men who, being sinners themselves, love to see self-professed virtue stray from the path of righteousness: a priest's gluttony, greed, or lust was funnier and more deserving of notice than a layman's because it conflicted so much more with his professional claims and status, not because it was necessarily more common or notorious. But people cannot laugh at or abuse their spiritual pastors for generations without losing all respect for them. There was thus much of that feeling which is generally summarised in the word anticlericalism. The higher clergy were disliked because they were wealthy and ostentatious; Wolsey provided a suitable epitome of this alleged trait. The lesser clergy—parish priests and unbeneficed men—earned contempt and dislike by rapacity and pretensions with which their intellectual equipment, material means, and private morality too rarely kept pace. Monks and nuns, hidden away in convents which—like all unfamiliar territory—were peopled by ignorance and lascivious imagination with all the abominations possible, gathered about them a reputation which was to make the most extravagant accusations credible and their overthrow easy.

Apart from reprobation of real or supposed immorality, there were more potent interests at work to turn the laity against the clergy. One was the latter's wealth, concentrated in the hands of the larger monasteries, the bishops, and some prosperous incumbents. The Church held probably about one third of all land in England, and the incomes of great abbeys like Glastonbury or St Albans, and of bishoprics like Winchester and Durham, exceeded the revenues of the greatest temporal lords. These lands the laity had for some time coveted, the more so since in the depression of the fifteenth century many monasteries had leased out their demesne lands to a local gentleman who thereafter wished to convert his leasehold into direct tenure by expropriating his landlords. If the lands of the Church were ill-administered, the argument ran that they could be put to better use in lay hands; if—as was now too rarely the case—they were efficiently exploited, the cries against rapacious and wicked lords were loud. Before the dissolution of the monasteries, many complaints were recorded of sharp practices with which the next generation charged the monks' successors in the lands; the growing difficulties and the glamour of the past quickly gave the dispossessed monks a reputation for exceptional fair-dealing which historians are still trying to dispel. The simple truth is that the Church, and especially the monasteries, were in the intolerable position of owning great wealth but having lost the respect and devotion which permitted and encouraged the accumulation. Instead they were surrounded by a laity which resented their wealth and in addition thought it could make better use of it.

People also objected to the exactions of the Church and to its courts. Tithe was a standing grievance. The payments due upon the probate of wills, and more particularly the mortuary payments demanded even of the poorest before a body could be buried in consecrated ground, had roused a vast and sullen resentment which only awaited a chance to show itself. But the chief grievance concerned the courts of the Church. Side by side with royal and baronial jurisdiction, England also harboured a great system of courts held by bishops, their officials, and archdeacons. To these not only the clergy itself but also the laity were subject in matters technically affecting their spiritual welfare. All testamentary and matrimonial causes fell under this head, as well as straightforward breaches of the moral law and heresy—itself a very wide term. Moreover, these courts enforced the financial demands of the Church. Thus large numbers of laymen came into contact with a jurisdiction which was particularly rapacious in fees, unreliable and dilatory in decision, and corrupt in procedure. It was alleged that frivolous charges were common, that citations from one diocese into another were resorted to for purposes of chicanery, that bribes were taken, that excommunication was applied for no reason at all, even that ecclesiastical lawyers (proctors) laid false information themselves in order to augment their business.[1] Of all the clergy, the archdeacon in his court and the summoner travelling around the country to serve summons on often innocent people were probably the most hated. When all the necessary reservations are made, it still remains beyond dispute that the Church courts, having ceased to serve a useful purpose, were an intolerable burden; their rapid decline after the Reformation demonstrated their essential superfluity well enough.

All in all, men were tired of being ruled or badgered by priests—that is what one means by speaking of the secular temper of the times. From the villager who did not see why the parson should castigate him for doing as he himself did, to the duke of Suffolk who smote the table with a great oath and cried that times were merry in England before there were cardinals, the laity wished to humble, dispossess, and discipline the clergy. Anti-clericalism may not have been general or equally strong everywhere, though it is difficult to avoid the conclusion that the clergy as such rarely commanded respect and obedience. But it was strongest in the south, and particularly in London—that is, in the most populous and politically most influential part of the country. There was nothing new in it either. Since the fourteenth century, at least, the gentry and merchants, and especially the citizens of London, had repeatedly expressed their dislike of clerical wealth and jurisdiction; plans to confiscate the one and curb the other were canvassed repeatedly during the 150 years preceding the Reformation—though not by the government. In his own day, Henry VIII witnessed an outburst which displayed the real feeling on the subject. In 1514, the bishop of London, Richard Fitzjames, arrested a prosperous London merchant, Richard Hunne, on a charge of heresy, and in December Hunne was found hanged in the bishop's prison. According to his supporters, his arrest had nothing to do with any suspicions of Lollardy but was meant to punish him for refusing to pay a mortuary fee and threatening to bring an action of præmunire against the priest who demanded it.[2] Fitzjames hoped to dispose of the issue by trying, sentencing, and burning Hunne's dead body for heresy, alleging that he had committed suicide; but a coroner's jury returned a verdict of murder against the jailer and the bishop's chancellor Horsey, a

[1] Especially in the 'Commons' Supplication against the Ordinaries' (1532), a document which embodied the genuine grievances of the laity.
[2] For præmunire cf. below, p. 109.

clerk in orders. The case caused an uproar and had political repercussions in parliament and before the king which shall be discussed in a moment. Its most striking immediate effect was to unleash the anti-clerical temper of the city to such a degree that Fitzjames begged the king not to let Horsey come to trial, for—he said—any London jury would convict him, were he as innocent as Abel; in the end, Horsey got off with a fine and removal from London. Sir Thomas More wrote a very effective piece of polemic on the side of the ecclesiastical authorities, but a recent investigation has left little doubt that Hunne was murdered.[1] Hunne's personal fate was less significant than the temper it revealed. Both London and the king were to remember Hunne when there came cause to attack the Church.

Such were the feelings in a nation which, though formally pious, had little esteem for its clergy; but was the Church really in so deplorable a condition? The answer to that question does not affect the other issue: people thought the Church corrupt, whether it was so or not, and their opinion is a factor in the history of the Reformation. In great part they spoke truly. The Church was full of weaknesses and abuses; reforms had been talked about for a very long time. The parish clergy were often ill-educated and ignorant, unable to understand and sometimes even to read the Latin of the services; often, too, they were wretchedly poor. Coming from the same class as their flocks, they could rarely command the respect which a better education or a little higher standard of living would have produced. The higher clergy were wealthy and worldly and resented by their own inferiors; many of them practised those abuses against which pope after pope, and council after council, had issued their edicts. There was plenty of pluralism (the holding of more than one benefice) and consequent non-residence which left many men without the consolations of religion; there were simony and nepotism; there were lapses from morality, ranging from money-grubbing to persistent incontinence. Monastic institutions were in a decline: of the roughly 800 religious houses in England few had more than twenty-five inmates, while the average of the 600 lesser houses was four to five. The monastic ideal was dying when masses for the dead could not be said for lack of men to take the vows. Here and there one can find genuine scandals: visitation records of pre-Reformation days show that accusations of vice, ill-discipline, and scandalous quarrels were not based on invention, though they also show that the allegedly general was often only exceptional. The

[1] A. Ogle, *The Tragedy of the Lollard Tower* (1949).

monasteries' real canker was worldliness. Abbots and priors lived the life of the rural gentry with whom they consorted, administering their estates, hunting, dining, and occasionally drinking. Too often monks took the vows before they were old enough to understand their meaning; naturally they might later find it impossible to forsake the world. Most of these men were decent folk and harmless, but they had no claim to the religious devotion of the commonalty and no justification for the wealth which past fervour had showered upon their predecessors. That these and other abuses existed was no secret; the best spirits of the age—among them men who were to die for the old religion and the papacy—clamoured insistently for reform. But the Church as a whole was content to ignore the coming day of retribution. The pope acted the Italian prince; the English bishops busied themselves with the king's affairs; the great cardinal put Church reform at the bottom of his long list of preoccupations. When Wolsey, with all his special powers and exceptional energy, failed to make the slightest advance towards genuine reform, it was settled that the Church could not put its house in order and that the state would have to do it instead.

The state had a special reason for interference: in the consolidation of royal power which Henry VII had fostered, the privileges of the Church remained virtually untouched. Yet these privileges and liberties hindered the full development of national kingship. To start with, they interfered with the restoration of order. Benefit of clergy, the outcome of Henry II's failure to defeat Becket, protected any man in orders against the consequences of his first crime: only after he had been deprived of his orders for a felony did he become subject to the king's courts. The rights of clerical sanctuary provided refuge for criminals, though they were thereafter forced either to surrender themselves to the law or abjure the realm. Neither privilege, in fact, was as serious an infringement on the king's powers as seems still to be thought, and both were in process of being whittled away before ever Henry VIII attacked the Church. An act of 1491 ordered convicted clerks to be burned in the hand, so that they should not escape the punishment for further crimes through the ignorance of the judges; another of 1512 restricted the privilege to clerks in major orders, thus removing its worst anomaly which had protected numbers of rogues who could claim brief acquaintance with the Church or the universities. In 1515, however, the problem suddenly rose from the ashes when Richard Kidderminster, abbot of Winchcombe, preached a sermon at St Paul's Cross in which he attacked the act of 1512 from the text 'Touch not Mine Anointed'. He was only interpreting a recent papal renewal of the claim, but, coming as he did into the middle of Hunne's case where a clerk was threatened with secular prosecution, he provoked an uproar. The laity in parliament petitioned the king, and Henry arranged for a disputation between Kidderminster and Henry Standish, a friar and well-known preacher. The royal theologian himself presided. Standish, putting the case for relative independence from papal decrees, had the better of the argument, only to see himself attacked and threatened with a heresy trial by convocation. Parliament exploded; the king summoned Standish and his accusers before the judges and himself; and the whole clergy in convocation were adjudged to have rendered themselves liable to the dread penalties of præmunire by appealing to a foreign jurisdiction in denial of the king's. 'Kings of England,' said Henry, 'have never had any superior but God alone.' These words, spoken as early as 1516, must be remembered. Wolsey, who had to ask pardon for the clergy, secured the rapid dissolution of this hotly anti-clerical parliament, but the lesson was not forgotten by the one man who mattered. Henry now knew from his judges that the law declared such reliance on Rome punishable by imprisonment at pleasure and forfeiture of goods. Benefit of clergy, won in the pope's triumph over Henry II, played a strange part in Henry VIII's rescinding of that triumph.

Sanctuary represented a different problem, largely because its ecclesiastical character was somewhat fortuitous. Truly ecclesiastical sanctuaries existed in every church and churchyard, but these mattered little in comparison with the great liberties, especially in the north, where the king's writ did not run. Due to a number of historical accidents, those that survived were mostly in the hands of the Church, as the archbishop of York's liberties at Ripon and Beverley, or the whole county palatine of Durham. In these places criminals found a refuge for life, provided they never left the sanctuary. Throughout the fifteenth century the judges had done their best to limit the privilege, and under Henry VII and Henry VIII parliamentary legislation carried on the good work on a somewhat larger scale. However, sanctuary was not fully abolished until various acts of the years 1530-40 destroyed it in one place after another, subjecting all monastic liberties, the county of Durham, and finally all England to the king's law.

Benefit of clergy and sanctuary were only aspects of the real difficulty posed by the Church—the problem of its dual allegiance. The clergy owed obedience and loyalty to the king, for they were Englishmen dwelling in his peace, holding their lands from him, and possessed of property and rights protected by his courts. They also owed loyalty and obedience to the pope, the supreme and absolute monarch in the Universal Church. Such double allegiance involved much difficult delimiting of spheres and much burdensome double taxation. Ordinarily, when king and pope were at peace, the Church was the real sufferer, for both these powerful potentates then combined in exploiting it. In England, king and pope had been working in harmony for a century and more before Henry VIII came to the throne. Earlier there had been trouble—the struggle over investitures between Henry I and Anselm, the bitter war over criminous clerks and clerical jurisdiction between Henry II and Thomas Becket, the decisive intervention of Innocent III in the affairs of John. The fourteenth century looked likely to bring matters to a head. With the defeat of Boniface VIII, with the 'Babylonish captivity' at Avignon, and finally with the papal schism when one pope at Rome and another at Avignon demanded the obedience of distracted and disgusted Christendom (1377), the stock of the papacy slumped badly. Throughout the reign of Edward III it was closely associated with the national enemy, France, and therefore liable to attack by the growing national fervour of which the Hundred Years' War was both expression and nurse. Typically enough, the quarrel took the highly practical form of a conflict over property rights in the issue of 'provisors'. Objection was taken to the papal habit (nourished by poverty) of 'providing' incumbents for benefices, especially bishoprics, all over Europe, a habit which was crystallising into a doctrine of the pope as the universal patron. In the course of the fourteenth century the English parliament passed successive statutes known as acts of provisors and of præmunire which protected the property of English patrons of benefices, prohibited papal interference with these rights, and punished those who either sought out or published papal bulls affecting them. The legislation culminated in the statute of 1393 which had a much more restricted scope than was once thought: it was not a general code against papal intervention in the affairs of the English Church, but a limited and practical summary of earlier legislation designed to protect the temporal rights of the laity (and especially the king) in appointments and advowsons.[1]

The legislation, significant as an expression of views hostile to

[1] W. T. Waugh, 'The Great Statute of Præmunire', *English Historical Review*, 1922; see also C. Davies, 'The Statute of Provisors of 1351', *History*, 1953. Advowsons—rights of presentation to benefices—were in England subject to the secular courts.

the papacy among the propertied classes represented in parliament, produced the writ of *præmunire facias* under which proceedings for infringements of these laws were to be taken, and the large penalties—forfeiture of property and imprisonment at the discretion of king and council—which were their sanction. The real significance of præmunire, as the whole complex of laws limiting papal encroachments on the king's 'crown and regality' came to be called, lay in its vagueness and dark threats. Largely because the Lancastrian kings needed papal support, and because the papacy of the schism was too weak to counterattack, the laws of the fourteenth century remained virtually dead. In the fifteenth century there were no more orthodox and papalist country and monarchy than those of England. The laity stood protected against the pope by laws which needed no application for the simple reason that popes were careful not to infringe them, and the kings down to Henry VIII—equally secure in their regal rights—had no difficulty in remaining on good terms with Rome. The victim of this happy harmony among its masters was, as usual, the English Church which paid heavy taxes to both king and pope and learned to dread the demands of their absolute sovereign at Rome even more than those of their limited sovereign in England. This long period of co-operation between crown and papacy culminated in Wolsey's legateship. Wolsey combined the powers of both king and pope, and—being an active autocrat as well as near at hand—brought home to the Church what papal powers could mean. At the same time, he revived the laity's dislike of a foreign potentate's pretensions. Few Englishmen had any objection to the pope's spiritual supremacy, and many rather enjoyed the discomfiture of the Church at the hands of its own champion, but none in an age when temporal nationalism first became a fully realised doctrine wanted to see an Italian prince interfere in their affairs. The duke of Norfolk summed it all up in answer to Wolsey's lament at his fall that his legacy was gone 'wherein stood all my high honour'. 'A straw for your legacy,' was the duke's reply, 'I never esteemed your honour the higher for that.' But, he added, he had reverenced Wolsey as archbishop of York and cardinal whose estate 'surmounteth any duke within this realm'. Where the pope was concerned, the anti-clerical passions which denounced the pretensions of the priesthood found an ally in nationalist prejudice and national interest.

However, in England none of these feelings were translated into religious opposition to Church or pope. Almost to a man, the English people, high or low, were content with orthodoxy. The stress so commonly laid in discussions of the Reformation's pre-history on intellectual or doctrinal disputes misleads entirely. This was, in any case, not a religious age, in the sense that men followed their faith rather than their material ambitions, as on the whole they were to do a century later. Nor was the Reformation of this reign greatly concerned with doctrinal changes. The peculiarly political and jurisdictional preoccupations of the English Reformation arose from the fact that it was made from above, by the government, but it could have been made in no other way in a nation which abhorred heresy and prided itself on its orthodoxy. The continental Reformation took its origin in the religious revolt of individual prophets, only to fall in its second stage into the hands of secular governments; in England, the government led the way, and it was only the political changes carried out which made possible and even necessary the subsequent religious transformation. It is a fact, however difficult to grasp, that an England which showed no deference to priests and much dislike of the papacy yet stood firmly by the mass; active anti-clericalism and doctrinal orthodoxy were somehow combined. At the same time it is worth noting at once that the success of the attack on the papacy brought in its train a swelling attack on orthodoxy: conservatism in doctrine and ritual seems to have lacked any deep roots. In part, the English were orthodox because they had had earlier experience of heresy. The Wycliffite and Lollard movements of the fourteenth century produced a violent reaction; because of them England had a law for burning heretics. No one now doubts that Lollardy played no part in the Reformation. Here and there it survived, mostly among the poorer artisans; in some places the Lollard bible was still read, and views were held which represented the last and crudest simplifications of Wycliffe's difficult scholastic arguments on the nature of the priesthood or the sacrament of the altar.[1] But these poor men of Cotswold villages and London shops had nothing to do with the movement which got under way when Henry VIII broke with Rome.

In the 1520s a different form of heresy began to appear, and the bishops, in trying to deal with it, often confused the two. The universities, especially Cambridge, began to respond to Luther's teaching on the continent. The official attitude found expression in the book *Assertio Septem Sacramentorum* which appeared over the name of Henry VIII in 1521 and won him the title of Defender of the Faith from a grateful pope. It is now commonly admitted that the book is not so learned as to preclude

[1] Cf. K. B. McFarlane, *John Wycliffe* (1953).

Henry's authorship, though he certainly had assistance from Bishop Fisher and Sir Thomas More. But among the younger generation of university dons, Lutheran views were received with much delight, and in the meetings of a discussion group dubbed 'Little Germany' in the White Horse Tavern at Cambridge one source of English protestantism has rightly been discerned. The leading English heretic was William Tyndale who fled abroad in 1524 to translate the Bible and conduct a vigorous pamphlet war with Thomas More, before he was betrayed to the imperial authorities and burned in 1536. England, too, saw some burnings. Wolsey, cardinal though he was, proved true to his secular temper by displaying much tolerance, though even he could not stomach heretical teaching at the universities. He was particularly unfortunate in that he inadvertently infected Oxford when he staffed his new college there with Cambridge men some of whom held Lutheran views. When Thomas More succeeded Wolsey as chancellor, and such bishops as Nix of Norwich and Longland of Lincoln (in whose dioceses the danger of heresy was greatest) could at last act on their own, a minor wave of persecutions followed; More's record in the matter is rather that of the convinced and high-minded sixteenth-century believer that he was, than that of the nineteenth-century moderate liberal he is so often made out to be. John Foxe found material here for his martyrs. They were men like Little Bilney—Thomas Bilney, who was orthodox on the pope and on the mass and most things, but died because he relapsed after recanting his views on saints and image worship—or John Frith who shared Tyndale's extremer views. As individuals they were harmless enough—sincere men of very limited influence; but in view of what had happened in Germany the Church could not afford to overlook even small-time heretics. These first rumblings of attack played no part in bringing about the Reformation; but for the political revolution they would have been stamped out.

Nor was the Reformation in England a result of the so-called intellectual Renaissance. That the fourteenth and fifteenth centuries saw a revival of classical learning spread from Italy to the rest of Europe is certainly true, though few historians today would regard it as the profound break with the past which it was once held to be. It effected a general shift of emphasis, the more marked because it coincided with a general decline in piety and deference to the Church. Which was cause and which effect is not a proper question; there was mutual interaction. Out of it grew humanism, a phenomenon of the schools like other medieval trends of thought;

in part, at least, it represented a revolt against a curriculum dominated by such outstanding teachers of an earlier generation as William Ockham and Duns Scotus, even as they had superseded their predecessors. Such sweeps of fashion are familiar in universities, and to universities and learned men the movement was throughout confined. Like all scholastic doctrine humanism appealed to authority, but the authority on which it relied was that of pre-Christian pagan writers rather than that of the writers of the Church. This dependence on authority, so natural to the age, prevented an appeal to independent reasoning; humanism did not mark the triumph of the individual mind over some collective system. Medieval schoolmen were on the whole more subtle and penetrating than their humanist successors; where they differed was not in powers or independence of thought but in preconceived notions and relevant subjects. The humanists' devotion to the classics opened whole new fields for study, and the high critical standards of the best ancient authors (whom they admired) supplied them with new and effective weapons against their professional opponents. In their own sphere, the humanists were as uncritical and credulous as any medieval believer in miracles and authority; the typical humanist, to take an example, would base his knowledge of a plant or an animal on Pliny, even if his own eyes could convince him that Pliny had erred. Men of genius like Leonardo da Vinci or Copernicus did not belong to the humanist movement proper. This was not the age of science but the great age of alchemy and astrology, an age of odd superstitions replacing a lost faith. Only in dealing with the assumptions and beliefs of their opponents—of those *obscuri viri* whom the great Erasmus satirised—were the humanists armed with well-tempered and sharp critical weapons from the armoury of Greece and Rome.

In England, humanism never acquired the pagan tinge of the Italian prototype. Its prophet was Erasmus of Rotterdam, a man of great learning, sharp insight, a satirical humour, and valetudinarian habits, who produced an edition of the text of the New Testament from the original Greek which corrected the Vulgate in places so as to undermine the scriptural authority of the priesthood and the papacy. Erasmus' work influenced heresiarchs like Luther and Tyndale, but Erasmus himself, though quarrelling with monks and friars and the 'old learning' in general (as a good university controversialist was bound to do), always remained orthodox and free from suspicion. In this his English associates followed him. Men like John Colet, dean of St

Paul's and the founder of St Paul's School, William Grocyn and Thomas Lineacre—Greek scholars both and the latter an eminent physician—and Thomas More were eager to apply the new learning to England in order to refresh the Church and its doctrine. It was an age of much intellectual activity. Young men questioned the syllabus of the universities; colleges were founded to promote new studies and old; royal and noble amateurs took much interest in the arts and sciences.[1] Henry VIII himself liked to have brilliant young men about; of a large number of exceedingly clever and highly trained humanists the brightest star was Thomas More whose *Utopia*—describing an imaginary commonwealth—is rightly regarded as the outstanding product of the early English humanism, before the Reformation came to turn that carefree playing with ideas into a sombre and serious business. More made a career in government service, rising ultimately (1529-32) to the office of lord chancellor, but his fame rests rather on his personality, his wit and genius, and his sacrificial death. In the history of English thought—indeed, of European thought—he is a figure of note; in the political history of his country, fate determined that his part should be small.

There was thus a good deal of 'new learning' in England, but it was not heretical. Colet and More, the churchman and the layman, wanted reform in a Church whose abuses More only started to deny when they were attacked by the Lutheran partisans whom he combated, but they stayed orthodox. No humanist of note joined the ranks of the protestants; on the contrary, in More and Fisher they supplied the leading martyrs of the papalist party. In the next generation, indeed, the potential link between new learning and protestantism was more evident: such men as Cranmer or, on a lower plane, the propagandists employed by Thomas Cromwell came under the influence of the new ideas in religion while at the university. But once again the essential relationship is the other way round: the new learning no more than Lutheran doctrine could work upon the English Reformation until the crown had led the way in the political and jurisdictional break of the 1530s. To see in those poor stirrings of protestantism which Little Bilney and his like represented, or in the humanistic new learning of Erasmus' friends and followers, anything that could cause or lead to the

[1] Thus Cardinal's College was founded by Wolsey. Christ's and St John's Colleges at Cambridge owed their foundation to John Fisher's influence with Lady Margaret Beaufort, Henry VIII's grandmother. The patron of English humanism was William Blount, Lord Mountjoy, a friend of Henry VIII.

Reformation in England is vastly to overrate the place of intellectuals in the sixteenth century, and vastly to misjudge the character of the revolution that actually took place.

Thus when Henry VIII began his attack on the papacy, he had in his favour the strong dislike of the clergy and of foreign interference in English affairs which animated certainly the politically effective part of the nation and was represented in parliament. He did not by an exercise of superhuman power and coercion drag a faithful people from the fold; rather he at last unleashed those passions which for years only the government's frown had been able to stem. Attacks on the Church, on its way of life and its great wealth (rumoured to be even greater than it was) were some 150 years old at least; and so was dislike of papal 'usurpations' and encroachments. But despite statutes of provisors and præmunire, the crown had stood good ally to Rome; the antipapal legislation remained a dead letter, and England's medieval history culminated in a royal minister who was also papal legate and who adapted his country's foreign policy to the needs of the pope. Until Henry fixed his desire upon Anne Boleyn, and Clement VII, to his despair, found himself a prisoner of Charles V, there was nothing to disturb the harmony of king and pope; and until their alliance was broken all the latent feelings which Henry VIII was to harness remained powerless. That is the place which the divorce occupies. It did not alone cause the Reformation; it did not even, if we like, play any large part in bringing about a movement which rested on national feeling and the scandal of a corrupt Church; but without it there would still have been no Reformation because the powerful intercession of the crown would have been against it and not for it.

It is, then, easy enough to see why Henry's war on the pope was accepted so readily by his people—though we shall see later that there was some opposition—and there is no need to postulate despotic action which anyhow would have been beyond Henry's means. It must still, however, be explained how the opponent came to be so weak as to make Henry's task relatively easy. He had to coerce the Church into obedience to himself, and to force the papacy either to give in to him or to withdraw from England. Not that he saw it in that light: as shall be shown, he had no idea of the outcome and no plan for the future when he first set out to get his divorce. All he knew was his will and desire which his conscience had turned into right and justice, and all he wanted was to achieve these. The pope, a weak man at other times but now rendered obstinate by his greater fear of Charles V and by his reluctance to endorse what amounted to a denial of the papal power to dispense, was no suitable opponent for the determined Tudor king whose physical resources were so much larger. Any danger that threatened from secular princes taking up the cause of Rome was removed by the unstable relations between France and the emperor which kept both at peace with England—though only the event was to prove right a calculation which the peace of Cambrai of August 1529 rendered unlikely. Indeed, one of the most striking things about Henry VIII's break with Rome was the ease with which it was accomplished: all the imposing façade of papal power and imperial displeasure vanished like the mirage it was once the king could take Thomas Cromwell's advice and act boldly.

As for the Church in England itself, much ingenuity has been spent on the question why it gave way so readily; yet the answer is not really so hard to find. As has already been said, the fall of Wolsey left it in a specially weakened state. Battered and badgered by the cardinal-legate, the bishops were the less willing or able to resist the demands of the king; disorganised and superseded as their administration had been during Wolsey's ascendancy, they could not hope to marshal opposition when attacked by the laity with the crown's connivance. The king alone had stood between the Church and its lay enemies; now that protector cheered on the hunt. In any case, the bishops were almost all king's men; their past predisposed them honestly to obey his will. Warham, of Canterbury, had made a conventional career, rising to the chancellorship from which Wolsey dislodged him in 1515. Longland of Lincoln was king's confessor before his promotion, Stokesley of London almoner and ambassador; both these men hated innovations in religion, but they obeyed the king against the pope. Not all had mortgaged their conscience: Standish of St Asaph, who had preached high royalist doctrine in 1516, took up Catherine's cause in 1527—but he was to consecrate Cranmer. There were exceptions, like Fisher of Rochester who had never had anything to do with politics; there was Tunstall of Durham who, while he avoided all action that might get him into trouble, yet did not surrender his independence and integrity to the habits of an old official of the crown. But the custom by which for over a century the way to the bench had lain through the king's service and good grace made of the leaders and guardians of the Church active or retired ministers of the crown rather than prelates obeying their spiritual head. Perhaps the bishops deserve a less lukewarm defence. The pope's spiritual headship was indeed unquestioned dogma, but the relations between Church and state and papal authority in the temporal sphere were much less certain than later definition has made them. In the fifteenth century the popes had fought a long battle against a constitutional movement in the Church which tried to replace monarchical by representative government—the conciliar movement; and though in the end the pope won hands down, the fact that Henry kept appealing from the pope to a General Council of the Church gave him a case in the eyes of men who, especially after their recent experience of Wolsey, were not over-ardent papalists. Altogether, as the legal and philosophical arguments of the time show, there was much to be said on the king's side, at least until 1533, even by those who did not hold with his later activities; it is unfair to condemn the English bishops, king-trained as they were, for not taking up a position which only events clarified, and which was never really as simple as the partisans of either side would make it. In addition, as we shall see, the government were careful to ensure obedience by skilful pressure.

3. THE PROGRESS OF THE DIVORCE TO WOLSEY'S FALL

All of this lay yet in the future when Henry VIII, in the spring of 1527, decided that he was living in sin with his wife, and that the marriage ought to be annulled. Who or what finally brought him to that view is not certain. The king himself put it about that the Bishop of Tarbes, on embassy from France, had cast doubts upon Mary's legitimacy and therefore on her usefulness in a dynastic marriage. Catherine, and Spain with her, believed Wolsey to be the origin of it all, but in this she was certainly mistaken. Though the cardinal did not like the queen and had fallen out with Charles V, he had nothing to gain from a plan which aimed at putting the Boleyns in the saddle; Anne herself had personal reasons for hating him, and her family represented very strongly that anti-clerical gentry of whom we have spoken. No one now believes that the Boleyns were Lutherans, but they and their party unquestionably approved of Luther's attack on the Church and of the secularisation of Church property. As the niece of the duke of Norfolk, Anne also commanded the powerful Howard interest, unshakably hostile to Wolsey. In all probability, there is no reason for depriving Henry himself of the credit, such as it is, for turning upon his innocent wife. In the whole sordid tale, Catherine stands out as the one person wronged but not wronging; no one has ever had anything but pity for her, victim as she was of a movement she could neither understand nor approve, and of a husband who could only dislike when he ceased to love. The people, especially of London, seem to have expressed a preference for her, but in these questions of popular attitude and reaction to Henry's doings the evidence is very shaky. Most of it comes from the reports of hostile observers, especially the imperial ambassador Eustace Chapuys who in those years used his office to plot for Catherine; his reports must be treated with the greatest care. Some men were charged with speaking vilely of Anne; but men who praised Anne and abused Catherine (if any there were) would not, of course, have got into trouble and therefore into the record. In general, much caution is needed in assessing a public opinion which undoubtedly mattered, especially if it appeared in parliament, but of which far too little is known.

The actual history of the divorce is extremely complicated and confused, full of twists and turns which it would be pointless to follow. At first, Henry thought he could get his divorce from the pope, the only proper authority, as others had done before him; the matrimonial adventures of his sister Margaret and his friend Suffolk, both of whom had been freed from inconvenient commitments by a compliant papacy, provided recent precedents, and, after all, the pope owed both king and cardinal a burden of gratitude. It all began with a secret collusive action in May 1527 when Wolsey summoned Henry before his legatine court to explain why he was living in sin with his brother's widow. He intended to establish a *prima facie* case for declaring the marriage invalid which would then be confirmed by the pope. But the apparently unexpected indignation with which Catherine received the news first arrested the easy progress of the matter; and when, late in May, the imperialist troops sacked Rome and took the pope prisoner the situation changed entirely. Wolsey, well aware that all his power depended on the successful accomplishment of Henry's desires, now proved full of invention, but at all points Clement VII, horrified at the quandary into which he had been put, was a match for him. In 1527, the cardinal proposed to act with the assistance of the Church without Rome—*capto papa*—a plan which was wrecked first by the failure of the French cardinals to back him up and then by the politic 'liberation' of Clement in December. In 1528, therefore, Wolsey concentrated on getting a sufficient commission from the pope which would enable him to dissolve the marriage and free Henry in all respects for re-marriage. The king insisted throughout on the safest dispensation that could be got: there must never be a shadow of doubt on his second marriage and the issue he hoped it would produce, and therefore full papal authority was necessary. He had thus no use for Clement's desperate suggestion that Henry should get himself divorced in England and in any way he liked, or even commit bigamy, as long as the papacy was not involved. Wolsey wanted a decretal commission virtually empowering him to declare the marriage void; instead the pope at last (April 1528) granted a commission to try the case as though it had not already been tried and settled in Henry's own mind. This public commission was made out to Wolsey and Cardinal Campeggio, bishop of Salisbury and protector of England at the papal curia. Further pressure, however, together with the French successes in Italy early in 1528, induced Clement to add a secret decretal commission which he entrusted to Campeggio with private instructions not to use it. By October, when Campeggio at last reached England, the situation in Italy had been completely reversed by the imperialist triumph at Genoa which once more persuaded the pope that his way lay with Charles V.

Campeggio now played a masterly game of delays and procrastinations, designed to keep Henry quiet without committing the pope. Wolsey, who understood better that the king was only being driven into anger and unpredictable action, was desperate but powerless; the signs were multiplying that his supremacy had nearly reached its end. At least one of the embassies dispatched to Rome had gone without his knowledge.[1] Early in 1528 he seriously displeased his master by persisting in his advocacy of an unsuitable candidate for the office of abbess of Wilton nunnery; Henry was beginning to speak sharply to 'his cardinal'. For the moment, the king still relied on him, but Wolsey knew that one failure would be enough. Well might he lament to Clement VII: the pope's hesitations, he wrote, were ruining the cardinal, and with the cardinal would fall the Church. But much as Clement desired to oblige the defender of the faith, much as he dreaded the spread of schism in the north, nothing could overcome the near presence and definite views of the emperor or the pope's primary interest in Italian affairs. So Campeggio dallied, suggesting various ways out (as that Catherine should retire to a nunnery), all of which were blocked by the queen's determination to have right done to her. The delays encouraged ribald rumours about these supposedly secret matters, till Henry found it advisable to hold a meeting of courtiers and city dignitaries at Bridewell Palace in November 1528 to announce to them his scruples of conscience and fears for the succession. It may be doubted whether this convinced those

[1] Knight in 1527; on the other hand, Gardiner and Foxe who extorted the legatine commission in 1528 were Wolsey's own agents.

of the people who—according to the chronicler—said that the king wanted another wife and therefore had summoned the legate to divorce him, or reassured the women who generally were on Catherine's side against Anne.

Even Campeggio's ingenuity could not have manufactured delay out of nothing, but in October 1528 the legate heard of a document whose importance to the case made a trial impossible until it had been thoroughly discussed. This was Julius II's brief of 1503 to Isabella of Spain in which he allegedly resolved the doubts raised by his dispensation for Catharine's second marriage; the Spaniards now announced its opportune discovery. Since the whole English argument depended on the insufficiency of the dispensation, the brief—if genuine—would have left them without a case, except to deny outright the pope's power to dispense, an extreme step they were reluctant to take; they naturally claimed it to be a forgery, and it is a fact that its authenticity has never been satisfactorily established. The English would not admit the brief until they had seen and studied it; the Spaniards would not entrust the precious document to men interested in its disappearance; one more deadlock was added to those already existing. But now Wolsey realised that the trial must open, for while his envoys failed to persuade the pope of the need to support Henry, the emperor was urging Clement to revoke the case to Rome[1]—and he seemed likely to succeed. Should Henry find himself summoned to Rome to answer for his marriage, his boundless wrath would be worth seeing; it would also sweep Wolsey into oblivion. Thus, on 31 March 1529, the court at last opened at Blackfriars. The proceedings dragged on; the queen made a deep impression by her impassioned pleas and steadfast bearing; Henry endeavoured to prove that her marriage to Arthur had been consummated, which she denied. The whole unsavoury business continued until 23 July when—a decision being confidently expected—Campeggio sprang his concealed mine: he announced that, since the court was part of the Roman consistory, it would have to keep the terms kept at Rome, and that it thus stood adjourned through the hot Italian summer until 1 October. It never met again: this desperate step, to which Wolsey had assented because he could see no good coming out of a decision, ended the matter as far as Henry was concerned. A day earlier Wolsey had heard that Clement had given in to Charles and revoked the case to Rome; a week later the peace of Cambrai, concluded without his knowledge, put paid to a last hope

[1] I.e. to order its trial at Rome instead of in the court of the legates commissioned in 1528.

that the Italian wars might take another turn, Clement be set free, and Wolsey's policy triumph.

This concluded the first stage of the divorce—the attempt to achieve it by co-operation with Rome. The second stage followed almost at once: Henry, still convinced that only the pope could legally free him from Catherine, now determined to exercise pressure at Rome. For three years he battered away with threats and hints of dire things to come. But before he felt free to attack he had to rid himself of the man who had failed him. Once the king had made up his mind, Wolsey's fall was headlong. When on 9 August writs went out for a parliament—in itself a threat to Wolsey—the cardinal was deprived of the control which his office of chancellor gave him. The king refused to see him or join him at his manor of the More, and the subtle barometer of courtierdom reacted quickly. Where all the councillors had thronged to hear the cardinal in the star chamber, leaving the king deserted, the opposite was now true: when the term opened in October, Wolsey found himself alone. On 9 October the blow fell: the attorney-general indicted him for præmunire in the king's bench. But the king would not ruin him entirely; he was saved by the memories of fifteen years and the possibility that he might yet again be useful. On the 18th he surrendered the great seal. On the 22nd he confessed his guilt in writing (for technically he was guilty) and was sentenced to the penalties of the statute. The bill of attainder brought against him in the parliament that met on 3 November was his special enemies' doing and not the king's; it therefore need not surprise us that it was thrown out.

Wolsey fell because he could not serve the man who had made him. His dependence on the papacy had only lost him the one favour that mattered; he had no prop but the king. All men of influence hated him—and women too, for he always thought that Anne Boleyn was instrumental in his overthrow. The pope, for whom he had waged many a diplomatic battle and real war, made no move to save him. By accepting the legatine commission from which so much of his power stemmed, and thus exercising a foreign authority to the detriment of the king's regality, Wolsey laid himself open to the charge of præmunire. That Henry had of course endorsed Wolsey's legateship mattered nothing. Papal power in England was already exercised only at the king's discretion. This must be remembered when it is said that Henry learned from Wolsey the possibility of combining all secular and ecclesiastical authority in one man: it seems rather that Henry was always fully persuaded that he was supreme and unchallengeable in England.

The king's mind was not of the kind that works out such matters in theory and then transforms them into action. As he saw it, he had such power that no man should gainsay it; but he had no idea how to apply that power to the problem in hand, or that it could be developed into a revolutionary theory of the state. All he did in the next three years showed that. If he learned anything from Wolsey it was the need to have the agreement of parliament, the folly of an over-enterprising foreign policy, and an enhanced opinion of his own sagacity. In the deeper aspects of statesmanship Henry learned nothing from Wolsey because the king was not a good pupil at any time, and because the cardinal had nothing to teach.

For Wolsey turned out to be the most disappointing man who ever held great power in England and used it for so long with skill and high intelligence. He survived for a year after his fall. Saved from imprisonment by Henry's unwonted mercy, restored to part of his preferments and property, he determined to devote himself to his archbishopric of York which he had never yet visited. But the pull of the great world proved too strong. He moved north slowly, casting longing glances over his shoulder; he continued to excite hostile comment by his lavish living; finally he involved himself in plots which his enemies turned against him. In November 1530 the council had him arrested and conveyed to London; he knew what was in store. By easy stages the ailing man reached Leicester; there, met by the captain of the king's guard, he died on the 24th. His fall had been tremendous, for he had risen to tremendous heights, and only pity will be excited by that famous death-bed in Leicester Abbey. But the historian must also ask what Wolsey had really achieved. His foreign policy, often brilliant and never negligible, had resulted in the isolation of England, the enmity of both Spain and France, and the king's failure to get his divorce; it had been based on a false estimate of English power and directed consistently to ends in which England had little interest. The administration, badly in need of reform, was on the contrary more confused than before; the reserves of treasure were gone, prosperity was declining, trade neglected. The Church, his special charge, Wolsey left in an unprecedented state of weakness, facing a most untempered storm in a freshly shorn condition. Only in the law he had done things that bore fruit, and much though he liked the work of a judge he would surely have been dissatisfied with a verdict that allowed him but this piece of success. And yet it is hard to see what else one can say. Embodying in himself the link with Rome and the height of the medieval polity, he pulled them down in his fall; his death marks the close of the old order with as much definition as any man's fate ever marks the fate of nations.

4. YEARS WITHOUT A POLICY, 1529-32

The government which replaced Wolsey did not make his mistakes, but it neither had his successes or brilliance. It was a stopgap without either brilliance or success, composed of second-rate men. The chancellorship went to Thomas More whom one can certainly not describe as second-rate; but More took office only on condition that he would not be involved in the divorce to which he was immovably opposed. Since the divorce naturally dominated the events of those years, the king's promise meant that he deprived himself of the services of far and away the ablest minister left after Wolsey's fall. More concentrated on some useful work in the court of chancery where he began the tradition of great common lawyers and laymen who, building on the foundations laid by the ecclesiastical chancellors of the middle ages, acclimatised this potentially alien court to the common law. As for the rest, he was rather more questionably active in searching out heretics and writing polemical works against Tyndale. The government was really in the hands—under Henry—of the triumvirate of Norfolk, Suffolk, and Wiltshire. The duke of Suffolk, an admirable sportsman, had no ability whatsoever in affairs; the duke of Norfolk,[1] a good soldier and competent administrator, never displayed sufficient originality of mind to rank as a statesman; the earl of Wiltshire, father of Anne Boleyn, owed his rise to noble rank to his daughter's place in the king's affections, though he too made a good enough agent of others. These were not the men to succeed where Wolsey had failed. For three years after August 1529 the conduct of government really depended on the king; in its uncoordinated vigour, piecemeal attack on problems, and essential bankruptcy in ideas it displayed Henry's mind to perfection.

When Henry decided that co-operation with Rome must be replaced by hostile pressure on Rome, he realised that to this end he had to have allies in England. The summoning of a parliament for 3 November 1529 was a very significant step. No parliament had met since 1523, and none had met since Wolsey rose to power without causing trouble to the government. In falling back on parliament, Henry therefore showed that he understood the nation he governed. He remembered the anti-clerical temper of 1515 and

[1] The third duke, son of the victor of Flodden (see above, p. 75).

saw that it could be turned to advantage against the independence of the Church. We may take it from what followed that Henry had two lines of attack in mind when he assumed the direction of affairs himself: he wished to reduce the Church to absolute obedience to himself, so as to prevent their natural allegiance to the papacy from weakening his case, and he wished to use parliamentary anti-clericalism to make the pope's fear of what might happen in England greater than his fear of what Charles V might do. Since Charles was near at hand and England far away, this policy was from the first without hope of success.

The parliament which met in November 1529 was no more packed than any other of Henry's parliaments. That is to say, it naturally contained a number of royal councillors and servants, for these usually had some standing in their own localities and—being in politics anyway—also some interest in being elected. The government presumably exercised such influence as it had in elections (not a great deal), and in other elections private patronage was undoubtedly at work. Contemporary statements about a packed or servile house of commons are exaggerations, often prompted by hostility to Henry's policy. The house was representative of the men of the middle sort, gentry and merchants and lawyers, on whose faithful support Tudor government depended and who were particularly hostile to the pretensions and exactions of the Church. The lords, of whom about half were bishops and abbots while many of the rest owed their elevation to the Tudor kings, were immediately less important: opposition was not to be feared from the lay peers, and the presence of the spiritual lords made the house as a body less useful in attacks on the Church. It was therefore in the commons that the critical events took place. Henry gave them full liberty to discuss what they would, and they replied by putting forward bills against abuses in the Church. Three of these—those limiting the fees taken for probate and mortuaries, and one against pluralism and non-residence—passed into statutes; another document, which attacked in the form of a petition the activities of the Church courts, remained in the hands of Thomas Cromwell, then a private member, when the session ended. It is quite certain that these measures of the first session were taken on the commons' own initiative: they attacked evils of great interest to themselves and of none to the king, and the documentary evidence is conclusive. Henry's decision to let loose the hatred of the Church which Wolsey had greatly augmented paid full dividends; the activities of the commons frightened the bishops and proved useful as propaganda material at Rome where

Henry's representatives were careful to point out the danger to the Church. The king would readily call off his dogs if only the pope agreed to his just demands: the point was taken, but the little finger of Charles V seemed thicker than Henry's thigh.

After six weeks the parliament was prorogued (16 December 1529), not to meet again until January 1531; plague and policy prevented an earlier recall, but meanwhile the king was not idle. He increased his diplomatic pressure at Rome, using an intellectual weapon which he found congenial. Following the advice tendered in August 1529 by Thomas Cranmer, an obscure Cambridge divine, Henry's agents spent the better part of 1530 gathering opinions from the universities of Europe in favour of the king's point of view on the canonical problem of his marriage. Oxford, Cambridge, and the French universities not unnaturally supported a view hostile to Spain; but even the great North Italian universities of Bologna, Padua, and Ferrara voted for the king. The rest of Italy and Spain, as well as Germany, decided for the other side. It was a typical piece of work: expensive in time and treasure, for bribery played its part, it could do no good. These opinions were to be used at Rome together with the threat of calling a General Council of the Church which would act if the pope did not. Faced by the hint of another conciliar movement even the weak Clement proved strong, though in any case no prince or Church in Europe was sincerely interested in reviving these ancient controversies; it took the Church forty years to assemble a council under papal guidance to deal with protestantism. The opinions of learned divines, too, could have no effect in a struggle in which power counted much more than argument. That Henry genuinely thought he could batter in the iron gates of Rome with such feeble weapons is evidence both of his failure to understand the situation and of his inability to find his own way out of the maze.

He proved rather more successful in the other part of his policy, for he managed to stifle opposition from his own clergy. The weapon employed was that used to destroy Wolsey, the statute of præmunire. From the summer of 1530 a number of bishops and leading clerics found themselves accused in the court of king's bench of having broken the statute by obeying Wolsey's legatine authority; it does not surprise to find that the men so attacked were connected with the queen's party, including for instance Bishops Fisher, Clerk, and Standish who had been her counsel at the legatine trial.[1] Significantly enough, these victims of Henry had

[1] I owe the information on these proceedings to Mr J. J. Scarisbrick.

also been Wolsey's victims; their alleged offence consisted in agreeing to pay part of their revenues to Wolsey as legate, an agreement which the cardinal had extorted by threats of the very same præmunire which their compliance was now judged to have fallen foul of. However, before these individual thrusts took effect, the government decided to extend the operation to the whole clergy, purposing both to cow and to amerce a body whose essential loyalty was beginning to weaken after the parliamentary attacks of 1529. In December 1530 the whole clergy were indicted of præmunire on the sweeping grounds that they had unlawfully exercised their spiritual jurisdiction.[1] Everyone understood the meaning of the threat; rather than forfeit its corporate property, the Church surrendered. In February 1531 the two convocations bought a royal pardon for their 'offence' by paying £100,000 and £18,000 respectively. Not content with this, Henry also demanded that they recognise him as their supreme head; after much opposition the aged Warham of Canterbury proposed an alternative title—'singular protector, only and supreme lord, and as far as the law of Christ allows even supreme head'—and took the ensuing silence for consent. What meaning the title of supreme head had at this time is far from clear. Since it involved spiritual as well as temporal supremacy only the pope was in strict law supreme head of the Church; this accounts for the opposition. Henry himself explained the words away and showed no sign, for two years, of understanding their implications; it is very likely indeed that it meant no more to him than the claim he had made in 1516 (when he had no quarrel with the pope) that the kings of England never had any superiors on earth. He simply wished to assert his control over the Church and remind it that its duty lay with him rather than the pope; as yet he had no thought of replacing the pope altogether. This conclusion is supported by his acceptance of the modifying clause which really invalidated the claim. In the canon law—the law of Christ—the king could not be supreme head of the Church in the technical sense, whatever his practical power might be. At the time, the heavy fine imposed was much more important than the nominal surrender, and more significant still was the fact that the parliament, in its session early in 1531, was asked to register the pardon in an act. Henry again indicated that he would rely on the temporality and its anti-clericalism, and he underlined this when he consented to a free pardon for the laity who had also

[1] As Mr Scarisbrick has shown, in work as yet unpublished, the common view that the charge was obedience to Wolsey's illegal authority rests on a mistake.

technically offended against præmunire by using the Church courts. Otherwise the session was barren of political interest.

Indeed, the year 1531 served to show up the weakness of the royal policy. Determined to render his second marriage as safe as papacy and canon law could make it, Henry persisted at Rome several years after that road had proved to be firmly blocked; his patience and the endurance of his love for Anne Boleyn are both a great deal more evident than his supposed sagacity and political skill. Clement VII forbade re-marriage in 1531, and though Spain could not as yet persuade him to declare the first marriage fully valid he also refused to release Henry. Catherine would not solve the problem by either giving in or dying. The king has even been praised for forbearing to poison her, though it is not likely that he ever thought of doing so, for Henry had a superstitious dread of poison in general; in any case, with all his faults he was not an assassin, and his conscience always required due forms of law in his murders. As 1531 drew to a close, the king's mental bankruptcy became increasingly apparent. Now and again he had hinted at Rome that England could at a pinch do without the pope, but that he had no plan ready for such desperate expedients was plain after his long frustrations. What he was after was probably the kind of concordat by which Francis I had in 1516 acquired very wide powers over the Church in France; but Francis had then merely exploited his position after Marignano and been negotiating from overwhelming strength. Henry, thundering from England, could not hope to achieve similar results. His ministers were broken reeds, without ideas to offer or sufficient skill even to take the burden of government from Henry's shoulders; as early as 1530 he had talked pointedly of recalling Wolsey. But Wolsey was dead, and these Norfolks and Wiltshires, Gardiners and Suffolks, had no answer to the royal perplexities. It was at this point that Henry discovered among his lesser councillors a man who knew exactly how the problem could be solved, and who was an even better administrator than Wolsey. In December 1531, Thomas Cromwell was promoted to the inner ring of the council, and the Tudor revolution was about to begin.

Chapter VI

THOMAS CROMWELL AND THE BREAK WITH ROME

1. THE NEW MINISTER

THOMAS CROMWELL was born about the year 1485 at Putney where his father had a small business as a smith and fuller; of his youth very little is known. He seems to have pursued a most adventurous and unorthodox career which took him abroad as a soldier of fortune in the Italian wars; later he became a merchant with interests and connections on the Antwerp market and somehow got enough learning in the common law to set up as an attorney. He himself told Cranmer that he had been quite a ruffian in his early days, and there survive a number of unreliable stories which only agree in showing that he knocked about Europe in surprising fashion. No doubt it was in these years that he acquired not only an understanding of men and the world, but also an outlook remarkably free from the prejudices of his time and country, and a wide knowledge of languages. He had a reputation for pleasant conversation and wit, for never forgetting old friends and benefactors, and for being a good master to his servants and protector to his clients. His naturally powerful intellect was developed by his unusual history into the most successfully radical instrument at any man's disposal in the sixteenth century; as a statesman he displayed cool indifference in destroying the old and perspicacious dexterity in constructing afresh. His temper was secular, sympathetic to the prevailing anti-clericalism of the time; dislike of the priesthood may have been magnified intc contempt for the papacy by what he saw in Italy. But he appears to have been virtually devoid of passion, even in his anti-clericalism: he did not hate priests as such, or as purveyors of bad religion, but simply objected to them as obstacles to his plans. Cromwell seems to have been incapable of merely negative opinions; everything he did was designed to achieve some positive end, some lasting result. His qualities made him the most remarkable revolutionary in English history—a man who knew precisely where he was going and who nearly always achieved the end he had in view. Though he was ruthless in affairs, he lacked cruelty; seeing little purpose in mercy, he yet had no trace of vindictiveness. Like all politicians of the age he took bribes and presents, but the wealth he accumulated he also spent: ostentation was as foreign to his nature as the pride which values the appearance of power above its reality.

However, he was essentially a cold man, and many who—curiously enough—find it easy to forgive Henry VIII his cruelties and murders because they were carried out in hot blood have nothing but execration for the man who killed for a purpose only and as rarely as possible, but who showed no weakness—attractive or otherwise—once he had decided on a course of action. The men of his day knew him as the all-powerful minister and held him responsible for everything done; he took then, and has since taken, the blame for the unpopular actions without the credit for the rest. Though he had many personal friends and political adherents, his enemies—who comprised all the victims of his devastating policy—were more numerous and more influential. In the last resort, Cromwell, like Wolsey, rested his power on the king's support only. Such popularity as attended him in life did not survive in history. The protestant martyrologist, John Foxe, made him his hero, but in the end Cromwell's fame collapsed in face of the reaction against the Reformation and of the renewed adulation of Henry VIII. The sentimental eighteenth century went maudlin over the ruins of the monasteries, and the Oxford Movement completed what 'sensibility' began. Desire to exculpate Henry VIII increased the burden of contumely heaped upon his minister.[1] By now, general opinion has accepted Thomas Cromwell as a 'Machiavellian', though it is doubtful if he ever read Machiavelli and certain that he did not learn his statecraft from any book; as the cruel, sly, and greedy servant of an imperious master, the wicked though clever destroyer of a civilisation, the unscrupulous builder of a despotism which justly destroyed him in the end.[2] Little of this is true, and even the truth has been distorted by exaggeration. Yet we must endeavour to understand Cromwell's character and aims aright, for in the last analysis it was he who

[1] The serious attack on Cromwell began with S. R. Maitland's *The Reformation in England* (1849), a formidable indictment of 'protestant' history, John Foxe, and the sixteenth-century iconoclasts. Moreover, the leading writers on the period in the last hundred years on the Protestant side (J. A. Froude and A. F. Pollard) were both admirers of Henry VIII and played down the importance of the king's advisers.

[2] The modern picture of Cromwell is derived from the attack made on him by his enemy, Cardinal Pole; though Pole was certainly an honest man, he was also a polemical writer in the medieval tradition which believed in heaping abuse, and he had personal reasons for hating Cromwell and his work which disqualify him as an impartial witness.

founded the modern constitutional monarchy in England and organised the sovereign national state.

Cromwell's travels ended round about 1512 when he appeared once more in England, engaged in legal and commercial affairs. By 1520 he had entered the service of Wolsey whose solicitor and general man of business he became; in this work, and especially in the dissolution of the monasteries used to found the colleges at Ipswich and Oxford, he earned much dislike. In Wolsey's entourage he rose to a leading position, but his patron's fall threatened to end his career. Unlike, for instance, Stephen Gardiner (who was to be his leading opponent), Cromwell did not desert the fallen cardinal; he continued to work for him. In this there was much loyalty but also some calculation, for he used Wolsey's affairs to bring himself to Henry's notice, and he knew that with the king a reputation for faithfulness would be worth having. However, he had to struggle hard before he rose to eminence. In November 1529, he managed to enter parliament pledged to support the king's policy, though he did not owe his seat to official patronage. He played a leading part in the anti-clerical debates of the first session and was rewarded soon afterwards by being taken into the king's service; towards the end of 1530 he was sworn of the council, and a year later he belonged to the inner ring. Throughout he displayed his astounding administrative ability, working his way up through the duties of a civil servant to the king's confidence. It was not until April 1532 that he obtained an office—that of master of the king's jewels. To this he added others: clerk of the hanaper (1532), chancellor of the exchequer (1533), principal secretary and master of the rolls (1534), and finally lord privy seal (1536). These offices he used to acquire wide and precise control of the administration; even at the height of his power he always supervised minutely every detail of government. What gave him power, of course, was not any office but the king's confidence, and this he first secured in the year 1532 when he came forward to cut the knot which none of Henry's other advisers could untie. Cromwell's suggestion for a way out of the king's difficulties had about it a kind of tremendous simplicity. He offered to make a reality out of Henry's vague claims to supremacy by evicting the pope from England. To the king this meant a chance of getting his divorce, and a chance of wealth; to Cromwell it meant the chance of reconstructing the body politic.

2. THE ROYAL SUPREMACY

Cromwell's advice was apparently too overwhelming to be fully accepted at once; nevertheless the parliamentary session of 1532 made it plain that a new temper had taken hold of the government. The uncertainties and futilities of the last three years were to give way to a definite plan and purpose. In this session both the English Church and the papacy were for the first time attacked with real weapons instead of with threats, and the measures used to do this are indisputably linked with Cromwell. In 1531 the Church had been compelled to acknowledge a so far meaningless title and agree to a heavy fine (much of which was never paid); in 1532, the constitutional independence of the Church was overthrown. The instrument employed for this was that petition against Church courts of which Cromwell had taken charge in 1529. As he revised it, a document originally representative of the genuine grievances of the commons concentrated on the one issue in it which affected the crown—the fact that the laws of the Church did not depend on royal sanction. The petition known as 'the Commons' Supplication against the Ordinaries' was introduced into a house exasperated by the king's demands for their assent to a bill strengthening his feudal rights; naturally, the commons took it up with relief and soon convinced themselves that they were debating their own proposals—as in a manner they were.

On 18 March the Supplication was presented to the king. It asserted the commons' orthodoxy, stressed their dislike of the Church's independent legislation, and recited at length many complaints against the practices of the ecclesiastical courts. Henry accepted it graciously and passed it to convocation who drew up a long and not ineffective answer, largely inspired by Gardiner. Henry, however, expressed himself dissatisfied with the answer and suggested to the commons that they might react likewise. Pressure thus having been kept up, the scene was set for the king's demands put before convocation on 10 May: the clergy were to enact no canons and ordinances without the king's licence, the existing canon law was to be examined by a commission of thirty-two men (half of them lay) whom the king would appoint, and the laws approved by them were to receive the king's assent. To impress convocation with the need for surrender, Henry next day summoned another commons' deputation and informed them that he had discovered the clergy to be but half his subjects since they took an oath to the pope; he asked the commons to consider what might be done. Rather than leave their fate and the fate of the canon law in the hands of parliament, convocation on the 15th surrendered them into the hands of the king by accepting his demands in a document known as 'the Submission of the Clergy'. The threat of parliament did more than the threat of præmunire, because there was now a minister in power who knew how to translate generalised assertions into severe practice. In 1531 the clergy had called Henry their supreme head (with vital reservations); in 1532 they accepted the king in the pope's place as their supreme legislator (without any reservations). From that point the English Church ceased to be a potential obstacle in the progress of the breach with Rome.

At the same time, the first direct attack on Rome itself was made. As the discussion in the commons of the government's bill concerning feudal rights made way for the Supplication, the lords began to consider the bill of annates. Annates were the payments made by the bishops to the pope on succession to their sees, rated at one third of a year's income; they had been a long-standing grievance in the whole Western Church. The bill proposed to abolish them on the ground that these payments involved a heavy loss to the nation; it also provided for the consecration of bishops-elect by English authority if the pope were to retaliate by refusing bulls of consecration. The bill thus contained a double-pronged attack: it removed the chief papal source of revenue from England, and it virtually destroyed one of the essential aspects of the pope's spiritual headship. However, the time for extremes had not yet come; Henry still hesitated to throw the pope out altogether; and so Cromwell drafted a clause which became famous. By it the operation of the act was held up until the king should confirm it by letters patent; in the meantime, he was to see what negotiations could do. From a double-edged sword, the first act of annates became a mere diplomatic counter: Henry told the pope that he had had the clause inserted so as to be able to stop the parliament's vigorous attack. In fact, parliament expressed its doubts. In both houses the bill led to a division, an unusual step especially in the commons; the king thought it advisable to be present on both occasions, though there is no reason to think that improper influence was exercised. The ostensible beneficiaries—the bishops and abbots—voted against it to a man; one may suspect that they were expressing their feelings over the progress of the Supplication rather than giving vent to their eagerness to pay taxes to Rome. The opposition in the commons is usually ascribed to the clause which delegated parliament's legislative authority to royal letters patent; there is no evidence for this, and it is at least as likely that the fears of reprisals (such as the stopping of the Flanders trade) which came out a year later were already at work. This interpretation certainly fits this house of commons much better than one which would make it jealous of its legislative powers in the best seventeenth-century manner.

Though fears in parliament and the king's desire to continue with his diplomatic pressure at Rome halted the attack in 1532, the signs were clear. The day after Henry received the clergy's Submission, Sir Thomas More resigned the chancellorship and retired into private life; at last he realised that his attempt to serve the king in everything except the one thing that mattered was putting him in an impossible position. He was succeeded by Sir Thomas Audley, an ally of Cromwell's and lately speaker of the commons. Cromwell himself spent 1532 consolidating his hold over the king and preparing for the real attack. In September, he accompanied Henry to his meeting with Francis at Boulogne, a meeting intended to confirm the Anglo-French amity upon which the foreign policy of these years rested. Francis was more than willing to support Henry at Rome against his own imperial enemy, but he quite failed to realise that the king, and especially the new minister, were beginning to think of more than a concordat with the pope. When Cromwell's policy developed in full the French interest turned against him. It is the mark of Cromwell's ability that he managed to combine a pro-Spanish foreign policy in the interests of English trade with the destruction of everything that Spain wanted to see preserved in England.

1532 declared the new policy; 1533 saw it put through. On 25 January Henry secretly married Anne Boleyn. The matter had become urgent: about this time it must have become certain that she was with child—that child Elizabeth who was to be born early in September—and the expected heir had to be legitimate. But the events of the next session had been planned before this; indeed, it is likely that the sudden pregnancy, after six years of delays, was the result rather than (as is commonly assumed) the cause of the policy embodied in the great statute passed, with an ease that surprised many, early in March 1533. This was the act in restraint of appeals to Rome which made possible the settlement of the divorce in England, as Cromwell had recommended. In August 1532 Archbishop Warham died; in January 1533, Henry appointed Cranmer to the see—Gardiner, who had been angling for it, was in disgrace after his opposition over the Submission of the Clergy—and secured him the papal bulls of consecration by means of the diplomatic threat contained in the conditional act of annates. All this time, and before Anne's pregnancy called for rapid action the act of appeals was drafting in Cromwell's hands; it proved a difficult document to compose and underwent many changes in a lengthy course of preparation. As finally enacted, it prohibited appeals in testamentary and matrimonial causes from the archbishops' courts to Rome. Thus enabled, Cranmer—the canonically appointed archbishop who was to lead the English Church away from Rome and into protestantism—opened his court at Dunstable and on 23 May delivered sentence. The marriage with Catherine was declared void, that with Anne true; the long business of the divorce was over. On 1 June Anne was crowned queen.

Henry had got his will, but what really mattered was the instrument of success, the great act of appeals, Cromwell's masterpiece in statute-making. The enactment confined itself to a practical issue; in effect, it extended the provisions of Richard II's statute of præmunire to appeals lodged at Rome. This was no new grievance: English courts had suffered, and the papal court had profited, from a practice which removed cases to Rome at the instance of one of the contending parties. Money left the realm, justice was delayed, a foreign jurisdiction exercised wide influence on English affairs. The immediate purpose of the prohibition was to enable an English court to free Henry for re-marriage: there had been a plan to pass an act for this specific purpose only, but Cromwell succeeded in getting a general statute which put all ecclesiastical jurisdiction in the king's control. The act of appeals was thus important enough as the most decisive single step towards Cromwell's goal—the expulsion of the papacy—but its famous preamble held even greater significance. This declared that 'this realm of England is an empire . . . governed by one Supreme Head and King', quoting in support the testimony of 'divers sundry old authentic histories and chronicles'. Basing itself on uncertain traditions, the act enunciated new doctrine: it stated as accepted facts that the king was supreme head and the realm a sovereign state free from all foreign authority. The full meaning of these assertions—which amounted to a fully fledged theory of the state—will be discussed in the next chapter. Cromwell's conservative revolution, a revolution resting on strict constitutionalism and dubious historical claims, was therewith really accomplished; it only remained to work out its detailed application. In that important work the enacting clauses of the statute of appeals played themselves a major part by defining the operation of the supremacy in the sphere of jurisdiction as the Submission had defined it in the sphere of legislation. When the annates act was put into force (July 1533), the pope had been deprived of all effective temporal authority in England.

For the rest, the year 1533 saw the fading away of the earlier conflicts, about to be subsumed in the total rejection of the papacy. The divorce—*fons et origo* though hardly any longer the main issue—was, as we have seen, settled by Cranmer, Henry's special archbishop. Cranmer's rise had been rapid. A Cambridge don of reforming tendencies (partly at least because he was given to matrimony), he had come to Henry's notice when he suggested to Gardiner that the theological opinions of the universities might be worth collecting. For twenty years after his sudden elevation to the primacy he was to play a leading part in the story of the English Reformation which in some ways is a fair reflection of his painful and sincere search for spiritual truth. He suited Henry, for he was somewhat unworldly and a change from the political prelates and ambitious laymen who surrounded the king; his gentle, scholarly temper and convinced adherence to the supremacy of the crown—obedience to which he held to be enjoined by the divine law—made him an agreeable leader of the new Church. He and Cromwell presided over the beginnings of the Church of England, and both have had many hard words for their pains; but while Cromwell continues to be maligned, Cranmer's good name has been saved by historians with more sympathy for scholarly hesitation and sincere doubts than for ruthless statesmanship and the truly secular temper.[1] In the Dunstable judgment Cranmer did as he was told, though he also believed the divorce to be just. In reply, the pope excommunicated Henry in July, holding the sentence over till September; Henry in turn confirmed the act of annates and in November lodged an appeal from the pope to a General Council of the Church. This annoyed Francis I who told Gardiner that while he was studying to win the pope the English as fast studied to lose him. Clearly he still failed to understand what was happening. These were but motions to be gone through; Cromwell—and Henry, under his influence—had no intention of winning the pope. The appeal to a general council was useful for propaganda purposes—in December the king's council decided so to employ it—but the reality lay in the preamble of the statute of appeals. The English government wound up its negotiations with the pope and prepared the measures which would put the implications of that preamble into operation.

[1] A. F. Pollard, *Thomas Cranmer and the English Reformation* (1905); C. H. Smyth, *Cranmer and the Reformation under Edward VI* (1926).

The work was done in the two parliamentary sessions of 1534. In the first (January to March) a further act of annates confirmed in full statutory manner the prohibition of these payments to Rome and laid down the procedure for the election of bishops and abbots. Election now became purely formal, the chapters and monasteries being bound by nominations given in the royal licence to elect.[1] The act against the payment of a small annual tax known as Peter's Pence cut off another source of papal revenue; it also transferred the granting of dispensations and licences from Rome to Canterbury, thus removing one further juridical link between the pope and England. The act for the submission of the clergy embodied in a statute the 1532 surrender of convocation and changed the course of appeals in ecclesiastical causes as laid down in the statute of appeals. There, the archiepiscopal courts had had the last word; now appeals were authorised from them to commissions appointed under the great seal, that is to the king in chancery. Thus the Church lost jurisdictional independence to the secular courts. Lastly, the first act for the succession registered the invalidity of the first and validity of the second marriage, drawing the logical conclusion that therefore Mary was illegitimate and the crown must descend to the children of Henry and Anne. More important than this declaration, precedents for which can be found in the reigns of Henry IV and Henry VII, was the clause which made it high treason 'maliciously' to deny or attack the second marriage 'in writing, print, deed, or act', while similar denial in words only was made misprision of treason, a milder offence which carried with it imprisonment and loss of property instead of the death penalty. The act proposed to bind the whole nation by a general oath to observe it; this, not specified in the statute but devised soon after, was intended as a political test of obedience to the new order and of adherence to the royal supremacy in the Church.

The session of November-December 1534 added, first of all, the act of supremacy. It is a short act, containing little of practical import, but it put Henry's full claim on the statute book. It did not make the king supreme head but acknowledged that he 'justly and rightfully is and ought to be Supreme Head of the Church of England', going on to enact that he shall be so 'taken, accepted, and regarded'. Further, it conferred authority to carry

[1] Such interference had been habitual for a long time: the act, by making it statutory, gave it a worse odour in the nostrils of the independent churchmen of today but did not, in fact, alter the contemporary position at all.

out visitations proper to the spiritual power, an indication that the later attack on the monasteries was already decided upon. Another statute showed how hollow had been the pretence that payments to Rome were forbidden as too burdensome to the Church: it ordered the payment of first fruits and tenths to the crown. First fruits meant the payment of one year's income by the new incumbent of any benefice, from episcopal sees to parish vicarages, and tenths an annual levy of one tenth the annual value of every benefice (that is, a ten per cent. income tax); in the event, the Church paid vastly more to the king than it had ever paid to Rome, even as the royal supremacy was in every way nearer home and more troublesome than the pope's had been. At this stage, at least, the Reformation was not the victory of the national Church over an alien domination, as its later champions have too readily imagined, but the victory of the state over the Church in any form. Lastly, the treason act of this session recited a number of treasons, mostly closer definitions of old ones, but it added calling the king or queen heretic or schismatic—which things were presumably being said. Moreover, it extended treason from intent expressed in deeds to intent expressed in words (maliciously). On this much ink has been wasted. Treason by words could be a terrible weapon in the hands of a government dominated by the determined Cromwell and the vengeful Henry, but it was not a new weapon. Throughout the fifteenth century, the judges had been forced by the insufficiency of the treason law of 1352 to 'construct' treasons—that is, to adjudge matters ostensibly outside the statute as falling within it—and words had been so interpreted. The act of 1534 embodied in parliamentary legislation a principle already developed by the common law. Of course, in these years of revolution when opposition had to be stamped out every extension or confirmation of treasons was so much further equipment for the government. But the picture so often drawn of a rule of terror based on a vast network of spies, of innocent men convicted for harmless words twisted against them, is not to be supported by the evidence and must be discarded.

These acts of 1534 completed the work of setting up the royal supremacy in the Church and of destroying the pope's power in England. In January 1535 Henry added the title 'Supreme Head of the Church of England' to his style. A final summary was published in the act of 1536, 'against the papal authority'; this was a good deal ruder to the 'bishop of Rome' but did not deprive him of anything further or add anything to the king's competence. It could not have done so: the work of transferring the papal powers to the crown, begun in the act of appeals, was completed by the enactments of 1534.

3. THE OPPOSITION

The revolution was carried out with the consent of parliament, given readily enough except when fears of papal retaliation through the cloth trade had to be reasoned away. Such fears delayed the first act of annates and the act of appeals; having twice been proved wrong, they did not recur. Some burgesses showed that they preferred Catherine to Anne, and some lords talked wildly to Chapuys of the support that Charles V would receive if he were to invade England; but though the ambassador—wishing to believe—was taken in, his master was not, and nothing ever came of it. The commons proved themselves capable of opposition by freely resisting demands for money and financial assertions of the prerogative, but that there was any real feeling against the king's ecclesiastical policy is denied by the smooth progress of events and cannot be deduced from the deluded hopes of enemies or from a later remark (1537) that the act of appeals passed only because members did not like to displease Cromwell. A little hesitancy there was in parliament, and some opposition—most of it hidden or sullen—outside it. Certainly the government equipped itself with formidable legal weapons against doubters and resisters, but—considering that we are dealing with a revolution—the astonishing thing is that there were so few victims. The reason is plain: this revolution was made and led by the government with the consent of the politically conscious and active classes, and with an almost finicky attention to constitutional propriety. Opposition was confined to those few whose objections rested on principle or conscience, and who moreover rated their consciences higher than anything else. The English Reformation under Henry VIII produced, one might say, no victims and only martyrs. Since among these martyrs there were also some of the most attractive personalities of the day, much attention has always been given to the opposition and its downfall, but the most impressive thing about it is its exiguous size. After the careful repression of the bishops and the Church in 1531-2, only the adherents of the so-called Nun of Kent (including Bishop Fisher), Sir Thomas More, and a few monks felt strongly enough to call into action the treason legislation passed to protect the revolution.

The fatal train was lit by Elizabeth Barton, a poor servant-girl afflicted with epilepsy and visions, who from about 1525 began to attract attention by her trances and prophecies. She was taken up by Dr Edward Bocking, a monk of Canterbury, and acquired a reputation for holiness throughout the county, being named the Holy Maid or Nun of Kent. Unfortunately for himself and his protégée, Bocking, who stage-managed her ravings, conceived the notion of using the Nun against the king's policy. She began to prophesy against the second marriage, alleging that the king would not survive for six months after putting away Catherine, and she actually forced her way into the royal presence to admonish Henry on his way of life. This was dangerous stuff to put about, especially as the Nun had many adherents among the simple folk of Kent (a shire notoriously volatile) and was in touch with the papal representatives. It is hardly to be wondered at that the government could not ignore her activities. She and the accomplices in her tragic farce were arrested and made to confess their impostures publicly in November 1533; in the February session of parliament that followed they were attainted; and in April the deluded woman was executed together with four of the men who had thought to use her for political ends. One's pity must be reserved for Elizabeth Barton; Dr Bocking and friends deserved their fate, and the government cannot be blamed for taking action against such treasonable talk.

But the talk was not yet treasonable in statute law, and this necessitated process by attainder in addition to a trial. Henry intended to use this attainder to attack more illustrious opponents of the divorce: the names of Fisher and More were included, though they were accused only of misprision of the Nun's treason by having kept silent about her doings. Fisher had played an equivocal part: as bishop of Rochester he was in a position to deal with the Nun, and as an eminently sane and learned man (of the famous new learning, too) he should have known better than listen to her with reverence. But listen he did. Perhaps he simply proved how wrong it is to equate humanism with scepticism and a critical attitude to the past; perhaps he allowed his dislike of the divorce to get the better of his judgment. He was lucky, at this time, to get away with a fine of £300. Thomas More, on the other hand, had always judged the Nun rightly, going so far as to call her 'the wicked woman of Canterbury'; his inclusion in the bill was indefensible and shows how Henry's liking for his ex-chancellor had turned to virulent hatred. The bill encountered strong opposition in the lords, but it took much entreaty on the part of his councillors to persuade Henry into leaving More's name out of the bill. More himself remarked that this was but deferring the issue.

The king, now growing ever more intolerant of opposition from his own subjects (parliament always excepted), was determined to pursue both Fisher and More to the death.

His chance came in April 1534 when commissioners began to administer the oath to the act of succession. The oath demanded adherence not only to the succession as laid down in parliament, but also condemnation of the first marriage and an implied denial of the papal supremacy. While Fisher and More were prepared to swear to the first—reluctantly, but after all it was a fact—they would not compromise their consciences to do the second. The resistance of these two well-known leaders of conservative opinion was felt to be deplorable, even though nearly all men, clergy as well as laity, took the full oath readily enough. Both Cranmer and Cromwell tried hard to save More from Henry and himself, but the differences were fundamental. Both men were lodged in the Tower for refusing the oath, until the treason act passed later in 1534 made possible a further attack. More, in particular, defended himself brilliantly in a trial scene as famous almost as that of Socrates, but by dint of declaring that the inclusion of 'maliciously' in the act was invalid, and by accepting the perjured evidence of Sir Richard Rich, the solicitor-general, who deposed to having tricked More into speaking treason, the judges commissioned for the trial felt able to convict him. Fisher, whom the new pope (Paul III) had very injudiciously elevated to the cardinalate in May 1535, was executed in June; More suffered in July; and Henry had demonstrated both his implacable cruelty and his determination to suppress opposition. Two months earlier five clerics, among them three Carthusians of the London Charterhouse, suffered similarly for the same reason, after unspeakable ill-treatment which failed to break their spirits; three more Carthusians followed More to the scaffold.

These executions, and especially those of More and Fisher, have always been considered the worst blot on Henry's record, and rightly so. The king must bear the responsibility. It was he who pressed for extreme measures throughout; baulked of his revenge in the attainder of Elizabeth Barton, he did not rest thereafter until his victims were dead. Cromwell seems to have had a real liking for More whose integrity, personal charm, gentle determination, and miserable fate make him the most attractive figure of the early sixteenth century (not a difficult achievement); for Fisher, his sympathy was less. In any case, Cromwell probably realised the folly of a policy which made martyrs of these well-known men. The brief sharp terror was successful in the short run, but it has since lain heavily in the balance against Henry VIII. Two things, however, must be noted. The country reacted as Henry had reckoned: Edward Hall, the chronicler, a lawyer and member of parliament, spoke for his important section of society when he thought Fisher 'wonderfully deceived' and reproved More solemnly for his excessive levity which could jest even on the scaffold. The victims died without exciting much sympathy in an England given over to loyalty and anti-papalism, though later generations have rehabilitated and even canonised them. The other point is that both Fisher and More were, in fact, dangerous to the government; in a measure, their condemnation was justifiable even though their trials were rigged and the law was twisted. Fisher had been in treasonable correspondence with the emperor's ambassador for some years, though the government were not aware of it; and More, in the fine speech he made after sentence had been passed, expressed his unshakable allegiance to the papal supremacy. These honourable men stood in the way of a revolution; it is tragic but not surprising that they had to be removed, even if the law could get at them only by chicanery. But no one need condone the determined blood-lust displayed by the king who resented opposition to his own will where Cromwell applied the dangerous but not indefensible principle of reason of state.

The case of the Carthusians was different. They suffered for the same reason and deserve even more sympathy because they were not, in fact, anything like as dangerous; also they were treated very badly indeed while More was handled with comparative gentleness. Torturous imprisonment instead of reasoned persuasion was applied to break them, but they did not break. Throughout one feels that this resistance from monks only angered everyone: no one had any patience with monks. The royal supremacy was achieved and opposition to it wiped out; it was time to consolidate the position by putting the supremacy to practical use. Cromwell turned his attention to the monasteries of England where the last centres of resistance might be suspected to be, and where there lay the wealth which the laity desired.

4. THE DISSOLUTION OF THE MONASTERIES

The attack on the monasteries has usually been regarded as the most important part of the great upheavals of the 1530s; but though it was unquestionably spectacular and had some consequences of note, it does not really merit the central position commonly allocated to it. In some ways it was almost the least revolutionary part of the revolution, for attacks on clerical property and piece-meal dissolutions had taken place at intervals over the centuries, whereas the royal supremacy differed altogether from whatever powers the king might previously have exercised over the clergy. The monastic institutions of England had always been in rather a special case, many of them enjoying independence from the bishops and answering for their conduct only to visitors appointed by the pope or by the superior of their own order. They were less national than the secular clergy and owed a special duty to Rome. It is not too much to say that throughout the middle ages regular orders of various kinds—monks as well as friars—had formed the papal vanguard; in the Jesuit order, they were to do so again in the sixteenth century. True, few monasteries or orders displayed any resistance to the royal supremacy, most of them taking the oath readily enough; but what resistance there was came largely from the orders. The six small houses of Observants (strict Franciscan friars) suffered dissolution in 1534 for their opposition, even though they had been Henry VII's favourite order; and apart from More and Fisher, the martyrs of 1535 were men who had taken the vows. The government could be pleased at the ease with which even the traditional papal strongholds had succumbed, but they could not risk a monastic revival in favour of the pope.

The orders collapsed so readily before the assault because monasticism in England was on its last legs. Riddled by worldliness and deadened by routine, the institution had lost all or nearly all meaning; the ideal was as near extinct as no matter, and the practice not such as to encourage sincere men. Sir Thomas More found it more congenial to wear his hairshirt outside a formal order. Intellectually, only the friars retained any vigour; for that reason they supplied so many leaders of the Reformation. An Austin friar led the way in Germany when Luther 'hopped from his habit', and in England, too, the leading heretic and preacher of the 1530s (Tyndale being exiled) was a friar of that order, Dr Robert Barnes. The laity had no respect left for monasticism, and quite a number of the monks themselves were interested only in getting out of vows they had taken before they were old enough to understand their meaning. Nor did the monasteries play a useful part in the community. Old notions of the kindly monks as gentle landlords have been disproved; where they administered their own estates they were quite as keen on making the most of things as laymen, and indeed it would have been dereliction of duty if an abbot or prior had neglected the welfare of his house. In any case, most monastic estates were by this time leased to local yeomen or gentlemen. Monastic charity and hospitality, too, played little part in sixteenth-century England: it has been calculated that the monks gave rather less than five per cent. of their net income to charitable purposes, and—except in the desolate north—the abbeys were no longer needed as places of refuge and refreshment. The people who used them as inns were not so much poor wayfarers (as sentimental writers think) but more commonly the great—men and women connected through patronage or honorary office with the abbeys, like the duchess of Suffolk who often visited Butley Priory in Suffolk to be entertained with dinner and a fox hunt. The monasteries' sole remaining purpose was also their original one. They still stood for a spiritual ideal (though too often their practice denied it), and they still prayed for the souls of the dead. But few men now included in their wills those bequests for prayers which in earlier centuries had testified to the real need served by monastic institutions. Their spiritual value cannot be assessed by the historian, outside whose competence this matter is; what he can say is that contemporaries had largely ceased to care about it, and that the monks themselves were often too few to carry out these duties.

Monasticism was, then, in such decline that its end might have come spontaneously, but the real reason for the attack on it lay elsewhere. It was the property of the orders that men desired—the lay lords and gentlemen as much as the government. Schemes of secularisation were of long standing: the whole property of the Church—between one fifth and one third of all land in England—had been under spasmodic attack for some two centuries. Plans were mooted to transfer all the lands to lay hands and pay bishops and incumbents a fixed stipend, but this was too vast a task to contemplate seriously. From an early date the government realised that it could bind the gentry and nobility to the new order by bribing them with lands which any reversal of policy would force them to restore. But Cromwell had a more urgent reason still for sequestrating the monasteries. The crown's finances were far from healthy. Cromwell inherited a financial problem from Wolsey who had not managed to keep the revenue on a level with his expenditure, and the exigencies of the years when the royal supremacy was established aggravated the situation. Regular revenue was dropping because of a decline in the wool customs; this reflected an increase in the amount of wool exported as cloth (which paid less duty than raw wool) and therefore an encouraging trend in English trade, but was nevertheless awkward for the government's finances. The years 1533-4 saw a determined effort to put England's defences in order against the possibility of an attack from Spain; affairs in Ireland, to be discussed hereafter, demanded heavy expenditure; and the French pension, which Wolsey had found so useful, was surrendered in 1534 as part of the diplomacy which tried to maintain friendship with France to balance the danger from Charles V. It was patently impossible to ask much from parliament at a time when its harmonious co-operation was desired in the expulsion of the pope. Cromwell succeeded in getting supplies in 1534, but they amounted to less than £200,000 payable over four years; he needed an increase in the regular revenue. For a time he made do with revivals of Henry VII's practices: distraint of knighthood appeared again, and he exploited the chance of mulcting the clergy collectively or individually in fines imposed for real or imaginary offences. The feudal rights of the crown came to the fore in the long battle for the statute of uses, not passed until 1536; this was intended to follow up Henry VII's recovery of prerogative rights by preserving the king's just claims upon a tenant's death from infringements by means of legal fictions and evasions. But all this, useful though it was, amounted to no more than temporary expedient and failed to solve the lasting problem of a static revenue in an age of rising costs.

Thus Cromwell turned to the Church. In 1534 he transferred to the crown the payment of first fruits and tenths, calculated as likely to yield an average annual income of about £40,000. There was to be a realistic assessment, and in January 1535 commissions issued for the valuation of all ecclesiastical property in England. The stupendous task was done within some six months, and it was done thoroughly and well; its product, the tax-book known as the *Valor Ecclesiasticus*, has been carefully tested by modern historians and found astonishingly good. The achievement spoke well for the administrative capacity of Tudor governments and the skill of the minister and his agents. Equipped with this detailed and complete knowledge of what there was to be had, Cromwell could proceed to the real attack. He had had it in mind for some time, and he had precedents to guide him: he himself had been trained by Wolsey's dissolutions in the technical details of the task. First one had to discover an official pretext: this was to be found in the monasteries' corruption and decay, established by means of the traditional ecclesiastical weapon of a visitation. The act of supremacy, which included a clause authorising the king as supreme head to visit all institutions of the Church in order to search out and correct abuses, superseded at will the disciplinary powers of the bishops and brought within the royal survey all houses hitherto free from control in England. In January 1535, Thomas Cromwell, appointed vicar-general by the supreme head, began to dispatch a group of visitors to gather evidence. These men have been the object of violent attack, even as they themselves violently and unfairly attacked the institutions they visited. Admittedly, they were hardly prepossessing characters, and they knew that they were expected to turn in damaging details. Dr Richard Layton, a cleric of salacious tastes, Dr Thomas Legh, an arrogant young man with a 'satraplike countenance' (as one of his colleagues put it), John ap Rice, a man of servility, Dr John London, a persecutor born: no one need admire these and their like. But the visitation, hostile though it was, followed precedent in everything, even in the speed of its work and the extremity of its conclusions. The only difference was in the ultimate outcome. The visitors brought questionnaires of the traditional type and imposed the sort of injunctions to obey the rules which bishops had time and again and with increasing weariness put to their charges; but Layton and Legh knew that they were to enforce the rules as to residence, asceticism, clean living, and obedience with all the rigour possible, so as to encourage monks to opt for a dispensation from their vows and the end of monasticism.

The whirlwind went through the country, sweeping up many discontented brethren, finding plenty of scandals (though hardly more than earlier visitors had done, so that one need not suspect fabrication), and providing much ammunition for the attack. Medieval propaganda relied on denigration; that is, it assembled every charge, silly or heinous, and flung everything—regardless of truth—at the accused. Cromwell's government acted likewise against the monasteries, not so much because these were so utterly corrupt—though by high-lighting the wicked the truth could be made to appear quite bad enough—as because they wished to prepare the ground for the dissolution. The visitation of 1535 was never intended to mend but always to end; it was an hypocritical weapon. Equally hypocritical was the pretence in the bill introduced into the parliament of February 1536 that only the lesser houses were corrupt; the bigger ones served religion, maintained discipline, and knew no vice. It appeared from the bill that the line between virtue and depravity followed with curious fidelity the line which divided £200 a year from incomes larger than this: realising well that he could not carry out the whole dissolution at one stroke, Cromwell first attacked only the smaller monasteries.

Another statute set up the court of the augmentations of the king's revenue which was to administer the transfer of their lands to the crown. The court started work at once. Throughout 1536 its officers went the rounds of the monasteries affected, dissolved the institutions, took surveys of the lands, made inventories of lead, gold, silver, and precious stones found, and disposed of the monks either by sending them to a bigger house of their own order or—if they wished to leave the religious life—by paying them pensions or finding them vicarages and benefices. The dissolution violently destroyed centuries-old communities and wiped out ancient landmarks; but it was carried through not only with efficiency but also with unexpected humanity and with a regard for property rights which, though typical of the age, is a little ludicrous in the midst of the great expropriation. Thus debts incurred by the monasteries were taken over by the government and paid, and the personal goods of monks were guaranteed to them.

In the midst of the dissolution a sudden storm of opposition took the government by surprise; for a time it looked likely to threaten not only Cromwell's policy but even perhaps Henry's throne. This was the northern rising, also known as the pilgrimage of grace, which convulsed Lincolnshire, Yorkshire, and finally all the north in the last three months of 1536. The movement was complex. The north had never yet been properly settled; conservative and dominated by old feudal allegiances, it resented the interference of the central government which was increasing under Cromwell. The gentry and nobility objected to successive attacks on 'liberties' and hated the statute of uses with its augmentation of royal rights. The influential Percy interest was discontented because of the downfall of the sixth earl of Northumberland who had wasted his substance and attempted to govern the north as the king's lieutenant in opposition to the king's interests. As always, there was an agrarian element in the unrest: cries were heard against enclosures and raised rents. The collection of the subsidy of 1534 and the enforcement of legislation for the better manufacture of cloth stirred up additional trouble among the well-to-do of the West Riding. The final impetus was given by religion. The attack on the old religion had barely begun, yet already it smacked of far too much heresy to the northern people, and the dissolution of the monasteries—of which Lincolnshire and Yorkshire were particularly full—proved the last straw. Resentment at the various commissioners who went round assessing for the subsidy, dissolving and pulling down abbeys, and administering to conservative parish priests the heterodox Injunctions of 1536 no be discussed later), was exacerbated by wild rumours: it was said, among other things, that many parish churches would also be put down, that the king would have all the gold in the country, that no one would be allowed to eat white bread, pigs, and capons without a licence. All this only shows how profoundly disturbed the north was. Trouble, signs of which multiplied during September, broke out at Louth in Lincolnshire on 1 October with a riot which soon spread further; in a few days the whole county rose, the gentry followed willy-nilly, Cromwell's commissioners were taken and manhandled. The rebels demanded that no more abbeys be suppressed, that Cromwell be handed over to the people, and that the heretical bishops (especially Cranmer) be dismissed. All through they declared themselves loyal to the crown; perhaps the most remarkable thing about the whole rising was the confidence of these deluded men that the king was on their side and they on his.

Although the rebels occupied Lincoln in force and the king's representative—the duke of Suffolk—had not a fortieth of their army, the Lincolnshire rising collapsed abruptly on 19 October when the king haughtily refused to listen to the demands of men under arms against his authority. But in the meantime more serious trouble began further north. Yorkshire was up, and here there appeared a leader in the person of Robert Aske, a country gentleman and lawyer. To Aske the rising was religious; it was he who popularised the banner with the five wounds of Christ and spoke of a pilgrimage. His followers took York where he set up in state, issued ordinances for the government of the north and received the adherence of great men like the archbishop (Edward Lee) and Lord Darcy. By the 24th he had 30,000 armed men at Doncaster, while the king's commanders had nothing. Suffolk was stuck in Lincolnshire which could not as yet be safely left without a royal army; Shrewsbury had rashly advanced too far with too few men and was useless; and Henry's ablest general, the duke of Norfolk (rapidly recalled from the retirement into which Cromwell had shunted him) was as yet collecting a force. On 27 October he met Aske at Doncaster Bridge and, unable to take action, agreed to communicate the rebels' demands to the king. He told Henry that he had no intention of keeping his promises; indeed, his conduct at this time does not suggest—as has been suspected—that he was secretly encouraging the rising in order to get rid of Cromwell. Instead he temporised, tricking Aske into disastrous delays. In any case, the rebel leader found it impossible to lead his followers south; they wished to stay near their homes, and there was no response to their appeals anywhere south of the Trent where the country remained firmly loyal. Furious at having to treat with rebels, Henry yet played his part well: he delivered an interim answer which kept the door open, while Norfolk rapidly increased his army. On 2 December Aske gathered a 'great council' at Pontefract to draw up the pilgrims' final terms; these repeated the earlier demands for an end to the dissolution, for the repeal of the statute of uses, and for the dismissal and punishment of Cromwell and his supporters, but added also the restoration of the papal jurisdiction and the liberties of the Church. In addition, Aske demanded a reformed parliament free from royal interference; this is remarkable enough as a recognition of the place held by parliament, though it differs little from past complaints on that score back to the reign of Richard II and reflects rather northern resentment at the activities of the Reformation parliament than that parliament's corruption and subservience, which it has been taken to prove.

However, the crisis was nearly over, for Aske had waited too long and trusted too well. Neither Norfolk nor Henry thought themselves bound by promises made to rebellious subjects. The duke met Aske again at Doncaster on 6 December; Norfolk promised vaguely to adhere to some of the demands and offered a full and free pardon. Thereupon Aske ended the pilgrimage. He declared himself the king's faithful subject and with great difficulty prevailed upon his followers to disperse. The king had won, seemingly at the cost of surrendering to the pilgrims on essential points, but he could bide his time. The unrest was not ended by Aske's resignation at Doncaster; throughout January and February 1537 there were minor riots and upheavals which were used to free the king from his promise and to exact his vengeance. In the first half of 1537, Norfolk, as Henry's lieutenant in the north, summarily executed men all over the northern provinces, distributing the hangings so as to impress all parts with the terror of the king's power. The leaders of the late rising were separately executed, including Lord Darcy, an old servant of the crown, and Aske who died at York after a travesty of a trial and despite promise of pardon. Altogether some 220 to 250 people suffered, not many by the standards of contemporary Europe but a sufficiently fearsome retribution. Moreover, it was made possible only by a wholesale breaking of promises. Yet, when all was done, the pilgrimage stood out for the futile, misdirected, and ill-considered venture it was. The grievances of the commons and especially the religious enthusiasm of some (Aske in particular) deserve respect and sympathy, but much of the spirit of the rising was sordid, self-seeking, and particularist. The pilgrimage achieved nothing. The one major protest against Cromwell's revolution and seemingly dangerous for a time, it was always confined to the backward and barbarous north. The tranquillity of the south demonstrated that Henry and Cromwell had the majority of their people behind them. Even the factions among leading politicians, profound though they appear, proved to be only superficial when Norfolk prevented the success of a movement designed to destroy his rival. Loyalty and obedience to the king, the guardian of peace and order and the symbol of the state, dominated everything. Even the rebels used the language of loyalty, though in the circumstances their protestations sounded odd. Five months of trouble resulted only in the reorganisation of the north, which will engage our attention later, and in a vigorous renewal of Cromwell's revolution both in the progress of the dissolution and in the seeking out and suppression of further malcontents in the next few years.

The rising had involved many monks—naturally enough, for they had most to gain by it. A number of abbots and priors lost their lives because they had participated in the Pilgrimage, though others, and many lesser brethren, were pardoned. But the executions of the abbots of Kirkstead, of Whalley and Jervaux, and of the ex-abbot of Fountains (March to May 1537) led the way in the attack on the bigger monasteries. Their suppression had always been intended, despite the kind words used about them in the act of 1536; now the collapse of the rising—their last hope—encouraged the greater houses to surrender themselves and their property into the king's hands. Furness, in Lancashire, led off early in 1537, and many others followed. In 1538, Cromwell's commissioners began another visitation of the abbeys yet standing, offering a prepared form of surrender which was commonly signed without protest. Action reinforced threats: apart from a general attack on the old religion which produced in 1538 a first burst of image-breaking and the suppression of relics, Cromwell took care to remind recalcitrant monks of the government's power by obtaining the conviction and execution of the abbot of Woburn for attacking the supremacy. The parliament which met in April 1539 passed an act securing to the crown all property that had come to it or would yet come by surrender or dissolution; in the autumn, the three great abbeys of Glastonbury, Colchester, and Reading were dissolved after their abbots had been hanged for treasons they probably contemplated but had barely yet committed; and when Waltham surrendered in March 1540 the monasteries were gone. In 1539 the friaries had been similarly absorbed, and in 1540

Cromwell added the preceptories (or branch establishments) of the Order of St John of Jerusalem. Therewith the vast secularisation was complete; monasticism had ended, and the crown and the laity had acquired a great mass of lands whose disposal was to have far-reaching effects on the social structure of England. The dissolution increased the revenue of the crown by well over £100,000 a year, roughly the total royal income at the beginning of Cromwell's ministry.

The wider effects of the dissolution belong to the story of economic change;[1] what were the immediate results? Much undoubtedly was destroyed. A whole form of religion was gone; England could not be protestant while the monasteries stood, and unquestionably—whatever the intention of Henry VIII—protestantism was brought nearer by the dissolution. There was destruction of buildings, works of art, and libraries, lamentable enough but neither complete nor without its compensations; many of England's finest buildings today—the great houses—would not exist but for the dissolution. The dissolution hardly aggravated the problem of poor relief: neither had the monasteries played a great part in supplying it, nor did the number of paupers much increase. The old pictures of exiled monks wandering about the roads of England to die in ditches were wildly inaccurate. The monks received pensions which were generally adequate and lavish for the late abbots and priors, though nuns and friars, whose houses were mostly poorer, did less well and often badly. But both monks and friars were as quickly as possible placed in livings, unless they preferred to be rid of their vows and take to a secular life. Some of the many servants employed in the monastic establishments no doubt went to swell the ranks of the poor, but many took service with the new owners who still had to till the lands and maintain their establishments.

The really surprising thing is not that there was some dislocation—even at times a good deal of it—but that the dissolution passed off so easily. Within a few years the monks were but memories, and as memories they soon acquired a glamorous reputation for holiness and kindliness which in their decline they had done little to earn. The effect of the great secularisation on the land market—the leases and sales—is a different matter. It had never been intended that the crown should keep all the lands, and from 1538 onwards Cromwell began to organise a judicious disposal. The men who carried out the dissolution—the vicar-general himself, the lord chancellor, and the officers of the court

[1] Below, Ch. IX.

of augmentations—were well rewarded with gifts, as were some courtiers. But others had to buy lands or take up leases on terms advantageous to the crown; certainly until Cromwell's fall there was no question of squandering the wealth with which he had equipped the king. In the Church itself the dissolution produced one commendable change. In 1540, Henry was at last able to carry out a plan of Wolsey's by establishing six new episcopal sees;[1] these were badly needed, for Lincoln and Lichfield were much too big to be properly administered. The dissolution destroyed the last possible refuge of papalism, enriched the crown, and anchored the new order firmly in the self-interest of the land-owning classes who purchased the estates. It did all this with the thoroughness and amazing ease (despite the pilgrimage of grace) which characterised all Cromwell's achievements.

5. FOREIGN POLICY AND RELIGION, 1536-40

The dissolution of the monasteries was far from being the only business to occupy the government in the years 1536-40. The break with Rome demanded the greatest care in relations with other countries; the correspondence of Chapuys is full of references to malcontents ready to rise if only the emperor will invade England, and though the ambassador was unquestionably prone to daydreams it cannot be doubted that Henry VIII took an enormous risk in the 1530s. Real action from the champions of the pope and Queen Catherine would, to say the least, have been most embarrassing to a country undergoing a revolution, however well-conducted and peaceful this was. On the other hand, the English war with Rome could hardly hope to go forward without some attention to other men elsewhere who were assailing the same target for very different reasons. Henry VIII himself wished to hold his nation to that orthodoxy of the catholic faith which he and they valued so much: he never saw any difficulty in remaining a good catholic without the pope and never envisaged the spread of protestantism which the break with Rome encouraged. From the first the few reformers in England raised joyful voices at the supreme head's doings, even though they equally miscalculated in thinking that Henry's anti-papalism would mean the speedy establishment of their own doctrines. The appointment to Canterbury of Cranmer, not so far a well-known protestant but known to have leanings that way, foreshadowed great changes; the

[1] Oxford, Chester, Gloucester, Bristol, and Peterborough endured; Westminster was abolished in 1550.

religious Reformation in England owed a great deal to Henry's strange whim in picking on this man as his primate and his stranger fidelity in supporting him against his enemies for fifteen years. Cromwell's position is more dubious. It is now fashionable to suppose that he had no religion at all, but that is as demonstrably wrong as the old notion that he was an inspired protestant. In a careless moment he once told some Lutheran envoys that he was on the whole of their opinion, but that 'as the world now stood he would believe even as his master the king believed'. This seems reasonable enough. He did not propose to push through a form of religion, or to die for it, in which he (as secular a man as has existed in a pre-scientific age) had at best a lukewarm interest; but to his logical mind the religion of all those who opposed the pope ought to be the same, that is to say, protestant in some fashion.[1] He held this the more strongly because throughout his ministry he overestimated the danger from abroad and therefore overvalued an alliance with foreign Lutherans or native reformers. After 1536, the question was no longer the defence of the royal supremacy against attack, but the growing faction strife between those who wished to establish a reformed Church and those who wished to keep the Church catholic. This struggle, in which diplomacy and religion were intricately entwined, is the story of the years 1536-58.

While Cromwell was establishing the king as supreme head, he had to rely on the alliance with France inherited from Wolsey's last years. This proved relatively easy until late in 1533 when Francis I, at last understanding where things were tending in England, began to waver. In consequence other feelers were put out. In 1533 Cromwell tentatively opened fruitless negotiations with the Lutheran princes of Germany; in 1534, Henry himself, forsaking the determined neutrality which he normally favoured after witnessing the collapse of Wolsey's policy of alliances, involved himself in the affairs of protestant Lübeck, a Baltic town which was trying to prevent the imperial nominee from ascending the vacant throne of Denmark. Nothing came of all this except ephemeral trouble; Charles V was hindered from succouring his aunt (whose treatment grew worse after 1533) not by English skill but by his commitments in the Mediterranean and his troubles in Germany. In 1535 things began to look black. France showed signs of turning from the understanding with England to friendship with Spain: the spectre of a union of the catholic powers

[1] I personally consider that his religion was rather more sincere than that, though it never interfered with his politics; but this is a point that cannot be developed here.

against schismatic England, which was to haunt Cromwell to his death, seemed for a time very real. Immediately, negotiations with the German Lutherans were resumed, though still to no purpose; this time it was hoped to get not only a political alliance but also the services of great reformers like Melanchthon. Melanchthon stayed at home, but Cromwell took advantage of some episcopal vacancies to promote well-known English protestants. In 1535 Hugh Latimer succeeded to Worcester and Nicholas Shaxton to Salisbury; these and others were the heretical bishops whose dismissal the pilgrims of grace demanded a year later. Cromwell clearly wished to face attack with Henry as the leader of a reformed country, but it is much less certain whether the king was with him in this. Henry seems to have understood the essential safety of England's isolated position. Cromwell was always much too inclined to practise the directness and thoroughness of his methods in the field of foreign affairs which required delays, waiting, and opportunism; he was temperamentally a worse foreign minister than the king.

Not only did the danger pass in 1535; the next year seemed to bring promise of complete success and a chance of getting Europe to accept the new England without engaging on either side in the increasing religious split. In January 1536 Catherine died, to the king's open and indecent (if understandable) rejoicing; and in May Anne Boleyn perished on the scaffold. Her fate had been creeping upon her for some time. Henry's passion, steadfast enough through six years of frustration, does not appear to have long survived its fulfilment, and in the great matter of the succession Anne proved a disappointment. The child born in September 1533 was a girl, named Elizabeth, and thereafter the dreary tale of miscarriages was resumed. Henry, like the gentleman he was, showed his disappointment openly and reminded his queen of her origin and his ability to humble her again. The story of her overthrow is confused. The king's conscience again came conveniently into play; there was a new candidate for queenly honours in Jane Seymour, a lady of the court; Anne's last safeguard died with Catherine during whose life the second marriage could not be repudiated without implying the validity of the first. Cromwell, whose alliance with the Boleyns had always been one of convenience only, decided the more readily to sever it because he was anxious to restore the Anglo-Spanish alliance and to break with the French understanding of which the Boleyns and Howards had been the protagonists. In April a secret commission was appointed to find evidence against Anne, and in May she was accused of manifold adultery, one of her alleged lovers being her own brother. That some of the charges—which included conspiracy to kill the king—were wild is certain; whether there was any truth in them at all has never been settled. At any rate, Anne and five men were put to death by due process of law because the king wished to marry again. Of all the victims of Henry VIII, Anne Boleyn—light-hearted and light-headed instrument of revolution—has had almost no sympathy; yet by her death and the manner of it she deserves it. Henry had now so far discarded scruple that to get his way he was prepared to appear as a cuckold and a victim of witchcraft. Anne died on 19 May; on the 17th Cranmer declared her marriage void, and on the 30th Henry married Jane Seymour.

These events cleared the deck. With Catherine and Anne both out of the way, England stood much better internationally, the more so as relations between Spain and France worsened noticeably during 1536. Henry was determined to continue in isolated neutrality, confident—rightly confident—that he was safe; Cromwell, on the other hand, fearing danger from abroad and even more perhaps the activities of the Francophile faction at home (led by his enemies Norfolk and Gardiner), attempted in vain to restore the alliance with the emperor. On one occasion he got into serious trouble with the king for acting precipitately. At the same time the religious problem grew pressing. The break with Rome had left the Church in a very uncertain state; some definition of the faith to be observed was urgently required, for the country was being set by the ears by wild teaching and revolutionary preaching. The pope gone, many thought the time had come for a full religious reform, but neither the king (who remained attached to the old faith) nor Cromwell and Cranmer (moderates in Church reform) were prepared to go as far as the extremists whose voices were loudest. In July 1536 the government issued the first formulary of the Church of England, the Ten Articles, a compromise between the old and the new. On the sacraments of the altar, penance, and baptism, and on good works, the Articles were orthodox; but they deemed no other sacraments necessary, and on the vexed problems of prayers to saints and prayers for the dead they cautiously advanced towards the Lutheran view that these were of no value. The document rested, of course, on the authority of the supreme head, not on that of convocation or parliament, and in August Cromwell, as the supreme head's deputy or vicegerent in spirituals (a title bestowed some time before January 1536) issued Injunctions making the Articles binding upon the clergy. The Injunctions also taught priests their business and ordered a bible in English to be placed in every parish church. The translation was already in hand, though not until 1539 were the first official bibles supplied—Matthew's Bible, as it is called, a compilation drawing on the work of two leading English protestants, William Tyndale and Miles Coverdale. But while there were signs of cautious reform, continental hopes, nourished by negotiations in 1535-6, that England would adopt the Lutheran faith were disappointed with the appearance in 1537 of a primer (or book of faith and instruction) called *The Institution of a Christian Man* or 'The Bishops' Book'. This 'found again' the four 'lost' sacraments of 1536 and generally defended catholic orthodoxy against innovation.

The reasons for these vacillations are partly to be found in the international situation. Late in 1536 war broke out between Charles V and Francis I, freeing Henry from all need to serve any interests but his own; and the king was as anti-Lutheran as ever. The 'Bishops' Book' may also reflect second thoughts after the pilgrimage of grace had demonstrated the great strength of conservative opinion in religion. Altogether, 1537 was a year of marking time and clearing up after the northern rising and the first act for dissolving the monasteries. Even Cromwell forbore to push his two schemes of alliance—a political and commercial understanding with Spain, and a religious rapprochement with the German League of Schmalkalden. In October, Henry at last had a son—Edward—and though his birth cost his mother's life, it seemed as if Heaven was blessing all the supreme head's enterprises. But not for long: 1538 saw the beginning of a crisis which first swept Cromwell away, outlived Henry and two of his children, and was only settled with great difficulty by Elizabeth. The struggle between the old religion and the new was joined in earnest, with the usual intricate interplay of foreign affairs and doctrinal reform. The vague factions crystallised: Norfolk and Gardiner assumed the virtual leadership of conservatism against the radicals led by Cromwell and Cranmer. For nearly two years Henry carefully felt his way between them before falling in with the orthodoxy with which his own sympathies lay; so far from directing this storm, he was determined to put his weight in the scales only after he knew where majority opinion tended.

The crisis really began late in 1537 with better relations between France and Spain which led to the peace of Nice in the summer of 1538. All Cromwell's fears revived, as his energetic activity throughout the year in restoring England's military defences proves clearly enough. Splendid isolation did not seem enough now, and the approach to Germany was resumed with vigour. From May to October 1538 German ambassadors tried to come to an agreement with Cromwell and Cranmer, but Henry's reluctance both to commit himself to a political alliance and to commit the country, whose temper was far from radical, to protestantism prevented a treaty. In his Injunctions of September 1538 the vicegerent renewed the war on 'popish and superstitious' practices: throughout the year, centres of pilgrimage were attacked, ancient wonder-working images were exposed as frauds and destroyed, even Becket's shrine at Canterbury was demolished and despoiled. The crown gained much treasure in gold and jewels, but the chief reason was religious: it was all part of the radical party's programme during its first brief ascendancy.

At the same time Cromwell proceeded against disaffection. The protagonist of the papal project to reconquer England was Reginald Pole, a kinsman of Henry VIII and a cardinal since 1536. Pole's activities provoked an attack on his family in England—who were also the last remnant of the old Yorkist faction. In August 1538, the Poles (Reginald's brothers Geoffrey, pardoned after he had supplied evidence against the rest, and Lord Montague, and his mother, the aged countess of Salisbury), as well as the marquess of Exeter (Henry Courtenay) and Sir Edward Neville, were arrested; in December all except the countess, who survived until 1541, were executed. The attack on them arose directly out of treasonable activities in defence of the pope and the old faith in which they had been engaged; but it also completed the dynastic policy of the first two Tudors by removing their last potential rivals. This second aim does not appear to have been deliberate; rather were the victims themselves induced to pit themselves against Henry's policy by their dynastic ambitions as much as by their religion. The onslaught caused an uproar abroad and much fear among the nobility at home who saw in it proof of Cromwell's contemptuous attitude to their order (a debatable point). The real leaders of the opposition to him—Gardiner and Norfolk, whom with misplaced generosity he spared from all attack—decided that only his death could make them safe. As 1538 closed and 1539 opened, the situation worsened. Attempts to reform the French alliance were rebuffed by Francis who would not let Henry find a wife among his subjects; the alternative—marriage with the duchess of Milan to secure the friendship of Spain—also collapsed when Spain and France renewed their amity in January 1539. Cardinal Pole went on a mission to these two countries in order to win support for a campaign to execute the bull of deprivation of

1535. This, calling upon all Christians to destroy Henry VIII, was put into effect late in 1538. All through 1539 Pole travelled over Europe, achieving nothing, narrowly escaping assassination, and keeping Cromwell apprehensive. Henry seems by this time to have believed himself invulnerable, and though such arrogant egotism deserved a worse reward he was proved right in his conviction that there was no danger to be feared from abroad which England could not weather on her own.

Cromwell thought differently, especially after a clash over religion which occupied most of the time of the parliament that sat from April to June 1539. His Injunctions of the previous year, which had attacked images and pilgrimages, ordered the reading of the English bible, and incidentally inaugurated the keeping of parish registers, marked an advance in radical reform. The reaction was not long in coming. By early 1539 it became clear that the country was being riven in two by a religious controversy which the supreme head would have to settle. Henry ordered the convocations, which met concurrently with parliament, to consider the matter, and after much debate conservative orthodoxy prevailed. The king waited upon the outcome rather than interfered to determine it:[1] the radicals were in a minority even among the bishops, and Cromwell and Cranmer gave way when they saw the trend of things. Even so Cromwell had a bad two months before he could recapture control from Norfolk and Gardiner who came very near to unseating him. The decision on religion was given force by a parliamentary statute appointing penalties for transgressors against the six articles agreed upon—the act of six articles. These articles embodied full catholic doctrine: they asserted transubstantiation, the need for auricular confession, the sanctity of monastic vows, communion under one kind only, the justness of private masses, and the illegality of clerical marriage. The act might have been a decisive weapon against the reformers had it ever been employed very widely, but while Cromwell lived it slept, and it was never fully operative. The radicals, with few exceptions (Latimer and Shaxton resigned their sees), accepted the verdict of king and parliament and awaited a better future. The importance of the act has been overestimated by both sides; it did not even signal the overthrow of Cromwell who recovered most of his strength by July.

However, the rough handling of these months and the continued danger from abroad now betrayed Cromwell into action fatal to

[1] This is not to deny that in the course of the discussions he proved himself interested and very knowledgeable in theology.

himself. A second Lutheran embassy had departed in May with even less satisfaction gained than the first; but there still remained the projected treaty with the duke of Cleves, no Lutheran himself but allied to Lutherans. To this alliance Henry showed himself inclined in March 1539 when even he began to have his doubts about England's isolation in Europe. Cleves, astride the lower Rhine, was a thorn in the emperor's side and a useful ally to have while Pole seemed likely to stir up a crusade against England. The situation changed in the course of the year, especially when the arrival in June of a French ambassador to England suggested hopes of ending the Franco-Spanish friendship. Nevertheless, Cromwell determined to force the king to his side, and in October he dragooned Henry into a marriage alliance with Anne of Cleves. Holbein, who painted a flattering portrait of Henry's fourth bride which deceived both king and minister, bears an ironical share of the responsibility for Cromwell's downfall. In January 1540 Anne came over; Henry, meeting her, was shocked by her plainness and bad manners; but, as he said, there was no cure—he had to put his neck in the yoke. From 6 January 1540, when the marriage was celebrated, Cromwell's position was in danger; though his mistakes were not beyond remedy, he had forced the king into a distasteful policy and an even more distasteful marriage both of which could most easily be discarded by getting rid of Cromwell.

The conservative faction now gathered its strength. In February, Norfolk went on embassy to France and, from a court conditioned to hate Cromwell by Gardiner's long residence there, brought back a virtual promise of friendship if only the vicegerent were removed. Late in March, Gardiner recovered his seat in the privy council by an attack on the Lutheran Dr Barnes, an overconfident and self-assertive reformer whose extravagances brought upon him the king's displeasure. Barnes was Cromwell's protégé, and though Cromwell was careful not to involve himself in the affair he could not but be displeased at Gardiner's success. Rumours of coming changes flew about the capital. When parliament reassembled in April Cromwell displayed his accustomed skill and leading position in steering through a subsidy bill and the confiscation of the lands of the Order of St John. On 17 April he was given fresh honours, being made earl of Essex and great chamberlain of England. But while he was busy at Westminster in parliament and council, his enemies gained the upper hand at Greenwich where the court was. Norfolk, taught nothing by the fate of his niece Anne Boleyn, succeeded in interesting the king in the charms of another niece, Katharine Howard, and so Henry's demand for a third annulment of a marriage was added to all the other problems. In the second half of May Cromwell counterattacked, at last seeking out his real enemies among the bishops; but though he seized Richard Sampson of Chichester and got evidence against unnamed others, it was too late. Even early in June Henry still trusted the man who had removed two queens from his path to bring off yet a third miracle, but Cromwell could not remove Anne of Cleves if it meant putting the Howards in the saddle. Thus, in stroke and counterstroke, the drama was played out. On 23 May Sampson was arrested and the conservatives felt their heads loose on their shoulders; on 10 June, the captain of the guard arrested Cromwell in the council chamber. By convincing Henry at the last that his vicegerent was an heretic and favourer of heretics, the Norfolk-Gardiner faction won the day. Cromwell was never heard in his own defence, being condemned for treason and heresy—and guilty of neither—by an act of attainder without trial, a procedure he is alleged to have invented for the countess of Salisbury (who, incidentally, was kept alive while he remained in power). After lingering in the Tower until his testimony should have enabled his grateful master to obtain a divorce from Anne of Cleves, he was executed on 23 July. On the scaffold he said that he died in the catholic faith.

Cromwell's fall and manner of death have provided much material for moralising. He had more enemies than friends: the nobles hated the upstart, the clergy the man who had disciplined them, the bishops the vicegerent, the conservatives the radical. Many had suffered in his eight years of power, and the hatred engendered rested on him; indeed, though the cruelty and vengefulness which there were must be laid at the king's door, Cromwell must bear his share of the heavy burden. A man of great mind and enormous ability, he had little gentleness and no mercy once his purpose was fixed. He was well fitted to carry out a revolution, and if—like most revolutionaries—he did not die in his bed, that is a matter neither for wonder nor for rejoicing. Nor must one's abhorrence of some of the means used blind one to the achievement. Cromwell lived in a violent age, but he used violence only when he thought it indispensable, and his habit of striking terror at the first and then easing up probably prevented the much worse bloodshed which commonly results from a procrastinating and vacillating policy in disturbed times. Unlike Henry, he preferred opponents to survive if they but ceased to trouble him; he would have liked to save More. Unlike Norfolk and Gardiner, he did not pursue personal vendettas in the guise of political campaigns. Among the men of that day he stands out not only by his ability, nor even by his undoubted ruthlessness, but by the singleminded purpose to which he put both ability and ruthlessness. In eight years he engineered one of the few successful revolutions in English history, and he achieved this without upsetting the body politic. The end does not indeed justify the means, but at least it explains and to some extent excuses it. When all is said and done, the fact remains that Cromwell's work endured and proved not only important but also beneficial. We must pity the victims, most of whom hardly knew what they were resisting; but we must also judge fairly the man who, directly or indirectly, caused their deaths. His own was to less purpose than theirs and did incalculable harm to the country and state he had served.

Chapter VII

THE TUDOR REVOLUTION: EMPIRE AND COMMONWEALTH

I. SOVEREIGNTY

THE changes described in the last chapter were so many and far-reaching that we have had no opportunity yet to investigate their real significance. They were revolutionary, if that term may be applied to any changes which profoundly affect the constitution and government of a state even when they do not involve the systematic and entire destruction of what there was before. The Tudor revolution grew from roots which can be traced well back in time, and it was peculiarly unrevolutionary in appearance because its makers insisted on the utmost show of legality and constitutional propriety. For everything they did, they claimed the authority of ancient prescription, and in everything they did they adhered to the forms of the old law. This made the revolution most conservative to look at, and out of this arose both its enduring permanency and its ready acceptance; but none of it makes it any less of a revolution. When Thomas Cromwell died, the state and kingship of England were very different from what they had been at the fall of Wolsey, the difference lying less in the real power exercised by the king—this depended largely on personality and circumstance, not on the forms of government—than in the potential power released by the establishment of national sovereignty. A revolutionary era commonly produces vast upheavals and immediate profound differences, only to see the old state of affairs creep back after a time: the faster men proceed at the start, the sooner they lose their momentum and the less securely they build. The revolution of the 1530s, on the other hand, proceeded by safe stages, never outrunning its own strength or breaking its lifeline with the past; as a result there was never anything like a successful reaction.

The essential ingredient of the Tudor revolution was the concept of national sovereignty. The philosophy underlying Cromwell's work was summarised brilliantly in his preamble to the act of appeals (1533), the operative clause of which reads as follows:

> This realm of England is an Empire, and so hath been accepted in

> the world, governed by one Supreme Head and King having the dignity and royal estate of the imperial Crown of the same, unto whom a body politic, compact of all sorts and degrees of people divided in terms and by names of Spirituality and Temporalty, be bounden and owe to bear next to God a natural and humble obedience.

The critical term is 'empire'. Kings of England had before this claimed to be emperors—the title occurs in Anglo-Saxon times and was taken by Edward I, Richard II, and Henry V—but the meaning here is different. Those earlier 'emperors' had so called themselves because they ruled, or claimed to rule, more than one kingdom, as Edward I claimed Scotland and Henry V France.[1] In the act of appeals, on the other hand, England by herself is described as an empire, and it is clear both from the passage cited and from what follows that the word here denoted a political unit, a self-governing state free from (as they put it) 'the authority of any foreign potentates'. We call this sort of thing a sovereign national state. The introduction of the term into the controversy can be brought home to Cromwell, but it had been used in that sense before. In the fourteenth century some exponents of the Roman law concluded that any state which did not acknowledge a superior was an empire (*imperium*); Cromwell, who has been falsely accused of wishing to introduce the Roman law in England, nevertheless may possibly have encountered the notion during his travels. He seems also to have been familiar with the parallel thought, on the subject, of Marsiglio of Padua who in the same century defended the authority of the medieval empire against the papal claim to 'fullness of power' (*plenitudo potestatis*). Since England was engaged in shedding papal power, the assertions of anti-papal authority made in preceding centuries obviously came in useful. The English attack on Rome therefore rested on the ancient claim that *imperium*—lay authority—derives as much from God as does the pope's authority, elaborated into an important theory of the state by the addition of Marsiglio's and the civilians' conclusion that *imperium* exists wherever a body politic governs itself without superior on earth.

The statute thus enunciated this doctrine: England is an independent state, sovereign within its territorial limits. It is governed by a ruler who is both supreme head in matters spiritual and king in matters temporal, and who possesses by grant divine ('by the goodness and sufferance of Almighty God') 'plenary, whole, and entire power, preeminence, authority, prerogative, and

[1] Richard II's use of the term is markedly like the Tudor use; much that that king thought and did anticipated Tudor ideas and practices.

jurisdiction to render and yield justice' to all people and subjects resident within the realm. This ruler is one part of the empire, or—as we should say—one part of the constitution; the other is a 'body politic' or nation composed of clergy and laity, each —the act goes on to show—authorised to administer justice under the king within its own spiritual or temporal sphere, without interference from outside the realm. The special preoccupations of an act concerned with prohibiting appeals from courts within the realm to courts outside the realm naturally put the stress in the preamble on such points of jurisdiction, but behind these particulars there stands the general theory of a sovereign state composed of those who live within the realm of England and owe exclusive allegiance to the holder of its 'imperial' crown who is also supreme head of its Church. It is this supremacy in the Church which, being quite new, stands out as apparently the chief characteristic of the revolution. But this is so only because the principle of national sovereignty was established in a struggle with the ecclesiastical authority of Rome; it is at least possible to imagine a state of affairs where the temporal authority of the English crown might have had to be defended against foreign encroachment while the king's control of the Church was not questioned, and where the stress would have been on kingship rather than supreme headship. The principle, which is much more important than the particular application, is the same: absence of outside authority or, to say it again, national sovereignty.

2. CHURCH OF ENGLAND

The royal supremacy over the Church virtually replaced the pope in England by the king. Papal power had been defined as of two kinds: *potestas jurisdictionis*, or rule of the Church's temporal sphere, and *potestas ordinis*, or the spiritual functions which the pope shared with any bishop. The former was transferred entirely into the king's hands with his acquisition of the rights to administer the Church, to tax it, to appoint its dignitaries and officials, to control its laws and to supervise its courts. The second Henry VIII never claimed, for he never claimed to be a priest: he never pretended that he could say mass or ordain priests. But he claimed the highest jurisdictional authority in the Church: he controlled legislation and administration, and by virtue of his headship he could and did determine doctrine and ritual. As supreme head, Henry VIII acquired all the administrative episcopal powers of the papacy and none of the sacerdotal ones: he was as much of a bishop as a man can be who is no priest. The appointment of Cromwell as vicar-general is good proof of this episcopal character of the supremacy: the title was one bestowed on the deputies of bishops and on no one else. If it is remembered that Henry VIII's supremacy meant episcopal but not sacerdotal rights and functions, its difficulties are more easily resolved.

These rights Henry claimed to hold by ancient prescription and grant from God: kings had always held powers which the papacy had then usurped. There has been much stress on the significance of the coronation oath, the anointing at the coronation, the power to touch for the king's evil, all of which seem to show the king as a quasi-sacerdotal person, but the full meaning of the Henrician position is often missed. Those points were part of that medieval line of thought which saw in the king—*rex et sacerdos*—a ruler who, deriving his powers from God, had certain spiritual (though, despite the term *sacerdos*, no priestly) functions and faculties. Henry VIII came to fulfil the doctrine of 'True Monarchy' which ultimately went back to Constantine the Great and his position in the Church; the frequent references to that emperor in the writings of the English Reformation demonstrate how conscious the descent was. What made these assertions of kingly powers so striking was the earlier failure of the doctrine of True Monarchy before the onslaught of the papalist doctrine which had certainly triumphed in England: in the writings of the early sixteenth century there is no trace that would suggest doubts about the papal supremacy. The rights and wrongs of it may be argued for ever. Certainly, kings of England had never exercised the episcopal functions of a *rex et sacerdos*; when they had interfered in the appointments of bishops and had taxed the clergy they had done so as temporal rulers, not as being bishops themselves. The doctrine of True Monarchy was developed for the benefit of German emperors and French kings; it was a curious accident that brought about its fulfilment by a king of England. The significance of these derivations is obvious. For one thing they explain how Henry VIII could persuade himself that he had rights in spiritual matters and how he—a layman—came to be accepted so readily as holding those rights. For another, they gave the respectability of ancient arguments to the revolution, once again displaying that careful traditionalism that distinguished these upheavals. But most significant is the fact that really these theories did not matter greatly. Though king, bishops, and propagandists might fill volumes with proofs and precedents from Constantine downwards, the strength of the storm lay not in this backward-looking justification and revival of a moribund doctrine, but in the forward-looking assertion of secular sovereignty.

Attempts have been made to link the supremacy with the legislative authority of parliament; it is still usual to assert that Henry's supremacy was a parliamentary one. But this was certainly not the way that Henry VIII and Cromwell saw it. According to the official doctrine, the royal supremacy was divinely ordained: it rested on direct grant from God. By virtue of his kingship, the king was automatically also vicar of Christ on earth, as far as his territorial dominions extended. The supremacy was personal, vested in the king by no earthly authority, and exercised by him without reference to any earthly authority. The king as supreme head not only issued injunctions for the doctrine and government of the Church (as the Ten and Thirteen Articles of 1536 and 1538); he was even able, by his own unaided power, to transfer all his spiritual authority to a deputy when by commission he appointed Cromwell vicegerent in spirituals. In that capacity, Cromwell not only carried out the visitatorial powers of the supreme head, as he had done as vicar-general (acting for his bishop like any vicar-general), but exercised all the king's spiritual functions (including, for instance, the determination of dogma) by delegation. Neither parliament nor convocation played any part in these manifestations of the supremacy. The supremacy was taken from the monarchical papacy, and it remained monarchical, even despotic. In the Church, the king, as supreme head, was an absolute ruler, the more so as there existed no single assembly of the English Church. The convocations of Canterbury and York were neither in theory nor in practice a limitation on the king's spiritual headship.

That these were revolutionary changes is perfectly obvious, though from that day to this attempts have been made to prove that the post-Reformation Church was identical with the pre-Reformation Church, attempts which incidentally involve a playing down of the king's share in Church government and religious regulation that is possibly very proper for the twentieth century but highly improper for the sixteenth. This is no place to enter into that controversy, but it must be stated briefly that the Henrician Reformation and the creation of the royal supremacy turned the Church *in* England (the archiepiscopal provinces of the Universal Church lying in the realm of England) into the Church *of* England. This does not affect the issue of the apostolic succession and canonical derivation of the English episcopate, preserved when Clement VII granted Cranmer's bulls in January 1533, nor the question of the English Church's claim to be catholic, but it does assert that the Henrician Reformation amounted to a schism. The act of supremacy of 1534 begged the question with the calm assurance characteristic of Cromwell's beautifully drafted preambles when it spoke of the 'Church of England called *Anglicana Ecclesia*'; this after all, need mean no more than English Church and ought rightly to be translated (before 1533) as 'the Church in England'. The act of appeals admitted as much when it mentioned 'that part of the body politic called the Spirituality, now being usually called the English Church'; the term *Anglicana Ecclesia* meant all the clergy (or spiritualty) in England, and not—as it did after the Reformation—a separate ecclesiastical institution called the Church of England. From 1533 or 1534 such an institution may be discerned and must be admitted: in Church affairs, where it began, the revolution of the 1530s is most obvious. The establishment of the royal supremacy and the creation of the Church of England are fundamental breaks with the past, giving the English Church a new unity, a new organisation, new authorities under God, though not as yet a new doctrine. It was a jurisdictional revolution in the Church, not a religious revolution.

3. PARLIAMENT

As has been said, the establishment of national sovereignty produced a new kind of political community with new potentialities and new duties. The precise character of that sovereignty and who it was that exercised it must now engage attention, the more so as the prevailing interpretation is demonstrably wrong. It is generally said that Henry, and especially Cromwell, planned to erect a despotism in the state to match the despotism of the royal supremacy in the Church. This they did not do; indeed, basing themselves on the past, on constitutional propriety, and on the law, they could not do it. It becomes necessary to investigate the place of parliament in the royal supremacy.

That the supremacy was parliamentary, depending either for its first authority or for its exercise on parliament, has already been denied; yet all through the 1530s every important step was embodied in statutes made by king, lords, and commons—for it must be remembered that the king was and is as much a part of parliament as are the commons. The accepted interpretation of this use of statute is distinguished by a kind of enthusiastic vagueness sometimes deviating into rhapsody.[1] It argues that Henry VIII's

[1] Especially in A. F. Pollard's *Henry VIII* and *Factors in Modern History*, the standard accounts of the view here combated.

turning to parliament proved his supreme political genius; that his deliberate decision to take the nation 'into partnership' was the most momentous step in the rise of parliament; that parliament, and especially the commons, were asked to endorse matters by enactment in order to make acceptance of the changes easier and advertise the unquestioned unity of king and people. It claims both much too much and, in some respects, rather too little. This becomes clear when we ask what parliament actually did and distinguish between the preambles and the enactments of statutes. Parliament 'does' only what is set out in the enactment. The preamble may explain and justify; it may—as in the act of appeals—outline a whole political philosophy, or—as in the act of supremacy—accept as given vast novel assertions; but it can never record what parliament has done. In the political legislation of the 1530s the form is quite plain: the preamble of the statute declares as fact some aspect of the Cromwellian revolution (as that England is an empire, or that the king rightly is supreme head), while the enactment draws administrative conclusions from this fact (that therefore appeals outside the realms must be forbidden, or that therefore the king ought to have certain taxes and how they are to be collected) and appoints penalties for transgressors. The acts of this time are declaratory in that they set out in their preambles as already in existence what the government really wishes the nation to accept; their preambles are propaganda. The acts are also administrative orders, laying down procedure and practices. But above all the acts are penal: they decree punishments. Parliamentary statute cannot create the supremacy which is conceived of as derived from God, but it alone can make the supremacy enforceable at law, in the law courts. Until parliament has decreed that certain activities (such as the denial of the supremacy or the seeking out of appeals at Rome) are criminal and carry appointed penalties, there is no way in which the supremacy can be enforced on the country, especially on the laity: the king has no means of forcible and extra-legal coercion, and only statute can add felonies and treasons, involving loss of life or member, to the body of law. This disposes of the notion sometimes encountered that Henry could have established his supremacy by proclamation: had he wished to do so he would have had to give to proclamations powers they had never had.

Parliament thus legalised the Reformation, not in the vague sense of giving the consent of the realm to what was done, but in the severely practical sense of making possible the prosecution at law of those who opposed the royal policy. The place of parliament in the Tudor revolution is both less and more than has been alleged. It is less because the supremacy did not depend for its existence on parliament but on divine appointment. It is more because parliament was not an agency of government propaganda but an essential element in the establishment of the whole revolution and its protection in law. Henry and Cromwell had to employ parliament and statute if they wished to make their revolution legally enforceable; no time need be wasted on admiring their penetration in choosing parliament as a partner because in fact they never had any choice. What does deserve praise and study is the skill with which these two men employed the means to hand in their tremendous task.

But the matter goes further than that. The Reformation statutes demonstrate that the political sovereignty created in the 1530s was to be a parliamentary one. There was no thought—no possibility—of a purely royal despotism. The highest authority in the land was recognised to lie in that assembly of king, lords, and commons whose decrees (by name of statute) commanded complete and universal obedience and could deal with any matter on earth, including even spiritual concerns hitherto reserved to spiritual authority. The Tudor revolution established the supremacy and omnicompetence of statute. That statute was the highest way in which the state (the laity) could pronounce law had been acknowledged since the reign of Edward III; but that there was no sphere of life closed to it—that it could do what it wished—was demonstrated only in the 1530s when statute extended to new fields. It is likely that few so far realised all this to the full; perhaps there were only two men who genuinely grasped the import of events. Thomas Cromwell certainly knew what he was doing; his immense labours in drafting the acts of the time and his great care in parliamentary management show him well aware of the supreme importance of statute and parliament in the revolution. The other man was Thomas More who declared that he could not obey an act of parliament when it went contrary to the law of Christendom. In this More represented the conception of a universal Christian law to which man-made law must conform, as well as the persistent fears of all thoughtful men at putting absolute legislative sovereignty in the hands of any human body. But however right More may have been in abstract philosophy and as a member of a Christian community, as a subject of King Henry VIII and his laws he was utterly wrong. When Cromwell, the first statesman to understand the potentialities of statute, used it to enforce great revolutionary changes through the courts of law, he demonstrated that in law and on earth there is nothing that an act of parliament cannot do. Of course, this truth was not at once put in so clear-cut a fashion; it took centuries of talk about the law divine and the law natural, with which the law made by man was supposed to be consonant, before men would admit in all its starkness the simple theory of Thomas Cromwell. To this day one may meet with attempts to discover some sort of morally binding restraint on the powers of parliament. But in the modern state there are, in fact, no limitations on the supremacy and competence of statute: parliament may forbear doing certain things because it is too sensible or too frightened to attempt them, but there is no one who can dispute its authority.

The Tudor revolution thus not only created national sovereignty; it also acknowledged the supremacy of statute on which the modern English state rests. That means that it established the sovereignty of the king in parliament, otherwise known as constitutional or limited monarchy. Whatever may have been the case before Cromwell's work—whatever Wolsey may have stood for—there was no Tudor despotism after it. Wittingly or not—and the present writer has no doubt that it was done wittingly—Cromwell established the reformed state as a limited monarchy and not as a despotism. He gave the king great power—power over the Church, power of the purse because for a time he was wealthy—and Henry VIII was at all times a formidable ruler whom it was difficult to limit; but the polity which Cromwell wanted rested not on the supremacy of the king, but on the supremacy of the king in parliament. Of course this was not totally new; all medieval development stood behind this flowering of parliamentary monarchy. But the Reformation freed the sovereign body of England not only from the authority of foreign potentates but also from the limitations of the laws divine and natural: from now on parliaments made laws. Because men's thoughts can take generations to catch up with reality, the 'declaratory' concept of law-making—pretending a discovery rather than a creation—survived for a time; in truth, however, the Reformation had shown once and for all that parliament, the king in parliament, exercised untrammelled powers of true legislation. The essential characteristic of medieval government was that it discovered the law and then administered it, while modern government first makes and then administers laws; thus the 1530s mark quite definitely the end of the medieval constitution and the beginning of the modern.

Though the rule of Henry VIII was strong, ruthless, at times very arbitrary, it could not be despotic because it always rested on the law—the law which was made by parliament and administered by the courts. The common law of England may nearly have suffered eclipse during Wolsey's rule, but, in contrast to his predecessor, Cromwell practised a policy of deference to it. He may have learned the idea of empire from the Roman law, and he may have wished at times to use its more autocratic weapons (as Gardiner alleged he did); but if we go by what was actually done, the triumph of the common law is manifest. Indeed, it was Cromwell's administration that saved the medieval common law, as it saved the medieval parliament, and used both in the service of the modern state. The use of parliament meant enforcement through the courts of the common law to whom the statutes of the 1530s opened up a great and important new field. Cromwell himself was a common lawyer, as were his chief assistants, especially Lord Chancellor Audley. At the same time, the judges' attitude to parliament changed. It is noticeable that from the 1530s onwards they began to obey statute in a way they had never done before. In the fifteenth century they had often merely taken statute as the basis for argument: as the crown's legal advisers they had themselves often 'made' acts of parliament and felt competent to interpret them—at times almost out of existence. A more rigid adherence to the letter of the act now became apparent, leading up to the modern principle that judicial interpretation means the strict application of the act, not an arbitrary explanation roughly within its limits.

Even where means of extra-parliamentary action existed and were lawful, the prevailing deference to statute comes out. Cromwell's whole attitude was consistent: he believed in statute above all else and would proceed nowhere without its sanction. His natural reaction to any problem of government was to draft a bill; in this he was so 'modern' that only the nineteenth century fully returned to his lavish law-making. In 1535 it was desired to stop the export of coin from the realm; Cromwell at once insisted on discovering a relevant statute, though he was glad to hear from the judges that, failing a statute, the king could in such a matter proceed by proclamation. The judges were perfectly correct: a government must be able to put out orders about immediate economic needs or temporary policies without having to await the meeting of an occasional body like the sixteenth-century parliament. Yet Cromwell remained unsatisfied, and four years later he introduced an act designed to give general legal sanction to royal proclamations. The act of proclamations (1539) was once wrongly considered the height of Henry's despotism. It ordered that proclamations (of the traditional type, unable to impose the death penalty or forfeiture of goods) should be obeyed 'as though they were made by act of parliament' and appointed machinery for their enforcement. There was never any intention of replacing statute by proclamation or of legislating without the consent of parliament; no one intended to wipe out the vital differences in standing and sanctity between the two. The act was simply meant to resolve such doubts as Cromwell himself had felt about the legality of any proclamation not grounded upon statute. Its practical significance lay in the clauses for its enforcement. Almost certainly Cromwell intended originally to let the common-law courts enforce proclamations (as they enforced statutes—this may well be the meaning of the phrase quoted above); opposition in the lords forced him instead to accept a council nominated in the act which proved quite incapable of doing the work. The statute was not employed for despotic purposes and its repeal in 1547 made no difference to the legality of royal proclamations: superfluous as a basis for proclamations, it is proof of Cromwell's veneration for statutory authority and therefore for parliament, not of any attempt to do without parliament and govern by proclamation.

The supremacy of statute meant the sovereignty of the king in parliament, and this raised difficult practical problems. If laws are to be made only by the consent of three partners—king, lords and commons—then agreement between them must somehow be secured or government will become impossible. This again was scarcely a new problem, for parliamentary legislation—the thing if not the name—had existed for some two centuries; but the constitutional revolution of the 1530s—the new stress laid on sovereignty and the newly expanded use of parliament—made it both more pressing and more constant. On the whole, Henry VIII and Cromwell had comparatively little difficulty, especially since on the main issue of the Church the royal policy represented very fairly the feelings and desires of the majority of those who sat in the parliament. The lords were a 'safe' house; with their Tudor lay peers and their cowed spiritual peers, few of them felt able to offer opposition. The commons were both able and willing to oppose. No full study of the parliaments of this reign has yet been made, but we know roughly that the members of the lower house were on the whole less independent than they were to become later, though there can be no question of subservience or intimidation. Many were servants of the king, forming a kind of government party in embryo around the privy councillors who sat in the commons. Numbers of substantial gentlemen sat for boroughs, instead of the local burgesses whose duty it ostensibly was to represent their towns and who in general had less independence of mind than knights and gentlemen; but this 'invasion of the gentry'—already well under way—had not yet produced the kind of commons familiar from the reign of Elizabeth onwards in which the gentry called the tune. Moreover, in this age when the property of the Church was under attack, the gentry's interest coincided with the government's. When they felt like it, the commons of the 1530s stood up to the crown readily enough; money grants were never easily obtained, and the bill of uses, designed to protect the king's feudal rights against the very people who sat in the house, took five long years to get through. Henry VIII allowed opposition in parliament; with all his imperious arrogance, he had little of the true tyrant's temper which will not listen to objections, and his councillors as well as his commons could generally speak frankly to him even when they advised against his desires. He permitted full freedom of speech in the first two sessions of the 1529-36 parliament because he knew that he would thus obtain ammunition for his attack at Rome; he never tried to prevent members even from defending Catherine or desiring him to take her back. Only on one occasion did a member of parliament get into serious trouble in those years. This was an advanced protestant from Calais who in 1539 was sequestered by the shocked house of commons itself for putting forward his extreme views on religion. Strode's Case of 1512 had established freedom of speech in parliament as far as the complaints of private persons were concerned;[1] the wider issue of freedom from interference by the crown did not arise in this reign because Henry avoided all attacks on such liberty. Both his genuine feelings and his diplomatic skill came out in the words he addressed to parliament in 1543 when he declared his pride in the fact 'that we at no time stand so highly in our estate royal as in the time of parliament'.

He could afford these sentiments the more readily because of the natural community of interests between him and his parliaments, but also because subtler means of management existed than frontal assault. The Speaker had for long been a royal nominee, despite the appearance of a free election by the commons, and the Speakers of the reign were all crown servants, like Sir Thomas

[1] Richard Strode was imprisoned for proposing some bills to regulate tin-mining and interfering with the stannary courts; the commons secured his release and enacted that no member should be sued in a court of law for anything said or done in parliament.

More (1523), Sir Thomas Audley (1529-32), Sir Humphrey Wingfield (1533-6), Sir Nicholas Hare (1539-40)—all common lawyers and king's legal counsel. The Speaker's control over the business of the house made him a useful instrument of royal influence. Similar tasks were performed by privy councillors sitting in the commons; it was Cromwell who first exploited the position of a government minister in the house in the manner which was to become typical in the reign of Elizabeth. Apart from managing matters by speech and answer, Cromwell also took up aspects of government management of whose previous existence there is so little evidence that one may say he virtually initiated them. He bestowed great care on a legislative programme; dozens of draft acts with his corrections all over them and many notes among his memoranda testify to the labour involved in putting before the house a series of well-designed measures. In 1529 and 1531 parliament largely discussed bills introduced by members of the house of commons, like those acts mending abuses in the Church which heralded the whole attack; but from 1532 onwards the houses mostly debated the bills produced by the government. Such a government legislative programme was something new, for the simple reason that no one had ever dreamt of establishing a complex of fundamental changes by means of acts of parliament. The new practice, soon to become normal and revived as normal after the interruptions of the seventeenth century, put upon government a heavy task of parliamentary management. Attendance in the house, organisation of opinion there, and the preparation of measures were important aspects of the art of management which Cromwell developed and in great part almost certainly invented.

His name is linked with another side of parliamentary history that was to play a great part in the centuries of the 'unreformed' house of commons. He was the first man to pay systematic attention to the composition of the house and to attempt to influence it in favour of the government. He saw to bye-elections, made necessary by the unprecedented length of time for which the Reformation parliament sat; he used royal influence, and the influence of loyal noblemen and crown officials, to secure favourable returns at general elections; he wrote letters to local authorities moving them to elect men agreeable to the crown. It will not do to speak of packing. Elections were not then 'free' in our sense (that is, limited to a choice between the nominees of official parties), nor were they to be so until the reforms of the nineteenth century. Free elections and the secret ballot reflect accurately the social structure of a democracy, but the England of the Tudors, Stuarts, and Hanoverians was characterised by the social dominance of the gentry and nobility (under the crown), and its parliamentary system did right to reflect that very different structure. Few constituencies returned members without listening to the orders of a borough patron or deferring to the wishes of the great shire families. Cromwell merely tried to organise these isolated examples of influence by making them all serve the interests of the crown. He did not 'pack' the house with nominees but employed the local powers of dukes and earls and knights to secure the return of men he wished to see elected, a practice continued by parliamentary managers down, at least, to 1867. In one case—the Canterbury election of 1536—he ordered the city to rescind their choice and return the two men previously named by the king; nothing is known of the circumstances which provoked so peremptory an order, and in any case one must not generalise from one instance. In 1539 Cromwell mobilised all the electoral resources of the crown and secured what he himself called a tractable parliament; but he did so by the use of perfectly proper influence—his own, or the king's, or the duke of Norfolk's, and so forth—and in a manner fully approved of by his age and by succeeding centuries.[1] Now that the commons had become an indispensable partner—even if not an always existing partner—in the sovereign nation state governed by the king in parliament, it was necessary to ensure harmony in the mixed sovereign; Cromwell first employed the methods used to achieve this in the centuries of the monarchical parliamentary state which endured from the Tudor revolution to the democratic revolution of the nineteenth century.

It is obvious, therefore, that in the history of parliament, too, the 1530s are of vital significance. Its importance increased, its procedure developed, its use by the king grew into a working alliance in which the crown was at this time much the more evidently powerful partner. The structure of the institution also developed. The house of commons had been a 'house'—an organised body—since the fourteenth century; from this time it was invariably a house of parliament, and any idea that a body meeting without the commons could be called a parliament was at an end. We hear for the first time of the use of committees, that remarkable expedient which was to turn the house from an assembly of critics into an efficient instrument of government. The seven years of the Reformation parliament, followed by two more elections in three

[1] Nor (as has been alleged) was he trying to get a parliament in his own interest; it was of course tractable to the king.

years, provided an invaluable training in co-operation, experience, political and personal friendship, even—as Pollard has shown—in the growth of a political class based on intermarriage. The house of commons never forgot those years, or the importance of the work on which it had been engaged. In 1543 the house acted directly to secure the release of a member (George Ferrers) imprisoned at a private suit and punished the officers of the City of London for contempt; thus began the long struggle of the commons for control over their own privileges and for the powers of a court in ordering their own affairs. For the lords, too, the period was one of consolidation into modern form: from being the parliament itself (as the great council of magnates) they now quite definitely turned into one of the houses of parliament. With this went many complicated developments in the law of peerage and blue blood, and a growing definition which deprived the crown of the right to summon whom it would, making the writ a matter of hereditary right. The act of 1539, 'for the precedence of the lords in the parliament chamber', marked an important step. The great council of magnates assembling around a core of professional councillors (judges, officers of the chancery, and so on) became a body consisting only of peers of the realm; the professionals lost first their voice in the house of lords and ultimately also the right to sit there.

Thus the second notable revolution of the 1530s is the establishment of the sovereignty of the king in parliament, and the effect this had on the three partners. Parliament's growth in importance had nothing to do with its making the king supreme head, for it did no such thing; but the working out of the royal supremacy produced the supreme statute and provided parliament with a novel eminence in the state. The crown grew in real power despite the constitutional limits placed upon it. That realisation was behind Henry VIII's pride in his place in parliament. By admitting the alliance of the nation represented in parliament, the Tudors made the powers of government—the powers of the king—so much more effective that the crown itself, whether the personal crown of the Tudors or the crown in commission of our day, can do much more than even the strongest medieval kings had dreamt of. Commons and lords developed into precise institutions, part of one sovereign body. Of the two, the lords, the more important socially, also retained for the time being greater political weight. This was especially proved during the reign of Edward VI. The commons experienced a few short and rather spurious years of primacy, at first (1529-31) because they were the natural mouthpiece of anti-clericalism, but then simply because Cromwell sat there. In 1536, Cromwell was made a baron just before parliament met, with a special provision that he was to retain his place in the lower house for the session, so that he might steer through the measures he had prepared for it. In 1539, when he sat in the lords, all the important bills were introduced there first, whereas in 1532-6 they had been introduced in the commons. For the history of the English parliament, and therefore of constitutional monarchy in England, it was of great importance that Henry VIII had an admirable political sense and knew how to work together with a representative institution. He deserves the more credit for this because he had not been brought up to it either by his father or by Wolsey. But it was even more important that he chose for his leading adviser at this time a man who had deliberately made a career in parliament, entering it in 1529 with the express determination to rise to power through it; a man who could see the potentialities of the institution and who knew how to exploit them; a man who realised what statute could do and how the statute-making body could be harnessed to the needs of a constitutional revolution. So far from attempting to build a despotism in England, Thomas Cromwell was that country's first parliamentary statesman.

4. CONSOLIDATION OF TERRITORY

If England was to be an empire 'governed by one Supreme Head and King', the pope's was not the only authority that stood in the way. The work of attacking franchises and semi-independent rights within the borders of the realm itself, which had gone forward since the days of Henry VII at least, was as yet unfinished. Cromwell resumed it with vigour and—typically—with a more systematic approach. In place of the piecemeal suppression of such franchises as caused trouble (like the Tynedale liberties abolished by Parliament in 1504), he wished to put forward a general statement of policy. This he achieved in the act of 1536, entitled 'for recontinuing certain liberties and franchises heretofore taken from the crown'. Despite this title the act was really meant to do away with all those franchises that prevented an effective dissemination of royal authority. The preamble, in Cromwell's usual style, stated a grievance in succinct and, for once, historically accurate terms:

Where divers of the most ancient prerogatives and authorities of

> justice appertaining to the imperial crown of this realm have been severed and taken away from the same by sundry gifts of the king's most noble progenitors . . . to the great diminution and detriment of the royal estate of the same and to the hinderance and great delay of justice . . .

The act reserved all pardons for treasons and felonies to the crown, laid down that judges and justices of all kinds anywhere in the realm (including counties palatine, Wales, and the marches thereof) could be appointed only by the king, provided that writs in counties palatine were to run in the king's name, and in general extended the operation of the royal justice and shire administration to all England. Though a few minor exceptions were made, in effect all franchisal rights of any consequence were destroyed: for the first time, the whole realm, without qualification, became subject to government from Westminster. In particular this ended the independence of the county of Durham which alone of all the great palatinates had escaped absorption into the Tudor crown lands.

The act played a part in the unrest which led to the pilgrimage of grace; in turn, the collapse of the rising gave the government a chance of effectively suppressing the liberties of the northern counties. The death of the earl of Northumberland put all his lands into the king's hand to whom they were mortgaged; Norfolk's executions broke the spirit of resistance; finally, in the summer of 1537, Cromwell devised a new council of the north, a permanent body dominated by royal officials and controlled from the centre which was to govern the five northern counties, suppress independence, and bring the north into line with the more advanced south. This permanent bureaucratic council, replacing the temporary and personal councils which had fitfully governed the north since Edward IV's day, achieved its aim; despite the rising of 1569, it may be said that the medieval history of the north came to an end in 1537 when its separatism fell before the centralisation of the modern state imposed by Henry VIII and Cromwell.

In Wales, too, Cromwell's policy of consolidation was thoroughly successful. He began in 1534 by securing the appointment of his friend Rowland Lee, bishop of Coventry and Lichfield, as president of the council in the marches; for the next six years, Lee concentrated all his notable energies on the task of reducing both the marches and Wales itself to order. Statutes were passed to equip him with better weapons. An act of 1534 transferred the trial of

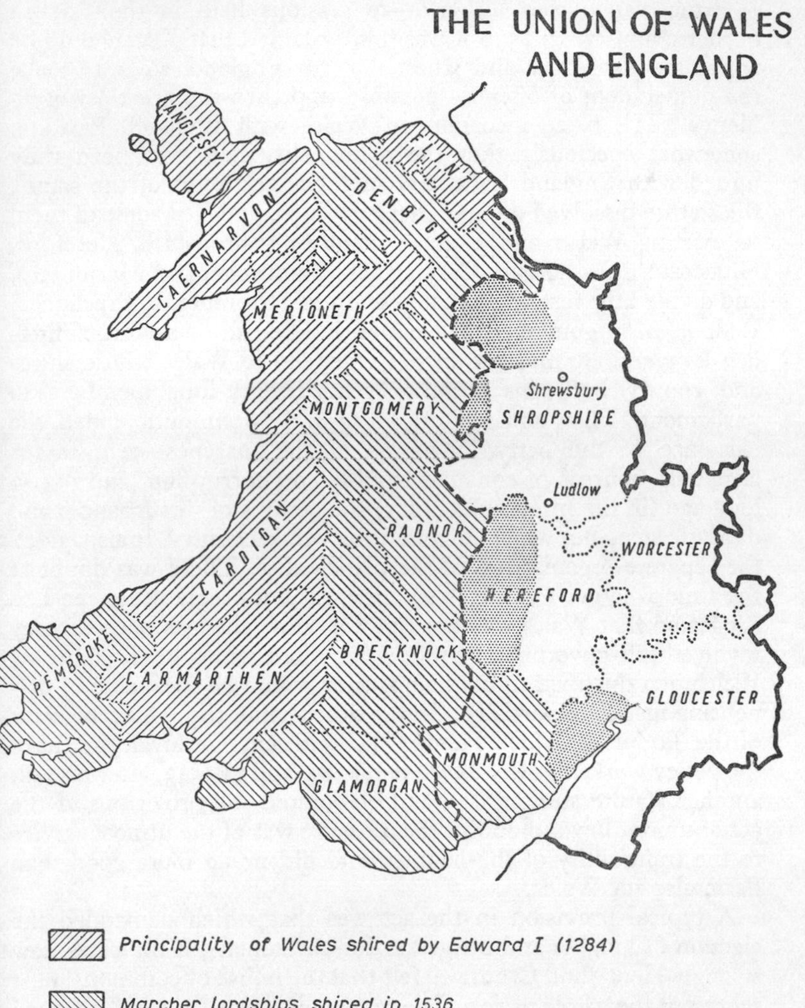
THE UNION OF WALES AND ENGLAND
ANGLESEY
FLINT
DENBIGH
CAERNARVON
MERIONETH
MONTGOMERY
Shrewsbury
SHROPSHIRE
Ludlow
CARDIGAN
RADNOR
WORCESTER
HEREFORD
PEMBROKE
CARMARTHEN
BRECKNOCK
GLOUCESTER
MONMOUTH
GLAMORGAN
Principality of Wales shired by Edward I (1284)
Marcher lordships shired in 1536
Approximate area of marcher lordships added to English shires
Administrative boundary of Wales 1542 - 1830
Boundary of area subject to the council in the marches of Wales

murders and felonies committed in the territories of marcher lords—virtual sanctuaries hitherto—to sessions held in the English border counties. In 1536 it was first ordained that J.Ps. should be appointed for Wales and Chester as for England, so as to make the punishment of offences possible, and then the great act of 27 Henry VIII, c. 26 incorporated Wales with England. Pleading somewhat speciously that the principality had ever been fully united with England 'as a very member and joint of the same', the statute dissolved the marcher lordships, annexed some of them to existing Welsh and English counties (Shropshire, Hereford, Gloucester, Glamorgan, Carmarthen, Pembroke, and Merioneth), and divided the rest into five new counties (Monmouth, Brecknock, Radnor, Montgomery, and Denbigh). The full operation of English laws and administration was extended to Wales whose shires and county boroughs were to send twenty-four members to parliament. This 'shiring' of Wales and Monmouth ended the existence of the petty kingdoms of the marches—refuges for criminals, sources of constant trouble and corruption, and not so long ago (in the fifteenth century) the centres of disturbances and dynastic struggles which engulfed the whole country. It also ended the separate organisation of the principality. There was doubt at the time whether Cromwell's policy was not premature; even Lee suggested that Wales was not ripe for these changes because they involved self-government by J.Ps., an office which he thought few Welshmen qualified to hold since they would be incapable of dispensing justice impartially. On the other hand, the Welsh ancestry of the Tudors provided Henry VIII with enough loyalty to make the policy workable; Cromwell persisted, and in 1543, after his fall, another statute summarised and elaborated the provisions of the act of union. Beyond doubt, the measure was of the utmost service to the tranquillity of the country and did much more good than harm also for Wales.

A typical provision in the act was that which demanded the election of knights and burgesses for parliament; it indicates how strongly Henry and Cromwell felt that the house of commons must represent the whole nation. The same policy was therefore adopted for Calais in 1536 when new ordinances for its government were ratified by statute; from 1536 to 1558 two burgesses sat for Calais in the English parliament. Chester similarly received two burgesses in 1543. The whole policy rested on the achievements of earlier kings in reducing or even suppressing independent rights and privileges of exemption, but now it was pursued not only more vigorously and on a larger scale but also in obedience to a general principle. Cromwell (or Henry—but Henry had not stirred until Cromwell was his chief minister) wished to turn the empire of England into a properly consolidated state, governed throughout by the king in council and subject to the legislative sovereignty of the king in parliament. This ended the kingdoms within the kingdom typical of the middle ages and made possible full national government. It is no denigration of the achievement of Henry VIII and Cromwell to recall that they started with the advantage of an unusually centralised medieval state where the king already held more real power than anywhere else in Western Europe.

In the history of Tudor relations with Scotland and Ireland the 1530s marked an interlude of comparative success. Scotland offered few problems at this time. It had to be kept quiet so as not to interfere with the delicate progress of the English Reformation. This was achieved easily enough as long as England remained on good terms with France, and when the French friendship wore very thin Henry kept his nephew James V at peace by refusing to take notice of such provocations as James's successive marriages to two French princesses, despite his uncle's preference for others. Cromwell had recommended peace with Scotland as long ago as 1523, and he practised it successfully in a period when no troubles arose to jeopardise it. Ireland, on the other hand, demanded attention. Since the departure thence in 1521 of the earl of Surrey, it had again reverted to the rule of local lords—Butlers at first and later Geraldines—with but the slenderest link of allegiance to England. Wolsey had neither time nor money to spare for Ireland; he attempted to control it by putting the Geraldine earl of Kildare in the Tower as a surety for the good behaviour of lesser Geraldines whom he appointed vice-deputies. Disorders continuing, Kildare was released in 1529, but the duke of Richmond became nominal lord lieutenant and the actual ruler of the country was the deputy, Sir William Skeffyngton, master of the ordnance and therefore nicknamed the gunner. Skeffyngton, an able soldier and conscientious official, was starved of the means to persuade the Geraldines and Butlers to peace, and in 1532 Kildare recovered the office of deputy. He used it in the accustomed fashion to pursue his feud with the Butlers and add to the disorders of the wild and unhappy country.

The beginning of the break with Rome made the question urgent; England could not afford a hostile Ireland where a papal counterattack might find a ready foothold. In 1533, complaints from Ireland led to Kildare's fall; he returned to the Tower where he died of natural causes in 1534. Even before this his son Thomas Fitzgerald, deceived by a rumour that his father had been executed, renounced his allegiance and called upon the pope and Charles V to assist him. But only the Geraldine faction rose, the towns held out, no help came from abroad, and the revolt collapsed before Skeffyngton's forces when 'the gunner' returned to Ireland in 1535. The final defeat was accomplished by Lord Leonard Grey who in January 1536 succeeded as deputy on Skeffyngton's death. Thomas Fitzgerald was promised his life on surrender, but five of his uncles were later arrested by treachery, and all six were ultimately executed in 1537. Therewith the Geraldine faction was destroyed, and Grey proceeded to enforce Cromwell's anti-papal policy on Ireland. How far Ireland remained attached to Rome simply because the break with Rome came from England will always remain in dispute. Grey was superficially successful, though his methods involved him in a quarrel with the Butlers ending in 1541 in his own execution—ostensibly for treason but really for failure. Before this, in December 1540, Henry adopted the title of king of Ireland. However, Ireland was far from pacified or reconciled, and the progress of the religious Reformation was to render futile all hopes of a genuine settlement.

5. ADMINISTRATIVE REFORMS

Cromwell was an administrator of genius. He could work harder at more details than seems quite believable; even in a century that boasted of Wolsey and Burghley, his ability and many-sidedness stand out. But it is more important still that he was also a natural reformer of administration. His temper was bureaucratic: he liked to organise and loved to record. Of this his devotion to statute is striking proof. It was well that he should do these things by preference, for the new state he was building demanded reform of precisely this kind. Cromwell took over a government dominated by that revival of household methods which had been Henry VII's great achievement. But the polity which Cromwell envisaged and largely achieved needed national government. Both household and national governments were of course the king's governments. But household methods meant that the king stood actively at the centre of things; they demanded a great deal of personal effort from the holder of the crown and relied on his immediate entourage for the driving power behind the machinery. National bureaucratic methods, on the other hand, while they still depended—in that age of monarchy—on the existence and power of the king, were freed from the personal activity of either king or entourage. The older system always broke down when there was no active or powerful king, or at least some deputy like Wolsey to play the king's part. Thus government collapsed in the fifteenth century, and it also declined very markedly after Henry VII's death. Such institutions as the council in star chamber or the general surveyors of crown lands appear to have been almost dormant for two or three years until stimulated into new life by Wolsey. The extrusion of the household from national affairs and its replacement by a series of bureaucratically organised institutions largely removed that danger and gave to modern government an air of permanency and independence from the accidents of politics. Cromwell was quite capable of copying Wolsey and governing in a highly personal fashion. Thus he himself acted as an informal treasurer for public money from 1532 to 1536 simply because he wished to have ready access to cash in the affairs of government. There are other examples of high-handed and irregular action, explicable only as manifestations of his commanding personal position. But in addition he spent much time and thought on reorganising the machinery of administration.

The financial system which Cromwell took over centred upon the general surveyors of crown lands and the treasurer of the chamber. Since he could not make sufficient use of an organisation so directly dependent on the crown, he tried to reduce the importance of the chamber and turn the general surveyors into a proper, but restricted, department of state. He began to deprive the chamber of revenue, much to the sorrow of its treasurer, Sir Brian Tuke, who was himself a civil servant of ability and responsible for much of the increasing bureaucratic organisation of his department. Soon Cromwell had to set up new agencies of finance as the additions he made to the revenue came to complicate the problem. The acquisition of the clerical first fruits and tenths in 1534 could have been handled by the chamber, as was originally intended, but Cromwell instead appointed a personal servant of his own, John Gostwick, as treasurer for this money, using him very much as his personal paymaster in affairs of state. The monastic lands raised much greater administrative difficulties which were solved by the erection of a separate and self-contained institution capable of acting both as a court (since litigation over the lands was bound to arise) and as a revenue department. It was modelled on the duchy of Lancaster whose simple accounting methods it copied. It seems that in about 1535 Cromwell decided on this policy of revenue courts, planning to allot the royal income properly to various departments whose reserves would be drawn upon indiscriminately by the government (himself) as need arose.[1] In 1535, an act of parliament made the general surveyors permanent —they had hitherto existed from one parliament to the next only— and deprived them of all chance of new revenues. Though it was not until 1542, after Cromwell's fall, that they were incorporated in a fully organised court, it is certain that Cromwell had meant them to develop in that way. In 1540 an act drafted by Cromwell but not passed until after his fall added the court of wards;[2] and a few weeks later the treasurer of first fruits also became treasurer of a proper court, a step which Cromwell had been reluctant to take because of the needs of his personal government.

The financial administration as reformed by Cromwell or under his immediate influence therefore consisted of six courts or departments of state, each fully organised with its own specialised officials, equipped with seals and habitat, and responsible for a particular kind of revenue. The exchequer administered the ancient revenues and especially the customs and parliamentary taxation; the duchy of Lancaster the body of lands belonging to it; the court of general surveyors the crown lands collected by Henry VII and Wolsey; the court of augmentations the monastic lands; the court of first fruits and tenths the revenue contributed by the Church; and the court of wards and liveries the feudal income of the crown. The system did not work with the admirable precision which this description suggests: nothing in the sixteenth century did. But such an organisation was the ideal aimed at, and it gave to the finances a management which did not involve either the excessive formality of the old exchequer or the excessive informality of the chamber system. Its drawback was the multiplication of departments whose sole unifying agent was Cromwell himself; his fall raised difficulties necessitating further reforms which, however, followed his principle of relying on bureaucratic institutions.

In the secretarial departments, too, Cromwell broke with tradition by relegating the royal seals to a secondary place and elevating the king's principal secretary to the position of chief executive and co-ordinating minister. Cromwell acquired the office in April 1534 and used it to make himself the master of the administrative machine. He set the example which the great Elizabethan secretaries were to follow. Wolsey was the last man who headed the

[1] These courts were statutory, since they were set up by acts of parliament, and not prerogative, as they are always being called.

[2] Turned into the court of wards and liveries in 1542 by the addition of the surveyor of liveries.

administration as chancellor; Cromwell's choice of the secretaryship foreshadowed the future. In his hands the office acquired control over everything: revenue and finance, home and foreign affairs, defence and religion—a hundred different tasks. He virtually took the secretary out of the household and made him an officer of state capable of standing side by side with the earlier executive ministers, such as the treasurer and controller of the household.[1] The change was described in an act of 1539 which included the secretary among the great officers of the realm. In April 1540 Cromwell surrendered the office for reasons both administrative and political; he was succeeded by two of his staff, Thomas Wriothesley and Ralph Sadler, who divided it between them. This division, designed to enable both Henry and Cromwell to dispose of the constant services of a secretary, was to endure, though for a time one secretaryship might occasionally be left vacant. In some ways, Cromwell's exploitation of the secretaryship was his chief contribution to English administration; the secretary of state has always been the executive mainstay of modern government. At the same time, Cromwell deliberately assisted the formalisation of all three royal seals. The privy seal lost its old place as the administrative centre and clearing-house of government orders; its functions were taken over by Cromwell himself as secretary and lord privy seal, acting through his own signed letters rather than by instruments under any seal. Both privy seal and signet were reduced to mainly formal functions which made their survival for another 300 years something of a triumph for official conservatism.

Lastly Cromwell saw to the organisation of the central government itself when, round about 1534-6, he transformed the inner ring of the king's council into a proper institution known as the privy council. The inner ring of important councillors, virtually dissolved while Wolsey ruled, came to the fore again after Wolsey's fall. So far from attempting to suppress it as his predecessor had done, Cromwell applied his usual bureaucratic methods to it. Building on the plans outlined in the 1526 Eltham Ordinance, he drew together the king's nineteen leading councillors as a separate board, provided them with a clerk, and continued to use them in the business of government. Admittedly, he also kept them firmly under his thumb, preparing their agenda and directing their deliberations: in this he instituted the normal relations between

[1] These were really already nominal titles; their holders exercised few functions in the household but acted as ministers without portfolio in council and government.

Tudor privy councils and Tudor principal secretaries. Admittedly, too, his personal standing prevented the complete emergence of the privy council which only in August 1540, soon after Cromwell's death, met to appoint an active clerk and inaugurate its register. But it was Cromwell who created the typical governing board of Tudor and early Stuart times, which in turn was to produce the modern cabinet. This reform resulted in the first institutional split in the king's council, so that for a few years we hear of 'ordinary' councillors—councillors who are not members of the privy council. By the reign of Elizabeth, however, the privy council was the sole survivor of the old council, except for the court of star chamber (itself largely composed of privy councillors) which achieved institutional separation as a result of the setting up of this small, tightly organised, and efficient conciliar board.

This brief summary of a very difficult and complicated subject should have proved the assertion that Thomas Cromwell reformed administration by replacing medieval household methods by modern national and bureaucratic methods. Of course, he did not create from nothing, but though he invariably and necessarily built up on what there was before him, he altered the very concepts and basic nature of things. His administrative reforms—many and enduring as they were—provided the machinery for governing the new state he had started to construct. In this as in everything he proved himself capable both of long views and of the detailed application: here too he displayed to the full a constructive statesmanship the like of which is seldom found.

6. PATERNALISM

So far we have considered the 'imperial crown' of England and what happened when Cromwell persuaded Henry to establish national and parliamentary sovereignty. But there were two sides to the constitution. The act of appeals spoke of the king and the body politic owing him obedience; more clearly, Henry himself defined the notion in 1543 when he spoke of the parliament 'wherein we as head and you as members are conjoined and knit together into one body politic'. The reformed polity rested on an organic view of the state. That is to say, it conceived of crown and subjects as living in natural harmony and mutual dependence. This indeed was good traditional doctrine, theorised about only a few years earlier by Edmund Dudley in his *Tree of Commonwealth* (1509) and practised, for instance, by Henry VII; however, Cromwell's administration both witnessed a renewed vigour in the practice and a closer definition in the theory because the Tudor revolution naturally raised all sorts of problems. The doctrine of the body politic knit together demanded obedience and assistance from the governed and put upon the government the duty of looking after the welfare of its subjects. It was once thought that this represented typically medieval doctrine with which the *laissez faire* principles that dominated the state from 1660 to 1906 could be usefully contrasted; more recent development has shown that attitudes to the state which regard it either as a natural protector or an unholy but necessary evil may alternate without regard to the categories of historical development. In fact, the Tudor revolution produced a much more effective example of the paternal state than anything the middle ages knew—something so effective that only the twentieth century has come to eclipse it. The sixteenth century called this sort of thing 'commonwealth' or 'common weal'. The term is almost as frequent in statements emanating from Cromwell's circle as is the word empire itself, and together these two—national sovereignty and paternalism—make up Cromwell's philosophy of the state which matters so much because he actually impressed it upon the realm and government of England. Commonwealth was to become the watchword of a group of social reformers in the 1540s; these 'commonwealth-men' had their predecessors in the 1530s among men working and thinking about the welfare of the community and putting their trust in Thomas Cromwell. The whole important subject has been little studied so far, and all one can do is to suggest a few points and stress the more obvious aspects of Cromwell's social policy.[1]

The group of commonwealth enthusiasts contained men well known as well as obscure, both men connected with the government and private individuals. Many of them were printers, a trade much given to pamphleteering in a century when the best way to get published was to own your own press and the best way to supply your press was to write your own material. Thus John Rastell, at first connected with the circle of Sir Thomas More but later with that of Cromwell, or William Marshall and Thomas Gibson, employed by Cromwell, were all printers who wrote on social and political questions. Others stuck to pamphleteering and took service under Cromwell, the great patron of political theorists; in this circle of men employed as propagandists and also sometimes

[1] The only relevant study is W. G. Zeeveld, *Foundations of Tudor Policy* (Harvard 1948) which discusses the political thought of some lesser writers. There is nothing on the social and economic investigations of the group.

as planning staff the names Thomas Starkey, Richard Morison, and Richard Taverner are the best known. The first two had been with Reginald Pole at Padua, which shows how closely progressive thought on the Romanist side was allied to its counterpart across the schism. Starkey was probably the abler theorist but Morison the more fertile pamphleteer; neither of them was an original thinker of note, though both could put into words the ideas of their patron and serve the ends of propaganda. They put forward interesting theories on the supremacy, on the state, and on social equality which indicate what Cromwell had in mind. They are more obscure but probably much more significant than the conservative defenders of the supremacy, such as Bishop Gardiner (*De Vera Obedientia*, 1535) or Bishop Edward Foxe (*De Vera Differentia Regiae Potestatis et Ecclesiae*, 1534). Gardiner and Foxe wrote to a brief they but partially subscribed to; they wrote in Latin; and they wrote scholastic and theological argument. The radicals, on the other hand, ordinarily wrote in English, discussed burning questions of the hour with a specific purpose (for which reason there is no point in quoting titles of their works),[1] and employed practical arguments. They were political and social reformers concerned with realities. When the whole question comes to be properly studied, it will at last be seen how the second generation of humanists supplied writers and propagandists for a theory of the state first developed and applied by the exceedingly practical Cromwell.

Of a different significance are the critics, men less closely tied up with the government and commonly more interested in economic and social problems than political. Here the outstanding name is Clement Armstrong, a London merchant (like so many of the active minds of the age) who wrote a number of treatises on questions of trade. (The identification of the authors of these commonly anonymous manuscript tracts presents often insuperable difficulties). More than anyone else, he anticipated the specific preoccupations of the later commonwealth-men. Hugh Latimer, bishop of Worcester and a violent (and unreliable) critic of religious and social complaisance, was also already active; he was to be the nominal leader of the movement in the 1540s. Gibson, already mentioned, may have been the man who produced a scheme for

[1] An exception should perhaps be made for Starkey's *Dialogue between Pole and Lupset* which has been much praised for its ideas on state and society; but Starkey never published the work which was first printed in 1871, and his contemporary importance really rested on the occasional pieces analysed by Mr Zeeveld.

erecting a standing army in which are included some criticisms of the dissolution of the monasteries—lack of alms and hospitality—which strongly remind one of Latimer's views in the next decade. There were critics among the lawyers, too, like the over-publicised Christopher St German who wrote some interesting treatises in which he investigated the royal supremacy from the point of view of the common lawyer and found it good, or the anonymous author of a draft act of parliament designed to establish an efficient police force in England under a committee known as 'Conservators of the Common Weal'. As the Henrician Reformation released a spate of theological speculation, so the concomitant revolution in the state produced an outburst of writings on political, social, and economic problems which was to swell from that day into an immense flood of printed stuff, most of it worthless and unreadable, which reached its height in the civil commotions of the seventeenth century. Men's minds were stirred up, and the printing press—so recently invented—stood ready to serve them. At the head of this stream we must put not a work like More's *Utopia* (1517), which is on its own both in literary merit and in irrelevance, but the propaganda put out to explain and justify Cromwell's revolution—the national constitutional monarchy and its duty to its subjects.

There was indeed much for pamphleteers and critics to write about, and the interesting thing is that most of the problems were economic. It is usual to call the age materialist, and certainly it displayed a quite modern preoccupation with the questions involved in getting a living. But very largely this was so because no thoughtful man could doubt that there was something seriously wrong with the daily life of the nation. Poverty seemed on the increase, trade was in difficulties, the sheep—it was thought—were driving the men from the land. As has already been pointed out, the early Tudors faced a problem arising out of increases in population and the amount of money circulating—a problem of unemployment and inflation. In the 1530s there was the additional difficulty that political factors made it impossible to satisfy the common people's desire for an end to enclosing without antagonising the gentry whose support in parliament was indispensable. Cromwell took a few steps against enclosures: an act of 1539 made possible a more effective prosecution of those who enriched themselves from depopulations, while other legislation attempted to prevent the commercial exploitation of land. The dissolution of the monasteries actually had little effect on rural life: enclosing and rack-renting, the two chief grievances, were not practised only by men who bought monastic estates. Nor did it make much difference to the already swollen ranks of the vagrant poor, though it rendered agrarian society unusually fluid through the sales and re-sales of land which did not really cease until about 1660.[1] Yet since it was thought that the dissolution had altered or even created the problem, and since people's views influence their actions, the resentment built up led to the pilgrimage of grace, and this in turn preserved even among adherents of the Reformation like Latimer a false picture of the causes of distress and of the excellence of monastic estate-management.

The outstanding social problem of the day was that of the poor, and during Cromwell's ministry an important step was taken towards its solution. The poor law of 1536 represents the one positive achievement of the commonwealth movement in the 1530s. In Tudor England, unemployment took the form of vagrancy. Those who could not find work at home took to the roads, at first no doubt because they hoped to be luckier elsewhere, but some of them soon because they began to prefer vagabondage and begging. The country was full—or comparatively full—of men, women, and children, moving from place to place, maintaining themselves by begging and living on charity, often organised into bands which were capable of terrorising isolated farmsteads or small villages. Many of them, especially those that drifted to London, were professional criminals. It is only necessary to recall the nursery rhyme which tells of the beggars coming to town to understand the light in which contemporaries were compelled to see the problem. The core of the begging bands were no doubt honest husbandmen fallen on bad days, but they were joined by many rogues, like the rufflers or swaggering vagabonds, often discharged soldiers from wars abroad or armed retainers whom royal policy had thrown out of work. There were, in fact, two kinds of poor—those capable of work but either unable or unwilling to find it (sturdy beggars), and those too old or sick to work (the impotent poor). It took the government quite some time to grasp this essential difference; the first reaction—as against the unfortunate gipsies then beginning a career of misery in England—was to hate and to punish and to wipe out by force. Whipping and branding seemed the only answer in an age which regarded suffering with indifference and idleness among the lower orders as wicked. How many such poor and vagrants there were it is quite impossible to say. The 'hundreds of thousands' sometimes so

[1] Monastic, episcopal, noble, and crown lands all came up for sale in stages, producing a fluid land market for some 120 years.

rashly alleged are certainly nonsense; we are dealing with a total population of less than three millions. If there were 20-30,000 workless the problem was quite big enough.[1]

Solutions and remedies were tried as early as the reign of Richard II, but all the acts down to 1531 did little except provide punishment for vagrants and order them to return to their homes, there to support themselves by begging. Charity remained private, and therefore insufficient. The act of 1531 for the first time made a clearer distinction between those able to work and those unable; it ordered the former to be whipped and the latter to beg under licences. The justices of the peace were coming to be used as the general executive agents of local administration; the poor act of 1501 had specifically saddled them with the punishment of beggars, and in 1531 they were given charge of the impotent poor permitted to beg. But the statute made no provision for the work which the sturdy beggars were to do, and the system of licences was excessively clumsy and impossible to control. Moreover, the spread of reformed ideas with their contemptuous attitude to good works was making respectable the general turning away from charity; it came to be held that all begging was bad and should be prevented. Of necessity, therefore, the state had to accept the responsibility for the failures and victims of society, and the admission and elaboration of this important principle mark the development of the effective poor law from 1536 to the great Elizabethan codifications in 1597 and 1601. In the autumn of 1535 Cromwell commissioned one of his assistants (probably William Marshall) to draft a poor law. Marshall produced a magnificently comprehensive scheme which displayed a real knowledge of the varied causes of pauperism and introduced three principles on which the poor law rested until its revision by the Utilitarians in 1834: work must be found for the unemployed that are able to labour, begging is wrong and the helpless must be a charge on the community, the unit responsible shall be the parish supervised by the justices of the peace. Marshall planned rather too well. He provided a general scheme of public works to absorb the unemployed, and a hierarchy of officials both local and national to administer both this and local relief. In the year designed for the dissolution of the monasteries, the government could not face such a task, and Cromwell contented himself instead with an enfeebled version of part of Marshall's draft. But though the

[1] It was incidentally a problem common to all Western Europe in the sixteenth century, not—as one might think from some statements—confined to a specifically brutal, capitalist, and anti-monastic England.

scheme of labour and even the parish overseers were dropped—so that little remained except some assertions of principle and policy—the act of 1536 still embodied the essential ideas on which the later poor law was to rest. Especially it still made the parish responsible for collecting alms, employing the fit, and relieving the needy. It was the real, though so far ineffective, beginning of that main achievement of Tudor paternalism, the Elizabethan poor law, and it arose out of the ideas of men who served Thomas Cromwell.

Cromwell himself was more interested and successful in the active encouragement of English trade. Himself once a trader with interests in the chief centre of English exports—Antwerp—and closely connected with the Merchants Adventurers of London, the great trading company which controlled the cloth export from London to Antwerp on which England's commercial prosperity largely depended, he was both inclined and qualified to do his best for trade. In this respect he initiated little that was new, but picked up the threads from Henry VII who had helped trade by commercial treaties, by encouraging alien merchants in order to increase the volume of trade, and by navigation acts designed to protect English shipping. Wolsey, on the other hand, showed himself both ignorant and careless of the intricacies of English commercial relations. The war of 1528 was rendered silly by the need to maintain friendly relations with the Netherlands while trying to fight their ruler, the emperor Charles V; even so, Wolsey bequeathed a legacy of bad blood. The danger grew more serious in the years 1529-32 when the emperor's desire to humble Henry VIII and the Brabanters' ambition to alter the reasonable terms of the existing treaties in their own favour co-operated in a general attack on England's monopoly of the cloth supply. The negotiations were protracted by the Netherlanders' chicanery, and not until Cromwell took over the direction of affairs in 1533 was the assault beaten off. Thereafter the trade continued in a flourishing condition despite the hostility between emperor and king; it cannot be doubted that Cromwell's often expressed preference for a Spanish alliance and an end to dallyings with France derived from his care for the English export trade.

It appears, however, that he had much more far-reaching plans, designed to enable England to exploit fully her favourable position as the chief supplier of unfinished cloth. Why should Antwerp be the centre of a trade which depended much more on English sellers than on Flemish buyers? The events of 1528-33 had shown how dangerous the English dependence on a foreign mart could be, and the years 1538-9, once more threatening attacks from abroad, drove the point home. There were thus good negative as well as positive reasons for attracting trade from Antwerp to London: England would profit from becoming the centre instead of the periphery of the whole trade, foreign merchants would be encouraged to resort to her in greater numbers, and at the same time the trade could be freed from the political pressure which was always to be feared while English merchants depended on a staple in Antwerp. These ends Cromwell hoped to gain by two measures. In 1539, a proclamation reduced the customs paid by merchants strangers to those payable by English merchants; in 1540, a great navigation act—amounting to a general code for English shipping and the sea-borne trade—confined the privileges of the proclamation to foreign merchants exporting English cloth in English ships. The effects were instantaneous. Foreigners flocked to England, the cloth export by merchants strangers rose at once without affecting the volume exported by Englishmen, and the navy and merchant marine derived all the benefits which a monopoly of the carrying trade could bestow. The effectiveness of Cromwell's policy is best illustrated by the violent reaction it provoked in the Netherlands where protests soon developed into an energetic attempt to get these measures rescinded. Cromwell's fall removed the one man of sufficient skill to carry through the attack on the Antwerp staple, and after two years of inept negotiations Henry VIII had to admit defeat—the first defeat in trade matters which an English government had suffered since 1485. It is an adequate comment on the abilities of Henry VIII when left to himself.

In one respect Cromwell's commercial policy was open to question. It concentrated on the interests of the Merchants Adventurers of London and thus encouraged their growing monopoly; Cromwell did nothing to arrest the decline of the once flourishing trades with Italy and Spain which had been mostly in the hands of the south-coast ports, especially Southampton. It was in the 1530s that the direct trade with Venice nearly ceased with the ending of the annual fleets which had been wont to sail up the Channel, and that the break with Rome terminated the prosperity of English merchants settled in Spain. The future seemed to lie with the Antwerp trade—easier, cheaper, safer, and larger than any other possible export trade—and here the Merchants Adventurers held a monopoly because the age believed in organising commerce in companies, and because these companies demanded a monopoly if they were to take all the risks. We shall have more to say about trading companies; here we may note that the events of the 1530s greatly assisted the development by which English trade put nearly all its eggs into the Antwerp basket. The obvious dangers of such a policy were shown up later when the Antwerp trade collapsed, but Cromwell at any rate had intended to prevent such troubles by transferring the mart and staple for cloth to London. That would have made the English cloth trade quite safe, secure in its hold over supply and selling at home to all comers; it was, once again, unfortunate that Cromwell's fall led to an abandonment of Cromwell's plans.

Chapter VIII

THE CRISIS OF THE TUDORS, 1540-58

1. THE LAST YEARS OF HENRY VIII

THOMAS CROMWELL'S fall marked something of a period in Tudor history. By depriving himself of his outstanding servant, Henry VIII destroyed the efficiency and the purpose of his government. For eighteen years—first under an ailing old man, then under a child, and finally under a woman—Tudor rule was tested to the utmost. That it survived at all was a tribute to the work of Henry VII, to the depth of king-worship and obedience to established authority which Henry VIII's terrifying personality had riveted upon an England anxious to avoid disorder, and also to the administrative reforms of Thomas Cromwell which up to a point made continued government possible even when the crown failed to play its part. But while Tudor rule survived, to be resuscitated by Elizabeth and her more than competent ministers, it underwent such vicissitudes in those years —was so rarely animated by a steady or intelligent purpose—that the total achievement would fill barely a page. The years served a purpose: passions played themselves out in the clashing of extremes which, having had their turn, retained the less strength to trouble the government of Elizabeth; but such an argument savours of the ancient heresy that all things work to the best of all possible ends and that success crowns the work. It also underestimates the degree to which the free play of passions, mostly religious, under Edward VI and Mary encouraged the growth of divisions which beset England in the second half of the century. It is impossible to say what would have happened but for the relaxation of good government between 1540 and 1558. The keynote of those eighteen years of somewhat purposeless turmoil is found in the development of the doctrinal changes which Henry VIII's constitutional revolution had set in motion despite his will. It is a story of the conflict of two extremes in religion alternately getting the upper hand, with a complicating admixture of international troubles and diversified by a gigantic economic crisis. This last deserves, and shall have, a chapter to itself.

Of all Henry VIII's follies none cost his country dearer than his illusion that he was an old and experienced king who knew his business and needed no one to do it for him. Cromwell had no successor, partly no doubt because the privy council after 1540 contained no one of his stamp or Wolsey's, but partly because the king thought a successor unnecessary. The council was from the first divided into two parties. The orthodox or conservative section naturally held the ascendancy immediately after Cromwell's fall. Its leaders were Thomas Howard, duke of Norfolk, a second-rate man skilled only in surviving adversity, and Stephen Gardiner, bishop of Winchester, a political ecclesiastic of great ability who was throughout handicapped by being a churchman and by an arrogance, masquerading as the patriotic Englishman's plain speech, which caused mistrust. Nevertheless, with Henry married to Norfolk's niece Katharine Howard (August 1540) and Cromwell dead, this party could feel secure. The radicals included on their right wing—the extremists, quite out of favour, did not count at this time—the archbishop, Thomas Cranmer, and Edward Seymour, earl of Hertford, whose influence owed much to the fact that he was the uncle of Henry's sole legitimate heir. Cranmer's hold on the king's friendship seems never to have weakened; it is either sign or cause of the curious fact that in his last years, and after the triumph in 1539-40 of religious conservatism, Henry moved away from the orthodoxy of his life's devotion to occupy a kind of middle position not dissimilar to that advocated by Cromwell in the 1530s.

The catholic success of 1540 was not complete. In August Henry signalled his neutrality between the parties by burning three reformers as heretics and executing three conservatives as papalist traitors, all on the same day. Cromwell was gone, but none of his side followed him to the scaffold; and Cranmer retained his crucial position at Canterbury. The Six Articles were still only patchily enforced. For a time, no further move was made towards establishing the true faith of the English Church; no parliament met until 1542 by which time the situation had changed again. In April 1541, memories of the pilgrimage of grace produced a desperate plot in Yorkshire to restore the old religion and overthrow what was felt to be Henry's tyranny; it was a plot of discontented men, restive under the even but heavy hand of the council of the North, which deserves little sympathy. The conspirators were betrayed and many executed; in their wake they dragged the old countess of Salisbury, in the Tower since 1539 and now beheaded as a warning to catholics, and Lord Leonard Grey, recently deputy in Ireland, who probably fell victim to his aristocratic connections rather than his alleged treasonable dealings with the Geraldines. Perhaps, however, this ominous clearance of the Tower had to do more with the king's plans for war than with the abortive Yorkshire conspiracy.

If the revival of catholic conspiracies undermined the standing of the orthodox party, the fall of Katharine Howard was a more serious blow still. In November 1541 the council obtained evidence that the queen had been unchaste before her marriage, and there were strong suspicions that her misbehaviour had not ended there. Henry was shattered by the discovery. After the political marriages with Jane Seymour and Anne of Cleves, he had re-discovered his youth with the lively and frivolous Katharine; indeed, he had given a somewhat ludicrous display which was yet touching in its happiness. But the queen was unquestionably very generous with her favours; at a court not especially noted for licentiousness (as courts went) she seems to have behaved with singular disregard for both morals and circumspection. Thus she was attainted by parliament—for treason!—and went to the scaffold in February 1542. With her she pulled down the Norfolk faction and really ended all chance of a full reaction in the sense favoured by Gardiner. The duke himself escaped by joining in his niece's condemnation, but his influence was pretty well gone. When Henry married once more, in June 1543, he chose Katharine Parr, herself a widow, who proved capable of dealing with the ever viler temper of an egoist soured thoroughly by ill health and by what he conceived to be his unmerited tribulations. Henry's last queen, who apparently had protestant sympathies, managed on the whole to keep out of politics, so that she survived her husband. She was a mild and moderately sensible woman much given to matrimony, but she scarcely merits the somewhat sanctimonious praise bestowed on her by the reformers and often echoed since.

In more than one way Henry demonstrated that he had recaptured the ardour of youth. Secure now in his triumphant establishment of the royal supremacy at home, free from the anxiety of ten years when foreign intervention was always threatening, he once again looked round for a way of displaying his greatness. In the summer of 1541, the amity of France and Spain which had driven Cromwell into the disastrous Cleves alliance cracked with a resounding report when the Spanish governor of Milan murdered two French envoys passing through his territory. With war imminent, England found herself the object of overtures from both sides. This suited Henry very well. Though he had avoided continental involvements while the situation created by the break with Rome made it desirable, he had always continued to harbour the ambitions which had led him into the wars of his younger days. Hostility to France and the hope of conquering Scotland still dominated his unoriginal mind. Scotland, indeed, could be said to be a danger, ruled as she was by a French and papalist faction led by the militant and immoral Cardinal Beaton. Diplomacy was tried first; Sir Ralph Sadler, one of Cromwell's young men, went north in 1540 to wean James V from his French associations and break Beaton's power. He was so far from successful that conditions on the border deteriorated, until in August 1542 an English raiding party was wiped out at Hadden Rig. In October 1542 Norfolk invaded Scotland, in order to compel acceptance of terms which would have made the northern kingdom England's satellite; the expedition achieved nothing and ended in an ignominious withdrawal. In November, James launched his counterattack. The better part of his forces, riven by internal dissensions, was met by a greatly inferior English army in the marshes of Solway Moss and destroyed in a rout. The English lost seven men killed and the Scots twenty, but hundreds more, including many nobles, surrendered. The news killed James V. His realm was left in the hands of the French party acting for the infant Mary, herself the daughter of James's second and French wife.

In the spring of 1543 Henry thus had a magnificent chance of achieving his ends in Scotland. He used the prisoners taken at Solway Moss to form the nucleus of an English party in Scotland; he encouraged a reaction there which overthrew Beaton and put the near-protestant earl of Arran temporarily in power; in July he forced upon the Scots the treaty of Greenwich which arranged for a peace to be cemented by the marriage of Mary Stuart to the prince of Wales. However, Henry's arrogance defeated itself. The spectre of English domination revived Scottish nationalism at its fiercest; Beaton escaped from imprisonment and re-established the French and catholic ascendancy; and Henry had to resume military action. But the activities of the earl of Hertford, who burnt Edinburgh and laid waste much country, only made the English party and policy more unacceptable. Even the murder of Beaton in 1546 did not alter the position; though the English party, protected by English naval strength, held Edinburgh Castle until after Henry VIII's death, the king's policy proved a failure. So far from achieving his great aim of subordinating Scotland to England by a marriage alliance, he only ensured the triumph of the French faction: the French might be unpopular, but the English were hated and much nearer.

In any case, with characteristic over-confidence, Henry had entered another war in 1543. Something might be said for the

Scottish enterprise which had an intelligent purpose behind it, though the execution of the design can earn little praise; but the only justification (such as it is) that can be found for the ultimatum which Henry delivered to France in 1543 is that he thought the Scottish war at an end. For two years imperial diplomacy had been trying to draw England into the continental war, while France had endeavoured to keep her out of it. In the end, traditional alignments combined disastrously with Henry's old desire to display his power in Europe. In actual achievement, the war proved modest but far from disgraceful. A small force of Englishmen, dispatched in 1543 to assist the imperial armies in Flanders, impressed knowledgeable observers on both sides. The real effort came in the following year when some 40,000 men invaded France from Calais in a move intended to combine with a Spanish thrust towards Paris. Henry would not be prevented from accompanying his army, though his old,[1] unwieldy, and diseased body had to be carried in a litter. The conduct of the campaign was in the hands of other old men, the dukes of Norfolk and Suffolk, who had first displayed their military skill thirty years earlier. In the event, the great army, too slow and cumbersome to sweep the undefended province of Picardy, was content with the rapid conquest of Boulogne. After this the alliance of Henry and Charles, each of whom wanted different things from the French, broke up, and Charles made peace. England would have joined in, but Henry's determination to keep Boulogne prevented agreement. The war, dragging on, now concentrated on the French effort to recapture the town from the sea, so that the only actions of note were naval engagements in the Channel. In the course of these operations the French actually rowed their galleys up the Solent, but the most serious English loss—that of the *Mary Rose*—occurred when the ship turned turtle in making a sharp turn with gunports open, and the only real result of it all was to enhance the reputation of the lord admiral, Sir John Dudley, Viscount Lisle. Like Hertford in Scotland a commander of the younger generation, he demonstrated that England would not always have to rely on her Suffolks and Norfolks.

Peace was finally concluded at Ardres in June 1546, largely because neither side saw much hope of decisive success. France once again promised to pay sizable pensions, and England was to retain Boulogne until 1554 when France would buy the town back. Henry could imagine that he had waged another successful war, but the gain was infinitesimal and the loss, especially to the crown,

[1] At fifty-four Henry was in fact an old man.

terrible. The wars had been astonishingly expensive, costing altogether well over £2,000,000—perhaps ten times as much as the first French war of the reign. The reasons are obvious now: the price rise of the period had driven up costs, a factor for which the government failed to allow, and in the absence of an efficient minister the administration of the war was wasteful and corrupt. To cover these costs Henry had recourse to several expedients. The years 1540-7 saw an unprecedented burden of taxation, some £650,000 being obtained in this way. In addition, forced loans and even illegal benevolences appeared again on the scene. It is a sign of Henry's increased power and of the hold he had over his nation that parliament voted subsidies, and the rich 'lent' sums which they knew would never be repaid, without any of the troubles which similar demands had caused in 1522-4. For the crown thus to pillage its subjects might have been politically dangerous, but it did little harm to a country which could well afford to pay. The same cannot be said for Henry's other methods of raising money. He sold crown lands, especially—though not exclusively—the property taken from the monasteries. The sales made before Cromwell fell had been few and carefully controlled. But from 1542 onwards vast quantities of crown lands were alienated, bringing some £800,000 into the court of augmentations. On the whole the crown still obtained fair value, though it is significant that it also began to sell the rights and rents originally reserved on the lands sold: all capital was being realised. The real trouble was that the money so obtained did no good; it was all poured into the war. Thus Henry VIII impoverished the crown only so recently enriched by Cromwell's financial policy, and he further burdened it by contracting great loans on the Antwerp money market, often at high interest (14 per cent., and never less than 10 per cent.), leaving some £75,000 in debts. Most disastrous of all, however, was the debasement of the coinage. By recoining the available bullion with more alloy, the mint increased the face-value of its output without spending more precious metal; in effect this meant an income of about £360,000 in Henry's last three years. But the result was to ruin England's coinage and destroy confidence in it; in exchange for immediate gain to himself, swallowed up by the insatiable war, Henry damaged the economic life of the country so seriously that even twenty years of varied efforts could barely retrieve the situation.[1] The sum total of Henry's last years of direct personal rule was therefore to undo the good work of his father

[1] The details of the debasement and its effect on prices are discussed in the next chapter.

and of Thomas Cromwell. In order to pursue his futile and ill-conducted wars, the king destroyed the financial independence of the crown and undermined the prosperity of his country.

While the king pursued dreams of imperial conquest in the north and effective intervention on the continent, he still had to deal with the problem of religious unity at home. The crisis of 1538-40 resulted in the fall of Cromwell and the temporary ascendancy of the conservative party; orthodoxy, which Henry favoured, triumphed in the act of six articles. But Cromwell's fall did not destroy the reforming party, and the conservatives suffered a set-back in the fate of Katharine Howard. The king continued to display that genius for cautious and opportunist adaptability, disguised as strong-minded decisiveness, which had already brought him far. Despite high words, he did not encourage the persecution of heretics which some of the bishops wanted.[1] The English Bible survived Cromwell's end, and Cranmer showed no inclination to return to strict orthodoxy. However, 1543—with its alliance with Spain—saw the balance once again turn to conservative views. The king was seriously perturbed by the manifold blasphemy reported from all over the country: God's Word was bandied about in taverns and ale-houses, and the scurrility which was always near the surface of medieval piety broke through in disconcerting fashion. The remedy adopted is most significant of the age. An act of 1543 limited the right of reading the bible to clerics, noblemen, gentry, and substantial merchants; women below gentle rank, servants, apprentices, and base people were forbidden to read what it was alleged they simply could not understand aright. Hierarchical paternalism—both contempt for the lower orders and fatherly care for their welfare—was here neatly and unquestioningly expressed by a government which—and this is typical too—thought it could do the impossible by legislative enactment. The act also promised a definition of doctrine, and this was achieved in the *Necessary Doctrine and Erudition for any Christian Man*, published in 1543. The book was the work of the bishops but the king had greatly influenced it; it deserves its name of the 'King's Book'. It came down entirely on the side of traditional orthodoxy, merely replacing the papal supremacy by the king's; those traces of

[1] The outstanding example of the sporadic persecution going on in Henry's last years was the torture, trial, and burning of Anne Askew, a gentlewoman who went to the stake for her denial of transubstantiation in July 1546. Attempts made to implicate others—especially Cranmer and Katharine Parr—led nowhere.

Lutheranism which had penetrated into the 'Bishops' Book' of 1537 had quite disappeared.

Gardiner and his party now thought their time come. The only obstacle to a firm stand on catholic doctrine seemed to be the suspected heretic at Canterbury. But once again they had misjudged their master. Henry had by now acquired a thorough dislike of episcopal pretensions very much at variance with his earlier attitude to Wolsey, and he never trusted Gardiner who, despite his modern defenders, can hardly be interpreted as anything but an overbearing and over-subtle schemer. It is probable that Henry's attachment to Cranmer, so strong despite their not inconsiderable differences in matters of theology, derived largely from Cranmer's refusal to engage in politics. At any rate, the catholic party three times between 1543 and 1545 devised plans for charging the archbishop with heretical opinions, and each time they were foiled by Henry's personal intervention. Secure in the king's protection, Cranmer busied himself along lines which might easily have lost it: he composed liturgical books which he was later to combine into the Book of Common Prayer. However, unable to get either convocation or the king to accept his own strong views against many ceremonies, he had to be content with the English litany of 1545. Henry determinedly stuck to a middle way which Cranmer was rapidly leaving behind.

In his famous address to parliament in December 1545, the king once more stated his own position. Making an impassioned plea for charity, the fierce and intolerant old man, who one way and another had shed so much blood, denounced the stiffness of both extremes—the intolerance of the old religion and the unquiet and disturbing curiosity of the new—and deplored their mutual recriminations. He wanted moderate orthodoxy: the old religion with some of those late-medieval excrescences in image-worship, pilgrimages, and ceremonies pruned away. But in a way it was already too late to hope for the maintenance of this compromise. A new generation was growing up; in court and council the division between conservatives and innovators came to coincide largely with the division between the older men and the younger. Hertford and Lisle, whose reputations were eclipsing those of the old dukes (Suffolk died in 1545), both favoured protestantism and were known to do so. For some reason which has never been satisfactorily explained, Henry permitted his son and heir to be brought up by reformist tutors; Edward VI was to be a bigoted protestant. Late in 1546 a temporary catholic ascendency in the council made way before the influence of Hertford and Lisle, returned from the wars; Gardiner, refusing to exchange some lands with the king, fell quite out of favour.

Worst of all for the conservatives, the reign did not close without another political upheaval, and this time the victims were the Howards, the secular mainstay of the orthodox party. Henry VIII had never lost the sense that his throne was somewhat insecure; throughout the reign, dynastic worries accounted for more illustrious victims than any other preoccupation. Buckingham, the Poles and Courtenays, the countess of Salisbury—whatever their immediate offence, connection with the White Rose was common to them all. Now the duke of Norfolk's brilliant young son, Henry earl of Surrey, thought fit to remember his own descent from Edward I and to display the arms of Edward the Confessor. Surrey himself probably leant nearer to protestantism than to orthodoxy, but the trouble did not arise over religion. At heart, everything turned on the personal rivalries and jealousies among the men who were getting ready to seize the inheritance of the dying king. The Howards had many enemies, and Surrey's indiscretion offered a ready handle. In December 1546 father and son were arrested; in January 1547 Surrey was executed for treason in displaying the royal arms; on the 27th the old duke was condemned to suffer likewise because he had concealed his son's offence. That night King Henry died and Norfolk escaped the scaffold; but the power of his house was broken, and as a child ascended the throne the protestant party looked to have it all its own way.

Henry VIII retained the reins of power to the very end; despite his physical decay there was no dotage. In his last months he concentrated on one thing only—the safe and peaceful succession of his son. He had long provided for the accession of a minor; an act of 1536 had authorised a king to revise all legislation passed during his minority, and the succession act of 1543—after settling the crown on Edward, Mary, and Elizabeth in that order—had reserved to the king the right of altering the succession by testament. In his will, Henry first repeated the terms of the act as far as his own children went; failing their heirs—a possibility which no one thought likely though in the end it came about—he then excluded the heirs of his sister Margaret (the Stuart line) and gave the crown to the heirs of his other sister Mary (the line of Suffolk). Determined to prevent trouble after his death, he had to decide between the parties and factions which for so long he had kept in strict subjection. The developments of the last two years of his reign—the rise of Hertford and Lisle, the fall at the critical time of the catholic protagonists—as well as a preference for laymen who could be better trusted than ecclesiastics to keep the royal supremacy intact, determined that his decision should advance the party of reform. In the end, Henry proved true to the two outstanding features of his reign—his own skilful opportunism and the triumph of the secular state—even though it meant the surrender of a lifetime's religious opinions.

Fifty-seven years old, King Henry VIII died on 27 January 1547, his hand in Cranmer's, convinced as he had always been of his own righteousness. The nation, informed three days later by Lord Chancellor Wriothesley (in tears), was stunned and frightened of the future. The follies of the last seven years made sure that the next reign would be burdened with an evil inheritance, but the earlier work of Henry VIII and his great ministers had not been done in vain.

2. EDWARD VI AND THE REVIVAL OF FACTION

The death of Henry VIII left the crown in the hands of a child nine years old. Since the Tudor constitution, like the medieval constitution whose development it was, required the presence of an effective king, this virtual lapse of the crown posed enormously difficult problems of government. In theory, of course, and also in his own opinion, Edward VI was a real king: his surviving diary and other papers show this boy adopting almost his formidable father's tone in his supposed dealings with ministers and events. In fact, as one might suppose, Edward played no part in his reign; his so-called opinions were those of his advisers, and his so-called acts were his endorsements of accomplished fact. Yet, since he was king and the nation pathetically worshipped all wearers of the crown, he could not be ignored and had to be persuaded, so that his character and views mattered a little. They were neither attractive nor promising. Edward was naturally haughty and arrogant, like all the Tudors; also like all his family, he had a marked intellectual ability which an appalling schooling had turned into a precocious passion for protestant theology. The king was a cold-hearted prig, a fact which not even the pathos of his miserable death can make one forget. Self-righteous, inclined to cruelty, and —need we wonder at it?—easily swayed by cunning men, he exercised such little influence as he possessed in favour of disastrous policies and disastrous politicians. Unable by reason of his years to support the kingly pretensions to which he was heir, he reduced the king-worship of the early sixteenth century to absurdity and broke the spell which Henry VIII had cast over the nation. The crown was never quite the same after Henry VIII died.

Of more real importance, especially in 1547, were those who actually ruled—the privy council. Henry VIII had tried to prevent friction by appointing a council for his son from which the extremists on the catholic side—Bishops Gardiner and Bonner—were absent, and to prevent the ascendancy of one man by laying down that all the council were equal. But the council at once broke Henry's last will by appointing the earl of Hertford, Edward's uncle, protector of the realm and duke of Somerset.[1] Somerset had secured Edward's person and the support of both the protestants and the civil servants in the council; his only possible rival was Lisle, now earl of Warwick; and that there needed a regent was not really in doubt. The man so chosen is one of the enigmas of a century whose personalities as a rule fall readily enough into obvious categories. Personally ambitious and rather haughty in manner, he was also liberal in ideas and generous in practice. An excellent and successful general in the field, he proved visionary, short-sighted, and incompetent in politics. Beyond question he was a man of ideals: as Sir William Paget, who originally supported and even stage-managed him, once wrote to him in despair, it was nothing but liberty with him. He sympathised with the poor and helpless, but to so little purpose that his sympathy in the end cost them dearer than other men's indifference. Always willing to make enemies among the powerful, and specially skilful in alienating the council who resented his assumption of a power above their own station, he deprived himself of any chance of putting through his ambitious programme of religious and social reform. Somerset is an attractive figure, with his frequent gentleness and relative unselfishness, especially in an age when the greed and unbridled self-seeking of others make him appear unique; but when all is said, he yet remains the type of the ignorant idealist, applying the wrong remedies to troubles wrongly diagnosed, who is the very worst man to be in charge of a state. As Pollard (who admired him) said, 'he took his office seriously and himself too seriously'; he was simply not up to managing the inheritance of Henry VIII.

That inheritance was admittedly a pretty burden. Henry left a heavy debt, a debased coinage, a shaken administrative system, and an example in spoiling the Church which the self-made men who filled court and council were eager to follow and enlarge upon.

[1] Paget, the secretary of state, produced a list of promotions which he said Henry VIII had intended to make. All the leading councillors moved up a step in the peerage: probably these were their rewards for acquiescing in Somerset's protectorate.

He left an unsettled doctrine and a nation divided in religion. He left an uneasy truce with France and a flaming war in Scotland. All these problems Somerset tackled in his two years' ascendancy. First he freed himself of all restraint when he removed the last notable catholic from the council by securing the fall of Lord Chancellor Wriothesley on a somewhat curious charge of exceeding his competence. That left a council of protestants and pliable indifferents. The protector then turned to the one task for which he was fitted, the war with Scotland. Here, too, his aims were visionary: he dreamt of a peaceful fusion of the two countries in one 'empire' of Great Britain. But though he wanted consent he saw no way of getting it except by war, especially as the Scots persisted in believing that the marriage between Edward VI and Mary Stuart, arranged by the treaty of Greenwich, would simply put their country into an English pocket. So Somerset crossed the border in September 1547 and won the bloody battle of Pinkie, retiring thereafter in the belief that the retention of a few strongholds and the sending of protestant missionaries would gradually win the Scots over. Pinkie, never followed up, marked the end of the Henrician policy in Scotland. In 1548, Mary Queen of Scots was sent to France and the ground prepared for her own personal tragedy as well as the long rule of the French at Edinburgh.

In the meantime, the burning question of the day was advancing towards a solution. Somerset had at once ended all persecution of protestants, and England now became for a few years the Mecca of continental reformers. Those that came were mostly of the Zwinglian persuasion—John à Lasco from Poland, Peter Martyr from Italy, Francis Dryander from Spain, Martin Bucer from Strassburg, and others. Their influence was to turn Cranmer more and more away from the moderate reforms of the Lutherans who refused his invitation to come over, but his own moderation always prevented the Church from fully embracing Zwingli's doctrines. Controversy centred largely on the nature of the eucharist, the sacrament of the altar, and with it on the quarrel between the mass and the communion service. The theological background to all the events of this period must be remembered even though space forbids a full exposition of it. Cranmer stood characteristically between the extremes, though precisely where is still a matter for some dispute. Somerset advanced the protestant cause he had at heart at first by allowing the Henrician legislation to lie dormant, and then by repealing it in the parliament which met in November 1547. Most of the treason and heresy laws of the last (and earlier) reigns, including the act of six articles, were repealed, together with the proclamations act of 1539 and the act which permitted Edward VI to repudiate all legislation passed during his minority. Unquestionably these measures were, and were intended to be, a manifesto of freedom, and Somerset invariably earns much praise for a liberalism commonly described as far in advance of his time. That phrase itself implies a censure, and his own fellow-councillors thought ill of these repeals. A policy which retains some strong weapons to check disorder but applies them with restraint deserves respect: this had virtually been the policy of Henry VIII from 1534 onwards. But a wholesale abrogation of such weapons at a time when a country ordinarily turbulent enough was about to be thrown into further confusion by the proposed religious changes was idealist folly—even criminal negligence.

The other measure of 1547 which merits attention was the act dissolving the chantries, the many small foundations for religious, charitable, and educational purposes which abounded in medieval England. This step had originally been planned by an act of 1545, but the death of Henry VIII interrupted the proceedings which Somerset now resumed with energy. In theory, the dissolution was justified by the new hostility to the doctrine of purgatory and to masses for the dead, the chief religious purpose of the chantries; in fact it was simply another stage in the secularisation of Church property. The lands and goods went to fill part of the large hole in the royal coffers, and then as rapidly passed out again by sale and grant to the eager purchasers who had already absorbed so much monastic property. Somerset himself profited notably. Some was used to found grammar schools: the old legend of Edward VI as the patron of schooling is now dead, though the newer legend of the great system of education available in the old chantry schools still awaits overthrow. The attack on the chantries involved an attack on some gild property in the towns which caused difficulty in and out of parliament, but on the whole the measure passed easily enough.

The chantries act and some others which almost incidentally introduced communion under both kinds and the appointment of bishops by royal letters patent indicated the way things were going. Even before, Cranmer had stirred up trouble by publishing *Homilies* contrary to the King's Book and *Injunctions* based on those of 1538, all of which Gardiner attacked as unconstitutional to such good purpose that he was for a time confined to the Fleet. The year 1548 saw the flood swell. The continental mentors continued to arrive and to spread their doctrines, especially at the universities. The protector and council issued orders and literature of a reforming kind. In June Gardiner was sent to the Tower for his public opposition, remaining there throughout the rest of the reign. The removal of Henry's restrictive legislation let loose a flood of preaching, teaching, and disputation, often of a scandalous and scurrilous character, but much of it also profound and searching. The new protestantism had the support of some of the clergy and bishops, especially Cranmer; Somerset and a few other councillors adhered to it; there may have been some real enthusiasm in London; but it seems never to have penetrated to the nation at large. Unlike the anti-clericalism of the previous reign, it struck no deep roots; its safest support came from those gentry and nobility who, disliking or ignoring its doctrines, yet felt themselves bound by their secular interests in monastic and chantry lands to oppose a conservatism which, by seeking the leadership of the Princess Mary and talking of the absent Cardinal Pole, threatened a return of the papal supremacy.

The first stage of the doctrinal Reformation culminated in the Prayer Book of 1549, enforced by a mild act of uniformity. The book represented a compromise intended to persuade catholics to accept it; the concessions made to them, especially in the matter of ceremonial, greatly disappointed Cranmer's Zwinglian friends. It was so darkly worded that Gardiner and Cranmer had no difficulty in interpreting it very differently; Gardiner virtually killed it by giving it an orthodox catholic reading which finally convinced the reformers that it was worthless. In its hesitant advance towards protestantism, in the mild measures taken for its enforcement, and in its general ineffectiveness, it well represented the policy of Somerset's government—laudably moderate in intent but also deplorably futile in execution.

Even so, the first Prayer Book was to cause trouble enough. The year 1549 was one of crisis in which religion formed one of the chief issues. The other was economic distress, especially agrarian grievances. Throughout the 1540s prices rose rapidly and poverty mounted. Enclosure for pasture revived as wool boomed; in particular, there were many encroachments on commons.[1] Even so, however, enclosure and its worst product, depopulation (the disappearance of whole villages as the sheep took over), were not so much the real cause of the dearness and destitution as the cause advanced by a number of reformers who composed what was called the commonwealth party.[2] They were mostly clerics—

[1] The 'agrarian revolution' will be discussed more fully in the next chapter.

[2] From their catchword, commonwealth or common weal. For their forerunners see above, p. 185.

moralising preachers like Hugh Latimer and Thomas Lever, skilful pamphleteers like Robert Crowley—but their expert was a civil servant, John Hales of Coventry, who may have been the author of the movement's literary monument, the *Discourse of the Common Weal of this Realm of England.* They believed that enclosures were at the root of the trouble, and that enclosures were simply the work of greedy money-grubbing landlords; and they convinced the lord protector. In 1547 Hales attempted to secure the passage of three bills dealing with enclosure and, more sensibly, with tenants' rights, but the house of commons, dominated by the lords of manors who were themselves driven on by economic necessity, would have none of such things. It showed its true temper by enacting the most savage of the century's poor laws by which vagrants were rendered liable to slavery. Baulked by parliament, Somerset turned to the weapons of conciliar government: in 1548 he condemned enclosures once again by proclamation and appointed commissions to investigate and enforce the laws against the practice. The only commission which seems to have taken action was that of which Hales was the moving spirit, but it dealt with the main enclosing counties—the Midlands from Leicestershire down to Buckinghamshire—and authorised the destruction of many enclosures, among them a park recently made by the earl of Warwick. When, in the year after, a great rising took place, the interests which Hales and Somerset had offended charged them with inciting the commons to riot and rebellion; but in truth, hedges fell and ditches were filled in all over England at different times throughout these and earlier years. Enclosure riots—protests on a small scale by individual villages or even only a few peasants—were frequent; what happened in 1549 was only the culmination of this sporadic and spontaneous movement.

Nevertheless, the commission of 1548 played an unwitting part in stirring up trouble. Somerset's deeds, and even more his words, created the impression that 'the good duke' would assist the poor against the local gentry, and the Norfolk rising of 1549—known from its leader as Ket's rebellion—was a definite attempt to enlist support from the centre against the ruling class of a county which was particularly ill-administered by its traditional magistrates. The rising seemed formidable: Ket at one time had some 16,000 men under arms on Mousehold Heath outside Norwich, controlled that city, and governed his territory and followers in an alarmingly independent manner. Early fears that the rising might by inspired by catholics eager to put the Princess Mary (who lived in the county) on the throne proved groundless; Ket's rebellion was the only major agrarian disturbance of the period with a protestant bias. But it came on top of an upsurge in Cornwall which was caused by the new Prayer Book: the insurgents wanted the old faith as well as the pope, pointing out that a service in English was as incomprehensible to them as one in Latin without even the merit of familiarity. The Cornishmen allowed themselves to be absorbed by a fruitless siege of Exeter, and Ket failed to seize his advantage because he was concerned only with Norfolk. The risings were suppressed with great violence, not by Somerset whose generous and muddled mind prevented him from taking action either way, but by the outraged representatives of the gentry. Russell and Herbert pacified the West, Warwick destroyed Ket; and by the autumn of 1549 England was once again at peace.

However different in their origins and aims, the troubles showed up the protector's failure to govern. His position had already been weakened by the execution for treason of his brother, the wayward Lord Admiral Thomas Seymour, for which justifiable act of stoicism he was much blamed; nor did it help that the French were besieging Boulogne with every appearance of an early success. Somerset did not deserve all the blame heaped upon him, and historians who have seen the cause of his fall in the self-interest of the great landlords opposing him and the specific ambitions of Warwick have seized upon the heart of the matter; yet there are things to be said on the other side. Somerset had talked much of liberty but had produced disorder; he had acted with the best intentions but without any sign of administrative ability or political sense; he had attempted to fill a position reserved to the crowned and anointed king, thus alienating his fellow-councillors whose feelings and ideas he persistently ignored. When the crisis came, he found friends among the poor and powerless; all men of standing were against him. This speaks well for his heart, no doubt, but his championship did the poor the less service because he had concentrated all the strong against them. In October 1549 he was arrested by a group of councillors supposed to favour catholicism, but by February 1550 his real rival, the earl of Warwick, got rid of the conservatives and released Somerset from the Tower, attempting fornearly two years to achieve co-operation on his own terms. He never took the title of protector, preferring to govern through his domination of the council and the young king over whom he acquired the ascendancy of an indulgent older man playing at grown-ups with a child. But Warwick wanted full power, and Somerset's popularity stood in his way. After preparing the ground in 1550, the earl attacked in 1551. He and his followers acquired new honours—Warwick became duke of Northumberland; the king was introduced into the council to work against his uncle; and in October Somerset was arrested on a frivolous charge of treason. In the following February, among impressive scenes of popular sorrow, he suffered under the axe. The story of these faction struggles need not be rehearsed in detail. Their occurrence, indeed, and their virulence are highly significant, for they demonstrate the decay of good royal government in Edward VI's minority; it is also important to note how long it took Northumberland to get rid of his rival, since in the end he proved to have left himself insufficient time to consolidate his triumph.

Thus Somerset, noble-minded and generous, but also ambitious, high-handed, and incompetent, made way for a man for whom no one has ever had a good word. Northumberland, son of that Edmund Dudley whom Henry VIII had executed in his early days, was the second of the young soldiers who came to the fore in the renewal of war after Cromwell's fall. A reputation then made was enhanced somewhat easily in the rout of Ket's half-armed followers at Dussindale in 1549. Unquestionably Northumberland was exceedingly ambitious of power and very greedy. He represented, at its worst, the type of man who was speculating in monastic property and the exploitation of land, and the businesslike landowning gentry looked to him to save them from Somerset's predilection for the peasants. The manner in which Northumberland and his followers grasped honours and lands from the powerless hands of a boy king demonstrates to the full that the evils of factious magnate rule were reviving under this upstart nobility. Their attitude to economic problems, embodied in legislation in 1553, was straightforward: they confirmed their own gains at the expense of the king and refused to be tied in any way in the use of their property. But in some ways Northumberland's rule marked an improvement on Somerset's. He recognised the evils of a debased coinage and did something to tackle them, and he undertook a thorough review of the dilapidated administration of the country. The financial reforms which the new lord treasurer, the marquess of Winchester,[1] carried through in 1554, and which provided the basis for sound finance in the reign of Elizabeth, were begun by Northumberland's government at the very time when we are

[1] Sir William Paulet (1485?-1572), successively Lord St John, earl of Wiltshire, and marquess of Winchester, was probably the outstanding example of the Tudor civil servant in high places who avoided the complications of politics. His life and work want studying. He himself accounted for his survival through four reigns by saying that he was sprung from the willow and not the oak.

commonly told that government was at its worst. They are no credit to Mary who merely permitted measures to develop which her brother's death had interrupted. It looks very much as though Northumberland had to cope with an administration allowed to rot by Henry VIII and Somerset, and as though he attempted genuine remedies, hampered as he admittedly was by his own and his party's selfish greed. Where Somerset was attractive as a man but disastrous as a ruler, Northumberland displayed every unpleasant personal characteristic but seems to have shown skill and penetration in public affairs. It is difficult to say who did more harm to the country they were supposed to govern.

However, Edward VI's reign is associated not only with the near-collapse of the Tudor system, but also with the progress of the protestant Reformation; and here Northumberland's part is even less easy to understand. In the end he affirmed that he had always been a catholic, and when he first attacked Somerset the conservative faction had hoped great things from him. Yet in between he directed a headlong advance towards full protestantism, overthrowing the compromise of 1549 and encouraging extremes in iconoclasm and doctrine which went even further than the settlement of 1552 which he sponsored. Very probably the reason must be sought not in any convictions he may have had, but in the designs which he and his like had on the property of the Church. Any retreat from the position of 1549 might have involved them in demands for the restoration of lands already acquired—the lands of monasteries and chantries; and if they wanted more, they had to turn to episcopal lands which the spread of protestant doctrine and the weak position of protestant bishops were, in fact, to deposit in their laps. Every bishop of the old persuasion deprived of his see meant a protestant successor whom the dominant party would only appoint after they had wrung material concessions from him. Henry VIII had pointed the way and Somerset had followed; but it was in these years of Northumberland's ascendancy that the Church was really ruined as the wealth of the bishops began to follow that of monasteries and chantries into lay hands.

Early in 1550 the reformers gained control of the council and set to to promote greater changes than any yet accomplished. More continental experts arrived, and Cranmer was swayed by Bucer and the Zwinglians. The catholic bishops fell in numbers: Gardiner, so far from being released from the Tower, was deprived of his see for his opposition (February 1551), and others of his persuasion followed. The appointments in 1550 of Nicholas Ridley at London and John Hooper at Gloucester greatly reinforced the extremer party. In Hooper the government came up against the first genuine representative of that puritanism which was to cause so much trouble later on. He had all the hallmarks: blazing sincerity, intolerable obstinacy, devotion to small points, bad manners, and utter confidence in his own judgment and conscience. Characteristically he had been in exile under Henry VIII, imbibing the pure Swiss doctrine and returning eager to establish it. An exasperated council and an uneasy Cranmer struggled with him over the question of priestly vestments, until Ridley persuaded him to compromise. 1550-1 witnessed a general attack. A new Ordinal (February 1550) simplified the rites of ordination and abolished minor orders; later embodied in the revised prayer book, it marked the change from catholic priest to protestant minister. In 1551, a controversy between Gardiner (sending his thunderbolts from the Tower) and Cranmer raised the central question of all, the sacrament of the altar. Cranmer rejected transubstantiation but accepted the real presence in a spiritual though not a corporeal sense; he held that the communion service was more than the mere commemorative act of the Zwinglians but that, unlike the mass, it contained no element of sacrifice. This satisfied the reformers to whom Latimer, hitherto a conservative in doctrine though a radical in policy, now adhered. Celibacy and priestly marriage, always a ticklish point, assumed importance in 1551 because of the appointment of John Ponet to Winchester and Robert Holgate to York, both of whom were rumoured to be married to wives with first husbands yet living. The story, which was true of Ponet but not of Holgate, did much to embarrass the reformed party and to weaken the standing of the Church at a time when it needed strength and good repute to resist the secularisers. In accordance with the Prayer Book of 1549 altars were replaced by communion tables, especially by Ridley in London; this caused irreverence on the one hand and unease on the other. There was, however, little enough opposition to the innovations. The Edwardian Reformation was superficial—imposed on a reluctant or indifferent people by a few ardent spirits and the politicians—but twenty-five years of royal control following upon a century and a half of obedience to papal direction had accustomed the nation to accept authority. One who did resist was the Princess Mary whom the council tried in vain to deprive of the mass.

It was not until after the fall of Somerset, when the last moderating influence had gone from the council, that the final step was taken. The 1549 Prayer Book had from the first been attacked by the protestants who abominated its attempts to compromise with the old religion; like most compromises in violently disturbed ages, it only succeeded in falling foul of everybody. Bucer, the most learned of the foreign divines, wrote a long commentary whose criticisms are fully reflected in the later revision, while John à Lasco set to work on Cranmer himself, claiming afterwards that he had persuaded him to Zwinglianism. Cranmer certainly moved further towards the Swiss position in these years, but it would seem more correct to accuse him of an eclectic mind which adopted parts of several systems; from its first archbishop the Anglican Church inherited not only a beautiful liturgy and a readiness to obey civil authority, but also a doctrine half-way between the extremes. The revised Prayer Book, published after much consultation in 1552 and enforced by an act of uniformity which appointed penalties for failure to use it as well as for positive attacks upon it, marked the arrival of the English Church at protestantism. The various 'popish' remnants in doctrine, gestures, and vestments, which had still attached to the communion service, were dropped, and even Hooper could be satisfied that the mass was abolished in England. One hurdle remained: the book demanded kneeling at the communion, and the extreme reformers had to be placated by the insertion of the so-called Black Rubric which stated that the practice denoted only respect for and not adoration of the sacrament. In 1553 Cranmer produced a statement of faith for the English Church in his Forty-two Articles which represented a compromise between the Lutheran and Calvinist (or Zwinglian?) creeds without attempting to accommodate the catholic faith except where the branches of Christianity did not, in any case, differ. The Prayer Book of 1552, the Ordinal of 1550 which it took over, the act of uniformity which made the Prayer Book the only legal form of worship, and the Forty-two Articles binding upon all Englishmen, clerical and lay—these between them comprehended the protestant Reformation in England. Matters had changed rapidly in the five years and few months since Henry VIII had died, an orthodox catholic still except for his break with the papacy; they had moved even faster in the two and a half years since Somerset's fall. Gardiner and the Henricians seemed utterly overthrown; the sees of England were filled by upstart protestants; there was rejoicing at Geneva and Zürich, and Cranmer was revolving further plans for uniting the dangerously divided protestant Churches.

In fact, the moves had been too rapid. The whole English Reformation depended on the life of Edward VI, and so did—

what mattered more to the man in charge—the ascendancy of Northumberland. Edward was probably the most ardent lay protestant in England; he was certainly the only complete adherent of the duke who had succeeded in making enemies of all men by his greed and arrogance. His party was held together by self-interest only; he had one only as long as he commanded wealth and patronage. In 1552, Edward's health, never good, took a turn for the worse; measles and smallpox attacked a frame constitutionally consumptive; and in the spring of 1553 the king contracted a cold which brought him to his death. Northumberland was faced by a sudden crisis. If Edward died his sister Mary would succeed him under the terms of the act of 1543 and of her father's will. Her accession would mean the end of the Reformation in England and as certainly the end of the duke who had tied his career to advanced protestantism. Out of this dilemma grew Northumberland's desperate and doomed attempt to pervert the succession in his favour. He persuaded Edward to set aside the will of Henry VIII, to declare both his sisters bastards and therefore incapable of inheriting the crown, and to bestow the succession upon the daughter of the duke of Suffolk, Lady Jane Grey, descended from Edward's aunt Mary and married to Northumberland's son Guildford Dudley. The council was coerced into supporting the plot which would leave Northumberland the real ruler of England as father-in-law to a helpless young queen. No attempt was made to abrogate the succession acts of 1536 and 1543, but in the event legal points mattered nothing. Failure was assured when the council failed to get possession of Mary's person: warned in time (oddly enough by Northumberland's younger son Robert), she fled into Norfolk, the stronghold—despite its protestant feelings—of the catholic Howards.

Edward died on July 6th; four days later Queen Jane was proclaimed in London, but Queen Mary was proclaimed in Norfolk. Much against his will, Northumberland set out to overcome her by armed force, only to find the country up in her favour and his troops melting away. Deprived of his strong hand the council ratted; in the end Suffolk himself told his daughter that she had ceased to be queen and proclaimed Mary on Tower Hill. The news reached Northumberland at Cambridge. Hoping to save his life he threw up his cap in the market place for Queen Mary. No sudden plots could take the crown from the Tudors where the passionate loyalty of the nation desired it to be: Mary's triumphant success owed everything to her being King Henry's daughter and very little to her catholic faith. This she quite failed to understand—

with dire results. But in the meantime all was rejoicing as she rode into London, acclaimed by the multitude which had pelted the captive Northumberland on his way to the Tower where he was soon joined by the rest of his party, including Lady Jane Grey, the innocent victim of his ambition.

3. MARY AND THE FAILURE OF REACTION

The reign of Mary Tudor lasted only five years, but it left an indelible impression. Positive achievements there were none: Pollard declared that sterility was its conclusive note, and this is a verdict with which the dispassionate observer must agree. Even the financial and administrative recovery, which has been noted,[1] owed nothing to the queen or her policy; planned in the previous reign, it was the work of Winchester who played no part in Marian politics. The decline of good government was accentuated by Mary's preference for a large council of nearly fifty members and her encouragement of cliques and cabals, not to mention the influence of Charles V's ambassador Simon Renard and of Mary's husband, Philip of Spain. For the first time in English history, a queen regnant occupied the throne, an event which on this occasion only served to prove right the fears which had gripped Henry VIII in the 1520s. After the rule of factions in the reign of a child, the accession of the wrong kind of queen nearly completed the ruin of dynasty and country. Yet Mary herself is often regarded as the most attractive of the Tudors. She was personally gentle and inclined to mercy, though her history—the vicious attack on her mother, her own bastardisation, the treatment of her religion and her person by her father and brother—ought to have turned her into a fearsome instrument of hatred and vengeance. She was also sensible and generous—altogether of a better character than was common in her family. But all her good qualities went for nought because she lacked the essentials. Two things dominated her mind—her religion and her Spanish descent. In the place of the Tudor secular temper, cool political sense, and firm identification with England and the English, she put a passionate devotion to the catholic religion and to Rome, absence of political guile, and pride in being Spanish. The result cannot surprise. Welcomed by the nation as a Tudor and a relief from the ambitions of selfish politicians and the extravagances of reforming divines, she died only five years later execrated by nearly all. Her life was one of almost unrelieved tragedy, but the pity which this naturally excites

[1] E.g. F. C. Dietz, *English Government Finance, 1485-1558.*

must not obscure the obstinate wrong-headedness of her rule.

Mary's own single ambition was to restore England to the papal obedience, to save—as she saw it—her country from mortal sin. This overriding issue was complicated—both advanced and retarded—by problems of foreign policy. Since Henry VIII's death England had played little part on the continent. In 1550 Northumberland gave up Boulogne whose neglect he had made one of the charges against Somerset. The emperor had been busy in Germany and in Lorraine where the French king (Henry II) had been making conquests; for once the Rhine, and not the Channel seaboard, had been the scene of the Habsburg-Valois struggle. But in 1553 the war between Spain and France had reached stalemate, and both sides began to look for additional strength. The accession of Mary, the emperor's cousin, seemed to promise a revival of that alliance between England and the Burgundian House which Henry VII had made the basis of English diplomacy, and which rested firmly on a common interest in the cloth trade between England and the Netherlands. Mary had been, as it were, the seal of that alliance, and even Henry VIII's behaviour to his Spanish wife had not destroyed it. Charles V now saw a chance of giving it still greater solidity. The question of Mary's marriage loomed large from the first. A few there were who thought that this woman of thirty-seven would do well to avoid trouble by not marrying at all; these included Cardinal Pole who was himself mentioned as a possible husband. (He was as yet but in deacon's orders, and a papal dispensation could have been secured.) But Mary herself was clear that she would marry a Spaniard and no one else, and Charles V decided upon his son and heir, Philip, at the time archduke of Burgundy. The marriage would add England to the Habsburg dominions; successful marriages had built these up so amazingly in the previous half-century that the idea seemed sensible enough and France had cause to fear it. London became the centre of a diplomatic battle between the great European powers in which England played barely the part of a pawn. To make matters more difficult still, few members of the council favoured Mary's own choice of a Spaniard for husband; Gardiner especially, released from the Tower to become lord chancellor and (at last) chief minister, sturdily opposed a policy which would reduce England to a Spanish colony. But the English candidate, Edward Courtenay, earl of Devonshire, was a weakling and a poltroon: the Spanish match seemed likely to come off.

Thus the reign started with every promise of trouble. A new set of councillors replaced those of Northumberland; the Henricians, led by Gardiner and Paget, were back in power. The queen's determination to spare bloodshed meant that only three men died on the scaffold for Northumberland's conspiracy, the duke himself vainly endeavouring to save his life by embracing the catholic religion. His recantation was the first move in a distressing game of chess. In its determination to reverse the Reformation and restore the papal power, the government sought to produce as many apostates from protestantism as it could because by lowering the reputation of that faith one could most quickly reduce the numbers of its followers; meanwhile the other side triumphantly chalked up each death of a steadfast believer on the principle—borne out by results—that the Church is fructified by the blood of its martyrs. Northumberland's death opened the score for the catholics and lost many recent converts to protestantism.

However, for the time being, the queen could do no more than rescue catholic councillors, deprive heretic bishops, and arrest Cranmer for treason. This eager daughter of Rome, this unswerving adherent of the papal supremacy in the Church, found herself inevitably saddled with the title of supreme head and compelled to resort to parliament in order to reverse her father's and brother's doings. Suggestions that she might restore the realm to Rome without parliamentary sanction were quashed by, among others, Gardiner. There were technical legal reasons for this, but a very practical problem existed also in the lands taken from the Church and absorbed by the laity since 1536. These Mary wished to recover, but she and everybody knew this to be impossible; any attempt to declare the Henrician and Edwardian legislation null and void—which, since it contravened canon law, Mary adjudged it to be—without giving parliament a chance to safeguard the interest of the new owners would lead to rebellion. It is most striking how everybody around the queen all the time smelled or feared uprisings; Mary herself, her ministers, Renard, and the French ambassador Noailles moved in an almost palpable fog of violent political disorder which in part was real but in large part only existed in their apprehensions. About the Church lands, however, they were right. The Reformation sat as yet lightly on most Englishman's minds, but the nobility, gentry, and yeomanry who had invested in those lands were not prepared to disgorge them, and their self-interest saved protestantism in England. It may also be noticed that the vigorous dislike of priests and priestly rule had not abated since 1529.

The first parliament of the reign met in October 1553 in an atmosphere disturbed by forthcoming events. Neither house made any bones about repealing the Edwardian act of uniformity, thus restoring the religious situation of the end of Henry VIII's reign—with this difference that, the heresy laws repealed by Somerset not being re-enacted, the state did not yet assist in the enforcement of catholic orthodoxy which Mary and Gardiner wished to put in train. It was also made plain to the queen that she could abandon all hope of returning the Church lands to their late owners and therefore of restoring the monasteries. Worse still, the commons sent a deputation to protest against the proposed marriage with Philip, a move which demonstrated that the relaxation of discipline since 1547 and the freedom enjoyed in Edward's reign had given the lower house a good conceit of itself. Mary expressed her angry displeasure and hurried into the match; it was concluded by proxy in October 1553. This brought discontent to a head in various plots secretly assisted by Noailles who still hoped to prevent England from acceding to the side of Spain. Only one of these conspiracies came to anything, but it turned out to be serious. In January-February 1554 Sir Thomas Wyatt, son of the poet, roused the gentlemen of Kent and beset the capital itself with some 3,000 men. Stopped at London Bridge he crossed the Thames at Kingston and penetrated as far as Fleet Street, but the desultory and confused fighting petered out against the government's superior forces (marshalled by Northumberland's late supporters rather than by Mary's party proper), and Wyatt surrendered. His enterprise had been inspired both by protestantism (Kent had a tradition of heresy) and by nationalist resentment at the proposed foreign king; it was so serious because it was the only rising in Tudor times to take place in the neighbourhood of the seat of government itself. The fright which the council had had was reflected in its actions. Mary's desire for mercy was overruled both by her advisers and by Charles V. Wyatt and many of his followers died in London and in Kent; the innocent Jane Grey and her husband were executed; the Princess Elizabeth, on whose behalf Wyatt had allegedly risen, narrowly escaped a like fate, though she did not escape imprisonment in the Tower.

In the meantime Mary was no nearer her real aim—the restoration of the papacy—and she found it difficult to stomach the cautious advice of Charles V who cared little for the healing of the schism but did not want to send his son into a country possibly torn by religious war. A second parliament met in March 1554, only to prove more troublesome than the first. Gardiner attempted to revive the heresy laws and the act of six articles, but was defeated in the lords; the reaction against the Reformation and the persecution of protestants had to continue to wait. Trouble arose over attempts to give Philip the protection of the treason laws and other privileges, though Wyatt's rebellion made sure that the marriage treaty itself was accepted without opposition. Philip, the commons thought, should be Mary's husband and might even bear the name of king, but he was not to be a real king and above all he was not to retain the crown if he survived his middle-aged wife. All this opposition came perhaps less from the nation than from a party in the council led by Paget who in this parliament won a marked victory over the clerics under Gardiner; the state of a government so badly and so publicly divided needs no comment. In July 1554 Philip at last arrived, and the marriage was celebrated. Mary, who persuaded herself into deep and real love with her unprepossessing husband (who did not reciprocate), had a brief interlude of happiness; the country looked on and disapproved.

Their disapproval was strengthened by the first real signs of ecclesiastical reaction which ensued upon Mary's failure to restore the link with Rome in her second parliament. The government began to eject a large number of beneficed clergy, nearly always because they had taken wives; if these married clergy had once been monks or friars they were forced to put their wives away as well. This deliberate concentration on those who had broken their vows of celibacy was inspired by the queen herself. Altogether probably a quarter of the English clergy were ejected from their livings—some 2,000 or so; but the figure itself contains a hint that the authorities could not be as rigorous as their words pretended. There were not enough ordained priests acceptable to the catholic party to fill so many vacancies. Many, in fact, reappeared in other parishes where their earlier history was unknown. Deprived Essex clergy have been traced in Gloucestershire, and so forth, though the task of tracing them all is hopeless. In more rural areas neighbouring priests sometimes exchanged parishes, changing back again when the accession of Elizabeth brought another turn of the wheel. Nevertheless, many suffered because they had taken women in marriage, especially in London where the Reformation had made most progress.

Protestantism had ceased to be the religion of the land, many old ceremonies and practices were again used in the churches, mass especially was again being said. But, except for the repeal of the

Edwardian laws on uniformity, all this had been done by Mary's authority as supreme head: England had not returned to the Roman communion, and the devout queen could only do what she thought right by the exercise of a power she held to be wrong and usurped. It was time that the schism was healed. Two things stood in the way: the impossibility of recovering the Church lands, and the refusal of the chosen instrument to admit defeat on this issue. That instrument was Reginald Pole, cardinal and papal legate. His was an obvious choice—the only English cardinal, related to the queen, a persistent fighter for the papal supremacy against the English schism. It was, however, also an unfortunate choice in some ways, for Pole lacked all diplomatic and statesmanlike abilities. His temper agreed most unfortunately with that of Queen Mary: both were personally kind and inclined to mercy, both put principle far above expediency, both believed earnestly and immovably in the necessity of exterminating heresy by fire. Neither was a match for the children of this world among whom it soon appeared that there had to be numbered not only Gardiner, Paget, and the Henricians, but also Mary's husband and father-in-law, and even the pope himself. Fearful of what he might do, Charles V delayed Pole's journey to England until he had accepted the necessity of surrendering the Church lands; then at last, in November 1554, Cranmer's successor in the see of Canterbury landed at Dover, bringing with him the absolution of the realm and reconciliation with Rome. His arrival coincided with the meeting of yet another parliament (November 1554) whose elections had been influenced by the government with sufficient success to bring about some degree of co-operation. The old heresy laws were re-enacted and ferocious new treason laws passed (a weapon which no effective sixteenth-century government could avoid); more important still, parliament at last agreed to repeal all the anti-papal and anti-ecclesiastical legislation passed since 1529. Pole and Mary much regretted the necessity of seeking parliamentary repeal of acts which they held to be inherently void as contrary to the laws of God and Holy Church, but even the defenders of the medieval Church had to imply acceptance of the principle that statute stood above all other law in England. As far as enactments could kill it, the Reformation was dead and Henry VIII and Cromwell need never have laboured; by and large there was reason to suppose that the country, some irreconcilables apart, would accept the fact.

This hope, however, was never more than an illusion. England had so far little sympathy for protestantism on the Edwardian model, but the anti-clerical and anti-papal nationalism which Henry VIII had exploited continued as strong as ever. It now found reinforcement from the government's activities against heresy. The responsibility for the persecution and burnings which are the best-remembered thing about Mary's reign is easily attributed. The Spaniards, with Philip and Charles V to give a lead, were against it, for reasons of policy. Gardiner and Bonner (in whose diocese of London the majority of the victims were found) went at it with a will, the latter especially displaying a coarse liking for the task; neither can be exonerated from a charge which seems more serious to the twentieth century than to the sixteenth, but neither also was the originator of the policy. It was the queen and the cardinal who inspired it, believing that only so the souls of Englishmen could be saved from eternal damnation. The trials opened in January 1555, and before the reign was out nearly 300 men and women were burnt for their faith. Most of them were humble folk—shopkeepers, artisans, and the like; most of the leaders of the Edwardian Church had taken the opportunities offered to flee abroad, but Hooper, Ridley, Latimer, and Cranmer died in the flames. The last-named suffered much perturbation of spirit at the end, being torn between his religious convictions and his lifelong adherence to the principle of obeying the civil power. But when he came to die he rejoiced the reformed and disappointed the government by revoking all his recantations and facing the fire as steadfastly as the others had done. These martyrs, celebrated by John Foxe in his *Acts and Monuments*, deserve no doubt no more and no less sympathy than the victims of Henry VIII or Elizabeth, but their importance is vastly greater. Mary burned few as compared with continental practice, but for English conditions and traditions her activities were unprecedented and left an ineradicable memory. More than all the denunciations of Henry VIII, the fires of Smithfield and the like places all over southern England created an undying hatred of the pope and of Roman Catholicism which became one of the most marked characteristics of the English for some 350 years. This in itself is an adequate comment on the activities of these earnest and good and rather stupid fanatics, and an answer to those who would always judge people's place in history by their personal morals rather than by the work they did

Her efforts on behalf of the faith had to be Mary's sole consolation from the middle of 1555 onwards, for after the appearance of triumph in the Spanish match and the absolution of the realm everything went wrong. In September 1555 Philip departed to take over his inheritance in Spain; he left behind him a disconsolate woman looking eagerly and hysterically (and in vain) for signs of the child upon whom all her hopes now centred. The parliament of October 1555 proved obstreperous to a degree, resentful of the persecution, eager to throw off government control—it even proposed a bill to exclude from membership all office-holders under the crown—and unwilling to grant the supplies which had been the real cause of its assembly. In November Gardiner died. Much maligned in the past, too much praised today, he had played a prominent part in thirty-five years of public life without ever attaining to the power and influence he craved. Henry VIII distrusted him, Somerset and Northumberland feared him, Mary found him too English for her taste. Yet he had stood for a certain continuity and for a definite party of conservative patriots. He was very able, learned (especially in the canon and civil law), and energetic, but overbearing and violent in manner. His few years of office and influence (1553-5) were spent in attempts to restrain and divert the one of his sovereigns with whom in general he was most in sympathy. His life achieved little, for even the continuity of the Anglican Church with pre-Reformation days owes more to Cranmer than to Gardiner. His death, however, deprived the government of the one man able to combat the influence of Pole and of Spain.

The Spanish match and England's virtual absorption into the Habsburg empire had played relatively little part until 1556 because domestic issues had then predominated upon which Philip and his advisers exercised little influence. Despite their studiously good behaviour they were hateful to the simple and virulent nationalism of the English, the more so as the Spanish alliance coincided with a decline in the Netherlands cloth trade (though it did not cause it) and did not lead to better trade for the English seamen trying to break the Iberian monopoly of transoceanic trade. In 1556 the Spanish connection began to have positively harmful effects. Philip quarrelled with the pope, Paul IV (a man whose violence of temper amounted to madness) over Italian issues, and Mary had the dreadful experience of seeing her husband excommunicated by her spiritual father. Pole, too, fell under the pope's displeasure; he was deprived of his legacy and accused of heresy. Into these distractions there dropped the renewal of war between Spain and France in 1557. Philip briefly returned to England—of which, after all, he was still king—in order to press for military assistance; the queen felt it her duty to provide it, and her council, more mindful of the constant rumblings of disaffection and of the crown's financial straits, resisted in vain. In June 1557, England declared a war on France in which she had no concern, of which the country disapproved, and which was singularly ill-managed. Empty coffers and the inadequacy of parliamentary grants (January 1558) compelled recourse both in 1557 and 1558 to forced loans and other expedients both desperate and illegal. Spain used English assistance, for instance at the battle of Gravelines in July 1558; but she treated English interests with contempt. All the fears that the alliance would but make England a Spanish province proved justified. The chief blow fell in January 1558 when the French overran the ill-defended Calais in a week; the last remnant of England's medieval empire in France, a base held for over 200 years, was virtually thrown away. Probably Calais—expensive and useless—was better lost than kept, but neither the nation nor Mary saw it that way. The failure broke her spirit and destroyed the last vestige of loyalty to her.

As 1558 dragged on it became clear that the queen's days were numbered, and all thoughts turned to the successor. Elizabeth was very nearly holding court before her sister died. Mary's last year was as tragic as all her life had been. Still thinking that she might yet have the child that would perpetuate her work, she mistook the symptoms of her disease; surrounded by the ruins of all she had striven for—self-produced ruins at that—she died on 17 November 1558. Twelve hours later Cardinal Pole followed her. It was a fitting close. The catholic reaction was over, though no one yet knew what exactly the Church and the religion of England were to be. The situation looked grim indeed. Church and state had decayed since the day on which King Henry was quick and dead. Neither Edward VI nor Mary lacked some of the qualities necessary in a Tudor sovereign. They had courage and intelligence, and they enjoyed the advantages of the king-worship of the day. But the rule, successively, of an incompetent idealist, a reckless adventurer, and a devout and devoted Spaniard had well-nigh ruined the achievement of the first two Tudors. Disorder at the top was again threatening the stability of the realm. The work of restoration was to prove relatively easy, because the foundations were much more solid than the years 1547-58 would suggest; but the real saving of England lay simply in the fact that Edward died young and Mary ruled for only five years. Good government came back in the nick of time. As for Mary, all she had achieved was to destroy both the old religion and the Spanish alliance by making them the heart of her policy. Even before the Council of Trent put it beyond doubt, the Marian reaction demonstrated that an anti-papal Church preserving the doctrine and ritual of pre-Reformation days was an impossibility; while the Spanish match began to teach Englishmen to see in Spain rather than France the national enemy. The main lines of Elizabeth's reign were determined from the start by her sister's disastrous failure.

Chapter IX

ENGLAND DURING THE PRICE REVOLUTION

NOTE. Of all the categories of historical writing those dealing with changes in economic and social life are least easily accommodated to ordinary critical divisions. In this chapter I shall therefore try to describe the main facts of sixteenth-century economic history, although this will involve much reaching back and forward from the point attained. This attempt to set out in outline the chief points of Tudor economic history is necessary—to avoid it would leave the picture very incomplete—but it is also doomed to some sort of failure. All over England research is going forward of the only kind that can ultimately tell us the truth—research into the economic and social history of individual localities and especially counties—and the results make the generalisations so confidently put forward by both past and present historians look ever more dubious. Yet we must have generalisations. These studies demand and use statistics; but Tudor statistics are bound to remain patchy and therefore very dangerous. This chapter is certainly not going to avoid all the pitfalls. All one can do is to sketch the broad lines of economic and social change in a particularly restless century, as they appear to one writer who has consulted the authorities and, while gratefully accepting most of what they say, feels compelled to dissent respectfully on some vital matters. The outstanding economic event of the period was an unprecedented inflation; prices—especially those of food—rose rapidly and persistently; and these changes were reflected in much upheaval, great distress, but also much opportunity for improvement. Not all the changes to be discussed were due to the price rise, and in many cases the effects of inflation were complicated by other factors; but the heart of the story is that increasing 'dearth' or dearness which contemporaries viewed with such dismay and so little comprehension.

1. THE INFLATION

AS has already been mentioned, the static or falling price levels which persisted for something like 150 years before the accession of the Tudors gave way round about the beginning of the sixteenth century to a gradual increase. Between 1500 and 1540 prices rose by a half; they then more than doubled in the next twenty years; thereafter the curve flattened, but by the end of the century prices were about five and a half times what they had been 100 years earlier.[1] Of course, this rise must not be thought of as a straightforward advance along a consistently climbing line. Occasional sharp lifts must still be ascribed to the ancient causes of famine and dearth; there were bad harvests in the 1530s and 1590s which produced perfectly natural sudden increases in prices. At times prices might even drop again a little. But despite local and temporary differences it is plain that they were constantly on the upgrade, that better harvests after a famine did not reduce the price of wheat to its former level, and that contemporary accounts of hardships reveal a persistent though uneven and not altogether calculable inflation.

The causes of the phenomenon were but little understood at the time. It was usual to think of the price of goods as stable, an opinion which the experiences of the later middle ages of course supported, exception being made only for times of shortage. But now men were faced with rising prices in an age of comparative plenty and they naturally thought, as men will, that the greed of unscrupulous individuals was responsible. Inexperience was reinforced by doctrine—the medieval doctrine of the 'just price'. This declared that everything had its proper price corresponding to an abstract value fixed by natural law and consisting of such components as the true value of the material, the labour, and the time which went to the making of the product. This just price was always and everywhere the same, except that a shortage, by increasing the value of the material, could increase the value of the total product. Since the age also supposed that the value of money represented the intrinsic value of the metal (its just price, as it were), it followed that prices were invariably stable unless men improperly and even blasphemously interfered with the natural order. Both doctrine, therefore, and the common desire of bewildered men to find a scapegoat led people to suppose that the price rise could be arrested if only the unlawful and selfish doings of the few were prevented from afflicting the many. The result may be seen in the numerous statutes against those who enclosed lands or rigged the market by forestalling and regrating, that is by buying goods cheaply on their way to market and holding them to sell when prices rose. It was a long time before thinkers recognised that an inflation which affected at least all Western Europe was likely to arise from deeper and more general causes. Not until 1574

[1] See Sir John Clapham, *Concise Economic History of Great Britain*, pp. 186-7.

did a French philosopher, Jean Bodin, at last relinquish entirely the doctrine of the just price by discovering what may be called the modern theory on prices. This is that prices represent the relationship between the goods available and the money available. If goods become scarce while purchasing power remains equal, prices will rise; this was the common experience of the middle ages in times of famine. Originally dearth and dearness meant the same thing. Bodin understood that the same result would come about if the amount of money in circulation increased while the supply of goods remained more or less stable; this in its turn has been the basic cause of most modern inflations resulting from the putting out of paper money. Bodin therefore argued that the sixteenth-century price rise was due in the main neither to the malpractices of greedy men, nor to shortages, but to a vast increase in minted bullion, and in this he was perfectly correct.

The amount of money in circulation can be increased by a number of factors. More coin may be available from freshly minted bullion, from hoarded treasure, or through debasement (making the existing bullion go further), and an increase in the amount of trade itself, by accelerating the circulation of money, may add to the effective amount of coin. The later middle ages had suffered from a chronic shortage of bullion which in fact hampered trade, though it also benefited it by encouraging the invention of credit instruments. The needs of merchants led in the late fifteenth century to a more energetic exploitation of the chief European silver mines in Germany and Bohemia. The beginnings of the price rise are commonly ascribed to this. Even at this date major changes in price levels could not be confined to one country; the organisation and operation of trade was sufficiently international to make sure that fluctuations in one place would soon show in another. This was particularly true of England whose commercial life was dominated by the export trade in raw wool and woollen cloth, changes in which affected all men from the king (much of whose revenue came from wool customs) and the big merchant exporters down to the primary producers, whether they were big sheep-ranchers like the Yorkshire monasteries or the least little peasant who sold the wool off the backs of his few animals. Thus England almost at once shared in the rising prices of Western Europe.

The first serious English inflation, however, in the reign of Henry VIII, was due to particular local causes. Henry's early wars and Wolsey's diplomacy by subsidy greatly increased government spending and in particular released the treasure laid up by Henry

VII. The worst effects resulted directly from the government's manipulation of the coinage. In 1526 Wolsey undertook a recoining in the course of which he increased the money in circulation by reducing the weight of silver coins—the first instance of a serious debasement since the Conquest. Wolsey's action had this to recommend it: that it merely brought English coins into line with continental money, thereby preventing the loss of silver which always takes place when one country's coinage is 'better' (richer in silver) than another's.[1] But unfortunately the example was remembered eighteen years later when Henry VIII, once more engaged in war, found himself desperately short of money. The series of debasements between 1544 and 1551 reduced English coins to an unexampled state of badness. They altered both in weight and in 'fineness' (the proportion in their alloy of precious metal to base) until the silver content of each coin was only about a sixth of what it had been under Henry VII. This meant, of course, that the available silver could be recoined at a much greater face value, so that the crown technically made an enormous profit—something like £500,000 in all. But it was only seen afterwards that the debasement was bound to drive up prices so disastrously that the advantages of the nominal increase of revenue were soon lost. Debasement achieves its worst effects when people treat money as possessing a real value. In the sixteenth century a shilling piece containing 90 per cent. of silver was thought of as worth about four times as much as a shilling piece containing 25 per cent.: Latimer, in one of his sermons, cried that he had almost mistaken this new 'pretty little shilling' for an old groat. Since, in consequence, sellers of goods would not accept the new coin as equal to the old, prices rose swiftly and appallingly. For once economists got on to the trouble quickly enough; by 1551 it was realised that prices could only be stabilised and confidence restored if the debased coin was called in and reminted with a proper silver content. Unfortunately the duke of Northumberland, planning to do this, made two mistakes; he decided to reap just once more the short-term advantages of debasement, and he announced the proposed improvement of the coinage four months in advance. Since he thus first made the problem much worse and then warned all men that they would lose most of the money they would take

[1] 'Bad money driving out good', a principle known as Gresham's Law. Its essence is that people will hoard good coin and spend bad, so that less and less good coin is used, with cumulative effects showing in lack of confidence and lack of readiness to accept bad coin. That is, prices will rise again.

before the recoinage, it cannot surprise that prices shot up again in the summer of 1551. However, Northumberland then began a stabilisation which Elizabeth completed, and by 1560 English coins had recovered a decent silver content and the confidence of the nation. These irresponsible manipulations had caused disastrous hardships to many, but at last it could seem that the bad period was over and that the price rise had been arrested.

But the price rise continued. It was much less violent than before; there were years of stability and even years of recession; but by and large prices still rose—by something over sixty per cent. in the reign of Elizabeth. The correct reason was stated by Bodin in his analysis of the phenomenon. The discovery of enormous new sources of silver and also gold in South and Central America added so vastly to Europe's total of coinage that the whole of the price rise has been—not unjustly—linked with this single cause. Quantities of gold and silver entered Europe from the first days of the Discoveries, and the finding in 1545 of what seemed an inexhaustible mine—a solid mountain of silver—at Potosi in Peru ensured a steady flow of precious metal to the old world. The effects were first felt by Spain since that country first imported and exported the American silver, but international trade quickly spread them around the rest of Western Europe. England felt them very early, partly because of a flourishing direct trade with Spain in the first quarter of the century, but largely because the English cloth trade concentrated on Antwerp which was also the financial centre of the Spanish Empire.

These, briefly and with some simplification, are the causes conventionally assigned to the price rise in Tudor England. There is some argument about them; some scholars feel less and less certain about the effects of American silver and more and more inclined to look for particular reasons here and there. In any case, inflation is the natural state of mankind. The times when prices have remained static are very few, and they were usually bad times. A little gentle inflation stimulates trade, encourages enterprise, and tends to increase national wealth. What was so serious about the Tudor price rise was its suddenness and violence, most marked in the years between 1547 and 1551 whose troubles were certainly due in the main to a foolish and selfish financial policy. The effects of that inflation were indeed wholly bad.

When a stable community is suddenly attacked by an impersonal economic movement of great violence and long endurance, when moreover the enemy is not really recognised or sought in the wrong quarter so that no valid remedies are applied, the effects are many and far-reaching. Taken in all, they amounted to a revolution. This remains true even though earlier views of the sixteenth century as one of pure revolution in economics and society are no longer tenable. This was not—as used to be supposed—the time when capitalism first arose, involving an economy based exclusively on money relationships, an industry centred on a primitive factory system, and the appearance of a so-called middle class. It is quite apparent by now that all these developments had a very respectable ancestry right back into the middle ages, and that on the other hand much sixteenth-century life remained nearly untouched by these supposedly modern features. But because existing tendencies towards change were enormously stimulated by the price rise, so that movements discernible before became indisputably visible, it is still possible to speak of a revolution, a great and often violent change in the fortunes and standing of individuals, and in the methods by which men earned their living. But the new never swept the old away even though it may have pushed it aside.

2. THE LAND

Sixteenth-century England was and remained a predominantly agrarian country. Nine-tenths of the people earned their living on the land, and the remaining tenth retained some connection with it. There were few entirely urban people, for even townsfolk still had their fields around the borough, and even workmen in the woollen and other industries continued to add to their livelihood by growing things in plots of land. London alone was a town in the modern sense, with a population perhaps twenty times that of the next town in the realm, Norwich.[1] Even the proud mercantile ports—the rising Bristol, the declining Southampton and Hull—or the so-called manufacturing centres—Norwich, Coventry (declining), Manchester (rising)—were at best country towns or, to our eyes, large villages. Thus the land ruled everything, for on and by it people lived, and the economic effects of the price rise on the land were far and away the greatest. The basic changes arose from this: the rise in prices compelled people to make more out of their lands if they could, and they would find this easiest if they could sell produce on the rising market. In other words, the price rise encouraged—even compelled—what is known as the commercial exploitation of land. The three main ways of achieving this were changes in agrarian organisation and land tenure, changes in

[1] London can be estimated very tentatively at about 300,000 in 1600.

the kind of product produced, and improvements in agricultural method.

Of these three—which incidentally are really always found in co-operation—the last is the most obvious and may be quickly disposed of. Better methods of husbandry engaged attention throughout the Tudor period. Books were written to instruct improving farmers how to go about it. Sir Anthony Fitzherbert, one of his Majesty's judges, published works on husbandry and surveying in 1523; the shrewd Thomas Tusser's *Five Hundred Points of Good Husbandry* went through five editions between 1557 and 1580. Other Elizabethan textbooks on the use of marl, the special problems of the newly introduced hops, and similar points indicate the strength of the desire for the better use of land and new inventions to exploit it. Gradually the horse replaced the ox before the plough and cart. But the advance was slow and far from general. Cumbersome and inefficient ploughing, harvesting methods which wasted much of the straw, and the persistence of the open field with its narrow strips prevented really large-scale innovations. Hops, for instance, as a new crop which required compact fields where a man could experiment, established themselves in Kent where fields had always been enclosed. But all reservations allowed for, it is a fact that many Tudor landlords, small and great, tried to improve the yield of their lands by becoming better farmers. The foundations were being laid for the scientific farming of the eighteenth century.

However, changes of this kind take their time, and Tudor landlords, pressed for money as their incomes dwindled, required more rapid returns. One way of achieving this was to concentrate on stock-rearing. One hears of cattle-ranching on a considerable scale in the hill country of the west. Almost a new profession arose with the graziers or owners of large herds, often themselves butchers and retailers as well, and frequently attacked for combining trades which gave them a monopolistic hold over meat supply. But more important and more famous than cattle are the sheep. As we shall see, the first half of the century in particular was a time of increasing demand for wool, and throughout a rising population[1] provided more mouths for mutton—London especially proved a ready market there. Sheep were easy to keep and to feed on England's extensive grasslands; they required little labour

[1] Population figures are largely guess-work, though the increase is a fact. Mr A. L. Rowse (*The England of Elizabeth*, p. 218) accepts 4½ million in 1558 and 5 million in 1603 as the nearest he can get to the truth; these estimates are higher by a million than most people would think safe.

since one shepherd, his boy, and his dog could look after a whole flock; and they yielded immense returns. There was therefore an increase in sheep-farming, even if the contemporary picture—in Sir Thomas More's graphic but unreliable phrase—of the sheep devouring the men must not be accepted too readily. But many men—if they could—turned from an unprofitable arable economy to pasture; large stretches of farmland in the Midlands went under grass in the earlier part of the century, with the result that some villages quite disappeared (the modest basis of fact for the hysterical complaints of depopulation raised by contemporaries); and in East Anglia the demands of the local textile industries even called forth a type of grazier who, owning no land, ran his flocks on commons and waste ground. England has a good deal of land unsuitable for extensive and intensive arable farming but admirably suited for the sheep; a gentry and yeomanry desperate for an increased income to set off increased costs turned naturally to this way out, sometimes with bad effects on rural economy, but by and large to the increase of the national wealth. There is really no evidence that the rising population went without food, except in years of bad harvests, though the fear that more sheep-farming would destroy food-supply was ever present to Tudor statesmen; throughout the century, England tended to export both grain and meat. In the present state of knowledge it looks as though the increase in pasture-farming started about the middle of the fifteenth century, continued steadily—despite government measures to arrest it—to a peak in the years 1540-55, and then declined, in part because the sheep had conquered about as much land as they could, and in part because the bottom dropped out of the wool-market. There are signs that more sheep were reared for mutton in Elizabeth's reign than in Henry VIII's.

These changes in the practice of farming, whether better husbandry or concentration on stock, could only be carried out efficiently by profoundly altering the distribution of land among the people. It is in this—the changes in land-tenure and the structure of the countryside—that the real agricultural revolution of the century lies. The new methods required consolidated holdings and individualistic exploitation which were not available under the medieval system of agriculture. Of course, the traditional view of one general manner of farming the land in use all over England in the middle ages—with open fields around the village divided into strips allotted to the villagers who necessarily adjusted themselves to a common plan—is no longer tenable: many parts of the country had never known this so-called classical open-field system. But the chief corn-growing area—the eastern Midlands from Leicestershire and Warwickshire down to Berkshire, as well as much of Yorkshire, Lincolnshire, East Anglia, and parts of the Home Counties—fell within the area of the open fields. It was here that the movement for enclosing mostly applied. 'Enclosure' is a very general term—and usually simply a term of abuse—which covers at least three distinct operations. There was the individual tenant, often of villein stock, who began to buy up strips adjoining his own, put a hedge round the field so created, and farmed land thus cut off from the open fields. The movement in that direction was strong in the fifteenth century, a time of peasant prosperity, and the whole practice of enclosing seems to have arisen first in this form of enclosure for better small-scale farming. Then there was the bigger man who somehow consolidated large stretches of open field—by evicting his tenants or by purchase—and put the land to pasture; this—depopulating enclosure—was the evil inveighed against by the preachers and pamphleteers and resisted by the government. This form of enclosure dominated the first half of the sixteenth century. Lastly, there was the enclosing of commons and wastes. Every medieval village, however it arranged its farming land, had a common—some stretch of ground usually under rough grass on which the villagers pastured their animals and geese, or with bits of timber which were also shared proportionately. It is not too much to say that a village deprived of its rights of commons could not survive, and the machinations of some lords of manors who successfully intrigued and bullied to get exclusive use of commons for their sheep were of all the forms of enclosure the most resented. In Ket's agrarian grievances they played the biggest part.

This, then, was enclosing, the great evil—so contemporaries claimed—of the first half of the Tudor century. The total area affected by one form of enclosure or another was not large, though it is hard to give figures; perhaps 30 per cent. of the arable in an enclosing county (Northants or Leicester, for instance), or some 3 or 4 per cent. of its whole area, would be a generous estimate. One need only remember the great enclosing movement of the eighteenth century to get things into proportion. Hedges were raised and ditches dug in the sixteenth century, now to mark off some strips of open field thrown together by a peasant on the make, then again to distinguish the sheep run, or (worse) the park, or the big arable farm of a greater landlord or leasehold tenant, or perhaps to prevent the villagers from driving their cattle on the common where a speculator grazed his sheep. But much the greater part of the open fields remained open for another two centuries. Yet the effect of the enclosure movement cannot fairly be measured by extent alone. Not only was it—or rather the outcry against it—a political factor of some magnitude, but it also embodied a very deep-going change in rural economy.

Once the activities of small tenants had shown the way, the chief source of land for enclosure was to be found on the manorial demesne. Originally, very nearly every manor possessed a demesne, or land reserved to the lord of the manor and not let out to tenants, whether free or bond. In the open-field area that demesne consisted of strips distributed among the tenants' strips; elsewhere it might be one consolidated home-farm. On it—in the 'pure' form of the manorial economy—the villeins had done the labour for which their lord recompensed them with their own bits of land. The total of the demesne—its lands, its rights of common and woods and meadows, its buildings, and the rights of rents or services attached to it—was naturally very much bigger than any other single holding in manor or village. By the fifteenth century lords of manors had gradually ceased to farm their own demesnes; many, particularly the greater lords who held many manors, found it best to let the demesne to rent on lease to some tenant who might quite possibly be the wealthiest local peasant. Monasteries often leased their demesnes to those same local gentlemen who later bought the lands at the dissolution. In this way the lords of manors got a steady income from fixed rents, while the tenant made what he could out of his leasehold. For him the temptation to enclose was considerable, especially because he held a block of land well worth throwing into a consolidated farm, and so enclosures for agricultural purposes extended further.

Upon this relatively stable society, where such changes as took place in the holding and exploitation of land were small and achieved by purchase and agreement, there impinged the price rise. All at once the life of a rentier ceased to suit the lord. What had been a handsome regular income became first barely adequate and soon much too little as prices and costs rose. These lords underwent the common experience of men living on fixed incomes in a time of inflation: they found it impossible to keep up their standard of living in a world in which everything grew dearer while their revenues remained the same. On the other hand, tenants holding lands on the old terms and selling produce on a rising market were very favourably placed. The price rise put money in the pockets of the actual producers but took if from those of whom the lands were held. Thus men who had hitherto been content to let their lands at fixed rents now tried to get more out of them. They could try to recover direct control of the farms and themselves pocket the profits which enterprising agriculture was yielding, or they could try to raise rents. The first expedient, where practicable, was closely bound up with the more energetic exploitation of land which has already been discussed. Gentlemen and yeomen turned from corn to wool and later in the century back again to corn; they endeavoured to increase the yield by enclosing and by such scientific farming as was known to them; they exploited any additional resources there might be by mining for coal and dabbling in industrial pursuits, if their lands offered a chance. Also they often endeavoured to add to their lands. The price revolution assisted enterprise and luck; a man who acquired capital, either in farming, or in trading, or in the law, or even in marriage or the exploitation of an office under the crown, would wish to buy land both because it alone gave social standing and because it was a sound economic investment. More land meant an additional source of income. Thus there was a large body of eager purchasers for any land on the market, ready to spend their accumulated capital, or if necessary to borrow on security from the growing class of men who were as yet moneylenders but would soon become bankers, or again to take advantage of the instalment system which the government operated on its land sales. Before these buyers there was spread the most fluid land market since the Conquest—the lands of monasteries and chantries, of traitors and felons, of the bishops and of the crown, and at times of the great aristocratic lords who in the reign of Elizabeth were selling either because they needed money or more often because they wished to consolidate their property around their most important manors and to dispose of those in distant counties. Between them, the great land market and the desire for land—the one the outcome of the crown's attack on the Church and its own later needs, the other of the price rise—caused a widespread redistribution of landed property. The social effects of this shall be discussed later.

The substitution of direct farming for letting to rent, and the acquisition of fresh property constituted two ways in which the hardpressed upper classes could make ends meet (or in which the successful could grow exceedingly rich). The more direct way was simply to raise the rents they got from their lands and to increase the fines charged when one tenant succeeded another. There were many complaints against rack-renting (as it was called), a grievance less spectacular but more widespread than that against enclosing. But in fact both the recovery of lands previously let out and the raising of rents came up against obstacles in the law. The economic life of the countryside was dominated as much by the legal problems involved in the possession of land and the relationship between lord and tenant, as by the purely economic questions of the use of land. Feudal law recognised only one owner of land—the king—from whom all land was held on varying terms. In practice, however, lands held by one of the free tenures—the tenure in knight's service of the nobleman or gentleman, or the socage tenure of the smaller freeholder—were pretty secure and barely distinguishable from true possession. They were subject to demands. The freeholder paid a rent, but this had been fixed long before and constituted a small and diminishing burden under the new conditions. Lands in knight's service bore the various feudal incidents which were much resented, but these after all only occurred exceptionally and not at the whim of the lord. The upper ranks of society could feel secure in their possession of lands which technically they only held in tenure, unless they undermined their security by extravagance or got involved in the pitfalls of Tudor politics, with confiscations and forfeitures waiting upon the false step. The real problem of security arose in the lower orders—among the manorial tenants of individual lords.[1] Leaseholders presented a simple case. Their contracts terminated at some fixed day—most Tudor leases were short—so that lords could revise the rents at intervals or, if they wished, could resume direct use of their lands. Before the sixteenth century, leasehold was largely confined to the manorial demesne; when it became difficult to live on rents, demesne lands were the first to be taken back by progressive lords. But the demands of the new agriculture—especially of sheep-farming—required larger units than those strips of demesne scattered among villagers' strips in the common fields; a lord who wished to enclose in the Midland area of the open field needed to acquire lands held from him by tenure and not upon lease. Hence the 'rack-renting' landlord came up against the tenants' rights of the peasantry.

Peasant is a general term which covers a variety of status, wealth, and security. The commutation of labour services for a money rent and the leasing out of the demesne had altered the condition of the peasantry a good deal before the end of the fifteenth century. Bondage itself, the low social status of the villein with few rights and tied to his village and manor, was disappearing;

[1] It may be as well to point out that 'lord' in the sense constantly used means only a man holding a manor and does not imply that he was noble or even necessarily gentle.

though a few cases are known in Tudor times, economic change and the hostility of the common law were to make all Englishmen free and equal before the law by the time that Elizabeth died. Land held originally in villeinage was now held in one of three basic ways. The tenant could be 'at will', that is, he held the land as long as his lord pleased and on his lord's terms. He might, on the other hand, be a customary tenant whose right was protected by the 'custom of the manor' enrolled in the manorial court roll, or, if he was lucky, he might possess a copy of the record and be a copyholder. At first the decisive difference between the copyholder and the merely customary tenant was that the former could defend his tenure in the king's court where his 'copy' was admitted as evidence, while the latter had no remedy outside the manorial court held by his own lord. But by the middle of the sixteenth century, manorial custom was generally enforced in the king's courts, and what mattered then was not the technical name of the tenure but the terms on which an individual peasant held his land. Ideally, a copyholder would have an 'estate of inheritance' with fine certain: that is, when he died his heir succeeded and the lord had no say either in the disposal of the land or the size of the fine. Such tenants were the lucky elite of the peasantry. But if the entry on the court roll (whether or not a copy had been granted to the tenant) provided for a life-interest only or for a fine arbitrary (at the will of the lord), that copyholder was no better off than a tenant-at-will: his heir had to pay what the lord asked or get out. The differences in manorial custom were so many and so large—and so doubtful—that they provided the basis for a vast deal of litigation, in chancery, requests, and also at common law, in which the peasants as often as not succeeded in asserting their rights. Thus lords soon began to dislike these tenures; throughout the reign of Elizabeth there was a movement to alter copyholds into leases. Pressure could be applied or agreement secured, for the tenant too might prefer the precision of a leasehold to the uncertainties of custom, and by the time that the first Stuart ascended the throne leasehold had replaced copyhold as the characteristic contract of the agrarian system.

When, therefore, need or greed—or both—compelled lords of manors to raise the rents and burdens by which their tenants retained their lands, they were faced by a problem so complex that only an account of individual fortunes would really describe it. The very fact that all freeholders and most copyholders and customary tenants could resist pressure concentrated the attack on the unfortunate tenants-at-will, in any case by and large the poorest section of the peasantry. There was bound to be pauperisation of some, just because others, legally and economically better off, were going ahead. Simple economic causes—the price rise and the needs of lords of manors—took effect through people of very varying character and temperament. Many lords, especially in the north, preserved the ancient society through pride and conservatism, even if it meant that they themselves remained at best backward and at worst poverty-stricken. The men who bought monastic lands sometimes did so as a speculation: they bought in order to make a profit—either by reselling or by direct exploitation—and they therefore naturally raised rents and enclosed to the destruction of the more helpless tenants. But the romantic indignation of so many writers is misplaced. The majority of the monastic lands went to the established gentry and yeomanry who added them to their own lands and treated them like the rest. Exploitation was neither new nor general. After the middle of the century rents rose very markedly, though whether they rose more slowly or faster than prices—whether in fact they were truly rack-rents—is still being debated. The movement on the land market must have assisted the break-up of rural society, but we must not ascribe the decline of the peasantry to the activities of the supposed villains who dabbled in buying and selling land. Complaints against enclosing and rack-renting were heard before the monasteries were dissolved. Furthermore, not only the agents but also the victims of change were various, in their different tenures and copyhold rights, in their different capacities and accidents of luck or fate.

Though generalised conclusions must be stated, they must not be thought of as more than guides to that true understanding which only the investigation of county after county can bring. The causes of the upheaval were the price rise, the demand for wool, the free market in land. Its phenomena were trade in land, enclosing for both agriculture and pasture, the raising of rents and entry-fines accompanied if need was by eviction, and the general application of the principles of leasehold. The results were the creation of a considerable class of landless men who either earned a living by working as day-labourers for wages, or (a few of them) went to the towns, or turned to vagabondage; the rise of the substantial farmer holding on lease; and an increase in the so-called capitalist attitude (by no means new) which treats land as a source of wealth rather than as the basis of political function and social degree. The changes affected only parts of the country and not even those wholesale. Yet their total outcome was prodigious. The sixteenth century began the destruction of the English peasantry (at least in the South) and laid the foundation for that characteristic structure of landlord, leasehold farmer, and landless labourer which has marked the English countryside from that day to this. Compared with this change, the innovations in the practice and organisation of farming itself, not inconsiderable though they were, pale into insignificance.

3. INDUSTRY AND TRADE

Until the Industrial Revolution of the eighteenth century, industry definitely took second place to commerce. The man who made things was commonly a small craftsman, either independent or in the employ of a big merchant; the man who sold things could reach the heights of wealth, power, and social standing. The big problem of earlier days was to sell products: markets were thought of as limited, and though such an idea has roused the hearty laughter of free traders, Manchester liberals, and other moderns, it was much nearer the truth than the books lead one to suppose. While populations remained small and poor, and while transport difficulties limited range, it was very difficult indeed to expand existing markets and add to the volume of trade. Consequently there was less interest in increasing production, whereas in modern times, with markets either unlimited or falsely thought of as limitless, this latter point has become the main concern of economists. However, English trade has always rested on a firm foundation of English industry—it has never specialised in merely importing from one direction and exporting in another, as the great Dutch traders were to do—and in the sixteenth century there took place a real widening of horizons with prospects of an expanding trade. Not only were there the new markets overseas, the newly discovered lands on the coasts of Africa and America, the end of the Venetian monopoly in the Near East; there was also a general shaking up of established trade routes and marts in Europe itself which offered chances for the enterprising. Furthermore, the closer definition of the national state and the cash needs of the government encouraged a policy of producing at home rather than importing from abroad. These various stimulants produced a notable increase in English industrial activity; new manufactures were introduced and old ones improved. It has almost become the fashion to speak of an industrial revolution in the sixteenth century, but that is to debase a very useful term. The changes, though considerable by comparison with the small amount of industry then in the country, were really on too small a scale to deserve such a resounding name.

The only two medieval industries pursued on a sufficiently large scale to require a major organisation were textiles and shipbuilding. (Building, which might have rivalled them, was in the hands of thousands of individual craftsmen.) Ships continued to be built in Tudor times near or in all the major ports; their number increased, though their size did not, and no change in method took place. In the clothing industry the chief developments to note are the introduction of new textiles and the adoption of a few pieces of machinery. The old staple products—woollens and worsteds—began to lose favour, partly because their export declined in the second half of the century and partly because fashion demanded finer and lighter cloths. Hence we find the so-called new draperies (bays and says) encouraged by the government; the use of cotton in fustian began in Lancashire (*c.* 1600); silk was attempted. Yet wool retained pride of place. England exported in the main unfinished or 'white' cloth—undyed and not treated to the point where the tailor would use it—to the industrial centres of Flanders and Brabant where the rough cloth was turned into the finest stuff in Europe. Of course, some cloth had always been finished in England for the home market, but the English finishers (even the elite among them, the dyers) were insufficiently skilled, and the Flemings refused to buy any but white cloth. Attempts to concentrate all cloth manufacture in England—to exploit industrially England's virtual monopoly of the raw material—thus proved only partially successful. The new inventions mattered little. Since at least the thirteenth century cloth had been fulled (beaten in water to felt the fibres) by water-driven mills; now there was added a gig-mill to raise the nap for shearing, a stocking-frame on which stockings could be knitted more rapidly than by hand, and the Dutch loom which made possible a sort of mass production of narrow goods like ribbons. All were resented by the workers as dangers to employment, and none amounted to more than a slight adjustment in one or two minor processes. More stockings were certainly produced and worn, and also more English-made ribbons, but this chief of England's industries was in the main remarkable for changing very little.

There was also virtually no change in organisation. As before, the yarn was spun in countless cottages and then woven into cloth by weavers on their hand-looms in their own houses. For a long time now, the industry had been dominated by capitalist clothiers—the putters-out—who supplied the yarn to the domestic weaver, took the finished product, and paid him wages. This early stage of capitalist organisation (the domestic system) seems to have conquered almost the whole field in the sixteenth century; cloth of whatever sort was produced in this manner—new draperies and old, woollens and worsteds and mixed, linens and cottons and silks. It used to be thought that some enterprising clothiers inaugurated the factory system by bringing their weavers under one roof, but even the factory of the celebrated Berkshire clothier, Jack of Newbury, has had doubts thrown on it. The industry was well past the truly domestic stage when a man's wife span for him the wool of his own sheep for him to weave; the clothiers, originally middlemen between weaver and merchant, had long established their firm hold on it. Bad times for them—and they were to be bad through most of Elizabeth's reign—meant unemployment for many, with complaints, even riots, and ineffective government interference to stimulate the trade which would set the looms going again. On the other hand, in those days before the building of textile mills, the various workers in the industry did not depend exclusively on wages. The domestic weaver usually had a patch of land; even this largest of all English industries, employing by far the biggest number of workers, did not involve the existence of a purely wage-earning class. To find that one must look to building, for since this occupation was both urban and migratory it offered none of the chances of independent side-lines which the cloth-worker still enjoyed.

Wool required capital, but the new industries developing in the century needed it even more. Mining, in particular, showed signs of remarkable life. Some coal had always been dug for use as fuel in the neighbourhood of the mine; now, with the decay of the great forests, coal was gradually replacing wood or charcoal as the main fuel in both domestic and industrial use. London imported some 15,000 tons a year in Elizabeth's reign—coal carried by colliers from the Newcastle fields and therefore dubbed sea-coal. Transport difficulties, however, restricted the spread of coal to the sea-board, and technical difficulties prevented its use in the industry which needed it most, iron smelting. The necessary process—the making of coke and its use in furnaces—was not invented till the beginning of the eighteenth century. But other industries used coal. The saltpans of Cheshire and the North-East needed much; one capitalist enterprise on the Wear, extracting salt from sea-water, employed some 300 men. Coal was used in the refining of sugar and the manufacture of glass, both processes introduced into the country in this century, and in soap-boiling which expanded enormously. Nor was coal the only product to be mined. Henry

VIII looked for gold in Wales, and some of the worn-out silver mines were investigated again by a government in need of cash. More particularly, however, the government concentrated on finding zinc-ore (calamine), a mineral vital to the manufacture of brass which in turn was needed for the new cannon. In the reign of Elizabeth, England began to export pieces of artillery to the continent. Saltpetre was sought and found for the making of gun-powder; alum for its use in the dyeing of cloth. The metal industries developed, though handicapped by the growing shortage of charcoal; rolling mills for the production of sheet metal and drawing mills for that of wire were built. The whole movement was still scattered, piecemeal, and confined to a small proportion of the population. But all these processes required equipment and therefore capital; their growth foreshadowed the growth of a genuine factory industry and provided both incentive and example for later expansion.

These major industries had one thing in common: they were not subject to the medieval gild organisation, either because they were new, or because they were pursued in the country. Gilds were associations of urban craftsmen, designed to protect their own interest by maintaining a local monopoly and (ostensibly) the customer's by maintaining a high standard of work. Many of them performed also social and religious functions; these suffered heavily from the legislation of Edward VI's reign which confiscated chantry and gild endowments made for 'superstitious' purposes. But on their economic side, too, as organisations of crafts and manufactures, the gilds declined in the sixteenth century. As early as the fourteenth, the various processes involved in cloth-making (though not the finishers), leaving the towns in search of the water power demanded by the new fulling mill, had emancipated themselves from gild regulations. Now with the rise of new crafts and with a growing disregard for the monopolies of gilds, the old organisations decayed. National legislation took the place of municipal legislation. Statutes dealing with the proper making of cloth or leather rendered superfluous the piecemeal enactments of gilds on which they very often rested. Thus the great statute of artificers of 1563, an industrial code which among other things wished to enforce a seven-years' apprenticeship in all trades including husbandry, was most effective when the local craftsmen's companies employed its assistance to enforce their own views on apprenticeship. The decline of the gilds was reflected in the tendency to amalgamate several widely different trades into one association; the Ludlow hammermen of 1511 controlled not only ironworkers but also masons, and the Hull goldsmiths' company included in 1598, among others, plumbers and basket-makers. Though the gilds survived for a long time they soon ceased to play a part in the structure of English industry; their last attempts to continue their control collapsed after 1660 when the state ceased to support their aspirations.

The organisation which prospered in the sixteenth century was the livery company, first seen in London whose twelve great companies, old and new, came to rule the city in this period. Companies of this sort, though nominally composed of certain trades (as the London mercers, fishmongers, goldsmiths, and so on), were less concerned with industrial and craft problems than with municipal politics; their members were the great men of the city, not its manufacturers, and they made their position as merchants.[1] Other towns soon copied the London example. Henry VIII, Elizabeth, and James I all chartered such companies who clamped a firm control on the affairs of their municipality. The expansion of industry and trade brought with it not a growing freedom for individual craftsmen and merchants, but an increasing complexity of monopolistic organisations which bought their privileges at heavy cost from an impoverished crown and recouped themselves by steering all possible profit towards their own members. These organisations fell into two groups. The so-called regulated companies were associations of individuals each working on his own with his own capital but licensed by his membership to pursue his trade and subject to the rules of his company. In industry gilds and their descendants, the great companies, represented this kind of organisation. By their side, the needs of an expansionist age raised companies based on joint-stock. The principle here was that several men put their capital into a common enterprise and either took it back with a share of the profits when the company wound up, or—if it carried on—drew a dividend (a share of the profits) proportionate to their investment. The advantages of this second kind of company were felt in affairs which required a considerable initial outlay of capital. They were more important in foreign trade, but industry could use them too, especially in the various mining experiments which required both the capital which only joint-stock could provide and the monopoly only to be got from a royal charter. Such were the Mines Royal Company and the Mineral and Battery Works, both incorporated in 1568 but developed from earlier

[1] Of the London 'Great Twelve' only the clothworkers were not mercantile, but many lesser craft-gilds continued a decreasingly influential existence.

enterprises in mining, the making of brass, and the casting of cannon.

There was thus plenty of life in English industry, so much so that one is in some danger of overrating the scale on which things happened. In economic growth the categories of reigns and political history are particularly meaningless, and the phenomena discussed really came to fruition under the early Stuarts. The sixteenth century merely laid foundations, even as the seventeenth only expanded these foundations upon which the genuine industrial revolution of the eighteenth was to build. Yet the growth of industry under the Tudors—the development of both old and new crafts, the expansion of coal and mineral mining, the elaboration of industrial organisation—is marked enough to require explanation. What stimulated all this? There was some profit inflation because prices rose faster than wages, so that the industrialists' costs lagged behind their increasing profits. This encouraged enterprise and the accumulation of capital for expansion. The profit inflation was not as great as was once supposed, and other things played their part, as for instance the new inventions, the greater purchasing power of the home market, England's freedom from internal war, and her ancient industrial traditions—though much greater traditions did not prevent the rapid decline in this period of the industries of Flanders, Germany, and Northern Italy. Mining developments owed much to the needs of gentlemen who had to exploit their lands in other ways than by farming. War stimulated especially the metal industries; the new brass manufactures depended on such factors as the government's need for artillery. The increasing population probably assisted the clothing industry whose periods of decline are attested only as far as exports are concerned, while we know nothing of its home market. Luxury trades in ribbons, silks, laces, and so forth received support from the growing ostentation of the upper classes trying to copy Italy and France and enabled to do so by the expansion of their own incomes as both agriculture and office-holding grew more and more profitable. All in all, the marked if limited expansion of the century resulted from as striking a mixture of causes as its own haphazard and varied character would lead one to believe. But among them the effects of the inflation, causing changes, forcing action, and rewarding efforts in all sorts of trades, must come first.

The story of trade is both more straightforward and much more important. The industrial changes already described in a manner reflect the vicissitudes of trade: the expansion of Elizabeth's reign, with its new industries and new organisations, in part resulted from the decline of the main export trade of the first half of the century. Admittedly, straightforward or not, the whole story cannot yet be told and may never in fact be fully known. In the first place, we know too little of internal trade; that is, we know that it took place, we suspect that it increased and that Elizabethan Englishmen bought more—were wealthier—than their Henrician fathers, but we can rarely measure it. The story is thus confined to goods exported and recorded in the various documents produced by the customs service. Here arises the second difficulty: except in London, there was a great deal of smuggling, often connived at or even encouraged by the customs officials, and the figures of exports which can be produced represent neither the total turnover of trade nor an accurate yardstick of industrial production, but merely the percentage of trade which paid its tribute to the royal coffers. The smuggling of this time concentrated not on the import of taxable luxury articles as it did in the classic age of smuggling literature, the eighteenth century; it concentrated on the free export of customable goods and of goods whose export was forbidden except under special licence from the crown—which licence had to be paid for. Thus foodstuffs—especially wheat and barley—were taken from the East Anglian ports to the continent; even in time of war the government could not stop the trade with France and Scotland. Coin and bullion, too, trickled through the leaky net of the customs controls, despite proclamations to the contrary. Sixteenth-century legislation must ever be regarded as evidence of intentions rather than as a policy rigidly carried out, and this is especially true of economic legislation and customs regulations. One can only hope—with some reason—that the proportion between legitimate and illicit trade remained much the same throughout, so that the known figures at least describe with some accuracy the trends and changes in English trade.

The chief English export was cloth; everything else—leather, hides, tin, lead, grain, coal, and later the new manufactures—came a long way behind. During the fifteenth century, cloth woven in England and exported mainly to the Netherlands to be there finished for re-export took over from the raw wool previously exported to the continental weaver. In the earlier sixteenth century the trade concentrated more and more on one channel—Antwerp. Flourishing trades with Italy and Spain decayed at this time as that great city rose to its commercial supremacy in the Habsburg empire and sat itself astride England's trade routes to the continental interior. Antwerp's monopoly called into being an English monopoly. To trade in the emperor's dominions, an English merchant needed a licence, and these imperially licensed 'merchant adventurers haunting Brabant' (that is, living and trading in Antwerp) soon captured most of the export of cloth—mainly of white cloth—from England. These Merchant Adventurers were based on London, being mostly freemen of the mercers' company, and they succeeded in the course of the first half of the century in destroying their English rivals at Southampton (once the centre of the trade with Italy and Spain) and Hull (which had traded directly with Scandinavia) by exploiting their monopoly of the easiest and cheapest route by which England's chief manufacture could be exported. The export of cloth from London increased about threefold between 1500 and 1550, a period of such mounting prosperity that trade could be freed far beyond the usual practices of the time. Restrictions on cloth export vanished, English merchants ceased to harry their German rivals of the Hanseatic League because there was trade enough for all, and the usury laws (which limited trading expansion and the investment of capital) collapsed until, in 1546, parliament admitted the propriety of taking interest upon loans. These fair conditions suffered occasionally from disruption by war, but, as we have already had occasion to point out, it was more usual for war and politics to accommodate themselves to the chief English and Flemish commercial interest. The cloth trade affected not only the Merchant Adventurers but also the clothiers who supplied the exporters, the weavers and spinsters in the clothier's employ, and everybody back to the man who owned and herded the sheep, the ultimate source of all this activity and wealth. Thus the alliance with the Habsburg rulers of the Netherlands—with the Emperor Charles V and therefore with Spain—rested on a mutual economic interest much stronger than the differences over Henry VIII's wives or religion.

This period of expanding trade was assisted, if not caused, by the price rise. In the 1520s direct trade with Spain brought generous profits as the wealth of America drove up prices there before the rest of Europe followed suit, so that English merchants could buy cheap at home and sell dear in Spain. Even when matters levelled out, England remained in a position of advantage. The flood of the price rise reached Antwerp before London—indeed, Antwerp was the chief means of extending the general rise beyond the Channel—so that the purchasing power of money always remained a little higher in England than on the continent. That meant that English merchants were persistently trading from a country of lower prices into one with higher—selling for more than they paid out—with results which encouraged them to develop the trade to the limit. Then, in the years 1550-2, artificial aids suddenly drove the cloth trade into an enormous and unhealthy increase. The debasement of the English coinage had its natural effect of stimulating exports because it lowered the exchange rate between London and Antwerp. Where £1 English was worth 32*s.* Flemish in 1522, it was worth 26*s.* 8*d.* in 1526 and only 13*s.* 4*d.* in 1551. In other words, an English merchant who bought a £1's worth of cloth in England and offered it for sale in Antwerp at what had been his usual profit seemed, to the purchaser, to be asking only half of what he had asked before. Naturally Antwerp rushed to buy, exports rose to amazing heights, and merchants welcomed the debasement. But in this they were alone. As has been seen, the debasement endangered the internal economy of England by destroying confidence in her coinage; it also ultimately ruined government finance, even though it began by aiding it in an unrepeatable manner. So unfavourable a rate of exchange closed the only way out when all possible profit had been made from land sales and recoinage—the raising of loans abroad. Natural causes (exchange rates tend to stabilise in time) and the desire of the government for sounder finance led to the activities of Northumberland and Elizabeth in restoring the coinage to some soundness and therefore the rate of exchange to near-normal. The agent employed by both Mary and Elizabeth to act for the government in Antwerp was Sir Thomas Gresham, a leading London merchant and financier who was to found the Royal Exchange. Gresham proved a skilful diplomatist who raised loans for his government at such unpropitious moments as the accession of Elizabeth, but his claim that he had restored the exchange and therefore solvency by his manipulations arose from a misunderstanding. The exchange rate recovered as the silver content of English coins recovered; for good English money the Antwerp exchangers would pay their 20*s.* or more of Flemish coin as they had done before the debasement.

The end of the disastrous inflation also ended the boom in the export trade. After 1552 the volume of cloth exported fell with a crash, and the third quarter of the century was full of slumps and depressions. The expansion of the half-century had led to an increase in sheep-farming and in the manufacture of cloth; now land had to revert to arable, and clothiers and weavers felt the pinch. Other causes assisted. The 'Spanish Fury' of 1576, which destroyed Antwerp, only sealed the steady decline which that vital commercial centre underwent with the accession of Philip II in 1555. Charles V had always protected the interests of the Netherlands, even at the risk of tolerating heresy. His son was to ignore this, the most prosperous and valuable part of his dominions, preferring instead to rely on the unproductive and disastrous wealth of America and to pursue a religious policy fatal to the interests of Flanders. During the reign of Elizabeth, for reasons which England could not affect, the simple steady trade of the first half of the century came to an end. Wars, religion, and politics now took precedence over commerce, at a time when the economic conditions had in any case turned against further expansion. The boom of the early 'fifties marked in effect the end of the Antwerp trade and the happy conditions when the Merchant Adventurers of London ran a hugely profitable business without having to obtain a formal monopoly or fight off foreign rivals because there was enough for everybody. The later 'fifties and the 'sixties were a time of depression when trade stagnated and the government was inundated with complaints from unemployed clothworkers. Both the needs of the trade and the permanent Tudor fears of unrest compelled the government to intervene at a time when the merchants began to look to restriction and rigid monopolies for their salvation. Trade had to do two things—to find new outlets if it could, and to be more dog-in-the-manger about the old. The reign of Elizabeth was an age of control and organisation, following upon a period of virtual free trade.

The Merchant Adventurers naturally suffered most from the difficulties which had arisen in the Netherlands trade. The closing of their staple at Antwerp compelled them to find a new continental depot; after many travellings and attempts to settle both on the Elbe and the Ems, from where they could easily have exploited the trade with Central Germany, they came to rest at Middelburgh in the Northern Netherlands in 1598. But their great days were really over.[1] Admittedly they seemed more powerful than ever and even increased their own exports. But this they could only do by driving all rivals from the field and monopolising the reduced amount of cloth exported each year.[2] They obtained government

[1] Mr A. L. Rowse, in reverting to a traditional but dubious view of the Merchant Adventurers, claims great things for them in the reign of Elizabeth (*The England of Elizabeth*, pp. 116, 149-50). He is right to warn us against judging the sixteenth century by the conditions of the nineteenth, but his rather airy account ignores the facts as recited by Unwin (cf. below, p. 248n.).

[2] In the last quarter of the century exports remained steadily about 20 per cent. below the high level reached in mid-century.

action against the German Hanse whose privileges were revoked in 1552, restored at Philip's request in 1554, and taken away by Elizabeth in 1558 after the Germans had broken off relations in high dudgeon. A long and fruitful association thus came to an end, but not until the usefulness of the German traders had nearly disappeared in the internal decay of their league and the decline of the English cloth trade. Worse still, the Merchant Adventurers limited the activities of their own members. They turned upon the so-called New Hanse within their ranks—provincial members admitted with reservations in 1497—and excluded them from the trade, while even the solid London core of the 'Old Hanse' was forced to adhere to a stint (or quota of exports) which prevented the company from promoting an expansion of the industry or acting (as it was once thought to have done) as the agent of a vigorous English penetration abroad. In 1564 the Merchant Adventurers at last obtained a royal charter granting them in effect a monopoly in the export to Europe of white cloth—the cloth with the readiest market—and thereafter they were content to maintain what they had won. Their monopoly did not remain unchallenged; especially towards the end of the reign, as the difficulties caused by the Spanish war began to diminish, numbers of 'free-traders' or 'interlopers'—merchants not of the company but trading in its territory—greatly annoyed the Adventurers who again and again pleaded for action with the government.

The Adventurers' monopoly was attacked both in their own day by interlopers and their representatives in parliament, and later by economic historians.[1] It has been shown that they failed to help the cloth industry to expand, and even to exploit to the full the potential it had displayed in the boom years. They did not promote the national interest but (understandably) those of some merchants whose profits they thought could only be maintained by limiting trade. Their own argument ran that markets were restricted: there was only so much trade to go round, and if they let others have a share they would go short themselves. Hence they set their faces against the German Hanse, their own New Hanse, and the interlopers. The idea that trade is naturally limited was anathema to Victorian freetraders, though perhaps it seems more convincing again now. In sixteenth-century conditions there was

[1] Especially George Unwin in his lectures on 'The Merchant Adventurers in the Reign of Elizabeth', *Studies in Economic History*, pp. 133ff. Although Unwin probably underrated the company's difficulties and failed to understand the position of the government, his work remains fundamental to the subiect.

something to be said for it: populations stood still or rose only slowly, while their wealth almost certainly declined in the wars of religion which swept the continent for a hundred years after 1550; transport difficulties stood in the way of opening up new trade; conflicts and nationalist barriers everywhere were ruining the freedom of the later middle ages. Conditions were, in fact, comparable to those of the twentieth century rather than the nineteenth; then, as now, depressions led to trade restrictions and attempts at self-sufficiency. Hampered by the small number of potential purchasers and the relatively small area they could cover, the Merchant Adventurers had quite a good case, but they overdid it, as the interlopers proved. The only really sound argument for the company is that in the unquiet conditions of the time only a strongly organised body, with authority and reputation to back it, could establish a steady trade; this view supposes that the interlopers cashed in on the position created by their enemies. With this point the Adventurers themselves made most play, but proof is difficult if not impossible. On the whole, taking into account that all Europe practised trade by companies and in the form almost of international treaties, one gives the Adventurers the benefit of the doubt: they were necessary. Nevertheless, their monopoly did not advance trade or help the clothing industry.

The government, too, have received much blame for permitting and licensing the monopoly. Here the answer is simple. Burghley, in particular, was fully aware of the disadvantages, and during the depression which followed the virtual breach with Spain in 1586 he tried to help trade by freeing it; but the interests opposed to free trade were too strong. The government, pressed by Gresham, had in the first place made the monopoly possible—by the break with the Germans and the charter of 1564—simply because it needed the money which only the Adventurers were in a position to advance. After 1558, when new customs rates raised the value of the cloth custom, the government depended financially on the good will of the chief cloth exporters. The whole policy of granting monopolies—the trading companies, the farming out of various customs (especially on wines), ultimately the granting of manufacturing monopolies (for instance in leather)—followed simply from the crown's penury: monopolies were sold and the purchaser paid heavily. It did not help that many courtiers profited from the practice and encouraged it without special regard to the needs of the crown, but the queen herself and her chief minister acted under financial duress. Especially was this the case with the Merchant Adventurers who offered their loans and assistance in return for special privileges. The price rise, which badly injured the finances of the crown, thus assisted the tendency towards monopoly and restriction which dominated the economic policy of Elizabeth's government. It may be added that in part at least this policy resulted also from a desire to put things in a rigid order and system. Fluid expansion and changeability were not welcome to Elizabethan statesmen with their passion for degree and order. Cromwell and the profiteers of Henry VIII's time had a better appreciation of the advantages of change than the rigid queen and her conservative ministers.

The story of the new companies seeking to open up new trades is rather more cheerful. The Elizabethan age witnessed England's entry into transoceanic trade. The collapse of the traditional market released production for new markets and in fact compelled search for them; the discoveries of the previous half-century showed the way; the inflation supplied both the capital needed for investment and the hope of large profits which drew forth that capital. The real story of Elizabethan commercial and geographical enterprise centres round these new routes and new organisations.[1] They, too, have been attacked as monopolistic and restrictive, and once again an abstract case can be made out against them. But it is a worse case than that against the Adventurers, for new trade with such distant lands as Russia or the coast of Africa required an organisation to start it. This was proved especially in India where the trading company had to act virtually as a sovereign power commanding armed forces and conducting diplomatic negotiations. However, the Tudor period only saw the beginnings of the vast expansion. A number of projects were started, some as regulated companies modelled on the Merchant Adventurers (for instance the Eastland Company—1579—trading with the Baltic), some as joint-stock. The first joint-stock enterprises were organised only for one journey: Hawkins' slaving expeditions to Africa in 1562-7 and Drake's circumnavigation in 1577-80 were famous Elizabethan examples of an extension of the partnership principle of which instances can be found earlier. A number of people—merchants, seamen, courtiers, country gentlemen, even the queen—put up the capital needed, taking it back with a share of the profits at the end of the voyage. But in 1555 Sebastian Cabot and a group of London merchants founded the Muscovy Company, the first trading company whose joint-stock remained in use from voyage to voyage, and in the same year individual enterprises in Africa culminated in the foundation of the Guinea Company. In

[1] The maritime side of the matter is discussed below, Ch. XII.

1581 there was added the Levant Company which mainly subsisted on a very lucrative monopoly of the trade in currants, and in 1600 some merchants of this company obtained a charter for trading in East India—the beginning of the East India Company, the greatest of them all. Similar organisations were used in the early colonial enterprises, such as Raleigh's Virginian settlements from 1584 onwards. The companies often passed through difficulties: the Levant Company suffered so severely from the Spanish war that it had to reorganise itself by 1589 as a regulated company, a more rigid body with less risk but also less chance of expansion. Greater days awaited both the trading and the colonising companies under the Stuarts, but handsome and notable beginnings were made in the reign of Elizabeth when English traders found their affairs forcing them to follow the romantics overseas.

In trade and commerce, too, the sixteenth century was a restless period, an age of marked advances and disastrous depressions, but in general of improvements. Trade expanded—at first through the old continental markets and later through new markets in the opening world. The difficulties of the government and the selfishness of established merchants encouraged a restrictive policy whose worst effects were only avoided because it could never be rigorously enforced. The age was not—as some would have us believe—one of unhindered and lavish expansion. Indeed, to the Elizabethans themselves it seemed dark and distressful, with war and depression destroying England's commerce and wealth. In fact it laid sound foundations for later expansion in industry and trade. To the best of our knowledge national wealth increased markedly. In part this resulted from legitimate trade and in part from the piracy which made up for the ruin it caused to trade by importing stolen bullion; but the most solidly prosperous part of English life was its booming agriculture. Altogether, the price inflation, while it brought much hardship and many problems, also offered fine chances which did not go begging.

4. SOCIAL CHANGES

In his account of the government of England, written in the first half of Elizabeth's reign, Sir Thomas Smith listed the various classes of men.[1] He divided them into four groups—gentlemen, citizens and burgesses, yeomen artificers, and labourers. Among

[1] He probably borrowed the whole section from William Harrison's *Description of England* (cf. *De Republica Anglorum*, ed. Alston, pp. xvi seqq.).

gentlemen he included the king and the nobility, classifying the latter into greater (aristocracy) and lesser (knights). These, together with esquires (those entitled to bear arms), make up the gentlemen—'those whom their blood and race doth make noble and known'—and Smith thought that the English manner of 'making gentlemen so easily' was an advantage to the realm. Citizens and burgesses are the substantial inhabitants of the towns. As for the yeomen, Smith equated them with the 40*s*. freeholders who had the vote in county elections and served on juries; he grew quite enthusiastic over their sterling qualities and happy condition. The rest he admirably defined as 'the fourth sort of men which do not rule'—husbandmen and labourers, craftsmen and artificers, and even all merchants and copyholders without free land. The principle of his classification, however, is exceedingly artificial. It is not by wealth: many a merchant could rival the proudest gentleman in England, and many a copyholder had more land than the average freeholder. Freehold was relatively rare, and Smith's definition of the yeomanry is much too narrow. At the same time, his definition of the gentry appears to be too wide for modern opinion which (as we shall see) has tried to find a class distinction between noblemen and gentlemen. His ascription of nobility to the knighthood falsifies the picture completely, though it may have made it more comprehensible to the French public for which he orginally wrote. Smith's fourth class includes both substantial men and the very poorest. Up to a point his catalogue rests on birth, but since birth—even by this time villein birth—was not in England an obstacle to advancement or deterioration in status he had to admit the ease with which men became gentle. Fundamentally his criterion is tenure and the duties that go with it, a criterion of much less significance in the sixteenth century than in earlier days.

Smith's list is antiquarian; it takes insufficient notice of the fluidity of a social structure buffeted by the price rise. But it is a reasonable beginning for an understanding of the problem, and it should act as a warning against the modern tendency to impose a class structure on the sixteenth century. The whole concept of class belongs to an industrial and urban society; it should be altogether discarded for a society which indeed rested on degree and differences in status but knew no economic divisions rigid enough to be called classes. The Tudor age is not the age of the rise of the middle class, let alone the bourgeoisie, both meaningless terms in the context. The story is much more subtle and difficult than that, and the only distinctions which it is perhaps worth making are three: the prince, those sort of people that took their part in government (nobility, gentry, even yeomanry in the widest sense, but also the merchants and lawyers commonly indistinguishable from the gentlemen), and those who took no part. A brief section of this sort cannot hope to clarify the whole question of English social structure in the sixteenth century: we shall treat of the effects of the price rise on the crown, the gentry, and the poor.

Nothing perhaps shows up Sir Thomas Smith's conservatism so much as his inclusion of the prince among his gentlemen. There was good reason in past history and in etymology for so doing, but it was contemporary nonsense. The Tudors had raised the crown to a place of lonely eminence which even its possession by a child and a couple of women could not threaten for long. Despite many authoritative statements to the contrary, the sixteenth century managed quite well to distinguish between the crown and its holder. A visible embodiment of state and nationhood was of enormous political value—indeed, it still is—but that does not mean that men could not grasp the mystical entity of the crown as an almost religious symbol and think of it apart from the human being to whom they paid such semi-religious honours because he (or she) was clothed in the majesty of monarchy. We must remember that a religious age has less difficulty in dealing in abstracts than a scientific age, though it will also make a less clear distinction between the abstract and the concrete, the mystical and the personal. Tudor king-worship came at times perilously near to idolatry, but commonly it embodied rather a natural confusion between the specific and the general attributes of the crown—the person on the one hand, the emblem of nationality and statehood on the other. It need surprise us the less that an unrelenting devotion to monarchy could go hand in hand with a decline in the powers of the crown in the second half of the century. The cause of the decline was simple: the inflation depressed the royal income and increased the royal expenditure.

During an inflation, as has already been pointed out, those who live on fixed incomes suffer because their revenues remain the same while everything they have to buy grows dearer. Of all people, the king (or queen) was most relentlessly pressed by that difficulty. The crown's finances had been established on a sound basis by Henry VII on the supposition that rents from lands were the best sort of income; these the price rise rendered progressively less valuable. Unlike other landlords the crown could not adapt itself: its lands were too vast and the income required too large to make direct exploitation of land feasible, while the practices of rack-renting and raising fines could hardly be pushed to extremes by the official guardian of the poor. As it was, rents and fines rose on crown lands, but never sufficiently to compensate for the price rise. The other foundation of the royal finances, the customs, suffered from unavoidable maladministration: not until 1558 was a realistic tariff put on the chief English export (cloth), while smuggling and the peculations of officials away from the administrative centre reduced the value of this source. The government of Elizabeth therefore resorted to farming: at intervals some or even all the customs revenue was sold to courtiers and syndicates who for a lump sum bought the right to extract the customs for themselves. This at least ensured a steady income and cut down administrative costs, but it meant that the elasticity of the customs revenue—its chief advantage—tended to benefit the farmer and not the crown. Parliamentary taxation proved less expedient under Elizabeth than under her predecessors because the commons and the queen wished to pursue different policies: rather than face them often, Elizabeth did without subsidies.

There were other ways of augmenting revenue. Crown lands were sold, licences and offices granted for money, episcopal property came to the crown. Many expedients both sensible and undesirable were resorted to, but the only effective one was rigid economy, the much-maligned 'parsimony' of Elizabeth and Burghley. Contrary to Tudor habit, the queen—a woman fond of show and glitter—had to cut and pare because she was poor. For while skilful and desperate administration succeeded in raising the ordinary income of the crown to two or three times what it had been under Henry VIII, expenditure kept easily ahead of this. The price rise vastly increased the cost of keeping up the royal palaces and household, the armed forces, the diplomatic service; all the unavoidable expenses of government rose steadily till towards the end of Elizabeth's reign Burghley estimated them at £200,000 at least, twice as much as the whole revenue of the crown in 1530 which had been adequate for all purposes. When on top of that there came war with Spain and the constant drain of Ireland, all Burghley's measures failed. Elizabeth died £400,000 in debt, leaving also a legacy of trouble over the financial expedients of her last years. Financially shaken, the crown faced a body of men—call them gentry or what you will—who were cashing in on the price rise and thus able to back with power their political and religious disagreements with the government. As the inflation did its work, the great achievement of the earlier Tudors began to divide: the strength of the nation increased while that of the crown declined. The price rise was not the cause of the conflicts between the Stuarts and their parliaments, but by redistributing national income it made the struggle possible. In the reigns of Henry VII and Henry VIII the two parties (had they existed) would have been so ill matched that parliament would not have stood a chance. Throughout the reign of Elizabeth the balance was being redressed.

That brings us to a problem at present much in dispute—the so-called rise of the gentry. In 1941 Professor R. H. Tawney put forward a brilliantly argued theory that between 1540 and 1640 a class whom he called the gentry rose to economic supremacy by effectively exploiting their increasing lands, while what he called the aristocracy declined since it could not adjust its extravagant mode of life to a decreasing revenue. Mr L. Stone then elaborated the second part of the theory till it appeared that the Elizabethan aristocracy was altogether on the rocks. This ingenious piece of special pleading was so obviously at variance with the vigorous splendour of the great Elizabethan and Jacobean families that the whole theory became suspect, and Mr H. R. Trevor-Roper then devoted several articles to overthrowing the Tawney thesis. His own suggestion is that there was both decline and rise in the gentry: land alone proved unprofitable, so that only those who could obtain office and its bye-products improved their position. He therefore sees a conflict between office-holding gentry (court gentry) and country gentry, leading straight to the civil war of the seventeenth century.[1] The matter is far from ended yet, but several points are already quite clear. The idea of a declining aristocracy cannot be maintained, nor can that of the gentry rising as a class; apart from everything else, Professor Tawney's original version fails to explain the civil war which was not a war between crown and gentry but a war between sections of the gentry supporting either crown or parliament. But Mr Trevor-Roper's ideas cannot stand either in entirety: there is ample proof that many men both noble and gentle built up sizable fortunes from land

[1] The controversy may be studied in the following papers: R. H. Tawney, 'The Rise of the Gentry', *Econ. Hist. Review*, vol. ix (1941); L. Stone, 'Anatomy of the Elizabethan Aristocracy', *ibid.* vol. xviii (1948); H. R. Trevor-Roper, 'The Elizabethan Aristocracy: An Anatomy Anatomized', *ibid.*, 2nd Ser. vol. iii (1951); L. Stone, 'The Elizabethan Aristocracy: A Restatement', *ibid.*, vol. iv (1952); H. R. Trevor-Roper, *The Gentry, 1540-1640* (Econ. Hist. Soc., 1953); R. H. Tawney, 'The Rise of the Gentry: A Postscript', *Econ. Hist. Review*, 2nd Ser. vol. vii (1954).

alone and that office or court-life might bring disadvantages as easily as advantages.

There are several misconceptions to which this discussion has given rise—not perhaps among the participants but certainly among readers. For one, no distinction can be made between aristocracy and gentry; Sir Thomas Smith realised this better than the modern student labouring among the artificial creations of Marxism. The upper ranks of English society in the sixteenth century included men of noble title as well as those who had none, and traffic from one to the other was brisk, partly because the principle of primogeniture forced younger sons downwards into the ranks of commoners or 'gentry', and partly because the crown could push men upwards into gentle or noble condition. The Tudors made relatively few noblemen (though they made some), but they made very many gentlemen and esquires. Rather unconvincing attempts have been made to find in the reign of Henry VIII a tendency to give the nobility the structure of a closed caste; whether one agrees or not that such ideas were about, the fact remains that nothing of the sort was ever carried through. The essence of this upper structure of Tudor society was not class but status—or as they termed it, degree. What mattered was not the group but individual personal condition. A nobleman exacted higher respect and obedience than a gentleman, a knight more than an esquire—but if the knight became noble (as well he might) his place in society was that of his noble peers and his acquaintances adjusted themselves accordingly. The correspondence of any of the many Tudor statesmen who ran the gamut from low to high rank will bear this out. This is not to deny that noblemen of older vintage resented upstarts, or that many men developed pride of birth and blood; but the truth remains that society was constructed on lines not of class but of degree, and that a man's place depended entirely on his personal status in an intricate scale of ranks—a status which fate or his prince might alter—and not on a kind of fixed group or class to which he belonged once and for all.

More serious still is the fact that no common economic factors can be discovered to mark off class from class. If it is sometimes far from easy to distinguish classes in an industrial society, with its wage-earners and employers, the task becomes hopeless in the mostly rural society of the sixteenth century. Landowners are of all kinds, great and small, and both great and small include some that are going up, some that are falling, and no doubt some that are standing still. Indeed, the whole controversy has been able to develop only because the gentlemen of Tudor England were of so many kinds that accidental or deliberate selection can find proof for a number of theories. Professor Tawney is right in stressing the activities of improving landlords, of men who exploited the mineral resources and industrial possibilities of their lands, the advantages of the price rise to the enterprising; Mr Trevor-Roper is right in stressing the advantages of court life, the chances provided by wardships and monopolies, the difficulties of the 'mere' country gentlemen. But, in Tudor times at least, these are not mutually exclusive versions: they are parts of one picture. The plain economic facts—inflation and the need for an income rising as prices rose—were the same for all, but they impinged on a highly diverse society. Some men had exploitable lands, some had none. Some had court connections, others temperamentally hated London and Westminster. Some suffered from accidents and ill luck—sudden death, disease, incompetence, lack of sons; some were lucky and married heiresses or found coal or took the queen's eye. The story is really quite as individualistic as that. When the fate of all or nearly all families that claimed to be gentle—their number runs into thousands—has been studied, it may be possible to trace accurately what happened to the gentry as a whole; at present this cannot be done. The 'lucky dip' principle of historical investigation produces only a succession of discarded theories. But sometimes it is necessary to proceed in that way, and no harm is done provided no one is led to believe that the truth is yet known.

The third difficulty is probably the most serious and the least realised. It results from the impression given (perhaps unintentionally) by any theory which seems to treat the 'rise of the gentry' in the sixteenth century as a new phenomenon. The rise of a new class—a 'middle' class or whatever one wishes to call it—is one of those repetitive instruments of historical generalisation which are in danger of losing all meaning. Every other generation can provide examples of men lamenting the invasion of the higher ranks by new men from below, and the essential truth of that observation has been obscured by historians trying to see in it the rise of classes. There are theories of a rising middle class in the fourteenth, sixteenth, eighteenth, and nineteenth centuries—and of course we can see the thing happening again today. The truth is rather that at all times men try to better themselves by approximating to a social ideal. Those that succeed (always a minority of those that hope and try) come as new men into established ranks, but in a society as flexible as that of England they generally get established in a generation or two, just in time to bewail in their turn the arrival of others from below. Now the social ideal of Tudor

England was the landed gentleman, and those that could—having made money in trade or the legal profession or by adding acre to acre—pushed through into that position. But this is not peculiar to the sixteenth century. If—after all this belabouring of generalisations—a vaster generalisation still may be hazarded, it is this: from the decay of feudalism proper round about the year 1300 to the rise of an industrial and urban society round about the year 1850, the social ideal of England was that of the landed gentleman.[1] These five hundred years may be called the age of the gentry. During them the gentry, and the nobility growing out of it, dominated English society, giving it its standards, its structure, its purpose, and its way of life. What, therefore, could be more natural than that men on the make should constantly be refreshing and enlarging the ranks of that gentry?

But five hundred years are a long time during which trends and movements may change direction and momentum. They were the age of the gentry, but the gentry is essentially not so much a class as a form of existence always drawing in new men and discarding failures by the wayside, frequently changing in character as circumstances change. In those 500 years the sixteenth century was a critical period when the gentry changed most radically and achieved a novel power. It grew in numbers, in self-consciousness, in political and religious and commercial vigour; it also incidentally for the first time produced great poets. The reasons are many. The restoration of peace and order by the Tudors was an essential condition, as was the consolidation of the national state. Protestantism may have been a cause or a symptom, a point too vast to discuss here. But one obvious factor stands out. The gentry rested its existence on land, and the sixteenth century witnessed the biggest transfer of land since the Conquest. When the great monastic estates came on the market, to be supplemented by other lands of both lay and ecclesiastical owners, many men could either acquire land for the first time or add to what they had. The great inflation provided the capital and the desire for investment. Thus in the century after 1540 the gentry spread and grew as it profited from the effects of an economic revolution, even though some of the gentry were also destroyed by this same revolution. What was new was not the gentry as a rising class nor the gentry as an ideal, nor even the gentry as a power in the land; what was new was the number of gentlemen and their power relative to other sections of

[1] Need I add that these dates are to be taken as the merest general guides? There are places today where the gentry, refusing to acknowledge itself dead, persists in a rearguard action.

the community. The redistribution of property meant that the middle sort of people—those between the crown and the great magnates on the one hand, and the landless and small farmers on the other—came into their own.

Lastly, what of the poor? It has been shown that the price rise assisted a sorting out in the lower ranks of society, some men becoming prosperous and sometimes rising through yeoman status even into the gentry, and others declining into genuine poverty. Something has also been said about the problem of vagrancy. It is extremely difficult to be accurate in these questions, for it is of the essence of the poor that they do not appear in history. Now and again they made themselves felt, as in the agrarian disturbances of the century; quarter sessions dealt with vagrants and recorded the harrying of these outcasts of society; there is comment from reformers, and there is government legislation. These last two have combined to make the issue appear unduly big. The times were harsh for poor people, but then they always are. Undoubtedly the price rise increased pauperism. It helped to add to the number of landless men and, through sheep-farming, to the number of rural unemployed. The depression in the clothing industry after 1560 raised another problem of unemployment. None of the attempts made to deal with all these difficulties were very successful. Various piece-meal enactments for labour culminated in the great code of 1563, the statute of apprentices or artificers, a comprehensive enactment which attempted to fix the structure at the bottom of society in an earlier mould. Men were to stay both in the locality and the work into which they were born. This was to be achieved by strictly controlling the movement of labour, by enforcing apprenticeship in all existing crafts and even in agriculture, by preventing idleness, and by having justices of the peace fix wages. None of these ideas were new; the statute summed up a long history of economic legislation both local and national. It was no dead letter: its apprenticeship clauses were invoked in crafts and trades, though not in agriculture, and wage assessments were made frequently. In the textile industries, where wage-earners suffered from unemployment and exploitation by clothiers, minimum wages were often fixed; in agriculture, where small employers suffered from the shortage and demands of labour, maximum wages were the rule. Professor Tawney has suggested that the purpose of the statute was rather to protect the small men and the poor than to exploit the labourer in the interests of farmer and capitalists, but in the main it embodied a stern if paternal concept of society. The statute seems to have done a little to preserve stability and maintain the supply of labour on the land, but it never achieved anything like the complete stabilisation it was intended to secure—a hopeless endeavour in that age of upheaval.

Stability and order were the government's chief concern; it was for their sake that it turned its attention to the unemployed, the vagrants and vagabonds. That their numbers have been quite astonishingly exaggerated has already been shown; the statute of apprentices offers further proof that the number of unemployed was not large, for even on the land the supply of surplus labour seems to have been so small that employers had to be stopped from paying higher wages. This is not the sort of thing that happens when many landless men press on a glutted labour market but can only occur when labour can make its own terms. The real problem of the poor was twofold. There were those who could not work and those who would not work; so at least contemporaries saw it, and there is really precious little evidence that those who wanted work but could not find it ever made up a sizable proportion of the wandering poor. After the beginnings of a considered poor law in 1536, various acts gradually elaborated a general system for providing charity, work, and punishments, a system which was codified in the two great acts summing up the Elizabethan poor law in 1597 and 1601. The duty of looking after the helpless, aged, and sick devolved upon the parish; it was administered by parish overseers and financed out of a compulsory rate levied upon householders. The parish was also to provide work for the genuinely unemployed by supplying stocks of hemp and similar material for them to work on; the incorrigibles who (can we blame them?) preferred the open road to beating hemp were punished by the justices of the peace. As the century drew on, the worst dislocations of the agrarian revolution began to wear off; new industries on the one hand, organised crime on the other, absorbed most of the workless poor; the problem became manageable, and the Elizabethan poor law proved satisfactory till the greater upheaval of the late eighteenth century raised entirely new difficulties.

More might be said about the poor, especially if one concentrated either on the protests—More's *Utopia* (1517) or Roderick Mors' *Complaynt* (1548) or Latimer's *Sermons* (1548 onwards)—or on the works of that journalist of genius, Robert Greene, who both recorded and invented the traditional Elizabethan rogue in his pamphlets on their practices. But we must observe a proper proportion. In the flourishing, reckless, enterprising, often disastrous and often very grim ebb and flow of Elizabethan society there is much light and dark; it is not easy to write about the period without seeming to ignore either one or the other. Many prospered, many failed; inconceivable poverty co-existed with solid wealth and showy display. An age of unexpected and unexplained inflation can be many things: it can bring trouble and decay as well as opportunity and advancement. But it cannot be humdrum and stable. The excessive preoccupation of the Elizabethans with the order of the universe and the fixed degrees of men reflects less (as has been argued) the memory of the disturbed politics of the fifteenth century than an awareness of the instability of their own day when society was being dragged from its moorings by new ideas, new worlds, and—most basically of all—by new wealth and new poverty. On balance, however, the gains enormously outweighed the losses, though this no doubt was small consolation to the losers. In its economic life, as in so much else, Tudor England broke loose from the past and prepared amid great turmoil for the easier prosperity and the wider horizons of succeeding centuries.

Chapter X

THE ELIZABETHAN SETTLEMENT, 1558-68

I. THE SITUATION IN 1558

THE young woman of twenty-five who ascended the throne of England on 17 November 1558 presented a much more formidable figure than her devout and blundering half-sister. A naturally imperious, self-willed and selfish character in the best Tudor tradition had been schooled by a hard childhood and adolescence into patience and calculation; even her rages were usually controlled by her mind. Elizabeth's character was of steel, her courage utterly beyond question, her will and understanding of men quite as great as her grandfather's and father's. She was a natural-born queen as her sister had never been—the most masculine of all the female sovereigns of history. At the same time she nourished several supposedly feminine characteristics. She was persistently dilatory, changed her mind as often as chance offered, exasperated everybody by her refusal to come to decisions, and charmed them all back again by some transparent piece of graciousness. Determined never to marry—her reasons seem to have been both political and personal—she developed two unpleasingly old-maidish traits: a show of permanent youthfulness and desirability on the one hand, on the other venomous jealousy of younger women who found husbands. Her parsimony has already been explained as the careful housekeeping of a poor queen faced with ruinous expenses, and it is certainly true that she needed to save all she could. But however justified she was in husbanding her resources, the shifts and deceits and broken promises she often resorted to came perilously near to genuine miserliness. She was a great queen and never less than queen: sagacious, brave, tolerant where it was wise, and tenacious of her rights where tolerance would have been weakness. But she fell far short of that standard of angelic perfection—that inability ever to do wrong—which some would like to ascribe to her, explaining even her errors of taste and judgment as superlative examples of political skill. After 350 years, the old spell is still at work.

What really matters, of course, is Elizabeth's ability in politics—her standing as a queen rather than her pretty obvious failings as a woman. One great difficulty in arriving at a fair verdict lies in her long association with her chief minister, Sir William Cecil, from 1571 Lord Burghley. The partnership began only three days after the queen's accession with Cecil's appointment as principal secretary; it was not dissolved till Burghley died in 1598, less than five years before his mistress. The son of a Northamptonshire gentleman who had risen to affluence as a courtier of Henry VIII, Cecil first obtained office in 1550 as a follower of the Protector Somerset. He showed much pliancy in the years that followed, serving Northumberland despite that duke's attack on his patron, and though he lost his place under Mary he preserved life and liberty by judicious attendance at the mass, even as the Princess Elizabeth did. The two had much in common. Both were by nature secular, holding religion to be a matter of conscience which need not interfere with affairs of state, though Elizabeth may have gone further in this than Cecil who held to a moderate but consistent protestantism. Both were naturally cautious, disinclined to stir up trouble by magnificent gestures, and careful of the limited resources of a poor monarchy. Cecil's mind was eminently judicious; he could never have committed a rash act. But if in this he was rather drabber than the brilliant queen, he could be brisk enough when the situation seemed to demand it and was free from her besetting sin of dilatoriness and her incurable fear of responsibility. Indeed, he suffered much from her, not only the occasional taunts and hard words with which all Tudor servants were familiar, but also the more insidious pangs of seeing things go wrong because the queen would not make up her mind. Whether queen or minister was responsible for the great successes of the reign is not at present a question we can answer; those who should know come to different conclusions, and there is no adequate study of Cecil. As a team they were superb, matching caution for caution, diplomatic *finesse* for administrative ability, and a marvellous capacity for keeping six balls in the air at once for an equal skill in keeping a dozen strings from getting entangled. In experience they grew old together. Of course, the queen ruled over all and Burghley was not her only servant: others often influenced her decisions which (when at last they came) were always her own. But except for occasional divagations, the government of England was for forty years in the hands of this partnership between queen and minister. Neither, incidentally, had the qualities of ruthless imagination leading to revolutionary action which had distinguished the 1530s. It was well so. That work was done; now it needed consolidation and development—the immensely important and difficult exploitation of achievements which eighteen years of bad government had put in jeopardy. For this the wayward but ultimately sensible genius of the queen and the steady, hardworking, eminently sane genius of Cecil were exactly right.

The immediate problem confronting the government was that of religion. The death of Mary left England technically catholic and reunited to Rome, but whether this would last depended on the new queen. Twice changes in rulers had produced changes in religion; it was likely that this would be so again. As the daughter of Anne Boleyn—as the visible pledge of Henry VIII's break with Rome—Elizabeth seemed bound to forswear her sister's religion. Rome did not recognise her legitimacy, though that was a snag which a papal dispensation could remove; Paul IV, fierce hater of heresy though he was, professed himself ready to consider the point. However, Mary's reign had really destroyed what hold Rome yet retained on Englishmen: the country had shown clearly enough what it thought of a religion which reimposed papal rule and added the dominance of Spain. Whatever the gentry's ardour for the new faith, they valued their new lands and continued to dislike priesthood and popes. While England and Europe waited for a sign from Elizabeth, English nationalism cast its vote by giving the new queen a vociferous welcome which implied a convinced condemnation of the old. Though some fond minds in Rome and Madrid deceived themselves into false hopes, the pope's power in England was from the start unlikely to endure. The further question whether Elizabeth would restore Henry VIII's religion or Edward VI's was less easy to answer. The least known factor of all was her own religious faith. Perhaps—as we are now commonly told, usually by way of commendation—she had none; certainly she had no patience with the quarrels of doctrine and wished to keep the peace. She would not, as she said, make windows in men's souls; her concern was that men, whatever they believed, should obey her government. Her personal taste was hostile to the mass but in favour of the pomp and splendour of the old religion; she liked candles and ornaments and vestments, and in another age might have liked images. But the situation was much too complicated to permit an indulgence in a personal bent.

As had been the case ever since Henry VIII broke with Rome, international involvements set the stage. England was still technically at war with France and allied to Spain, though the peace negotiations were nearing conclusion, despite English reluctance to give up Calais. In Scotland, the regent Mary of Guise ruled for her young daughter who was both queen of Scots and dauphiness of France. The ancient friendship between France and Scotland thus looked like turning into a personal union which would put England squarely between the jaws of a nutcracker—the deplorable outcome of Henry VIII's overhasty and overbearing attempt to dominate Scotland from London. Against this threat England's only protection seemed to lie in a continuance of the Spanish amity, and a genuine alliance with Philip II could hardly be combined with anything but catholicism at home. Again, if Spain and France came to terms the two leading catholic countries would be free to turn their combined strength on any heretic power: England might find herself alone against both her old ally and her old foe. Either way, the state of Europe counselled caution; a less astute and daring diplomat than Elizabeth might even have thought it compelled her to accept her sister's religion. Since, however, her own and her people's wishes definitely prevented a continued submission to the papacy, she rightly decided that she could only save herself by preserving Philip's benevolent neutrality while at the same time drifting away from Rome.

Such a course not only demanded uncommon diplomatic skill but also implied that the settlement of religion could not be too rapid or too radical. But here Elizabeth came up against the pressure of organised protestant opinion. On the news of Mary's death, a stream of exiles began to flow back with ever increasing speed, bringing with them very definite ideas about the establishment of religion. Definite these ideas were, but unanimous they were not, and in this lay the queen's chance of victory. Protestantism benefited by its martyrs, but if all its adherents had followed Cranmer's and Ridley's example it would have remained little but a memory. Many ardent protestant divines, and a few equally ardent laymen, fled therefore to various reformed communities on the continent as soon as Pole brought back Rome and the stake, rightly saving themselves against the day of triumph. Free from the relative moderation which a half-hostile England and a sense of responsibility to the government had previously induced, these English protestants were soon among the most extreme of their faith. As extremists will, they fell out amongst themselves. The quarrels centred on Frankfort where John Knox, lately King Edward's chaplain, tried to establish a Calvinist community but was defeated in the end by Richard Cox whose faction adhered to the specifically English system of the second Edwardian Prayer Book. Knox returned to Geneva with a band of extremists. There were other exile groups, but the Frankfort and Geneva sections—Coxians and Knoxians—were the ones that mattered. Both supported a religion 'purified' of all the works of Rome and therefore acquired the name of puritans, but the latter wanted the complete Calvinist system with the Geneva 'discipline' (or order of Church government and service) which put power over the laity in the hands of the ministers. The Coxians were the first to return to England, together with such moderate protestants as Edmund Grindal who had spent his exile in Strassburg, the late Martin Bucer's stronghold. The Geneva group found the queen hostile from the start: Knox, a Scotsman, was never allowed to stay in England again. Elizabeth objected to them partly because of Knox's unfortunate *First Blast of the Trumpet against the Monstrous Regiment of Women*, a violent attack on female sovereigns directed against Mary Tudor and Mary of Guise which proved a stumbling-block in the way of agreement with the equally female but much more protestant Elizabeth. In general, too, the Genevan ideals went counter to her ideas of a hierarchical and state-controlled Church.

However, if Knoxians were insufferable, Coxians were none too agreeable. Alliance with them closed the road to a restoration of the Henrician Church—a Church catholic in doctrine but divided from Rome. It meant upsetting the many to whom the old faith was still the most congenial, even if they had no wish to see the pope back. Yet despite Elizabeth's own sympathy with this point of view, the alliance could not be avoided. Where was she to find her bishops? Unlike her father she could not take the existing episcopate with her on the road away from Rome. Thirty years of strife and increasing protestantism had taught the Marian bishops the folly and indecency of yet another change of front, and with remarkable solidarity they all but one refused to accept the new state of things. Of the twenty-six sees—ten, including Canterbury, were conveniently vacant by death—Elizabeth had to fill twenty-five; she simply had to accept clergy of an Anglican or more definitely protestant hue. While she could set her face against the extreme puritans from Geneva, she could not do without the moderate puritans from Frankfort; some purification—some move towards Edwardian protestantism at least—was unavoidable.

What really tied Elizabeth's hands, however, was a phenomenon full of portent for the future. Puritanism in the clergy one might cope with; puritanism in the laity was another matter altogether. For the first time since 1529, the government found itself following instead of leading the nation as represented in parliament. From Elizabeth's very first parliament onwards, the puritan faction commanded a formidable support in the commons. A group of Marian exiles, including Sir Francis Knollys (himself a privy councillor) and Sir Anthony Cooke (father-in-law to two other privy councillors), co-operated with puritan divines outside the house in pressing for a protestant settlement. Such pressure in parliament was a serious matter. Parliament had played an important part in the Henrician Reformation: it had not erected the royal supremacy but it had enforced it. In consequence, the very existence of the supremacy—the structure of the Church—came to be bound up with statute. Edward VI's parliaments had really enacted the Prayer Books, not merely appointed penalties for refusal to use them; the 1552 act of uniformity spoke of 'a very goodly order set forth by authority of parliament'. The distinction which Henry VIII and Cromwell had so carefully made between preamble and enactment vanished as Somerset and Northumberland blithely permitted phrasing which implied that the royal supremacy was to be exercised in and with parliament only. Mary found that she could not restore catholicism and repair the break with Rome without parliamentary enactment; worse, she could not even divest herself of that shirt of Nessus, the Supremacy title itself, until parliament had spoken. In the violent changes of religion which agitated England between 1547 and 1558, parliament established a claim to participation which would have horrified Henry VIII and was to drive Elizabeth to distraction. She tried hard to preserve the original notion that the government of the Church was for the sovereign alone, while statute must be used to create penalties for offences against the order established by the crown, but the pass had been sold before she came to the throne.

Parliament's invasion of the sphere of Church government became a danger only as the crown lost the initiative. Elizabeth wished to adhere to her settlement, but even in this settlement—as we shall see—she had to go further than she intended because of puritan pressure in the commons. The puritans were far from satisfied, and the reign resounded with the battles waged by their dynamism in the commons against the static policy of the queen. This ominous alliance between advanced religion and the house of commons depended for its success on the constitutional growth of the house itself. If the puritans there were to make their views felt they had to be able to express them freely and without fear of the consequences. Thus the struggle seemed to turn on the privileges of parliament, especially those which guaranteed freedom from arrest and freedom of speech. By 1558 the house of commons had secured recognition of certain powers over its own members which gave it a corporate and effective existence; in this development of the house as a 'court' lay the foundation of its modern greatness. An act of 1515 transferred to the house itself the right to license absentees which the crown had hitherto exercised. Ferrers' Case (1543), when the commons by their own authority punished some city officers of London who had arrested a member, established their right of direct action and the sufficiency as warrant of their serjeant's mace. The crucial right of free speech has a more difficult and doubtful history. Medieval Speakers had petitioned for free speech for themselves—the right, that is, to inform the king of what had been discussed and agreed in the commons, without prejudice to themselves. The first reliable instance of the genuine privilege—the right of members to speak freely in the house—seems to date from Sir Thomas More's Speakership in 1523; it is supposed, with some probability, that More was himself responsible for this important advance in the claims of parliament.

By 1558 the request was regularly included in the Speaker's petition at the beginning of each parliament: it had become matter of form. But its precise meaning was still unsettled. Henry VIII adhered to a policy of persuasion, refusing to punish members' words even when they plainly attacked his plans or invaded his prerogative. However, leading parliament as he did he could afford to let a little opposition have its way; Elizabeth, trying to maintain a much-attacked *status quo*, felt unable to be as tolerant. She also displayed a more self-conscious awareness of her dignity and rights, and a more imperious contempt for the opinions of those presumptuous men who would teach her her business. The fact that crown and commons came to pursue divergent policies in religion, the most touchy matter of all, made certain that freedom of speech would become a battleground. The queen defined her concept of it most clearly towards the end of the reign, in the lord keeper's speech of 1593 in which it was said that 'to say yea or no to bills, God forbid that any man should be restrained or afraid to answer to his best liking, with some short declaration of his reasons therein, and therein to have a free voice.' Members were free to speak about all matters submitted to them, provided they preserved decorum and avoided license. There was much to be said for this view on grounds of precedent, and it was far from ungenerous. As a corollary Elizabeth refused the house the right to discuss her 'prerogative' without permission, for which limitation again precedent and the law were on her side; but in this prerogative she included ecclesiastical matters and matters affecting her person, as her marriage and the problem of the succession. In other words, she put precisely those things out of bounds which the opposition wished to discuss. They retaliated with a wider notion of freedom of speech, culminating in the theory of Peter Wentworth that the house had the right freely to discuss all matters affecting the common weal and to introduce legislation concerned with it. Such complete freedom of speech could not be reconciled with the queen's politic desire to keep 'mysteries of state' in her own hand; the quarrel was fundamental and insoluble.

Such, then, was the position in 1558. Elizabeth had to settle the Church and religion before she did anything else. Her own inclination and the international situation rendered it dangerous not only to establish a genuinely protestant Church, but even to restore Henry VIII's system. The situation in the country worked the other way. If she broke with Rome, as she meant to do, she would have to accept an alliance with protestant Churchmen: Henrician anglo-catholicism was out of the question. Moreover, she had to work through and with parliament if the settlement was to be constitutional and enforceable, and parliament was now a much less manageable ally. A house of commons accustomed by thirty years' work to participate—even, it seemed, to authorise—in high matters of state and growingly conscious of its rights, privileges, and powers, was dominated from the start by a minority of puritans who knew what they wanted. It must have appeared to the queen and Cecil that every solution must fail. The history of the previous two reigns offered no encouragement. How the government, stepping delicately and with a purpose, threaded its way through these troubles, how its actions were affected by pressure from both sides, and how its achievement was preserved both by its own skill and the folly of its enemies—all this must now be told.

2. THE CHURCH OF ENGLAND RESTORED

Elizabeth's claim to the throne was not a bad one, resting as it did on act of parliament (1543) and Henry VIII's will. If statute had once declared her a bastard, Mary's fate had been the same. London received her with joy and acclamation. But others there were who felt differently. The hint from Rome that her mother's irregular marriage might yet be put right also implied that until this was done she could not properly inherit the crown. Mary Stuart stood in the wings to take over as the catholic candidate. Philip II, through his envoy de Feria, an arrogant and stiffnecked fool, tried to claim all credit for Elizabeth's peaceful accession; he was firmly convinced that the new queen would have to depend on Spain as the old queen had done, and for some months he planned to marry Elizabeth himself. On the other hand, there were murmurings at the failure to remove the Marian bishops by prerogative action; though Elizabeth picked Cecil for her chief councillor she made no clean sweep of Mary's council; caution and circumspection, in any case her favourite attitude, were the necessary order of the day. To begin with she succeeded in allowing all men to believe what they wished while she kept herself free to act. Pope Paul IV, badgered by Spain, professed to believe it possible that she would yet prove faithful to Rome; Philip II persuaded himself readily into the same opinion because he wished to continue his sway in England; her catholic subjects saw with relief that she was no second Northumberland. But protestants knew better and hoped more eagerly. Her title was made to end in a mysterious etcetera: she was queen of England, France, and Ireland, she was defender of the faith, 'etc.' Thus she neither called herself supreme head nor clearly relinquished that critical name.[1] Each man might make of it what he would. This game could not be played for long. The queen would have to attend divine service, and then some of the matter at least would become plain. Nothing Elizabeth did was ever plain, and she invariably succeeded in talking herself out of even the most definite action, but hints soon appeared. On Christmas Day 1558 Bishop Oglethorpe of Carlisle, saying mass in the royal chapel, was ordered to refrain from elevating the host for the adoration to which reformers so strenuously objected; he refused, and the queen walked out before that point in the service. As a result she had great difficulty in finding a bishop to crown her, but in the end Oglethorpe again obliged. Elizabeth took every opportunity on this 15 January 1559 for a little significant playacting. She received the English Bible with dramatised fervour; she again withdrew before the elevation of the host. As far as she might she had signalled her acceptance of some sort of reformed faith, while her carefully obscure talk kept Spain and Rome in wilful delusion.

The crisis approached with the meeting of parliament, called for 25 January. The queen's control over the lords was weaker than was usual in the sixteenth century because the sixteen Marian bishops and one Marian abbot proved solid against all the government's blandishments. Tunstall of Durham made his excuses on the score of age and Goldwell of St Asaph received no summons because he was actually being translated to Oxford at the time; but these and other absentees gave proxies to staunch conservatives,

[1] Mary had used the device for the opposite reason.

especially Nicholas Heath, archbishop of York, only just replaced as lord chancellor by Nicholas Bacon, Cecil's brother-in-law.[1] The lay peers were mostly Mary's but they had been Edward's before that; a few new creations rewarded friends of Elizabeth's hard days but did not pack the house. The queen indulged in none of the practices—creations, orders to stay absent—which might have been used to secure an obedient house; she was hardly safe enough to do so as yet. Nor were the commons packed; there seems to have been less influence exercised on elections than usual, as one would expect from a government that had yet to find its feet. About a third of the members had sat in Mary's last parliament (with which she had managed well enough) and undoubtedly there were many good catholics; but there were certainly also several exiles and other ardent protestants. Religion was not the only subject before this parliament, but religion was the issue that mattered. Several eager pamphleteers submitted their ideas to Cecil and Elizabeth. One of these writing—the 'Device for the alteration of religion'—agrees so well with the final outcome that it used to be considered the basis for the government's action, but in fact Elizabeth favoured something much more gradual and piecemeal than the immediate establishment of a protestant Church of England. Her ideas were in accord rather with the exceedingly cautious advice given by Richard Goodrich and Armigail Waad, a lawyer and an official. Divines she never liked.[2]

On 25 January 1559 the parliament met. The convocation of Canterbury sat at the same time; its only action was to assert the full catholic position on the papal supremacy and on dogma, on 28 February. It played no part in the settlement, a fact which caused much trouble in the nineteenth-century Church but need not worry us here. The commons, on the other hand, showed their anti-papal inclination from the start when they tried to impugn Mary's legislation on the grounds that she had dispensed with 'supreme head' in her title, and to force Elizabeth to expand her etcetera into the full glory of Henry VIII's invention. These were skirmishings. Issue was joined on 9 February when the government introduced a supremacy bill in the commons which

[1] Bacon held the lesser dignity of keeper of the great seal. Elizabeth was fond of this compromise which saved money and the need of a peerage, both of which she disliked bestowing.

[2] The following account of events in Elizabeth's first parliament is based on J. E. Neale's analysis in *Eng. Hist. Rev.*, 1950, and in *Elizabeth I and her Parliaments 1559-1581*, pt. I. His interpretation has successfully overthrown views of long standing.

embodied Elizabeth's original plan. It would have revived the Henrician legislation by repealing Mary's second statute of repeal, would have enforced Elizabeth's title of supreme head by an oath to be taken by all the clergy, and would furthermore have permitted communion under both kinds. Thus it would have returned to conditions as they were in 1547; Somerset had also proceeded gradually, first permitting protestant doctrine and only later establishing protestant worship by law. To start with, Elizabeth wanted neither a prayer book nor an act of uniformity. However, she was not permitted to get away with so little. Strenuous opposition in committee forced alterations into the bill which came back to the commons as the second supremacy bill on 21 February. It is probable that this made the penalties for refusing the oath harsher and revived the 1552 prayer book. There was no chance of the queen permitting such extremism on the part of the protestant commons, and the lords soon reduced the bill to its original form. Even so Heath protested against the title of supreme head, especially because a woman could in no circumstances be head of the Church. The commons (whose leaders were working in close contact with the returned clergy, especially Cox, Grindal, and Edwin Sandys) saw all hope of a protestant establishment fading in face of the queen's desire to remain uncommitted; in despair they rushed through a bill which would at least have granted toleration to anyone practising the religion of Edward VI's last year. They had no hope of getting this past the lords, let alone the queen, but intended to impress the government with the strength of protestant feeling.

Whether it was impressed by this move or not, the government had by this time realised that the issue would have to be faced. Easter was near (26 March), and it had been intended to dissolve parliament before then; the second supremacy bill was ready for the queen's assent on 22 March. At the last moment she changed her mind, took no action over the bill, and prorogued parliament till early April. She had received the news that peace was concluded at Cateau-Cambrésis between Spain, France, and England. This meant that the powers recognised her as queen: for the moment she was secure and could afford to come off the fence. The turmoil in parliament had decided on which side she would descend. During the recess consideration began of the form of religion to be enforced. On 31 March a discussion was staged in Westminster Hall between some Marian bishops and some protestant divines. It served no purpose except to reduce the votes of the spiritual peers in parliament: White of Winchester and Watson of Lincoln were sent to the Tower for speaking against the supremacy. Meanwhile the various parties set about the production of a prayer book. There was no formal revision by a committee of clergy early in the year, as used to be thought; instead, negotiations took place between the queen, Cecil, and the protestants. The queen wanted the first Edwardian Prayer Book, the divines and the commons were barely satisfied with the second. The Prayer Book of 1559 is a compromise in which the queen conceded most. She had to accept the 1552 book with slight modifications of which the chief were the dropping of the 'Black Rubric'[1] and the addition of an ornaments rubric which ordered the wearing of vestments as in 'the second year' of Edward VI (1548); interpretation of this last was to provoke a major conflict.

Before the book was agreed parliament had reassembled (3 April). On the 10th the government produced a third supremacy bill identical with the second except that it substituted for the title of supreme head of the Church that of 'supreme governor as well in all spiritual or ecclesiastical things or causes as temporal'. The widespread feeling against a female head had taken effect. In this form the bill was passed rapidly through the commons and more slowly through the lords. On the 18th the commons gave a first reading to the uniformity bill which authorised the agreed Prayer Book; within a few days it had passed both houses—the lords by a majority of only three with the spiritual peers solidly against it and several lay peers also opposing the government—and on 8 May Elizabeth, dissolving this momentous parliament, gave her assent. The Elizabethan settlement was made. It now consisted of an act of supremacy enforcing the renewed break with Rome and the queen's position as supreme governor of things temporal and spiritual, and an act of uniformity enforcing a protestantism not quite so clear-cut as that of 1552 but much more extreme than that of 1549. It is usual to call this settlement a compromise, and so it was—but not quite in the sense commonly supposed. Contemporaries did not think that the established Church rested halfway between the rival denominations: they thought this was a protestant Church. Episcopacy had not yet become an issue: even Knox accepted bishops. It was only the further development of puritanism (whose Coxian representatives were moderately content in 1559), as well as Elizabeth's diplomatic suggestions to a number of deliberately blind Spanish and French emissaries that her protestantism was after all quite like catholicism, that disguised the nature of the settlement. The compromise was between

[1] See above, p. 212.

the queen and her protestant subjects represented in parliament, and it involved greater concessions from her than from them. In this first round of the long parliamentary struggle over religion, the queen came off worst; the puritan minority displayed their characteristic tenacity and tactical skill; and England at once got a protestant Church despite Elizabeth's desire for a gradual exploration of the way.

The settlement involved two constitutional issues worthy of attention. In the first place, it assigned to parliament a place which it did not hold under Henry VIII but had acquired under Edward VI. The act of supremacy—like Henry's similar act—gave to the sovereign all such jurisdictions and powers 'as by any spiritual or ecclesiastical power or authority hath heretofore been . . . exercised' in the government of the clergy; but it further expressly participated in the use of such powers by authorising their delegation. The act of uniformity stood on the principle first accepted in 1549 that the recognised legal form of worship was not only enforced but actually authorised by statute. Neither Cromwell's vicariate-general or vicegerency, nor the settlement of doctrine by such royal instruments as the King's Book of 1543, was therefore possible under the new dispensation. When Elizabeth delegated her ecclesiastical powers to successive commissions, those commissions' doings could be challenged by reference to the act of 1559; this happened and caused much trouble. Similarly, the Prayer Book could not be altered without parliament, and parliament had a perfectly sound case for claiming a share in deciding the official ritual and doctrine: it had done so once at the queen's invitation, and it was difficult to prevent ardent men in the commons from supposing that it could do so again on their unofficial initiative. The statutory character of the settlement—which could not be avoided—and the phrasing of the act of uniformity ended the queen's exclusive control of Church and religion, whatever she might say.

Elizabeth's position was therefore weaker than her father's. It is now usual to allege that there was no difference between the supreme head and the supreme governor—that the latter name merely saved the consciences of catholics and of those who remembered the Pauline injunction against women in the Church, without lessening the queen's control of ecclesiastical government. Contemporaries said the same: the Spanish ambassador and Elizabeth's very protestant ambassador in France, Sir Nicholas Throckmorton, were agreed on this. Yet they were wrong. Though she had a harder task in fighting off the interference of puritans in clergy and laity, Elizabeth governed the Church in practice as firmly as Henry had done; but that was because hers was as formidable a character. There was an essential difference between head and governor. The first was, so to speak, himself an ecclesiastical person partaking (as we have seen) of episcopal characteristics; the second stood outside the clergy. Henry as supreme head was himself the highest ecclesiastical dignitary in the realm; his deputy, a lay vicegerent in spirituals, took precedence over archbishops in convocation. Elizabeth ruled the Church from outside, through her archbishops and commissioners. Unlike her father, Elizabeth was no pope in England, not only because she was a woman but also because no such quasi-ecclesiastical character appertained to the supreme governorship. While the queen lived it made little practical difference, but the change profoundly affected the position of her successors. The Elizabethan settlement created a Church protestant in doctrine, traditional in organisation, and subject not to a lay pope but to the queen-governor in parliament. Statute had triumphed in this field also, with the natural consequence that the difficulties inherent in a 'mixed sovereign' were bound to show in the most contentious sphere of all.

Parliament had spoken; now the country had to be brought into line—for the third time in a dozen years. The oath of supremacy was the test; not to take it meant deprivation. By January 1560 all the Marian bishops except Kitchen of Llandaff were deprived. Their solidarity and refusal to bow to circumstances deserve praise, nor could they know beforehand that Elizabeth would treat them with a leniency which they themselves had failed to show during their ascendancy. Most of them lived out their lives under a mild and private surveillance; even Bonner, whose death was widely demanded in revenge for his bloody doings, was only imprisoned a trifle more rigorously and lived to embarrass the government in 1567 with shrewd thrusts at the legality of the act of supremacy. There had been hopes of taking some of the bishops along. The venerable Tunstall was wooed by Cecil, but Tunstall was content to have held Durham for twenty-nine years; in any case he survived his deprivation by only a few weeks. Thus twenty-five sees had to be filled. Elizabeth was lucky to have a man to hand for Canterbury who fulfilled exactly her idea of an ecclesiastical commander-in-chief. This was Matthew Parker, a Cambridge don of moderately protestant opinions in the Cranmer tradition. A believer in authority and monarchy, opposed to all extremes and disorder, and one who devoted his intellectual abilities to history rather than theology, he was at the same time an admirably firm and dispassionate administrator. On 17 December 1559 he sat consecrated—canonically, because some Edwardian bishops survived—in the late Cardinal Pole's place, and the Church of England had again a leader. The other sees were filled, some with bishops deprived in 1553, but more with those Marian exiles who had organised the puritan attack on the queen's ecclesiastical plans in parliament. Richard Cox took Ely, Edmund Grindal London, John Jewel Salisbury, Edwin Sandys Worcester, James Pilkington Durham, Robert Horne Winchester. These were the leaders of Frankfort and their allies. But Elizabeth had no choice: the new bishops stood high above the general level of the English clergy, and because of the Marians' firmness there were no other possible candidates. Episcopacy, administrative duties, and the experience of responsibility soon sobered down their puritanism, but some were to find it difficult to combine office with the memories of the past.

The lesser clergy gave little trouble. They had expressed their attachment to Rome, transubstantiation, and so forth under Bonner's guidance in convocation's protest early in 1559; a year later, as the bishops' visitors went about administering the oath, few only refused. The exact figures are in dispute: the most likely estimate reckons that some 240-300 beneficed clergy out of a total of about 8,000 were deprived in the years 1560-6. The government acted without rigour; evasion of the rules was for the moment winked at and the mass permitted to survive in remoter districts. This mercy was, of course, politic but none the less attractive for that; the type of writer who sneers at Elizabeth's moderation because it was calculated and praises Mary's intolerance because it rested on principle either cannot have much experience of persecution or feels sure that he would have been on the right side of the fiery divide. The settlement gradually took root in England. Men could not be sure but that another turn of the wheel might come any day; in the meantime, this moderate and moderately imposed system could be borne by nearly all. The threat to the re-established protestant Church came rather from abroad. The great triumph of Elizabeth's policy in her first few years was the elimination of the Scottish danger.

3. THE REFORMATION IN SCOTLAND

At Elizabeth's accession England was unbelievably weak. Her military strength had declined so disastrously that she entirely depended on the international situation for the minimum of national safety. Her finances were disorganised and her credit gone. Much was done in a single year to recover from this collapse for which Mary's reign must be held largely responsible: Cecil laboured successfully at the restoration of armed forces, the development of armament industries, and—with the assistance of Gresham in Antwerp—at the rebuilding of financial stability. Nevertheless, much continued to depend on factors outside English control, so that the first decade of the reign was filled with a bewildering complex of diplomatic negotiations both avowed and secret. The treaty of Cateau-Cambrésis (April 1559) confirmed Elizabeth's recognition by the continental powers, but it also ended for a time the rivalry of Spain and France on which England had for so long relied. Ultimately England was to be offered even better opportunities for fishing in troubled waters by the religious wars which destroyed French power for nearly half a century, and by the revolt of the Netherlands which fatally weakened Spain. It was the crowning irony of Elizabeth's reign that she, the champion of monarchy and avowed enemy of all who resisted authority, was to achieve her triumph in making England a great power by supporting rebellion in other princes' lands. She never liked doing it: a feeling of solidarity with all crowned heads remained a potent factor in her conduct of affairs. But, realist that she was, she always ultimately sacrificed it to the more obvious interests of her country.

The immediate result of Cateau-Cambrésis was the death of Henry II of France in the tournament which celebrated the peace. His successor, Francis II, fifteen years old, was husband of the seventeen-year old Mary Queen of Scots. Dominated by the great catholic family of Guise, he caused much apprehension in Spain. The duke of Guise and his brother, the cardinal of Lorraine, ruled France; their sister Mary governed Scotland as regent for her daughter; the Guises had thoughts of asserting their protégée's claims to the throne of England. The fear of a French empire stretching from Inverness to the Pyrenees kept Spain on England's side and prevented concerted catholic action against the heretic queen. Elizabeth and Cecil thought themselves reasonably safe from attack across the sea, but the northern border constituted a very imminent danger. Two things helped. In the first place, the French had outstayed their welcome in Scotland. Since 1550, when Northumberland abandoned the policy of Henry VIII, the regent, assisted by French troops and French officials, had ruled that country almost as a province of France. Scottish nationalism, which had frustrated Henry, now turned against the Guises. In this it found an ally in protestantism, for the Guises were the foremost champions of the Counter-Reformation. In December 1557 a number of Scottish lords, calling themselves the lords of the congregation, combined in an association which they named the Covenant. It might be only another of the traditional 'bands' formed by Scots nobles against their feeble monarchs, but it rested on religion and for a century was to be a powerful factor in Scottish politics.

Here was Elizabeth's chance. In May 1559 John Knox was permitted to return through England to Scotland, and wherever he went Rome fell before Geneva. A few months later the queen of England encouraged the Scottish opposition by smuggling out of France and sending north the Hamilton claimant to the Scottish throne, the earl of Arran, after first inspecting and rejecting this incipient lunatic as a candidate for her own hand. The lords of the congregation gathered their forces and attacked the French garrisons. These proved much too strong for the more numerous but untrained Scots, and by the end of 1559 it was clear that the revolt would collapse unless England did more than cheer on from the sidelines. Elizabeth, as always, was hard to persuade into action, but in the end she gave way in the face of the obvious Scottish need, the growing weakness of the Guises in France in face of Huguenot unrest, and the persuasion of Cecil, assisted by the one statesman thrown up by the Scottish lords, Maitland of Lethington. An English squadron under William Winter blockaded the Scottish East coast; an army under Lord Grey de Wilton joined the forces of the Covenant in besieging the French at Leith. Admirably led by the regent, the French resisted the amateurish assaults of Grey and the covenanters, but in June Mary of Guise died and Cecil arrived to see what could be done by negotiation. The result was the treaty of Edinburgh, concluded in July 1560, by which most French troops and all French influence were expelled from Scotland whose government passed into the hands of the lords of the congregation and the protestants—of Lethington and Knox. The Reformation was established, the threat removed; and for the first time in history an English army recrossed the border sped on its way by the cheers and gratitude of the Scottish nation. What centuries of arrogant claims to suzerainty had not been able to achieve was accomplished by community of religion and the reluctantly extorted assistance of the least arrogant English sovereign who ever interfered in Scotland.

Gloomy and hopeful prognostications that Elizabeth had let herself in for trouble were disappointed: France and Spain had been too preoccupied with matters nearer home to intervene—France with the growing divisions between religious parties, and Spain with troubles in the Mediterranean and Burgundian parts of her empire. Yet difficulties of another kind soon threatened. In December 1560 Francis II died, leaving his Stuart wife a mere queen-dowager at eighteen. For the moment the power of the Guises was broken, and her mother-in-law, Catherine de Médicis, had no intention of allowing this daughter of Mary of Guise any further part in French affairs. Reluctantly—for she loved France where she had spent most of her young life and dreaded the gloomy northern kingdom with its Calvinism—Mary turned to go back to Scotland and take up her crown. It remains impossible so to speak about Mary Queen of Scots that all are satisfied; she had to the utmost the Stuart ability of attaching men's loyalties to herself despite the most outrageous and the most foolish of deeds. Of her famous beauty her surviving portraits provide little evidence. She was passionate, wilful, intelligent, given to violent moods of exaltation and depression, and entirely without common sense—one might say, entirely without moral sense. It was too much to expect that this young woman, reminder of the recently overthrown French domination and ardently catholic, should bring peace to the land. Early fears that she would revive the French and catholic policy of her Guise mother were allayed by her readiness to accept the protestant party; Lethington and Lord James Stuart (soon to be earl of Murray) continued her chief ministers, John Knox preached at her in a tactless fashion which has needlessly distressed her sentimental partisans, and she took lessons in Calvinism from George Buchanan. Not religion but dynastic policy was her immediate concern: she wished to assert her claim to the English throne, inherited from Margaret Tudor, daughter of Henry VII who had married James IV of Scotland.

This half-French claimant north of the border drove Elizabeth into the most obvious diplomatic blunder of her reign when she drifted into assisting the Calvinist Huguenots in the first French war of religion, which broke out in 1562. It seemed a good idea to promote protestant revolt in the country which still constituted the gravest threat to her security; it seemed an even better idea to link this help with a revival of claims to Calais and other French territory. Whether Elizabeth herself favoured this extravagance, so much at variance with the moderation displayed in Scotland, is not known: it was bound to be a popular move. In effect it ensured failure. The English did little to affect the war but they occupied Le Havre, and when, after the assassination of the duke of Guise,

Catherine succeeded in opening negotiations for peace, the terms upon which Elizabeth had helped rapidly cemented an alliance between the French parties. Huguenots and catholics combined against the English at Le Havre and expelled them after a gallant defence ill-supported from home. In 1563 Elizabeth replaced her ambassador in France, the violently anti-catholic Throckmorton, by that elderly moderate Sir Thomas Smith who at once entered upon the negotiations which in the end led to England shifting her continental alliance from Spain to France. Her experiences confirmed Elizabeth in her dislike of continental commitments, especially on behalf of Huguenots; the campaign also ended for all time the English ambitions for continental conquest.

The problem of Mary remained. She had to marry: it was expected of every queen, and while Elizabeth showed how the question could stay unanswered, Mary was not likely to remain celibate for long. A plan to give her Philip's degenerate son, Don Carlos, for husband was foiled by England and France together for fear of spreading Spanish influence to Scotland. Elizabeth offered Lord Robert Dudley, created earl of Leicester for the occasion, whom rumour credited with being her own lover; the Scots considered this an insult—which it was. But in 1564 the man was found in Henry Lord Darnley, son of the earl of Lennox and grandson, by her second marriage, of Mary Stuart's own Tudor grandmother. To this vague link with the Tudors Darnley added birth on English soil which, by English law, enabled him to inherit in England, as Mary could not; thus their marriage, following upon Mary's ready falling in love with the tall, handsome man whose contemptible character was not yet known, greatly strengthened the Stuart claim to the English throne. Elizabeth had opposed it and was furious at Mary's defiance; nor did she much welcome the birth of a son, James, in 1566. It was a fateful business. In the short run it destroyed Mary; in the long run it put the Stuarts on the English throne and destroyed the Tudor state. Immediately, however, it reinforced the clamour in England for the queen to marry and settle the succession, for how could protestant England contemplate without horror an heir to the throne who was not only a foreign potentate but also a catholic?

4. MARRIAGE AND SUCCESSION

When Elizabeth came to the throne it was taken for granted that she would soon marry and produce an heir. The need was generally recognised both among the people and in the council.

Yet the problem of where her choice should fall stared them all in the face, for they had just experienced the troubles to which a queen's marriage could lead. Mary Tudor's example was a manifestly bad one, so manifest indeed that one can only wonder at Philip II's effrontery in offering to take the younger sister on as well for the sake of keeping the kingdom. Elizabeth thankfully used his offer to keep him quiet during the critical first months and then turned it down (January 1559); his subsequent marriage to Elizabeth of Valois threatened a Franco-Spanish alliance, but that was an ever-present danger which never materialised. The difficulties which confronted the queen were enormous—bigger than her sister's just because her sister had shown the danger. In the circumstances it was perhaps as well that Elizabeth privately determined never to marry. But while she would not marry, she also would not say so; she had no intention of depriving herself and England of one of the best diplomatic counters available in that age of dynastic marriages. The courtships of Queen Elizabeth were the joke and the despair of her time; we shall only understand them aright if we remember that to her they were not only a substitute for the emotional life which, despite everything, she missed, but also a vital part in the game of international politics, and a part in which she excelled.

Whether she married or not, the succession was a separate problem. As things stood, easily the best claim rested with the Stuarts, and Mary Stuart was not only a catholic but married to the dauphin, soon King Francis II. The Suffolk line, which Henry VIII's will had preferred to the Stuarts, had had its try in the person of Lady Jane Grey; its surviving representative was another woman, Lady Catherine Grey. It is astonishing how everything turned on females, and it was unfortunate that it did, for women claimants meant husbands and difficulties with dynastic marriages. When Catherine Grey clandestinely married the earl of Hertford, son of the Protector Somerset (1561), she became the pawn of a protestant faction in the council (who feared Elizabeth's entanglement with Robert Dudley) and the object of vigorous dislike to the queen herself. The fact that she disliked both Mary Stuart and Catherine Grey played its part in Elizabeth's refusal to contemplate the determination of the succession. A third candidate existed in Henry Hastings, earl of Huntingdon, descended from the Poles; he too was offered as a protestant alternative to the queen of Scots, and he too would have made a plainly unsatisfactory king. The problem thus seemed virtually insoluble. If Elizabeth died the succession would be disputed between several equally impossible claimants; that dispute could only be avoided if the queen agreed to say who should succeed; yet the choice was such that one cannot blame her for not saying. In addition, of course, there was Elizabeth's steadfast and at times almost hysterical refusal even to consider the matter. Judging from some obscure hints dropped by her, her own experience as 'second person' (heir apparent) in Mary's reign had left her deeply reluctant either to saddle herself with a similar incubus or to impose on anyone else the strain of becoming the centre of intrigues against the reigning sovereign. Elizabeth's position is fully understandable; but so is that of her subjects who dreaded the disorders of a disputed, and abominated the probability of a catholic, succession. No one could know that Elizabeth would solve the problem by living long beyond the normal Tudor span.

Though she rebuked the commons in 1559 for presuming to ask her to marry, she proceeded to raise hopes in the years that followed. The earl of Arran was summoned, looked at, and discarded; Philip II's suggestion of a German Habsburg led to negotiations with the Archduke Charles, son of the emperor Ferdinand. A crisis came late in 1560. When Cecil returned from Edinburgh he found himself in disgrace and the queen entirely taken up with Robert Dudley, son of the duke of Northumberland, a handsome vigorous man with very little sense and a lawfully wedded wife. When the latter, Amy Robsart, died in circumstances suggesting murder, it was freely rumoured that Dudley had had her killed with Elizabeth's knowledge so as to clear the way for his marrying the queen. The story—true or not—was enough to make Elizabeth recover her balance, if indeed she had ever lost it. The intimacy with Dudley (soon after created earl of Leicester) simmered down into the ordinary relations of queen and favourite; Cecil recovered control; politics and responsibility had triumphed over a particularly unsuitable infatuation. The contrast with Mary Stuart's later goings-on is instructive. Elizabeth returned to her diplomatic courtships, Eric of Sweden—another incipient madman—being the latest candidate (1561). Then, in the autumn of 1562, Elizabeth fell very ill of the smallpox and nearly died; though she made a surprising recovery, the problem of the succession loomed enormously large when the second parliament of the reign met in January 1563.

There is again no evidence of particular influence being exercised in the elections for this parliament; several new boroughs sent members, being authorised to do so by their recent charters, but this reflected rather the desire of local patrons for representation in the commons than an attempt at packing. The result was as unfortunate as could be. The lords were now a reasonably safe house, for the Anglican bishops supported a government which their popish predecessors had opposed; but in the commons there was a body of some forty or fifty very active members, mostly with puritan sympathies, who dominated the less independent men and were not afraid even of taking issue with the privy councillors who represented the queen and government. The unofficial leader of this 'choir', as a contemporary called them, was Thomas Norton, the first of the great puritan parliament-men and the hero of the two sessions of this parliament. Other business, of course, occupied much time. This was the parliament which passed the great statute of artificers, already mentioned;[1] an important act for poor relief and an attack on the government's right of purveyance absorbed energies; religion and the fear of papists grew vocal. The chief issue was the succession, together with the queen's hoped-for marriage. A new and dangerous phenomenon made its appearance: the leaders of the opposition met privately before and during the session to concert their moves. The consequences were seen in the revolutionary and highly effective tactics employed against the queen—in all loyalty, of course. Elizabeth often denounced, at this time and later, the discussion of affairs of state in taverns and the like; in the same way her father had denounced talk of religion, also without being able to stop it.

Parliament assembled on 12 January 1563; on the 16th a member raised the subject of the succession. On the 26th it was proposed to petition the queen to marry and permit the nomination of a successor. The first part of this request clearly invaded the queen's private life and was therefore improper; the second, however, could be based on the precedents of Henry VIII's reign when parliament several times declared the succession, and even on precedents going back to Henry IV. On the other hand, such action had never been taken except on the initiative of the crown, and Elizabeth had a tolerable case in constitutional law for refusing to allow the matter to be treated in the house. Her real reasons were the political inadvisability and emotional impossibility of a definite statement. The commons on their side were driven by fear of the queen's death into ever more extreme and unrelenting pressure for an answer. Elizabeth received the commons' petition on the 28th and a parallel one from the lords on 1 February; hiding her anger, she promised an answer which she had no intention of giving. Gentle reminders failed to stir her, till on 10

[1] Above, p. 259.

April she came to close the session. Because she could not give a positive reply and would not risk a plain no, she prorogued parliament rather than dissolve it; the speech she made on the subject of the petition is in her best—that is, her most mystifying—vein. She said that the rumour of her determination never to marry was false: 'for though I can think it best for a private woman, yet do I strive with myself to think it not meet for a prince.' Then she turned to the succession, but her words, sonorous though they were, carried no meaning that anyone could get hold of. With this experience of their queen in a mood familiar to her councillors and more familiar still to foreign ambassadors, the commons had for the moment to be content.

Parliament stood prorogued for over three years, an interval during which stories of marriage continued while the succession remained unsettled and the queen of Scots tried to assert her claims. The Archduke Charles's desultory negotiations for Elizabeth's hand carried on until 1567; there was never much in it on either side. A pamphlet war between the supporters of the Suffolk (Grey) line and the Stuart claim exacerbated feelings and annoyed the queen extremely. If she hoped that time would render the 'choir' more amenable she was sadly astray, the more so as these energetic protestants represented a growing public opinion. Finally, in the autumn of 1566, shortage of money—the heritage of her Scottish and French policy—forced Elizabeth to recall parliament. The move was the more dangerous because she was asking for supplies in peacetime, an unpopular step in itself. The houses reassembled on 30 September, the commons having to elect a new Speaker since the old one had died during the recess; this led to a quite unprecedented clash as the opposition challenged the official nominee (Richard Onslow) who was elected by only twelve votes in a house of 152. The real shock came when the government introduced the subsidy bill. On 18 October a Mr Molyneux made his mark in history by proposing to make supply depend on the queen's favourable answer to the three-years-old petition about the succession. Despite all the councillors could do, the house agreed. The lords, asked to co-operate, sent a deputation to the queen which received the full blast of Elizabethan invective. The parliament could do as they pleased; their bills had no effect without her authority. But, surprisingly, the lords stood firm and joined the commons' manœuvre. Elizabeth, deserted by all and pressed on every side, was beside herself, so much so that she even confided her anger and distress to the Spanish ambassador, de Quadra. They would not have dared to treat her father thus, she said with much justification; and she worked off her fury at court where even Leicester discovered that a queen's favour could be withdrawn. But political sense soon overcame mere anger. On 5 November she anticipated further petitions by summoning representatives of both houses and speaking her mind. She would marry, but the time was 'not convenient' for talking of the succession. It was 'a strange thing that the foot should direct the head in so weighty a matter'. She angrily rebutted their fears: 'I care not for death, for all men are mortal.' Nor would she surrender to pressure. 'Though I be a woman, yet I have as good a courage, answerable to my place, as ever my father had. I am your anointed queen. I will never be constrained to do anything. I thank God I am endued with such qualities that if I were turned out of the realm in my petticoat, I were able to live in any place in Christendom.' When she had a mind to, Elizabeth could speak as plainly as anyone.

Unfortunately her speech was watered down by Cecil in his report to the commons who, undeterred, revived the agitation. The queen's patience gave way and she took steps which immediately provoked a major constitutional row—the first of many which in the end led to the breach between the Stuarts and their parliaments. On 9 November she commanded the commons to cease discussion at once and content themselves with her promise to marry. After two days the reply came. Paul Wentworth, burgess for Buckingham, moved three questions to the house. First, was the queen's command 'a breach of the liberty of free speech of the house'? Secondly, was the authority of the privy councillors who had communicated the order sufficient to bind the house? Thirdly, if the command was proper and binding, what offence would it be for a member 'to err in declaring his opinion otherwise' (that is, flatly to contradict the queen)? The house listened approvingly; battle was joined; the specific issue of the succession had led to a wide break between the queen and the commons. Elizabeth repeated her order, with a hint that anyone who disagreed might be summoned to argue the matter before the privy council. She was sure of the lords again, but she underestimated the tenacious courage of the lower house. The commons composed an address which, though humble enough in tone, did not withdraw an inch. They thanked the queen for her promise to marry, stressed that a decision on the succession had only been postponed, and affirmed their right of free speech which they felt sure the queen had never meant to attack. The address was never presented. Elizabeth saw that she had gone too far. Rather than face a real conflict over the liberties of the house she surrendered: on 25 November she graciously revoked her commands. The commons were delighted, especially when she followed this up by stopping proceedings against a member, James Dalton, who had made a speech offensive to the Scottish ambassador and was being examined by the council. Now at last she hoped to get her supplies and, to hurry them up, she remitted one third of the money asked. Cheerful after all their troubles, the commons rapidly passed the bill. However, Norton's 'choir' were not to be caught so easily. As a last attempt to pin the queen down over the succession they proposed a preamble for the subsidy bill which registered the queen's promise to marry and decide her successor. It was a skilful but impudent move. Elizabeth's reaction practically scorched the paper on which she scribbled it: 'I know no reason why any my private answers to the realm should serve for prologue to a subsidies-book . . . if these fellows were well answered and paid with lawful coin, there would be fewer counterfeits among them.' The preamble of the act as passed is short and innocuous.

The memorable session was not yet over; further trouble arose over religion—which shall be dealt with in the next section—and the queen could not be rid of her unwelcome advisers until after Christmas. When she dissolved parliament she made, as usual, a masterly speech, rebuking the forwardness of the commons but also acknowledging their loyalty and good will. The tie between crown and parliament was far from broken, but it had been strained very severely. Elizabeth had had to try every expedient to combat the determined and skilful attack of the commons' leaders. She had used patience with persuasion, to no purpose; she had commanded in her most imperious manner, again without avail; finally she had surrendered, pocketed her pride, given up much needed money, and restored the commons to good humour. On the immediate issue she had won, for the succession was not decided and her marriage remained a promised mirage. But she had experienced a new thing—the opposition of the house of commons on a major matter of state, an opposition well led, well disciplined, and based on principle. Worst of all, she had provoked a quarrel over the privileges of the house. The succession would settle itself as time went on; free speech remained to trouble her and later kings. When Elizabeth had acquired more experience she displayed greater tactical skill: never again would she keep in being a house of commons which had proved as refractory as that of 1563, and in future her calculated and always successful surrenders would be timed better. However, while she could stall opposition on marriage and succession by promises and tactics, she could not put off the problem of the Church in or out of parliament.

5. THE SETTLEMENT SECURED

In 1559 the settlement of the Church seemed satisfactory enough; in 1560 doubts began to appear. There were many, bishops and lesser clergy and laity, who thought the act of uniformity but an interim measure; the queen, on the other hand, held that it embodied the complete system. In the general view of the age all subjects of the imperial crown of England were joined with the holder of that crown in one body politic whose secular aspect might be called state or (more commonly) Commonwealth, while its spiritual aspect was comprised in the Church. In such a body, religious nonconformity was naturally the same thing as political opposition and, in extreme cases, as treason. The issue is confused by the fact that the term Church continued to be used for the clergy only, but that was a loose use. The puritans, or precisians, were not a nonconformist body outside the Church (though in time such bodies arose), but a movement within the Church—comprising both clergy and laity—which desired to 'purify' the Church of popish remnants and render it more 'precise'—like heir ideal of the Early Church, or in effect like Geneva. The radical wing within the Church was a threat to Elizabeth's settlement which had proved its strength in 1559 by bringing the Church more rapidly to a protestant condition than she had hoped. She was therefore compelled to keep a wary eye on the other wing—the conservative, catholic, even Romanist wing. The England which she came to rule was predominently catholic; of this there can be no doubt. Yet by about 1570 the catholics—those that looked to Rome rather than Canterbury—had been reduced to a hard core of no more than 150,000, at which number they roughly remained for the rest of the reign.

The reason for this decline was twofold. On the one hand, the queen's government treated this large body of Englishmen with deliberate and calculated moderation in order not to drive them from the fold. On the other, the catholic powers of Europe, including the pope, who should have succoured the catholics in England, left them in the lurch for over ten years. In that time the catholic cause was lost in England. Philip II at first persisted in treating England as his subject protégé; a papal emissary (Parpaglia) dispatched in 1560 to invite Elizabeth to the Council of Trent was prevented by Philip from crossing the Channel on the ground that he was pro-French, a step which saved the queen much embarrassment. Even as it became plain that the Church of England had broken with Rome for good, both the king of Spain, in the interests of his policy, and the pope (the gentle Pius IV who succeeded the fierce Paul IV in 1559) under Spanish pressure continued in their conciliatory attitude. Pius IV sent another messenger to England in 1561, the abbot Martinengo; since Philip did not oblige by stopping him too, Elizabeth had to show her hand by forbidding him to enter the country. In consequence the pope joined France at Trent in pressing for Elizabeth's excommunication, but Spain and the Empire resisted on the grounds that the sentence would do more harm than good since no one could carry it out. Their attitude was sensible, but it prevented the English catholics from receiving a clear lead from Trent. Since they were given no official indication that Elizabeth was a heretic and her Church damnable, most of them saw no difficulty in compromising their consciences by attending Anglican services. When to this feebleness from abroad there was added the studied moderation of the government at home—refusing to enforce the oath of supremacy too rigidly, careful not to enquire after fines for recusancy (refusal to attend at church) in notoriously catholic districts like Lancashire—the winning over of the catholic majority proved easy. As usual the queen was milder than her council and her parliaments. In 1563, the obstreperous commons forced upon her an act which sharpened the penalties for catholics: to support Rome by word, writing, or deed was made punishable by præmunire, while a second refusal to take the oath was made treason. The queen countered by ordering Parker not to tender the oath a second time, despite the clear tenor of the statute. Skilfully handled by a queen who continued to use cross and candles in her chapel and to drop hints of a possible return to Rome before credulous ambassadors, deserted moreover by their friends abroad, and without priests of their own before 1575, most of the English catholics accepted the new state of things and became Anglicans.

This gentle treatment of catholics naturally exasperated those to whom all Romish things were of the devil. Since the most vigorous and intelligent of the Anglican clergy inclined to puritanism, the bishops, who had to reanimate a Church fallen into deplorable ways of idleness, ignorance, and corruption, were in a quandary. Those clergy who answered to the official standard of behaviour tended to be those who opposed the official policy. In 1562, Bishop Jewel published his *Apology*, the leading defence of the settlement for some thirty years; in it he opposed to the puritan demand for a 'pure' Church on the primitive pattern the argument that the English Church had been rebuilt in accordance both with Apostolic principles and with the best teaching of the Church's history. The controversy came into the open in 1563. In convocation, which met at the same time as parliament, the puritans tried to pass measures making the settlement more radical, but failed. The commons signalled their sympathy by opposing a bill designed to improve the navy because it involved a compulsory fast-day on Wednesdays (to encourage the fishing industry) which they held to be a popish practice. However, the bill passed and 'Cecil's Fast' became law. The positive achievement of 1563 was the passage through convocation of the Thirty-nine Articles, a definition of doctrine based on Cranmer's Forty-two and sufficiently indeterminate to conciliate catholics and exasperate puritans. Even so the queen would not have them enacted by parliament: her diplomacy demanded a free hand.

The French treaty of 1564 and the growing strength of the queen of Scots turned Elizabeth more catholic and drove her into action against the puritans. The occasion of this first overt quarrel was the ornaments rubric of the prayer book which had spoken of the vestments of the second year of Edward VI. It probably meant those of the Prayer Book of 1549 which included not only the surplice but the alb and cope as well. Puritan ministers, on the other hand, objected to all distinctive dress and wished to conduct their services in their plain 'Geneva' gowns. There was thus much failure to conform to the rule, and for some years Parker and the queen shut their eyes to it. But in 1564 Elizabeth ordered action, first against the masters of two Oxford colleges—the universities were the chief breeding grounds of puritanism—and then, in January 1565, a general enquiry into the prevailing laxity. In March 1566 Parker published his *Advertisements*—the queen's refusal to accept responsibility delayed them by two years—in which he laid down rules on costume and other matters connected with worship. The Vestiarian Controversy was joined. It expressed itself in pamphlet warfare and puritan appeals for support from abroad which were unsuccessful: the old high-priest of English nonconformity, Henry Bullinger at Zürich, counselled submission to authority, though Theodore Béza, Calvin's successor at Geneva, was rather more friendly. Parker kept the bishops in line and at their task, and by early 1567 the controversy was over; even London, the centre of puritanism and too gently administered by the sympathetic Grindal, had been compelled to conform. However, the residue was worse than the actual trouble, for the affair left a strong bitterness with many against the bishops. So far English puritanism had not been noticeably anti-episcopalian, but the necessary appearance of the bishops as agents of a policy dubbed popish, and as the agents of the queen with her cross and candles, made them objectionable in the eyes of the precise. Though one could not afford to attack the queen, one could attack the bishops whom the queen herself treated with scant courtesy. The unfortunate prelates, assailed by the puritans, despoiled by the supreme governor and her courtiers, and reviled by Elizabeth both for not acting quickly enough and for acting at all, were the real losers in the controversy.

Defeated in convocation and the pulpit, the puritans took the significant step of transferring their agitation to parliament. In 1566 the long wrangle over the succession and the subsidy delayed matters, but early in December no less than six unofficial bills were introduced, imposing various reforms in the quality and practices of the clergy. The commons dropped all except one which gave statutory authority to the articles of 1563. Elizabeth held firmly to the view that the administration of religion was for the supreme governor with the advice of the clergy in their convocations; parliament could participate only if requested to do so. The opposition in the commons insisted that the precedents of the past thirty-odd years justified parliament in taking the initiative as well. Both sides had a case, the queen's being rather the better as the constitution stood. The issue could not have been made plainer than it was in 1566: Elizabeth had no real objection to the substance of the commons' bill, but she would on no account permit them to discuss religious measures at all. A word of command stopped the bill in the lords; so the commons tried blackmail by holding up a government bill which renewed eleven uncontroversial but necessary acts of the last parliament.[1] Both sides stood firm: the government lost its eleven acts, but the commons lost their bill on religion.

That session of 1566 contained in it all the ingredients of the long struggle between crown and parliament: the fundamental issues (succession, religion), the skilful tactics on both sides, the financial weapon, the sudden concentration on constitutional points and the liberties of the house. Above all it demonstrated

[1] It was common for acts to be made valid until the end of the following parliament, so as to provide a chance for revision; that next parliament would then simply extend the operation of the laws.

the strength of an organised and well-led puritan opposition in the commons and foreshadowed the triumph of puritanism through parliament and the laity rather than through convocation and the clergy. The clergy, so much reduced in numbers since the Reformation had abolished monasticism and the minor orders below deacon, were never again to rule the roost in England; but even as the secular state triumphed it found itself involved in the resurgence of religious feeling which the Reformation produced. The plainly secular Elizabeth could not abide a preaching and mouthing laity, and she seems never to have understood that the strength and toughness of the opposition she encountered derived from the conscience and religion of puritan laymen. There was much wrong with puritanism—it was narrow, intent on inessentials, incapable of generosity or tolerance—but it gave religion a positive content and stiffened character as nothing else could. In the midst of that pushing, self-seeking, and bootlicking society it served a most necessary purpose.

6. THE FALL OF MARY QUEEN OF SCOTS

In 1567 it might seem as though the worst was over; Elizabeth could imagine that she had ridden out the storm. France was fast drifting into civil war, Spain began to be absorbed by rebellious subjects in the Netherlands, in Scotland the catholic claimant to the English throne was being rendered harmless. At home, catholicism was rapidly turning into allegiance to the Church of England and puritanism had been defeated; as for parliament, economy in money and better management of elections might deal with that. In fact, however, the real crisis of the reign was only just approaching. Three events of the next few months laid the foundation for much trouble. Late in 1567 Thomas Cartwright returned to Cambridge, soon to be Lady Margaret professor of divinity and to give English puritanism a new lease of life. In 1568, William Allen, an English exile ultimately to become a cardinal, founded at Douai in the Spanish Netherlands a seminary for the training of missionary priests to keep the faith alive in England. And also in 1568, Mary Stuart was driven from Scotland, to remain a danger and an embarrassment to Elizabeth for close on twenty years.

The Darnley marriage quickly turned out a mistake. That young man, twenty when he became king of Scots, combined in himself all the worst features of the Stuart character—stupidity, arrogance, moodiness, obstinacy, licentiousness, unreliability. Mary's genuine love for him barely survived the year, but it sufficed to infect her with his wilful pride; she altered her sensible policy of peace with the congregation and circumspection towards protestants. In 1565 the earl of Murray, leader of the protestant lords, was forced to flee abroad, and Mary began to display her attachment to catholicism and dislike of the restraint so far put upon her. But in that queen's life politics were ever intermingled with private affairs. Disgusted with her husband, alienated from the Scottish politicians, she began to put her trust in a private secretary, the Italian David Riccio, with whom her relations may have been innocent. Darnley, wild with jealousy, broke into the queen's chamber with a gang, dragged Riccio out, and murdered him (1565). Mary was then with child, the later King James. She determined to be avenged. Dissembling sufficiently to extract from the idiot to whom she was married the details of the affair, she drove out his accomplices and welcomed back Murray. But when the year 1566 proved clearly that Darnley's one remaining usefulness—his help in asserting the Stuart claim to the English throne—was not likely to be great in view of the English parliament's attitude to the succession, his fate was sealed. He fell ill towards the end of the year; in February 1567 his devoted wife conveyed him to the house of Kirk o' Field near Edinburgh and left him there to be murdered and his body blown up with the house by a conspiracy of Scottish lords led by the wildest of them all, James Bothwell. Her complicity in the plot has never been proved or disproved; that she wished Darnley dead and suspected he might not return from Kirk o' Field is the least one must say.

In any case, it was her utterly mad behaviour after the murder that mattered. She allowed herself to be taken by Bothwell to Dunbar where they lived together until he was divorced and they could be married (by protestant rites) in May. This was the end of Mary Queen of Scots. Catholic Europe stood horrified and refused her countenance and assistance. The Scots went further. A murderous and adulterous queen, tainted moreover with the wrong sort of religion, was more than they could stomach. She who has had so many ardent defenders since her death had none to succour her at this critical point in her life, and whatever excuses one might make for the woman none can be made for the queen. Incidentally, her taste and sense must also be impugned, for she married both the imbecile and vicious Darnley and the wild, dissolute, and untrustworthy Bothwell for love. All the Scots factions combined against her. In June she was imprisoned at Loch Leven where she was forced to abdicate in her child's favour and to nominate Murray as regent. Bothwell, true to form, deserted her, fleeing to Denmark. But Mary's spirit was unbroken. Refusing to renounce her third husband, she managed to escape from Loch Leven in May 1568. Her attempt to recover the crown ended in the skirmish of Langside; she fled to England to appeal to Elizabeth for help against those whom she termed rebels.

It is often said that the move showed her open and trusting nature, while the consequences display the dark meanness of Elizabeth. In fact, Mary had nothing else left—Spain and France were still too shaken by her earlier exploits to be friendly—and Elizabeth was put in the most difficult position imaginable. Her deep-seated reverence for royalty inclined her to the side of a sister queen, the more so as Mary had for the time ceased to be a danger. To restore Mary she would have to overthrow her own best friends in Scotland; if she did not assist, she would give ready offence in the rest of monarchical Europe. Small wonder that even her resources of duplicity and procrastination were taxed to the limit. She kept Mary at Carlisle, under the discreet surveillance of that staunch puritan, Sir Francis Knollys, though even he seems to have fallen under the spell of that impossible woman. Elizabeth then proceeded to give vague promises to Mary and to encourage Murray to suppress Mary's partisans in Scotland. What was she to do with the refugee? She could not return her to power in Scotland without ruining the English cause there; she could not let her go to France, as Mary suggested, without reviving the situation of 1560; she could not keep her in England without providing a centre for any disaffection going. Perhaps the second course would have been best, but it would have involved a known risk which she was not prepared to take.

Thus the business dragged on in devious negotiations and spurious promises. In the end Elizabeth offered to hear both sides: the Scottish lords led by Murray were to produce their proofs of murder and adultery against Mary who was to defend herself and give proof of rebellion, not indeed in a formal trial but in a general examination of the case. Commissioners for all three parties—Mary, Murray, and Elizabeth—met first at York and then at Westminster (October-January 1568-9). Murray and Lethington produced the famous 'Casket' letters, documents allegedly found after Mary's flight which proved her to have been Bothwell's mistress and involved in the plot against Darnley even before Kirk o' Field. Whether these letters were genuine or forgeries has become the subject of almost a special branch of historical science; Mary's partisans have of course refused to admit them, but the truth is that they alter matters very little. On no grounds can Mary be absolved of completely reckless and foolish behaviour, and if she was not actually immoral she did her best to appear so. She sacrificed her place, her country, and herself to an exceedingly unprepossessing passion. At Westminster she refused to answer Murray, and Elizabeth in the end declared that no case had been made out against the Scottish lords while that against Mary lacked completeness. It was a damning enough verdict. Murray returned to Scotland as regent; Mary, long since brought south from Carlisle, began her long years in English prison-castles; and Elizabeth had saved the budding unity between the two parts of Great Britain.

She had weathered this particular trouble well enough, but only at the cost of saddling herself with an appalling burden. The queen of Scots had been a nuisance to Elizabeth in Scotland; she was a permanent and lively danger in England. There was always the possibility that she might escape and head a catholic conspiracy; she became the centre, usually innocent, of plot after plot; she caused trouble between Elizabeth and her parliaments. Too fearful of the Stuart claim to send Mary packing, too scrupulous of the divinity inherent in royalty and too averse to bloodshed to countenance either open execution or secret murder, Elizabeth lived for nineteen years under the shadow of her prisoner.

Chapter XI

THE GROWING CONFLICT, 1568-85

FROM the arrival of Mary Stuart in 1568 to the outbreak of war in 1585, England passed through a phase in which international complications played a greater part than ever before. Elizabeth was trying to preserve peace and her freedom of action in a tumultuous situation and without the positive strength which would have enabled her to stand aloof in safety. Her own inability to take a decision and adhere to it, and the growing split in the council between a peace-faction favouring agreement with Spain (Burghley, Sussex, and Crofts) and a war-faction seeking a protestant alliance with Dutch rebels and French Huguenots and moderates (Walsingham, Leicester, and Bedford) weakened the purposes of English policy. Spain was held back from decisive action by difficulties in the Netherlands, while France was kept divided and therefore ineffective by religious and political factions. Scotland, whose unstable politics maintained a Marian party against the successive regents for James VI who necessarily looked to England, added a further complication. A new aggressive policy from Rome and a new ardent protestantism in England raised problems both religious and constitutional at home, while far away from the turmoil, but playing their part in it, English seamen began the great expansion overseas. Elizabeth, Philip, and Catherine de Médicis were all opposed to war but prepared to work against one another behind the scenes in a manner which would have precipitated war at almost any other period of history. These seventeen years are therefore filled with a mass of negotiations, changes of front, agreements made and broken, secret and barely traceable doings, through which it is difficult to thread one's way. In the end, a clear enough situation emerged. England grew stronger as Spain grew weaker; their old friendship vanished as Spain became the champion not only of catholicism but also of Mary Stuart; and the old enmity with France was replaced by a partial though uneasy reconciliation secure enough in France's distracted state to prevent at all times the dreaded catholic alliance against England. When at last war came, in 1585, Elizabeth, Burghley, and Walsingham had brought their country to such strength and into so favourable a position that England could take on and defeat the greatest power of the day.

1. THE END OF THE SPANISH AMITY

From the marriage of Prince Arthur with Catherine of Aragon (1501) to the marriage of Queen Mary with Philip of Spain (1554), the Spanish alliance was the guiding star of English foreign policy. Often endangered and at times apparently dissolved, it had yet recovered time and again under the double stimulus of the cloth trade and French hostility. Not even Elizabeth's deliberate attack on Spanish susceptibilities from 1558 onwards provoked Philip into active enmity; on the contrary, mindful of the Channel route to the Netherlands and yet hopeful of recovering England for the Church and Spain by peaceful means, he played a leading part in shielding her from the consequences of the renewed schism. Nevertheless, throughout the 1560s, events were undermining the amity which had endured so long. Both sides were guilty of acts which in easier conditions and with sovereigns less bent on peace would unquestionably have resulted in war. Elizabeth permitted her subjects to volunteer assistance to the disaffected Netherlands, received the thousands of refugees who fled from the energetic restoration of order by the duke of Alva's 'council of blood', and sheltered the pirates who infested the Channel. Philip, on the other hand, offered secret assistance to the English catholics and permitted the Inquisition to ill-treat protestant Englishmen in the prisons of the New World and of Seville. The Spanish embassy in London became the centre of plots against the government under the egregious de Quadra, ambassador from 1559 to 1566, and—after the tenure of the discreet Guzman de Silva (1566-8)—under the meddling Guerau de Spes (1568-73) who did his successful best to ruin Anglo-Spanish relations. Even the commercial link with the Netherlands weakened as the revolt there gathered force. Under pressure from the Merchant Adventurers, Cecil promoted an attack on Flemish privileges which in 1563-4 led to a temporary interruption of the trade. Calvinist riots in 1566 and Alva's terror in 1567-8 began the ruin of the Flemish economy which was completed by the destruction of Antwerp in the Spanish 'Fury' of 1576. Overshadowing all other disagreements, however, were the English incursions into Spain's cherished monopoly in the New World, culminating for the time being in the treacherous attack on Hawkins and Drake at San Juan de Ulua (September 1568); news of this event had a direct influence on events in Europe.[1]

The arrival of Mary in England opened a new chapter in

[1] For the full story of English maritime expansion see Ch. XII.

relations with Spain. It ended the danger of a vast Guise empire which had kept Philip to his English policy, and it offered an opportunity for a catholic crusade against the heretic queen, the Jezebel of the North. In his endeavour to restore Spanish power in the Netherlands, Alva had run up against the unquestionable if unofficial intervention of England on the rebels' side, and he hoped to use the Spanish Netherlands as a spring-board for a counter-attack. Overt hostile action came first from England: in December 1568, the queen confiscated a large shipment of bullion despatched by Philip's Genoese bankers for the payment of Alva's troops. The ships, which had been driven into English harbours by fear of Huguenot pirates, offered a splendid opportunity for avenging San Juan de Ulua. When she discovered that the treasure would not be Philip's property until it was delivered to Alva, Elizabeth promptly borrowed it herself from the Genoese and thus forestalled all Spanish protests. Alva nevertheless replied with an embargo on all trade with England and seized English goods; Cecil in turn imposed heavy penalties and seized all Spanish property. In this game Alva was the loser by a margin, but both sides soon had reason to regret it. It was, however, highly significant of the true power and position of the two contestants that England's apparently irresponsible act led to nothing more than a five years' interruption in the Flanders trade.

Unwilling to risk war, Spain had to rest satisfied with fomenting and supporting English discontent which came to a head in the three years' crisis of 1569-72. De Spes, in touch with Mary Stuart and with a set of disgruntled noblemen led by the duke of Norfolk and the earl of Arundel, wrote wildly optimistic letters to Alva in which he demanded assistance for plot after plot whose folly and lack of substance were more sensibly assessed by that great soldier. The Norfolk faction had several grievances of which the main seems to have been hatred of the upstart Cecil. Through Roberto Ridolfi, a Florentine merchant settled in England, they approached de Spes early in 1569 with suggestions for the overthrow of Cecil, the subjugation of Elizabeth to their will, the restoration of catholicism, and the proclamation of Mary as heir to the throne. Unconvinced by de Spes' imaginative description of masses of English catholics only waiting for liberation, Alva refused to move until the conspirators could show some concrete result; the plot collapsed. Norfolk, the only duke in England and very conscious of the difference between his pretensions and his position, was a vain and feeble man, too ready to enter into secret machinations and equally ready to desert them in a panic. He hoped to marry Mary himself, but though the council was not opposed the queen put a stop to the idea. The duke fled to his Norfolk estates, intending to rise in conjunction with the earls of Northumberland and Westmoreland who had grievances of their own. Then, in September 1569, he was summoned to London and his courage left him; he tamely surrendered to the government and sent a soothing message north.

There, however, events were in the hands of more resolute men. The north had not forgotten the pilgrimage of grace, though it seems to have forgotten the outcome of that brave enterprise. Since Cromwell's death, the border country had tended more and more to fall back into magnate hands; Sussex, as president of the council of the north, found himself almost unsupported when the crisis came. The word of a Percy, a Neville, or a Dacre still counted for much more than the word of a Tudor. At this time the heads of these houses had special grievances whose character may be illustrated by the fact that Northumberland especially resented his loss of a valuable copper mine to the queen. Religion played little part in the disaffection, though it supplied a useful cloak. It would appear that the earls' plans for a rising had almost been put by even before Norfolk's arrest, but when Elizabeth then summoned Northumberland and Westmorland to London fear revived the movement. The earls called out their followers, entered Durham Cathedral where they said mass and tore up the English Prayer Book and Bible, and marched south with their demands. Catholicism was to be restored, Cecil brought to trial, Norfolk freed, and Mary (restored to Scotland) recognised heir to the English throne. Their attempt to liberate Mary was frustrated when the government rapidly removed their prisoner from Tutbury. Before the gathering forces of the queen the rebel host melted away; the leaders escaped into the Scottish borders. A belated rising by Leonard Dacre was destroyed by Lord Hunsdon. The north was swept by the queen's vengeance: some 800 men, all of little account, suffered death. Though the rising of the earls seemed a serious matter at the time, it really ended feudalism in the north. Exile, executions, and confiscations broke it, and under its new president, the puritan earl of Huntingdon, the reconstituted council of the north set about its task of wiping out the line of the Trent which since the Norman Conquest had divided England into two markedly different halves.

The government's victory had in part been eased by Alva's refusal to accept the rebels' offer of Hartlepool as a port of entry, but more important still had been the support given to Elizabeth by Murray, the Scottish regent. It will be as well to anticipate a little in order to explain how this northern 'postern gate' of Scotland, as Walsingham called it, came to be secured in the next few years. Murray was assassinated in January 1570, in the middle of the northern troubles, and there seemed a danger of the Marian party gaining the upper hand. However, with English support, successive regents—first Lennox, then Mar, and finally Morton—maintained the Anglophil protestant rule which Elizabeth desired, so that by February 1573 Mary's supporters had shrunk to a small force holding Edinburgh Castle. This happy development saved Elizabeth from a bad stain on her reputation because it rendered unnecessary a plan for handing Mary over to Mar who was to have her executed; before Mar's scruples (and Morton's after him—Mar died in October 1572) could be overcome, the dispersal of Mary's faction ended the civil war in Scotland. An English force was needed to compel the surrender of the Edinburgh garrison, but once this was achieved in May 1573 Scotland ceased to be a threat. Morton's interests were closely linked with England, and though Elizabeth's parsimony made it impossible to bind the Scots nobles firmly to the English interest by the only means they acknowledged—frequent bribes—the 'postern gate' was now in reasonably friendly hands.

The failure of the northern rebellion was a bad blow to Guerau de Spes whose activities in the matter had already attracted the attention of the English government. Reluctant as Cecil was to break with Spain, even he had to acknowledge the unlikelihood of enduring peace. It therefore became necessary for England to prepare for the worst by seeking better relations with France. Since the treaty of 1564, civil war in France had prevented true amity between the catholic Valois and the protestant Tudor. A chance of better things came in 1570 when the peace of St Germain ended the third war of religion and freed Elizabeth from the—to her—unpleasant necessity of supporting the Huguenots, rebels as they were but after all protestants and enemies to Spain, against their lawful king. Charles IX now called the Huguenot leader, the Admiral Coligny, into his council, while Catherine de Médicis began to listen favourably to the suggestion from England that Elizabeth might find her long desired husband in Catherine's second son, the duke of Anjou. In 1570 Francis Walsingham entered upon his long and distinguished career when he was dispatched to France to conduct the negotiations for an alliance and marriage. Since both Elizabeth and Catherine were pastmasters in procrastination, reversals of policy, and dark ways, the negotiations dragged on interminably. Elizabeth for a time maintained the pretence of wanting to marry Anjou, but ended the matter when it suited her by refusing any concessions in religious matters to this most bigoted of the Valois. Walsingham, greatly discouraged, nevertheless continued the negotiations for an alliance, and his endeavours resulted at last in the treaty of Blois (April 1572) by which the two countries bound themselves to mutual defensive assistance. The treaty, soon rendered nearly valueless by events, was nevertheless something of an achievement. At a critical time it removed all danger of a general continental alliance against England to carry out the bull of excommunication and deprivation which the pope had issued in 1570.[1]

The Anjou courtship had served to keep France friendly at a time when Cecil was wrestling with the most serious threat arising out of the northern rebellion and Spanish animosity. This was the so-called Ridolfi plot. Ridolfi—one of those business men who long to manipulate the strings of state affairs—had had a hand in the abortive plotting of 1569, and he took the opportunity of Norfolk's release from the Tower (August 1570) to renew his machinations. Travelling to and fro between England and the continent, he spun a somewhat unsubstantial web round a projected rising which was to get rid of Elizabeth and put Mary, married to Norfolk, on the throne of England. Mary, the bishop of Ross (her agent in France), Philip, the pope, and Norfolk were all involved; Alva alone remained sceptical. Cecil soon received information from such divers places as Scotland and Tuscany, and by September 1571 all the details had been secured by threats and torture. Nearly every conspirator—the queen of Scots leading —hastened to throw the onus on someone else. Norfolk was re-arrested, tried for treason, and sentenced to death (January 1572), but Elizabeth's reluctance to execute England's premier nobleman preserved his life for some months. However, in May 1572 parliament took a hand. The country was deeply stirred by the revelations of treason and danger to the queen, and the puritan faction did not hesitate to point out that none of this would have occurred but for the existence of Mary Stuart, herself heavily implicated. The demand was raised for her death as well as for the carrying out of the sentence on Norfolk. In the prolonged debates that followed, these partisans of Elizabeth soon found themselves gravely at odds with the object of their solicitude. But though the queen resisted even at the risk of another clash with the commons, she had to accept a compromise in the end. Mary

[1] See below, p. 303.

she saved, but Norfolk went to the block in June, victim of his weak vanity and irresolute ambition rather than of more positive and more dangerous qualities.

The crisis thus passed away in the summer of 1572, except that trade with the Netherlands was still at a standstill. The queen's enemies at home were down, her friends in Scotland were improving their position, France had signed a treaty, even Spain seemed ready for peace. In March 1572, ostensibly to conciliate Philip, Elizabeth ordered the closing of English ports to the Dutch 'sea-beggars'. Their leader, La Marck, Orange's admiral in theory and pure pirate in practice, thereupon descended upon the port of Brill. Its capture gave the rebels their first foothold on Spanish territory and immediately provoked a widespread revolt in the northern Netherlands. Town after town threw off the Spanish rule, until four of the thirteen provinces stood united under William of Orange. The revolt of the Netherlands was to provide the chief problem of international politics for the next sixteen years, as well as Elizabeth's best chance of fighting Philip by proxy. It does not seem likely—despite argument and some dubious evidence to the contrary—that she intended any such consequences when she expelled La Marck, but the result was bound to be pleasing though often perplexing.

However, the immediate outcome was to weaken the new alliance with France. In pursuance of Coligny's Huguenot policy, and cheered on by Walsingham, Charles IX encouraged a Huguenot raid into the Spanish Netherlands which was cut to pieces by Alva in July 1572. A violent revulsion at once took place. In order to save himself from war with Spain, Charles deserted Coligny, fell back upon the Guises, and permitted the carrying out of his mother's violent plans which culminated in the massacre of St Bartholomew in August. Walsingham was distraught and England horrified. The plaudits of the catholic world, from the pope downwards, confirmed the worst fears of Englishmen: this was the sort of thing they could expect if Rome and Mary Stuart triumphed. The massacre renewed the religious wars in France and revived Elizabeth's difficulties: she could not afford either to abrogate the treaty of Blois or to desert the Huguenots on whose aid she relied to keep France away from Spain. She did the customary thing by secretly assisting La Rochelle while publicly remaining neutral. Time eased the situation, though the massacre was never forgotten. In 1573, Charles IX made peace after failing to capture La Rochelle and resumed friendly relations with England. As usual, these were expressed in a courtship: the suitor now was the duke of Alençon the youngest of Catherine's sons. For the moment little came of this because Alençon involved himself in domestic intrigues and landed in prison (1574), but the suit was to be resumed later and afford Europe years of incredulous amusement. Also in 1574 Charles IX died; his brother Henry III (late the duke of Anjou) was expected to give rein to his known fanatical catholicism, but in the end, after much trouble and further secret assistance from England to the Huguenots, he confirmed Blois and received the Garter (April 1575). If less of an ally than had seemed likely in 1572, France was yet no enemy, and new internal disruptions were to prolong her inability to intervene in European affairs.

With Spain, too, Elizabeth now came to terms. One of the hopes of Blois had failed to bear fruit. It had been planned to transfer the centre of the cloth export from Antwerp to France, but French jealousy of English merchants and the lack of Antwerp's facilities prevented the trade from expanding. With the clothiers' lamentations at their 'lack of vent'—their inability to find a market—dinning in his ears, Burghley was eager to restore normal traffic. Alva had been ready for some time, but the plots encouraged by de Spes (who was expelled in 1572) had delayed matters. Finally Burghley, opposed to Leicester's French policy, recovered his ascendancy in the council with the news of the massacre and promoted better relations with Spain. The resumption of traffic was followed by a general settlement of the rival claims arising out of the confiscations of 1568-9 in the treaty of Bristol (August 1574), and by an agreement with Alva's successor Requesens be which the Spaniards expelled the English refugees from thy Netherlands and Elizabeth closed her harbours to Dutch rebels and forbade Englishmen to assist them in any way (March 1575). It was not to be a lasting agreement, but it once again postponed the conflict which men like Walsingham thought to be not only inevitable but even desirable. Spain needed a respite to deal with the Netherlands; as for England, she could well do with more years of preparation if the panic of July-October 1570 is anything to go by. In those months the double passage up and down Channel of a Spanish convoy escorting Philip's bride to Spain caused the calling out of the fleet and the musters at an expense which—in view of Elizabeth's feelings on that point—measures the depth of the scare. More particularly, Elizabeth and her government wanted a rest from involvements abroad because they needed time and a free hand to guard the Church at home against attacks from both sides.

2. THE CATHOLIC THREAT

The various scares and plots of the years 1569-72 have so far been viewed as accidental to a general problem of foreign policy, but they were this largely because they arose out of the first positive reaction from Rome to the English schism. This was the bull *Regnans in Excelsis*, proclaiming Elizabeth's excommunication and deposition, which Pope Pius V issued in February 1570. In many ways it was an unfortunate document. It was incorrect in canon law, inasmuch as it failed to give Elizabeth a chance to defend herself and pronounced the deposition at once instead of letting a year pass after excommunication; the explanation that Elizabeth was only a 'pretended' queen was made nonsense of by the recognition she had received from Rome between 1559 and 1570. The bull displayed a painful ignorance of English affairs, denouncing Elizabeth for taking a title (supreme head) which she had been careful to avoid. The pope published it without reference to Spain, thus depriving himself of the only champion remotely capable of executing it; Philip was greatly annoyed both at the bull and at the discourtesy to himself. Pius V, an austere and passionate Dominican, acted from conviction rather than sense. Political considerations did not enter his head: he did what he thought his duty against the heretic queen, but he did it with a precipitancy and neglect of proper form which gave men a chance of evading the issues he had raised. In the event Elizabeth had little difficulty in representing the pope as the aggressor, a view still held by reputable historians. Yet the truth is that Rome had valiantly ignored a series of blatant defiances and concealed attacks: for over ten years catholicism had been outlawed in England, and though the government were careful to mitigate the rigour of the law in its execution it is impossible not to admit that Rome had a real grievance and had at first shown much misguided patience. The rash, ill-conceived, and far-reaching step of February 1570 reversed the position.

The bull declared Elizabeth excommunicate, called upon all faithful sons of the Church to remove her, and absolved Englishmen from their oath of allegiance. It therefore contained a threat to the queen's position which was quite decisive if the pope found anyone to carry it out. This explains the fears of that summer of 1570 when a Spanish armament sailed down the Channel: it was thought, with some reason, that Philip had come to put the bull into effect. It explains the activities of Ridolfi, the plots of de Spes, the hopes of Mary and the fears of Cecil. It explains Walsingham's desire for a protestant alliance to forestall the dreaded association of Guisard France with Habsburg Spain and Burgundy which must destroy England. It explains Elizabeth's reaction to the massacre of St Bartholomew which was generally thought to be the first step in a concerted catholic action against all protestant countries. In reality the situation was nothing like as dangerous. Philip had always had his doubts about the possibility of carrying out a sentence of excommunication and deprivation; he had stopped Pius IV from passing one in the early 1560s and he was rendered no readier to act as the papacy's secular sword by Pius V's single-handed proceedings. France, whether under the direction of Coligny or Guise or Catherine de Médicis, was too distracted and too persistently distrustful of Spain to become an effective partner in a crusade. In effect, the bull fell flat. When the great attack at last came, in 1588, it was barely remembered and played a very minor part. As far as rousing Christendom against the defiant heretic was concerned, Pius V had flung his bolt in vain.

But the bull had its effects—in England. It involved the English catholics in a dreadful dilemma by ending the long years of compromise. The pope's claim to be able to absolve subjects from their allegiance struck at the core of the national state. A man was now virtually compelled to choose between his country and his religion, a choice which, of course, was at the heart of the whole struggle between Reformation and Counter-Reformation. Adherence to the queen meant denial of the bull and the papacy; obedience to Rome meant rejection of Elizabeth and active or passive treason. Most Englishmen, even those who still cherished the old faith, chose the side of the state, seizing eagerly on the technical shortcomings of the bull to save their consciences or taking the step over to the national Church. The government, however, could not afford to wait upon the event. All those who acknowledged the authority of Rome in any particular were now potentially hostile to the state and would have to be dealt with accordingly. The bull ended the period of temporising and the queen's hope of gradually making the Anglican Church comprehensive. From 1570 onwards the number of English catholics altered little, for those who stayed with Rome now chose deliberately. The stragglers, the compromisers, the many who had contrived to think little about it, dropped off.

But if the pope had hoped to rouse the mass of the nation against a heretic and excommunicate queen, he was quickly disappointed. At Rome, and up to a point also in Spain, English affairs were seen through the eyes of the catholic refugees most of whom had fled the country before 1567-8 when the dangers created by Mary Stuart and the Spanish quarrel induced the government to intensify its control over disaffected subjects. Assisted by the fantastic miscalculations of men like de Spes and Ridolfi, these exiles spread the impression abroad that England was ready to revolt and only waiting for a clear call. Instead the nation expressed its passionate revulsion against a hostile power which threatened to break the bonds between ruler and ruled. The bull's clauses shocked a nationalist and king-worshipping generation; from it dates the instinctive English reaction which equates popery with subtle and poisonous treason. The feeling found expression in the parliament of 1571. Led by the puritans, recovering under the Roman stimulus from their earlier defeats, the commons demanded legislation more vigorous than the queen would allow, though the council were on the commons' side rather than hers. An act was passed making it treason to introduce or publish any papal bulls in England, but only the queen's opposition prevented further statutes which, by vastly increasing fines for recusancy and compelling attendance once a year at the Anglican communion, would have rendered the lot of English catholics desperate. Another act deprived of their property all those who had fled abroad and failed to return within a year. The law of treason was reinforced by a third act which included in the offence any affirmation that Elizabeth was not queen or was a heretic and schismatic; the opposition wished specifically to deprive the Stuarts of the succession but failed. The uncovering of the Ridolfi plot added fuel to the flames in the next parliament, but Elizabeth continued to stand out against parliamentary interference.

The queen had shown her attitude: she still refused to admit the conflict to be inevitable. She would punish all those who actively threatened her and her realm, but she would not force her loyal subjects into a choice which might lead many of them into an opposition they did not desire. This policy might have been successful but for one thing: the English catholics were at last about to receive succour and spiritual guidance from abroad through the missions of catholic priests which from 1575 added so romantic—but also so important—an element to the great jurisdictional quarrel. In 1568 William Allen founded his college at Douai in the Netherlands for the training of priests to go and maintain the faith in heretic England. The seminary flourished with the influx of young and ardent students from England and under the guidance of a man who, though clumsy in politics, was a great teacher. After Requesens had been forced to expel the exiles they settled down at Rheims whence their most lasting achievement—an English translation of the Vulgate—derives its name of the Rheims Bible. In 1579, another college was founded at Rome; it soon came under the sway of the Jesuit order and produced, by a most carefully planned and rigorous course of training, a succession of men longing for martyrdom at the hands of the heretic government. Other colleges grew up later in Spain. The whole movement was a testimony to the vigour of English catholicism and to the efficiency of Allen's and the Jesuits' single-minded training. The Douai and Rheims priests first landed in 1575 and rapidly established contact with catholic families eager for the ministrations of which they had been deprived since 1559, but it was after the arrival of the Jesuits from 1580 onwards that the missions achieved their great successes. They made few converts: the numbers of English catholics did not increase. But they arrested their decline and ended the government's hopes of destroying popery and drawing all Englishmen into the English Church. By their vigorous opposition to all compromise, their denunciation of the lax practices of semi-conformity which had grown up in the priest-less years, the missionaries consolidated the catholic minority into a body able to survive persecution and erected a firm barrier between the Churches of Rome and Canterbury.

The missionaries' first task was a spiritual one, and they and their later defenders claimed that they confined themselves to it. Elizabeth and her government naturally saw it differently. Popish priests were popish as well as priests: they were bound to support the policy of the bull—which was treason. It is certain now that the English government's natural suspicions—that the priests acted as political agents stirring up disaffection—were unjustified. Their instructions ordered them not to meddle in politics, to avoid talk against the queen, and not to permit such talk. The missions were not supposed to carry out the bull. Nevertheless, they could not avoid the subject. If they were asked point-blank by their flock how a man was to reconcile his duty to God and his loyalty to the queen they could only evade the question—a difficult thing to do which might lose them influence—or admit the necessity of pursuing the overthrow of Elizabeth. The problem was a very real one, and the first Jesuit missionaries, Robert Parsons and Edmund Campion, raised it at Rome before their departure for England (1580). Gregory XIII, Pius V's successor, replied that the bull was not binding on catholics until it could be executed; thus obedience to the state in power was not to lead to spiritual censures despite the clear tenor of the bull. This sophistry provoked much scorn and subsequent heartburning, but it did save the English catholics from an intolerable position (into which, of course, they had first been pitchforked by Rome) and the priests from having to pronounce on political issues. It also made more difficult the task of the government in repelling the missions.

Throughout the 1570s and 1580s the persecution of catholics—'mass-priests' and their aiders and abettors—went on with growing vigour. Before 1580 priests could be charged with having brought in the bull and therefore with having committed treason under the act of 1571; the first martyr of the missions, Cuthbert Mayne, suffered for this in 1577. Few of those who landed in the creeks and on the deserted foreshores of southern, eastern, and western England escaped the government for long; the protestant zeal of magistrates and the self-interest of informers saw to that. The missionaries came to glory in martyrdom, and the English government—after vain attempts to moderate the rigour of the law—obliged. Elizabeth always claimed that no one was persecuted in England for his religion: the trials of catholic priests were always for treason. It was a sound enough argument on the surface, but specious withal; for the priests did not in fact commit treason except inasmuch as they were priests, and therefore, though Englishmen, emissaries of a foreign power. After Gregory XIII's decision on the bull it was no longer so easy to try them under the act of 1571, and the usual charge became one of conspiring against the queen, which was thought proved if the accused could be shown to have come from Rome or Rheims. At a time when the threat of foreign invasion seemed always about, when the presence in the realm of Mary Stuart encouraged frequent plots endangering both the life of the queen and the safety of the state, the government could act in no other way. But it had to twist the law to do it, and the men it caught were the victims of political issues in which, deliberately but of course unavailingly, they endeavoured not to engage. Edmund Campion, the most saintly and most attractive of all the Jesuit missionaries, was executed in 1581 for treason committed by simple adherence to the queen's enemies (under the basic treason law of 1352); although he had done nothing except preach the faith, he had clearly adhered to the pope who was pursuing an active war against England. Parsons, a much abler and more dangerous but also much more dubious character, escaped to carry on the war from Rome and Spain by pamphlets and intrigues. An act of 1581 heavily increased the fines for recusancy to £20 and made it treason to convert and be converted to Rome.

The last provision was designed to catch the missionaries now that the bull had dropped out of the argument; it preserved the political character of the persecution by expressly equating conversion with withdrawal of allegiance. Some 250 men died altogether in the reign for the catholic faith—or for treason, according to the point of view—and of them over fifty died in prison. The numbers are very small by sixteenth-century standards and no other contemporary government bothered to keep inveterate opponents alive in permanent imprisonment, as did that of Elizabeth when it created a special depository of priests at Wisbech in Norfolk. This was part of the policy which tried to make the recusants a profit to the state by touching their pockets rather than martyrs by seeking their deaths: it, too, was at most moderately successful in protecting the realm against Rome. Enough died, and more suffered torture and barbarous treatment in the course of the persecution, to remind us that we are dealing with a life-and-death struggle in which many very ugly weapons were freely employed by both sides.

A few attempts were made by the papacy itself to give effect to the bull by direct action. In 1572 the ardent and unpolitical Pius V was succeeded by Gregory XIII, as determined to extinguish heresy and recover the Western world for Rome but less troubled by moral scruples about the means employed. He was always hatching plots, planning action, driving others to take up the sword for Rome, but he displayed no ability to develop a single effective scheme. Rashness and foolish optimism characterised all his doings, and his impulsiveness—as in his 'explanation' of the bull in 1580—destroyed much of the moral basis on which the papacy might have acted. He saw the value of the Jesuit missions and encouraged them, but he wanted more immediate and more warlike results as well. The powers having shown themselves unready or unable to carry the crusade into Elizabeth's country, the pope himself undertook the fitting out of expeditions to carry out the *empresa*—the enterprise against England—of which papal and Spanish documents are full. He got his chance through the condition of Ireland where Elizabeth's policy of continuing the subjection of the country had roused savage opposition led by James Fitzmaurice, a Geraldine of the unruly province of Munster. Failing to secure Spanish help, Fitzmaurice went to Rome, and in 1578 an expedition was despatched by Gregory. Its leader, Sir Thomas Stukeley, one of the most extraordinary figures of the day, was an English renegade who had led a brilliant and adventurous military career all over Europe. He had had a hand in Irish troubles before this, had fought at Lepanto, had won and lost the confidence of Philip II. Gregory, sanguine and eager as usual, fell under Stukeley's spell, but the adventurer promptly diverted the papal armament to assist Portugal in Morocco (where he died at Alcazar) and the expedition came to nought. In 1579, however, Fitzmaurice himself, accompanied by the propagandist Nicholas Sanders as legate, landed with a scratch force at Smerwick in Ireland. For some time it looked as though a successful revolt might be raised, though Fitzmaurice was soon killed; Spanish reinforcements arrived in 1580, and Sanders was turning Irish hostility to England into zeal for the Church. But late in the year the English deputy (Grey de Wilton) captured Smerwick, putting to death as pirates the Spanish troops who had held it—for Philip had disowned them. That was the end of the last independent action by the papacy. Grey's savagery at Smerwick was justified by the law and standards of the time, though it was far from commonly copied: it shows starkly the state of mind into which these religious wars were driving all nations.

The hopes of Rome thus once again concentrated on Spain on the one hand and on the missions on the other. Spain was tardy, and the devoted priests were suffering terrible losses: Rome's hopes did not stand very high in the early 1580s. The priests are the more to be pitied because in fact they were pursuing a hopeless quest. They never touched more than a minority of Englishmen, and of that minority few only would in the last resort put their faith before their country. Throughout those years the international situation was growing darker and the name of Spain more obnoxious to Englishmen. When the crisis came the country stood united behind Elizabeth: the first thirty years of her reign, by preserving the peace and by judiciously mingling severe repression with prudent blindness to evasions, gave back to England a solid unity which she had not known since Henry VIII broke with Rome. To English catholics the failure of the Armada was only a sign that Spain was not God's chosen instrument, a point which they had long suspected. The catholic attack preserved the catholic faith in England, but it failed to shake the protestant state and in fact assisted, by reaction, in the growth of a more ardent and uncompromising protestantism.

3. THE GREAT AGE OF ELIZABETHAN PURITANISM

As has been seen, the Vestiarian Controversy ended in the technical defeat of the puritan opposition, but the real losers were the bishops and with them discipline in the Church. After 1568 the queen's preoccupation with the catholic threat gave the puritans a breathing space, while their denunciation of popish ways and their attacks on popish remains in the Church of England attracted to their side those who thought the protestant settlement in danger. For a time, the extreme wing of the Church seemed to represent all that was best and most principled in it; the moderates seemed too lukewarm, too tarred with the brush of Rome. Thus the movement for purifying the Church revived, and more and more voices were raised against the shortcomings of pluralist, worldly, and unlearned clergy. In their struggle the ecclesiastical radicals found allies in the press and in parliament; until the imposition of a stricter censorship in 1586 puritan pamphlets and manifestoes flooded the country, and every meeting of parliament offered an opportunity for airing puritan views and putting forward puritan bills for Church reform. The council was either indifferent or downright friendly: Leicester and Walsingham both favoured puritanism, the former probably because it demanded the war with Rome in which he hoped to distinguish himself. Sir Francis Knollys and Sir Walter Mildmay, privy councillors and regular government representatives in the commons, were of the same colour. The queen continued to abominate puritanism, an attitude in which she probably represented the views of the inarticulate majority of the people rather than those of the educated and politically active minority. In these years between the bull and the Armada puritanism had its ups and downs, but in the end it was shown to have lost the battle for control of the Church and to have won a substantial and highly significant following in the lay gentry. Kept out of the higher ranks of the Church and driven from official place, the puritan ministers found refuge in the chaplaincies and rectories which puritan gentlemen or municipalities like the city of London bestowed on them.

The most significant development in puritanism was its closer definition. It had hitherto been a somewhat amorphous movement, gaining cohesion from a general opposition to things thought popish, and it had therefore expressed itself in quarrelling over such inessentials as vestments and church ornaments. For another dozen years there were many both clergy and lay who thought that the Church needed reform and wished to alter some of its practices, but who stopped short of adopting the full Calvinist theology and constitution. By the side of this moderate puritanism there grew up after 1568 a definitely presbyterian movement—a movement, that is, which wished to reform the Church by abolishing bishops and putting in their place the Genevan system of government by ministers and elected elders, through a hierarchy of synods ranging upwards from local congregational bodies to a national assembly. The English prophets of this movement were Thomas Cartwright and Walter Travers, and its organisers were the young London ministers John Field and Thomas Wilcox. Cartwright, a Cambridge don of great influence in his circle, was appointed Lady Margaret professor of divinity in 1569. He devoted his courses to a general attack on the constitution of the English Church, fell out with John Whitgift, the master of his college (Trinity), and went into exile at Geneva. Refreshed by draughts from the fountain-head he returned just in time to join Field and Travers in the preliminary manœuvres before the session of 1572. These culminated in the publication of the *First Admonition to the Parliament* (June 1572) which attacked the state of the Church and asked parliament to introduce the Genevan model of discipline and government as the only one properly based on Scriptural authority. A shrewd and passionate appeal, it led to a prolonged pamphlet warfare, with Whitgift's *Answer*, Cartwright's *Reply*, and a *Second Admonition*. The presses on which this puritan propaganda was printed were secret, but so far the government's censorship could not prevent a liberal output of hostile writings. Direct methods proved more effective: Cartwright was once more driven from England in 1573, and Travers followed him a year later. They continued to put out numerous pamphlets and books defending the presbyterian system and attacking episcopacy; of these, the most significant was Travers's *De Disciplina Ecclesiastica*, a detailed exposition of presbyterianism with its organisation of ministers, deacons, and ruling elders, which remained the text-book of English presbyterians. Edmund Dering, the most outspoken preacher of his time who had not hesitated to accuse the queen to her face of permitting the abuses with which he charged the clergy and the patrons of livings, died in 1576; Field and Wilcox confined themselves to parish duties; the vigorous leadership of extreme puritanism was dispersed.

The movement then entered a new phase. Militancy, nourished by the catholic plots of 1569-72, had failed to carry the Church by storm; now moderate means, well disguised as merely moral reform, were to attempt the conversion of the Church from within to a quasi-presbyterian condition. The chance offered because in 1575 Matthew Parker died, after sixteen years of honest and diligent labour in the service of a queen who had done her best to render his task of establishing uniformity difficult by her delays and her failure to back him up. The obvious successor, Cox of Ely, was married and therefore anathema to the queen; the choice fell in 1576 on Grindal of York, a man who since his Strassburg days under Queen Mary had displayed a consistently mild temper and a readiness to approve of the reforming ideas of puritans. It was a serious mistake to make and one that surprises, for Elizabeth rarely picked the wrong man. Grindal was at once confronted with a development among certain of the clergy which went by the name of 'prophesyings'. These were regular meetings to expound the Scriptures with discussions on the expositions offered. Round them there might grow up, as there did at Northampton, a virtually puritan cell within the Church, supported by the lay magistrates and spreading Calvinist teaching among clergy and laity alike. To Grindal, the movement seemed innocuous and even meritorious, for it certainly helped to bring learning and skill in preaching to a clergy who were in general notoriously deficient in both. The archbishop wished to encourage the spread of such spontaneous reform; the queen who, with much justification, suspected the seeds of a presbyterian organisation ordered him to prohibit prophesyings. He refused, respectfully but definitely, and in June 1577 he was suspended from the exercise of his authority. To have publicly removed him would have caused a scandal which the Church could not afford; in the event Canterbury remained virtually vacant till Grindal died in 1583, on the point of at last resigning. In the meantime, disorder reigned. Some bishops, especially John Aylmer of London, the centre of puritanism, did something to enforce conformity, but others encouraged the prophesyings. The council continued to give support to moderate puritanism behind the queen's back, while Elizabeth insisted on not being involved actively at all despite her strong opinions on the subject.

The dangers of weakness were shown in the rise of a further division with the growth of separatism, a movement affecting individual congregations who wished to elect their own ministers and pursue their own way to salvation without any superior authority. There had been such bodies in the London of the 1560s; in 1581, a more serious deviation occurred at Norwich under Robert Browne and Robert Harrison. Browne, a preacher and pamphleteer of great ability, had hopes of converting the whole Church to congregationalist ideas but had to be content with leading a separatist movement. Here the authorities did not hesitate, for neither Anglicans nor presbyterians had any sympathy with splinter groups. The Brownists were driven to take refuge at Middelburgh in Holland (1582) where the inherent instability of such organisations soon produced quarrels. Excommunicated by his own Church and badly disillusioned, Browne retired into a country parish in England where he spent forty-two conforming years (1591-1633) to live down his revolutionary past. But his example survived his retirement. Brownists were soon rivalled by Barrowists, the followers of Henry Barrow of London who actively organised separatist groups from his prison where he spent seven years before he was hanged in 1594 for sedition. Separatist groups were to have a great future, to dominate puritanism in the next century, and—as Independents—to win the civil war and set up their own government in England, but under Elizabeth their influence and importance were small.

In any case, the government turned to a more energetic repression of nonconformity from about 1580 onwards. In that year the various ecclesiastical commissions, established at intervals since 1559 to seek out and destroy failure to conform to the official Church and worship, were consolidated into the regular court of the high commission for ecclesiastical causes. In 1583, Whitgift succeeded Grindal at Canterbury. An uncompromising opponent of puritanism since his Cambridge quarrels with Cartwright, he was just the man for the queen's purpose. Unlike Parker he does not seem to have been greatly troubled by Elizabeth's evasions and refusals to commit herself, but went ahead, using the high commission to destroy the puritan organisation. Out of the prophesyings had grown what is known as the 'classical movement', that is an unofficial but effective organisation of 'classes' upon which a further organisation of provincial and national synods was to be erected. The Dedham classis began it in about 1582. The movement threatened at one time to engulf the lower clergy, but it began to break up from within as some classes showed themselves less presbyterian than others. Field, the movement's organiser and real inspiration, died in 1588, and the general synods of that year and of 1589 proved to be agreed only in their desire for an ill-defined presbyterian model. When it came to action there was a split between those who wanted to attack the bishops and those who were content to resist passively. The extremists did the movement little good, especially when the publication of the violent and scurrilous, but clever and amusing, 'Martin Marprelate' tracts (1588-9), attacking the bishops, provoked the active anger of the queen. Leicester died in 1588 and Walsingham in 1590, and with them passed away the puritan party in the council. The defeat of the Armada also played its part by robbing puritanism of its specifically patriotic appeal: it ceased to profit from its out-and-out opposition to catholicism when the whole country was at war with catholic Spain. Furthermore, the established Church was now, after some thirty years' existence, at last acquiring a firmer hold on the country. Exploiting all these factors, Whitgift, ably assisted by Richard Bancroft who acted as detective-in-chief to the high commission, steadily continued his work of routing out and suppressing nonconformity. In 1571 three articles had been devised as tests for conformity—acknowledgement of the royal supremacy, the 1559 prayer book, and the Thirty-nine Articles. In the interval, many clergy had evaded the duty of subscribing to these, but Whitgift now revived and applied them consistently in examinations before the high commission. By the end of the period under review Elizabethan puritanism was past its peak. It had failed to capture the Church, first by the attack of militant presbyterianism, then by alliance with Grindal and through the peaceful means of prophesyings; the classis was dead or conforming; and the movement had entered upon a decline which made it, after its failure to exploit James I's accession, a permanent minority opposition outside the Church.

There its strength lay in the laity, especially the gentry and the city of London. Outmanœuvred and defeated in the Church, it found a refuge in parliament. Even in these middle years of the reign, when the commons were on the whole amenable, a minority of puritan members continued the struggle by bills for Church reform and pleas for a purer clergy. The growing Spanish menace assisted them: they represented the genuine fears of Spanish and popish influence at court which found nourishment in the queen's enigmatic policy. The opposition which had grown up round constitutional issues in the 1560s continued into the 1570s and after. The spark was fanned into flame by the arrival of the greatest of the Elizabethan 'parliament-men', Peter Wentworth.

4. THE CONSTITUTIONAL QUESTION

With such stalwarts as Thomas Norton, Walter Strickland, and William Fleetwood, the precedent-hunting recorder of London, surviving from earlier parliaments, and with Peter Wentworth sitting for the first time in 1571, the puritan faction continued strong. But there is a difference about the opposition. The frequent protests that no disloyalty is intended to the queen now truly represent the curious double feeling of these ardent parliament-men: their fear for the future of the country and their passionate devotion to the crown. Even Wentworth, a constant thorn in Elizabeth's side, a contentious and often unreasonable obstacle in the path of smooth government, in all his violent attacks on the queen's policy never intended any attack on the queen's person. As he put it on one occasion:

> I will never confess it to be a fault to love the queen's majesty, while I live; neither will I be sorry for giving her majesty warning to avoid her dangers, while the breath is in my belly.

Elizabeth rightly thought herself as fit to notice danger as this puritan gentleman from Northamptonshire whose blunt but eloquent speeches and constant readiness to see offences against the rights of parliament both greatly helped to develop the doctrine of free speech and greatly hindered the discharge of parliamentary business. To the queen he was nothing but a nuisance; while appreciating his stand on principle and admiring so uncompromisingly consistent a career, we should also remember the fact that in the policy he advocated Wentworth was almost invariably wrong and often captious. This goes for the whole tribe of parliamentary puritans. One may understand their fears as they looked round and saw Spain stronger, the protestant Dutch in sad straits, the queen dallying with a French catholic suitor; but one can now see that England was safer in Elizabeth's hands than she would have been in those of Wentworth and his associates.

The earlier problem of the queen's marriage barely evoked an echo after 1571. Elizabeth was soon into her forties, so that there seemed the less point in asking her to marry. Even so, she was once more provoked into a reference to the matter, in the speech with which she closed the 1576 session. In it she again stressed her natural inclination to the single state and her readiness to sacrifice preference to the interests of the country. The long-drawn negotiations with Alençon seemed to bear her out and kept the commons quiet. Of the succession, on the other hand, they could hardly forbear to speak, with the queen of Scots in the country and plots being uncovered (and many more suspected) all around her. There was an outburst in the 1572 session, when parliament demanded Mary's head in revenge for her part in the Ridolfi plot, only to have to content itself with Norfolk's and a characteristic evasion on Elizabeth's part. Refusing either to approve or to veto a bill for the execution of Mary Stuart, she promised to adhere faithfully to the courteous formula which normally masked the royal veto: *la reine s'avisera*—the queen will think about it. This aptly literal interpretation left the commons—and the council—baffled and preserved Mary's life for another fifteen years. In 1584 parliament hastened to embody in an act the spontaneous association formed the year before whose members were sworn to protect the queen and to avenge her death by the punishment of anyone who had shared in its guilt. This, a reaction to the assassination of William of Orange, was designed to prevent the succession of Mary, but no positive statement depriving her or settling the succession in any way could be got in the face of Elizabeth's continued refusal to touch the matter. Thus these delicate topics, not forgotten but passing out of mind, gave place to other issues. By and large, all the conflicts of these years fall into one of two constitutional categories—those concerned with the privilege of freedom of speech and its application, and those illustrating the growing and growingly touchy selfconsciousness of the house.[1]

In 1571, after some preliminary manœuvres, Walter Strickland introduced a bill for the reform of the prayer book. For this—as she saw it—plain invasion of her prerogative, the queen had him called before the council and forbidden to attend the house. This raised a storm: despite the efforts of the privy councillors present, members protested against this unexplained semi-arrest of one of their number and raised the question of privilege. Warned of the excitement, the queen realised her mistake, and before matters could go further Strickland was permitted to return to his place. It was a tactful and timely withdrawal which tacitly acknowledged the commons' freedom from any sort of arrest during a session; but the bill was dropped and Elizabeth had preserved her prerogative and protected her Church.

However, there was one in the house now who remembered such things and pondered them during and between sessions, wrestling in the best puritan fashion with his soul and invariably coming up (as puritans were and are liable to do) with some unpleasant but necessary duty in which clearly he delighted. Peter Wentworth did little in this first parliament in which he sat, but that little was significant. The point which struck him was the frequent mention of the queen's displeasure—rumours went about that the queen had said such and such, while in turn the queen herself received garbled rumours from the house. He unburdened himself of all this in a violent attack on Sir Humphrey Gilbert, the explorer, himself a member, who had made a speech needlessly flattering to

[1] The following parliaments sat in this period: 1571, 1572 (prorogued to 1576 and again to 1581), 1584-5, 1586-7.

the sovereign and hinting at improper channels of information. Wentworth recurred to the point in the next parliament, in 1572, when Mr Snagge complained that a speech of his had been twisted into an attack on the lords. Wentworth enthusiastically followed the lead, and the Speaker, Robert Bell, who as a private member had suffered similarly in the previous parliament, lent his support. The grievance, such as it was, had some body in it. It was one of the unacknowledged duties of privy councillors in the house to keep the queen informed of what went on there, and their fellow-councillors in the lords naturally shared in the information. In the process, no doubt, many a rash word might be inconveniently preserved, and the queen's reaction, as conveyed in hints and rumours, might act as a serious limitation on members' liberty to speak their minds. In 1572 the matter blew over, after a vigorous debate and protests to the lords, but with Wentworth it rankled.

When the house reassembled in 1576, Wentworth immediately opened a prepared oration on freedom of speech which he had composed as much as three years earlier. It is one of the great classics of parliamentary oratory. Taking as his text the words 'sweet indeed is the name of liberty and the thing itself a value beyond all inestimable treasure', he complained of seeing free speech infringed in the two sessions during which he had attended parliament. He argued that the commons were in duty bound freely to discuss all matters affecting God's honour and everything 'commodious, profitable, or in any way beneficial for the prince or state'—that is, those points of ecclesiastical legislation and affairs of state which Elizabeth determinedly reserved for the prerogative. Else the parliament were no parliament. There were two things very hurtful to its privilege. One was the sort of rumour which said that 'the queen's majesty liketh not of such a matter; whosoever preferreth it, she will be much offended with him' or alternatively that she would resent opposition to a matter she liked. The other was that messages came to the house, ordering or inhibiting some action. 'I would to God, Mr Speaker, that these two were buried in hell: I mean rumours and messages.' He elaborated these points at length, indulging in so much of his own desired freedom of speech that the house sat aghast. 'Certain it is . . . that none is without fault: no, not our noble queen. Since, then, her majesty has committed great faults . . .' Such language was unheard of.

Wentworth was stopped in mid-career, and the house considered what to do with him. In the end they committed him to the serjeant-at-arms and had him interrogated by a powerful committee. In this examination Wentworth—it is his report alone that we have—acquitted himself nobly, defending his attacks on the queen's policy and his rude references to Mary Stuart as well as his remarks about rumours. The house was deeply disturbed. Wentworth had clearly gone too far, and they were both angry at his attack on one who had already become an idol and apprehensive of what she might do. Realising that she could for once trust the commons to do all that was needful, Elizabeth kept out of the affair. Wentworth was committed to the Tower by the house itself; there he spent four unrepentant weeks—his first but by no means his last sojourn there. He had been presumptuously rude by the standards of the time, but no more so than puritans thought it right to be; that other puritan, Sir Francis Walsingham, frequently lectured the queen as frankly—though not, of course, as publicly—which may account for her dislike of him. But Wentworth had raised a genuine point of principle, and his fate showed that there was something in it. The commons would not be really free in their speech while the crown exercised subtle influence through 'rumours and messages'. That without some such contact affairs of state might resolve themselves into an intolerable series of unexpected conflicts is plain and was to be lamentably proved by the Stuarts. The problem of how to provide free speech for those who thought it their duty to oppose, without ruining the co-operation of crown and parliament on which English government rested, was yet far from solved.

In 1581 Wentworth kept fairly quiet, and the problems that arose were minor ones. As if to illustrate his brother's point, Paul Wentworth moved for a general fast; Elizabeth took this to be an encroachment on her control of ecclesiastical affairs and forced the commons to apologise humbly for letting the matter go forward. Thomas Norton had a last fling in trying to make even fiercer the fierce recusancy act of that year. Before the next parliament met, he died (1584) after nearly twenty-five years in the commons. A ready debater, skilful tactician, and strongly-principled puritan, he more than anyone had nursed and shaped the parliamentary opposition of the reign. His reward was a general fame as 'Master Norton the parliament-man', though it is only recently, after being for long overshadowed by the more assertive and dramatic Wentworth, that he has come into his own again.[1]

In 1584-5 Wentworth did not sit, but the parliament of 1586-7

[1] Norton is the real hero of Professor Neale's *Elizabeth I and her Parliaments 1559-81*.

saw him revive the agitation for free speech. He got his opportunity when Anthony Cope introduced his 'bill and book'—a bill for the repeal of the prayer book and its replacement by the puritan book of discipline and worship which he offered instead. It was an impudent move, but one which found the house in sympathy in that desperate year before the queen of Scots was dead and while a Spanish descent on England seemed only too likely. The queen ordered the Speaker to render up both book and bill, which he did. Thereupon Wentworth submitted ten articles which he wished the Speaker to put to the house for its resolution. In them he asked whether parliament was not necessary for the existence of the state as the only maker and abrogator of laws, and whether free speech was not granted by law since parliament could not operate without it. He went on to attack his old targets. It was injurious to the order and liberties of the house for messages to be carried to and fro; the house would be failing in its duty if it permitted such messages and rumours; anyone who infringed the liberties of the house was to be regarded as an enemy to God, the prince, and the state. The language of this remarkable document reads astonishingly like the pronouncements of Stuart parliaments; Wentworth was rapidly travelling towards an opposition so intransigent—and so puritanically biblical in expression—that his place as the forerunner of such men as Eliot or Pym becomes unmistakable. The Speaker showed the paper to a privy councillor, and in consequence Wentworth spent another spell in the Tower. This time the council—that is the queen—committed him. Others followed, including Cope, but it seems that they were arrested for their activities in improperly concerting a parliamentary campaign before the session opened rather than for anything they did in the house. The ten articles were Wentworth's last word on privilege. In his attempts to get past Elizabeth's obstructionist tactics to a reform of religion he had been driven into an unprecedently complete doctrine of free speech. Though for a time he seemed defeated, his example was not forgotten when crown and commons began to clash without the shock-absorbing interposition of an essential loyalty to the wearer of the crown.

While the struggle for freedom of speech centred on—indeed, emanated from—the heroic and craggy figure of Peter Wentworth, the signs of the commons' growing self-consciousness centred on the egregious, ill-tempered, and rather petty Arthur Hall. Hall attracted attention when he spoke in favour of Norfolk and Mary Stuart in 1572: from first to last he was always out of tune with the feeling of the house, though despite this ill-timed if honourable championship he was no catholic himself.[1] Round him there revolved a storm in the session of 1576 which is known as Smalley's Case. It arose in a private quarrel of Hall's which ended in one of his servants, Edward Smalley, being sued for debt. Smalley got himself arrested during the session in order to secure his release on grounds of privilege and thus baulk the debt. When Hall moved for his servant's release, the house ordered the serjeant-at-arms to fetch Smalley from prison, but the serjeant objected that the correct thing to do was to obtain a writ of privilege from chancery. Here the matter stuck, for chancery refused to issue a writ, on the sufficient grounds that a man once arrested for debt and then released could not be proceeded against thereafter—the very reason, of course, for which Smalley had sought arrest in the first place. Oddly enough the house did not use Ferrers' Case as a precedent for freeing Smalley;[2] one may suspect that Hall's unpopularity made them reluctant to find a way out. In the end, however, the serjeant was ordered to bring Smalley to the bar of the house. The rest of the story concerns the attempts of the commons to defeat Hall's and Smalley's conspiracy by forcing payment of the debt: arbitration having failed they went so far as to send Smalley (freed from his original arrest) to the Tower, but Hall, furious at being shown up, would not allow his servant to pay until his wife saved him from himself by settling the affair behind his back. Out of this unsavoury business there arose a further precedent for the right of the commons to secure a release from arrest by warrant of the mace—that is, by order of the house—without the intervention of chancery—that is, the crown.

Hall continued to brood over his injuries and, unfortunately for himself, vented his spleen in two pamphlets in which he not only published the proceedings of the house—a serious offence in itself—but attacked the pretensions of the commons to ancient powers and privileges. Describing them as a 'new person in the Trinity' of crown, lords, and commons, he rightly denied the false history by which the Elizabethan parliamentarians were creating for their institution prescriptive rights and powers, perhaps the most significant sign of the new spirit in parliament and a portent of the future. That Hall was right is beyond doubt, but his sound

[1] Another member who defended Mary was a conservative married to a catholic, Francis Alford. The existence of such men and their liberty to express their views should warn us to remember that the puritans never composed more than a minority—a loud and influential minority—of the house, and that the Elizabethan commons were a varied crowd, very different from the regimented supporters of party we are accustomed to.

[2] See above, p. 174.

history only added to the wrath to come. In the next session (1581) he was arrested, sentenced to fine and imprisonment, and expelled the house. He submitted with an ill grace, and the queen spared him the fine and the six months in the Tower, but though he was re-elected in 1584 he did not take his seat for fear of reviving the agitation against himself. Choleric and sulky though he was, he deserves some pity as the first victim of the commons' use of privilege to protect their exalted opinion of themselves. In the course of his troubles he had helped inadvertently to increase their powers by confirming that the house could release by its own mere order prisoners who claimed privilege, could expel members and by implication exercise exclusive control over them, and could inflict punishments in the manner of a court. They claimed to do these things by ancient privilege; in fact these powers, if not unprecedented, were of such recent origin that only the story of Arthur Hall really marked their establishment.

The commons' assertiveness also came out in several clashes with the lords, a rather ominous development. There existed machinery for the settling of such disputes: joint committees of both houses had met on occasion since 1529 to discuss difficulties. The queen naturally used the lords' readiness to support her in order to weaken the commons' chances of thwarting her, and from 1572, when Burghley sat in the upper house, the chief architect of legislation could no longer control at first hand the discussions in the less amenable house. Since bills were often introduced in that house which contained the councillor concerned with them, the commons were on occasion presented with a controversial bill already discussed and passed by the lords, a procedure they resented. Thus they objected to two bills in 1576, and minor quarrels recurred at other times. None of it was very serious—conciliation prevailed—but it was significant enough of a new temper in the lower house. Beyond question, the commons, resentful of anything that savoured of dictation by lords, council, or queen, had become a factor to be reckoned with. Even in these years when she had at last found a parliament (1572-81) which was so far from obstreperous as to make its retention for nine years agreeable, Elizabeth could never relax her vigilance. Her and her councillors' skill in management was constantly called for, and she employed all her arts, from threats and persuasions to the appearance of gracious surrender.

The strength of the commons lay in the fact that they represented accurately the uneasiness, even fear, of protestant England in face of foreign threats and—as it seemed and often was—

domestic irresolution. England was far from puritan, but it was becoming more definitely protestant, and in this movement the extremists naturally took the lead. When men fear an enemy they prefer to follow those who denounce that enemy most strongly rather than those who chart a middle course. These events at home—action against catholics, the struggle with the puritan clergy, disputes in parliament—took place against the background of a darkening international situation.

5. ALENÇON AND THE NETHERLANDS

We left the realm at peace in 1575: agreements had been concluded with both Spain and France, and Scotland was in the safely Anglophil hands of the regent Morton. But the centre of disturbance remained untouched. Since the beginning of the revolt in the Spanish Netherlands (1572) the prince of Orange had maintained his hold on the provinces of Holland and Zeeland and his stubborn resistance to the forces of Alva's successor, Don Luis de Requesens. Though willing to stay on good terms with Spain—in 1575 she even expelled Dutch refugees from England—Elizabeth could not avoid involvement in the affairs of the Channel seaboard, the less so because, if she refused to assist, Orange was ready to turn to France. And French control of the Netherlands was, if anything, more intolerable than Spanish because it could not be limited by a return to the relative independence which the Netherlands had enjoyed under Charles V and which Elizabeth tried to secure for them under Philip II. Thus, despite the treaty of Blois and France's abandonment of Mary Stuart, France also remained a danger-spot. There the tripartite division into the Guise faction of ardent catholics intent on alliance with Spain, the Huguenot section determined to secure religious toleration and co-operate with the protestant powers, and the court of Henry III dominated by his mother Catherine who was trying to play off the factions, preserved a general instability which made France an incalculable element. In the late 1570s, the Huguenots, disorganised after the massacre of 1572 and the loss of their leaders, began to revive under Henry of Navarre and to find a successor to Coligny's ambitions, though not to his ability, in Catherine's youngest son, Francis duke of Alençon and Anjou.[1] The French court party were eager to be rid

[1] Alençon succeeded to the dukedom of Anjou on his brother's acceptance of the Polish crown in 1574, but it is usual to avoid confusion by referring to him throughout under his earlier title, a practice which shall be followed here.

of Alençon and he wished to carve a kingdom for himself: his restless activities in 1578-84 provide the thread which runs through Elizabeth's policy in those years.

In 1575-6 the queen was so much opposed to renewing trouble for herself by assisting the Dutch that, early in 1576, the two countries were even involved in a minor commercial and naval war. But the situation was changed by the death of Requesens and the wild excesses of his unpaid soldiers who devastated the Netherlands in the summer of 1576. After the sack of Antwerp, Orange's arguments at last prevailed with the southern provinces, and in November the Netherlands were reunited in the Pacification of Ghent. The arrival of a new Spanish governor, Don John of Austria, threatened to lead to further trouble, but in February 1577 Don John, by the so-called Perpetual Edict, accepted the Pacification on the terms offered by the States General. These included the removal of all Spanish troops. Don John complied, but with a heavy heart. One of the foremost soldiers of his day—the victor of the great battle of Lepanto against the Turks (1571)—this natural son of Charles V had not come north to act as figurehead for a parcel of commercial and industrial provinces. In fact, he was planning, with Philip's approval, to restore order in the Netherlands and then carry out the much heralded *empresa* against England. Elizabeth had done much to forward the Perpetual Edict, but in July 1577, when Don John recovered his freedom of action by a military *coup d'état*, she was forced back on Orange. The prince alone had not joined in the rejoicings of February, and now that his suspicions were proved correct he more than ever seemed the only hope of the distracted provinces. In turn, his only hope seemed to be Elizabeth, as reluctant as ever to enter the war. The queen pursued a futile policy, spending good money on the leader of a mercenary army, Duke John Casimir of the Palatinate, whom at intervals she had subsidised to assist both Huguenots and Dutch but who never achieved anything. She also negotiated direct with Spain, a move which seemed to promise success when diplomatic relations were resumed in 1578. However, the new Spanish ambassador, Bernardino de Mendoza, was a foolishly arrogant and blustering man, sent less to represent his country than to organise the moves against Elizabeth.

Negotiations failed to arrest the progress of Don John in 1578: Orange was once again confined to his northern fastness and his plight was desperate. Since Elizabeth would not help, he turned to Alençon. The duke re-entered European politics in 1578 with an offer, received with suspicion and reluctance, to take charge of the

Dutch revolt; at the same time, in order both to advance his own ambitions and to conciliate English opposition, he resumed his courtship of Elizabeth which had died a quiet death in 1576. The second Alençon courtship was Elizabeth's last fling in this field, and it was the most ardent, most tricky, and—to all appearance—most serious of all her amorous manœuvres in the interests of diplomacy. She was forty-five, but Burghley argued that she might easily and without danger yet have children, and she herself may have been making a last attempt to secure a normal family life for herself. Thus Alençon's suit, encouraged by his mother and brother, prospered. In October 1578 Don John died suddenly and with him, it seemed, died the Spanish project for the conquest of northern Europe. Alençon became protector of the Netherlands by a treaty with the States General, but his enjoyment of his position was limited by the arrival of another Spanish governor, Alexander Farnese of Parma, far and away the ablest general and diplomatist in Philip's employ. The short storm of Don John's meteoric career was over; there began the slow but more certain reconquest by Parma and the ill-concerted opposition offered to his steady advance by Orange, Alençon, and Elizabeth.

From all points of view it seemed best that the last two should link forces and do so by marriage. Early in 1579 Alençon sent his friend, Jean de Simier, to plead his cause with the queen, and there followed scenes of public affection which seemed indecorous even to that age. Elizabeth showed herself her father's daughter by abandoning affairs of state in favour of a round of amusements mixed with dalliance. She excelled at the game and Simier was her match: undoubtedly there was no more in it than a high-spirited delight in her own skill. But it served Alençon's turn. Elizabeth added the two to her menagerie of pet names: Simier became her ape and Alençon—a short, slightly misshapen figure with a pock-marked face—her frog. In August 1579 he arrived in person—secretly, but it was a well divulged secret. When he left after three weeks of ardent wooing, the marriage seemed very near. The country took alarm: few wanted a French prince. A puritan gentleman, John Stubbs, with the honest but ill-considered vigour of his kind, published an attack on the match for which he and the printer lost their right hands. The scene has become famous: the silent multitude, sullenly hostile to the queen's angry revenge, Stubbs shouting his 'God save the Queen' before fainting, the printer's cry that he had left there the hand of a true Englishman. Enmeshed in the toils of the Alençon courtship, Elizabeth was in danger of losing touch with her people. It is easy to understand and to pity her. Her greatness lay in that she recovered her senses before it was too late. She quarrelled with her council in a series of temperamental scenes in October 1579, but a few weeks after Alençon left the marriage was really dead: no one any longer seriously wanted it.

At this point circumstances revived it, but now it was much more a diplomatic manœuvre and much less a serious affair of Elizabeth's heart. In 1580 there arose the problem of the Portuguese succession. The king of Portugal, a cardinal-archbishop, died in that year, and the claimant with not only the best right but also far and away the greatest power to enforce it was Philip of Spain. He quickly overran the country, thus combining the two largest empires of the day and conjuring up a spectre of overwhelming Spanish power. In consequence the anti-Spanish countries took up the cause of a native Portuguese claimant, Don Antonio. Elizabeth toyed with the idea of sending Drake to the Azores, where Antonio had retained a foothold, but she wanted French assistance which was delayed until she dropped the plan. In 1582 the French tried by themselves, only to be heavily defeated in the naval battle of Terceira. Unable to exploit the Portuguese succession in her endeavour to involve Spain in sufficient distraction to prevent a descent on England, Elizabeth was forced to assist Alençon in the Netherlands and thus to revive the game of his courtship. She hoped to win success in her Dutch policy by using him as an agent and without spending either blood or treasure herself. He revisited England in November 1581 and to all appearance Elizabeth was as enamoured of him as ever. She publicly kissed him and proclaimed her desire to marry him. Behind the scenes, however, things stood rather differently. Alençon was wanted in the Netherlands where Parma's success in bringing the southern provinces under Spanish control endangered the whole war of liberation; instead he dallied for three months and was then finally persuaded with difficulty to return to his place in the country whose sovereignty he had accepted in 1580. The marriage project was over, despite mutual protestations to the contrary; the party of Leicester and Walsingham, who had consistently opposed it as dangerous to the protestant alliance they hoped for, had triumphed. In 1582 Alençon proved his utter incapacity in a series of disastrous encounters with Parma and even more disastrous quarrels with the States General; his part in the Dutch revolt was virtually ended by January 1583, although he survived until May 1584. His death affected Elizabeth deeply; she had all the rather facile emotion of her age and family, but her sorrow was never prolonged or so sincere as to cloud her judgment.

Elizabeth's dealings with the Netherlands were constantly bedevilled by her refusal to sink money in that country without such securities as the ports of Flushing or Brill which the Dutch were equally determined to keep out of foreign hands. But her attitude will be the more readily condoned—exasperating though it was both to Orange and the English war party—when it is remembered that the queen was virtually fighting on three fronts: or rather, was desperately involved on three fronts in an effort to avoid fighting. Relations with Spain, superficially normal, were threatened by the distant exploits of Drake and his fellows, and more by England's involvement with the Dutch; it seemed in 1580-1 that the great attack of Pope Gregory XIII would be carried on Spanish wings. In reality Philip still hesitated quite as much as did Elizabeth to take an irrevocable step, but like her he was ready to do all he might to undermine English power by secret means. After all, there was always Mary Stuart, still alive, still a centre of plots, still an obvious candidate for the English throne if only the *empresa* succeeded. To Rome the cautious attitude of Spain suggested the need of readier allies, especially after the failure of the Irish expedition. Thus after 1580 there was added to the trouble centre in the Netherlands the so-called Lennox-Guise plot, a revival of the earlier alliance between France and Scotland against England. Into it the Spanish threat was also woven, as well as the ambitions of Mary Stuart. The story began in Scotland.

Here the friendly government of Morton ended abruptly in 1578 when the regent, after several ups and downs, had to resign and James VI, at the age of twelve, became nominally king in person. Next year there arrived from France Esmé Stuart, sieur d'Aubigny, soon created earl of Lennox, who with the assistance of Captain James Stewart (later earl of Arran) won his way to the control of king and kingdom. Morton was arrested late in 1580 and executed, despite vigorous English protests, next year. Lennox and Arran were now supreme, and they represented the French interest. Lennox was in fact in close touch with the French League, a catholic association dominated by the duke of Guise and determined to destroy protestantism in alliance with Spain. He hoped to restore Scotland to the Roman Church and Mary to her throne. English relations with France, always endangered by Elizabeth's persistent secret support of Huguenot ambitions, were not improved by Walsingham's embassy of July 1581; charged to negotiate a treaty of alliance and the Alençon marriage, he was prevented from achieving either by Elizabeth's rapid changes of mind. His failure increased the League's influence at court. With Lennox well established, the plot got under way. Two Scottish Jesuits arrived in 1581, full of illusions about the support which an invasion from the north would receive in England; Guise prepared to attack from the south. But the machinations were well known in England where Walsingham's intelligence service—often overrated in both size and perspicacity—for once did all that was required of it. Nevertheless, it was the internal feuds of Scotland that ruined the plot. In August 1582, some protestant lords abducted James in the Raid of Ruthven and drove Lennox and Arran from the country. Elizabeth joyfully seized the occasion to seek a close alliance which would restore English supremacy at Edinburgh. The English diplomats found James much readier to abandon his mother than they had expected; this somewhat precocious and selfish young man was only interested in securing his own throne in Scotland and succession in England. From 1583, sixteen years old, he played a real part in the rapidly changing faction strife of Scotland. The Ruthven party lost control in June 1583 and Arran returned; Walsingham himself, sent north, failed to achieve much beyond annoying James whose self-confidence did not take kindly to the elderly statesman's lectures; then England found an ally in an intriguer even more skilful than Arran. This was the Master of Gray with whose help the French party was finally destroyed in October 1585. Arran was exiled; James, who had tried to use French influence in order to blackmail Elizabeth into nominating him her successor, gave in; and the treaty of Berwick (July 1586) ended at last all threats from the north and the ancient disunion in the island.

It came none too soon, for other things were in train. When the Ruthven raid put a stop to Lennox's plans, the Guise interest, in alliance with Spain, the pope, and Mary Stuart decided to attack direct across the Channel. The plans were long maturing. Walsingham knew that something was up but for a long time, blinded by the Scottish troubles, failed to track the right game. In 1583, however, he almost accidentally stumbled over an unsuspected link in the conspiratorial chain. This was Francis Throckmorton, an English catholic, who acted as intermediary between Mary and the Spanish ambassador, Mendoza. At once, all the secretary's resources were switched from the innocent French ambassador to the guilty Spanish envoy. Torture made Throckmorton reveal all he knew, and the plot was broken. Mary, whose part is understandable but was nevertheless very real and dangerous, once again escaped the consequences of her action, while those whom religion, chivalry, or self-interest involved in her affairs suffered as usual. In January 1584 Mendoza was called before the council, informed that his part in all these doings was fully known, and told to leave the country within a fortnight. He exploded in a rage and eased his gall with an outburst of threats, but he left in disgrace—the second Spanish ambassador of the reign to be expelled from England for plotting against the queen to whom he was accredited. The exceeding latitude which the time allowed to diplomats and governments in working against each other while nominal peace reigned can only be understood if it is remembered that we are dealing with a conflict of ideologies in an age in which international law had barely begun. The rules governing relations between sovereign states were even more obscure and less tested than they are today.

Mendoza's expulsion brought war very close. In the Netherlands Spain was advancing under the able leadership of Parma, and the events of 1584 at last compelled Elizabeth to come into the open. In May Alençon died, leaving the headship of the rebellious provinces empty; in June a much worse calamity befell the Dutch cause when, after several attempts, an assassin at last managed to kill William of Orange. The deed found much praise in catholic countries, then the home of the doctrine of tyrannicide—and among tyrants heretic rulers stood high—even as it shocked England into horror and probably exaggerated fears. The result was the bond of association formed to protect the queen and avenge her if need arose, to which parliament gave its blessing in 1585. The long-drawn period of unquiet peace was nearly over; all those twists of diplomacy, secret assistance and open avowals, plots and conspiracies and treacheries, in which both sides had indulged, were at last to be subsumed in real war. Elizabeth, who hated the folly and waste of war, could not for ever resist the determination of Rome and its allies to have her down and the determination of her people to defend the protestant religion. Least doctrinaire of rulers and averse in temper and thought to the bigotry of either side, she was yet doomed to lead a war of religion.

Not that religion alone caused the war. In Europe the power politics of Spain, France, and England had played round the Channel coast and the Netherlands, and had exploited the internal dissensions of France and Scotland. To Elizabeth and to most of her contemporaries those seemed the stages that mattered. But the story is very incomplete without an investigation of what was going on across far oceans where England and Spain clashed—distantly but with reverberating effects on the narrow scene in Europe—in the first great colonial and naval struggle of modern times.

Chapter XII

SEAPOWER

IT was in the sixteenth century that the seeds were sown which were to grow into English seapower and the British empire. The discovery of America turned the Atlantic from the edge of the world into a busy traffic centre; command of the sea routes superseded control of overland roads in deciding the fate of nations; the distant island off the north-western corner of the Eurasian landmass automatically acquired immense possibilities. Medieval England had had her seamen: an island must have shipping. But such part as the kings of England had played in wider affairs had depended on their continental possessions and ambitions, and on the military prowess of their land-based armies. Under the Tudors the ancient military traditions—the memories of Crécy and Agincourt—were being replaced by a new national folklore of sea-heroes. The military past was a long time a-dying: its memories dominated the wars of Henry VIII and frustrated under Elizabeth the revolutionary notions of the new naval school of strategists. Nowadays, when the Elizabethan age seems to be obviously dominated by its Drakes and Hawkinses, when the defeat of the Armada overshadows all other warlike events of the time, when attention so readily concentrates on the distant exploits of explorers, colonists, traders, privateers, and pirates—nowadays it is necessary to remind oneself at every step that these men stood only at the opening of an era. Their mistakes, their irresolutions, their frequent folly and vicious selfishness cannot otherwise be understood, nor can due praise be given to their remarkable achievements. The traditions of maritime England, of England's navy and England's empire, go back no further than the Tudor century. They began hesitantly in the reign of Henry VII and received but partial advancement under Henry VIII; it was not until the second half of the period that a real start was made.

1. THE ROAD TO ASIA: FROM CABOT TO FITCH

Whatever the various motives that led to the wonderful movement known as the early explorations—and thirst for knowledge, the desire to convert the heathen, and military ambitions all played their part—the driving force was supplied by trade and the search for wealth. Although the Portuguese had for some time been carrying on a brisk trade with the west coast of Africa—Upper Guinea and Benin Bay—the story really began when various men determined to investigate the possibility of direct commercial relations with the sources of silks and spices and other goods in South Asia. It is alleged that Henry VII might have had the honour of employing Columbus who spent a long time looking for a government to finance his enterprise; but even if the king had been at liberty in 1490 to listen to the Genoese visionary, it does not follow that England lost what Spain gained. If Columbus had sailed from Bristol in 1490, as John Cabot did seven years later, he would have reached the inhospitable shores of Nova Scotia (as Cabot did), and not the promising islands of the Caribbean: the winds would have seen to that. In considering these early voyages we must rid our minds entirely of the knowledge that there lie between the western shore of Europe and the eastern shore of Asia two great oceans and a huge continent. What may be called the western school of navigators supposed that the route to the west would reach China and the Spice islands—known from a curious amalgam of accurate information, garbled reports, and pure legend—more quickly than the Portuguese were progressing in their laborious search for the southern end of Africa. Columbus died in the belief that he had found some barbaric islands only ust off the coast of civilized Asia, and when John Cabot, a Genoese seaman settled in Bristol since 1490, offered his services to Henry VII he promised a route straight to Cipango (Japan) from which, by laying a south-westerly course, he would reach Cathay (China).

In March 1496 Henry responded by granting a charter to a syndicate of Bristol merchants, headed by Cabot and his sons, permitting them to sail east, north, or west to discover lands so far not known to Christians. By this time the step had been taken which was to render all maritime enterprise politically dangerous. In 1493 Pope Alexander VI, himself of Spanish descent, issued a bull which divided the discoveries between Spain and Portugal along the line of the meridian passing through the Azores.[1] The bull spoke of lands 'west and south' of this meridian, which is nonsense, and the best interpretation—adhered to, for instance, by Philip of Spain as long as he was king of England—reserved only lands west of the meridian, and south of the parallel, of the Azores. Henry's grant was thus careful to prevent any incursion

[1] The precise details were worked out by the two powers in the treaty of Tordesillas in 1494.

into pre-empted territory by excluding exploration southwards and by prohibiting Cabot from landing on soil already visited by European seamen. Cabot sailed in May 1497, reaching land to the westward which he called the new-found land, and which was probably Nova Scotia. Of course, he was convinced that he had found Asia, and the trend of the coastline confirmed his notion that by following it he would strike Cathay with all its riches. In 1498 he set out again, never to return. There are indications that he got some way south in his coasting, sufficient to alarm the Spaniards: he may, in view of the savage lands he passed, have realised that he was nowhere near China. But his death, Henry's preoccupations in England, and an international situation which made it inadvisable to fall foul of Spain, for a time ended the official enterprise. England had got off to a good start in exploring but none at all in trading, and so the matter virtually dropped. In 1501 and 1502 licences were granted to groups of Bristol merchants who continued to interest themselves in discovering new markets, but little is known of activities which do not seem to have produced much profit. The only result of these early voyages was to establish the great Newfoundland cod fisheries, found by Cabot; from that time onwards they were visited regularly by fleets from England and France.

Meanwhile the Spaniards had realised that Columbus' discoveries were not in Asia; by 1500 the existence of the new continent was known. This did not kill the hopes of finding a westerly route to Asia, the less so because the Portuguese had established by now a monopoly of the eastern route—Vasco da Gama reached India in 1498 and all Europe knew it a year later—which was so enormously profitable that it encouraged everyone to try to break it. The way east was blocked by the papal bull, the Portuguese forces, and most convincingly of all by Portugal's carefully guarded exclusive knowledge of the charts. In the west there lay a landmass whose breadth was unknown until Balboa saw the Pacific in 1513, but which it was thought might be outflanked. Here was the origin of that famous and disastrous chimera, the north-west passage, which was to bedevil the history of voyages almost to the end of the seventeenth century. Its first prophet was John Cabot's son Sebastian, a navigator of ability and boundless faith in himself, equipped with a conveniently selective memory and a gift for telling the tale. He made his first attempt under Bristol auspices in 1509; when he failed and found enthusiasm on the wane in England, he left to make a career in Spain.

For some forty years after this England took little part in the movement. While Cortez and Pizarro proved that Columbus' discoveries had led Spain to vaster power and wealth—as it seemed—than she could ever have obtained if he had really found a route to Asia, England stood aloof. Committed to the Spanish alliance, she could not afford to interlope, especially after the break with Rome which made every additional provocation mere folly. Her statesmen had other matters to think of. Most important of all, the merchants of England who had taken the lead in the 1490s found in these years that the flourishing cloth trade absorbed about all their energies. A booming trade in Europe left little inclination to risk capital in dubious enterprises. In 1521, when Henry VIII tried to form a national company for exploration, it was the opposition and lethargy of the London commercial community which frustrated the project. They had had recent experiences of such follies when a group of lawyers and men about town, led by John Rastell (Thomas More's brother-in-law), had fitted out an expedition for America, only to come to grief in Ireland. At Bristol, the memory of Cabot's last voyage and the petering out of the subsequent trading ventures seems to have sufficed.

England at large cared little for explorations, and even individuals, whether statesmen or traders, who might have been interested, failed to share in the spirit which in the 1520s was driving Spanish power across Central and Southern America. A few men's imaginations caught a little of the flame: More's *Utopia* reflects an intelligent man's interest in this astonishing widening of the horizon, and Rastell used his own experience in a play—*A New Interlude of the Four Elements* (1519)—to popularise knowledge of the new continent. But the only Englishmen who really knew what was going on were those who traded and often settled in Spain. Many did so in those halcyon days when Spain and England were allied and before the religious schism destroyed the easy terms on which they lived with their Spanish neighbours and the Spanish government. Quite a colony of them existed near Seville, the centre of the Indies trade in which they shared. One of them, Robert Thorne, was the first significant English propagandist for overseas expansion. In 1525 Ferdinand Magellan discovered the straits to the south of America and a possible western route to the Spice Islands. Political circumstances and the difficulties of the voyage persuaded the emperor to forego this new addition to his dominions and to offer it for sale. The English ambassador in Spain consulted Thorne who replied with a pamphlet, *A Declaration of the Indies*, in which he spoke of hitherto undiscovered islands in the Pacific, rich in spices, pearls, and gold, and suggested that the shortest route to them from England was by way of the North Pole. England's position, he argued, indicated that God meant her to build an empire by using that road. Like many men then and later, Thorne underestimated the arctic ice: all calculations were based on the ice-free conditions of north-west Europe which, of course, are due to the gulf stream. He died in 1532, back in England and disappointed of his hopes. Few would enterprise into distant seas and in the teeth of Spanish disapproval, at this time when the Flanders trade was going well and Spain must not be provoked. An exception was William Hawkins, of Plymouth, who in the 1530s initiated a profitable trade in dyestuffs with the coast of Brazil; if others there were they have left no trace.

The initial impetus given by the voyages of Henry VII's time thus seemed to have died when it was revived in the middle of the century by the trade slump of the 1550s and the ambitions of the energetic and enterprising speculators who had already exhausted the possibilities of the land market. The duke of Northumberland, commonly (and rightly) belaboured by historians, here appears as the guardian angel of the maritime movement: after his time it never relapsed again. In 1548 Sebastian Cabot returned to England, after thirty-five years of profitable and honourable service under the Spanish crown, and from 1551 we can trace the remarkable career of John Dee, the power behind the scenes of early English exploration. Astrologer, necromancer, mathematician, and geographer, Dee was that mixture of genuine scientist and credulous charlatan so typical of the sixteenth century. But apart from his more dubious activities, he entered heart and soul into the movement for expansion. He became the prophet of the north-east passage and later of the fabled southern continent—the great Terra Australis Incognita supposed to lie to the south of the Pacific Ocean and to stretch from Cape Horn to the East Indian islands. It was the best opinion of the time that such a continent must exist to counterbalance the northern land masses and prevent the earth from toppling over. The new—rather belated—interest of England in the discoveries was shown by the inception of propaganda literature. In 1553 and 1555 Richard Eden published translations of continental works which he entitled *Treatise of the New India* and *Decades of the New World or West India*. There began now that fruitful co-operation of merchants, sailors, and moneyed gentry (including members of court and council) which was to lead to such splendid results in the days of Drake. In the first place the older but petty beginnings of direct trade with Africa were exploited. In 1551 and 1552 Thomas Wyndham led expeditions to the Barbary coast—the Atlantic coast of Morocco—and in 1553 he went right down the Guinea coast into Benin Bay. He himself died on his last voyage, but the survivors brought back so much gold that London went into raptures, and another and even more profitable venture was undertaken next year by John Lok. The Portuguese protests, allowed by Mary's government under Philip's influences, were ignored after 1558 on the grounds that the holding of a few forts on a coast a thousand miles long did not constitute effective occupation, and the Guinea merchants continued to bring in their gold and ivory.

The real goal, however, was still distant Asia, especially the Spice Islands (the Moluccas). The southern route round Africa being closed, and that round South America being both difficult and in Spanish hands, there remained the northern latitudes where, as Thorne had pointed out, England started with a special advantage. Cabot favoured the north-west passage round North America: it was supposed that once the channel was found the coast would trend south-westwards and lead straight to China. Dee thought well of the north-east passage, holding (falsely) that no part of Asia reached higher than the North Cape of Norway: once this was turned travellers would have an easy passage in icefree waters to the eastern extremities of Asia. In 1552 Northumberland formed a large joint-stock company to carry out Dee's plan, and an expedition sailed next year under the leadership of Sir Hugh Willoughby and Richard Chancellor. Cabot had contributed the experience of a seafaring life, Dee the theoretical knowledge of the geographers, and some 200 capitalists, led by the duke himself, the necessary money. The journey was only half successful. Willoughby, held up by storms, died with all his crew when he tried to winter on the coast of Lapland, but Chancellor entered the White Sea, found the village of Archangel, and established contact with the distant Czar of Moscow. He returned in 1554 with stories of the court of Ivan the Terrible and with the promise of a lucrative trade. In 1555 the Muscovy Company was formed to exploit these beginnings. Although further voyages by Chancellor and Stephen Borough ended in disaster—Chancellor failed to return in 1557—so that the north-east passage remained undiscovered, the accidental by-product of a new cloth trade straight into Central Russia remained to bring profit to merchants, training to seamen, hope to explorers, and assistance to the government in their struggle to break the Hanse's monopoly in the

Baltic whose shipping stores of timber, cordage, and pitch now began to assume the importance they were to have for some two centuries.

In the 1560s interest switched to a new theatre of operations—the Caribbean—which shall be dealt with in the next section. A more or less regular trade now existed with Muscovy and the Guinea coast; the Newfoundland fisheries grew yearly in value; England's maritime interests were firmly established, and more and more men, especially from the west coast ports of Plymouth and Bristol, were seeking wealth and adventure across the seas. The route to Asia, not yet found, remained to tease men's ingenuity. In 1566 Sir Humphrey Gilbert wrote his famous *Discourse for a Discovery for a New Passage to Cathay* which, with its mixture of sense and nonsense, remained the stand-by of north-western explorers. Dee preached his faith in the Southern Continent whose spectre was to haunt geographers until James Cook finally disproved its existence in the eighteenth century. In 1574 a Devon syndicate led by Sir Richard Grenville laid plans for an enterprise through the Straits of Magellan and for the Terra Australis, but that was the year in which Burghley was trying to make peace with Spain and the project was forbidden by the government. There ensued a tug-of-war between the advocates of the north-west passage and those of the Straits. Since to go north was to keep out of Spanish preserves, Burghley favoured that route, and despite the opposition of the Muscovy Company (who feared for their monopoly) an expedition commanded by Martin Frobisher sailed in 1576. He discovered a strait which he named after himself and which he claimed was the passage, though he had barely entered it: it was, in fact, a narrow and longish inlet. He also brought back some curious ore which sanguine hope and some highly peculiar assaying immediately declared to be gold-bearing. The outcome was a magnificent bubble: speculation in the mythical gold of the arctic wastes ran high, and Frobisher was dispatched on two more voyages in 1577 and 1578 to explore his strait and bring more ore. The moving spirit behind all this was Michael Lok, half visionary and half speculator, who was completely ruined by the collapse of the bubble; for, not surprisingly, no more gold was found. Frobisher discovered Hudson's Strait and entered Hudson's Bay whose shore, trending to the south-west, seemed to confirm that here was the northern shore of North America. But other enterprises and war distracted both government and investors; the Bay remained unexplored till the next century; the passage remained still a hope; and Frobisher, a rough, cantankerous, and at this time a needy man, conceived a lasting grudge at the neglect of his discoveries and the popular acclamation of Drake. The southern project, kept alive by Grenville, later fell into Drake's hands, so that Grenville was another who cherished resentment against this most famous of the great Elizabethan seamen.

One last Elizabethan attempt to find the north-west passage may be recorded here. In 1585 a small expedition sailed from Dartmouth under the command of John Davis, a seaman of that port. He had the backing of Sir Humphrey Gilbert's brother Adrian who had secured the patent, of William Sanderson, merchant of London, who supplied the money, and of Raleigh and Walsingham who represented the court interest. In three voyages (1585-7) Davis achieved remarkable things for geographical discovery, but nothing of commercial value. Together with the Armada threat of 1588 this explains why his efforts were not followed up. He was in many ways one of the most attractive of the Elizabethan explorers —eminently competent, a genuine scientific investigator, untainted by those touches of money-grubbing and piracy which hang around the others. As a single-minded discoverer he excelled them all. He established that Greenland is separate from America, sailed high into Baffin's Bay, and alone of all sixteenth-century seekers for the passage avoided the false turnings (Hudson's Straits, Frobisher's Straits, Cumberland Sound). The way he pointed was much later to prove the right one, though contrary to expectations the passage was ultimately found in latitudes too northerly to make it a practicable highway to Asia.

The west failing, the east beckoned once more. In 1580 the Muscovy Company, assisted by William Borough and John Dee, despatched a fleet to the north-east under Arthur Pett and Charles Jackman. Their purpose was to seek the passage to China, trade in cloth, and probably also to make contact with Drake, then in the Pacific. Ice, as always, stopped them. More profitable was the resumption of trade with the Levant: it is one of the curiosities of English naval history that the Caribbean and the Arctic were familiar to English seamen before they really got to know the Mediterranean. In 1581 the Turkey Company was incorporated, the title being later changed to Levant Company. And in 1583 John Newbery and Ralph Fitch made their memorable journey overland to India. They reached Portuguese Goa and, with difficulties, were permitted to trade; they visited the court of the Great Mogul, Akbar; they then parted, Newbery planning to return through Persia while Fitch headed east. Newbery vanished without trace, but Fitch travelled through Bengal, Burma, Siam,

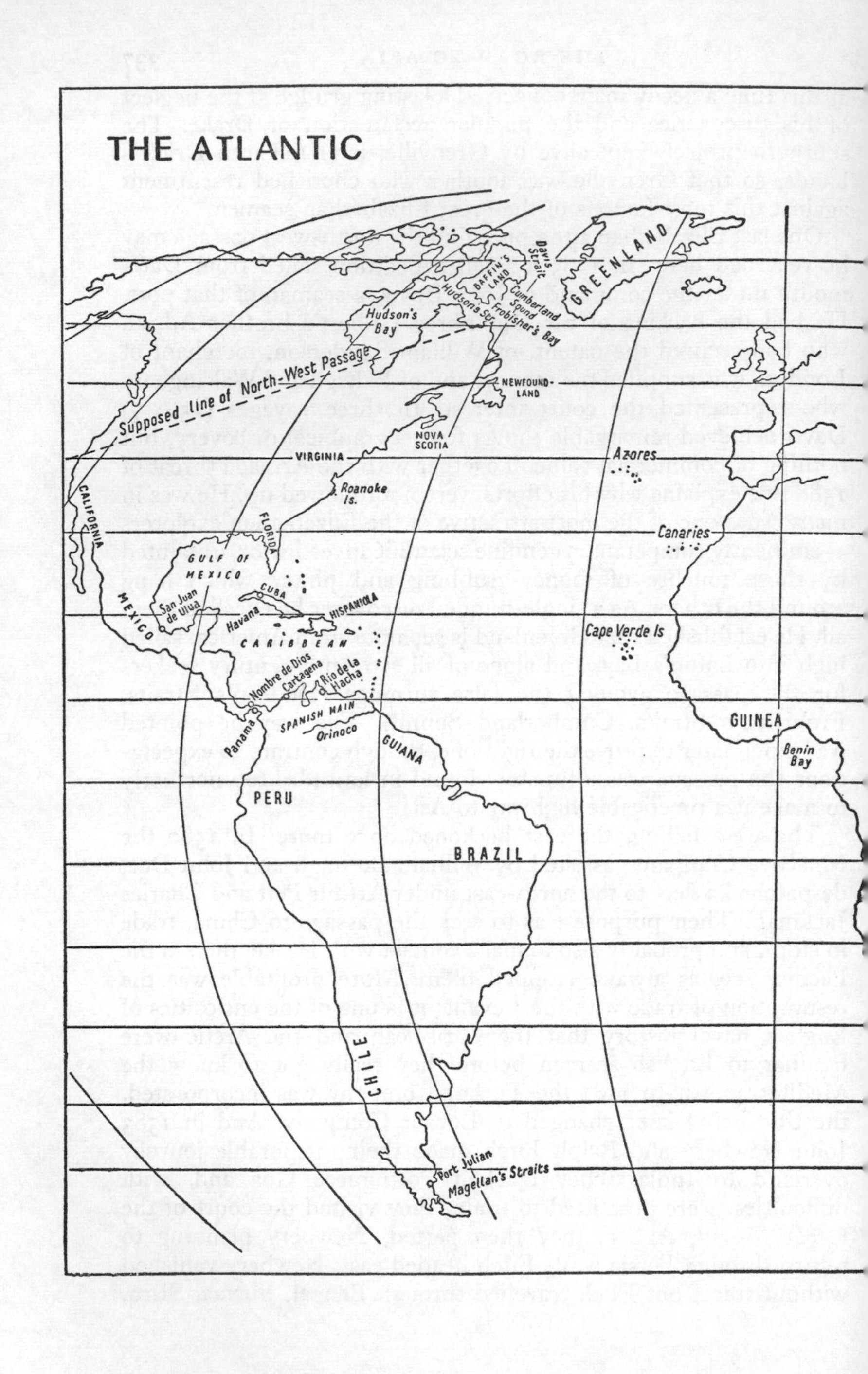
THE ATLANTIC
GREENLAND
Davis Strait
BAFFIN'S LAND
Cumberland Sound
Hudson's Str
Frobisher's Bay
Hudson's Bay
Supposed line of North-West Passage
NEWFOUND-LAND
NOVA SCOTIA
VIRGINIA
Azores
Roanoke Is.
CALIFORNIA
FLORIDA
Canaries
GULF OF MEXICO
CUBA
MEXICO
San Juan de Ulua
Havana
HISPANIOLA
CARIBBEAN
Cape Verde Is
Nombre de Dios
Cartagena
Rio de la Hacha
Panama
SPANISH MAIN
Orinoco
GUIANA
GUINEA
Benin Bay
PERU
BRAZIL
CHILE
Port Julian
Magellan's Straits

and the Malayan sultanates, to return in 1591 with the most remarkable traveller's tales of any in that age so full of wonders. Out of his journey was to grow the English East India Company and all that followed from it. As Chancellor secured trading privileges by treaty from Ivan the Terrible, so Fitch came to some sort of agreement with Akbar, or said he did; trade with settled countries always took the form of diplomatic negotiations. By now, English interests were spreading round the globe, but legitimate trade with the East and voyages of discovery were the smaller part of English maritime enterprise. Immediate returns were much larger from semi-piratical expeditions, or from the more respectable but barely more legal participation in the trade with the Spanish empire in the west.

2. THE CARIBBEAN: HAWKINS AND DRAKE

Of all the great discoveries, those of Spain were by far the most fabulous and profitable. By the middle of the sixteenth century the crown of Castile had established and organised a great empire in America, comprising Mexico, Peru, and Chile, and centring upon the islands and the mainland of the Caribbean. Here it preserved a jealous and rigid monopoly. No foreigner was allowed to settle or trade in the Spanish colonies without a royal licence which was rarely granted. All goods shipped to the Indies had to be registered at Seville, the seat of the central authority for the colonies (the Council of the Indies). Local officials, from viceroys downwards, could not act without direct orders from a government 3,000 miles—or anything from two or five months—distant. A notable part of the Spanish crown revenue consisted of the bullion mined in America and transported to Europe by two regular annual fleets: the *flota* which sailed by way of the Azores to San Juan de Ulua on the Gulf of Mexico to bring back the Mexican treasure, and the *galleones* which similarly reached Nombre de Dios on the Isthmus of Panama to collect that from Peru. These two great convoys and the many ships carrying contributions toward the collecting centres powerfully attracted men interested in a little piratical wealth. On the other hand, the insufficiencies of Spanish merchant shipping deprived the colonists of many badly needed commodities—above all of slaves to work their plantations—and rendered them willing to trade with anyone who could supply their wants in spite of the home government's vigorous and unswerving policy. In the middle of the century, the Spanish empire—immensely wealthy, too vast and too rapidly grown for efficient administration, and very ill protected—was ripe for exploitation by outsiders.

Though Robert Reneger of Southampton captured a treasure ship as early as 1545, it was French seamen from the Atlantic ports who first put the matter to the test. Spain and France were intermittently at war from 1521 to 1559, during which time French sails became a dreaded sight in the scattered Spanish settlements. Many of the privateers were Calvinists who both inflicted and suffered horrible things in the dominions of his Catholic Majesty. English maritime relations with Spain deteriorated after the break with Rome led to attacks on the English merchants in Andalusia. War in the 1540s added English privateers to French and gave a chance to men like Reneger. The Spanish ascendancy of 1553-8 delayed matters, but the beginnings of the conflict have been traced to the reign of Henry VIII. The treaty of Cateau Cambrésis (1559), which ended the Habsburg-Valois struggle in Europe, explicitly exempted the region beyond 'the lines'—the meridian of the Canaries and the tropic of Cancer—from its operation; it established the principle that diplomacy did not control the oceans. The wars of religion encouraged privateering by French, Dutch, and English in European waters. And the diplomatic situation was changing: the government of Elizabeth and Cecil, while reluctant to provoke Spain, saw much less cause to pander to her than Mary's had done and was ready to shut both eyes to West Indian enterprise if only it were not involved. Throughout the century hundreds of unrecorded sailings took place from the ports and creeks of the south and west coasts. Many a man sought to make his fortune in the fabled lands of the west, and many a ship left England never to return. Many others no doubt came back, some with wealth and some without, but only the greater enterprises and those which by chance left a record in the English admiralty court or the Spanish and Mexican Inquisitions have found their way into history.

Out of this confused situation grew the voyages of John Hawkins, one of the founding-fathers of England's naval tradition. The son of William Hawkins of Plymouth who had traded with Brazil in the 1530s, he was a man of commanding presence and intellect, of outstanding abilities as a seaman, administrator, fighter and diplomat, and endowed with such charm that even his opponents in the Spanish colonies could only remark ruefully that once you let Hawkins talk to you you would end up by doing his will. In the early 1560s, inspired by the French example and by his own wide contacts with both Spaniards and English at Seville and in the Canaries, he conceived a plan for peacefully invading the Spanish monopoly. Although he lacked a licence he had some reason to hope for favourable treatment: his queen was allied to the king of Spain, quite a few Englishmen were still trading from Seville to the New World, and he proposed to offer essential goods. His plan required capital which he gathered by moving his headquarters to London and forming a syndicate in that city where maritime enterprise was at last attracting speculators. Even his first company included men like Sir William Winter and Benjamin Gonson (whose daughter he married), both officials of the queen's navy. In October 1562 Hawkins set out for West Africa where he bought slaves from the native rulers—by fair means, though the local Portuguese officials, to hide their complicity, later pretended that he had used superior force. He then crossed with the trade winds to the West Indies. On this occasion he landed on the island of Hispaniola (Haiti) where he tactfully overcame official reluctance and did a roaring trade. Two of his vessels were confiscated when he sent them into Spanish ports, and despite his best efforts he never secured compensation; that he did send them there indicates that he was not trying to act clandestinely.

Even with these losses his voyage showed sufficient profit to encourage both him and his backers to persist. The second voyage (1564) was a much grander affair. The shareholders included not only Cecil, Leicester, and the lord admiral, but even the queen who contributed a naval vessel, the famous *Jesus of Lubeck*, a high-charged, impressive, and wellnigh unseaworthy ship. It was a gift in the true Elizabethan manner, though admittedly the queen could hardly risk her best ships in so speculative a cause. At any rate, Hawkins was now in her service: his voyage had official standing. It seems clear that both the queen and the captain hoped to make these voyages regular by offering to police the Caribbean against pirates in return for trading privileges. But these hopes foundered on Spain's intransigeance and her recovery of control in the West Indies after a general reorganisation in the 1560s and 1570s. As far as trade went, Hawkins was even more successful in his second voyage. He followed the same route and practice as on the first occasion, except that he made for the

[1] It may still be necessary to defend Hawkins because he went in for slaving at a time when few thought negroes human. Moreover, the men he sold in the West Indies were slaves in Africa before he bought them and may have been saved from worse treatment by their transhipment into an area where they represented valuable property. By the standards of age Hawkins, who valued seamen's lives and cared for his men, was exceptionally humane.

Spanish Main—the north coast of South America—instead of the islands. After the usual collusive display of intimidation, designed to save the faces of the Spanish officials, he filled his holds and sailed for Havana, which (lacking both map and pilot) he missed, and Florida where he called on a French colony a few weeks before its destruction by the Spaniards. He took in fish in Newfoundland and returned to Plymouth, paying a profit of 60 per cent. on the shares of the company.

Hawkins' second voyage established his route and his methods, but it was really the end of a very promising venture. Relations between England and Spain were deteriorating. Hawkins' scrupulous behaviour availed little when the officials with whom he had dealt covered their disobedience by blackening his character with accusations of piracy, murderous bombardment, and heresy, and when other English seamen were preying on Spanish shipping in European waters. Instead of accepting Hawkins' notion of peaceful and mutually profitable relations, Philip II launched vigorous protests at London and got down to mending the gaps in his imperial defences. Throughout 1565 energetic measures were in train to stiffen the backs of Spain's imperial agents and prevent the colonists from breaking the strict trading laws, so that John Lovell, who followed in Hawkins' footsteps in 1566, found the ports closed against him. Unable to emulate his model's diplomatic skill, he returned empty-handed from a voyage worth recording only because it served to introduce Francis Drake to the Caribbean. Drake, born about 1540 and therefore Hawkins' junior by some eight years, was an altogether different man. Of west country stock, he was raised at Chatham where his father was chaplain in the dockyard, and learned his seamanship in the wild and pirate-infested Channel. He surpassed Hawkins as a commander in war and in controlled if reckless-seeming enterprise, but lacked the older man's polish and diplomatic skill. Passionately protestant and given to preaching the gospel to his shipmates, he approached the Spanish empire from the first as a crusader against popish wickedness and Spanish arrogance rather than as a merchant bent on his peaceful pursuits.

In 1567 Hawkins equipped his third fleet, and this time Drake accompanied him, ultimately commanding the small *Judith* of fifty tons. It was the biggest enterprise yet, and the queen again held shares, but things went badly from the start. The Portuguese were watching the Guinea coast more carefully and Hawkins had to get his slaves by war: he assisted a negro king in the capture of a stronghold and took those for slaves whom his allies spared. When he reached the Main he found the Spaniards ready to resist him, so that he had to force his trade upon them. The officials, beaten off by a display rather than the use of force, stood aloof, and some trade took place. Then, as Hawkins turned to set course for England, disaster struck him. A hurricane so damaged the ancient *Jesus* that she would either have had to be abandoned or repaired in harbour. To his credit, Hawkins determined on the latter course: she was, he said, the queen's ship, and he would think it shame not to try to save her. His attitude was the more remarkable as he stood to lose by it. By the terms of the contract the queen would suffer the loss if any of her ships sank at sea, while those returned had to be repaired at the expense of the whole syndicate of which Hawkins was a leading shareholder. The storm left Hawkins only with the hope of putting into San Juan de Ulua where the treasure fleet from Spain was expected—that is, with the prospect of helplessly facing a much superior force. He did his best: he took possession of a fortified sandbank which commanded the harbour, and when the Spanish fleet appeared agreed to let them enter only on condition that he retained his hold on that vital point. The fleet was carrying the new viceroy of New Spain who deeply resented this heretic corsair making conditions to him on the threshold of his dominion; from the first it was intended to break the agreement. A treacherous attack led to confused and bitter fighting from which Hawkins came off with the loss of all his ships except the *Minion* and Drake in the *Judith*. In the morning the *Judith* was gone; she arrived in England a few days before Hawkins, but nothing at all is known of her journey or the reasons for Drake's desertion. Hawkins never reproached him for it. He himself made a terrible voyage home. The *Minion* carried at first more than twice her proper complement of men, so that some hundred demanded to be put on shore where they fell into the hands of the Inquisition; the remainder, very short of food, sailed on, but only fifteen out of over a hundred reached Plymouth.

San Juan de Ulua marked a turning point. The treachery—beyond question it was that, though of course Hawkins had no right by Spanish law to be in the Caribbean at all—was not forgotten for generations. It ended all possibility of peaceful trade with the Spanish empire and ushered in open attacks on Spanish cities and treasure ships. Hawkins' seagoing days were over after his tragic third voyage, for Burghley employed him to reconstruct the navy. The hero of the new phase was Drake, now about to launch out on twenty years of daring and continuously successful enterprise which made his name a terror to Spain and a by-word in England. He may have visited the Caribbean in 1570 and was certainly there in 1571, gathering booty from coastwise shipping and information for his projected attack on Nombre de Dios and the *galleones*. English relations with Spain were bad at this time when the effects of the quarrel with Alva and the mutual trade embargo still lingered, and it is possible (as had been argued) that Drake's expedition of 1572 represented an underhand but official policy of the queen's. It certainly represented Drake's vengeance for San Juan and his desire to be at the popish enemy. With two ships, seventy-five men, and a carefully prepared plan of attack he set sail from Plymouth in May 1572. He made for a harbour in Panama which he had chosen the previous year, hoping in vain to keep it secret from Spain. There he built three pinnaces from components brought from England and coasted up towards Nombre de Dios. The attack on this place, a town of some size, by his seventy men was completely successful, but a tropical storm held up the invaders, and in the end they drew off without treasure when Drake, wounded in the leg, collapsed from loss of blood. However, the enterprise was far from over. After some months spent in sweeping along the Main, looting and terrorising the local shipping, Drake heard news of a treasure train about to cross the Isthmus from Panama. Allying himself with the Cimaroons, a mixed tribe of runaway negro slaves and Indians who roamed the inaccessible interior of this narrowest part of America, Drake laid two ambushes of which the second, almost under the eyes of Nombre de Dios, succeeded. Thus he returned, carrying some £40,000 worth of Spanish silver and having left his mark on the Spanish colonies (and on history). By modern standards, his action was that of a pirate, but by the standards of the time it was that of a patriot taking advantage of the distinction between European and American conditions. It is now commonly alleged that the activities of Drake and his imitators, so far from bringing wealth into the country, harmed England by ruining her trade with Spain and the Spanish dependencies. But Anglo-Spanish relations were bad before ever the seadogs set out, and Anglo-Spanish trade was in the doldrums before the middle of the century. The government at least welcomed these much needed draughts of ready cash.

When Drake reached England with his booty in 1573 he found the government trying to restore good relations with Spain and realised that this was no time to advertise his doings. He therefore vanished from view: his track is lost for about two years at the end of which he reappeared in Ireland (1575). But the news spread among the west country seamen, and several expeditions attempted to emulate his achievements. Some are recorded, more are doubtless forgotten. The most famous of them was John Oxenham's disastrous voyage of 1576. Oxenham had been with Drake in 1572-3 and had then worked out a grandiose plan for capturing temporary control of the Isthmus: he wanted to attack the unarmed Spanish shipping in the Pacific and then retreat at leisure to the Caribbean shore. Taking only fifty men and relying on the alliance already made with the Cimaroons, Oxenham carried out the first part of his plan. But while he crossed the Isthmus and collected his treasure, the Spaniards found and destroyed his ships and prepared to capture him on his retreat. Oxenham behaved very differently from Hawkins and Drake, going out of his way to display a crude protestantism and showing himself carelessly over-confident. In the end he was surprised, lost most of his men and all his gains, and fell into the hands of the Inquisition who hanged him at Lima. Some of his men died with him, while others went into slavery in Spanish galleys. The stories of the treatment meted out to English protestants and interlopers by the Spaniards stirred up an enduring passion in England. The Spanish courts, and especially the Inquisition of Mexico, acted with perfect though merciless justice according to their lights and laws, by which the English were strictly pirates as well as heretics; but the cruelties and extravagances of the Spanish administration cannot be explained away and were severe even by the not very exacting English standards of the time. It was memories of this sort that induced Grey to massacre the Spaniards at Smerwick: there was little tolerance or gentleness to be found anywhere, though Hawkins always avoided illegality and fighting if he could, and Drake invariably treated his prisoners with courtesy and mercy.

Oxenham's failure ended the project of the Isthmus, the more so as the Spanish authorities now virtually exterminated the Cimaroons. But the vulnerability of the Pacific coast had been shown up: there could be no stopping the men who wanted to get at this easy target. The leading scheme was that put forward by Grenville: to pass through the Straits of Magellan, raid the west coast, and come back through the north-west passage the eastern end of which Frobisher claimed to have found. Its western opening was thought to be about the fortieth parallel of latitude. To this Dee added his desire for the discovery of Terra Australis. The possibility of following Magellan's route to the Moluccas was also considered. Drake learned of these schemes in Ireland from Thomas Doughty, a dabbler in the science of the day and an adventurer whom the event proved to be but an indifferent seaman and explorer. Thus when the government took up the idea in 1577, forming a powerful syndicate with the queen again contributing her share, Drake's reputation and his relations with Burghley caused him to be chosen for the command in preference to Grenville. The expedition set sail in November 1577, with three ships and with Doughty sharing the lead with Drake. To begin with, things did not go too well. The men had believed that they were making for Alexandria, and when Drake sailed to Cape Verde and then, turning west, got becalmed in the hitherto unfamiliar doldrums, the muttering began. From the first Doughty was an impossible subordinate and a bad colleague, and when the ships at last reached Port Julian, just north of the Straits of Magellan, Drake had to try him for mutiny and execute him. He rightly held that command had to be absolutely in one man's hands if these enterprises were to succeed, but it was a long time before the practice of appointing a council of commanders in naval expeditions finally disappeared. Having established control, Drake attempted the passage and covered its 300 miles in the remarkably short time of sixteen days. No sooner, however, had his fleet reached the Pacific than they were met by appalling weather from the north which for months prevented them from making any headway. In the course of this time Drake lost his other two vessels, remaining alone with the *Golden Hind* which was at one point driven so far south that he may have sighted Cape Horn. If geographers had not been so convinced of the existence of the southern continent, Drake's observations ought to have destroyed the notion, but, though some began to doubt, with many the conviction remained.

At last in November 1578 the gales abated and Drake sailed north. The whole vast and unprotected Spanish empire lay open before him. His single ship's guns could destroy anything the Spaniards could put against him, a notable early example of the rôle of gun-power in naval warfare. Thus he raided up and down, till in the end he struck lucky with the capture of a great carrack, the *Cacafuego* and her cargo of silver (March 1579). The exploit secured the financial success of the voyage, and Drake proceeded to carry out his other instructions.[1] Sailing north along the coast of California he made a hurried search for the passage to the Atlantic, taking the opportunity to claim possession of California by the name of New Albion. He got well above latitude forty before

[1] It appears from his own statements that the order to attack the Spanish empire was endorsed by Elizabeth herself but kept secret from Burghley.

deciding that the geographers were once more wrong and turning west for the islands of Asia. After an easy passage he reached the Moluccas in July 1579. Here he bought three tons of the precious cloves and made a so-called trading treaty with the sultan of Ternate who hoped to use the English against the Portuguese. The passage out of the rock-infested and uncharted archipelago nearly proved fatal to the *Golden Hind*—she struck a submerged rock and the cloves as well as some guns had to be jettisoned—but after that the rest was easy. Sailing round the Cape of Good Hope, up to Sierra Leone, and from there along a familiar trade route, Drake reached Plymouth in September 1580. His famous first question—was the queen alive—reflected not only his patriotic loyalty but also his wish to know whether his fantastic doings would be recognised or disavowed. He had completed the second circumnavigation of the globe—the first by an Englishman—and easily the most notable achievement of Elizabethan maritime enterprise.

While Drake was on his three years' journey the protests had been coming in thick and fast, but by this time Elizabeth was less careful of Spanish susceptibilities. In any case, Drake's exploits had made him a national hero whom she could not disavow, let alone punish, without risking a serious storm in the country. Nor did she wish to do any such thing. In April 1581 she visited Deptford and there, on the deck of the *Golden Hind*, by way of publicly proclaiming her approval of his work and her acceptance of the profit, she had him knighted by Alençon's ambassador—so as to commit the French to the same policy. But while England resounded with the news, and while men were dreaming of a new age of commercial prosperity—with easy profits off the west coast of America and lucrative trade with the Moluccas—the truth is that Drake's return marked the end of the heroic, the carefree, stage of Elizabethan maritime endeavour. In 1581 it was hoped to employ him to capture the Azores for Don Antonio of Portugal and establish a base across the path of the Spanish treasure fleets: nothing came of this, and the defeat of a similar French attempt at Terceira sobered everybody. Spain was not as decrepit as the fire-eaters had thought. A company formed to exploit Drake's treaty with Ternate sent a well-found fleet east, but memories of Drake's exploits stirred up trouble on board: the crews, eager to find more *Cacafuegos*, demanded to be taken west through the straits, and the proud expedition returned with nothing but loss. There were other lesser voyages. Spanish reorganisation was making the Caribbean anything but a pleasant hunting-ground, the Straits of

Magellan were very rarely passed as easily as by Drake,[1] and the approaching danger of war compelled the government to keep the best seamen of England close at hand. The scene narrowed down from the wonderful prospects opened by Hawkins and Drake to the immediate problem of defence against Spain.

3. PROPAGANDA AND COLONISATION

Vigorous as the maritime movement of the early Elizabethan age was, two aspects of it foreshadowed achievement rather than accomplished it: writings on the explorations and attempts at settlement. Stories of fabulous lands rich in gold, silver, ivory, spices, and pearls, as well as wonders for the curious and adventure for the restless, were now gaining a growing audience in England. The works of Thorne, Eden, and Gilbert, and the activities of John Dee have already been mentioned, but there is no harm in stressing them once again—especially the last, for without his constant output of mathematical and navigational memorials, of geographical speculation, of map-making and studies of instruments, the whole great movement would never have developed. A lesser man of the same ilk was Richard Hakluyt the Elder, a lawyer whose informed interest in trade and navigation resulted in learned and sensible memoranda which greatly assisted, for instance, the work of the north-eastern explorers. Altogether, the second half of the century witnessed an astonishing output of geographical literature, some of it original but most of it translated from the works of Italian, Spanish, Flemish, and German writers, mathematicians, and map-makers. The libraries of learned men as well as gentlemen's houses were filling with works on the new science of cosmography.

The greatest of Elizabethan propagandists did not write until the 1580s. This was Richard Hakluyt the Younger, cousin of the elder Hakluyt (1552?-1616). A clerk in holy orders, he received his initiation into geographical enthusiasm from his cousin and then proceeded to study and teach the subject at Oxford, before diplomatic employment—he was chaplain to the embassy in France—widened his view, introduced him to yet more continental learning, and suggested to him the lines on which he was to work. Inspired more by scientific interest but not unmindful of the commercial

[1] The prevailing westerly winds made the Straits a very difficult proposition, while the Cape Horn route suffered from the additional disadvantage of not supplying the penguins with which the ships commonly replenished their stores of provisions.

preoccupations which moved the elder Richard, the younger found his real vocation in collecting and publishing the adventures of others. In his first collection—*Divers Voyages touching the Discovery of America* (1582)—he gathered material both English and foreign on the early discoveries. *A Discourse of Western Planting* followed in 1584, one of a number of pamphlets connected with the colonising movement. But Hakluyt established his lasting fame with the volumes of his *Principle Navigations, Voyages, and Discoveries of the English Nation*, first published in 1589 and greatly enlarged in 1598-1600. It was Hakluyt's aim to counter the taunt that the English had done nothing to deserve a share of the world's discoveries, and to record for posterity the exploits of the great navigators of his day. Usually he collected his stories at first hand, and many of them are in fact preserved in the very words of the actors. Thus the only record we have of Hawkins' last voyage is his own rather terse report, happily preserved by Hakluyt. With such material, and writing Tudor prose at its best, Hakluyt could hardly go wrong.

Perhaps the most interesting of Hakluyt's tracts discussed, as has been indicated, the desirability of English settlement in America. While merchants and seamen of merchant descent (or less) supported the movement for an expanding trade and encouraged or carried out the attack on Spanish treasure, the movement for colonisation was in the hands of the gentry, and in particular of a small group of Devon gentlemen—Sir Humphrey Gilbert, his half-brother Sir Walter Raleigh, and their cousin Sir Richard Grenville. These three had had strikingly similar careers. Educated at the universities and inns of court, in the best manner of the Elizabethan gentry training for their tasks of local government, they had taken part at various times in the constant Irish warfare which proved so remarkable a nursery of soldiers, adventurers, and colonisers.[1] From the late 1570s the ideas of propagandists began to take effect. Of all North America, Englishmen were well acquainted only with the Newfoundland fishing banks, and these they knew only during the summer. Ignorant of the effects of the gulf stream, they thought reasonably enough that a coast which stretched down to Mediterranean latitudes should provide plenty of good land and fine conditions for European settlement. Unemployment and vagabondage at home provided a spur. The idea got about that England was overpopulated and, it was thought, could no longer feed or employ her people. Just how serious the situation was is not known—though certainly

[1] Ireland really belonged to the sphere of foreign countries which Elizabethan statesmen wished to colonise. See below, pp. 389f.

contemporaries exaggerated wildly—but the middle of Elizabeth's reign probably saw population at a height, before the return of plague and bad harvests, and the effects of war, once more put a brake on expansion in the 1590s. But colonies would do more than draw off the surplus. American settlements (as Spain had shown) were sources of wealth, or (as France had tried to show) might be a standing threat on the flank of the Spanish treasure route; one would find precious metal, it was thought, in any part of the New World; some held that another isthmus existed in the neighbourhood of Virginia which ought to be occupied as a stage on the road to Asia, in preference to the bootless search for the north-west passage. Above all else, of course, it was the example of the colonising powers which excited the rampant nationalism of the age to demand equal exertion and performance.

In 1578, Anthony Parkhurst, who had made a thorough study of Newfoundland, wrote two reports in which he advocated a settlement there: a permanent station would help the fishing industry, there were iron and copper waiting to be mined, the forests could provide naval stores, and—he argued—the climate was mild enough to grow crops on the English pattern. Gilbert, who had thought of colonies as early as 1572, took the matter up. In 1578 he got a royal patent authorising the settlement of North America, but difficulties in finding men and money, as well as his own inclination to do a little raiding à la Drake first, held up operations until 1582. Associated with him were the inevitable Dee, Sir Philip Sidney, and a catholic gentleman, Sir George Peckham, who hoped to found a refuge for his co-religionists. Queen and court gave their support; the elder Hakluyt wrote notes and the younger offered his *Divers Voyages* (dedicated to Sidney); hopes ran high. But only very formidable men—men like Drake and Hawkins—could handle the wild, lawless, and gold-hungry adventurers who alone would be persuaded to make up the crews and part of the higher ranks of these expeditions. Gilbert, a man of spirit with the wide if somewhat unstable interests usual among the Elizabethans, lacked the essential qualities of leadership and the power to drive discordant elements in harness. He lost his largest ship two days out of Plymouth: her captain simply turned back. Even so, the fleet reached Newfoundland, formally took possession of St John, and then explored southwards. But when the ships carrying the prospective colonists were wrecked off this uncharted coast, there was nothing left but to return. In his enthusiasm Gilbert had put every penny he possessed into the venture; had he returned he would have been both bankrupt and discredited. Fate proved kinder. He made the passage back in the tiny *Squirrel* of ten tons and was lost in a storm off the Azores, having won himself lasting renown with those famous words of stoicism—'we are as near to heaven by sea as by land'. Even the lesser of these Elizabethan adventures were truly heroic at heart.

Gilbert's mantle fell upon Raleigh, an altogether more important figure. A brilliant fighting soldier but only moderate in command, one of the masters of English prose, an accomplished dilettante in poetry and science, warrior and courtier and man of intellect, he epitomised the Elizabethan ideal—even down to his tragic death after worldly success. By 1583 he had made his fortune and marred his life by gaining the favour of the queen who showered him with wealth and advantages but deprived him of all chance of active enterprise. All he could do was to put his enthusiasm, knowledge, and wealth behind the voyages of others. In 1584 he obtained a new grant for a projected settlement to the south of Gilbert's site and dispatched a fleet under Philip Amadas and Arthur Barlow. It followed the usual route to the Caribbean but then struck north. Amadas made his landfall in the islands off the North Carolina coast, established contact with the Indians who in their awe were uncommonly friendly, and spent a few highly idyllic weeks of pleasant intercourse on Roanoke Island. Confident that they had found an earthly paradise, the expedition returned, bringing with them two Indians; Raleigh, playing the courtier, named the colony Virginia in the queen's honour. Though Elizabeth was naturally pleased and flattered, she never put anything into these ventures. A voyage of trade and looting, with a promise of immediate rich reward was one thing; these visionary, expensive, and profitless schemes of settlement were quite another. Undoubtedly, placed as she was in Europe, she could do no other.

Raleigh despatched his second expedition to consolidate the discoveries of the first in 1585. The command was entrusted to Sir Richard Grenville, so far better known as a soldier than as a sailor, but one who had already displayed vision and interest in those South Sea plans of 1573-5 from which Drake had in the end profited. Grenville was a man to whom the habit of command came easily, but he lacked Hawkins' humanity to his men and Drake's inspiration, so that he never recorded achievements worthy of his abilities. He put the colonists ashore on Roanoke under their governor Ralph Lane who unfortunately had none of the qualities necessary to a pioneer. The most striking thing about all those early settlements is the overconfidence of the adventurers: it was all thought much easier than it turned out to be. Of course, the

Spanish conquest of mighty empires by a handful of men and in a few years gave the wrong impression. The first Virginian colonists were not settlers but soldiers: they expected to live the life of a garrison supplied by the local natives and an annual fleet from home. Unfortunately the Indians, who during Amadas' summer visit had been so lavish, themselves had little enough and nothing to spare at other seasons. They also lost their awe and respect for the white visitors when they found them to be but mortal and moreover permanent neighbours. Lane could do nothing to establish a colony on a sound footing, and when Grenville failed to appear in April 1586 the settlers began to talk of going. A little later Drake arrived at the colony from his last raid in the Caribbean. In his most generous manner he offered a ship and supplies to tide them over till the relief arrived, but a storm endangered his ships in Roanoke's unsafe anchorage while the colonists debated among themselves, and in the end they accepted a passage home. Only a few days afterwards Grenville reached the deserted colony. He left a token force of fifteen to preserve the English claims; none of these men were ever seen again.

The first attempt to colonise Virginia thus ended in disaster and with Raleigh too impoverished to contemplate further activity. He leased his rights to a London syndicate who in 1587 despatched a new body of men under John White to re-settle Roanoke Island. The plans were sounder—it was intended to distribute land and encourage genuine settlement—but the execution was worse. White was forced to return for supplies, leaving the colonists under uncertain and divided leadership. Then came the years 1588-9 when all English shipping concentrated on the Spanish war, and it was not until 1591 that White managed to return. He found the colony abandoned, but it looked as though the men had gone peaceably into the interior, whereas Grenville's fifteen had certainly been killed in a fight with the Indians. White's men, eager to seek for treasure, would not permit him to investigate, and Raleigh, tired by this time of the whole project, had other things in mind. Thus the mystery of the second Virginia colony was never solved. The sole outcome of all the high hopes, manifold hardships, and considerable expense was an abandoned stockade on an island off the unknown continent. Or so it seemed: in fact the memory of that beginning was never lost, and Lane brought home knowledge of the great Chesapeake Bay round which the ultimate settlement of Virginia was to grow up. Gilbert, Grenville, and Raleigh, with all their failures, and Dee and Hakluyt with all their miscalculations, remain the founders of the British empire.

4. THE NAVY

The voyages into distant countries trained a new breed of seamen and laid the foundations of England's maritime ascendancy. In time of war, merchant ships as well as private vessels built to be able to give battle composed the bulk of the nation's fighting force at sea, but they were collected around a nucleus of royal ships. The king's navy is said to date from the time of Alfred, but its history was discontinuous until the Tudors constructed ships, trained and employed officers, and set up shore installations. Henry VII, finding the Lancastrian navy dispersed, built a few ships, two of them at least—the *Regent* and the *Sovereign*—of real value. It may be noted that even before the Reformation English ships, unlike those of Spain, did not bear the names of saints: the common opinion which sees in this the influence of protestantism appears to be mistaken. These modest beginnings, designed rather to protect England from invasion than to provide a weapon for aggressive war, were continued on a much more impressive scale by the second Tudor. Whatever his shortcomings as an administrator, it appears that Henry VIII put much energy and considerable knowledge into the building of a fleet. As soon as he came to the throne, the problem of military strength occupied him: he wanted a navy which could hold the Channel and blockade the enemy while he invaded France. There were two periods of intensive naval building in his reign. By 1515 he had created an effective fleet containing as well such unwieldy monstrosities as the famous *Great Harry* or *Henry Grace à Dieu* of 1,500 tons, the pride of king and country alike but purely a prestige vessel which never saw action. Then again, in the later 1530s, when the threat of invasion from the continent grew serious, Henry and Cromwell rebuilt the navy on more efficient lines. It was this fleet that fought the naval actions of the 1542-6 war, a war marked by an unusual bustle of naval engagements because both the contending kings had paid much attention to their ships. At Henry's death the navy consisted of some fifty-three seaworthy ships, a considerable number of them of larger size.

The typical ship of the time was the carrack or high-built ship, very short in proportion to her beam and with a pronounced tumblehome above the waterline to carry the huge forecastles and poops, several stories high, which provided the accommodation for her fighting crew. For naval actions continued to be based on the tactics of laying-to and boarding; each ship carried a considerable number of soldiers who did the actual fighting once the sailors—

inferior creatures that they were—had transported them to the scene of action. Assaults of this sort profited from high towers which enabled archers and handgun-men to fire down upon the enemy. Until Henry VIII's reforms, ships' artillery consisted of very many (200-300) small calibre guns which fired chain and canister to sweep the opposing decks; there was no attempt to sink the enemy, and before the reign of Elizabeth the Tudor navy lost only one capital ship at sea—the *Mary Rose* which sank turning into the wind and not because of enemy action. Henry is credited with the invention of the heavy-calibre broadside. It is true that he believed in big guns placed in the castles and the waist of these high-charged ships, but there is in fact no sign that naval tactics had yet changed. In home waters, close to ports and supplies, the carrack with her very large complement could serve a purpose; but she was unfit to take to the oceans where her clumsy build, topheaviness, and problems of provisioning were shown up. The Spaniards had already abandoned her in favour of the more seaworthy galleon—longer in proportion to her beam, with a low poop and no raised forecastle—but until the 1570s English naval construction, based on Mediterranean models, generally lagged behind that of Spain and France.

Henry's reign was more successful in producing a better supply and repair organisation for the navy. Portsmouth and Dover being exposed to French raids (and the latter repeatedly silted up), Henry founded dockyards in the Thames (at Woolwich and Deptford) for the building and laying up of his cherished fleet. A series of experiments resulted in 1546 in the creation of the navy board, consisting of the treasurer of the navy, controller of the navy, surveyor of ships, master of the ordnance, and clerk of the ships, which under the lord admiral was to administer the royal navy until later Stuart times. Henry's fleet was not so magnificent as he thought, but he had assisted at the laying of sure foundations. Under his immediate successors his achievement was endangered by the general decay which overtook the administration. Peculation and neglect between them ruined Henry's proud battle-fleet: by 1558 its strength had declined from fifty-three to twenty-four, and in tonnage from 11,000 to 7,000. What was worse, many of the ships that remained were so badly decayed that they had ceased to be seaworthy. Wooden ships demanded regular overhauls to test for dry rot and check the caulking, while hempen rope immersed in water had a short life and ships' riggings needed constant attention. Although Northumberland had first-hand experience of naval fighting—he was Henry VIII's last and best admiral—and attempted to arrest the decline, Elizabeth inherited a fleet which as near as made no difference had ceased to exist. Northumberland's only achievement was the building of Chatham dockyard in the safe reaches of the Medway: here was to be the nerve-centre of the Elizabethan navy.

During the first twenty years of her reign Elizabeth—or rather Burghley—could do little for the navy except attempt piecemeal improvement. The end of the French danger removed the most pressing need, and financial difficulties dictated a policy of dangerous parsimony. During this time the navy board was dominated by Sir William Winter, surveyor of ships and master of ordnance, while its nominal head was Benjamin Gonson, Hawkins' father-in-law. The Winters were a family of sea-captains and merchants, and Sir William had earned a just reputation for competence in both respects. But the whole naval administration suffered from the bane of Elizabethan government—minor peculation. The work got done—things were not as bad as under Edward VI and Mary—but it got done too expensively, and since the money available was limited not much got done. Burghley knew too little of the technicalities to stop practices by which the queen's timber was sold back to her or used for Winter's own vessels, cordage and pitch and other stores were charged more highly than they should have been, and queen's ships were employed for the navy board's private profit. When the *Revenge* was built in 1575 she cost the queen £4,000, though the true cost had been nearer £2,200. Aware that things were not as they ought to be, Burghley was helpless until he found in John Hawkins a professional adviser. After 1569 Hawkins left seagoing to others: under pressure from queen and treasurer he turned his skill to the reconstruction of the navy. It was he above all who enabled the English fleet to face and defeat the Armada.

In a way this was itself ironical, for Hawkins saw little purpose in concentrating on Channel defence. He wanted to base English strategy on the treasure routes. His experience had shown him that Spain could be kept helpless if the supply of American silver was cut off: on this revenue, some ten per cent. of his total, Philip II relied for the maintenance of his fleet and armies. Hawkins therefore proposed to cut the routes, either in the Caribbean or at the Azores, and for this he needed an ocean-going fleet. The *Jesus* stuck in his memory as an awful warning. In the place of out-of-date carracks he wished to put improved galleons; instead of the traditional floating castles he wanted to build fast-sailing and manœuvrable fighting ships which would rely on seamanship and fire-power. He owed his survival at San Juan de Ulua to the better gunnery of his ships: even in confined waters the broadside had proved more effective than boarding tactics. Hawkins' ideas met with violent opposition from the navy board whose members had had no experience of war outside the narrow seas, but Burghley trusted Hawkins. The *Revenge* was the first ship to be built to Hawkins' plans, and she was Drake's favourite among all the queen's ships, the one he picked as his flagship during the Armada campaign. But in order to build more ships like her Hawkins had to break the navy board; he had to obtain money and he could get it only by saving from the existing allocation, for there was no hope of more. Thus he convinced Burghley of Winter's corruption, was appointed treasurer of the navy in 1578, and next year took over the running of it for a lump sum, under the terms of a contract known as the 'first bargain'. He had promised an annual saving of £4,000, and he very nearly achieved it. Labouring under great difficulties, and hampered by the hostility of his colleagues who (since they held by patent for life) could not be removed from the board, Hawkins thoroughly reformed the administration of navy and dockyards. A 'second bargain' in 1585 gave him dictatorial powers which he used for a programme of new building. The outcome of it was that in 1587, when he laid down his office, the queen's navy consisted of twenty-three ships and eighteen ocean-going pinnaces,[1] all of them eminently seaworthy and representing a formidable fighting force. Among them was the great *Ark Royal* which the queen had bought from Raleigh and which was the last word in naval construction. Hawkins reduced the proportion of men to tonnage, with happy results. He wanted cleanliness and air on board to avoid disease, and he knew that an overmanned ship, short of supplies, was only a nuisance to an ocean-going fleet; but again he had to fight traditions grounded on Channel fighting with its near-by supply bases. He even succeeded in getting naval pay raised, so as to attract a better type of man; knowing what Elizabeth was, one may think this his highest achievement. And he had done it single-handed, against his colleagues though supported by Burghley. In the end, however, the famous Hawkins charm produced a lasting reconciliation with the Winter party. Rebuilt, renewed, and ready, the queen's navy was waiting at its anchorages in 1587, while rumours and threats of invasion were flying up from the south.

[1] Pinnaces were small oared vessels with a sail, very necessary for dispatch-carrying and the investigation of unfamiliar shores.

Chapter XIII

WAR, 1585-1603

1. ENGLAND AT WAR

FROM the moment of Elizabeth's accession, war was always impending. For twenty-seven years the queen managed to postpone its outbreak, but during the last eighteen years of the reign England was continually at war. Not indeed that moments of rest and something like peace did not intervene in this long period: like all the wars of the time this one too was very desultory, brief vigorous campaigns alternating with long-drawn sieges and months of stagnant inactivity, while armies rested and typhoid and dysentery did more efficiently what the enemies' weapons could not accomplish. Yet at all times during those eighteen years the drain on men and money went on inexorably. England was really engaged on four fronts. Defence of the realm came first: even after the defeat of Spain's greatest effort (as it proved) in 1588, the danger of invasion remained ever present, and repeated alarms—both true and false—underlined the necessity for constant vigilance, especially in the sea lanes. The war at sea went on without ceasing, a story of privateers and search for contraband in neutral shipping broken only by the occasional big expedition and more sizable action. Further, England was engaged on the continent of Europe. From 1585 to the end of the reign, Elizabeth maintained an expeditionary force in the Netherlands as well as garrisons in the towns of Flushing and Brill—the 'cautionary towns'—which were ceded by the Dutch into temporary English keeping as a guarantee of good faith and as safe ports of entry for English reinforcements. Ostend and Bergen, also garrisoned by English troops but outposts against the enemy rather than rear-guard towns, completed a quartet of fortified places that over the years came almost to look like English colonies. In addition, English expeditions sailed to the support of Henry IV of France between 1589 and 1596. Fourthly and lastly, the biggest battlefield of all lay in Ireland, a danger spot from the beginning of the reign and nearly fatal to Elizabeth's policy after 1595 when rebellion there joined hands with the national enemy.

The effort required by such a war was naturally prodigious, and the results obtained were really very slight in proportion. After the repulse of Spain's attack in 1588 England never again won a decisive battle, though she continued to score successes in minor actions and an occasional exploit. On the whole the war lacked clear purpose or incisive action, but in this it merely conformed to sixteenth-century type. Nevertheless, much criticism has been levelled at the queen and her ministers. Elizabeth, it is alleged, was constitutionally incapable of conducting a war: she displayed qualities of indecision, procrastination, variability of mind, and cheeseparing parsimony which went far to ensure the failure of the various enterprises attempted. She prevented the effective use of England's resources, held up her admirals when they wished to sail, restrained them with foolishly rigorous and ill-considered instructions, and left the continental forces in the lurch when the timely despatch of reinforcements could have crowned great efforts with success. One school of commentators has concentrated on the alleged mistake of frittering away England's strength in continental expeditions, to the detriment of the war at sea where lay—as later history was to show—her best chance of triumph. The naval strategy had its exponents at the time, especially in Sir John Hawkins. In 1579 he recommended the despatch of a squadron to catch the plate fleet in the Azores and raid the Caribbean; in 1584 he proposed to cripple Spain by sweeping her shores in support of Don Antonio, the Portuguese claimant; in 1589 he submitted a grand strategical concept relying on a permanent force maintained by relays in the Azores, to cut for ever the flow of treasure which enabled Spain to make war. Though less articulate, Drake also supported a policy of concentrating on Spain's supply lines by means of sea-going squadrons. Much of this was at times attempted: the accusation against the queen is that too often she neglected this side of the war, insisted (with a landsman's failure to understand sea warfare) on keeping the navy in home stations to protect the Channel, and wasted time on continental actions. There is some truth in this comprehensive indictment. Elizabeth was often impossibly dilatory and wayward; as she grew older, her old tricks of indecision became an unbreakable habit. She hated war and was usually ready to seek her ends by other means, and neither she nor Burghley—unrepentant civilians—ever fully grasped the realities of military action. But the accusers miss their mark: the government did much better than alleged, and often the soldiers and sailors bore the guilt for failure. This will appear from an examination of the difficulties faced by England in those long years of war.[1]

In the first place, there is the problem of manpower: where did England get the men to fight her wars? As European populations went, the country ranked low: her 3,500,000 (at a rough estimate) represented perhaps a quarter of the French nation, less than half that of Spain, and stood even below the numbers of the United Provinces (the rebellious Netherlands). She had no standing army. The old feudal levy had proved its futility, though Henry VIII, for instance, still tried to fight his wars by summoning the leading nobility and gentry with their tenants and retainers. Financial difficulties as well as national considerations forbade the hiring of mercenaries, the expedient which had helped Henry VII to establish his throne. There remained volunteers, an uncertain and fluctuating source of supply, and the county militia, reorganised by statute in Mary's last year. All Englishmen between the ages of sixteen and sixty were liable to muster once a year for a review of the forces available, a check on equipment, and training. But exceptions were readily made; those of the militia that promised best—the 'trained bands'—were kept at home to defend the realm; and the armies overseas could be recruited only from the untrained men. In strict law the militia could not be compelled to serve overseas, though the government solved the legal problem by ignoring it and came down heavily on murmurings in the 1590s when the burden of the war began to tell. When men were needed, the usual practice was to send special commissioners to the shire musters to take what they required; these might be experienced officers like Sir John Norris who went recruiting in 1589, or more commonly the lords lieutenants of the counties. Thus in driblets reckoned by hundreds the total force was gradually assembled at the ports of embarkation. The numbers available were not large: in 1591 it was calculated that the whole amounted to some 104,000 men of whom only 42,000 were both trained and equipped —and these, of course, had to await the Spaniard at home. Yet out of such unpromising circumstances the government produced, according to the best estimates, some 20,000 men for France (of whom barely half returned), rather more than that for the Netherlands, perhaps 25,000 for Ireland, and new levies for the three great naval expeditions of 1589, 1596, and 1597 to a total of 17,000.

[1] For hostile views of Elizabeth's conduct of the war see e.g. E. P. Cheyney, *History of England from the Defeat of the Armada to the Death of Elizabeth*, and J. Corbett, *Drake and the Tudor Navy*. A useful corrective is applied, e.g. in J. E. Neale's *Queen Elizabeth*.

The armies so collected were far from satisfactory. Over the years, no doubt, the survivors turned into veterans: the performances of English detachments under such men as Sir John Norris in Brittany, Sir Roger Williams in Normandy, or Sir Francis Vere in the Netherlands were perfectly creditable. But they started as raw recruits, pressed men who did their best to desert on the march to the ports, or during the long waits while transport was assembled, or even abroad. As pressure mounted, it became more and more necessary to recruit criminals, prisoners, and vagabonds; the best military material from among the yeomen, ploughmen, and farmers was wanted to till the soil. Problems of supply, victualling, arming, and pay continued throughout the war, though experience gradually improved the services. Thus the council produced a ration organisation in the Netherlands after 1588, with regular contractors and warehouses, which was copied in Ireland in 1598. The ration scales were generous and varied, but the food often rotted before it reached the soldiers. Supplies of ordnance, powder, match, balls, armour, and so forth came partly from the ordnance office in the Tower and partly from county arsenals; here, too, organisation improved, though the practice of charging powder and match upon a soldier's pay (partly to prevent wastage) naturally led to a somewhat unwarlike reluctance to fire muskets at all. The men were supplied with winter and summer uniforms; here contractors had a field-day in the supply of ill-fitting and unserviceable shoes, cloaks, stockings, and so on. Most of these difficulties were to recur in all wars down to modern times; what is remarkable is that the Elizabethan privy council, starting from scratch and ever hampered by lack of money, yet produced some order out of complete chaos, and in the end sent English soldiers into action better equipped and fed than was usual even among the military powers of the continent.

Only one problem proved quite intractable. Corruption in the army itself could not be stamped out. It centred mostly on the captains of companies, responsible for allocating supplies and pay to their men, who with the assistance of the company clerks took their improper share of everything that passed through their hands. The common practice of returning more men on strength than actually existed produced the concession known as 'dead pays': for every ninety men under his command the captain drew a hundred men's pay, the difference being his perquisite. Even this did not satisfy the greed of these men, and illegal dead pays continued to appear on the returns. The overwhelming impression is of a government trying its best in the face of the criminal irresponsibility, negligence, self-seeking, and lack of public spirit of nearly all the men on the spot, from generals to privates.

These armies—and navies too, where conditions of life were of course even worse—were not, on the whole, led by any great commanders. Almost of necessity, the small and scattered English army never produced generals to compare with the best the continent could show—men like Alexander of Parma, Maurice of Nassau, or even Henry IV of France—though as the wars went on many English commanders became very competent warriors of the second rank. In one form of war the English acquired genuine mastery: that was the guerilla warfare of the Irish bogs and forests where they were held at bay, off and on, for forty years. Here men like Sir Henry Sidney and Lord Mountjoy displayed remarkable abilities as colonial conquerors. Mountjoy may be the exception to the rule: he succeeded even against trained Spanish infantry, though they were rather out of their element at the time.[1] At sea, the early years of the war saw the decline and passing away of a great generation of admirals. Grenville died in 1591, Frobisher in 1594, Drake and Hawkins—shadows of their real selves—in 1595; and though many hardy and skilful sailors still set out from Plymouth and Bristol and London, those heroes found only lesser (though still at times notable) successors in such men as Howard of Effingham, Lord Thomas Howard, or Sir Walter Raleigh. Worst of all in its effects on the war was the flashing career of the young earl of Essex, despite all his zeal and gallantry; this will appear in the course of the story. Almost all the actions of the war were marked by unbelievable courage, reckless enterprise despite all odds, fierce fighting, and too little skill in the higher reaches of military science.

With such men, such armies, and such physical difficulties in supply and transport, it ought to be evident that discussions of strategy cannot be based on the possibilities of a technically more advanced age. Sixteenth-century navies, for instance, always found it hard to keep at sea for more than two months. Victualling and watering were insoluble problems, for the large number of men required to work the sails of the day kept crews big. All operations away from home waters involved almost insuperable risks, as the Spaniards learned in 1588 and the English in 1589. The consequent need for a land base in hostile country led to much inevitable dissipation of time and energy in preliminary operations. Those careful plans that we hear so much about do not even seem to have taken sufficient account of the ordinary difficulties of navigation.

[1] See below, p. 393.

The ships of the time were seaworthy enough in the sense that they could outride most storms, but their primitive rig meant that they could not sail very close to the wind or at all into it. The various expeditions were held up in English harbours at least as much by the prevailing winds from the south-west as by the queen's changes of mind; and in a gale the only thing to do was to run before the wind. Bad weather thus invariably scattered a fleet, and a ship caught on a lee shore was lost for certain. None of the naval forces sent out by either side ever came back in a body; there was only one Armada simply because three others sent in the 1590s were driven back by storms before they got into English latitudes. All this helps to indicate how unusually difficult such actions as Hawkins advocated really were: both he and Drake drew on experience gained with small compact forces against very shaky defences and tended to overrate the skill of the English and the weakness of Spain. It is not even clear that either they or later writers were correct in ignoring the problem of Channel defence which the queen insisted upon. Since that day the best defence of English shores has often lain in attacks elsewhere, but in 1588 the English were nearly caught defenceless, and in 1597 only storms prevented a major Spanish descent while the English fleet was still straggling back from the Azores.

Above all else it was lack of money that limited England's effectiveness in the war. As always, war fantastically increased government expenditure, the more so because it was in this period that England came into line with continental practice by abandoning the long-bow and equipping her infantry with muskets, calivers (light handguns), and pikes. Precisely how much the war swallowed up it is hard to say since different documents give different amounts for the same items; figures can only be tentative. A soldier's pay was 8*d*. a day; the cost of raising a horseman with his equipment rose from £25 to £30; one winter uniform in Ireland cost £3 14*s*. 4*d*. For the 7,600 men sent to the Netherlands in 1585 the queen contracted to pay £126,000 a year, and this proved too low an estimate; something over £2,000,000 was spent there before Elizabeth died. The small expedition to Brittany, with reinforcements, absorbed about £280,000. The mobilisation for the Armada more than doubled the ordinary outlay on the navy, and the two expeditions to Cadiz and the Azores (1596-7) were calculated to have cost some £170,000. As for Ireland, Robert Cecil alleged in 1599—before the biggest campaign there—that £4,300,000 had been spent on it since 1588; but even on a lower estimate less influenced by desire to extract supplies, the Tyrone rebellion alone (1596-1601) accounted for little short of £2,000,000. These are staggering sums for sixteenth-century conditions. When Elizabeth died the Dutch owed her debts of nearly £800,000 (of which about half was in the end paid to James I), while Henry IV's debts were nearly £300,000 of which he never repaid more than a quarter. All this throws a flood of light on Burghley's desperate economies and on Elizabeth's care of her resources and her frequent complaints that she was pouring away her treasure to no purpose. In those years Spain defaulted with such regularity that the matter became a joke, while Elizabeth never went bankrupt; but the struggle for survival left a heavy burden of debt to the next reign.

After all, the ordinary revenue of the crown amounted to only £200,000 a year, augmented in the war years by rigorous exploitation to £300,000. Out of this the ordinary government of the realm and the expenses of court and household had to be covered. None the less, Burghley had built up by 1585 a reserve of £300,000 which served to support the war down to the Armada year. Thereafter the government were of necessity back to the hand-to-mouth existence of Henry VIII and his immediate successors. Elizabeth showed no hesitation to call parliament to aid her: every one of the six war-parliaments (1585, 1587, 1589, 1593, 1597, 1601) was asked for subsidies, and every one granted them, on the whole with surprising readiness. Members grumbled after 1593, and the taxpayers made even more noise, but there was no serious or lasting opposition. In those sixteen years the queen obtained about £2,000,000 in direct and extraordinary taxation, and even this unprecedented burden, which—since the assessment did not reflect national wealth at all accurately—was borne with some difficulty, came nowhere near to meeting the cost. Ready cash was always short, for taxes took their time coming in. Everything was tried. The government extracted more from the customs, mainly by returning to farming; it sold crown lands, thus once again impoverishing the crown in the long run; rents and recusancy fines were exploited more stringently; forced loans and benevolences were revived. But none of this sufficed, and Elizabeth was forced to borrow on interest, to skimp the war, and to conduct it by the curious expedient of joint-stock companies financed partly by herself and partly by private persons. Small wonder that she thought more of the possible profit when her ships sailed for Lisbon or Cadiz, than of the military problems involved; small wonder that a loss on such an expedition, which at the least was expected to pay for itself, was more than she would put up with.

The queen, Burghley, and after his death in 1598 Robert Cecil and Lord Buckhurst, did wonders; the country paid more, and more readily, than it had ever done; but even so shortage of money dogged every step. The war laid the foundation for that shaky financial position which the Stuarts, who made it worse without a war, were to find the biggest obstacle to autocratic government.

In truth, England entered the conflict without being in the least ready for it, Hawkins' navy always excepted. Not for 150 years had the country fought a major war, and things had changed beyond recognition since the days of Joan of Arc. England's economy was not organised for war; she had neither an efficient armed force nor experienced leaders; dangers threatened in too many places at once. All that England had were numbers of eager, brave, foolhardy men willing to fight, as well as many willing to plunder, and more reluctant conscripts whom war occasionally turned into good soldiers; she had a queen and council, inexperienced indeed in such matters, but willing and—as the event proved—well able to learn; and she had the advantage of a fierce protestant spirit among her best men which drove them into the breach at Cadiz, across the oceans, and into the bloody skirmishes round Ostend and Brest with more passion than mere discipline or the desire for booty would ever account for. As it is, those sixteen years nearly turned the English into a military people—militant they had always been. When Elizabeth died the treasury might indeed be empty, but she had an army and a navy which, despite many failures and too few decisive successes, could look back upon performances which by the standards of the time were creditable. As for the queen, she never ceased to think the war a calamity or to hope for its cessation; and of course she was right.

2. THE BEGINNING OF THE WAR, AND THE END OF MARY STUART

The assassination of William of Orange (June 1584) ended the queen's hopes of continuing her policy of peace. The earlier death of Alençon and the besotted incapacity of Henry III of France meant that she could no longer use French intervention to maintain Dutch resistance to Spain. Throughout 1584 and 1585 the prince of Parma was carrying all before him in the Netherlands; in August 1585, the great city of Antwerp, left without succour, fell into Spanish hands, and the Dutch cause stood at its lowest. Moreover, in January 1585 the Guise faction formed an alliance with Spain and raised rebellion against their king; by June the Catholic League dominated France. If Spain was to be held at bay and protestantism was to be saved, England would have to take an open part in the war. The decision proved difficult and the negotiations dragged on. Relations with Spain had been bad since the expulsion of Mendoza, but many—including Burghley—still hoped to be able to come to terms with her. However, in May 1585 Philip ordered the seizure of all English ships in Spanish harbours, thus ending the opposition of English merchants to a step which would destroy their trade with Spain, and the fall of Antwerp clinched matters. In August 1585 Elizabeth concluded a treaty of alliance with the Dutch States General by which she promised to maintain an army in the Netherlands at her own cost until the end of the war, while the Dutch handed over Flushing and Brill. The queen refused the sovereignty of the Netherlands, vacant since Alençon's death, but accepted the title of protector. After further delays, due largely to financial difficulties or the queen's parsimony—according as one sees it—Leicester sailed in December with some 7,600 men and a showy retinue. Though it remained undeclared, war with Spain was a fact.

Leicester's campaigns in the Netherlands proved both disastrous and humiliating. At this time England was in no position to wage successful war on land, and Leicester himself, now in his fifties, displayed little except arrogance, quarrelsomeness, and incompetence. A figure-head was needed, but this figure-head wished to act. The queen had strictly forbidden any arrangement which might suggest an English administration in the Netherlands: she was an ally, not a ruler. Yet the first thing Leicester did was to accept the title of governor. Elizabeth's fury nearly finished him and the whole enterprise; only the impossibility of deserting the Dutch so soon prevented his recall. The cost of the expedition was reckoned not far short of half the crown's annual revenue, yet Leicester wasted his supplies, arbitrarily increased officers' wages (including his own), and did nothing to stop the rampant peculation. Instead he complained of the government's parsimony, an unjustified charge which was to stick for 350 years.[1] The actual campaign of 1586 produced no positive results except some individual deeds of valour of which Sir Philip Sidney's death after the battle of Zutphen is the best remembered. Leicester quarrelled with his own best captains and his Dutch allies; in November 1586 he returned to England; the war, so eagerly begun by the English fire-eaters and so well received by the hardpressed Dutch threatened to end in mutual hostility, with ignominy for the former and disaster for the latter.

[1] It was proved groundless by J. E. Neale in *Eng. Hist. Rev.* (1930).

While the continental engagements yielded neither glory nor profit, English feats at sea amazed all Europe and raised Sir Francis Drake to the status of a legendary figure. The Spanish seizure of English property in May 1585 provoked a counter-stroke which was originally and officially intended to secure compensation, but was turned into a general attack on Spain's American empire. As early as 1579 Hawkins had suggested the despatch of a small mobile squadron to intercept the treasure fleet in the Azores and then to raid the Caribbean: in his opinion no harbour or shipping there need escape pillage and destruction. It was in effect to carry out this plan that Drake sailed in September 1585. He had with him nearly thirty ships and a force of over 2,000, both mariners and soldiers; the expedition was equipped by a joint-stock of £6,000 to which the queen contributed £1,000; he had official backing and instructions. Leaving Plymouth in great haste, for fear of countermanding orders from the queen, with watercasks half-filled and victuals taken on all anyhow, Drake made for Vigo. Here, on Spanish soil, he completed the fitting out of his fleet; although he did only very little material damage to Spain, Philip's prestige suffered a heavy blow, and since financial credit depended on prestige Drake's visit affected Spain's power to make war. He missed both the plate fleets of 1585, touched at the Cape Verde Islands where the fleet picked up a virulent fever, and made for the West Indies where his exploits were daring and eminently successful. In brilliant amphibious actions, he captured and sacked San Domingo, the capital of Cuba, and Carthagena, the capital of the Main. Losses by fever forced him to break off the enterprise sooner than intended, and he took insufficient booty to pay a profit, but if as piracy the voyage was a failure it did great things as an act of war. The Spanish West Indies were crippled—short of ships and guns—and Philip, forced to restore them and to pay a higher interest on his Italian loans, had to divert precious resources from the Netherlands where they could be ill spared. Parma's troops remained unpaid and therefore inactive: Drake in the Caribbean had done more than Leicester in Zeeland to ease the pressure on the Dutch.

The success of 1586 was not followed up, a fact for which Drake's financial failure and the needs of the Netherlands are quite enough to account. At the same time, Elizabeth and some of her councillors, continued to look for the possibility of peace. Throughout these years contact with Spain was maintained in devious ways, and the queen was ever ready to seize any chance of ending the war. That that chance never came was probably due to Philip.

As the king of Spain grew older he changed from a politician to a fanatic: the cause of the Church began to dominate all his plans. With Parma successful in the Netherlands and the League keeping France pro-Spanish, he was moreover free at last to turn his full power on that island whose protestant queen had thwarted him for thirty years. England seemed to have been behind every move against the Habsburg ascendancy since the abdication of Charles V, and although such a view underestimated the normal hostility of France it accurately interpreted the situation in the 1580s. Peace was out of the question. Elizabeth cannot be blamed because at this stage she did not concentrate on wiping out Spanish sea-power and obtaining a stranglehold on the treasure routes. England was on the defensive: the tone was set by Spain, immeasurably the stronger power, as it seemed to all men at the time.

However, before we turn to the great Spanish assault, we must follow up the story of one disturbing element in the first half of Elizabeth's reign. The imprisoned queen of Scots was drawing near to her tragic fate. Ever since Elizabeth saved her, in 1571-2, from the consequences of the Ridolfi plot and the nation's wrath, Mary had been a potential danger and an active centre of conspiracy. Until 1585 she was kept in Sheffield Castle, guarded by the earl of Shrewsbury and inflicted with the earl's formidable wife, Bess of Hardwick. But her imprisonment, though close, had been honourable; she was treated as a queen and permitted free contact with the outer world. The treaty of Berwick ended the plotting which centred on Scotland, but from France her relatives, the Guises, continued to buoy up her hopes. However, the discovery of the Throckmorton plot, the assassination of William of Orange, the parliamentary association to protect the queen, all combined to bring matters to a head. In January 1585 Mary was transferred to Tutbury Castle into the custody of Sir Amyas Paulet, a stern puritan who treated her as an immoral and dangerous woman, and not as a queen. Almost immediately another plot was uncovered, or as some would have it, manufactured. A Dr William Parry was executed in March for conspiring against Elizabeth. Parry was a thorough scoundrel who had escaped hanging for burglary by entering Walsingham's secret service. He even got back into favour and respectability sufficiently to sit in the parliament of 1584. But he either involved himself with Mary's partisans abroad, or else was sacrificed by Walsingham who employed him as an *agent provocateur*. In any case, he deserved hanging more than most of the political victims of the reign. One result was that Walsingham was induced to pay closer attention to the English catholic refugees in France and so to come upon the track of the Babington conspiracy which terminated the life of Mary Stuart.

That there were men plotting to free Mary and kill Elizabeth was certain, but Walsingham wanted proof of Mary's complicity since he was convinced that the danger could only end if the rival queen were dead. To that purpose he so arranged matters that ever since men have been found to say that he invented the plot for which Mary was executed. The truth is that Mary was guilty, but Walsingham tricked her into giving herself away. In December 1585 he had her transferred to Chartley Manor, and there, with the assistance of Paulet and a renegade catholic, persuaded her that she had found a safe way to communicate with France. In reality, every letter to and fro passed through the secretary's hands. By the middle of 1586 the new conspiracy was taking shape in the mind of Anthony Babington, a young man of more devotion than sense, and by July Mary was in Walsingham's toils. Babington wrote her a full account of the plot—which involved the assassination of Elizabeth—and asked her approval. There is both drama and disgust in the scene that followed, with Walsingham and his agents tensed in their wait for Mary's answer. It was delayed and all seemed lost; at last it came, and the queen of Scots was seen to have given her approval to everything. It was the end. By September the conspirators were executed—to the joy of the populace—and in October a special commission tried Mary and found her guilty. Guilty she was, but Elizabeth felt no more inclined now than earlier to exact the penalty. A fellow queen whose links with France made her execution a serious international matter—all Elizabeth's humane and political instincts rose up against the action. But the nation and the council were determined. Once more parliament, pressing for Mary's death, was put off with an 'answer answerless', but on 1 February 1587 Elizabeth yielded and signed the warrant. She would not let it go; she tried to get Paulet to act in secret which that narrow but upright man refused angrily; then the council, acting without her knowledge, despatched the warrant. On the 7th Mary mounted the scaffold in Fotheringay Castle and welcomed martyrdom, expiating her sins and also creating a legend and a continued attachment which no other death could have produced. Elizabeth was distraught. Her rage overtopped all previous experiences of that awesome natural phenomenon. All the council were in disgrace: there was talk of prosecuting them for murder. William Davison, the second secretary of state who had let the warrant out of his keeping, was

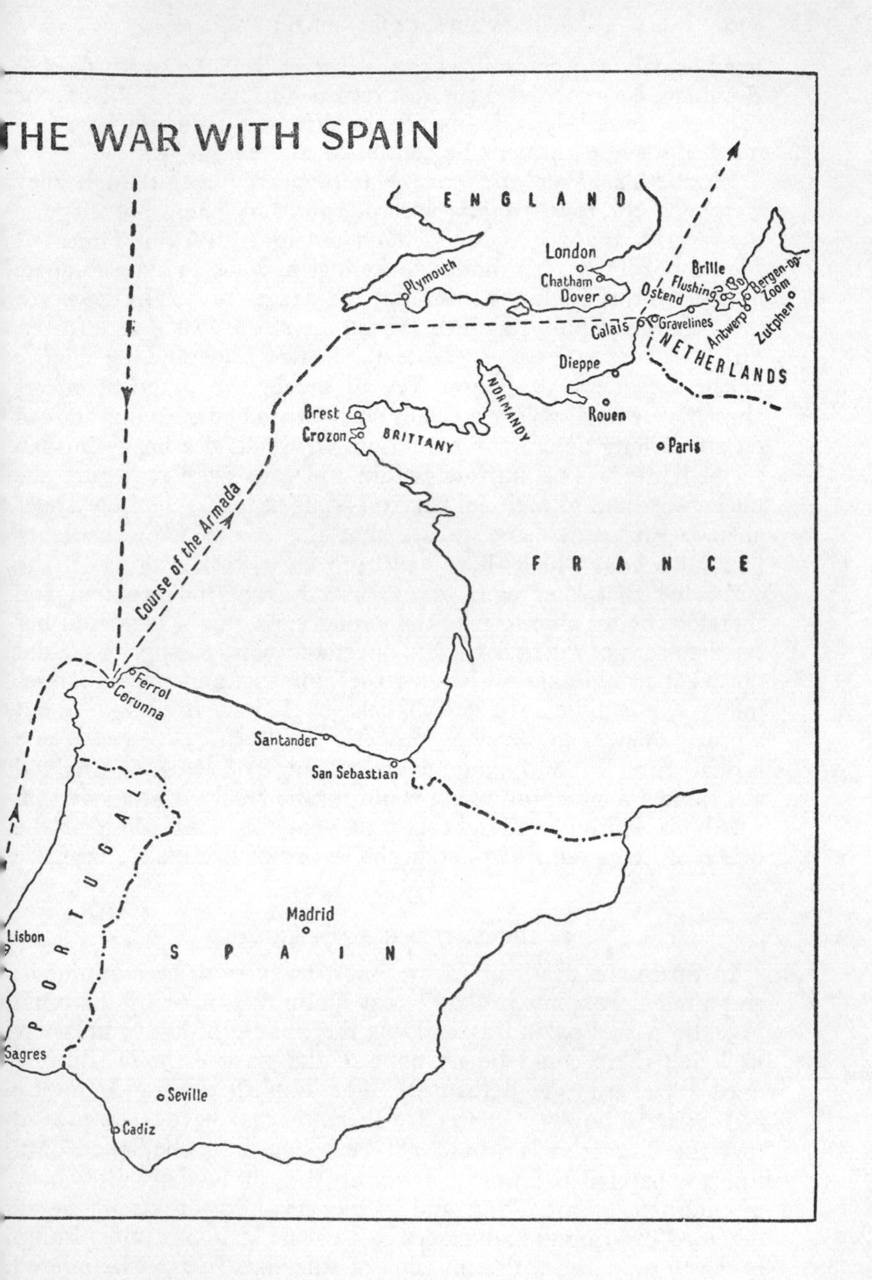
THE WAR WITH SPAIN
ENGLAND
London
Chatham
Dover
Plymouth
Brille
Flushing
Ostend
Bergen-op-Zoom
Calais
Gravelines
Antwerp
Zutphen
NETHERLANDS
Dieppe
NORMANDY
Rouen
Brest
Crozon
BRITTANY
Paris
Course of the Armada
FRANCE
Ferrol
Corunna
Santander
San Sebastian
PORTUGAL
Madrid
Lisbon
SPAIN
Sagres
Seville
Cadiz

fined heavily and committed to the Tower. But the wrath passed. Burghley, Leicester, and the rest returned to favour; Davison, the scapegoat, was released, his fine remitted, and though he relinquished his appointment he continued to draw his fee.

Elizabeth's anger and sorrow (temporarily real though they were) and the royal funeral accorded to Mary could not disguise the facts to anyone. Scotland burst out in a fury, but James VI soon subordinated his moderate feelings as a son to his passionate interest in the English succession; the danger of war in the north melted away rapidly. France, where the storm was even greater, proved harder to appease: the death of Mary cemented the alliance of the League with Spain. Yet all in all, the practical effects abroad were negligible, especially since Spain had been determined on attack long before the execution. In England a heavy burden seemed lifted. The traitors within the gate were frustrate, the queen—symbol of national survival—safe at last. When her anger abated, Elizabeth came to see that the council's disobedience had cut a knot which there had been no way of untying. If she suspected that later ages, more distant from the problem and therefore better able to take the wrong view, might condemn her for the death of the unfortunate queen of Scots, one hopes she did not let it trouble her. Whatever the moralists and the romantics may say, it is difficult to see what else could have been done about a proven danger to the state, properly and lawfully convicted of a capital crime. From the moment that Mary took refuge in England she created a situation which could not be resolved in a way that was both sensible and moral. And yet—the martyrdom of the queen of Scots remains to stain the record of Elizabeth's reign.

3. THE ENTERPRISE OF ENGLAND

In Spain the death of Mary Stuart acted both as a stimulant and a relief. It seems probable that Philip had made up his mind to settle with England as early as the middle of 1585; he knew well that there could be no hope of the great catholic triumph until Elizabeth was dethroned. The English assistance to the Netherlands, however ineffective Leicester may have been, proved that the Netherlands would not be reduced to obedience until England had fallen. Thus while Elizabeth continued her diplomacy of alternate negotiations and demonstrations of strength—all designed to bring the adversary to a pacific state of mind—Philip began to prepare for the invasion of England. In 1585 he offered himself to Pope Sixtus V as the sword of the Church, provided the

Church put up the money. Sixtus, outstanding among the Counter-Reformation popes, remained sceptical. Unlike the northern protestants with their fevered imaginations, he knew enough about Philip and Spain's religious policy to doubt the king's devotion to the catholic cause. What was more, he had a healthy respect for England whose growing power he divined and admired. When Drake set Europe talking of his exploits, the pope, oddly enough, was among his leading admirers, and it was not only an Italian delight at seeing the haughty Spaniard humbled. Sixtus suspected Philip's intentions because he thought that the catholic king was more interested in succeeding to the throne of England than in fighting the battles of the Church, in which conclusion he seems to have been right. In February 1587, when Mary's fate was sealed, Philip declared that James of Scotland, as a heretic, could not inherit, and that therefore he would assert his own rights.[1] Thus Mary's removal meant that Philip could enjoy both the practical advantages of an enterprise undertaken in his own interest and the asset of a good cause represented by his anger against the adulterous, illegitimate, heretic regicide who had usurped the English crown.

The preparations proceeded apace. Late in 1586 the pope gave a cautious blessing and an even more qualified financial assistance. In the meantime, the admiral, the marquess of Santa Cruz, busied himself in getting together the great fleet which was to bring England to her knees. His own plan, which envisaged a direct seaborne invasion, had to be abandoned because Philip could not afford the enormous expense it involved; instead it was decided to send a fleet which would win command of the English Channel and so ensure the safe transport of 3,000 veterans under Parma from the Netherlands to England. Throughout 1586 and 1587 the west coast ports of the Iberian peninsula were full of vessels being got ready for the enterprise, and stores were collected from all parts of the Spanish dominions in the Mediterranean. It was now that Drake's Caribbean raid of 1585-6 took effect by making it harder for Philip to raise the necessary loans; also, Spain depended for naval stores on the Baltic, the route whither was blocked by Dutch and English squadrons. Nevertheless, the English government, kept abreast of developments by Walsingham's foreign intelligence, knew soon enough that it was facing a formidable threat and made counter-preparations. The musters were brought up to date and the militia trained; measures against catholic priests

[1] He had a species of hereditary claim and also alleged that Mary Tudor had willed the realm to him.

were intensified and a strenuous watch was kept. Late in 1586, while Hawkins was at sea intending to raid Spain, he was kept by the queen plying up and down the Channel; there was a rumour-induced panic which soon passed over. In June 1587, after long negotiations, Elizabeth reluctantly agreed to send Leicester back to the Netherlands; she neither wanted to renew the war nor deprive herself of the earl's company, but treaty obligations and the pressure of a united council, most of them anxious to see Leicester out of England, secured his return to the post of duty. He was, if anything, less successful than on his first visit: he failed to save Sluys from Parma, quarrelled with everybody both Dutch and English, and was recalled in November 1587, leaving the Netherlands and the English forces there in a pretty confusion.

The heavy drain and the failures of the Dutch war explain sufficiently why Elizabeth wished to open negotiations with Parma, but the threat from Spain could not be overlooked. The naval experts had long clamoured to be allowed to take counter-measures, and in April 1587 Drake had his way. Sailing with a strong fleet to tackle any Spanish armament (if one were on its way to England) and to cut up the treasure convoys, but also to 'distress the ships within the havens' themselves, he reached Cadiz on the 19th and went straight in before the Spaniards knew what was upon them. In a brilliant action he destroyed some thirty ships. Then he captured the fort and anchorage of Sagres near Cape Vincent from where for nearly two months he preyed on the ships carrying supplies for the Armada. A challenge to Santa Cruz to come out and fight having been sensibly declined, Drake took his disintegrating force—disease, lack of victual, and indifferent discipline doing their accustomed work—to the Azores where he captured a great carrack and secured a financial profit for the expedition which had been equipped by the usual joint-stock company. The material loss to Spain was great—many ships destroyed, naval stores burned, supplies taken away—but worse still was the blow to Philip's reputation and credit inflicted by an English squadron based on Spanish territory itself. Nevertheless the king remained undaunted. The preparations were resumed, and, since Elizabeth either would or could not try again, the sailing of the Armada was delayed by only one year. Even so England gained much when Santa Cruz died in February 1588, for Philip had no other experienced seaman to serve him.

Thus the initiative returned to Spain, though this proved no advantage to her. In May 1588 the lord admiral, Lord Howard of Effingham, a competent officer who displayed unusual skill in making the great sea-dogs work amicably under his command, took over, with nearly all the fleet, at Plymouth. Both he and his chief advisers—Drake, Hawkins, Frobisher—wished to sail to Spain and attack, especially when it became known that the Armada, having sailed in March, had been driven by storms into Corunna. The queen and council have usually been blamed because in their ignorance of sea-fighting they kept the fleet at home for fear that the Spaniards might slip past it and attack a defenceless England; Corbett even thought that Howard had to be driven by Drake into more seamanlike action. But it is now realised that all the commanders were for attacking, and that they were probably wrong in this: off Spain the English ships would have been in the position in which the Armada was soon to be. Drake's exploit of 1587 offers little guidance—though no doubt it influenced him at the time—because the Spanish defences had since then been greatly strengthened and because a Spanish fleet was now actually on the high seas. As it was, the weather defeated Howard's three attempts to reach Spain in May and June. The same winds which drove him back into Plymouth brought the Armada north. On 19th July it sighted the Lizard. The news caught the English imprisoned by a contrary wind in Plymouth harbour, but while the Armada shortened sail to take up its predetermined formation the English beat out of Plymouth Sound and in the night of the 20th sailed across the Spanish fleet to win the weather gauge.

The two fleets were in every way better matched than used to be supposed. On both sides there were rather less than fifty effective fighting ships with some eighty others. The Spaniards were unhandier and taller, with a much heavier short-range armament and burdened with an army intended both to fight at sea and to join Parma's forces for the invasion. The English ships —Hawkins' navy supported by some warlike merchantmen of the Turkey Company—sailed much better and were more skilfully handled, but against this the Armada put its tight line-abreast formation (its 'crescent moon') which nullified the new English tactics of line-ahead sailing with the concentration of superior fire-power on individual ships. In gunnery the English had the advantage of more and better long-range guns and better trained gunners, though the Spaniards had learned much in this respect; neither side carried sufficient ammunition. In the outcome the English were surprised by the tough resistance encountered which differed greatly from what the corsairs were accustomed to find in the Caribbean: it is too easily forgotten that Spain was still the foremost military power in Europe who could not help but be formidable when she concentrated her resources, skill, and discipline on one particular task. The greatest handicap imposed on the Armada's commander, the reluctant duke of Medina Sidonia, was strategic rather than tactical. His orders forbade him to capture a harbour in England: he was to make for the Netherlands to join with Parma. But Parma, too, could offer the Armada no safe anchorage: the only port suitable for the manœuvre which Philip had in mind was Flushing, and that was in English hands.

The Spanish progress up-Channel developed into a nine days' running battle, with the English ships sailing rings round the ponderous Armada but unable to make any noticeable impression on its militarily tight formation. This was maintained by sailing at a speed of barely three knots, which in turn enhanced the advantages of English manœuvrability. There was a good deal of rather piecemeal fighting with two bigger engagements off Portland Bill and the Isle of Wight when the English knowledge of the tides enabled them to bring the Armada to action on disadvantageous terms. But although the Armada lost two ships and suffered much superficial damage, it was still an almost undiminished fighting force when it arrived off Calais on 27th July. Both sides had used up much more powder and shot than they could afford, but the Spaniards—far from home, friends, and supplies—suffered worse. It was the enforced recourse to Calais sands which was to finish the Armada; the fatal error which had overlooked the necessity for a proper anchorage prepared the way for the English victory. On the 27th Howard dropped anchor a mile offshore. There he was joined by Seymour's squadron which had been blockading Parma; now at last the lord admiral had the full strength of the fleet and parity with the Spaniards. On the night of the 28th, the English launched six fire-ships which were so well handled that the tight formation, which had defied the English long-range tactics, at last broke up. In a panic most of the Spaniards cut their cables and drifted away in the night. When morning came, all but Medina Sidonia's own ship with three or four more were seen to be scattered to the north-east. The battle which followed is known as that of Gravelines. Though the duke fought courageously, restoring something like a fleet in the course of several hours' vigorous bombardment, the Armada was virtually destroyed. Only four ships were lost, but the rest took a terrible battering from the English gunfire and lost thousands of men.

What the guns had begun the weather completed. A rain squall from the north-east ended the fight and threatened to drive the Spanish hulks on to the Flemish sands, until at the last moment the wind shifted back to the south-west. Before it the Armada took flight. There was no question of returning through the Channel, let alone of carrying out the junction with Parma who had long given up all hope of the plan's success. Medina Sidonia determined to make his way round the north of the British Isles. Though empty of ammunition, Howard followed as far as the Firth of Forth. Its final fate yet awaited the Armada. As it doubled the north of Scotland it met the Atlantic gales which threw the unseaworthy ships in scores upon rocks and headlands or sank them in mid-ocean. Some half struggled back to Spain in 1589; the fate of most of the rest was never known. All round the northern shores of Scotland and Ireland there lay the wrecks of the galleons and the bodies of the seamen and soldiers killed by the savage sea and (supposedly) by the yet more savage natives of those parts.

The disappearance of the Armada into the northern mists left everything uncertain. Rome and Spain rejoiced over false rumours of a great victory, before the truth turned all to sorrow and reviling. Philip alone received Medina Sidonia, disconsolate but blameless, with kindness and without reproaches. The commander had done his best—a good best. He was defeated by better ships, better seamanship, a needlessly rigid plan, and at the last the weather. That the storms rather than the English had destroyed the Armada was a legend fostered by the English themselves in an endeavour to claim the Almighty for their side. 'Afflavit Deus,' said Elizabeth's medal, 'et dissipati sunt': God blew and they were scattered. The queen expressed disappointment at the small number of ships taken, and neither she nor her advisers thought England safe—so much so that the defence force was mustered at Tilbury ten days after Gravelines. Lest this be thought the folly of landsmen who could not tell a victory at sea, it must be noted that the naval commanders were similarly disappointed. They grumbled at the shortage of powder. The first onslaught had been 'more coldly done than the service required', and to the end the Armada never sank before the English guns. Used to the small-scale actions of raids and piracy, Drake and his fellows underestimated the powers of defence of which a large compact fleet was capable. Howard expressed all their awe and wonder when he wrote: 'All the world never saw such a force as theirs was.' What with all this surprise and shock, the English undervalued their own achievement. The plain fact was that the Armada reached Calais a fighting force, if slightly battered and growing seriously short of ammunition. After the fire-ships had given the English guns their chance, the scattered fleet which fled before the kindly south-west wind was a collection of defenceless hulks, incapable of doing any further harm. No doubt, if the English shortage of powder could have been remedied, the guns might have anticipated the work of the gales. But the victory was won at Gravelines, by human agency. England's mood of sober rejoicing and thanksgiving to God was a creditable one and reflected moreover the knowledge that the defeat of the Armada did not end the war. Indeed, in a measure it proved its beginning and the renewal of Spanish power. Yet all this must not hide the fact that in the first great naval battle of modern times the English navy won a victory based on its superior skill and advanced tactics, as well as on the qualities of the new-style fleet of seaworthy, handy ships fighting long-range gun-actions rather than engaging at short range and boarding the enemy.

4. THE WAR WITH SPAIN, 1589-1603

The defeat of the Armada seemed to open the way to some decisive counter-stroke, though it may be said at once that this view has been more popular with historians than it was with the men who had to work out the details. They knew that Spain was not on her knees and felt rather inclined to underrate the extent of their victory. However, by December 1588 a plan had been formed. A counter-armada was to sail, commanded by Drake as admiral and Norris as general—each the leading man in his profession—and designed to break Spain at one great blow. The enterprise came to be known as the Portugal expedition, though Portugal was not among its original objectives. It was a dismal failure, made worse by the initial hopes and the enthusiasm which sent thousands of volunteers to swell the ranks of the adventurers. That failure has customarily been put entirely at the queen's door: after all, how could military men of the calibre of Drake and Norris possibly be responsible for such egregious errors? A recent review of the evidence has altered the picture considerably.[1] The queen has been accused of halfheartedness in support (so that the expedition had to be fitted out by a joint-stock company instead of being a properly financed national undertaking), of causing the fatal delay in sailing from February to April 1589, of a parsimony which despatched the fleet short of victuals, of instructions either uncertain or fatuous which compelled the commanders to waste time on side issues. But the truth is that the queen had neither ships

[1] R. B. Wernham, 'Queen Elizabeth and the Portugal Expedition of 1589', *Eng. Hist. Rev.* (1951).

nor men nor money of her own to equip such a fleet, so that the normal method of a partnership with private enterprise was inevitable; in any case, Drake and Norris, who had conceived the whole notion, as well as other gentlemen and financiers wanted their share of the expected profits. The delays were due to a quarrel with the Dutch, arising out of the projected withdrawal of seasoned troops from the Netherlands for the expedition; though originally caused by Elizabeth's highhandedness, it was prolonged beyond February by Willoughby, the English commander in the Netherlands, who did not wish to lose so many of his best men. Victuals were short because the commanders foolishly allowed popular eagerness to swell the numbers of the fleet far beyond the original estimate. But the crux of the matter was the purpose of the voyage.

The Armada had been scattered but not wiped out, and early in 1589 some forty vessels had found refuge in the ports of the Biscayan coast of Spain, especially Santander and San Sebastian. The queen, preoccupied as always with the defence of England rather than raids in distant waters, intended that these should be destroyed before anything else was attempted. Against this, the adventurers argued that those ports in the eastern end of the Bay were impossible to sail back from; they would not endanger the whole fleet by getting themselves caught in that pocket. They therefore put forward a plan for Portugal, based on the claims of Don Antonio with the exploitation of which Drake had toyed since 1581. Why should they not capture the Azores and Lisbon, stimulate a national rising, and take all Portugal? Elizabeth and Burghley had rather less faith in Antonio and a problematic uprising, but even as Philip II never ceased to hope for a catholic revolt against Elizabeth so Drake fell victim to the Portuguese exile's deluded hopes. The excuse put forward against going to Santander was but a cloak for his insistent ambitions to strike a really big blow: the Spaniards themselves had no difficulty in getting their ships round to Ferrol after refitting. Elizabeth was right: the first objective should have been the elimination of the Spanish fleet while it was yet helpless. However, as a mere shareholder she had to compromise: the final instructions ordered Drake to attack the Biscay ports and then to capture an island in the Azores, while they left the possibility of an attack on Lisbon open.

Even so, the expedition did not obey orders. It got away in April 1589, but instead of making for Santander it went to Corunna which could just about be considered a Biscayan port and which harboured one Armada galleon. Here the fleet delayed a vital fortnight, taking the town but failing before the citadel and, worst of all, failing to revictual thoroughly. Only incompetence, induced perhaps by a divided command and a mistaken confidence in Spanish weakness, can explain such behaviour. Early in May they set sail for Lisbon, completely ignoring instructions. On the way they were joined by the queen's favourite, the young earl of Essex, who had stolen away without leave to satisfy his thirst for adventure and had thus drawn upon the expedition Elizabeth's personal rancour. Lisbon was reached, but the delay at Corunna had given plenty of warning, and the attack itself was carried out very inefficiently. Combined naval and military operations are always difficult since they depend on experience and faultless timing; here Drake and Norris made things harder by losing contact with each other. All the gallantry in the world could not overcome bad strategy; the expected Portuguese rising entirely failed to happen; and by the end of the month there was nothing for it but to re-embark. Even the lucky capture of a large Hanse convoy, carrying contraband, which was used to return the sick and wounded to England, only marked a tiny break in the lowering clouds. The biggest cloud was gathering at court: the queen's letters denounced the expedition's doings and demanded the return of Essex. The fleet now began to disintegrate and its action lost purpose. A raid on Vigo was followed by a desultory invasion of the Azores, and by the end of June what was left of the great enterprise—they had lost many men though few ships—had straggled back to Plymouth. None of its aims had been achieved. Philip had suffered great annoyance and a little damage, but the ships of the late Armada were being got ready for action, Antonio remained an exile, no captures worth the telling had been made, and financially the whole affair was a total loss. Naturally Elizabeth made no secret of her thorough displeasure, and Drake and Norris remained for some years in a disgrace which it is hard, on the evidence, to suppose undeserved.

Unavoidable continental commitments now began to absorb all the resources of the crown. The war at sea continued, but for a time it remained in the hands of private persons, with an occasional queen's ship in the larger fleets. Throughout the war privateers of various kinds, equipped with royal letters of marque and commissions to prey on Spain, roamed the seas; the earl of Cumberland, for instance, had at least one such ship and usually many more at sea all the time. It appears that an average of from 100 to 200 privateering ventures set sail from England every year after 1585, bringing in prizes to an annual value of £150,000-£300,000. The main backers were merchants, especially the great men of the Barbary, Guinea, and Levant Companies. The weight of enterprise shifted from the west country to London and it acquired a much more thorough organisation. Though the regular trades, such as that in cloth, suffered by the war, imports of prize goods increased enormously, especially of sugar in which England came near to establishing a European monopoly. Shipbuilding boomed. Altogether, though the crown and perhaps the country made little out of it, the mercantile community seems to have enjoyed considerable profits from privateering.[1] The better-known voyages brought less gain. In 1590 and 1591 Frobisher, Hawkins, and Cumberland all had squadrons in the Azores on the look-out for treasure ships. No captures were made, mainly because Philip II had stopped the 1591 *flota* from sailing; although he thus greatly added to his own difficulties, he also robbed the English raiders of all profit. In 1591 the Spaniards had their one naval success of the war. A fleet from Ferrol—the ex-Armada vessels which Drake had omitted to destroy in 1589—sailed to the Azores to bring home the delayed plate fleet. At Flores it surprised a squadron commanded by Lord Thomas Howard which got away, except for the *Revenge* under Sir Richard Grenville. To this day it is uncertain whether Grenville's failure to escape was due to folly, braggadocio, or misfortune. The vessel's heroic day-long fight against the whole Spanish fleet has become legendary. When the *Revenge* surrendered, Grenville was dying and all the crew were dead or wounded. But glorious as the action was it was also probably unnecessary, and it really marked the triumph of the new Spanish convoy system which made both her empire and her treasure fleets much more difficult to attack. The only English success of the time was the taking of the great East India carrack, the *Madre de Dios*, in 1592. The ship was so ruthlessly and carelessly plundered on their own behalf by officers and men of the capturing squadron that her treasures in pearls, jewels and specie vanished beyond hope of recovery into private pockets; during the search the candles of the gold-crazed horde started fires no less than five times. The hull with its immensely valuable cargo (£800,000) was nearly left behind in the rush, and though the queen got a very fair return on her outlay she felt, with some justification, that indiscipline had

[1] These facts and conclusions (which go contrary to some received notions) are derived from the printed summary of an unprinted London thesis: K. R. Andrews, 'Economic Aspects of Elizabethan Privateering', *Bulletin of the Institute of Historical Research* (1952).

robbed her of more. The *Madre de Dios* played the part for a new generation which the *Cacafuego* had played for their elders: hopes of another such capture kept the ships at sea.

In the meantime the real centre of affairs shifted to France. Here the assassination of Henry III in 1589, in revenge for his earlier murder of Henry of Guise, had brought to the throne Henry of Navarre who as a Huguenot was quite unacceptable to the powerful catholic League but on the other hand was a necessary and valuable ally to England. In his plight he appealed for assistance, and Elizabeth responded promptly. In part she was moved by fear of a common enemy, but she also hoped to revive English claims to a French town—preferably Calais—and her demands for a 'cautionary town' on the Dutch model were to lead to much tricky negotiating and bad blood between the allies. Henry IV needed English help, especially in money, but he wished to secure his own throne and rule a united France, not burden his reign with the ignominy of having given away French territory. In 1589 he got a loan of £20,000 and an English force under Willoughby which proved quite useful, though disease forced its withdrawal after three months. Henry's successes in 1590 (the battle of Ivry) brought about Parma's first invasion of France from the north, which in turn eased the pressure on England's other ally, the Dutch, ably assisted by an English army under Vere. While things thus looked brighter in Picardy, the situation was complicated in October 1590 by the invasion of Brittany by a Spanish force in alliance with the League. The Spaniards in Brittany called up visions of important Channel bases in enemy hands, and Elizabeth did not hesitate to despatch an expeditionary force under Norris (recalled from his disgrace) which spent little short of five years in generally rather indecisive fighting. Unsupported by the French, weakened by disease and the withdrawal of troops to other theatres, though also at times reinforced by new levies, Norris and the deputies he left in charge during his occasional absences at court at least prevented Spain from obtaining a foothold in Brittany.

In the same year (1591) another English force came to Henry's assistance in Normandy. Its leader was Robert Devereux, earl of Essex, at this time barely twenty-six years old. A tall handsome man gifted with great charm of manner but also the moody testiness of the spoiled child, he touched nothing that did not decay. He was a brilliant and able enough fighter, though incompetent in command, given to foolish gestures which earned him the contempt of the professionals and the acid tongue of Elizabeth. Thus he challenged the Spaniards to come out and fight off Lisbon in

1589, and in 1591 crossed 100 miles of enemy-held territory with a splendid train to impress the glamour of his orange-tawny on the shabby and warstained Henry IV. The ageing queen found it difficult to refuse him things, but she also tried hard to instil some discipline and order into a mind potentially great but never trained to discretion, consistency, or sound judgment. One need pay no attention to the stories which would turn her feelings for this favourite—just of an age to have been the son she never had—into a matter of disgusting elderly passion. In any case, Elizabeth never forgot that she was queen, not even with Essex. No Tudor would ever let a man grow great without reminding him that he who could make could also break; but Essex, rash fool, thought that his greatness lay in himself.

At this time he only wanted to share in the war, and he persuaded Elizabeth to sanction an expedition to Normandy. She tried to get Henry to promise Le Havre and Rouen, both in League hands, to the English, but to no avail. In the end Essex went proudly, allowed his army to rot away, joined in a fruitless siege of Rouen, and returned in January 1592, to brave a more formidable foe in Elizabeth's displeasure and sarcasm. Sir Roger Williams, a genuine soldier, stayed behind at Dieppe until the end of the year. The war in France and the Netherlands dragged on without decision, until Henry IV yielded to long persuasions and changed his religion (July 1593). With that the French opposition to him collapsed, but the war against Spain continued and friendly relations with England remained important. Though in fact all English troops were withdrawn from French soil by February 1595, negotiations for a closer alliance resulted in a treaty ratified in January 1597 to which the Netherlands acceded. For years Walsingham (who died in 1590) had dreamed of just such a protestant alliance against Spain (and Rome); now that at last it had come one of the partners had ceased to be protestant.

The continental war no sooner showed signs of letting up than naval projects were revived. Late in 1594 Drake at last got back into favour, and he and Hawkins joined hands once more. The third great sailor of their generation was dead: in 1594 Frobisher lost his life in a combined operation in Brittany when Norris captured the fortess of Crozon from its Spanish defenders. Drake and Hawkins planned another powerful raid into the Caribbean. Though a minor descent on Cornwall by the Spaniards expelled from Brittany (July 1595) and the outbreak of rebellion in Ireland held up their departure, they sailed in August 1595 with a great armament and a greater reputation. But the outcome was sad: a sorry ending to two wonderful careers. Drake was now about fifty-five and Hawkins in his sixties; thirty years had passed since they first invaded the Spanish empire, and while things had changed much they had only grown old and set in their ways. It does not appear that they found it easy to work together, and the whole voyage was a series of misfortunes. Their intention was to capture a big treasure ship which was known to have had to put into Porto Rico, and to raid the Main and attack the Isthmus. All this was known long before they reached the West Indies, and the new spirit of active defence which they encountered played havoc with their memories of superior skill and easy conquest. Hawkins fell ill and died at sea as the fleet neared Porto Rico; the attack on the harbour there was beaten off with ease; raids along the Main brought very little booty because the inhabitants had been forewarned and had withdrawn with their valuables; and the march across the Isthmus was prevented by superior Spanish forces. Mortified by all these failures Drake fell a victim to dysentery and died at Porto Bello. Sir Thomas Baskerville buried him at sea and brought the disconsolate fleet home. Thus ended the lives and careers of the two greatest of Elizabethan seamen, but these shadows at the latter end cannot dim the splendid achievements of their manhood.

The failure of the 1595 expedition did, however, mark the end of large-scale enterprises into the West Indies, though individual privateers continued to do well for themselves in those waters. With the land war still languishing, the energies and greed of the adventurers thus once more concentrated on the coast of Spain and on the Azores. In 1596 Essex, Howard of Effingham (who was to survive them all and to die, at eighty-eight, in 1624), and Francis Vere combined to plan an invasion of Spain herself. Somewhat reluctantly the queen gave her blessing—together with instructions to Howard to prevent Essex from needlessly exposing himself to danger. They were distracted for a time by a sudden Spanish investment of Calais. Essex wished to relieve it, but the queen would only act if Henry IV agreed to hand the place over to her. In consequence Calais fell in April 1596, and Essex set sail for Spain in June. The fleet was the best equipped in the war: nearly 150 vessels, forty-eight of them warships, with 6,000 troops on board, and led by Essex, Howard, Vere, and Raleigh. For once the Elizabethan warriors proved capable of complete success. Cadiz was taken in a brilliant combined land and sea action and held for a fortnight during which time it was thoroughly plundered and rather inefficiently burned. Though for a time Essex wished to establish a permanent base, the queen's objections and the difficulties of supply forced him to depart on an ineffectual cruise for booty. The fleet returned in triumph but little the richer. Elizabeth, ever harder pressed, resented its failure to obtain financial profit, but the earl's reputation stood at its highest. Moreover, Philip had suffered a very serious blow indeed as well as the most complete of his frequent bankruptcies. The supremacy of the English at sea could not have been more convincingly proved, nor the essential inability of the Elizabethan navy, even at its most successful, to bring the war to a close.

Old though he was, the king of Spain reacted with vigour: indeed, the capture of Cadiz put some long-missed energy into him. Within a month or two he had launched a new armada which was to invade Ireland in support of the rebellion there. There was again something like panic in England, but the fleet had been equipped and despatched in too great a haste and storms off Cape Finisterre ended the threat. In turn, Elizabeth recognised the need of, and Essex pressed for, a repetition of the brilliant stroke of 1596. The earl had had to contend with the queen's displeasure for some time: she had tried to reduce the swollen head brought on by popular clamour by disciplining him a little and advancing his rivals, Robert Cecil and Raleigh. Early in 1597 Essex made his peace with these, and the queen also forgave him his sulks, so that the expedition of 1597 was commanded by the same quartet as that of 1596. Its fate, however, was very different. The queen wished it to attack the Spanish ships which had been scattered the year before and now lay at Ferrol and Corunna, and then to intercept the treasure fleet in the Azores. Storms drove the expedition back in July, but when it sailed in August it ignored Ferrol and made straight for the Islands. Here some rather disconnected raiding resulted in the capture of a few small islands, but sheer incompetence permitted the *flota* to pass through into the safety of Terceira. The oft-desired success had never been nearer, nor had Spain throughout the whole war a more narrow escape from a really decisive disaster. Instead the English fleet could only return disconsolate in October. It ran into north-east gales which, as usual, scattered it widely; but they also turned back another Spanish armada, for the ships so foolishly left to refit at Ferrol had set sail in autumn. At one time two fleets—one Spanish and one English, the former well-found and the latter distressed—were approaching England's undefended shore on converging lines.

The fright which this danger, when it was known, gave to queen and council, together with the failure of the Islands voyage, sufficed to end the age of great naval expeditions. Essex's reputation with the people—ready as ever to overlook incompetence when it was accompanied by generosity, display, and charm—continued high, but the queen was very angry, and the Islands voyage played its part in his ultimate downfall. In May 1598 Henry IV made peace with Spain at Vervins, somewhat against the terms of his treaty with England. In August Burghley, hoping for peace, died, and a few weeks later Philip II followed him. But peace remained to seek, for Essex and his like had little interest in it, nor could the Dutch yet lay down arms since Spain still refused to recognise their independence. Thus for the next five years small but veteran English forces under Vere continued to assist Maurice of Nassau in his gradually complete conquest of the Northern Netherlands. It was as well that the war with Spain made only small demands in those years, for Elizabeth could hardly have spared it much attention. In 1598 English fortunes in Ireland entered a phase of extreme danger.

5. THE CONQUEST OF IRELAND

Throughout the reign Ireland presented a military rather than a civil problem. We have seen how Henry VII could do little to clear the way to the establishment of royal authority, and how Henry VIII displayed energy there only during the short time of Cromwell's ascendancy.[1] Cromwell destroyed the power of the house of Kildare, and his nominee, Lord Leonard Grey, did much to overcome Irish resistance, but after 1540 the island once more drifted out of control. Henry exchanged the title of lord of Ireland for that of king (1540) and continued the old policy of anglicising the Irish chiefs by turning them into earls: to the Geraldine earls of Kildare and Desmond and the Butler earl of Ormonde, he added the Burke earl of Clanricard, the O'Brien earl of Thomond, and the O'Neill earl of Tyrone. In Mary's reign the Pale was extended by the creation of King's County and Queen's County out of tribal lands in Leix and Offaly, but these new shires were far from securely held when Elizabeth ascended the throne. English authority in Ireland had once again reached a very low ebb. The country was divided into English and Irish territory of which the former included only the enlarged Pale and the towns of the south and west (Waterford, Youghal, Cork, Limerick, and Galway).

[1] Above, pp. 30ff., 179f.

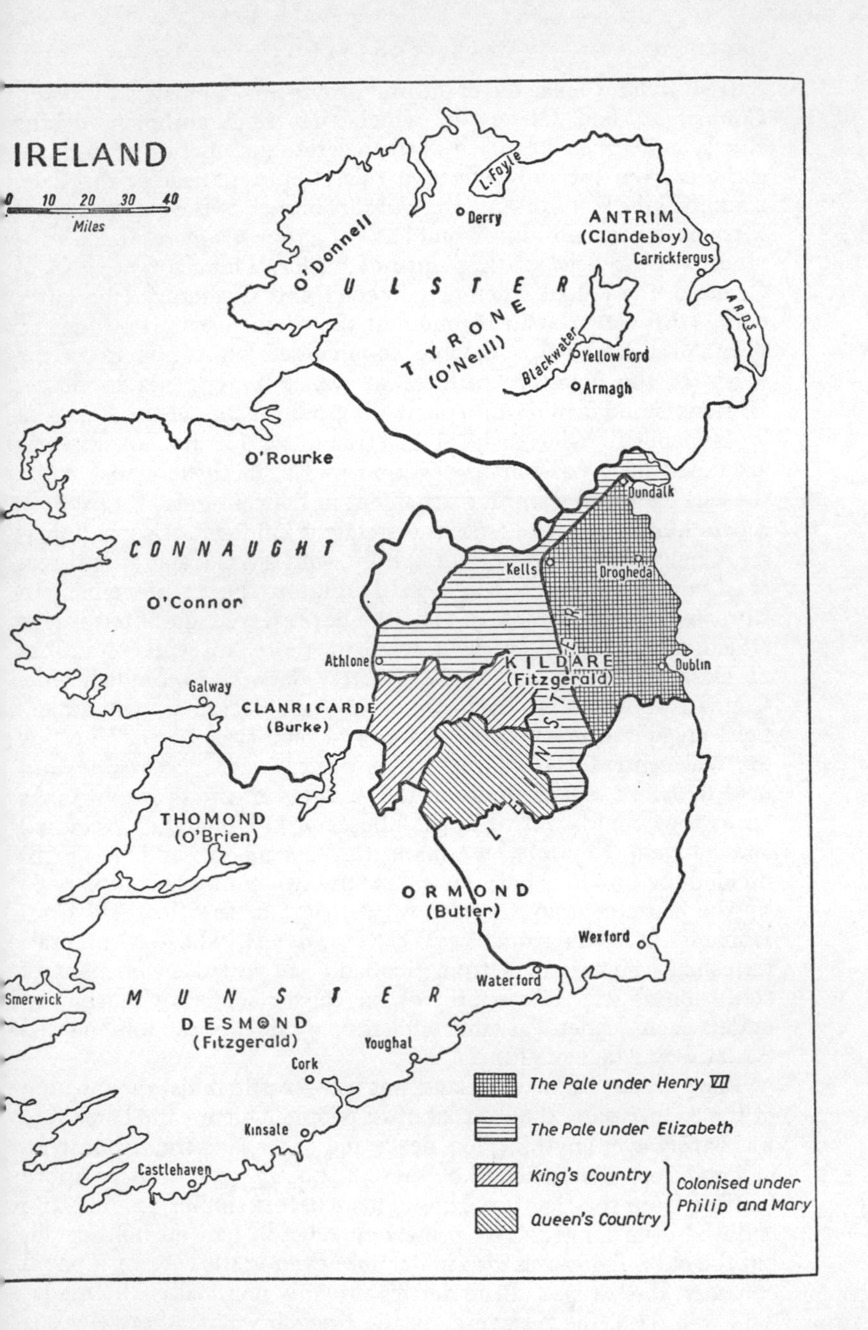
IRELAND
0 10 20 30 40
Miles
O'Donnell
ULSTER
L. Foyle
Derry
ANTRIM
(Clandeboy)
Carrickfergus
ARDS
TYRONE
(O'Neill)
Blackwater
Yellow Ford
Armagh
O'Rourke
Dundalk
CONNAUGHT
Kells
Drogheda
O'Connor
Athlone
KILDARE
(Fitzgerald)
Dublin
LEINSTER
Galway
CLANRICARDE
(Burke)
THOMOND
(O'Brien)
ORMOND
(Butler)
Wexford
Waterford
Smerwick
MUNSTER
DESMOND
(Fitzgerald)
Youghal
Cork
Kinsale
Castlehaven
The Pale under Henry VII
The Pale under Elizabeth
King's Country
Queen's Country
Colonised under Philip and Mary

Irish Ireland consisted of the four provinces—Leinster, Munster, Connaught, and Ulster—in which the tribal authority of the chiefs, sometimes disguised as the palatine jurisdiction of nominal earls, exerted the only effective rule. Leinster, nearest the Pale, contained the lands of Kildare, but this branch of the great house of Fitzgerald gave no more trouble. The other magnate of the province was the head of the house of Butler, Thomas tenth earl of Ormond, the feudal ruler of Kilkenny and Tipperary (the latter part of Munster), who throughout the reign proved the queen's most loyal Irishman. An able commander who understood the needs of the country, ruthless in war but generous in peace, Ormond stood firm despite many disappointments at the hands of lords deputies who disliked all Irishmen; for his loyalty was grounded on a passionate devotion to Elizabeth of whose court the earl had been a shining ornament in his young days. Elizabeth repaid him with a firm trust and frequent kindness. Also in Leinster, County Wicklow—wooded, hilly, wild—was a standing threat of disaffection, much too near Dublin to be comfortable. In Munster, the O'Briens of Thomond preserved an intermittent attachment to the government, while the more powerful Geraldines of Desmond were one of the greatest dangers to English rule. Connaught was wild Irish, practically unaffected by the superficial anglicisation of south and east; Ulster was worse. Here lay the real centre of Irish resistance, pretty well inaccessible and held by tribes still virtually in the savagery of the bronze age. As far as they could control it, the houses of O'Donnell (Tyrconnel) and O'Neill (Tyrone, Fermanagh, Monaghan, and Armagh) divided the province between them; the situation was complicated by the settlement in Clandeboy (Antrim) of the Scottish MacDonalds, invaders from the Western Islands, who—at intervals refreshed by accessions from Scotland—provided an element of confusion as well as a source of mercenary soldiers (Redshanks) under such leaders as the enchantingly if improbably named Sorley Boy MacDonald.

The ordinary state of Ireland was war—cattle raids, the burning of the countryside, the murder of its people. Outside the Pale there was hardly ever anything like peace and order, and the tribes lived in conditions reminiscent of 'heroic' poetry and perhaps more familiar from the Scottish Highlands where a similar mode of life endured even longer. The protestant religion had no hold at all, but the old religion was also in decline: even in the eyes of a papal emissary, the savages of the north were only nominally Christians. To begin with, the resistance to the English was neither religious nor national; it was simply the struggle of one form of civilisation (if it deserved the name) against the superior power of another. That so far no really energetic attempt had been made to subdue these menaces to settled government was due in the main to English preoccupation elsewhere: it was easier to leave Ireland alone. But the Elizabethan break with Rome necessitated action. Ireland now became a possible landing-place for hostile forces, and in the end indeed a part of the Spanish war. In the process, the old religion gained a new vigour, partly as a counterblast to the English invader, partly because Rome was a potential ally in the struggle, but largely because of the devoted labours of a few missionaries. At the beginning of the reign Ireland was virtually ungoverned and heathen; by the end it was firmly under English control and Roman Catholic.

The first task confronting Elizabeth's government was that of conquest. Before anything could be done to give Ireland an effective civil administration or to establish the Elizabethan Church there, the power of the chiefs had to be broken in battle. As it turned out, this task occupied all the reign: final victory was won almost on the day of the queen's death. The country offered all the conditions for successful guerilla warfare. Broken by woods, hills, and bogs, it easily absorbed the elusive Irish who rarely stood to give battle but harassed the royal forces on the march and closed behind them again to wipe out the illusory successes of one army after another. Not until Tyrone created an Irish army in the 1590s could Irish levies ever confront with any hope of success even half-trained Englishmen, and even in Tyrone's day they were more commonly defeated than victorious. Bad discipline and inferior weapons were the chief reasons. But, on the other hand, the war could never be brought to an end. Pacifications never lasted. Time and again a rebellious chief 'came in' to make terms; time and again, obeying the rules of tribal life, he rebelled anew. Without the bases provided by the towns and the assistance of loyal Irishmen, the government forces would have been driven into the sea in the first ten years of the reign. But no single Irishman—not even Tyrone of whom this has been alleged—ever rose to the concept, much less the fact, of national resistance; at all times the ancient feuds and rivalries prevented unity and gave the English commanders their chance. With few exceptions, these last were able and energetic men, though often ruthless and savage in the murderous manner of Irish warfare. To the existing difficulties of the Irish landscape, the prevalence of malaria which killed thousands of soldiers, and the Irish character which kept the situation ever changing, the English sometimes added by folly and rashness, leading to defeats which roused the whole country, or by arrogance which lost them the support of men willing to be loyal. Worst of all, for a long time the government at home thought it could conquer Ireland on the cheap. Until 1596 the forces at the disposal of Irish viceroys were as a rule amazingly small—a few thousand, and at times less. Time and again one reads of forts garrisoned—and successfully held, for the Irish never learned about siege warfare —by twenty or thirty men. Elizabeth's chronic procrastination too often left the country without an effective governor at critical times, and her parsimony, however explicable, ultimately wasted much treasure and blood which more energetic action at the start might have saved. The government learned their lesson the hard way: in the last stages, in Essex's army and especially in that of Mountjoy, all the necessaries—troops, stores, organisation—were supplied with a ready and efficient hand. But by then the miserable country had lived through thirty-five years of war and devastation.

The story is a long one, full of fascinating details like the bottle of whiskey which assisted Mountjoy in his great victory at Kinsale;[1] but it cannot here be told in any way to do justice to an extended episode which, however small its scale, yet involved great national and international issues and much heroism. Out of the welter of skirmishes and raids, four main occasions stand out: the rebellion of Shane O'Neill (1559-66), the Fitzmaurice confederacy in Munster (1569-72), the Desmond rebellion (1579-83), and the great or Tyrone's rebellion (1594-1603).

The first trouble arose with predictable ease out of the attempt to convert the chief of the Clan O'Neill into the earl of Tyrone. In 1559 a succession quarrel broke out between the claimants by Irish and English law, and since the former—Shane O'Neill—was much the more forceful man he soon established himself. Three uneasy years during which the lord lieutenant, the earl of Sussex, tried to maintain the English nominee ended with a compromise in 1562: Shane was permitted to retain the reality of power as captain of Tyrone, while the young heir to the earldom—Hugh O'Neill—was taken to England to be educated at court. Of all Elizabeth's Irish opponents Shane was probably the most primitive—a true savage who has been described as 'a drunkard

[1] An Irish chief in Tyrone's army whose supply of whiskey had given out, sent to ask for more to Mountjoy's second-in-command, Sir George Carew, whom he had known in better days; during the proceedings Mountjoy discovered the enemy's intentions.

even by contemporary Ulster standards', but a formidable warrior. He next spent four years of horrible war and tyranny, winning control over all Ulster; by 1566 he was so far successful that he boasted himself greater than any earl, got in touch with Rome in the hope of finding allies against the English overlordship, and appealed for help to France. This compelled the new lord deputy, Sir Henry Sidney, to take action, and in one great march through Ulster with greatly inferior forces he destroyed the power of Shane. He was assisted in this by the hatred which the O'Neill had aroused in his triumphant but barbarous conquest. Shane's army was actually destroyed by Hugh O'Donnell, in revenge for the treatment earlier meted out to Tyrconnel, and Shane himself was killed by the Antrim Scots with whom he took refuge and who, after first welcoming him, later remembered his devastating attack on them a few years earlier. The O'Neill was a great man, as savages go, but his overthrow benefited most of all his own Irish neighbours. The chieftaincy of Tyrone passed to Tirlagh Luineach O'Neill, a man who through nearly thirty years of moderate ambitions and hard drinking proved the wisdom of a cunning policy and the preservative qualities of Irish whiskey. Though never quiet, and never conquered, Ulster ceased to be an active threat.

Soon after, trouble started in the south, in Munster. Here Desmond, whom Sidney called 'a man both void of judgment to govern and will to rule', tyrannised over some of the best land in Ireland to such a degree that murder and famine were the daily lot of the people. A feud with Ormond in Tipperary, and the conjoint activities of the younger Burkes in Connaught, as well as such other wolves as the MacCarthy More and O'Sullivan Beare in Kerry, kept the whole area in despair. Sidney took such action as his means permitted and removed Desmond to the Tower; he also set up presidents of Munster and Connaught to break the local power of the chiefs and had plans for anglicising both provinces. But in 1569, a Geraldine of more ability than the imprisoned earl of Desmond, James Fitzmaurice Fitzgerald, interrupted the lord deputy's plans by raising all Munster against him. Militarily his success was shortlived and the hoped-for assistance from the continent never came; Ormond and Humphrey Gilbert (knighted for his services) suppressed the rising, and Fitzmaurice submitted in 1572. Much trust was at this time put in projects of colonisation —'plantings'—of which one was attempted in Munster and Leinster (1568-70) by a group of west country gentlemen including Sir Richard Grenville; this came to little because of the determined resistance of all Irish leaders, of whatever allegiance. Two more promising ventures in Ulster—Thomas Smith's settlement in Ards (1572-3) and the earl of Essex's colony in Clandeboy—were wiped out by the MacDonalds some of whom Essex had quite needlessly massacred. The only outcome was a general state of desultory war, full of mutual brutality, in south-east Ulster and all over the west. In 1575 Sidney returned for a second spell of duty, and in an impressive progress through all Ireland proved his remarkable qualities of command: his was the true proconsular cast. When he left in 1578—no deputy stayed longer in that barbarous country than he could help—Ireland seemed almost on the road to peace and order; his policy of controlling the whole country by English presidents of provinces, and of turning Irish chieftains into landowners by accommodating their rights to English legal arrangements, was bearing fruit.

However, he had no sooner gone than another outbreak occurred, though it is some reflection of his achievement that this time there needed outside assistance. James Fitzmaurice, who had fled the country in 1575, had since been trying to gain help in those manœuvres at Rome and Madrid of which mention has already been made. The fate of Stukeley, the landing of papal forces, the death of Fitzmaurice, the slaughter at Smerwick, have been described.[1] But though the invasion failed, the response in Ireland was such as to involve the country once more in several years of war. The earl of Desmond, back in Ireland since 1573, gradually drifted into rebellion; Viscount Baltinglass rose in the Pale itself; the newly arrived deputy, Lord Grey de Wilton, incurred a needless defeat which fanned the flames. Happily for the English, Tirlagh O'Neill stayed quiet in Ulster. Grey and Ormond swept Munster with fire; Smerwick was taken (November 1580), Baltinglass driven abroad, and Desmond 'turned into a wood-kerne', the usual description of those forced to take to outlawry in the hills; but it was not until late in 1583 that Ormond, in charge during a vacancy of the deputyship, finally hunted the earl down. Desmond was killed in an inter-tribal affray, and with him really died the great house of Fitzgerald. His lands were confiscated and 'planted' by a syndicate of which Sir Walter Raleigh was the head; this 'Munster Plantation', a larger and more promising scheme than those that had preceded it, vanished in the conflagration of the Tyrone rebellion.

Ulster had been unnaturally quiet for a long time—a long time as peace went in Ireland—though of course minor depredations with their crop of attendant atrocities had occurred. But this

[1] Above, pp. 308f.

respite really hid the gathering of trouble. Old Tirlagh Luineach seemed at last to be declining, though he surprised everyone by lasting till 1595, and it became obvious that the next man to dominate Ulster would be Hugh O'Neill, earl of Tyrone. He returned to Ireland in 1585, ostensibly a good friend to the English but from the first ambitious to make himself free master of his territories—and more. Tyrone was a man of considerable abilities, a great organiser of troops who turned the irresponsible Irish forces into something like a disciplined standing army, and a subtle statesman who was ever ready to bide his time. In negotiations he repeatedly overreached his adversaries who would have sworn that Tyrone was loyal when Tyrone was plotting his deepest. But Tyrone lacked vigour; his exceptional, and by Irish standard unnatural, patience had its counterpart in a tendency to hesitate in a crisis. Because the earl rarely acted with open decision and continued at all times to protest his loyalty—he was invariably polite and deferential to the queen's authority against which he bore arms—it is difficult to assign a precise date to his rebellion. The situation deteriorated rapidly in Ulster in 1593 with the rise of Hugh Roe O'Donnell who dominated Tyrconnel. This chief, a young man of nineteen (Tyrone was already in his forties), bore a personal grievance against the English, to which he added religious fervour (which with Tyrone was but a pretence) and the ardent bellicosity of an Ulster clansman. More than Tyrone, he was a soldier and leader of men, but it was Tyrone who alone could turn a local rising into a coherent rebellion.

O'Donnell declared himself ready to fight to the death in 1593; two years later, after much shilly-shallying, frequent encounters and withdrawals, and several reverses for the English army, Tyrone came into the open. He disposed of a trained army of 6,000, to which Sir William Russell, deputy since 1594, could oppose perhaps 1,100. The government acted promptly, dispatching reinforcements under Sir John Norris who was given a special command in Ulster. This led to friction between Russell and Norris; Tyrone's guerilla tactics proved fully effective; and Norris came near to sinking his reputation in the Irish bogs. In May 1597 Lord Burgh replaced Russell, in December Norris died, a month later Burgh followed him. Affairs were in this unsatisfactory state when disaster struck. When a temporary truce ended in mid-1598, Ormond, once again temporarily in charge, stayed in Wicklow to protect Dublin and his own estates and sent Sir Henry Bagenal (an old personal enemy of Tyrone's) to relieve the Blackwater Fort which protected the Pale against invasion from Ulster. At the

Yellow Ford across the Callan brook, a tributary of the Blackwater, Bagenal ran into Tyrone and was utterly defeated, he himself being killed with about 1,500 men (August 1598) It was the biggest defeat—the only serious defeat—of English arms in all the Irish wars, and it could have been avoided by more intelligence on the spot. The worst of it was that for a time the government had virtually no forces in Ireland: Dublin stood wide open, panic reigned, everybody except Ormond disgraced themselves to the queen's violent and well-expressed disgust. But Tyrone wasted his chance. All along he had insisted that nothing could be achieved without Spanish support, but the attempts of 1596 and 1597 to send a force to Ireland were, as has been seen, shattered by the wind. The earl continued to wait rather than act.

Even so the Yellow Ford had serious consequences. All Munster rose under a Geraldine offspring called the 'Sugane' (strawrope) earl of Desmond, while Hugh Roe established himself in Connaught. Raleigh's plantation was washed away in blood. The English hold on Ireland hung by a hair. The queen, whose failure for eighteen months to appoint a successor to Burgh had done something to bring about this state of affairs, now acted at last; indeed, the government's behaviour for the next three years deserves all praise for steadfast nerves, energy, and purpose. The reason for the long delay was the earl of Essex who, wishing to redeem himself after the Islands voyage and in any case unwilling to let someone else earn the glory of settling Ireland, demanded the post as of right. The queen hesitated. She did not want to risk a man whose presence delighted her in that graveyard of men and reputations; with her uncanny skill in judging ability even in those she favoured, she seems to have doubted his fitness for the job; above all, the post had become a matter of dispute among the court factions, which obliged her to tread warily. Meanwhile Ireland suffered. But at last she gave in: Essex arrived in Dublin in April 1599, with the largest and best equipped army yet sent there. He missed his chances shamefully. Though he impressed everyone by his bearing, his charm, and his personal courage, he failed more abysmally than any of his less well-provided predecessors. Instead of following the queen's instructions and tackling the root of the trouble in Ulster, he went on an imposing but pointless progress in Munster. Having achieved precisely nothing, he grew despondent and committed his crowning folly by entering into negotiations with Tyrone. That seasoned diplomat found Essex easy meat: a truce was concluded which left him everything he had and a breathing space in which to recruit his strength and await the Spaniards. In the meantime Essex's splendid army wasted away in disease. The letters from court grew more acid; no one could boast in Elizabeth's hearing of what he would do and hope for compassion when he completely failed to live up to his high words. But Essex, increasingly suspicious and moody, alleged that the queen was listening to his detractors. So, in September 1599, he left his post without leave to rush travel-stained into the queen's presence at court and put his side of the case. It was the virtual end of him and his career, but that does not concern the present matter.

For the English cause in Ireland Essex's desertion was a blessing. The man who replaced him proved to be the man to do the job. Charles Blount, Lord Mountjoy was a general of the stamp of Wellington: thorough, tenacious, careful, and yet capable of that calculated rashness which wins battles. Though he suffered from indifferent health he displayed astonishing energy; contrary to all the practice of the time he even fought winter campaigns which vanquished the plan upon which Tyrone proceeded. Without the winter in which to sow their grain and raise their cattle, the Irish forces could not live off the land—that is, they could not live at all. While Sir George Carew settled Munster by weaning chief after chief away from rebellion, the lord deputy himself tackled Connaught and Ulster. Sir Henry Docwra was established in a new fort at Derry, near Lough Foyle; from here, assisted by disaffected O'Neills and O'Donnells, he soon subdued Tyrconnel and cut Ulster in two. By the end of 1600 the rebellion was virtually extinguished, the Sugane earl a fugitive (he was captured in May 1601), and Tyrone driven into the fastness of his own country. At that point the long-awaited Spanish aid arrived, too late now to alter the outcome but in time to prolong the struggle. In September 1601 a force of 4,000 trained infantry under de Aguila occupied the port of Kinsale on the south coast. Mountjoy reacted with typical vigour; in no time he had concentrated his and Carew's forces at Kinsale and invested that small and ill-protected town. By December the Irish forces had also arrived, free now to break out of Ulster, and Mountjoy at last saw his chance to bring them to battle. His army, between two fires, was in a bad way with disease and lack of supplies but quite undaunted, and the victory over a much more numerous enemy was won by great superiority in skill and dash. O'Donnell fled to Spain; Tyrone, his army shattered, reached temporary sanctuary among his own mountains. It was all over. De Aguila surrendered with the honours of war in January 1602; Carew, Docwra, and the rest mopped up what remained of rebels in the course of that year, and in March 1603 Tyrone gave himself up. His actual surrender took place after Elizabeth's death, but she knew of it before she died. He was ultimately pardoned and restored by James I, but fled to Rome in 1607 and died there in 1616.

The conquest of Ireland was complete, but the work of settlement could not begin until the reign of the first Stuart. The country had suffered dreadfully; Munster, the richest province, was twice burned completely, not to mention minor afflictions. Grey, Ormond, Sidney and others—but also O'Donnell, Tyrone, and many lesser chieftains—had time and again carried death and destruction from one end of the island to the other. Only the recuperative powers of a purely agrarian community in a naturally fertile country prevented the effects from lasting for years. The conquest was necessary. England could not permit the existence of this turbulent neighbour, only nominally subject to her and a standing invitation to her enemies. As for Ireland, only conquest by England gave her a chance of emerging from the prehistoric welter of tribal warfare, with its blood-feuds, raidings, and constant killings. It was England's triumph that made possible the growth of an Irish nation, even as it was the fact of conquest that really established the firm adherence of Ireland to the Church of Rome.

Chapter XIV

THE STRUCTURE OF THE AGE: CONSERVATISM

I. CONSERVATISM

THE question is sometimes raised whether the age of Elizabeth belonged to the middle ages or modern times. Some scholars, looking at the prevailing conceptions of nature and the universe, assert confidently that an age so blatantly 'pre-scientific' cannot be modern. Others, allowing their eyes to follow Drake and the rest across the uncharted oceans, or contemplating the activities of merchants and industrialists, make no doubt that the middle ages had been left behind. Did people think in terms of progress, the individual, and the power of man's reason? Or did they preach the fall from grace, the organic and orderly society, the ineluctability of sin? The answer is that they did a little of the first and a great deal of the second. Medieval notions, we are then told, continued strong in the Elizabethan age. If this means that the period, like every other, witnessed a mingling of the old and new, the thought is hardly worth expressing; if it is to imply that ideas to do with science, rationalism, individual claims, and progress are modern, while the middle ages thought only of religion, mysticism, the society, and the decline from a golden age, then the notion is plain nonsense. The labels medieval and modern cannot be usefully attached to ideas. But they may, with reservations, be attached to things, especially to institutions; and in that respect, the age of Elizabeth, coming after the revolution of the 1530s, was modern. All surviving limitations upon the national state notwithstanding, Elizabethan England looked much more like what was to come after than what came before.

As for the prevailing attitude of the period, it is more useful to enquire whether it was directed towards change or towards stability. The reign of Henry VIII provided violent changes in part at least because a revolutionary spirit was abroad. In contrast the age of Elizabeth stood for consolidation rather than invention, for preservation rather than revolution. That which was to be preserved was 'modern'—the national Church, the sovereign state, the bureaucratic organisation of government. Elizabeth herself was a conservative in the sense that she disliked and avoided change, and she represented a very strong feeling among her people. The chief concept of the age—often unconscious, never questioned—was that of order and degree. It came as easily to the Elizabethan to suppose that all things, man included, had their place in an eternally fixed scheme of things, and that there existed degrees among men, as it comes to the present day to think that there is neither order nor purpose in the universe, or that all men are equal. These last two propositions would have struck the sixteenth century not only as blasphemous but as manifestly absurd. The world which God had created had its settled laws, and in the great 'Chain of Being' every created thing, from the angels at the top to the animals and plants and metals at the bottom, had its assigned place. These ideas took a 'medieval' form: that is, they found expression in phrases and thoughts inherited from centuries of speculation and writing.[1] But that fact has no profounder meaning: ideas are rarely expressed in entirely new language, and conservative ideas never.

An age which insisted on degree could not think in radical terms or welcome the break-up of any established thing. The words of Shakespeare's Ulysses, often quoted, may yet be cited once again:

> Take but degree away, untune that string,
> And hark! what discord follows; each thing meets
> In mere oppugnancy: the bounded waters
> Should lift their bosom higher than the shores
> And make a sop of all this solid globe:
> Strength should be lord of imbecility,
> And the rude son should strike his father dead:
> Force should be right; or rather, right and wrong—
> Between whose endless jar justice resides—
> Should lose their names, and so should justice too.

Without degree, with the natural order of things disturbed, the moral order itself would dissolve. Sanctionless, right would fall before might. The statesmen of the age held this view with cold passion, and every means of propaganda was employed to preach order, obedience, and humble acquiescence in one's station. Cranmer's *Homily on Obedience* (1547)—an official sermon read in all churches—justified the existing political order as part of that universal order which the 'Chain of Being' exemplified. That the political order of 1547 was a very different thing from that of 1527 there was no need to admit: the Henrician revolutionaries always pretended to be preservers of the proper order. Afterwards,

[1] Cf. E. M. W. Tillyard, *The Elizabethan World Picture* (1943).

however, the new order was to be really preserved unaltered. The political common-place book of the Elizabethan period, the *Mirror for Magistrates* (first published in 1559 and frequently reprinted), a collection of tales about kings and others who came to a sticky end through offending against the universal order, preached both the supremacy of degree and the duty of obedience. Even evil rulers are for God to deal with, and not for man. Rebellion is the great political sin because it disturbs degree which is man's only right condition.

That such doctrines served a very practical need is obvious. An age of agrarian and political unrest was only just passing away; many of its feelers stretched right through the queen's reign. In such times the powers that be tend to inculcate the duty of obedience and wickedness of rebellion with a fervour born of self-interest. No doubt; but the matter went further. Even the rebels tended to be tarred with the same brush. Even the puritans, however much they might dislike the official hierarchy, did not question the queen's rule, the reality of degree, or the universal order of which both men and society must be reflections. If there were egalitarian ideas about, they spread among the lowly and have left no record. No matter whether men profited or suffered from the existing state of affairs, their minds were coloured by conservative preconceptions. It is impossible to define forty-five years so crowded with great men and great events in a phrase. Towards the end of the century, especially, speculation turned into different channels. Men said later that they had waited for the old queen's death before embarking on new enterprises; people can grow tired of a worthy and cautious conservatism. Such men as Raleigh and Bacon have been taken as prototypes of modern rationalism—and certainly Raleigh's *History of the World* and Bacon's *Novum Organum* seem to breathe a different spirit from the *Mirror of Magistrates*. Nevertheless, they were hardly rationalists, for they remained firmly within the religious mould of a far from pious age,[1] and influenced by the barely conscious general acceptance of the notion of order. If that was to be medieval then Newton was medieval whose greatest scientific discoveries were made in the desire to prove the rational order of God's universe; then men have never ceased to be medieval. In a sense this is

[1] 'The orthodox scheme of salvation is pervasive in the Elizabethan age,' is Dr Tillyard's comment. Before rationalism received the support of physical science, only religion could offer any sort of explanation of the universe and of life, and whether Elizabethans were pious or not, formally Christian or not, they thought in terms of a world made and ruled by God.

true; but what then is the value of so meaningless a definition?

Thus, exceptions and modifications allowed for, and in the knowledge that many may dissent, it can be said again that the reign of Elizabeth, especially when compared with that of Henry VIII, was a conservative rather than a radical period. This came out in its political thinking, the structure of its government, and the history of its Church.

2. THE CROWN AND SOVEREIGNTY

As has already been stressed, Tudor rule depended in the first place on a full, even fulsome, recognition of the prince as the visible embodiment of the state. Elizabeth maintained this tradition by carefully cultivating her own appeal as a queen and a woman, and by the splendour and ceremonial of her court. She entertained no small opinion of her place, and the words 'my prerogative' were frequently in her mouth. Compared with Henry VIII's calm assurance her attitude almost protested too much, but then she had to overcome the double handicap of a growingly vocal opposition and of her sex. About her capacity to govern opinions have differed greatly; perhaps one may say that no one can be consistently lucky for half a century unless there is more than luck in it. In many ways she was an unpleasant woman. Our age probably objects not at all to her coarseness, elementary sense of humour, or secular temper—all of which tended to distress the Victorians—but still dislikes her unfairness, occasional vindictiveness, frequent rages, and constant vacillation. Like her father she may not have been capable of an original thought, and like her grandfather she may have been a little too fond of treasure; but kings can be great without being great statesmen in their own right, and poor rulers ought to set a value on money. On the whole the light eclipses the shadow. She deserves admiration for her competence, good sense, lack of bigotry, and shrewdness. In any case, she was the queen; of her overwhelming personality, her unceasing personal activity, and her all-pervading presence there must be no doubt. Surrounded by a court as brilliant in show as in intellect, served with a ceremonial which set her permanently apart,[1] she

[1] Sir Thomas Smith noted, and foreign observers confirmed it with surprise, that no one spoke to the queen except on his knees, unless she deigned to raise him up. One of the minor problems of Elizabethan history is whether the queen could ever have had a hot meal. She dined in private (unlike her father), but the public ceremonial was still gone through, and she seems to have received the dishes at least half an hour after they had been carried in procession from the kitchen.

completely fulfilled the first duty of monarchy—to appear as the symbol of the nation and the sum of all earthly allegiance.

On the queen or those whom she might appoint depended the running of affairs. 'The prince,' said Sir Thomas Smith, 'is the life, the head, and the authority of all things that be done in the realm of England.' Administration in peace time as well as the needs of war and diplomacy were in his hands; he could act at need without reference to advisers or parliaments because he must be able to act at once and in secrecy for the safety of the realm; and he enjoyed certain financial benefits to equip him for his task. These special rights of the crown are its famous prerogatives among which Smith enumerated the making of peace and war, the appointment of the privy council, the administration of martial law, the minting of money, dispensations from the operation of the law (in the exercise of which prerogative 'equity requireth a moderation to be had'), the appointment of all chief officials in the realm, the administration of justice, and the collection of feudal dues of wardship and the like. The crown's prerogatives made sure that Tudor government, like medieval government before it and modern after it, should be the king's government.

But government is not identical with the state. The prince can be a symbol and even the ultimate source of all action, without thereby becoming identified with the state itself. This question of the nature of the state really raises the question of sovereignty, for the sovereign (in John Austin's classical definition) is that man or body of men whose every dictate is habitually obeyed by a given community. We are told that the medieval and modern states differ in this that the former is an association of all its parts (the famous 'body politic' metaphor) for a moral purpose, while the latter embodies a sovereign will (wherever it may be found) and serves the purposes of power.[1] It is a valuable distinction, though in practice a rather unreal one. Political bodies have always obeyed some will and depended on power, however much moral purposes may have been talked about; the differences lie, firstly, in the nature of the sovereign will and secondly in the absence of restraint which the discarding of the 'moral purpose' theory brings about. Once the facts of political life gained admission to the writings of the theorists—and here the sixteenth century, through Machiavelli and Bodin, achieved much—the new absence of theoretical limitations on the physical power of states and rulers encouraged a larger practical exploitation of forces which themselves were far from new. The modern state has been assisted by a description which

[1] E.g. W. S. Holdsworth, *History of English Law*, iv.196.

gives to it unrestricted and irresponsible sovereignty, and it has therefore been readier to act in a manner which at one time would have had to seek a cloak to satisfy the unquestioned belief in a moral purpose. It is at least doubtful whether that moral purpose really played a larger part in the middle ages than it does today.

The distinction is then unreal in practice, but its value lies in the fact that it summarises two different attitudes to the problem of political organisation. The question now is whether Tudor England believed in the allegedly medieval notion of the harmonious body politic or the allegedly modern notion of sovereignty. Scholars have inclined to treat these concepts as mutually exclusive because they have concentrated on the potential conflict between the law-giver and the subject. Yet another answer is possible. The principle of representation makes it possible to combine the idea of sovereignty with that of harmony. The attitude implicitly adopted by the Tudor revolution of the 1530s was this: the state is a harmonious unity of head and members, of king and subjects, which is quite independent of all outside authority; and this unity is represented in the parliament of the realm whose decrees therefore embody the common will and inevitably override all other orders as far as concerns the commonwealth. The supremacy of statute, divested in practice by Cromwell of all limitations, embodies botn a full doctrine of internal sovereignty and the 'medieval' notion of harmony, because it acknowledges the existence of a mixed sovereign comprehending within it by representation every individual and every individual will. It was one of the great moments in human history when the most centralised monarchy in Western Europe thus adapted the ideas of consent and representation to the demands of sovereignty.

But the concept of sovereignty, however implicit, did not persist into Elizabethan thought. The idea of parliament as representing the body politic became a commonplace. John Aylmer, later bishop of London, declared in 1559 that the government of England was a mixed monarchy 'the image whereof, and not the image but the thing in deed, is to be seen in the parliament house' with its three estates; in 1565 Sir Thomas Smith said that 'the highest and most absolute power of the realm of England consisteth in the parliament' because 'every Englishman is intended to be there present, either in person or by procuration and attorneys . . . from the prince . . . to the lowest person in England. And the consent of parliament is taken to be every man's consent'; in the 1590s Hooker employed very similar language, saying that the parliament was 'even the body of the whole realm', that it consisted of the king and all his subjects, and that from it depended 'the very essence of all government within this kingdom'. Practising statesmen recognised the omnicompetence of statute. Cromwell based his work on this interpretation; Burghley is reported to have remarked that 'he knew not what an act of parliament could not do in England'; Francis Bacon acknowledged that an act of parliament could not bind 'the supreme and absolute power' of future parliaments.

This deference to parliament ought to have resulted in the acceptance of a full doctrine of sovereignty—legislative supremacy—vested in king, lords, and commons. The reasons why Elizabethan theorists and politicians never took this final step were two, both of them essentially conservative. One was the old notion that no human sovereignty is possible—that there exists a law above man's will which regulates the behaviour of the universe and by which man-made law must be judged. In addition to this 'law of nature' the Elizabethan age inherited from centuries of speculation and practice the more humdrum fact of the law of England which defined the rights and place of every man, king or peasant. A sound doctrine of sovereignty was impossible until these two points had lost their force. In practice they were already dying: the Reformation, achieving unheard-of alterations through act of parliament, had, as has been seen, asserted an implicit doctrine of sovereignty. But men's thoughts had not yet caught up, and the law of nature—the traditional defence against an entirely man-ruled community—experienced a determined revival in the sixteenth century. In Henry VIII's reign, Christopher St German knew it, though he called it the law of reason; Hooker based his whole magnificent structure on the existence of a universal law giving unity and purpose to God's creation; and, late in the century, Edward Coke began to argue his narrow case which identified the law of nature or reason with the English common law and thus transmuted the inherent moral restraints on behaviour into the highly practical restraint of the positive law of the land.

This revival of natural law marked a conservative reaction against the makers of the Henrician Reformation which was assisted by the practice of the second half of the century. It has been rightly pointed out that a theory of parliamentary sovereignty was made no easier by the rarity of parliament's existence. Cromwell's belief in parliamentary sovereignty expressed itself in the fact that parliament met almost every year after his accession to power, and Henry VIII followed the precept down to his death. Elizabeth, on the other hand, called parliament only thirteen times in forty-five years; unlike Cromwell, she and her ministers were not so much concerned with the making of law as with its enforcement—with government rather than legislation. It is only when law-making becomes a reasonably regular expression of the state's functions that the problem of sovereignty enters politics at all; the decline of legislative pressure after 1559—though laws continued to be made, neither their number nor their importance can compare with those of the 1530s—revived a condition in which the state expressed itself mainly in administration. Elizabethan thinkers thus had the less reason to seek for the seat of sovereignty. Parliament continued to be seen as a high court—which it was—rather than as the legislative assembly which the Reformation had proved it to have become; it was a very honourable, even an important, part of the constitution, but it was hard to see in so intermittent an organisation a regular part of government.

Thus while the Tudor state in practice worked on the principle that statute was supreme—that parliament was sovereign—conservatism prevented a full realisation of what may be called the native theory of sovereignty. The man to free sovereignty from the trammels of natural law was Jean Bodin (1566), and he—arguing from French conditions—placed it in the hands of the prince alone. His monarchical theory spread in England after 1570, to encounter there not a rival, parliamentary (king-in-parliamentary) theory of sovereignty but a vacuum. Confronted with the idea of a king truly sovereign—a personal law-giver whose dictates are obeyed—English writers did not reply that in England sovereignty rested with a mixed body. They reacted in one of two ways. Either they used this imported notion to justify and exalt the autocratic tendencies which the strong kings of England had often displayed. Traces of such truly royalist doctrines appear in the writings of some, especially courtiers, but Elizabeth was not interested in theoretical claims and their full development had to await the coming of James I with his indefeasible divine right. Alternatively, being aware of the limitations on English kings—limitations which as lawyers they sought in the law rather than in a doctrine of representation—the theorists got into a muddle. Unable to see Bodin's sovereign either in the limited king of England or in the occasional sessions of the king-in-parliament, they tried instead to give to the English crown some sovereign and some not so sovereign attributes. Following a lead given already by Fortescue in the fifteenth century, they distinguished between an 'absolute' and an 'ordinary' prerogative, using absolute in the sense of discretionary. Since naturally they could not define limits to powers whose very essence was a vagueness depending on the demands of the moment, 'absolute' and 'ordinary' remained unresolved terms, reappearing in the next century in those murky discussions about emergency powers and the king's 'different persons' which tried to justify Stuart despotism.

In truth, these attempts to suit an imported concept of royal sovereignty to the facts of parliament's existence and the crown's subordination to the law mark the gradual breakdown of the Cromwellian polity which had ignored the idea of natural law and had given expression to the harmonious commonwealth in a sovereign king-in-parliament. The new theories really began to postulate an inherent conflict between monarch (sovereign?) and people; they defined royal power by trying to find its limits, either exalting it by itself or nibbling it away with 'safeguards'. The truer English doctrine exalted the power of government because it represented the joint will of an organic body politic.[1] With arguments of double nature and the like we approach the temporary collapse of the constitution which was to be the Stuarts' main achievement. In Elizabeth's parliaments, despite their loyalty, harmony was preserved with greater difficulties than in Henry VIII's, for interests once at one had begun to diverge. Confronted with the evidence of political squabbles and failing to see behind them the possibility of a mixed sovereign, the thinkers of the time either tended to miss the notion of sovereignty altogether or to revive the supremacy of natural law.

It is therefore hard to say that any well-developed doctrine of the state and the ruler was held in Elizabethan England. The queen, representing the crown, commanded loyalty, allegiance, devotion, even adulation. She herself clung to high views of her prerogative but avoided definition; on the other hand, though she may have stretched a point here and there, she never pretended that she was not a 'limited' monarch, dependent on parliament for taxes and laws and compelled to govern according to 'the law', not her will. The lawyers—Smith and his like—took over the theory of a constitutional monarchy from the previous century without ever grasping the full implications of mixed sovereignty. Those who, like Hooker, thought deepest also thought in terms of a divine order and a universal law which imposed a moral nature on the state and limited discussion of it as it really was. In practice everyone saw that of the parts of parliament the crown mattered much more than the lords and commons, so that discussions of power and sovereignty were sidetracked into attempts to define the position

[1] If the theory of 'safeguards' is Whig (as it is), that of the organic body politic is Tory. That makes Thomas Cromwell a Tory!

of the prerogative or to limit the supposed autocratic tendencies of the ruler. Few writers opposed the queen. In Mary's reign protestants like John Ponet (*Short Treatise of Politic Power*) and John Knox (*First Blast of the Trumpet against the Monstrous Regiment of Women*) had developed doctrines of justifiable resistance which in Ponet's remarkable book culminated in the right to kill tyrants. But though some catholic writers—especially Parsons—took up such themes in the next reign, English writers in general returned to the original protestant position of doing honour to 'the magistrate'—of obedience to secular authority. Ardent puritans were to find it difficult to 'tarry for the magistrate' when that magistrate was the immovable Elizabeth, but for most men political speculation began and ended with reliance on the safety of a strong crown in the hands of so competent a ruler.

Failure to define rights and prerogatives, and to delimit the spheres of what the crown could only do in parliament and what it could do by its 'absolute' power did not so much lay up trouble for the future as avoid, in the sound tradition of good government, the posing of insoluble problems. When political and religious difficulties, as well as private follies, put those questions squarely before the nation, the result was civil war. The weakness of the Tudor theorists lay not in their ignoring the concept of sovereignty but in their inability to develop the theme on a native basis by admitting the unrestricted sovereignty (not only the supremacy under the law) of the crown in parliament. Thus they permitted the conflict between improper and alien theories which wished to ascribe true sovereignty either to the king or to the commons alone. The practice of the Cromwellian constitution collapsed after 1603; it may be argued that its underlying theory remained obscure in the sixteenth century and did not come to be accepted more generally until Burke's revival of the organic body politic.

3. GOVERNMENT

This discussion of theories has not advanced an understanding of Elizabethan government which must rather be sought in the institutions of government themselves. The reign of Elizabeth was not one of reform but of exploitation and consolidation. After the vast but incomplete overhaul of the machinery which was part of Cromwell's amazing achievement, what was needed was a little development but in the main use; and these the great Elizabethan administrators provided.

Though the queen reigned, and though the queen may even

have ruled, it was the privy council that governed. Consolidated by Cromwell out of the vague 'inner ring', it made its first formal appearance in August 1540 when, in order to cope with the eclipse of its maker, it agreed to a more bureaucratic organisation by appointing a clerk and a minute-book. Thereafter this board of (originally) nineteen men underwent some vicissitudes which reflected the political upheavals of the times of crisis. From the first it was far from united because membership, being essential to participation in affairs, was, in that age of the Reformation, sought by and granted to men of very different religious views. Both Cranmer and Gardiner belonged to it in the 1540s. Henry VIII held the balance without difficulty, so that the ascendancy of one side or the other expressed itself not in the expulsion of the loser but in his temporary absence from the board. However, after the old king's death the faction leaders began to pack the council with their supporters and to remove their opponents from the council chamber to the Tower or, in extreme cases, to the block. The temporary ascendancy of the new nobility, aping their Lancastrian predecessors, was well displayed in a council of forty under Edward VI and forty-four under Mary. Many held no office: they joined the council to advance not the king's government but their patrons' or their own interests. A large council cannot govern: thus the privy council broke up into committees to which both Northumberland and Mary tried to give permanence. In the latter's reign Spanish influence worked for the creation of an inmost 'council of state' on continental lines; this would have destroyed the efficiency of the privy council itself and added to the irresponsibility of both councillors and crown. Elizabeth's accession ended these experiments which in truth marked only a decline of royal control over the government. Cecil took up where Cromwell left off—that was to be their relation throughout—and a small council of eighteen, at times reduced to twelve, was to govern England for forty-five years.

The Elizabethan privy council was a well-defined bureaucratic organisation. It had a staff of clerks which grew from one to four; it had ushers and messengers. Minutes were kept, though some meetings were so secret that the clerk was excluded from them and no record survives. It met at regular times and in regular places—regular but not fixed. Early in the reign, the council met on Tuesdays, Thursdays, and Saturdays, expecting to get its work done in the mornings; this left Wednesdays and Fridays free as star chamber days. But business increased, especially when the war was added to other concerns. In the last decade of the century hardly a day passed on which the council did not sit; even Sunday brought no respite. As for place, the council met wherever the queen was, which meant at one of the palaces she usually inhabited (White Hall, Windsor, Greenwich, Oatlands, Nonesuch), or in whatever mansion she might be putting up during her frequent progresses. Not indeed that all the council were always present: most of the routine business was handled by some four to six regular attendants. And most of the business was routine.

The privy council concerned itself quite simply with everything that went on in England, and it often dealt with these matters directly, though at other times it delegated them to a particular member (in the main, the principal secretary), a lesser official, or a different court. No mere summary can give an idea of the all-pervasive interests and influence of the council, but here is a list of the sort of things that came before it: war and peace, foreign affairs and diplomatic negotiations, military and naval matters, finance, religion and the Church, order and police duties, crown patronage in lands and offices, local government, private affairs, disputes, and suits for favour. The most vital concerns of the state rubbed shoulders with the petty troubles of individuals. On one typical day (5 September 1581) the council considered the catholic Lady Stonor's house arrest, trade with Spain, a minor land dispute in Guernsey, a poor man's complaint against the bishop of Hereford, various matters connected with recusants, the report that a man had spoken in favour of Edmund Campion, a land dispute between the earls of Northumberland and Bedford, a merchant's losses through Turkish pirates, Sir Peter Carew's debts, seven passports to foreign vessels released from embargo, and the provision of post horses for a messenger. Although there existed specific courts to attend to their wants, suitors continued to pester the privy council itself on the sound principle that one ought always to go as high as possible. Some judicial work the council necessarily retained: it could not afford to pass to a public court the interests of queen and state, whether they concerned the latest treasonable plot or the financial rights of the prerogative. Its own members, too, naturally exploited their position to advance their affairs through the authority of the council board. But at least one might discourage others from doing the same: hence repeated orders that 'the multitude of private suitors resorting daily to her majesty's privy council' should stop annoying their lordships and take their petty concerns to the courts properly appointed for the purpose. The repetition (1582, 1589, 1591) proves their futility. The courts of law and equity sat relatively rarely and grew more and more behindhand in their work; the structure of Tudor society compelled privy councillors to advance the interests of their clients and adherents; the interests of the age concentrated on litigation and pot-hunting; altogether it proved impossible to stop private suits from taking up the council's time and thus hindering it in its attempts 'to attend and proceed in such causes as do concern her majesty'.

The lords of the council resented these swarms of suitors the more because they were all men of importance, with affairs of state and affairs of their own absorbing quite enough time. The Elizabethan privy council always included a mixture of nobility and gentry who were also office holders—the great officers of the realm (lord chancellor, lord treasurer, lord privy seal, perhaps lord admiral and lord great chamberlain), the leading officers of the household (steward, chamberlain, treasurer, controller, master of the horse), the principal secretaries, and others—but also, especially at first, men of the same stamp who might hold no office. The judges had been excluded by Cromwell, and this valuable distinction between judicial and ordinary administration was maintained under Elizabeth. A curious case is presented by the bishops. Their presence was desirable in the middle of the religious Reformation when the council often discussed affairs of Church and faith, but with the accession of Elizabeth the clerical element disappeared from the council. This is usually thought to have been policy—the queen's deliberate assertion of the triumph of secular rule—but it may have been no more than an accident. Matthew Parker had no wish to take part in the government of the realm, while the other new bishops were, by and large, much too radical for Elizabeth's taste. When she got an archbishop in Whitgift whom she really liked she put him on the council (1586): it looks as though personal preference rather than policy brought about the exclusion of the bishops. It was assisted by the fact that the Church now definitely ceased to hold any of the offices of state: if in nothing else, the age was secular in reserving government to the laity.

All these councillors were technically equal and united in their desire to advise the queen and do their duty by the commonwealth; in practice they were neither. At nearly all times the council divided into parties and there was much personal rivalry. Unless a man sat on the council he could take no part in affairs: the Elizabethan system knew no place for the private favourite, the closet confidant. When the earl of Essex decided to transfer his ambitions to the scene of 'domestical greatness' he had to seek membership of the council (1593); by then he had been a special favourite of the queen's for six years without enjoying a voice in government. The two great struggles of the reign—between Burghley and Leicester, and later between Robert Cecil and Essex—are full of parallels: in each case a statesman opposed a courtier, in each case the fight had personal reasons behind it, in each case matters of public policy gave respectability to disagreement, in each case Elizabeth supported the man of sense against the man of charm. In that small and close-knit society rivalries often looked like family quarrels; at times they were nothing else. The two promising sons of lord keeper Nicholas Bacon, Anthony and Francis, originally belonged to the Cecil interest since Burghley was their uncle by marriage. But when the lord treasurer showed that his own son's career was nearest his heart they moved to the opposition, Francis especially hoping to become the intellect of the Essex faction. The purest example of the intellectual intriguer that the age supplies, he was a man of superlative gifts of the mind (though poetry was not among them), a great lawyer and potentially a great statesman, but also a singularly cold fish whose subtle calculations in politics were only matched by his lack of success. He did, of course, much better under James I.

The factions and rivalries dominated much of the inner history of the reign. A fuller account of them than is possible here would make Elizabethan politics more real, rather less heroic, and much more interesting. Not that everything depended on personal ambitions only. Walsingham's career provides an outstanding example of principles dividing the council. He began very much under the Burghley ægis; from Burghley he learned the scope of the secretaryship and the details of secret service and intelligence, all of which he was to bring to a fine point. But since the personal quarrel between Burghley and Leicester took the form of a contest between a moderate peace policy and a protestant war policy, Walsingham's passionate attachment to the protestant cause drove him into Leicester's camp. He was not even advancing his own interests: Elizabeth preferred Burghley's policy to Leicester's, and there is reason to think that by the later 1570s she even preferred the lord treasurer personally to the earl. Relations between Walsingham and his first patron, though of course disturbed by their disagreement over affairs, were never really hostile, and as soon as developments forced war upon the country they worked together again in perfect amity. But fanatics like Walsingham were rare at the queen's court: she saw to that, though she did not object to using his great abilities even if she disliked his temperament. Nor did she mind the existence of factions in the council. In that way dangerous personal cross-currents played themselves out away from her and a disunited council preserved her personal control. Her father, for much of his reign, had relied on a single great minister and had thus often ceased to be the determining factor in affairs; but she learned the lesson of his last years when the absence of such a minister and the existence of council factions gave greater freedom of action to the crown. The Elizabethan privy council was never a restraint on royal authority, and Elizabeth resembled rather Henry VII than Henry VIII in the practice of government—though when it suited her she could forcefully remind her hearers whose daughter she was.

The councillors were not equal because they included great men as well as lesser, and because the leaders of faction naturally loomed larger than the followers. More important for good government was that they did not all attend with equal zeal. The ordinary work was in fact done by a smaller group of executive ministers. Among these must be mentioned the treasurer and controller of the household whose titles represented sinecures; they were in effect ministers without portfolio available for any work that needed doing. That solid man, Sir Francis Knollys, cousin of the queen, supporter of puritanism, government spokesman in the house of commons, and one of the most regular attendants at the council board, held the office of treasurer of the household for a quarter of a century (1572-96). The executive agent was the principal secretary, as Cromwell had decided he should be. When Cromwell gave it up in 1540 the office lost somewhat in weight. The secretaries of the Tudor crisis either lacked the force and ability to be more than important civil servants, or else they left the office rapidly to seek higher promotion, as did Thomas Wriothesley (1540-4) who became chancellor, or William Paget (1543-52) who preferred the privy seal. It was William Cecil who resuscitated the Cromwellian secretaryship. In the fourteen years that he held it (1558-72) he once again made it the keystone of government. From this position it was not to decline, though the secretaries of the reign differed in standing and influence. At times only one was appointed, as when William Cecil, Walsingham, and Robert Cecil all preferred to avoid competition, and at other times—as after Walsingham's death (1590-6)—the queen kept the place vacant. But all in all, it was in the principal secretary that the activating force of Elizabethan government lay. He prepared the council's agenda and carried out the council's decisions;

in his hand met all the strands of domestic and foreign affairs.

Financial administration concentrated upon the lord treasurer. Here there had been certain changes since Cromwell's fall. The great reformer, as has been seen, had multiplied organised offices of state as need arose, so that when he fell in 1540 the management of the revenue was troublesome and expensive on account of the numbers of officials involved. The financial and administrative difficulties of the years 1540-58, aggravated by war, debasement, corruption, and inefficiency, produced further reforms which really embodied the Cromwellian system in one organisation independent of such accidents as his own death had been. The two men responsible were William Paulet, from 1550 marquess of Winchester, who had proved his great bureaucratic ability since 1526, and (probably) Sir Walter Mildmay, a somewhat humdrum but very sound civil servant whose fame rests on the foundation of Emmanuel College at Cambridge and the puritan sympathies which this act evinced, but ought to rest on the forty-four years of his labours in the courts of augmentations and the exchequer (1545-89). The lives of men like Paulet and Mildmay, spanning the reigns and devoted to the details of administration, explain the astonishing stability and marked success of Tudor government, behind the superficial disturbances of politics.[1]

The reforms which they carried out solved the problem by re-uniting most of the crown's finances under the exchequer. In 1547 the courts of general surveyors and augmentations were fused into a new court of augmentations which in effect administered all the Tudor crown lands except those of the duchy of Lancaster. In 1554, the courts of first fruits and augmentations were abolished, their business being transferred to the exchequer. The court of wards remained separate because it was a difficult organisation to subordinate to the exchequer, but also because its master was a friend of Queen Mary's; the duchy remained separate because of its own interests. Augmentations and first fruits did not, as is sometimes said, continue as separate departments in the exchequer, but they preserved some identity and the new work was done according to the better new methods. Even so the 1554 reforms marked a certain retracing of steps: Winchester's failure totally to conquer the conservatism of the civil service left the exchequer

[1] Other men similarly long in office were Sir Ralph Sadler, once Cromwell's secretary and active in finance, the secretariats, and diplomacy from 1533 to 1587; William Mill, clerk of the star chamber from 1572 to 1608; Nicholas Bacon whose legal career began in 1537 and ended in 1579; or of course Burghley himself, Elizabeth's guiding hand for most of the reign and an official for forty-eight years (1550-98).

with annoying relics of medieval practices which clogged efficiency until the court's abolition in 1833. Throughout the reign of Elizabeth pressure mounted for a further return to the old ways, but Winchester and Burghley resisted with sufficient success to prevent the administration deteriorating. No more structural reforms were made after 1554: here, too, the queen's reign was an age of consolidation not of alteration. The exception to this rule is to be found in the customs which the national administration was so incapable of exploiting that both ministers had to resort to farming.[1]

The chief effect of the 1554 reforms was to give to the lord treasurer, departmental head of the exchequer, almost complete control of the finances. The drawback of Winchester's failure to incorporate the court of wards was overcome by Burghley simply enough: he also held the mastership of that court (1561-96). This office, which administered the feudal rights of the crown, became the centre of speculation for courtiers and landed gentry desirous to profit from the wardships and lands which it had to sell; bribery by suitors made it also a centre of corruption, so that even the upright Burghley could not maintain really rigorous standards. Its mastership was a profitable office which, it was alleged (somewhat exaggeratedly), made Burghley wealthy; when Robert Cecil took over from his father, both corruption and the cheating of the crown for private profit increased. Administratively, the exchequer was now the only financial department that mattered. Winchester's reforms created the modern ascendancy of the lord treasurer and his chief assistant, the chancellor of the exchequer. In this reign, Winchester himself continued to administer the exchequer until his death in 1572, proving the while his training in the Cromwell school by further plans of reform which his successor abandoned in favour of stabilisation. Burghley held the treasurership from 1572 until 1598; his papers are full of the details of finance, as they are full of all the details of government. His successor, Thomas Sackville Lord Buckhurst (1599-1608), not a trained administrator, yet maintained the honourable traditions of Tudor treasurers. As Cromwell had begun and the Cecils continued the organisation of the secretary's office out of which grew the departments of the secretaries of state, so Burghley's private office

[1] The various expedients which culminated in the Great Farm of the customs in 1604 (cf. A. P. Newton in *Transactions of the Royal Historical Society*, 1918) are often praised; but it seems to me that by preferring an easy, if safe, return from the customs and leaving the enormous profits possible to the private farmers, they abdicated responsibility and failed to serve the financial interests of the crown.

laid the foundations for the department of state known as the treasury, which became fully established under the later Stuarts.

While the lord treasurer and the secretary thus embarked on careers of great promise, two other executive officers of the past dropped out of administration. The office of lord privy seal underwent a decline in this reign which reflected its future position as that of a ministry without portfolio. Throughout the period it was held for prestige and money by men who did the work of other real offices, in the main the secretaryship. The lord chancellor had by now quite gone over to his judicial functions, a point which introduces the subject of the courts. A very large number of these existed and not all can here be discussed. Thus the court of admiralty expanded with the business brought in by exploration, piracy, and war. The household court of the steward and marshal exercised its restricted jurisdiction over the 'verge' of the court—the area twelve miles each way from where the court happened to be. There were the courts christian, the courts of the Church, by no means yet dead. Many kinds of local courts flourished, whether franchisal (a few survived, as in Durham) or delegations from the centre (as the assizes), not to mention the declining sphere of the manorial courts and the growing sphere of quarter sessions. Locally one might find special courts, like the stannary courts of Cornwall, or the council courts of the north and the Welsh marches. Everywhere special commissions of magistrates were dealing with cases remitted to them to decide or merely to investigate and report upon. The important central courts were chancery, the conciliar courts of star chamber and requests, and the three courts of the common law. As has already been said, the earlier Tudors created a system in which common law and special (or prerogative) jurisdiction existed side by side; though in some ways they covered different things, they also overlapped a good deal.

Of the rivals to the common-law courts, the court of chancery was the oldest. Moreover, it had originally built up its jurisdiction by filling in the gaps of the common law: equity began and continued as a supplement rather than an enemy to the older law. Development was straightforward in the Tudor century. Wolsey represented the old type of chancellor who governed as chief minister, but also the new type who was first of all a judge. With Sir Thomas More (1529-32) there began the modern line of great lawyer-chancellors—chancellors bred to the common law who were to bring to the gradually crystallising principles of equity enough of the air of the inns of court to make a partnership possible. Thomas Audley (1532-44) and Richard Rich (1547-51) were of the same stamp, though neither such eminent lawyers nor such admirable men. Thomas Wriothesley (1544-7), a civil servant turned politician, and Thomas Goodrich (1551-3), a reforming bishop, marked irrelevant interludes. Mary's reign, on the other hand, produced bishop-chancellors who reverted to the medieval type in Stephen Gardiner (1553-5) and Nicholas Heath (1556-8). Here, too, the reign of Elizabeth declared itself on the modern side: all Elizabeth's chancellors were judges, and nearly all were trained lawyers. Nicholas Bacon (1558-79), the father of two brilliant sons but noteworthy in his own right, was succeeded by Sir Thomas Bromley (1579-87), probably the first chancellor to be known as nothing but a lawyer. More surprising was the appointment of Sir Christopher Hatton (1587-91) who had caught the queen's eye by his qualities as a courtier and a wit. However, he turned out a very sensible chancellor: he used his common sense where it sufficed, and where it did not he adjourned the case till he could have consulted the experts. His career proves that equity was still in the fluid stage, subject to the individual views of each chancellor. Sir John Puckering (1592-6) and Sir Thomas Egerton (1596-1617) revived the lawyers' hold on the office. In Egerton Elizabeth picked perhaps the greatest chancellor of the century, though only James I was to bestow the full title together with the barony of Ellesmere.[1] In his long tenure he went far towards defining the body of law known as equity by freeing it from the uncertainty and caprice which had beset it. More important still, he was to preside over chancery when its quarrel with the law courts was composed. Though chancery had at first interfered but little with the sphere of the common law, from Wolsey's time onwards its injunctions had taken away much business especially from the court of common pleas. The resentment of the common lawyers at this interference could do little till the revival and reforms of the later sixteenth century encouraged the common-law courts to take the offensive. The matter was not settled until the next reign when James I decided a quarrel between Chief Justice Coke and Lord Chancellor Ellesmere in the latter's favour. As far as chancery was concerned, the sixteenth century established it as a regular court, instituted its regular body of law, and enabled it to survive the attack of the common law to remain one of the courts of the realm until the reforms of the nineteenth century.

[1] Elizabeth preferred to appoint lord keepers of the great seal who could do all a chancellor's work without his great salary. This naturally assisted in the relative decline of the office. Bacon, Puckering, and Egerton were keepers.

The conciliar courts proper had a stormier career, although under the Tudors they seemed even more firmly founded. Both the court of requests and the court of star chamber originally were no more than specifically judicial sessions of the council or some councillors; both had a history of gradual growth, repeated starts, and occasional lapses under Henry VII and Wolsey; and for both the organisation of the privy council in the 1530s marked the beginning of permanent institutional existence. Requests, concerned with civil cases brought by 'poor men' and crown servants, administered a species of equity much like that of chancery but distinguished perhaps by a greater liking for the Roman law. Its advantages were cheapness and speed. In any case, the upheavals of the century—the agrarian changes and the rapid movement of land—provided plenty of work for two equitable courts. After 1536-40 the councillors who sat as judges in the court no longer belonged to the council proper, the privy council. In the reign of Edward VI the situation was stabilised by the creation of two permanent masters of requests, later, as pressure of business increased, augmented by two extraordinary (or unpaid) masters. The office was profitable in fees and pickings and one of the few rewards a doctor of civil law could hope for; the presidency of the admiralty court was the ultimate prize of his profession. Though conciliar in origin and in its own claims, the court lacked the prestige which the presence of privy councillors gave to star chamber, so that it fell an easy victim to the common law's counter-attack. In the 1590s common pleas began to inhibit requests from proceeding with cases brought there, and in 1599 the judges denied that this body of men sitting in the White Hall 'had power of jurisdiction' —that is, they deprived its actions of legal force. Nevertheless, simply because its work was still demanded by litigants, the court of requests continued to sit until the great rebellion; the only trouble was that if a defeated party cared to take the matter to the common law, the decision made by requests would prove unenforceable.

Star chamber has been a difficult problem to historians, but no purpose would here be served by entering into the tricky questions raised by it: one must be content with a brief and perhaps rather dogmatic statement.[1] It has already been shown that the court

[1] In this short discussion of star chamber I am relying in part on my own researches and in part—especially for the reign of Elizabeth—on the unprinted thesis by Miss E. Skelton [Mrs J. E. Neale] ('The Court of Star Chamber in the Reign of Elizabeth', London, 1930) which is the only satisfactory treatment of the subject in existence.

grew out of the immemorial jurisdiction of the king's council, especially in criminal matters. As far as is known it rested on no specific order, and certainly not on any statute. In the reign of Henry VII the council began to hold regular meetings in the council chamber of the palace of Westminster, which was known as the star chamber, to adjudicate upon petitions and especially to enforce the king's policy of restoring peace and order. A lapse in this work after Henry VII's death did not prevent its revival, on a vastly increased scale, by Wolsey. When in 1540 the new privy council rounded off its organisation by appointing a clerk and keeping records, the institutional differentiation between these two so-called offsprings of the council was complete. In fact there was only one offspring—the smaller council which at times composed the board known as the privy council and at times sat in the open and regular court known as the star chamber. They were two entirely separate institutions staffed by the same people (or nearly the same people) but with different officers attending upon each. Star chamber consisted of all the privy councillors but it could, and usually did, summon others: thus two of the judges, commonly the two chief justices, attended to provide knowledge of legal matters, though the privy councillors always remained the real judges in star chamber. The chancellor presided and dominated; in a very real sense, as chancery was his court of civil jurisdiction, so star chamber was his court of criminal jurisdiction. The court met on Wednesdays and Fridays during the sixteen weeks of the four law terms, and usually on the day after the end of each term. It was in every sense an ordinary court of the realm: public, with its fixed rules of procedure, a known body of law administered in it.

Nevertheless, traces of its conciliar origin continued to cling to it. The presence there of the queen's government—all or part of the council—gave to the court both a high standing and a somewhat unjudicial appearance. It was, said Coke, 'the most honourable court (our parliament excepted) that is in the Christian world, both in respect of the judges of the court and of their honourable proceeding according to their just jurisdiction and the ancient and just order of the court'. Star chamber dealt in the main with two matters—riots, and the enforcement of proclamations. On the interpretation that anything that might lead to a breach of the peace constituted a riot, the court had extended the first part of its competence to include conspiracy, fraud, perjury, subornation of perjury, forgery, threats, attacks on men in authority, waylaying, and challenges to duels—a generous field of criminal jurisdiction which covered many gaps in the common law and altogether provided even under Elizabeth still the best way of preserving the peace. Proclamations were enforced in star chamber because they were issued by the queen in council and therefore seemed naturally subject to the council sitting in judgment:[1] thus such matters as the censorship of the press, the control of building in London, or the temporary orders regulating trade and prices, came to be star chamber matters. But in all this the council acted as a court, and common views of the star chamber's 'continuing conciliar functions' arise from misunderstandings. The star chamber room was used by the privy council in public sessions: things not done on star chamber days—which includes the allegedly non-judicial actions—were not star chamber doings. Nor was star chamber employed in political matters by the Tudors; the state trials of the period were held before special commissioners of oyer and terminer, usually of course—since high matters of state were at issue—themselves leading councillors. Star chamber did not employ torture, as the privy council sometimes did in its investigations. But star chamber could impose unusual punishments more effective than those available to the common law: it could fine very heavily, imprison, whip and mutilate, or at need use weapons of ridicule like the pillory. It could not order the death penalty.

Two things only happened in the court of star chamber which were not straightforwardly judicial. It published orders which looked like proclamations, and its final session each term was at times used for a public address on the queen's policy. But those orders always arose out of a judicial decision in a case; they were in fact specially vigorous and solemnly pronounced precedents for future guidance, rather than the equivalent of legislation in council. The chancellor's or lord keeper's address at the end of term, to an assembly which often included justices of the peace as well as many officials, was given more regularly at the beginning of the reign when it was felt that these useful occasions might be improved by a little instruction to an as yet unsettled country; they tended to be dropped later as the need for them lessened. On the whole, it remains true that privy council and star chamber, comprising much the same membership, existed as two different organisations ('courts', as the sixteenth century would have said) from that day in August 1540 when the councillors at the board, and the same

[1] An attempt to transfer them to the common-law courts, made (it is conjectured) by Cromwell in 1539, was defeated in parliament, and the lapse of the mutilated act of proclamations in 1547 left the whole problem in a mess from which it was rescued by the action of the council in star chamber, irrespective of authority or right.

councillors in star chamber, found themselves recorded by different clerks in a different series of archives. The court of star chamber, however exceptional in its judges and solemn in its rather self-conscious authority, was still only a court like all the rest.

Chancery, requests, and star chamber employed a procedure greatly influenced by the civil law—especially in the use of written documents and witnesses, though they were in the English tradition by being open and by demanding verbal pleadings—but the law they administered was the law of England. At no time was there any question of the common law being superseded. But it needed expanding and amending; it had to be brought up-to-date and made more flexible. The work might be done by statutes enforceable both in the common-law courts and in star chamber; it might be done by equity, in chancery, requests, and later also in the exchequer; it might be done by proclamations enforced in star chamber, though these could produce only minor and commonly temporary changes; it might, finally, be done in the common law itself if it reformed its ways. This is a highly technical subject which it is unnecessary to enlarge upon here. Suffice it to say that from perhaps 1580 onwards the three courts of common law—king's bench, common pleas, and exchequer—began to revive in the hands of men who valued the old law and the old institutions but saw the need for change. The greatest of these was Sir Edward Coke, an unattractive but impressive character, who in his work as a judge and a writer recast and revivified the common law under the pretence of describing it. This revival produced, as has been said, a conflict with the newer courts in which chancery survived and requests succumbed; star chamber remained untouched in its majesty until the follies of Stuart kings and ministers destroyed the popularity of the most efficient and most impartial court of Tudor times.

Such then, in outline, was the central government of Elizabeth's day—a well-designed series of institutions presided over and co-ordinated by the small body of privy councillors, and given life and vigour by the even smaller group of great secretaries and treasurers who did the work of turning advice and direction into action. Nothing in it was new, but much of it was less old than some would have it; it was not medieval government, but the first phase of modern government, resting on principles and offices given a new twist in the 1530s and now in need of acquiring endurance through usage. This, as well as much hard labour, hard thought, skill and subtlety, Burghley, Walsingham, and the rest provided. If they lacked originality (as I think they did), it must also be said that originality can be overvalued, and that the startling outburst of originality associated with Thomas Cromwell gave his successors quite enough to do.

The same careful and inspired exploitation of what was given, rather than invention of new weapons, marked the diffusion of central authority through the realm. This is local government, another huge subject which can only be touched on here. The council kept its eye on the localities in various ways. Special commissions for enquiries, for the taking of witnesses' depositions, even for trials, were constantly going out under the great seal, in the same way as a steady stream of reports and informations made their way from local magistrates to the government. The unit not only of administration but also of social life was the shire on which Elizabethan government acquired a tight hold by developing to the full the office of lord lieutenant. Local noblemen had occasionally been commissioned, with that title, to organise the military forces of the shire in the reign of Henry VIII; under his successors the institution became regular, permanent, and extended to all counties. Too useful to be employed only about military duties, the lord lieutenant was entrusted also with the preservation of the peace and a generial supervision of his region by bei ng put at the head of the magstrates. To equip him with judicial powers he was always included in the commission of tnal peace: in fact, he was as a rule made *custos rotulorum*, a nomihe office technically charged with the keeping of the records of the county justices, but in practice the title bestowed on the senior magistrate.

The justice of the peace, from the first the best weapon of Tudor rule, was exploited almost shamefully by Elizabethan administrators. To his original police duties the century added an ever expanding burden of administration and the enforcement of statutes. To take only two examples: the statute of apprentices (1563) made justices fix wages, while the poor laws of 1597 and 1601 entrusted them with the general and particular supervision of relief and welfare. The commission itself was revised in 1590 in a form which was to endure until 1875; thus the institution inherited from the past was insensibly transformed into something almost new. The commission increased to thirty or forty men in each shire, so that all those of the nobility and gentry who felt it their right to take a share in government could be accommodated. At the same time, to obviate the disadvantages which this influx of amateurs brought with it, the institution of the 'quorum' made the justices capable of efficiently discharging their duties: some of them were specified of whom (*quorum*) one at least had to be present at all formal exercise of authority, and the men so named were those with official or legal experience. The use of unpaid justices in local administration had its advantages for an impecunious government. The council's hold over the justices was at the same time hardly less secure than a salary could have made it. No one had a right to be appointed to the commission: the queen alone decided, and since to be dropped from it meant social death the council could usually discipline a recalcitrant or negligent justice. It failed where conscience or excessive self-interest intervened, as in the standard case of the Lancashire justices who, catholics themselves, would not enforce the recusancy laws, or in the difficulties encountered with smugglers; but justices fixed wages and protected the poor contrary to the alleged interest of their so-called class and in accordance with express government policy. Under the strict, active, and intelligent privy council of Tudor times local government by local men was a success. It exploited local knowledge and loyalties in the interests of the state, a thing no centralised bureaucracy could hope to achieve, and it provided a training in self-government which was in the end to express itself in the self-reliance and skill of the parliamentary opposition. The Tudors preferred to enlist the abilities of the gentry even at the cost of foregoing a despotism they neither needed nor wanted; but only great administrators and rulers could make the system consistently successful.

The same conservatism is apparent in the remaining institutions of local government which need concern this summary. For the purpose of its welfare legislation—the relief of the poor, the provision of work for the unemployed, the care of the sick—the Elizabethan poor law employed the parish. Two overseers of the poor were appointed in each, to do all this and collect the poor-rate which financed their work. This use of the parish and this careful organisation were indeed in a sense new; the whole poor law, the great achievement of the paternal state in action, was in practice the product of the Elizabethan administration. But it borrowed the parish from the old ecclesiastical organisation (if that is not too strong a word) of charity, and it built up once again on ideas which were first worked out, though not then put into practice, in the 1530s.

The two councils which administered the outlying parts of the realm were also taken over as reorganised by Cromwell. That of the north did much good work under that honest puritan and able man, the earl of Huntingdon, after the suppression of the 1569 rising, while that of Wales became little but a law court. Like the privy council itself, these local councils acted both as conciliar courts and as administrative boards. As has already been said, they were not offshoots of the central council but parallel bodies which received from Cromwell the institutional organisation which made them such excellent instruments for the administration of disturbed regions. A third council, that of the west, established in 1538 to deal with Devon and Cornwall, disappeared about 1543, its work done. The great success of these councils, modelled on the central administration, in close touch with it, and as it were extending its arm, appeared in the fact that by the end of the century the ancient separateness of the Scottish border and the Welsh marches had well-nigh vanished. Different still in some ways of life and social structure, they were yet shire ground where the queen's writ ran effectively.

A great deal has had to be left out in this survey of Elizabethan government; in particular it has not been possible to show it at work. Elizabethan government was good government; this was as well because by any standards except those of the last fifty years Elizabethan England was a much governed country. It needed to be, not only because it was passing through upheavals of its own but even more so because it had to cope with the legacy of the past in bringing England into the new age of centralised national states expanding overseas. Much of that legacy was good and was preserved—as the rule of law, the particular position of the English crown, the place of parliament, the nation-state built up of local and lesser units. But some of it was bad—the disorder, the disaffection, the particularism, the ascendancy of a fighting aristocracy. The sorting had been done under Henry VII and Henry VIII, and in particular by the revolutionary genius of Tudor times, Thomas Cromwell; without the long labours, the years of drudgery, the high and honest endeavour of the Elizabethans no amount of revolutionary genius would have sufficed.

4. THE CHURCH

In the reign of Elizabeth, the Church was still an organ of government. It was now an instrument of the state which had established its dominance under Henry VIII; since the supremacy of 1559 was much less definitely ecclesiastical than that of 1534 it may be argued that the Elizabethan Church admitted even more completely to the primacy of the temporal power. This does not mean that the age was indifferent to religion: on the contrary, an age whose thought and values were all animated by religious ideals saw no difficulty in according to the temporal power a quasi-religious deference. In theory, state and Church were one: to the queen, her councillors, and the majority of her people the Church of England coincided with the nation of England. The Church appeared as the spiritual manifestation and organisation of the state: as the queen governed in secular matters through councillors, judges, and the like, so she governed in ecclesiastical affairs through archbishops, bishops, and the rest of the clergy. That was the meaning of her title—'Supreme Governor . . . as well in all spiritual or ecclesiastical things or causes as temporal'. This straightforward theory did not in practice turn out so simple. The notion of one realm, one people, ruled over by one queen and ministered unto by two sets of officials in its secular and ecclesiastical affairs, implied beyond question that by Church was meant the body of all Christians. Yet by the side of this meaning, as old as the Christian religion itself, there had long stood another meaning—which during the middle ages had carried more weight—of the Church as the body of clergy, the mediators between man and God. The English clergy inherited from the past not only an aura of priesthood (which at different times has been differently regarded and stressed) but also the dislike and contempt which the late-medieval priesthood had inspired. The defeat of the papacy, the victory of an anti-clerical laity, reduced the clergy in circumstances without, however, removing all the scorn and distrust which the old clerical pretensions had produced.

Admittedly, it was difficult to feel enthusiastic about a clergy which included too many ignorant men of doubtful morals. The Elizabethan clergy were a mixed lot. They inherited from pre-Reformation times a burden of poor parishes served by men manifestly unfit in learning and behaviour, not to mention piety, to act as spiritual guides to their congregations; the situation was aggravated by secular raids on Church property, especially the inroads on bishops' lands made by Northumberland and Elizabeth; and their best men, most eager on bettering things, fell foul of the queen because they thought improvement possible only by following continental example. At the top the Church was not ill-served. Elizabeth's bishops, though neither so splendid nor so influential as her father's, included able scholars and administrators in men like Parker and Cox, Aylmer and Sandys. They also included men like Grindal—good but ineffective—and weak fools like Richard Cheyney who allowed Gloucester diocese to go to rack and ruin for twenty years. By and large, however, the Elizabethan episcopate displayed those qualities of mind which have become typical of the bench: sound learning, moderate zeal, honest conscientiousness, and a certain necessary pliability towards the secular authority. Whitgift, a hard vigorous man of few scruples when he saw his way clear, brought a different air with him: he swept along on the prophetic storms of conflict and persecution rather than on the gentle winds of indifference and accommodation which more correctly interpreted the queen's own attitude to the vexed question of uniformity in religion.

If the bishops did not lack worthy men, neither did the lesser clergy. There were saints like Richard Greenham, parson of Dry Drayton near Cambridge, a puritan whose fame was known to all England. Always in the first place a good shepherd to his flock, he spent all he had in time, energy, and money to bring the gospel to an unreceptive crowd of rustics. It was said of him that in his own parish he 'had pastures green but sheep full lean'. There were supporters of the establishment, like the great Richard Hooker, a man of so gentle and shy a temper that the vigour of his writings and the force of his opinions came as a great surprise; a scholar of unusual attainments and even more unusual charity in controversy, he also lived a life of genuine humility and example. But these were the fine flowers of their respective wings in the Church; the generality hardly came up to such standards. Not all were as bad as Thomas Powell, chancellor of the diocese of Gloucester for twenty years (1559-79), whose greed, corruption, and disgraceful private life brought the bishop's court, and with it all ecclesiastical authority, into utter contempt. Gloucester, like the other border dioceses, was probably worse than the average, but plenty of testimony survives of an unlearned, unpreaching, incontinent, and worldly clergy in all parts of the country. Most of this testimony comes from the compilations of puritans and has therefore been thought suspect; but after all, the puritan movement derived much of its strength from the inadequacy of the clergy whom it hoped to reform, and while those zealous men might at times exaggerate they certainly at most painted a dark enough picture in unrelieved black.

Yet this same clergy not only claimed spiritual authority but also continued to exercise a direct sway over the laity. The whole system of Church courts was still in existence, and they were still active—from the archbishop of Canterbury's appeal court of the Arches (sitting in St Mary-le-Bow in London) down through episcopal consistory courts to the judicial and visitatorial authority of archdeacons. Before the Reformation these courts had formed a second and all-pervasive system of jurisdiction by the side of the royal courts. They had indeed lost much since then, in particular much valuable jurisdiction over testamentary cases which the conciliar courts were taking to themselves;[1] but moral delinquencies and all matrimonial affairs as well as the enforcement of the clerical rights (such as the ever hated tithe) continued to be dealt with in the Church courts. Where they really declined was not in activity or business but in authority. The powers of the ecclesiastical judges rested upon spiritual penalties, especially the imposition of penances and excommunication. Both these were losing—in many places had lost—their terrors. The denial of purgatory and the spread of a Calvinist theology which firmly separated salvation from works removed the spiritual fears upon which such penalities had had to depend. More important still—for at no time did the majority of men take the thunders of the Church in quite such dread as the more sensitive spirits believe—was the new refusal of the state to support ecclesiastical censures with the more physical action of imprisonment and fine. To this must be added the growing abuse of the spiritual sanctions by the ecclesiastical courts themselves. Not all of them may have gone as far as Powell at Gloucester who generously commuted penances for money paid to himself, but it is doubtful whether the many penances imposed—public expressions of penitence, standing in a sheet, and so on—were often carried out, and it is certain that excommunication, often used for the merest trifles, was generally disregarded. As a result many culprits cited before the courts simply failed to appear, and ecclesiastical jurisdiction relaxed its ancient hold upon the laity.

Out of this general muddle which left a lay population still largely given to religious beliefs and observances without spiritual guidance, there grew the puritan movement and its quarrel with the official leadership of the Church. As has already been said, it is not easy to define puritanism. All its manifestations shared a desire to purify the Church in two respects: to stamp out abuses and thus render it fit to assume the moral leadership which was its due, and to remove the remaining traces of popish practice and traditions. The first of these aims was shared by all respectable and thinking clergy, and especially by the bishops; it was in the end to be accomplished without involving the march down the inviting but dangerous road to Geneva. To follow the example of the 'best

[1] Probate of wills was not removed from the ecclesiastical courts until 1857.

reformed Churches' became the ambition of men who saw their ideal of clerical life and spiritual authority embodied in the practice of Calvinism, but an unprejudiced observer must feel relief at their ultimate defeat.

Puritanism was not in the main a theological movement: it produced no original ideas in theology and almost no treatises on divinity. It borrowed these things from abroad, at first from the Zwinglians and later from Calvin and Béza. Its main characteristics have been analysed into four.[1] The first was a strong moral consciousness, a practical desire to counteract the chances offered to irresponsibility by the doctrine of predestination which in theory rendered a man's behaviour immaterial to his ultimate fate. In theory and practice, the puritan held firmly to an absolute moral standard. Among their best men this produced something like saintliness; among the not so great it could result in that inquisitorial and long-faced nosey-parkering which, unfairly perhaps, has come to be thought of as the hallmark of the puritan. It was secondly a movement which stressed at one and the same time the importance of the individual and the necessity of a social conscience—what Mr Knappen has called 'collectivist individualism'. In nothing else, perhaps, does the essential conservatism of English puritanism come out so well: at this time, at any rate, it preached and worked against anti-social selfishness and the self-assertive individual in a manner commoner among medieval friars and old-fashioned men like Latimer and Lever a generation earlier, than among the doctrines of the nonconformist commercialism of the future. Next, it was a zealous movement: it abominated compromise, gentle and perhaps devious advances to the desired end, and anything but absolute certainty of itself. Lastly, it was strongly clericalist, intent upon putting the clergy back in the saddle. Though not especially theological and always keen on solving the problems of this world, it kept the other-wordly end of salvation firmly in view and came at times near to a pride in priesthood which would have been very distressing to its sectarian offspring in the age of Oliver Cromwell.

None of these things necessarily brought puritanism into conflict with the established Church, except perhaps the zeal which rejected the time-serving, semi-secular policy of the queen and her bishops. When the possibility of an internal transformation of the Church ended with the appointment of Whitgift and the energetic persecution of the puritans (1583), there was precious

[1] M. M. Knappen, *Tudor Puritanism* (1939), the standard work on the subject where the whole problem may be found further discussed.

little between the sides. Both wanted an active clergy, a moral laity, a society harmonious rather than selfishly disintegrated. Both were zealous and uncompromising. Both were solidly Calvinist: not even Cartwright believed more firmly in predestination and the doctrine of the elect than did Whitgift himself.[1] The difference was political: it concerned rival views of the structure and government of the Church. Cartwright and his followers desired a presbyterian Church, resting upon a hierachy of individual congregations, provincial assemblies, and national synods, and administered by a democracy of ministers and an oligarchy of lay elders. Other puritans—the sectarians of Brownist and Barrowist allegiances—went so far as to deny the need for a general national Church. Against this the queen stood firm on the principle of an episcopal Church, with authority percolating from the top downwards—from the supreme governor, through archbishops and bishops, down to the parish clergy—and she found in the Calvinist Whitgift a staunch defender of this organisation which the other side dubbed popish.

This violent political disagreement rested ultimately on a deeper spiritual and intellectual conflict over the nature of authority. The puritans were above all else the people of the Book. What united all puritans was their belief in the Bible as the sole authority; what produced the many sects and divisions of puritanism was the varied interpretation to which the Bible may be subjected. Nothing matters so much in the history of the English Church and its derivatives as the English translation of the Bible. From William Tyndale (1525-31) and Miles Coverdale (1535-7), through the Great or Matthew's Bible which was officially sanctioned (1539), down to the wonderful achievement of the Authorised Version (1611), there was hammered out the chief—indeed the only—weapon of an exclusively English form of Christianity. To the puritan, everything—not only religion and theology, but also secular and ecclesiastical government as well as the rules of personal conduct and private life—was laid down in the Bible. He held that the Scriptures needed no interpreter, each man being able to understand them for himself, and that interpretation must be literal. Medieval scholasticism, inspired by St Augustine, had attempted to resolve the obvious contradictions contained in the

[1] Whitgift endorsed predestinarianism in the Lambeth Articles of 1595, but even then a contrary trend existed in the Church of England which was to culminate in the anti-Calvinist Arminianism of the next century. Richard Bancroft rather than Whitgift was the true forerunner of William Laud.

body of sacred writings partly by discovering different senses in difficult passages—ascribing to them figurative or allegorical meanings often the exact opposite of the literal meaning—and partly by recourse to the pronouncements of later authorities—the fathers, the early councils, the Church, the papacy. The true puritan would have none of this. Nevertheless, since he thus involved himself in serious difficulties, he was driven at times into attempts at interpretation and differentiation which conflicted with his basic belief in the universal and literal authority of the whole Bible. He might have recourse to a species of historical analysis, testing the Old Testament by reference to the New; he might fall back on later authority in order to reconstruct the early Church by working backwards; he might appeal to a different authority altogether by citing the example of 'the best reformed Churches'. But none of this altered his fundamental position. The only real authority was in the Bible where no one could find the episcopal structure of the Church: this was the abomination of Rome which must be purged away.

The puritan position had the advantage of simplicity and the strength that goes with it. The half-hearted objections of official defenders could be swept away every time with a demand to have the opponent's tenet proved from Scripture. Uncertain of itself, strongly influenced by continental protestantism of the same kind as that appealed to by the puritans, conscious of the political and uninspired nature of the settlement, the Church at first offered nothing to arrest the rapid advance of presbyterian puritanism. Especially the younger generation at the universities—in the main at Cambridge—took to the simple and authoritarian teaching of men like Cartwright with the readiness always displayed by certain young men to whom practical politics and compromise are anathema. Even so, the Anglican position was quite well defended in John Jewel's *Apology* (1562) which successfully justified the Church's renunciation of Rome but did not offer sufficient positive content for the Church of England's *via media*. Throughout the reign, many writings appeared which here and there managed to controvert the attacks of both catholic and puritan pamphleteers, but on the whole the presbyterians dominated the intellectual side of the English Church with their Calvinist theology and their insistence on Scriptural authority. It was not until the latter years of the queen's reign that puritanism as the leading movement within the Church fell on evil days. Its intellectual strength was undermined by Richard Hooker, while its organisation and practical resistance were destroyed by John Whitgift.

Hooker's greatest work, *The Laws of Ecclesiastical Polity*, appeared in stages—four books in 1593, the fifth in 1597, the remaining three after his death in 1600. Within its extended length there may be found a total view of the Church, the state, and the divine order of things which makes this obscure don and parish priest one of the great thinkers of the century and his book —the bye-product of a controversy—one of the important writings of political and religious thought. His insistence on natural law as the expression of God's world and his view of the state have already been touched upon. He derived much of his thought from predecessors like St Thomas Aquinas and Marsiglio of Padua; indeed, a notable part of Hooker's greatness is his learning and the way in which he applied tradition to the creation of something new—the doctrine of the protestant Church of England. For his theology proves him to have been a protestant; there is nothing, for instance, in his teaching on the sacraments with which any puritan could have found fault. But against the puritans' exclusive insistence on Scripture, Hooker put forward the claims of tradition, authority, and the Church. He summarised his position in four 'propositions' in which he listed those rites and observances which may be justified even if they cannot be deduced from the Scriptures: 'such things as are apparently, or can be sufficiently proved, effectual and generally fit to set forward godliness . . . may be reverently thought of'; things whose fitness is not evident or easily proved may yet be rendered fit by tradition and the judgment of antiquity; innovation is proper because not 'all things could be of ancient continuance which are expedient and needful for the ordering of spiritual affairs', and 'the Church . . . hath always power . . . no less to ordain that which never was than to ratify what hath been before'; lastly, if necessity or common utility so require, the Church may dispense from ordinances otherwise profitable. Hooker thus gave back to the Church the authority to interpret and guide which puritanism denied it. He based his argument on such wide and cogent knowledge, so thoroughly informed by an all-pervading historical sense, that the book was immediately successful and remained the basis for every later justification of the Church of England. The 'judicious' Hooker—the adjective is John Locke's—had just the spirit and learning necessary for the justification of the *via media*, the one religious position of the sixteenth century that had within it the germ of toleration.

There was nothing judicious about Whitgift or his vigorous campaign to stamp out puritan divagation in the Church. The weapon employed was the court of high commission. It grew out of the commissions for the enforcement of the royal supremacy of which that granted to Cromwell as vicegerent in spirituals (1535) was the first. A body composed of bishops, privy councillors, civil and common lawyers, it was appointed and sat at intervals until 1580 when it was turned into a court. Its work had hitherto been mainly visitatorial—to seek out and punish failure to conform. Now it became judicial—cases were decided between party and party. In the manner familiar from the history of star chamber, the high commission court rapidly developed a regular body of judges, a regular procedure, and a regular province of jurisdiction. Its judges were in the main bishops and ecclesiastical lawyers. Unlike an ordinary ecclesiastical court it covered the whole realm and, because of the standing of its judges, it could make its decisions felt; thus it grew popular and attracted much business, mainly among clerical litigants. In 1583 Whitgift published his twenty-four articles which he desired to impose upon the clergy; since they prohibited 'prophesyings', reinforced the rules about clerical dress, demanded subscription to the Prayer Book and Parker's *Advertisements*, and supported the authority of bishops, they amounted to a declaration of war on puritanism. The high commission, so far simply an important Church court, now became the instrument with which Whitgift made his articles effective. Using the procedure of the *ex officio* oath, by which a man could be compelled to incriminate himself, he harried the puritans into submission, deprivation, or even death. His activities caused much anger. Burghley protested in a famous letter (and in exaggerated language) that these proceedings smacked too much of the popish Inquisition; the lawyers—always good allies to the puritans—assailed the legality of the court; there were attacks in parliament. But Whitgift, who knew he had the queen behind him, went on undeterred. By the end of the reign, puritanism as a movement in the Church was dead. Its synodal organisation had been destroyed, its propagandists silenced, its ministers made to conform to the episcopal standard. That the movement began at the same time to increase its formidable hold over influential parts of the laity was nothing to do with Whitgift. He could not prevent its future development, but he could and did prevent it from subverting the Church from within.

Thus when Elizabeth died, the Church stood strong and, to all appearance, secure. Founded as a political compromise—though never as purely a compromise or as purely political as its attackers then and later pretended—it had established itself in the faith and the affections of the majority. It had fought off assaults from catholics and puritans. It had developed its own doctrine and philosophy. Altogether it was an achievement of which the many who had contributed to it in various ways might well be proud—Parker, Grindal, and Whitgift, Jewel and Hooker, Burghley and the queen herself. Perhaps Elizabeth had been its most consistent defender, especially in the days, now distant, when the firebrands of puritanism and anti-popery seemed to carry all before them. To the queen as much as to anyone was due the eminently conservative character of the achievement. She had gone as far as she would in 1559, and she had really not moved forward from there. In any case, forward and backward are misleading terms. There is something to be said for holding that the most progressive, least conservative, religious movement of the age was the Church of Rome after the Council of Trent. All the English movements looked back: the idea of progress did not occur to them, and they could not believe in the perfectability of man. The Anglican based himself consciously on tradition of which he claimed to be the only true inheritor; the puritan went further back and sought his model in the dawn of Christianity. Neither side claimed to innovate even where they did, for authority—whether confined to the Bible or not—was the guiding star, not man's sovereign reason. Of course, the puritan movement demanded an advance away from 1559, but it was an advance dominated by backward-looking tenets. In religion, as in government, the age of Elizabeth tried hard to stand still, to consolidate, and to preserve the links with the past; and even its rebels were essentially as conservative as the things they rebelled against.

Chapter XV

THE STRUCTURE OF THE AGE: RENAISSANCE

FEW words today are more apt to rouse historical passions than the word Renaissance. It is therefore advisable to preface this chapter with a warning that the use of the term implies no claim that in the sixteenth century the influence of the classics and of Italian models produced, at a stroke, an outburst of the 'modern spirit'. At one time all art and literature, politics and international affairs, religion and morals, economics and philosophy and history were regarded as coming to the end of their medieval forms about 1500 and as turning out different and new under the influence of the Renaissance. That view is now as dead as it deserves to be, though its corpse, decked out in a semblance of life, may yet be met with in some books. However, the question is whether in rightly denying the Renaissance in politics and affairs, and in tracing with great learning the persistence of 'medieval' ideas and modes of thought, historians have not fallen into the error of opposing outright denial to an untenable outright assertion. The Master of Jesus College, Cambridge, who has himself done much to popularise the notion of the Elizabethan age as dominated by the intellectual temper of the past,[1] has recently reconsidered the question of a Renaissance in literature.[2] Though his arguments on this point carry less than perfect conviction, it is yet hard to escape his conclusion that in sixteenth-century England something happened in the arts that cannot be explained without the use of some such term as Renaissance. There are certain activities of mankind which, being of the mind and subject to fashion, do accommodate themselves to the intellectual categories discerned—or devised—by the observer. Whatever may be true of the mental climate of the period and the majority of men, the achievements in literature and the arts fulfilled a deliberate purpose. How far they derived from classical and Mediterranean models may become apparent as they are discussed; that there was a Renaissance in the strictest sense—a rebirth of English poetry in particular—the merest glance at the writings of the day will confirm beyond question.

[1] See above, p. 396 and n.
[2] E. M. W. Tillyard, *The English Renaissance—Fact or Fiction?* (1952).

1. INTELLECTUAL BACKGROUND

The basis of the revival was a movement in education to which the name humanism is commonly given. It has already been explained that humanism was not the coming of light after darkness; it was, however, a break with the over-formal, over-abstracted dialectics of the later middle ages. The inspiration came from such diverse sources as the Italian passion for the classics, Erasmus' intellectual attack on scholasticism, the introduction of Greek into England by William Grocyn (1446?-1519) and Thomas Lineacre (1460?-1524), and the religious doubts which drove people like Tyndale to the Greek text of the Bible. The ideal of education changed from the theological to the rhetorical, from the training of priests and scholars to the training of accomplished gentlemen serving the state. Cicero dominated sixteenth-century education—they were for ever citing 'Tully' for the example of his oratory and the wisdom of his *De Officiis*—until a reaction against verbosity towards the end of Elizabeth's reign replaced him by the models of the Jacobeans, Seneca and Tacitus. This Ciceronian tradition was far from dead through most of the middle ages; the movement was really new only in that it demanded intellectual attainments in the lay leaders of society. By combining classical learning with medieval knighthood it created the ideal of the gentleman, that powerful civilising influence of the next 400 years: of that ideal, Sir Philip Sidney, who fused knightly 'courtesy' with humanistic learning and the Elizabethan courtier's love of poetry, stands as the first English embodiment.

An early exposition of these aims (partly taken from Italy) occurs in Sir Thomas Elyot's *The Governour* (1531), a training-scheme for a ruling class. But the most influential figure in practice was Sir John Cheke (1514-57), the first professor of Greek at Cambridge, provost of King's College, secretary of state, and tutor to Edward VI whom he imbued with protestant beliefs. Cheke's personal standing as a scholar and a man of affairs saved the new learning from the contempt of practical men; his principles, which rested on a firm belief in the 'usefulness' of learning and its application to the service of the state, became standard theory. It was from Cheke that Roger Ascham (1515-68) traced his intellectual descent, and Ascham was not only the foremost Greek scholar of his day and tutor to two queens (Lady Jane Grey and Elizabeth), but also, as author of *The Scholemaster* (1570), the leading exponent of the theory of education. The book is full of sound advice on the practice of teaching—it deprecates the prevailing brutality of the schools and prefers the late-developing solid intelligence to flashy precocity—as well as some rather hysterical warnings against the atheistical and evil influence of Italy on visitors from the north. Another who came under Cheke's influence was Thomas Wilson (1525?-81) whose *Art of Rhetorique* (1553) describes the sort of training in ready speech and sharpened reason that humanists thought best. Scholarship, especially in Greek studies, rather declined later in the century (Whitgift had no Greek), but the education provided by schools and universities in the reign of Elizabeth was firmly based on the ideals developed earlier. Sir Humphrey Gilbert's *Queen Elizabeth's Academy* (1572), the first 'modernist' protest against the classical syllabus, describes an ideal school where modern languages, mathematics, law, and military exercises rival the study of Latin and Greek; but it did nothing to undermine the humanist method. The century imposed on English education that exclusive attention to the classics and the rhetorical treatment of language that did service down to very recent times. The consequent permeation of all thought with allusions to classical history and mythology was to produce a kind of *lingua franca* of poetry.

It ought perhaps to be pointed out that the secular ideal of education—the accomplished gentleman—did not stand alone. It was accompanied by the traditional professional training for the clergy in their various capacities. In the reign of Elizabeth the gentry invaded both the universities and the inns of court, not to become scholars and lawyers but to acquire the equipment and polish which contact with scholarship and law alone could give; but their invasion did not drive out those who went there for professional reasons. The universities remained always in part at least schools for experts and a road to employment. In this century they were doing well as new foundations increased their size and variety. The humanism of the earlier years produced, at Cambridge, Jesus College (1496), Christ's College (1505), and St John's College (1511), and at Oxford Brasenose College (1509), Corpus Christi College (1517), and Cardinal College (later Christ Church: 1525). The ambitions of lay founders added Magdalene (1542), Trinity (1546), and Emmanuel (1584) at Cambridge, and Jesus at Oxford (1571). Many of these foundations played a leading part in the Reformation: thus St John's was a breeding ground of early protestantism, it and Trinity produced Cartwright, and Emmanuel was founded as a puritan college. Gresham College (1596) in London, financed from the bequest of Sir Thomas Gresham, began the liberal and anti-classical tradition of the capital's academic training. Schools, too, made their appearance: the activities of that brutal but efficient teacher, Nicholas Udall, at Eton (1534-41) and Westminster (1554-6) were matched by those of his brilliant pupil Richard Mulcaster, first headmaster of Merchant Taylors (1561-86). Other new schools included Repton, Rugby, Uppingham, and Harrow, all founded between 1559 and 1590.

If this vigorous educational activity was one pillar of the intellectual revival, another must be sought in the development of printing. William Caxton (1422?-91), who began printing in England in 1476, also founded the tradition by which printers doubled their activities with authorship. The good work was carried on by his apprentice Wynkyn de Worde and by a succession of king's printers of whom Thomas Berthelet and Richard Grafton, under Henry VIII and Edward VI respectively, are the best known. Thereafter there was no holding the press. Licensed or unlicensed (like the secret presses that produced the Marprelate Tracts), it poured out a stream of books and pamphlets, created a book trade and the profession of publisher, and provided the ground for the first genuine literary movement. Much of the poetry of the age was not printed at the time—some even yet remains in manuscript—but a vast deal appeared in book form, stimulating demand and making possible mental contact and cross-fertilisation. It is a commonplace, but none the less true for that: though without the printing press there might still have been a revival in literature, it would not have been so fruitful and lavish and would certainly have been less rapid in producing perfection.

Another striking aspect of the age was its renewed interest in history. The great medieval tradition of historical writing declined in the fourteenth and fifteenth centuries into a series of undistinguished chronicles. The historic importance of the wars of the Roses, as well as foreign example, resulted in worthier attempts to write history proper. Polydore Vergil (1470-1555), an Italian who as papal collector was long resident in England, set a new standard with his *Anglica Historia*; employing the training of Italian humanism, he displayed an organising faculty and a critical acumen of which English history stood in much need. Of the native chroniclers of the earlier period, Edward Hall (*The Union of the Two Noble and Illustre Famelies of Lancastre and Yorke*, published in 1548) deserves special mention. He proved himself possessed of a vigorous personal style and genuine insight, transferred to the vernacular chronicle some of Vergil's literary quality, and was one chief source for the encyclopædic chronicle of Richard Holinshed (1578) on which the dramatists mainly relied. All these, and others like Richard Grafton (1568) and John Stow (1580), were eclipsed by William Camden, a genuine historian of great dramatic power whose *Annales Regnante Elizabetha* (1615)—though in Latin—are the highwater mark of Elizabethan historical studies. Modern biography began with Thomas More's *History of Richard III* (*c.* 1514), can claim a fine if homespun example in George Cavendish's *Life of Wolsey* (1557), and achieved a masterpiece in Francis Bacon's *Henry VII* (1622). The interest in history spread to local studies like Stow's *Survey of London* (1598), William Lambarde's *Perambulation of Kent* (1570), and Richard Carew's *Survey of Cornwall* (1602). General surveys of England, mixing historical and geographical knowledge, were produced by John Leland (*Itinerary*, *c.* 1540), William Harrison (*Description of England*, 1577), and especially by Camden in his monumental *Brittania* (1586). The catalogue could be extended beyond all patience, but even as it stands it may give some inkling of the enormous output of an age whose interests ranged from the Anglo-Saxon studies of Archbishop Parker and the foundation of a Society of Antiquaries before the end of the century to contemporary history chronicled in John Foxe's *Acts and Monuments*, popularly known as the *Book of Martyrs* (first edition in 1563).

There was much other serious writing. The main work of Francis Bacon belongs to the next century, but the *Essays* appeared first in 1597. They are a collection of philosophical and moral reflections, distinguished by flashes of thought and a severely elliptical style; the present writer has never been able to understand the praise showered both on their manner and matter. The geographical works of Dee and Hakluyt have already been noted; to them one may add the surveys with maps of which John Speed's *Theatre of the Empire of Great Britain* was the finest. Yet all this was only a part of the writing done—the lesser, and to contemporaries perhaps the less important, part. If this account concentrates on the secular literature of the age it is not because the output of theology was small: on the contrary. Religion and writings about religion loomed very large indeed, But, except for the occassional masterpiece like Hooker's, the literary quality and the intellectual interest are greater among the secular productions. In any case, these are significant of something new. Together with a number of treatises on hawking, archery (Ascham wrote a well-known one, the *Toxophilus*), husbandry, courtly life, and all the rest of it, they display a vigorous intellectual interest in matters rarely hitherto touched by literature. With creditable ease, the age accommodated a genuine feeling for spiritual things with an equally genuine devotion to the possibilities of secular life. No one can say how this fruitful turmoil was related to the outburst of great music and poetry. A view, still not uncommon, which seeks to explain Shakespeare and his fellows out of the intellectual zest of the age, tries too much. The activity in education, printing, and secular studies here described is not to be thought of as the cause of the artistic developments to which we must now turn. Rather is it an aspect of the same thing—the great increase, leading in the end to a unique manifestation, in the workings of the human mind and spirit which distinguish the sixteenth century in England.

2. THE FINE ARTS

The Tudor age delighted in colour and lavish display, as any portrait of—say—Henry VIII or Elizabeth makes plain. The lively brashness of an exuberant time often fell short of good taste, but its brightness and richness—even its bizarre touches—are signs of sprouting life. The moralists and legislators—the latter trying by sumptuary laws to limit the worst indulgence in silks, velvets, and jewellery to those who could afford them—fought a losing battle against the slashed doublets, wide ruffs, enormous (and very unsightly) breeches, massive chains and delicate feathers, the idiotically tall hats and high heels of the dandies who infested Elizabeth's court. The simpler fashions of the earlier reigns, even if often they went in for a sort of tough virility with their unnaturally broad shoulders and tight hose, are beyond question preferable. Women's fashions were rather less gorgeous, except in the hands of the very wealthy and especially the queen herself, but they were even more objectionable: the huge hooped skirts rendered movement difficult, while the tight bodices and deep stomachers squeezed vital organs in a way not exceeded by the worst Victorian tight-lacing. But beautiful or not, sensible or not, all the clothes that mattered were designed to dazzle and overwhelm.

It is therefore a little astonishing to find that this taste for colour did not produce any great painting. Much Tudor painting seems to have disappeared; what there is is practically all portraits and the best of it by foreigners. Several important painters were brought to England by royal patronage, as for instance the Italian Vincent Volpe, the Flemings Hans Eworth and Antonio Moro, and the German Gerlach Flicke. The greatest painter to work in England in that century was Hans Holbein the younger, from Basle, whose splendid portraits—especially the series of drawings preserved at Windsor—have made the reign of Henry VIII the first age we fancy we know intimately. Holbein's work influenced others; despite the later impact of Italian, Flemish, and Spanish styles of portraiture, a trace of his purely linear style survived to the end of the century. Among a number of competent portraitists, he was the only artist of real genius, and the fact that he worked under Henry VIII has obscured the actual development from feeble beginnings early in the century to a genuine mastery of technique learned from abroad in the reign of Elizabeth. However, though there are many good portraits of the second half of the century, few succeeded in depicting character as Holbein's did. The later Elizabethan painters concentrated more and more on the careful description of detail—dress, jewellery, and the Renaissance accessories of the background—while contenting themselves with a linear suggestion of the features. This is particularly marked in pictures of the queen herself after 1584 when George Gower received a monopoly for royal portraits: most people are therefore liable to think of her as a stiff cone of brocade hung with pearls and surmounted by elaborately bejewelled red curls. Only in the field of miniature painting was there a native tradition. Growing out of the art of illuminating manuscripts and developed by the many craftsmen who 'limned' royal portraits in the initial letters of public documents, it reached astonishing heights of beauty in the work of Nicholas Hillyard and his slightly inferior successor Isaac Oliver. These artists combined a 'modern' technique of portraiture and mastery of perspective with the 'medieval' technique of illumination. Their colours in particular recall the vivid blues and golds of medieval manuscripts. By and large, the vogue for portraits represents less a genuine interest in the arts than a genuine interest in one's own face: the portrait painters—full-scale or miniature—did the work of the photographic studio.

More native traditions and more notable achievements may be recorded in building. Here the Reformation made an obvious difference: it ended the great era of church-building. The early Tudor period was the last age of Gothic—the age of late perpendicular. Opinions on this differ: some speak of decadence, arguing that the fretted stone-work which reduced the windowless wall-area to the least possible before the invention of steel-girders, the non-functional ribs of the fan-vaulting, the plentiful ornamentation (often heraldic), show that the purpose of the building had been lost sight of. It is true enough that a perpendicular chapel like that of King's College, Cambridge (the finest example of the style) creates less of a mystical gloom than does the solidity of thirteenth-century Early English, but it would be wrong to argue from this that it represents irreligion. The late perpendicular is sometimes mechanical and uninspired, but at its best it is a very high achievement in craftsmanship and architectural technique. The stained glass of the late fifteenth and early sixteenth century was the finest ever made.

Some of these early Tudor buildings, ecclesiastic and secular, owed much to foreign artists and workmen. The Italian sculptor Torregiano built Henry VII's tomb at Westminster, Wolsey employed Flemings at Hampton Court, Sir Richard Weston's typical early-Tudor palace at Sutton Place in Surrey was probably designed by another Italian, Trevisano. Nevertheless the domestic architecture of the period was strictly indigenous, owing little to foreign models. It marked the development of the rather cramped medieval castle, designed with at least one eye to defence, into the more comfortable palaces and manor houses of monarchy and gentry. The new inherited some points from the old. The central hall—once the sole public room—is a notable feature in them all; it still survives in college architecture. So is the quadrangle, developed as outhouses grew up around the hall and complete when these became additional dwelling-chambers. The great gatehouses with their crenellated turrets are a distinctive part of early-Tudor palace building; vestigial remains of embattled castles, they may be seen at Hampton Court, or at Queen's and St John's Colleges in Cambridge. The growing use of brick, the employment (for lesser houses) of half-timbered walls even where stone was found locally, the improvements in fire-places which appear in the sprouting of the famous Tudor chimney stacks (again very noticeable at Hampton Court), are other typical points. All over the country, palaces and manor houses were built; in the towns wattle-and-daub gave way to half-timbered buildings; a growing wealth and the needs of the new landowners after the Dissolution encouraged a vigorous activity. A few names may be cited: Henry VII's old palace at Sheen (Richmond) now covered up by Stuart alterations, Wolsey's Hampton Court, Henry VIII's St James's Palace, Haddon Hall in Derbyshire, Wollaton Hall in Nottinghamshire, Kirby Hall in Northamptonshire. And dozens more: many an Elizabethan manor house survives today as a farmhouse.

More remarkable, however, than painting and even architecture was the development of music. Of this nothing like enough can be said here, partly for lack of space, partly because the present writer can lay no claim to expert knowledge at all. The idea of all England as a nest of singing-birds, popular with writers of romantic history, may indeed be rather exaggerated—there are signs that it is coming under attack—but there is no doubt at all both of the extremely high level reached by the many great composers of the century and of the widespread interest in music shown by all classes and especially by the court, the centre of culture. Kings and queens, courtiers and poets, played and sang and many composed, especially Henry VIII whose efforts have, however, found little favour with the experts.[1] In music, too, one finds the familiar mixture of the traditional and the new. In particular, while much music continued to be written specifically for an ecclesiastical purpose—settings of services, and here the Reformation made almost no difference, especially because some leading composers were catholics—the reign of Elizabeth also witnessed the growth of a wonderful corpus of secular music, especially for voices. The great composers of the mid-century—Christopher Tye (1500?-73), Robert White (1530?-74), and especially Thomas Tallis (1505?-85) —produced church music of magnificent quality, but so far little worthwile secular music was written. The change came with the introduction from Italy of the madrigal and the canzonetta, the pupils soon outstripping the teachers. Good opinion holds that Elizabethan part-song and solo-song reached the highest point possible in that field. Helped by the great poetry of the age, the composers achieved an unsurpassed marriage of music and words. Between 1588 and 1630 more than eighty collections of songs appeared in print, containing little short of 2,000 pieces, and others as beautiful remained in manuscript.

The great names here are John Wilbye (*d.* 1614), the supreme writer of madrigals, John Dowland (1563-1626) who wrote accompanied solo-songs, Thomas Campion (*d.* 1619), a poet who set his own verses, and Thomas Morley (1557-1602) who could do all kinds and was responsible, for instance, for 'Now is the month of maying'. Greater even than these in passionate intensity were two men whose fame rests mostly on their church music: Orlando Gibbons (1583-1625), the first composer of Anglican services, and the supreme master William Byrd (1543-1623) who must rank with the very highest, with Palestrina and Bach. In his long life Byrd produced a great deal of music. His attempts at secular songs are comparative failures; he seems to have needed the words of devotion, and especially of the services, to bring out his power of mystical thought and absorption in the remotest realm of musical language. There were others, barely less remarkable than those named. Not all madrigals are good, nor need one necessarily like

[1] E. Walker, *A History of Music in England* (1952), p. 45, describes the king, rather gratifyingly, as 'an eclectic of the feeblest kind'.

madrigals at all; but no one can resist Byrd's *Cantiones Sacrae*, Wilbye at his best, or Dowland's sad, sweet songs. In the reign of Elizabeth, England reached the highest concentration of musical genius in all her history and led Europe in this field.

3. LITERATURE

Any attempt to summarise here the work of the writers, poets, and dramatists who made of the sixteenth century one of the few really great periods of literature must obviously be hopeless. It was in language and its use that the English Renaissance mainly expressed itself. The visual arts played little part in it; music recorded astonishing achievements but for technical reasons remained a restricted expression of the age; in poetry, on the other hand, no more remarkable work has ever been done. Within the short space of some sixty years, and thanks to the labours of a few men of genius and many men of unusual talent, the English language shed the awkwardness and insufficiency which clung to it and became the flexible and all-competent instrument of an incomparable out-pouring. The greatest of all poets (perhaps in any language) was part of that band, but others beside Shakespeare added their efforts—more than can be listed here. Another difficulty is raised by the fact that the death of Queen Elizabeth marked a date of no importance in this story. There are differences between the Elizabethans and Jacobeans, but the significant years are really 1580-1630. Yet we cannot include here the whole reign of James I. As far as possible we shall therefore confine ourselves to work done before Elizabeth died and to men who were prominent before 1603, taking three subjects in turn—prose, lyrical poetry, and the drama.

Prose has always been later to reach perfection than poetry because poetic language is always the first to undergo the discipline of literary treatment. The age of Elizabeth is no exception. Some decent literary prose appeared under Henry VIII, though most of it was cumbersome and long-winded; under the influence of their Greek and Latin studies, Cheke and Ascham wrote a clear if rather pedestrian style; but when the literary men really got hold of prose they did terrible things to it. Dissatisfied with the plainness of daily speech and the artlessness of his predecessors, John Lyly, in his two romances *Euphues* (1579) and *Euphues his England* (1580), developed a style of his own which, by the name of Euphuism, became the model and bane of English writing. Its essence lay in a laborious display of rhetorical devices; Lyly was particularly fond of pointless but well-balanced antitheses, frequent alliteration, a prodigality of similes arranged in wearisome strings, and rhetorical questions. Sir Philip Sidney's *Arcadia* (*c.* 1580) suffers from much the same faults, though they are less glaring; oddly enough—in view of the large number of versified romances that ought to have been in prose—the episodic and often exalted *Arcadia* would be better all in rhyme than in a mixture of both. Unlike Lyly, Sidney (who after all was a minor genius) could turn out good prose within the limits of his convention, but too often he was guilty of conceits like the following description of a piece of sewing:

> The needle itself would have been loth to have gone fromward such a mistress but that it hoped to return thitherward very quickly again, the cloth looking with many eyes upon her and lovingly embracing the wounds she gave.

This stuff was popular for a time, but that it palled is evident both from the way in which Shakespeare later parodied it and from the career of Robert Greene (1560?-92), perhaps the first professional journalist, who always wrote in the fashion. Thus he produced a lesser *Euphues*, pastoral romances in the manner of Sidney, and—when realism grew in vogue—the splendid pamphlets, mostly of low life, on which his fame rests: *Notable Discovery of Cozenage*, *A Quaint Dispute between Velvet-Breeches and Cloth-Breeches*, and others (1590-2). Here the style has become racy, straightforward, and English. The main achievement of this greater freshness was Thomas Nash's *The Unfortunate Traveller* (1594), a picaresque novel full of humour and incident. Nevertheless, even at its best Elizabethan literary prose makes hard going and proves how much less universal prose is than verse.

The best prose of the day is probably found elsewhere—among the translators, among those who merely wished to convey their ideas without regard to the refinements of Latin and Italian example, in prose passages in plays, and in letters. The sixteenth century was a great age for translations; a list of the authors communicated to the English is some indication of the debt owed by this Renaissance to foreign inspiration. The Italians in particular made their appearance in strength: Boccaccio, Ariosto, Machiavelli's *Art of War*, the tales of Bandello, and others were all translated. In prose translations the restraint imposed by the original compelled the writer to drop the tasteless refinements and adornments which beset English prose in its youth, with such outstanding results as Lord Berners' *Froissart* (1523-5), Thomas North's *Plutarch* (1579), and John Florio's *Montaigne* (1603). Above all, of course, one must here mention the *Authorised Version* of the Bible (1611), whose perfection, achieved by a committee of rather dreary divines, is as good a proof of direct inspiration as one can find. The needs of controversy exercised a similarly salutary influence: those who wrote to convince could not afford the graces and obscurities indulged in by those desiring to amuse. Not that the vast pamphlet literature of the century was always written in good English; much of it was unrhythmical, crude, prolix, and tedious. But much also reached remarkable heights. A useful study of the development of English prose might trace the controversial style from the rather awkward plainness of Thomas More to the accomplished ease of Hooker. Take these two passages, one from More's *Apology* of 1528, the other from Hooker's *Ecclesiastical Polity* of 1594:

> But yet for that I have myself seen and by credible folk have heard, like as ye say by our temporalty that we be as good and as honest as anywhere else, so dare I boldly say that the spiritualty of England, and especially that part in which ye find most fault, that is to wit that part which we commonly call the secular clergy, is in learning and honest living well able to match and (saving the comparisons be odious I would say further) far able to overmatch, number for number, any nation christened.

This Doric, good of its kind, looks back to medieval writings; in Hooker, on the other hand, we can hear the true English prose of the centuries to come.

> He that goeth about to persuade a multitude that they are not so well governed as they ought to be shall never want attentive and favourable hearers, because they know the manifold defects whereunto every kind of regiment is subject; but the secret lets and difficulties, which in public proceedings are innumerable and inevitable, they have not ordinarily the judgment to consider.

Thus far had skill moved in the space of some sixty years.

The most interesting, characteristic, and vigorous prose is found where there is least artifice. The common speech of the age, as reported in law-suits and transformed by Shakespeare into a species of poetry, reached a remarkable standard of succinct and lively expressiveness: in that respect every succeeding century has produced only progressive deterioration. The measured solemnity exemplified in a threat uttered in 1534, during a quarrel over the fixing of meat prices—'I will advise you not to meddle with the said weight of flesh, for if you do it shall be to your pain'—becomes, in the hands of the poet, the magnificent pathos of Mistress Quickly's threnody on Falstaff: 'Nay sure, he's not in hell; he's in Arthur's bosom if ever man went to Arthur's bosom', and the rest of it. And then there are the letters, to prove that few in the century could fail to write well when they had something to say and no need to clothe it in artificiality. Here is Thomas Cromwell, gravely rebuking Bishop Shaxton, one of his own party:

> My lord, you had showed yourself of much more patience—I will not say of much more prudency—if ye had contented yourself with their lawful appeal and my lawful injunctions and rather have sought fully to instruct me in the matter than thus to desire to conquer me by shrewd words, to vanquish me by sharp threaps [assertions] of Scripture which, as I know to be true, so I trust to God—as great clerk as ye be—ye allege them out of their place.

Queen Elizabeth, taking James VI to task for double-dealing:

> How may it be that you can suppose an honourable answer may be made me when all your doings gainsay your former vows? You deal not with one whose experience can take dross for good payments, nor one that easily will be beguiled.

And these two were hardly expert stylists, unlike Sir John Harington, that good Elizabethan, describing some goings on at a masque at James I's court in a manner which explains why Elizabeth once referred to him as 'that witty fellow, my godson':

> Now did appear, in rich dress, Hope, Faith, and Charity: Hope did essay to speak, but wine rendered her endeavours so feeble that she withdrew and hoped the king would excuse her brevity. Faith was then all alone, for I am certain she was not joined with good works, and left the court in a staggering condition. Charity came to the king's feet and seemed to cover the multitude of sins her sisters had committed . . .

In this field, as in every other aspect of prose, the century witnessed a marvellous growth of ease, rhythm, vocabulary, and general skill; one of the finest tools of human thought, instruction, and amusement was thus fashioned by the English Renaissance.

In poetry, the revival and change are very marked, and the part played by Italian (and French) models is unquestioned. As the century opened, the traditions of Chaucer were well-nigh dead. When historians of literature have to fall back on the tedious and clumsy Alexander Barclay, whose *Ship of Fools* (1509) imported from Germany a fashion in heavy-handed satire, English poetry was in a parlous state. Nor can much more be said for John Skelton (1460?-1529), not the last poet-laureate hardly to deserve the first part of his title, though his idiosyncratic doggerel breathed vigour, a crude humour, and—especially in his attacks on Wolsey (*Speke*, *Parrot* and *Why Come Ye Nat to Courte?*, 1522-3)—a genuine savagery. As he said himself:

> For though my rhyme be ragged,
> Tattered and jagged,
> Rudely rain-beaten,
> Rusty and moth-eaten,
> It hath in it some pith.

But the man who could think of commending a lady with the pedestrian lines

> How shall I report
> All the goodly sort
> Of her features clear
> That hath none earthly peer?

or another with these words—

> By St Mary, Lady,
> Your mammy and your daddy
> Brought forth a goodly babby,

was a very long way from true poetry. A revival was certainly called for.

It came late in Henry VIII's reign with two poets who formed the mainstay of a collection known as *Tottel's Miscellany* (1557)—Sir Thomas Wyatt (1503-42) and Henry Howard, earl of Surrey (1517-47). Their fame once rested on the fact that they introduced the sonnet into England, thereby both giving a new strictness and form to the sprawling genius of English poetry and laying the foundations for that mass of sonnet-cycles later in the century with which we must bear because to that fashion we owe Shakespeare's sonnets. If they had done nothing else the old view which ranked Surrey higher would have been justified: Wyatt's sonnets are clumsy, with an often atrocious misuse of English rhythm (once he scans harbour as an iambus, for instance), and altogether less accomplished. But Wyatt was the greater poet. Surrey's work —his conventional love lyric, his translations of Virgil and the Psalms—is meritorious, nice-sounding, unreal, and dull; Wyatt's lyrics are among the finest because they sprang from genuine feeling. The impressive thing about Wyatt is not his imitation of Petrarch—though he could produce a good sonnet like *The Hind* (his resignation of Anne Boleyn to the king, with the famous final couplet '*Noli me tangere* for Caesar's I am, and hard for to hold though I seem tame')—but his poetry in the English tradition, a tradition going back to the anonymous *Alison* (*c.* 1300). The man who could write

And wilt thou leave me thus?
Say nay, say nay, for shame!
To save thee from the blame
Of all my grief and grame.
And wilt thou leave me thus?
  Say nay, say nay!

or

What should I say,
Since faith is dead
And truth away
From you is fled?
Should I be led
With doubleness?
Nay, nay, mistress!

was a great poet in his own right. The themes and the atmosphere of Wyatt—the inconstancy of women, the corruption of courts and attractions of rural life, the vigorous melancholy—became poetic commonplaces and were worked to death; but with him they were real and personal.

Much of Wyatt's best work owed, to all appearance, nothing to foreign example; he was 'in the tradition'. So were all the great poets of the age. What is one to make of Sir Walter Raleigh, beyond doubt one of the most learned of men, deeply read in all Europe could offer, and the author of one of the best of Elizabethan sonnets ('Methought I saw the grave where Laura lay'), who could yet write that haunting ballad-type poem *Walsinghame*?

> As you came from the holy land
> Of Walsinghame,
> Met you not with my true love
> By the way as you came?
>
> How shall I know your true love,
> That have met many one
> As I went to the holy land,
> That have come, that have gone?
>
> . . . . .
>
> But love is a durable fire
> In the mind ever burning;
> Never sick, never old, never dead,
> From itself never turning.

It may be, as we are told, that he was here allegorically lamenting his lost court favour (though who can see it and what does it matter?) but in any case the mood and manner are the real thing, and the echoes are of folksong and Walter de la Mare! The 'Renaissance' did not produce an entirely new poetry, but gave to native genius new competence in expression, new vigour of thought, new metres (very important, this), a new language, and up to a point new subjects. There is no question of an Italianate poetry, but an invigorating stream came from the south. No rational explanation can fully account for the wonderful outburst of poetry that ensued after Wyatt and Surrey and has lasted, with interruptions, to the present day. But though one cannot explain, the fact of a rebirth is patent.

The impetus given by the authors printed by Tottel soon spent itself among the products of minor poets like Barnaby Googe (1540-94) and George Turberville (1540-1610). The best of that generation was Thomas Sackville, later Lord Buckhurst and earl of Dorset (1536-1608), who when he was about twenty wrote the very fine introduction to the *Mirror of Magistrates* and then abandoned poetry for politics and administration. He sounded a new note which was to find many to repeat it, a note of didactic solemnity expressed in sound metre and worthy language, the note (if one may say so) of Augustan poetry. Lines like these seem to find their nearest echo in Gray's *Elegy:*

> Here puled the babes, and here the maids unwed
> With folded hands their sorry chance bewailed,

Here wept the guiltless slain, and lovers dead
That slew themselves when nothing else availed;
A thousand sorts of sorrow here that wailed
With sighs and tears, sobs, shrieks, and all yfere
That oh, alas, it was a hell to hear.[1]

But despite Wyatt, Surrey, and Sackville, English poetry was once again settling into a rut of imitation when the mould was burst and made anew with the appearance of Spenser's *The Shepherd's Calendar* (1579), Sidney's *Defence of Poesy* (1582-3), and Sidney's sonnet-sequence *Astrophel and Stella* (1584, published 1591).

The place of Sir Philip Sidney (1554-86) and Edmund Spenser (1552?-99) is assured, but the present writer finds it rather difficult to do justice to them. Sidney's critical work—the first really fruitful piece of literary criticism in the language—contains such misconceptions as an attack on rhyme and an insistence on the classical unities in drama; it is one of the best known ironies in English literature that the great age of Elizabethan poetry which followed immediately upon the book's publication triumphed by neglecting most of its advice. But by taking poetry seriously and really thinking about it Sidney did good work, and he saved it from such futilities as the ideas of the Cambridge pedant Gabriel Harvey who wanted to introduce the hexameter into English and nearly stopped Spenser from writing his genuine poetry because it was not classical in cast.[2]

Spenser's output consists in the main of *The Shepherd's Calendar* (1579), a set of twelve eclogues or pastoral poems; the *Faerie Queene* (1589 and 1596), a long allegorical poem written in the 'Spenserian' nine-line stanza; the satires *Mother Hubberd's Tale* and *Colin Clout Come Home Again* (1595) in which he attacked his enemies at court and the present state of poetry; and the lyrical poetry of the *Amoretti*, *Epithalamion*, and *Prothalamion* (1595-6). All his work is suffused by a high poetic spirit and displays intense imagery and a superb mastery of words; the *Faerie Queene* is in many ways the most highly charged of all English poems, and it was this quality that prompted Keats to describe Spenser as 'the poet's poet'. But even his greatest poem, rich and

[1] 'Yfere' means together. The last two lines are well outside Gray's grasp.

[2] How wrong even sensible men could be when they followed the classical fashion is shown by Roger Ascham's praise for the appalling hexameters of Thomas Watson's translation of the *Odyssey*, beginning:

All travellers do gladly report great praise of Ulysses,
For that he knew many men's manners and saw many cities.

splendid as it is, is marred by a failure in purpose. Spenser himself intended it as a manual for the training of gentlemen, and his allegories are so badly mixed that at times it is hard to see whether his meaning is moral and didactic, or political and in praise of Gloriana, or both, or neither. Spenser also lacked humour—that is, he is usually elevated and invariably over-solemn—and was the first to try the invention of a poetic language based on archaisms, but all these faults are as nothing when he is at his best, as in the rapt and inspired lyric of his marriage poems. All his work, too long to quote, loses by extraction, but one may cite the refrain from *Prothalamion*—

> Against the bridal day, which is not long:
> Sweet Thames, run softly, till I end my song—

or a few lines from *Epithalamion:*

> Ah! my dear love, why do ye sleep thus long,
> When meeter were that you should now awake,
> T' await the coming of your joyous make
> And hearken to the bird's love-learned song,
> The dewy leaves among?

Sidney could not aspire to the same height of poetic passion, but he wrote much fine lyric verse, and his sonnets, influenced by Petrarch and Ronsard, provoked a flood of imitators. The 1590s are the years of the sonneteers, one and all copying the conceit of a mistress (nearly always imaginary) whose fickle love must be wooed though fulfilment is out of the question. Sidney's *Stella* found successors in Henry Constable's *Diana*, Samuel Daniel's *Delia*, Fulke Greville's *Caelica*, Thomas Lodge's *Phyllis*, Michael Drayton's Unknown of the *Ideas' Mirror*, and many others. Spenser wrote the *Amoretti* to his future wife; above all Shakespeare produced the 154 poems of the greatest sonnet cycle ever written. The value of this mass of poetry varied enormously. At their not uncommon worst, the sonneteers wrote mechanical stuff, full of conventional attitudes and unfelt borrowings. At their best they reached the heights of 'Farewell, thou art too dear for my possessing', 'When to the sessions of sweet silent thought', 'When I have seen by Time's fell hand defaced', 'Let me not to the marriage of true minds', and all the other masterpieces of concentrated thought and poetical perfection with which Shakespeare honoured the sonneteering fashion. Only one other is commonly thought worthy to rank with these—Drayton's 'Since there's no help, come let us kiss and part'.

Elizabethan poetry was not confined to sonnets, and this section may close with a brief consideration of two styles—the long narrative poem and the true song. Of the former Michael Drayton's (1563-1631) are the representative examples. In a long life, Drayton—with all his versatility—always adhered to the spirit of the late Elizabethan age and showed no sign of the revolution wrought by John Donne whom (though he started to write in the 1590s) we must here exclude, since he is essentially Jacobean and a man must make an end (to quote a much more recent poet). Drayton's long patriotic poem-chronicles—*The Barons' Wars*, *The Legend of Great Cromwell*, *Poly-Olbion*—contain some fine passages but also a terrible amount of sheer dross: versified prose which would have been more suitable, because more pithy and painless, if left in prose. At his best, however, as in the celebrated *Agincourt*, he produced a combination of noble thought and vigorous language which raised the patriotic poem to some height:

> Fair stood the wind for France
> As we our sails advance
> Nor now to prove our chance
> Longer to tarry;
> But, putting to the main,
> At Caux, the mouth of Seine,
> With all his martial train,
> Landed King Harry.

(Even here, the sixth line, though justified in the story, reminds one of Wordsworthian bathos.)

As for the songs, they were truly legion, and no bare idea even can be given of them. All the poets of the day wrote verse which was clearly meant to be sung and in many cases was published with music. Of the song-books, the most famous is *England's Helicon* (1600), containing contributions by Sidney, Spenser, Drayton, Greene, Lodge, Nicholas Breton, George Peele, Shakespeare, Sir Edward Dyer, Raleigh, Marlowe, and many others. Once again the secular lyric reached its height in Shakespeare's incidental songs in his plays:

> Under the greenwood tree
> Who loves to lie with me
> And turn his merry note
> Unto the sweet bird's throat,

Come hither, come hither, come hither!
Here shall he see
No enemy
But winter and rough weather.

Or, in another typical mood:

Come away, come away, death,
And in sad cypress let me be laid;
Fly away, fly away, breath;
I am slain by a fair cruel maid.
My shroud of white, stuck all with yew
O prepare it!
My part of death, no one so true
Did share it.

Technically, the interest of the songs lies in their extraordinary variety and ingenuity of metre, in their vitality and sincerity, in a tunefulness which almost never declines into mere prettiness, and in the sheer verbal beauty of even the tritest. Apart from those already mentioned, one name stands out—Thomas Campion, who wrote both words and music for many lovely songs, lovely despite his own preposterous objection to rhyme:

Rose-cheeked Laura, come;
Sing thou smoothly with thy beauty's
Silent music, either other
Sweetly gracing.

On the other hand, the age produced little religious lyric, a form which the next century was to bring to perfection. The only poet always quoted in this context is the catholic martyr Robert Southwell (1561-95) whose work certainly shines with genuine ardour but lacks the technical accomplishment of the secular poetry. He seems to have escaped the influence of the great change made by Sidney and Spenser, and his rather plain, sometimes awkward, diction endows even the much-praised *Burning Babe* with a certain pedestrian quality which is very different from the simplicity of great poetry.

One could go on for ever. From about 1580 onwards, poet after poet contributed work of imperishable beauty to this great age of English poetry. It culminates in Shakespeare: no one else even approaches his concentrated thought, his consistent beauty of language, and especially his ability to use concrete imagery so as to render real the passions and ideas which in others too often seem insincere because they are cast in conventional phrases. But if they were not all men of supreme genius, they all assisted in this rebirth of a literature.

Much the same is true of drama, except that here the achievement is even more astounding. There have been other ages of great lyric poetry, but—even including Periclean Athens?—never anything like the thirty years which produced the work of Marlowe, Shakespeare, Jonson, Dekker, Webster, and their lesser contemporaries. Moreover, while there was a real English tradition of poetry, however moribund, it is hard to discover anything in pre-Tudor times that deserves to rank as the ancestor of Tudor drama. The miracle plays and moralities (allegorical dialogues) of the middle ages, the mummings and disguisings that accompanied popular festivals, no doubt provided a certain tradition of acting and the staging of spectacles, but they are a very long way indeed from true drama. The early Tudor plays, such as they were, still were very close to these beginnings. In the main they are associated with a group centring on Thomas More's household: More himself, as a young man, seems to have had a fondness for acting and may even have composed a comedy. But these 'interludes'—like John Rastell's *Interlude of the Four Elements* (1519)—are little more than dramatic discussions in which personified abstractions —Vice and Virtue, Nature and Humanity, Experience and Ignorance—exchange views on given topics. John Heywood (1497-*c.* 1580) injected into this tedious art form some skilful writing and much really funny humour, in his *Play of the Weather*, *Play of Love*, *Witty and Witless*, and especially *The Four PP*, a discussion between a palmer, a pardoner, a potecary, and a pedlar. These plays are much closer to the literary dialogue exemplified in the *Discourse of the Common Weal* (1549), in which a knight, a merchant, a husbandman, and a doctor debate the state of the realm, than to true drama.

The inspiration which turned this somewhat barren tradition to new uses came from the classical past. Humanistic teaching stressed the practice of Latin speech, and several enlightened schoolmasters saw that the result could best be obtained by the acting of plays. Thus Mulcaster had his boys act even at court, and Udall himself wrote the first English comedy constructed on a classical pattern—*Ralph Roister Doister*, not uninfluenced by Plautus' *Miles Gloriosus*. Latin plays were specially written for performance at the universities, and the queen's visits to Cambridge

(1564) and Oxford (1566) stimulated eager activity on those lines. Cambridge can claim the first important rustic comedy, *Gammer Gurton's Needle* (*c.* 1560), which has the honour of having invented the traditional Mummerset speech of the English stage. At the Inns of Court, too, play-acting grew very popular after the middle of the century. Here the influence of Seneca's plays, marked in Sidney's *Defence of Poesy*, was paramount. The plays were full of dumb-shows and other effects borrowed from Italy; the two productions that deserve mention were *Supposes* (1566), a prose comedy adapted from Ariosto's *Gli Suppositi* by the prolific George Gascoigne, and the first blank-verse tragedy in English, *Gorboduc* (1561), a sanguinary chronicle from British prehistory. In this play two lawyers more familiar in other fields collaborated —Thomas Sackville and Thomas Norton; it causes no surprise to find that *Gorboduc* ends with a veiled but impassioned plea to the queen not to let the succession go unsettled!

But still true drama was to seek, and only developments after 1575 were to make it possible. Two lines must be followed: the growth of the court play and the development of the public stage. The first was mainly in the hands of John Lyly, whose Euphuistic novels had, in their dialogue, given promise of much dramatic ability. When he turned to comedy, Lyly produced a series of plays adapted to a fairly sophisticated taste in which he used a flexible prose. *Campaspe* (1584) is the best of a cycle based on classical mythology and history: it is the story of the rivalry for a captive girl's love between Alexander the Great and the painter Apelles. (The painter won.) The court grew very fond of plays; the office of revels developed into a theatrical company, and the lord chamberlain began his association with stage-licensing and censorship. Outside the court the movement was even more vigorous, with the growth of several companies of actors under noble patrons and the building of theatres. The earls of Leicester and Pembroke, the lord chamberlain and lord admiral, and others lent their names to famous players' companies. In 1576, James Burbage, father of the great actor Richard Burbage, built the *Theatre* in Shoreditch; the *Curtain* followed. Later the actors escaped the hostility of the City by crossing over to Bankside; there they erected the *Rose* (1587), the *Swan* (1594), and the *Globe* (1598). Conditions were ripening for the outburst of genuine dramatic writing. The theatres, players, and public existed; noble and even royal patronage smiled on the play; the example of ancient Romans and modern Italians had transformed the interlude.

The first man to take advantage of these conditions was Thomas Kyd (1558-95?) whose *Spanish Tragedy* (*c.* 1585) initiated a series of 'revenge' plays of which *Hamlet* was to be the acme. Kyd excelled in stagecraft and the construction of plots but lacked any vestige of poetry. The vogue caught on, and for several years plays turned on nothing but sudden death and the accumulation of corpses. When old stories of cruel wrongs and savage revenge gave out, one could use the stories of more recent murders, as in the anonymous *Arden of Feversham* (1592) and *A Warning to Fair Women* (1599). But more plentiful blood-letting mixed with the comforting moral was to be found in history: hence the chronicle play, so popular in the 1590s. Plays appeared on King John, on Henry V, on King Leir (as it is spelled there), all of which provided material for Shakespeare. The chronicle play could find material in recent history, as in *Thomas Lord Cromwell*, a straightforward 'dramatisation of the book' (Foxe's *Martyrs*), or the better-constructed *Sir Thomas More*. An entirely different element was added to these rather obvious examples of popular taste by the work of Christopher Marlowe (1564-93), the first great English poet to write for the stage. Like Kyd, Marlowe was a man of education who applied the teaching of the schools to dramatic work; unlike Kyd, he was weak on plot but strong on verse. The four great plays—*Tamburlaine the Great* (1590), *The Jew of Malta* (1589-90), *Edward II* (1591?), and *The Tragical History of Doctor Faustus* (1592)—are full of weaknesses in the story, absurd inconsistencies in character, and inadequate psychology; but they also contain the finest poetic writing of any English plays, outside Shakespeare. Marlowe took the halting blank-verse of his predecessors and gave it grandeur and fervent colour, now savage and now tender. But despite good opinion which reckons that his early death may have cut short the growth of one as great as Shakespeare, one may venture to suggest that Marlowe's verse is the weapon of the rhapsodist rather than the dramatist.

One other group must be mentioned—the so-called university wits. These men—especially Robert Greene, George Peele, and Thomas Nash—all came to London from Cambridge; they wrote plays (as well as other things) which are distinguished by a certain graceful ease, much wit, and experimentation with material; but they did not write very good drama and clearly belong to the second rank. Greene's well-known jealous remarks about Shakespeare illustrates the rivalry between the professionals of the London stage and these university wits, but neither his *Friar Bacon and Friar Bungay* (influenced by Marlowe's *Faustus*), nor

Peele's charming *Arraignment of Paris* and lively *Old Wives' Tale*, are major achievements.

Out of all this, and yet out of nowhere, came the genius of William Shakespeare, inexplicable but in no need of explanation. As he excelled his fellow sonneteers, as he wrote more consistently perfect songs than anyone else, so he stood high above all other playwrights. Of Shakespeare as of the *Authorised Version*, an amateur of literature cannot speak without simply repeating the encomium of ages, nor is there any need to discuss him at length when there are so many good books on him—and when he has written a better than any of these. The cycle of thirty-seven plays contains much hack-work, a good deal that is tedious or stop-gap or ranting, but all in all it represents the greatest achievement of both the poetic and the dramatic spirit in human history. Shakespeare surpassed all his contemporaries at their own specialities: his plots are much better constructed than Kyd's, his humour is profounder and funnier than Greene's, he was a much greater poet than Marlowe. In addition, he had what can only be described as the Shakespearian quality—a universality, embracing and understanding all men, mixed with a wonderful gift for the creation of character and a language so unique that in any collection of blank verse it stands out unmistakably. What he did with and to blank verse is nothing less than a miracle. He found it a rather stiff but impressive medium for dramatic verse; he left it so thoroughly exploited that after him no one could ever use it again in any form without danger of losing part of his individuality, a danger which perhaps only Milton overcame. The ending of *King John* is good enough verse and would have made the fortune of any other Elizabethan dramatist:

> This England never did nor never shall
> Lie at the proud foot of a conqueror
> But when it first did help to wound itself.
> Now these her princes are come home again,
> Come the three corners of the world in arms
> And we shall shock them. Nought shall make us rue
> If England to itself do rest but true.

But, with its regular beat, so deadening in the long run, this is lacklustre dullness by the side of Shakespeare's mature work—for instance the spiritual and poetic excitement of Lear's death:

> And my poor fool is hang'd! No, no, no life!
> Why should a dog, a horse, a rat, have life

And thou no breath at all? Thou'lt come no more,
Never, never, never, never, never!
Pray you, undo this button: thank you, sir.
Do you see this? Look on her, look, her lips,
Look there, look there!

Of all poets Shakespeare at his peak was the most sovereign, using his weapons at will and never at the mercy of his material in matter or manner. And of all poetic dramatists he was the only one in whom poetry and drama met in perfect marriage.

Shakespeare must be read or seen, and not talked about. He marks the height not only of Elizabethan drama but of all drama, and in a way he fittingly closes this chapter. But there were others who must not be omitted, though—like Shakespeare—they did their best work after 1603. Ben Jonson (1573-1637), more learned but less miraculous than Shakespeare, in his Elizabethan days almost revived the allegorical tradition with such plays as *Every Man in his Humour* (1598) and *Every Man out of his Humour* (1599), the 'humours' of traditional medicine standing for the embodied qualities of men. He did better work later in his satires (for instance *Volpone* and *The Alchemist*) and the realistic *Bartholomew Fair*. Thomas Dekker's (1570?-1641) *Shoemaker's Holiday* comes from the same stable. The rest—George Chapman, John Webster, Cyril Tourneur, Francis Beaumont and John Fletcher—are more completely Jacobean, and if that division is arbitrary it must still be obeyed here. The English Renaissance produced much magnificent poetry and many excellent plays. Even without Shakespeare it would have been an age of greatness; with him and because of him it moves into the realm of timeless magnificence, to be judged not by the standards of its own conventions but by the eternal criteria.

Chapter XVI

THE LAST YEARS

THE year 1588 has long been recognised as at most a stage in the military history of Elizabeth's reign, but in domestic events it continues to be thought of as a date of great significance. The view expressed by A. F. Pollard some forty years ago still holds the field: 'It opened a new chapter in the political and constitutional history of England. . . . The Tudor period is dissolving into the Stuart.' The dominant personalities passed from the stage—Leicester died in 1588, Walsingham in 1590, Burghley, a shadow of his old self, in 1598. The queen herself showed signs of her age, and in the end signs of the coming dissolution. The new men did not approach the stature of their predecessors. Robert Cecil may have matched his father in political skill and managerial dexterity, but he lacked both his profound sagacity and his unselfish honesty. The rest of the council were second-rate men. The great sea-dogs found only lesser epigones. Raleigh, who might have bridged the gap between the generations, was unpopular with the people who believed him to be an atheist and sorcerer; worse, he lost the queen's favour in 1592 when he was discovered to have seduced, and subsequently to have secretly married, one of her ladies-in-waiting—it is not clear which act Elizabeth thought the more heinous. As for Essex, he defies definition and stands apart. In the Church, Whitgift's stern Calvinism was growing old-fashioned before the sophisticated High Church tendencies of Lancelot Andrewes and Bancroft. What looked like a new spirit of restlessness and defiance appeared in parliament: control of the commons became more difficult, the government—and even the queen—were openly contemned, attacks were made on the prerogative. In 1604 the house told James I that they had held their fire before Elizabeth's death 'in regard to her sex and age which we had great cause to tender', and in expectation of 'freer times' under her successor. All this seems to support the view that the end of national danger in 1588 released the realm from the fears which alone had made it acquiesce in Tudor autocracy.

But this is not so. The Elizabethans did not realise that all danger had passed in 1588, any more than they could have thought of their period as 'dissolving into the Stuart'. While it is true enough that one must beware of marking too deep a break in 1603, it is wrong to treat the last years of Elizabeth as a kind of anticipation of what was to come; one must look at them for their own sake and not allow after-knowledge to exert its misleading fascination. The 1590s differed from earlier decades for perfectly plain and valid reasons. There was a war going on, demanding an unprecedented and crippling outlay of money. After the prosperous trading years of 1575-90, England now experienced a period of economic difficulties only very partially accounted for by the activities of pirates. The harvests of 1592-6 were very bad: such a run of disastrously wet summers had not occurred in living memory. Famine, or near-famine, brought with it a sudden rise in prices as well as the return of plague which had mercifully left England alone for most of the reign. War, plague, and economic distress produced social and administrative difficulties. The standing problem of vagrancy was aggravated by the bands of sick, wounded, discharged, and deserting soldiers, so that comprehensive legislation became necessary in 1597 and 1601. The needs of the national economy provoked, on the one hand, a more stringent application of controls which annoyed the gentry and the merchants, while on the other they showed up the inadequacies of Tudor government and led to complaints. It all boiled up in parliament—because parliament was the proper arena for the airing of grievances, and because the demands of war finance prevented Elizabeth from following her earlier policy of calling as few parliaments as possible. Even so, all except the last parliament were really less determined in their opposition than those of the 1560s had been, and the issues were really less fundamentally constitutional. Among those who departed the scene in these years was Peter Wentworth, and with him went the one man who could turn everything to constitutional profit.

More significant than the alleged foreshadowings of later troubles are the continuities with the past. Of course, as Elizabeth enters her sixties, as the familiar figures vanish, as men begin to think of the queen's successor, it is hard not to feel that an age is coming to an end. Yet except on the personal side, little was changing. The issues and problems of the reign—the Church and its adversaries, the constitutional questions, the voyages of exploration—dominated also these dying years of a great generation.

1. THE CHURCH'S ADVERSARIES

In the history of the Church of England, the 1590s were a time of consolidation and mounting triumph.[1] The internal enemy—puritanism—was subdued; the external enemy—catholicism—wasted its strength in private dissensions. The Marprelate attacks of 1589 succeeded only in rousing official anger to a pitch of grim determination and in alienating moderate opinion. Whitgift's work in the high commission has already been noted. The death of Field and Leicester in 1588 robbed the movement of its organiser and its leading patron. Cartwright survived, to know prison in 1590-2, to publish a last blast in his *Apology* of 1596, and to disappear into ineffectualness and semi-exile in Guernsey where he died in 1604. Even in parliament the puritan cause found fewer defenders and little support. In 1593 James Morrice, attorney of the court of wards and therefore a crown official, revived memories of Strickland and Cope by introducing two bills attacking ecclesiastical jurisdiction and especially the 'tyrannical' practices of the high commission. Although Sir Robert Cecil's reminder that Elizabeth would resent such an invasion of the prerogative met with little response, Speaker Coke was compelled to divulge the matter to the queen and bring back notice of her anger: he was charged, on his allegiance, to permit the reading of no bill concerning ecclesiastical causes. It seems that a command which in earlier days would have stung the puritan 'choir' into action moved no one in the house; Morrice underwent a spell in prison, and the last attempt by the Elizabethan commons to take the initiative about the Church fell by the wayside.

While the presbyterian movement thus entered upon a decline from which only Scottish support rescued it for a time during the civil war, the sectarian or separatist movements seemed to gain in strength. No one except themselves had any patience with these splinter groups: Cartwright was as opposed to them as was Bancroft, though he used rather less violent language and had no chance of emulating the bishop's violent deeds. The parliament that witnessed Morrice's failure also passed a vicious act against sectaries, though admittedly it toned it down from the even more devastating plans of the government. By this statute failure to conform was punished with imprisonment, to give the offender time to think it over; if he proved obstinate after three months he

[1] This fact, in such marked contrast with the troubles of the Church after 1603, is worth noting in connection with the theory that the period really anticipated Stuart times.

had to abjure the realm. Refusal to go into exile, or unlicensed return from it, meant death for felony. In the same year (1593) three leading sectaries suffered death—Henry Barrow and John Greenwood for seditious writings, and John Penry for treason. It may be that the executions were designed to create an impression. At any rate, the act did its work, and the London congregation which Barrow had organised moved to Amsterdam, as Browne's Norwich congregation had gone to Middelburgh some years earlier. Continuing to copy its predecessor, the group at Amsterdam soon fell prey to internal strife. But they were never dispersed entirely, nor did the survivors lose their fervour: it was from among them that the movement started which a generation later took the *Mayflower* to New England.

Thus puritanism in the Church, presbyterian and separatist, collapsed before the determined onslaught of the hierarchy, supported by the state. No one thought that it had been wiped out, and Bancroft came to hold that its hard core was irreconcilable and should be driven forth. However, while Elizabeth lived the theory at least of uniformity was preserved: she would have no two ecclesiastical bodies in one state. The government found it easier to adopt these energetic measures because they no longer required the aid of the zealots against the threat from Rome. The war with Spain not only confirmed the protestantism of the majority of Englishmen; it also discovered the patriotism of the catholic minority. To offset the attack on puritanism, another act of 1593 made a catholic's life truly unbearable: he was forbidden to move more than five miles from his residence, and inability to pay the heavy recusancy fines resulted in exile. Many catholics began to think of ways in which to convince the government of their essential loyalty and thus obtain relief. Even though Philip of Spain carried papal blessing, they had much difficulty in seeing in him God's chosen instrument. As early as 1590, a priest had publicly asked whether English catholics could lawfully defend the realm against Spain, and he had answered himself by saying that they could because Philip, being merely intent on his own ends, was no true defender of the faith. Not surprisingly, his doctrine met with no success at Rome, but it became clear that a split was developing. The moving spirit behind the Spanish attack were the Jesuits, especially Robert Parsons who had become Philip's adviser and propaganda expert on England. Between the Jesuits and the secular priests no love was lost, and when in 1594 Parsons published a pamphlet which, by pressing the claims of the Spanish Infanta before the Stuart claim to the English throne, seemed to confirm all the old suspicions of Habsburg ambition, the united front of English catholicism collapsed. The seculars rebelled against the Jesuits' ascendancy in the English college at Rome and among the imprisoned priests at Wisbech in Norfolk, and feelings ran very high.

In this unhappy situation the death of Cardinal Allen (1594) produced all the difficulties of a disputed succession. The pope had to appoint someone to rule the English catholic community: whom would he choose? Jesuit influence was so high at Rome that the outcome need not surprise, though it also displayed the Roman proclivity for compromise. The pope refused the seculars' request for a bishop elected from among their ranks, but appointed as archpriest one George Blackwell who was himself a secular, but a secular with a difference. He had pronounced leanings to the Jesuit ideal and the Jesuit habit of autocracy; to cap it all, he was instructed to follow the Jesuit lead. For six years the conflict raged as the seculars refused to accept the archpriest's authority. In the end, after many appeals, the court of Rome confirmed its original decision and left the secular clergy at the mercy of Jesuits and Spaniards, unless they could make their peace with the queen. The ensuing negotiations showed that the government, too, were far from united on the issue. Bancroft, for ecclesiastical reasons, and Cecil, on political grounds, hoped to bring about the submission of the catholics, but these would only agree to swear loyalty if freedom of worship were granted. Bancroft would have consented, but Elizabeth, mindful of the reaction this would have produced among the people, refused. Her attitude may have been intolerant, but how wise and necessary it was appears plainly enough from the unhappy history of James I and Charles I whose gentle treatment of catholicism did more than any other single thing to bring them into odium with their own subjects. No one at this time could afford to tolerate Rome in England without arousing suspicions of treason; Bancroft's attitude—he practised secret and unlawful toleration—shows how far the 'high' movement in the Church had gone thirty years before the heyday of William Laud.

The queen's statesmanlike obstinacy seemed to end the chance of splitting the catholic ranks by exploiting the archpriest controversy, but in fact it secured such a split without surrendering to catholic demands and by a typically Elizabethan manœuvre. In November 1602 a proclamation ordered all priests out of the country but permitted seculars to stay if they swore allegiance to the crown. Thirteen of them did, much to the government's satisfaction; they thus advertised the divisions within the catholic Church in England, branded the Jesuits as supporters of Spain rather than religion, and destroyed two legends—Spain's pose as a crusading power, and the idea that English catholics were waiting to welcome her armadas. Elizabeth did not survive this submission for long, but the signs were clear. Catholicism was rendered innocuous, even as puritanism had been driven out of the Church. What neither she nor the two parties could foresee was that the next dynasty would fall over backwards in trying to make up to catholicism for what it had suffered under Queen Elizabeth, thus provoking a vast revival of puritanism and making anti-popery the only sure-fire cry in a century of political strife.

2. THE CONSTITUTIONAL QUESTION AGAIN

The queen's difficulties with her parliaments also continued, though the older problems caused little stir at this time. As has been seen, Morrice's bills of 1593 were the only positive reminder of the old puritan tactics in parliament. Free speech did not again become an issue, but this was because its champion, Peter Wentworth, had discovered another outlet for his furious energies. He picked on the question of the succession, decently interred for some twenty years, but now—he thought—urgent again because the queen was growing old. Wentworth did not stand alone in thinking about the succession—it would be fair to say that few politicians thought of much else as the 1590s drew on—but only he dreamt of bringing it up in parliament. As early as 1587 he became convinced that unless the queen agreed to settle the succession on safely protestant lines, the danger of a catholic claimant would grow potent. He composed his *Pithy Exhortation to her Majesty for Establishing the Succession* in which, with his usual freedom of language, he urged the queen to regard the country's interest. Only an unaccustomed touch of caution, or failure to find a printer fool enough, prevented him from publishing the pamphlet. In 1591 his agitation got him into trouble with the council who rewarded his zeal with six months in prison. Baulked out of parliament, Wentworth returned to his proper sphere of action in 1593. But he discovered that his day was past. With much energy and ingenuity he did his best to organise a campaign on the succession issue; yet even Morrice, himself ready to brave the queen's anger on other matters, tried to dissuade him. Nearly thirty years had passed since Norton and his fellows had fought tooth and nail on this issue; if anything, the queen's age made

Wentworth's agitation more reasonable than theirs had been. But no cock crew. His scheming outside parliament during the session constituted a constitutional impropriety—faction making—and the outcome was his last imprisonment in the Tower. There he survived until 1597, undauntedly refusing to give the promise to cease his agitation which would have released him and still writing on the state. Seventy-three years old he died, undefeated and unvictorious, a crotchety nuisance but also a martryr in a cause which a subsequent generation was to understand better. His violence and rigidity had deprived him of real influence in parliament; not only privy councillors thought him a needless complication. But he had raised the issue of free speech to the high pinnacle of principle which it deserved; he had begun the deliberate organisation of opposition; and he had lived and died for his beliefs in a manner which makes him a fit forerunner of the seventeenth-century parliamentarians.

The real problem of the 1590s was money. War expenditure demanded a constant and unusually heavy burden of taxation.[1] In practice only the demands of 1593 roused serious opposition: the war was too obvious an emergency and too obviously expensive to make the levies anything but reasonable. But out of this problem of taxation and finance grew two serious constitutional quarrels which reflected the commons' self-confidence and the dangers inherent in the unsettled relations between the three parts of parliament. These quarrels were a conflict between the commons and the lords in 1593, and an attack on the prerogative in finance and the making of grants in 1597 and 1601.

In the parliament of 1593, the commons made heavy weather over the granting of supply, largely because they had granted unusually large subsidies four years earlier and were not yet used to the persistence of such needs in the long war. In the end they offered two subsidies, as in 1589. However, this seemed insufficient to the government who tried to use their unquestioned control of the lords to extract more. The upper house therefore asked for a conference at which Burghley, explaining some details of expenditure, declared that the lords would insist on giving three subsidies. This occasioned a vigorous debate on the question of privilege. Francis Bacon, in whom throughout this session the lawyer and statesman triumphed over the ambitious politician (partly at least because in attacking the subsidy he was attacking the Cecil interest), pointed out that the commons alone had the right to decide on the amount to be granted: the lords were to be warned

[1] For the details of the subsidies see above, p. 363.

off. It was therefore suggested that the commons should protect their privilege by themselves offering the three subsidies deemed necessary by Burghley. The ensuing debate was distinguished by the number of eminent men who took part in it and by the expression of bewilderingly diverse views on the country's ability to pay. In a speech which cost him the royal favour for six years, Bacon asserted that if the proposal went through the gentlemen would have to sell their plate and the farmers their brass pots; some others seemed to think that the country had never been so rich; others again suggested new, ingenious, and largely impracticable methods of taxation. In the end the grant passed—three subsidies to be paid within three years—but in this serious clash between the houses—the first in the century—the commons had successfully protected their right to initiate all money bills.

The attack on the prerogative, culminating in the very stormy session of 1601, arose out of the question of monopolies. Of course, the prerogative had been involved in all those debates about the Church, the succession, and the control of policy which had disturbed earlier parliaments; but it was only when its financial effects came under review that it succeeded in creating something like a unitedly resistant house of commons. One of the undoubted powers of the crown was to make grants for the regulation of trade, a power which in this period took the form of establishing monopoly rights by letters patent. The rights differed in kind. A man might be licensed to perform certain things notwithstanding (*non obstante*) statutory provisions to the contrary: thus he might be permitted to export goods otherwise forbidden or to evade the laws regulating the manufacture of cloth or leather. He might hold a grant entitling him to sell licences to others: in 1588 Raleigh obtained the privilege of licensing all taverns for thirty years. Or he might be permitted a monopoly in the manufacture and sale of certain articles, such as salt and sugar, or in the import of others—as Raleigh's famous monopoly of playing-cards.[1] Some of these monopolies did only the work of the modern patent laws—that is, they protected a legitimate interest in new inventions. But most of them were noxious. Those of the *non obstante* type raised the issue of the crown's control of legislation: could the prerogative

[1] Though he blushed for it on one occasion, Raleigh rather specialised in monopolies. A contemporary lampoon alleged that

'He seeks taxes in the tin,
He polls the poor to the skin,
Yet he swears 'tis no sin;
Lord for thy pity!'

dispense with a law at pleasure? In practice, Tudor statesmen employed the licensing system both to maintain control of economic life and to extract money, and when not carried to excess some such flexibility was essential if the rigid regulations were not to be disastrous or stultified. Worst, however, were the monopolies of the last kind. Granted as favours to courtiers and for payment to syndicates of capitalists, they were widely exploited at the expense of the public by raising prices. Their enforcement caused the greatest annoyance. The monopolist was commonly authorised to protect himself against interlopers by wide powers of search and punishment, and the resultant arrogant dealings and invasions of privacy led to much trouble. The queen liked monopolies because they enabled her to reward services and show favour at little cost to herself; more farseeing men like Burghley had often objected to them. In the depression of the 1590s they became a serious grievance, made especially intolerable because there was no redress in the courts.

Discussions started in the parliament of 1597 when it was proposed to petition the queen to abolish burdensome monopolies. Elizabeth, as usual, made a fair answer but had no intention of doing anything. This time that policy did not pay. Within four years she had to face another parliament. It opened with an inauspicious muddle: the better part of the commons, arriving at the parliament chamber for the opening of the session, found the door accidentally locked against them. Thereafter nothing would go right. The session was marked by a constant undercurrent of touchiness, jealousy, and discontent. Few would say 'God save your majesty' when Elizabeth passed through their crowded ranks after the Speaker's installation; members' servants created much noise and disturbance around St Stephen's Chapel; the two houses bickered; debates were frequently interrupted as unpopular speakers endeavoured to make themselves heard above the laughing, hawking (clearing of throats), and spitting with which the Elizabethan commons liked to express their disapproval. The Speaker and the privy councillors could hardly preserve a modicum of order and entirely failed to keep control of the proceedings: the house seems to have grown a little tired of Sir Robert Cecil's guidance and was not to be appeased by his overworked favourite opening in which, time and again, he declared that he had not really meant to intervene at all. Up to a point the impression of special turbulence in this parliament may be due to the fuller information available about it; but there can be no doubt that it was a troublesome session.

Monopolies provided the issue, and they were more than merely a convenient pretext. Without the exasperation produced by their abuse and the queen's transparent evasions, there is little reason to suppose that this parliament would have been more of a nuisance than any other. It had no sooner met than the subject was revived; this time, several members introduced bills against monopolies one of which was only twelve lines long but allegedly sweeping. The commons were trying to legislate about the prerogative; all the makings of a pretty show-down were assembling. Bacon, explaining that the queen's prerogative enabled her 'to set at liberty things restrained by statute law and otherwise' and to 'restrain things which be at liberty', warned the house that it was putting itself in the wrong and advocated established practice: 'the use hath ever been to humble ourselves unto her majesty, and by petition desire to have our grievances remedied, especially when the remedy toucheth her so nigh in point of prerogative.' The fact that a year or so before he had at last succeeded in putting his great gifts at the service of the crown ought not to obscure the truth of his view. The debate turned less on the proposed bills—apart from a few extremists, the commons were not really yet ready to flout the prerogative—than on the evils of monopolies. One member recited a list of over twenty commodities, many of them in common use, which were involved; this provoked young William Hakewill (who was to make a forceful speech against the Stuart prerogative in 1610) into the only half facetious suggestion that bread would next be added unless the house took action. Cecil magisterially rebuked members for behaving in a manner 'more fit for a grammar-school than a court of parliament', but his only positive suggestion was to wait till the committee already appointed should report to the house.

At this point, after days of debate, Elizabeth realised the danger. However autocratic in manner she might be, she knew better than to stand obstinately on her prerogative and refuse redress for justified grievances. Her master-stroke in parliamentary management did all the commons wanted yet saved the prerogative from the bills before the house and herself from either risking a serious quarrel or appearing to act under pressure. She professed herself much surprised and angered that grants she had made should have proved oppressive to the people and declared her intention immediately to review the situation and abolish all bad monopolies. A proclamation to that effect appeared at once: many monopolies were withdrawn and others put under the law by permitting people who had grievances to sue against them in the courts. This gracious and skilfully timed surrender immediately changed the whole temper of the house. They had been behaving like wayward children rather than determined politicians: the queen's concession turned all to smiles and acclamation. On 30 November 1601 Elizabeth received a large deputation from the commons who came to express their thanks; she answered them in the most famous oration of her reign—her 'golden speech' in which, like Prospero, she took farewell of her arts.

> Though God hath raised me high, yet this I count the glory of my crown, that I have reigned with your loves. . . . I was never so much enticed with the glorious name of a king or royal authority of a queen, as delighted that God hath made me his instrument to maintain his truth and glory and to defend his kingdom from peril, dishonour, tyranny, and oppression. . . . Though you have had and may have many mightier and wiser princes sitting on this seat, yet you never had nor shall have any that will love you better. . . . And I pray you, Mr Comptroller, Mr Secretary, and you of my council, that before the gentlemen depart into their counties you bring them all to kiss my hand.

The humility of this speech has provoked scepticism, but its measured clarity contrasts so strongly with Elizabeth's usual style that, patently, she must have been sincere. On this occasion, the last on which she was to address her people, she recorded the proud faith and humble gratitude of a ruler who, with all her faults, had been as well and as deservedly loved and served as any in history. With equal pride and humility she could look back on the long years of her own devoted service to her people. As the commons passed by to kiss the old woman's hand, the strength and glory of the Tudor state stood visibly embodied.

The difficulties experienced with these last parliaments might suggest that something had gone wrong in the matter of management. There is certainly no sign that the government tried harder either to secure a pliable house of commons or to weaken the commons' independence of action. But that was not due to any failure on the part of Elizabeth's councillors: rather it expresses the truth that management was at all times just that and nothing equivalent to control. Difficulties, grievances, conflicts could not be avoided—no one thought they could—but only minimised, adjusted, or in the last resort given way to. Elizabethan elections were largely free; that is, they were influenced by local powers only, such as the great families in the shires or the patrons and municipal authorities in the boroughs. Occasionally, the council tried to obtain the election of nominees. An early example of this occurred in 1553 when Mary's council sent out a circular letter with nominations attached in the hope of getting a parliament which would reverse the Reformation. More commonly these council circulars merely asked that men fit for the place be elected, and the two Elizabethan letters which went further—one of 1584 asking for members well-affected to the queen, and one of 1586 suggesting the re-election of the last parliament's knights and burgesses—had little effect. No one at this time tried deliberately to create a government party, though members sitting for the few crown boroughs and the rather more numerous seats controlled by councillors and courtiers formed a reliable unofficial body of support for the privy councillors in the house who represented the queen and managed policy. The powers of the Speaker—always a government nominee—and the authority of the councillors, as well as natural awe of the queen, generally kept things in order in the commons themselves; but in a house growingly developed in its procedure[1] and growingly aware of its opportunities for opposition, nothing could be done to maintain a really safe ascendancy. This was so from the start of the reign; the last parliaments do not mark a new spirit of independence but rather a change of subject and at most a growing feeling that the younger generation ought to have its say. The Stuarts failed to cope with their parliaments because they were less skilful and less adaptable than Elizabeth, not because their problems were more insoluble, or because they were confronted by a new kind of commons of which the first signs might conceivably be looked for in the four parliaments after 1588.

3. MORE NAVIGATIONS

Though the war occupied most of the ships and seamen of England, some of them continued to go further afield. Of course, whether they sailed into American and Asian waters or hung around the islands of the Azores, they were often preying on the enemy; but the greater voyages really carried on from the exploits of Drake, Hawkins, Frobisher and their like before 1588, so that they deserve separate treatment here. The journeys of the 1590s followed the tracks already marked out. Now that war had broken out and the susceptibilities of Spain did not have to be regarded any longer, the dangerous and futile attempts to reach Asia by a

[1] The very interesting and important subject of parliamentary procedure is too detailed to be treated here. It may be read up in J. E. Neale's *Elizabethan House of Commons*, chs. XIV-XXI.

northern route were abandoned in favour of following Drake into the South Seas. Asia—the Spice Islands in particular—continued to be the real target, with two ways there available: some went westward, as Drake had done, while others began to find the Portuguese route round Africa more promising. There was also another project on the American mainland, again in the hands of Raleigh.

Of those who went westward, Thomas Cavendish proved at first the most successful: in 1586-8 he became the second Englishman to circumnavigate the globe. His exploit reads like a copy of Drake's, with the spectacular success left out. He crossed the Atlantic from Sierra Leone to Brazil, sailed down the coast to the Straits, and after a seven week's passage entered the Pacific. Despite the capture of one rich prize coming from Manila with silks and spices, his raiding along the west coast brought little profit. An easy crossing of the South Seas and a prosperous voyage home led him to underestimate the difficulties, and when he sailed again, in 1591, he took too little care. On this occasion he was joined by John Davis. From the first, lack of preparation had the expedition in trouble—short of victuals and full of unrest. Cavendish, who seems to have suffered from the ungovernable temper that distinguished so many Elizabethans, quarrelled with his officers, took refuge on Davis's ship, then returned to his own. In the face of violent winds they failed to make the passage of the Straits, after which the ships parted company because Cavendish had not provided for so obvious a danger. He re-appeared in Brazil, trying to gain treasure by fighting; but he had to draw off empty-handed and died, only thirty-two years old, on the return voyage. In the meantime Davis, hampered by a half-mutinous crew, tried to find his commander in and out of the Straits; in the course of these sailings he performed such incredible feats as taking the vessel safely at night through rock-infested waters which he had memorised on a single previous passage. But in the end he had to return with a ship soon populated by little more than ghosts. His was another of those dreadful voyages which wind, weather, the sea, and scurvy made so common before the eighteenth century.

There was one more attempt to attack the Pacific coast of Spain's empire. The news of Cavendish's failure had not reached England before, in 1593, another small fleet set out under Richard Hawkins, old Sir John's son. They made the Pacific all right but found the Spanish defence so thoroughly reorganised that that safe hunting-ground had become a graveyard. Chased by better-equipped vessels built to exploit the light winds of those latitudes, Hawkins and his men avoided capture once but were in the end defeated and taken. Hawkins, treated with respect, was sent to Spain and did not see England again until 1602, long after his father and Drake had died at sea in their last disastrous invasion of the Caribbean, which has already been described.

The high old times of plundering a defenceless Spanish empire in the west were clearly over: only a sizable and well-found fleet could now hope to make an impression on the forces which the viceroys of Peru and Mexico could send out, and at this time—with so much to do near at home—there was no prospect of one going all that way. A little more promising, though at the time equally beset by shipwreck and disaster, the eastern route attracted the merchants of London. In 1591 the Levant Company equipped a fleet of three ships one of which, under John Lancaster, reached the Malacca Straits after touching at Zanzibar. As sickness struck, his crew forced him to abandon his intention of cruising around on the look-out for spice ships, and another expedition returned very bedraggled and with nothing but loss to report. However, the Levant merchants could afford an occasional financial disaster. Driven on by hopes of emulating the Dutch who were then rapidly pushing their trade into India, the London capitalists kept up the good work. In 1600, after a few more profitless voyages, the East India Company received its charter and dispatched a trading fleet commanded by Lancaster and guided by Davis. With its departure a new era began in English expansion. Trade—peaceful trade—was at last ousting privateering, raiding, and plain piracy as the first preoccupation of sailors and navigators. The story of that further expansion belongs to the Stuart century and cannot here be followed up.

One last Elizabethan enterprise remains—Raleigh's attempt to establish an English base off the Spanish Main and discover the legendary gold mines of Eldorado. The presence of much gold and the absence of any gold mines in Peru had early raised the question of the real source of this precious metal, and by the late sixteenth century Spanish explorers had narrowed its supposed site down to the inaccessible mountains of Guiana, stretching between the basins of the Orinoco and the Amazon. Raleigh's imagination was fired by what he heard and read, and when in 1592 his disgrace left him with nothing else to do he devoted himself to the project. In 1595 he sailed for Trinidad where he established a base. The only way into the mountains seemed to be up a tributary of the Orinoco, but all these were barred by formidable waterfalls where they precipitately descended from the range to the river basin. After four weeks of far from reckless enterprise Raleigh gave up, disgusted with the heat and dirt and worn out by hardships which were slight by the standards of the Spanish explorers. He was nearly forty-five: his life at court had not equipped him for this work; and, as always with Raleigh, the last obstinacy was lacking. Although he sent another fleet a little later to investigate the Guiana coast itself for access to the interior, the whole project must be added to the many which Raleigh took up in his generous enthusiasm but failed to carry through. This is quite apart from the fact, of course, that the country of Eldorado, its magnificent city of Manoa, and its gold-mines amounted to a myth.

The 1590s thus marked a decline in real maritime enterprise after the glowing achievements of the previous thirty years. In part this was because so much money and energy concentrated on sea-warfare—whether the small privateering expeditions or the great attacks on Cadiz and the Azores—and in part because the heroes were going out and finding only successors of a lesser stamp. But the chief reason lay deeper. English mariners and merchants were only beginning to grasp that their real future lay not in the search for rapid enrichment—the capture of treasure ships, the plundering of gold-exporting shores—but in the ordinary pursuit of a trade whose horizons had grown enormously in those hundred years. And while they sought profit at the expense of Spain, they found Spain growing stronger. The defeat of the Armada and Philip's failure in the Netherlands had indeed heralded the decline of Spain, but the greatest empire of the day could still give a good account of itself in defence. In the last analysis the rather sombre note which hangs over the naval story of the 1590s describes only the difficulties encountered by a somewhat slapdash and over-confident attacker in the face of a resistance whose competence was novel and surprising.

4. THE TRAGEDY OF ESSEX

Before the violent century closed it witnessed yet another violent incident. There was in England one whose arrogant pride, assurance of high place, hold over Elizabeth's affections, and complete command of popular favour made him a standing danger to the state. Essex—'a nature not to be ruled'—could not live as anything but the first of men. He looked down upon Elizabeth as an old woman jealously frustrating his greatness; he ever thought that others—especially Cecil and Raleigh—were plotting against his fortunes; the just retribution of his follies he ascribed to their burrowings. In the end these feelings turned to a pathological hatred. The pity of it was that Essex had it in him to be a great man; he had vision, generosity, courage, and vigour—as well as charm. But he lacked in character and ability; rash, unstable, ungovernable, and not very clever, he dug his own grave with persistent skill. Any Tudor except Elizabeth would have had his head much sooner and saved much trouble; she hoped that discipline and temporary setbacks would make another man of him. But with him her sure touch deserted her. His meteoric rise to fame, favour, and fortune, and the plaudits of a sycophantic entourage, gave Essex such a conceit of himself that the queen's repeated attempts to tighten the reins only exacerbated his recklessness. There was a famous scene, soon after his return from the Islands voyage, when he discourteously turned his back on her: she boxed his ears and told him to go and be hanged, whereupon in a blind passion he half-drew his sword. Essex completely misjudged the old lady: he had yet to learn that she was a statesman and a queen before she was a woman.

After Essex's unauthorised and mud-bespattered return from Ireland in September 1599 things took their fatal course. He was committed to the keeping of Sir Thomas Egerton; for six months he was closely imprisoned and for another six in easier confinement, before he regained a measure of liberty. All this time the evidence of his popularity accumulated. London was crowded with officers who had deserted from the Irish army to follow their leader—a dangerous crew, desperate for profit and advancement, absolutely reckless as to means. The people, especially of London, shouted for the earl and poured scorn on his rivals. Impecunious gentlemen, kept out of office and favour by the ascendancy of the Cecil faction (or so they thought)[1], rallied round Essex. The earl himself does not appear to have done any party-building at this time; eating his heart out in prison, full of the festering self-pity which brought on the last fatal outburst, he devoted his thoughts to his own fate and as far as he plotted plotted ineptly. Elizabeth wanted to bring him to public trial in the star chamber; very sensitive to his popular appeal which rivalled her own, she hoped

[1] After six years of power without office, Sir Robert Cecil was appointed to the vacant secretaryship in 1596. His character is only a mystery if his libellers are believed, for then his own actions and protestations clash with their picture of a Machiavellian near-devil. He was ambitious, able, clear-sighted, not over-scrupulous, and extremely hardworking—a suitable and typical Tudor minister, which Essex was not. His meagre personal appearance told against him with the queen, but she trusted his judgment and his loyalty, and she never made mistakes in such matters.

to recover sole possession of her subjects' affections by publicly exposing his guilt. But wiser counsels and Essex's humble submission spared him the public disgrace. In June 1600 he was brought before a commission sitting in private. He was charged on five main counts: desertion of his post, failure in Ireland, his making of knights and appointing Southampton as general of horse despite the queen's orders, the presumptuous tone of his letters, and his private interview with Tyrone. The commissioners, who were eager to spare him, persuaded him with some difficulty to forego his defence and throw himself on the queen's mercy. He was deprived of most of his offices, suspended from the privy council, and confined to Essex House (in the Strand). A promise of ultimate restoration to favour was not given but allowed to hang in the air.

Unfortunately for Essex, he had at last aroused the old Tudor distrust. Humble appeals availed nothing now. In September the queen failed to renew his monopoly of the import of sweet wines on which single pillar his tottering finances rested; despair grew on him. In private he expressed views of the queen, of Cecil, of the rest of his supposed detractors, which inflamed his followers and came near treason. He lost all sense of proportion and succumbed to the influence of the wild adventurers who surrounded him. Growing convinced that Cecil was plotting to put the Spanish Infanta on the throne after the queen's death, he entered into negotiations with James of Scotland and tried to get Mountjoy to bring over the Irish army to restore himself to power and secure the Stuart succession. Luckily for himself, Mountjoy (away from the influence of his mistress, Essex's sister Penelope Lady Rich) was too cautious for such folly, and Elizabeth ignored what came to her of the business in the knowledge that Ireland would purge him of treason and employ him usefully. At Essex House, however, the plots grew ever thicker and more absurd. Puerile schemes were evolved for seizing Essex's enemies and 'freeing' the queen. In February 1601 the council at last took notice and summoned him to attend; this lit the fuse. One evening some of his followers paid Shakespeare's company forty shillings to perform *Richard II* at the Globe—a play fraught with meaning for these hotheads who saw in their Essex another Henry Bolingbroke. When on 8th February four privy councillors, all rather his friends, came to Essex House in the queen's name, the earl arrested them and with a crowd of two hundred gentlemen, armed only with swords, issued forth to raise the city.

It was a mad and pointless thing and came to the end it deserved.

Crying, 'for the queen, for the queen! there is a plot against my life', Essex rode up Fleet Street, Ludgate Hill, and Cheapside. All who would listen were told how Raleigh, Cecil, and Cobham were aiming to murder him and were exhorted to come to the rescue of queen and Church. No one moved. Instead the Lord Mayor began to barricade Essex's following, while from court there came troops and heralds to proclaim him traitor. The aimless riot petered out. Essex began to lose all control, displaying something very like persecution mania; for fifteen minutes he held a city official's horse by the bridle while he poured out to the astonished man his grievances and imaginary injuries—'looking wildly up and down'. At last he let himself be pushed down to the river and returned to Essex House. Here he found that the man he had put in guard over his hostages had lost his nerve and let them go. It was over. In the late evening he came out with the earls of Southampton and Rutland to surrender; the whole band was soon under lock and key. After the events of the day the end could be in no doubt, and no satires about

> Little Cecil tripping up and down,
> He rules both court and crown,
> With his brother Burghley clown,
> In his great fox-furred gown.
> With the long proclamation
> He swore he saved the town.
> Is it not likely?[1]

or later laments such as the *Lamentable Ditty composed upon the death of Robert Lord Devereux, late Earl of Essex* ('Sweet England's pride is gone—welladay, welladay'), could alter the fact that Essex had firmly placed his head on the block when he rode into the Strand on 8 February. Within nine days he was brought to trial, Coke and his old follower Francis Bacon appearing against him, and the sentence was carried out as rapidly. Southampton, also found guilty, was spared sentence; Rutland escaped even trial but paid a heavy fine, as did many others. Only a few of Essex's lesser followers, among them those who had really stirred him up, suffered for their treason; as usual, the queen's vengeance was moderate.

[1] Thomas Lord Burghley, the old treasurer's somewhat boorish elder son, had led the troops that pushed Essex out of the city; the proclamation in question was that issued next day to declare the earl's treason. As for who saved the city, the satirist was right in implying that it did not need saving.

The significance of Essex's rising is too often explained in purely personal terms. Admittedly, it is a story of high ambitions and headlong fall, given even greater interest by the play between earl and queen. E. P. Cheyney thought Essex worth pity; he put everything down to Elizabeth's jealousy of his popularity.[1] If a wider significance is found at all, the rising is usually described as an example of belated feudalism. But in truth it was a far from belated example of bastard feudalism. Essex acted as an 'over-mighty subject', or more specifically as one of those leaders of affinities whose military power had been broken by Henry VII, but who continued to play their part in politics right down to the end of the eighteenth century. In effect he attempted to revive the military side of the social system which depended on clientage and the great 'connexion'—the grouping around a magnate of gentlemen and lesser men eager for advancement. There was nothing territorial about Essex's power: he was no feudal lord. But the charges against him (which Cheyney, for instance, thought absurdly insignificant) assume their real meaning if we remember the nature of bastard feudalism. Those Irish knights he had made amounted to a body of personal retainers; altogether, his behaviour in Ireland looked far more like a king-maker's than a crown servant's. There was plenty of discontent and disappointed ambition for him to fashion a party from: 'swordsmen, bold confident fellows, men of broken fortunes, discontented persons, and such as saucily use their tongues in railing against all men'. In that light the queen saw it, and the event so proved it. At the end of her reign Elizabeth had to turn once more to the original task of her house and suppress the overpowering ambitions of one individual who was creating a private following for himself. Unhappily for her, the individual was a man she would have liked to favour and cherish; happily for the state he was a man without political sense without patience, and afflicted by a mental instability which even expressed itself in bouts of nervous sickness. The career of Essex is a tragedy in the Shakespearian sense because potential greatness was wrecked by a flaw in the man himself.

5. THE END

The passing of the Essex storm left all in a strange quiet. Mant bewailed his fate, but none felt constrained to do anything about it Cecil now ruled everything, though Raleigh unsuccessfully tried to

[1] *History of England*, ch. 44. It may be as well to remark that Lytton Strachey's *Elizabeth and Essex* is perhaps best left unread.

dispute the ascendancy with him. As for the queen, it appears that she was certainly growing old and rather weary. But not yet: it was not Essex's death that depressed her, but the gradual disappearance of all those with whom she had lived a long lifetime together. Her old skill and vigour appeared undimmed in the story of the 1601 parliament. She continued to enjoy dancing and hunting with an energy remarkable in one approaching her seventieth year and only to be explained by her persistent refusal of her physicians' ministrations. Nevertheless, everyone saw that the reign was drawing to a close and began to make preparations. With the skill which had enabled him to ride out several storms and make his way despite physical handicaps, Cecil established himself in the good graces of the only really likely heir, James VI of Scotland. Though he feared the queen's anger and therefore tried very hard to keep the negotiations secret, she knew what went on but said nothing. It is probable that she favoured the Stuart succession—indeed, it is difficult to see whom else she could have favoured—but true to her principle of naming no successor she kept silent, until on her deathbed she pronounced for James—if she did and was not only said to have done so by those in whose hands lay the management of a quiet succession. As the year 1602 progressed, melancholy and a sense of being unwell took possession of her, though in reality her health continued good; her mind remained unaffected to the very end, but she preferred devotion and 'old Canterbury tales' to politics. In March 1603 it became plain that she had lost the desire to live; everyone waited for the end, with sorrow, but also with a lively anticipation of the future. At last, on 24 March 1603, sixty-nine years and six months old, the great queen died quietly, at rest with this world.

The Tudor age was over, for there were no more Tudors. The new reign about to open inherited its problems, and 1603 is a date of only limited significance in the history of England. But it remains true that much of the Stuart trouble was due to Stuart incompetence, and that much of the Tudor success had been due to the skill of the dynasty. It was a wonderful family, and its achievements—aided by the work of many others—were impressive. A country once ravaged by internal war and depression was now, despite external war and more depression, on the way to becoming a major power. Peace at home had brought order and law, a rising prosperity, a spreading over the globe, great things in the arts, a remarkable people. No one would pretend that the sixteenth century was an ideal age. Poverty and disease and cruelty abounded; life was hard and often short for high and low alike. Its politics were too often violent and repulsive, though also full of intelligent vigour. Its religion, though in the end more sincere than that of the late middle ages, also indulged in more intolerance and persecution. Its people were too often hard of face and harder of heart. Yet the state was built anew, government restored and reformed, enterprise encouraged, faith rekindled. The good past survived, the bad past died. In those hundred and twenty years of unremitting labour by monarchs and ministers, merchants and mariners, gentlemen and yeomen, writers and poets and thinkers, a new and greater England emerged from the day-to-day turmoil of life.

BIBLIOGRAPHY

THIS is no attempt at an exhaustive bibliography but only a collection of the more important writings in which the subject may be pursued further. I have tried to give particular attention to recent publications not to be found in earlier lists. I see no point in attempting to choose among the many printed sources for the sixteenth century, but three books shall be mentioned because they will offer an easy and painless introduction to contact with the age. *The Thought and Culture of the English Renaissance*, ed. Elizabeth M. Nugent (Cambridge 1956) assembles a great variety of excellent Tudor prose; the introductory prefaces vary in value but are in general helpful. R. H. Tawney and E. Power, *Tudor Economic Documents* (3 vols., London 1924), supply much detail to illumine the complexities of economic affairs. And any edition of Shakespeare's *Works*, supplemented perhaps by the *Oxford Book of Sixteenth Century Verse*, is a *sine qua non*. For a full discussion of the literature I refer to Conyers Read, *Bibliography of British History: Tudor Period* (2nd ed., Oxford 1959). Useful lists are found in (4), (5), and (13) below.

A. General

1. S. T. Bindoff, *Tudor England* (London 1950).
   The best short survey and a brilliant achievement of compression. Particularly good on economic questions.

The Political History of England:

2. H. A. L. Fisher, *Vol. V: 1485–1547* (London 1913).
3. A. F. Pollard, *Vol. VI: 1547–1603* (London 1910).
   Still in some ways the best account, though both detail and general interpretation require revision.

The Oxford History of England:

4. J. D. Mackie, *The Earlier Tudors 1485–1558* (Oxford 1952).
5. J. B. Black, *The Reign of Elizabeth* (2nd ed., Oxford 1960).
   Include sections on economic, constitutional, and cultural matters not found in (2) and (3). Certainly worth consulting, especially for the sake of their excellent bibliographies.
6. J. A. Williamson, *The Tudor Age* (2nd ed., London 1959).
   Good on maritime affairs.

B. Political History

(*a*) *Henry VII*

7. W. Busch, *England under the Tudors: Henry VII* (London 1895).
   Remains the best detailed history, but is seriously out of date in its discussion of government and finance.
8. K. Pickthorn, *Early Tudor Government: Henry VII* (Cambridge 1934).
   Analytical discussion of government, mainly from a lawyer's point of view. Though not superseded, clearly in parts no longer acceptable in the light of more recent research.
9. G. R. Elton, 'Henry VII: Rapacity and Remorse', *Hist. Journal* 1958.
   Elaborates approach of chapters I and II above. Has led to a controversy: J. P. Cooper, 'Henry VII's Last Years Reconsidered', *ibid.* 1959; G. R. Elton, 'Henry VII: A Restatement', *ibid.* 1960.

See also (32), (34), (35).

(*b*) *Henry VIII*

10. K. Pickthorn, *Early Tudor Government: Henry VIII* (Cambridge 1934).
This exchanges the analytical for the chronological method and in effect becomes a history of the reign with some valuable *obiter dicta* on government.
11. G. R. Elton, *Star Chamber Stories* (London 1958).
Six cases of Henry VIII's reign, throwing light on several aspects of its history.
12. A. F. Pollard, *Henry VIII* (London 1905).
The best life. Tends to overestimate the king's ability and to sentimentalise the constitutional problems.
13. A. F. Pollard, *Wolsey* (London 1929).
P.'s greatest work: embodies vast knowledge and penetrating judgment. Particularly good on Wolsey's activities as a judge.
14. R. W. Chambers, *Thomas More* (London 1935).
Of the many lives of More, this is certainly the one best worth reading. Imaginative and sympathetic, but also fair.
15. A. G. Dickens, *Thomas Cromwell and the English Reformation* (London 1959).
To this brief but excellent modern appraisal, which destroys many false views, add three papers by G. R. Elton, the basis for much said in chapters VI and VII above: 'King or Minister? The Man behind the Henrician Reformation', *History* 1954; 'Thomas Cromwell's Political Creed', *Trans. R. Hist. Soc.*; 1956 'Thomas Cromwell's Decline and Fall', *Cambridge Historical Journal* 1951.
16. J. A. Muller, *Stephen Gardiner and the Tudor Reaction* (London 1926)
Workmanlike, but tends to take Gardiner at his own valuation.

(*c*) *Edward and Mary*

The best outline is in (3); (1) is valuable for a summary of the economic background.

17. A. F. Pollard, *England Under the Protector Somerset* (London 1900).
Much too kind to Somerset and the author's weakest book—but that still makes it a good one.
18. S. T. Bindoff, *Ket's Rebellion* (Historical Association Pamphlet 1949).
19. H. F. M. Prescott, *Mary Tudor* (London 1952).
Rather crowded and a trifle romantic, but sound and readable.
20. E. H. Harbison, *Rival Ambassadors at the Court of Queen Mary* (Princeton 1940).
Detailed discussion of foreign affairs and the activities of the French and Imperial ambassadors; based on much useful material, but it does go on.
21. F. G. Emmison, *Tudor Secretary* (London 1961).
Painstaking biography of Sir William Petre; throws much light on politics and government, as well as on the notorious new gentry of the age.

(*d*) *Elizabeth*

22. A. L. Rowse, *The England of Elizabeth* (London 1950).
Discusses, with an overwhelming wealth of detail, the land, people, government, and Church of the period. Indispensable for the social structure and history of the time. The author's obtrusive prejudices must be discounted.
23. M. Creighton, *Queen Elizabeth* (London 1899).
Judicious: by a notable historian of the last pontifical school. Interpretation perhaps too purely political.
24. J. E. Neale, *Queen Elizabeth* (London 1934).
The outstanding modern life. A little indulgent towards Elizabeth.
25. J. E. Neale, *Elizabeth I and her Parliaments* (2 vols.; London 1953, 1957).
A brilliant and remarkably full narrative of parliamentary affairs, indispensable to an understanding of the political, constitutional, and ecclesiastical history of the reign.

26. E. P. Cheyney, *History of England, from the Defeat of the Armada to the Death of Elizabeth* (2 vols.; New York 1914, 1926).
Intended as a continuation of J. A. Froude's great *History of England 1529–88*, but both much sounder and much duller. Good on the agencies of government; unduly hostile to Elizabeth.
27. *Elizabethan Government and Society*, ed. S. T. Bindoff, J. Hurstfield, C. H. Williams (London 1961).
A collection of valuable papers by various authors; the most important ones are separately noted in the right place. Note here: W. T. Maccaffery, 'Place and Patronage in Elizabethan Politics'; J. Hurstfield, 'The Succession Struggle in Late Elizabethan England'.
28. Conyers Read, *Mr Secretary Walsingham and the Policy of Queen Elizabeth* (3 vols.; Oxford 1925).
The main study of Elizabethan foreign policy; also useful on the office of secretary. Exceedingly detailed with very full quotations.
29. Conyers Read, *Mr Secretary Cecil and Queen Elizabeth* (Oxford 1955); *Lord Burghley and Queen Elizabeth* (Oxford 1960).
Despite its enormous detail and vast quotations, this is not the badly needed biography of Burghley, but rather a companion work to (28). Concentrates predominantly on foreign affairs and Scotland.
30. L. Stone, *An Elizabethan: Sir Horatio Palavicino* (Oxford 1956).
Interesting life of an out-of-the-way character—merchant, financier, diplomatist, gentleman, upstart.

C. Government
31. G. R. Elton, *The Tudor Constitution: Documents and Commentary* (Cambridge 1960).
Replacing J. R. Tanner's *Tudor Constitutional Documents* (Cambridge; 2nd ed. 1930), this contains a concise analytical account of Tudor government and its instruments, with a detailed guide to the bibliography.

(*a*) *Finance*
32. F. C. Dietz, *English Government Finance 1485–1558* (Univ. of Illinois 1920).
33. F. C. Dietz, *English Public Finance 1558–1642* (New York 1932).
The only comprehensive studies of revenue and expenditure. However, both leave too many administrative questions unanswered and are often unreliable in their figures; a new study would not come amiss. There is much on finance in (26), (34), (35), (36).

(*b*) *Administration*
34. G. R. Elton, *The Tudor Revolution in Government* (Cambridge 1953).
Deals with financial administration, the seals and secretaries, the council, and the king's household, mainly during Thomas Cromwell's tenure of office.
35. W. C. Richardson, *Tudor Chamber Administration 1485–1547* (Baton Rouge 1952).
Product of much difficult research and especially useful for Henry VII. Conclusions differ somewhat from (34).
36. G. R. Elton, 'The Elizabethan Exchequer: War in the Receipt', in (27).
37. H. C. Bell, *Introduction to the Court of Wards and Liveries* (Cambridge 1953).
Deals thoroughly with the administrative but not with the social aspects of this court.
38. J. Hurstfield, *The Queen's Wards* (London 1958).
More than a history of the court of wards under Elizabeth: rather an important study of Elizabethan social history. For other aspects of the subject see the same author's 'The Revival of Feudalism in Early Tudor England', *History* 1952; 'Lord Burghley as Master of the Court of Wards', *Trans. R. Hist. Soc.* 1949.

39. F. M. G. Evans, *The Principal Secretary of State* (Manchester 1923).
In the main after 1580. See also (28) and (34).

(*c*) *The Law*

40. W. H. Holdsworth, *History of English Law* (13 vols.; London 1903 onwards).
Vol. i contains the best account of the various courts; vols. iv and v the history of law in the sixteenth century. Vol. iv also includes a remarkable survey of the constitution, which, however, needs ample correction in many parts.
41. J. P. Dawson, *A History of Lay Judges* (Harvard 1960).
Although the book ranges from the ancient Greeks to the nineteenth century, its core consists of excellent studies of English central and local jurisdiction in the fifteenth to seventeenth centuries.

(*d*) *The Council*

The older accounts of the privy council are practically worthless, at least as far as the history of the council is concerned: they still offer something towards an understanding of its working. E. R. Turner, *The Privy Council*, vol. i (Baltimore 1927) needs a red flag of warning. The subject is dealt with in (31); it may be pursued further in (34) and (26), together with the following:

42. *Cases in the Council of Henry VII*, ed. C. G. Bayne (London, Selden Society 1958).
Valuable introduction; for a criticism see G. R. Elton in *Eng. Hist. Rev.* 1959.
43. A. F. Pollard, 'Council, Star Chamber, and Privy Council under the Tudors', *English Historical Review* 1922 and 1923.
44. W. H. Dunham, Jr., 'Henry VIII's Whole Council and Its Parts', *Huntington Library Quarterly* 1943.

(*e*) *Parliament*

A. F. Pollard's *Evolution of Parliament* (2nd ed., London 1925) is interesting and contains some valuable points, but it is so unreliable in parts and so badly constructed that its use is not recommended except to the expert. Thus there are no books on parliament before 1558, but useful discussions will be found in (8), (10), (12), and (31). The following articles, the basis of several points made in this book, may help further:

45. G. R. Elton, 'Parliamentary drafts 1529–40', *Bulletin of the Institute of Historical Research* 1952 (classifies the surviving drafts into aspects of government planning and examples of private enterprise); 'The Evolution of a Reformation Statute', *Eng. Hist. Rev.* 1949 (discusses the growth of the act of appeals and Cromwell's drafting of legislation); 'The Commons' Supplication of 1532', *ibid.* 1951 (describes the development of the measure and analyses the parliamentary manoeuvres involved; has been subjected to some partially constructive criticism by J. P. Cooper, 'The Supplication against the Ordinaries Reconsidered', *ibid.* 1957).

About the parliaments of Elizabeth we are well informed thanks to J. E. Neale (also [25] above).

46. J. E. Neale, *The Elizabethan House of Commons* (London 1949).
Very important. An analysis of elections, membership, and procedure.
47. J. E. Neale, 'The Commons' Privilege of Free Speech in Parliament', *Tudor Studies presented to A. F. Pollard* (London 1924).
48. W. Notestein, *The Winning of the Initiative by the House of Commons* (London 1924).
Changes in Commons' procedure late in the reign.

(*f*) *Local Government*

On this much has been written; there are good summaries in (8), (25), and (34).

49. G. Scott Thompson, *Lords Lieutenants in the Sixteenth Century* (London 1923).

50. C. A. Beard, *The Office of Justice of the Peace* (New York 1924).
No more than a bare introduction.
51. R. R. Reid, *The King's Council of the North* (London 1921).
Exhaustive and sound. A useful short account is F. W. Brooks, *The Council of the North* (Historical Association Pamphlet 1953).
52. P. Williams, *The Council in the Marches of Wales under Elizabeth I* (Cardiff 1958).
Gives also a succinct account of the council's earlier history and an excellent description of the social situation in the Marches.
53. J. A. Youings, 'The Council of the West', *Trans. R. Hist. Soc.* 1960.

(*g*) *Thought on Government and Politics*

54. Sir Thomas Smith, *De Republica Anglorum* (ed. L. Alston, Cambridge 1906).
A most valuable contemporary survey. In English, despite its title.
55. C. Morris, *Political Thought in England from Tyndale to Hooker* (Oxford 1953).
A brilliant summary with many original and interesting suggestions to make. Contains a really first-class bibliography which makes a long list superfluous here.
56. J. W. Allen, *Political Thought in the Sixteenth Century* (London 1928).
Weighty and authoritative. Covers thought in all Western Europe.
57. F. Le V. Baumer, *Early Tudor Theory of Kingship* (Yale 1940).
Full survey, rather cut and dried.
58. W. G. Zeeveld, *Foundations of Tudor Policy* (Harvard 1948).
A study of the obscure men who defended the Cromwellian revolution. Z. probably overestimates their importance, but the book is most interesting and revealing.
59. E. T. Davies, *The Political Ideas of Richard Hooker* (London 1946).

Not in (55) and therefore worth mentioning separately:

60. J. H. Hexter, *More's Utopia: the biography of an idea* (Princeton 1952).
The sanest and least engaged analysis of a famous book. But see also (14).
61. C. H. McIlwain, *Constitutionalism Ancient and Modern* (New York 1947).
Often splendid essays by an old master which the present writer finds progressively less convincing. Chapter 5 deals with the transition from 'medieval' to 'modern'.
62. G. L. Mosse, *The Struggle for Sovereignty in England* (Michigan State College Press 1950).
Mostly on the early Stuarts, but with a useful though controversial summary of late Tudor thought.

D. Economic History

At present there is no full-scale economic history of this period, but (63) and (64) provide something like a survey.

(*a*) *General*

63. E. Lipson, *An Economic History of England*, vol. ii (London 1931).
Unreliable on agrarian and social questions; still useful on trade and industry.
64. J. H. Clapham, *Concise Economic History of Britain* (Cambridge 1949).
An admirable introduction.

(*b*) *Agriculture*

65. R. H. Tawney, *The Agrarian Problem in the Sixteenth Century* (London 1912).
Much of this famous pioneering work now needs supplementing with later studies, but the book remains the basis of all agrarian history in the period.

66. M. Beresford, *The Lost Villages of England* (London 1954).
Tries to trace the sites of deserted villages, as well as the occasion and cause of their abandonment. Seeks to re-establish the view that enclosure for sheep-farming resulted in widespread depopulation c. 1450–1520 and makes some telling points; but the question remains fairly open.
67. Joan Thirsk, *Tudor Enclosures* (Historical Association Pamphlet 1959).
Best recent summary of the present position.
68. W. G. Hoskins, *Essays in Leicestershire History* (Liverpool 1950).
An outstanding example of the growing body of 'local' historical writing directly relevant to large national problems. Important for the effects of enclosure and the fate of the yeoman.
69. M. Campbell, *The English Yeoman under Elizabeth and the Early Stuarts* (Yale 1942).
Deals in detail with the social and economic circumstances of the subject.
70. E. Kerridge, 'The Movement of Rents 1540–1640', *Economic History Review* 1953.
Perhaps the beginning of a new view on rack-renting, but so far has remained in somewhat doubtful isolation.

(*c*) *The Gentry*

71. R. H. Tawney, 'The Rise of the Gentry', *Economic History Review* 1941.
72. H. R. Trevor-Roper, *The Gentry 1540–1640* (Cambridge 1953).
The two main contributions to the controversy outlined above, pp. 255ff. There have been further moves since that section was written, on the whole bearing out the tentative verdict there recorded. See e.g.: M. Finch, *Five Northamptonshire Families* (Oxford 1956); A. R. Batho, 'The Finances of an Elizabethan Nobleman', *Econ. Hist. Rev.* 1957; H. R. Trevor-Roper, 'The General Crisis of the Seventeenth Century', *Past and Present* 1959; P. Zagorin, 'The Social Interpretation of the English Revolution', *Journal of Economic History* 1959. The business has ceased to be fruitful.

(*d*) *Trade*

73. G. D. Ramsay, *English Overseas Trade during the Centuries of Emergence* (London 1957).
Extends beyond the sixteenth century, but provides the best introduction to Tudor trade.
74. G. Schanz, *Englische Handelspolitik gegen Ende des Mittelalters* (Leipzig 1881).
Despite its age still the standard account of early Tudor commercial affairs. Some of its tables and arguments are corrected by P. Ramsay, 'Overseas Trade in the Reign of Henry VII', *Econ. Hist. Rev.* 1954.
75. A. A. Ruddock, *Italian Merchants and Shipping in Southampton 1270–1600* (Southampton 1951).
The last part covers the decline of Southampton's Italian trade under the early Tudors.
76. G. Connell-Smith, *Forerunners of Drake* (London 1954).
A thorough investigation of Anglo-Spanish trade from the treaties of Henry VII to its decline in the 1540s.
77. F. J. Fisher, 'Economic Trends and Policy in the Sixteenth Century', *Economic History Review* 1940.
Important analysis of the ups and downs of the cloth trade.
78. W. R. Scott, *The Constitution and Finance of English, Scottish, and Irish Joint Stock Companies* (3 vols.; Cambridge 1910–12).
A badly arranged monumental work which contains a vast deal of information on trade.

79. G. Unwin, 'The Merchant Adventurers' Company in the Reign of Elizabeth', *Studies in Economic History* (London 1927).
The classic deflation of the M.A. For a different but unconvincing view see (22). The great days of the M.A. in the early sixteenth century still await their historian.
80. T. S. Willan, *The Early History of the Russia Company* (Manchester 1956).
81. A. C. Wood, *A History of the Levant Company* (London 1935).
82. T. S. Willan, *Studies in Elizabethan Foreign Trade* (Manchester 1959).
In addition to a detailed study of the Morocco Company, this contains valuable essays on interlopers and the outports.
83. A. E. Feavearyear, *The Pound Sterling* (Oxford 1931).
The best account of the coinage and its manipulation. See also appendix in (4).

(*e*) *Industry*
84. G. Unwin, *Industrial Organisation in the Sixteenth and Seventeenth Centuries* (Oxford 1904).
Mostly on the seventeenth, but important, especially together with the same author's *Guilds and Companies of London* (London 1908).
85. J. U. Nef, 'Technology and Industry, 1540–1640', *Economic History Review* 1934).
Controversial, as are the same author's 'Prices and Industrial Capitalism in France and England, 1540–1640', *ibid.* 1937; 'War and Economic Progress 1540–1640', *ibid.* 1942; and *Industry and Government in France and England 1540–1640* (American Philosophical Society Memorials, Philadelphia 1940).
86. E. Lipson, *English Woollen and Worsted Industries* (2nd ed., London 1953).
87. J. U. Nef, *The Rise of the British Coal Industry* (2 vols., London 1932).

(*f*) *Social Policy*
88. G. R. Elton, 'State Control in Early Tudor England', *Economic History Review* 1961.
Throws doubt on the present state of knowledge and confident assertions based on it.
89. S. T. Bindoff, 'The Making of the Statute of Artificers', in (27).
90. R. K. Kensall, *Wage Regulation under the Statute of Artificers* (London 1938).
91. R. H. Tawney, 'The Assessment of Wages in England by the Justices of the Peace', *Vierteljahrschrift f. Sozial–u. Wirtschaftsgeschichte* 1913
92. M. G. Davies, *The Enforcement of English Apprenticeship* (Harvard) 1956.
Between them, these last four make the statute of artificers one of the better known Tudor topics; (92) has wider implication for the whole problem of law enforcement.
93. E. M. Leonard, *The Early History of English Poor Relief* (Cambridge 1900).
It is time that this old standard work were superseded, at least for the period before 1572 and especially as to the practical working of poor relief. See also G. R. Elton, 'An Early Tudor Poor Law', *Econ. Hist. Rev.* 1953.
94. W. K. Jordan, *Philanthropy in England 1480–1660* (London 1959).
Contains a vast deal of most valuable (and largely unsuspected) information concerning testamentary charity and charitable foundations. Unfortunately the argument raised on the facts, supported by statistics which take no account of the changing value of money, cannot be accepted without serious reservations.
95. R. H. Tawney, *Religion and the Rise of Capitalism* (London 1926).
The fundamental work on economic thought in the period. Has led to much controversy and is, indeed, more convincing for the seventeenth than the sixteenth century. But remains one of the outstanding historical works of the present century.

96. Thomas Wilson, *A Discourse on Usury*, ed. R. H. Tawney (London 1925).
The long introduction provides the fundamental study of money and credit in the sixteenth century.

E. The Church

A small selection from a huge mass of writings.

97. J. Gairdner, *The English Church in the Sixteenth Century from Henry VIII to Mary* (London 1903).

98. W. H. Frere, *The English Church in the Reigns of Elizabeth and James I* (London 1904).
These two volumes, part of a series, cover the period. Both are sound enough on fact, but while (98) is judicious and to be recommended, (97) is marked by a distorting dislike of the Reformation, and its opinions and interpretations must be used with great care. The same applies more forcibly still to Gairdner's *Lollardy and the Reformation* (4 vols., London 1908–13).

(*a*) *The Reformation*

See also n.2 on p. 99 above.

99. T. M. Parker, *The English Reformation to 1558* (Oxford 1950)
The best brief survey, questionable here and there on the constitutional side.

100. H. Maynard Smith, *Pre-Reformation England* (London 1938).

101. H. Maynard Smith, *Henry VIII and the Reformation* (London 1948).
Both these are interesting and lucid accounts, rather lightweight in treatment and only ordinary on the political side. (100) gives a good view of the state of the Church, for which see also (13) and (102).

102. P. Hughes, *The Reformation in England* (3 vols., London 1950–4).
The inevitable bias of this catholic history does nothing to lessen the importance of vol. i; the other two volumes need more critical care in use. However, throughout it contains much important and unusual discussion not found elsewhere.

103. G. Constant, *The Reformation in England* (2 vols., London 1934), 1942; translated from the French).
Sound account of little independent value; based on very wide reading among printed materials; commonly rated too high. Vol. ii (on Edward VI), with valuable analyses of theological questions, is the more important.

104. A Ogle, *The Tragedy of the Lollards' Tower* (Oxford 1949).
Mainly a study of the case of Richard Hunne. Proves that he was murdered, and argues that his case was the basis of the commons' attitude and work in 1529–32. Its thesis has some support from (45).

105. A. G. Dickens, *Lollards and Protestants in the Diocese of York* (Oxford 1959).
Throws a quite new light on the religious situation and attitude of Yorkshire.

106. F. W. Maitland, 'The Anglican Settlement and the Scottish Reformation', *Old Cambridge Modern History*, vol. ii.
Still in many ways far and away the best account of the years 1558–68; part of the story must be revised in accordance with J. E. Neale's 'The Elizabethan Acts of Supremacy and Uniformity', *Eng. Hist. Rev.* 1951.

107. J. V. P. Thompson, *The Supreme Governor* (London 1940).
A useful, if rather slight, summary of Elizabeth's policy towards the the Church.

108. J. Mozley, *William Tyndale* (London 1937).

109. A. F. Pollard, *Thomas Cranmer and the English Reformation* (London 1905).
The best of several lives of Cranmer.

110. H. Darby, *Hugh Latimer* (London 1953).
Straightforward; interesting on account of its subject.

(*b*) *The Monasteries and the Deprivations*

F. A. Gasquet's *Henry VIII and the Monasteries*, despite the notion, not so long ago expressed by Cardinal Gasquet's biographer, that it still sets the standard in the field, is best ignored.

111. D. Knowles, *The Religious Orders in England: The Tudor Age* (Cambridge 1959).
Not only just the best book on the subject, but a truly excellent one.

112. G. Baskerville, *English Monks and the Suppression of the Monasteries* (London 1937).
Marred slightly by too ready a hostility to the monks, and heavily by a needless flippancy, this book still retains some independent value by the side of (111) because it is more able to see the anti-monastic point of view.

113. A. Savine, *English Monasteries on the Eve of the Dissolution* (Oxford 1909).
Very important. A detailed investigation of the condition of the houses, based in the main on an analysis of the *Valor Ecclesiasticus*.

114. H. Grieve, 'The Deprived Married Clergy in Essex', *Trans. R. Hist. Soc.* 1940).

115. C. H. Garret, *The Marian Exiles* (Cambridge 1938).
Valuable facts, doubtful deductions.

(*c*) *Catholic, Puritan, and Anglican*

116. A. O. Meyer, *England and the Catholic Church under Elizabeth* (London 1916; translated from the German).
A scholarly investigation—thorough, unimpassioned, and in a neutral tone; but readable. Easily the best thing on the subject.

117. A. C. Southern, *Elizabethan Recusant Prose* (London, n.d.).
Mainly a study of writings, but also a valuable contribution to the history of Elizabethan Catholicism.

118. M. M. Knappen, *Tudor Puritanism* (Chicago 1939).
Now the standard work. Deals with the subject in all its forms, from Tyndale to the Separatist movement.

119. A. F. Scott Pearson, *Thomas Cartwright and Elizabethan Puritanism* (Cambridge 1925).

120. P. Collison, 'John Field and Elizabethan Puritanism', in (27).

121. R. G. Usher, *The Reconstruction of the English Church* (2 vols., New York 1910).
Book I of vol. i deals with the state of the clergy and the attack on puritanism late in the reign.

122. R. G. Usher, *The Rise and Fall of the High Commission* (Oxford 1913).
Fair example of the constitutional history of a court.

(*d*) *Special Studies suggested for Reading*

123. E. G. Rupp, *Studies in the Making of the Protestant Tradition* (Cambridge 1947).
Admirable essays on the Lutheran influence in the Henrician Reformation.

124. E. T. Davies, *Episcopacy and the Royal Supremacy in the Church of England in the XVI Century* (Oxford 1950).
Interesting analysis of the teaching of the formularies; weak on the actual working of the relationship.

125. H. C. Porter, *Reformation and Reaction in Tudor Cambridge* (Cambridge 1958).
Goes well beyond the implications of the title in investigating the nature and effect of theological disputes.

126. F. D. Price, 'Gloucester Diocese under Bishop Hooper 1551–3', *Transactions of the Bristol and Glos. Archaeol. Soc.* 1938; 'An Elizabethan Church Official—Thomas Powell, Chancellor of Gloucester Diocese', *Church Quarterly Review* 1939; 'Abuses of Excommunication and the Decline of Ecclesiastical Discipline under Queen Elizabeth', *Eng. Hist. Rev.* 1942.
These three papers give a very good idea of the state of the Church in a badly run diocese, but though Gloucester may have been particularly bad it was not untypical.

127. C. Hill, *Economic Problems of the Church from Archbishop Whitgift to the Long Parliament* (Oxford 1956).
Though mainly concerned with the early Stuart period, this book is valuable for the condition of the Elizabethan Church and clergy.

F. NAVAL AND MILITARY MATTERS

A good general account may be extracted from (6)

(*a*) *The Navy*

128. M. Oppenheim, *History of the Administration of the Royal Navy* (London 1896).
The fundamental study.

129. W. Monson, *Naval Tracts*, ed. M. Oppenheim (6 vols., Navy Record Society 1902–14).
Important Introductions.

For the navy under Elizabeth see also (135), 137), and (141).

(*b*) *The Army*

130. C. G. Cruickshank, *Elizabeth's Army* (Oxford 1946).
Good introductory study, with useful bibliography. The first chapters of (144) add important detail on the army in Ireland; and see (49) for the militia.

(*c*) *Explorations*

131. J. A. Williamson, *Maritime Enterprise 1485–1558* (Oxford 1913).
An older standard work, now to be amended and extended by (132), (133), and especially (76) which shows that naval depredations by Englishmen began much sooner than used to be thought.

132. J. A. Williamson, *The Voyages of the Cabots and the English Discovery of North America under Henry VII and Henry VIII* (London 1929).

133. E. G. R. Taylor, *Tudor Geography 1485–1583* (London 1931).
Important study of geographical learning and practice. Must be read, even though the material has hardly been turned into a book.

134. A. L. Rowse, *The Expansion of Elizabethan England* (London 1955).
Valuable for its picture of the countries on the fringe of England.

135. J. A. Williamson, *The Age of Drake* (London 1946).
The best survey of the second half of the century, rather more critical of Drake than—

136. J. S. Corbett, *Drake and the Tudor Navy* (2 vols., London 1898–9).
Still a very important work much of which cannot be found elsewhere. Undoubtedly prejudiced in Drake's favour.

137. J. A. Williamson, *Hawkins of Plymouth* (London 1946).
Probably the author's masterpiece, it supersedes his own earlier *Sir John Hawkins* (Oxford 1927). Particularly good for the history of the navy.

138. A. L. Rowse, *Sir Richard Grenville* (London 1937).
Good both as biography and history; throws much light as well on the social structure of the south-west (for which see also the same author's *Tudor Cornwall* [London 1947]).

139. D. B. Quinn, *Raleigh and the British Empire* (London 1947).
Very useful on both subjects, and lists the more important of the many lives of Raleigh, to which might now be added W. M. Wallace, *Sir Walter Raleigh* (Princeton 1959).
140. J. A. Williamson, *The Ocean in English History* (Oxford 1941).
Less narrative than this author's other work, it contains in particular a fine summary of the work of the propagandists.

(*d*) *The War*
Thoroughly dealt with in (26) and (134); much detail also in (135–9).
141. G. Mattingly, *The Defeat of the Spanish Armada* (London 1959).
Exciting, in part overdone; a brilliant synthesis of English and Spanish contributions which places the campaign in the larger setting of war and politics.
142. R. B. Wernham, 'Queen Elizabeth and the Portugal Expedition of 1589', *English Historical Review* 1951.
Important revision of the traditional version, as given, e.g., in (26).
143. R. B. Wernham, 'Elizabethan War Aims and Strategy', in (27).
Continues the rehabilitation of the queen's policy.
144. C. Falls, *Elizabeth's Irish Wars* (London 1950).
Thorough and fascinating, with a good bibliography.

G. SCOTLAND, WALES, AND IRELAND
(*a*) *Scotland*
Both (4) and (5) are strong on this.
145. P. Hume Brown, *History of Scotland* (3 vols., Cambridge 1911).
The standard history.
146. G. Donaldson, *The Scottish Reformation* (Cambridge 1960).
Important revision of traditional views; stresses the gradual establishment of the Reformation and the initial absence of presbyterianism.
147. Lord Eustace Percy, *John Knox* (London 1937).
148. T. F. Henderson, *Mary Queen of Scots* (London 1905).
Generally accepted as the best biography: there are many. Read's *Bibliography* lists well over a hundred items directly concerned with the Queen.
149. D. H. Willson, *King James VI and I* (London 1956).

(*b*) *Wales*
See especially (52).
150. C. A. J. Skeel, 'Wales under Henry VII', *Tudor Studies presented to A. F. Pollard* (London 1924).
151. W. Ll. Williams, *Making of Modern Wales* (London 1919).
Collection of important studies on Tudor Wales.
152. J. F. Rees, 'Tudor Policy in Wales', *Studies in Welsh History* (Cardiff 1947).
A lucid summary with an excellent map. See also W. Rees, 'The Union of England and Wales', *Transactions of the Cymmrodorion Society* 1937.

(*c*) *Ireland*
153. R. Bagwell, *Ireland under the Tudors* (3 vols., London 1885–90).
Another standard work.
154. B. Fitzgerald, *The Geraldines* (London 1953).
Brief and rather popular, but sound.
155. R. Dudley Edwards, *Church and State in Tudor Ireland* (Dublin 1935).
The impact of the Reformation on Ireland; see also the same author's 'Ireland, Elizabeth I, and the Counter-Reformation', in (27).
156. E. W. L. Hamilton, *Elizabethan Ulster* (London 1919).
Together with (144), a good account of Ireland under Elizabeth.

H. Literature and the Arts

(4) and (5) give adequate summaries and good biographies.

157. F. Caspari, *Humanism and the Social Order in Tudor England* (Chicago 1954).
Discusses, fully and in detail, the educational thought of some leading Tudor humanists; valuable bibliographical footnotes.

158. E. M. W. Tillyard, *The Elizabethan World Picture* (London 1943).
A polished account of the traditional element in Elizabethan thinking.

159. *The Cambridge History of English Literature* (reprint of 1932), vols. iii–vi.
A most valuable compilation, covering all aspects of literature in considerable detail. The chapters, written by different people, vary enormously: some are excellent, others the last word in literary murder.

160. C. S. Lewis, *English Literature in the Sixteenth Century, excluding Drama* (Oxford 1954).
A brilliant, often provocative, survey which illumines much darkness.

161. F. P. Wilson, *Elizabethan and Jacobean* (Oxford 1945).
A highly illuminating analysis of the great age.

162. F. S. Boas, *An Introduction to Tudor Drama* (Oxford 1933).
Deals with the drama before Shakespeare.

163. M. M. Reese, *Shakespeare: his world and his work* (London 1952).
A discussion of all aspects of Shakespeare and a useful introduction to the enormous literature of the subject. For this see also the annual surveys edited by A. Nicol.

164. E. Walker, *A History of Music in England* (3rd ed., revised by J. A. Westrup, Oxford 1952).
The standard work, not exciting, but sound.

165. T. Garner and A. Stratton, *The Domestic Architecture of England during the Tudor Period* (2 vols., London 1929).
Plentiful pictures and illuminating comment; jejune off the field of architecture.

166. Erna Auerbach, *Tudor Artists* (London 1954).
Important. Concentrates on miniature painting, but gives also summaries of portrait painting on a larger scale and the work done by artists in heraldry and for the royal revels. Valuable biographical details and a very full bibliography.

167. Erna Auerbach, *Nicholas Hillyard* (London 1961).

INDEX